MW01620899

NIGHTSHADE TAVERN

OBSIDIAN BUTTERFLY
NARCISSUS IN CHAINS

Laurell K. Hamilton

Publication History: Ace hardcover, January 2000
Ace paperback, October 2000

Publication History: Ace hardcover, October 2001
Ace paperback, September 2002

First SFBC Fantasy Printing: November 2005

Published by arrangement with:
The Berkley Publishing Group
a division of Penguin Putnam Inc.
375 Hudson Street
New York, NY 10014

Visit The SFBC online at http://www.sfbc.com

ISBN 0-7394-6121-4

Printed in the United States of America.

Contents

OBSIDIAN BUTTERFLY

Acknowledgments

Michael Miller who told me more about guns, and weapons in general, than I'd ever hoped to know. To Masaad Ayoob, who caught last-minute gun mistakes. He did not have the opportunity to read the entire book before final edit, so any missed gun mistakes are mine and mine alone. Steve (S. M.) and Jan Stirling who read the book over to make sure I'd captured the flavor of the Santa Fe area. To all the people who made me feel so welcome in Santa Fe and Albuquerque while I wandered around asking questions and absorbing the atmosphere. And for my husband, Gary, who took care of our daughter Trinity while I was in New Mexico. And for Trinity, who shared my office chair while I finished the last third of this book. Chuck Holmes of the Bernallio County Sheriff's Department who answered my last-minute questions. To Deborah Millitello, who deserves special thanks for braving the wilds of New Mexico with me, sprained ankle and all. As always to my writing group, the Alternate Historians, who have been with me from the beginning: Deborah Millitello, Mark Sumner, Sharon Shinn, Marella Sands, Tom Drennan, N. L. Drew, and W. Augustus Elliot. Due to time constraints not everyone got to read this book, so it will be new to you guys, as well. What a switch.

This one is for all the Edwards fans, who by their letters, questions, and sheer interest let me know that they were as interested in knowing more about him as I was.

Author's Note

For those of you who have never read an Anita Blake novel before, let me tell you a bit about her world.

It's just like the world we all live in—except that the creatures of the night—vampires, werewolves, zombies and such—are not the stuff of fiction. They are here-and-now. We co-exist with them—not always happily, not always peacefully.

And sometimes we get to know them all too well . . .

1

I WAS COVERED in blood, but it wasn't mine, so it was okay. Not only was it not my blood, but it was all animal blood. If the worst casualties of the night were six chickens and a goat, I could live with it, and so could everyone else. I'd raised seven corpses in one night. It was a record even for me.

I pulled into my driveway at a quarter 'til dawn with the sky still dark and star-filled. I left the Jeep in the driveway, too tired to mess with the garage. It was May, but it felt like April. Spring in St. Louis was usually a two-day event between the end of winter and the beginning of summer. One day you were freezing your ass off and the next day it'd be eighty plus. But this year it had been spring, a wet gentle spring.

Except for the high number of zombies I'd raised, it had been a typical night. Everything from raising a civil war soldier for a local historical society to question, a will that needed a final signature, to a son's last confrontation with his abusive mother. I'd been neck deep in lawyers and therapists most of the night. If I heard, "How does that make you feel, Jonathan (or Cathy, or whoever)?" one more time tonight, I'd scream. I did not want to watch one more person "go with his or her feelings" ever. At least with most of the lawyers the bereaved didn't come to the graveside. The court-appointed lawyer would ascertain that the zombies raised had enough cognitive ability to know what they were signing, then he would sign off on the contract as a witness. If the zombie couldn't answer the questions, then no legal signature. The corpse had to be of "sound" mind to sign a legally binding signature. I'd never raised a zombie that couldn't pass the legal definition of soundness, but it happened sometimes. Jamison, a fellow animator at Animator's Inc., had a pair of lawyers come to blows on top of the grave. What fun.

The air was cool enough to make me shiver as I walked down the sidewalk to my door. I could hear the phone ringing as I fumbled the key into the lock. I hit the door with my shoulder because no one ever calls just before dawn unless it's important. For me that usually meant the police, which meant a murder scene. I kicked the door closed and ran for the phone in the kitchen. My answering machine had clicked on. My voice died on the machine and Edward's voice came on.

"Anita, it's Edward. If you're there, pick up." Silence.

I was running full out and skidded on my high heels, grabbing the receiver as I slid into the wall and nearly dropped the phone. I yelled into the receiver as I juggled the phone, "Edward, Edward, it's me! I'm here!"

Edward was laughing softly when I could finally hear him.

"Glad I could be amusing. What's up?" I asked.

"I'm calling in my favor," he said quietly.

It was my turn for silence. Once upon a time Edward had come to my aid, been my backup. He'd brought a friend, Harley, with him as more backup. I'd ended up killing Harley. Now, Harley had tried to kill me first, and I'd just been quicker, but Edward had taken the killing personally. Picky, picky. Edward had given me a choice: either he and I could draw down on each other and find out once and for all which of us was better, or I could owe him a favor. Some day he would call me up and ask for me to be his backup like Harley. I'd agreed to the favor. I never wanted to come up against Edward for real. Because if I did, I was pretty sure I'd end up dead.

Edward was a hit man. He specialized in monsters. Vampires, shapeshifters, anything and everything. There were people like me that did it legal, but Edward didn't sweat the legalities, or hell, the ethics. He even occasionally did a human, but only if they had some sort of dangerous reputation. Other assassins, criminals, bad men, or women. Edward was an equal opportunity killer. He never discriminated, not for sex, religion, race, or even species. If it was dangerous, Edward would hunt it and kill it. It's what he lived for, what he was—a predator's predator.

He'd been offered a contract on my life once. He'd turned it down and had come to town as my bodyguard, bringing Harley with him. I'd asked him why he hadn't taken the contract. His answer had been simple. If he took the contract, he only got to kill me. If he protected me, he thought he'd get to kill more people. Perfect Edward reasoning.

He's either a sociopath or so close it makes little difference. I may be one of the few friends that Edward has, but it's like being friends with a tame leopard. It may curl on the foot of your bed and let you pet its head, but it can still eat your throat out. It just won't do it tonight.

"Anita, you still there?"

"I'm here, Edward."

"You don't sound happy to hear from me."

"Let's just say I'm cautious," I said.

He laughed again. "Cautious. No, you're not cautious. You're suspicious."

"Yeah," I said. "So what's the favor?"

"I need back up," he said.

"What could be so terrible that Death needs backup?"

"Ted Forrester needs backup from Anita Blake, vampire executioner."

Ted Forrester was Edward's alter ego, his only legal identity that I was aware of. Ted was a bounty hunter that specialized in preternatural creatures that weren't vampires. As a general rule vamps were a specialty item, which was one of the reasons that there were licensed vamp executioners but not licensed anything else executioners. Maybe vampires just have a better political lobby, but whatever, they get the most press. Bounty hunters like Ted filled in the blanks between the police and the licensed executioners. They worked mostly in rancher-run states where it was still legal to hunt down varmints and kill them for money. Varmints still included lycanthropes. You could shoot them on sight in about six states as long as later a blood test proves they were lycanthropes. Some of the killings had been taken to court and were being contested, but nothing had changed yet on a local level.

"So, what does Ted need me for?" Though truthfully I was relieved that it was

Ted asking and not Edward. Edward on his own probably meant illegal, maybe even murder. I wasn't quite into cold-blooded murder. Not yet.

"Come to Santa Fe and find out," he said.

"New Mexico? Santa Fe, New Mexico?"

"Yes."

"When?" I asked.

"Now."

"Since I'm coming as Anita Blake, vamp executioner, I can flash my executioner's license and bring my arsenal."

"Bring what you want," Edward said. "I'll share my toys with you when you arrive."

"I haven't been to bed yet. Do I have time to get some sleep before I get on a plane?"

"Get a few hours sleep, but be here by afternoon. We've moved the bodies, but we're saving the rest of the crime scene for you."

"What sort of crime scene?"

"I'd say murder, but that's not quite the right word. Slaughter, butcher, torture. Yes," he said, as if trying the word over in his mind, "a torture scene."

"Are you trying to scare me?" I asked.

"No," he said.

"Then stop the theatrics and just tell me what the hell happened."

He sighed, and for the first time I heard a dragging tiredness in his voice. "We've got ten missing. Twelve confirmed dead."

"Shit," I said. "Why haven't I heard anything on the news?"

"The disappearances made the tabloids. I think the headline was, 'Bermuda Triangle in the Desert.' The twelve dead were three families. Neighbors just found them today."

"How long had they been dead?" I asked.

"Days, nearly two weeks for one family."

"Jesus, why didn't someone miss them sooner?"

"In the last ten years almost the entire population of Santa Fe has changed. We've got a huge influx of new people. Plus a lot of people have what amounts to vacation homes up here. The locals call the newcomers Californicators."

"Cute," I said, "but is Ted Forrester a local?"

"Ted lives near the city, yeah."

A thrill went through me from the soles of my feet to the top of my head. Edward was the ultimate mystery man. I knew almost nothing about him, really. "Does this mean I get to see where you live?"

"You'll be staying with Ted Forrester," he said.

"But you're Ted Forrester, Edward. I'll be staying at your house, right?"

He was quiet for a heartbeat, then, "Yes."

Suddenly, the whole trip seemed much more attractive. I was going to see Edward's house. I was going to be able to pry into his personal life, if he had one. What could be better?

Though one thing was bothering me. "When you said families were the victims, does that include kids?"

"Strangely, no," he said.

"Well, thank goodness for small blessings," I said.

"You always were a soft touch for the kiddies," he said.

"Does it really not bother you to see dead children?"

"No," he said.

I just listened to him breathe for a second or two. I knew that nothing bothered Edward. Nothing moved him. But children . . . every cop I knew hated to go to a scene where the vic was a child. There was something personal about it. Even those of us without children took it hard. That Edward didn't, bothered me. Funny, but it did.

"It bothers me," I said.

"I know," he said, "one of your more serious faults." There was an edge of humor to his voice.

"The fact that you're a sociopath, and that I'm not, is one of the things I take great pride in."

"You don't have to be a sociopath to back me up, just a shooter, and you are that, Anita. You kill as easily as I do, if the circumstances are right."

I didn't try and argue, because I couldn't. I decided to concentrate on the crime instead of my moral decay. "So Santa Fe has a large transient population."

"Not transient," Edward said, "but mobile, very mobile. We have a lot of tourism, and a lot of people moving in and out on a semi-permanent basis."

"So no one knows their neighbors," I said, "or what their schedules should be."

"Exactly." His voice was bland, empty, with that thread of tiredness underneath, and under that was something else. A tone—something.

"You think there's more bodies that you haven't found yet," I said. I made it a statement.

He was quiet for a second, then said, "You heard it in my voice, didn't you?"

"Yeah," I said.

"I'm not sure I like that. You being able to read me that well."

"Sorry. I'll try to be less intuitive."

"Don't bother. Your intuition is one of the things that's kept you alive this long."

"Are you making a joke about women's intuition?" I asked.

"No, I'm saying that you're someone who works from your gut, your emotions, not your head. It's a strength for you, and a weakness."

"Too tenderhearted, am I?"

"Sometimes, and sometimes you're just as dead inside as I am."

Hearing him state it like that was almost scary. Not that he was including me in the same breath as himself, but that Edward knew something had died inside of him.

"You ever miss the parts that are gone?" I asked. It was the closest thing to a personal question I'd ever asked him.

"No," he said. "Do you?"

I thought about that for a moment. I started to say yes, automatically, then stopped myself. Truth, always truth between us. "No, I guess I don't."

He made a small sound, almost a laugh. "That's my girl."

I was both flattered and vaguely irritated that I was "his girl." When in doubt, concentrate on the job. "What kind of monster is it, Edward?" I asked.

"I've no idea."

That stopped me. Edward had been hunting preternatural bad guys years longer than I had. He knew monsters almost as well as I did, and he'd traveled the world killing monsters, so he had first hand knowledge of things I'd only read about.

"What do you mean, you have no idea?"

"I've never seen anything kill like this, Anita." I heard an undercurrent in his voice that I'd almost never heard—fear. Edward, whose nickname among the vamps and shapeshifters was Death, was afraid. It was a very bad sign.

"You're shook, Edward. That's not like you."

"Wait until you see the victims. I've saved you photos of the other scenes, but the last one I kept intact, just for you."

"How did the local law enforcement like putting a ribbon around a crime scene and wrapping it up just for little ol' me?"

"The local cops all like Ted. He's a good ol' boy. If Ted tells them you can help, they believe him."

"But you're Ted Forrester," I said, "and you're not a good ol' boy."

"But Ted is," he said, voice empty.

"Your secret identity," I said.

"Yeah," he said.

"Fine, I'll fly into Santa Fe this afternoon, or early evening."

"Fly into Albuquerque instead. I'll meet you at the airport. Just call me and give me the time."

"I can rent a car," I said

"I'll be in Albuquerque on other business. It's not a problem."

"What aren't you telling me?" I asked.

"Me, keeping secrets?" There was a thread of amusement in his voice again.

"You're the original mystery man, Edward. You love keeping secrets. It gives you a sense of power."

"Does it?" he made it a question.

"Yeah, it does."

He laughed softly. "Maybe it does. Make the ticket reservations and call me with the flight times. I've got to go." His voice went low as if someone else had come into the room.

I hadn't asked what the urgency was. Ten missing, twelve confirmed dead. It was urgent. I hadn't asked if he'd be waiting for my call. Edward, who never spooked, was scared. He'd be waiting for my call.

2

IT TURNED OUT that the only flight I could get that wasn't full was a noon flight, which meant I got about five hours of sleep before I had to get up and run for the airport. I also missed Kenpo class, a type of karate that I'd just started a few weeks ago. I'd have much rather been in class than on a plane. I hate to fly. I'd driven to as many of the out of town appointments as possible, but I'd been doing a lot of flying lately. It had lessened the actual terror, but I was still phobic. I hated to be in a plane being flown by someone I didn't know, who I had not personally drug tested. I just wasn't the trusting sort.

Neither are the airlines. Carrying a concealed weapon on a plane was a pain in the ass. I'd had to take the two-hour FAA course on carrying concealed on a plane. I had a certificate to prove I'd taken the course. I could not get on the plane without the certificate. I also had a letter stating that I was on official business that required me to carry a gun. Sergeant Rudolf (Dolf) Storr, head of the Regional Preternatural Investigation Team, had faxed me the letter on taskforce letterhead, alway impressive. Someone who was a real policeperson had to give me something to legitimize my status. If it were real police business, even if Dolf weren't directly involved, he'd usually give me what I needed. If Edward had called me in to help in an unofficial case, i.e., illegal, I would have avoided Dolf. Mr Law and Order wasn't real fond of Edward, a.k.a. Ted Forrester. "Ted" was around a lot when there were bodies on the ground. It made Dolf not trust him.

I did not look out the window. I read and tried to pretend I was on a very cramped bus. I'd finally figured out that one of the reasons I didn't like to fly was that I also have claustrophobia. A 727 full of people was close enough to make it hard to breathe. I turned the little fan above my seat on high and read. I was reading Sharon Shinn. She was an author that I trusted to hold my attention even hundreds of feet above the ground with a thin metal sheet between me and eternity.

So I can't tell you what Albuquerque looks like from the air, and the little walkway that led into the airport was like every other one I'd ever walked through. Even in the tunnel you could feel the heat pressing like a giant hand hovering over the thin plastic. It may have been spring in St. Louis, but it was summer in Albuquerque. I scanned the crowd for Edward and actually looked past him once before realizing it was him. Part of it was the fact that he was wearing a hat, a cowboy hat. There was a fan of feathers tucked into the front of the hat band, but it had the look of a hat that had been worn well. The brim was curved back on both sides as if he'd worked at the stiff material until the brim had formed a new shape under the constant run of his hands. His shirt was white and short-sleeved like something you'd get at any department store. It was matched with dark blue jeans that looked new and a pair of hiking boots that weren't.

Hiking boots? Edward? He'd never impressed me as a country boy. No, definitely a city fellow, but there he stood, looking sort of down-homey and comfortable. It didn't look like Edward at all until I met his eyes. Wrap him up in whatever disguise you want, you could dress him like Prince Charming on a Disney float, but as long as you could glimpse his eyes, you would still run screaming.

His eyes are blue and cold as winter skies. He is the epitome of WASP breeding with his blond hair and slender paleness. He can look harmless if he wants to. He is the consummate actor, but unless he works at it, his eyes give him away. If the eyes are the mirror to the soul, then Edward's in trouble because no one is home.

He smiled at me, and it thawed his eyes to something close to warmth. He was glad to see me, genuinely glad. Or as glad as he ever was to see anyone. It wasn't comforting. In a way it was unnerving because one of the main reasons Edward liked me was that together we always got to kill more than we did apart. Or at least I did. For all I knew, Edward might have been mowing down entire armies when he wasn't with me.

"Anita," he said.

"Edward," I said.

The smile turned into a grin. "You don't seem happy to see me."

"You being this happy to see me makes me nervous, Edward. You're relieved I'm here, and that scares me."

The grin faded, and I watched all the humor, all the welcome, drain out of his face like water leaving a glass through a crack—empty. "I'm not relieved," he said, but his voice was too bland.

"Liar," I said. I would have liked to say it softly, but the noise of the airport was like the crash of the ocean, a continuous roar.

He looked at me with those pitiless eyes and gave one small nod. An acknowledgment that he was relieved I was here. Maybe he would have verbalized it, but suddenly a woman appeared at his side. She was smiling, her arms sliding around him until she cuddled against him. She looked thirtyish, older than Edward appeared, though I wasn't sure of his actual age. Her hair was short, brown, a no-nonsense style, but flattering. She wore almost no makeup, but was still lovely. There were lines at her eyes and mouth that had made me jump her from thirty to forty something. She was smaller than Edward, taller than me, but still petite, though she didn't look soft. She was tanned darker than was healthy which probably explained the lines on her face. But there was a quiet strength to her as she stood there smiling at me, holding Edward's arm.

She wore jeans that looked so neat they must have been pressed, a white short-sleeved shirt that was sheer enough that she'd put a spaghetti strap tank top under it, and a brown leather purse almost as large as my carry-on bag. I wondered for a second if Edward had picked her up from a plane, too, but there was something too fresh and unhurried about her. She hadn't come off a plane.

"I'm Donna. You have to be Anita." She held out her hand, and we shook. She had a firm handshake, and her hand wasn't soft. She'd worked, this one had. She also knew how to shake hands. Most women never really got the knack of it. I liked her instantly, instinctively, and mistrusted the feeling just as quickly.

"Ted's told me so much about you," Donna said.

I glanced up at Edward. He was smiling, and even his eyes were full of humor. The entire set of his face and body had changed. He slouched slightly, and the smile was lazy. He vibrated with good ol' boy charm. It was an Oscar-winning performance, as if he'd traded skins with someone else.

I looked at Edward/Ted and said, "He's told you a lot about me, has he?"

"Oh, yes," Donna said, touching my arm while still holding onto Edward. Of course, she would be a casual toucher. My shapeshifter friends were getting me accustomed to touchie-feelie stuff, but it still wasn't my best thing. What the hell was Edward—Ted—doing with this woman?

Edward spoke, but there was a slight Texas-like drawl to his voice like an old accent almost forgotten. Edward had no accent whatsoever. His voice was one of the cleanest and hardest to place I'd ever heard, as if even his voice was never touched by the places and people he saw.

"Anita Blake, I'd like you to meet Donna Parnell, my fiancee."

My jaw dropped to the carpet, and I just gaped at him. I usually try and be a little more sophisticated than that, or hell, more polite. I knew that astonishment, nay shock, showed, but I couldn't help it.

Donna laughed, and it was a good laugh, warm and chuckly, a good mom laugh. She squeezed Edward's arm. "Oh, you were right, Ted. Her reaction was worth the trip."

"Told ya, honey-pot," Edward said, hugging her and planting a kiss on the top of her head.

I closed my mouth and tried to recover. I managed to mumble, "That's . . . great. I mean really . . . I . . ." I finally extended my hand and said, "Congratulations." But I couldn't manage a smile.

Donna used the handshake to draw me into a hug. "Ted said you'd never believe he'd finally agreed to tie the knot." She hugged me again, laughing. "But, my god, girl, I've never seen such pure shock." She retreated back to Edward's arms and his smiling Ted face.

I am not nearly as good an actor as Edward. It's taken me years to perfect a blank face let alone outright lying by facial expression and body language. So I kept my face blank and tried to tell Edward with my eyes that he had some explaining to do.

With his face slightly turned from Donna, he gave me his close, secretive smile. Which pissed me off. Edward was enjoying his surprise. Damn him.

"Ted, where are your manners. Take her bag," Donna said.

Edward and I both stared at the small carry-on bag I had in my left hand. He gave me Ted's smile, but he said Edward's line, "Anita likes to carry her own weight."

Donna looked at me for confirmation as if this couldn't possibly be true. Maybe she wasn't as strong and independent as she appeared, or maybe she was a decade older than she appeared. A different generation, you know.

"Ted's right," I said, putting a little too much emphasis on his name. "I like to carry my own bags."

Donna looked like she'd have liked to correct my obviously wrong thinking but was too polite to say it out loud. The expression, not the silence, reminded me of my stepmother Judith. Which made me push Donna's age over fifty. She was either a mightily well preserved fifty-something, forty-something, or a sun-aged thirty-something. I just couldn't tell.

They walked ahead of me through the airport, arm in arm. I followed behind them, not because my suitcase was too heavy but because I needed a few minutes to recover. I watched Donna bump her head against Edward's shoulder, her face turning to him, smiling, glowing. Edward/Ted bent over her, face tender, whispering something that made her laugh.

I was going to be sick. What the hell was Edward doing with this woman? Was she another assassin, as good an actor as he was? Somehow I didn't think so. And if she was exactly what she appeared—a woman in love with Ted Forrester, who didn't exist—I was going to kick Edward's metaphorical ass. How dare he involve some innocent woman in his cover story! Or—and this was a very strange thought—was Edward/Ted really in love? If you'd asked me ten minutes ago, I'd have said he wasn't capable of such depth of emotion, but now . . . now I was just plain confused.

The Albuquerque airport broke my rule that all airports look nearly identical and you can't really tell what part of the country, or even the world, that you're in just from the airport. If there are decorations, they're usually from a different culture entirely, like inland bars having seaside motifs. But not here. Here there were hints of a southwestern flavor everywhere. Multi-colored tile or paint leaning to turquoise and cobalt blue lined most of the shops and store fronts. A small covered stand sold silver jewelry in the middle of the large hallway leading from the gates to the rest of the airport. We'd left the crowd behind and with it the noise. We moved in a world of nearly ringing silence, heightened by the white-white walls and the large windows on either side. Albuquerque stretched outside those windows like some great flat plain with a ring of black mountains at the edge, like the backdrop to a play, somehow unreal. The heat pressed down even through the air conditioning, not really hot, but letting you know it was going to be. The landscape was totally alien, adding to my sense of having been cut adrift. One of the things I liked about Edward is that he never changed. He was what he was, and now Edward, dependable in his own psychotic way, had thrown me a curve ball so wild I didn't even know how to swing at it.

Donna stopped and turned, drawing Edward with her. "Anita, that bag is just too heavy for you. Please let Ted carry it." She gave him a little good-natured push in my direction.

Edward walked towards me. Even his walk was a rolling sort of gait like someone who spent a lot of time on horseback or on a boat. He kept Ted's smile on his face. Only his eyes slipped and showed through the mask. Dead those eyes, empty. No love shone in them. Damn him. He actually leaned over, his hand started to close over mine and the handle.

I hissed, "Don't." I let that one word hold all the anger I was feeling.

His eyes widened just a bit, and he knew I wasn't talking about just the carry-on bag. He straightened up and called back to Donna, "She doesn't want my help." He put emphasis on the "my."

She tsked under her breath and walked back to us. "You're just being stubborn, Anita. Let Ted help you."

I looked up at her and knew my face wasn't neutral, but I couldn't drain all the anger out of my face.

Donna's eyes widened just a bit. "Have I offended you in some way?" she asked.

I shook my head. "I'm not upset with you."

She looked at Edward. "Ted, dear, I think she's angry with you."

"I think you're right," Edward said. His eyes had gone back to sparkling with love and good humor.

I tried to salvage the situation. "It's just that Ted should have told me about the engagement. I don't like surprises."

Donna put her head to one side, giving me a long considering look. She started to say something, then seemed to think better of it. "Well, I'll try and make sure you don't get any more surprises from me." She settled herself a little more securely on Edward's arm, and the look in her brown eyes was just a tad less friendly than it had been before.

I realized with a sigh that Donna now thought I was jealous. My reaction wasn't normal for a mere friend and business acquaintance. Since I couldn't tell her the real reason I was upset, I let it go. Better she think Ted and I had been an item once, than the truth. Though Heaven knew she'd probably prefer we'd been lovers to the real truth about her "Ted." She was in love with a man who did not exist, no matter how real the arm she was holding happened to be.

I tightened my grip on my bag and moved up so I was walking on the other side of Donna as we moved up through the airport. She wasn't comfortable with me trailing behind so I'd keep up. I'm not good at small talk at the best of times, but now, I couldn't think of a damn thing to say, so we moved in a silence that grew progressively uncomfortable for me, and for Donna. Her, because she was a woman and naturally friendly. Me, because I knew silence would make her uncomfortable. I didn't want to make her more uncomfortable.

She broke first. "Ted tells me you're an animator and vampire hunter."

"I prefer vampire executioner, but yeah." In a desperate attempt to be polite I asked, "What do you do?"

She flashed me a brilliant smile that showed the smile lines on either side of her mouth like a frame for her thin, oh-so-slightly lipsticked mouth. I was glad I'd worn no makeup. Maybe that would help her realize I wasn't after Edward/Ted. "I own a shop in Santa Fe."

Edward added, "She sells psychic paraphernalia." He gave me a smile over her head.

My face hardened, and I fought to keep it blank. "What sort of paraphernalia?"

"Crystals, tarot decks, books, everything and anything that catches my fancy."

I wanted to say, "But you're not psychic," but I didn't. I'd met people before that were convinced they had psychic gifts when they didn't. If Donna was one of the successfully deluded, who was I to burst her bubble? Instead, I said, "Is there much of a market for that sort of thing in Santa Fe?"

"Oh, there used to be a lot of shops like mine. The new age was really big in Santa Fe, but the property taxes have skyrocketed and most of the new psychics have moved further into the mountains to Taos. Santa Fe's energy has changed in the last five years, or so. It's still a very positive place, but Taos has better energy now. I'm not sure why."

She talked about "energy" like it was an accepted fact, and didn't try to explain it, as if I would understand her. She was assuming, like so many people did, that if you raised the dead for a living you were psychic in other areas, too. Which was often true, but not always. What she called "'energy," I called the "feel" of a place. Some places did have a "feel" to them, good or bad, energizing or draining. The old idea of *genius loci* was alive and well in the new age movement under a different name.

"Do you read cards?" I asked. It was a polite way of finding out if she believed she had powers.

"Oh, no," Donna said. "My gifts are very small. I'd love to be able to read cards or crystals, but I'm only a proprietor. My talent in this life is helping others discover their strengths."

It sounded like something a therapist who believed in past lives would have said. I'd been meeting enough of them at graveside to know the lingo. "So you're not a psychic," I said. I just wanted to be sure she knew it.

"Oh, heavens no." She shook her head for emphasis, and I noticed her small gold earrings were ankhs.

"Most people that go into the business usually are," I said.

She sighed. "The psychic I'm going to now says that I'm blocked in this life because of misuse of my gifts last time around. She says I'll be able to work magic next time."

Again, she assumed I believed in reincarnation and past life therapy, probably because of what I did for a living. Either that or Edward/Ted had been lying to her about me just to amuse himself. But I didn't point out that I was a Christian and didn't believe in reincarnation. There are, after all, more religions on the planet that believe in reincarnation than ones that don't. Who am I to quibble?

I just couldn't help the next question. "And have you met Ted before in a past life?"

"No, actually he's brand new to me, though Brenda says he is a very old soul."

"Brenda, your psychic?" I asked.

She nodded.

"I'll agree with the old soul part," I said.

Edward gave me a look over her head where she couldn't see him. It was a suspicious look.

"You've felt it, too, then, the way he resonates. That's what Brenda calls it, like a great heavy bell in her head whenever he's around."

Alarm bells more likely, I thought. Aloud I said, "Sometimes you can make your soul heavy in one lifetime."

She gave me a puzzled look. She wasn't stupid. There was intelligence in those brown eyes, but she was naive. Donna wanted to believe. It made her an easy mark for a certain kind of liar like would-be psychics and men like Edward. Men who lied about who and what they were.

"I'd like to meet Brenda before I go home," I said.

Edward's eyes widened where she couldn't see them.

Donna smiled delightedly. "I'd love to introduce the two of you. She's never met an animator before. I know she'd get a kick out of meeting you."

"I'll bet," I said. I did want to meet Brenda, because I wanted to see if she was truly a psychic or just a charlatan. If she was professing to abilities she didn't possess, it was a crime, and I'd turn her in. I hated seeing supposed psychics take advantage of people. It was always amazing to me with the number of genuine talents around, how many fakes still managed to prosper.

We were passing a restaurant decorated in more blue and fuschia tiles with small daisy-like flowers painted in the edges. There was a mural on one wall showing Spanish conquistadors and breechcloth-clad Native Americans as we came down the escalators. I was still managing to balance my carry-on without any trouble, all that weightlifting I guess.

There was a bank of pay phones set to one side. "Let me try to get hold of the kids one more time," Donna said. She kissed Edward's cheek and moved off towards the phones before I could react.

"Kids?" I said.

"Yes," he said, voice careful.

"How many?" I asked.

"Two."

"Ages?"

"Boy, fourteen; girl, six," he said.

"Where's their father?"

"Donna is a widow."

I looked at him, and the look was enough.

"No, I didn't do it. He died years before I met Donna."

I stepped close to him, turning my back so that Donna wouldn't see my face from the phones. "What are you playing at, Edward? She has children and is so in love with you, it makes me gag. What on God's green earth could you be thinking?"

"Donna and Ted have been dating for about two years. They're lovers. She expected him to propose so he did." His face was still smiling Ted, but the voice was matter of fact and totally unemotional.

"You're talking like Ted's a third person, Edward."

"You're going to have to start calling me Ted, Anita. I know you. If you don't make it a habit, you'll forget."

I stepped into him in the relative silence, lowering my voice to a furious whisper.

"Fuck that. He is you, and you're fucking engaged. Are you going to marry her?"

He gave a small shrug.

"Shit," I said. "You can't. You cannot marry this woman."

His smile widened, and he stepped around me holding his hands out to Donna. He kissed her and asked, "How are the munchkins?" He turned her in his arms so he was half-hugging her, and had her turned away from me. His face was Ted, relaxed, but his eyes were warning me, "Don't screw this up." It was important to him for some reason.

Donna turned so she could see my face, and I fought to give blank face. "What were you two whispering about so urgently?"

"The case," Edward said.

"Oh, pooh," she said.

I raised eyebrows at Edward. Oh, pooh. The most dangerous man I'd ever met was engaged to a mother of two that said things like, "Oh pooh." It was just too weird.

Donna's eyes widened. "Where is your purse? Did you leave it on the plane?"

"I didn't bring one," I said. "I knew I'd have the bag and pockets."

She looked at me as if I'd spoken in tongues. "My god, I wouldn't know what to do without my monstrosity in tow." She pulled the huge purse around in front of her. "I'm such a pack rat."

"Where are your kids?" I asked.

"With my neighbors. They're a retired couple and are just great with my little girl, Becca." She frowned. "Of course, nothing seems to make Peter happy right now." She glanced at me. "Peter's my son. He's fourteen going on forty, and seems to have hit his teenage years with a vengeance. Everyone told me a teenager was hard, but I never dreamed how hard."

"Has he been getting into trouble?" I asked.

"Not really. I mean he's not into anything criminal." She added the last a little too quickly. "But he's just stopped listening to me. He was supposed to come home two weeks ago from school and watch Becca. Instead, he went to a friend's house. When I came home after the shop closed, the house was empty, and I didn't know where either of them were. The Hendersons had been out so Becca wasn't there. God, I was frantic. Another neighbor had taken her in, but if they hadn't been home, she'd have just had to wander the neighborhood for hours. Peter came home and just wasn't sorry. By the time he came home, I'd convinced myself he'd been abducted by someone and was lying dead in a ditch somewhere. Then he just comes strolling in as if nothing's wrong."

"Is he still grounded?" I asked.

She nodded, face very firm. "You bet he is. Grounded for a month, and I've taken every privilege I can think of away from him."

"What does he think of you and Ted getting married?" It was a sadistic question, and I knew it, but I just couldn't help myself.

Donna looked stricken, truly stricken. "He's not too keen on the idea."

Keen? "Well, he's fourteen, and a boy," I said. "He's bound to resent another male coming into his turf."

Donna nodded. "Yes, I'm afraid so."

Ted hugged her. "It'll be all right, honeypot. Pete and I will come to an understanding. Don't you worry."

I didn't like Edward's phrasing on that. I watched his face but couldn't see anything behind his Ted mask. It was as if for minutes at a time he just vanished into his alter ego. I hadn't been on the ground an hour and his Jekyll/Hyde act was already beginning to get on my nerves.

"Do you have any other bags?" Edward asked.

"Of course, she does," Donna said. "She's a woman."

Edward gave a small laugh that was more his own than Ted's. It was a small cynical sound that made Donna glance at him and made me feel better.

"Anita isn't like any other woman I've ever met."

Donna gave him another look. Edward had phrased it that way on purpose. He'd caught her jealous reasoning just as I had, and now he was playing to it. It was one way to explain my strange reaction to the engagement news without risk of blowing his cover. I guess I couldn't blame him, but in a way I knew it was payback for my lack of social skills. His cover was important enough to him to let Donna think we'd been a couple, which meant it was pretty important to him.

Edward and I had never had a single romantic thought about each other in our lives.

"I've got luggage," I said.

"See," Donna said, tugging on his arm.

"The carry-on bag wouldn't hold all the guns."

Donna stopped in the middle of saying something to Edward, then turned slowly to stare at me. Edward and I stopped walking because she had stopped. Her eyes were a little wide. She seemed to have caught her breath. She was staring at me, but not at my face. If it had been a guy, I might have accused him of staring at my chest, but that wasn't exactly what she was looking at. I followed her gaze and found that my jacket had slipped back over my left side exposing my gun. It must have happened when I readjusted the bag coming off the escalator. Careless of me. I'm usually pretty careful about exposing my arsenal in public. It tends to make people nervous, just like now. I shifted the bag so that my jacket slid back over the shoulder holster like a curtain dropping back in place.

Donna drew a quick breath, blinked, and looked at my face. "You really do carry a gun." Her voice held a sort of wonderment.

"I told you she did," Edward said in his Ted voice.

"I know, I know," Donna said. She shook her head. "I've just never been around a woman that . . . Do you kill as easily as Ted does?"

It was a very intelligent question, and meant that she'd been paying more attention to the real Edward than I'd given her credit for. So I answered the question truthfully. "No."

Edward hugged her to him, eyes warning me over her head. "Anita doesn't believe shifters are animals. She still thinks the monsters can be saved. It makes her squeamish sometimes."

Donna stared at me. "My husband was killed by a werewolf. He was killed in front of me and Peter. Peter was only eight."

I didn't know what reaction she expected so I didn't give her one. My face was neutral, interested, far from shocked. "What saved you?"

She nodded slowly, understanding the question. A werewolf tore her husband apart in front of her and her son, yet they were still alive and the husband wasn't. Something had interceded, something had saved them.

"John, my husband, had loaded a rifle with silver shot. He'd dropped the gun in the attack. He'd wounded it but not enough." Her eyes had gone distant with remembering. We stood in the bright airport, three people huddled in a small circle of silence and hushed voices and Donna's wide eyes. I didn't have to look at Edward to know that his face was as neutral as mine. She'd fallen silent, the horror still too fresh in her eyes. The look was enough. There was worse to come, or worse to her. Something she felt guilty about at the very least.

"John had just showed Peter how to shoot the week before. He was so little, but I let him take that gun. I let him shoot that monster. I let him stand his ground in the face of that thing, while I just huddled on the floor, frozen."

That was it. That was the true horror for Donna. She'd allowed her child to protect her. Allowed her child to take the adult role of protector in the face of a nightmare. She'd failed the big test, and little Peter had passed into adulthood at a very tender age. No wonder he hated Edward. Peter had earned his right to be man of the house. He'd earned it in blood, and now his mother was going to remarry. Yeah, right.

Donna turned those haunted eyes to me. She blinked and seemed to be drawing herself back from the past as if it were a physical effort. She hadn't made peace with the scene, or it wouldn't have remained so vivid. If you can begin to make peace, you can tell the most horrible stories as if they happened to someone else, unemotional. Or, maybe you haven't made peace, but you still tell it like it was an interesting story that happened a long time ago, nothing important. I've seen cops that had to get drunk before the pain spilled out into their stories.

Donna was hurting. Peter was hurting. Edward wasn't hurting. I looked up at him, past Donna's softly horrified face. His eyes were empty as he looked at me, as waiting and patient as any predator. How dare he step into their lives like this! How dare he cause them more pain! Because whatever happened, whether he married her or didn't, it was going to be painful. Painful for everyone but Edward. Though maybe I could fix that. If he fucked up Donna's life, maybe I could fuck up his. Yeah, I liked that. I'd spread the rain around all over his parade.

It must have shone in my eyes for a second or two, because Edward's eyes narrowed, and for a moment I felt that shiver he could send down my spine with just a glance. He was a very dangerous man, but to protect this family I'd test his limits, and mine. Edward had finally found something that pissed me off enough to maybe press a button that I'd never wanted to touch. He had to leave Donna and her family alone. He had to get out of their lives. I'd see him out of their lives, or else. And there is only one "or else" when you're dealing with Edward. Death.

We stared at each other over Donna's head while he hugged her to his chest, stroking her hair, mouthing soothing words to her. But his eyes, his face were all for me, and I knew as we stared at each other that he knew exactly what I was thinking. He knew the conclusion I'd come to, though he might never understand why his involvement with Donna and her kids was the straw that broke the camel's back. But the look in his eyes was enough. He might not understand why, but he knew the camel was broken in fucking two and there was no way to fix it except to do what I wanted him to do, or die. Just like that, I knew I'd do it. I knew I could look down the barrel of a gun and shoot Edward, and I wouldn't aim to wound. It was like a cold weight inside my body, a surety that made me feel stronger and a little lonelier. Edward had saved my life more than once. I'd saved his more than once. Yet . . . yet . . . I'd miss Edward, but I'd kill him if I had to. Edward wonders why I'm so sympathetic to the monsters. The answer is simple. Because I am one.

3

WE WALKED OUT INTO the heat, and it blasted against our skin on the edge of a hot wind. It had the feel of a serious heat, and considering that it was only May, it probably would be a real barnburner when true summer finally hit. But it is true that eighty plus without humidity isn't nearly as miserable as eighty plus with humidity, so it wasn't horrible. In fact, once you blinked into the sunlight and just got adjusted to the heat, you sort of forgot about it. It was only attention-getting for the first, oh, fifteen minutes or so. St. Louis would probably be ninety plus by the time I got home, and with eighty to a hundred percent humidity. Of course, that meant I'd be going home. If I really drew down on Edward, that was a debatable option. There was a very real possibility that he'd kill me. I hoped, seriously hoped, that I could talk him out of Donna and her family without resorting to violence.

Maybe the heat didn't seem bad because of the landscape. Albuquerque was a flat empty plain running out and out to a circle of black mountains, as if everything of worth had been strip-mined away and the waste had been lumped into those forbidden black mountains like giant mounds of coal. Yeah, it looked like the world's largest strip-mining operation, and it had that feel to it of waste and desolation. Of things spoiled, and an alien hostility as if you weren't quite welcome. I guess Donna would say, bad energy. I'd never felt anyplace that had such an instant alienness to it. Edward was carrying both my suitcases that had come off the carousel. Normally, I'd have carried one, but not now. Now I wanted Edward's hands full of something besides guns. I wanted him at a disadvantage. I wasn't going to start shooting on the way to the car, but Edward is more practical than I am. If he decided I was more danger than help, he might be able to arrange an accident on the way to the car. It'd be tough with Donna in tow, but not impossible. Not for Edward.

It was also why I was letting him lead the way and putting me at his back instead of him at mine. It wasn't paranoia, not with Edward. With Edward it was simply good survival thinking.

Edward got Donna to go ahead of us and unlock the car. He dropped back to walk beside me, and I put some distance between us so that we were standing in the middle of the sidewalk staring at each other like two old-fashioned movie gunfighters.

He kept the suitcases in his hands. I think he knew that I was too keyed up. I think he knew if he dropped the suitcases, I was going to have a gun in my hand. "You want to know why I wasn't bothered with you following behind me?"

"You knew I wouldn't shoot you in the back," I said.

He smiled. "And you knew I might."

I cocked my head to one side, almost squinting into the sun. Edward was wearing sunglasses, of course. But since his eyes rarely gave anything away, it didn't matter. His eyes weren't what I had to worry about.

"You like the personal danger, Edward. That's why you only hunt monsters. You have to be taking the big risk every time you come up to bat, or it's no fun."

A couple came walking by with a cart full of suitcases. We waited in silence until they passed us. The woman glanced at us as they hurried past, picking up on the tension. The man jerked her back to face front and they pushed past us.

"You have a point?" Edward asked.

"You want to know which of us is better, Edward. You've wanted to know for a long time. If you take me from ambush, the question will never be answered and that would bug you."

His smile both widened and faded, as if it wasn't a humorous smile anymore. "So, I won't shoot you in the back."

"That's right," I said.

"So why go to so much trouble to fill my hands and make me walk in front."

"This would be a hell of a time to be wrong."

He laughed then, soft and vaguely sinister. That one sound said it all. He was excited about the idea of going up against me. "I would love to hunt you, Anita. I've dreamed about it." He sighed, and it was almost sad. "But I need you. I need you to help solve this case. And as much as I'd like the big question answered, I'd miss you. You may be one of the only people in the world that I would miss."

"What about Donna?" I asked.

"What about her?" he asked.

"Don't be cute, Edward." I looked past him to find Donna waving to us from the parking lot. "We're being paged."

He glanced back towards her, lifting one of the suitcases to make a vague wave. It would have been easier to do if he'd dropped one of the cases but in his own way, Edward was being cautious, too.

He turned back to me. "You won't be able to do your job if you're looking over your shoulder for me. So a truce until the case is solved."

"Your word?" I asked.

He nodded. "My word."

"Good enough," I said.

He smiled, and it was genuine. "The only reason you can take my word at face value is that if you give your word, you'll keep it."

I shook my head and started closing the distance between us. "I keep my word, but I don't take most people's oaths very seriously." I was even with him and could feel the weight of his gaze even through the black lens of the sunglasses. He was intense, was Edward.

"But you take mine."

"You've never lied to me, Edward, not once you've given your word. You do what you say you'll do, even if it's a bad thing. You don't hide what you are, at least not from me."

We both glanced back at Donna, and started walking side by side toward her as if we'd discussed it. "How the hell did you let it get so far? How could you have let Ted propose?"

He was quiet for so long, I didn't think he'd answer. We walked in silence in the sun-warmed heat. But finally, he did answer, "I don't know. I think one night I just got too caught up in my role. The mood was right and Ted proposed, and I think for just a second I forgot that I'd be the one getting married."

I glanced at him. "You've told me more personal shit in the last half hour than in the entire five years I've known you. Are you always such a jabberbox when you're on Ted's home turf?"

He shook his head. "I knew you wouldn't like Donna being involved. I didn't know how strongly you'd react, but I knew you wouldn't like it. Which meant to keep the peace I had to be willing to talk about it. I knew that when I called you."

We stepped off the curb, both of us smiling and me waving to Donna. I said through the smile like a ventriloquist, "How can we know each other this well, and would miss each other if we died, yet still be willing to pull the trigger? I know it's the truth, but I don't understand it."

"Isn't it enough to know it's true? Do you have to explain it?" he asked as we wove through the cars toward Donna.

"Yes, I need to explain it."

"Why?" he asked.

"Because I'm a girl," I said.

That made him laugh, a surprise burst of sound, and it made my heart ache because I could count on one hand the number of times I'd heard Edward surprised into laughter. I valued the sound of that particular laugh because it was like an old sound from a younger, more innocent Edward. I wondered if I was the only one that could force that laugh from him. How could we be talking calmly about killing each other? No, it wasn't enough to know we could do it. There had to be a why to it, and saying we were both monsters or sociopaths wasn't enough explanation. At least not for me.

Donna looked at me rather narrowly as we walked up. She made a big show of kissing him and when he sat the suitcases down and had his hands free, she put on an even better show. They kissed, hugged, and body-pressed like a couple of teenagers. If Edward was in any way reluctant, it didn't show. In fact, he slipped off his hat and melded into her like he was happy to be there.

I stood, leaning against the side of the car close enough to touch them. If they wanted privacy, they could get a room. It went on long enough that I wondered if checking my watch would be hint enough, but resisted the urge. I decided that leaning against the car, arms crossed over my stomach, looking bored might be hint enough.

Edward drew back with a sigh. "After last night, I wouldn't think you'd be missing me this much."

"I always miss you," she said in a voice halfway between sultry and a giggle. Donna gazed at me, hands still encircling him, very possessive. She looked right at me and said, "Sorry, didn't mean to embarrass you."

I pushed away from the car. "I don't embarrass that easy."

The happy light in her eyes turned to something fierce and protective. The look and her next words were not friendly. "And just what would it take to embarrass you?"

I shook my head. "Is this my cue to say, a lot more than you've got?"

She stiffened.

"Don't worry, Donna. I am not now, nor have I ever been interested in . . . Ted in a romantic way."

"I never thought . . ." she started to say.

"Save it," I said. "Let's try something really unique. Let's be honest. You were worried about me with Edward," I changed it very quickly to, "Ted, which was why you did the teeny-bopper makeout session. You don't need to mark your territory for my sake, Donna." The last was said in something of a rush because I hoped she hadn't noticed my slip on the names, but of course she had, and I knew Edward had. "Ted's too much like me to ever consider dating. It'd be like incest."

She blushed even through the tan. "My, you are direct."

"She's direct even for a man," Edward said. "For a woman she's like a battering ram."

"It saves time," I said.

"That it does," Edward said. He drew Donna into a quick but thorough kiss. "I'll see you tomorrow, honeypot."

I raised eyebrows at that.

Edward looked at me with Ted's warm eyes. "Donna drove her own car in so we could spend part of the day together. Now she's going to drive home to the kiddies, so we can do business." Donna turned from him, giving me a long searching look. "I'm taking you at your word, Anita. I believe you, but I'm also picking up some strange vibes from you like you're hiding something."

I was hiding something, I thought. If she only knew.

Donna continued, face very serious. "I'm trusting you with the third most important person in my life. Ted is right behind my kids for me. Don't screw up the best thing I've had since my husband died."

"See," Edward said, "Donna knows how to be blunt, too."

"That she does," I said.

Donna gave me one last searching look, then turned to Edward. She drew him away towards a car three down from us. They talked quietly together while I waited in the still, dry, heat. Since Donna had tried for privacy, I gave it to them, turning away and gazing off at the distant mountains. They looked very close, but it's always been my experience that mountains are seldom as close as they appear. They're like dreams, distant things to set your sights on, but not truly to be trusted to be there when you need them.

I heard Edward's boots crunch on the pavement before he spoke. I was facing him, arms crossed lightly over my stomach, which put my right hand nicely close to the gun under my arm. I believed Edward when he said we had a truce on, but . . . better cautious than sorry.

He stopped by the car one slot over, leaning his butt against it, arms crossing to mirror me. But he didn't have a gun under his arm. I wasn't sure that a bounty hunter's license was enough to get him through an airport metal detector, so he shouldn't have been able to have a gun or large blade on him. Unless of course he'd picked it up from one of the cars, where he'd hidden it. It would be something that Edward would do. Better to assume the worst and be wrong than assume the best and be wrong. Pessimism will keep you alive, optimism won't, not in our line of business anyway.

Our line of business. Strange phrase. Edward was an assassin. I wasn't. But somehow we were in the same business. I couldn't quite explain it, but it was true.

Edward gave me a pure Edward smile, a smile meant to make me uneasy and suspicious. It also usually meant that he meant me no harm and was just yanking my chain. Of course, he knew I knew what the smile usually meant, so he might use it to lull me into a false sense of security. Or it could mean just what it seemed to. I was overthinking things and that was bad all on its own. Edward was right, I was at my best when I let my gut work and kept my higher functions in the background. Not a recipe for going through life, but a good one for a gunfight.

"We have a truce," I said.

He nodded. "I said, we did."

"You make me nervous," I said.

The smile widened. "Glad to hear you're still scared of me. I was beginning to wonder."

"The day you stop being afraid of the monsters is the day they kill you."

"And I'm a monster?" He made it a question.

"You know exactly what you are, Edward."

His eyes narrowed. "You called me Edward in front of Donna. She didn't say anything, but you are going to have to be more careful."

I nodded. "I'm sorry, I caught it, too. I will try but I'm not half as good a liar as you are. Besides, Ted is a nickname for Edward."

"Not if the full name on my driver's license is Theodore."

"Now, if I can call you Teddy, maybe I'd remember."

"Teddy is fine," he said, voice totally unchanged.

"You are a very hard man to tease, Ed . . . Ted."

"Names don't mean anything, Anita. They're too easy to change."

"Is Edward really your first name?"

"It is now."

I shook my head. "I'd really like to know."

"Why?" He gazed at me from the black sunglasses, and the weight of his interest burned through the glass. The question wasn't idle. Of course, Edward seldom asked any question he didn't want an answer to.

"Because I've known you for five years, and I don't even know if your first name is real."

"It's real enough," he said.

"It bugs me not to know," I said.

"Why?" he asked again.

I shrugged and eased my hand away from my gun because it wasn't necessary, not right this minute, not today. But even as I did it, I knew there would be other days, and for the first time I really wasn't sure that both of us would see the end of my little visit. It made me sad and grumpy.

"Maybe I just want to know what name to put on the tombstone," I said.

He laughed. "Confidence is a fine trait. Overconfidence isn't." The laughter faded and left his face around the glasses cool and unreadable. I didn't have to see his eyes to know they were cold and distant as winter skies.

I pushed away from the car, hands empty at my sides. "Look, Edward, Ted, whatever the hell you call yourself, I don't like being invited here to play monster bait, and find you dating the new age mom of the year. It's thrown me, and I don't like that either. We have a truce until the case is solved, then what?"

"Then we'll see," he said.

"You couldn't just agree to stop being engaged to Donna?"

"No." His voice was small, careful.

"Why not?" I asked.

"I'd need to give her a good enough reason to break her heart and the kids'. Remember, I've been spending a lot of time with the kids. How would it look to just vanish on them?"

"I think her son wouldn't mind. Peter, wasn't it? I think he'd love it if Ted would vanish."

Edward turned his head to one side. "Yeah, Peter would love it, but what about Becca? I've been in her life for over two years and she's only six. Donna trusts me to pick her up after school. I drive her once a week to dance lessons so Donna doesn't have to close the shop early." His voice and face never changed as he spoke, as if it was just facts and meant nothing.

Anger tightened my shoulders and traveled down my arms. I put my hands in fists just to have something to do with my body. "You bastard."

"Maybe," he said, "but be careful what you ask me to do, Anita. Just walking out could do more damage than the truth."

I stared at him, trying to see behind that blank face. "Have you thought about telling Donna the truth?"

"No."

"Damn you."

"Do you really think she could handle the truth, the entire truth about me?" he asked.

I thought about that for nearly a full minute while we stood in the heat-soaked parking lot. Finally, I said, "No." I didn't like saying it, but truth was truth.

"You're sure she couldn't play wife to an assassin? I mean you've only met her for half an hour. How can you be so sure?"

"Now you're teasing me," I said.

His lips twitched almost a smile. "I think you are exactly right. I don't think Donna could handle the truth."

I shook my head, hard enough that my hair lashed my face. I literally threw my hands in the air. "Fuck it, for now. I didn't get on a plane at a moment's notice to stand in the heat and discuss your love life. Don't we have a crime to solve or something?"

"We could discuss your love life," he said. "Werewolf or vampire, which are you fucking now?" There was something close to bitterness in his voice. It wasn't jealousy, but utter disapproval. You killed the monsters. You did not date them. It was one of Edward's rules, and used to be one of mine. Just another example of my moral downfall.

"Neither, actually, and that is all I'm going to say on the subject."

He lowered his sunglasses enough so I could see his pale blue eyes. "You dumped them both?" He actually sounded interested.

I shook my head. "If I feel like sharing, I'll let you know. Now tell me what the hell you've dragged me into besides your sordid love life. Tell me about the murders, Edward. Tell me why I'm really here."

He slipped the glasses back over his eyes and gave a small nod. "Okay." He opened the driver's side door and left me to let myself into the passenger side. He'd held Donna's door for her, but that wasn't the kind of relationship Edward and I had. If we might have to start shooting each other, I'd get my own doors.

4

THE CAR BELONGED to Ted, even though Edward was driving it. It was a square and big something between a Jeep, a truck, and an ugly car. It was covered in red clay mud as if he'd been driving through ditches. The windshield was so dirty only two fans of clear space remained where the windshield wipers had washed away the mud, everything else had dried to a reddish-brown patina of dirt.

"Gee, Edward," I said, as he opened the back hatch, "what have you been doing to this poor whatever it is. I've never seen a car so dirty."

"This is a Hummer, and cost more than most people's houses." He raised the hatch and started putting my bags inside. I offered him my carry-on, and when I was close could smell that new car smell, which explained why the carpeting in back was still nearly pristine.

"If it costs that much, then why doesn't it rate better care?" I asked.

He took the carry-on and put it on the new carpet. "I bought it because it could go over almost any terrain in almost any weather. If I didn't want it to get dirty, I'd have bought something else." He slammed the hatch shut.

"How can Ted afford something like this?"

"Actually, Ted makes a fine living off varmint hunting."

"Not this good," I said, "not off of bounty hunting."

"How do you know what a bounty hunter makes?" he asked, peering around the filthy car at me.

He had a point. "I guess I don't."

"Most people don't know what a bounty hunter makes so I can get away with some purchases that might be out of Ted's price range." He walked around the car toward the driver's side, only the top of his white hat showing above the mud-caked roof.

I tried the passenger side door, and it opened. It took a little bit of work to climb into the seat, and I was glad I wasn't wearing a skirt. One nice thing about working with Edward was that he wouldn't expect me to wear business attire. It was jeans and Nikes for this trip.

The only business thing I was wearing was the black jacket slung over my cotton shirt and jeans. The jacket was to hide the gun, nothing more. "What are the gun laws like in New Mexico?"

Edward started the car and glanced at me. "Why?"

I put on my seatbelt. Evidently, we were in a hurry. "I want to know if I can ditch the jacket and wear my gun naked, or whether I'm going to have to hide the gun for the entire trip."

His lips twitched. "New Mexico lets you carry as long as it's not concealed. Concealed carry without a permit is illegal."

"Let me test my understanding, I can wear the gun in full view of everyone with or without a carry permit, but if I put a jacket over it, concealing it, and don't have a carry permit, it's illegal?"

The twitch turned into a smile. "That's right."

"Western state gun laws are always so interesting," I said, but I started sliding out of the jacket. You can wiggle out of almost anything while remaining seatbelted in a car. Since I always wear a seatbelt, I'd had a lot of practice.

"But the police may still stop you if they see you walking around armed. Just make sure you're not here to kill anybody." He half smiled when he said the last.

"So I can carry as long as it's not concealed, but not really, not without getting questioned by the police."

"And you can't carry a gun of any kind, even unloaded, into a bar."

"I don't drink. I think I can avoid the bars."

A wire fence edged the road he pulled onto, but did nothing to take away the flat, flat distances and the strange black mountains. "What are the mountains called?"

"Sangre del Cristo—the blood of Christ," he said. I looked at him to see if he was kidding. Of course, he wasn't. "Why?"

"Why what?"

"Why call them the blood of Christ?"

"I don't know."

"How long has Ted lived out here?"

"Almost four years," he said.

"And you don't know why the mountains are named Sangre del Christo? Do you have no curiosity?"

"Not about things that don't affect the job."

He didn't say, a job, but the job. I thought it was odd phrasing. "What if this monster that we're hunting is some kind of local bugaboo? Knowing why the mountains are named what they're named may mean nothing, or it may have to do with a legend, a story, a hint about some great blood bath in the past. There are very localized monsters, Edward, things that only come above ground every century or so like really long-lived cicadas."

"Cicadas?" he asked.

"Yeah, cicadas. The immature form stays in the ground until every thirteen or seven or whatever their cycle is years, they climb out, molt, and become adults. They're the insects that make all that noise in the summer time."

"Whatever did those people wasn't a giant cicada, Anita."

"That's not the point, Edward. My point is that there are types of living creatures that stay hidden, almost totally hidden, for years, then resurface. Monsters are still a part of the natural world. Preternatural biology is still biology. So maybe old myths and legends would give us a clue."

"I didn't bring you down here to play Nancy Drew," he said.

"Yes, you did," I said.

He looked at me long enough to make me want to tell him to watch the road. "What are you talking about?"

"If you just wanted someone to point and shoot, you'd have brought in someone else. You want my expertise, not just my gun. Right?"

He'd turned back to the road, much to my relief. There were small houses on either side, most of them made of adobe, or faux-adobe. I didn't know enough about it to judge. The yards were small but well-tended, running high to cacti and huge lilac bushes with surprisingly small bundles of pale lavender flowers on them. It looked like a different variety from the lilacs in the Midwest. Maybe it took less water.

Silence had filled the car and I let it, watching the scenery. I'd never been to Albuquerque, and I'd play tourist while I could. Edward finally answered me when he turned onto Lomos Street. "You're right. I didn't ask you down here just to shoot things. I already have backup for that."

"Who?" I asked.

"You don't know them, but you'll meet them in Santa Fe."

"We're driving straight to Santa Fe now? I haven't eaten yet today. I was sort of hoping to catch some lunch."

"The latest crime scene is in Albuquerque. We'll catch it, then lunch."

"Will I feel like eating afterwards?"

"Maybe."

"I don't suppose I could talk you into lunch first then."

"We've got a stop before we hit the house," he said.

"What other stop?" I asked.

He just gave that small smile, which meant it was going to be a surprise. Edward loved to try my patience.

Maybe he'd answer a different question. "Who's your other backup?"

"I told you, you don't know them."

"You keep saying them. Are you saying that you already have two people for backup, and you still needed to call me in, too?"

He didn't say anything to that.

"Three people backing you on this. Geez, Edward, you must be desperate." I'd meant for it to be a joke, sort of. He didn't take it that way.

"I want this case solved, Anita, whatever it takes." He looked grim when he said it. So much for my sense of humor.

"Do these two backups owe you a favor?"

"One does."

"Are they assassins?"

"Sometimes."

"Bounty hunters like Ted?"

"Bernardo is."

At least I had a name. "Bernardo is a sometimes assassin and a bounty hunter like Ted. You mean he uses his bounty hunting identity like you use yours as a legal identity?"

"Sometimes he's a bodyguard, too."

"A man of many talents," I said.

"Not really," he said. Which was a strange thing to say.

"What about the other guy?"

"Olaf."

"Olaf, okay. He's sometimes an assassin, not a bounty hunter, not a bodyguard, and what else?"

Edward shook his head.

His noncommittal answers were beginning to get on my nerves. "Do either of them have any other special abilities besides being willing to kill?"

"Yes."

He'd reached my limit on "yes, no" answers. "I didn't come down here to play twenty questions, Edward. Just tell me about the other backups."

"You'll meet them soon enough."

"Fine, then tell me where the other stop is."

He gave a small shake of his head.

"Look, Edward, you're getting on my nerves, and you've already pissed me off, so cut the mysterious crap, and talk to me."

He glanced sideways at me, a glimpse of eyes from the edges of the dark glasses. "My, my, aren't we touchy today."

"This isn't even close to touchy for me, Edward, and you know it. But keep up the noncommittal crap and you are going to truly piss me off."

"I thought you were already pissed off about Donna."

"I am," I said. "But I'm willing to get interested in the case and forget to be continuously pissed. But I can't get interested in the case if you don't answer questions about it. As far as I'm concerned your backup is part of the case, so either start sharing info or drive me back to the damn airport."

"I didn't tell Olaf and Bernardo you're shacking up with a vampire and a werewolf."

"Actually, I'm not dating either of them anymore, but that's not the point. I don't want to know about their sex life, Edward. I just want to know why you called them in. What are their areas of expertise?"

"You broke up with Jean-Claude and Richard both?" For one of the few times since I'd met him I heard real curiosity in his voice. I wasn't sure if it was nice to know or disturbing that my personal life interested Edward.

"I don't know if we broke up, it's more like we aren't seeing each other. I need some time away from them before I decide what to do."

"What are you thinking about doing to them?" And there was a note of eagerness now.

Edward was only eager about one thing. "I am not planning to kill either of them, if that's what you're hinting at."

"I can't say I'm not disappointed," Edward said. "I think you should have killed Jean-Claude yourself before it all got too deep."

"You're talking about killing someone who has been my lover off and on for over a year, Edward. Maybe you could strangle Donna in her bed, but I'd lose sleep over something like that."

"Do you love him?"

The question stopped me, not because of the question but because of who was asking it. It seemed a truly odd question coming from Edward. "Yeah, I think I do."

"Do you love Richard?"

Again, it seemed odd talking about my emotional life with Edward. I have a few male friends, and most of them would rather have a root canal than to talk about "feelings." Of all my male friends I was talking to the one I thought would never discuss love with me. It just wasn't my year for understanding men.

"Yes, I love Richard."

"You say, you think you love the vampire, but you simply answer yes about Richard. Kill the vampire, Anita. I'll help you do it."

"Not to put too fine a point on it, Edward, but I'm Jean-Claude's human servant. Richard is his animal to call. The three of us are bound by vampire marks into a nice little ménage à trois. If one of us dies, we may all die."

"Maybe, or maybe that's what the vampire tells you. It wouldn't be the first time he's lied to you."

It was impossible to argue without looking like a fool, so I didn't try. "When I want your advice on my personal life, I'll ask for it. Until people start ice skating in hell, save your breath. Now, tell me about the case."

"You get to tell me who to date and who not to, but I can't return the favor?" he asked.

I looked at him. "Are you angry with me about my stand on Donna?"

"Not exactly, but if you get to give me advice on dating, why can't I return the favor?"

"It's not the same thing, Edward. Richard doesn't have kids."

"Children make that big a difference to you?" he asked.

I nodded. "Yeah, they do."

"I never figured you as the maternal type."

"I'm not, but kids are people, Edward, little people trapped by the choices the adults around them make. Donna's old enough to make her own mistakes, but when you screw her, you're screwing her kids, too. I know that doesn't bother you, but it bothers me."

"I knew it would. I even knew how you'd react, but I don't know why."

"Well, you're one ahead of me. I never dreamed you were boffing new age widows with munchkins. I figured you more for the pay as you go plan."

"Ted doesn't pay for it," he said.

"How about Edward?"

He shrugged. "It's like eating, just another need."

The cold bluntness of it was actually reassuring. "See, that's the Edward I've grown to know and be afraid of."

"You're afraid of me, but yet you'd come against me for a woman you just met and two kids you don't even know. I'm not even planning to kill any of them and yet you'd push the ultimate question between us." He shook his head. "I don't understand that."

"Don't understand it, Edward. Just know it's true."

"I believe you, Anita. You're the only person I know, except for me, that never bluffs."

"Bernardo and Olaf bluff?" I gave it that extra little lilt, making it a question.

He shook his head and laughed. The tension that had been building eased with that laugh. "No, I'm not giving you anything on them."

"Why?" I asked.

"Because," he said, and he almost smiled.

I looked at his careful profile. "You're enjoying this. You're enjoying Olaf and Bernardo meeting me." I didn't try and keep the surprise out of my voice.

"Just like I enjoyed you meeting Donna."

"Even though you knew I'd be pissed," I said.

He nodded. "The look on your face was almost worth a death threat."

I shook my head. "You're beginning to worry me, Edward."

"Just beginning to worry you? I must be losing my touch."

"Fine, don't tell me about them. Tell me about the case."

He pulled into a parking lot. I looked up to find a hospital looming over us. "Is this the crime scene?"

"No." He pulled into a parking spot, and shut the engine off.

"What gives, Edward? Why are we at a hospital?"

"The survivors are here."

My eyes widened. "What survivors?"

He looked at me. "The survivors from the attacks." He opened his door, and I grabbed his arm, holding him in the car.

Edward turned slowly and looked at my hand on the bare skin of his arm. He looked at my hand a long time with his disapproval at the touch radiating from him, but it was a trick I'd pulled myself more than once. If the person makes it known that they don't want to be touched, most people that don't mean you violence will back off. I didn't back off. I dug my fingers into his skin, not to hurt, just to let him know he wasn't getting rid of me that easily.

"Talk to me, Edward. What survivors?"

He shifted his gaze from my hand to my face. I had an urge to snatch the sunglasses from his face but fought it. His eyes wouldn't show me anything anyway.

"I told you there were injured people." His voice was mild.

"No, you didn't. You made it sound like there were no survivors."

"My oversight," he said.

"My ass," I said. "I know you enjoy being mysterious, Edward, but it's getting tedious."

"Let go of my arm." He said it the way you'd say, hello, or nice day, no inflection at all.

"Will you answer my questions if I do?"

"No," he said, still with that same pleasant empty voice. "But if you make this a pissing contest, Anita, I'll feel compelled to make you let go. You wouldn't like that."

The voice never changed. There was even a slight smile to his mouth. But I let go, slowly, drawing back into my seat. If Edward said I wouldn't like it, I believed him.

"Talk to me, Edward."

He gave me a big ol' smile. "Call me Ted." Then the son of a bitch got out of the car. I sat in the car, watching him walk across the parking lot. He stopped at the edge with the hospital just across a small road from him. He took off the sunglasses, slipped one of the ear pieces into his shirt front, and stared back at the car, waiting.

It would serve him right if I didn't get out. It would serve him right if I went back to St. Louis and let him clean up his own mess. But I opened the door and got out. Why, you might ask. One, he'd asked me for a favor, and being Edward he'd reveal all in his own sadistic time. Two, I wanted to know. I wanted to know what had finally cut through all that coldness and scared him. I wanted to know. Curiosity is both a strength and a weakness. Which one this particular curiosity was wouldn't be answered for a while. I was betting on weakness.

5

SAINT LUCIA HOSPITAL was big and one of the few buildings of any size in Albuquerque that I'd seen that didn't have a southwest theme to it. It was just big and blocky, generic hospital. Maybe they didn't expect the tourists to see the hospital. Lucky tourists.

As hospitals go, it was nice, but it was still a hospital. A place I only go when things have gone wrong. The only up side this time was that it wasn't me or anyone I knew in the rooms.

We were in a long pale corridor with lots of closed doors, but there was a uniformed police officer in front of one of them. Call it a hunch, but I figured that was our room.

Edward walked up to the policeman and introduced himself. He was at his good ol' boy best, harmless and jovial, in a subdued hospital sort of way. They knew each other on sight which should have sped things up considerably.

The uniform looked past Edward to me. He looked young, but his eyes were cool and gray, cop eyes. You have to be on the job a while before your eyes go empty. But he looked at me too long and too intently. You could almost feel the testosterone rising to the surface. The challenging look said that either he was insecure in his own masculinity, his own copness, or that he hadn't been on the job all that long. Not a rookie, but not much beyond it either.

If he expected me to squirm under the scrutiny, he was going to be disappointed. I faced him, smiling, calm, eyes blank and close to bored. Passing inspection had never been my favorite thing.

He blinked first. "The lieutenant is inside. He wants to see her before she goes inside."

"Why?" Edward asked, voice still likable.

The officer shrugged. "I'm just following orders, Mr. Forrester. I don't question my lieutenant. Wait here." He opened the door and slipped inside without giving much of a glimpse inside. He shut the door behind him, not waiting for the weight and hinges to do it for him.

Edward was frowning. "I don't know what's going on."

"I do," I said.

He looked at me, raising an eyebrow, as if to say, go ahead.

"I'm a girl and technically a civilian. A lot of cops don't trust me to do the job."

"I vouched for you."

"Gee, Ed . . . Ted, I guess your opinion doesn't carry as much weight as you thought it did."

He was still frowning at me with Edward's eyes when the door swung open. I was watching his face as he transformed into Ted. The eyes sparkled, the lips curved, the entire set of his face remade itself, as if it were a mask. His own personality vanished like magic. Watching the show this up close and personal made me shiver just a bit. The ease with which he switched back and forth was just plain creepy.

The man in the doorway was short, not many inches above me, maybe five foot six at best. I wondered if their police force didn't have a height requirement. His hair was a golden sun-streaked blond cut very short and close to his square-jawed face. He was tanned a nice soft gold, as if it were as dark a tan as his pale skin were capable of. First Donna, now the lieutenant. Didn't anyone sweat skin cancer here? He looked at me with green-gold eyes, the color of new spring leaves. They were beautiful eyes with long golden lashes and softened his face to an almost feminine appearance. Only the masculine jut of the jaw saved him from being one of those men who is beautiful instead of handsome. The jaw both ruined his face and saved it from perfection.

The eyes may have been lovely, but they weren't friendly. It wasn't even the coolness of cop eyes. It was hostile. Since I'd never met him before, it had to be the fact that I was a woman, a civilian, and/or an animator. He was either a chauvinist or superstitious. I wasn't sure which I preferred.

He let me have a nice long dose of glaring. I just gave blank face, waiting for him to get tired of it. I could stand there all day and be peacefully blank. Standing in a nice safe hospital corridor wasn't even close to the worst thing I'd had to do lately. It was always sort of peaceful when no one was trying to kill me.

Edward tried to break the stalemate. "Lieutenant Marks, this is Anita Blake. Chief Appleton called you about her." He was still using Ted's happy voice, but there was a set to his shoulders that was stiff and not so happy.

"You're Anita Blake." Lieutenant Marks managed to sound doubtful.

I nodded. "Yep."

His eyes narrowed. "I don't like civilians messing in my case." He jerked a thumb at Edward. "Forrester here has proven himself valuable." He pointed a finger at me. "You haven't."

Edward started to say something, but Marks cut him off with a sharp movement of his hand. "No, let her answer for herself."

"I'll answer a question if you'll ask one," I said.

"What's that supposed to mean?"

"It means you haven't asked a question yet, Lieutenant. You've just made statements."

"I don't need shit from some fucking zombie queen."

Ah, he was prejudiced. One mystery solved. "I was invited down here, Lieutenant Marks. I was invited to help you solve this case. Now if you don't want my help, fine, but I'll need someone from the city government to explain to my boss why the hell I got on a plane to New Mexico when I wasn't sure of my welcome."

"I don't treat you right and you run to powers that be, is that it?"

I shook my head. "Who got your panties in a twist, Marks?"

He frowned. "What?'

"Do I remind you of your ex-wife?'

"I'm married to my only wife." He sounded indignant.

"Congratulations. Is it the voodoo that I use to raise the dead? Are you nervous around the mystical arts?"

"I don't like black magic." He fingered the cross-shaped tie tack that was standard police issue almost everywhere, but somehow I thought Marks was serious about it.

"I don't do black magic, Marks." I drew on the silver chain around my neck until the crucifix spilled into the light. "I'm Christian, Episcopalian actually. I don't know what you've heard about what I do, but it's not evil."

"You would say that," he said.

"The state of my immortal soul is between God and myself, Lieutenant Marks. Judge not lest ye be judged yourself. Or do you skip that part and just keep the parts you like?"

His face darkened, and a vein in his forehead started to pulse. This level of anger, even if he was a right-winger Christian extremist, was over the top. "What in hell is behind that door to have you both so spooked?" I asked.

Marks blinked at me. "I am not spooked."

I shrugged. "Yeah, you are. You're all bent out of shape about the survivors and you're taking it out on me."

"You don't know me," he said.

"No, but I know a lot of policemen, and I know when someone's scared."

He stepped close enough to me that if it had been a fight, I'd have stepped back, put space between us. Instead, I stood my ground. I wasn't really expecting the lieutenant to take a swing at me.

"You think you're so fucking tough?"

I blinked at him, close enough that if I'd risen on tiptoe, I could have kissed him. "I don't think, Lieutenant. I know."

He smiled at that, but not like he was happy. "You think you can take it, be my guest." He stepped to one side, making a sweeping motion towards the door.

I wanted to ask what was behind the door. What could possibly be so horrible that it had Edward and a police lieutenant this shaken? I stared at the closed door, smooth, hiding all its secrets.

"What are you waiting for, Ms. Blake? Go ahead. Open the door."

I glanced back at Edward. "I don't suppose you'd give me a hint."

"Open the door, Anita."

I muttered, "Bastard," under my breath and opened the door.

6

THE DOOR DIDN'T LEAD directly into the room. It led into a small antechamber with another sealed, mostly glass door beyond. There was a hush of air circulating through the room as if the room had its own separate air supply. A man stood to one side wearing green surgical scrubs complete with little plastic booties over his feet, a mask hanging loose from his neck. He was tall and slender without looking weak. He was also one of the first New Mexicans that I'd met without a tan. He handed me a pile of scrubs. "Put this on."

I took the clothes. "Are you the doctor on this case?"

"No, I'm a nurse."

"You got a name?"

He gave a small smile. "Ben, I'm Ben."

"Thanks, Ben. I'm Anita. Why do I need the scrubs?"

"To guard against infection."

I didn't argue with him. My expertise was more in the line of taking lives, not preserving them. I'd bow to the experts. I put the scrubs over my jeans, tying the string tie as tight as it would go. The legs of the pants still bagged around my feet.

Ben the nurse was smiling. "We weren't expecting them to send us a policeman so . . . petite."

I frowned at him. "Smile when you say that."

His smile brightened a flash of white teeth. The smile softened the face and made him seem less like Nurse Cratchet and more like a human being.

"And I'm not a cop."

His eyes flicked to the gun in it's shoulder holster. The gun was very black and very noticeable against the red shirt. "You're carrying a gun."

I slipped a short-sleeved shirt over my head, and the offending gun. "New Mexico law says I can carry as long as it's not concealed."

"If you're not a policeman, then why do you need the gun?"

"I'm a vampire executioner."

He held a long-sleeved gown out towards me. I slipped my arms through the sleeves. It tied in the back like most hospital gowns. Ben tied it for me. "I thought you couldn't kill a vampire with bullets."

"Silver bullets can slow them down, and if they're not too old or too powerful, blowing a hole in their brain or heart works. Sometimes," I added. Wouldn't want Ben to get the wrong idea and try to take out an intruding vamp with silver ammo and get munched because he trusted my opinion.

We had some trouble getting my hair up under the little plastic hair thing but finally managed it, though the thin ridge of elastic that held it in place scraped the back of my neck every time I moved my head. Ben tried to help me with the surgical gloves, but I put them on myself, no problem.

He raised eyebrows at me. "You've put on gloves before." It wasn't a question.

"I wear them at crime scenes and when I don't want blood under my fingernails."

He helped me tie the mask around my neck. "You must see a lot of blood in your line of work."

"Not as much blood as you see, I bet." I turned with the mask over my mouth and nose. Only my eyes were left uncovered and real. Ben looked down at me, and his face looked thoughtful. "I'm not a surgical nurse."

"What is your specialty?" I asked.

"Burn unit."

My eyes widened. "Are the survivors burned?"

He shook his head. "No, but their bodies are still like open wounds, just like a burn. The protocol is similar."

"What do you mean their bodies are an open wound?"

Someone tapped on the glass behind me, and I jumped, turning to see another man in an outfit just like mine glaring at me with pale eyes. He hit an intercom button, and his voice came clear enough to hear the irritation in it. "If you're coming inside, then do it. I want to sedate them again, and I can't do that until you've had a chance to question them, or so I'm told." He let go of the button and walked further away behind a white curtain that hid the rest of the room from view.

"Gee, I'm just on everybody's happy list today."

Ben put on his mask and said, "Don't take it personally. Doctor Evans is good at what he does, one of the best."

If you want to find a good doctor in a hospital, don't ask other doctors or referral services. Ask a nurse. Nurses always know who's good and who's not. They may not say the bad stuff aloud, but if they say something good about a doctor, you can take it to the bank.

Ben touched something on the wall that was a little too big to be called a button, and the doors whooshed open with a sound like an air lock opening. I stepped inside, and the doors hushed closed behind me. Nothing but the white curtain now.

I didn't want to pull that curtain aside. Everyone was too damned upset. It was going to be bad. Their bodies were like open wounds, Ben had said, but not a burn. What had happened to them? As the old saying goes, only one way to find out. I took a deep breath and pushed the curtain aside.

The room beyond was white and antiseptic looking, a very hospital of a hospital room. Outside this room there had been some attempt at pastels and a pretense that it was just a building, just hallways, just ordinary rooms. All pretense ended at the curtain, and reality was harsh.

There were six beds, each with a whitish plastic hood/tent over the head of the beds and the upper bodies of the patients. Doctor Evans was standing beside the nearest bed. A woman in matching scrubs was further into the room, checking one of the many blinking, beeping pieces of equipment that huddled around each bed. She glanced up, and the small area of her face that showed was a startling darkness. African American, female, and not fat, but beyond that and height I couldn't tell anything underneath the protective clothing. I wouldn't recognize her again without the scrubs. It was strangely anonymous and disturbing. Or maybe that was just me. She dropped her gaze and moved to another bed, doing the same checks, writing something down on a clipboard.

I walked towards the closest bed. Doctor Evans never turned around or acknowledged me in any way. White sheets formed tents over each patient, held up by some sort of frame work to keep the sheet from touching them.

Doctor Evans finally turned to one side so I could see the face of the patient. I blinked and my eyes refused to see it, or maybe my brain just rejected what I was seeing. The face was red and raw as if it should be bleeding, but it didn't bleed. It was like looking at raw meat in the shape of a human face, no meaty skull. The nose had been cut off, leaving bloody holes for the plastic tubes to be shoved inside. The man rolled brown eyes in his sockets, staring up at me. There was something wrong with his eyes beyond the lack of skin around them. It took me a few seconds to realize his eyelids had been cut off.

The room was suddenly warm, so warm, and the mask was suffocating me. I wanted to pull it off so I could breathe. I must have made some movement because the doctor grabbed my wrist.

"Don't take anything off. I'm risking their lives with every new person that comes in here." He let go of my wrist. "Make the risk worth it. Tell me what did this."

I shook my head, concentrating on breathing slowly in and out. When I could talk, I asked, "What's the rest of the body look like?"

He stared at me, his eyes demanding. I met his gaze. Anything was better than looking at what lay in the bed. "You're pale already. Are you sure you want to see the rest?"

"No," I said, truthfully.

Even with just his eyes visible I could see the surprise on his face.

"I would like nothing better than to turn and walk out of this room and keep walking," I said. "I don't need any new nightmares, Doctor Evans, but I was called in here to give my expert opinion. I can't form an opinion without seeing the whole show. If I thought I didn't need to see it all, trust me, I wouldn't ask."

"What do you hope to gain by it?" he asked.

"I'm not here to gape at them, Doctor. But I'm looking for clues to what did this. Most of the time the clues are on the bodies of the victims."

The man in the bed made small jerks, head tossing from side to side as if he were in a great deal of pain. Small helpless noises came from his lipless mouth. I closed my eyes and tried to breathe normally. "Please, Doctor, I need to see." I opened my eyes in time to see him rolling back the sheet. I watched him roll it back, folding it carefully, revealing the man's body an inch at a time. By the time I saw him to the waist, I knew that he'd been skinned alive. I'd hoped it was just the face. That was awful enough on its own, but it takes a hell of a long time to skin a grown man's entire body, a long screaming eternity to do it this well and this thoroughly.

When the sheet rolled back over the groin, I swayed, just a little. It wasn't a man. The groin area was smooth and raw. I glanced back up at the chest. The bone structure looked male. I shook my head. "Is this a man or a woman?"

"Man," he said.

I stared down and couldn't keep from staring at the groin and what was missing. "Shit," I said softly. I closed my eyes again. It was so hot, so very hot. With my eyes closed, I could hear the hiss of the oxygen, the whisper of the nurse's booties as she came towards us, and small sounds from the bed as he twitched and strained against padded restraints at his wrist and ankles.

Restraints? I'd seen them but hadn't really registered them. All I could see was the body. Yes, body. I couldn't keep thinking of the man as a "he." I had to distance myself or I was going to lose it.

Concentrate on business. I opened my eyes. "Why the restraints?" My voice was breathy but clear. I glanced down at the body, then back up, giving Doctor Evans the most complete eye contact I'd ever given. I'd stare at him until I memorized the light crows-feet around his eyes, if I just didn't have to keep looking at what lay on the bed.

"They keep trying to get up and leave," he said.

I frowned, not that he could see it under the mask. "Surely, they're too hurt to get far."

"We've got them on some very strong painkillers. When the pain dies down, they try to leave."

"All of them?" I asked.

He nodded.

I made myself look back to the bed. "Why isn't this just a case of a serial . . . not killer. What would you call it? A serial . . ." I shook my head. I couldn't think of a word for it. "Why was I called in? I'm a preternatural expert, and this could have been done by a person."

"There are no blade marks on the tissue," Doctor Evans said.

I stared up at him. "What do you mean?"

"I mean that no blade did this because no matter how good they are at torture, there are always telltale signs of the instrument used. You're right when you say the bodies of the victims have the best clues, but not these bodies. It's almost as if their skin just dissolved away."

"Any corrosive agent that could take someone's skin and soft tissue like nose and groin wouldn't just stop at the skin. It would keep eating through the body."

He nodded. "Unless it was washed off immediately, but there's no residue of any known corrosive agent. More than that, the body isn't patterned on an acid burn. The nose and groin were torn away. There are signs of tearing and damage that aren't present elsewhere. It's almost as if whoever did the skinning, skinned them then tore off the extra pieces." He shook his head. "I've traveled all over the world to help catch torturers. I thought I'd seen it all, but I was wrong."

"Are you a forensic pathologist?" I asked.

"Yes."

"But they're not dead," I said.

He looked at me. "No, they're not dead, but the same skills that let me judge a dead body work here, too."

"Ted Forrester said there were deaths. Did they die from the skinning?" Now that I was "working," the room didn't seem so hot. If I concentrated very carefully on the business stuff, maybe I wouldn't throw up on the patients.

"No, they were cut into pieces and left where they fell."

"Blade marks on the cut up bodies, I assume, or you wouldn't have used the word cut."

"There were marks of a cutting tool, but it was like no knife or sword, or hell, bayonet that I'd ever seen. The cuts were deep but not clean, something less refined than a steel blade was used."

"What?" I asked.

He shook his head. "I don't know. The blade didn't cut through the bones, though. Whoever cut the bodies up pulled the bodies apart at the joints. No human would have the strength to do that, not multiple times."

"Probably not," I said.

"You really think a human being could have done this?" he asked, motioning at the bed.

"Are you asking me if a person could do this to another person? If you travel the world testifying in cases of death by torture, then you know exactly what people are capable of doing to each other."

"I'm not saying a person wouldn't do this," he said. "I'm saying I don't think it would be physically possible to do it."

I nodded. "The cutting and tearing, I think might have been human, but I agree with the skinning. If it were done by a human, then there would be tool marks of some kind."

"You say tool marks, not blade marks. Most people assume it takes a blade to skin someone."

"Anything that holds an edge can do it," I said, "though it's slower and usually messier. This is strangely clean."

"Yes," he said, nodding. "Yes, that's a good phrase for it. As horrible as it is, it's still very neatly done, except for the extra tissue that was removed. That was not neatly done, but brutally done."

"Almost like we have two different . . ." I kept wanting to say killers, but these people were still alive. "Perpetrators," I said finally.

"What do you mean?"

"Cutting up a body with a dull tool that isn't strong enough to tear through bone, then pulling a person apart with bare hands is something more in the line of a disorganized serial killer. The careful skinning is something an organized serial killer might do. Why go to the trouble of carefully skinning the face and groin, then pulling off the pieces? It's either two different mutilators, or it's two different personalities."

"A multiple personality?" He made it a question.

"Not exactly, but not all serial killers are so easy to put in one category or another. Some organized criminals have moments of savagery that resemble the disorganized killer, and some organized minds become more disorganized as they escalate their killing. The same isn't true of a disorganized killer. There aren't enough brownies in the pan for them to ape organized methods."

"So either an organized killer with savage moments of disorganization, or . . . or what?" The good doctor was talking very reasonably to me, not angry anymore. I'd either impressed him or at least hadn't disappointed him. Not yet, anyway.

"It could be a pair of killers, an organized killer being the brains of the operation and the disorganized being the follower. It's not that unusual to find killers working in tandem."

"Like the Hillside Strangler or rather Stranglers," he said.

I smiled behind the mask. "There have been a lot more cases than just that one where we had two killers. Sometimes it's two men. Sometimes it's a man and a woman. In that case the man is the dominant personality. Or at least in every case I've ever heard of, except one. Either way one is dominant and the other is to a lesser or greater degree in the control of the other. It can be a near complete domination so that the other person is unable to say no, or it can be more of a partnership. But even in more equal relationships one person is primarily dominant while the other is the follower."

"And you're sure it's a serial mutilator?" he asked.

"No," I said.

"What do you mean?"

"The serial mutilator idea is the most normal solution I can come up with, but I'm a preternatural expert, Doctor Evans. I'm rarely called in when the answer wears a human face, no matter how monstrous. Someone thinks this wasn't done by human hands, or I wouldn't be here."

"The FBI agent seemed very sure," Doctor Evans said.

I looked at him. "Have I just wasted both our times here? Did the Feds come in and say pretty much what I just said?"

"Pretty much," he said.

"Then you don't need me."

"The FBI is convinced that it's a serial mutilator, a person."

"Sometimes the Feds can be very sure of themselves, and once they've committed themselves, they don't like to be wrong. Policemen in general can be like that. It is usually the easy answer when it comes to crime. If a husband dies, the wife probably did do it. Cops aren't encouraged to complicate a case. They're encouraged to simplify it."

"Why aren't you taking the simple solution?" he asked.

"Several reasons. One, if it was a serial anything, a human, I'd think the police, Feds, whatever would have some clues by now. The level of fear and uncertainty among the men is too high. If they had a clue to what was happening, they'd be less panicked. Two, I don't have a superior to report to. No one's going to slap my hand or demote me in rank if I guess and I'm wrong. My job and income don't depend on pleasing anyone but myself."

"You do have a boss to answer to?" he said.

"Yeah, but I don't have to give regular written reports. He's more a business manager than anything. He doesn't give a rat's ass how I do the job, as long as I do it and don't insult too many people along the way. I raise the dead for a living, Doctor Evans. It's a specialized skill. If my boss gives me too much grief, there are two other animating firms in this country that would take me in a hot minute. I could even go freelance."

"You're that good?" he said.

I nodded. "I seem to be, and that frees me from a lot of the red tape and politics that the police have to mess with. My goal is to keep this from happening to anyone else. If I look a little foolish or indecisive along the way, that's just fine. Though I'll probably get some pressure to make up my mind and pick a bogeyman. Not from my boss, but from the police and the Feds. Solving something like this could make a cop's career. Being wrong and failing to solve it could be the end of a career."

"But if you're wrong, you aren't hurt," Evans said.

I looked at him. "If I'm wrong, then no harm, no foul. If everybody's looking in the wrong direction, me, the cops, the Feds, everybody, then this is going to keep on happening." I looked down at the man on the bed. "That will hurt."

"Why? Why will it hurt you?"

"Because we're the good guys, and whoever or whatever is doing this, is the bad guy. Good is supposed to triumph over evil, Doctor Evans, or what's a Heaven for?"

"You're Christian?"

I nodded.

"I didn't think you could be Christian and raise zombies."

"Surprise," I said.

He nodded, though I wasn't sure what he was agreeing with. "Do you need to see the others, or is this enough?"

"You can cover him back up, but yeah, I should at least look at the others. If I don't, then I'll wonder if I missed something by not looking."

"No one else has made it all the way around the room without having to leave, and that includes me the first time I walked in here." He was walking to the next bed as he spoke. I followed behind, not happy to be there, but feeling better. I could do this if I just concentrated on solving the crime and shoved my empathy in a tight dark box. At that moment sympathy was a luxury I couldn't afford.

The second man was almost identical to the first except for height and eye color. Blue eyes this time, and I had to look away. If I locked gazes with any of them, they'd become people, and I'd run screaming.

The third bed was different. The wounds on the chest seemed different somehow, and when Doctor Evans rolled the sheet over the groin, I realized it was a woman. My gaze went back to her chest where something had ripped away her breasts. Her eyes rolled wildly, mouth opening and closing, making small sounds, and I saw for the first time why no one was talking. The tongue was just a ruined stump, rolling like a butchered worm in that lipless, skinless opening.

Heat washed over me in a rush. The room swam. I couldn't breathe. The mask molded itself to my open, gaping mouth. I turned and went for the doors. I walked slowly. I didn't run, but if I didn't get out of there I was going to lose what little I had on my stomach or maybe faint. Of the two I think I preferred throwing up. Doctor Evans pressed the pad that opened the door without a word. The doors opened, and I went through.

Ben the nurse turned to me, mask hastily held in place with a gloved hand. When the doors shut behind me, he let the mask drop. "You all right?"

I shook my head, not trusting my voice. I jerked the mask off my face and still couldn't seem to get enough air. It was too quiet in the little room. The only sound the soft hush of the air whooshing in, recycling. The small movement of cloth as Ben moved towards me. I needed noise, human voices. I needed out of there.

I jerked the plastic thingie off my head. My hair fell around my shoulders, brushed my face. I still couldn't get enough air. "I'm sorry," I said, and my voice sounded distant. "I'll be back." I opened the outer door and escaped.

7

THE HALL FELT COOLER, though I knew it wasn't. I leaned beside the closed door, eyes closed, breathing in great draughts of air. The corridor was full of noise after that silent hissing room. People walking, moving, and Lieutenant Marks' voice, "Not so fucking tough after all, eh, Ms. Blake."

I opened my eyes and looked at him. He was sitting in the chair that had probably been brought up for the uniform guarding the door. The uniformed officer was nowhere to be seen. Only Edward leaned against the far wall, hands behind his back. He was watching my face, watching me, as if he'd memorize my fear. "I made it through three patients before I had to leave the room. How many did you see before you had to go outside, Marks?"

"I didn't have to leave the fucking room."

"Doctor Evans said that no one has made it through the room, all the way through the room without having to run out. That means you didn't make it either, Marks. So piss off."

He was on his feet now. "You . . . you witch." He spat the last word at me as if it were the worst insult he could come up with.

"Don't you mean bitch?" I said. I was feeling better out here in the hallway. Trading insults with Marks was a cakewalk compared to my other choices.

"I said what I meant."

"If you don't know the difference between a real witch and an animator, no wonder you haven't caught the thing that's doing this."

"What do you mean 'thing'?" he asked.

"Thing, thing, monster."

"The Feds think it's a serial mutilator," he said.

I glanced at Edward. "Nice of someone to tell me what the Feds said."

Edward didn't look guilty in the least. He gave me pleasant, unreadable, and I turned my attention back to Marks. "Then why aren't there any tool marks from the skinning?"

Marks glanced down the corridor where a nurse was pushing a small cart. "We don't discuss an ongoing investigation in the open, where anyone can hear us."

"Fine, then after I've gone back in there and looked at the last three . . . bodies, we'll go some place more private and talk about the case."

I think he paled just a bit. "You're going back in there?"

"The victims are the clues, Lieutenant. You know that."

"We can take you to the crime scenes," he said. It was the nicest thing he'd ever said to me.

"Great, and I need to see them, but right this moment we're here and the only possible clues are inside that room." My breathing had returned to normal and the sick sweat had dried on my forehead. Maybe I was a touch pale myself, but I was mobile and felt almost normal.

I walked into the middle of the hall and motioned Edward over to me, as if I had something for his ears alone. He pushed away from the wall and came toward me. When he was close enough, I faked a low kick. He looked down for just an instant, reacting to it, and the second, higher kick caught him in the jaw. He went backwards hard. He had his arms up to defend his face. He knew enough to defend the vital areas, and worry about standing later.

My heart was thudding in my chest, not from exertion, but from adrenaline. I'd never used my new-found Kenpo skills in a fight. Trying it out for real for the very first time on Edward was probably not my best idea, but hey, it had worked. Though truthfully, I was a little surprised it had worked that easily. In the back of my head a voice wondered if Edward had let me take him down. The front of my head said that he had too much ego for that. I believed the second voice. I stayed where I was in a modified horse stance. It was pretty much the only stance I knew well enough to go back to once a kick was launched. I had my fists up, waiting, but didn't move in.

When Edward figured out I wasn't going to do anything else, he lowered his arm and stared at me. "What the hell was that?" There was blood on his lower lip.

"I've been taking Kenpo," I said.

"Kenpo?"

"It's sort of like Tae-kwon-do with fewer kicks and more fluid movements, a lot of hand work."

"A black belt in Judo wasn't enough?" he asked, and it was Ted's voice asking.

"Judo's great exercise, but it's not great for self-defense. You have to close with the bad guy and grapple. This way I can stay out of reach and still do damage."

He touched his lip and came away with blood. "I see that. Why?"

"Why did I kick you in the face?" I asked.

He nodded, and I think he winced ever so slightly. Great.

"Why didn't you warn me about the victims? Tell me what I was up against?"

"I walked in on them cold," he said. "I wanted to see how you handled it cold."

"This is not a pissing contest, Edward. Ted. I am not competing with you. I know you're better than me, tougher than me, colder than me. You win, okay? Stop with the macho bullshit."

"I'm not so sure," he said, softly.

"Not sure about what?" I asked.

"Who's tougher. Remember, I didn't make it through the whole room either."

I stared at him. "Fine, you want to go one on one, great, but not now. We are supposed to be solving a case. We are supposed to be making sure that what happened to those people doesn't happen to anyone else. When we're back on our own time, then you can get competitive. Until we solve this, cut it the fuck out, or you are going to seriously piss me off."

Edward got slowly to his feet. I backed away out of reach. I'd never seen him use martial arts before, but I put nothing past him.

A sound made me back up further until I could see Edward and Marks without looking away from Edward. Marks was making a small sniggering sound. It took me a moment to realize he was laughing, laughing so hard his face was purplish and he seemed to be having trouble breathing.

Edward and I both stared at him.

When Marks could finally talk, he said, "You kick a man in the face, and that's not seriously pissed off." He straightened, hand to his side like he had a stitch in it. "What the fuck do you call seriously pissed?"

I felt my face going blank, my eyes going empty. For just an instant I let Marks see the gaping hole where my conscience was supposed to be. I didn't really mean to, but I couldn't seem to help it. Maybe I was more shaken up from the room and its survivors than I thought. It's the only excuse I can give.

Marks' face went from fading laughter to something like concern. He gave me cop eyes, but underneath that was an uncertainty that was almost fear.

"Smile, Lieutenant. It's a good day. No one died."

I watched the thought spill through his face. He understood exactly what I meant. You should never even hint to the police that you're willing to kill, but I was tired, and I still had to go back into the room. Fuck it.

Edward spoke in his own voice, low and empty, "And you wonder why I compete with you?"

I turned eyes that I knew were just as dead as his to meet his gaze. I shook my head. "I don't wonder why you compete with me . . . Ted. I just told you to stop doing it until the case is solved."

"And then?" he asked.

"Then we'll see, won't we?"

I didn't see fear on Edward's face. I saw anticipation. And that was the difference between us. He enjoyed killing. I didn't. What really scared me was the thought that that might be the only difference between us now. It wasn't enough of a difference for me to throw stones in Edward's direction. I still had more rules than Edward did. There were still things that he would do that I wouldn't, but even that list had been growing shorter of late. There was something close to panic fluttering in my stomach. Not fear of Edward or anything he could do, but wondering when I'd turned the corner and become just another monster. I'd told Doctor Evans we were the good guys, but if Edward and I were on the side of the angels, then what was left to be on the other side?

Something that could skin a person alive without using a tool of any kind. Something that would jerk the penis off a man and the breasts off a woman with its bare hands. As bad as Edward was, as bad as I'd become, there were worse things. And we were about to go hunting one of them.

8

I DID GO BACK into the room, and no, I didn't learn a damn thing from the last three victims. All that wasted bravery for nothing. Well, not exactly for nothing. I proved to myself that I could go back into the room without throwing up or fainting. I didn't care if it impressed Edward or Marks. It impressed me. If you can't impress yourself, then no one else really matters.

I either impressed Doctor Evans, or he needed a restorative cup of tea because he invited me back to the doctors and nurses lounge. There's no such thing as truly undrinkable coffee, but I hoped the tea was better for Evans' sake. Though I doubted it. The coffee came out of a can, and the tea was from little bags with strings on them. There's only so much you can hope for from prepackaged tea and coffee. At home I grind my own beans, but I wasn't home and I was grateful for the bitter warmth.

I added cream and sugar and noticed that the coffee was trembling in the cup, as if maybe my hands weren't quite steady. I was also cold. Nerves, just nerves.

If Edward had nerves, you couldn't tell it as he leaned against the wall, drinking his coffee black. He'd scorned sugar and cream, tough he-man that he was. He winced as he sipped, and I don't think it was the scalding liquid. His lip was swelling slightly from where I'd kicked him. It made me feel better. Childish but true.

Marks had taken a place on the room's only couch, blowing on his coffee. He'd taken cream and sugar in his. Evans settled down into the only chair that looked halfway comfortable, sighing as he stirred his tea.

Edward watched me, and I finally realized that he wouldn't sit down until I did. Screw it. I sat down in a chair that was far too straight-backed to be comfortable, but was placed so I could watch everyone in the room, including the door. There was a small, but full-size, refrigerator against the far wall. It was an older model, done in an odd shade of brown. A small L-shaped cabinet area housed a coffee maker, a second coffee maker with nothing but hot water in it, a sink, and a microwave oven.

Doctor Evans had used the hot water for his tea. There were white plastic spoons in an open packet, and a mug of those useless little coffee stirrers. There'd been a choice of sugar, Nutrasweet, and some other artificial sweetener that I'd never heard of. There was a circle of artificial creamer that had dried into a round crusty ridge where someone had sat a mug down in it. I concentrated on the minutia of the cabinet, trying not to think. For just a few moments I wanted to sip my coffee and not think. I still hadn't eaten today, and now I didn't want to.

"You said you had some questions for me, Ms. Blake." Doctor Evans spoke into the silence.

I jumped, and so did Marks. Only Edward stayed half-leaning against the wall, unmoved, blue eyes watching us all as if he were apart from the tension and the horror. Maybe he was, or maybe it was just an act. I just didn't know anymore.

I nodded, trying to focus. "How did they all survive?"

He tilted his head to one side. "Do you mean technically how did they survive? Medical detail?"

I shook my head. "No, I mean, one person surviving this much trauma, or even two, I'll buy. But most people wouldn't survive it, or am I wrong?"

Evans pushed his glasses more securely on his nose, but nodded. "No, you aren't wrong."

"Then how did all six of them survive?" I asked.

He frowned at me. "I'm not sure I understand exactly what you're trying to say here, Ms. Blake."

"I'm asking what are the chances that six people of varying sex, background, physical fitness, age, etc. . . . would all be able to survive the same amount of trauma. My understanding is that all the victims that were just skinned have survived, right?"

"Yes." Doctor Evans was watching me closely, pale eyes searching my face, waiting for me to go on.

"Why did they survive?"

"They're tough sons of bitches," Marks said.

I glanced at the lieutenant, then back to Evans. "Are they?"

"Are they what?" the doctor asked.

"Are they tough sons of bitches?"

He lowered his eyes as if thinking. "Two of the men worked out regularly, one of the women was a marathon runner. The other three were just ordinary. One of the men is close to sixty, and didn't have a regular exercise routine of any kind. The other woman is in her thirties but didn't . . ." He looked at me. "No, they aren't particularly tough individuals, not physically anyway. But I've found that it's often the people who aren't physically strong or outwardly tough that survive the longest under torture. The he-men are usually the first to cave."

I forced myself not to glance at Edward, but it was an effort. "Let me test my understanding, Doctor. Have any people that have been skinned like the six in that room died?"

He blinked and again looked into the distance as if remembering, then he looked at me. "No, the only deaths have been those people torn apart."

"Then I ask again, why are they all alive? Why didn't at least one of them die from shock, blood loss, or a bad heart, or hell, the pure terror of it."

"People don't die from terror," Marks said.

I glanced at him. "Are you absolutely sure of that, Lieutenant?"

His handsome face looked petulant, stubborn. "Yeah, I'm sure."

I waved the comment away. I'd argue with Marks later. Right now I was chasing a point. "How did all six of them survive, Doctor? Not why this six, but why all of them?"

Evans nodded. "I see what you mean. How could all of them have survived it?"

I nodded. "Exactly. Some of them should have died, but they didn't."

"Whoever skinned them is an expert," Marks said. "He knew how to keep them alive."

"No," Edward said. "No matter how good you are at torture, you can't keep everybody alive. Even if you do exactly the same thing to each of them, some people die and some people live. You're not always sure why some make it, and some don't." His voice was very quiet, but it filled the hush of the room.

Doctor Evans looked at him, nodding. "Yes, yes, even an expert can't make people survive what was done to these six. You should lose some of them. For that matter I don't know why they're all still alive. Why hasn't one of them contracted some secondary infection? They are all remarkably healthy."

Marks stood so abruptly, he spilled coffee over his hand. He cursed, striding to the sink and throwing the cup and all in the sink. "How can you say they're healthy?" He looked over his shoulder at the doctor while he ran his hands under the water.

"They are still alive, Lieutenant, and for their condition that is very healthy indeed."

"Magic would do it," I said.

Everyone looked at me.

"There are spells that can keep a person alive during torture so that the torture can be prolonged."

Marks tore too much paper towel off the roll and turned on me, wiping his hands with small abrupt movements. "How can you say you don't do black magic?"

"I said there are spells that will do it, not that I did the spells," I said.

It took him three tries to get the paper towel in the waste basket. "Just knowing about such things is evil."

"Think what you like, Marks, but maybe one of the reasons you had to call me in is that you've kept yourself so lily white that you don't know enough to help these people. Maybe if you were more interested in solving crime than in saving your own soul you'd have wrapped this up by now."

"Saving a soul is more important than solving crime," he said. He was striding towards me now.

I stood up, coffee cup in my hand. "If you're more interested in souls than crime then become a minister, Marks. What we need right now is a cop."

He stalked towards me, and I think would have come close enough to exchange blows, but I watched him remember what I'd done out in the hall. I watched him remember caution, and he walked far around me to get to the door.

Doctor Evans glanced from one to the other of us, as if wondering what he'd missed.

Marks turned at the door, pointing a finger at me. "If I have my way, you are going to be back on a plane tonight. You can't ask the devil to help you catch the devil." With that he closed the door behind him.

Evans spoke into the silence. "There must be more in you, Ms. Blake, than mere toughness, something I haven't seen yet."

I looked at him and took a drink of the cooling coffee. "What would make you say that, doctor?"

"If I didn't know better, I'd say Lieutenant Marks is afraid of you," he said.

"He's afraid of what he thinks I am, Doctor Evans. He's jumping at shadows."

Evans looked up at me, his tea forgotten in his big hands. The look was a long considering one. I had an urge to squirm under such scrutiny, but fought it down.

"Perhaps you are right, Ms. Blake, or perhaps he has seen something in you that I have not."

"When you spend all your time worrying that the devil is right behind you, eventually you start seeing him whether he's there or not," I said.

Evans stood, nodding. He rinsed his coffee mug in the sink, washing it out with a fresh paper towel and soap. He spoke without turning around. "I do not know if I will ever see the devil, but I have seen true evil, and if there is no devil behind it, still it is evil." He turned and looked at me. "And we must put a stop to it."

I nodded. "Yes," I said, "we must."

He smiled then, but his eyes stayed tired. "I will work with my colleagues here that are more accustomed to working with the living instead of the dead. We will try and discover why these six survive."

"And if it's magic?" I asked.

He nodded. "Do not tell Lieutenant Marks, but my wife is a witch. She has traveled the world with me seeing such things. Sometimes what we find is more up her alley than mine, not often, mind you. People are quite able to torment one another without aid of magic. But occasionally it has been more."

"Don't take this wrong," I said, "but why haven't you called her in before this?"

He took in a long breath and let it out. "She was out of the country on another matter. Why, you may ask, didn't I call her home sooner?"

I shook my head. "I wasn't going to ask."

He smiled. "Thank you for that. I reasoned that my wife was needed elsewhere, and the FBI seemed so sure it was a person." He glanced at Edward then back to me. "The truth is, Ms. Blake, something about all this frightens me. I am not a man who is easily frightened."

"You're afraid for your wife," I said.

He stared at me as if he could look into my mind with those pale eyes. "Wouldn't you be?"

I touched his arm, gently. "Trust your instincts, doctor. If it feels wrong, send her away."

He drew away from my touch, smiling, tossing the paper towel into the trash can. "That would be terribly superstitious of me."

"You've got a bad feeling about your wife's involvement with this thing. Trust your gut. Don't try to be reasonable. If you love your wife, listen to your heart, not your head."

He nodded twice then said, "I will think about what you said. Now I really must be going."

I held out my hand. He took it. "Thanks for your time, doctor."

"My . . . pleasure, Ms. Blake." He nodded to Edward. "Mr. Forrester."

Edward nodded in return, and we were left in the silence of the lounge. "Listen to your heart and not your head. Damn romantic advice, coming from you," Edward said.

"Drop it," I said. I had my hand on the door handle.

"How would your love life be if you took your own advice?" he asked.

I opened the door and walked out into the cool white hallway without answering him.

9

MARKS' OFFER OF ESCORTING me to the crime scene seemed to have evaporated with his temper. Edward drove me. We drove in almost complete silence. Edward never sweated small talk, and I just didn't have the energy for it. If I could have thought of something useful to say, I'd have said it. Until then, silence was fine. Edward had volunteered that we were on our way to the latest crime scene, and we'd meet his other two backups in Santa Fe. He told me nothing else about them, and I didn't press it. His lip was still swelling because he'd been too macho to put ice on it. I figured the busted lip was all the slack Edward was going to give me for one day. I'd told him in the strongest terms I could manage, short of pulling a weapon, to stop the competitive crap, and nothing would change that, least of all me.

Besides, I was still riding in a ringing bell of silence as if everything echoed and nothing was quite solid. It was shock. The survivors, if that was the word for them, had shaken me down to my toes. I'd seen awful things, but nothing quite like that. I was going to have to snap out of it before we had our first fire fight, but frankly if someone had pulled a weapon on me right that second, I'd have hesitated. Nothing seemed truly important or even real.

"I know why you're afraid of this thing," I said.

He glanced toward me with the black lenses of his eyes, then back to the road, as if he hadn't heard. Anyone else would have asked me to explain, or made some comment. Edward just drove.

"You don't fear anything that just offers death. You've accepted that you're not going to live to a ripe old age."

"*We*," he said. "*We've* accepted that *we* aren't going to live to a ripe old age."

I opened my mouth to protest, then stopped. I thought about it for a second or two. I was twenty-six, and if the next four years were anything like the last four, I'd never see thirty. I'd never really thought about it in so many words, but old age wasn't one of my biggest worries. I didn't really expect to get there. My life style was a sort of passive suicide. I didn't like that much. It made me want to squirm and deny it, but I couldn't. Wanted to, but couldn't. It made my chest squeeze tight to realize that I expected to die by violence. Didn't want it, but expected it. My voice sounded uncertain, but I said it out loud. "Fine, *we've* accepted that *we're* not going to make it to a ripe old age. Happy?"

He gave a slight nod.

"You're afraid that you'll live like those things in the hospital. You're afraid of ending up like them."

"Aren't you?" His voice was almost too soft to hear, but somehow it carried over the rush of wheels and the expensive purr of the engine.

"I'm trying not to think about it," I said.

"How can you not think about it?" he asked.

"Because if you start thinking about the bad things, worrying about them, then it makes you slow, makes you afraid. Neither of us can afford that."

"Two years ago, I'd have been giving you the pep talk," he said, and there was something in his voice, not anger, but close.

"You were a good teacher," I said.

His hands gripped the wheel. "I haven't taught you all I know, Anita. You are not a better monster than I am."

I watched the side of his face, trying to read that expressionless face. There was a tightness at the jaw, a thread of anger down the neck and into his shoulders. "Are you trying to convince me or yourself, . . . Ted?" I made the name light and mocking. I didn't usually play with Edward just to get a rise out of him, but today, he was unsure, and I wasn't. Part of me was enjoying the hell out of that.

He slammed on the brakes and screeched to a stop on the side of the road. I had the Browning pointed at the side of his head, close enough that pulling the trigger would paint his brains all over the windows.

He had a gun in his hand. I don't know where in the car it had come from, but the gun wasn't pointed at me. "Ease down, Edward."

He stayed motionless but didn't drop the gun. I had one of those moments when you see into another person's soul like looking into an open window. "Your fear makes you slow, Edward, because you'd rather die here, like this, than survive like those poor bastards. You're looking for a better way to die." My gun was very steady, finger on the trigger. But this wasn't for real, not yet. "If you were really serious, you'd have had the gun in your hand before you pulled over. You didn't invite me here to hunt monsters. You invited me here to kill you if it works out wrong."

He gave the smallest nod. "Neither Bernardo or Olaf are good enough." He laid the gun very, very slowly on the floorboard hump between the seats. He looked at me, hands spread on the steering wheel. "Even for you, I have to be a little slow."

I took the offered gun without taking either my eyes or my gun off of him. "Like I believe that's the only gun you've got hidden in this car. But I do appreciate the gesture."

He laughed then, and it was the most bitter sound I'd ever heard from Edward. "I don't like being afraid, Anita. I'm not good at it."

"You mean you're not used to it," I said.

"No, I'm not."

I eased my own gun down until it wasn't pointing at him, but I didn't put it up. "I promise that if you end up like the people in the hospital I'll take your head."

He looked at me then, and even with the sunglasses on I knew he was surprised. "Not just shoot me or kill me, but take my head."

"If it happens, Edward, I won't leave you alive, and taking your head we'll both be sure that the job's done."

Something flowed across his face, down his shoulders, his arms, and I realized it was relief. "I knew I could count on you for this, Anita, you and no one else."

"Should I be flattered or insulted that you've never met anyone else cold-blooded enough for this?"

"Olaf's blood is plenty cold enough, but he'd just shoot me and bury me in a hole somewhere. He'd have never thought about taking my head. And what if shooting didn't kill me?" He took off his glasses and rubbed his eyes. "I'd be in some stinking hole somewhere alive because Olaf would never think to take my head." He shook his head as if chasing the image away. He slid the glasses back on, and when he turned to look at me, his face was blank, unreadable, his usual. But I'd seen beneath the mask, further than I'd ever been allowed before. The one thing I'd never expected to find was fear, and beneath that, trust. Edward trusted me with more than his life. He trusted me to make sure he died well. For a man like Edward there was no greater trust.

We would never go shopping together or eat an entire cake while we complained about men. He'd never invite me over to his house for dinner or a barbecue. We'd never be lovers. But there was a very good chance that one of us would be the last person the other saw before we died. It wasn't friendship the way most people understood it, but it was friendship. There were several people I'd trust with my life, but there is no one else I'd trust with my death. Jean-Claude and even Richard would try to hold me alive out of love or something that passed for it. Even my family and other friends would fight to keep me alive. If I wanted death, Edward would give it to me. Because we both understand that it isn't death that we fear. It's living.

10

THE HOUSE WAS a two-story split-level ranch that could have been anywhere in the Midwest, in any upper-middle-class neighborhood. But the large yard was done in rock paths running high to cacti and a circle of those small flowered lilacs that were so plentiful. Other people had tried to keep their lawns green as if they didn't live on the edge of a desert, but not this house. This house, these people had landscaped for their environment and tried not to waste water. And now they were dead and didn't give a damn about environmental awareness or rainfall.

Of course, one of them could be a survivor. I didn't want to see pictures of the survivors before they'd been . . . injured. I was having enough trouble keeping my professional distance without color photos of smiling faces that had been turned into so much naked meat. I got out of the car, praying that everyone had died in this house, not my usual prayer at a crime scene. But nothing about this case so far was usual.

There was a marked police car sitting out in front of the house. A uniformed officer got out of the marked car as Edward and I walked towards the yard. He was medium build but carrying enough weight for someone taller, a lot taller. His weight was mostly in the stomach and made his utility belt ride low. His pale face was sweating by the time he'd walked the five feet to us. He put his hat on as he walked towards us, unsmiling, thumb hooked in his utility belt.

"Can I help you?"

Edward went into his Ted Forrester act, putting his hand out, smiling. "I'm Ted Forrester, Officer . . . " he took the time to read the man's name tag, "Norton. This is Anita Blake. Chief Appleton has cleared us both to see the crime scene."

Norton looked us both up and down, pale eyes not the least bit friendly. He didn't shake hands. "Can I see some ID?"

Edward opened his wallet to his driver's license and held it out. I opened my executioner's license for him. He handed Edward's back, but squinted at mine. "This license isn't good in New Mexico."

"I'm aware of that, Officer," I said, voice bland.

He squinted at me, much as he had the license. "Then why are you here?"

I smiled and couldn't quite make it reach my eyes. "I'm here as a preternatural advisor, not an executioner."

He handed the license back to me. "Then why the hardware?"

I glanced down at the gun very visible against my red shirt. The smile was genuine this time. "It's not concealed, Officer Norton, and it's federally licensed so I don't have to sweat a new gun permit every time I cross a state line."

He didn't seem to like the answer. "I was told to let the two of you in." It was a statement, but it sounded like a question, as if he wasn't quite sure he was going to let us in, after all.

Edward and I stood there trying to appear harmless, but useful. I was a lot better at looking harmless than Edward was. I didn't even have to work at it most of the time. He was better at looking useful, though. Without seeming dangerous in the least he could give off an aura of purposefulness that police and other people responded to. The best I could do was look harmless and wait for Officer Norton to decide what our fate would be.

He finally nodded, as if he'd made up his mind. "I'm supposed to escort you around the scene, Miss Blake." He didn't look happy about it.

I didn't correct him that Miss Blake should have been Ms. Blake. I think he was looking for an excuse to get rid of us. I wasn't going to give him one. Very few policemen like civilians messing around in their cases. I wasn't just a civilian, I was female, and I hunted vampires; a triple threat if ever there was one. I was a civvie, a woman, and a freak.

"This way." He started up the narrow walkway. I glanced at Edward. He just started following Norton. I followed Edward. I had a feeling I'd be doing a lot of that in the next few days.

Quiet. The house was so quiet. The air conditioner purred into that silence reminding me of the recycled air in the hospital room. Norton came up behind me, and I jumped. He didn't say anything, but he gave me a look.

I moved out of the entry hall and into the large high ceilinged living room. Norton followed me. In fact he stayed at my heels as I moved around the room like some obedient dog, but the message I was getting from him wasn't trust and adoration. It was suspicion and disapproval. Edward had settled into one of the room's three comfortable-looking powder blue chairs. He'd stretched himself full length, legs crossed at the ankles. He'd left his sunglasses on so he looked the picture of ease in the midst of that careful living room in that too silent house.

"Are you bored?" I asked.

"I've seen the show," he said. He'd toned down his Ted act and was more his usual self. Maybe he didn't sweat Norton's reaction, or maybe he was tired of playacting. I knew I was tired of watching the show.

The room was one of those great rooms which meant the living, dining, and kitchen were all one shared space. It was a large space, but I'm not really comfortable with the open floor plan. I like more walls, doors, barriers. Probably a sign of my own less than welcoming personality. If the house was any clue to the family that had lived in it, they'd been welcoming and somewhat conventional. The furniture was all purchased as sets: a powder blue living room set, a dark wood dining room set to one side with a bay window and white lacy drapes. There was a new hard back southwestern cook book on the kitchen cabinet. The receipt was still being used as a bookmark. The kitchen was the smallest area, long and thin with white cabinets and a black and white cow motif down to a cookie jar that mooed when you took its head off. Store bought cookies, chocolate chip. No, I didn't eat one.

"Any clues in the cookie jar?" Edward asked from his chair.

"No," I said, "I just had to know if it really mooed."

Norton made a small sound that might have been a laugh. I ignored him. Though since he was standing about two feet from me the entire time, ignoring wasn't easy. I changed direction in the kitchen abruptly, and he nearly ran into me. "Could you give me a little more breathing space?" I asked.

"Just following my orders," he said, face bland.

"Did your orders tell you to stand close enough to tango or just to follow me?"

His mouth twitched, but he managed not to smile. "Just to follow you, ma'am."

"Great, then take about two big steps back so we do this without bumping into each other."

"I'm supposed to make sure you don't disturb the scene, ma'am."

"The name's Anita, not ma'am."

That earned me a smile, but he shook his head and fought it off. "Just following orders. That's what I do."

There was something just a touch bitter about that last. Officer Norton was on the down side of fifty or looked it. He was close to putting in his thirty years, and he was still a uniform sitting in a car outside a crime scene following orders. If he'd ever had dreams of more, they were gone. He was a man who had accepted reality, but he didn't like it.

The door opened, and a man came through with his tie at half-mast, the white sleeves of his dress shirt rolled up over dark forearms. His skin was a dark solid brown, and it didn't look like a tan. Hispanic or Indian or maybe a little of both. The hair was cut very short, not for style, but as if it were easier that way. There was a gun on his hip and a gold shield clipped to the waist band of his pants.

"I'm Detective Ramirez. Sorry I'm late." He smiled when he said it, and there seemed to be genuine cheerfulness, but I didn't trust it. I'd seen too many cops go from cheerful to hardcore up in your face too many times. Ramirez would try to catch his flies with honey instead of vinegar, but I knew the vinegar was there. You didn't get to be a plainclothes detective without that streak of sourness. Or maybe a loss of innocence was a better phrase for it. Whatever you called it, it would be there. It was only a matter of how far under the surface it was.

But I smiled and held my hand out, and he took it. The handshake was firm, the smile still in place, but his eyes were cool and noticed everything. I knew that if I left the room now he'd be able to describe me in detail down to my gun, or maybe up from my gun.

Officer Norton was still behind me like a pudgy bridesmaid. Detective Ramirez' eyes flicked to him, and the smile wilted just a touch. "Thank you, Officer Norton. I'll take it from here."

The look Norton gave him was not friendly. Maybe Officer Norton didn't like anybody. Or maybe he was white and Ramirez wasn't. He was old and Ramirez was young. He was going to end his career in uniform and Ramirez was already in plainclothes. Prejudice and jealousy are often close kin. Or maybe Norton was just in a bad mood.

Whatever, Norton went out like he'd been told, shutting the door behind him. Ramirez' smile went up a notch as he turned to me. I realized that he was cute in a young guy sort of way, and he knew it. Not in an egomaniac way, but I was a female, and he was cute, and he was hoping that that would cut him some slack with me. Boy, was he shopping in the wrong aisle.

I shook my head, but smiled back.

"Is something wrong?" he asked. Even the slight frown was sort of boyish and endearing. He must practice it in the mirror.

"No, Detective, nothing's wrong."

"Please call me Hernando."

That made me smile more. "I'm Anita."

The smile flashed bright and wide. "Anita, pretty name."

"No," I said, "it's not, and we're investigating a crime, not out on a blind date. You can tone the charm down just a touch, and I'll still like you, Detective Ramirez. I'll even share clues with you, honest."

"Hernando," he said.

It made me laugh. "Hernando. Fine, but really, you don't have to work this hard to win me over. I don't know you well enough to dislike you yet."

That made him laugh. "Was it that transparent?"

"You make a good good-cop, and the little boy charm is great, but like I said, it's not necessary."

"Okay, Anita." The smile went down a watt or two, but he was still open and cheerful somehow. It made me nervous. "Have you seen the entire house yet?"

"Not yet. Officer Norton was trailing a little too close for comfort. Made it hard to walk."

The smile closed down, but the look in the eyes was real. "You're a woman and with that black hair probably part something darker than the rest of you looks."

"My mother was Mexican, but most people don't spot it."

"You're in a section of the country where there's a lot of mixing going on." He didn't smile when he said it. He looked serious and a little less young. "The people that want to notice will."

"I could be part dark Italian," I said.

A small smile that time. "We don't have a lot of dark Italians in New Mexico."

"I haven't been here long enough to notice one way or another."

"Your first time to this part of the country?"

I nodded.

"What do you think so far?"

"I've seen a hospital and part of this house. I think it's too early to form an opinion."

"If we get a breather while you're here, I'd love to show you some of the sights."

I blinked at him. Maybe the boyish charm wasn't just a cop technique. Maybe he was, gasp, flirting.

Before I could think of an answer, Edward came up behind us in his best good ol' boy charm. "Detective Ramirez, good to see you again."

They shook hands, and Ramirez wasted a smile on Edward that looked just as genuine as Edward's. Since I knew Edward was play-acting, it was sort of unnerving how similar the two expressions were.

"Good to see you, too, Ted." He turned back to me. "Please, continue looking around. Ted's told me a lot about you, and I hope for all our sakes that you're as good as he says you are."

I glanced at Edward. He just smiled at me. I frowned. "Well, I'll try not to disappoint anybody." I walked back out into the living room trailed by Detective

Ramirez. He gave me more room to maneuver than Norton had, but he watched me. Maybe he did want a date, but he wasn't watching me like a potential date. He was watching me like a cop to see what I did, how I reacted. It made me think better of him that he was professional.

Edward had lowered his sunglasses enough to give me a look as I passed by him. He was smiling, almost grinning at me. The look said it all. He was amused at Ramirez' flirting. I flipped him off, covering the gesture with my other hand so only he would see it.

It made him laugh, and the sound seemed at home here in this bright place. It was a place meant for laughter. The silence filled in behind his laughter like water closing over a stone, until the sound vanished into a profound quiet that was more than quiet.

I stood in the middle of the bright living room, and it was as if it were a display home waiting for the real estate agent to come through with a tour of potential home owners. The house was so new, it felt like a freshly unwrapped present. But there were things that no real estate agent would have allowed. A newspaper was spilled over the pale wood coffee table with the business section folded into fourths. The business section had *New York Times* written across the top of it, but some of the other pieces said *Los Angeles Tribune*. A business person recently moved from Los Angeles, maybe.

There was a large colored photo pushed to one corner of the coffee table. It showed an older couple, fiftyish, with a teenage boy. They were all smiling and touching each other in that posed casual way photos often use. They looked happy and relaxed together, though you can never really tell with posed photos. So easy to fool the camera.

I looked around the room and found smaller photos scattered throughout on numerous white shelves that took up almost all available wall space. The photos sat among souvenirs, mostly with an American Indian theme. The smaller more candid shots were just as relaxed, just as smiling. A happy, prosperous family. The boy and man, tanned and grinning on a boat with the sea in the background and a huge fish between them. The woman and three small girls covered in cookie dough and matching Christmas aprons. There were at least three photos of smiling adult couples with one or two children apiece. The little girls from the Christmas photo; grandchildren, maybe.

I stared at the couple and that tall, tanned teenager, and hoped they were dead because the thought of any of them up in that hospital room turned into so much pain and meat was . . . not a comfy thought. I didn't speculate. They were dead, and that was comforting.

I turned my attention from the photos to the Indian artifacts lining the shelves. Some of it was touristy stuff: reproductions of painted pots in muted shades, too new to be real; Kachina dolls that would have looked just as at home in a child's room; rattlesnake heads stretched in impotent strikes, dead before their murderer opened their mouths to appear fearsome.

But in among the tourist chic were other things. A pot that was displayed behind glass with pieces missing and the paint faded to a dull gray and eggshell color. A spear or javelin on the wall above the fireplace. The spear was behind glass and had remnants of feathers and thongs, beads trailing from it. The head of the spear looked like stone. There was a tiny necklace of beads and shells under glass with the worn edges of the hide thong that bound them together showing. Someone had known what they were collecting because every piece that looked real was behind glass, cared for. The tourist stuff had been left out to fend for itself.

I spoke without turning around, staring at the necklace. "I'm no expert on Indian artifacts but some of this looks like museum quality."

"According to the experts it is," Ramirez said.

I looked at him. His face had gone back to neutral, and he looked older. "Is it all legal?"

That earned me another small smile. "You mean is it stolen?"

I nodded.

"The stuff we've been able to trace was all purchased from private individuals."

"There's more?"

"Yes," he said.

"Show me," I said.

He turned and started walking down a long central hallway. It was my turn to play follow the leader though I gave him more room than either he or Norton had given me. I couldn't help noticing how nicely his dress slacks fit. I shook my head. Was it the flirting, or was I just tired of the two men in my life? Something less complicated would have been nice, but part of me knew that the time for other choices was long past. So I admired his backside as we walked up the hall and knew it meant nothing. I had enough problems without dating the local cops. I was a civilian surrounded by police, and a woman, too. The only thing that would earn me less respect in their eyes was to date one of them. I would lose what little clout I had and become a girlfriend. Anita Blake, vampire executioner and preternatural expert, had some ground to stand on. Detective Ramirez' girlfriend would not.

Edward trailed behind us, but far enough back that we were at the far end of the hallway when he was barely in the corridor. Was he giving us privacy? Did he think it was a good idea to flirt with the detective, or was any human better than a monster, no matter how nice the monster was? If Edward had any prejudice, it was against the monsters.

Ramirez stood at the end of the hallway. He was still smiling as if he were giving me a tour of some other house for some other purpose. His face didn't match what we were about to do. He motioned to the doors to either side of him. "Artifacts to your left, gory stuff to the right."

"Gory stuff?" I made it a question.

He nodded, still pleasant, and I moved closer to him. I stared into those dark brown eyes and realized that the smile was his blank-cop face. It was cheerful, but his eyes were just as unreadable as any cop's I'd ever seen. Smiling blankness, but still blankness. It was unique and somehow disquieting. "Gory stuff," I said.

The smile stayed, but the eyes were a little less sure. "You don't have to play the tough girl with me, Anita."

"She's not playing," Edward said. He'd finally joined us.

Ramirez' eyes flicked to him then back to study my face. "High compliment coming from you, Forrester."

If he only knew, I thought. "Look, Detective, I just came from the hospital. Whatever is behind the door can't be worse than that."

"How can you be so sure?" he asked.

I smiled. "Because even with the air conditioner on, the smell would be worse."

The smile flashed bright and I think real for a moment. "Very practical," he said, voice almost laughing. "I should have known you'd be practical."

I frowned at him. "Why?"

He motioned at his own face. "No make-up," he said.

"Maybe I just don't give a damn."

He nodded. "That too." He started to reach for the door, and I beat him to it. He raised eyebrows at me, but just stepped back and let me open the door. Which also meant I got to walk in first, but hey, only fair. Edward and Ramirez had both already seen the show. My ticket was fresh and hadn't been punched yet.

11

I EXPECTED TO FIND a lot of things in the bedroom: blood stains, signs of a struggle, maybe even a clue. What I did not expect to find was a soul. But the moment I entered that pale white and green bedroom I knew it was there, hovering near the ceiling, waiting. It wasn't the first soul I'd sensed. Funerals were always fun. Souls often hung around the bodies as if unsure what to do, but by three days' time the souls were usually gone to wherever souls were supposed to go.

I stared up at this soul and saw nothing. If a soul has a physical shape, you couldn't prove it by me, but I knew it was there. I could have sketched the outline of it in the air with my hand, knew about how much space it was taking up as it floated near the ceiling. But it was energy, spirit, and though it took up space, I wasn't entirely sure it took up the same kind of space as I did, as the bed did, as anything else did.

My voice came out hushed, as if I spoke too loudly, I'd scare it away. "How long have they been dead?"

"They aren't dead," Ramirez said.

I blinked and turned to him. "What do you mean they're not dead?"

"You saw the Bromwells in the hospital. They're both still alive."

I looked into his serious face. The smile had vanished. I turned back to gaze at that slow hovering presence. "Someone died here," I said.

"No one was cut up here," Ramirez said. "According to the Santa Fe PD that's the method of killing that this guy is using. Look at the carpet. There's not enough blood for anyone to have been cut up."

I looked down at the pale green carpet, and he was right. There was blood like black juice soaked into the carpet, but it wasn't much blood, just spots, dabs. The blood was from the skinning of two adults, but if someone had been torn apart limb from limb there would have been more blood, a lot more. There was still the faint rank smell where someone's bowels had let go either under torture or death. It was pretty common. Death is the last intimate thing we ever do.

I shook my head and debated on what to say. If I'd been at home with Dolph and Zerbrowski and the rest of the St. Louis police that I knew well, I'd have just said I saw a soul. But I didn't know Ramirez, and most cops spook around anyone that can do mystical stuff. To tell or not to tell, that was the question, when noises from the front room brought us all around to stare behind us at the still open door.

Men's voices, hurried footsteps, coming closer. My hand was on my gun when I heard a voice yell, "Ramirez, where the hell are you?"

It was Lieutenant Marks. I eased away from my gun and knew I wasn't telling the police that there was a soul hanging in the air behind me. Marks was scared enough of me without that.

He stepped into the doorway with a small battalion of uniforms at his back, almost as if he expected trouble. His eyes were both harsh and pleased when he looked at me. "Get the fuck off my evidence, Blake. You are outta here."

Edward stepped forward, smiling, trying to play peace maker. "Now, Lieutenant, who would give such an order?"

"My chief." He turned to the cops behind him. "Escort her off the property."

I held up my hands and started moving towards the door before the uniforms could move in. "I'll go, no problem. No need to get rough." I was at the door almost abreast with Marks.

He hissed close to my face, "This isn't rough, Blake. You come near me again and I'll show you rough."

I stopped in the doorway, meeting his gaze. His eyes had turned a swimming aqua blue, dark with his anger. The doorway wasn't that big, and standing in it we were almost touching. "I haven't done anything wrong, Marks."

He spoke low, but it carried, "Thou shalt not suffer a witch to live."

I thought of a lot of things to say, and do, most of which would have gotten me dragged out by a bunch of uniforms. I didn't want to be dragged out, but I wanted to make Marks suffer. Choices, choices.

I rose on tiptoe and planted a big kiss on his mouth. He stumbled back, pushing away from me so hard that he fell into the bedroom and left me pushed into the hallway beyond. Masculine laughter filled the hallway. Two bright spots of color flamed on Marks' cheeks as he lay panting on the carpet.

"You're lying in your evidence, Marks," I said.

"Get her out of here, now."

I blew Marks a kiss, and left through a grinning parade of policeman. One of the uniforms offered to let me kiss him any time. I told him he couldn't handle it and left through the front door to laughter, catcalls, and masculine humor mostly at Marks' expense. He didn't seem to be a popular guy. Go figure.

Edward stayed inside for a few moments, probably trying to soothe things over like a good Ted would do. But in the end he came out of the house, shaking hands with the cops, smiling, and nodding. The smile vanished as soon as he turned so that I was his only audience.

He unlocked the car and we got in. When we were safe inside of its mud-stained windows, he said, "Marks has gotten you kicked off the investigation. I don't know how he did it, but he did it."

"Maybe he and the chief go to the same church," I said. I had snuggled down into the seat, as far as the seatbelt would allow. Edward looked at me as he started the engine. "You don't seem upset."

I shrugged. "Marks isn't the first right-wing asshole to get up in my face, and he won't be the last."

"Where's that famous temper of yours?"

"Maybe I'm growing up," I said.

He shook his head. "What did you see in the corner of the room that I didn't? You were looking at something."

"A soul," I said.

He actually lowered his sunglasses so I could see his baby blues. "A soul?"

I nodded. "Which means that someone in that house did die, and within three days."

"Why three days?" he asked.

"Because three days is the limit for most souls to hang around. After that they go to heaven or hell or wherever. After three days you may get ghosts, but you won't get souls."

"But the Bromwells are alive. You saw them yourself."

"What about their son?" I asked.

"He's missing," Edward said.

"Nice of you to mention that." I wanted to be angry at him for the game playing, but I just couldn't find the energy. No matter how blasé I was about Marks, it did bother me. I was Christian, but I'd lost count of the number of fellow Christians who'd called me witch or worse. It didn't make me angry anymore, just tired.

"If the parents are alive, then the boy probably isn't," I said.

Edward pulled out onto the road, easing his way among the plethora of marked and unmarked police cars brought with him. "But all the other murder vics were cut up. We didn't find any body parts in the house. If the boy is dead, then it's a change in the pattern. We haven't figured out the old pattern yet."

"A change in pattern may give the police the break they need," I said.

"You believe that?" he asked.

"No," I said.

"What do you believe?"

"I believe that the Bromwells' son is dead, and whatever skinned and mutilated his parents took his body, but didn't cut it up. However the son was killed, it wasn't being torn apart or there would have been more blood. He was killed in a way that didn't add blood to the room."

"But you're sure he's dead?"

"There's a soul floating around the house, Edward. Someone's dead, and if there are only three people living in a house, and two of them are accounted for . . . You do the math." I was staring out the car window but wasn't seeing anything. I was seeing that young tanned face smiling in the pictures.

"Deductive reasoning," Edward said. "I'm impressed."

"Yeah, me and Sherlock Holmes. By the way, now that I'm persona non grata, where are you taking me?"

"To a restaurant. You said you hadn't had lunch."

I nodded. "Fine." Then after a moment, I asked, "What was his name?"

"Who?"

"The Bromwells' son, what was his first name?"

"Thad, Thaddeus Reginald Bromwell."

"Thad," I said softly to myself. Had he been forced to watch while his parents were skinned alive, mutilated? Or had they watched him die before they bled? "Where's your body, Thad? And why did they want it?" There was no answer. I hadn't expected one. Souls weren't like ghosts. To my knowledge there was no way to communicate with them directly. But I would have answers and soon. It had to be soon. "Edward, I need to see the pictures from the other crime scenes. I need to see everything the Santa Fe PD have. You said only this last case was in Albuquerque, so screw them. I'll start from the other end."

Edward smiled. "I've got copies at my house."

"Your house?" I sat up straighter and stared at him. "Since when do the police share files with bounty hunters?"

"I told you the Santa Fe police like Ted."

"You said the Albuquerque police liked you, too," I said.

"They do like me. It's you they don't like." He had a point. I could still see the hatred in Marks' eyes when he hissed at me, "Thou shalt not suffer a witch to live." Sweet Jesus. That was actually the first time I'd ever had that particular verse quoted at me. Though I suppose someone would have gotten around to it sooner or later, being who I am and what I do. I just didn't expect it from a police lieutenant during a murder investigation. It lacked a certain professionalism.

"Marks won't be able to solve this case," I said.

"Without you, you mean?"

"It doesn't have to be me, but someone with some expertise is going to be needed. We are not dealing with a human killer here. Normal police work is not going to do the job."

"I agree," Edward said.

"Marks needs to be replaced," I said.

"I'll work on it," he said. Then he smiled. "Maybe with that nice Detective Ramirez that found you sooo fascinating."

"Don't go there, Edward."

"He does have one thing over your other two boyfriends."

"What?" I asked.

"He is human."

I'd have liked to argue but couldn't. "When you're right, you're right."

"You're agreeing with me?" He sounded surprised.

"Neither Jean-Claude nor Richard are human. As far as I can tell, Ramirez is human. What's to argue about?"

"I was teasing you, and you go all serious on me."

"You have no idea how refreshing it would be to be with a man that just wanted me for me, without any Machiavellian plots."

"Are you saying that Richard has been plotting behind your back, just like the vampire?"

"Let's just say I'm no longer sure who the good guys are, Edward. Richard has become something harder and more complex because his role as Ulfric, Wolf King, has demanded it of him. And God help me, partly I think because I demanded it of him. He was too soft for me, so he's become harder."

"And you don't like it," Edward said.

"No, I don't like it, but since it's partially my fault, it's hard to bitch."

"Then dump them both, and date some humans."

"You make it sound so simple."

"It's only hard if you make it hard, Anita."

"Just dump the boys and start dating other men, just like that."

"Why not?" he asked.

I opened my mouth sure I had an answer, but for the life of me couldn't come up with one. Why not date other people? Because I loved two men already and that seemed one too many without adding anyone else. But what would it be like to be with someone who was human? Someone who wasn't trying to use me to consolidate his power like Jean-Claude. Both Richard and Jean-Claude huddled around my humanity like it was the last fire at the end of the world and all the rest was icy darkness. Richard especially clung to me because I was human, and having a human girlfriend had seemed to help him retain human status. Though lately how human I was, was up for debate. At least Richard had been human until he became a werewolf. Jean-Claude had been human until he became a vampire. I'd seen my first soul when I was ten at my great-aunt's funeral. I'd raised my first dead by accident when I was thirteen. Of the three of us I was the only one who had never been truly human.

What would it be like to date someone "normal"? I didn't know. Did I want to find out? I realized with a shock that I did. I wanted to go out on a normal date with a normal guy and do normal things, just once, just for a while. I'd been vampire's lover, werewolf's mate, zombie queen, and for the last year I'd been learning ritual magic so I could control all the rest, so I guess you could add apprentice witch to the list. It had been a weird year even for me. I'd called a break to the romance with both Richard and Jean-Claude because I needed a breather. They were overwhelming me, and I didn't know how to stop it. Would one date with someone else really hurt? Would going out with someone who was just a guy really bring the world crashing down around my ears? Would it? The answer was probably no, but the very fact that I wasn't sure meant I should have run from Ramirez and any other nice guy who asked me out. I should have said no, and kept saying no, so why did part of me want to say yes?

12

IT WAS ONLY AS Edward was searching for a parking spot on the rock-covered parking lot behind Los Cuates that I realized it was a Mexican restaurant. The name should have been a clue, but I just hadn't been paying attention. If my mother had liked Mexican food, she hadn't lived long enough to pass it on to me. Blake was an English name, but before my great-grandfather came through Ellis Island it was Bleckenstien. My idea of ethnic cuisine was wiener schnitzel and sauerbraten. So I was less than enthused as we crossed the gravel to the rear entrance of the restaurant. For someone who didn't like Mexican or southwestern cuisine, I was in the wrong part of the country.

The back entrance led through a long shadowed hall, but the main restaurant was bright with white stucco walls: bright wall hangings, fake parrots dangling from the ceiling, and strings of dried chilies everywhere. Very touristy, which usually means the food won't be authentic or very good. But a lot of the diners were Hispanic and that boded well. Whatever the food, if the actual ethnic group liked the restaurant, then the food was authentic and likely good.

A woman that actually looked Hispanic asked if we'd like a table. Edward smiled and said, "Thanks, but I see our party."

I looked where he was looking and saw Donna at a booth. There were two kids with her, one girl about five or six and a boy in his early teens. Call it a hunch, but I was betting I was about to be introduced to her kiddies. Introduced to Edward's potential step-children. Can you stand it? I was almost sure I couldn't.

Donna stood and gave Edward a smile that would have melted a lesser man into his socks. It wasn't the sex, though that was in there. It was the warmth, the perfect trust that only true love can give you. That first romantic love that may not last, but while it does, wow. I knew that he was probably giving as good a look as he was getting, but his wasn't real. He didn't mean it. He was lying with his eyes, something I'd only managed to learn recently, and part of me is sad about that. It's one thing to know how to lie, but to be able to lie with your eyes says you are someone not to be trusted. Poor Donna. She was with two of us.

The little girl scooted out of the booth and came running towards us, arms outstretched, chestnut braids flying. She gave a glad shriek of, "Ted!" and flung herself into his arms. Edward scooped her up and tossed her towards the ceiling. She laughed that joyous full-blown sound that children eventually grow out of, as if the world bleeds the joy from them. Unless we're very lucky, the world teaches us to laugh more quietly, more coyly.

The boy just sat staring at us. His hair was the same rich chestnut brown as the girl's, cut short with a wave of bangs that hung into his eyes. The eyes were brown and dark and not friendly. Edward had said the boy was fourteen, but he was one of those boys that look younger. He could have passed for twelve easily. He looked sullen and angry as he watched Edward and Donna hug, the little girl still in Edward's arms so it was a family hug. Edward whispered something in Donna's ear that made her laugh and pull away blushing.

He swung the girl to his other arm and asked, "How's my best girl?"

She giggled and started talking in a high excited voice. She was telling some long complicated story about her day that involved butterflies and a cat and Uncle Raymond and Aunt Esther. I assumed they were the neighbors that had played babysitter for the day.

The boy turned his hostile eyes from Edward to me. The frown did not lessen, but the eyes went from angry to curious, as if I wasn't what he'd expected. I actually get that a lot from men of all ages. I ignored the happy family stuff and held out my hand to him. "I'm Anita Blake."

He gave me his hand half hesitating as if most people didn't offer. His grip was unsure as if he needed practice, but he said, "Peter, Peter Parnell."

I nodded. "Good to meet you." I would have said his mother said good things about him, but that wasn't strictly true, and Peter struck me as someone who respected truth.

He nodded vaguely, eyes flicking to his mother and Edward. He didn't like it, not one little bit, and I didn't blame him. I remembered how I'd felt when my father brought Judith home. I'd never really forgiven my father for marrying her only two years after my mother's death. I hadn't finished my grieving and he was moving on with his life, being happy again. I'd hated him for it and hated Judith more.

Even if Edward had truly been Ted Forrester, and his intentions honorable, it would have been a difficult situation. As it was, it sucked.

Becca was wearing a bright yellow sundress with daisies on it. She had yellow ribbons at the end of each neat braid. The hand she put over her mouth to smother a giggle still had that soft, round baby look to it. She was looking at Edward as if he was the eighth wonder of the world. In that moment I hated Edward, hated that he could lie to the child so completely and not understand that it was wrong.

Something must have shown on my face because Peter was giving me a strange considering look. Not angry, but thoughtful. I forced my face blank and met his eyes. He held my gaze for a few seconds, but finally had to look away. Probably not fair to bring out my full stare on one angry fourteen-year-old boy, but to do less would imply that he was less, and he wasn't, just young. And time would cure that. Donna took Becca back from Edward's arms and turned towards me smiling. "This is Becca."

"Hi, Becca," I said and smiled because she was one of those children that made it easy to smile.

"And this is Peter," she said.

"We've met," I said.

Donna gave a funny look from Peter to me and back to me. I realized she thought we'd literally met before. "We introduced ourselves already," I said.

She relaxed and gave a nervous laugh. "Of course. Silly of me."

"You were just too busy to notice," Peter said, and his voice held what the actual words did not: scorn.

Donna looked at him as if she didn't know what to say, and finally, said, "I'm sorry, Peter."

She shouldn't have apologized. It implied she'd done something wrong, and she hadn't. She didn't know that Ted Forrester was an illusion. She was holding up her end of the bargain for happily ever after. Apologizing makes you sound weak, and from the look on Peter's face Donna needed all the strength she could get.

Donna slid into the booth first, then Becca, and Edward on the outside, with one leg hanging out from the booth. Peter had already sat down in the middle of his side of the booth. I sat down beside him and he didn't move over, so I found enough seat to be comfortable and ended with the line of our bodies touching from shoulder to hip. If he wanted to play sullen teenager with Edward and his mom, great, but I was not playing.

When Peter realized I wasn't moving over, he finally scooted over with a loud sigh that let me know it had been an effort. I did feel sorry for Peter and his plight, but my sympathy is never endless, and the sullen teenager routine might use it up pretty quick.

Becca was sitting happily between her mother and Edward. She was swinging her legs, and her hands were out of sight, maybe holding a hand of each of them. Her contentment was large and complete as if sitting between them not only was she happy, but she felt safe the way you're supposed to feel with your parents. It made my chest tight to see her so pleased with the situation. Edward was right. He couldn't just leave without some explanation. Becca Parnell more than her mother deserved better than that. I watched the little girl sit there and shine between them and wondered what excuse would be good enough. Nothing came to mind.

A waitress came to the booth, handed plastic menus all around even to Becca which pleased her, and then went away while we looked at them. Peter's first comment was, "I hate Mexican food."

Donna said, "Peter," in a warning voice.

But I added my two cents worth, "Me, too."

Peter looked at me sideways, as if he didn't trust my show of solidarity with him. "Really?"

I nodded. "Really."

"Ted picked the restaurant," he said.

"Think he did it just to be irritating?" I asked.

Peter was looking directly at me, eyes a little wide. "Yeah, I do."

I nodded. "Me, too."

Donna had an open-mouthed astonished look on her face. "Peter, Anita." She turned to Edward. "What are we going to do with the two of them?" Her appealing to Edward for help over such a small thing made me think less of her.

"You can't do anything with Anita," he said, and he turned cool blue eyes to Peter. "I'm not sure about Peter yet."

Peter wouldn't meet Edward's gaze, and the boy squirmed just a bit. Edward made him uncomfortable on more than one level. It wasn't just that Edward was doing his mom. It was more than that. Peter was just a little afraid of Edward, and I was betting that he hadn't done anything to earn it. I was betting that Edward had tried very hard to win Peter over as he'd won Becca over, but Peter wasn't having any of it. It had probably started out as just the normal resentment of anyone his mom dated, but the way he sat there now with his gaze carefully avoiding Edward's let me know it was more now. Peter was more nervous than he should have been around Ted, as if he somehow had picked up the real Edward under all the fun and games. It was both good for Peter and bad for him. If he ever guessed the truth and Edward didn't want it known . . . Well, Edward was very practical.

One problem at a time. Peter and I bent over our menus and made disparaging comments about nearly every menu item. By the time the waitress had come back with a basket of bread, I'd actually seen him smile twice. My own younger brother Josh had never been sullen, but I'd always gotten along with him. If I ever had children, not that I was planning on it, I wanted boys. I was just more comfortable with them.

The bread wasn't bread, but some fluffed pastry thing called a sopapilla. There was a plastic container of honey on the table especially for them. Donna spread honey on a small corner and ate that. Edward spread honey across one entire end of his bread. Becca put so much honey on her bread that Donna had to take it away from her.

Peter took a sopapilla. "It's the only good part of the meal," he said.

"I don't like honey," I said.

"Me, either, but this isn't bad." He spread a minute amount of honey and ate the small bite he'd spread it on, then repeated the process.

I got one and followed his example. The bread was good, but the honey was very different, stronger, and with an undercurrent that reminded me of sage. "This honey tastes nothing like honey back home."

"It's sage honey," Edward said. "Stronger flavor."

"I'll say." I'd never had anything but clover honey. I wondered if all honey took on the flavor of the plant the bees used. It seemed likely. Learn something new every day. But Peter was right. The sopapillas were good, and the honey wasn't bad in small, nay, microscopic amounts.

I finally ordered chicken enchilada. I mean, what could they possibly do to chicken to make it uneatable. Don't answer that.

Peter had plain cheese enchiladas. Both of us seemed to be going on the less is better plan.

I was on my second sopapilla when everyone else, including Peter, had finished their two a piece, when I saw bad guys come into the restaurant. How did I know they were bad guys? Instinct? Nope, practice.

The first one was six foot and almost obscenely broad through the shoulders. His arms swelled against the sleeves of his T-shirt as if the cloth couldn't contain him. His hair was straight and thick, tied back in a loose braid. I think the braid was for effect because the rest of him was so ethnic, he could have been the poster boy for the American Indian *GQ*. The cheekbones were high and tight under the dark skin, a slight uptilt to his black eyes, a strong jaw, slender lips. He wore blue jeans that were tight enough that you could tell his lower body had not had the workout that his upper body had. There is only one place where a man will put that much effort into his upper body and ignore his lower: prison. You don't lift weights in prison to get a balanced effect. You lift weights so you look like a complete badass and can hit with everything you got when the time comes. I looked for the next clue, and the tattoos were there. Black barbwire chased the swell of his arms just below the sleeves of the T-shirt.

There were two other men with him, one taller, one shorter. The taller one was in better shape, but the shorter had a wicked-looking scar that nearly bisected his face giving him the more sinister look. All the three of them needed was a sign above their heads that flashed "bad news." Why was I not surprised when they started walking toward us. I looked at Edward and mouthed, "What's up?"

The strangest part was that Donna knew them. I could tell by her face that she knew them and was scared of them. Could this day get any stranger?

13

PETER LET OUT A soft, "Oh, my God."

His face showed fear. He put his angry sullen look up like a mask, but I was close enough to see how wide his eyes were, how his breathing had quickened.

I glanced at Becca, and she had curled back into the seat between Edward and Donna. She peered out around Edward's arm with wide eyes. Everyone knew what was happening except me.

But I didn't have long to wait. The threatening threesome came right up to the booth. I tensed, ready to stand if Edward did, but he stayed seated though his hands were out of sight under the table. He probably had a gun out. I dropped my napkin accidentally on purpose and when I came out from under the table, the napkin was in one hand, and the Browning Hi-Power was in the other. The gun was under the table out of sight, but it was pointed at the bad guys. From under the table the shot probably wouldn't kill anyone, but it would make a big hole in someone's leg, or groin, depending on how tall the person was who happened to be standing in the wrong place at the wrong time.

"Harold," Edward said, "you brought backup." His voice was still Ted's voice, more lively than his usual, but it was no longer a pleasant voice. I couldn't have told you what had changed in the voice, but it raised the tension level another notch. Becca scooted back until she couldn't see the men, hiding her face against Edward's sleeve. Donna reached for her, drawing her away from Edward and into her arms. Donna's face was openly fearful like the girl's. Edward's was open, almost smiling, but his eyes had gone empty. His real eyes peeking out. I'd seen monsters, real monsters, pale under that gaze.

The short one with the scar shifted from foot to foot. "Yeah, this is Russell," he motioned at the Indian, "and this is Newt."

I almost said, "Newt," aloud, but figured we had enough problems without me being a smart-ass. And people say I don't know when to keep my mouth shut.

"Tom and Benny still in the hospital?" Edward asked, voice still conversational. So far we hadn't attracted too much attention. We were getting some glances but not much else, yet.

"We're not Tom and Benny," Russell said. His voice matched the smile on his face, but I was reminded that smiling is just another way of baring teeth, another way to snarl.

"Bully for you," I said.

His gaze swiveled to me. His eyes were so black that the iris and pupil had melted into one black hole. "You another psychic bleeding heart trying to keep the Indian lands safe for us poor savages?"

I shook my head. "I've been accused of a lot but never of being a bleeding heart." I smiled up at him and thought that if I pulled the trigger, I would take out most of his thigh, and maybe cripple him for life. He was standing that close to the table. Close enough that I wanted him to back up, but I was waiting on Edward, and he seemed just fine with them towering over us.

"You should leave now," Edward said, and his voice was beginning to sound like Edward. Ted was leaking away, leaving his face a blank, cold mask, his eyes empty as a winter sky. His voice was without inflection as if he were saying something totally different. Edward was emerging from his Ted mask like a butterfly pulling free of a chrysalis, though I wanted something less pretty, less harmless for the analogy, because what was pulling free into the light wasn't harmless, and if things went wrong it wasn't going to be pretty at all.

Russell leaned over the table, large hands spread across the top. He leaned way over so he would be close to Donna's face, ignoring both Edward and me. Either he was stupid, or he figured we wouldn't draw first blood in a public place. He was right about me, but I wasn't so sure about Edward.

"You and your friends stay out of our way, or you are going to get hurt." He wasn't smiling when he said it. His voice was flat and ugly. "You've got a cute little girl there. Be a shame if something happened to her."

Donna paled and clutched Becca tighter. I don't know what Edward had planned because it was Peter who spoke. "Don't you threaten my sister." His voice was low and angry, no fear showed through.

Russell's gaze flicked to Peter, and he leaned over into his face. Peter sat unmoving, until their faces were inches apart but his eyes flickered back and forth like they were trying to escape. His hands gripped the seat edge as if he were literally holding on to keep from backing down.

"And what are you going to do about it, little man?"

"Ted?" I made it a question.

Russell's eyes flicked to me, then back to Peter. He was enjoying the boy's fear and the show of bravado. Hard to be tough muscle if you can't make a fourteen-year-old boy back down. He'd finish scaring Peter then turn to me. I don't think he considered me a threat. His mistake.

I couldn't see Edward through Russell's bulk, but I heard his voice, cold and empty, "Do it."

No, I didn't shoot him. That wasn't what I'd asked permission to do or what Edward had given the go ahead on. How did I know this? I just did. I switched the gun to my left hand, and let out a breath, long and soft, until my shoulders were relaxed. I centered myself like I learned for years in Judo, and now Kenbo. I visualized my fingers going into his throat, through the flesh. When fighting for real, you don't visualize hitting someone. You visualize throwing the punch through them and out the other side. Though I would hold back a little. You can collapse a man's windpipe with this move, and I didn't want to go to jail over this. I dropped my right hand down to the seat beside me and brought my hand up with two fingers like a spear pointed. Russell saw the movement, but didn't react in time. I drove my fingers into his throat coming to my feet with the strength of the blow.

He gagged, hands going to his throat, half collapsing on the table. I used my right hand to drive his face into the table, once, twice, three times. Blood spurted from his nose, and he slid bonelessly across the tabletop to end up on the floor, staring up at the ceiling, gagging, trying to breathe through his injured throat and the smashed nose. I think if he could have breathed better, he'd have passed out, but it's hard to pass out when you're gagging. He rocked on the floor, gagging, eyes rolled back into his head, not focused.

I was standing beside the booth, staring down at him. My gun was still in my left hand, at my side, unobtrusive against my black jeans. Most people wouldn't even see the gun. They'd see the blood and the man on the floor.

Harold and the tall Newt were standing there, frozen, staring down at Russell. Harold shook his head sadly. "You shouldn't have ought to have done that."

Edward was standing beside the booth, blocking their view of Donna and Becca. He spoke softly, so his voice wouldn't carry much beyond our little circle. "Don't ever threaten these people again, Harold. Don't come near them for any reason. Tell Riker that they are off limits, or the next time it won't just be a broken nose."

"I see the guns," Harold said, voice low. He bent down beside Russell. The big man's eyes still weren't focused. His blue T-shirt had turned purple with blood. Harold was shaking his head. He looked up at me. "Who the hell are you?"

"Anita Blake," I said.

He shook his head again. "Don't know the name."

"I guess my reputation does not proceed me," I said.

"It will," Harold said.

I said, "Peter, get some napkins."

Peter didn't ask questions. He just got a double handful of napkins from the dispenser on the table and handed them my way. I took them with my right hand and held them out to Harold. He took them, watching my face, eyes flicking to the gun still bare against my leg.

"Thanks."

"Don't mention it."

He shoved the napkins against Russell's nose and took one arm. "Get his other arm, Newt."

There was a distant wail of sirens coming closer. Someone had called the cops.

Russell was still unsteady on his feet. They'd shoved napkins into his flattened nose, and he looked both silly and grotesque with the bloody napkins sticking out of his nose. He had to clear his voice twice before he could speak, his voice sounded rough, clogged, painful, "You fucking bitch! I am going to hurt you so bad for this."

"When you can stand without help and you've got your nose packed at the nearest emergency room, give me a call. I'd love a rematch."

He spat in my general direction but didn't have the aim, so it splattered harmlessly into the floor. Gross, but not very effective.

"Come on," Harold said. He was trying to move the show towards the door. The sirens were very close now.

But Russell wasn't finished. He turned, forcing the other two to turn with him. "I am going to fuck your bitch, and leave the girl and boy for the coyotes."

"Russell is not a fast learner," I said.

Becca was crying now, and Donna was so pale, I was worried she was going to faint. I couldn't turn around enough to see Peter's face without turning away from the bad guys, so I don't know what he looked like. But it wasn't a pretty scene.

The cops spilled in with Harold still trying to get Russell out the door. Edward and I used the confusion to put up our guns. The two uniforms were a little unsure whom to arrest, but the people actually testified to having heard Russell's threats, and seeing him "menace" us before I hurt him. I'd never seen so much witness cooperation. Most of the time people are deaf and dumb, but having a small, pretty little girl in tears helped people's memories. Technically, Russell could press assault charges on me, but everyone was jumping over themselves to say that he'd been threatening us. One man claimed he'd seen Russell pull a knife. Amazing how quickly details are added to a story. I could not corroborate the knife, but I had enough witnesses to the threats that I didn't think I'd be going to jail. Edward pulled out his Ted ID, and the officers knew him by reputation if not by sight. I pulled out my executioner's license and my gun carry permit. Technically, I was carrying concealed when my permit wasn't for this state. I explained I'd worn the jacket to keep from distressing the children. The cops nodded, wrote it down, and seemed to accept it all.

It helped that Russell was being verbally abusive to the officers and was so obviously a badass, and I was so harmless looking, so small, so feminine, and so much less scary than he was. Edward gave them his address, said I'd be staying with him, and we were free to go.

The restaurant offered us a different table, but strangely Donna and the kids had lost their appetites. I was still hungry, but no one asked me. Edward paid for the food, and declined a takeout order. I put the tip on the bloodstained table, way overtipping to try and make up for the mess. Then we left, and I still hadn't eaten today. Maybe if I asked nicely, Edward would run through a drive-up window at McDonalds. Any port in a storm.

14

DONNA STARTED CRYING OUT in the parking lot. Becca joined her. Only Peter stayed silent and apart from the general hysteria. The more Donna cried, the more panicky the girl got, like they were feeding off each other. The girl was crying in those great hiccuppy sobs bordering on hyperventilation. I looked at Edward and raised my eyebrows. He looked blank. I finally gave him a push. He mouthed, "Which one?"

"Girl," I mouthed back.

He knelt by them. Donna had settled down on the bumper of his Hummer cradling Becca in her lap.

Edward knelt in front of them. "Let me take Becca for a little walk."

Donna blinked up at him, as if she saw him, heard him, but wasn't really understanding. He reached for Becca and started prying her from her mother's arms. Donna's arms were limp, but the girl clung to her mother, screaming.

Edward literally pried her small fingers away, and when she was free of her mother, Becca turned and clung to him, burying her face in his shoulder. He looked at me over the girl's head, and I shooed him away. He never questioned, just walked towards the sidewalk that edged the parking lot. He was rocking the girl slowly as he moved, soothing her.

Donna had covered her face with her hands, collapsing forward until her face and hands met her knees. Her sobs were full-blown almost wails. Shit. I looked at Peter. He was watching her, and the look on his was disgusted, embarrassed. I knew in that instant that he'd been the adult in more ways than just shooting his father's killer. His mother was allowed hysterics, but he wasn't. He was the one who held together in a crisis. Damned unfair, if you ask me.

"Peter, can you excuse us for a few minutes?"

He shook his head. "No."

I sighed, then shrugged. "Fine, just don't interfere." I knelt in front of Donna, touching her shaking shoulders. "Donna, Donna!" There was no response, no change. It had been a long day. I got a handful of that short thick hair and pulled her head up. It hurt, and it was meant to. "Look at me, you selfish bitch."

Peter moved forward, and I pointed a finger at him. "Don't." He settled back a step, but he didn't leave. His face was angry, watchful, and I knew that he might interfere regardless of what I said if I went much further. But I didn't have to go further. I'd shocked her. Her eyes were wide, inches from mine, her face drenched with tears. Her breathing was still coming in small chest-heaving gulps, but she was looking at me, she was listening.

I released her hair slowly, and she stayed staring at me with a horrible fascination on her face as if I were about to do something cruel, and I was. "Your little girl has just seen the worst thing she's ever seen in her life. She was calming down, taking it in stride, until you started on the hysterics. You're her mother. You're her strength, her protector. When she saw you fall apart like that, it terrified her."

"I didn't mean . . . I couldn't help . . ."

"I don't give a shit what you feel or how upset you are. You're the mommy. She's the child. You are going to hold yourself together until she is not around to see you fall apart, is that clear?"

She blinked at me. "I don't know if I can do that."

"You can do it. You're going to do it." I glanced up but didn't see Edward yet. Good. "You are the grownup, Donna, and you are by God going to act like it."

I could feel Peter watching us, could almost feet him storing it away for later playback. He would remember this little scene and he would think on it, you could feel it.

"Do you have children?" she asked, and I knew what was coming.

"No," I said.

"Then what right do you have to tell me how to raise mine?" She was angry now, sitting up straighter, wiping at her face with short harsh movements.

Sitting up on the bumper, she was taller than I was kneeling. I looked up into her angry eyes and told the truth. "I was eight years old when my mother died, and my father couldn't handle it. We got a phone call from a state trooper that told us she was dead. My father dropped the phone and started to wail, not cry, wail. He took me by the hand and walked the few blocks to my grandmother's house, wailing, leading me by the hand. By the time we got to my grandmother's we had a crowd of neighbors, all asking what was wrong, what was wrong. I was the one who turned to my neighbors and said, "My mommy's dead." My father was collapsed in the bosom of his family, and I was left standing alone, uncomforted, unheld, tears on my face, telling the neighbors what had happened."

Donna stared at me and there was something very close to horror on her face. "I'm sorry," she said in a voice that had grown soft and lost its anger.

"Don't be sorry for me, Donna, but be a mother to your own daughter. Hold it together. She needs you to comfort her right now. Later when you're alone, or with Ted, you can fall apart, but please, not in front of the kids. That goes for Peter, too."

She glanced at him, standing there, watching us, and she flushed, embarrassed at last. She nodded her head too rapidly, then visibly straightened. You could actually see her gathering herself. She took my hands, squeezing them. "I am sorry for your loss, and I apologize for today. I'm not very good around violence. If it's an accident, a cut, no matter the blood, I'm fine, honestly, but I just can't abide violence."

I drew my hands gently from hers. I wasn't sure I believed her, but I said, "I'm glad to know that, Donna. I'll go get . . . Ted and Becca."

She nodded. "Thank you."

I stood, nodding. I walked across the gravel in the direction Edward had gone. I liked Donna less now, but I knew now that Edward had to get away from this family. Donna wasn't good around violence. Jesus, if she only knew who, what, she'd taken to her bed. She'd have had hysterics for the rest of her life.

Edward had walked down the sidewalk to stand in front of one of the many small houses. They all had gardens in front, well tended, well planned. It reminded me of California where every inch of yard is used for something because land is such a premium. Albuquerque didn't look nearly as crowded and yet the yards were crowded.

Edward was still holding Becca, but she was looking at something that he was pointing at, and there was a smile on her face that showed from two houses away. A tension I hadn't realized I was carrying eased from my back and shoulders. When she turned so that her face was full to me, I saw a sprig of lilac tucked into one of her braids. The pale lavender flower didn't match the yellow ribbons and dress, but hey, it was cute as hell.

Her smile faltered around the edges when she saw me. There was a very good chance that I wouldn't be one of Becca's favorite people. I'd probably scared her. Oh, well.

Edward put her down, and they walked towards me. She was smiling up at him, swinging his arm a little. He smiled down at her, and it looked real. Even to me it looked real. You might have really believed he was Becca's adored and adoring father. How the hell were we going to get him out of their lives without screwing Becca over? Peter would be pleased if Ted went poof, and Donna . . . She was a grown-up. Becca wasn't. Shit.

Edward smiled at me and said in his cheerful Ted voice, "How are things?"

"Just dandy," I said.

He raised eyebrows, and for a split second his eyes flinched going from cynical to cheerful so fast it made me dizzy.

"Donna and Peter are waiting for us."

Edward turned so that the girl was between us. She glanced up at me, and her gaze was questioning, thoughtful. "You beat up that bad man," she said.

"Yes, I did," I said.

"I didn't know girls could do that."

That made my teeth hurt. "Girls can do anything they want to do, including protect themselves and beat up bad guys."

"Ted said that you hurt that man because he said bad things to me."

I glanced at Edward, but his face was all open and cheerful for the child and gave me nothing.

"That's right," I said.

"Ted says that you'd hurt someone to protect me just like he would."

I met her big brown eyes, and nodded. "Yes, I would."

She smiled then and it was beautiful, like sunshine breaking through clouds. She reached out her free hand to me, and I took it. Edward and I walked back to the parking lot, holding the child's hands while she half-walked, half-danced between us. She believed in Ted, and Ted had told her that she could believe in me, so she did. The odd thing was that I would hurt someone to protect her. I would kill to keep her safe. I looked across at Edward and for just a moment he looked back at me from the mask. We stared at each other over the child, and I didn't know what to do. I didn't know how to get us all out of the mess that he had made.

Becca said, "Swing me."

Edward counted out, "One, two, three," and swung her up and out, forcing me to swing her other arm. We moved across the parking lot, swinging Becca between us while she gave that joyous, full-throated laugh.

We sat her down laughing in front of her mother. Donna was composed and smiling. I was proud of her. Becca looked up at me, shining. “Mommy says I’m too big to swing now, but you’re strong, aren’t you?”

I smiled at her, but I looked at Edward when I said, “Yes, I am.”

15

DONNA AND EDWARD DID a tender but decorous good-bye. Peter rolled his eyes and scowled as if they'd done a lot more than a semi-chaste kiss. He'd have had a cow if he could have seen them smooching earlier at the airport. Becca kissed Edward on the cheek, giggling. Peter ignored it all and got in the car as soon as he could as if afraid "Ted" might try to hug him, too.

Edward waved until the car turned onto Lomos and out of sight, then he turned to me. All he did was look at me, but it was enough.

"Let's get in the car and get some air conditioning going before I grill you about what the hell is going on," I said.

He unlocked the car. We got inside. He started the engine and the air conditioner, though the air hadn't had time to cool yet. We sat in the expensive hum of his engine with the hot air blowing on us, and silence filled the car.

"Are you counting to ten?" he asked.

"Try a thousand and you'll be closer."

"Ask. I know you want to."

"Okay, we'll skip the tirade about you dragging Donna and her kids into your mess and go straight to who the hell is Riker and why did he send goons to warn you off?"

"First, it was Donna's mess, and she dragged me into it."

My disbelief must have shown on my face because he continued, "She and her friends are a part of an amateur archeology society that tries to preserve Native American sites in the area. Are you familiar with how an archeological dig is done?"

"A little. I know they use string and tags to mark where an object is found, take pictures, drawings, sort of like you do for a dead body before you move it."

"Trust you to come up with the perfect analogy," he said, but he was smiling. "I've gone with Donna on weekends with the kids. They use freaking toothbrushes and tiny paint brushes to gently clean the dirt away, or dental picks."

"I know you have a point," I said.

"Pot hunters find a sight that is already being explored, or sometimes one that hasn't been found, and they bring in bulldozers and backhoes to take out as much as possible in the least amount of time."

I gaped at him. "But that destroys more than they can possibly take out, and if you move an object before its site is recorded, it loses a lot of its historical value. I mean the dirt it's found in can help date it. What is found near an object can tell all sorts of things to a trained eye."

"Pot hunters don't care about history. They take what they find and sell it to private collectors or dealers who aren't too particular about how an object was found. A site that Donna was volunteering on was raided."

"She asked you to look into it," I said.

"You underestimate her. She and her psychic friends thought they could reason with Riker, since they were pretty sure it was his people behind it."

I sighed. "I don't underestimate her, Edward."

"She and her friends didn't understand what a bad man Riker is. Some of the really big pot hunters hire bodyguards, goon squads, to help take care of the bleeding hearts, and even the local law. Riker is suspected of having been behind the deaths of two local cops. It's one of the reasons that things went so smoothly in the restaurant. All the local cops know that Riker's a suspected cop killer, not personally, but of hiring it done."

I smiled, not a pleasant smile. "I wonder how many traffic tickets he and his men have acquired since it happened."

"Enough that his lawyer filed a harassment suit. There is no proof that Riker's people were involved, just the fact that the cops were killed at a dig that had been partially bulldozed, and an eye witness that saw a car with a partial plate that might have been one of his trucks."

"Is the witness still among the living?" I asked.

"My, you do catch on quick."

"I take it that's a no."

"He's missing," Edward said.

"So why come after Donna and her kids?"

"Because the kids were with her when she and her group formed a protest line protecting a site that was on private land that Riker had gotten permission to bulldoze. She was their spokesperson."

"Stupid, she should not have taken the kids."

"Like I said, Donna didn't understand how bad a man Riker was."

"And what happened?"

"Her group was manhandled, abused, beaten. They fled. Donna had a black eye."

"And what did Ted do about this?" I was watching his face, arms crossed over my stomach. All I could see was his profile, but it was enough. He hadn't liked it, that Donna had gotten hurt. Maybe it was just that she belonged to him, a male pride thing, or maybe . . . maybe it was more.

"Donna asked me to have a talk with the men."

"I take it that would be the two men that you put in the hospital. I seem to remember you asking Harold if two guys were still in the hospital."

Edward nodded. "Yeah."

"Only two in the hospital, and none in a grave. You must be slipping."

"I couldn't kill anyone without Donna knowing, so I made an example of two of his men."

"Let me guess. One of them would be the man who gave Donna the black eye."

Edward smiled happily. "Tom."

"And the other one?"

"He pushed Peter and threatened to break his arm."

I shook my head. The air had begun to cool, and it raised goose bumps even through my jacket, or maybe it wasn't the cold. "The second guy has a broken arm now?"

"Among other things," Edward said.

"Edward, look at me."

He turned and gave me his cool blue gaze.

"Truth, do you care for this family? Would you kill to protect them?"

"I'd kill to amuse myself, Anita."

I shook my head, and leaned close to him, close enough to study his face, to try and make him give up his secrets. "No jokes, Edward, tell me the truth. Are you serious about Donna?"

"You asked me if I loved her and I said, no."

I shook my head again. "Dammit, don't keep evading the answer. I don't think you do love her. I don't think you're capable of it, but you feel something. I don't know exactly what, but something. Do you feel something for this family, for all of them?"

His face was blank, and I couldn't read it. He just stared at me. I wanted to slap him, to scream and rant until I broke through his mask into whatever lay underneath. I'd always been on sure ground with Edward, always known where he stood, even when he was planning to hurt me. But now suddenly, I wasn't sure about anything.

"My God, you do care for them." I slumped back in my seat, weak. I couldn't have been more astonished if he'd sprouted a second head. That would have been weird, but not this weird.

"Jesus, Mary, and Joseph, Edward, you care for them, all of them."

He looked away. Edward, the stone cold killer, looked away. He couldn't or wouldn't meet my gaze. He put the car in gear and forced me to buckle my seat belt.

I let him pull out of the parking lot in silence, but when we were sitting at the stop sign waiting for the traffic to clear on Lomos, I had to say something. "What are you going to do?"

"I don't know," he said. "I don't love Donna."

"But," I said.

He turned slowly onto the main street. "She's a mess. She believes in every new age bandwagon that comes along. She's got a good head for business, but she trusts everyone. She's useless around violence. You saw her today." He was concentrating very hard on the driving, hands gripping the wheel tight enough for his knuckles to be white. "Becca is just like her, trusting, sweet, but . . . tougher, I think. Both the kids are tougher than Donna."

"They've had to be," I said, and couldn't keep the disapproval out of my voice.

"I know, I know," he said. "I know Donna, everything about her. I've heard every detail from cradle to the present."

"Did it bore you?" I asked.

"Some of it," he said carefully.

"But not all of it," I said.

"No, not all of it."

"Are you saying that you do love Donna?" I had to ask.

"No, no, I'm not saying that."

I was staring so hard at his face that we could have been driving on the far side of the moon for all the attention I gave the scenery. Nothing mattered more right that second than Edward's face, his voice. "Then what are you saying?"

"I'm saying that sometimes when you play a part too long, you can get sucked into that part and it becomes more real than it was meant to be." I saw something on his face that I had never seen before, anguish, uncertainty.

"Are you saying that you are going to marry Donna? You're going to be a husband and a father? PTA meetings, and the whole nine yards?"

"No, I'm not saying that. You know I can't marry her. I can't live with her and two kids and hide what I am twenty-four hours a day. That good an actor I'm not."

"Then what are you saying?" I asked.

"I'm saying . . . I'm saying that part of me, a small part of me, wishes I could."

I stared at him opened-mouthed. Edward, assassin extraordinaire, the undead's perfect predator, wished he could have not a family, but this family. A trusting new age widow, her sullen teenage son, and a little girl that made Rebecca of Sunnybrook Farm look jaded, and Edward wanted them.

When I trusted myself to be coherent, I said, "What are you going to do?"

"I don't know."

I couldn't think of anything helpful to say, so I resorted to humor, my shield of last resort. "Just please tell me they don't have a dog and a picket fence."

He smiled. "No fence, but a dog, two dogs."

"What kind of dogs?" I asked.

He smiled and glanced at me, wanting to see my reaction. "Maltese. Their names are Peeka and Boo."

"Oh, shit, Edward, you're joking me."

"Donna wants the dogs included in the engagement pictures."

I stared at him, and the look on my face seemed to amuse him. He laughed. "I'm glad you're here, Anita, because I don't know a single other person who I'd have admitted this to."

"Do you realize that your personal life is now more complicated than mine is?" I said.

"Now I know I'm in trouble," he said. And we left it on a lighter note, on a joke, because we were more comfortable that way. But Edward had confided in me about a personal problem. In his way he'd come to me for help about it. And being who I was, I'd try to help him. I thought we would solve the mutilations and murders, eventually. I mean violence and death were our specialties. I was not nearly so optimistic about the personal stuff.

Edward did not belong in a world with a woman who had a pair of toy dogs named Peeka and Boo. Edward was not now, nor ever would be, that cutesy. Donna was. It wouldn't work. It just wouldn't work. But for the very first time I realized that if Edward didn't have a heart to lose, that he wished he had one to give. But I was reminded of the scene in *The Wizard of Oz* where Dorothy and the Scarecrow bang on the Tin Man's chest and hear the rolling echo. The tinsmith had forgotten to put in a heart. Edward had carved his own heart out of his body and left it on a floor somewhere years ago. I'd known that. I just never knew that Edward regretted the loss. And I think until Donna Parnell came along, he hadn't known it either.

16

EDWARD DID TAKE ME through a drive-up window, but he didn't want to stop. He seemed anxious to get to Santa Fe. Since he was rarely anxious about anything, I didn't argue. I requested we go through a carwash while I ate my French fries and cheeseburger. He didn't say a word, just drove into one beside the highway that let us ride through in the car. When I was little, I'd loved watching the suds slide down the windows and the huge brushes roll by. It was still nifty, though not the thrill a minute it had been when I was five. But the carwash did mean that I had a clear view out all the windows. The dirty windows had made me feel ever so slightly claustrophobic. I'd finished my food before we left Albuquerque. I sipped on my soda as we drove out of town and towards the mountains. These were not the black mountains, but a different range that looked more "normal." They were jagged and rocky looking, with a string of glittering light near their base.

"What's with the light show," I asked.

"What?" Edward asked.

"The glitter, what is it?"

I felt his attention shift from the road, but he was wearing his sunglasses, and I couldn't really see his gaze shift. "Houses, the sun is hitting the windows on the houses."

"I've never seen sunlight on windows glitter like that."

"Albuquerque is at 7,000 feet. The air is thinner than you're used to. It makes light do strange things."

I stared at the sparkling windows like a line of jewels imbedded in the mountains. "It's beautiful."

He moved his whole head. This time so I knew he was really looking at it. "If you say so."

After that we stopped talking. Edward never did idle chatter, and apparently he had nothing to say. My mind was still reeling from Edward being in love, or as close as he would probably ever get. It was just too weird. I couldn't think of a single useful thing to say so I stared out the window until I thought of something worth saying. I had a feeling it was going to be a long quiet drive to Santa Fe.

The hills were very round, covered in dry brownish grass. I had the same feeling I'd had when I stepped off the plane in Albuquerque—desolate. I'd thought the hills were close until I spotted a cow standing on one. The cow looked tiny, small enough for me to cover with two fingers held up, which meant the "hills" were really small mountains and not nearly as close as they appeared to the road. It was late afternoon or early evening depending on how you looked at it. It was still daylight, but you could feel night looming even in the brightness. The day had worn away like a piece of candy sucked too long. No matter how bright the sunshine, I could feel the darkness pressing close. Partly it was my mood—confusion always makes me pessimistic—but it was also an innate sense of the coming night. I was a vampire executioner, and I knew the taste of night on the breeze just as I knew the feel of dawn pressing against the darkness. There had been times when my life had depended on dawn coming. Nothing like near death experiences to hone a skill.

The sunlight had begun to fade to a soft evening gloom when I'd finally had enough of the silence. I still had nothing helpful to say about his personal life, but there was the case. I'd been asked here to help solve a crime, not to play Dear Abby, so maybe if I just concentrated on the crime, we'd be okay.

"Is there anything about the cases that you've withheld from me? Anything I'm going to be pissed that I didn't know beforehand?"

"Changing the subject?" he asked.

"I wasn't aware we were on a subject," I said.

"You know what I meant."

I sighed. "Yeah, I know what you meant." I slumped in my seat as far as the seatbelt would allow, arms crossed over my stomach. My body language was not happy, nor was I. "I don't have anything to add to the Donna situation, or nothing helpful."

"So concentrate on business," he said.

"You taught me that," I said, "you and Dolph. Keep your eye and mind on the important stuff. The important stuff is what can get you killed. Donna and her kiddies aren't a threat to life and limb so put them on the back burner."

He smiled, his normal close-lipped, I-know-something-you-don't-know smile. It didn't always mean he knew something I didn't. Sometimes he did it just to irritate. Like now. "I thought you said you'd kill me if I didn't stop dating Donna."

I rubbed my neck against the expensive seats and tried to ease a tension that was beginning at the base of my skull. Maybe I had been invited here to play Dear Abby, at least in part. Shit.

"You were right, Edward. You can't just leave. It would screw up Becca for one thing. But you cannot keep dating Donna indefinitely. She's going to start asking for a date for the wedding, and what are you going to say?"

"I don't know," he said.

"Well, neither do I, so let's talk about the case. At least with that we've got a solid direction."

"We do?" he glanced at me as he asked.

"We know we want the mutilations and murders to stop, right?" I asked.

"Yes," he said.

"Well, that's more than we know about Donna."

"Are you saying you don't want me to stop seeing her?" he asked, and that damn smile was back. Smug, he looked smug.

"I'm saying I don't know what the hell I want you to do, let alone what you should do. So let's leave it alone until I get some brilliant idea."

"Okay," he said.

"Great," I said. "Now back to the question I asked. What haven't you told me about the crimes that you think I should know, or rather that I think I should know?"

"I don't read minds, Anita. I don't know what you'll want to know."

"Don't be coy, Edward. Just spill the beans. I don't want any more surprises on this trip, not from you."

He was quiet for so long, I thought he wasn't going to answer. So I prompted him, "Edward, I mean it."

"I'm thinking," he said. He moved in his seat, shoulders tightening and loosening as if he were trying to get rid of tension, too. I guess, even for him, this had been a stressful day. Odd to think of Edward letting anything truly stress him. I'd always thought he walked through life with the perfect Zen of the sociopath, so that nothing truly bothered him. I'd been wrong. Wrong about a lot of things.

I went back to watching the scenery. There were cows scattered close enough to the road that you could make out color and size. If it wasn't a Jersey, a Guernsey, or a Black Angus, I didn't know it. I watched the strange cows standing at impossible angles on the steep hillsides and waited for Edward to finish thinking. Twilight seemed to last a long time here, as if the light of day gave up the fight slowly, struggling to remain and keep the darkness at bay. Maybe it was just my mood, but I wasn't looking forward to darkness. It was as if I could sense something out there in those desolate hills, something waiting for the night, something that could not move during the day. It could be just my own over-active imagination, or I could be right. That was the hard part about psychic abilities: sometimes you were right, and sometimes you weren't. Sometimes your own anxiety or fear could poison your thinking and make you, almost, literally see ghosts where there were none.

There were, of course, ways to find out. "Is there a place where you can pull over out of sight of the main road?"

He looked at me. "Why?"

"I'm . . . sensing something, and I just want to make sure I'm not imagining it."

He didn't argue. When the next exit came up, he took it. We took a side road from the exit. It was dirt and gravel and full of huge dry potholes. The shocks on his Hummer took the road like silk flowing down hill, comfy. A soft roll of hills hid us from the main highway, but the road was very flat in front of us, giving a clear view of the road as it went almost straight towards a distant rise of hills. There were a handful of tiny houses on either side of the road, the major cluster some ways ahead with a small church sitting to one side by itself, as if it were part of the houses and not. The church had a steeple with a cross on top of it, and I assumed a bell inside of it. Though we were too far away to be sure. The town, if it were a town, looked down on its luck but not empty. There were people there and eyes to see us. Just our luck, the land had been so empty and the road we go down has a town.

"Stop the car," I said. We were as far from the first house as we could get without backtracking.

Edward pulled over to the side of the road. The dust rose in a cloud to either side of the car, settling over the clean paint job in a dry powder.

"You guys don't get much rain up here, do you?"

"No," he said. Anyone else would have elaborated, but not Edward. Even the weather wasn't a topic of conversation unless it affected the job.

I got out of the car and walked a little way into the dry grass. I walked until I could no longer sense Edward or the car. When I looked back, I was yards away. Edward was standing on the driver's side door, arms crossed on the roof, hat tilted back so he could watch the show. I don't think there was another person I knew who wouldn't have asked at least one question about what I was about to do. It would be interesting to see if he asked any questions afterwards.

Darkness hung like a soft silken cloth, hanging against the sky, and the dying light. It was a soft comfortable twilight, an embracing dark. A breeze blew across the open land and played with my hair. Everything felt fine, good. Had I imagined? Was I letting Edward's problems get to me? Was the memory of the survivors in their air-compressed hospital room making me see shadows?

I almost just turned around and walked back to the car, but I didn't. If it were my imagination, then it wouldn't hurt to check, and if it wasn't . . . I turned and faced away from the car, away from the distant houses, and looked out into the emptiness. Of course, it wasn't really empty. There was grass rustling in the wind, it sounded so dry, like corn in autumn just before it's harvested. The ground was covered in a thin layer of pale reddish-brown gravel with paler dirt showing through. The ground ran until it met the hills that continued on and on towards the darkening sky. Not empty, just lonely.

I took a deep cleansing breath, let it out and did two things at once: I dropped my shields and spread my arms wide, hands reaching. I was reaching with my hands, but it wasn't just my hands. I reached outward with that sense I have—magic, if you like the word. I don't. I reached outward with that power that let me raise the dead and mix with werewolves. I reached outward towards that waiting presence that I'd felt, or thought I'd felt.

There, there like a fish tugging on my line. I turned to face the direction of the road. It was in that direction, going towards Santa Fe. It—I had no better word. I felt its eagerness for the coming night and knew that it could not move in daylight. And I knew that it was large, not physically, but psychically, because we were not close to it, and yet I'd picked it up miles away. How many miles I couldn't say, but far, very far to have sensed it. It didn't feel evil. That didn't mean it wasn't evil, just that it didn't think of itself as evil. Unlike people, preternatural entities are rather proud of being evil. They embraced their malignancy because whatever this was, it wasn't human. It wasn't physical. Spirit, energy, pick a word, but it was up ahead, and it was not contained in any physical shell. It was free floating. No, not free . . . Something slammed into me, not physically, but as if a psychic truck had run me down. I was on my butt in the dirt, trying to breathe, as if someone had hit me in the chest and knocked the wind out of me.

I heard Edward's running footsteps, but I couldn't seem to turn around. I was too busy relearning how to breathe.

He knelt by me, gun in hand. "What happened?" He was looking out into the thick twilight, not at me, searching, searching for the danger. His sunglasses were gone, and his face was very serious as he searched for something to shoot.

I gripped his arm, shaking my head, trying to talk. But when I finally had air enough, all I said was, "Shit, shit, shit!" It wasn't helpful, but I was scared. Most of the time when I get this scared, I get cold, shocky, but not when it's psychic shit. When something goes wrong with "magic," I never go shocky or get cold, I stay warm. If anything it's like tingling, warm, as if I'd stuck my finger in a light socket. Whatever "it" was, had sensed me and shut me down.

I pulled my shields around me like clutching a coat against a blizzard, but strangely it had backed off. Though if that one swat of power was any indication, it could slice me, dice me, and serve me on toast if it wanted to. It hadn't wanted to. I was glad, thrilled, but why hadn't it hurt me worse? How had I sensed it from so far away, and how had it sensed me? Usually, my greatest talent is with the dead. Did that mean whatever "it" was, was dead, or had something to do with the dead? Or was this one of the new psychic abilities that my teacher, Marianne, had warned me might crop up. God, I hoped not. I didn't need more strange shit in my life. I had plenty.

I forced myself to stop the useless cursing, and said, "Put up the gun, Edward. I'm all right. Besides, there's nothing to shoot and nothing to see."

He put a hand under my arm and pulled me to my feet before I was ready. I'd have been very happy to stay sitting for a while. I leaned on him, and he started moving us back towards the car. I stumbled and finally had to tell him, "Stop, please."

He held me up, still searching the new dark, gun still in hand. I should have known he'd keep the gun out. It was his security blanket—sometimes.

I could breathe again, and if Edward stopped dragging me on, I might be able to walk. The fear had faded because it was useless. I'd tried a bit of "magic," and I hadn't been good enough. I was learning ritual magic, but I was a beginner. Power isn't enough. You've got to know what to do with it, like a gun with the safety on. It makes a fine paperweight, but that's about it unless you know what to do with it.

I slid into the car, had my door closed and locked before Edward opened his door. "Tell me what happened, Anita."

I looked at him. "It would serve you right if I just looked at you and smiled."

Something crossed his face, a frown, a snarl, quickly lost to that perfect blankness he could manage. "You're right. I've been a secret-loving bastard, and it would serve me right. But you're the one who said we needed to stop the pissing contest and solve the crime. I'll stop if you will."

I nodded. "Agreed."

"So," he said.

"Start the car and get us out of here." Somehow I didn't like sitting on the nearly deserted road in the freshly spilled darkness. I wanted to be moving. Sometimes movement gives you the illusion that you're doing something.

Edward started the car, turned around in the weeds and drove back towards the highway. "Talk."

"I've never been to this area before. For all I know what I sensed is always here, just some local bugaboo."

"What did you sense?"

"Something powerful. Something that's miles away towards Santa Fe. Something that may be connected to the dead in some way, which would explain why it called to me so strongly. I'm going to need to find a good local psychic to see if this thing is always around or not."

"Donna will know some psychics. Whether they're good, I can't say, and I'm not sure she can either."

"It's a place to start," I said. I snuggled into my seatbelt, hugging myself. "You got any local animators, necromancers, anyone who works with the dead? If it is something connected to my type of power, then an ordinary psychic might not sense it."

"I don't know of any, but I'll ask around."

"Good."

We were back out on the highway. The night was very dark, as if thick clouds hid the sky. The headlights seemed very yellow against the blackness.

"Do you think this whatever-it-is has anything to do with the mutilations?" he asked.

"I don't know."

"You don't know a hell of a lot," he said. He sounded grumpy.

"That's the problem with psychic shit and magic. Sometimes it's not very helpful."

"I've never seen you do anything like what you just did. You hate the mystical crap."

"Yes, I do, but I've had to accept what I am, Edward. This mystical crap is a part of who and what I am. I can't run from it because it is me. You can't hide from yourself, not forever, and you can't ever outrun yourself. I raise the dead for a living, Edward. Why should it be a shock that I may have other abilities?"

"It's not," he said.

I glanced at him, but he was watching the road, and I couldn't read his face. "It's not," I said.

"I called you in to be backup not just because you're a shooter, but because you know more about preternatural stuff than anyone else I know, that I trust. You hate the psychics and the mediums, because you are one, but you still deal in reality, and that makes you different from the rest of them."

"You're wrong, Edward. I saw a soul today hovering in that room. It was real, just as real as the gun in your holster. Psychics, witches, mediums, they all deal in reality. It's just not the same reality that you deal with, but it is real, Edward, it is very, very real."

He didn't say anything to that, just let the silence fill the car, and I was content with silence because I was tired, terribly, terribly tired. I'd found that doing psychic shit sometimes exhausted me a hell of a lot faster than physical labor. I ran four miles every other day, lifted weights, took Kenbo class, and Judo, and none of it made me as tired as having stood in that field and opened myself to that thing. I never sleep in a car because I don't trust the driver not to have a wreck and kill me. That is the truth about why I don't sleep in cars, no matter what I say out loud. My mother was killed in a car accident, and I've never really trusted cars since.

I settled down in my seat, trying to find a comfortable place for my head. I was suddenly so tired, so tired my eyes burned. I closed my eyes just to rest them, and sleep dragged at me like a hand pulling me under. I could have fought it, but I didn't. I needed the rest, and I needed it now, or I wouldn't be worth shit soon. And the thought crossed my mind as I let myself relax that I did trust Edward. I really did. I slept huddled in the seat and didn't wake until the car stopped.

"We're here," Edward said.

I struggled to sit up, feeling stiff, but rested. "Where?"

"Ted's house."

I sat up straighter. Ted's house? Edward's house. I was finally going to get to see where Edward lived. I was going to snoop and strip some of his mystery away. If I didn't get killed, finding out Edward's secrets would make the entire trip worthwhile. If I did get killed, I'd come back and haunt Edward, see if I could make him see ghosts after all.

17

THE HOUSE WAS ADOBE and looked old or genuine, not that I was an expert, but there was a feel to the house of age. We unloaded my luggage from the back of the Hummer but I had eyes mostly for the house. Edward's house. I'd never really hoped to see where he lived. He was like Batman. He rode into town, saved your ass, then vanished, and you never really expected an invitation to see the Bat Cave. Now here I was standing in front of it. Cool.

It wasn't what I'd pictured. I'd thought maybe a high-tech condo in the city. LA maybe. This modest appearing adobe house hugging the land was just not what I'd had in mind. It was part of his secret identity, his Tedness, but still, Edward lived here, and there had to be more reason than just Ted would have liked it. I was beginning to think I really didn't know Edward at all.

The light over the front door switched on, and I had to turn away, shielding my night vision. I'd been staring right at it when it glared to life. I had two thoughts: one, who had turned on the light; two, the door was blue. The door was painted a blue-violet, a rich, rich color. I could also see the window nearest the door. Its trim was painted the same vibrant blue.

I'd seen it at the airport, though with more flowers and an addition of fuchsia. I asked, "What's with the blue door and trim?"

"Maybe I like it," he said.

"I've seen a lot of doors painted blue or turquoise on a lot of houses since I've been here. What gives?"

"Very observant."

"A failing of mine. Now explain."

"They think witches can't cross a door painted blue or green."

I widened my eyes. "You believe that?"

"I doubt most of the people who paint their doors believe it anymore, but it's become part of the local style. My guess is that most people who do it, don't even remember the folklore behind it."

"Like putting out a jack o' lantern at Halloween to frighten the goblins away," I said.

"Exactly."

"And because I am so observant, who turned on the porch light?"

"Either Bernardo or Olaf."

"Your other backups," I said.

"Yes."

"Can't wait to meet them."

"In the spirit of cooperation, and no more surprises, Olaf doesn't like women much."

"You mean he's gay?"

"No, and implying that to him will probably mean a fight, so please don't. If I'd known I'd be calling you in, I wouldn't have called him in at all. The two of you in the same house on the same case is going to be . . . a fucking disaster."

"That's harsh. You think we can't play nice together."

"I'd almost guarantee it," he said.

The door opened, and our conversation cut off abruptly. I was wondering if it was the dreaded Olaf. The man in the doorway didn't look much like an Olaf, but then what does an Olaf look like?

The man was six foot, give or take an inch. It was hard to tell his exact height because his lower body was completely covered by a white sheet that he had clutched in one hand at his waist. The sheet spilled around his feet like a formal dress, but from the waist up he was anything but formal. He was lean and muscular with a very nice set of abs. He was tanned a lovely even brown, though some of that was natural color because he was American Indian, oh, yes, he was. His hair was waist length falling over one shoulder and across the side of his face, heavy and solid black, tosseled from sleep, though it was early to be in bed. His face was a soft, full triangle, with a dimple in his chin, and a full mouth. Was it racist to say that his features were more white than Indian, or was it just true?

"You can close your mouth now," Edward said near my ear.

I closed my mouth. "Sorry," I mumbled. How embarrassing. I didn't usually notice men this much, at least men I didn't know. What was wrong with me today?

The man folded the sheet over his free arm until his legs showed and he could come down the two steps without tripping. "Sorry, I was asleep, or I'd have come out to help sooner." He seemed perfectly at ease in his sheet, though he was going to a lot of effort to spill it over the same arm that was holding it in place, so he could grab a suitcase.

"Bernardo Spotted-Horse, Anita Blake."

He was holding the sheet with his right hand, and he looked mildly perplexed as he dropped the suitcase and started the process of switching everything to the other hand. The sheet slipped down in front, and I had to turn my head away, fast.

I kept my head turned because I was blushing and wanted the darkness to hide it. I waved my hand vaguely behind me. "We'll shake hands later when you're wearing clothes."

Edward's voice. "You flashed her."

Great, everybody noticed.

"I'm sorry," Bernardo said, "truly."

"We can get the luggage," I said. "Go get a robe."

I felt someone move up behind me, and I wasn't sure how I knew, but I knew it wasn't Edward. "You're modest. I expected a lot of things from Edward's descriptions but not modesty."

I turned around slowly, and he was standing too close, invading the hell out of my personal space. I glared at him. "What were you expecting? The Whore of Babylon?" I was embarrassed and uncomfortable and that always made me angry. The anger showed in my voice.

The half-smile on his face faded round the edges. "I didn't mean any offense." His hand came up as he said it, as if he'd touch my hair.

I stepped back out of reach. "What's with the touchie-feelie routine?"

"I saw the way you looked at me in the doorway," he said.

I felt the heat ride up my face, but I didn't turn away this time. "If you want to come to the door looking like a Playgirl centerfold, don't blame me for staring. But don't make more of it than it is. You're nice eye candy, but the fact that you're coming on this strong isn't flattering to either of us. Either you're a whore, or you think I am. The first I'm willing to believe. The second I know isn't true." I walked up to him now, invading his space, the blush gone, leaving me pale and angry. "So back off."

It was his turn to look uncertain. He stepped back, put the sheet into as much of a cover as it could be, and bowed. It was an old-fashioned, courtly movement, as if he'd done it before and meant it. It was a nice gesture with his hair spilling all around, but I'd seen better. Not for six months, but I had seen better.

He raised up, and his face was solemn. He looked sincere. "There are two kinds of women that hang around with men like Edward, like me, that know what we are. The first are whores, no matter how many guns they own; the second is strictly business. I call them Madonnas because they never sleep with anyone. They try to be one of the guys." The smile played along his lips again. "Forgive me if I'm disappointed that you're one of the guys. I've been here for two weeks, and I'm getting lonely."

I shook my head. "Two weeks, poor baby." I pushed past him and grabbed my overnight case. I looked at Edward. "Next time remind me about everybody's little foibles."

He raised his hand in a Boy Scout oath. "I have never seen Bernardo do that with any woman at first meeting her, I swear it."

My eyes narrowed, but I looked into his eyes, and believed him. "How did I get the honor?"

He picked up my suitcase, and did smile. "You should have seen the look on your face when he came down the steps in the sheet." He laughed and it was very masculine. "I've never seen you that embarrassed."

Bernardo came up next to us. "I really, honestly, didn't mean to flash you. I just don't wear anything to bed so I threw this on."

"Where's Olaf?" Edward asked.

"Pouting that you're bringing her in."

"Great," I said. "One of you thinks he's a Lothario, and the other one won't talk to me. That's just perfect." I turned and followed Edward toward the house.

Bernardo called from behind us. "Don't mistake Olaf, Anita. He likes women in his bed, and he's not nearly as particular as I am about how he gets them there. I'd be more careful of him than of me."

"Edward," I said.

He was just inside the door. He turned back and looked at me.

"Is Bernardo right? Is Olaf dangerous to me?"

"I can tell him about you what I told him about Donna."

"What's that?" I asked.

We were all still in the doorway, not quite in the house. "I told him if he touched her, I'd kill him."

"If you come to my rescue, then he'll never work with me, never respect me," I said.

Edward nodded. "That's true."

I sighed. "I'll handle it on my own."

Bernardo had moved up behind me, closer than I wanted him. I used the carry-on bag to accidentally move him back a step or two. "Olaf has been in prison for rape."

I looked at Edward and let my disbelief show on my face. "Is he serious?"

Edward just nodded. His face had gone to its usual blankness. "I told you in the car that I wouldn't have invited him if I'd known you were coming in on this."

"But you didn't mention the rape conviction," I said.

He shrugged. "I should have."

"What else should I know about good ol' Olaf?"

"That's it." He looked behind me to Bernardo. "Can you think of anything else she needs to know?"

"Only that he brags about the rape and what he did to her."

"All right," I said, "you've both made your point. I only have one question."

Edward just looked at me expectantly, Bernardo said, "Shoot."

"If I kill another one of your backups, do I owe you another favor?"

"Not if he deserves it."

I dumped the bag on the doorsill. "Shit, Edward, if you keep putting me together with fucking crazies and I keep having to defend myself, I'll be owing you favors until we're in our graves."

Bernardo said, "You're serious. You really killed his last backup."

I glanced at him. "Yeah, I'm serious. And I want permission to off Olaf if he gets out of hand, without having to owe Edward another pound of flesh."

"Who'd you kill?" Bernardo asked.

"Harley," Edward said.

"Shit, really?"

I walked up to Edward, invading his space, trying to read past the blank blue of his eyes. "I want permission to kill Olaf if he gets out of hand, without owing you another favor."

"And if I don't give it?" he asked, voice low.

"Drive me to a hotel because I'm not staying in a house with a bragging rapist if I can't kill him."

Edward looked at me for a long slow moment, then gave a small nod. "Done, as long as he's in this house. Outside the house, play nice."

I would have argued, but it was probably the best I was going to get. Edward was very protective of his backups, and since I was one of them, I could appreciate the attitude. I picked up my bag from the floor, and said, "Thank you. Now where's my room?"

"Oh, she's going to fit in just fine," Bernardo said, and there was something in his voice that made me look at his face. His handsome face had thinned to a blankness, an emptiness that left his dark brown eyes like two burned holes in his face. It was as if he'd dropped his mask and let me see inside because I'd proven myself monster enough to handle it. Maybe I had. But I knew one thing: Olaf or Bernardo, either one, better not walk in their sleep.

18

THERE WAS A FIREPLACE against the far wall, but it was narrow and white, formed of the same smooth whiteness as the walls. There was an animal skull mounted over the fireplace. I would have said deer, but the skull was heavier than that and the horns long and curving. Not a deer, but something close kin, and not from this country. The narrow mantlepiece held two tusks, as in elephant tusks, and smaller animal skulls. A low white couch faced the fireplace. A large block of unpolished marble sat to one side of it with a small white china lamp on it. A small alcove above the lamp held a huge chunk of white crystal. There was a black lacquered table against the far wall between two doorways. A second larger lamp sat on the table. Two chairs sat facing each other in front of the fireplace. They had carved arms with winged lions on the arms and legs. They were black leather and looked vaguely Egyptian.

"Your room is this way," Edward said.

"No," I said, "I've waited a long time to see your home. Don't rush me."

"Mind if I take your luggage through to your room while you explore?"

"Help yourself," I said.

"Gracious of you," he said, and put an extra touch of sarcasm into his voice.

"Don't mention it," I said.

Edward picked up both my bags, and said, "Come on, Bernardo. You can get dressed."

"You didn't let us look around on our own," Bernardo said.

"You didn't ask."

"It's one of the joys of being a girl and not a guy," I said. "If I'm curious, I just ask."

They went through a far door, though the room was small enough that "far" was relative. There was wood to one side of the fireplace in a woven basket of pale, almost white reeds. I ran my hand down the smooth coolness of the black marble coffee table that sat nearest the fireplace. There was a black vase on the table full of what looked like either small wild flowers or large black-eyed-Susans. The deep yellow gold and the brown center didn't really match anything in the room. Even the Navajo rug that took up most of the floor was in shades of black, white, and gray. There were more flowers in an alcove between the far doorways. The alcove was large enough to be a window except it didn't look out on anything. The flowers spilled from the opening like a mass of gold and brown water, a huge riotous bouquet.

When Edward came back into the room, without Bernardo, I was sitting on the white couch with my feet stretched out underneath the coffee table. I had my hands clasped over my stomach and was trying to picture a roaring fire and a cold winter evening. But somehow the fireplace looked too clean, too sterile.

He sat down beside me, shaking his head. "Happy?"

I nodded.

"What do you think?"

"It's not a restful room," I said, "and for Heaven's sake look at all the wall space. Get some paintings."

"I like it this way." He had settled down on the couch beside me, feet stretched out, hands on his stomach. He was mimicking me, but even that couldn't ruin my mood. I was going to see every room in detail before I left. I could have tried to be cool about it, but I didn't sweat being cool with Edward. We'd moved beyond that in our strange friendship. I really wasn't trying to play king of the hill with Edward. The fact that he was still playing the game with me just made him look silly. Though I hoped the game-playing was over for this trip.

"Maybe I'll get you a painting for Christmas," I said.

"We don't buy Christmas presents for each other," Edward said.

We were both staring at the fireplace as if visualizing that make-believe fire. "Maybe I'll start. One of those big-eyed children or a clown on velvet."

"I won't hang it if I don't like it."

I glanced at him. "Unless it's from Donna."

He was very still suddenly. "Yes."

"Donna added the flowers, didn't she," I said.

"Yes," he said.

"White lilies, or an orchid maybe, but not wild flowers, not in this room."

"She thinks they brighten up the place."

"Oh, they do," I said.

He sighed.

"Maybe I'll tell her how much you love those pictures of dogs playing poker and she can buy you some prints."

"She wouldn't believe it," he said.

"No, but I bet I could come up with something that she would believe that you'd hate just as much."

He stared at me. "You wouldn't."

"I might."

"This sounds like the opening to blackmail. What do you want?"

I stared at him, studying that blank face. "So you're admitting that Donna and her crew are important enough for you so that blackmail would work."

He just looked at me with those pitiless eyes, but the blank face wasn't enough now. There was a chink in his armor big enough to drive a truck through. "They're hostages, Edward, if anyone ever thinks of it."

He looked away from me, closing his eyes. "Do you really think you're telling me something I haven't thought about?"

"My apologies, you're right. Like teaching your grandmother to suck eggs."

"What?" He turned and was half-laughing.

I shrugged. "Just an old saying. It means that I'm lecturing someone who taught me what I'm lecturing about."

"And what have I taught you?" he asked, humor dying, face turning serious.

"You can't take all the credit. My mother's death started the lesson early, but I learned that if you care for people, they can die. If other people know you care for someone, they can use that person against you. You ask why I don't date humans. Hostages, Edward. My life is just too damn violent for cannon fodder to be near and dear to my heart. You taught me that."

"And now I've broken the rule," he said, voice soft.

"Yep," I said.

"And where does that leave Richard and Jean-Claude?" he asked.

"Oh, I make you uncomfortable and now it's my turn."

"Just answer the question."

I thought about it for a second, or two, then answered truthfully, because I'd spent a lot of the last six months thinking about it, about them. "Jean-Claude is so *not* cannon fodder. If anyone I've ever met knows how to take care of himself, it's Jean-Claude. I guess you can't be a four-hundred-year-old anything without being a survivor."

"And Richard?" Edward was watching my face as he asked, studying me as I so often studied him, and I wondered for the first time if my face was empty more often than it was full, if I hid my emotions, my thoughts, even when I wasn't meaning to. How can you really tell what your own face shows?

"Richard can survive a shotgun blast to the chest with non-silver shot. Can you say the same about Donna?" It was blunt, maybe too blunt, but it was truthful.

His eyes shut down like curtains had pulled, hiding, hiding. There was no one home. It was the face he wore when he killed sometimes, though sometimes when he killed he wore the most joyous expression I ever saw on his face.

"You told me that they huddle around your humanity. Are you saying you huddle around their monstrousness?" he asked.

I looked into that so carefully unreadable face, and nodded. "Yeah, it took me a while to realize it and longer to accept it. I've lost enough people in my life, Edward. I'm tired of it. The chances are very good that both the boys will outlive me." I held up my hand before he could say it. "I know that Jean-Claude isn't alive. Trust me. I probably know that better than you do."

"You guys look serious. Talking about the case?" Bernardo walked into the room wearing blue jeans and nothing else. He'd tied all that hair back in a loose braid. He padded barefoot towards us, and it made my chest tight. It was one of Richard's favorite ways to walk around the house. He only put shoes and a shirt on to go out or if company was coming over.

I watched a very handsome man walk towards me, but I wasn't really seeing him. I was seeing Richard, missing him. I sighed and struggled to sit up straighter on the couch. Call it a hunch but I was betting that Edward didn't have heart to heart talks with Bernardo, at least not about Donna.

Edward had also straightened. "No, we weren't talking about the case," he said.

Bernardo looked from one to the other of us with a smile playing on his lips. But his eyes didn't match. He didn't like the serious air and it not being about the case, and him not knowing what it was about. I'd have asked. Edward wouldn't have told me, but I'd have still asked. Sometimes it was good to be a girl.

"You said you had the files on the Santa Fe cases," I said.

Edward nodded, standing. "I'll bring them to the dining room. Bernardo, show her the way."

"My pleasure," he said.

Edward said, "Treating Anita like a girl would be a mistake, Bernardo. It would piss me off to have to replace you this late in the game." With that, Edward left through the far right door. There was a wash of night air and a buzz of insects before he closed the door behind him.

Bernardo looked at me, shaking his head. "I've never heard Edward talk about any woman the way he talks about you."

I raised eyebrows at him. "Meaning?"

"Dangerous. He talks about you like you're dangerous." Intelligence showed in his solid brown eyes, an intelligence that had been hiding behind his good looks and charming smile. An intelligence that didn't show when he had his monster face on. For the first time I thought that it might be a mistake to underestimate him. He was more than just a gun for hire. How much more remained to be seen.

"What, I'm supposed to say I am dangerous?"

"Are you?" he asked, still studying me with that intense expression.

I smiled at him. "Well, you get to go down the hall first."

He tilted his head to one side. "Why don't we go together, side by side?"

"Because the hall's too narrow, or am I wrong?"

"You're not wrong, but do you really think I'll shoot you in the back?" He spread his arms wide and turned a slow circle. "Do I look armed?" He was smiling when he faced me again, charming.

I didn't buy it. "Unless I run my hands through all that thick hair and down your pants, I don't know you're unarmed."

The smile faded a touch. "Most people don't think about the hair." Which meant that he did have something hidden away. If he was truly unarmed, he'd have teased and offered me a chance to search.

"It's got to be a blade. The hair isn't thick enough to hide a gun, not even a derringer," I said.

He reached behind his head and drew out a slender blade that he'd woven through his hair. He held it up, then flipped it hilt to blade, back and forth, dancing it through his long slender fingers.

"Isn't it an ethnic stereotype that you're good with a knife?" I asked.

He laughed, but not like it was funny. He bounced the blade once more in his hand, and it made me tense. I was still standing behind the couch, but knew that if he were really good, I'd never get behind cover or draw my gun in time. He was just too damn close.

"I can cut my hair and put on a suit, but I'm still going to be an Indian to most people. If you can't change it, might as well embrace it." He slipped the knife back into his hair, making it look smooth and easy. I'd have had to use a mirror and even then I'd have probably cut off half my hair.

"You try to play in corporate America?" I asked.

"Yeah," he said.

"So now you don't do corporate stuff."

"I still play in corporate America. I protect the suits that want flashy muscle. Something exotic to impress their friends about what a big shot they are."

"You do the knife act on command?" I asked.

He shrugged. "Sometimes."

"I hope it pays well," I said.

He smiled. "It either pays well or I don't do it. I may be their token Indian, but

I'm a rich token Indian. If you're as good as Edward thinks you are, you'd do better at bodyguard work than I do."

"Why?" I asked.

"Because the majority of protective work wants their bodyguard to blend in. They want you not to be flashy or exotic. You're pretty, but it's more a girl next door pretty, nothing too beautiful."

I agreed with him, but said, "Oh, that won you a lot of brownie points."

"You've pretty much told me I don't have a chance so why should I bother lying?"

I had to smile. "Point taken."

"You may be a little dark around the edges, but you can pass for white," Bernardo said.

"I'm not passing, Bernardo. I am white. My mother just happened to be Mexican."

"You got your father's skin?" he asked.

I nodded. "Yeah, what of it?"

"No one's ever got up in your face about it, have they?"

I thought about it. My stepmother's hurried comments to strangers that I was not hers. No, I wasn't adopted. I was her stepdaughter. Me and Cinderella. The really rude ones would ask, "What was her mother?"

Judith would always answer quickly, "Her mother was Mexican." Though lately it was Hispanic-American. No one could accuse Judith of not being politically correct on the issue of race. My mother had died long before people had worried about political correctness being in vogue. If someone asked, she always said proudly, "Mexican." If it was good enough for my mother, it was good enough for me.

That memory I didn't share. I'd never really shared it with my father. I wasn't about to start with a stranger. I chose another memory that didn't hurt quite so much. "I was engaged once until his mother found out my mother had been Mexican. He was blond and blue-eyed, the epitome of WASP breeding. My future-in-law didn't like the idea of me darkening her family tree." That was a brief, unemotional way to say some very painfully things. He had been my first love, my first lover. I thought he was everything to me, but I wasn't everything to him. I'd never let myself fall so completely into anyone's arm before or since. Jean-Claude and Richard were both still paying the bill for that first love.

"Do you think of yourself as white?"

I nodded. "Yeah. Now ask me if I think I'm white enough?"

Bernardo looked at me. "Are you white enough?"

"Not according to some people."

"Like who?"

"Like none of your damn business."

He spread his hands. "Sorry, didn't mean to step on your toes."

"Yes, you did," I said.

"You think so?"

"Yeah," I said. "I think you're jealous."

"Of what?"

"That I can pass and you can't."

He opened his mouth and emotions flowed over his face like water; anger, humor, denial. He finally settled on a smile, but it wasn't a happy one. "You really are a bitch, aren't you?"

I nodded. "You don't pull on my chain and I won't pull on yours."

"Deal," he said. The smile flashed wider. "Now, allow me to escort your lily white ass to the dining room."

I shook my head. "Lead on, tall, dark, and studly, as long as I get to watch your ass while we walk down the hall."

"Only if you promise to tell me how you like the view."

I widened my eyes. "You mean give you a critique on your butt?"

He nodded and the smile looked happy now.

"Are you this big an egotist or just trying to embarrass me?"

"Guess."

"Both," I said.

The smile spread to a grin. "You are as smart as you look."

"Just get moving, Romeo. Edward doesn't like to be kept waiting."

"Damn straight."

We went down the short hallway; him leading, me following. He put an extra glide into his walk, and yes, I watched the show. Call it a hunch, but I was betting Bernardo would actually ask me for the critique, probably out loud in front of other people. Why is it when you have a sure thing to bet on, there's never anyone around to take your money?

19

THERE WERE MORE heavy dark beams in the dining room, more off-white walls. If the chairs were a clue, the dining table was black and silver. But the table was hidden under a tablecloth that looked like another Navajo rug. Though this one had some color, dull red stripes running with black and white. There was even a black metal candelabra with red candles in the middle of the table. It was nice to see some color that hadn't been added by Donna. It had taken me years to break Jean-Claude of his fixation on black and white decor. Since I was just Edward's friend and nothing more, it wasn't my business how he decorated.

There was a fireplace in the corner nearly identical to the one in the living room except for a black piece of wood set into the white stucco. I would have called it a mantel, but it didn't stick out that far. The true mantel was decorated in more red candles of every shape and size, some sitting with their waxy bottoms directly on the mantel, some in black metal holders. There were two round ones that stuck up above the rest on the kind of holders where you spear the candle to hold it into place. A silver-edged mirror that looked antique was hung behind the candles so that when they were burned, you'd get their reflection. Strange, I hadn't thought Edward was the candlelight type.

There were no windows in the room, just a molded doorway leading out the other side. The walls were utterly white and utterly blank. Somehow the lack of decoration made the room seem more claustrophobic rather than less.

A man appeared in the far doorway. He had to bend over to keep his bald head from smacking the top of the door. He was taller than Dolph, who was six foot eight, which meant he was the tallest person I'd ever met. The only hair on his head was heavy black eyebrows and a shadow of beard along his chin and cheeks. He was wearing the draw string bottoms of men's pajamas. They were black and looked satin. He had on slippers, the kind that have no heels and always seem in danger of falling off. Olaf, because who else could it be, moved in the slippers like they were part of his flesh. Once he got over stooping through the door, he moved like a well-oiled machine, muscles rippling under his pale skin. He was tall, but there wasn't an ounce of fat on him. It was all hard, lean, muscle. He walked around the table towards us, and I moved without thinking to keep the table between us.

He stopped moving. I stopped moving. We stared at each other across the table. Bernardo was at the end of the table, nearest the door, watching us. He looked worried. Probably wondering if he was supposed to come to my rescue if I needed one. Or maybe he just didn't like the tension level in the room. I know I didn't.

If I hadn't moved away as he walked in, would the tension level have been lower? Maybe. But I'd learned long ago to trust my gut, and my gut said, to stay out of reach. But I could try and be nice. "You must be Olaf. I didn't catch your last name. I'm Anita Blake."

His eyes were dark brown set deep in the bones of his face like twin caves, as if even in daylight his eyes would be shadowed. He just looked at me. It was as if I had not spoken.

I tried again. I'm nothing if not persistent. "Hello, Earth to Olaf." I stared into his face, and he never blinked, never acknowledged my words in any way. If he hadn't been glaring at me, I'd have said he was ignoring me.

I glanced at Bernardo, but kept my gaze on the big man across the table. "What gives, Bernardo? He does talk, right?"

Bernardo nodded. "He talks."

I turned my full attention back to Olaf. "You're just not going to talk to me, is that it?"

He just glared at me.

"You think not hearing the dulcet sounds of your voice is some kind of punishment? Most men are such jabber mouths. Silence is nice for a change. Thanks for being so considerate, Olaf, baby." I made the last word into two very separate syllables.

"I am not your baby." The voice was deep and matched that vast chest. There was also a guttural accent underneath all that clear English, German maybe.

"It speaks. Be still my heart."

Olaf frowned. "I did not agree with your being included on this hunt. We do not need help from a woman, any woman."

"Well, Olaf, honey, you need help from someone because the three of you haven't come up with shit on the mutilations."

A flush of color crept up his neck into his face. "Do not call me that."

"What? Honey?"

He nodded.

"You prefer sweetheart, honeybun, pumpkin?"

The color spread from pink to red, and was getting darker. "Do not use terms of endearment to me. I am no one's sweetheart."

I'd been all set to make another scathing remark, but that stopped me, and I thought of something better. "How sad for you."

"What are you talking about?"

"How sad that you are no one's sweetheart."

The color that had been fading from his face flushed dark now, almost as if he were blushing. "Are you feeling sorry for me?" His voice rose a notch, not yelling but like the low growl of a dog just before it bites. As he got more emotional, the accent got thicker. Very German, very lowland. Grandmother Blake was from Baden-Baden, on the border between Germany and France, but great-uncle Otto had been from Hapsburg. I couldn't be a hundred percent sure, but it sounded like the same accent.

"Everyone should be someone's sweetheart," I said, but my voice was mild. I wasn't angry. I was baiting him, and I shouldn't have. My only excuse was that all the talk of rape had made me scared of him, and I didn't like that. So I was doing something that was actually very masculine. I was pulling the tail of the beast to make myself feel braver. Stupid. The moment I realized why I was doing it, I tried to stop.

"I am no one's fool, and that means I am no one's sweetheart." He spoke carefully, enunciating each word but his accent was thick enough to walk on. He had started to move slowly around the table, muscles tense like some big predatory cat.

I flashed my jacket on the left side, showing the gun. He stopped moving forward, but his face was furious. "Let's start over, Olaf," I said. "Edward and Bernardo here told me what a big bad guy you were and that made me nervous, which made me defensive. When I'm defensive, I'm usually a pain in the ass. Sorry about that. Let's pretend that I wasn't being a smart ass, and you weren't being all big and bad, and start over."

He stilled. That was the only word I had for it. The quivering tension in his muscles eased like water running down hill. But it wasn't gone, just shoved away somewhere. I had a glimpse into Olaf. He operated from a great dark pit of rage. That it was directed mostly at women was accidental. The rage needed some target or he'd turn into one of those people that drive their cars through restaurant windows and start shooting strangers.

"Edward has been most insistent that you are to be here, but nothing you will say can make me like it." His words were pulling free of the accent as he regained control of his temper.

I nodded. "Are you from Hapsburg?"

He blinked, and for an instant puzzlement replaced the sullenness. "What?"

"Are you from Hapsburg?"

He seemed to think about it for a second or two, then gave a small nod.

"I thought I recognized the accent."

The scowl was back full force. "You are an expert on accents?" He managed to sound sarcastic.

"No. My Uncle Otto was from Hapsburg."

He blinked again, and the scowl wilted around the edges. "You are not German." He sounded very sure.

"My father's family is; from Baden-Baden on the edge of the Black Forest, but Uncle Otto was from Hamburg.

"You said only your uncle had the accent."

"By the time I came along, most of the family, except for my grandmother, had been in this country so long there was no accent, but Uncle Otto never lost his."

"He's dead now." Olaf made it half question, half statement.

I nodded.

"How did he die?"

"Grandma Blake says Aunt Gertrude nagged him to death."

His lips twitched. "Women are tyrants if a man allows it." His voice was a touch softer now.

"That's true of men or women. If one partner is weak, the other partner moves in and takes charge."

"Nature abhors a vacuum," Bernardo said.

We glanced at him. I don't know what the expressions were on our faces, but Bernardo held his hands up and said, "Sorry to interrupt."

Olaf and I went back to looking at each other. He was close enough now that I might not be able to draw the Browning in time. But if I moved away now, all my peace-making efforts would be for nothing. He'd either be insulted or see it as weakness on my part. Neither reaction would be helpful. So I stood my ground and tried not to look as tense as I felt, because no matter how calm I sounded, my stomach was in one hard knot. I had one chance to make this work. If I blew it, then the rest of this visit was going to be an armed camp, and we needed to be solving the crime, not fighting each other.

"You are either a leader or being led," Olaf said. "Which are you?"

"I'll follow if someone's worth following."

"And who decides, Anita Blake, who is worth following?"

I had to smile. "I do."

His lips twitched again. "And if Edward put me in charge, would you follow me?"

"I trust Edward's judgment, so yeah. But let me ask you the same question. Would you follow me if Edward put me in charge?"

He flinched. "No."

I nodded. "Great, we know where we stand."

"And where is that?" he asked.

"I'm sort of goal-oriented, Olaf. I came down here to solve a crime and I'm going to do that. If that means at some point taking orders from you, so be it. If Edward puts me in charge of you, and you don't like it, take it up with him."

"Just like a woman to put the responsibility off on a man's shoulders."

I counted to ten, and shrugged. "You talk like your opinion matters to me, Olaf. I don't give a damn what you think of me."

"Women always care what men think of them."

I laughed then. "You know I was starting to feel insulted, but you are just too funny." I meant it.

He leaned towards me trying to use his height to intimidate. It was impressive, but I've been the smallest kid around for as long as I can remember. "I will not take it up with Edward. I will take it up with you. Or don't you have the balls to stand up to me?" He gave a harsh laugh. "Oh, I forgot, you don't have balls." He reached for me in a quick motion. I think he meant to grope me, but I didn't wait to see. I threw myself backward into the floor and was drawing the Browning before my butt hit the floor. Drawing the gun meant I didn't have time to slap my hands down and take the impact the way you were supposed to. I hit hard and felt the shock all the way up my spine.

He'd drawn a blade as long as his forearm from somewhere. The blade was coming down, and the Browning wasn't quite pointed at his chest. It would be a race to see who drew first blood, but it was almost a guarantee that we'd both bleed. Everything slowed down to that crystalline vision, as if I had all the time in the world to point the gun, to avoid the blade, and at the same time everything was happening too fast. Too fast to stop it or change it.

Edward's voice cut through the room. "Stop it! The first one to draw blood, I will personally shoot."

We froze in mid-action. Olaf blinked, and it was as if time had resumed normal flow. Maybe, just maybe, we weren't going to kill each other tonight. But I had the gun pointed at his chest, and his hand was still upraised with the knife. Though knife seemed too small a word, sword was more like it. Where had he pulled it from?

"Drop the knife, Olaf," Edward said.

"Have her put up the gun, first." I met those hard brown eyes and saw a hatred there like what I'd seen earlier in Lieutenant Marks' face. They both hated me for being things that I could not change: one for an innate God-given talent, and the other because I was a woman. Funny, how one unreasoning hatred looks so much like another.

I kept the gun very steadily pointed at his chest I'd let all the air go out of my body, and was waiting, waiting for Olaf to decide what we'd be doing tonight. Either we'd be fighting crime, or we'd be digging a grave, maybe two if he was good enough. I knew what my vote was, but I also knew that the final vote wasn't mine. It wasn't even Olaf's. It was his hatred's.

"You drop the knife, and Anita will put up the gun," Edward said.

"Or she will shoot me while I'm unarmed."

"She won't do that."

"She is afraid of me now," Olaf said.

"Maybe," Edward said, "but she's more afraid of me."

Olaf looked down at me, a glimmer of puzzlement rising up through the hatred and anger. "I am going to shove this blade inside her. She fears me."

"Tell him, Anita."

I hoped I knew what Edward wanted me to say. "I will shoot you twice in the chest. You may get a slice of me before you fall to the ground. If you're really good, you might even slit my throat, but you'll still be dead." I hoped he made up his mind soon because it was awkward holding a shooting stance while sitting on your butt. I was going to get a crick in my back if I didn't get to move soon. The fear was fading, leaving only a dull emptiness behind. I was tired, and the night was still young. Hours to go before I'd sleep. I was tired of Olaf. I had a feeling if I didn't shoot him tonight, I'd get another chance.

"Who are you more afraid of, Anita—Olaf or me?" Edward asked.

I kept my gaze on Olaf and said, "You, Edward."

"Tell him why."

It sounded like a teacher telling his student what to say, but from Edward I'd take it. "Because you would have never let me get the drop on you like this. You would have never let your emotions compromise your safety."

Olaf blinked at me. "You do not fear me?" He made it a question and seemed disappointed. There was something almost little-boyish about his disappointment.

"I'm not afraid of anything I can kill," I said.

"Edward can be killed," Olaf said.

"Yes, but can he be killed by anyone in this room? That's the question."

Olaf looked at me, puzzled now more than angry. He began to lower the blade, slowly.

Edward said, "Drop it," in a quiet voice.

Olaf dropped the blade to the floor. It hit with a ringing clang.

I got to my knees and then scuttled backwards along the edge of the table, lowering the gun as I moved. I got to my feet at the head of the table near Bernardo. I looked at him. "Move over around by Edward."

"I didn't do anything," he said.

"Just do it, Bernardo. I need a little space right now."

He opened his mouth as if to argue, but Edward cut him off. "Do it."

Bernardo did it.

When they were all at the other end of the room, I put the gun up.

Edward had an armful of cardboard box. It was overbrimming with files. He set it down on the tabletop.

"You didn't even have a gun," Olaf said.

"I didn't need one," Edward said.

Olaf pushed past Edward to the hallway beyond. I hoped he was going to pack and leave, but doubted we'd get that lucky. I hadn't known Olaf for an hour, and I already knew why he was no one's sweetie.

20

A MURDER ALWAYS BREEDS a lot of paper, but a serial murder, you can drown in the paperwork. Edward, Bernardo, and I were swimming upstream. We'd been at it for about an hour, and Olaf hadn't come back. Maybe he had decided to pack up and go home. Though I hadn't heard any doors or cars, but I wasn't sure how soundproof the house was. Edward didn't seem bothered by Olaf's absence, so I didn't give it much attention either. I had read one report through back to front. One to get an overview and see if anything jumped out at me. One thing did. There were slivers of obsidian in the cut up bodies. An obsidian blade, maybe. Though we were in the wrong part of the world for it, or were we?

"Did the Aztecs ever get up this far?" I asked.

Edward didn't treat it like a weird question. "Yes."

"So I'm not the first one to point out the obsidian clue might mean Aztec magic?"

"No," he said.

"Thanks for telling me that we're looking for some sort of Aztec monster."

"The locals cops talked to the leading expert in the area. Professor Dallas couldn't come up with any deity or folklore that would account for these murders or the mutilations."

"You sound like you're quoting. Is there a report around here somewhere?"

He looked out over the mound of papers. "Somewhere."

"Isn't there an Aztec deity that the priests skinned someone as an offering, or is that Mayan?"

He shrugged. "The good professor couldn't make a connection. That's why I didn't tell you. The police have been looking into the Aztec angle for weeks. Nothing. I brought you down here to think different thoughts, not follow old ones."

"I'd like to talk to the professor all the same. If that's okay with you." I made sure he got the sarcasm.

"Look at the reports first, try to find what we've missed, then I'll introduce you to Professor Dallas."

I looked at him, trying to read behind those baby blues and failing as usual. "When do I get to see the professor?"

"Tonight."

That raised my eyebrows. "Gee, that is quick, especially since you think I'm wasting our time."

"She spends most nights in a club near Albuquerque."

"She, being Professor Dallas," I said.

He nodded.

"What's so special about this club?"

"If your career was Aztec history and mythology, wouldn't you just love to interview a real live Aztec?"

"A live ancient Aztec in Albuquerque?" I didn't try and keep the surprise out of my voice. "How?"

"Well, maybe not live," he said.

"A vampire," I said.

He nodded again.

"Has this Aztec vamp got a name?"

"The Master of the City calls herself Itzpapalotl."

"Isn't that like an Aztec goddess?" I asked.

"Yes, it is."

"Talk about delusions of grandeur." I was watching his face, trying to catch a hint. "Did the cops talk to the vamp?"

"Yes."

"And?"

"She wasn't helpful."

"You didn't believe her, did you?"

"Neither did the cops. But she was on stage at her club during at least three of the murders."

"So she's cleared," I said.

"Which is why I want you to read the reports first, Anita. We've missed something. Maybe you'll find out what, but not if you keep looking for Aztec bogeymen. We raised that rock, and as much as the police would like it to be the Master of the City, it isn't."

"So why the offer to take me down to see her tonight?"

"Just because she's not doing the murders, doesn't mean she can't have information that could help us."

"The police questioned her." I made it a statement.

"Yeah, but funny how vampires don't like talking to the police, and how much they like talking to you."

"You know you could have just told me that we were seeing the Master Vamp of Albuquerque tonight."

"I wasn't going to take you down there tonight unless you got bitchy about it. I was actually hoping you wouldn't make the Aztec angle until you'd read everything first."

"Why?"

"I told you, it was a blind alley. We need new ideas. Things we haven't thought of, not things the police have already crossed off the list."

"But you haven't crossed this Itza-whatever off your list, have you?"

"The goddess will let you call her by her English translation, Obsidian Butterfly. It's also the name of her club."

"You think she's involved, don't you?"

"I think she knows something that she might share with a necromancer, but not a vampire executioner."

"So I go down off duty, so to speak."

"So to speak."

"I'm Jean-Claude's human servant, one third of his little triumvirate of power. If I go visiting the Master of this City without police credentials, then I'll have to play vamp politics. I hate vamp politics."

Edward looked out over the table. "When you've read your hundredth witness report tonight, you may change your mind. Even vampire politics look good after reading enough of this shit."

"Gee, Edward, you sound almost bitter."

"I'm the monster expert, Anita, and I don't have a fucking clue."

We looked at each other, and again I had the sense of his fear, his helplessness, things that Edward just didn't feel. Or so I'd thought.

Bernardo came in with a tray of coffees. He must have caught something in the air because he said, "Did I miss something?"

"No," Edward said, and he went back to the papers in his lap.

I stood and started sorting papers. "You haven't missed anything yet."

"I just love being lied to."

"We're not lying," I said.

"Then why is the tension level so high in here?"

"Shut up, Bernardo," Edward said.

Bernardo didn't take it as an insult. He just shut up and handed out the coffee.

I sorted out all the witness reports I could find, then spent the next three hours reading them. I'd read one report back to front and found out nothing the police and Edward hadn't known weeks ago. Now I was looking for something new, something that the police, Edward, the experts they'd called in, nobody had found. It sounded egotistical, but Edward seemed sure I'd find it, whatever it was. Though I was beginning to wonder if it was confidence in me or sheer desperation on Edward's part that made him so sure I'd find something. I'd give it my best shot, and that was all I could do.

I looked down at several stacks of witness reports and settled in to read. I know most people read each report in full, or almost in full, then move to the next, but in a serial crime you were looking for a pattern. On serial murders I'd learned to divide the files up into parts: all the witness statements, then all the forensic reports, then the pictures of the crime scene, etc. . . . Sometimes I did the pictures first, but I was putting it off. I'd seen enough in the hospital to make me squeamish. So the pictures could wait, and I could still do legitimate work on the case without having to see all the horrors. Procrastination with a purpose, what could be better?

Bernardo kept making us all coffee and continued to play host, going back and forth when the coffee ran low, offering food, though we both declined. When he brought me my umpteenth cup of coffee, I finally asked, "Not that I'm not grateful, but you didn't strike me as the domestic type, Bernardo. Why the perfect host routine? It's not even your house."

He took the question as an invitation to move closer to my chair until his jean-clad thigh was touching the arm, but it wasn't touching me so that was fine. "You want to ask Edward to go for coffee?"

I looked across the table at Edward. He didn't bother to look up from the papers in his hands. I smiled. "No, I was more thinking I'd get my own."

Bernardo turned and leaned his butt against the table, arms crossed over his chest. Muscles played in his arms as if he were flexing just a bit for my benefit. I didn't think he was even aware he was doing it, as if it were habit.

"Truthfully?" he asked.

I looked up at him and sipped the coffee he'd brought me. "That would be nice."

"I've read the reports more than once. I don't want to read them again. I'm tired of playing detectives and wish we could just go kill something, or at least fight something."

"Me, too," Edward said. He was watching us now with cool blue eyes. "But we have to know what we're fighting, and the answer to that is in here somewhere." He motioned at the mounds of papers.

Bernardo shook his head. "Then why haven't we, or the police found the answer in all this paper?" He ran his finger down the nearest stack. "I don't think paperwork is going to catch this bastard."

I smiled up at him. "You're just bored."

He looked down at me, a little startled expression on his face, then he laughed, head back, mouth wide as if he were howling at the moon. "You haven't known me long enough to know me that well." Laughter was still sparkling in his brown eyes, and I wished it were a different pair of brown eyes. My chest was suddenly tight with missing Richard. I looked down at the papers in my lap, not sure if it would show in my eyes. If my eyes showed sorrow, I didn't want Bernardo to see it. If my eyes showed longing, I didn't want him to misinterpret it.

"Are you bored, Bernardo?" Edward asked.

Bernardo turned at the waist so he could see Edward with a minimum of movement. It put his bare chest facing me. "No women, no television, nothing to kill, bored, bored, bored."

I found myself staring at his chest. I had an urge to rise up out of my chair, spill the papers to the floor and run my tongue over his chest. The image was so strong, I had to close my eyes. I had feelings like this around Richard and Jean-Claude, but not around strangers. Why was Bernardo affecting me like this?

"Are you all right?" He was bending over me, face so close that his face filled my entire vision.

I jerked back, pushing the chair and rising to my feet. The chair crashed to the floor, papers spilled everywhere. "Shit," I said with feeling. I picked up the chair.

He bent down to help pick up the papers. His bare back made a firm curved line as he started shoveling the papers back into a pile. I watched the way the small muscles in his lower back worked, fascinated by it.

I stepped away from him. Edward was watching me from across the table. His gaze was heavy, as if he knew what I was thinking, feeling. I knew it wasn't true, but he knew me better than most. I didn't want anyone to know that I seemed to be unwarrantedly attracted to Bernardo. It was too embarrassing.

Edward said, "Leave us alone for a while, Bernardo."

Bernardo stood with a bundle of papers, looking from one to the other of us. "Did I just miss something?"

"Yes," Edward said, "Now get out."

Bernardo looked at me. He looked a question at me, but I gave nothing back.

I could feel my face unreadable and empty. Bernardo sighed and handed me the papers. "How long?"

"I'll let you know," Edward said.

"Wonderful, I'll be in my room when Daddy decides to let me come out." He stalked through the nearest door where Olaf had vanished through.

"No one likes being treated like a child," I said.

"It's the only way to deal with Bernardo," Edward said. His gaze was very steady on my face, and he looked way too serious for comfort.

I started sorting the papers in my hands. I used the cleared space on the table that I'd made hours ago when I was still leaning over the table instead of slumping in the chair to read. I concentrated on sorting and didn't look up until I felt him beside me.

I looked then and found his eyes weren't blank. They were intense, but I still couldn't read them. "You said you hadn't been dating either of the guys for six months."

I nodded.

"Have you been dating anyone else?" he asked.

I shook my head.

"No sex, then," he said.

I shook my head again. My heart was beating faster. I so did not want him to figure this out.

"Why not?" he asked.

I looked away then, unable to meet his eyes. "I don't have any moral high ground to preach from anymore, Edward, but I don't do casual sex, you know that."

"You're jumping out of your skin every time Bernardo comes near you."

Heat climbed up my face. "Is it that noticeable?"

"Only to me," he said.

I was grateful for that. I spoke without looking at him. "I don't understand it. He's a bastard. Even my hormones usually have better taste than that."

Edward was leaning against the table, arms crossed over his white shirt. It was exactly how Bernardo had been sitting, but it didn't move me, and I didn't think it was just the shirt. Edward just did not affect me in that way and never had.

"He's handsome, and you're horny."

The heat that had been fading, flared until it felt like my skin would burn. "Don't say it that way."

"It's the truth."

I looked at him then, and let the anger show in my eyes. "Damn you."

"Maybe your body knows what you need."

I widened eyes at him. "Meaning what?"

"A good uncomplicated fuck. That's what I mean." He still looked calm, unmoved as if he'd said something entirely different.

"What are you saying?"

"Fuck Bernardo. Give your body what it needs. You don't have to go back to the monsters to get laid."

"I cannot believe you said that to me."

"Why not? If you were having sex with someone else, wouldn't it be easier to forget Richard and Jean-Claude? Isn't that part of their hold on you, especially the vampire. Admit it, Anita. If you weren't celibate, you wouldn't be missing them as much."

I opened my mouth to protest, closed it, and thought about what he'd said. Was he right? Was part of the reason I was still mooning over them the lack of sex? Yeah, I guess it was, but it wasn't just that. "I miss the sex, yeah, but I miss the intimacy, Edward. I miss looking at them both and knowing they're mine. Knowing I can have every inch of them. I miss Sunday after church and having Richard stay over to watch old movies. I miss watching Jean-Claude watch me eat a meal." I shook my head. "I miss them, Edward."

"Your problem, Anita, is that you wouldn't know an uncomplicated fuck if it bit you on the ass."

I wasn't sure whether to smile or be mad, so my voice was a little amused and a little angry. "And your relationship with Donna is so uncomplicated?"

"It was at the beginning," he said. "Can you say that about either of yours?"

I shook my head. "I'm not a casual person, Edward, not in anything."

He sighed. "I know that. When you give your friendship, it's for life. When you hate someone, it's forever. When you say you're going to kill someone, you do it. One of the things making you squirm about your boys is the fact that for you, love should be forever."

"And what's wrong with that?"

He shook his head. "Sometimes I forget how young you are."

"And what does that mean?"

"It means you complicate your life, Anita." He raised a hand before I could say it, and said it for me. "I know I've screwed up with Donna, but I went into it meaning to be casual, meaning it to just be part of the act. You always go into everything like it's life or death. Only life and death are life and death."

"And you think that sleeping with Bernardo would fix all that."

"It'd be a start," he said.

I shook my head. "No."

"Your final word?" he asked.

"Yes," I said.

"Fine, I won't bring it up again."

"Great," I said and looked into that blank, Edward face. "Being with Donna has made you more personal, more warm and fuzzy. I'm not comfortable with the new Edward."

"Neither am I," he said.

Edward went back to his side of the table, and we both started reading again. Usually, silence between us was companionable and not strained. But this quiet was full of unsaid advice: me to him about Donna, and him to me about the boys. Edward and I playing Dear Abby to each other. It would have been funny if it hadn't been so sad.

21

AN HOUR LATER, I'd finished the witness reports. I stretched my lower back while still sitting in the chair, just bending slowly at the waist until my hands touched the floor or almost touched the floor. Three stretches, and I could press my palms flat to the floor. Better. I got up and checked my watch. Midnight. I felt stiff and strange, estranged from this quiet room and the peaceful surroundings. My head was filled with what I'd read, and what I'd read hadn't been peaceful.

Standing, I could see Edward. He'd moved to the floor, lying flat on the floor, holding the reports up in front of his face. If I had lain down, I'd have been asleep. Edward always did have a will of iron.

He glanced at me. I got a glimpse of what he was looking at. He'd moved on to the pictures. Something must have shone on my face because he placed the pictures face down on his chest. "You finished?"

"With the witness reports, yeah."

He just looked at me.

I went around the table and sat in the chair he'd started the night in. He stayed lying on the floor. I would have said like a contented cat, but there was something more reptilian about him than feline; a coldness. How could Donna miss it? I shook my head. Business, concentrate on business.

"The majority of the houses are isolated ones, mostly because of the wealth of the owners. They've got enough money to give them land and privacy. But three of the houses were located in developments like the Bromwells' with neighbors all around. Those three attacks occurred on one of the few nights that all the neighbors were gone."

"And?" he said.

"And I thought this was going to be a brainstorming session. I want your ideas."

He shook his head. "I brought you down here for a set of fresh eyes, Anita. If I tell you all our old ideas, it may lead you down the same wrong paths we've already taken. Tell me what you see."

I frowned at him. What he said made sense, but it still felt like he was keeping secrets. I sighed. "If this was a person, I'd say he or they stake out the houses night after night, waiting for that one night when all the neighbors were out of the way. But do you know the odds of an entire street clearing out on any given night in the suburbs?"

"Long odds," Edward said.

I nodded. "Damn straight. A few people had plans for that night. One couple went to a niece's birthday party. Another family had their once a month dinner with the in-laws. Two couples from different crime scenes were both working late, but the rest of the people didn't have plans, Edward. They just all left home about the same time on the same night for different reasons."

He was watching me, eyes blank, but steady, intense, and neutral at the same time. From his face I didn't know whether I was saying something he'd heard a dozen times before, or something brand new. Detective Sergeant Dolph Storr likes to stay neutral and not influence his people so I was kind of used to it, but Edward made Dolph seem positively loaded with influence.

I continued, but it was like slogging through mud without any feedback at all. "The detective in charge of the second case, he noticed it, too. He went out of his way to ask why they left their houses. The answers are almost identical where the police take the time to ask details."

"Go on," Edward said, face still blank.

"Dammit, Edward. You've read all the reports. I'm just repeating what you already know."

"But maybe you'll end up someplace new," he said. "Please, Anita, just finish your thought."

"They all got restless. A spur of the moment trip to get ice cream with the kids. One woman decided to go grocery shopping at eleven o'clock at night. Some of them just got in their cars and went for a drive, no place in particular. Just had to get out for a while. One man described it as cabin fever.

"A woman, Mrs. Emma . . . shit. I've read too many names in too short a space of time."

"Was it an unusual name?" Edward asked without a single change of expression.

I frowned at him and leaned across the table, lying on it to reach the reports. I shuffled through them until I found the one I wanted. "Mrs. Emma Taylor said, 'The night just felt awful. I just couldn't stand being inside.' She goes on to say, 'Outside the air was suffocating, hard to breathe.' "

"So?" he asked.

"So I want to talk to her."

"Why?"

"I think she's a sensitive, if not a psychic."

"There's nothing in the reports that say she's either."

"If you have the gift and you ignore it or pretend it's not real, it doesn't go away. Power will out, Edward. If she's a strong sensitive or a psychic that has neglected her powers for years, then she'll be either depressed or manic. She'll have a history of treatment for mental illness. How serious will depend on how gifted she is."

He finally looked interested. "You're saying that having psychic ability can drive you crazy?"

"I'm saying that psychic ability can masquerade as mental illness. I know ghost hunters that hear the voices of the dead like whispers in their ears, one of the classic symptoms of psycophernia. Empaths, people who draw impressions from other people, can be depressed because they're surrounded by depressed people, and they don't know how to shield themselves. Really strong clairvoyants can spend their lives getting visions from everything they touch, unable to turn it off, again seeing things that aren't there. Psycophernia. Demonic possession can mask itself as multiple personality. I could give you examples for the next hour matching mental illness with different types of power."

"You've made your point," he said. He sat up and didn't seem the least bit stiff. Maybe the floor was good for his back. "I still don't understand why you want to talk to this woman. The report was taken by Detective Loggia. He was very thorough. He asked good questions."

"You noticed that he took more time with why people left than the rest of the cops, just like I noticed it."

Edward shrugged. "Loggia didn't like the way everyone cleared out. Too damn convenient, but he couldn't come up with anything that tied the people together into a conspiracy."

"A conspiracy?" I almost laughed then stopped at the seriousness in his face. "Did someone actually suggest that an entire upper-middle-class to more-than-middle-class neighborhood conspired together to kill these people?"

"It was the only logical explanation for why they all left within thirty minutes of each other on the night of the murders."

"So they investigated all these people?" I asked.

"That's where some of the extra paperwork comes from."

"And?" I said.

"Nothing," Edward said.

"Nothing?" I made it a question.

"A few neighborhood squabbles over kids destroying the flowers, one affair where the husband that turned up dead was banging the next door neighbor's wife." Edward grinned. "The neighbor was lucky that the other man got cut up in the middle of a string of serial killings. Otherwise, he'd have been the top of the hit parade."

"Could it have been a copycat?" I asked.

"The police don't think so, and believe me they tried to make the pieces fit."

"I believe you. The police hate to let a good motive slide since most of the time motive isn't even one of their top priorities. Most people kill over stupid things, impulse, screw motive."

"Do you have a logical reason why all these people would vacate their houses just at the right time for the killer, or killers, to make their move?"

I nodded. "Yep."

He looked up at me, a slight smile on his face. "I'm listening."

"It's very common in hauntings for people to be uncomfortable in the area where the ghost is strongest."

"You're saying ghosts did this?"

I waved a hand. "Wait, wait until I'm done."

He gave a small nod. "Dazzle me."

"I don't know if it's dazzling, but I think it's how it was done. There are spells that supposedly can make a person uneasy in a house or a place. But the spells I read in college were for one person or one house, not a dozen homes and twice that many people. I'm not even sure a coven working together could affect that big an area. I don't know that much about actual witchcraft of any flavor. We'll need to find a witch to ask. But I think it's moot. I just mentioned it as a possibility."

"It's a possibility the cops haven't come up with yet."

"Nice to know I haven't entirely wasted the last five hours of my life."

"But you don't think it was witches," Edward said.

I shook my head. "Witches of almost any flavor believe in the threefold rule. What you give out comes back to you threefold."

"What goes around comes around," Edward said.

"Exactly, and no one is going to want this shit coming back on them three-fold. I would have said they also believe in 'do what you will, only harm none,' but you can have bad pagans just like you can have bad Christians. Just because your belief says something is wrong doesn't mean someone's not going to break the rules."

"So what do you think caused them all to leave their homes just when our killer needed it?"

"I think whatever is doing this, is big enough and powerful enough to simply arrive on the spot and want the people to go, and they went."

Edward frowned at me. "I'm not sure I understand what you mean."

"Our monster arrives, knows which house it wants, and he fills the rest of the houses with dread, driving the other families out. That takes a hell of a lot of power, but to then turn around and shield the murder house so that that one family doesn't flee, that's truly impressive. I know some preternatural critters that can throw a sense of unease around them. Mostly I think to keep hunters at bay. But I don't know anything that can cause this kind of controlled panic."

"So you're saying you don't know what it is," he said, and there was just a tinge of disappointment in his voice.

"Not yet, but if this is true, then it rules out a hell of a lot of things. I mean some vampires can throw out fear like this, but not on this large a scale, and if they could do the other houses, they couldn't shield the murder house."

"I know a vampire kill when I see it, Anita, and this isn't one."

I waved my hands in the air as if clearing it. "I'm just throwing out examples, Edward. Even a demon couldn't do this."

"How about a devil?" he asked.

I looked at him, saw he was serious, so I gave him a serious answer. "I won't go into how long it's been since anyone saw a devil, a greater demon, above ground, but if it were anything demonic, I'd have felt it today in the house. The demonic leave a stain behind, Edward."

"Couldn't one that was powerful enough hide its presence from you?"

"Probably," I said. "I'm not a priest, so probably, but whatever is mutilating these people doesn't want to hide." I shook my head. "It's not demonic, I'd almost bet the farm on it, but again I'm not a demonologist."

"I know that Donna can help us locate a witch tomorrow. I don't think she knows any demonologists."

"There are only two in the country. Father Simon McCoupen, who has the record in this century in this country for number of exorcisms performed, and Doctor Philo Merrick, who teaches at the University of San Francisco."

"You sound like you know them," Edward said.

"I attended a class taught by Merrick, and a talk given by Father Simon."

"I didn't know you were that interested in demons."

"Let's just say that I'm tired of running into them without knowing much about them."

He looked at me, sort of expectantly. "When did you run into a demon?"

I shook my head. "I won't talk about it after dark. If you really want to know, ask me again tomorrow when the sun is shining."

He looked at me for a second or two, as if he wanted to argue, but he let it go. Which was just as well. There are some stories, some memories, that if you tell them after dark, they seem to gain weight, substance, as if there are things listening, waiting to hear themselves spoken of again. Words have power. But even thinking about them is sometimes enough to make the air in a room heavy. I'd gotten better over the years at turning off my memories. It was a way to stay sane.

"The list of what our murderer isn't is getting longer," Edward said. "Now tell me what it is."

"I don't know yet, but it is preternatural." I leafed through the pages until I found the part I'd marked. "Four of the people now in the Santa Fe hospital were only found because they wondered outside their homes at night, skinned and bleeding. Neighbors found them both times."

"There's a transcript of the 911 call somewhere in this mess. The woman who found the Carmichaels had hysterics over the phone."

I thought about what I'd seen in the hospital and tried to imagine finding one of my neighbors, perhaps a friend, in that condition in the middle of the street. I shook my head and chased the image back. I did not want to imagine it. I had enough nightmares of my own, thank you very much.

"I don't blame her," I said. "But my point is this: how could they walk around in that condition? One of the survivors attacked his neighbor when the man came to help. He bit his shoulder so badly that the man was taken to the hospital with the mutilation victims. Doctor Evans said that they have to restrain all the patients in Albuquerque or they try to get up and leave. Don't you find that strange?"

"Yes, it's all strange. Is there a point in here somewhere?" And I heard that thread of tiredness in his voice.

"I think that whatever skinned them was, is, calling them."

"Calling them how?" he asked.

"The same way a vampire calls a person he's bitten and mind-raped. The skinning or something about it gives the monster a hold over them."

"Why doesn't the monster just take them with him the night he skins them?" Edward asked.

"I don't know."

"Can you prove that the skinned victims are being called by some bogeyman?"

"No, but if the doctors would okay it, I wonder where one of the survivors would go, if no one stopped him. Maybe the mutilation victims could lead us right to the thing."

"You saw the hospital today, Anita. They are not going to let us take one of their patients and set him free. Between you and me, I'm not sure I could stand to watch it myself. "

"Well, the great Edward, afraid at last," another voice said.

We both turned to see Olaf standing in the far doorway. He was wearing black dress slacks, and a black polo-style shirt, the shirtsleeves a little short for his long arms. I guess there just aren't a lot of choices when you wear Jolly Green Giant sizes.

He glided into the room, and if I hadn't spent so much time around vampires and shapeshifters, I'd have said he was good at gliding. For a human, he was very good.

Edward stood as he spoke. "What do you want, Olaf?"

"Has the girl solved your mystery?"

"Not yet," Edward said.

Olaf stopped at the edge of the table closest to us. "Not yet. Such confidence you have in her. Why?"

"Four hours and that is the best question you can come up with," I said.

Olaf turned to me with a snarl. "Shut up!"

I took a step forward, and Edward touched my elbow. He shook his head. I stepped back, gave them some room. Truthfully, I wasn't up to arm wrestling Olaf, and I couldn't really shoot him just for yelling at me. It kind of limited my options.

Edward answered Olaf's question. "When you look at her, Olaf, you see just the surface, just the small, attractive packaging. Underneath all that prettiness is someone who thinks like a killer, and a cop, and a monster. I don't know anyone else who bridges all three worlds as well as she does. And all the preternatural experts you find are specialists; they're witches, or clairvoyants, or demonologists." He glanced at me as he said the last, then back to Olaf. "But Anita is a generalist. She knows a little about most of it and can tell us whether we need to find a specialist, and what kind of specialist we need."

"And what kind of magical specialist do we need?" He put a lot of sarcasm into that question.

"A witch, someone who works with the dead." He'd remembered my earlier request about finding out what I'd sensed on the road. "We're making a list."

"And checking it twice," I said.

Edward shook his head.

Olaf turned to me. "Was that a joke?"

"A little one, yes."

"Perhaps you should not try to make jokes."

I shrugged.

He turned back to Edward. "You told me all this before she came. You waxed eloquent about her abilities. But I have worked with your magical people in the past, and you never talked about them as you speak of her. What is it about her that is so God damned special?"

Edward glanced at me, then back to Olaf. "The Greeks believed that once there were no male and female, that all souls were one. Then the souls were torn apart, male and female. The Greeks thought that when you found the other half of your soul, your soul mate, that it would be your perfect lover. But I think if you find your other half, you would be too much alike to be lovers, but you would still be soul mates."

I was fighting hard to keep my face from showing the growing surprise at this little speech. I hoped I was succeeding.

"What are you trying to say?" Olaf demanded.

"She is like a piece of my soul, Olaf. "

"You are mad," Olaf said, "a lunatic. Soul mates, bah!"

I kind of agreed with Olaf on this one.

"Then why is the thought of giving her a gun while I hunt her one of my greatest fantasies?" Edward asked.

"Because you are mad," Olaf said.

Hear, hear, but I didn't say it out loud.

"You know that I have no greater compliment to give than that," Edward said. "If I wanted to kill you, Olaf, I would just do it. The same with Bernardo because I know that I'm better than both of you. But with Anita I'll never be sure unless we do go up against each other for real. If I die without knowing which of us is better, I'll regret the not knowing."

Olaf stared down at him. "You cannot mean to say that this girl, this die Zimtzicke of a girl is better than Bernardo or me."

"That's exactly what I mean."

Die Zimtzicke meant a quarrelsome or bitchy woman. Couldn't really argue with that one. I sighed. Olaf had hated me before. Now he was going to feel forced to be competitive. This I did not need. And compliment though it was, it was not reassuring to know that Edward fantasized about killing me. Oh, excuse me, hunting me while I was armed to see which of us was better. Oh, yeah, that was much more sane.

I checked my watch. It was 1:30 A.M. "Frankly, boys, I don't know whether to be flattered or frightened, but I do know one thing. It's late, and I'm tired. If we are really going to see the big bad vampire tonight, then it has to be now."

"You just don't want to look at the pictures tonight," Edward said.

I shook my head. "No, not just before trying to sleep. I don't even want to read the forensic reports tonight. I'll look at the gory remains first thing tomorrow."

"Afraid," Olaf said.

I met his angry eyes. "I need some sleep if I'm to function well while I'm here. If I see the pictures right before bedtime, I can't guarantee sleep."

He turned back to Edward. "Your soul mate is a coward."

"No, she's just honest."

"Thank you, Edward." I went to stand closer to Olaf, so that I had to crane my neck back to see his face, and he loomed over me. There was really no way to get decent eye contact, so I stepped back to a more comfortable angle for my neck, and settled for meeting his deep-set eyes. "If I'd been a man I'd have probably felt compelled to look at the pictures, to prove myself worthy of all Edward's praise. But one of the good things about being a woman is that my level of testosterone poisoning is lower than most men's."

"Testosterone poisoning?" Olaf looked confused. Probably not a new sensation for him.

"Show me to my room, then explain it to him, Edward. I want to get some extras if I'm going to be interviewing vamps tonight."

Edward led me past the brooding Olaf and out the door that everyone seemed to disappear through. The hallway was white and so unadorned it looked unfinished. He pointed out Bernardo's room as the first door and Olaf's was right beside mine.

"Do you really think Olaf and I bunking next door to each other is a good idea?"

"By putting you right beside him, it shows him I'm not afraid for you."

"But I am," I said.

He smiled. "Just take some basic precautions. You'll be fine."

"Nice to know one of us confident. If you hadn't noticed, he outweighs me by like a ton."

"You're talking like it would be a standup fight. I know you, Anita. If Olaf comes through your door tonight, you'll just shoot him."

I studied his face. "Are you setting him up so I will kill him?"

He blinked, and I saw for a moment that I'd surprised him. "No, no. I meant what I said to Olaf. If I wanted him dead, I'd just kill him. I put you next door to him because I know how he thinks. He'll think it's a trap, too easy, and he'll behave himself tonight."

"What about tomorrow night?"

Edward shrugged. "One night at a time."

I shook my head and opened the door. Edward called to me before I could go inside or even turn on the light. I turned back to face him.

"You know most women get all mushy when a man tells them they're his soul mate."

"I'm not most women."

His smile widened. "Amen to that."

I looked at him. "You know what you said in there scares me. The thought that you fantasize about hunting me and killing me. That's creepy, Edward."

"Sorry," he said, but he was still smiling, still amused.

"But honestly if you'd said the soul mate stuff and meant it like lovey-dovey, that could have scared me more. I've known since we met that you might kill me some day, but fall in love with me . . . that would be just too weird."

The smile faded a notch or two. "You know if we could love each other, our lives would be less complicated."

"Truth, Edward. Have you ever had a romantic thought about me?"

He didn't even have to think about it. He just shook his head.

"Me, either. I'll meet you out front by the car."

"I'll wait for you here," he said.

I looked at him. "Why?"

"I don't want you smarting off to Olaf on your way out if I'm not there to stop the fight."

"Would I do that?"

He shook his head. "Get the extra firepower and let's start the drive. I'd like to get to bed before dawn."

"Good point." I went into the room, closing the door behind me. There was a knock on the door almost immediately. I opened it back up, slowly, but was pretty sure it was Edward. It was.

"We'll take you into the club as my guest, just a friend. If the vamps don't know who you are, they might be more careless around you, let something slip that would make sense to you, that wouldn't make sense to me."

"What happens if I get outted during the evening? Think Her Worship will resent you sneaking the Executioner into her club?"

"I'll tell her that you wanted to see the best show in town and thought that they might not want the Executioner around, but that you're strictly there in an unexecution work mode."

"Will you say it just like that, unexecution work mode?"

He smiled. "Probably. She likes her men to be either very serious or very cute."

"She. You talk like you know her."

"Ted only kills rogues. He is very welcome in a lot of the local monster hangouts."

"Edward the actor," I said.

"I do good undercover work."

"I know you do, Edward."

"But it always makes you uncomfortable to see me do it."

I shrugged. "You're such a good actor, Edward, sometimes it makes me wonder which act is real."

The smile faded, leaving his face blank, and empty like some of him had slithered away with his smile. "Go get your gear, Anita."

I closed the door with him still standing there. In some ways I understood Edward better than either of the men I had been dating. In other ways he was the biggest mystery of all. I shook my head, literally shaking it off, and looked around the small bedroom. If we came back here at dawn, I'd be tired, and tired could mean careless. I decided to make some changes now while I was fresh.

The room's only chair would go under the doorknob, but not until I was in for the night. I moved a line of miniature Kachina dolls from the dresser to the windowsill. If anyone opened the window, one or more of the dolls would fall. There was a small mirror on the wall that was framed by deer antlers. I placed it under the window, just in case the dolls didn't fall. I'd leave my suitcase to one side of the door entrance so if the door did somehow manage to open without knocking the chair over, Olaf might trip over the suitcase. Of course, I was almost as likely to trip over it trying to get to the bathroom on the way out. The moment I thought of it, I had to go. I'd hit the bathroom on the way out. Edward could stand outside and make sure Olaf didn't interrupt.

I searched through my suitcase. It was illegal for me to carry my vampire gear without a court order of execution. Carrying it without one was like premeditated murder. But no law against carrying a few extras. I had two thin vials of holy water with little rubber caps. You hit the cap with your thumb and it popped open, sort of like a grenade, but only dangerous to the vamp. Which made it a lot more user friendly than a grenade.

I slipped the holy water into each of my back pockets. They barely showed through the dark cloth. I already had my cross, but I'd had crosses ripped off of my throat before, so I had backups. I put a plain silver cross with chain in one front pocket of my jeans, and another one in the pocket of the black dress jacket. I opened the box of new ammunition that I'd packed.

I'd had to leave my apartment almost two years ago now. When I'd lived in my apartment, I'd put Glazer Safety Rounds in my guns because I didn't want my neighbors to take a stray bullet. Glazers will not go through walls, but as Edward and some of my police friends had pointed out, I'd been lucky. Glazers will shatter bone, but don't really go through bone, the difference between a shotgun and a rifle round, sort of. Edward had actually come into town just to take me out to the shooting range and test fire stuff. He'd asked me questions about specific gun fights, and what I'd learned was that the reason the Glazers had done what I wanted them to do was mostly being almost point blank every time I used them for a kill. What I needed was something that was a reliable kill from a safer distance than arm's length. It also might explain why I'd hit some older vamps from a distance, but they hadn't stopped. Maybe not. Maybe they were just that old, but . . . Edward had been very convincing. Something with more penetrating power, more stopping power, ammo meant not to wound but to kill. Because let's face it: when was the last time I'd wounded anyone that I hadn't meant to kill? Wounding was an accident for me. Killing was the goal.

I'd settled on the Hornady Custom XTP handgun ammo. To be exact the 9 mm Luger, 147 JHP/XTP, silver-coated of course. There were other hollow point bullets that will expand to a bigger mass, but some of them don't penetrate nearly as far into a body mass. With a vamp you need to make sure you hit something vital, not just that you make a big hole. There were even bullets that penetrated further into a mass, which meant they'd reliably go through a body and out the other side. But all the Hornady XTPs were designed to penetrate the target, but not so far as to pass through the target object and "create a hazard." That last was a quote from some of the Hornady Manufacturing literature. The ammo followed the FBI penetration requirements. The Feds, even more than little ol' me, have to worry about what happens when a bullet hits the bad guy and keeps traveling. Is it going to hit a kid, a pregnant woman, a nun out for her morning stroll? Once a bullet hits the mark and keeps traveling, you really never know where it will end up. So the plan is to make sure it doesn't leave the target, but that the target doesn't get up either.

Of course, Edward had made his own recipe for killing. He'd taken silver hollow points and filled the end with holy water and mercury, then sealed the top with wax. I'd been afraid that the wax would make the bullets jam in a gun, but they ran through like silk—smooth, dependable, like Edward himself. The ammo was a hell of a show. So Edward had told me. I hadn't used Edward's homemade surprise yet. I was still vaguely wary of them. He shouldn't have told me that they might jam the gun. Or maybe, I would have been nervous of them anyway. With these even if you hit in a non-lethal area, missed the heart, the head, everything vital, you still did damage. The holy water and silver mercury would explode through the vamp's body, burning where they touched. The holy water would eat through the body like acid. Hit a vamp even in a leg or arm with this shit, and they might lose all interest in killing you and just want to stop the pain.

I stared at the two boxes of ammo, and finally loaded up with the Homady XTP, Edward's specials in their box. If I did have to shoot any vamps tonight, I had no court order of execution, and carrying the homemade seemed too much like premeditation. Premeditation is the difference between first degree murder, and second degree murder or even manslaughter if you had a good lawyer and a sympathetic jury. There were people in jail at this very moment for killing vamps. I did not want to be one of them. Besides, we were just going down there to ask questions, nothing major. So I told myself as I closed the suitcase and left the other bullets behind.

But I knew better than most that what should be simple always grows complex when you add a vampire. Add a Master of the City, any city, and you never really know what you're walking into. I'd killed three Masters of the City: one with a sword, one with fire, one by killing their human servant. Never just a straight on shoot out. I probably wouldn't be shooting anyone tonight, but . . . I loaded up my extra clip with the bullets. I'd only use them if I'd used up the first clip. If I emptied thirteen of the XTPs into something and it didn't go down, all bets were off. I'd worry about murder charges later, after I survived. Survival first. Try to stay out of jail second. My priorities in order, I slipped the extra clip into the right pocket of my jacket and went off to find Edward. He was, after all, the one who had taught me my priorities.

22

I WAS COOLING my heels in the living room when Bernardo and Olaf came out of the far rooms. They had both changed clothes.

Bernardo was in white dress slacks with a sharp crease and a roll of cuff. A white vest showed off his darkly muscled arms. He'd added heavy silver arm bracelets at mid-bicep, and matching ones at each wrist. A silver saint's medallion glittered against the smooth darkness of his chest. Most of his hair fell like a black dream around all that white, except for a braid on one side. It was a thick braid because he just had that much hair, and he'd woven silver chains with tiny bells here and there in his hair, so he stalked into the room to the sound of gentle chimes. He looked at me through a curtain of blackness caressing one side of his face, the other graced by the silver on black glint of the braid. It was, to say the least, eye-catching.

It was a little bit of a struggle to tear my gaze from Bernardo and look at Olaf. He had gone for a black shirt that seemed utterly sheer. To hide his shoulder holster, he'd put on a leather jacket. It was way too hot for leather. Though admittedly, with his totally shaved head, black jeans, and black boots with silver toes and heels, the leather jacket looked about the right speed.

"You guys look spiffy. What's the occasion?"

"We're going to a club," Bernardo said, as if that explained it.

"I know that," I said.

He was frowning now. "You should change."

I pushed to my feet from the couch. "Why?"

He walked toward me. I caught glimpses of dark flesh above his white leather loafers and the hem of his pants, no socks. He stopped at the edge of the couch, as if I'd pulled back, or made some other sign that I wasn't happy. "I know you can look as good as we do." He gave a little self-deprecating smile. "Or as good as Olaf here. Maybe not as good as me." He smiled, and it was a good smile, meant to melt something a little lower than my heart. But I'd been working on my reaction to him. I was not a slave to my libido. Richard and Jean-Claude could attest to that.

I looked at him in all his light and dark glory. "If I can't look as good as you, why try at all?"

The smile widened to a grin that made his face look somehow more real and less handsome. Less handsome, less practiced, but I liked it more. He took a step closer, and that teasing, practiced look was back. This was a man who knew how to flirt. But if anything will turn me off, it's a very practiced approach, as if the man has done it a thousand times before, to a lot of different women. Which always seems to imply that I am no different from all the rest. Not flattering.

"I think you might, might, be able to approach my glory, if you tried."

Even knowing it was an act, I had to smile. "I just don't want to work that hard, Bernardo."

"If I am forced to change, then everyone changes," Olaf said.

I looked at him. Was he handsome? Not really, but he was striking. If he could tone down the bad boy routine, he could probably pick up plenty of girls at the club, or maybe even if he didn't tone it down. It always amazes me how many women like dangerous men. Men who almost from the moment you meet them, you know are bad news. Me, I prefer my men kinder, gentler, nice. Niceness is highly underrated by most people.

"I don't remember anyone putting you in charge, Olaf. When Edward asks me to change clothes, I'll change."

He took a step towards me, but whatever he was going to say or do, stopped when Edward came into the room. He was wearing a red tank top with a short-sleeved silk shirt that matched the tank. The shirt would hide his shoulder holster if he were careful. His jeans were new and black, and with his yellow hair grown out enough to have a little curl to it, he actually looked sort of cute. Edward never looked cute.

I knew when I was beaten. I raised hands in surrender and started walking towards the bedrooms. Then stopped. I turned back to him. "I thought the point to taking me down there without cops was that the monsters might talk to Anita Blake, vamp executioner. So that means no undercover crap."

"Why would changing clothes be undercover for you?" Bernardo asked.

I looked at him, then looked at Edward. "If you want my services, you take whatever the hell I'm wearing. I don't dress up outside the office."

Edward said, "Let's go down there with you a little under wraps. Look around the club, meet the monsters, before they find out who you are."

"Why?"

"You know the answer."

"You want me to look around, use my expertise, before they know I have any expertise."

He nodded.

"But you also want me to be Anita Blake and impress the monsters."

"Yes," he said.

"Hard to do both."

"Be a tourist until they make you, then be yourself."

"The best of both worlds," I said.

"Exactly."

I looked at him. "Is this all your plan? No hidden agenda?"

He smiled, and it was Ted's smile, slow, lazy, innocent. "Would I do that to you?"

I just shook my head and started for the bedrooms. "Forget I asked. I'll change into something more . . . festive," I said without turning around.

Edward didn't call me back and say no need to change so I kept walking. We were undercover tonight apparently. I hate undercover work. I am just so damn bad at it.

I had also not packed with an eye for club hopping. I changed into the newest, blackest jeans I had. The Nikes would have to do because I hadn't brought anything else. Except more Nikes. All my shirts were just different colors of one or two styles. If I find something comfy, I've learned to buy doubles if I really like something, and multiple colors if I really, really like a style. This means I am usually wearing last year's style long after the fashion trend has moved on, but it's not like I care.

I had a royal blue cotton tee with a scoop neck. Almost all the shirts I'd packed had a scoop neck. The blue was a little softer than the rest of the colors. I added a touch of eye shadow, enough eyeliner to be dramatic, enough mascara so that the eyeliner didn't overwhelm my eyelashes, a hint of blush, and some kiss-ass red lipstick.

I couldn't really get a good look in the room's small mirror, but at least the makeup looked good. The shoulder holster was very black against the blue shirt, but the black suit jacket took care of that. Since I couldn't take the jacket off without flashing the guys, I added my wrist sheaths with matching silver knives. If I was going to be stuck with the jacket all night, I might as well carry them. Besides, you never know when you'll need a good blade. I ran a brush through my hair and called it done.

Apparently, I looked okay because Bernardo said, "I take it back. If you'd packed a dress, you'd be prettier than I am."

I shook my head. "No, I wouldn't, but thanks for saying it."

"Let's go," Edward said.

"She is showing too much breast," Olaf said.

I looked at his completely sheer black shirt. "I can see your nipples."

His face darkened. I think he was actually blushing. "Bitch."

"Yeah, sure, you and the horse you rode in on," I said.

Edward moved between us, soothing the big man. To me, he said, "Don't tease him unless you want the trouble."

"He started it," I said.

He looked at both of us, his face that icy gaze that I'd seen him wear when he killed. "I don't care who starts it, but I will finish it. Is that clear?"

Olaf and I looked at Edward, then at each other. Slowly, we both nodded. "It is clear," Olaf said.

"Crystal," I said.

"Good." His face transformed into a smiling face, somehow appearing years younger. How did he do it? "Then let's go."

We went.

23

OBSIDIAN BUTTERFLY, THE CLUB, was located between Santa Fe and Albuquerque. The club was set back from the road like one of the Indian casinos. It had high-class tourist trap written all over it. The parking lot was so full we had to circle to find a spot.

The building was done in faux-Aztec temple. Or for all I knew real Aztec temple. But the outside of the building looked like a movie set. Red neon traced square carved faces, and the name was traced in more red neon. There was a line stretching around the corner of the building and out into the hot summer dark. This was not my town. I didn't know the manager, so I couldn't jump the line. I also did not want to stand in the line.

Edward walked up the line, confident, as if he knew something I didn't. We followed him like obedient puppies. We weren't the only foursome trying to get into the club. We were the only foursome that wasn't made up of couples. To blend in we needed at least one more woman. But Edward didn't seem to be trying to blend in. He walked up to the head of the line where a large, broad-shouldered man of very Indian descent stood bare-chested, wearing what looked like a skirt but probably wasn't, and a heavy faux-gold collar that covered most of his shoulders like a mantle. He was wearing a crown covered in macaw feathers and other smaller feathers that I couldn't identify.

If this was just the bouncer at the door, I was actually interested in seeing the show. Though I hoped they had access to lots and lots of pet parrots and hadn't actually slaughtered birds just for the outfits.

"We're Professor Dallas's party. She's expecting us," Edward said in his best hail-fellow-well-met voice.

The feather and gold bedecked man said, "Names." He uncrossed his arms and looked at a clipboard that had been in his hand the entire time.

"Ted Forrester, Bernardo Spotted-Horse, Olaf Gundersson and Anita Lee." The new last name stopped me. Apparently, he was serious about me going in incognito.

"IDs."

I tried very hard to keep my face blank, but it was an effort. I didn't have any fake ID. I looked at Edward.

He handed his driver's license to the man, then still smiling, said, "And now aren't you glad that I didn't let you leave your license in the car." He handed a second license to the man.

He looked at both for longer than I thought he should have, as if he suspected something. My shoulders were actually tight, waiting for him to turn to me and say, ah-hah, fake ID, but he didn't. He handed both licenses back to Edward, and turned to Bernardo and Olaf. They waited with their licenses out, as if they'd done this before.

Edward moved back to stand by me and handed me the license. I took it and looked at it. It was a New Mexico license with an address on it that I didn't know. But it was my picture, and it said Anita Lee. The height, weight, and the rest were accurate, just the name and address was wrong.

"Better put it in your pocket. I may not be around to find it next time," he said.

I slipped it in my pocket along with my other license, a lipstick, and some money, and an extra cross. I wasn't sure whether to be flattered or insulted that Edward had set up a secret identity for me. Of course, maybe it was just the license, but knowing Edward there'd be more to it. There usually was.

The big double doors were opened by another large muscled guy in a skirt, though he didn't have a feather crown or a nifty collar. A lesser bouncer, apparently. The doors led into a darkened room thick with an incense I didn't recognize. The walls were completely covered with heavy drapes, only another set of double doors showing the way.

Another bouncer, this one blond and tanned the color of thick honey, opened the door. He had feathers woven into his short hair. He winked at me as we went through the door, but it was Bernardo he watched the closest. Maybe he was looking for weapons, but I think he was watching Bernardo's butt. He wouldn't see a weapon from the back. Bernardo had transferred his gun to a front cross draw because the gun had showed a lump at the back. Which told you how snug the pants fit in back.

The room we entered was large, stretching out and out into the near darkness. People sat at square stone tables that looked suspiciously like altars to me. Or at least what Hollywood is always using for altars. The "stage" took up most of the far left wall, but it wasn't a stage, not really. It was being used as a stage, but it was a temple. It was as if someone had sliced off the top of a pyramid temple and transported it here to this night club, in a city so far removed from the lush jungles where the building began that the stones themselves must be lonely.

A woman appeared in front of Edward. She looked as ethnic as the first doorman with high sculpted cheekbones, and a fall of shiny black hair that fell to her knees as she moved through the tables. She had menus in her dark hands, so I assumed she was the hostess. But her dress was red with a black design, and I knew silk when I saw it. The dress was vaguely oriental and didn't match the decor of the room, or the waitresses hurrying to and fro in odd loose dresses made of some rough material. The waitresses struggled along in loose-fitting sandals, while the hostess glided before us in high heels the same scarlet as her dress and perfectly manicured nails.

She was beautiful in a tall, slender, graceful fashion, like a model, but she was a discordant note, as if she belonged to a different theme. She showed us to a table that was in the very front with a view dead center of the temple. There was a woman at the table, who stood and offered us her hand as we sat down. Her handshake was firm, and her hand was about my size. It takes practice to have a firm handshake with hands this small.

Professor Dallas, call me Dallas, was shorter than I was, and so petite that in the right clothes she'd have looked prepubescent. She wore tan Docker pants, a white polo shirt, with a tweed jacket complete with leather elbow patches, as if she'd read the dress code for college professors and was trying to conform. Her hair was shoulder length, a baby fine, medium brown. Her face was small and triangular and as pale and perfect as God had intended it to be. Her glasses were gold wire frames and too large for the small face. If this was her idea of party clothes, someone needed to take her shopping. But somehow I didn't think the good doctor gave a shit. I like that in a woman.

A man stepped out of the odd-shaped door at the top of the temple. The moment he stepped out, silence fell in rings around him, spreading out and out into the murmuring audience until it was so quiet I could hear the pulse of my own blood. I'd never heard a crowd this large go so quiet so quickly. I'd have said it was magic, but it wasn't, not exactly. But this man's presence was a sort of magic. He could have worn jeans and a T-shirt and he'd still have commanded your attention. Of course, what he was wearing was pretty eye-catching all on its own.

His crown was a mass of thin, long feathers, a strange greenish, bluish, goldish color, so that as he moved they shifted color like a trapped greenish rainbow hovering in a fan of colors above his forehead. His cape hung nearly to his knees and seemed to be formed of the same feathers as his headdress, so that he moved in a wave of iridescence. The body that showed was strong, square, and dark. I was sitting close enough to tell if he was handsome or not, but staring at him, I wasn't sure. It was impossible to separate his face from that presence, and so the face didn't matter much. He was attractive, not because of the length of a nose or the turn of a chin, but just because.

I found myself sitting up a little straighter in my seat, as if coming to attention. The moment I did it, I knew that even if it wasn't magic, it was something. I had to fight to tear my gaze from him and look at the others at the table.

Bernardo was gazing at him, as was Doctor Dallas. Edward was gazing out over the hushed crowd. Olaf was studying the doctor. He watched her, not as a man watches a woman, but as a cat watches a bird through cage bars. If Dallas noticed, she ignored it, but somehow I think she didn't notice. I think even with the man's presence filling the room, his rich voice riding the air, I'd have felt Olaf's gaze like a cold wind down my spine. That Dallas was oblivious to it made me worry about her, just a little, and made me very sure that I never wanted Olaf alone with her. Her survival instincts just weren't up to it.

The man, king or high priest, talked in rich tones. I caught part of it. Something about the month of Toxcatal, and a chosen one. I could not concentrate on his voice, any more than I could gaze upon him because to give him too much of my attention meant I was caught up in the spell he was weaving over the crowd. It wasn't a spell in the true sense of the word, but there was power in it, if not magic. The difference between magic and power can be very small. I'd been forced to accept that fact in the last two years.

The high priest was human, but there was a taste of ages to him. There are just not that many ways for a human to last centuries. One way is to be the human servant of a powerful master vamp. Unless Obsidian Butterfly was more generous about sharing her power than most of the Masters of the City that I'd met, the high priest belonged to her. He was too powerful an echo of his master to be endured unless she was that master. Master vamps have a tendency to either destroy or own that which is powerful.

The high priest had been powerful in life, a charismatic leader. Now centuries of practice had turned that charisma into a kind of magic. I'd had full-fledged vamps not affect me this much. If this was the servant, how scary was the master going to be? I sat there at the stone table, flexing my shoulders to feel the tightness of the shoulder holster. I was glad I'd packed an extra clip of bullets. I moved my wrists just enough to feel the knives resting against my arms. I was very glad I'd brought the knives. You can stab vamps and keep them alive, but still make your . . . point.

I was finally able to separate the power of his voice from the words. Most vamps, when they can, do tricks with their voices. The words themselves hold the key. They say *beautiful*, and you see beauty. They say *terror*, and you feel afraid. But this voice had little to do with the words. It was just an overwhelming aura of power like a great white noise hum. The audience may have thought that they were hanging on every word, but the man could have recited a grocery list with similar effect.

The words were, "You saw him as the god Tezcathpoca in our opening dance. Now see him as a man." The lights had been dimming as the priest spoke, until he was left in near darkness, only the iridescent gleam of feathers showed as he moved. The light came up on the other side of the stage, revealing a man, pale skin that glowed in the lights from his bare feet to equally bare shoulder. His back was to the audience and for a moment I thought he was nude. There was nothing to break up the curve of his body from the swell of his calves, to his thighs, the tight roundness of his buttocks, the lean waist, the spread of shoulders. His hair looked black under the lights, cut so close to his head that it looked shaved. He turned slowly, revealing the barest of G-strings, a color so close to his skin that you knew the illusion of nudity was a planned effect.

His face shone unadorned like a star, starkly beautiful. He looked somehow pure and perfect, which wasn't possible. No one human was perfect. But he was pretty. A line of black hair ran down the center of his chest and stomach to vanish into the thong. Our table was close enough, and his body white enough, that I could see the thin line of hair encircling his nipples to meet that thin line down his chest like the soft arms of a T.

I actually had to shake my head to clear it. Maybe it was being celibate, or maybe there was more magic in the air than just the voice of the human servant. I looked back at the stage and knew that it was only a trick of the light that made his skin seem to glow. I looked over at Professor Dallas. She had her head bent very close to Edward, talking to him in whispers. If she saw the show almost every night, it was nothing new to her, but the lack of attention that she paid the man made me turn and search the dim tables around us. Most eyes, especially the women, were turned rapt to the stage. But not all eyes. Some were drinking, holding hands with their dates, doing other things. I turned back to the stage and just looked at him, drinking in the lines of his body. Damn, it was just me. Or rather, it was just a normal human reaction to a nearly naked and attractive man. I'd have preferred a spell. At least then I could blame someone else. My hormones, my fault. I needed more hobbies, that was it, more hobbies. That would fix everything.

The lights came up slowly until the Priest was visible once more. "It was traditional that twenty days before the great ceremony, brides would be chosen for him." I caught a glimpse of fur, and for just an instant I thought it was a line of shapeshifters in their half-human, half-beast guise. But it was men dressed in leopard skins. Not hanging loose like cloaks but as if the skins were sewn around their bodies. Some of them were too tall for the skins so that a foot or more of bare leg showed below the animal feet, or out of the clawed arms. They moved among the tables in a strangely graceful line, encased in fur with their faces framed through the open jaws of the dead animals.

A man passed within touching distance of our table, and I saw the black rosettes that decorated the golden skin more closely, and it wasn't leopard. I was spending a lot of time with St. Louis' wereleopards. I'd killed the wereleopard leader because he was trying to kill me, among other things. But I'd left the leopards without a leader, and shapeshifters without a leader are anyone's meat. So I was de facto leader until we could work something else out. I'd been learning how to forge them into a stronger unit, or pard. One of the ways you did that was sheer physical closeness, not sex, but closeness. I stared at the skin, and my hand went out without thinking. The man's movement stroked my hand over the once living fur. The spots were larger. The markings weren't as neat somehow. I watched the cat heads on the men, and the heads were more square, not the rounded almost feminine line of leopard. Jaguars, they were jaguars, which made perfect sense with the Aztec motif, but, like the bird feathers, I wondered how they'd obtained the skins, and was it legal. I knew it wasn't right. I don't believe in killing for decoration. I wear leather because I eat meat, just using the whole animal. Nothing wasted.

The man turned and looked at me. His eyes were blue, his face tanned a pale gold that matched the line of belly fur just before it turned white. The moment he looked at me energy danced down my skin like a hot breath. A shapeshifter, great. There was a time, not long ago, that that much power this close would have drawn an answering energy from me, but not this time. I sat there staring at him, and I was safe behind my shield that squeezed down a layer of energy that stood between me and all the psychic shit. I gave him innocent brown eyes, and he moved off through the tables as if I was no longer interesting. Which was fine with me.

I didn't reach out for it, but the energy came here and there from them. It would have been so much worse without the shielding. They had to be werejaguars or the costumes were like the ultimate false advertising. Somehow, this didn't strike me as a show that promised anything it couldn't deliver.

The werejaguars picked women from the audience, took them by the hand and led them towards the stage. A petite blonde was pulled from her seat giggling. A short, square woman with skin the color of tanned leather was pulled solemn-faced and didn't seem to be nearly as pleased, but she let herself be led to the stage. A taller more slender Hispanic woman was next, with long black hair that shimmered as she moved like an ebony curtain. She stumbled on the steps, and only the werejaguar's arm saved her from falling. She laughed as he steadied her, and I realized she was drunk.

A figure appeared in front of me, blocking my view of the stage. I looked up into a dark face framed by snarling jaws. The jaguar's golden glass eyes rode above the man's face, as if the dead animal were staring at me, too. The man reached a square, dark hand out to me.

I shook my head.

The hand stayed, pale palm up, waiting.

I shook my head again. "No, thanks anyway."

Dallas leaned around Edward, across the table, having to nearly crawl on it to get close to me. It stretched her body in a long line, her long ponytail pooling on the stone. Olaf's hand hovered over that spill of hair, and the look on his face was strange enough to distract me from everything else. Her voice made me look at her face instead of Olaf's. "They need someone your size and body type to round out the brides. Someone with long hair." She was smiling. "Nothing bad is going to happen." She gave me a cheerful smile that made her look even younger.

The man leaned over me and I could smell the fur and . . . him. Not sweat, just his scent, and that made my stomach contract, made me have to concentrate on holding my shields, because the part of me that was tied to Richard and his beast wanted to respond, wanted to spill outward and wallow in that scent. The animal impulses, true animal impulses, always threw me.

The man's voice was thickly accented, and sounded unsuited to whispering. It was a voice for shouting orders. "Do nothing that you do not wish to do, but please come to our temple."

Maybe it was the please or the accent or the absolute seriousness in his face but I believed. I still might not have gone with him, but Edward leaned into me, and said, "Tourist, think tourist." He didn't say, "Play along, Anita. Remember, we're undercover," because with a shapeshifter this close he'd hear anything that was said at the table. But Edward had said enough. I was a tourist. A tourist would go.

I gave the man my left hand and let him pull me to my feet. His hand was very warm. Some lycanthropes seem to adopt their alter ego's body temperature. Even Richard's skin grew warmer near the full moon, but that couldn't be it tonight. We were only days away from the dark of the moon, as far from the shining fullness that called the beasts as we could get. The man was just warm. Too hot for fur.

The priest in his feathers encouraged the audience to applaud as the last reluctant bride, me, joined the grouping around the nearly naked man. The were-jaguar stood me on the side with the giggling blond. The smell of beer was strong enough that I knew the giggling wasn't just nervousness. Perfect.

I looked past the man, doing my best to ignore him, to the two women on the other side. The tall one with all the hair was swaying slightly on her spike heels. Her skirt was leather, and the blouse looked like a red camisole. The other woman was that solid that some people call fat, but it isn't. She was square and wore a loose black shirt over black pants. She caught my eye, and we shared a moment of discomfort. Audience participation was great as long as the audience wants to participate.

"These are your brides," the priest said, "your reward. Enjoy them."

The solid woman and I both took a step back as if it were choreographed. The blonde and the tall one with all the hair melted into his arms, cuddling and laughing. The man played to them, but it was their hands that wandered over his body. He was very careful where he touched them. I thought at first it was just fear of being sued, but there was a stiffness, a tightening of his body when their hands wandered over his bare buttocks that said he wasn't having as good a time as it looked. From the audience you'd have never noticed. He came away from them with orange-red lipstick like a wound on his pale skin and pale pink like a patch of glitter down his face.

He reached out to us, and both of us shook our heads. We took another step back, and a step closer together. Solidarity. She offered me her hand, not to shake, but to hold, and I realized she was scared, not just nervous. I was neither, just not happy. She whispered, "I'm Ramona." I gave her my name, and what seemed to matter more, held her hand. I felt like Mommy on the first day of school when the bullies are waiting.

The priest's voice came. "You are his last meal, his last caress. Do not deny him."

Ramona's face changed, grew soft. Her hand fell away from mine. The fear was gone. I called, softly, "Ramona." But she moved forward as if she never heard me. She moved into the man's arms. He kissed her with more tenderness than he'd shown the other two. She kissed him back, with a passion and a strength that made anything the other two had done seem pale and watered down. The other two women had gone to their knees on either side, either because they couldn't stand upright anymore, or the better to run their hands over both the man and the new woman. It looked like a mild version of a pornographic four-way.

He drew back from Ramona, laying a second kiss on her forehead as if she were a child. She stayed unmoving, eyes closed, face slack. It was illegal to force anyone to do anything against their will by use of magic. I looked at Ramona's empty face, waiting, waiting for what came next, all decision, all choice, washed away. If I'd been myself tonight instead of whoever the hell I was supposed to be, I'd have called them on it. I should still turn them in to the cops. But truthfully, unless they did worse, I wasn't going to turn them in if the Master of the City could help us solve the mutilation murders. If the murders stopped, a few mind-games could be overlooked.

There was a time when I wouldn't have tolerated it, when I wouldn't have looked the other way for any reason. They say everyone has their price. Once I thought I was the exception to the rule, but if it was a choice of letting this nice woman be made to do some things she didn't want to do, or seeing another crime scene, another survivor, they could have the woman. Not have in the true sense of the word, but to my knowledge mind-magic by a human servant wasn't permanent. Of course, until tonight I hadn't known a human servant could do mind-rape. I really didn't know how much danger this woman was in, and yet . . . and yet I would risk her, as long as nothing worse happened. If they told her to strip, all bets were off. I had rules, limits. They just weren't the same ones they'd been four years ago, or two years, or a year ago. The fact that I let them mind-rape her and didn't complain, bothered me, but not enough.

The blonde woman leaned into the man and bit his butt, not hard but enough to make him jump. His back was to the audience, so I was probably the only one who saw the anger that showed for just a moment in that handsome face.

The priest stayed on his side of the stage, as if he didn't want to distract from the show, but I knew he'd turned his attention to me. The full force of him was like pressure against my skin.

His voice. "A most reluctant bride to leave him lonely in his hour of need." I felt his power and now that power was wedded to the words. When he said, "need," I felt need. My body tightened with it, but I could ignore it. I knew I could stand there and be unmoved, that he could do his worst and I could stand against it. But no human could have done it. Anita Blake, vamp executioner, could stand firm, but Anita Lee, undercover party-goer, well . . . If I just stood there, the game was up. At the very least they'd know I wasn't an ordinary tourist. Times like these are one of the reasons I hate undercover work.

I ignored the priest's rich voice and just walked toward the man. He was having trouble keeping the blonde's hand out of the front of his G-string. The other woman knelt in a pool of her own dark hair, hanging on his leg, one hand playing with the side strap of the G-string. Only Ramona stood there, face blank, hands at her sides, waiting for orders. But the priest was concentrating all his energies on me. She was safe until he finished with me.

The dark-haired woman got the strap to slide over the smooth bone of his hip, and the blonde used it as a chance to plunge her hand under the cloth. His eyes closed, head going back, body reacting automatically, even as his hand grabbed her hand and tried to pull her hand out of his pants. Apparently, she was hanging on, not hurting him exactly, but not letting go.

I doubted the club would have tolerated this level of abuse if the performer had been a woman and the audience member a man. Some forms of sexist double standards do not work in a man's favor. A woman they would have rushed on stage and saved her, but he was a man, and he was on his own.

I touched Ramona's shoulders and moved her to one side like she was furniture. She moved where I put her, eyes still closed. Made me feel worse that she was that pliant. But one problem at a time. I put my hand on top of his and moved his hand away from the blonde's wrist. His hand didn't move at first, then he looked at me, really looked at me. His eyes were large, a soft pure gray with a circle of black around the iris like someone had used the same eye pencil to trace his eyes that they'd used on the sweep of eyebrow and dark lashes. Strange eyes. But whatever he saw in my eyes seemed to reassure him because he let go of the blonde. There's a nerve in the arm about three fingers down from the bend of the elbow. If you hit it right, it's pretty painful. I dug my fingers into her flesh, as if I'd find that nerve and drag it to the surface. I was pissed, and I wanted to hurt her. I succeeded.

She gave a small scream, her hand opened, and I was able to move her arm back, fingers digging into the nerve. She didn't struggle, just whimpered and stared up at me with large unfocused eyes, but the pain was chasing the liquor away. If I kept it up long enough, I could have sobered her up in, oh, fifteen minutes or so, if she didn't pass out first.

I spoke low, but my voice carried. The stage had great acoustics. "My turn."

The tall Hispanic woman crawled away from the man, scuttling in her tight skirt until she fell flat on her face. You have to be pretty drunk to fall from a crawling position. She got to one elbow, and her voice came thick, but panicked. "He's yours."

I drew the blonde a few steps further away from the man, and slowly let go of her arm. I told her, "Stay." She cradled her arm against her body, huddling over it. The look she gave me was not friendly, but she didn't mouth off. I think she was afraid of me. I wasn't having a great night. First, I let the nice lady be mind-raped, then I terrorize drunken tourists. I would have said, how could the night get worse, but worse was waiting. I looked back at the nearly naked man and didn't know what to do with him.

I walked back over to him because I couldn't figure a graceful way off stage. I'd probably blown my cover as a tourist, but Edward had let me bring a gun and knives into the club. In fact, we were all loaded for bear or vampire or whatever. The bouncers, unless they were idiots, had to have seen some of the weapons. I was just not supposed to be a vamp executioner, but I've never played victim well. I should never have come on stage, but too late now.

The man and I stood facing each other, his back still to the audience. He leaned into me, breath warm against my hair. He whispered, "My hero, thank you."

I nodded, and that small movement brushed my thick hair against his face. My mouth was dry, and it was hard to swallow. My heart was suddenly beating too hard, too fast, as if I'd been running. It was a ridiculous reaction to a strange man. I was horribly aware of how close he was, how little he was wearing, and how my hands just hung at my sides because to move at all would brush against him. What was the matter with me? I had not been noticing men this badly in St. Louis. Was there something in the air in New Mexico, or was it just lack of oxygen from the elevation?

He rubbed his face against my hair, whispered, "I am César." That small movement put the curve of his jaw, the skin of his neck next to my face. There was a trace of the women's perfume mixing along his face, overlaying the clean scent of his skin, but underneath it all was a sharper scent. It was the smell of warmer flesh than human, slightly musky, so rich it was almost a damp smell, as if you could bathe in the scent like water, but the water would be hot, hot as blood, hotter. The scent was so strong that I swayed, and for a second I could feel the brush of fur against my face like rough piled velvet. The sensory memory poured through me, and overwhelmed all my careful control. The power poured upward in a spill of heat along my skin. I'd managed to cut the direct links to the boys so that I was alone in my own skin, but the marks were still there, coming to the surface at odd moments, like this one. Shapeshifters always recognize each other. Their beasts always know, and though I had no beast of my own, I had a piece of Richard's. That piece reacted to César. If I'd been expecting it, I might have been able to prevent it, but it was too late now. It wasn't dangerous, just a spill of heat, pulsing along my skin, a dance of energy that didn't belong to me.

César had jerked back from me as if I'd burned him, then he smiled. It was a knowing smile like we shared a secret. He wasn't the first shapeshifter to mistake me for one of them. To my knowledge I was one of only two humans in the world that had this close a tie to a shapeshifter. The other man's tie was to a weretiger, not a werewolf, but the problems were similar. We were both part of a vampire's triumvirate, and neither of us seemed happy.

César's hands went to either side of my face, hesitating just above my skin. I knew he was feeling the push of that otherworldly energy like a veil that had to be pushed aside to touch. Except he didn't. He spilled his own power into his hands, so that he held me in a pulsing shell of warmth. It made me close my eyes, and he hadn't even touched me yet, not with his hands.

I opened my mouth to tell him not to touch me, but as I drew breath to speak his hands touched my face. I wasn't ready. He pushed his power into mine. It hit like a jolt of electricity, raising the small hairs on my body, tightening places low on my body, raising gooseflesh in a wash down my skin. The power flowed towards César like a flower turning towards the sun. I couldn't stop it. The best I could do was ride the power instead of letting it ride me.

He bent his face towards me, still cradling my face between his hands. I put my own hands on top of his as if I was going to hold on. Power poured from his mouth as he hovered over my lips. The power ran through my body and spilled out of half-parted lips like a hot wind. Our mouths met and the power flowed into each of us, mingling as it brushed like two great cats rubbing furred sides along each other's bodies. The warmth grew to heat, until it almost hurt to stay tied to his lips, as if any second now our flesh would burn into each other, melting through skin, muscle, bone, until we fell into the center of each other like molten metal cutting through layers of silk.

The energy had turned sexual, as it usually did . . . for me. Embarrassing but true. We drew back from the kiss at the same time, blinking at each other like sleepwalkers awakened too early. He gave a nervous laugh and leaned into me as if to kiss me again, but I put a hand on his chest, and held him away. I could feel his heart thudding against my palm. I could suddenly feel the blood racing in his body. My eyes were drawn to the big pulse in his throat. I watched that rapid rise and fall in the side of his neck as if it were some sort of jewel, something to watch sparkle and glitter in the lights. My mouth was suddenly dry, and it wasn't sex. I actually stepped into him, pressed my body down the front of his, brought my face close to his neck and that jumping beat of life. I wanted to go down on that soft skin, sink teeth into his flesh, taste what lay beneath. I knew with a knowledge that was not mine that his blood would be hotter than a human's. Not warm but hot, a scalding rush of life to warm cold flesh.

I had to close my eyes, turn my head, step away with my hands over my eyes. I had no direct link to either of the men, but I held their power in me. Richard's burning warmth, and Jean-Claude's cold hunger. For a space of heartbeats I had wanted to feed on César. This when I had walled up the marks, boarded them up, chained them, locked them with everything I had. When the marks were open between the three of us, the desires that ran through me, the things that I thought, were too horrible or maybe just too alien. Not for the first time I wondered what piece of me each of them held in their bodies. What dark desire or strange urge did I leave behind? If I ever talked to either of them again, maybe I'd ask, or then again, maybe I wouldn't.

I felt someone hovering close. I shook my head. "Don't touch me."

"Let us get back stage, then I can apologize." It was the priest's voice.

I lowered my hands and found him standing beside me. He held out his hand to me. I didn't touch him. "We meant no harm." I laid my left hand in his and found his skin quiet. There was nothing but human warmth and the solid feel of him. He led me towards an area to the far left of the stage. César was already there with the three other women.

The werejaguars were there like guards, and it seemed to have made the blonde and the one with all the hair brave again. They were pawing César, and he was kissing Ramona, who was kissing him back with enthusiasm.

The priest led me towards them, and I hung back. I whispered, "I can't." I meant that I couldn't touch César again so soon. I didn't trust myself, and I didn't want to have to say it out loud. I didn't have to. The priest seemed to understand.

He leaned close. "Please, just stand near them. No one will touch you."

I don't know why I believed him, but I did. I stood near the near-orgy, trying not to look as uncomfortable as I felt. Then a large white screen came down out of the ceiling, and before it was solidly in place, the priest drew me to one side. A woman my size with hair my length appeared and moved towards the mini-orgy. I watched her join the group, and a jaguar dragged the blonde out. A woman that matched the blond came to take her place. They replaced everyone, even César, with actors, who did a shadow orgy against the white screen, thrown large for the audience. The actresses matched all the women chosen, at least for a shadow play. Which is what Dallas had meant when she said they needed someone my size with long hair to complete the brides.

The actors weren't really doing anything, but it must have looked awful from the audience's point of view. Clothes flew and the women were topless. I wondered if the shadows looked as topless as the real thing.

The priest drew me away until we stood in a small curtain area. He spoke low but clearly, so I guess we could talk without being heard on stage. "You would never have been chosen if we didn't think you human. Our deepest apologies."

I shrugged. "No harm done."

He looked at me and there was a weight of knowledge in his eyes that I couldn't lie to. "You are frightened of what lies inside you, and you have not made peace with it."

That much was true. "No, I haven't made peace with it."

"You must accept what you are, or you will never know what your true place in the world is, your true purpose."

"Don't take this wrong, but I don't need a lecture tonight."

He frowned at that, and there was a flash of anger. He wasn't used to being talked to like that. I was betting that everyone was afraid of him. Maybe I should have been, but what fear I had of him or them had vanished when I realized I wanted to take a bite out of César's neck. That scared me more than anything they could do to me tonight. All right, almost anything they could do tonight. Never underestimate the creativity of a being that is hundreds of years old. Most of them know more about pain than we poor humans will ever know. Unless we are very, very unlucky. I was either feeling lucky or stupid.

He made a small motion and the werejaguar that had chosen me came to us. He dropped to one knee, head bowed. The priest said, "You chose this woman."

"Yes, Pinotl."

"Did you not feel her beast?"

His head lowered even more. "No, my lord, I did not."

"Choose," the priest said.

The kneeling man drew a knife from his belt. The handle was turquoise in the shape of a jaguar. The blade was about six inches of black obsidian. The man held the blade up to the priest who took it as reverently as it had been offered. The man undid some hidden catch on the jaguar skin, and pushed the hood back so that his head was bare. His hair was thick and long, tied in a long club at the back of his head. He raised a dark face that was so square and chiseled, it looked like he could have poised for Aztec temple carvings. If you were into Meso-Americans, his profile was perfect.

He raised his face up to the priest. His face was empty of all expression, just a calm waiting.

There was a roar from the audience that made me glance at the actors, but I turned back to the priest and the man before I'd really seen anything. I had a glimpse of seminude bodies, and an impression of something large and phallic strapped around the man. Normally, that would have made me take a second glance, just to make sure I was seeing what I thought I'd seen, but no matter what was happening out there, the real show was here. It was in the serene, upturned face of the man, and the serious eyes of the priest, the dull gleam of the black blade. They could use all the props they wanted, no matter how big, but it wouldn't come close to the two men and the quiet intensity stretching between them.

I didn't know exactly what was about to happen, but I had an idea. He was being punished because he'd chosen a lycanthrope from the audience, instead of a human. But I was human, or at least not a lycanthrope. I couldn't let him get sliced up, not even if it meant admitting who I was. Could I?

I touched the priest's arm, lightly. "What are you going to do to him?"

The priest looked at me, and his eyes seemed like deep caves, a trick of shadows. "Punish him."

My fingers tightened on his arm, trying to feel it through the slick softness of feathers. "I just want to make sure you're not going to slit his throat or something really dramatic."

"What I do with our men is my business, not yours." The force of his disapproval was strong enough that I took my hand off his arm. But I was worried now what he was going to do. Damn Edward and his undercover idea. It never worked for me, pretending. Reality always screwed it up.

The priest laid the blade point against the man's cheek. There was no fear in his face, nothing but an eerie serenity that made my throat tight, and a thrill of fear slide down my spine. God, I hated zealots, and that's what I was seeing.

"Wait," I said.

"Do not interfere," the priest said.

"I'm not a lycanthrope," I said.

"Lies, to save a stranger," nothing but contempt in his voice.

"I'm not lying."

The priest called, "César."

He appeared like a well-trained dog coming to his master's call. Maybe the analogy was unfair, but I wasn't feeling particularly charitable right now. If I blew our cover, had to say who I was, I didn't know if I was going to be blowing something that Edward had planned. By saying who and what I was, I didn't know if I was endangering us. Edward hadn't shared enough of his plans, which I would take up with him when the evening was over, but my first concern was safety. Was saving a stranger from being sliced up worth our lives? No. Was keeping a stranger from being killed worth maybe risking our lives? Probably. I had so many unanswered questions and so little real information that I felt like I must be killing brain cells thinking around all the things I didn't know.

César appeared beside me, on the far side of me away from the priest. I think he'd spotted the blade. "What has he done?"

"He picked her out of the audience and did not sense her beast," the priest said.

"I don't have a beast," I said.

César laughed, and it was too loud, He covered his mouth with his hand for a moment, as if to remind himself we had to be quiet. "I saw the hunger in your face." He said hunger like it should have been in capital letters. Great, more shapeshifter slang that I didn't know.

I tried to think of a short version that would make sense. I made two starts, before I finally said, "There is too much. I will sum up." I even threw in the bad Spanish accent.

The priest's face stayed blank and unhappy. He did not get the movie reference. César choked back another laugh. He'd probably seen *The Princess Bride*. "The hunger you saw was not from some beast," I said.

The priest gave his full attention to the man kneeling in front of him. It was as if I'd been dismissed. He sliced the man's cheek open. The thin cut spread and blood welled in liquid lines down the dark skin.

"Shit," I said.

He placed the knife against the man's other cheek. I grabbed his wrist. "Please, listen to me."

The priest turned his dark eyes to me. "César."

"I am not your cat to call," César said.

The priest's dark gaze slid from me, to the man beside me. "Be careful that what is pretense does not become real, César."

It was a threat, though I didn't understand exactly what the threat had been, but I knew a threat when I heard one. César moved up beside me. "She merely wishes to speak, my lord Pinotl. Is that so much to ask?"

"She also touches me." They both stared at my hand on his wrist.

"I'll let go if I have your word that you won't cut him until you've heard me out."

Those eyes came back to rest fully on my face, and I felt the force of him thundering down on me. I could almost feel his skin vibrate under my hand. "I can't let you bleed him for something that wasn't his fault."

He never said a word, but I felt movement behind me, and I knew it wasn't César, because he turned toward the movement. I looked back and found two of the jaguar men coming towards us. They were probably not going to hurt me, just stop me from interfering. I turned back to the priest, met his eyes. I let go of his wrist. I had a few seconds to decide whether to draw a gun or a knife. They weren't trying to kill me, so the least I could do was return the favor. I slipped a knife out, holding it against my leg, trying to be unobtrusive. I'd made the decision to go for the knife and not the gun. I hoped it was the right decision.

One of jaguars was the tanned, blue-eyed one. The other was the first African American I'd seen in the club, his face very contrasting with all the pale spotted fur. They advanced on me in a roil of energy, a low growl escaped from one of their throats, the faintest of threats. That one faint sound raised the hair at the back of my neck. I backed up, putting the kneeling man between me and the two jaguars.

The priest had laid the obsidian blade against the man's right cheek. He hadn't started cutting yet. "Are you just going to cut each cheek, is that it? Will it stop there?"

The blade tip bit into his cheek. Even in the dark I could see the first liquid drop, a faint gleam, like a dark jewel. "If you just want to slice him up a little, fine. It's your business. I just don't want to see him mutilated or killed for something he couldn't have sensed."

The priest sliced the other cheek, slower this time. I think I was making things worse. I asked it out loud, of everyone and no one. "Am I making things worse?"

The cheek closest to me began to heal, the skin reknitting as I watched. I had an idea. I stepped closer to the priest and the kneeling man. I kept an eye on the two jaguars across from them, but they just stood watching. They'd backed me off, maybe that's all they were supposed to do.

I touched the kneeling man's chin, turned his face towards me. The other cheek was completely healed. I'd never seen an obsidian blade used and hadn't been a hundred percent that it didn't act like silver. But it didn't. Shapeshifters healed the damage. The priest was still holding the obsidian knife upright in his hand.

The audience broke into thunderous applause, the sound rising like thunder through the small backstage area. The actors were pouring away from the white screen. The act was almost over. Everyone had turned at the noise and the movement, even the priest. I put my finger against the tip of the obsidian knife and pressed. The tip was like glass, the pain sharp and immediate. I drew back with a hiss.

"What have you done?" the priest demanded, and his voice was too loud, it must have carried out into the crowd.

I spoke lower. "I won't heal, not as fast as he did. It'll prove that I'm not a lycanthrope."

The priest's anger filled the air like something hot and touchable. "You do not understand."

"If someone would talk to me, instead of hugging their secrets so damn close, I wouldn't be blundering into things."

The priest handed the blade back to the kneeling man. He took the knife and bowed his forehead to it. Then he licked the blade, carefully around the sharp edges, until he came to the point and my blood. Then he slid the tip between his lips, into his mouth, sucking it down like a woman taking a man into her mouth. His mouth worked around the blade and I knew it was cutting him, as he swallowed it. I knew it was cutting him up, but he made it look as if it were something wonderful, orgasmic, as if he were having a very good time.

He watched me as he did it, and his eyes weren't serene anymore. They had filled with heat. It was the same heat you could see in any man's eyes when he was thinking about sex. But not when the man was sucking on a glass sharp blade, cutting his mouth, tongue, throat, drinking his own blood, with a taste of my blood as a chaser.

Someone grabbed my hand, and I jumped. It was César. "We must be on stage. You must take your seat." He was watching the kneeling man, all the men, carefully. He eased me around the group of them, and all eyes followed me like I was some wounded gazelle.

The other three women were already in place, standing behind the now dim white screen. They'd taken off some clothing. The giggling blonde was down to pale blue bra and panties, still laughing her head off. The Hispanic had taken off her skirt and was down to a pair of crimson panties that matched the red camisole she was still wearing. She'd kept the matching red high heels. She and the blonde were leaning against each other, swaying and laughing. Ramona wasn't laughing. She still stood quietly, unmoved and unmoving.

The priest's voice came from backstage. "Disrobe for our audience." His voice was soft, but Ramona grabbed the bottom of her shirt and lifted. Her bra was an ordinary bra, white and simple. It wasn't meant to be lingerie, and I doubted she'd planned on anyone seeing it tonight. She let her shirt fall to the floor. Her hands went to the top button of her pants. I pulled away from César and grabbed Ramona's hands. "No, don't."

Her hands went slack in mine, as if even that small interference had broken the spell, but she didn't look at me. She didn't see what was in front of her, just the internal landscape that I couldn't see.

I picked her shirt back up and placed her hands over it. She clutched it automatically, covering most of the front of her.

César took my arm. "The screen is going up. There is no time."

The screen began to slowly lift.

"You can't be the only one dressed," he said. He tried to slide the jacket from my shoulders, and bared the shoulder holster.

"We'll scare the audience," I said.

The screen was to our knees. He grabbed the front of my shirt, jerking it out of my pants, baring my stomach. He dropped to his knees and was licking my stomach as the screen came up completely. I tried to grab a handful of hair to pull him off me, but there wasn't enough hair to grab. The hair was much softer than it looked, much softer than my hair would have been if you shaved it to stubble. His teeth bit gently into my skin, and I put my hand under his chin, raising his face, so that he either had to take his teeth out of my skin, or bite deeper. He let go, let me raise his face to stare upward at me. There was a look in his eyes that I couldn't read, but it was something large and more complex than you see in a stranger's eyes. Complex I didn't need tonight.

He was on his feet in a movement so liquid and graceful that I knew that Edward would spot him for what he was, not human. He went to the one with all the hair first, giving her a tonsil-cleaning kiss, as if he'd crawl into her from the mouth down. Then he spun her like a dance move, and jaguar men were there to escort her and her arm full of clothes back to her table. The blonde was next. She kissed him, running pale nails down his back. She gave a little jump and wrapped her legs around his waist, forcing him to hold her weight or fall. The kiss was long, but she was in control of it. César walked her to the edge of the stage, still clinging to his body like a limpet.

The jaguar men pried her away from his body, one pale limb at a time, until they had to carry her above their heads while she struggled, and then finally went limp, laughing as they carried her back to her table.

Ramona seemed to wake up. She blinked around her as if she'd woken and wasn't sure where she thought she should be. She stared down at her blouse clutched to the front of her and screamed. César tried to help her on with her blouse, and she slapped at him. I went to her, trying to help her, but she seemed afraid of me, too, now, as if her panic had spread to include all of us.

The jaguar men tried to help her off stage, and she fell trying to keep them from touching her. It was finally a man from her table who came and escorted her out of the lights, out of the ring of strangers.

She was crying and speaking softly in Spanish as he led her back to the table. I would have to talk to someone about her. I couldn't leave town without knowing that the mind tricks weren't permanent. If it had been a vampire with a one on one call like that, he could have called her any time, any night, and she would answer his call. She would have no choice.

César stood in front of me. He raised my hand, I think to kiss it, but it was the hand that I'd cut to prove I wouldn't heal. Not that anyone had cared. César raised my hand and stared at the small wound in the tip of my finger. It was a small cut and didn't bleed much, but it wasn't healing either. If I'd been a lycanthrope, the small prick would have closed up and healed by now.

He looked at me over the still bleeding finger. "What are you?" he whispered.

"Long story," I whispered back.

He kissed the wound like a mother with a child's scrape, then his mouth slid over my finger, down to my hand. He drew it slowly back out. Fresh blood welled to the tip of my finger, bright and sparkling under the lights. His tongue flicked out, rolling the drop of blood into his mouth. He leaned close as if to kiss me, but I shook my head and moved towards the steps that would lead me off the stage and away from him.

The jaguar men were there to help me off the stage, but I looked at them, and they backed off, letting me walk down the steps by myself. Edward held my chair for me, and I let him. Food had been served while I was on stage. Edward handed me a linen napkin. I wrapped it around my finger, holding pressure to it.

Dallas actually got up from her chair and came to talk to me, hanging over the back of my chair. "What happened back there? I've been a volunteer before, and I've never seen anyone hurt."

I looked up at her, her face close in the dimness, all serious and concern. "If you think no one gets hurt, then you haven't been paying attention."

She frowned, looking puzzled.

I shook my head. It was too late, and I was suddenly too tired to try and explain. "I cut myself shaving."

She frowned harder, but also got the point that I didn't want to talk. She sat back down, leaving me to Edward. He leaned into me, laying his mouth against my ear and whispering so low it was like he was breathing into my ear. He knew how good a shapeshifter's hearing was, not to mention vamps. "Do they know who you are?"

I turned, putting my mouth against his ear, having to raise on one knee in my seat, putting my body in a line against his. It looked intimate, but it allowed me to whisper to him in a voice so low I wasn't sure he would hear. "No, but they know I'm not human, not a tourist." I put my arm across his shoulders, one hand on his shoulder, holding him because I didn't want him to move away. I wanted the next question answered. "What are you planning?"

He turned to me, a look on his face that was far too intimate, too teasing for the conversation. He leaned into me, mouth pressed so close to my ear that it must have looked to the others like he had his tongue down it. "No plan, just thought you being you might scare the monsters from talking to us."

It was my turn to whisper, "No plan, you promise?"

"Would I lie to you?"

I jerked back from him and slugged him in the shoulder, not hard, but he got my point. Would Edward lie to me? Would the sun rise tomorrow? Yes to both.

The actors that had taken our places were finally on stage, in robes. The priest in his feathers was introducing them, getting the applause they deserved. I was glad they ruined the effect and didn't leave poor Ramona convinced she'd done terrible things. I was actually surprised that they'd spoiled the trick, like a magician revealing his secrets.

"We'll allow you to eat before the next and last act of our show."

The lights came up, and we all turned to our meals. I'd thought the meat was beef, but when I put the first bite in my mouth the texture told me I was wrong. The waitress had brought me an extra napkin, and I used that to spit the bite into.

"What's wrong?" Bernardo asked. He was eating the meat and enjoying himself.

"I don't eat . . . veal," I said. I took a forkful of an unrecognizable vegetable, then realized it was sweet potatoes. I didn't recognize the spices in them. Of course, cooking wasn't exactly my area of expertise.

Everyone was eating the meat except me, and strangely, Edward. He'd taken a bite, but then he concentrated on the flat bread, and the vegetables, too.

"You don't eat veal either, Ted?" Olaf asked. He put another bite in his mouth and chewed slowly, as if trying to draw every ounce of flavor.

"No," Edward said.

"I know it's not moral indignation about the poor little calves," I said.

"And you worry about the poor little calves?" Edward said. He gave me a long look as he asked. I couldn't read his eyes, but they weren't blank, I just couldn't read them. What else was new?

"I don't approve of the treatment of the animals, no, but truthfully I just don't like the texture."

Dallas was watching us all as if we were doing something a lot more interesting than discussing meat. "You don't like the texture of . . . veal?"

I shook my head. "No, I don't."

Olaf had turned to the other woman. He took his latest bite of meat and offered it to her on the end of his fork. "You like veal?"

She got a strange little smile on her face. "I eat veal here almost every night." She didn't take his bite that he offered but took another bite from her own fork.

I felt like I was missing something, but before I could ask, the lights went down again. The final act was about to begin. If I was still hungry, surely there'd be something open on the way home. There usually was.

24

THE LIGHTS WENT DOWN until the room was left in darkness. A dim spotlight cut the darkness. The light was only a faint white gleam when it finally stopped at the far, far end of the darkened room.

A figure stepped into that pale gleam. A crown of brilliant red and yellow feathers was bent towards the light. A cloak of smaller feathers covered the figure from neck to the edge of the light. The crown raised, revealing a pale face. It was César. He turned his face to one side, giving profile and showing that he had earrings going from lobe to halfway up the edge of his ear. Gold glittered as he moved his head, and the light grew stronger. He lifted something in his hands and a note of music filled the near dark. A thin trilling note like a flute, but not. The song was beautiful, but eerie, as if something lovely were crying. A jaguar man lifted off the feathered cloak and vanished into the darkness. A heavy gold collar lay across his shoulders and chest. If it were real, it was a fortune in precious metal. Hands came from either side of the darkness, appearing in the light, taking the feathered crown without ever showing themselves.

César walked slowly, and halfway up the room I could see what he was playing. It looked like a panpipe, but not exactly. The song cut through the darkness, crawled through it, one moment uplifting, the next mournful. It looked like he was truly playing it, and if so it was impressive. Jaguar men stripped him of everything he was carrying: a small shield; a strange stick that looked sort of like a bow, but not, a bag of short arrows or something like them. He was close enough now that I could see the jade decoration that he wore in front of his kilt, though I knew it wasn't a kilt, but skirt wasn't right either. The front was covered in feathers; the rest, some rich cloth. More hands came into the light to undo the garment and take it and the jade away. They were close enough now that the darkness and light couldn't hide that the hands belonged to the jaguars. They stripped him down to the flesh-colored G-string he'd worn before, or one like it.

The song rose into the dimness as he neared the last few rows of tables. You could almost see the notes rising upward like birds. I don't usually wax poetic about music, but this was different. Somehow you knew it wasn't just a song, just something to listen to and forget, or hum in odd moments. When you think of ritual music, you think of drums, something with a beat to remind us of our hearts, and the ebb and flow of our bodies. But not all ritual is made to remind us of our bodies. Some of it's made to remind us of why the ritual is happening. All ritual at its heart is for the sake of divinity. All right, not all, but most. Most of it is us yelling, hey God, look at me, look at us, hope you like it. We are all just children at heart, hoping Dad or Mom likes the present we picked out.

Of course, sometimes Mom and Dad can have quite a temper.

César let the flute or pipes hang from a thong around his neck. He knelt and removed his own sandals, then handed them to a woman at the nearest table. There was a shifting in the dimness as if she wasn't sure she wanted them. Maybe after the earlier show she was afraid to take them. Couldn't really blame her on that one.

He stopped at the table just behind that one and spoke quietly to another woman. She stood and removed one of the gold earrings from his ear. Then he went from table to table, and let sometimes men, but mostly women take the last of his decoration from his body. Which probably explained why the earrings were the least expensive, least authentic pieces he'd been wearing. Except for the last earrings. A medium sized jade ball set in each earlobe, but it was the figurines that dangled beneath, moving as his head moved, swaying as he walked, that made the earrings special. Each figure was nearly three inches high, brushing his shoulders like the hair he did not have. As he got closer, you could see the green stone was intricately carved into one of those squat deities the Aztecs were so fond of.

He stopped at our table, and I was surprised because he'd carefully ignored the other "brides" on this walk. He raised me to my feet with one hand in mine, then turned his head so I could reach the earring. I didn't want to stop the show, but they were too expensive a gift to accept unless they were fake. The moment I touched the cool stone, I knew it was real jade. It was too heavy, too smooth to be anything else.

I don't wear earrings, and I've never had pierced ears, so I was left feeling the back of his ear in the near dark, trying to figure out how to undo the earring. He finally reached up and helped me, hands doing quickly and almost gracefully what I'd been fumbling at. By watching him I realized that they unscrewed, and when he turned his head I was able to get the second one out myself. I knew enough about jewelry to know that the screws were modern. It was real jade, real gold, but it wasn't an antique, or at least the clasps were modern.

The stones rested heavy and very solid in my hands. He leaned over and whispered, breath warm against my cheek. "I will get them back from you after the performance. Don't interfere." He laid a gentle kiss on my cheek and walked to the bottom step. He took the flute from around his neck and broke off one of the many reeds, scattering it on the step.

I sat back down, the jade gripped in my hands. I leaned into Edward. "What's about to happen?"

He shook his head. "I've never seen this particular show."

I looked across the table at Professor Dallas. I wanted to ask her what was going on, but she had all her attention on the stage. César had broken part of the flute on every step as he walked up them. Four jaguar men were waiting at the top, grouped around a small, roundish stone. The priest was there, too, but without the cape. He was even broader through the shoulders than he'd seemed, and though not tall you got the impression of sheer strength, sheer physicality. He seemed more warrior than priest.

César had made it to the top of the temple. The four jaguar men grabbed him, by wrist and ankle, lifting him over their heads, steadying his body with their hands. They paced the stage with him held above their heads, showing him to the four corners of the stage, even the one that faced away from the audience. Then they brought him to the small round stone and laid his body across it, so that his head and shoulders leaned back, and the lowest part of his chest and upper stomach were curved over the stone.

I was on my feet before I saw the obsidian blade in the priest's hand. Edward grabbed my arm. "Look to your left," he said.

I glanced and found two of the jaguar men waiting. If I made a run for the stage, I bet they'd try and stop me. César had said that he'd come for the earrings after the performance. Which implied he'd be alive to do it. He'd warned me not to interfere. But dammit, they were going to cut him up. I knew that now. What I didn't know, was how badly they were going to cut him up.

Dallas had gotten from her seat and was at my other arm, whispering, "It's part of the show. César plays sacrifice twice a month. Not always this exact sacrifice, but it's part of his job." She spoke low and soothingly like you talked to a crazy person on a ledge. I let her and Edward ease me back into my seat. I was gripping the jade earrings so hard the edges dug into my hands.

Dallas knelt beside me, keeping a hand on my arm, but she watched the stage. The jaguar men held him, and you could see their grip tighten, see them take in their collective breaths. César's face showed nothing, not fear, not anticipation, just waiting for it.

The priest drove the blade into the flesh just below the ribs. César's body jerked in reaction, but he didn't cry out. The blade tore across him, digging into the meat, widening the hole. His body danced with the wound, but he never made a sound. Blood poured across César's pale skin, bright and almost unreal under the lights. The priest reached his hand into the wound nearly up to his elbow, and César cried out.

I grabbed Dallas's arm. "He can't survive without his heart, not even a shapeshifter can survive that."

"They won't take his heart, I swear it." She stroked my hand where it gripped her like you'd soothe a nervous dog.

I leaned in close to her, and whispered, "If they take his heart when I could have stopped it, I'll have your heart on a knife before I leave New Mexico. You still willing to swear?"

Her eyes had gone wide. I think she was holding her breath, but she nodded. "I swear it."

The funny thing was that she believed the threat instantly. Most people you tell them you're going to cut their heart out and they won't believe you. People believe you'll kill them, but get too graphic and they take it like a joke or an exaggeration. Professor Dallas believed me. You could see it in her face. Most college professors wouldn't have. Made me wonder about Dallas more than I already did.

The priest's voice came into the utter silence that had filled the room. "I hold his heart in my hand. In the long gone days we would have torn it from his chest, but those days are gone," and you heard, felt the regret in his words. "We worship as we can, not as we would." He slid his hand out slowly, and I was close enough to hear the wet, fleshy sound as his hand pulled out of the wound.

He raised a hand covered in blood above his head, and the audience cheered.

They cheered. They fucking cheered.

The jaguar men lifted César from the altar and tossed him down the steps. He tumbled bonelessly coming to rest on the floor directly in front of the steps. He lay on his back, gasping, fighting to breathe and I wondered if the priest had damaged a lung or two when he went fishing for the heart.

I just sat there, staring at him. He did this twice a month. It was part of his job. Shit. Not only didn't I understand it, I didn't want to. If he was into pain and death, I didn't need to know anything else about him. I was eyeball deep in sadomasochistic wereleopards back home. I didn't need another one.

The priest was talking, but I didn't hear him. I didn't hear anything but a great roaring like white noise in my ears. I watched the wereleopard twitch, body jerking, blood pouring down his sides, across the floor, but even as I stared, the blood was slowing. It was hard to tell through all the blood and torn flesh, but I knew he was healing.

Two of the human bouncers came and picked him up, one taking his ankles, the other lifting under his arms. They carried him through the tables, past us. I stood, stopping them. Dallas stood with me, as if afraid of what I'd do. I stared into César's eyes. There was real pain there. He wasn't having a good time or didn't seem to be. But you don't do shit like this on a regular basis unless you enjoy it on some level. His hands were lying on his chest, as if he were trying to hold himself together. I pried one hand up. The skin was slick with blood. I pressed the jade earrings into his hand, closed his fingers around them.

He whispered something, but I didn't bend down to hear. "Don't ever come near me again."

I sat back down, and they carried him away. I started to reach for a napkin to wipe my hands, but Dallas grabbed my arm. "She's ready to see you now."

I hadn't seen anyone talk to her, but I wasn't questioning it. If she said it was time, fine. We could meet the Master of the City and get the hell out of here.

I started to reach for the napkin again, but she moved it out of reach. "It is fitting that you meet her with the blood of sacrifice on your hands."

I looked at her and grabbed the napkin out of her hands. She actually struggled to keep it, and we had a little tug of war before I jerked it away from her. But a woman appeared at my elbow. She wore a red-hooded cloak and came up only to my shoulder, but even before she turned her head so I could see the face that lay inside that cloak, I knew what she was. Itzpapalotl, Obsidian Butterfly, Master of the City, and self-proclaimed goddess. I hadn't felt her coming. I hadn't heard her or sensed her. She just appeared beside me like magic. It had been a long time since a vampire had been able to do that. I think I stopped breathing for a second or two as I met her eyes.

Her face was as delicate as the rest of her, her skin a milk-pale brown. Her eyes were black, not just brown, but truly black like the obsidian blade she was named for. Most master vamp's eyes are like drowning pools, things to fall into and be trapped, but her eyes were like solid black mirrors reflecting back, not something to fall into, but something to show you the truth. I saw myself in those eyes, a miniature reflection perfect in every detail like a black cameo. Then the image split, doubling, tripling. My face stayed in the center with a wolf's head on one side, and a skull on the other. As I watched, the three images grew closer until the wolf and skull were superimposed over my face, and for a split second I couldn't tell where one image left off and the others began.

One image floated above the rest. The skull rose above the first two, spilling upward through the blackness, filling her eyes until the skull filled my vision, and

I was able to stumble back, nearly falling. Edward was there, catching me. Dallas had moved to stand beside the vampire.

Bernardo and Olaf were at Edward's back, and I knew in that instant that if he'd given the word, they'd have both drawn guns and fired. It was a comforting thought. Suicidal, but comforting. Because I could feel her people now, which meant she had to have been blocking me, hiding them. I felt the vampires underneath the building, around it, through it. There were hundreds of them, and most of them were old. Hundreds of years old. And Obsidian Butterfly? I glanced at her but was careful not to meet her eyes this time. It had been years since I'd had to avoid a vampire's eyes. I'd forgotten how hard it is to look someone in the face without making eye contact, like some elaborate game. Them trying to catch my glance and bespell me, me trying to keep away.

She had a fall of straight black bangs, but the rest of her hair was pulled back from her face to reveal delicate ears set with jade ear spools. She was a delicate thing, petite even standing next to me and Professor Dallas, but I wasn't fooled by the packaging. What lay inside was a vampire not that old. I doubted she was a thousand years yet. I'd met older, much older, but I'd never met any vampire under a thousand that echoed in my head with the power that this one did. Power breathed off her skin like a nearly visible cloud, and I'd learned enough of vampires to know that the echo of power wasn't on purpose. Some of the masters with special abilities, like causing fear or lust, just gave off that power constantly like steam rising from a pot. It was involuntary, partially at least. But I'd never met one that leaked power, pure power.

Edward was talking to me, probably had been talking to me for a while. I just hadn't heard. "Anita, Anita, are you all right?" I felt the press of a gun not pointed at my back, but drawn, using my body to shield it from the room. Things could get ugly really fast.

"I'm all right," but my voice didn't sound all right. It sounded hollow and distant, like I was in shock. Maybe I was, a little. She hadn't exactly rolled my mind, but she knew things about me in that first contact that most vampires never figured out. I realized suddenly that she knew what kind of power I was. That was her gift, to be able to read power.

Her voice when it came was heavily accented and much deeper than that fragile throat should have held, as if the voice was an echo of that immense power. "Whose servant are you?"

She knew I was a vampire's human servant, but not whose servant I was. I liked that, made me feel better. She read only power, not details, unless of course, she was only pretending not to know. But somehow I didn't think she'd pretend ignorance. No, this was one that liked showing off her knowledge. She breathed arrogance as she breathed power. But why not be arrogant? She was, after all, a goddess, self-proclaimed anyway. You'd have to be either absolutely arrogant or crazy to claim godhood.

"Jean-Claude, Master of the City of St. Louis."

She cocked her head to one side as if listening to something. "Then you are the Executioner. You did not give your true name at the door."

"Not all vampires will talk to me if they know who I am."

"What is it you wish to speak with me about?"

"The mutilation murders."

Again, she turned her head to one side as if listening. "Ah, yes." She blinked and looked up at me. "The price for an audience is what lies on your hands."

I must have looked as puzzled as I felt, because she elaborated. "The blood, César's blood. I wish to take it from you."

"How?" I asked, just call me suspicious.

She simply turned and started walking away. Her voice came like the sound to a badly dubbed film, sound long after it should have been heard. "Follow me, and do not clean your hands."

I glanced at Edward. "Do you trust her?" I asked.

He shook his head.

"Me either," I said.

"Are we going or staying?" Olaf asked.

"I vote for going," Bernardo said. I hadn't really looked at him since the sacrifice began. He was looking a little pale. Olaf wasn't. Olaf looked fresh and bright-eyed, as if he were enjoying the evening.

Dallas said, "It would be a grave insult if you refuse her invitation. She rarely gives personal interviews voluntarily. You must have impressed her."

"I didn't impress her. I attracted her," I said.

Dallas frowned. "Attracted her. She likes men."

I shook my head. "She may have sex with men, but what attracts her is power, Professor."

She looked at me, searching my face. "You have that kind of power?"

I sighed. "We'll find out, won't we?" I started walking in the direction that the cloaked figure had gone. She hadn't waited for us to decide. She'd just walked away. Like I said, arrogant. Of course, we were about to follow her into her private lair. That was arrogance, too, or stupidity. Arrogance or stupidity, sometimes there's not much difference between the two.

25

I DIDN'T KNOW where to go, but Dallas did. She led us to a small door set to one side of the temple steps, hidden by curtains. The door was still open, like a black mouth. Steps led down. Where else? Just once I'd like to see a vamp whose major hideout was up instead of down.

Dallas walked down the steps with a spring in her step and a song in her heart. Her ponytail bounced as she skipped down the steps. If she had a single misgiving about going down into that darkness, it didn't show. Dallas confused me. On one hand she didn't see that Olaf was dangerous, and she wasn't afraid of any of the monsters in the club. On the other hand, she'd believed me when I told her I'd cut her heart out. I'd seen it in her eyes. How could she believe that threat from a total stranger and not see the other dangers? Didn't make sense to me, and I didn't like what I didn't understand. She seemed utterly harmless, but her reactions were weird, so I put a question mark by her. Which meant, I wouldn't be turning my back on her or treating her like a civilian until I was convinced that that was what she was.

I was going too slowly for Olaf. He pushed past me and followed Dallas's bouncing ponytail down the stairs. He had to stoop to keep from bumping his head on the ceiling, but he didn't seem to mind. Fine with me. Let him take the first bullet. But I followed them down into the dark. No one had offered me violence, not really, not yet. So it seemed rude to have a gun naked in my hand, but . . . I'd apologize later. Unless I knew the vampire personally, I liked having a loaded gun in hand the first time I paid a call. Or maybe it was the narrow stairs, the close press of stone as if it would close around us like a fist and crush us. Have I mentioned that I'm claustrophobic?

The stairs didn't go down very far, and there was no door at the end of them. Jean-Claude's retreat in St. Louis was something of an underground fortress. The barely hidden doorway, the short stairs, no second door—arrogance, again.

Olaf blocked my view of Dallas, but I saw him reach the dimly lit doorway at the bottom. He had to stoop even further to get through the door and hesitated before standing up on the other side. There was a sense of movement around him or rather to either side of him. Quick, almost not there, like things you see out of the comer of your eyes. It reminded me of the hands that had stripped César as he walked between light and darkness.

He stayed just in the doorway, his body nearly filling it completely, blocking what little light there had been. I caught the faintest edge of Dallas. She led him away from the door further into the firelit dark.

I called down, "Olaf, are you okay?"

No answer.

Edward tried. "Olaf?"

"I am fine."

I glanced back at Edward. We had a moment of staring into each other's eyes, both of us thinking the same thing. This could be a trap. Maybe she was behind the murders. Maybe she just wanted to kill the Executioner. Or maybe she was a centuries-old vampire, and she just wanted to hurt us for the hell of it

"Could she make Olaf lie?"

"You mean mind tricks?" I asked.

He nodded.

"Not this fast. I may not like him, but he's stronger than that." I looked at him, searching his face in the dim light. "Could they force him to lie?"

"You mean a knife at his throat?" Edward said.

"Yeah."

He gave a faint smile. "No, not this quick, not ever."

"You're sure of that?" I asked.

"My life on it."

"We're betting all our lives on it."

He nodded. "Yes, we are."

But if Edward said that Olaf wouldn't sell us out on fear of death or pain, then I believed him. Edward didn't always understand why people did what they did, but he was usually right about the fact that they were going to do it. Motive evaded him, but he was seldom wrong. So . . . I kept walking down the steps.

I strained my peripheral vision, trying to see on either side of the doorway as I walked through it. I didn't have to bend over to go through. The room was square and small, maybe sixteen by sixteen. It was also packed nearly corner to corner with vampires.

I put my back against the wall to the right of the door, gun clutched two-handed, pointed at the ceiling. I wanted badly to point it at someone, anyone. My shoulders ached with the tension of not doing it. No one was threatening me. No one was doing a damn thing except standing, staring, milling around the way people do. So why did I feel like I should have entered the room shooting?

Tall vampires, short vampires, thin vampires, fat vampires, every size, every shape, and almost every race, moved around that small stone room. After what had happened upstairs with their master, I was careful not to make eye contact with any of them. My gaze swept over the room, taking in the pale faces, and getting a quick head count. When I got over sixty, I realized the room was at least twice the size I'd originally thought. It had to be just to hold this many of them. It only looked small because it was packed so tight. The torchlight added to the illusion, flickering, dancing, uncertain light.

Edward stayed in the doorway, his back to the doorframe, shoulder touching mine lightly. His gun was up like mine, his eyes searching the vamps. "What's wrong?"

"What's wrong? Look at them." My voice was breathy, not because I was trying to whisper—that would have been useless—but because my throat was tight, my mouth dry.

He scanned the crowd again. "So?"

My gaze flashed to him, then back to the waiting vampires. "Shit, Ed . . . Ted. Shit." It wasn't just the number of them. It was my own ability to sense them that was the problem. I'd been around a hundred vamps before, but they hadn't affected me like this. I didn't know if having walled off my link to Jean-Claude made me more vulnerable to them, or if my necromancy had grown since then. Or maybe Itzpapalotl was just that much more powerful than the other master had been. Maybe it was her power that had made them so much more than most vamps. There were close to a hundred in this room. I was getting impressions from all of them, or most of them. My shields were great now, I could keep out a lot of the preternatural stuff, but this was too much for me. If I had to guess, there wasn't a vamp in the room under a hundred. I got flashes from individual ones if I looked at them too long, a slap in the face of their age, their power. The four females in the right corner were all over five hundred years old. They watched me with dark eyes, dark-skinned, but not as dark as they would have been with a little sun. The four of them watched me with patient, empty faces.

Her voice came from the center of the room, but she was hidden behind the vampires, shielded by them. "I have offered you no violence, yet you have drawn weapons. You seek my aid, yet you threaten me."

"It's not personal, Itz . . ." I stumbled over her name.

"You may call me Obsidian Butterfly." It was odd talking to her without being able to glimpse her through the waiting figures.

"It's not personal, Obsidian Butterfly. I just know that once I put up the gun, chances of drawing it again before one of your brood rips my throat out is damn small."

"You mistrust us," she said.

"As you mistrust us," I said.

She laughed then. Her laughter was the sound of a young woman, normal, but the strained echoes from the other vampires were anything but normal. The laughter held a wild note to it, a desperation, as if they were afraid not to laugh. I wondered what the penalty was for not following her lead.

The laughter faded away, except for one high pitched masculine sound. The other vampires went still, that impossible stillness where they seem like well-made statues, things made of stone and paint, not real, not alive. They waited like a host of empty things. Waited for what? The only sound was that high, unhealthy laughter, rising up and up like the sounds the movies have you hear in insane asylums, or mad scientists' laboratories. The sound raised the hair on my arms, and it wasn't magic. It was just creepy.

"If you put up your guns, I will send most of my people away. That is fair, is it not?"

It was fair, but I didn't like it. I liked having the gun naked in my hands. Of course, the gun only worked if shooting a few of them would stop the rest from rushing us, and it wouldn't. If she said, go to hell, they'd start digging a hole. If she told them to rush us, they most certainly would. So the guns were just a security blanket, a delaying tactic before the end. It took only a few seconds to think it through, but that awful laughter kept going like it was one of those creepy dolls with a laugh track inside of it.

I felt Edward's shoulder pressing against mine. He was waiting for me to give the answer, trusting my expertise. I hoped I didn't get us killed. I put the gun back in its holster. I rubbed my hand against my leg. I'd been holding the gun too long, and too damn tight. Me, nervous?

Edward put his gun up. Bernardo was still in the stairway, and I realized that he was making sure nothing came down the stairs and blocked our retreat. It was kind of nice working with more than just two people and knowing everyone on your side was willing to shoot anything that moved. No bleeding hearts, no empathy, just business.

Of course, Olaf was off to one side with Dallas. He had never pulled a gun. He had waded into this many vampires, following her bouncing ponytail to destruction. Or at least to potential destruction.

The vampires drew a breath, each chest rising as one, as if they were many bodies with one mind. Life, for lack of a better term, flowed back into them. Some of them looked almost human, but many of them were pale and starved, and weak. Their faces were too thin, as if the bones of their skull would push out through the sickly skin. They were all pale, but the natural skin color of many was darker than Caucasian, so even pale, they weren't the ghostly paleness I was used to seeing. I realized with something like shock that most of the vampires I knew were Caucasian. Here, white skin was the minority. A nice reversal.

The vampires began to glide towards the door. Or some of them glided. Some of them shuffled as if they didn't have energy to pick their feet up, as if they were truly ill. To my knowledge vampires couldn't catch any disease. But these vampires looked sick.

One of them stumbled and fell at my feet, landing heavily on hands and knees. He stayed where he was, head hanging down. His skin was a dirty white like snow that had lain too long by a busy road, a greyish white. The other vampires moved around him as if he were a bump in the road. They flowed past him, and he didn't seem to notice. His hands looked like the hands of a skeleton, barely covered with skin. His hair was a blond so light, it looked white, hanging down around his face. He raised his face up, slowly, and it was like looking at a skull. His eyes had sunk so far into his head that they seemed to burn at the end of long black tunnels. I wasn't afraid of looking in this one's eyes. He didn't have enough juice to roll me with his eyes, I could tell that just standing here. The bones of his cheeks pushed so hard against the thin skin that it looked like they should tear through.

A pale tongue slid from between thin nearly invisible lips. His eyes were a pale, pale green, like bad emeralds. The thin walls of his nose flared as if he were scenting the air. He probably was. Vamps didn't rely on scent the way shapeshifters did, but they had a much better sense of smell than humans. He closed his eyes in the middle of drawing a deep breath. He shuddered and seemed to swoon, faint. I'd never seen a vamp act like this. It caught me off guard, and that was my fault.

I saw him tense, and my hand was going for the Browning, but there was no time. He was less than a foot away. I never even touched the gun before he slammed into me. He knocked the breath from my body. His hand was on my face, turning my head to one side, baring my neck, before I had time to breathe. I had a sense of movement even though I couldn't see him. I felt his body tense and I knew he was coming in for a strike. He made no effort to control my hands. I kept going for the gun, but I would never get it out and pointed in time. He was going to sink fang into my neck, and I couldn't stop it. It was like a car accident. I just had time to see it coming and to think, "I can't stop it." There wasn't even time to be afraid.

Something jerked the vampire backwards. His hand curled in my jacket, and didn't let go. His desperate grip nearly pulled me off my feet, but I got the gun out before I worried about staying on my feet.

A large, very Aztec-looking vamp had the skeletal vamp, holding him pinned against his body, only that one arm with its clutching hand not pressed to the larger man's body.

Edward had his gun out pointed at the vampires. He'd gotten to his gun first, but then he hadn't been shoved up against a wall and manhandled. Or would that be vampire-handled?

The big vamp jerked the thin one hard enough that he nearly pulled me off my feet, but that one clutching hand stayed curled in my jacket, catching on the shirt underneath. I had the Browning pointed at the vamp's chest, though I wasn't sure if the Hornady ammo was safe to shoot at arm's distance into one target pressed directly in front of another person. I wasn't sure if the ammo would go through the first vamp and into the second. The second vamp had saved me. It really wouldn't be nice to blow a hole in him.

The other vampires were leaving the room in a hurrying line to get past us and up the stairs, out of harm's way. Cowards. But it was thinning out the ranks, which would be great. Eventually, I'd care that there weren't so damn many vamps in the room, but right now the world was narrowed down to the vamp that had hold of me. First things first.

The big vamp kept backing up, trying to get the skeletal one to let go of me. We kept moving further into the room. Edward paced us, gun held two-handed pointed at the vampire's head. I finally put the barrel of my gun underneath the vamp's chin. I could blow his brains up without hitting the second vampire.

Obsidian Butterfly's voice slashed through the room like a whip. The sound made me wince, shoulders tightening as if it had been a blow. "These are my guests. How dare you attack them!"

The skeletal vampire started to cry, and his tears were clear, human. Vampire's tears are tinged red. They cry bloody tears. "Please, please let me feed, please!"

"You feed as we all feed, as befits a god."

"Please, please, mistress, please."

"You disgrace me before our visitors." Then she spoke low and rapidly in a language that was sort of Spanish sounding, but it wasn't Spanish. I don't speak Spanish, but I've heard it spoken often enough to know it when I hear it, and this wasn't it. Whatever she was saying, upset both vampires.

The big one pulled so hard that he finally jerked me off my feet because the other vamp was still holding on. I ended up on my knees, my jacket and shirt dangling from the vamp's hand, one arm pulled up at an awkward angle. My gun was pressed into his stomach now, and again I wondered if at point blank range the new ammo would kill both vamps? It was a miracle that I hadn't accidentally shot his head off. Edward was still there, gun pointed at the vamp's head. The first hint I had that something else had gone wrong was a faint glow. The glow grew into something pure and white. My cross had spilled out of my shirt.

The vampire kept his grip on me, but started to scream in a high pitiful voice. The cross flared bright and brighter until I had to turn my head and shield my eyes. It was like having magnesium burning around your neck. So bright, it only got this bright when something very bad was near. I didn't think the something bad was the thing still hanging onto me. I was betting the cross was glowing for her benefit, maybe others' but mostly hers. A lot of things in the room could kill me, but nothing else in the room was worth this much of a light show.

"Let him go to his destiny," she said.

I felt the arm that was still pulling so desperately, go limp. I felt him kneeling, felt it through the barrel of the gun still pressed against him.

Edward said, "Anita?" It was a question, but I didn't have an answer yet.

I blinked past the light, trying to see. The vampire put a hand on either side of my shoulders. His eyes were squeezed shut against the light. His face stretched wide with pain. The white white light glistened on fangs as he moved in to feed.

"Stop, or die," I said.

I'm not sure he even heard me. His hand caressed the edge of my cheek, and it was like being touched by fleshy sticks. His hands didn't even feel real. I yelled, "I'll kill him."

"Do so. It's his choice." Her voice was so matter of fact, so uncaring, that it made me not want to do it.

His hand grabbed my hair, tried to twist my face to one side. His head was drawn back for a strike, but he couldn't push past the glare of the cross. But he might work up to it. As weak as he was, he should have run screaming from this much holy light.

"Anita," Edward's voice and it wasn't a question now, more a preview.

The vampire let out a scream that made me gasp. His head threw back, then down, and his face moved in a white blur towards me. The gun went off before I realized I'd squeezed the trigger, just a reflex. A second gun echoed so close on my shot that it sounded like a single gunshot. The vamp jerked, and his head exploded. Blood and thicker things sprayed half my face.

I knelt in a sudden deafening silence. There was no sound, nothing but a fine, distant ringing in my ears, like tinny bells. I turned in a sort of slow motion to see the vamp's body sprawled on its side, I got to my feet and still couldn't hear anything. Sometimes that's shock. Sometimes it's just gunshots going off next to your ears.

I scraped at the blood and thicker pieces on the left side of my face. Edward handed me a white handkerchief, probably something Ted would carry, but I took it. I started trying to scrape the stuff off of me.

The cross was still glowing like a captive star. I was already deaf. If I didn't stop having to squint around the light, I was going to be blind as well. I looked around the room. Most of the vamps had fled up the stairs away from the cross's glow, but what was left huddled around their goddess, shielding her, I think, from us. I blinked through the glare, and I think I saw fear on one or two faces. You don't see that often on several hundred years worth of vampire. It might have been the cross, but I didn't think that was it. I slipped the cross back into my shirt. The cross was still cool silver. It never burned unless vampire flesh touched it. Then it would flare into actual flame and burn the vamp and any human flesh that happened to be touching it at the same time. Usually, the vamp would jerk away before you got past second degree burns so I'd never gotten a scar from one of my own crosses.

The vampires stayed in front of their mistress, and the fear was still there on at least one face. The cross could keep them at bay, but that wasn't what they feared. I looked down at the body. The entrance hole was just a small red thing, with black scorch marks around it, but the exit hole was nearly a foot in diameter. There was no head on the body, only the lower jaw and a thin rim of back brain left. The rest had been blown in a wide spray across the floor and across me.

Edward's mouth was moving, and sound came back in a kind of Doppler shift, so that I heard only the end of it. ". . . ammo are you using now?"

I told him.

He knelt by the body and inspected the chest wound. "I thought the Hornady XTP wasn't supposed to make this much of a mess going out."

His voice still sounded like it was distant, tinny, but I could hear again. It meant that my hearing would go back to normal eventually. "I don't think they did any firing tests at point blank range."

"It makes a nice hole at point blank range."

"In like a penny, out like a pizza," I said.

"You had questions about the murders?" Obsidian Butterfly said. "Ask them."

She was standing in the middle of her people, but no longer shielded. I don't know if she decided we weren't going to shoot her, or if she thought it was cowardice to hide behind others, or if we'd passed some kind of test. But if she were willing to answer my questions, then I'd take it any way I could get it.

I saw Dallas and Olaf to one side of the vamps. Dallas had her face hidden against his chest, and he was holding her, comforting her, helping her not see the mess on the floor. Olaf was looking down at her as if she were something precious. It wasn't love, more the way a man will look at a really nice car that he wants to own. He looked at her like she was a pretty thing that he'd wanted but hadn't expected to get. He stroked her hair, running his fingers through the long dark ponytail over and over, playing with her hair, watching it fall against her back.

I wasn't the only one watching them. "Cruz, take the professor upstairs. I think she's seen enough for one night."

A short male vamp, very Hispanic, went to them, but Olaf said, "I'll take her upstairs."

"No," Edward said.

"I don't think so," I said.

Itzpapalotl said, "That will not be necessary."

The three of us exchanged a glance, though I didn't meet her eyes dead on. But there was an understanding between us, I think. Olaf needed to stay away from the professor. Maybe a state or two away from her.

Cruz pulled Dallas out of Olaf's reluctant arms and led the crying woman up the stairs, and away from the horror we'd stretched out on the floor. Though we hadn't made the vampire a horror, we just killed him. Itzpapalotl had starved him until he faced a glowing cross for the chance to feed. Starved him until he'd let two humans point guns at him and not even try to get away. He'd wanted to sink fangs into human flesh more than he'd wanted to live. I don't usually feel sorry for vampires that try to feed off of me, especially without permission, but this one time I'd make an exception. He'd been pitiful. Now he was dead. Pity has never stopped me from pulling a trigger, and Edward didn't feel pity. I could stare down at what was left of that skeletal body and think, poor thing, but I felt nothing about the death. It wasn't just that I didn't feel regret. I felt nothing, absolutely nothing.

I looked at Edward, and he looked at me, and I'd have given a great deal for a mirror right that second. Staring into Edward's blank face, those empty eyes that felt nothing, I realized that I didn't need a mirror. I already had one.

26

MAYBE I'D HAVE BEEN afraid of that revelation, but the vampires began to flow out towards us. Survival first, moral issues later. Richard might say that was one of my biggest problems. Jean-Claude wouldn't. There's more than one reason why Richard and I haven't settled down to a happy ever after life, and there's more than one reason why I haven't cut Jean-Claude loose.

Itzpapalotl glided forward still shrouded in the scarlet cloak. It was so long that you couldn't see her feet and she moved so smoothly that it looked like she was on wheels. There was something artificial about her.

The four silent women moved on her left, and something bothered me about the way they moved. It took me a second or two to realize what it was. They were moving in utter unison, perfect step. One lifted a hand to brush a strand of black hair from her face, and all the others followed the movement like puppets, though there was no stray hair on their faces. From the breaths that raised their chests, to the small jerk of a finger, they imitated each other. No, not imitated, that was too mild a word. They were like one being with four bodies. The effect was eerie because they didn't look alike. One was short and square. One was tall and thin. The other two were delicate and did look something alike. All of them had paler skin than Itzpapalotl, as if in life they hadn't been much darker than they were now.

The tall vamp that had tried to pull the starving vamp off me walked to her right. He was the tallest of the ones that looked pure Aztec, six feet at least, with shoulders and muscles to match. His hair fell in a black wash down his back, held from his face by a crown of feathers and gold. His nose was pierced though that was too mild a word for the three inches of thick gold that bisected his face. Gold earplugs stretched his earlobes to a thin line of flesh. His skin was the color that old ivory sometimes gets, not a pale gold, but a pale copper, palest bronze. It was a striking color with the coal black hair and the perfectly black eyes. He moved two steps back, at her right, and like the women he moved as if this had always been his place.

Three male vamps moved a little distance from the man. They were all that shining ivory white that I was used to seeing. They were dressed in the same clothing as the bouncers, those skirt/thong bathing suit thingies. But they had no adornment. Their arms and legs were pale and empty. They were even barefoot. I knew servants when I saw them or prisoners maybe.

One was medium height with curly brown hair cut short, and a darker brown line of beard and mustache outlining the perfect whiteness of the skin. The eyes were pale blue. The second man was shorter with short hair turned salt and pepper as if he'd died after the hair had gone grey. The face was lined, but strong, and the body still muscular, so that his age at death was hard to tell. Older than the others, fortyish, though I was no judge of age of death in vamps. His eyes were the dark gray of storm clouds, echoing his hair color. He held a leash in one hand, and on the end of that leash the third man crawled, not on all fours, but on his hands, and his feet, legs hunched monkey like, or like a whipped dog. His hair was short and a surprising yellow, curling soft. It was the only thing on him that looked alive. His skin was like old paper, clinging and yellowed to his bones. His eyes were sunk so far back into his head that I couldn't tell what color they were.

The end of the entourage was five very Hispanic, Aztecy bodyguards. Bodyguards are bodyguards regardless of the culture, the century, or state of life, or would that be death? I knew muscle when I saw it, and the five vamps were muscle, even carrying obsidian blades, and obsidian-edged clubs, and looking somewhat less than serious in feathers and jewelry. They exuded that aura of badass.

Olaf had moved back to stand with us, and the three of us faced them. Bernardo had stayed near the stairway, making sure our retreat wasn't cut off. So nice to work with other professionals. Olaf had his gun out now, too, and was watching the vamps with a look that wasn't neutral. It was hostile. I didn't know why, but he seemed pissed. Go figure.

The vamps stopped about eight feet from us. The dead vampire lay on the floor between us. The body had already stopped bleeding. When you take a head off of a vamp, they bleed just like a human, quarts and quarts of the red stuff. It is a freaking mess when you decapitate someone. But this vampire had bled only a small odd-shaped space on the stone floor, barely a foot across, and a second even smaller pool under the chest. Not nearly enough blood for what we'd done to him.

The silence seemed thicker than it should have, and Olaf filled it. "You can check his pulse if you want."

"Olaf, don't," Edward said.

Olaf shifted, either uncomfortable, or fighting down the urge to do something worse than mouthing off. "You're the boss," he said, but not like he meant it.

"I doubt this one had a pulse," I said, and I was looking at the vampires while I said it. "It takes energy to make a vamp's heart beat and he didn't have any."

"You feel pity for him," Itzpapalotl said.

"Yeah, I guess I do."

"Your friend does not."

I glanced at Edward. His face showed nothing. It was nice to know there were still some differences between us. I felt pity. He didn't. "Probably he doesn't."

"But there is no regret in either of you, no guilt."

"Why should we feel guilty? We just killed him. We didn't turn him into a crawling, starved thing."

Even under the masking cloak, I could feel her grow still with that awful stillness that only the old ones have. Her voice came warm with the first thread of anger. "You presume to judge me."

"No, just stating facts. If he hadn't been starved worse than any vamp I've ever seen outside of a coffin prison, he would never have attacked me." I also thought that they could have tried harder to get him off of me, but didn't say it out loud. I really didn't want to piss her off with eighty or so vamps waiting upstairs between us and the door. That wasn't even taking into account the werejaguars.

"And if I told my starved ones that they could feed off of you, all of them, what would they do?" she asked.

The starved vamp on the leash, looked up at that. His eyes never stayed on anyone too long, flitting from face to face to face, but he'd heard her.

My stomach jerked tight in a knot hard enough to hurt. I had to blow out a breath to be able to talk around the sudden flutter of my pulse. There'd been at least ten, fifteen of the starved ones. "They'd attack us," I said.

"They would fall upon you like ravening dogs," she said.

I nodded, hand settling more securely on the butt of my gun. "Yeah." If she gave the order, my first bullet was going between her eyes. If I died, I wanted to take her with me. Vindictive, but true.

"The thought frightens you," she said.

I tried to see her face in that hood, but some trick of shadow left only her small bowed mouth visible. "If you can feel all these emotions, then you can tell a lie from a truth."

She lifted her face, a sudden defiant movement. A look passed over her face, the barest flicker across that calmness. She really couldn't tell lie from truth. Yet she sensed regret, pity, fear. Truth and lie should have come in there somewhere.

"My starved ones are useful from time to time."

"So you starve them deliberately."

"No," she said. "The great creator god sees they are weak and does not sustain them as he sustains us."

"I don't understand."

"They are allowed to feed as gods feed, not as animals."

I frowned. "Sorry, I still don't get it."

"We will show you how a god feeds, Anita." She said my name like it was meant to be said, making it a rolling three syllable word, making of the ordinary name something exotic.

"Shapeshifter coming down," Bernardo said. He had his gun up and pointed.

"I have called a priest to feed the gods."

"Let him come down," I said. I looked at that delicate face and tried to read what was there, but there was nothing home that I could talk to, nothing I could understand. "I don't mean to be insulting, my apologies if I am being insulting, but we came here to talk about the murders. I would like to ask you some questions."

"Your vast knowledge of things arcane and things Aztec has brought us to you," Edward said.

I fought not to raise eyebrows at him, just nodding. "Yeah, what he said."

She actually smiled. "You still believe I and my people are merely vampires. You do not truly believe that we are gods."

She had me there, but she couldn't smell a lie. "I'm Christian. You saw that when the cross glowed. That means I'm a monotheist, so if you guys are gods, then it's something of a problem for me." That was so diplomatic, even I was impressed.

"We will prove it to you, then we will offer you hospitality as our guests, then we will talk business."

I've learned over the years that if someone says they're a god, you don't argue with them unless you're better armed. So I didn't try and get the business moved up. She was nuts and had enough muscle backing her in this building to make her brand of craziness contagious, or even fatal. So we'd do arcane vampire shit, then when the self-proclaimed goddess was satisfied I'd get to ask my questions. How bad could it be, watching them prove they were gods? Don't answer that.

The werejaguar that came through the door was the blue-eyed blond with his golden tan that had first passed so near our table that I'd touched his fur. He came through the door with a neutral face, empty-eyed as if he wasn't entirely sure he wanted to be here.

His gaze took in the room, and hesitated over the dead vamp in the middle. But he fell to one knee in front of Itzpapalotl, his back to us and our guns, fur-covered head bowed. "What would you have of me, holy mistress?"

I fought to keep my face blank. Holy mistress? Good grief.

"I want to show our visitors how a god is fed."

He looked up then, looking into her face. "Who am I to worship, holy mistress?"

"Diego," she said.

The brown-haired vampire startled at the name, and though his face was blank, empty, I knew he wasn't happy. "Yes, my dark goddess, what would you have of me?"

"Seth will offer sacrifice to you." She caressed a delicate hand across the fur of the man's hood.

"As you like, my dark goddess," Diego said. His voice was as empty as his face tried to be.

The werejaguar, Seth, crawled on all fours, mimicking the animal whose skin he wore. He pressed his forehead to his hands, lying nearly prostrate at Diego's feet.

"Rise, priest of our dark goddess, and make sacrifice to us."

The werejaguar stood, and he was nearly half a foot taller than the vampire. He did something on the front of the jaguar skin, and it opened, enough for him to lift the headpiece over his head, so that the animal's sightless glass eyes stared back at us over the man's shoulders. The head flopped bonelessly like a broken-necked thing. His hair was a rich honey blond, sun-streaked, held back in a long club, woven back and forth so that it looked like a lot of hair, but held close to his head so the jaguar skin would slip on easily. It was just like the hairdo on the one who had gotten cut up by the priest back stage.

"Turn so our visitors can see all," Itzpapalotl said.

The men turned so we had a side view. The werejaguar's earlobes were covered in thick white scars. He drew a small silver knife from his belt, the hilt was carved jade. He placed the sliver blade against his earlobe, steadying it with his other hand and sliced it open. Blood spilled in scarlet lines on his fingers, down the blade, to drip on the shoulders of the jaguar skin.

Diego went to the taller man, putting a hand behind his neck, and another at the small of his back. It looked oddly like a kiss, as he drew the werejaguar's head downward. The vampire's mouth sealed around the earlobe, drawing it and some of the ear into his mouth. His throat worked as he swallowed, sucking on the wound, drawing it down. The pale blue of his eyes had spread to a sparkling fire like palest sapphires sparkling in the sun. His skin began to glow as if there was white fire inside. The brown of his hair darkened, or maybe that was illusion because of how glowing white his skin had become.

The werejaguar had closed his eyes, head thrown back, breath catching in his throat, as if it felt good. One of his hands lay on the vampire's bare shoulder, and you could see the pressure of his fingers in that pale, glowing flesh.

Diego drew back, flashing fangs. "The wound closes."

"Another offering, my cat," she said.

The vampire moved back just enough for the other man to use the silver blade on the other ear. Then he fell on him, like a lover long refused. He drew back, eyes sparkling with blue light. He looked blind and heavy-lidded as he drew back from him. "The wound closes."

It was actually interesting that the wound closed as fast as it did. Vamps had an anticoagulant in their saliva that should have kept it flowing, and silver should have forced the shapeshifter to heal human normal, but the wound was closing pretty fast, not fast enough to make me comfortable, but a lot faster than it should have. The only thing I could figure was that Itzpapalotl had somehow given her shapeshifters even more healing ability than a normal shapeshifter. Maybe normal silver bullets wouldn't work on them, not to kill them anyway. It was something to think about, just in case.

"I want them to see what it is to be a god, Diego. Show them, my cat."

The werejaguar opened a seam on the fur that looked almost like it was Velcroed shut. He slit open the front of the fur, having to stop and undo the belt that held knives and a small pouch. The belt dropped to the floor, and he slipped the fur down his body. The golden tan was an all over tan, complete with . . . um, you know. Nude sun bathing, how unhealthy.

The jaguar slipped out of the skin until he stood completely nude. He still had the silver knife in his hand. I didn't have a clue what he was about to use it on, but having to strip couldn't be a good sign. He cupped his own penis, and it had come out of the fur smooth and hard, excited. He put the point of the blade against that delicate skin and drew it in a thin crimson line. His breath ran out in a ragged gasp.

It was echoed by me and Olaf. Bernardo said, "Shit!" Eeeyah. I don't think I had as much sympathy as the guys, but that had to hurt. Edward was the only one of us who hadn't made a sound. Either he knew what was coming, or nothing surprised him.

"Diego," Itzpapalotl said, "show them what it means to be a god." There was a thread of warning in her voice, as if she were warning him to do his job. I wasn't sure why because Diego had seemed to thoroughly enjoy the ear sucking. Why wouldn't he do this?

Diego dropped to his knees, and his face was very close to the offered blood, all he had to do was reach out and take it. But he stayed kneeling, staring at the cut flesh with eyes that still blazed pale blue fire. He stayed kneeling until the cut began to heal, and finally vanish as if the flesh had absorbed it. I'd never seen a shapeshifter heal silver that well. Never.

Seth looked over his shoulder, one hand still around his naked penis, though it was beginning to wilt a little. "Holy mistress, what do you wish me to do?"

"Sacrifice," she said, and there was enough heat in that one word to make me shiver.

Seth put the blade point to his flesh again. It seemed harder to get a clean cut when he wasn't fully erect, but he managed. Blood spread in fine rivulets over his skin, staining his fingers with tiny bits of red.

Diego stayed kneeling, but made no move to feed. The fire faded from his eyes, the glow leeched out of the skin, leaving him still lovely, a contrast of pale skin, dark hair, and blue eyes, but he looked defeated somehow, hands limp in his lap.

The four women moved around behind Itzpapalotl, gliding as a unit until they stood in a half-circle behind the kneeling vampire. "You have disappointed me again, Diego," the goddess said.

He shook his head and bowed it, eyes closing. "I am sorry for that, my dark goddess. I would not disappoint you for the sun and the moon itself." But his voice was tired when he said it, like it was a memorized line but his heart wasn't in it.

The four vamps surrounding him pulled black leather bound rods from their belts, and lifted leather bags off the ends. Dozens of thin leather cords spread out from each bag like obscene flowers. Silver balls were braided in the cords so that they sparkled in the torchlight. It was a cat o' nine tails, except it had a lot more tails.

"Why do you insist on refusing this honor, Diego? Why do you make us punish you?"

"I am not a lover of men, my dark goddess, and I will not do this. I am sorry that my refusal pains you, but this one thing I will not do." Again, his voice was tired, as if he'd said all of it before, many times before.

He was about five hundred years old, like the four women that surrounded him. Had he been turning the "honor" down for five centuries?

The four women watched their goddess, not glancing even at the vampire at their feet. Itzpapalotl gave a small nod. Four arms went back, flaring the cat o' nine tails in a fan of silver and leather. They whirled it through the air like they knew what they were doing. They hit him in sequence, right to left, each whip landing a blow, then the next, the next, the next. The blows fell so close together it was like the sound of hard rain, except that this rain was smacking into flesh, and you could hear it thudding home. They whipped him until they drew blood, then they stood motionless around him, waiting.

"Do you still refuse?"

"Yes, my dark goddess, I still refuse."

"When you raped these women long ago, did you dream of the price you would pay?"

"No, my dark goddess, I did not."

"You didn't believe in our gods, did you?"

"No, my dark goddess, I did not."

"You thought your white Christ could save you, didn't you?"

"Yes, my dark goddess, I did."

"You were wrong."

His head hunched between his shoulders as if he were trying to draw into himself like a turtle. The metaphor was funny. The gesture was not. "Yes, my dark goddess, I was wrong."

She gave another nod, and the women began to whip him in a blur that made the whips gleam silver like lightning in their hands. Blood ran in streamers down his back, but he never cried out, never asked for mercy.

I must have made some movement, because Edward stepped close to me, not grabbing my arm, but touching it. I met his eyes, and he gave the barest shake of his head. I wouldn't really risk our lives for a vampire I didn't know, really I wouldn't, but I didn't like it.

Olaf made a small sound. He was watching it with glowing eyes like a child at Christmas who comes down to find that he'd gotten exactly what he wanted. He'd put up the gun, his big hands clasped in front of him, clasped so hard they were mottled, and a fine tremor ran up his arms. I might not like it, but Olaf did.

I glanced at Edward, sort of nodding to the big man. Edward gave the barest of nods. He saw it, too, but he was ignoring it. I tried. I caught Bernardo's eyes. He was staring at the big man, a look very close to fear on his face. He turned and concentrated on the stairs, turning his back on everything in the room. I'd have liked to join him, but I couldn't turn away. It wasn't just macho crap, you know. If Edward could stand to watch it, then so could I. Though there was a little of that. Mostly it was if Diego could endure it, I could watch it. If I wasn't going to stop it then I had to at least watch. To do nothing to help him and to turn away would have been too much cowardice for me to swallow. I'd have choked on it. The best I could do was try to watch other things around him. The way the women's arms went up and down like machines, as if they would never tire.

The five guards stood impassive, but the vamp that walked at Itzpapalotl's right side watched it with half-parted lips, eyes intent as if afraid to miss even the smallest movement. He was almost as old as the goddess herself, seven, eight hundred years, and for five hundred of those years he'd been watching this particular show, and he still enjoyed it. I knew in that moment that I never wanted to make an enemy of the creatures in this room. I never wanted to be at their mercy. Because they had none.

The other two Spanish survivors had moved back to stand against the far wall, as far from the show as they could get. The one with salt and pepper hair stared at the ground as if there was something of great interest there. The starved one on his leash had curled into a fetal position, as if he were trying to disappear altogether.

The women turned Diego's back into bloody ribbons. A red pool formed at his feet. He curled his upper body over his legs until he was like a little ball of pain. Blood began to drip down his shoulders to form a second puddle in front of him. He was weaving, even that low to the ground, as if he might pass out. I hoped he passed out soon.

I finally did take a step forward, and Edward grabbed my arm. "No," he said.

"You feel pity for him," Itzpapalotl said.

"Yes," I said.

"Diego was one of the strangers that came into our lands. He thought we were barbarians. We were things to be conquered, robbed, raped, slaughtered. Diego never saw us as people, did you, Diego?"

There was no answer this time. He wasn't exactly unconscious but close enough that he was beyond words. "You didn't think we were people, did you, Cristobal?"

I didn't know who Cristobal was, but there was a high keening sound. It was the vampire on the leash. He unrolled from his tight fetal ball. The keening ended in that same awful laughter that I'd heard earlier. The laughter rose up and up until the vampire holding the leash jerked it tight, pulling him like you'd discipline a dog. I realized that the leash was a choke collar. Shit.

"Answer me, Cristobal."

The vampire let up on the leash enough for the starved one to get a ragged breath. His voice, when it came, was strangely cultured, smooth and sane. "No, we did not think you were people, my dark goddess." Then the ragged laughter came from those thin lips, and he huddled around himself again.

"They broke into our temple and raped our priestesses, our virgin priestesses, our nuns. Twelve of them raped these four priestesses. They did unspeakable, vile things to them, forced them with pain and threats of death to do whatever the men wanted them to do."

The women's faces never changed during the speech, as if it were about someone else. They had stopped whipping the man. They just stood there watching him bleed.

"I found them dying in the temple from what had been done to them. I offered them life. I offered them vengeance. I made them gods, and then we hunted down the strangers that had raped them, the ones that left them for dead. We took each of them, made them one of us, so their punishment would last forever. But my teyolloquanies were too strong for most of them. There were twelve of them once. Now only two remain."

Itzpapalotl looked at me, and there was a challenge in her face, a look that demanded an answer. "Do you still feel pity for him?"

I nodded. "Yes, but I understand hate, and revenge is one of my best things."

"Then you see the justice here."

I opened my mouth, Edward's hand tightened on my arm, until it was painful. He forced me to think before I answered. I'd have been careful, but he didn't know that.

"He did a terrible, unforgivable thing. They should have their revenge." In my head I added, though five hundred years of torment seemed a bit much. I killed people when they deserved it, anything beyond that was up to God. I just didn't think I was up to making decisions that would last five hundred years.

Edward eased up on my arm and started to let go of me, when she said, "So you agree with our punishment?" His hand locked back onto my arm, if anything tighter than before.

I glared up at him, hissing under my breath, "You're bruising me."

He let me go, slowly, reluctantly, but the look in his eyes was warning enough. Don't get us killed. I'd try not to. "I would never presume to question the decision of a god." Which was true. If I ever met a god, I wouldn't question their decision. The fact that I didn't believe in any god with a little "g" was beside the point. It wasn't a lie, and it sounded perfect for the situation. When you're prefabricating as fast as you can, it doesn't get better than that.

She smiled, and she was suddenly young and beautiful like a sudden glimpse of the young woman she must have been once. It was almost more of a shock than the rest. I'd expected a lot of things, but not Itzpapalotl to have retained even a shred of her humanity.

"I am very pleased," she said, and she looked it. I'd pleased the goddess, made her smile. Be still my heart.

She must have made some sign because the whipping continued. They beat him until the white of his spine showed through in places where the flesh had worn completely away. A human would have died long before they got that far, or even a shapeshifter, but the vampire was as alive as when they started. He had collapsed into a little ball, his forehead on the floor, arms trapped under his body, his weight resting on his legs. He was unconscious, but the body didn't fall over. It was propped up by its own weight.

Olaf was making a high-pitched hiss under his breath, fast and faster. If the circumstances had been different, I'd have said he was working up to an orgasm. If that was what he was doing, I so didn't want to know. I ignored him, or did my best to.

The werejaguar stood there through it all, nude, body going limp, the cut long healed as he watched the vampire's body torn apart. He watched it with a neutral face, but occasionally when a blow was particularly vicious, or when the first hint of bone showed through, he winced, gaze sliding away, as if he didn't want to watch but was afraid to actually turn his head away.

"Enough." That one word, and the whips stopped, drooping like wilted flowers. The silver balls had all turned crimson, and blood dripped from the end of the whips in slow spatters. The women's faces had never changed, as if the faces were just masks, and what lay underneath was inhuman and held all the emotions that the masks could not show. As if the monstrousness inside was more human than the human shells they wore.

The four women walked in a line to a small stone basin in the far comer. They dipped each whip into the water in turn, then ran their hands over each lash almost lovingly.

Olaf tried twice to speak, had to clear his throat, and finally said, "Do you use saddle soap and mink oil on the leather?"

The four women turned as one toward him. Then they all looked at Itzpapalotl. She answered for them. "You sound knowledgable about such things."

"Not as knowledgable as they are," he said, and he sounded impressed, like a cellist seeing Yo-Yo Ma perform for the first time.

"They have had centuries to perfect their craft."

"Do they use their craft just on the bodies of the men who hurt them?" he asked.

"Not always," she said,

"Can they speak?" he asked. He was watching them as if they were something precious and lovely.

"They have taken a vow of silence until the last of their tormentors is dead."

I had to ask. "Are they executing them periodically?"

"No," she said.

I frowned, and the question must have shown on my face.

"We do not execute them. We merely harm them, and if they die of their injuries, then so be it. If they survive, then they live to see another night."

"So you're not going to give Diego any medical attention?" I asked.

Edward's hand had never let go of me during the torture as if he truly didn't trust me not to do something heroic and suicidal. His hand dug into me again, and I'd had my fill. "Let me the fuck go, now, or we are going to have a disagreement . . . Ted." I wasn't feeling good about watching Diego bleed. I was feeling worse because it hadn't bothered me as much as I thought it should have. I'd have helped him if I could have, as long as it wasn't suicide. He was a stranger and a vampire. I wasn't risking our lives for him, and that was that. Had there been a time when I would have risked us all, even for a strange vampire? I just didn't know anymore.

"Diego has survived far worse than this. He is the strongest of all of them. We broke all the others before they died. They did everything we asked them in the end. Except Diego, and still he fights us." She shook her head, as if dismissing it all. "But we must show you how it is to be done properly. Chualtalocal, show them how the sacrifice is to be embraced."

The vamp that stood at her right hand stepped forward. He walked around the fallen Diego as if he were a pile of trash to be avoided, and left for someone else to clean up. He faced the werejaguar as Diego had faced him, but things had changed. Seth had been all pumped up from having his ears sucked when he first stripped, hard and eager to please. Now he was just naked, and his eyes kept going to the bloody mess that Diego had become as if he was wondering when his turn was coming.

"Make your offering, my cat," she said.

Seth was looking from Diego's body to the vampire in front of me. "My holy mistress, I am willing, you know I am, but I . . . I seem to be," he swallowed hard enough that I heard it even over the still faint ringing in my ears. "I seem to be . . ."

"Make your sacrifice, Seth, or suffer my wrath."

The four sisters weird had hung their cat o' nine tails on small hooks in the wall, all in a row like a sadomasochistic version of the seven dwarves with their identical possessions. They glided back towards us all, like sharks scenting blood in the water.

Seth seemed to know they were there. He actually grabbed himself and started trying to get some attention going, but his eyes were flicking wildly through the room as if looking for an escape. He was making the effort, but nothing was happening.

Edward wasn't holding onto my arm anymore, maybe that was it, or maybe I'd just had enough for one night. "You've scared him shitless. It's hard to get it up when you're scared."

She and Chualtalocal looked at me, and their black eyes held nearly identical expressions, not that I chanced looking into the eyes long, but it was still there, disdain. How dare I interfere?

Edward made as if to grab me again. I held up a hand to him. "Don't touch me."

He let his hand fall back, but his eyes were not happy with me. Fine, I wasn't happy with anyone right now.

"And are you offering to help him overcome his fear?" Itzpapalotl asked. The look on her face said plainly that she didn't expect me to offer.

"Sure," I said.

I don't know who looked the most surprised, but I think it was Edward, though Bernardo was a close second from the doorway. Olaf just watched me like a fox watching a rabbit through the fence, who's just spotted a hole big enough to crawl through. I ignored him. It was probably best to always ignore Olaf, if possible. Ignore him or kill him. That was my vote.

I held my hand out to the werejaguar. He hesitated, glancing from the vamp in front of him, to me, to the goddess behind him. I wiggled my fingers at him. "Come on, Seth. We don't have all night."

"Go with her, do as she says, as long as you offer fitting sacrifice."

He took my hand, tentatively, and though he was a six foot plus, naked, man, there was something very little boyish on his face. Maybe it was the near panic in his baby blues. He was scared, scared that he was going to end up on the floor, meat for the four sisters weird. I didn't blame him for worrying. I think if I hadn't stepped in, that was exactly what was about to happen. But I'd had all the torture I could handle for one night. It wasn't moral outrage. It was just plain outrage. I wanted to ask my questions and get the hell out of here. Vampires can live a very long time, theoretically forever, which means their idea of getting down to business can be damn leisurely. The vamps might have had eternity. I didn't.

I led Seth the werejaguar off to the other side of the room. The easiest thing would have been to work him by hand, but I was like so not doing that. The option I was voting for wasn't that simple, but it was something I was willing to do. I was going to call that part of me that was Richard's mark. Not the connection to him—that was safely walled away. I'd packed it so tight, I wasn't even sure I could open to the mark even on purpose. But I held a part of it inside me. The same part that had recognized César, the same part that let me deal with the wereleopards back home. That electric rush of energy was a turn on to wereanimals. I'd discovered it accidentally. Now I was going to try and do it on purpose.

But it wasn't like a switch. Maybe someday it would be, but right now it took some preparation to get it going. It was maddening that something that came out at odd moments when I didn't want it, would refuse to come out when I did, but psychic shit is like that, unpredictable. It's one of the reasons it's so hard to study in laboratory conditions. X does not always equal Y.

I put my hands on my hips and looked at him, from head to foot, and didn't know where to start. My life would be both easier and harder if I was into casual sex, but for better or worse, it wasn't my cup of tea.

"Can you undo your hair?"

"Why?" He sounded suspicious, and I didn't blame him.

"Look, I could have let her turn you over to her pet torturers, but I didn't. So work with me here."

His hands went to the knot at the back of his head. He pulled long pins out of his hair, and finally a comb that was made of bone. The hair uncurled slowly as if it were stretching from some long sleep, sliding down his back in a heavy mass. I walked behind him and he started to turn and watch me. I touched his shoulder, made him face front. "I'm not going to hurt you, Seth. I'm probably the only person in this room that won't."

He kept his face front, but there was a tension to his shoulder, his back that said he didn't like it. I didn't care. We needed to do this fast. Call it hunch but the goddess didn't strike me as patient.

I unrolled his hair, helping it slide down his back. The colors were extraordinary, bright yellow, rich gold, a pale almost white, all of it streaked together, each color blending into the next the way sea water blends one color into the next, distinct but making a whole. I ran my hands through the thick warmth of his hair until it lay spread across his back, an inch past his waist. I grabbed two handfuls of hair and pressed it to my cheek. There was the close smell of sweat and the scent of the fur he'd worn. He had a cologne, faint on his skin, something so sweet, it smelled like candy. I spread the hair apart until I could see the skin of his back, and laid my face against the warmth of him. He smelled warm, as if you could sink your teeth into him like something fresh from the oven. I walked around him, hands trailing lightly over his skin, touching mostly the fall of that sun-streaked hair.

I came to stand in front of him, looked up into those wide, still half-afraid eyes, but a glance down his body showed that I'd made some progress, not enough, but some.

I didn't look at the vampires, or Edward, or anybody. I concentrated just on the man in front of me. To look elsewhere was to lose ground. I took his hand, and that pale golden tan looked darker against the paleness of my skin. I lowered my face over his hand as if I'd kiss it, but I brushed my lips barely against his skin, moving up his arm, breathing in the scent of his skin. I opened my mouth, laying my breath like a warm touch just above the skin of his arm. It raised the pale hairs on his arm in a march of goosebumps.

He flexed the hand I was holding, rolling me into his body with my back resting against the front of him. His other arm wrapped around from the other side, enfolding me in the warmth of his body. He laid his face on the top of my head, and a spill of his hair fell across me like a warm sweet scented curtain. The firelight danced through the gold of his hair, turning it into an amber cage, carved of light. He kissed the top of my head, then laid a gentle kiss against my temple, the top of my cheekbone, my cheek. He was so tall that in bending over he enveloped me in his body, covering me in the feel of him. The candy smell of his cologne breathed along his skin, and my body constricted with it. The smell was the key. The power spilled upward in a warm liquid rush that brought me to tiptoe, made me luxuriate against his body like a cat with catnip, wanting to roll my body in the scent. My body writhed against his as the power rode in almost painful waves, so warm, it was almost hot, rising off my body like invisible steam.

One hand stayed around my waist, the other touched my chin, turning my face back to meet his mouth. He kissed me, and for a second I stiffened, but I'd learned that if you called the power, you didn't fight it. You embraced it. If you fought it, then you had less control. I kissed him back. I expected the power to push out my mouth into his like it had with César, but it didn't. The kiss was nice, but it was just the feel of his lips on mine. His warmth pushed against mine, his power like a trembling shadow spilling along mine. We stood wrapped in a curtain of his hair, a circle of arms, and a vibrating blanket of that skin-dancing power that was all shapeshifter.

He shuddered against me, arms hugging me close. I could tell he was ready for sacrifice without looking, but I had to glance down anyway. He was ready. I pulled free of him, gently. "You're ready to go back to the vamps, Seth. I think you're ready to make a sacrifice." I made myself look him in the eyes.

He bent and kissed my forehead, gently. "Thank you."

"You're welcome."

We walked back to the vamps hand in hand. But it wasn't the vampires that made me uncomfortable as we crossed the room. It was the humans. Bernardo looked like he was reconsidering my status as untouchable Madonna. Olaf had an almost hungry look on his face. It was closer to the way werewolves looked at you on the night of full moon than the way a man looks at a woman. Edward had a slight frown between his eyes, which for him meant he was bothered by something. The vampires looked about like I'd expected. Itzpapalotl looked serious, as if she hadn't known I could call the power up on purpose. It's why they'd apologized for dragging me up on stage earlier.

I gave Seth over to Chualtalocal like a father handing the bride to the groom. Then I moved back to stand by Edward. He looked at me, as if he was the one trying to read me for a change, and failing. It was almost worth it, if I could confuse Edward.

"Did you enjoy yourself, my cat?" the goddess asked.

"Yes, holy mistress, I did."

"Are you ready to make sacrifice?"

"Yes, holy mistress."

"Then do so." She looked past him to me, as if she didn't like what she saw. Something about what I'd done with Seth had disturbed her. Had she expected me to take him off in the comer and just do him by hand like a fluffer in a porno movie? Had the fact that I'd used power as well as mild sex disturbed her? Or had she seen something I hadn't, or understood something I did not? No way of knowing short of asking, and admitting that kind of ignorance to master vamps is a good way to get killed. So no questions about magic, just eventually, hopefully about the case.

Seth picked up the small silver blade again. He cradled his flesh in his hand and set the tip of the blade against himself. I caught Bernardo turning back towards the door. The blade tip bit into flesh, and I looked away. I think we all did, except for Olaf. It might have startled him the first time, but he was over the shock. Blood was being spilled, flesh being cut. Olaf couldn't miss that.

He watched the cutting, but then I caught him turning away out of the corner of my eye, and I had to look. I had to see what was bad enough for Olaf not to be able to stomach it.

The vampire had gone to his knees. I guess maybe I'd expected him to just lick the blood off, but he wasn't. He was sucking at it the way that Diego had sucked at Seth's ears, except this wasn't an ear. The vampire had covered almost every inch of Seth with its mouth. Seth's eyes were closed, and there was a look of concentration on his face.

I looked away again and found myself meeting the dead eyes of the four fallen nuns. Those empty, angry faces were almost harder to stare at than a vampire going down on someone. I literally turned my back on all of them and found that Olaf had done the same thing. He was hugging himself and staring at nothing. His discomfort rose off of him in almost visible waves. Even with his back turned, the sounds carried. I wished for the ringing in my ears to get worse.

Soft, sucking sounds, wet sounds, the sound of flesh in flesh, and the sharp intake of breath that was probably Seth. His breath came in three fast pants, and he spoke, "Please, holy mistress, I am not sure of my control tonight."

"You know the punishment," she said. "Surely, that is incentive enough to hold yourself in check."

I glanced back then and found that Seth was staring back over his shoulder at the four women in the corner. When he turned back, he looked scared. The vampire was still feeding, sucking, throat swallowing. Surely, the wound had healed by now, unless they'd made a second wound while I was being embarrassed and not looking.

Seth dug his fingernails into the palms of his hands. His hands paled with the force of squeezing nails into his own flesh. He threw his head back suddenly, breath coming fast, faster, fastest. The vampire pulled off of him, leaving him hard and still intact. "The wound has closed."

Chualtalocal stood and went back to his mistress. The moment there was room, Seth collapsed to his knees, opening his hands slowly as if they hurt. There were bloody half-moons where his nails had bitten into his palms. But it had worked. Any distraction to keep him out of the clutches of the goddess's pet freaks.

"I offer you hospitality, to you and your friends. You may have Seth if you like and finish him as his body seems to so badly need."

I suddenly knew what she meant by hospitality. Somehow I didn't think that was Aztec culture, though if I remembered correctly, hadn't some of the Aztecs sent Cortes and his men women along with food and gold? Maybe this wasn't any different. But I didn't want to mess with it.

"Dawn is coming. I can feel it pressing against the darkness like a weight about to tear the night apart."

She turned her head to one side and seemed to think, or maybe she was sensing the night, the air, something. "Yes," she said, "I feel it, too."

"Then if it isn't too large an insult, can we skip the hospitality for tonight and get to the murders?"

"Only if you give me your word that you will return and taste our hospitality before you go back to Saint Louis."

I glanced at Edward. He shrugged. I guess it was up to me. What else was new when it came to monster? "I don't agree to having sex with your people, but I'll agree to a return visit."

"You seemed to like Seth. I would offer you César, who your power seemed to like even more, but he does not make sacrifice, nor does he act as hospitality. It is his price for letting us come so near killing him twice a month."

"You mean because he lets you nearly tear his heart out twice a month, he doesn't have to make sacrifice or all the other stuff?"

"That is what I mean."

It made me think better of ol' César. I'd seen his show, and now I'd seen some of the behind the scenes stuff, and I had to say that it was a close call which was worse. Letting someone cut your chest open and touch your still beating heart, or letting vamps suck blood off of tender body parts and be offered for sex to strangers. No, come to think of it, I'd have rather had my chest cut open, as long as I knew I'd heal completely every time.

"It's not that Seth isn't lovely to look at. I'm sure it would be a pleasure to be with him, but I don't do casual sex. Thanks for thinking of me though. I know the police spoke with you."

"They did. I do not think they learned anything of value from me."

"Maybe they didn't ask the right questions," I said.

"And what are the right questions?"

I was about to do something that the police wouldn't like at all. I was about to tell the monsters, someone they had suspected at one point of being the murderer, details of the crime. But she needed specific details or how was she to recognize the marks of some Aztec bogeyman? I knew how the cops had done it. They'd been so general, it was almost useless to show up. I understood why they did it that way. Once I opened my mouth and let out details to Itzpapalotl, then she was contaminated. They'd never be able to slip her up in an interrogation, because she got the secret details from me.

What I knew and the police couldn't was that they'd never interrogate the truth out of her. She was the kind of vamp that could sit in a dark room and watch the colors on the inside of her own eyeballs and be content. The only thing they could threaten her with was the death penalty, and if she was behind the murders, it was already a death penalty. One of the downfalls to a swift and certain punishment was that it took a lot of the give and play out of an interrogation. Once someone knows they are going to be executed, you can't bargain with them.

"Can we clear the room out a little?"

"What do you mean?"

"Can we have fewer of your people in here? I'm going to share confidential police information with you, and I don't want it to get out."

"Whatever you say in this room remains in this room. No one here will talk of it to anyone else. I can promise you this." She was utterly sure of herself, arrogant. But why not? All of her people were terrified of her. If what happened to Diego was commonplace, then think what the exotic stuff must be. If she dictated that the secrets were safe, they were safe.

Edward stepped close to me. He lowered his voice though he didn't try and whisper. "Are you sure about this?"

"I'm sure, Edward. She can't help if she doesn't have enough information." We looked at each other for a few seconds, then he gave a small nod. I turned back to the waiting vampire. "Okay," I said, and I told her about the survivors, and the dead.

I don't know what I expected, maybe for her to be titillated, or to go, a-ha, and recognize the monster responsible. What I got was serious attention, good questions at the right places, and a glimpse at a very intelligent mind behind all the games. If she wasn't a delusional, sadistic, megalomaniac, would-be goddess, she might have been likable.

"The skins of men are valuable to Xipe Totec and Tlazolteotl. The priests would flay the sacrifice and wear the skin. The heart had many uses for the gods. Even the flesh was used, at least in part. Sometimes, the insides of a sacrifice would have some strange thing inside it, and be an omen. Then the other organs might be kept for a time and studied, but it was rare."

"Can you think why they would cut out the tongues?"

"To keep them from speaking the secrets they have seen." She said it, like of course that was the reason. It made sense ritually, I guess.

"Why cut off the eyelids?"

"So they can never not see the truth, even though they cannot speak it. I do not know if this is why they have done these awful things."

"Why would someone remove the outward secondary sex characteristics?"

"I do not understand," she said, and she was holding the cloak close about her, as if she were cold. We'd been talking long enough, I had to remind myself not to look directly in her eyes.

"The genitalia on the men, the breasts on the women, were removed."

She shuddered, and I knew something I hadn't before. Itzpapalotl, the goddess of the obsidian blade, was frightened. "It sounds like some of the things the Spanish did to our people."

"But the flaying and taking the organs, that's more Aztec, than European."

She nodded. "Yes, but our sacrifices were messengers to the gods. We caused pain only for sacred purposes, not for cruelty or a whim. All blood was holy. If you died at the hand of a priest, you died knowing it served a greater purpose. Literally, your death helped the rain to fall, the maize to grow, the sun to rise in the sky. I do not know of any god that would flay people and leave them alive. Death is necessary for the messenger to reach the gods. Death is part of the worship of the deity. The Spaniards taught us to kill for the sake of killing, not as a sacred trust, but just for slaughter." She stared past me at the four women that waited patiently for her to notice them, for her to give them a purpose. "We have learned the lesson well, but I would rather have stayed in a world where it was not true." I saw in her face that she had some clue to what she'd lost, to what her vampires had lost when she decided they would become as cruel as their enemies. "The Spaniards killed so many of our people along the road to Acachinanco that they tied white handkerchiefs over their noses because of the stench of rotting bodies."

She looked at me then, and the hatred in those eyes burned along my skin. After five hundred years, she still carried a grudge. You had to admire someone who could hold on to hate like that. I thought I knew how to hold a grudge, but looking into her face, I realized I was wrong. There was room in me for forgiveness. In Itzpapalotl's face there was room for only one thing, hatred. She'd been angry about the same thing for over five hundred years. She'd been punishing people for the same crimes for five hundred years. It was impressive in a psychotic sort of way.

I hadn't learned much more about the murders than when I'd stepped through the doors. I'd mostly learned negatives. A genuine Aztec didn't recognize the murders as the work of any god or cult associated with the Aztec pantheon. It was good to know, something to cross off the list. Police work is mostly negatives. Finding out what you don't know, so you can decide what you do. I didn't know anything positive about the murders, but I knew one thing for absolute certain as I listened to the outrage in her voice about atrocities older than the entire country we were sitting in. I never wanted this woman mad at me. I'd told people that I'd chase them into hell to have my vengeance, but I probably didn't mean it. Itzpapalotl would mean every word.

27

IT WAS STILL DARK as Edward drove us homeward. Still night, true dark, the vampires still roamed, but that soft edge in the air let you know the light is coming. If we hurried, we'd make it into bed before true dawn. If we dawdled, we'd get to see the sun come up. None of us seemed to be dawdling. We sat in the car in a silence that no one seemed willing to break.

We left the club behind and drove out into the hills beyond towards Santa Fe. Stars spread like a blanket of cold fire across the soft black silk of the sky. The sky had that larger than life, empty quality it gets over large bodies of water or in the desert.

Olaf's voice came out of the darkness, low and strangely intimate the way voices can be in a car at night. "If we'd accepted their hospitality, do you think I could have had the vampire they whipped?"

I raised an eyebrow. "Define have?" I said.

"Have, to do with as I liked."

"What would you have done with him if they had?" Bernardo said.

"You don't want to know, and I don't want to hear it," Edward said. He sounded tired.

"I thought you liked women, Olaf," Bernardo said it. I didn't say it, honest.

"For sex I like women, but so much blood. It shouldn't have gone to waste." He sounded wistful.

I turned in my seat and tried to see his face in the dark. "So it's not just women who have to be careful around you, is that it? Does it just have to bleed to be attractive?"

"Leave him alone, Anita. About this, leave him the fuck alone."

I turned to look at Edward. He rarely cussed, and he rarely sounded as tired and almost overwhelmed as he did now. "Okay, I mean, sure."

Edward glanced in the rearview mirror. There wasn't a car in either direction for miles. I think he was looking at Olaf. He stared into the mirror a long time. I think they had some major eye contact going.

He finally blinked and went back to staring at the road, but he didn't seem happy.

"What aren't you telling me?"

"Us," Bernardo said. "What isn't he telling us?"

"All right, what aren't you telling us?"

"It's not my secret to tell," Edward said, and that was all he'd say. He and Olaf had a secret, and they weren't willing to share.

We finished the rest of the drive in silence. The sky was still black, but it was a paler black, the stars dim in it. Dawn was tremblingly close when we went into the house. I was so tired, my eyes burned. But Edward took me by the arm and led me down the small hallway away from the bedrooms. He kept his voice low. "Be very careful of Olaf."

"He's big and bad. I get it."

He dropped his hand from my arm, shaking his head. "I don't think you do."

"Look, I know he's a convicted rapist. I saw the way he looked at Professor Dallas tonight, and I saw his reaction to the blood and torture. I don't know what you're not telling me, but I know that Olaf would hurt me if he could. I know that."

"You're afraid of him?"

I took a breath. "Yeah, I'm afraid of him."

"Good," Edward said. He hesitated then said, "You fit his vic profile."

"Excuse me?"

"His favorite victims are petite women, usually Caucasian, but always with long dark hair. I told you I would never have brought him in on this case if I'd known you were coming down, too. It isn't just because you're a woman. You're his physical ideal for a victim."

I stared at him for a few seconds, mouth opened, then closed it, and tried to think what to say. "Thanks for telling me, Edward. Shit. You should have told me this up front."

" I was hoping he could hold his act together, but I saw him tonight, too. I'm worried that he'll snap. I just don't want you to be the one in the way when it happens."

"Send him back to wherever he came from, Edward. We don't need him if he adds to the problem."

He shook his head. "No, he's got a specialty that's perfect for this case."

"And that specialty would be?"

He gave that small smile. "Go to bed, Anita. It's already dawn."

"No," I said, "almost, but not quite."

He studied my face. "You can really feel the sunrise without looking?"

I nodded. "Yep."

He looked at me, and it was as if he were trying to read me now. For the first time I felt that maybe, just maybe, Edward was as puzzled by me as I was by him, sometimes. He escorted me to my room and left me at the door like an overprotective date.

I was glad I'd prepared the room for safety before I left. If someone came through the window, they'd knock the dolls over or step on the mirror with its antlers. The door would have a chair and the suitcase in front of it. The room was as safe as it was going to get. I undressed, putting the guns and knives on the bed until I could decide exactly what was staying where for overnight. A man's extra large T-shirt that hung past my knees came out of the overnight bag. I'd started keeping one change of clothes, nightclothes, and toiletries in the overnight bag ever since the airline lost my luggage on a business trip. The last thing I pulled out of the overnight bag was my toy penguin Sigmund. I used to only sleep with Sigmund every so often, but lately, he'd been my constant companion under the sheets. A girl needs something to cuddle with at night.

The Browning Hi-Power was my other constant companion. At home it stayed in a holster I'd rigged to my headboard. Here I put it under my pillow, making very sure the safety was on. It always made me slightly nervous to put a loaded gun under my pillow. Seemed less than safe, but not nearly as unsafe as being unarmed if Olaf came through the door. I had brought four knives with me. One of them went between the mattresses. I put the Firestar back into the suitcase. I wanted something bigger than a handgun. I had a sawed-off shotgun and a mini-Uzi. Normally, I'd have brought more big guns, but I knew Edward would have more and better, and he would share. I finally decided on the mini-Uzi with a modified clip that held thirty rounds with enough humph to cut a vampire in half. It was a gift from Edward so the ammo was probably illegal, but then so was the gun. I'd been almost embarrassed about carrying it at first, but one night last August I used it for real. I'd pointed it at a vampire, pulled the trigger, and cut him in half. It had looked like his body was torn in half by some giant hand. His upper body had fallen slowly to one side. His lower body collapsed to its knees. I still had the vision of it like a slow motion image. There was no horror or regret. It was just a memory. The vampire had come with a hundred of his friends to kill us. I'd tried to kill one of them as messily as possible to get the rest to leave us alone. It hadn't worked, but that was only because the vampires were more afraid of their Master of the City than of me.

Maybe the Uzi was overkill for a human being, but if by some chance I emptied the Browning into Olaf's chest and he didn't go down, I wanted to make sure he didn't reach me. I'd cut him in half and see if the pieces could crawl.

28

IT WAS AFTER FIVE when I finally closed my eyes. Sleep sucked me under like a roll of black water, dragging me deep, and instantly into a dream. I stood in a dark place. There were small stunted trees everywhere, but they were dead. All the trees were dead. I could feel it.

Something crashed over to my right, something large moving through the trees, and a sense of dread rode before it like a wind. I ran, hands up to protect my face from the dry branches. I tripped over a root and went sprawling. There was a sharp pain in my arm. It was bleeding. Blood poured down it, but I couldn't find a wound.

The thing was getting closer. I could hear tree trunks snapping with sharp explosions. It was coming. It was coming for me. I ran, and ran, and ran, and the dead trees stretched out forever and there was no escape.

A typical chase dream, I thought, and the moment I thought it, I realized it was a dream, and the dream changed, faded into another dream. Richard standing in nothing but a sheet, one tanned muscled arm reaching out to me. His brown hair falling in a froth of waves around his face. I reached for him, and as my fingertips brushed his, a smile curving his lips, the dream shattered, and I woke.

I woke, blinking into a patch of sunlight that spilled across the bed. But it hadn't been the light that had woken me. There was a light tapping on my door. A man's voice. "Edward says get up."

It took me a moment to realize it was Bernardo's voice. It didn't take Freud to analyze the dream at the end with Richard in a sheet. I was going to have to be careful around Bernardo. Embarrassing, but true.

I sat up in bed, yelling through the door, "What time is it?"

"Ten."

"Okay, I'm coming."

I listened but didn't hear him walk away. Either the door was more solid than it looked, or Bernardo was quiet. If it had just been Edward, I'd have thrown on a pair of jeans under the over-sized T-shirt, and had some coffee. But there was company in the house and it was all male. I managed to get into the bathroom and dress without meeting anyone in the hallway. I was wearing dark blue jeans, a navy blue polo shirt, white jogging socks, and my black Nikes. Normally, I'd left the guns off until I went out into the big bad world, but at Edward's house the big bad world was staying in the next room, so I put the Firestar 9 mm in an inner pants holster, set for a right-handed cross draw. Brushed, cleaned, and armed, I wandered toward the smell of bacon.

The kitchen was small and narrow and white. But all the appliances were black, and the starkness of the contrast was almost too much first thing in the morning. There was another bouquet of wild flowers in the middle of a small white wooden table. Donna had struck again, but truthfully I agreed with her. The kitchen needed something to soften it.

The two men sitting at the table did nothing to humanize the room. Olaf had shaved so that the only hair left were the black lines of his eyebrows. He wore a black tank top, black dress slacks. Couldn't see the shoes, but I was betting on a monochrome look. He was also wearing a black shoulder rig with a big automatic of some kind. I didn't recognize the brand. A black-hilted knife was in a holster under his left arm.

Shoulder holsters chaff when you wear them with tank tops, but hey, it wasn't my problem.

Bernardo wore a white short-sleeved T-shirt and black jeans. He'd pulled the top layer of his hair back on either side with a large multi-colored barrette. There was still plenty of hair to fall down past his shoulders, stark and black against the pure whiteness of his shirt. He was wearing a ten mil Beretta just in back of his right hip. I couldn't see a knife on him, but I was betting it was there.

Edward was at the stove, emptying a pan of scrambled eggs onto two plates. He was also wearing black jeans with matching cowboy boots, and a white shirt that was a twin of the one he'd worn yesterday.

"Gee, guys, do I have to go back to my room and change?"

They all looked at me, even Olaf. "What you're wearing is fine," Edward said. He carried the plates to the table and put one in front of each of the empty chairs. There was a plate of bacon in the center of the table beside the flowers.

"But I don't match," I said.

Edward and Bernardo smiled. Olaf didn't. Big surprise. "You guys look like you're in uniform," I said.

"I guess we do," Edward said. He sat down in one of the empty chairs.

I sat in the other one. "You should have told me there was a dress code."

"We didn't do it on purpose," Bernardo said.

I nodded. "Which is what makes it funny."

"I am not changing clothes," Olaf said.

"No one's asking you to," I said. "I was making an observation." My eggs had bits of green and red things in them. "What's in the eggs?"

"Green peppers, red chilies, and diced ham," Edward said.

"Gee, Edward, you shouldn't have." I liked my scrambled eggs the way God intended them, plain. I pushed the eggs around with my fork, and reached for the bacon. Half the plate was barely cooked, the other half done to a crisp. I went for the crisp.

The bacon on Olaf's plate was the crispy kind, too. Oh, well.

I said grace over the food. Edward kept eating, but the others hesitated, uncomfortable with their mouths full. It's always fun to say grace at a table with people who don't. That uncomfortable silence. The panic while they wonder whether to keep chewing or to stop. I finished praying and took a bite of bacon. Yum. "What's the game plan for today?" I asked.

"You haven't finished looking at the files," Edward said.

Bernardo groaned.

"I think it is a waste of time," Olaf said. "We have gone over the files. I do not believe that she will find anything new."

"She's already done that," Edward said.

Olaf looked at him, a piece of bacon half way to his mouth. "What do you mean?"

Edward told them.

"That is nothing," Olaf said.

"It's more than you came up with," Edward said, quietly.

"If I am such a burden on this job, maybe I should leave," Olaf said.

"If you can't work with Anita, maybe you should."

Olaf stared at him. "You would rather have her as backup instead of me?" He sounded astonished.

"Yes," Edward said.

"I could break her in half over my knee," Olaf said. The astonishment was turning to anger. I suspected that most emotions turned into anger for Olaf.

"Maybe," Edward said, "but I doubt she'd give you the chance."

I held up my hand. "Don't make this a competition, Edward."

Olaf turned to me, slowly. He spoke very slowly, very clearly. "I do not compete with women."

"Afraid you can't measure up?" I asked. The moment I said it, I wished I hadn't. The momentary satisfaction wasn't worth the look on his face as he rose from his chair. I leaned into the table and drew the Firestar, pointing it in his general direction under the table.

Olaf stood, looming over me, like a muscular tree. "Edward has spent the morning talking to me about you. Trying to convince me that you are worth listening to." He shook his head. "You are a witch and I am not. The thing we hunt may be magical and we need your expertise. Maybe this is all true, but I will not be insulted by you."

"You're right," I said, "I'm sorry. It was a cheap shot."

He blinked at me. "You are apologizing?"

"Yes, on the rare, rare occasions when I'm wrong, I can apologize."

Edward was staring at me across the table.

"What?" I asked.

He just shook his head. "Nothing."

"Olaf's hatred of women is sort of a handicap, and I try not to make fun of people with handicaps."

Edward closed his eyes and shook his head. "You just couldn't leave it alone, could you?"

"I am not a cripple."

"If you hate anyone or anything with an unreasoning, uncompromising hatred, then you are blind where that hatred is concerned. The police kicked me out of a crime scene yesterday because the cop in charge is a right-winger squeaky-clean Christian, and he considers me devil spawn. So he'd rather more people get killed and mutilated than have me help him solve the case. He hates me more than he wants to catch this monster."

Olaf was still standing, but some of the tension had drained way. He seemed to actually be listening to me.

"Do you hate women more than you want to catch this monster?"

He looked at me, and for once his eyes weren't angry. They were thoughtful. "Edward called me because I am the best. I have never walked away from a job until the quarry was dead.

"And if it takes my preternatural expertise to help kill the monster, can you deal with that?"

"I don't like it," he said.

"I know that, but that's not what I asked. Can you handle my expertise helping you kill the monster? Can you take my help if it is the best thing for the job?"

"I don't know," he said. At least he was being honest, even reasonable. It was a start.

"The question, Olaf, is which do you love more: the kill or your hatred of women?"

I could feel Edward's and Bernardo's stillness. The room held its collective breath waiting for the answer.

"I would rather kill than do anything else," Olaf said.

I nodded. "Great, and thank you."

He shook his head. "If I take your help, it does not mean that I consider you my equal."

"Me either," I said.

Someone kicked me under the table. I think it was Edward. But Olaf and I nodded at each other, not exactly smiling, but I think we had a truce. If he could control his hatred, and I could control my smart-ass impulses, the truce might last long enough for us to solve the case. I managed to reholster the Firestar without him noticing, which made me think less of him. Edward had noticed, and I think, so had Bernardo. What was Olaf's specialty? What good was he if he didn't know where the guns were?

29

AFTER BREAKFAST WE HEADED back into the dining room. Bernardo had volunteered to do the dishes. I think he was looking for any excuse to get out of the paperwork. Though I was beginning to wonder if Bernardo had been as badly spooked by the mutilations as Edward had been. Even the monsters were afraid of this one.

Last night I'd been ready to look at the forensic reports next, but in the clear light of day I could admit that it was cowardice. Reading about it was not as bad as seeing it. I so did not want to look at the photos. I was afraid to see them, and the moment I admitted that to myself, I moved them to the top of the list.

Edward suggested we stick all the pictures on the walls of the dining room.

"And put pin holes in your nice clean walls," I said.

"Don't be barbaric," Edward said. "We'll use sticky putty." He held up a small packet of the pliable yellow rectangles. He peeled off some and handed it to Olaf and me.

I squeezed the stuff between my fingers, rolling it into a ball. It made me smile. "I haven't seen this stuff since elementary school."

The three of us spent the next hour putting the pictures up on the wall. Just handling the sticky putty made me remember fourth grade and helping Miss Cooper hang Christmas decorations on the walls.

We'd hung cheerful Santas, fat candy canes, and bright balls. Now I was hanging vivisected bodies, close-ups of skinless faces, shots of rooms full of body parts. By the time we had one wall covered I was mildly depressed. Finally, the pictures took up almost all the empty white wall space.

I stood in the center of the room and looked at it all. "Sweet Jesus."

"Too harsh for you?" Olaf asked.

"Back off, Olaf," I said.

He started to say something else but Edward said, "Olaf." It was amazing how much menace he could put into one ordinary word.

Olaf thought about it for a second or two, but in the end he let it go. Either Olaf was getting smarter or he was afraid of Edward, too. Guess which way I was voting.

We'd grouped the photos by crime scene in large clusters. This was my first glimpse of the bodies that had been torn apart.

Doctor Evans had described the bodies being cut by a blade of unknown origin, then disjointed by hand. But that had been a very clean description of what had actually been done.

At first, all my eyes could see was blood and pieces. Even knowing what I was looking at, my mind refused to see it at first. It was like looking at one of those 3-D pictures where at first it's just colors and dots, then suddenly you see it. Once you see it, you can't unsee it. My mind was trying to protect me from what I was looking at by just simply not allowing me to make sense of it. My mind was protecting me, and it only does that when it's bad, really, really bad.

If I had just walked out now before my eyes made sense of it, I might escape the full horror of it all. I could turn on my heel and march out of here. I could just refuse to take one more terror into my brain. Probably a good idea for my own sanity, but it wouldn't help the next family that this thing got hold of. It wouldn't stop the mutilations, the deaths. So I stood there and made myself stare up at the first picture, waiting to see what was really there.

The blood was brighter than movie blood, a cherry red. They'd gotten to this scene before the blood had started to dry.

I spoke without turning around. "How did the police find the bodies so quickly in this house? The blood is still fresh."

Edward answered, "The husband's parents were supposed to meet them for an early breakfast, before work."

I had to look away from the picture, at the floor. "You mean his parents found him like this?"

"It gets worse," Edward said.

"How could it possibly get worse?" I asked.

"The wife told her best friend she was pregnant. The breakfast meeting was to tell the husband's parents they were about to be grandparents for the first time."

The rug swam in my vision, like looking at it through water. I reached back for a chair and eased my way into it. I put my head between my knees and breathed very carefully.

"You all right?" Edward asked.

I nodded without raising up. I waited for Olaf to make a sarcastic remark, but he didn't. Either Edward had warned him off or he thought it was horrible, too.

When I was sure I wasn't going to throw up or faint, I spoke with my head still between my knees. "When did the parents arrive at the house? What time?"

I heard paper rustle. "Six thirty."

I rested my cheek against my knee. It felt good. "When did the sun come up?"

"I don't know," Edward said.

"Find out," I said. Gee, the rug on the floor was kind of pretty.

I raised up slowly, still practicing nice even breaths. The room did not swim. Good. "The grandparents-to-be arrived at six-thirty. It takes what, ten minutes, less, for them to recover enough to call the cops. Then uniforms arrive on the scene first. It could take thirty minutes or an hour, more, for a crime scene photographer to arrive, and yet the blood is still fresh. It hasn't dulled yet, let alone started to brown."

"The parents nearly walked in on it," Edward said.

"Yeah," I said.

"What difference does that make?" Olaf asked.

"If dawn was close to six-thirty, then the critter can be out in daylight, or it went to hole close to the murder scene. If it wasn't close to dawn, then it may be limited to darkness."

Edward was smiling down at me like a proud parent. "Even with your head between your knees, you're still thinking about the job."

"But what does it gain us," Olaf said, "if the creature is limited to darkness or daylight?"

I looked up at him. He was looming over me again, but I kept sitting down. Wouldn't look very macho if I stood up and fell down. "If it's limited to darkness, then it may help us figure out what kind of critter it is. There really aren't that many preternatural creatures that are limited exclusively to darkness. It would help narrow the list."

"And if it holed up near the first murder scene," Edward said, "we might find some traces."

I nodded. "Yeah."

"The police tramped over that area within an inch of its life," Olaf said. "Are you saying you can find something that they can't?" His arrogance was showing.

"With the first murder, especially, the police were looking for a human perpetrator. If you're looking for a human being, you look for different things than if it's a monster." I smiled. "Besides, if we didn't all think we could find things that the police couldn't, we wouldn't be here. Edward wouldn't have called us in, and the police wouldn't have shared the files with him."

Olaf frowned. "I have never seen you smile like this, Edward, unless you are pretending to be Ted. You took like a proud teacher whose pupil is doing well."

"More like Frankenstein with his monster," I said.

Edward thought about it for a second, then nodded and grinned, pleased with himself. "I like that."

Olaf frowned at both of us. "You did not create her, Edward."

"No," I said, "but he helped make me the woman I am today."

Edward and I looked at each other, and the smiles faded from both our faces, leaving us solemn. "Am I supposed to apologize for that?" he asked.

I shook my head. "Do you feel like apologizing for it?"

"No," he said.

"Then don't. I'm alive, Edward, and I'm here." I stood and didn't sway at all. Life was good.

"Let's find out if any of the killings took place after daylight. When I've looked at all this shit, let's go see some murder scenes." I looked at Edward. "If that's all right with you. You is the boss."

He gave a small nod. "That's fine, but to keep Ted working with the Santa Fe PD, we'll need to include them at the murder sites."

"Yeah," I said, "police don't like civvies mucking up their murder scenes, makes them testy."

"Besides, you're already persona non grata in Albuquerque," Edward said. "We've got to keep some of the cops willing to talk to you."

"And that's really bugging me," I said. "I'm barred from the freshest crime scenes, the newest evidence. I don't need another handicap on a case like this."

"You don't know what it is either, do you?" Edward said.

I shook my head, and sighed. "Not a damn clue." Bless his chauvinistic heart, but Olaf didn't say, I told you so.

I went back to staring at the pictures, and suddenly I could see it. I let out a breath, and said, softly, "Wow." The room seemed hot. Dammit, I was not going to have to sit down again. I put my fingertips on either side of the wall, steadying myself, but it must have looked like I was trying for a closer look. Trust me, I was as close as I ever wanted to get. I finally had to close my eyes for just a few seconds. When I opened them, I was okay or as okay as I was likely to be.

Body parts scattered like flower petals, stirred into a red mess. My eye flicked from one blood-covered lump to another. I was almost sure that was a forearm, and the ball of a knee joint showed whitely amid all the red. I'd never seen so many pieces before. I'd seen bodies torn apart before, but that had been for food or punishment. But there was a terrible completeness to this . . . destruction. I moved on to a shot of the same image but from a slightly different angle. I tried to put the body together in my head, but kept coming up short on parts.

I finally turned around. "There's no head and no hands." I pointed at small lumps in the blood. "Unless those are fingers. Was the body completely disjointed even down to the finger bones?"

Edward nodded. "Every victim has been almost completely dismembered down to the joints."

"Why?" I asked. I looked at Edward. "Where's the head?"

"They found it down the hill behind the house. The brain was missing."

"How about the heart?" I asked. "I mean there's the spine, almost intact, but I don't see any viscera. Where are all the internal organs?"

"They didn't find them," Edward said.

I leaned back, half-sitting on the table. "Why take the internal organs? Did they eat them? Is it part of some magical ritual? Or is it just part of the ritual of the killing itself, a souvenir?"

"There are a lot of organs in the body," Olaf said. "You put them all in one container and they can be heavy, bulky. They also rot very quickly unless you put them in some form of preservative."

I looked at him, but he wasn't looking at me. He was looking at the pictures. He hadn't given a lot of detail, but something in the way he said it made him sound like he knew what he was talking about.

"And how do you know how heavy the internal organs of a human body can be?"

"He could have worked in a morgue," Edward said.

I shook my head. "But he didn't, did you, Olaf."

"No," he said, and now he was looking at me. His eyes had been turned into two dark caves by the deep set of his face and a trick of light, or would that be darkness. He stared down at me, and without seeing his eyes I could feel the intensity of that stare, as if I were being studied, measured, dissected.

I kept my gaze on Olaf, but asked, "What is his specialty, Edward? Why did you call him in on this particular case?"

"The only person I've ever seen do anything close to this, is him," Edward said.

I glanced at him, and his face was calm. I turned back to Olaf. "I was told you went to jail for rape, not murder."

He looked right at me and said, "The police arrived too soon."

A cheerful voice called out from the front of the house. "Ted, it's us." It was Donna, and the "us" could only mean the kids.

Edward left at a goodly walk, trying to head her off. I think Olaf and I might have still been staring at each other when she walked in on us, but Bernardo came in, and said, "We're supposed to hide the pictures."

"How?" Olaf asked.

I took the candelabra off the table and said, "Put the table cloth over the door." I stood aside and let Bernardo drag it off the table.

Olaf said, "Aren't you going to help him? You are one of the boys, after all."

"I'm not tall enough to hold it up over the entire door," I said.

He gave a small smile, derisive, but he moved up to help Bernardo block the open doorway with the tablecloth.

I was left standing behind them with the black iron candelabra in my hands. I stared at the tall, bald man and was half-regretful that I wasn't tall enough to smash the heavy iron candelabra into his skull. Just as well. I'd owe Edward another favor if I killed one of his backups just because he'd scared me.

30

I COULD HEAR EDWARD in his best consoling Ted voice, trying to convince her that she didn't need to say Hi to everyone. She argued, polite, but firm, that of course she did. The more he tried to keep her away, the more she wanted to see. Call it a hunch, but I was betting it was me she wanted to see. The house was arranged so that you couldn't enter the three guest bedrooms without going through the dining room. Donna wanted to make sure where I was, and that I hadn't been in anyone's bed but my own. Or at least not in Ted's. Did she think that I was racing ahead of them to my room to throw clothes over my nakedness? Whatever the motive, she was coming this way. I heard Becca's voice.

Shit. I ducked under the rug across the door and nearly ran into them. Donna stopped walking with a small oomph of surprise. Her eyes were wide as she looked at me as if I'd scared her. Peter was watching me with cool brown eyes, as if it was all too boring for words, but underneath the perfect teenage boredom was a light, an interest. Everybody wondered why the tablecloth was in front of the doorway.

It was Becca who said it. "Why is the rug in front of the door?" I kept calling it a tablecloth because that's what Edward was using it for, but it still looked like a rug. Kids stick to the basics.

Donna looked at Edward. "Yes, Ted, why is the tablecloth in front of the door."

"Because we're holding it," Bernardo said from behind the improvised curtain.

She stepped close to the cloth. "And why are you holding it?"

"Ask Ted," Bernardo and Olaf said together.

Donna turned back to Edward. I usually know what Edward will say, but with Donna I was out of guesses.

"We've got the pictures from the case spread all over the room. They aren't something I want you or the kids to see." Gee, he went for the truth. It must be true love.

"Oh," she said. She seemed to think about it for a second or two, then nodded. "Becca and I will take the goodies through to the kitchen." She lifted a white, string-wrapped box, took Becca by the hand and went towards the kitchen. Becca was straining backwards, saying, "But, Mommy, I want to see the pictures."

"No, you don't, sweetie," Donna said, and very firmly led the child away.

I thought that Peter would follow but he stood there, looking at the doorway, then glanced at Edward. "What kind of pictures?" he asked.

"Bad ones," Edward said.

"How bad?"

"Anita," Edward said.

"Some of the worst I've seen, and I've seen some awful stuff," I said.

"I want to see," Peter said.

I said, "No."

Edward said nothing, just looked at him.

Peter scowled at us. "You think I'm a baby."

"I wouldn't want your mom to see them either," Edward said.

"She's a wimp," he said.

I agreed with him, but not out loud.

"Your mother is who she is," Edward said. "It doesn't make her weak. It just makes her Donna."

I stared at him, trying very hard not to gape, but I wanted to. I'd never heard him cut anyone any slack for anything. Edward was not just judgmental. He was a harsh judge. What chemical alchemy did the woman have to have won him over? I just did not get it.

"I think what . . . Ted is trying to say is that it isn't your age that makes us not want to show you the pictures."

"You think I can't handle it," Peter said.

"Yeah," I said, "I think you can't handle it."

"I can handle anything that you can handle," he said, arms crossed over his thin chest.

"Why? Because I'm a girl?"

He actually blushed, as if embarrassed. "I didn't mean that." But of course he had. But, hey, he was fourteen. I'd let it slide.

"Anita is one of the toughest people I've ever met," Edward said.

Peter squinted at him, arms still hugging his chest. "Tougher than Bernardo?"

Edward nodded.

"Tougher than Olaf?" And I thought more of the kid that he'd put the two men in that order. He knew instinctively which was the scariest man, or maybe it was just Olaf's size. No, I think Peter had a feel for the bad guys. It's something you either have or you don't. It can't really be taught.

"Even tougher than Olaf," Edward said.

There was a disgruntled sound from behind the rug. The sound of Olaf's ego getting bruised.

Peter looked at me, and the look had changed. You could almost see him thinking, trying to put my petite female self in the same category as Olaf's aggressive male presence. He finally shook his head. "She doesn't look as tough as Olaf."

"If you mean arm wrestling, I'm not."

He frowned and turned back to Edward. "I don't understand."

"I think you do," Edward said, "and if you don't, I can't explain it to you."

Peter's frown deepened.

"Part of the problem with the tough-guy code," I said, "is that a lot of it can't be explained."

"But you understand it," Peter said. He sounded almost accusatory.

"I've spent a lot of my time around very tough guys."

"That's not it," Peter said. "You're different from any girl I've ever met."

"She's different from any girl you will ever meet," Edward said.

Peter looked from one to the other of us. "Mom's jealous of her."

"I know," Edward said.

Bernardo's voice came from inside the room. "Can we lower the rug now?"

"Don't tell me you tough he-men are getting tired," I said.

"Lactic acid builds up in everybody's muscles, chickie," Bernardo said.

I'd started the name calling so I let the "chickie" comment go. "You need to join your mom and Becca in the kitchen," I said.

"Do I?" He was looking at Edward, and I realized he was appealing to Edward, asking permission.

"Yes," I said and looked at Edward, trying to tell him with my eyes, not to do this.

But he had eyes only for the boy. They stared at each other, and something passed between, some knowledge, something. "Drop the cloth," Edward said.

"No," I said and grabbed Peter's arm. I spun him around, so his back was to the door. I'd caught him by surprise, so he didn't struggle. Before he could decide what to do about me, Edward spoke. "Let him go, Anita."

I looked at him around Peter's shoulder and realized he was taller than me by a few inches. "Don't do this."

"He wants to see. Let him see."

"Donna won't like it," I said.

"Who's going to tell her?"

I looked into Peter's dark eyes. "He will when he gets mad enough at you or her or both."

"I wouldn't do that," Peter said.

I shook my head. I didn't believe him, and that more than anything made me let go of his arm and back off. If Edward showed Peter this little corner of hell and word got back to Donna, it might be enough to break them up permanently. I was willing to trade some of Peter's innocence for that. Harsh, but true.

The rug fell away on Olaf's side first, then Bernardo was left holding the rug in his arms like a limp child. He looked at Edward and shook his head, but he stepped back beside Olaf and let Peter walk into the room. I followed behind him and Edward.

Olaf had moved back near the far door. Bernardo laid the cloth on the table and stepped back to the far end of the table. I took up station to the far wall, almost mirroring Olaf, but at the opposite door. We'd all moved to separate corners of the room, and all of us tried to separate ourselves from what was happening. I don't think even Olaf approved.

Peter took in all the pictures, turning around and around. He paled, and his voice was a little breathy. "Are those people?"

"Yes," Edward said. He stayed right beside Peter, not touching, not too close, but very definitely with him.

Peter walked to the nearest wall, to the pictures I'd just been looking at. "What happened to them?" he asked.

"We don't know yet," Edward said.

Peter looked at the pictures, eyes flicking from one horrible image to another. He didn't walk the room or study any one picture as closely as I had, but he looked, he saw what was there. He didn't scream or faint or throw up. He'd proven his point. He wasn't a wimp. I wondered if I should warn him about the possibility of nightmares. Nay, he'd either have them or he wouldn't.

He was still pale, with a light dew of sweat on his upper lip, but he was mobile, and his voice was breathy, but calm. "I better help Mom in the kitchen." He walked out still hugging his arms around himself as if he were cold.

No one said a word as he walked out. When I was pretty sure he was out of ear shot, I walked up to Edward. "Well, that went better than I thought it would."

"It went about the way I thought it would," Edward said.

"Shit, Edward, the kid is going to have nightmares."

"Maybe, maybe not. Pete's a tough kid." He was looking out through the doorway as if he could still see the boy. His gaze was faraway.

I stared at him. "You're proud of him. Proud of the fact that he looked at this," I motioned at the pictures, "and didn't freak."

"Why shouldn't he be proud?" Olaf asked.

I looked at him. "If Edward were Peter's dad, maybe. But he's not." I turned back to Edward. I stared at him. His face was its usual blankness, but there was a flinching around the eyes.

I touched his arm, and the touch was enough. He looked at me. "You're treating him like a prospective son." I shook my head. "You cannot have this family."

"I know that," he said.

"I don't think you do," I said. "I think you're actually beginning to think about doing it, for real."

He dropped his gaze, not meeting my eyes.

"Shit, Edward, shit."

"I hate to admit it, but I agree with her," Olaf said. "If it was just the boy, then I would see no problem. I think you can make of him what you will, but the woman and the girl . . ." He shook his head. "It will not work."

"I don't understand why you even want a family," Bernardo said.

"For different reasons. Neither of you believe in marriage," Edward said.

"True," Olaf said, "but if men like us do marry, it should not be a woman like Donna. She is too . . ." he struggled for a word, and finally said, "innocent. And you know that I do not say that about many women."

"Maybe that's one of her attractions," Edward said, and he seemed as truly puzzled as the rest of us.

"You're already screwing her. Why marry her?" This from Bernardo.

"If all I wanted was sex, I'd have gone elsewhere," Edward said.

"She any good?" Bernardo asked.

Edward just looked at him, one long look.

Bernardo raised his hands. "Sorry, sorry, just curious."

"Don't be curious about Donna," Edward said. He turned to me. "You believe in marriage. Underneath all that toughness is a midwestern girl that still believes in the white picket fence."

"I do believe in marriage, but not for people like us, Edward."

I don't know what he would have said to that, because the phone rang and he went to answer it.

"Saved by the bell," I said.

"He intends to marry this woman," Olaf said.

I nodded. "I'm afraid so."

"If he wants to marry her, it's his business," Bernardo said.

Olaf and I stared at him until the smile on his face faded to a look of puzzlement.

"What?"

"Olaf may be a serial rapist, Bernardo, or even a serial killer, but in his own twisted way he has more scruples than you do. Doesn't that worry you?"

Bernardo shook his head. "No."

I sighed.

Edward came back into the room. His face was back to his normal "Edward face," as if all the near revelations of just a minute ago had never happened. "The monster did another couple in Albuquerque last night."

"Shit," I said. "Are you going without me?"

Edward was watching my face just a little too closely, so I knew there was a surprise coming. "Your presence has been requested on site."

I could feel the surprise on my face. "Is Lieutenant Marks not in charge anymore?"

"It was him on the phone."

"You're kidding me," I said.

Edward shook his head and smiled.

"I don't get it."

"I'd guess that someone up the feeding chain chewed his ass for kicking you out. They probably gave him a choice of working with you, or being off the case."

I had to smile. "A case like this can make a career."

"Exactly," Edward said.

"Well, we know Marks' price now."

"Price?" Bernardo asked. "You guys bribed him?"

"No," I said, "but his principles that he so kindly spat in my face yesterday weren't as precious to him as his career. Always nice to know how strong a person's convictions are."

"Not that strong," Edward said.

"Apparently not," I said.

I heard Donna coming down the hallway, talking loudly to Becca, but I think it was to warn us that they were coming. The men grabbed the rug and went for the doorway. Edward said in his loud, cheerful Ted voice, "Saddle up, boys and girls. We got work to do."

I went for my room. If we were going to go outside the house, I needed more weapons.

31

I SAT IN THE front seat beside Edward. It was probably my imagination but I could feel someone staring at the back of my neck. If I wasn't imagining it, I was betting on Olaf.

I'd added the shoulder holster complete with Browning Hi-Power. Usually, it was the only gun I wore until someone tried to kill me, or some monster showed in the flesh. But I'd kept the Firestar in its inner pants holster. Too many pictures of dismembered corpses for comfort. I even took all the knives, which tells you how insecure I was feeling. Being stared at hard enough to bore a hole through my flesh was beginning to get on what nerves I had left. It wasn't my imagination. I could feel it.

I turned in the seat and met Bernardo's eyes. There was a look on his face when I turned around that was nothing I wanted to see. I had an uncomfortable thought that he was fantasizing and I just might be in the starring role.

"What are you staring at?" I asked.

He blinked, but it seemed to take a long time for his eyes to really focus on me rather than whatever was inside his head. He gave a slow, almost lazy smile. "I wasn't doing anything."

"Like hell," I said.

"You can't tell me what to think, Anita," he said.

"You're presentable enough. Go get a date."

"I'd have to wine and dine her, and then I couldn't count on sex at the end of the evening. What good is that?"

"Then get a hooker," I said.

"I would if Edward would let me out on my own."

I turned and looked at Edward.

He answered the question without me having to voice it. "I've forbidden Olaf from . . . dating while he's here. Olaf resented it, so I told Bernardo the same thing."

"Very even handed," I said.

"It is totally unfair to punish me because Olaf is a psycho," Bernardo said.

"If I cannot meet my needs, then why should you be able to?" Olaf said. There was something in his voice that made me look at him. He was staring straight ahead, no eye contact to anyone.

I turned around in my seat and looked at Edward. "Where do you come up with these people?"

"The same place I find vampire hunters and necromancers," he said.

He had a point. Enough of a point that we finished the drive to Albuquerque in silence. I felt I had enough moral high ground to throw stones, but evidently

Edward disagreed. Since he knew Olaf better than I did, I wasn't going to argue. At least not now.

People talk of ranch-style houses, but this really was a ranch. A ranch as in cowboys and horses. It was a dude ranch for tourists so whether it counted as a really real ranch, I wasn't sure. But it was the closest thing to an actual working ranch that I'd ever set foot on.

The ranch really wasn't in Albuquerque, but in the middle of nowhere. In fact the house and corrals sat in the middle of a whole lot of nothing. Empty space with bunches of dry grass and strange palish soil stretching out and out to the horizon. Hills ringed the ranch like smooth piles of rock and brush. Edward drove us under an entrance that had a cow's skull nailed to it and said, "Dead Horse Ranch." It was so similar to a hundred western movies I'd seen on television that it seemed vaguely familiar.

Even the corral full of horses spilling in an endless nervous circle seemed stage-managed. The house wasn't exactly what I had pictured, being low to the ground and made of white adobe much like Edward's house but newer. If you could have just erased the plethora of police cars, emergency units, and even some fire rescue equipment, it would have been picturesque in a lonesome down-on-the-prairie sort of way.

A lot of the police cars had revolving lights, and the crackle of police radios was thick in the air. I wondered if it was the lights, the noise, or just this many people making the horses nervous. I didn't know much about horses, but surely rushing back and forth around their pen wasn't normal behavior. I wondered if they had been running in circles before the cops came or after. Were horses likes dogs? Could they sense bad things? Didn't know, didn't even know who to ask.

We were stopped just inside the gate by a uniformed cop. He took our names and went off to find someone who would let us pass, or find someone to tell him to kick us out. I wondered if Lieutenant Marks was here. Since he'd issued the invite, it seemed likely. What kind of threat to his career had they used to get him to invite me back?

We waited. None of us spoke. I think we'd all spent a lot of our adult lives waiting for one uniform or another to give us permission to do things. It used to get on my nerves, but lately I just waited. Maturity, or was I just getting too worn down to argue over small stuff? I'd have liked to say maturity, but I was pretty sure that wasn't it.

The uniform came back with Marks trailing behind him. Marks' pale tan suit jacket flapped in the hot wind, giving a glimpse of his gun riding just behind his left hip. He stared at the ground as he walked, briskly, all business, but he was careful not to look at us, at me, maybe.

The uniform got to us first, but he stood a little back from the open driver's side door and let the lieutenant catch up. Marks finally got there, and he looked fixedly at Edward, as if he could exclude me by just not looking at me.

"Who are the men in the back?"

"Otto Jefferies, and Bernardo Spotted-Horse." I noticed that Olaf had to use an alias, but Bernardo got to keep his real name. Guess who was wanted for crimes elsewhere.

"What are they?"

I wouldn't have known how to answer that question but Edward did. "Mr.

Spotted-Horse is a bounty hunter like myself, and Mr. Jefferies is a retired government worker."

Marks looked at Olaf through the glass. Olaf looked back. "Government worker. What sort of government worker?"

"The kind that if you contacted the state department, they'd confirm his identity."

Marks tapped on Olaf's window.

Olaf rolled the window down with the nearly silent buttons on the door handles. "Yes," he said in a voice that was totally devoid of his usual German burr.

"What did you do for the state department?"

"Call them and ask," Olaf said.

Marks shook his head. "I have to let you and Blake inside my crime scene, but not these two." He jerked a thumb at the back seat. "They stay in the car."

"Why?" Bernardo said.

Marks looked at him through the open window. His blue green eyes were mostly green right now, and I was beginning to realize that meant he was angry. "Because I said so, and I've got a badge and you don't."

Well, at least it was honest.

Edward spoke before Bernardo could do more than make inarticulate noises. "It's your crime scene, Lieutenant. We civilians are just here on your sufferance, we know that." He twisted in his seat to give the two men direct eye contact, but turned so Marks couldn't see his face well. I could, and it was cold and full of warning. "They will be happy to stay in the car. Won't you, boys?"

Bernardo slumped in his seat, arms crossed on his chest, sulking, but he nodded. Olaf just said, "Of course, whatever the good officer says." His voice was mild, empty. The very lack of tone was frightening, as if he were thinking something very different from the words.

Marks frowned but stepped back from the car. His hand hovered around his body as if he had a sudden desire to touch his gun, but didn't want to appear spooked. I wondered what had been in Olaf's eyes when he spoke those mild words. Something not mild, that I was certain of.

The uniformed cop had detected something in Marks. He stepped closer to his lieutenant, one hand on the butt of his gun. I didn't know what had changed in Olaf, but he was suddenly making the cops nervous. He hadn't moved. Only his face was turned towards them. What was he doing with just his facial expression that had them so jumpy?

"Otto," Edward said softly, so that the sound didn't carry outside the car. But as he had in the house when he said, Olaf, that one word carried a menace, a promise of dire consequence.

Olaf blinked and turned his head slowly towards Edward. The look on his face was frightening, feral somehow, as if he'd let down his mask enough to show some of the madness inside. But as I looked at him, I thought this was a face to deliberately frighten people, a sort of tease. Not the real monster, but a monster that people could understand and fear without thinking too hard.

Olaf blinked and looked out the far window, face bland and as inoffensive as it got.

Edward turned the car off and handed his keys to Bernardo. "In case you want to listen to the radio."

Bernardo frowned at him, but took the keys. "Gee, thanks, Dad."

Edward turned back to the police officers. "We're ready to go when you are, Lieutenant." He opened his door as he said it. The door swinging open made Marks and the uniform take a step or so back.

I took it as my cue and got out on my side. It wasn't until I came around the front of the Hummer in full sight that Marks finally paid attention to me. He stared at me, and his face was harsh. He could manage not to show outright hatred in his face, but he couldn't manage neutral. He didn't like me being here. He didn't like it one little bit. Who had twisted his tail in a knot hard enough to force him to let me back on board?

He opened his mouth as if he'd say something, closed it, and just started walking towards the house. The uniformed officer followed at his heels, and Edward and I trailed behind. Edward had his good ol' boy face on, smiling and nodding to the police officers, the emergency workers, everyone and everything in his path. I just stayed at his side, trying not to frown. I didn't know anybody here, and I'd never been comfortable greeting strangers like long-lost friends.

There were a lot of cops outside in the yard. I spotted at least two different uniforms, enough plainclothes to open up a discount men's store, and some plainclothes detectives that stood out. I don't know what they do during FBI training that is different from anywhere else, but you can usually spot them. The clothes are slightly different, more uniform, less individual than with regular cops, but it's more an aura about them. An air of authority as if they know that their orders come straight from God and yours don't. I used to think it was insecurity on my part, but since I'm rarely insecure, that can't be it. Whatever "it" was, they had it. The Feds had arrived. That could speed things up, be a big help, or slow things to a crawl and fuck up what little progress had already been made. It depended almost entirely on how the police in charge got along with each other, and how protective everyone was of their turf.

These crimes were gruesome enough that we might actually see some cooperation between jurisdictions. Miracles do happen.

Usually, when there's a body on the ground, the police of whatever flavor are inside at the scene walking on the evidence. But there were too many people out here. There couldn't possibly be that many more inside the house. The house was big, but not that big.

Only one thing would keep them out in the New Mexico heat. The scene was a bad one. Gory, piteous, frightening, though no one will admit out loud to that one. Pick an adjective, but the police milled around the yard in the heat with their ties, the women in high heels on the loose gravel. Cigarettes had appeared in a lot of hands. They talked in small hushed voices that didn't carry above the crackle of radios. They huddled in small groups, or sat alone on the edge of cars, but not for long. Everyone kept moving, as if to remain still was to think and that was a bad thing. They reminded me of the horses nervously running in circles.

A uniformed police officer was sitting at the open doors of the ambulance. The emergency medical technician was bandaging his hand. How had he gotten hurt? I hurried to catch up with Marks. If he were the man in charge, he'd know what had happened. Edward just fell into step behind me, no questions, just following my lead. He had ego problems with me sometimes, but on the job there was nothing but the job. You left the shit outside the door. You could always pick it up on your way back out.

I caught up with Marks on the long narrow wraparound porch. "What happened to the uniform that's getting his hand bandaged?"

Marks stopped in mid-stride and looked at me. His eyes were still a hard, pitiless green. You always think of green eyes as being pretty or soft, but his were like green glass. He had a big hate on for me, a big one.

I smiled sweetly and thought, fuck you, too. But I'd learned lately to lie even with my eyes. It was almost sad that I could lie with my eyes. They really are the mirror to the soul, and once they go, you are damaged. Not beyond repair, but damaged.

We stared at each other for a second or two, his hatred like a fine burning weight, my pleasant smiling mask. He blinked first, like there'd been any doubt. "One of the survivors bit him."

My eyes widened. "Are the survivors still inside?"

He shook his head. "They're on their way to the hospital."

"Anybody else get hurt?" When you ask that at a scene where vics are down, you almost always mean other cops.

Marks nodded, and some of the hostility drained from his eyes leaving them puzzled. "Two other officers had to be taken to the hospital."

"How bad?" I asked.

"Bad. One nearly got his throat ripped out."

"Have any of the other mutilation vics been that violent?"

"No," he said.

"How many vics were there?"

"Two, and one dead, but we're missing at least three other people, maybe five. We've got a couple unaccounted for, but other guests heard them talking about a picnic earlier. We're hoping they missed the show."

I looked at him. He was being very helpful, very professional. "Thank you, Lieutenant."

"I know my job, Ms. Blake."

"I never said otherwise."

He looked at me, then at Edward, then finally settled his gaze on me. "If you say so." He turned abruptly and walked through the open door behind him.

I looked at Edward. He shrugged. We followed Marks in, though I noticed we'd lost the uniformed officer somewhere in the walk across the yard. No one was spending more time inside than they had to.

The living room looked as if someone had taken white liquid and poured it down to form the sloping walls, the curved doorways leading away into the house, the freeform fireplace. There was a bleached cow skull above the fireplace. A brown leather couch wrapped a huge nearly perfect square in front of the cold fire. There were pillows with Native American prints on them. A huge rug that looked almost identical to one of Edward's took up most of the center of the floor. In fact the entire place looked like an updated version of Edward's place. Maybe I still hadn't seen Edward's sense of style. Maybe this was just a type of southwestern style that I'd just never seen.

There was a large open section that had been a dining room area. The table was still there. There was even a chandelier formed of what looked to be deer antlers. There was a pile of white, red-soaked cloth to one side of the table. Blood was seeping out of the bottom of the cloth bundle, leaking across the polished hardwood floor in tiny rivulets of crimson and darker fluids.

A photographer was snapping pictures of something on the table. My view was hidden by three suit-covered backs. Panic clawed at my throat, and it was suddenly harder to breathe. I didn't want the men to move. I did not want to see what was on the table. My heart was pounding in my throat, and I had to take a deep, shaking breath, clearing my throat. The deeper breath had been a mistake. The smell of fresh death is like a cross between an outhouse and a slaughterhouse. There was an acrid stink, and I knew the intestines had been perforated. But there was another smell under the almost sweet smell of too much blood. A smell of meat. I'd tried to find other words for it, but it was the closest I could come to describing it. It was like drowning in the scent of raw hamburger. Meat, a person reduced to so much meat.

That one smell made me want to run. To just turn on my heel and walk away. This was not my job. I was not a cop. I was here as a favor to Edward. If I left now, he could bill me. But of course, it was too late. Because I wasn't here just because of a favor to anyone now. I was here to help stop this from happening again. And that was more important than any nightmares I was about to accumulate.

A thin heavy line of liquid oozed off the edge of the table and fell slowly to the floor with a sparkle of crimson from the bright chandelier. The short man in the middle turned and caught a glimpse of us. His face was grim, but when he caught sight of us, of me, something close to a smile curled his lips. He left the others grouped around the table and came towards us. He was short for an FBI agent, but Special Agent Bradley Bradford walked with a confident swinging stride that covered ground and made taller men sometimes have to hurry to keep up.

We'd met over a year ago in Branson, Missouri, on a vampire case that had turned out to be vampires plus a little something older and less local. People had died, but mostly the monsters had died. Bradford must have been happy with my performance because he kept in touch. I knew that he was now assigned to the new FBI preternatural division. Last I heard they were calling it the Special Research Section, just like the Serial Killer Profiler unit was now called Investigative Support. The FBI tries to avoid sensational buzzwords like serial killer or preternatural or monster. But call it what you like, a spade's a spade.

He started to put his hand forward to be shaken, then stopped. His hands were encased in plastic gloves splattered with blood, and a spot on one side that was too black, too thick, to be blood. He smiled an apology as he lowered his hands.

I knew who had twisted Marks' tail and gotten me back in the ball game. I took shallow, even breaths and tried not to embarrass him. I hadn't thrown up at a murder scene in nearly two years. Be a shame to spoil my record now.

"Anita, it's good to see you again."

I nodded and felt myself smile. I was happy to see Bradley, but . . . "We really need to start meeting when there aren't bodies on the ground." See, light, joking, I could be cool. I was also delaying the final walk to what lay on the table. I could do semi-clever repartee all damn day if I just didn't have to see what was bleeding in the dining room.

Why was this one getting to me so badly? No answer, but it was.

Another agent joined us. He was tall, slender, skin actually dark enough to be called black. His hair was cut close to his head in a low, well-groomed wedge. He straightened his tie, and settled his coat in place with long-fingered hands that seemed to dance even in these small movements. I'm not one of those women who notices hands usually, but there was something about his that made me think poet, musician, as if he did other things with them besides shooting practice.

"Special Agent Franklin, this is Ted Forrester and Anita Blake."

He shook hands with Edward, but didn't answer the Ted smile with one of his own. He turned serious eyes to me. His hand was enough longer than mine that shaking was a little awkward, but we managed. But it was somehow an unsatisfying handshake as if we still didn't have the measure of each other. Some men still use a handshake as a way of sizing you up.

"How long have you been in the house, Ms. Blake?" he asked.

"Just got here," I said.

He nodded as if it were important. "Bradford has painted a glowing picture of you." There was something in his voice that made me say . . .

"I take it you don't share Bradford's opinion of me." I smiled when I said it.

He blinked and looked startled, then his shoulders relaxed just a touch, and a very small smile played across his lips. "Let's say I'm skeptical of civilians with no special training coming into a crime scene."

I raised eyebrows at the "no special training." Edward and I exchanged glances. The Ted face was slipping, letting some of his own natural cynicism leak into those blue eyes, that nearly boyish face.

"Civilians," he said softly.

"We don't have badges," I said.

"That must be it," he said, voice still soft, and vaguely amused.

Franklin frowned at us. "Are we amusing you?"

Bradford stepped between us almost literally. "Let's let them look at the scene, then we'll decide things."

Franklin's frown deepened. "I don't like it."

"Your objection has been noted, Franklin," Bradford said, and there was a tone in his voice that said he'd had enough of the younger man.

Franklin must have heard it too, because he smoothed his perfect tie once more and led the way towards the dining room. Bradford followed him. Edward looked at me, asking a question with his eyes.

"I'm coming," I said. Once I'd tried being more macho than the police. Nothing phased me. I was heap-big-vampire-slayer. But lately, I just didn't give a crap. I didn't want to do this anymore. It was almost a shock to realize that I really didn't want to be here. I'd seen too many horrors in too short a space of years. I was burning out, or maybe I'd already burned out and hadn't realized it.

Panic tightened my stomach into a hard knot. I had to get it under control. I had to separate myself from the task ahead, or I was going to lose it. I tried to take a few calming breaths, but the smell came thick on my tongue. I swallowed, wished I hadn't, and stared at the tips of my shoes. I stared at the ends of my Nikes as they touched the fringe of the dining room rug until the knot in my gut eased, and I felt calm. There was still a soft flutter in my chest, but it was the best I could do.

Agent Franklin said, "Ms. Blake, are you all right?"

I raised my eyes and saw what lay on the table.

32

I LET OUT a low, "Wow."

"Yes," Bradford said, "wow is good."

The table was pale natural pine, a pale, almost white wood. It matched the walls and the rest of the decor and made a dramatic showpiece for the thing on the table. Thing, it, no other pronouns would do. Distance, distance, mustn't think that this was once a human being.

At first all I could see was the blood and pieces of meat. It was like a jigsaw puzzle with pieces missing. The first thing I was sure of was the neck. I could see the broken edge of the spine sticking up above the flesh of the neck. I looked around for the head, but none of the blood-covered lumps was the right size. But there was a leg nearly perfectly whole, only ripped away from the hips, but it was intact. It had not been disjointed. Once I saw that, I found a hand lying on its back, fingers cupped as if cradling something.

I bent closer, hands in my pockets because I'd forgotten my own surgical gloves back in St. Louis. How unprofessional of me. I leaned over the hand and I wasn't smelling the stink anymore. I wasn't thinking oh, my, God, how awful. The world narrowed down to a nickel-sized lump cupped in the hand. I saw what was there. The hand had long, carefully groomed fingernails, some broken off, as if she'd struggled. She. I looked to the ring finger and found a wedding band set that looked heavy and expensive, though to be sure I'd have to move the hand and I wasn't ready for that yet. I registered all the information as if from a great distance because I'd found a clue. I concentrated on that like it was a life line, and maybe it was.

"There's something in her hand. It may be only a piece of cloth, but . . ." I bent so low over it that my breath caressed the skin and brought a scent up from it to me. Musty, an animal smell. My breath did one other thing. It moved the edge of the thing in her hand. The one tiny edge wasn't as blood-logged, and it moved as I blew across the hand.

I straightened. "I think it's a feather." I looked around the room trying to see where it could have come from. Except for the antler chandelier nothing else in the room seemed made of animals.

Bradford and Franklin looked at each other. "What?" I asked.

"What made you say her?" Franklin asked.

"The nails, the wedding ring set." I glanced up at the rest of the body. The only other clue that this had been a woman was maybe the size of the neck, dainty. "She was small, about my size, maybe a little smaller." I heard myself say it and felt nothing. I felt empty like a shell thrown up on the sand, empty and echoing. It felt a little bit like being in shock, and I knew that later I'd pay for it. Either I'd have screaming hysterics once I had some privacy, or . . . I'd broken something in myself that might never come back, might never fix.

"Besides the fact that it's female, what else do you see?" Franklin asked.

I didn't like being tested, but somehow I just didn't have the energy to bitch about it. "The other vics were disjointed down to their finger bones. This one isn't. When I first heard that survivors were being carefully skinned, then mutilated, and that the dead were all torn apart, I thought we might be dealing with a pair of killers. One very organized and in charge, the other disorganized and following. But the bodies weren't torn up. They were very carefully dissected. It was organized, very thought out. But this . . ." I motioned at the thing on the table. "This was not organized. Either our organized killer is beginning to dissolve and become less coherent, or we have two killers like I originally thought. If we have two killers, then the organized one in charge has lost control over his follower. This murder was not well planned. That means mistakes, which will help us. But it may also mean that anyone that crosses paths with this thing is dead. Higher body count from here on out, more frequent kills maybe, maybe not."

"Not bad, Ms. Blake. I even agree with you on most of it."

"Thank you, Agent Franklin." I wanted to ask what parts didn't he agree with, but was pretty sure where we disagreed. "You still think this is a human serial killer?"

He nodded. "I do."

I looked at the remains like lumpy red paint tossed across the table. The bloodstains had spread until I was standing in the edge of it. The cops hated to have you tracking blood everywhere. I stepped back, and the stain spread out towards me. I took another step back. My foot crunched in something. I knelt and found salt on the floor. Someone had gotten messy during lunch. I stood up.

"This is fresh kill, Agent Franklin, real fresh. How long would it take a person, even two people, to reduce another human being to this?"

His long hands played over his tie again. I wondered if he knew he did that when he was nervous. If he didn't, I'd play poker with him any day. "I really couldn't give an estimate, not and be accurate."

"Fine. Do you really think a person is strong enough to tear someone apart like this quickly enough to have the blood this fresh? The damn thing's bleeding like it's still alive, it's so damn fresh. I don't think a human being could do this much damage this quickly."

"You are entitled to your opinion."

I shook my head. "Look, Franklin, it was logical for you to assume the killer, or killers, were human. It usually is human in your line of work. I'm assuming you're with the Investigative Unit."

He nodded.

"Great. See, you hunt people. That's what you do. They are monsters but not real monsters. I don't hunt people. I hunt monsters. That's just about all I do. I don't think I've ever been called into a case where the perp was human, or at least where magic wasn't involved."

"Your point," he said, very stiff, eyes angry.

"My point is that if they had thought this was a monster to begin with, they'd have sent it over to Bradford's new unit. But they didn't, did they?"

His eyes were a little less angry, more uncertain. "No, they didn't."

"Everyone thought it was human, so why shouldn't you assume the same thing? If they'd dreamt that it was non-human, they wouldn't have sent it to you, right?"

"I suppose so."

"Great. Then let's work together, not at cross purposes. If we split our manpower between looking for people and looking for monsters, it will cost time."

"And if you're wrong, Ms. Blake, if it is a human being doing these terrible things and we stop investigating down that avenue it could cost more lives." He shook his head. "It's not my initial report I'm standing by, Ms. Blake. It's the chance that it is a human perpetrator. We will continue to treat this as a normal investigation." He looked at Bradford. "That is my final recommendation."

He turned to Edward. "And you, Mr. Forrester, are you going to dazzle me with your profiling abilities?"

Edward shook his head. "No."

"What do you offer to this investigation then?"

"When we find it, I'll kill it."

Franklin shook his head. "We are not judge, jury, and executioner, Mr. Forrester. We are the FBI."

Edward looked at him, and most of Ted's good ol' boy charm seemed to have seeped out of his eyes, leaving them cold and uncomfortable to meet. "I have two men with me out in the car, one of them is an expert on this type of crime. If this was done by a person, then he'll be able to tell us how it was done." His voice had gone bland, smooth, and empty.

"Who is this expert?" Franklin asked.

"Why is he still out in the car?" Bradford said.

"Otto Jefferies, and because Lieutenant Marks wouldn't let him in," Edward answered.

"By the way," I said, "thanks for getting me back on the case, Bradley."

Bradley smiled. "Don't thank me. Help us solve the damn thing."

"Who is Otto Jefferies?" Franklin asked.

"He's a retired government worker," Edward said.

"How does a retired government worker have expertise on this type of killing?"

Edward looked at him until Franklin began to fidget, smoothing his hands down not just his tie but his suit coat. He even checked his cuffs, though to make the movement really effective you needed cufflinks. Buttons just didn't do it.

"I'm sure you are implying something by your so pointed gaze, but my question stands. What kind of government worker would have this kind of expertise?"

Franklin may have been nervous but he was also stubborn.

"Call the state department," Edward said. "They'll answer your questions."

"I want you to answer my questions."

Edward gave a small shrug. "Sorry, if I told you the truth, I'd have to kill you." He said the last with a good ol' boy smile, and an awe-shucks shine to his eyes. Which probably meant he was serious.

"Bring your men in," Bradley said.

"I must protest involving more civilians in this case," Franklin said.

"Duly noted." Bradley looked at Edward. "Bring them in, Mr. Forrester. I'm agent in charge on site." Edward went for the door.

"For now," Franklin said.

Bradley looked up at the taller man. "I think you need to be elsewhere, Franklin."

"Where would I be of better use than overseeing the crime scene?"

"Anywhere that is away from me," Bradley said.

Franklin started to say something, then looked at both of us in turn, and finally at Bradley. "I won't forget this, Agent Bradford."

"Nor will I, Agent Franklin."

Franklin turned abruptly and walked out, hands sliding over his clothes. When he was out of earshot, I said, "He doesn't seem to like you."

"Making a new division for preternatural crimes wasn't a popular move with everyone. Until now the Investigative Division has been handling them."

"Gee, and I thought the FBI was above such petty disputes."

Bradley laughed. "God, don't I wish."

"This is a really, really fresh scene, Bradley. I don't mean to tell you your job, but shouldn't we be searching the area for the creature?"

"We did a ground search, turned up nothing. We've still got the helicopter up. We also sent off for geology maps of the ranch in case there's a cave we missed."

"Would a geology survey cover man-made ruins?" I asked.

"What do you mean?"

"This area of the country is supposed to be lousy with ruins. Just because nothing's visible from above ground doesn't mean there won't be something buried. A room, or even a kiva."

"What's a kiva?" Bradley asked.

"A sacred underground room for ceremonial magic. It's one of the few things that most of the southwestern tribes, or pueblos, have in common."

Bradley smiled. "Don't tell me you're also an expert on Native American religious practices, too?"

I shook my head. "Nope. I had a brief overview in my comparative religion class in college, but I didn't take Native American as one of my electives. Knowing that kiva do exist and their general use pretty much exhausts my knowledge of the southwestern tribes. Now if you need to know details about the Sioux sun worshipping rituals, those I remember."

"I'll check with the surveying company and see if they mark man-made structures."

"Good.

"The locals called in some tracking dogs. The dogs wouldn't come in the house. They refused to track."

"Were they bloodhounds?" I asked.

Bradley nodded. "Why?"

"Bloodhounds are a very friendly breed. They are not attack dogs. Sometimes on the preternatural bad stuff they refuse the trail. You need some trollhunds."

"Troll-what?" Bradley asked.

"Trollhunds. They were originally bred to hunt the Greater European Forest Trolls. When the trolls went extinct, the breed almost died out. They're still a rare breed, but they are the best you can find for tracking preternatural bad guys. Unlike the Bloodhound they will attack and kill what they trail."

"How do you know so much about dogs?" Bradley said.

"My dad's a vet."

Edward had reentered with Olaf and Bernardo at his back. He'd heard the last. "Your dad, a doggie doctor. I didn't know that."

He was looking intently at me, and I realized that Edward didn't really know much more about me then I did about him.

"Are there any trollhunds in this area?" Bradley asked it of Edward.

He shook his head. "No. If there were I'd know it. I'd have used them."

"You knew about troll-whatsits, too?" Bernardo asked.

Edward nodded. "If you're a varmint hunter, so should you."

Bernardo frowned at the criticism, then shrugged. "I do more bodyguard work than critter killing these days." He was looking at everyone, everything but the table and contents.

"Maybe you should go back to guarding other people's bodies," Edward said. I don't know what I'd missed, but Edward was angry with him.

Bernardo looked at him. "Maybe I should."

"No one is stopping you."

"Damn you, . . . Ted," and Bernardo walked out.

I looked at Olaf, as if for a clue to what had just happened, but Olaf had eyes only for the remains. His face was transformed. It took me a few seconds to realize what the expression on his face was, because it was wrong. It did not match what was happening. He stared down at the remains of that woman with enough raw lust in his eyes to burn down the house. It was a look that should have been saved for privacy, to be shared between your beloved and yourself. It was not a look for public consumption, when you were looking at the bleeding remains of a woman you did not know.

Staring into Olaf's face, I was cold, cold all the way down to my Nikes. Fear, but not of the monster, or rather not of that monster. If you had given me a choice between whatever was doing these killings or Olaf, right that moment I wouldn't have known who to pick. It was sort of like choosing between the tiger and the tiger.

Maybe I was standing too close, I don't know. He just suddenly turned his head and looked full at me. And just like I'd known in the car what Bernardo was thinking, I knew that Olaf was looking for a star in his own little fantasy.

I held my hands up, shaking my head, and backed away from him. "Don't even go there, . . . Otto." I was beginning to really hate all these aliases.

"She was almost exactly your height." His voice had a soft, almost dreamy quality.

Drawing a gun and shooting him was probably overkill, but I certainly didn't have to stand there and help his imagination. I turned to Bradley. "Someone said there were other bodies. Let's go see." Five minutes ago, you'd have had to drag me into the next chamber of horrors. Now I grabbed Bradley's arm and half pulled him, half let him lead me deeper into the house. I could feel Olaf's gaze against my back like a hand, hot and close. I didn't look back. Nothing ahead of me could be worse than watching Olaf paw through the woman's remains, knowing that he was thinking of me while he did it.

33

BRADLEY LED ME to a door that had been half-torn out of its hinges. Something big had pushed through here. Bradley had to use both hands to get the door to one side. It seemed to have settled into the carpet, wedging itself. He jerked back, and I jumped, pulse in my throat.

"Damn splinters." He held up the palm of his gloved hand and there was a small crimson spot on the plastic. He jerked the glove off. The splinter seemed to have come off with the glove, but it was bleeding freely.

"Some splinter," I said.

"Dammit." Bradley looked at me.

"You better let somebody look at it."

He nodded, but didn't turn to go. "Don't be insulted, but not everyone is happy with me forcing you back on this case. I can't leave you alone in here with evidence. If there were ever questions raised, it would be hard to explain."

"I've never pocketed evidence from a crime scene in my life."

"I'm sorry, Anita, but I can't take the chance. Will you follow me out to the ambulance?"

He was having to cup one hand under the other to catch the blood so it didn't reach the carpet. I frowned, but nodded. "Fine."

He started to say something, then turned and walked back to the living room. We were about a fourth of the way through the room when Edward asked, "Otto wants to open the table cloth and see what's inside."

"I'll send the photographer and Agent Franklin in to oversee it." Bradley kept going for the door having to hurry a little to keep his own blood from contaminating the scene.

Neither Edward nor Olaf nor the uniform that had magically appeared to watch them fondle the evidence, asked how he'd hurt his hand. Maybe no one cared.

I followed Bradley across the gravel turn-around to the ambulance. There were still too many people milling around outside. Shouldn't they be out searching for the creature? It wasn't my job to tell them their job, but this was the freshest crime scene yet, and there just didn't seem to be enough frantic activity to suit me.

Bradley sat down at the end of the ambulance and let the techs treat his wound. Because it was a wound. Splinter, my ass. He'd stabbed himself. I tried to be a good girl and just stand there, but I think my impatience showed, because Bradley started talking.

"We did send people out to search when we arrived, and we arrived damn quick."

"I didn't say anything."

He smiled, then grimaced as the EMT did something to his hand that hurt. "Walk far enough away from the house to give a 360 look. Then come back and tell me what you see."

I looked at him. He motioned me off with his good hand. I shrugged and started walking. The heat was like a weight across my shoulders, but without humidity it just wasn't as bad. The gravel crunched under my feet, louder than it should have been. I walked in the opposite direction from the horse corral. The horses were still running in their endless chase like a maniac merry-go-round. I threaded my way through the cars, marked and unmarked. The fire truck had driven away. I wasn't sure why it had been here in the first place. Though sometimes when you call 911, you get more emergency vehicles than you need, especially if the caller panics and isn't specific enough.

I stopped beside the silent revolving lights of a car. Who had called the police? Did we actually have a witness? If we did, why hadn't anyone mentioned it? If we didn't, then who had called for help?

I walked until the hot dry wind rustling through the clumps of grass was louder than the electric squawk of radios. I stopped and turned back towards the house. The cars were small enough that 1 could have covered one of them with my hand. I'd probably walked farther out than I needed to go. Far enough out that if I yelled for help, they might not hear me. Not bright. I should walk further in, but I needed to be clear of it for awhile. I needed to be out in the wind alone. I compromised. I drew the Browning and put off the safety, pointing the barrel at the ground, one-handed. Now I could enjoy the solitude and still be safe. Though, truthfully, I wasn't sure if what we were chasing gave a damn about bullets, silver or otherwise.

Bradley had said to look. I looked. The ranch lay in a large round valley or maybe a plateau, since we'd had to drive up some hills to get here. Whichever, the land stretched flat and smooth for miles to the rim of distant hills. Of course, I'd been surprised by distances here, so maybe the hills were really mountains, and the land stretched for a very long way in every direction. There were no trees. There was almost no vegetation above thigh height to me. Whatever had taken that door out had been big, bigger than a man, though not by much. I turned in a slow circle, scanning the ground, and there was nowhere for something that large to hide. They'd walked this ground when they first arrived, full of confidence that the creature couldn't have gotten far. They marched out, and out, and out, and found nothing. The helicopter buzzed overhead, high enough that it didn't disturb the wind, but low enough that I was pretty sure it was looking at me. They were looking for anything unusual, and I was standing out here by myself, unusual enough.

The helicopter circled a few times, then buzzed off to search somewhere else. I looked out at the empty land. There was nowhere to hide. Where had it gone? Where could it have gone?

Underground, maybe, or it flew away. If it flew away, I couldn't help them find it, but if it went underground . . . Caves, or an old well, maybe. I'd suggest it to Bradley, and probably be told that they'd checked it. But hey, I was here to offer suggestions, wasn't I?

I heard someone behind me and whirled. I had the gun halfway up when I recognized Detective Ramirez. He had his hands up and to each side, away from his gun. I let out the breath I'd been holding and holstered the gun. "Sorry."

"That's okay," he said. He was wearing another white dress shirt with the sleeves rolled back over dark, strong forearms. The tie was a different color, but it still hung loose like a necklace, and the top two buttons of his shirt were open so that you could see the smooth hollow of his throat.

"No it's not. I'm not usually this jumpy." I hugged myself, not because I was cold. Far from it. But because I badly wanted someone to hold me. I wanted to be comforted. Edward had many uses. Comfort was not one of them.

Ramirez came up beside me. He didn't try and touch me, just stood very close and looked out over the land where I was looking. He spoke still staring out in the distance. "The case getting to you?"

I nodded. "Yeah, I don't know why."

He gave a sharp laugh and turned to me, face halfway between astonishment and humor. "You don't know why?"

I frowned at him. "No, I don't."

He shook his head, smiling, but his eyes were gentle. "Anita, this is an awful case. I've never seen anything this bad."

"I've seen things as bad as the vivisected victims, the ones that died."

His face sobered. "You've seen things that bad before?"

I nodded.

"What about the mutilations?" he asked. His face was very serious now. His smooth nearly black-brown eyes watched my face.

I shook my head. "I've never seen anything like the survivors." I laughed, but it wasn't a happy sound. "If survivor is the word for them. What kind of life are they going to have, if they live?" I hugged myself tighter, staring at the ground, trying not to think.

"I've been having nightmares," Ramirez said.

I looked up at him. Police don't admit things like that often, especially not to civilian consultants that they've just met. We looked at each other, and his eyes were so gentle, so genuine. Unless he was a much better actor than I thought he was, Ramirez was letting me see the real him. I appreciated it, but didn't know how to say it out loud. You don't verbalize something like that. The best you can do is return the favor. The trouble was, I wasn't sure what the real me was anymore. I didn't know what to put in my eyes. I didn't know what to let him see. I finally stopped trying to pick and choose, and think I settled for confused, bordering on scared.

He touched my shoulder lightly. When I didn't say anything, he moved into me, wrapping his arms across my back, holding me against him. I stayed stiff in his arms for a second or two, but didn't pull away. I relaxed against him in inches, until my head rested in the curve of his neck, my arms tentatively around his waist.

He whispered, "It will be all right, Anita."

I shook my head against his shoulder. "I don't think so."

He tried to see my face but I was standing too close, at too awkward an angle. I pulled back so he could see my face, and suddenly I felt awkward standing there with my arms around a stranger. I pulled away, and he let me go, only keeping the fingers of one hand grasped in his. He gave my hand a little shake. "Talk to me, Anita, please."

"I've been doing cases like this for about five years. When I'm not looking at the messily dead, I'm hunting vampires, rogue shapeshifters, you name it."

His was holding my hand solidly now, wrapped in the warmth of his skin. I didn't pull away. I needed something human to hold onto. I tried to put into words what I'd been thinking for awhile now. "A lot of cops never use their guns, not in thirty years. I've lost count of how many people I've killed." His hand tightened on mine, but he didn't interrupt. "When I started out, I thought vampires were monsters. I really believed it. But lately I'm not so sure. And regardless of what they are, they look very human. I could get a call tomorrow that would send me down to the morgue to put a stake through the heart of a body that looks every bit as human as you and me. Once I've got a court order of execution, I am legally sanctioned to shoot and kill the vampire or vampires in question, and anyone that stands in my way. That includes human servants or people with just a bite on them. One bite, two bites, they can be healed, cured. But I've killed them to save myself, to save others."

"You did what you had to do."

I nodded. "Maybe, maybe, but that doesn't really matter anymore. It doesn't matter whether I'm right to do it, or not. Just because it's a righteous kill doesn't mean it doesn't affect you. I use to think that if I was right, it would be enough, but it's not."

He drew me a little closer with his hand. "What are you saying?"

I smiled. "I need a vacation."

He laughed then, and it was a good laugh, open and joyous, nothing special about it but his own astonishment. I'd heard better laughs but none when I needed it more. "A vacation, just a vacation?"

I shrugged. "I don't see myself taking up flower arranging, Detective Ramirez."

"Hernando," he said.

I nodded. "Hernando. This is part of who I am." I realized we were still holding hands, and I drew away from him. He let me, no protest. "Maybe if I take a break, I'll be able to do it again."

"What if a vacation isn't enough?" he asked.

"I'll cross that bridge when I come to it." It wasn't just the brutal day in and day out of the job. My reaction to Bernardo's body and letting a perfect stranger comfort me were so unlike me. I was missing the guys, but it was more than that. When I left Richard, I left the pack, all my werewolf friends. When I left Jean-Claude, I lost all the vamps, and strangely one or two of them were friends. You can be friends with a vampire as long as you remember that they are monsters and not human beings. How you can do both at the same time, I can't really explain, but I manage.

I hadn't just cut myself off from the men in my life for six months. I'd cut myself off from my friends. Even Ronnie, Veronica Sims, one of my few human friends had a new hot romance. She was dating Richard's best friend which made socializing awkward. Catherine, my lawyer and friend, had only been married two years, and I didn't like to interfere with her and Bob.

"You're thinking something very serious," Ramirez said.

I blinked and looked at him. "Just realizing how isolated I am even back home. Here, I am so . . ." I shook my head without finishing it.

He smiled. "You're only isolated if you want to be, Anita. I've offered to show you the local sights."

I shook my head. "Thanks, really. Under other circumstances, I'd say, yes."

"What's stopping you?" he asked.

"The case for one. If I start dating one of the local cops, then my credibility goes down the tubes, and I'm not too high on some lists already."

"What else?" He had a very gentle face, soft, as if he would be very gentle in everything he did.

"I've got two men waiting back home. Waiting to see who I'm going to choose, or if I'm dumping both of them."

His eyes widened. "Two. I'm impressed."

I shook my head. "Don't be. My personal life is a mess."

"Sorry to hear that."

"I can't believe I just told you all that. It isn't like me."

"I'm a good listener."

"Yeah, you are."

"May I escort you back?"

I smiled at the old-fashioned phrasing. "Can you answer some questions first?"

"Ask." He sat down on the ground in his dark brown pants, lifting the pants legs so they wouldn't bunch.

I sat down beside him. "Who called the police?"

"A guest."

"Where is he or she?"

"Hospital. Severe shock brought on by trauma."

"No physical injuries?" I asked.

He shook his head.

"Who were the mutilation vics this time?"

"The wife's brother and two nephews, all over twenty. They lived and worked on the ranch."

"What about the other guests? Where were they?"

He closed his eyes, as if visualizing the page. "Most of them were off on a planned outing, an overnight camping trip into the mountains. But the rest borrowed the ranch cars that are kept for the guests' use and left."

"Let me guess," I said. "They just felt restless, jittery, had to get out of the house."

Ramirez nodded. "Just like the neighbors around all the other houses."

"It's a spell, Ramirez," I said.

"Don't make me ask you again to use my first name."

I smiled and looked away from the teasing look in his eyes. "Hernando, this is either a spell or some sort of ability the creature possesses to cause fear, dread, in the ones it doesn't want to kill or hurt. But I'm betting on a spell."

"Why?"

"Because it's too selective to be a natural anxiety like a vampire's ability to hypnotize with its eyes. A vamp can bespell one person or a room full of people, but it can't do an entire street except for one house. It's too exact. You need to be able to organize your magic for this, and that means a spell."

He picked one of the rough-looking blades of grass, running it between his fingers. "So we're looking for a witch."

"I know something about wiccan and other flavors of witchcraft, and I don't know any way a lone wiccan, or even a coven could do this. I'm not saying there isn't a human spell worker involved somewhere, but there is definitely something otherworldly, nonhuman, at work here."

"We got some blood traces off the broken door."

I nodded. "Great. I wish someone would tell me when we find a clue. Everyone, including Ted is playing it so close to the chest, I've spent most of my time going over ground that someone else has already figured out."

"Ask me and I'll tell you anything you want to know." He tossed the grass blade to the ground. "But we better be getting back before you get a worse reputation than just dating me."

I didn't argue. Put any woman in an area run mostly by men and rumors will fly. Unless you make it very clear that you are off limits, there is also a certain competitiveness that sets in. Some men are either trying to run you out of town or get into your pants. They don't seem to know any other way to deal with a woman. If you're not a sexual object, you're a threat. Always makes me wonder what kind of childhoods they had.

Hernando stood brushing grass and dirt off the back of his pants. He seemed to have had a dandy childhood, or at least he'd turned out well. Congrats to his parents. Someday he'd bring home a nice girl and have nice children in a nice house with yard work on the weekends, and every Sunday dinner at one set of grandparents or another. A nice life if you can get it, and he still got to solve murders. Talk about having it all.

What did I have? What did I really have? I was too young for a mid-life crisis, and too old for an attack of conscience. We started walking back towards the cars. I was hugging my arms again, and had to force myself to stop. I lowered my arms to my sides and walked along beside Ramirez . . . ah, Hernando, like nothing was wrong.

"Marks said that one of the first cops on the scene had his throat nearly bitten out. How did that happen?"

"I wasn't here for the first rush. The lieutenant waited to call me in." There was a trace of harshness in his voice. He was gentle, but not if you pushed him. "But I heard that the three living victims attacked the cops. They had to subdue them with batons. They just kept trying to take pieces out of them."

"Why would they do that? How would they do it? I mean you skin most people and rip off pieces, they aren't going to feel like fighting."

"I helped pick up some of the earlier survivors, and they didn't fight. They just lay there and moaned. They were hurt and they acted hurt."

"Have they ever traced down Thad Bromwell, the son of the first scene I saw?"

Hernando's eyes widened. "Marks didn't call you?"

I shook my head.

"He is such a shithead."

I agreed. "What? Did they find the body?"

"He's alive. He was away on a camping trip with friends."

"He's alive," I said. Then whose soul had I seen hovering in the bedroom? I didn't say it out loud because I'd forgotten to mention the soul to the police. Marks had been ready to chase me out of town. If I'd started talking about souls floating near the ceiling, he'd have gotten matches and a stake.

But someone had died in that room, and the soul was still confused about where to go. Most of the time if the soul hovers, it hovers over the body, the remains. Only three people lived in the house, two of them mutilated, and the boy somewhere else.

I had an idea. "These new mutilation victims, they kept fighting, kept trying to take bites out of the officers?"

He nodded.

"Are you sure about the bites, not just hitting, but like they were trying to feed?"

"I don't know about feeding, but it was all bite wounds." He was looking at me strangely. "You've thought of something."

I nodded. "I may have. I have to see the other body, the one behind the door first, but then I think it's time to go back to the hospital."

"Why?"

I started walking again, and he grabbed my arm, turned me to face him. There was fierceness in his eyes, an intensity that trembled down his arm. "You've only been here a couple of days. I've been dealing with this for weeks. What do you know that I don't?"

I looked at his hand until he let me go, but I told him. He was having nightmares about this shit, and I hadn't gotten to that point yet. "I'm an animator. I raise zombies for a living. My specialty is the dead. One thing that the living dead have in common with one other from zombie, to ghoul, to vampire, is that they must feed off the living to sustain themselves."

"Zombies don't eat people," he said.

"If a zombie is raised and the animator that raised it can't control it, then it can go wild. It becomes a flesh-eating zombie."

"I thought that was just stories."

I shook my head. "No, I've seen it."

"What are you saying?"

"I'm saying that maybe there are no survivors. Maybe there are just dead and the living dead."

He actually went pale. I touched his elbow to steady him, but he stood straight. "I'm all right. I'm all right." He looked at me. "What do you do with a flesh-eating zombie?"

"Once it's gone amok, there isn't anything anyone can do except destroy it. The only way to do that is fire. Napalm is good, but any fire will do."

"They'll never let us roast these people."

"Not unless we can prove what I'm saying is true."

"How can you prove it?" he asked.

"I'm not sure yet, but I'll talk to Doctor Evans and we'll come up with something."

"Why would the earlier vics be docile and these new ones be vicious?"

"I don't know, unless the spell or the monster is changing, maybe growing stronger. I just don't know, Hernando. If I'm right about there being no survivors, then I've had my brilliant idea for the day."

He nodded, face very serious. He stared at the ground. "Jesus, if they are all dead, then that means that this thing we're after is making more of itself?"

"I'd be surprised if it was ever human but maybe. I don't know. I do know that if it is growing stronger and the skinned ones are growing more violent, then the creature may be controlling them."

We looked at each other. "I'll call the hospital and get more men down there."

"Call the Santa Fe hospital, too."

He nodded and broke into a half-run across the gravel, moving through the cars like he had a purpose. The other cops were watching him, as if wondering what the rush was. I hadn't asked Hernando if they'd checked for underground hiding places. Shit. I went to find Bradley and ask him. Then I'd go back into the house one last time, see the last body, and then . . . off to the hospital to answer the age-old question: what is life and when is death a sure thing?

34

THE MAN'S FACE stared up at me, eyes wide, glazed, unseeing. His head was still attached to his spine, but the chest had been split open as though two great hands had dug into his rib cage and pulled. The heart was missing. The lungs had been ripped, probably when the rib cage gave. The stomach had been punctured, giving a sour smell to the smaller room. The liver and intestines lay in a wet heap to one side of the body as if they had all spilled out at the same time. The lower intestine still curled down inside the lower end of the body cavity. By smell alone I was pretty sure that the intestines hadn't been pierced.

I sat back on my heels beside the body. Blood had splattered the lower half of the man's face, drops of it scattering across the rest of his face and into his graying hair. Violent, very violent, and very quick. I stared into his sightless eyes and felt nothing. I was back to being numb and I was not complaining. I think if I'd seen this body first, then I'd have been horrified, but the remains in the dining room had just used me up for the day. This was awful, but there were worse things, and those things were in the next room.

But it wasn't the body that was interesting. It was the room. There was a circle of salt around the body. A book lay within the circle covered so thickly in blood that I couldn't read the pages it was opened to. They'd taken all the pictures and videos they were going to in this room so I used borrowed gloves to raise the book up. It was bound with embossed leather, but there was no title. The middle half of the book had soaked so much blood up that the pages were sticking together. I didn't try and pry them apart. The police and the Feds had technicians for delicate work. I was careful not to close the book and lose the place the man was probably reading from. For all I knew the book had been on the desk that the man shoved against the door, and it had simply fallen to the floor, opening on its own. But to think that meant we had no clue, so we'd all pretend we were sure that the man had deliberately opened the book. In the middle of being chased by a monster that had just butchered his wife, he went for this book, opened it, started to read. Why?

The book was hand-written and I read enough to know that it was a book of shadows. It was the spell book, sort of, of a practicing witch. One that followed an older or more orthodox tradition than the neo-pagan movement. Gardian or Alexandrian, maybe. Though again I couldn't be sure. I'd had one semester in college on comparative witchcraft, though now I'm sure they called it comparative wiccan. Of the wiccan practitioners I knew personally, none of them practiced anything this traditional.

I put the book carefully back where'd I'd found it and stood. The bookshelves against the near wall were full of books on psychic research, the preternatural, mythology, folklore, and wicca. I had some of the same books at home, so the books alone weren't proof of much. But the clincher was the altar. It was an antique wooden chest with a silk cloth over the top. There were silver candlesticks with partially burned candles in them. The candles had runes carved into them. Other than the fact that they were runes, I couldn't read them.

There was a round mirror with no frame sitting flat between the candles. There was a small bowl of dried herbs to one side, a larger bowl of water, and a small carved box tight shut.

"Is that what I think it is?" Bradley asked.

"An altar. He was a practitioner. I think that book is his book of shadows, his spell book for lack of a better term."

"What happened here?"

"There's salt in the floor of the dining room."

"That's not unusual," Bradley said.

"No, but a salt circle is. I think he was somewhere further back in the house. He heard his wife screaming or heard the monsters. Something alerted him. He didn't come running with a gun, Bradley. He came running with a handful of salt. Maybe he had something else in his hands or on his person, some charm or amulet. I don't see it, but that doesn't mean it's not here."

"Are you saying he threw salt at this thing?"

"Yes."

"Why, for god's sake?"

"Salt and flame are two of our oldest purifying agents. I use salt to bind a zombie back into its grave. You can throw it on fairies, fetches, a whole host of critters, and it will make them hesitate, maybe not much more."

"So he threw salt and maybe some charm at the creature, then what?"

"I think that's why the monster stopped, and why the tablecloth full of trophies is still sitting by the table."

"Why didn't the monster go back and get the trophies after he killed the man?"

"I don't know. Maybe he finished the spell before he died. Maybe he drove it from the house. I'd like to get a real wiccan in here to look over the scene."

"Wiccan, you mean witch."

"Yes, but most of them prefer the term wiccan."

"Politically correct," Bradley said.

I nodded. "Yeah."

"What could a real wiccan tell us that you can't?"

"She might know what spell he used. If the spell drove the thing from the house, then we might be able to use a version of the same spell to trap or even destroy it. Something this man did drove the creature out of this house before it was ready to go. He forced it to leave behind its goody bag and to leave without gutting his body. It's the first weakness we've seen in this thing."

"Franklin won't like bringing in a witch. Neither will the locals. If I force everyone to bring this wiccan in, and it doesn't work or she talks to the media, then the next time you see me I won't be an FBI Agent."

"Aren't you supposed to try every angle to solve this crime? Isn't that your job?"

"The FBI doesn't use witches, Anita."

I shook my head. "How the hell did you get me in then?"

"Forrester had already brought you in on the case. All I had to do was stand up to Marks."

"And Franklin," I said.

He nodded. "I outrank Franklin."

"Then why is he so snotty?"

"It seems to be a natural talent of his."

"I don't want to get you fired, Bradley." I went to the overturned desk and started opening the drawers. There was a gun cabinet in the living room. Most people who had a cabinet full of them kept one for personal protection.

"What are you looking for?" he asked.

I opened the larger bottom drawer, and there it was. "Come here, Bradley."

He came to peer into the drawer. The gun was a 9 mm Smith and Wesson. It lay on the side of the drawer where it had fallen when the desk tipped over. Bradley stared down at the gun. "Maybe it's not loaded. Maybe he had the ammo locked in the living room."

"Can I touch it?"

He nodded.

I lifted it, and just by the weight I was pretty sure it was loaded, but it wasn't a gun I was familiar with, so I popped the clip and showed it to Bradley.

"Full," he said, voice soft.

"Full." I slid the clip back inside the gun, hitting it sharply with the palm of my hand to make it click. "He had a loaded 9 mm in his desk, but he grabbed salt and his book of shadows. He didn't waste time grabbing for the gun. He either knew what the thing was, or he sensed something about it and knew the gun wouldn't work, and that the spell would." I raised the gun up so that Bradley looked at it, the barrel pointed at the ceiling. "The spell worked, Bradley. We need to know what it was, and the only way to know that is to get a witch in here."

"Can't you take the book and just show her pictures?"

"What if the position of the book is important? What if there are clues to the spell in the circle itself? I don't practice this kind of ritual magic, Bradley. For all I know if you get someone in here, they may be able to sense something that I can't. Do you really want to take the chance that pictures and just seeing the book in their own home will be just as good as seeing it here like this?"

"You're asking me to risk my career."

"I am asking you to risk your career," I said, "but I'm also asking you to not risk any more innocent lives. Do you really want to see this done to another couple, another family?"

"How can you be so sure that this is the key?"

"I'm not sure, but it's the closest thing we've seen to a break in this case. I'd hate to lose it because of career jitters."

"It's not just that, Anita. If we use anything more exotic than psychics and we fail, then the entire unit could be disbanded."

I placed the gun in his hand. He stared at it. "I trust you to do the right thing, Bradley. That's why you're one of the good guys."

He shook his head. "And to think I blackmailed Marks to get you back on the case."

"You knew I was a pain in the ass when you fought to get me back on the case. It's one of my many charms."

That earned me a weak smile. He was still holding the gun flat across his hand. His fingers tightened around it. "You know any witches in the area?"

I grinned at him. "No, but I bet Ted does." I shook my head. "I've never hugged an FBI agent, but I'm tempted."

That made him smile, but his eyes stayed cautious, unhappy. I was asking a lot from him. I touched his arm. "I wouldn't ask you to bring in a witch if I didn't think it was our best shot. I wouldn't ask just on a whim."

He gave me a long look. "I know. You are one of the least whimsical people I've ever met."

"I would say you should see me when I'm not neck deep in corpses, but it doesn't really matter. I don't get much lighter than this."

"I've checked the cases you've helped the St. Louis PD solve, Anita. Gruesome stuff. How old are you now?"

I frowned at the question then answered it. "Twenty-six."

"How long have you been helping the police?"

"About four years."

"The Bureau switches its agents off the serial killer shit about every two years. Whether they want to transfer or not. Then after a break, they can come back."

"You think I need a break?"

"Everyone burns out eventually, Anita, even you."

"Actually, I'm thinking about a vacation when I get home."

He nodded. "That's good."

I looked up at him. "Do I look like I need a break?"

"I've seen it before in other agents' eyes."

"Seen what?" I asked.

"Like your eyes are a cup, and every horror you see is another drop added. Your eyes are full of the things you've seen, the things you've done. Get out while there's still some room for things that don't bleed."

"That is damn poetic for an FBI agent."

"One friend stayed with it until he had a heart attack."

"I think I'm a little young for that," I said.

"Another friend ate his gun."

We stared at each other. "I'm not the suicidal type."

"I also don't want to see you in jail."

My eyes widened. "Whoa. I do not know what you're talking about."

"The state department confirmed Otto Jefferies is a retired government worker, but they couldn't access the rest of his file at the present time. I've got a friend at the state department with a level two secret clearance. He couldn't access Otto Jefferies' files either. He's a total black out, which means he's a spook of some kind. You do not want to get involved with the spooks, Anita. If they try to recruit you, say no. Don't try to find out who Otto really is, or what he did. Don't get nosy or you'll end up in a hole somewhere. Just work with him, leave him alone, and move on."

"You sound like you're talking from personal experience," I said.

He shook his head. "I'm not going to talk about it."

"You brought it up," I said.

"I told you just enough to get your attention, I hope. Just trust me on this. Stay the fuck away from these people."

I nodded. "It's okay, Bradley. I don't like . . . Otto. And he hates women, so don't worry. I don't think it would occur to him to try and recruit me."

"Good." He put the gun back in the desk drawer and closed it.

"Besides," I said, "what would the top secret set want with me?"

He looked at me, and it was a look that I wasn't used to getting. The look said, I was being naive. "Anita, you can raise the dead."

"So?"

"I can think of a half a dozen uses for that one talent alone."

"Like what?"

"Prisoner dies in interrogation. Doesn't matter. Raise him up again. A world leader is assassinated. We need a few days to get our troops ready, raise the leader for a few days. Give us time to control the panic, or stop the revolution."

"Zombies are not alive, Bradley. They couldn't pass for a country's leader."

"From a distance, for two or three days, don't even try and say you couldn't pull that off."

"I wouldn't do it," I said.

"Even if it meant that hundreds of lives could be saved, or hundreds of Americans could be evacuated in safety."

I looked at him. "I . . . I don't know."

"No matter how good the cause seems at the beginning, Anita, eventually it won't be. Eventually, when you're so far in you can't see daylight, they'll ask things of you that you won't want to do."

I was hugging myself again, which irritated me. No one had approached me to do anything on an international level. Olaf thought I was good for only one thing and that did not include helping the government. But it did make me wonder how Edward had met him. Edward was spooky, but was he a spook?

I looked up at Bradley's so serious face. "I'll be careful." Then I had a thought. "Did someone approach you about me?"

"I was thinking about offering you a job with us." I raised eyebrows at him.

He laughed. "Yeah, after looking through your file, it was decided that you're too independent, too much a wild card. It was decided that you would not thrive in a bureaucratic setting."

"You got that right, but I am flattered you thought of me."

His face went back to serious, and there were lines in his face that I hadn't seen before. It made him look forty plus. Most of the time he didn't. "Your file got flagged, Anita. It got moved up the line. I don't know where to or who asked for it, but there is government work out there for the independent wild card if they have specialized enough skills."

I opened my mouth, closed it, and finally said, "I'd say you were joking, but you're not, are you?"

He shook his head. "I wish I was."

Edward had said that he wouldn't have brought Olaf in if he'd known I was coming. It made it sound like Olaf had been invited in, not volunteered, but I'd ask Edward. I'd make sure.

"Thank you for telling me, Bradley. I don't know much about this stuff, but I know you're taking a chance telling me at all."

"I had to tell you, Anita. You see it was me that pulled your file in the first place. I was the one that pushed to get you invited in. I brought you to someone's attention. For that I am heartily sorry."

"It's okay, Bradley. You didn't know."

He gave a small shake of his head, and the look on his face was bitter. "But I should have."

I didn't know what to say to that. It turned out I didn't have to say anything. Bradley walked out of the room. I waited a second or two, then followed him out. But I couldn't shake the unease. He'd meant to scare me, and he'd succeeded. It was all Big Brother watching and paranoia. He already had me wondering if Olaf had invited himself, or even if Edward could have been asked to recruit me. It wouldn't surprise me that Edward worked for the government, at least part time. He took money from anyone.

It would have seemed silly if I hadn't seen the look on Bradley's face. If he hadn't told me about my file. He said file, like everyone had a file. Maybe they did. But someone had requested my file. I had a sudden image of my life, my crimes, all printed in neat type crossing one shadowy desk after another until it reached, where? Or would the question be who?

Blake, Anita Blake. It even sounded funny. Of course, the federal government has never been known for its sense of humor.

35

EDWARD LET ME drive his Hummer to the hospital. He stayed behind to wait for the witch. She was Donna's friend so he'd play Ted and hold her hand through the crime scene. It would be her very first crime scene. Talk about being thrown in at the deep end to sink or swim. Even I'd had a gentler introduction to police work than this.

Olaf stayed to commune with the bodies. Fine with me. I did not want to be in a car, or any small confined space with Olaf without Edward along to chaperone. I think the police and the Feds would have gladly given him to me for the ride, though. All he'd really done was confirm my supposition that the killer would not have willingly left his trophies behind, though Olaf knew less about magic than I did. He didn't know why the killer left. I was the only one with a scenario for that, and even I would be relieved if the wicca practitioner seconded my opinion. If she didn't, then we were truly out of guesses.

In fact, almost no one wanted to go with me. Franklin thought I was nuts. What did I mean, the survivors weren't survivors, but the living dead? Bradley wasn't willing to leave Franklin as the ranking agent on site. The geology maps were on the way, and I don't think he wanted Franklin in charge of the search. Marks wouldn't leave the scene to the Feds, and he also thought I was nuts. Ramirez and one uniform followed me in an unmarked car.

I didn't really think they'd find the monster. There had been no track. No tracks meant either it could fly or it dematerialized. Either way they weren't going to find it, not on foot, not with maps. So I felt free to go to the hospital.

Another reason to go into Albuquerque was that Edward had found me a name. A man who was known as a brujo, a witch. Donna had only given "Ted" the name on the condition it would not be used to harm the man. She'd only been given the name on the strict understanding that no harm would come to him. The one who gave up the name didn't want the brujo to come back and hurt her. He would work evil spells for money, as well as personal vengeance. If you could prove in court that he performed real magic for nefarious purpose, it was an automatic death sentence. His name was Nicandro Baco, and he was supposed to be a necromancer. If he were, he'd be the first one, other than me, that I'd ever met. The name came with one other warning. Be careful of him. He was much more dangerous than he looked. Just what I needed—a necromancer with an attitude. Oh, wait, I was a necromancer with an attitude. If he got shitty with me, we'd see who was the bigger fish. Was that a chip on my shoulder or overconfidence? We'd see.

Oh, and Bernardo went with me. He sat in the passenger seat slumped down until the seatbelt I'd insisted he wear cut across his neck. His handsome face was set in a scowl, arms crossed over his chest. I think he'd have crossed his legs if he'd had room. Words like *closed-off*, *brooding*, came to mind.

Shadows stretched across the road, though there were no trees or buildings to cast them. It was like the shadows just spilled out of the earth itself to lie across the road like a promise of the night to come. If you went by the watch on my wrist, it was early evening. If you went by the level of daylight, it was late afternoon. We had about three hours of daylight left. I drove through the gathering shadows with a feeling of urgency pressing against me. I wanted to be at the hospital before dark. I didn't know why, and I didn't question it. We were being followed by a police car. Surely, they could fix the ticket.

It was frightening how quickly and smoothly the car went over eighty without me noticing it. There was something about the roads and the way they spilled out and out across the empty landscape that made lower speeds seem like crawling. I kept it at a solid eighty, and Ramirez kept up with me. He seemed to be the only one who believed me. Maybe he felt the urgency, too.

The silence in the car wasn't exactly companionable, but it wasn't uncomfortable either. Besides, I had enough problems without playing crying shoulder for one of Edward's sociopathic friends.

Bernardo broke the silence. "I saw you and that detective getting it on out there in the grass."

I frowned at him. He was watching me with hostile eyes. I think he was trying to pick a fight, though I didn't know why. "We were not 'getting it on,'" I said.

"Looked pretty cozy to me."

"Jealous?" I asked.

His face hardened, thinning into angry lines. "So you do sleep around. Just not with us bad guys."

I shook my head. "It was a comforting hug, not that it's any of your business."

"Didn't think you were the comforting hug type."

"I'm not."

"So," he said.

"So this case is getting to me."

"I hear that," he said.

I glanced at him. His face was turned away, only a thin rim of profile showing through his hair like the moon just before it goes dark.

I turned back to the road. If he didn't want eye contact, fine with me. "I thought you were avoiding the pictures and forensic stuff," I said.

"I've been here two weeks longer than you have. I've seen the pictures. I've seen the bodies. I don't need to see it all again."

"What exactly did you and Edward quarrel about today?"

"Quarrel," he said and gave a low chuckle. "Yeah, you could say we quarreled."

"What about?"

"I don't know why the hell I'm here. Tell me what or who to shoot, and I'll do it. I'll even guard bodies if the price is right. But there's nothing to shoot at. Nothing but dead bodies. I don't know shit about magic."

"I thought you were a licensed bounty hunter that specialized in preternatural critters."

"I was with Edward when he cleaned out a nest of lycanthropes in Arizona. Fifteen of them. We mowed them down with machine guns and grenades." He had an almost wistful tone to his voice. Ah, the good ol' days. "Before that I'd killed two rogue lycanthropes, but afterwards I got a lot of calls for this shit. I took the ones that were basically just hits. The only difference was that the vic wasn't human. Those I could handle, but I am not a detective. Call me in when the kill is in sight, and I'll be there, but not this. This fucking waiting around, looking for clues. Who the hell looks for clues? We're assassins, not Sherlock Holmes."

He shifted in his seat, and struggled to sit up straighter, arms still holding himself tight. He did the headshake to get the hair back away from his face. The headshake is a very feminine gesture. A man has to be muy macho for it not to be. Bernardo managed.

"Maybe he assumed that since you helped him out with the shapeshifters that you'd be useful with this."

"He was wrong."

I shrugged. "Then go home."

"I can't."

I glanced at him. I could see most of his profile, and it was a nice one. "You owe him a favor, too?"

"Yes."

"Mind me asking what sort of favor?"

"Same as you."

"You killed one of his other backups?"

He nodded, and had to run his hands through his hair to slide it back from his face.

"Want to talk about it?"

"Why?" He looked at me, and his face, for one of the few times, wasn't teasing, but serious, even solemn. He looked less handsome without the smile and glow in his eyes, but he also seemed more real. Being real will get me into trouble faster than any amount of charm. "Do you want to talk about how you killed Harley?" he asked.

"Not really."

"Then why did you ask?"

"You seem uptight. I thought it might help to talk, or is that just a girl thing?"

He smiled, and it almost reached his eyes. "I think it's a girl thing because I don't want to talk about it."

"Okay, let's talk about something else."

"What?" He was staring out the far window now, one shoulder pressed against the glass. The road went down between two hills, and the world was suddenly dark gray. We were literally running out of daylight. But this last attack had most definitely been a daylight attack. So why was I so worried about the coming night? Maybe it was just years of hunting vampires, where darkness meant that we humans no longer had any advantage. I hoped it was just old habits, but the fluttering in my stomach didn't think that was it.

"How long have you known Edward?" I asked.

"About six years."

"Shit," I said.

He looked at me then. "What's wrong?"

"I've known him for five. I was hoping you'd known him longer."

He grinned at me. "Wanting to pump me for information, eh?"

"Something like that."

He turned in the seatbelt until most of his body was facing me, one leg drawn up into the seat. "Let me pump you, and you can pump me all you want." His voice had dropped a notch or two. His head was to one side, the hair sweeping across the seat like black fur.

I shook my head. "You're horny, and I'm available. That isn't very flattering, Bernardo."

He moved back in his seat, sweeping his hair back to his side of the seat. "Now that is a girl thing."

"What is?"

"Complicating things, needing the sex to be about something more than sex."

"I don't know. I know a guy or two that make it just as complicated."

"You don't sound happy with him or them."

"Did Edward call you before Olaf or after?" I asked.

"After, but you're changing the subject."

"No, I'm not. Edward is an expert on people. He knows who to call for any given situation, for any kill. Olaf makes sense. I make sense. You don't make sense. He knows that this isn't your type of crime."

"You lost me."

"Edward encouraged me to sleep with you."

Bernardo looked at me, shocked, I think. Nice to know he could be. "Edward match making. We are talking about the same Edward, right?"

"Maybe Donna has changed him," I said.

"Nothing changes Edward. He's a mountain. He's just there."

I nodded. "True, but he wasn't encouraging me to pick out curtains with you. He said, and I quote, 'What you need is a nice uncomplicated fuck.' "

Bernardo's eyebrows went up into his hair. "Edward said that?"

"Yeah, he did."

He was looking at me now. I could feel his gaze on me even while watching the road. It wasn't sexual now. It was intense. I had his attention. "Are you saying that Edward brought me on to tempt you?"

"I don't know. Maybe. Maybe I'm wrong. Maybe it's just a coincidence. But he's not happy with my choice of lovers."

"First, there are no coincidences when it comes to Edward. Second, who could you possibly be sleeping with that would bother Edward? He wouldn't care if you were doing your dog."

I ignored the last comment, because I couldn't think of a comeback for it. Though notice I didn't disagree. Usually, Edward just wanted to know if you could shoot. Anything else was not important. "I'll answer your question, if you answer mine first."

"Try me."

"You may look like the cover boy for the Native American GQ, but there's no sense of you coming from a different culture?"

"Too white for you?" and his voice was angry. I'd touched the chip on his shoulder.

"Look, my mother's family is Mexican American, and you have a sense of their culture when you interact with them. My father's family is German, and they'll say things, do things that are sort of European or have a foreign flavor to them. You don't seem to have any specific culture or background. You talk like generic middle America, like television or something."

He looked at me, and he was angry now. "My mother was white. My father was Indian. I'm told he died before I was born. She gave me up at birth. No one wanted a little mixed baby, so I went from one foster home to another. When I was eighteen, I joined the army. They found out I could shoot. I killed things for my country for a few years. Then I went freelance. And here I am." His voice had grown increasingly bitter until it almost hurt to hear it.

Saying I was sorry would have been insulting. Saying I understood would have been a lie. Thanks for answering the question seemed wrong, too.

"Nothing to say?" he asked. "Shocked? Sorry for me? Give me a little pity sex."

I looked at him then. "If someone has sex with you, it isn't out of pity, and you damn well know it."

"But you don't want to have sex with me."

"It's not because of your ethnicity, or lack thereof, or your background. I've got two guys waiting for me at home. Two is one too many. Three would be ridiculous."

"Why doesn't Edward like them?" Bernardo asked.

"One's a werewolf and the other is a vampire." My words were bland, but I watched his face long enough to see the reaction. He gaped at me.

He finally closed his mouth, and said, "You're the Executioner, scourge of the undead. How can you be doing a vampire?"

"I'm not sure I can answer that question, even to myself. But currently, I'm not doing him at all."

"Did you think the werewolf was human? Was he trying to pass?"

"At first, but not for long. I knew what he was when I took him to my bed."

He let out a low whistle. "Edward hates the monsters. But I didn't think he'd give a damn if one of his backups slept with them."

"He cares. I don't know why, but he does."

"So he thought what? That one night with me would change your religion? Make you swear off the monsters?" He was staring at me now, studying my face. "I've heard that shapeshifters can change the shape of their bodies at will. Is that true?"

"Some of them can," I said. We were in the outskirts of Albuquerque. Strip malls and fast food restaurants.

"Can your boyfriend?"

"Yes."

"Can he change the shape of all his body, at will?"

I felt the blush roll up my neck into my face and couldn't stop it.

Bernardo laughed. "I guess he can."

"No comment."

He was still laughing softly to himself, a very masculine chuckle. "Is your vampire an old one?"

"Four hundred years and counting," I said. We'd left the strip malls behind and turned into a residential area. We were coming up to the first landmark on the directions Edward had given me. We'd used up nearly an hour of daylight. I almost drove past the turnoff to Nicandro Baco's place, but if I was right, if the thing we were dealing with was another type of undead from any that I'd ever heard of, then another necromancer might be nice to have around. For all I knew, this type of undead was a regional specialty, and Baco would know more than I did. I turned, checking the rearview to see that Ramirez was still behind me. We were actually all going the speed limit.

"Can you read the directions to me?" I asked.

He didn't answer, just picked the piece of paper up off the dashboard, and began reading off street names. "You're safe on the directions for a little bit. Let's get back to our little talk."

I frowned at him. "Do we have to?"

"Let me get this straight," Bernardo said. "You've been shacking up with a shapeshifter that has such fine control of his body that he can make any one part of it . . . bigger."

"Or smaller," I said. I was counting streetlights, under my breath. Didn't want to miss the turn. We had time to see this guy and get to the hospital before dark, but not if we got badly lost.

"No man makes things smaller during sex. I don't care what he is, he's still male."

I shrugged. I was not going to discuss Richard's size with Bernardo. The only person I had discussed it with had been Ronnie, and that had been over much giggling, while she shared embarrassing facts about her boyfriend, Louie. It has been my experience that women tell more intimate details to their friends than men do. Men may brag more, but women will talk the nitty-gritty and share the experience more.

"So, where was I?" Bernardo said. "Ah, you're doing this shapeshifter that has such fine control of his body that he can make any part bigger or smaller at will."

I squirmed in the seat, but finally nodded.

Bernardo smiled happily. "And you're doing a vampire that has been having sex for over four hundred years." He suddenly sounded faux-British. "Can one assume that he is well-skilled by now?"

The blush that had been fading came back with a burn. I'd almost have welcomed darkness to hide behind. "Yes," I said.

"Shit, girlfriend, I may be good, but I'm not that good. I am just a poor mortal boy. I can't compete with the lord of the undead and the wolfman."

We were in a section of town that seemed nearly deserted. Gas stations with bars on the windows and graffiti spread across everything like a contagious disease. The storefront across from it had boarded up windows and more graffiti. The afternoon was still thick with reflected sunlight, but somehow the light didn't quite reach the street, as if there was something here that kept it at bay. The skin on my back crept so hard, I jumped.

"What's wrong?" Bernardo asked.

I shook my head. My mouth was suddenly dry. I knew we had arrived before he called out, "There it is, Los Duendos, the dwarves."

The air was thick and oppressive with the weight of magic. Death magic. Either they had just killed something to gain power for a spell or they were actively working with the dead right at this very moment. Since the sun was still up, that was a trick. Most animators couldn't raise the dead until after dark. Theoretically, I am powerful enough to raise the dead at high noon, but I don't. I was told once that the only reason I couldn't do it was that I believed I couldn't do it. But Nicandro Baco didn't seem to share my doubts. Maybe I wouldn't be the biggest fish after all. Now I got an attack of the doubts. Too late to get Edward down here for backup. If Baco got a whiff of police, he'd either run, be uncooperative, or try to hurt us. His power breathed along my body, and I was still sitting in the car. What was he going to be like in person? Bad. How bad? As the old saying goes, only one way to find out.

36

I'D PULLED INTO a deserted parking lot about two blocks down and around the corner from the bar. Ramirez had pulled in beside me, and he and the uniform, Officer Rigby, walked over to us. Rigby was medium height, well built, and moved like he worked out. He had an easy confidence, and a ready smile that went all the way to his eyes. He was entirely too comfortable in his own skin, as if nothing really bad had ever touched him. He lacked entirely that air that most policemen have of having been ridden hard and put up wet. He looked older than I was, but his eyes were younger, and I resented that.

Ramirez had spent his drive time checking out Nicandro Baco, alias Nicky Baco. He was suspected of murders, but witnesses had a strange way of disappearing or forgetting what they'd seen. He was associated with a local biker gang, ah, club. Biker gangs now preferred the more politically correct term of club, according to Ramirez. The local "club" was called Los Lobos. "Not to be confused with the music group," Ramirez said.

I'd blinked at him. Then I got the joke. "Oh, yeah, Los Lobos, the music group."

He looked at me. "Are you all right?"

I nodded. Even two blocks away I could feel a touch of Baco's magic. I was betting if someone took the time, they'd find spells, charms, wards, set up here and there in the surrounding area. I didn't think he was aware of me yet. I think the only reason I'd sensed him so strongly was he was in the middle of a spell. The charms were scattered around the neighborhood to give off a certain unease. He might have literally driven the other businesses out of business. Illegal, as well as unethical. Of course, why he'd want to destroy the entire economy of the area surrounding his bar was a mystery to me. I'd worry about it later. Murder and mayhem first. Possible real estate scam later. Some days you just have to prioritize.

"The Lobos are small and local, but they've got a bad rep," Ramirez said.

"How bad?" I asked.

"Drug running, murder, murder for hire, assault, assault with a deadly, attempted murder, rape, kidnapping."

Bernardo said, "Kidnapping?" As if the other crimes were to be expected but not the last.

Ramirez looked at him, and his eyes went from friendly to cool. He didn't like Bernardo for some reason. "We think they abducted a teenage girl, but nobody ever surfaced, and the only witness just saw her being dragged into a van that looked like one that their leader, Roland Sanchez, owned at the time. But a lot of people own gray vans."

"Have you had a lot of disappearing teenage girls?" I asked.

"Our share, but no, we haven't noticed a pattern of young women being abducted by the gang. I'm not saying they won't do it, but they're not making a habit of it."

"Glad to hear it," I said.

Ramirez smiled. "You're armed, and . . ." He handed me a slender cell phone. "Press this button and it'll call this phone." He held up a matching phone. "Rigby and I will come running with backup."

My eyes flicked to Rigby, who actually tipped his hat at me. "At your service, ma'am."

Ma'am? Either he was five years younger than he looked, or he used ma'am for all women. I turned from his peaceful eyes to Ramirez. His eyes were kind, but they weren't peaceful. He'd seen too much of life for true tranquility. I liked his eyes better. "You're not going to try and argue me out of just Bernardo and I walking into the bar?"

"We suspect Baco of using magic to kill people. That is an automatic death sentence. If he gets a whiff of police, then he'll clam up and start asking for a lawyer. If you want information from him, you'll have to play ordinary citizen. Now, if you planned to go in there alone without Bernardo or some man with you, then I'd argue."

I frowned at him. "I can take care of myself."

He shook his head. "In the world that this gang runs in, women do not exist except through men."

My frown deepened. "You've lost me."

"All women are either someone' s mother, daughter, wife, sister, girlfriend, lover. They would not know what the hell to do with you, Anita. Go in as Bernardo's girlfriend." He had his hand up, stopping me from interrupting before I could even open my mouth and try. "Trust me on this. You need to have some sort of status that they can grasp quickly and easily. Flashing your animator's license is too close to a badge. No woman in her right mind would just wander in there for a drink. You have to be something." He glanced at Bernardo not like he was happy. "I'd go in with you as your boyfriend, but like it or not, I look like a cop, or so I've been told."

I looked at him. I wasn't sure what it was about most policemen, but after a while they really did look like cops, even off duty sometimes. It was partially the clothes, partially some indefinable air of authority or bad attitude or something. Whatever "it" was, Ramirez had it. Rigby was in uniform, and I wouldn't have taken him as backup anyway. He made me nervous with his air of contentment. Policemen should never be that well pleased with themselves. It means they haven't had much experience yet.

I looked at Bernardo's smirking face. "Agreed, under protest."

"Good," Ramirez said, but he was looking at Bernardo, too, like he didn't like the look on his face. He held a finger up near the taller man's face. "You get out of line in there with Anita, and I will personally make you sorry for it."

Bernardo's eyes drifted from amused to cool. It reminded me of the way Edward's eyes lost emotion until they were empty and somehow harsh.

I stepped between them, enough to get both of them looking at me. "I can take care of myself when it comes to Bernardo, Detective Ramirez. Thanks anyway." I'd used his title to remind Bernardo who and what he was. Even Edward treaded soft around the cops.

Ramirez's face had closed down, empty. "Suit yourself, Ms. Blake."

I realized that he thought I'd used his title because I was angry with him. Shit. Why was I always ass deep in male egos in the middle of any given crisis? "It's okay, Hernando. I just like to remind everyone that I'm a big girl." I touched his arm lightly.

He looked at me, and his eyes softened. "Okay." That was male short hand for apology and apology accepted. Though truthfully if one of the parties involved hadn't been female, the short hand would have been shorter.

I stepped away from both of them and changed the subject. "Amazing how many bad guys and monsters will talk to me and not the police."

He nodded, face still serious. "Amazing. That's one word for it." The look he gave me was so studied, so searching, that I wondered if he'd been checking me out as well as Baco.

I didn't ask. I didn't really want to know. But he was right about Baco. If he was what people said, then he wouldn't want the police anywhere near his homes or his work area. They were not kidding about the automatic death penalty. The last execution in this country of a spell caster had been two months ago. It had been in California, which is not a death penalty state for any other crime.

They'd tried and convicted a sorcerer, or would that be sorceress, of trafficking with the demonic. She'd used a demon to kill her sister so she'd inherit the parents' estate. They suspected she'd also killed her parents, but they couldn't prove that. And who cared? They could only kill her once. I'd read some of the trial transcript. She'd been guilty. I had no doubt on that point. But it had been three months from arrest, to conviction, to the carrying out of the sentence. It was unheard of in the American justice system. Hell, it usually takes longer than that to get a hearing date, let alone a full-blown trial. But even California had learned its lesson a few years back. They'd arrested a sorcerer for very similar crimes. They'd tried to give the sorcerer the usual wait for a trial because some congressman or other was arguing that the death penalty shouldn't be allowed even in cases of magical assassination.

That sorcerer had called a greater demon in his cell. It killed every guard on the cellblock, and some of the prisoners. He'd finally been tracked down with the help of a coven of white wiccans. The death total had been forty-two, forty-three, something like that. He was killed during the capture attempt. He took thirty slugs, which meant people had emptied their clips into his body once it went down. For none of the police to get caught in the crossfire, they must have been standing over him, pointing down. Overkill, you bet, but I didn't blame them. They never did find all the body parts of the guards at the prison.

New Mexico was a death penalty state. I was betting that they would be able to beat California's three months turn-around from arrest to completion of sentence. I mean, after all, in this state they might actually put you to death for a good old-fashioned murder. Add magic to it, and they'd be scattering your ashes to the wind faster than you could say Beelzebub.

The actual method of execution is the same for everyone. America does not allow burning at the stake for any crime. But after you're dead, they burn the body to ash if you were convicted of a crime involving magic. Then they scatter the ashes, usually into running water. Very traditional.

There are parts of Europe where it's still legal to burn a "witch" at the stake. There's more than one reason that I don't travel outside the country much.

"Anita, are you still with us?" Ramirez asked.

I blinked. "Sorry, just thinking about the last execution in California. I don't blame Baco for being worried."

Ramirez shook his head. "Me, either. Be very careful. These are bad people."

"Anita knows about bad people," Bernardo said.

The two men looked at each other, and again I got that hint that Ramirez didn't like him. Bernardo seemed to be teasing him. Did they know each other?

I decided to ask. "Do you guys know each other?"

They both shook their heads. "Why?" Bernardo asked.

"You guys seem to have some sort of personal shit going on."

Bernardo smiled then, and Ramirez looked uncomfortable. "It's not personal with me," Bernardo said.

Rigby turned away, coughing. If I hadn't known better, I'd have said he was covering a laugh.

Ramirez ignored him, all attention for Bernardo. "I know Anita knows how to handle herself around the bad guys, but a knife blade in the back doesn't care how good you are. The Lobos pride themselves on using blades instead of guns."

"Guns are for sissies," I said.

"Something like that."

I had the black suit jacket on over the navy blue polo shirt. If I buttoned two buttons, the jacket hid the Firestar in front and still left me plenty of room to reach for it, and the Browning. In fact the slender cell phone swinging in the right side pocket was more noticeable than the guns. "I just love taking a gun to a knife fight."

Bernardo had thrown a black short-sleeved dress shirt over his white T-shirt. It fanned in back and covered the Beretta 10 mil on his hip. "Me, too," he said and smiled. It was a fierce smile, and I realized that this may have been the first time in weeks that he was going up against something flesh and blood and killable.

"We're going in for information, not to do the OK Corral. You do understand that?" I said.

"You're the boss," he said, but I didn't like the way his eyes looked. They were anticipatory, eager.

I'd felt paranoid this morning when I slipped the knife in its spine sheath. Now I moved my head a little back and forth feeling the handle against my neck. It was comforting. I almost always carried the wrist sheaths and their matching knives, but the spine sheath was optional. One minute you're paranoid and packing too much hardware, the next you're scared, and underarmed. Life's like that, or my life's like that.

"Do you know what los duendos are?" Ramirez asked.

"Bernardo said it meant the dwarves."

Ramirez nodded. "But around here it's folklore. They're small beings that live in caves and steal things. But they're supposed to be angels that got left suspended between Heaven and Hell during Lucifer's revolt. So many angels were leaving Heaven that God slammed the gates shut and los duendos got trapped outside of Heaven. They were suspended in limbo."

"Why didn't they just go to Hell?" Bernardo asked.

It was a good question. Ramirez shrugged. "The story doesn't say."

I glanced at Rigby standing behind Ramirez. He was standing so easy, ready, prepared like a grown-up Boy Scout. He didn't seem worried about anything. It made me nervous. We were about to go into a bar that was thick with bikers, bad guys. There was a necromancer inside so powerful that it made my skin crawl from blocks away. The rest of us looked confident, but it was a confidence born of having been there and done that and survived. Rigby's confidence struck me as false, not false confidence, but based on a false assumption. I couldn't know for sure without asking, but I was betting that Rigby had never really been in any situation where he thought he might not come out the other side. There was a softness to him despite the lean muscles. I'd take a few less muscles and more depth to the eyes any day. I hoped that Ramirez didn't have to come in with Rigby as his only backup. But I didn't say it out loud. Everyone loses their cherry sometime, somewhere. If things went wrong, tonight might be Rigby's night.

"Did you tell us that little story for a reason, Hernando? I mean you don't really think that Baco or this biker gang are los Duendos?"

He shook his head. "No, I just thought you might want to know. It says something about Baco to name his bar after fallen angels."

I opened the driver's side door of the Hummer. Bernardo took the hint and went for the passenger side door. "Not fallen angels, Hernando, just caught in limbo."

Hernando leaned into the open window of the car. "But they're not in Heaven anymore, are they?" With that last cryptic comment he stepped back and let me raise the window. He and Rigby watched us drive off. They looked sort of forlorn standing there in the abandoned, broken parking lot. Or maybe it was just me feeling forlorn.

I looked at Bernardo. "Don't kill anyone, okay?"

He slid back in his seat, snuggling against the leather. He looked more relaxed than I'd seen him in hours. "If they try to kill us?"

I sighed. "Then we defend ourselves," I said.

"See, I knew you'd see things my way."

"Don't start the fight," I said.

He looked at me with eager brown eyes. "Can I finish it?"

I looked back at the road searching for a parking space. Whatever spell Baco had been working was over. The atmosphere was a little easier to breathe. But there was still something in the air like close lightning waiting to strike. "Yeah, we can finish it."

He started humming under his breath. I think it was the theme from "The Magnificent Seven." To quote an overused movie line, I had a bad feeling about this.

37

BY THE TIME I found a parking space, Bernardo and I had a plan. I was an out of town necromancer wanting to talk shop with one of the only other necromancers I'd ever heard of. If it hadn't been so damn close to the truth, it would have been a lousy cover story. Even being the truth, almost, it sounded weak. But we didn't have all day, and besides, I don't think being sneaky was a strong suit for either of us. We were both more comfortable with the bust-the-door-down-and-start-shooting school, than the concoct-a-good-cover-story-and-infiltrate.

Bernardo reached his hand out for me just before we crossed the street. I frowned at him.

He waggled his hand at me. "Come on, Anita, play fair." He was holding his right hand out to me. I stared at the offered hand for a heartbeat, but finally took it. His fingers slid around my hand a little slower, and a little more proprietarily than necessary, but I could live with it. Lucky for us that I was right-handed, and Bernardo was left-handed. We could hold hands and not compromise either of our gun hands. Usually, I was the only one armed when I was cuddling, so it was only my gun hand we had to worry about.

I've dated men that I couldn't walk hand in hand with, like an awkward rhythm between us. Bernardo was not one of those men. He slowed his pace to let me catch up to his longer legs, until he realized I was a step ahead of him, tugging on his hand. I have a lot of tall friends. No one ever complains that I can't keep up.

The door to the bar was black and blended so well with the building's facade that you almost missed it. Bernardo opened the door for me, and I let him. It might blow our cover to argue over who got to hold the door for who. Though if he had been my real boyfriend, we'd have had the discussion. Ah, well.

The minute I stepped inside the bar, no, the second I stepped inside the bar, I knew we were not going to blend in. So many things had already gone wrong. We were not so much overdressed as wrongly dressed. If Bernardo had ditched the black dress shirt and just worn the white T-shirt, and if it hadn't looked fresh out of the box, then he might have mingled. I was *so* the only suit jacket in the room. But even the polo shirt and jeans seemed a little much beside what some of the women were wearing. Can you say, short-shorts?

A girl near us, and I meant girl—if she was eighteen, I'd eat something icky—looked at me with hostile eyes. She had long brown hair that swung past her shoulders. The hair was clean and shiny even in the dim light. Her makeup was light but expertly applied. She should have been deciding who to take to prom. Instead, she was wearing a black leather bra with metal studs on it and matching shorts that looked like they'd been painted over her narrow hips. A pair of those clunky platform high-heels completed the look. Those platform shoes had been ugly in the seventies and eighties, and they were still ugly two decades later, even if they were back in style.

She was hanging all over a guy that had to be thirty years or more her senior. His hair and ragged beard were gray. At first glance you'd think he was fat, but he was fat the way an offensive lineman was fat, flesh with muscle under it. His eyes were hidden behind small round sunglasses, even though the bar was cast in permanent twilight. He sat at the table closest to the door, big hands resting on the wood. He was totally at rest, but you still got a sense of how very large he was, how physically imposing. The girl was slender and shorter than I was. I hoped she was his daughter, but doubted it.

He stood, and a wave of energy moved off of him in a curling, almost visible roil of power. It was suddenly hard to breathe, and it wasn't the cigarette smoke rolling like a low fog through the room. I'd come in expecting to meet a necromancer. I had not expected a werewolf. I couldn't be a hundred percent sure of the type of animal, but call it a hunch—los lobos—had to be werewolves.

I looked out over that room full of people, and felt their power raise like invisible hackles. Bernardo put his right hand on my shoulder and drew me towards the bar, slowly. It took almost all the restraint I had not to reach for one of the guns. They had not offered us violence. They probably always did this show to unwanted tourists. Almost anyone would get the message and leave. Leaving actually sounded like a really good idea. Unfortunately, we had business, and a really good threat display was not reason enough to stop us. Pity. Because they would not like the fact that we didn't leave. What if this afternoon's little display wasn't the norm? What if they were trying to chase us away because something illegal was going down? Worse and worse.

The long wooden bar had cleared out as we moved towards it. Fine with me. I didn't want to be outflanked. The bartender was a woman, surprise, and a dwarf, ah, little person. I couldn't see over the bar, but she had to have something she was standing on. She had short, thick hair, dark, shot through with strands of white. Her face was the typical rough square, but her eyes were as hard as any I've ever seen. Her face was heavily lined not with age, but with wear and tear. One eyebrow was bisected by a heavy white scar. All she needed was a sign above her head that said, "I've had a hard life."

"What do you want?" she asked. Her tone matched the rest of her, harsh.

I half expected Bernardo to answer, but his attention was all for the room and the growing air of hostility. "We're looking for Nicky Baco," I said.

Her eyes never flickered. "Never heard of him."

I shook my head. Her answer had been automatic. She didn't even have to think about it. I could have asked to see anyone in the room and the answer would have been the same. I lowered my voice, though I knew most of the things in the room would hear even the barest whisper. "I'm a necromancer. I heard that Baco is one, too. I've met a lot of zombie raisers, but never another necromancer."

She shook her head. "Don't know what you're talking about." She started to rub the top of the bar with a stained rag. She wasn't even looking at me now, as if I'd become something totally without interest.

They'd stall for a while, then they'd get impatient and try to kick us out. Unless we were willing to start shooting people, they'd succeed. When in doubt, tell the truth. Not my usual ploy, but hey, I'll try anything once.

"I'm Anita Blake," and that was all I got out before her gaze snapped upward, and she really looked at me for the first time.

"Prove it," she said.

I started to reach inside the jacket for my ID. I heard the gun click underneath the bar, as she pulled the hammer back. Just from the sound I'd say it was an old fashioned shotgun, sawed-off or it wouldn't have fit under the bar.

"Slowly," she said.

I caught Bernardo's movement out of the corner of my eye. Turning towards us, maybe going for a gun. "It's okay, Bernardo. It's under control."

I don't think he believed me.

I said, "Please."

I didn't say please often. Bernardo hesitated but finally turned back to watch the gathering werewolves. He hissed, "Hurry up."

I did what the lady with the shotgun pointed at my chest said, I moved very, very slowly, and handed her my ID.

"Lay it on the bar."

I laid it on the bar.

"Hands flat on the bar. Lean into it."

The bar top was sticky, but I kept my hands on it and leaned into it, in a sort of push-up position. She could have just asked me to assume the position. It was a leg width away from it.

"Him, too," she said.

Bernardo had heard her. "No," he said.

Something passed through her eyes that would have made Edward proud. I knew she'd do it. "Either do what she says or get the fuck out of here," I said.

He moved so he could watch the room at large, and see me and the lady behind the bar. He was beside the outer door. One quick move and he could be out in the afternoon sunlight. He didn't go for the door. He looked at me. His eyes flicked to the woman behind the bar. I think he saw in her face what I'd seen because he sighed enough that his shoulders slumped. He shook his head, but he moved towards the long bar. He moved stiffly, as if each small movement pained him. His posture, his face, all screamed that he didn't like doing this, but he leaned beside me against the bar.

"Legs further apart," she said. "Lean into it like you want to see that pretty face in the polish."

I heard Bernardo take a hissing breath, but he spread his legs and leaned close enough to see the varnish on the scarred bar. "Can I just say now that this is a bad idea?" he said.

"Shut up," I said.

The woman opened the ID on the bar top, one hand still hidden under the bar. They had the shotgun attached underneath the bar somehow. I wondered what other surprises they had.

"Why do you want to see Nicky?" she asked.

She hadn't told me to stop leaning, so I didn't. "I told the truth. I want to talk to another necromancer."

"Why didn't you tell me who you were up front?"

"I work with the cops sometimes. I thought it might make you nervous." I had to roll my eyes up to see her face. I was rewarded with a smile. It looked almost awkward on her harsh features, but it was a start.

"Why do you want to talk to another necromancer?"

I let the truth spill out of my mouth without concentrating on the fact that I planned to stop before I'd told all of it. I mean Nicky Baco was a necromancer, and if necromancy was involved in the killings . . . So only part of the truth until I knew whether he was a bad guy. "I've got a little problem that involves the dead. I wanted a second opinion."

She laughed then, a harsh sound like the caw of a crow. I jumped, and I swear I could feel the werewolves behind me flinch. If I hadn't known better, I'd have said they were just a little afraid of this small woman. I know I was.

"Nicky'll love that. The famous Anita Blake coming to consult him. Oh, he will just fucking love this." She motioned with her head. "Who's he?"

"This is Bernardo, he's . . . a friend."

Her eyes hardened. "How good a friend?"

"Close, very close," I said.

She leaned across the bar, putting her face next to mine, her hand still under the bar on the shotgun. "I should kill you. I can feel it. You'll hurt Nicky." I looked into her eyes from inches away. I expected to see anger or even hatred, but there was nothing. It was the very emptiness that clued me in. If she pulled the trigger on me, it wouldn't be the first time.

My pulse was suddenly thudding in my throat. Blown away by a psychotic dwarf bartender, how ironic. I kept my voice low and even the way you talk to jumpers on ledges, and people with guns pointed at you. "I don't plan to hurt Nicky. I honestly just want to consult with him, one necromancer to another."

She just kept looking at me, not even blinking. She raised up slowly. "If you move, I'll kill you. If he moves, I'll kill you." The way she said it promised that whatever was about to happen, was something we weren't going to like.

She turned her gaze to Bernardo and leaned down so that her head was sideways looking at him, her ear almost pressed to the bar. "Did you hear me, boyfriend?"

"I heard you," he said, and his voice was low and calm, too. He'd seen it, too. She wanted an excuse to kill me. I'd never met her before, so it couldn't be personal. But personal or not, I'd be just as dead.

"We don't let outsiders bring guns into our house."

"No disrespect intended," I said. "I always go armed. Nothing personal."

She leaned back down next to Bernardo's face. "How 'bout you? You always go armed?"

"Yes," he said. He frowned, then went back to staring at the bar. Lucky he'd worn a hair barrette today or his lovely hair would have been covered in sticky gunk. My hands felt like they were becoming permanently glued to the wood.

"Not in here you don't," she said.

It was the big man in front who searched us. Somehow I'd known it would be. His power beat against my back like a nearly solid wall of power. Shit. He patted me down like he'd done it before. He found the knives at my wrist and back, as well as the guns. He also found the cell phone but placed it on the bar in front of me instead of taking it.

You could see the effort it took for Bernardo to let the man touch him, pat him down, take his gun. He also took a knife out of one of Bernardo's boots. Anything was an improvement over the last crime scene, but the day really wasn't going well.

"Can we stand up now?" I asked.

"Not yet," she said.

Bernardo gave me a look that said plainly if he died, he was coming back to haunt me because it was all my fault.

I kept my voice calm, tried to make sense. "You know I'm Anita Blake. You know why I'm here. What else do you want?"

"Harpo, check the man's wallet. Find out who he is," she said.

Harpo? The big man, the vibrating mountain of mystical energy was named Harpo. I said none of this out loud. I really am getting smarter.

Harpo took out Bernardo's wallet. He'd stuffed Bernardo's ten mil down the side of his pants and my Browning on the other side. I didn't see the Firestar or the knives. Maybe he'd stuffed them in his pockets. "The driver's license says, Bernardo Spotted-Horse, but there ain't no credit cards, no pictures, no nothing."

The woman's eyes had gone back to pitiless. "You say he's a close friend?"

"Yes," I said. I was beginning to get scared again.

"He your lover?" she asked.

If she hadn't had a shotgun pointed at me, I'd have told her to go to hell, but she did, so I answered. "Yeah." I was trusting that Ramirez knew what he was talking about, that I needed to belong to a man. I hoped the lie was the right answer.

"Prove it," she said.

I raised eyebrows at her. "Excuse me?"

"Excuse me," she mimicked, and that brought low rumbling laughter from the rest of the room.

"Is he circumcised?" she asked.

I hesitated. I couldn't help it. The question caught me too far off guard. I swallowed, and said, "Yes." I had a fifty-fifty chance, and being American and under forty I had a better than even chance.

She smiled, but it left her eyes like empty glass. "You can stand up now."

I fought the urge to wipe my hands on my pants. Didn't want to insult her cleanliness, but I also wanted desperately to wash my hands. I moved closer to Bernardo, as if I wanted a hug. I even put my left arm around his waist, though I wondered if I was getting his nice white shirt dirty. His arm slid over my shoulders, but I'd really just wanted out of the line of fire of the damned shotgun. I was betting it was on a stationary mount and not a swiveling one. I hoped I was right.

Her hands were back in plain sight. A good sign. "Drop your pants, Bernardo," she said.

I felt him tense beside me. We both looked at her. I started to say excuse me again, but Bernardo said, "Why?"

I'd have asked her to repeat it, just to make sure I'd understood her. He just asked why, as if this had happened to him before.

"So we can see if you're circumcised."

I moved my hand out from behind Bernardo's back, standing close together but not entangled in each other's arms. We might be in for a fight after all. "I said he was. Isn't that enough?"

"No. You see, you're right. You do work with the cops a lot. You alone might have been okay to see Nicky, but him, we don't know anything about him. If he's your lover, then fine, but if he's not, then maybe he's a cop."

Bernardo laughed, and the sound startled all of us, I think. "Now that is a new one. Me being mistaken for a cop."

"What are you, if you're not a cop?" she asked.

"Sometimes I'm a bodyguard. Sometimes I'm someone you need to guard the body against. Depends on who's paying better." His voice sounded very sure of itself, very matter of fact.

"Maybe you are, and maybe you're not. Drop the pants, and we'll see."

He started unbuckling his belt. I moved away from him, though not too far. Didn't want to get back in front of the shotgun again.

"What's wrong? You've seen him without his pants before," she said. I was beginning to think she didn't believe me.

"Not in a crowd, I haven't," I said. I let the righteous indignation blaze in my voice. It got more laughter from the crowd.

The women were starting to chant, "Take it off, take it all off," and worse. The girl that had been hanging on Harpo was just behind him, watching the show with glittering excited eyes.

Bernardo didn't complain or blush. He just undid his pants and pushed them to about mid thigh, and stood there. My look away was automatic. The women screamed, and whistled. One voice yelled, "Big daddy, yes!" The men joined in. The men were congratulating him and speculating on how we did it without hurting me.

I had to look. I just couldn't help myself. I had to know if I'd guessed right, and frankly I just had to look. Embarrassing but true. It took me a few seconds to register that he was circumcised because what I saw first was sheer size. He was well, well endowed.

I was blushing, and I couldn't help that. But I knew if I just stood there and gaped that the lies would all be for nothing. I tried to act as if it were Richard or Jean-Claude standing there. What would I have done? I'd have covered them up.

I moved to stand in front of him, though was careful not to touch. I admit though that I couldn't seem to look anywhere else. Richard was impressive. Bernardo had passed impressive and gone over to scary. I shielded him from view with my body, putting my hands on either side of his waist to steady myself. I was blushing so hard, I was dizzy.

I looked at her, still shielding him from the room. "Good enough?" I asked. Even my voice sounded strangled with discomfort.

"Give him a kiss," she said.

I looked at her. "Let him put his pants up and I will."

She shook her head. "I didn't say kiss his lips."

If I blushed any harder, my head was going to explode. I turned around so I couldn't see him anymore. "We are so not doing this."

"I think you'll do anything we want," she said.

I don't know what I would have said to that because a man's voice sounded. "Enough games, Paulina. Give them back their weapons, and let them go."

We all turned. Coming from the dim back of the room was another dwarf, little person. He was maybe half a head taller than the bartender, Paulina, and he was more obviously Hispanic and younger. His hair was a rich black, his skin tanned and unlined. He looked twenty-something, but the aura of power that spread outward from him like an overwhelming perfume felt older.

"I am Nicandro Baco, Nicky to my friends." The crowd parted for him like a curtain being drawn back. He held his hand out to me, and I took it, but he didn't shake hands. He raised my hand to his lips and kissed it. But he kept his eyes rolled up to see my face as he did it, and something about the way his eyes looked, his mouth on my skin, reminded me of much more intimate places for a man's mouth to be. I took my hand back as soon as I could and still be polite.

"Mr. Baco, thank you for seeing me." It sounded so businesslike, as if Bernardo wasn't standing behind us with his pants around his thighs.

"Get dressed," he said. He barely glanced at Bernardo. But I heard him pulling up his pants, struggling to get everything back in place, though frankly I was surprised his jeans could fit over everything.

"Why are you here, Ms. Blake?"

"I really did want to talk to another necromancer."

"It sounds like you've changed your mind," he said. He watched me minutely, studying my face. When I moved a hand to touch my hair, his eyes tracked it.

"The grandstanding has taken up all my time. I've got an appointment with the police that I can't really miss." I'd added the police part on purpose because I had a feeling that Baco had known exactly what was happening out here. They hadn't really hurt us, just embarrassed us or me. He came in just in the nick of time. Yeah, right.

"Like the two policemen that are waiting outside for you."

I felt the knowledge flinch across my face, not much of a reaction, but it was enough. "Do you blame us for backup?"

"Are you saying you are afraid of us?" That brought a low rumble through the room, as if they had all drawn a breath together.

"I would be a fool if I wasn't," I said.

He cocked his head to one side in an almost bird-like movement. "And you are not a fool, are you, Anita?"

"I try not to be."

He motioned to the woman still standing behind the bar. "Paulina does not like you. Do you know why?"

It was my turn to shake my head. "Nope."

"She's my wife."

I must have still looked blank. "Sorry, I don't understand."

"She knows I have a weakness for women with power."

I frowned at him. "She doesn't have to worry. I'm sort of taken."

He smiled. "No more lies, Anita. You and he are not lovers." He took my hand again and gazed up at me with those black eyes. I realized for the first time that he considered himself a ladies man. And that his wife had reason to worry, not about me, but about other women. It was there in his eyes, the way he stroked my hand.

I drew my hand away from him and moved back to stand with Bernardo. I actually reached out my hand, and he took it. Both our hands were sticky from the bar, but I clutched at him.

Baco was half a body-length shorter than I was, but he made me nervous. Part of it was the push of his magic like a thick curtain filling the room. But part of it was the way any man can make you nervous. I didn't like how blatant he was, with us unarmed. I glanced at Paulina, and her harsh face was stricken. Was it a game he played with her? Tormenting her? Who knew, but I wanted out of here.

"I need to be somewhere before dark. If you don't want to talk to me, fine. We'll go." I started moving backwards, using my body to push Bernardo behind me towards the door.

"Without your weapons?" Baco made it a question, his voice lilting upward.

Bernardo and I froze. We were close enough to the door that we could have made a rush for it, probably made it, but . . . "Our weapons would be nice," I said.

"All you had to do was ask," Baco said.

I said, "May we have our weapons back?"

He nodded. "Harpo, give them back."

Harpo never questioned it, just gave us back the guns, the knives. Then he stepped back to join the rest of the silent watchers. The guns and wrist knives were easy to slide into place. The knife in its spine sheath was another matter. I had to use my left hand to feel for the sheath, then feel the blade's tip at the mouth of the sheath. I'd gotten in the habit of closing my eyes so that all I concentrated on was touch. It actually took only a few seconds now to put it away. The real trick was not chopping off a hunk of my hair as the blade slid home.

When I opened my eyes, Baco was looking at me. "So nice to see a woman who doesn't rely exclusively on sight. Touch is such an important sense for intimate occasions."

Maybe being armed again made me brave, or maybe I was just tired of the tension level. "Men who turn everything into a sexual come on are such bores."

Distaste, anger filled his face, turning his charming eyes to black mirrors, like the eyes of a doll. "Too good to fuck a dwarf?"

I shook my head. "It's not your height that's the problem, Baco. Where I come from, you don't do shit like this in front of your wife."

He laughed then, and it sparkled through his eyes, his face. "The sacrament of marriage? You're offended for my wife's sake? You are a funny girl."

"Yeah, me and Barbra Streisand."

The humor faded a little from his face. I don't think he got the joke. Strangely, it was the young girl in her short-shorts that met my eyes. I think she got the joke. If she liked early Streisand movies, maybe she wasn't a completely lost soul.

Bernardo touched my shoulder, and I jumped. "We're leaving now, Anita."

I nodded. "I'm with you."

"You never asked your questions," Baco said.

"Have you felt it?" I asked.

His face was suddenly serious. "There is something new here. It is like us. It deals in death. I have felt it."

"Where?" I asked.

"Between Santa Fe and Albuquerque though it began closer to Santa Fe."

"It's moving closer to Albuquerque, to you," I said.

For the first time he looked uncertain, not quite afraid, but not happy either. "It knows that I am here. I have felt that, too." He stared up at me, and now there was no teasing in his eyes. "It knows that you are here, too, Anita. It knows you are here, too."

I nodded. "We might be able to help each other, Nicky. I've seen the bodies. I've seen what this thing does. Trust me, Nicky. You don't want to go out that way."

"What do you propose?" he asked.

"That we pool our resources and see if we can stop this thing before it gets here, to you. And that we stop playing games. No more teasing. No more power plays."

"Just business between us?" he said.

I nodded. "We don't have time for anything else, Baco."

"Come back later tonight, and I will do what I can to help you. Though the police will not want you to share information with me. I am a very bad man, you know."

I smiled. "You're a bad man, Nicky, but not a stupid one. You need me."

"As you need me, Anita," he said.

"Two necromancers are better than one," I said.

He nodded, face solemn. "Come back tonight when you are finished with your police business. I will be waiting."

"It may be late," I said.

"It is already later than you think, Anita. Pray, if you are the praying sort, that it is not too late."

"Anita?" Bernardo said.

"We're going." I let Bernardo back us out the door, his hand on my shoulder guiding me backwards. I got to watch the room, trusting him to make sure nothing was coming up behind us through the door. The werewolves just watched us, not happy, but willing to take orders. Baco had to be their vargamor, their resident witch. I'd just never met a pack that feared its vargamor before.

It was Paulina's face that stayed with me. She was staring at Baco, and the hatred on her face was raw. I knew in that instant that once she had loved him, really loved him, because only true love could twist to such hatred. I'd looked into Paulina's eyes across the barrel of a gun. I think Nicky Baco had more problems than just monsters in the desert. If I were him, I'd be sleeping with a gun.

38

WE ARRIVED AT THE hospital with the world wrapped in a heavy blue dusk. A twilight so solid it was like cloth, something you could wrap around your hands or wear like a dress. I'd called ahead using Ramirez' cell phone. How do you prove that someone is really dead? I'd seen the "survivors." They drew breath. I assumed they had a heart beat or the doctors would have mentioned it. Their eyes looked at you and seemed to be aware. They reacted to pain. They were alive.

But what if they weren't? What if they were only vessels for a power that made Nicky Baco and I look like backstreet charlatans? There might have been a spell to prove it, but you couldn't take the results of a spell to court and get permission to burn the bodies. And that was what I wanted.

I finally came up with brain waves. I was betting that the higher functions of the brain weren't working. It was the only thing I could think of that might show that something was wrong with the survivors other than not having skin and missing body parts.

Unfortunately, Doctor Evans and company had done monitored brain wave activity long ago. They all had higher brain functions. So much for my brilliant idea. Doctor Evans had wanted to talk in the doctor's lounge, but I'd insisted we talk closer to the survivors' room than that. We talked in low tones in the hallway. He wouldn't let me talk in front of the survivors about the fact that they might be dead. Because if I was wrong, it might cause them distress. He had a point. But I didn't think I was wrong.

The survivors already at the hospital had become agitated and violent, snapping at the hospital staff like dogs on chains. No one had been hurt, but the timing coincided with the last murders. Why had the skinned ones been more violent? Was it the spell used to banish whatever it was from the home? Had that upped the ante somehow? Maybe frightened the creature that we were on to it? I didn't know. I just didn't know.

All I did know was that I could feel the darkness pressing like a hand about to crush us all. It was a heaviness in the air like before a thunderstorm, but worse, closer, harder to breathe through. Something bad was coming, and it was tied to the darkness. I wasn't able to convince Doctor Evans that his patients were dead, but my urgency must have been persuasive because he did give permission for the two officers that were already at the hospital to guard inside the room instead of out. The only proof I had that there were cops inside the room was a hat lying on one of the chairs outside the door.

I wanted to go into the room myself, but by the time I got suited up in gown and mask it would be full dark. It was that close, like a trembling line. So I stood in the hall and pretended that I was okay with it, because there was nothing else I could do.

Since Officer Rigby and Bernardo were new, they got the standard lecture about not shooting inside an oxygen atmosphere. It would be bad, though it wouldn't explode, which is what I thought it would have done. It would be the flash fire to end all flash fires, turning the room into a lower circle of hell for the few moments it took to use up all the oxygen or fuel in the room. But it wouldn't explode in a shower of glass and plaster. Nothing too dramatic, just deadly.

Rigby asked, "And if they try to eat us, what are we supposed to do? Spit on them?"

"I don't know," Evans said. "All I can tell you is what you shouldn't do, and you shouldn't fire a gun into a room full of oxygen."

Bernardo drew a knife from somewhere. He hadn't bent down near his boot, which meant it was a different knife, and one the werewolf in the bar had missed. He held the blade up to the light, letting it gleam. "You cut them."

Darkness fell like a lead curtain, almost clanging in my head like the roll of thunder. I waited for the door to the room to open. I waited for the screaming to start because that's what I was expecting. Nothing happened. Then the pressure that had been building for hours vanished. It was as if something had swallowed it up. I was just suddenly standing in the hallway feeling light, empty, better. I didn't understand the change, and I don't like what I don't understand.

We all waited for a few tense heartbeats, then I couldn't stand it. I spilled a knife into my own hand and reached for the door. The door swung outward. I jumped back. The male nurse that I'd been introduced to earlier paused in the door staring at the naked blade in my hand.

He never took his eyes off me, but he talked to Evans. "Doctor, the patients are quiet, quieter than they've been all day. The police officers are wanting to know if they can step out of the room for a while."

"The survivors are quieter than they've been all day?" I asked.

Ben the nurse nodded. "Yes, ma'am."

I took two steps back from the door, and let out the tension in my body in a long breath.

"Well, Ms. Blake?" Evans asked. "Can the officers come out?"

I shrugged and looked at Ramirez. "Ask him. He's ranking officer on site. But truthfully, I guess so. Whatever I've been feeling seemed to fade when darkness fell. I don't understand it." I slid the knife back into its sheath. "I guess there's not going to be a fight."

"You sound disappointed," Bernardo said. His knife had vanished to wherever he'd gotten it from.

I shook my head. "Not disappointed, just confused. I felt a great deal of power building for hours, and it just vanished. That much power doesn't just vanish. It went somewhere. Apparently, not into the survivors, but it's off somewhere tonight doing something."

"Any ideas what it's doing and where?" Ramirez asked.

I shook my head. "Not really."

He turned to the doctor. "Tell the men they can come outside."

Ben the nurse looked to Doctor Evans for confirmation. Evans nodded. The nurse ducked back inside, the door closing slowly behind him.

Evans turned to me. "Well, Ms. Blake, looks like you hurried over here for nothing."

I shrugged. "I thought we'd be ass deep in man-eating corpses by now." I smiled. "It's nice to be wrong once in a while."

We all smiled at each other. The tension spilled out of all of us. Bernardo gave that nervous laugh you sometimes give when the emergency is over, or the bullet passed you by.

"I'm very glad you were wrong, this time, Ms. Blake," Evans said.

"Me, too," I said.

"Me, three," Bernardo said.

"I'm happy, too," Ramirez said, "but it is disappointing to find out you're not perfect."

"If you don't know I'm not perfect after forty-eight hours of working with me on a police investigation, then you are not paying attention."

"I'm paying attention," Ramirez said, "close attention." There was a weight to his gaze, an intensity to his words that made me want to squirm. In trying not to squirm I caught Bernardo's eyes. He was smiling at me, enjoying my discomfort. Glad someone was.

"If you were wrong about this, you may be wrong about them being dead," Evans said.

I nodded. "Maybe."

"You admit you may be wrong, just like that?" Evans seemed surprised.

"This is magic, not math, Doctor Evans. There are very few hard and fast rules. There are even fewer rules the way I do it. Sometimes I think two and two is going to add up to five, and I'm right. Sometimes all you get is four. If it lowers the body count, I don't mind being wrong."

The door opened, and two men came out dressed in Albuquerque uniforms. They'd headed for the door as soon as Ben the nurse told them they could go. I didn't blame them one bit.

Their eyes looked haunted. The tallest one was blond and built all of squares. Broad shoulders, thick waist, heavy legs, not fat, just solid, strong. His partner was shorter and almost completely bald except for a ring of brown curls low on his head. Apparently, it was his hat sitting in the chair by the door.

Doctor Evans said, "Excuse me." He moved past them into the room.

The short one said, "He can have it."

The blond looked at me, eyes narrowing, not friendly. "Well, if it isn't the wicked witch of the Midwest. I hear we have you to thank for us sitting in there for the last hour."

I didn't recognize him, but apparently he knew me on sight. "I suggested it, yes."

The blond moved closer, using his size to intimidate me, or he tried. Size just isn't as impressive as most men think it is. "Maybe Marks was right about you."

Ah hah. He must have been one of the officers on site when Marks kicked me out. I felt Ramirez start to move up, probably to step between us. I put my hand on his shoulder. "It's all right."

Ramirez didn't move back the step he'd taken, but at least he didn't move forward. It was probably the best I would get out of him. But it meant that I was sandwiched between the two men. The blond's eyes flicked to Ramirez behind me.

The look on his face was enough. He wanted a fight and didn't really care who it was with.

He was glaring at Ramirez now, and I could almost feel the testosterone rising on every side. Enough testosterone to get the officer in trouble, maybe suspended when all he needed was to blow off some steam. He was trying to cleanse himself of the horrors in that room.

Both his partner and Bernardo were staying back. I didn't know what the partner was doing, but Bernardo was enjoying the show.

"You must have been one of the officers that helped Marks throw me out," I said. I was looking way up at the man, and he was looking over me at Ramirez.

It took him a second to blink and look at me. He frowned at me, and it was a good frown. I bet it made a lot of bad guys run like hell.

His partner came up behind him. "Yeah, Jarman and I were both there." The partner sounded calm, and I think worried about his partner. Good partners look after more than just your physical health.

"And you are?" I asked. I asked it like his partner, Jarman, wasn't about to pick a fight with everyone in the hallway.

He introduced himself like everything was normal, too. "Jakes."

"Jarman and Jakes?" I made it a question.

He nodded, smiling. "J and J at your service."

I felt the tension easing in the big man in front of me. Hard to stay pissed when you're being ignored, and everyone else is behaving themselves. I pressed my back into Ramirez, trying to urge him to back off. He took the hint, stepping back a little.

Officer Rigby came bounding down the hallway. He'd gone to the car to get something less explosive than his gun. What he was carrying was a Tazer gun. It would send a charge of 30,000 to 60,000 volts through a suspect. Theoretically, it could put someone down for the count without the danger of killing him. Unless you get very unlucky, like the perp has a pacemaker.

Ramirez was shaking his head. "What the hell is that for?"

Rigby looked at the Tazer. "I can't use my gun so I'll use this."

"Rigby," Jarman said, "a Tazer makes a spark."

Rigby looked puzzled. "So?"

"If the spark when we fire a gun will set off the oxygen in the room, so will the spark from a Tazer," Ramirez said.

"Go back to the car and find something else," Jarman said.

Jakes and I had moved to one side, watching Ramirez and Jarman ream the rookie. No one was mad anymore, derisive, condescending, but not mad. When Rigby had disappeared through the doors at the far end of the hall, Jarman turned to Ramirez. "Is Rigby all Marks gave you for backup?"

Ramirez nodded, then shrugged. "He'll learn."

"And get someone killed doing it," Jarman said.

Jakes held his hand out low, palm up. He was smiling. I gave him a low five. I was smiling, too, but not because his partner hadn't belted a detective. I was just happy that I'd been wrong. I'd had my fill of corpses for the day. Hell, for the year.

Bernardo was leaning against the opposite wall. He seemed puzzled by my interaction with the cops. I doubt it ever occurred to Bernardo to make friends with them.

The two uniforms had batons stuck in their utility belts. Ramirez looked unarmed except for his gun. "Where's your baton, Hernando?"

"Oooh, Hernando," Jakes said.

"Yeah, Hernando," Jarman said, rolling the name off his tongue, "where's your baton?" That they were willing to give Ramirez shit meant that under normal conditions he and Jarman got along. There is a different flavor to teasing when it's hostile. Rigby's teasing was close to hostile, not quite, as if they weren't sure if he were really one of them yet.

Ramirez took a short metal rod out of his hip pocket. He made a small sharp movement with his wrist, and the rod telescoped into a solid piece of metal about two feet long.

"An asp," I said. "I didn't notice you carrying one when we met. I'm usually pretty aware of weapons."

He flicked the rod back into its compact size. "An asp is pretty small when it's put away. How do you know I wasn't carrying one?"

I opened my mouth, then closed it, and looked at him. He was grinning at me. I debated on whether to rise to the bait, or let it pass. Hell, this was the most fun I'd had all day. "Are you implying that I was staring at your butt?"

"How else would you know I didn't have something about the size of a pen in my back pocket?" His eyes were sparkling like dark jewels, shiny with humor.

I shrugged. "Just checking for weapons."

"That's what they all say."

Jarman said, "Wanna check me for weapons?"

I looked at him. "I can see your weapon from here, Jarman."

He puffed his chest out a little, managing to strut without moving his feet an inch. "When you're my size, it's hard to miss."

I looked at every man in turn and had to really fight the urge to linger on Bernardo. I was willing to bet that his "weapon" was the biggest in the hallway. "Oh, I don't know, Jarman. You know what they say. It's not size that matters. It's talent." Again, I had to fight the urge to stare at Bernardo.

Jarman smiled happily. "Trust me, baby. I've got the talent and the size."

"Easy to brag when you know you'll never have to prove it," I said, and yes, I was baiting him.

Jarman swept his hat off and gave me a look. I think it was supposed to be a come hither look. His scary frown was better than his sexy look, but hey, I bet he got a lot more opportunity to practice scary than sexy.

"Let's find some privacy, babe, and I will prove it."

I shook my head, smiling. "And what would your wife say about you taking me out for a test drive. Nice wedding band, by the way."

He laughed, a good-natured rumble.

Jakes answered for him. "His wife would feed him his dick on a stick."

Jarman nodded, still chuckling. "Yeah, my Bren has a temper, that she does."

He said it like it was a good thing, a thing he valued. He looked at me. "My Bren would have kicked Marks in the balls, not kissed him."

"I thought about it," I said.

"Why didn't you hit him?" Ramirez asked. The humor still sparkled in his eyes but his face was more serious. I think he wanted a real answer, not a joke.

"He was expecting me to hit him. Maybe even wanted me to hit him. He could have pressed assault charges, gotten me behind bars for awhile."

I expected one of the three men to say Marks wouldn't do that, but no one did. I looked from one suddenly serious face to another. "No one going to defend the lieutenant's honor? Protest that he wouldn't do such a dastardly thing?"

Jarman said, "Nope."

Jakes said, "Dastardly. You talk real pretty for a devil-worshipping assassin."

I blinked at him. "Pass that by me again, slowly."

Jakes nodded. "According to the lieutenant, you're suspected in the disappearances of several citizens, as well as dancing naked in the moonlight with the devil himself."

"Marks didn't say that last part."

Jakes grinned. "Can't blame a man for wishful thinking." He wiggled his eyebrows at me.

I laughed. They laughed. A good time being had by all. Except Bernardo, who leaned against the wall apart from the general goodwill. He was watching me as if he'd never really seen me before. I'd surprised him in some way.

"Marks tried to get you arrested for magical malfeasance, so the rumor mill says," Jarman said.

I stared at him. Magical malfeasance could carry a death sentence. I stared at Ramirez. "Did you know he was trying to do that?"

Ramirez touched my arm. We moved down the hallway to the distant rumble of masculine laughter. The two officers were probably still giving each other good-natured shit. From the caliber of the laughter, if it was about me, it was probably something I didn't want to hear. There is always a line to the teasing that must be carefully avoided. I wanted to be a female one of the guys, not get a reputation for being a slut. A thin line to walk sometimes.

Probably best to be out of earshot, but I didn't want to be alone with Ramirez right now. It bothered me that he hadn't told me what Marks had said about me. He was a virtual stranger. He didn't owe me anything, but it made me think less of him.

An African-American nurse walked past us and went into the room. Since all I'd seen were her eyes the first time, I couldn't be sure if she was the same nurse I'd glimpsed earlier in the room. She was small, about the right size, but in full surgical scrubs, who knew?

The men had fallen silent as she walked past. As soon as the door closed safely behind her, the laughter sounded again.

Ramirez looked at me with that honest face, a line of concern between his eyebrows like a tiny wrinkle of discontent. He looked even younger when he frowned. "Doesn't that bother you?" he asked.

"What?" I asked.

He glanced back at the two officers. They were still smiling. "Jakes and Jarman."

"You mean the teasing?"

He nodded.

"When I kissed Marks in front of all of them, I sort of invited a little teasing.

Besides, I sort of started it, or rather you did." I shrugged. "It blows off steam, and we all need that right now."

"Most women don't see it that way," Ramirez said.

"I'm not most women. But frankly, one reason a lot of women don't stand for any teasing is that some men don't know when teasing crosses the line to harassment. If I had to work day in and day out with them, I might be more careful. But I don't, so I can afford to push the line a little."

"What is your line, Anita?" He was standing just a little too close for comfort.

"I'll let everyone know when they've reached it. Don't worry." I stepped back from him, giving myself the distance I wanted.

"You're mad at me." He sounded surprised.

I half-smiled. "Believe me, Detective, when I'm mad at you, you'll know it."

"Detective. Not even Ramirez. Now I know you're upset. What did I do?"

I looked at him, studying that open, honest fact. "Why didn't you tell me what Marks said about me? What he was telling the other cops about me? It could carry a death sentence."

"No way was Marks going to push that through, Anita."

"You still should have told me."

He looked puzzled for a moment, then shrugged. "I didn't know I was supposed to."

I frowned. "I guess not." But I wasn't happy with his answer.

He touched my arm again, every so lightly. "I didn't believe that Marks could get you arrested. I was right. Isn't that enough?"

"No," I said.

He let his hand fall away from me. "What good would it have done to tell you? You'd have worried for nothing."

"I don't need my feelings protected. I need to feel that I can trust you."

"You don't trust me because I didn't tell you everything that Marks said?"

"Not as much as I trusted you before."

The first hint of anger hardened his eyes. "And you told me everything that happened in Los Duendos? You didn't hold anything back about your interview with Nicky Baco?" His eyes weren't kind now. They were cool and searching, cop eyes.

I looked down once, then fought to maintain eye contact when what I desperately wanted to do was duck my head and say, aw shucks, you caught me. Push me into a corner, and I usually get angry. But somehow looking into his deep brown eyes, I couldn't pull up much moral indignation. Maybe it was having no moral high ground to stand on. Yeah, that might be it.

"I didn't kill anybody, if that's what you're implying." It was one of my usual comments with less than my usual force.

"That's not what I'm implying and you know it, Anita."

There was something familiar, almost intimate about the conversation. We'd known each other for two days, and yet we interacted as if we'd known each other much longer. It was unnerving. I didn't usually bond this quickly with people or monsters.

But if it had been my longtime police friend Sergeant Rudolph Storr himself standing in front of me, I'd have lied. If Nicky Baco got a whiff of cops, he'd back off, and he'd never trust me again. People like Baco don't give second chances when it comes to the police.

"Baco knew you and Rigby were outside the bar, Hernando. He has the entire area wired with magical . . ." I waffled my hand back and forth, seeking the right word ". . . wards, spells. He knows what happens in his streets. If I go back in with police as backup, no matter how distant, he won't help us."

"Are you so sure he can help?" Ramirez asked. "He may just be stringing you along, trying to find out what you know."

"He's scared, Hernando. Baco is scared. Call it a feeling, but I don't think much frightens him."

"You've just told me you're withholding information from an ongoing murder investigation."

"If you wire me up or insist on sending someone under cover with me, we'll lose Baco. You know I'm right on this."

"We may lose Baco, but you're not right," he said, and the anger was back. A frustrated anger that I'd seen before in other men that I'd known longer and in more intimate ways. That anger that I can't just be a good girl and play by their rules, and be what they want me to be. It made me tired to hear that thread in Ramirez's voice after only two days.

"The most important thing to me right this second is stopping these murders. That is my goal. That is my only goal." I thought about what I'd said, and added, "And staying alive. But other than that I don't have any other agenda. Stop the bad guys. Stay alive. It makes things simple, Hernando."

"You told me earlier that you wanted your life to change, to be more than blood and horror. If you want that to change, you are going to have to complicate your life, Anita. And you are going to have to start trusting people, really trusting them again."

I shook my head. "Thanks for using my moment of weakness against me. Now I remember why I don't confide in strangers." I was finally angry myself. It felt good. It felt familiar. If I could just stay angry, I could stop being so damned confused.

He grabbed my arm, and the grip wasn't gentle this time. It didn't hurt, but I could feel the press of his fingers in my flesh. For the first time since I'd met him, he let me see the hardness underneath. That core of harshness that you either have or acquire if you stay with the cops. Without that core to protect yourself, you may stay on the job, but you won't thrive.

I smiled. "What next, rubber hoses and bright lights?" It was meant to be a joke, but my voice wasn't light when I said it. We were both angry now. Underneath all those smiles and mild manners was a temper. We'd see whose was worse, his or mine.

He spoke low and carefully, the way I do sometimes when to do anything else will start me yelling. "I could just tell Marks about the meeting. Tell him you're holding out on us."

"Fine," I said, "do it. Marks will probably have him arrested, search his bar. He might even find enough magical paraphernalia to get him jailed on suspicion of magical malfeasance. And what will that get us, Detective? Baco in jail, and a few days from now more people dead. More bodies gutted." I leaned into his angry face and whispered, "How will your dreams be then, Hernando?"

He let me go so abruptly that I stumbled. "You really are a bitch, aren't you?"

I nodded. "If the situation warrants it, you bet."

He shook his head, rubbing his hands up and down his arms. "If I hold out on this and it goes wrong, it could be my career."

"Just say you didn't know."

He shook his head. "Too many people know I was your police escort." He managed to make the last two words heavy with irony. "You've got another meeting planned with him, haven't you?"

I tried to keep the surprise off my face, but a blank face was just as bad. It was like when you were asked if you were sleeping with someone, and you refused to answer. Not answering was as good as a yes.

He stalked from one side of the hallway to the other. "Dammit, Anita, I can't sit on this."

I realized he meant it. I stood in his path, so he had to stop pacing and look at me. "You can't tell Marks. He'll screw it up. If he thinks I'm dancing with the devil, he'll have hysterics when he meets Nicky Baco."

The anger was beginning to leak from his eyes. "When's the meeting?"

I shook my head. "Promise first that you won't tell Marks."

"He's in charge of the investigation. If I don't tell him and he finds out, I might as well hand in my badge."

"He doesn't seem very popular around here," I said.

"He's still my superior."

"He's your boss," I said. "He is in no way your superior."

That earned me a smile. "Flattery will get you nowhere with me."

"It's not flattery, Hernando. It's the truth."

He was finally quiet, standing there looking at me. His expression was almost his normal one, or what I thought was normal for him. For all I knew he dissected puppies in his spare time. All right, I didn't believe that, but I didn't really know him. We were strangers, and I was having to remind myself of that. I kept wanting to treat him like a friend or better. What was the matter with me?

"When is the meeting, Anita?"

"If I won't tell you, then what?"

A shadow of that hardness seeped into his eyes. "Then I tell Marks you're withholding evidence."

"And if I tell you?"

"Then I'll go with you."

I shook my head. "No way."

"I promise not to show up looking like a cop."

I looked at him from shined shoes to short, clean hair. "In what alternate reality would you NOT look like a cop?"

I heard the door open behind us, but neither of us turned. We were too busy making major eye contact.

Jarman yelled, "Ramirez!"

There was a tone in that one word that whirled us both around. Doctor Evans was leaning against the wall, holding his wrist upright. Blood gleamed like a scarlet bracelet around his arm.

Ramirez and I started running at the same time down that short space of hallway as if we had farther to go and less time to get there. Jarman and Jakes were disappearing through the door. Bernardo hesitated at the door, holding it open long enough for the screams to cut through the hospital silence. Low and wordless and panicked, and I knew without knowing that it was a man screaming. I was almost at the door, almost to Bernardo, Ramirez pacing me like a shadow.

Bernardo said, "This is a bad idea." But he went through the door, a heartbeat before we reached it. God, I hated being right all the time.

39

THE WHITE STERILE ROOM had been a quiet corner of hell. Now it was a loud, chaotic corner of hell. A skinless hand snatched at me. I slashed at it with the big blade that I'd pulled from the spine sheath. The hand bled and jerked back. They could feel pain. They bled. Good.

I had the blade raised for a neck blow as the corpse came at me again. Ramirez blocked my arms. "They're civilians!"

I looked at him, then back at that raw thing that was held to the bed only by one last wrist restraint. It launched at me again, slashing the air with its bloody hand, screaming wordlessly, butchered tongue flopping like a worm in the lipless ruin of its mouth.

"Just stay out of reach," he said and pulled me past it.

I had time to say, "They're corpses, Ramirez, just corpses."

He held up the asp. "Don't kill them." He moved into the fight, though it wasn't a fight yet. Most of the corpses were still restrained to the beds. They struggled, screaming, wailing, jerking their ruined flesh to bloodier ruin against the restraints, bodies bucking as they thrashed to free themselves.

Ben the nurse was beating at the head of one patient. It had sunk teeth into his arm so deeply that he couldn't free himself. Jarman was with him, beating the thing's head with his batton from far back like you'd hit a baseball. You could hear the soft, melon-like thunk even over the screaming.

Jakes and Bernardo were at the last bed near the windows. The African-American nurse was held in the embrace of a corpse that still had one hand and one ankle attached to the bed. Its head was buried into her chest. Blood plastered her gown to her body like someone had spilled a can of red paint down her. Where the thing was gnawing shouldn't have been a killing spot, but there was too much blood. It had reached something vital.

Jakes was beating at the thing's head so hard that he was rising on tiptoe, his body almost leaving the ground with each blow. The corpse's head was bleeding, cracking, but it wasn't letting go. Its head was buried into her chest like a monstrous child, feeding.

Bernardo was stabbing the corpse in the back over and over. The blade came free in a spray of blood, but it didn't matter. The one by the door had reacted to pain, but once they started feeding, they were just meat. You couldn't hurt meat, and you sure as hell couldn't kill it.

I walked between the beds with the corpses screaming, bodies writhing, and all the eyes looked the same. It was as if there was only one personality looking out of every pair of eyes. Their master, whatever that was, watched me walk between the beds, watching me go to the far bed, away from Ramirez, and his cautions. He still didn't understand what was about to happen when they all freed themselves. We had to be out of this room before that happened.

I moved in beside Bernardo, moving him back a step. I wiggled the blade underneath the thing's jaw. I took a deep breath, centered myself the way you do in martial arts class just before you break something big and permanent-looking. I pictured the blade coming out the top of the skull, and that's what I tried for. I tried to shove it through its head. The blade went through the soft tissue under the jaw with a sharp, wet, movement, then the tip hit the bone at the roof of the mouth, and kept going. The blade didn't come out of the top of its head, but I felt it shove into the strange emptiness of the sinus cavities.

It reared back from the woman, its jaws trying to open around the gleam of the blade. It clawed at its mouth with the one free hand, letting the nurse fall back onto the bed. We got our first glimpse of the wound. There was a hole in the middle of her chest. Broken ribs jutted outward like the broken sides of a frame. The hole was just the size for a human face to shove deep. I stared down into that dark, wet hole, and half her heart was gone, eaten away.

"Oh, God!" Jakes said.

The thing in the bed had freed its other hand. It was tugging at the hilt of the blade, trying to pull it free. Jakes, Bernardo, and I exchanged a look between us. One look, no words, and we turned towards the rest of the room with one goal in mind: get to the door any way we could. There was nothing human in this room but us.

I looked up and found Ramirez and Jarman at the far door with the male nurse sagging between them. Great. I yelled, "Run!"

We tried. I sensed movement and turned in time for the corpse to hit me full on and send us both crashing to the floor. I stabbed for the jaw, trying to pin its teeth like I had the other one, but it moved and I only got the throat. Blood splashed across my face in a hot liquid rush. It blinded me for a second. I could feel it moving over my body, legs straddling my waist. I kept my hand pushed into raw shoulder, holding it back, while it strained over me. I wiped the blood out of my eyes with the back of my hand that held the knife. It snapped at me like a dog, and I screamed. I cut its cheek so deep the blade scraped on teeth. It screamed and sank its teeth into my hand. I screamed as it shook its head like a dog with a bone. My hand opened, and the knife fell.

It came at me, mouth open, pale blue eyes so impossibly wide. It went for my throat. There was no time to try for the last knife. I went for its eyes. I plunged my thumbs into its eyes, and its own momentum pushed them deeper than I could have gotten them. I felt the eyeballs rupture, exploding in warm fluid and thicker things.

It screamed, whipping its head back and forth, hands clawing at its face. Bernardo was suddenly there, pulling it backwards, throwing it one-armed across the room to skid into the wall. Amazing what you can do when you're terrified.

I was on my knees, drawing the last knife. Bernardo dragged me to my feet, and we were almost to the door. Rigby was there with an ax, hacking at the corpses. Hands and less identifiable bits littered the ground around him. Ramirez shoved his asp into one's mouth, so hard the dull tip showed through the back of its throat.

Jakes was dragging Jarman by his wrists, leaving a thick red trail behind him. Jarman's body was wedged in the door. Rigby's ax had chopped two of the corpses into enough pieces that they were down. Two of the corpses were still held to the bed with one last restraint. Ramirez was wrestling with the one that was trying to swallow his asp. A corpse threw itself at Rigby, and the ax sliced air.

I heard the scrambling behind me before Bernardo yelled, "Behind . . ."

I was on the way down to the floor with the thing riding my back, before I heard Bernardo yell, ". . . you."

I tucked my head, trying to protect my neck. Teeth bit through my shirt, drawing blood, but having trouble gnawing through the strap of the shoulder holster and spine sheath. It dug its teeth into my flesh, but the leather straps acted like a sort of armor. I drove the knife back into its thigh, once, twice. It didn't care.

Suddenly, there was a wash of air, and a heavy blow, blood spilled across my hair, shoulders, and back, in a scalding wash. I scrambled out from under the corpse and found it was headless.

Rigby stood over it with the bloody ax and a wild look in his eyes. "Go, get out. I'll cover your back." His voice was high-pitched, fear dripping from it, but he stood his ground and started moving us all towards the door.

One of the corpses was on Bernardo's back, but it wasn't trying to eat him. It pounded his head twice into the floor, hard. It looked up at me. There was something in its eyes that hadn't been in any of the others. It was afraid. Afraid of us. Afraid of being stopped. Afraid, just maybe, of dying.

It scrambled through the open glass doors and brushed past Jakes, as if it had somewhere to go and something else to do. And I knew it had to be stopped, knew if it escaped that it would be very bad. But I put a hand under Bernardo's arm and started dragging him for the door. Ramirez took his other arm and it was suddenly easy to drag him through that glass door.

There was a sudden rush in the room behind us. Rigby stumbled back against the button that closed the door. It slid closed with Ramirez beating on it. I saw Rigby swing the ax, then a corpse came in from both sides. Ramirez reached for the button to open the door, but either Rigby's weight had jammed it or something else had.

Ramirez screamed, "Rigby!"

There was a gigantic whoosh of air as if a giant had drawn a breath, and the room filled with fire. Flames licked the glass like orange-gold water through the glass of an aquarium. I could feel the heat beating against the glass. Fire alarms went off with a high-pitched scream. I threw myself to the floor on top of Bernardo, covering my face, waiting for that tremendous heat to crack the glass and spill over all of us.

But it wasn't heat that spilled over me. It was coolness, water. I raised my head to the sprinklers that were filling the room. The glass was blackened, and smoke and steam curled against the glass like fog as the water killed the fire.

Ramirez reached for the button, and the doors opened in a sound of rushing water. The alarm was louder now, and I realized that it was two different alarms now, mixing together in one nerve-jangling screech. Ramirez stepped into the room, and I heard his voice over the maddening noise. "Madre de Dios."

I stood with the water pounding me, soaking my hair, clothing. I didn't follow him into the room. Rigby was beyond any help I could give him. We still had one more corpse on the run. I laid my fingertips on Bernardo's neck just under the jaw. The screech of the fire alarms seemed to make it hard to feel his pulse, but it was there, strong and sure. He was down for the count, but he was alive. Jakes was kneeling beside Jarman, tears streaming down his face. He was trying to stop a wound in Jarman's neck with his bare hands. The pool of blood that had spilled to either side of Jarman's head was being washed away by the sprinklers. His eyes were fixed and staring, unblinking as the water poured down on him.

Shit. I should have grabbed Jakes and said, "He's dead. Jarman is dead." But I couldn't do it. I got to my feet. "Ramirez."

He was still staring into the room at whatever was left of Rigby.

"Ramirez!" I yelled it, and he turned, but his eyes were unfocused as if he wasn't really seeing me.

"We've got one more corpse to catch. We can't let it get away."

He stared at me with dull eyes. I needed some help here. I took those few steps to stand in the doorway by him, and I slapped him hard enough that my hand stung with the blow. Harder than I'd meant to hit him.

His head whipped back, and I braced for him to hit me back, but he didn't. He stood there, hands in tight fists, shaking with the urge, eyes blazing with a rage that was just looking for someone to rain all over. It wasn't me hitting him. It was everything.

When he didn't slap me back, I said, "The bad thing went that way." I pointed at the door. "We need to go after it."

He started to talk very rapidly in Spanish. I couldn't understand the majority of it, but the anger came through just fine. I caught one word that I did know. He called me a bruja. It meant witch.

"Fuck this," I opened the door, having to edge around Jarman's body. The sprinklers were on in the hallway, too. Evans was still sitting with his back to the wall. He'd pulled his mask down, as if he couldn't get enough air.

"Where did it go?" I asked.

"Down the fire stairs, end of the hall." He had to raise his voice over the sound of fire alarms, but his voice was dull, distant. Maybe later if I was good, I could go into shock, too.

I didn't hear the door open behind me, but Ramirez yelled, "Anita!"

I half-turned as I ran for the door. "I'm taking the stairs, you take the elevators."

He yelled, "Anita!"

I turned, and he tossed one of the cell phones to me. I caught it one-handed awkwardly against my chest.

"If I get to ground and haven't found it, I'll call," he said.

I nodded, jamming the phone into my back pocket, running for the door. I found it. I had the Browning out now. There was no oxygen-filled room now. We'd see if bullets worked as well as knives. I pushed the heavy fire door with my whole body, until it was flat against the wall, and I knew the thing wasn't behind the door. Then I hesitated on the concrete landing. The sprinklers were going in here, too, like waterfalls down the concrete steps. The fire alarms filled the space with high-pitched echoes. I looked up at the rising stairs, then down. I had no idea which way it had gone. It could have gotten off on any floor above or below me.

Dammit, I needed to find this thing. I wasn't sure why it felt so urgent that it not get away, but I'd been right about the coming dark and the corpses. I'd trust my judgment. They were just animated corpses, just a kind I'd never seen before. But they were dead, and I was a necromancer. Technically, I could control any form of the walking dead. I could sometimes sense a vampire when it was near. I took a breath and centered myself in a solid line, drew my power in, flung it out, searching, my back to the door, the water pouring down on me, the scream of the fire alarms so piercing it was hard to think. I sent that "magic" outward, up the stairs, down the stairs like an invisible line of fog.

I jerked upright. I'd felt something like a pull on the end of a fishing line. Down, it had gone down. If I was wrong, there was nothing I could do about it. But I didn't think I was wrong. I started running down the wet cement steps, one hand on the banister to catch myself when I slipped, the other with the gun pointed upward. There was a woman crumpled outside the next landing, lying across the door, motionless, but breathing. I turned her face to the side so she wouldn't be drowned in the sprinklers, and kept going. Down, it was going down, and it wasn't taking time to feed. It was running, running away from us, running away from me.

I got to my feet, sliding on the wet steps, only my death grip on the slippery metal banister catching me before I fell. I lost my connection to the creature when I slipped. I just couldn't hold the concentration and do everything else. The sprinklers stopped abruptly, but the fire alarms went on and on, more piercing without the water to muffle it. I pushed to my feet and started running again. Very distant, far down below, there was a scream. I vaulted the next turn of banister, sliding down the wet metal, almost going head first over the next turn of railing. I was going as fast as I could, faster than was safe. I ran and slid and stumbled down the stairs, and all the time the growing sense that I was going to be too late. That no matter how fast I ran, I wouldn't get there in time.

40

I COULDN'T REGAIN the link with the thing without stopping and concentrating. I made the decision to keep chasing, and hoped I didn't miss it as I ran past the doors. Besides, on the 19th floor there was a huddled group of water-soaked patients with a nurse. They all pointed wordlessly down. At 17 there was a man with a bouquet of flowers with a bloody lip that babbled at me and pointed down. The door opened on 14, and nurse in a pink smock rushed out and ran into me. She screamed, jerking back against the wall, staring at me with huge eyes. She had a baby in each arm, in those little blankets. One even had its little pink knit hat still in place. Both babies were screaming, their high cat-like wails competing with the fire alarm.

The nurse just stared at me, unable to speak or afraid to. Maybe it was the gun, or maybe not all the blood had washed away in the sprinklers. I raised my voice above the noise, "Is it on this floor?"

She just nodded. She was mumbling something over and over. I had to lean into her to understand it. "It's in the nursery. It's in the nursery. It's in the nursery."

I didn't think my adrenaline could get any higher. I was wrong. I could suddenly feel the blood rushing through my body, feel my heart like a painful thing in my chest. I opened the door, scanning the hallway with the Browning. Nothing moved. The corridor stretched long and empty with too many closed doors for comfort. The fire alarm was still screaming, making my skin tight with the noise. But even over the screech of the alarm I could hear the babies . . . crying . . . screaming.

I slipped the phone out of my pocket, hit the button he'd told me to hit earlier, and started jogging down the hallway towards the sounds. Ramirez answered it in the middle of the first ring. "Anita?"

"I'm on maternity. It's the 14th floor. A nurse says the thing is in the nursery." I was at the first corner. I threw myself against the far wall, but didn't really stop. I'm usually more cautious around corners, but the crying was getting closer, more piteous.

"I'm on my way," Ramirez said.

I hit the button that cut us off, but still had it in my hand when I came around the next corner. There was a body pushed through a pane of wired safety glass. I could tell it was a man, but that was about all. The face looked like hamburger. I stepped on a stethoscope on the floor below him. Doctor or nurse. I didn't check for a pulse. If he was alive, I didn't know how to help him. If he was dead, it didn't matter. One last door, then a long expanse of window. But I didn't need to see the long window to know it was the nursery. I could hear the babies crying. Even over the fire alarm the sound of those panicked cries made my heart flutter, made me want to run and help them. A hard wiring response that I hadn't even known I had made me reach for the door. I still had the phone in my left, and made one attempt to shove it in my pocket. The bite on my left hand made me awkward. The phone slipped, and I let it fall to the floor.

The handle turned, but the door stopped just inches open. I put my shoulder into it, and realized it was a body, an adult body. I backed off and hit it again, moving it by painful inches. There was a woman screaming, not just the babies. I couldn't open the door. Dammit!

Then the window crashed outward in a spray of glass and a body. A woman hit the ground and lay there sprawled and bleeding. I left the wedged door and went for the window. There were shards of glass like small swords on the bottom of the break. But I'd taken falls in Judo higher than this. I'd practiced falling for years. I glanced in to check one thing. The herd of little plastic cribs was pushed to either side. I had room. I took a running leap at it and threw myself over the broken glass, rolling as I fell. I only had one free hand to slap the floor with and take the impact of the fall, but I wanted the gun in my hand ready to fire. I hit the floor, and the force of my blow, the jump, whatever, was still there, still rolling me. I used it to come to my feet before I even knew what was in the room.

I didn't so much see what was happening as take pictures of isolated things. I registered the overturned cribs: a tiny, tiny baby lying on the floor like a broken doll, the center of its body eaten away, like the center sucked out of a piece of candy; cribs still standing upright splattered with blood, some with tiny twisted bodies inside, some empty except for the blood; then in the far corner was the monster.

It held a tiny blanket-wrapped bundle. Tiny fists waving in the air. I couldn't hear it crying. I couldn't hear anything. There was nothing but sight, and that skinless face bending over the baby. My first bullet took it through the forehead, the second through the face as its head was thrown back by the impact of the first shot. It raised the struggling baby up in front of its face, and our eyes locked over the tiny form. It looked at me. The bullet holes in its face filled in like soft clay. I fired into its stomach because that's what I could hit without endangering the baby. It jerked back, but it threw itself to the floor. It didn't fall. I hadn't really hurt it. It took cover behind a row of tiny cribs. They were all on thin-legged wheels. I dropped to a crouch and sighted through that forest of thin metal legs, and saw it crouching, bringing the baby to its mouth.

There was no clear shot. I fired anyway, shooting into the wall beside it. It flinched, scuttling away, but didn't drop the baby. I fired through the legs of the wheeled cribs, keeping it moving. Where was Ramirez?

It stood and ran straight at me. I fired into its body. It shuddered but kept coming. The baby was naked except for a little diaper now, but it was alive. The thing threw the baby at me. It wasn't even a decision. I just caught it, cradling it to my chest, both hands compromised. The monster smashed into me. The momentum took us all back through the window I'd come through. We landed with the monster on bottom as if we'd flipped in midair. My gun barrel was pressed into its stomach, and I started pulling the trigger with my right hand before I even started cradling the baby tight with my left.

The creature jerked like a broken-backed snake. I got to my knees beside it, firing until the gun clicked empty. I dropped the Browning and went for the Firestar. I had it almost pointed when it hit me with the back of one hand, and the blow sent me crashing into the wall. I'd tried to protect the baby from the impact and had taken more of it than was good for me. I was stunned for a second, and it grabbed me by the hair, turning me towards it.

I fired into its chest and stomach. Each bullet made the body jerk, and somewhere around the sixth or seventh shot, it let go of my hair. A bullet later and the Firestar clicked empty. It stood over me, and that lipless mouth smiled.

The fire alarm stopped. The sudden silence was almost frightening. I could hear my heart pounding in my head. The baby in my arms was suddenly piercingly loud, more frantic sounding. The thing tensed, and I knew a second before it came that it was going to rush me. I used that second to try and put the baby on a clear piece of floor. I was half-turned when it picked me up and flung me into the opposite wall. I didn't have the baby to worry about anymore. I slapped my hands and arms into the wall taking as much of the impact as I could. When it closed the distance, I wasn't stunned. It grabbed one upper arm, and I struggled to keep it from grabbing the other.

I knew how to grapple, but not with something that was slick and skinless. There was nothing to grab onto. It picked me up by my shirt, the other hand under my thigh, and dead lifted me like a barbell. I hit the wall as though it had tried to throw me through it. I tried to protect myself, but I slid to the floor, stunned, unable to breathe or think for a space of heartbeats.

It knelt beside me, tearing my shirt out of my pants, baring my stomach and my bra. It put a hand under my back and lifted me almost gently, bowing my back, raising me up, and lowering its face towards my bare flesh, as if it meant to kiss me. I heard a voice in my head. It whispered, "I hunger." Everything seemed distant, dreamlike, and I knew that I was close to passing out. I raised my hand and almost didn't feel like it was mine. But I moved it. I caressed that slick, fleshless face. And it rolled those strange lidless eyes up at me as it lowered its mouth to feed. My thumb slid along the flesh, feeling, feeling for the eye. It didn't stop me. It bit into my upper stomach, as my thumb slid into its eye. We both screamed.

It reared back, dropping me to the floor. It was a short fall, and I was on my knees, edging away from it when the first bullet whirled it around. Ramirez came down the hallway from the direction of the fire stairs, firing in a two-handed stance as he advanced down the hall.

The body jerked, but the wounds were closing faster and faster, as if the more we shot it, the better the flesh was at healing the damage. I expected the thing to attack Ramirez or me, or escape, but it didn't. It leaped into the broken window of the nursery. And I knew what it meant to do. It wasn't trying to escape. It was trying to take as many lives as it could before we destroyed it. Its master was feeding off the deaths.

Ramirez went to the door that I'd tried earlier. I left him banging against it with his shoulder. I pulled myself up to the window. It was tearing the blanket off of another baby, like unwrapping a present. I didn't know where my guns were. I had nothing left to throw at it. It turned in silhouette, and the baby was grabbing for the air with tiny matchstick arms. The monster's mouth widened showing a mouth already red with blood.

Ramirez had gotten the door open enough to slip inside. He shot at its legs and lower body, afraid to try a head shot so close to the baby. The monster ignored him, and everything slowed down to a crystalline crawl. The face lowered, mouth wide to take that tiny heart. I screamed, and I put all my rage, all my helplessness into that shout. I pulled that power that let me raise the dead, I pulled it around me like a shining thing and flung it outward. I could actually see it in my mind like a thin white rope of fog. I threw my aura, my essence around the thing. I was a necromancer, and all this fucking thing was, was a corpse.

I screamed, "Stop!"

It froze in mid-motion, the baby almost at its mouth. I felt the power that animated it. I felt it inside that dead shell. Its master's power was like a dark flame inside it. I had a hand outstretched as if I needed it to point my power. I opened my hand and flared that white rope over the corpse. I covered it in my aura like growing a new body. I closed my aura like a fist around the thing and severed it from the power that made it move. The corpse shuddered, then collapsed instantly like a puppet whose strings had been cut.

I felt its master. I felt him like a cold wind across my skin. I felt him coming for me, following the line of my own aura towards me, like a string through a maze. I tried to pull it back, tried to fold it into myself again, but I'd never tried anything like this before, and I wasn't fast enough. Your aura is your magical shield, your armor. When I lashed out at the corpse, I'd opened myself to anything and everything. I thought I'd understood the risks, but I was wrong.

The master's power lashed out at me like fire following a trail of gasoline, and when it hit, there was a moment where I threw back my head, and I couldn't breathe. I felt my heart flutter and stop. I felt my body fall to the floor, but it didn't hurt, as if I were already numb. My vision went gray, then black, and there was a voice in the blackness. "I have many servants. That you stopped this one is nothing to me. I will feed through others. You die in vain."

I tried to form words to answer that voice and found that I could. "Fuck you."

I felt his anger, his outrage that I could defy him.

I tried to laugh at him, at his impotence, but there wasn't enough left of me to laugh. The darkness became something thicker. I passed beyond the master's voice, beyond my own, then there was . . . nothing.

41

THE FIRST HINT I had that I wasn't dead was pain. The second was light. My chest was burning. I jerked back to consciousness, gasping for air, trying to pull the burning things off of me. I blinked up into a burning white light, then voices.

"Hold her down!"

Weight on my arms and legs, hands holding me down. I tried to struggle, but couldn't feel my body enough to be sure I was moving at all.

"BP sixty over eighty and dropping fast."

I saw shapes, blurred with light moving around me. A sharp jab in my arm, a needle. A man's face swam into view, blond, wire-framed glasses. His face slid back out of sight into a white-rimmed fog.

Gray spots slid like greasy streamers across my vision, and I felt myself sinking backwards, downwards, outwards.

A man's voice, "We're losing her!"

Darkness rolled over me taking the pain, and the light. A woman's voice floated through the dark, "Let me try." Then silence in the dark. There was no alien voice this time. There was nothing but the floating dark and me. Then there was just the dark.

42

I WOKE UP SMELLING sage incense. Sage for cleansing and ridding you of negativity, or so my teacher Marianne was fond of telling me when I complained about the smell. Sage incense always gave me a headache. Was I in Tennessee with Marianne? I didn't remember going there. I opened my eyes to see where I was, and it was a hospital room. If you wake up in enough of them, you recognize the signs.

I lay there blinking into the light, happy to be awake. Happy to be alive. A woman came to stand by the bed. She was smiling. She had shoulder-length black hair, cut blunt around a strong face. Her eyes seemed too small for the rest of her face, but those eyes stared down at me like she knew things I didn't, and they were good things or at least important ones. She was wearing something long and flowing, violet with a hint of red in the pattern.

I tried to talk, cleared my throat. The woman got a glass from the small bedside table, her many necklaces clinking as she moved. She bent the straw so I could drink. One of the necklaces was a pentagram.

"Not a nurse," I said. My voice still sounded rough. She offered the water again, and I took it. I tried again, and this time my voice sounded more like me. "You're not a nurse."

She smiled, and the smile turned an ordinary face into something lovely, just as the burning intelligence in her eyes made her striking. "What was your first clue?" She had a soft rolling accent that I couldn't place; Mexican, Spanish, but not.

"You're too well dressed for one thing, and the pentagram." I tried to point at the necklace, but my arm was taped to a board with an IV running into my skin. The hand was bandaged, and I remembered the corpse biting me. I finished the gesture with my right hand, which seemed unharmed. My left arm seemed to have a sign over it that said cut here, bite here, whatever here. I moved the fingers of my left hand to see if I could. I could. It didn't even really hurt, just tight, as if the skin needed to stretch a little.

The woman was watching me with those eyes of hers. "I am Leonora Evans. I believe you've met my husband."

"You're Doctor Evans' wife?"

She nodded.

"He mentioned you were a witch."

She nodded, again. "I arrived at the hospital in the . . . how do you say, nick of time, for you." Her accent thickened when she said, how do you say.

"What do you mean?" I asked.

She sat down in the chair beside the bed, and I wondered how long she'd been sitting there, watching me. "They restarted your heart, but they couldn't keep life in your body."

I shook my head, and the beginnings of a headache was starting behind my eyes. "Can you put out the incense? Sage always gives me a headache."

She didn't question it, just got up and moved to one of those little folding tables on wheels that they have in hospitals. There was incense stuck in a small brazier, a long wooden wand, a small knife, and two candles burning. It was an altar, her altar, or a portable version of it.

"Don't take this wrong, but why are you here and a nurse isn't?"

She spoke with her back to me as she quenched the incense. "Because if the creature that attacked you tried to kill you a second time, the nurse would probably not even notice it was happening until it was too late." She came and sat back down by the bed.

I stared at her. "I think the nurse would notice if a flesh-eating corpse came into the room."

She smiled and it was patient, even condescending. "You and I both know that as horrible as its servants are, the true danger is in the master."

My eyes widened. I couldn't help it. Fear thudded in my throat. "How did you . . . know that?"

"I touched his power when I helped cast him out of you. I heard his voice, felt his presence. He was willing you to die, Anita, draining you of life."

I swallowed, my pulse still too fast. "I'd like a nurse now, please."

"You're afraid of me?" She smiled when she said it.

I started to say no, but then . . . "Yeah, but it's not personal. Let's just say after my brush with death, I'm not sure who to trust, magically speaking."

"Are you saying I saved you because this master allowed me to save you?"

"I don't know."

She frowned for the first time. "Trust me on this, Anita. It was not easy to save you. I had to encircle you with protection, and some of that protection was my own power, my own essence. If I had not been strong enough, if the names I called on for aid had not been strong enough, I would have died with you."

I looked up at her and wanted to believe her, but . . . "Thank you."

She sighed, settling the skirt of her dress with fingers aglitter with rings. "Very well, I will fetch you a familiar face, but then we must talk. Your friend Ted told me of the marks that bind you to the werewolf and the vampire."

Something must have shown on my face because she said, "I needed to know in order to help you. I'd saved your life by the time he arrived here, but I was trying to fix your aura, and I couldn't." She passed a hand just above my body and I felt that trail of warmth that was her power caressing over mine. She hesitated over my chest, over my heart. "There is a hole here as if there is a piece of yourself missing." Her hands slid further down my body and hesitated low on my stomach, or high on my abdomen depending on how you looked at it. "Here is another hole. They are both chakra points, important energy points for your body. Bad places to have no ability to shield from magical attack."

My heart was back to beating faster than it should have. "They are closed. I've worked for the last six months to close them up."

Leonora shook her head, taking her hands gently back from me. "If I understand what your friend told me of this triumvirate of power you are a part of, then these spaces are like electrical sockets in the wall of your aura, your body. The two creatures have the plugs that fit their respective sockets."

"They aren't creatures," I said.

"Ted painted a very unflattering picture of them."

I frowned. It sounded like something Edward would do. "Ted doesn't like the fact that I'm . . . intimate with monsters."

"You are lovers with both then?"

"No. I mean . . ." I tried to think of a quick version. "I was sleeping with them at separate times. I mean for a little while I was . . . dating them both at the same time, but it didn't work out."

"Why did it not work?"

"We were invading each other's dreams. Thinking each other's thoughts. Every time we had sex, it was worse, as if the sex was tying the knots tighter and tighter." I stopped talking, not because I was finished, but because the words weren't enough. I started over. "One night the three of us were alone, just talking, trying to work things out. A thought popped into my head, and it wasn't mine, or I didn't think it was mine, but I didn't know whose thought it was." I looked up at her, trying to will her to understand the moment of sheer terror that had been for me.

She nodded, as if she did, but her next words said she'd missed the point. "That frightened you."

"Yeah," I said, making the word two syllables so she'd catch the sarcasm.

"The lack of control," she said.

"Yes."

"The lack of individual privacy."

"Yes," I said.

"Why did you take on these marks?"

"They would have died if I hadn't done it. We might all have died."

"So you did it to save your own life." She sat there, hands crossed in her lap, perfectly at ease while she probed my psychic wounds. I hate people who are at peace with themselves.

"No, I couldn't lose them both. I might have survived losing one, but not both, not if I could save them."

"The marks gave you all enough power to overcome your enemies."

"Yes."

"If the thought of sharing your life with them is so terrifying, then why did their deaths loom so large?"

I opened my mouth, closed it, tried again. "I loved them, I guess."

"Past tense, loved, not love?"

I was suddenly tired. "I don't know anymore. I just don't know."

"If you love someone, then your freedom is curtailed. If you love someone, you give up much of your privacy. If you love someone, then you are no longer merely one person but half of couple. To think or behave any other way is to risk losing that love."

"It's not like having to share the bathroom, or argue over which side of the bed you get to sleep on. They're trying to share my mind, my soul."

"Do you really believe that last about your soul?"

I settled into the pillow, and closed my eyes. "I don't know. I guess not, but it . . ." I opened my eyes. "Thank you for saving my life. If I can ever return the favor, I will, but I don't owe you an explanation of my personal life."

"You're quite right." She straightened her shoulders as if pulling herself back, and suddenly she seemed less intrusive, more businesslike. "Let's return to my analogy of the holes being like light sockets, and the men being the plugs that fit them. What you did was spackle over the holes, cover them with plaster. When the master attacked you, his power tore off the plaster and reopened the holes. You cannot close these holes with your own aura. I cannot imagine the amount of effort it took to put patches over them. Ted said you were learning ritual from a witch."

I shook my head. "She's more psychic than witch. It's not a religion, just natural ability."

Leonora nodded. "Did she approve of you closing the holes the way you did?"

"I told her I wanted to learn how to shield myself from them, and she helped me do that."

"Did she tell you it was a temporary repair?"

I frowned at her. "No."

"Your hostility flares every time we approach the fact that you have given these two men in effect the keys to your soul. You cannot block them permanently, and by trying to you weaken yourself, and probably them as well."

"We'll all just have to live with it," I said.

"You almost didn't live with it."

She had my attention now. "Are you saying that the reason the master was able to almost kill me was the weakness in my aura?"

"He would have hurt you badly, even without them, but I believe the holes made you unable to resist him, especially with them freshly opened as they were. Think of them, perhaps, as wounds, freshly opened wounds that any preternatural infection can enter you through."

I thought about what she was saying. I believed it. "What can I do?"

"The holes are meant to be filled by only one thing, the auras of the men you loved. Your auras must now be like jigsaw puzzles with pieces missing, and only the three of you together are a whole now."

"I can't accept that."

She shrugged. "Accept it or not, but it is still the truth."

"I'm not ready to give up the fight just yet. Thanks anyway."

She stood, frowning. "Do as you will, but remember that if you come up against other preternatural powers, then you will not be able to protect yourself from them."

"I've been like this for a year. I think I can manage."

"Are you that arrogant, or just that determined not to talk about it any more?" She looked down at me as if she expected an answer.

I gave her the only one I had. "I don't want to talk about it anymore."

She nodded. "Then I will get your friend, and I'm sure the doctor will want to speak with you." She turned and walked out.

The room was very quiet, full of that hush that hospitals are so fond of. I looked at her makeshift altar and wondered what she'd had do to save me. Of course, I only had her word for that. The moment I thought it, I was sorry. Why was I so distrustful of her? Because she was a witch, the way Marks hated me because I was a necromancer? Or was it just that I didn't like the truth she was telling me? That I couldn't shield myself from magical critters until the holes in my "aura" had been filled in. It had taken me most of the last six months to fill up those holes. Six months of effort, and they were raw again. Shit.

But if they were open, why didn't I sense Jean-Claude and Richard? If the marks were truly unshielded again, then why wasn't there a burst of closeness? I needed to call my teacher Marianne. I trusted her to tell me the truth. She'd warned me that simply blocking off the marks was only temporary. But she helped me do it because she felt I needed some time to adjust, to accept. I wasn't sure I had another six months of meditative prayer, psychic visualization, and celibacy in me. It had taken all that and power, energy. Hers and mine.

Of course, Marianne had taught me other things, and one of those meant I could check myself. I could run my hand down my own aura and see if the holes were there. The trouble was I needed my left hand for that, and it was wrapped in bandages, strapped to a board with a tube in it.

Now that I was alone and not being pestered with hard questions, I began to feel my body. It hurt. Every time I moved my back, it hurt. Some of it was the dull ache of bruises, but there were two spots that had the sharp bite of things that had bled. I tried to remember how I could have cut my back. The glass in the window when the corpse took us back through it, that had to be it.

My face ached in a line from jaw to forehead. I remembered the corpse hitting me backhand. It had been almost casual, but it had knocked me half-senseless. Just once I'd like to meet a type of walking dead that wasn't stronger than a living person.

I lifted the loose neck of my hospital gown and found little round pads stuck to my chest. I glanced at the heart monitor beside the bed, giving that reassuring sound that said my heart was still working. I had a sudden memory of the moment when my heart had stopped, when the master had willed it to stop. I was suddenly cold, and it wasn't the overly ambitious air conditioner. I'd come very close to dying yesterday . . . today? I didn't know what day it was. Only the sunshine pressing against the drawn blinds let me know it was day and not night.

There were red patches on the skin of my upper body like bad sunburns. I touched one, gently. It hurt. How the hell had I gotten burns? I lifted the gown until it made a cave and I could see down the line of my body, at least until mid-thigh where the weight of the covers hid me from view. There was a bandage just below my rib cage. I remembered the thing's mouth opening over my skin while he cradled me, gently. The moment when he bit down . . . I pushed the memory away. Later, much, much later. I checked my left shoulder, but the scrape marks from teeth had already scabbed over.

Scabbed over? How long had I been out?

A man came into the room. He seemed familiar, but I knew I did not know him. He was tall with blond hair and silver-framed glasses. "I'm Doctor Cunningham, and I am very glad to see you awake."

"Me, too," I said.

He smiled and started checking me over. He used a penlight and made me follow the light, his finger, and kept staring into my eyes so long, he had me worried. "Did I have a concussion?"

"No," he said. "Why? Does your head hurt?"

"A little but I think it's from the sage incense."

He looked embarrassed. "I am sorry about that, Ms. Blake, but she seemed to think all this was very important, and frankly I don't know why you almost died to begin with, or why you didn't just keep on dying, I let her do what she wanted."

"I thought my heart stopped," I said.

He tucked his stethoscope into his ears and pressed it to my chest. "Technically, yes." He stopped talking, listening to my heart. He asked me to breathe deeply a couple of times, then made some notes on the chart at the foot of my bed. "Yes, your heart did stop, but I don't know why it stopped. None of your injuries were that serious, or for that matter, that kind of injury." He shook his head and came back to stand by me.

"How did I get the burns on my chest?"

"We used the difibulator to start your heart. It can leave mild burns."

"How long have I been here?"

"Two days. This is your third day with us."

I took a deep breath and tried not to panic. I'd lost two days. "Have there been any more murders?"

The smile wilted on his face, leaving his eyes even more serious than they had been. "You mean the mutilation murders?"

I nodded.

"No, no new bodies."

I let out the breath. "Good."

He was frowning now. "No more questions about your health? Just about the murders?"

"You said you don't know why I almost died, or why I didn't go ahead and die. I assume that means Leonora Evans saved me."

He looked even more uncomfortable. "All I know is that once we allowed her to lay hands on you, your blood pressure started to go back up, your heart rhythm steadied out." He shook his head. "I simply don't know what happened, and if you knew how hard it is for a doctor, any doctor, to admit ignorance, you'd be much more impressed with me saying that."

I smiled. "Actually, I've been in the hospital before. I appreciate you telling me the truth and not trying to claim credit for my miraculous recovery."

"Miraculous is a good word for it." He touched the one thin knife scar on my right forearm. "You have quite a collection of war injuries, Ms. Blake. I believe you have seen a lot of hospitals."

"Yeah," I said.

He shook his head. "You're what, twenty-two, twenty-three?"

"Twenty-six," I said.

"You look younger," he said.

"It's being short," I said.

"No," he said, "it isn't. But still to have these kinds of scars at twenty-six is not a good sign, Ms. Blake. I did my residency in a very bad section of a very big city. We used to get a lot of gang members. If they lived to see twenty-six, their bodies looked like yours. Knife scars . . ." He leaned across the bed and raised the sleeve of the gown enough to touch the healed bullet wound on my upper arm. ". . . bullet wounds. We even had a shapeshifter gang, so I've seen the claw marks and bites, too."

"You must have been in New York," I said.

He blinked. "How did you know?"

"It's illegal to purposefully give lycanthropy to a minor even with their permission, so the gang leaders were put under a death sentence. They sent in special forces along with New York's finest to wipe them out."

He nodded. "I left the city just before they did that. I'd treated a lot of those kids." His eyes were distant with remembering. "We had two of them shapechange during treatment. Then they wouldn't let them in the hospital anymore. If you wore their colors, you were left to die."

"Most of them probably lived anyway, Doctor Cunningham. If the initial wound doesn't kill them immediately, they probably aren't going to die."

"Are you trying to comfort me?" he asked.

"Maybe."

He looked down at me. "Then I'll tell you what I told all of them. Get out. Get out of this line of work or you will not live to see forty."

"I was actually wondering if I was going to make it to thirty," I said.

"Was that a joke?"

"I think so."

"You know the old saying, half in jest, all in seriousness?" he asked.

"Can't say I've heard that one."

"Listen to yourself, Ms. Blake. Take it to heart and find something a little safer to be doing."

"If I was a cop, you wouldn't be saying this."

"I have never treated a policeman that had this many scars. The closest I've ever seen outside the gangs was a marine."

"Did you tell him to quite his job?"

"The war was over, Ms. Blake. Normal military duty just isn't that dangerous."

He looked at me, all serious. I looked back, blank-faced, giving him nothing. He sighed. "You'll do what you want to do, and it's none of my business anyway." He turned and walked towards the door.

I called after him. "I do appreciate the concern, Doctor. Honestly, I do."

He nodded, one hand on either side of his stethoscope like it was a towel. "You appreciate my concern, but you're going to ignore my advice."

"Actually, if I live through this case, I'm planning to take some time off. It's not the injury rate, doctor. It's the erosion of the ethics that's beginning to get to me."

He tugged on the stethoscope. "Are you telling me that if I think you look bad, I should see the other guy?"

I gazed down, sort of taking it all in. "I execute people, Doctor Cunningham. There are no bodies to look at."

"Don't you mean you execute vampires?" he said.

"Once upon a time, that's what I meant."

We had another long moment of looking at each other, then he said, "Are you saying you kill humans?"

"No, I'm saying that there's not as much difference between vamps and humans as I used to tell myself."

"A moral dilemma," he said.

"Yeah," I said.

"I don't envy you the problem, Ms. Blake, but try to stay out of the line of fire until you figure out the answer to it."

"I always try and stay out of the line of fire, Doctor."

"Try harder," he said and walked out.

43

EDWARD CAME IN the door before it had time to swing closed. He was wearing one of those short-sleeved shirts with little pockets on the front. If it had been tan, I'd have said he looked dressed for a safari, but the shirt was black. So were his freshly pressed jeans, the belt that encircled his narrow waist, down to the black-over belt buckle, so it wouldn't shine in the dark and give you away. The belt buckle matched the shoulder holster and gun that outlined his chest. There was a line of white undershirt at the open neck of the shirt, but other than that it was unrelieved blackness. It made his hair and eyes look even paler. It was the first time I'd seen him without the cowboy hat out of doors since I arrived.

"If you're dressed for my funeral, it's too casual. If it's just street clothes, then you must be scaring the tourists."

"You're alive. Good," he said.

I gave him a look. "Very funny."

"I wasn't being funny."

We looked at each other. "Why so serious, Edward? I asked the doc, and he said there hadn't been any more murders."

He shook his head and came to stand at the foot of the bed, near the makeshift altar. I ended up looking down the length of the bed at him, and it was awkward. I found the button controls with my right hand and raised the head of the bed slowly. I'd been in enough hospital beds to know where everything was.

"No, there haven't been any more murders," he said.

"Then what's with the long face?" I was paying attention to my body while the bed raised, waiting for it to hurt. I ached all over, which you tend to do after being thrown into walls. My chest hurt, and it wasn't just the burns. I stopped when I was sitting up enough to see him without straining.

He gave a very small smile. "You nearly die, and you ask what's wrong?"

I raised eyebrows at him. "I didn't know you cared."

"More than I should."

I didn't know what to say to that, but I tried. "Does this mean you won't kill me just for sport?"

He blinked, and the emotion was gone. Edward was standing there staring at me, his usual amused blankness showing on his face. "You know I only kill for money."

"Bullshit," I said. "I've seen you kill people when you weren't getting a paycheck."

"Only when I'm with you."

I'd tried to play it tough and guylike. He wasn't having any of it. I tried for honesty next. "You look tired, Edward."

He nodded. "I am."

"If there haven't been any more murders, why do you look so beat?"

"Bernardo only got out of the hospital yesterday."

I raised eyebrows at him. "How bad was he hurt?"

"Broken arm, concussion. He'll heal."

"Good," I said.

There was still an air to him of strangeness, more than normal Edward strangeness, as if there was more to tell and he didn't want to tell it. "Drop the other shoe, Edward."

His eyes narrowed. "What do you mean?"

"Tell me what's got you all bothered."

"I tried to see Nicky Baco without you or Bernardo."

"Bernardo tell you about the meet?" I asked.

"No, your detective friend, Ramirez, told me."

That surprised me. "Last time I talked to him, he was sort of insisting that he go along with me to meet Baco."

"He still wanted to come along, but Baco wouldn't see any of us. He insisted that you and Bernardo, or at least you, had to be there."

"You're not upset just because Nicky wouldn't dance with you," I said. "Just tell me."

"Do you really need Baco, Anita?"

"Why?"

"Just answer the question." I knew Edward well enough to know he meant it. I answered his question or he wouldn't answer mine.

"Yeah, I need him. He's a necromancer, Edward, and whatever this thing is, it is just a form of necromancy."

"But you're a better necromancer than he is, stronger."

"Maybe, but I don't know much about ritual necromancy. What I do is actually closer to voodoo than traditional necromancy."

He gave a dim smile, shaking his head. "And what exactly is traditional necromancy, and how are you so sure that Baco practices it?"

"If he was an animator, I'd have heard of him. There just aren't that many of us. So he doesn't raise zombies. But you and everyone else in the metaphysical community in and around Santa Fe say that Baco works with the dead."

"I only know his reputation, Anita. I've never seen him do shit."

"Fine, but I've met him. He doesn't do vaudun, voodoo. I've seen that enough to know the trappings and the feel of it. So if he's not a zombie raiser or a vaudun priest, and people still call him a necromancer, then he must do ritual necromancy."

"Which is?" Edward said.

"To my knowledge it's raising the spirits of the dead for sort of divination purposes or to get questions answered."

Edward shook his head. "Whatever Baco does, it has to be worse than raising a few ghosts. People are scared of him."

"Nice of you to mention that before I met him the first time," I said.

He took a deep breath, hands on hips, not looking at me. "I was careless."

I looked at him. "You're a lot of things, Edward. Careless isn't one of them."

He nodded and looked up at me. "How about competitive?"

I frowned at him, but said, "Competitive, I'll give you. But what does that have to do with Baco?"

"I knew that his bar was the hangout for the local werewolves."

I stared at him, just stared at him. When I closed my mouth, I said, "You competitive shit. You let Bernardo and me walk in there unprepared. You could have gotten us killed."

"You're not even going to ask why I let you walk in blind?" he asked.

"Let me take a wild guess. You wanted to see how I'd handle it cold, or maybe how Bernardo would handle it, or maybe both."

He nodded.

"Fuck, Edward. This isn't a game."

"I know that."

"No you don't. You've been keeping things from me from the moment I stepped off the plane. You keep testing my nerve to see if it's better than yours. It is so junior high, so damned . . ." I struggled to find the right word, ". . . such a guy thing to do."

"I'm sorry," he said, and his voice was soft.

The apology stopped me, drained some of the righteous indignation. "I've never heard you apologize for anything, Edward, not to anyone."

"It's been a long time since I said I was sorry to anyone."

"Does this mean the games are over, and you'll quit trying to see who is the biggest, baddest person?"

He nodded. "That's what it means."

I lay there and looked at him. "Is it just being with Donna, or is something else starting to open you up?"

"What do you mean?"

"If you don't stop all this sentimental shit, I'll begin to think you're just a mere mortal like the rest of us."

He smiled. "Speaking of immortals," he said.

"We weren't," I said.

"I'm changing the subject," he said.

"Okay."

"If this monster really is an Aztec boogey-man, then it is a hell of a coincidence that the Master of the City, who just happens to be an Aztec, doesn't know anything about it."

"We talked to her, Edward."

"Do you think a vamp, even a master vamp, could do all the things we've been seeing?"

I thought about it, but finally said, "Not just from vampiric powers, no, but if she were some kind of Aztec sorcerer in life, she might retain her powers after death. I just don't know that much about Aztec magic. It doesn't come up a lot. She was different from any vampire I've ever met. It could mean that she was a sorcerer in life."

"I think you need to see her again."

"And what, ask her if she's involved in the murder and mutilation of some twenty people?"

He grinned. "Something like that."

I nodded. "Okay. When I get out of the hospital, a visit to vampire central goes up to the head of my list."

His face went very blank.

"What is it, Edward?"

"Do you really need Baco?" he said.

"I sensed this thing the first night I arrived or first day. It sensed me right back, and it shielded itself. I haven't picked it up that strongly since, and I've driven past the spot where I felt it. Baco can sense it, too, and he's afraid of it. So yeah, I want to talk to him."

"You don't think he's behind it?"

"I've felt this thing's power. Baco is powerful, but he's not that powerful. Whatever this thing is, it's not human."

He sighed. "Fine." He said it like he'd made a decision. "Baco says you have to meet him before ten this morning or don't bother coming."

I searched the room until I found the clock on the wall. It was eight. "Shit," I said.

"The doc says you need at least another twenty-four hours in here. Leonora says that if the monster tries for you again, you won't make it."

"You have a point to make," I said.

"I almost didn't tell you."

I was beginning to get pissed. "I don't need you to protect me, Edward. I thought you of all people knew better than that."

"Are you sure you're up to it?"

I almost just said yes, but I was so tired. It was a bone weariness that had nothing to do with lack of sleep. I was hurt, and it went beyond the bruises and cuts that I could feel. "No," I said.

He blinked. "You must feel like shit to admit that."

"I've felt better, but something's scaring Baco. If he says meet before ten this morning, we meet. Maybe the great bad thing is coming to get him at eleven today. Can't miss that, can we?"

"I've got a bag of fresh clothes out in the hall for you. They cut your shoulder holster off of you in the emergency room, and the spine sheath."

"Shit," I said, "that spine sheath was a custom job."

He shrugged. "You can order a new one." He went to the door, stepped out a moment, then came back in with a small overnight bag. He came around to the side of the bed that Leonora's chair was on. The other side of the bed was a little too crowded with equipment for visitors to stand.

He opened it and started laying out the clothes. His button-down black shirt didn't fit perfectly smoothly around his ribs. He laid out the clothes in neat piles: black jeans, black polo shirt, black socks, even the underwear and bra matched the theme. "What's with the funerary color scheme?"

"The dark blue polo shirt and jeans were trashed. All you had left was black, red, and purple for shirts. We need something dark today, authoritative."

"Why are you in black, then?" I was watching the way the shirt lay when he moved. It wasn't a gun. I didn't think it was knives. What was under his shirt?

"White shows blood."

"What's under your shirt, Edward?"

He smiled and unbuttoned the middle buttons. He had what looked like a modified belly band holster strapped across his upper body. But it wasn't a gun. It was metal pieces, too big to be ammo, and too oddly shaped on the end I could see. They looked like teeny-tiny metal darts . . . "Are those some sort of itty-bitty throwing knife?"

He nodded. "Bernado said that if you took out an eye the flayed ones didn't like it."

"I poked out eyes on them twice, and each time it seemed to hurt and disorient them. Truthfully, I didn't think Bernardo noticed what I was doing."

He smiled and started buttoning his shirt up. "You shouldn't underestimate him."

"Could you really hit an eye throwing one of those things?" He slipped one out of its little holster and threw it into the wall in one flick of his hand. He pierced one of the tiny designs on the wallpaper across the room.

"I can't hit shit with something like that."

He retrieved it from the wall and replaced it on his chest, and walked back to me. "You can even have your very own flamethrower, if you want it."

"Gee, and it isn't even Christmas."

He smiled. "Not Christmas, more like Easter."

I frowned up at him. "I don't get the Easter reference."

"You came back from the dead, or didn't anyone tell you?"

I shook my head. "Tell me what?"

"Your heart stopped three times. Ramirez kept it going with CPR until the doctors got to you. But they lost you twice. You were going down for the third time when Leonora Evans convinced them to let her try and save you with some of that good old time religion."

My heart was suddenly beating too hard, and I could have sworn that the inside of my ribs hurt with each beat. "Are you trying to scare me?"

"No, just explaining the Easter reference. You know, Christ rose from the dead."

"I get it, I get it." I was suddenly scared and angry. I am rarely one without being the other.

"If you still believe in it, I'd light a candle or two," he said.

"I'll think about it," I said, and my voice sounded defensive even to me.

He was smiling again, and I was beginning to distrust his smile almost as much as the rest of him. "Or maybe you should talk to Leonora and ask her who she asked for help to get you back. Maybe it's not a church candle you need to light. Maybe you need to slaughter a few chickens."

"Wiccans do not kill things to raise power."

He shrugged. "Sorry, they don't teach comparative religion or metaphysics in assassin school."

"You've scared me, reminded me how hurt I am, and now you're yanking my chain, teasing me. Do you want me to get up out of this bed and meet Baco or not?"

His face was all serious, the last of the humor draining away like ice melting down a hot plate. "I want you to do whatever you need to do, Anita. I thought I wanted to get this son of a bitch at any price." He touched my right hand where it lay on the sheet. He didn't hold it, just touched it, then pulled away. "I was wrong. Some things I'm not willing to pay."

Before I could think of anything to say, he turned and left. I wasn't sure which was confusing me more: this case, or the new and more emotional Edward. I caught sight of the clock. Shit. I had an hour and forty minutes to get dressed, check out of the hospital against doctor's orders, and drive to Los Duendos. I was betting arguing with Doctor Cunningham was going to take longer than either of the other two.

44

I PRESSED THE BUTTON to slowly raise the bed. The closer I got to a sitting position, the more I hurt. My chest ached as if the muscles around my ribs had been overused. The cuts on my back did not like sitting up and would probably like walking even less. There was a certain tightness to the skin, like a shoe laced too tightly, that said I had stitches on my back. They would be a pain all their own when I insisted on moving. Nothing feels quite like stitches. I wondered how many I had in my back. It felt like a lot.

When I was in a sitting position, I waited for a few seconds listening to my body complain. I usually don't get this hurt until the end of a case. I hadn't even met the great-bad-thing face to face yet. It had nearly killed me from a nice supposedly safe distance.

I let myself think about that for a few minutes. I'd almost died. Seems like I should get a few days of grace before having to crawl back into the trenches. But crime and tide wait for no woman, or something like that. I'll admit I thought about just staying put, just letting someone else be heroic for a change. But the moment I seriously thought it, I flashed on the nursery and those red-splashed cribs. I couldn't just lie here and trust that everyone would muddle through without me. I just couldn't do it.

I had my gown halfway down my arms when I realized I couldn't just yank the sticky pads that connected me to the heart monitor. Just yanking them off would give the hospital staff just a little too much excitement.

I finally pressed the nurse call button. I had to get unplugged from all the drips and machines.

The nurse came almost immediately, which either meant the hospital had more nurses on staff than most hospitals could afford these days, or I was really hurt and they were paying extra attention to me. I was hoping for a surplus of nurses, but wasn't betting on it.

The nurse was shorter than I am, very petite, with blond hair cut short and sort of bouncy. Her professional smile wilted when she saw me sitting up with the gown obviously coming off.

"What are you doing, Ms. Blake?"

"Getting dressed," I said.

She shook her head. "I don't think so."

"Look, I'd prefer help getting all the tubes and wires off me, but it is all coming off because I'm checking out."

"I'll get Doctor Cunningham." She turned and walked out.

"You do that," I said to the empty room. I got a death grip on the little wires that attached to the sticky pads and pulled. It felt like I'd pulled a foot worth of skin off with them, a sharp, grinding ache, like it would hurt to touch the skin. The high pitched scream of the machine let people know my heart was no longer going pitty-pat on the other end of the wires. The sound reminded me uncomfortably of the fire alarm, though it was much less obnoxious.

The pads had left large circular welts on my skin, but they were not nearly as big as they felt. The fact that the welts hurt enough to rise above all the other aches and pains lets you know how raw my skin felt.

Doctor Cunningham came through the door while I was still working on the tape that bound my hand to the IV board. He turned the screaming heart monitor off.

"What do you think you're doing?" he asked.

"Getting dressed."

"Like hell you are."

I looked up at his enraged face and just didn't have any anger to throw back at him. I was too tired and too hurt to waste energy on anything but the process of getting up and getting out of this bed.

"I have to go, Doctor." I kept picking at the tape and wasn't making much progress. I needed a knife. "Where are my weapons?"

He ignored the question, and asked one of his own. "Where could you possibly need to go badly enough to climb out of this bed?"

"I need to get back to work."

"The police can handle things for a few days, Ms. Blake."

"There are people who will talk to me that won't talk to the police." I'd gotten an edge of tape up.

"Then your friends in the hallway can talk to them." Doctor Cunningham got points for realizing that Edward and company were the kind of men that people who avoided the police might talk to.

"This particular person won't talk to anyone but me." I finally stopped picking at the tape. "Can you please get this off of me?"

He took a breath, to argue, I think, but what he said was, "I'll help you check out if you let me show you something first."

I must have looked as suspicious as I felt, but I nodded.

"I'll be right back," and he left the room. Everyone seemed to be doing that today. He was gone long enough that Edward came in to see what the hold up was. I lifted the taped arm, and he produced a switchblade from his pocket. The blade cut through the tape like paper. Edward always did take good care of his tools.

I was still left with having to peel the tape off my arm, and the IV itself had to come out, mustn't forget that.

"If you want it fast, I'll do it," Edward said.

I nodded, and he ripped the tape off my arm along with the IV. "Ow!"

He smiled. "Sissy."

"Sociopath."

Doctor Cunningham came in carrying a large hand mirror. His gaze flicked to Edward and my now free arm. It was not a friendly look. "If you'll step back for a moment, Mr. Forrester?"

"You're the doctor," Edward said, moving back to the foot of the bed.

"Nice of you to remember that," Doctor Cunninghmn said. He held the mirror in front of my face.

I looked startled, eyes too wide and so dark they looked black. I'm naturally pale, but my skin was ghost-white, ethereal like flexible ivory. It was what made my eyes look even darker than normal, or maybe it was the bruise.

I'd known my face hurt, and I'd even known why. Being hit hard enough to slam into a wall should leave a mark.

The bruise went up to the edge of my cheek, just under the eye, and catty-corner down to my jaw line just under the ear. My skin was a rainbow of purple-black with a core of red skin with darker red scattered across it. It was one of those really deep bruises that probably hadn't even shown much of a mark for the first day, but it would go through all the color changes once it started. I had shades of green, yellow, and brown to look forward to. If I hadn't had three vampire marks on me, I'd have had at least a broken jaw, or maybe a broken neck.

There were moments when I'd give almost anything to be free of the marks, but staring at the bruise, knowing that I healed faster than normal for a human and it still looked this bad, was not one of them. I was grateful to be alive.

I said a brief silent prayer while I stared at my face. "Thank you, dear God, for me not being dead." Aloud, I said, "Nasty," and handed the mirror to the doctor.

He frowned; obviously it wasn't the reaction he'd wanted. "You've got over forty stitches in your back."

My eyes went wide before I could stop them. "Gee, that's a record even for me."

"This isn't a joke, Ms. Blake."

"It might as well be funny, doctor."

"If you start moving around, you're going to rip the stitches open. Right now, if you're careful, the scars won't be bad, but if you start moving around, you'll scar."

I sighed. "It'll have plenty of company, doctor."

He stood there, shaking his head slowly, face set in harsh lines. "Nothing I can say is going to make any difference, is it?"

"No," I said.

"You're a fool," he said.

"If I stay in here until I'm healed, what am I going to say to myself when I'm staring down at the next round of bodies?"

"Saving the world is not your job, Ms. Blake."

"I'm not that ambitious," I said. "I'm just trying to save a few lives."

"And you truly believe that only you can solve this case?"

"No, but I know that I am the only one that . . . this man will talk to." I'd almost said Nicky Baco, but I didn't want Doctor Cunningham calling the police and telling them where we were going. Not that he would do that, but better safe than sorry.

"I told you that I'd check you out if you looked at your injuries. I keep my word."

"I appreciate that in a person, Doctor Cunningham. Thank you."

"Don't thank me, Ms. Blake. Don't thank me." He moved towards the door, giving both the makeshift altar and Edward a medium-wide berth, as if both made him uncomfortable. At the door he turned. "I'll send a nurse in to help you dress because you will need the help." He walked out before I could say thank you again. Probably just as well.

Edward stayed until the nurse arrived. It was a different nurse, tall, light brunette, if that wasn't an oxymoron. Her gaze stayed on my bruised face longer than was politic, and when she helped me slip out of the gown, she gave a low hiss at my back. It was unprofessional and sort of unnurselike. They were usually blankly cheerful to the point of nausea when you were hurt, or blunt. Anything to cover that what had happened to you bothered them.

"You'll never be able to wear a bra over the stitches in your back," she said.

I sighed. I hated to go without a bra. It always made me feel underdressed no matter what else I was wearing. "Let's just get the shirt on."

She held it and helped me slip it over my head. Putting my arms up to go through the sleeves made the pain in my back sharp and immediate, as if the skin would pull apart if I moved too quickly. I wondered if that would have been the analogy that I'd chosen if Doctor Cunningham hadn't warned me about the stitches pulling apart. I'd have shrugged if I hadn't been sure it would hurt.

"I normally work in the nursery," the nurse said as she helped me straighten the shirt, buttoning the first two buttons.

I looked up at her, not sure what to say. But I didn't need to worry. She knew exactly what to say. "They called me in after you destroyed the monster. For the . . . cleanup." She helped me sit on the edge of the bed. I sat there for a few seconds with my legs dangling off the edge, letting my body adjust to the fact that we were getting dressed, we were going to stand . . . in just a second.

"I'm sorry you had to see it," I said, because I had to say something. I wasn't even comfortable with her saying I'd "destroyed" the monster. It made it sound entirely too heroic, and what it had felt like was desperate. Desperation is the true mother of invention, at least for me.

She started to help me into the black panties, but I took them from her hands. If I couldn't even put on my own underwear, I was in serious trouble. And if I was truly that hurt, I needed to know it. It would cut down on my urge to be heroic.

I started to simply bend at the waist, but it just wasn't that easy. I lowered myself downward a little bit at a time, and I was still nowhere near low enough.

"Let me start them up your legs, so you don't have to bend all the way down," the nurse said.

I finally let her, and even pulling them only part way up my body turned my back into one great big hurt. I leaned against the bed when they were on, and didn't even argue when she bent down to put on my socks. She never argued that I was too hurt to be leaving. It was too obvious to argue about it.

"I'd worked with Vicki for two years. It was Meg's first job." Her eyes were dry, wide, and I noticed the dark circles under them like purplish smudges, as if she hadn't slept much in the last three days.

I remembered the body that had blocked the door into the nursery, and the nurse that had been thrown through the window. Vicki and Meg, though I'd probably never know which had been which, not that it mattered. They were dead and didn't care, and the nurse helping me slip into a pair of black jeans looked too fragile for questions. My job was to listen, and make encouraging noises where needed.

I slipped the jeans over my butt without help, buttoned them and zipped them all by myself. Things were looking up. I'd tried tucking the shirt into my pants out of habit, but that required more back movement than I thought. Besides, untucked, my braless state would be a little less noticeable. I was really too well endowed to go without, but my modesty wasn't worth the pain, not today.

"Every time I close my eyes, I see the babies." She was kneeling with one of my shoes in her hands, when she looked up. "I keep thinking I should be dreaming about my friends, but I only see the babies, their little bodies, and they cry. Every time I close my eyes, I hear the babies screaming. I wasn't there, and I hear them, every night." The tears were finally there, sliding soundlessly down her face as if she didn't know she was crying. She slid the shoe on my foot and looked down, paying attention to what she was doing.

"See a councilor or a priest or whoever you trust," I said. "You'll need help."

She got my other shoe off the bed, and gazed up at me, the tears drying in tracks down her pale cheeks. "I heard that there's some sort of witch making these corpses, causing them to attack people."

"Not a witch," I said. "What's behind all this isn't human."

She slipped the shoe on me, frowning. "Is it immortal like a vampire?"

I didn't do my usual lecture about how vamps aren't immortal, only hard to kill. She didn't need that particular lecture. "I don't know yet."

She laced my shoe solid, but not too tight, as if she did this regularly. She looked up at me with those strange empty eyes of hers, tear tracks still visible on her face. "If it's not immortal, kill it."

Her face held that absolute trust that is usually reserved for small children or people that are not quite all there. There was no questioning in her shocked eyes, no doubt in that pale face. I answered that trust. Reality could wait until she was ready for it. I said what she needed to hear. "If it can die, I'll kill it."

I said it because she needed to hear it. I said it because after what I'd seen it do, that was the plan. Maybe it had been the plan all along. Knowing Edward it probably had been. He said solve the case when what he usually meant was kill them, kill them all. As a plan, I'd heard worse. As a way of life, it lacked a certain romance. As a way to stay alive, it was just about perfect. As a way to keep your soul intact, it sucked. But I was willing to trade a piece of my soul to stop this thing. And that was perhaps my biggest problem. I was always willing to compromise my soul if it would take out the great evil. But there always seemed to be another great evil coming down the road. No matter how many times I saved the day and took out the monster, there was always another monster, and there always would be. The monster supply was unlimited. I was not. The parts of myself that I was using up to slay the monsters was finite, and once I used it all up, there would be no going back. I'd be Edward in drag. I could save the world and lose myself.

And staring down into the woman's face, watching that perfect faith fill her lost eyes, I wasn't sure the bargain was a good one, but I was sure of one thing. I couldn't say no. I couldn't let the monsters win, not even if it meant becoming one of them. God forgive me if it was arrogance. God protect me if it wasn't. I got up out of bed and went in search of monsters.

45

I WAS BUCKLED into the front seat of Edward's Hummer, holding myself stiff and careful, glad the ride was smooth. Bernardo and Olaf were in the back seat, dressed in someone's idea of assassin chic. Bernardo was in a leather vest. His cast looked very white and awkward, right arm at a forty-five degree angle, a white strap going from arm to around his neck. His long hair was done in a vaguely oriental style, with one large, deceptively loose knot held back with what looked like two long gold chopsticks. It held back the sides of his hair, but left most of the length swinging free down his back. Black jeans of a looser cut with holes worn through across his knees, and the black boots I'd seen him wear since I arrived. But who was I to complain? I had three pairs of black Nikes, and I had brought all three with me,

There was a swollen bump to the side of his forehead and bruises like a pattern of modern art tattoos down one side of his face. His right eye was still puffy around one edge. But he managed not to look pale or ill like I did. In fact, if you could ignore the cast and bruises, he looked dandy. I hoped he felt as good as he looked, because I looked like shit and felt worse.

"Who did your hair?" I asked, because with only one good arm, I knew he hadn't.

"Olaf," he said, and that one word was very bland, very empty.

I widened my eye and looked over at Olaf.

He sat beside Bernardo on the side behind Edward, as far from me as he could get and still be in the car. He hadn't spoken a word to me since I walked out of the hospital room and the four of us walked to the car. It hadn't bothered me at the time because I'd been too busy trying to walk without making small pain noises under my breath.

Whimpering while you walked was always a bad sign. But now I was sitting down and as comfortable as I was likely to get for a while. I was also in a momentously bad mood because I was scared. I felt physically weak and not up to a fight. Psychically, my hard-won shields were crap again, full of holes, and if the "master" tried for me again, I was in very deep shit.

Leonora Evans had given me a woven silk cord with a little drawstring bag on it. The little bag was lumpy, packed full with small hard objects that felt like rocks, and dry crumbling things that were probably herbs. She'd told me not to open the bag because that would let all the goodness out. She was the witch, so I did what she told me.

The bag was a charm of protection, and it would work without my believing in its power. Which was good since except for my cross I didn't believe in very much. Leonora had been making the charm for three days, since she saved me in the emergency room. She had not intended it to be a cure all for the holes in my defenses, but it was all she had to give me on such short notice. She was almost as angry with me as Doctor Cunningham had been for leaving the hospital early.

She had taken one of her own necklaces and placed it over my head. It was a large piece of polished semiprecious stone. A strange dark gold color. Citrine for protection and to absorb negativity and magical attacks directed at me. To say that I wasn't a big believer in crystals and the new age was an understatement, but I took it. Mainly because she was so angry and so sincerely worried about me out in the world with my aura hanging open for the bad guys to munch on. I knew I had holes in my aura. I could feel them, but it was all just a little too hocus pocus for me.

So I turned in my seat, feeling the stitches in my back tighten, adding a little push to the pain I was already feeling, and stared at Olaf. He was staring out the window as if there was something fascinating in the rows of small houses on that side of the car.

"Olaf," I said.

He never moved, just watched the passing scenery.

"Olaf!" It was almost a yell in the small confines of the car. His shoulders twitched, but that was all. It was like I was some kind of insect buzzing around him. You might wave a hand at it, but you wouldn't talk to it.

It pissed me off. "Now I understand why you don't like women. You should have just said you were homosexual, and my feelings wouldn't have been so hurt."

Edward said, softly, "Jesus, Anita."

Olaf turned very slowly almost in slow motion as if each muscle in his neck were pulling him around in small jerks. "What—did—you—say?" Each word was rage-filled, hot with hatred.

"You did a great job on Bernardo's hair. You made him look very pretty." I didn't believe that particular sexual stereotype, but I was betting that Olaf did. I was also betting that he was homophobic. A lot of ultramasculine men are.

He undid his seatbelt with a noticeable click and eased forward. I pulled the Firestar out of the holster that was sitting in my lap. The pants that Edward had brought to the hospital were a little too tight for my innerpants holster. I watched Olaf's hand vanish underneath the black leather jacket. Maybe he hadn't understood the movement when I'd unholstered the gun. Maybe he expected me to raise the gun and sight along the back of the car. I pointed the gun between the small space between the seats. It wasn't a perfect angle, but I had my gun pointed first, and that counted in a gun fight.

He'd pulled his gun out from under the jacket, but it wasn't pointed yet. If I'd meant to kill him, I'd have won.

Edward slammed on the brakes. Olaf slammed into the back of the seat, gun at a bad angle, driving his wrist backwards. It wasn't being thrown into the seatbelt, and nearly the dashboard that hurt. It was the being flung backwards into the seat. My breath went out in a sharp gasp. Olaf's face ended up very close to the space between the seats, and he saw the gun barrel pointed, now, at his chest. I was hurting so bad that my skin twitched with the need to writhe, but I kept my hand tight around the gun, using my free hand to brace myself and make sure I didn't move. I had the drop on him, and I was keeping it.

The Hummer skidded to a stop against the curb. Edward had his seatbelt off and was whirling around in his seat. I caught the flash of a gun in his hand and had a heartbeat to decide whether to try and take the gun off Olaf and try for Edward, or keep the gun where it was. I kept the gun on Olaf. I didn't think Edward would shoot me, and Olaf might.

Edward shoved the barrel of his gun against the back of Olaf's bald head. The tension level in the car skyrocketed. Edward went to his knees, gun never moving from Olaf's head. I could see Olaf's eyes rolled up. We looked at each other, and I saw that he was afraid. He believed that Edward would do it. So did I, though I didn't know why, and with Edward there was always a why, even if it was only money.

I had a sense of Bernardo sitting very stiff on his side of the seat, trying to pull back from the mess that was about to spill all over the car.

"Do you want me to kill him?" Edward asked. His voice was quiet and empty, as if he'd asked, did I want him to pass the salt. I could do an empty uninterested voice, but not like Edward. I could never be that dispassionate, not yet anyway.

I said, "No," automatically, then added, "not like this."

Something passed through Olaf's eyes. It wasn't fear. It was more like surprise. Surprise that I hadn't said, yeah, shoot him, or surprise about something else I couldn't fathom. Who knew?

Edward took the gun from Olaf's hand, then clicked the safety off on his own gun, and leaned back still on his knees in the driver's seat. "Then stop baiting him, Anita."

Olaf sat back in his seat, slowly, almost stiffly as if afraid to move too quickly. Nothing like having a gun to your head to teach you caution. He smoothed his hands down the leather jacket, which still looked like way too much to wear in the heat. "I will not owe my life to any woman." His voice was sort of subdued, but it was clear.

I eased the Firestar back out from between the seats, and said, "Consistency is the hobgoblin of little minds, Olaf."

He frowned at me. Maybe he didn't get the quote.

Edward looked at both of us, shaking his head. "You're both scared, and that makes you both stupid."

"I'm not scared," Olaf said.

"Ditto," I said.

He frowned at me. "You just crawled out of a hospital bed. Of course, you're scared. Wondering if the next time you meet the monster will be your last."

I looked back at him, and it was not a friendly look.

"So you picked a fight with Olaf because you'd rather fight him than be scared."

"Just like a woman to be so irrational," Olaf said.

Edward turned to the big man. "And you, Olaf, you're afraid that Anita is tougher than you are."

"I am not!"

"You've been quiet ever since we saw the mess at the hospital. Ever since you heard what Anita did, how much damage she took and survived. You're wondering just how good is she? Is she as good as you are? Is she better?"

"She is a woman," Olaf said, and his voice was thick with some dark emotion as if he was choking on it. "She cannot be as good as I am. She cannot be better than I am. That is not possible."

"Don't make this a competition, Edward," I said.

"Because you will lose," Olaf said.

"I'm not going to arm wrestle you, Olaf. But I will stop picking on you. I'm sorry."

Olaf blinked at me as if he couldn't quite follow the conversation. I didn't think I'd overstepped his English, more like his logic circuits were overloading. "I do not need your pity."

I moved up from being "she" or "a woman" to a neuter pronoun. It was a start. "It's not pity. I acted badly. Edward's right. I'm scared, and fighting with you is a nice diversion."

He shook his head. "I don't understand."

"If it's any consolation, you confuse me, too."

Edward smiled, his Ted smile. "Now kiss and make up."

We both frowned at him and said simultaneously, "Don't push it," and "I do not think so."

"Good," Edward said. He looked at Olaf's gun in his hand for a second, then handed it back with a lot of heavy-duty eye contact. "I need you to be my backup, Olaf. Can you do that?"

He nodded once and took the gun slowly from Edward's hand. "I am your backup until this creature is dead, then we will talk."

Edward nodded. "I look forward to it."

I glanced at Bernardo, but his face told me nothing, nothing except that it had gone blank and empty and confirmed what I was thinking. Olaf had just warned Edward that when the case was over, he would try and kill him. Edward had agreed to it. Just like that.

"Just one big happy family," I said into the thick silence that had filled the car.

Edward turned around in his seat and buckled back in. He gave me sparkling Ted eyes. "And just like family we'll fight among ourselves, but we're much more likely to kill an outsider."

"Actually," I said, "the vast majority of murders are done by your nearest and dearest blood relatives."

"Or spouse, don't forget the spouse," Edward said and put the car in gear, pulling carefully out into the sparse traffic.

"Like I said, your nearest and dearest."

"But you said blood relative, and there's no blood between husband and wife."

"Sharing one body fluid or another, doesn't seem to matter. We kill those we're closest to."

"We are not close," Olaf said.

"No, we are not close," I said.

"But I hate you all the same," he said.

I spoke without turning around. "Right back at you."

"And I thought the two of you would never agree on anything," Bernardo said. His voice was cheerful, joking. No one laughed.

46

THE BLACK-PAINTED FRONT of the bar looked tired in the morning sunlight. You could see where the paint was cracked and beginning to peel. The front of the bar looked almost as neglected as the rest of the street. Maybe Nicky Baco hadn't tried to run the other businesses off. Maybe it had been an accident. Standing there in the soft heat of morning, I felt something I hadn't felt at night. It was as if the street had been used up in a mystical sense. I'd felt very strongly when I'd been here last time that Baco had drained the street of vitality, caused this to happen, but if that were true, then it hadn't been enough energy to sustain him. Or maybe all that negativity was finally coming home to roost. Most systems of magic or mysticism have rules of conduct, things you do and things you do not. You break the rules at your peril. The wiccans call it the threefold law: what you do to others comes back to you threefold. Buddhists call it karma. Christians call it answering for your sins. I call it what goes around comes around. It really does, you know.

I had the Firestar tucked into the front of my pants, minus the innerpants holster, because the gun could ride higher and not dig in as much. Edward had loaned me a paddle holster for the Browning, and I had ended up with it in front, so that I looked like one of those wild west gunslingers with two guns crossed over my hips. Though actually the black polo shirt came down low enough to hide both guns. Untucked, most shirts are too long on me. It looked sloppy, but it did hide the guns if you weren't looking too close. The polo shirt was a little too close to the body not to show telltale lumps, though Edward had been thoughtful enough to bring my black suit jacket, which helped camouflage the lumps. Last time I'd been here with guns I'd had the police backing me, but now we were taking guns into a bar, very illegal in New Mexico. Strangely, it wasn't a big worry, but I did hope the cops didn't choose today for a raid.

I still had the wrist sheaths plus knives on my wrists. Ramirez had collected all my knives from the inferno and given them to Edward, who had scrubbed, cleaned, oiled, and sharpened them to an inch of their lives. I'd had to leave the big blade in the car because I couldn't figure out how to carry it concealed, and carrying what amounted to a small sword barehanded seemed a little too aggressive.

Edward had even given me an incendiary grenade for my jacket pocket. It helped balance out the derringer in my right hand pocket so that the jacket didn't swing too funny as I walked. The derringer had been his idea, too, though I had brought it with me from St. Louis. I wasn't sure I really needed it today, but I'd learned never to argue with Edward when he gave me a weapon. If he thought I might need it, I almost certainly would. Scary thought on the grenade, isn't it?

At some unknown signal, Olaf moved up and tried the bar door. It was locked.

He knocked twice hard enough to rattle the door. He also stood right in front of the door. After staring down a sawed-off shotgun the last time I came to the bar, I might not have stood facing front at that black door. Either Olaf hadn't heard about the shotgun, or he didn't care. Maybe he was trying to be muy macho for my benefit or maybe for his own benefit. If he'd been more secure in himself, then he wouldn't have been so easy to piss off.

Even standing off to one side, the sound of the locks being drawn back was loud. Good, solid locks just from the sound of it. The door pushed open, slowly, showing a thick slice of darkness like a cave pressing against the sunlight. The door continued to push slowly open as if on its own power. Only at the very last did a large beefy arm come into view, spoiling the illusion.

Harpo stood in the doorway peering out at us, eyes hidden behind the same small black sunglasses he'd been wearing the first time I saw him. He had changed clothes, though. He was wearing a jean vest open over a very hairy chest and stomach. He looked more like a bear than a werewolf. He looked like a great big sleepy bear that had rolled out of bed, pulled on some clothes and rumbled out to the door. Even his otherworldly energy seemed dimmer than last time.

But he blocked the door with his bulk, and growled out, "Anita, but not the others."

I moved around Olaf, and he actually moved back so I could face Harpo. Either Olaf was being nicer, or he figured better me than him in the door. "Nicky said I could bring some friends."

Harpo peered down at me. "Looks like you need better friends."

I didn't touch the bruise. It wouldn't help. "Let's just say I was relying on police backup and they were late." Which was true, and I still wanted to know where the hell Ramirez had been while I'd been playing lone ranger. I like policemen, but I knew the comment would please Harpo.

It did. He smiled a quick baring of teeth that flashed wolf fangs in the thickness of his beard. He had definitely been spending too much time in wolf form. There was a low murmuring voice, male. Harpo turned to look over one massive shoulder towards the voice. Then he turned back to me. The smile was gone.

"Boss says you were invited but not the others."

I gave a very small shake of my head because a big one would have hurt. "Look, Nicky invited me here. He said I could bring friends. I brought them. I'm here before ten in the fucking morning. I came down here to talk about our common problem, not to be dicked around at the door."

"This ain't dicking around," Harpo said, hand cupping his groin. "I can show you dicking around."

I held up a hand. "Fine, my mistake for using the wrong word. I didn't come down here to be stopped at the door."

He was still rubbing himself, getting into it or trying to piss me off. He'd succeeded on the last. I was so not standing here with forty-plus stitches in my back watching some werewolf ape jack off before I'd even had coffee.

"I am too tired for this shit," I said.

He started to get a little body language into it, smiling at me.

I raised my voice so it would carry into the open door of the bar. "I am not going anywhere today without my friends here. If you're waiting for me to give in on that point, then we're wasting each other's time."

There was no answer from inside the bar. Harpo had gotten a little hip action into his show. I'd had enough. "When the monster sucks your life out, Nicky, don't worry. It doesn't really hurt. Have a nice day."

I turned to my friends. "They're not going to let us see Nicky."

Edward nodded. "Then let's go." He made a small motion, and Bernardo and Olaf moved off down the sidewalk. Edward lagged a little behind with me. I think we were both hoping that Harpo would call my bluff. Except it was only partially a bluff. We could have forced our way in there with weapons, but Nicky wouldn't talk at the end of a gun. I needed a dialogue, not an interrogation.

I started walking away. Edward fell into step behind me, but kept an eye on our backs. I wasn't flexible enough to do much back trailing without turning my entire body around which was awkward. Besides I trusted Edward to watch our backs.

I admit there was a tension between my shoulder blades, waiting for Harpo to come running out and say come back, let's talk. But he didn't. So I kept walking. Olaf and Bernardo were beside the Hummer waiting for Edward to unlock the doors.

We were actually getting in the car when Harpo appeared on the sidewalk and started to walk towards us. He looked unarmed, but not happy.

I sat in the seat, and closed the door. "Start the engine," I said.

Edward did what I told him.

Harpo started jogging towards us waving those big arms. Some shapeshifters run like their animal counterparts, all grace and God-given motion. Harpo was not one of those. He ran awkwardly, as if he hadn't done it in a while, at least not in human form. It made me smile.

"You just wanted to see him run," Edward said. "Petty."

"Yeah, it's petty. Fun though," I said.

He put the car in gear, and Harpo put on a burst of awkward speed. He got to the car as Edward was starting to pull away. He actually slammed a big meaty hand on the hood.

Edward stopped. My window glide down, and I looked up at Harpo. There was sweat beading on his naked chest. His breath came harsh and too quick. "Fuck," he said.

"Did you want something?" I asked.

"Boss says—that you can all—come inside." He was leaning his hands against the Hummer while he got his breath back.

"Okay," I said.

Edward pulled the car back into the curb, while Harpo moved so there was room. We all got back out of the car. Harpo was still not breathing right. "Aerobic exercise is the key to good cardiovascular health," I said, sweetly, as we waited for him to start walking back to the bar.

"Fuck you."

I thought about getting back in the Hummer, but I'd played the game as far as I was willing to go. I wanted to talk to Baco, but only with backup. Harpo had said I could do both. I'd achieved my goal. Anything else was pure childishness. I was feeling petty, but not that petty.

When he recovered, he was once again the sunglass-wearing muscle man, face impassive. He strode back, hands in loose fists, doing his best impression of a moving mountain of flesh. His otherworldly energy prickled along my skin. Just a whisper of power, as if it were leaking out without him meaning for it to. Which probably meant he was pissed. Strong emotions made it harder to hold all that vibrating energy inside.

None of us spoke on the short walk back. Men are usually not good at useless small talk or don't see a need for it, and I was just too busy concentrating on walking normally without giving away just how much it hurt to sweat chitchat.

Harpo held the door for us. I glanced at Edward. He gave me blank eyes back. Fine. I walked inside and the others followed. Three days ago I'd have been nervous stepping into that dark with the vibrating energy of werewolves rising like an invisible tide. But that was three days ago, and there just wasn't that much fear left in me. My body hurt, but the rest of me was oddly numb. Maybe I'd finally crossed that line that Edward seemed to live behind. Maybe I'd never really feel anything again. When even that thought didn't scare me, I knew I was in trouble.

47

IT TOOK A SECOND for my eyes to adjust to the dark interior, but it wasn't my eyes that told me something was wrong. It was the skin on the back of my neck. I didn't argue with it. I had my hand on the Browning underneath the shirt and didn't care if it gave away the fact that I was carrying a gun. They'd be fools to think we'd come in here unarmed. Los Lobos Biker Club might have a lot of faults, but being that kind of fool wasn't one of them.

Nicky Baco was lying on the bar with his hands tied to his ankles so that the ropes formed a sort of handle like he was some kind of carry-on bag. His face was bloody and bruised, and the injuries were a lot fresher than mine.

I had the Browning out, and I felt rather than saw the other three fan out until we were the corners of a box, and each corner held a gun. Each corner watched its section of the room, and whether we liked each other or not, I trusted all of us to take care of our sections of the room, even Olaf. It was good to be sure.

My part of the room included the bar with Nicky on it; a tall man with a beard, and a curl of waist-length pony tail over one shoulder; two wolves the size of ponies; and a man's body staring sightless at the room, his throat cut like a second mouth red and screaming.

I had a peripheral sense of the how full the room was of crowding bodies. The energy was thick enough to choke on. I heard a noise to the right and did three things almost simultaneously. I pointed the Browning at the noise, drew the Firestar left-handed to point at the man with the ponytail, and let my eyes flick to the side to see what I'd heard. Good that I'd been practicing left-handed firing drills. The heavy slithering sound came again from behind the bar. The bar was in my section of the room. It was my ball, so to speak. I felt the others surging forward like a trembling tide about to swallow us all. We could shoot a lot of them, but there had to be over a hundred in this room and we were dead if they all came at once.

Fear tightened my stomach, jerking my pulse into my throat. Just like that the numbness was gone, chased away by adrenaline, and the musky scent of wolves. There were more wolves than just the two in front of me out in that packed, darkened room. I could smell them. My stomach jerked again, but not from fear. The mark that tied me to Richard, tied me to his pack, was alive again. It flared in my body like a tiny flame reborn, waiting to be fed so it could grow. Great, just great. I had to worry about it later. My concentration was all used up.

The ponytailed man just stood there smiling. He was handsome in a rough around the edges, tattooed prison sort of way. Even in the dimness his eyes flashed wolf amber, not human. I also knew what, or would that be who, I was looking at. This was their Ulfric, their wolf king. He stood in a space of emptiness with most of the pack huddled further back into the room, and yet his power made up for theirs. His power filled the nearly empty side of the room with a flesh-creeping energy like thunder just before it strikes.

The tension was thick enough that I had to swallow some of it before I could speak. "Greetings, Ulfric of the Los Lobos clan. What's shaking?"

He threw his head back and laughed, a big hearty, good-natured sound that ended with a howl that crawled out of his human throat and down my spine.

"Nice effect," I said, "but this is an official police investigation into the mutilation murders. I'm sure you've heard about them."

He turned those startling pale eyes to me. "I've heard."

"Then you know that we aren't investigating your pack."

He laid a casual hand on Nicky, who whimpered even though I don't think it really hurt. "Nicky is my vargamor. If the police wish to speak with him, then they must ask me first." He smiled, and I was close enough to notice that his teeth were human, no fangs for the Ulfric.

"Sorry. The only other pack I've ever met that had a vargamor doesn't make you talk to the Ulfric first. My apologies on the oversight." I hoped whatever we were doing was going to be over soon, because I couldn't keep up the gun in each hand stance for long. I'd practiced left-handed, but it was still my weak hand, and the bite in it was already starting a faint tremble in the muscles. I had to be able to lower my hand soon or it would begin to shake.

"If you were the police, then I would accept your apologies. We are always ready to help the police." That last brought a wave of snickers from the packed house. "But I don't see any police in this room."

"I'm Anita Blake. I'm a vampire executioner . . ."

He cut me off. "I know who you are. I know what you are."

I didn't like that last, made me nervous. "And just what am I?"

"You are the lupa of the Thronnos Roke clan, and you have come to my clan for help, but you have not honored me or my lupa. You enter my lands without permission. You contact my vargamor without talking to me first, and you give us no tribute." His power grew with every sentence until it was like standing in warm water up to your chin, knowing that if it got much deeper you'd drown.

But I understood the rules now. I'd insulted him, and he had to wipe out that insult. I'd try sweet reason, but I didn't have much hope for it. Besides, my left arm was getting tired. Hell, so was my right. Whatever was behind the bar moved in a huge roll of motion that you could feel and hear. It sounded bigger than a werewolf.

"I flew down here on police business. I did not enter your lands as lupa of the Thronnos Roke clan. I came down here as Anita Blake, the Executioner, that's all."

"But you contacted my vargamor." He slapped Nicky's thigh, and that did seem to hurt, because he closed his eyes and writhed at the touch, straining through his gag to scream.

"I didn't know Nicky was your vargamor until after I'd talked to him. No one told me that this bar was your lair. You're Ulfric. You can smell that I'm not lying."

He gave a small nod. "You tell the truth." He looked at the small man on the bar, running his hand over his body the way you'd stroke a dog, though the dog doesn't usually wince and try to pull back. "But he knew that he was my vargamor. Nicky knew that you were a lupa of another clan. It was the hot topic for a while, a human lupa."

"Lupa's often just another word for the Ulfric's girlfriend," I said.

He turned those golden eyes to me, more gold because of the heavy black eyebrows that framed them. "Nicky agreed to help you without asking me later, or even telling me about your visit." He gave a low growl that refreshed the fading goosebumps on my skin. "I am Ulfric. I lead here." He slapped Nicky and fresh blood trickled from his nose.

I badly wanted to put a stop to the abuse, just out of principle, but I didn't want it badly enough to die for it, so I waited and watched Nicky Baco bleed. I didn't like it, but I let it happen. My left hand was beginning to cramp. I needed to either start shooting people or put my guns up. Even holding my arms out for this long was putting a strain on my back and chest.

"Anita," Edward said, and just the tone of my own name was enough. He was quietly telling me to hurry it up.

"Look, Ulfric, I didn't mean to walk into some inner pack squabble. I'm just trying to do my job. Trying to keep more innocent people from being killed."

"Humans are fun," he said. "Sex and a meal and you never have to leave your car. But-you-do-not-make-them-your-queen!" His voice rose until with the last word he was screaming. Howls echoed him from the mob that was pressing close and closer.

"Anita," Edward said, and this time there was more of a warning to his voice.

"I'm working on it, Edward."

"Work faster," he said.

"You're a racist, Ulfric," I said.

He stared at me. "What?"

"I'm human so I'm good enough to fuck, good enough to kill but not good enough to be your equal just because I'm human. You're a racist chauvinistic big bad wolf."

"You come into my lands, ask aid of my pack, give no tribute to me or my lupa, and now you're calling me names." I don't know if he made some kind of psychic signal or his anger was enough, but the two giant wolves at his feet began to stalk forward on stiff legs.

My left hand was beginning to shake, visibly. Whatever was behind the bar thrashed, sounding large and bestial. My left hand was threatening to give out completely, and I needed both hands. "You die first, Ulfric," I said.

"What?" and he sort of laughed when he said it.

"The first thing that jumps any of us, and I shoot you. No matter what else happens today, you'll be dead. Your two pony wolves better stop right where they are."

"Your hand is shaking so badly, I don't think you've got it in you to kill anyone."

It was my turn to laugh. "You think my hand is shaking because I feel remorse about the thought of shooting you. Boy, have you got the wrong girl. Look at my right hand, Ulfric. It's not shaking. A walking corpse took a bite out of my left hand a couple of days ago, so I'm a little shaky with my left, but trust me. I hit what I aim at." This is usually when I give my victim full eye contact and let them know I'm not bluffing, but I was divided between the Ulfric and his entourage, and the bar. "How many of your wolves are you willing to sacrifice for your wounded pride?"

"If we fight, Anita, you and your friends will die."

"And you'll die, and some of your best people, so wouldn't it be nice to avoid the carnage and have you tell me what the hell you want from me. You know I'm telling the truth. I didn't know that I was stepping on your toes. If Nicky is making some kind of power play behind your back, I didn't know it. So, tell me what you want to make this . . . social gaffe okay between us. Tell me before my left hand starts spasming so badly that I start shooting things just because I have to."

He was watching me very narrowly, and I saw intelligence behind all the bragging and pride. There might be somebody home to bargain with. If there wasn't, then we were going to die. We were going to die, not because of the case but because I had been at one time Richard's girlfriend. It was a stupid reason to die.

"Tribute, I want the lupa of the Thronnos Roke Clan to give me tribute."

"You mean a gift," I said.

He nodded. "If it's the right kind of gift, yeah."

If I'd been coming to Albuquerque with Richard on personal business I'd have expected to make a gift to the local pack. The gift was usually a freshly killed animal, jewelry for the lupa, or something mystical. Death, jewelry, or magic. I didn't have any jewelry on me except Leonora's necklace, and I wasn't exactly sure what it would do for someone other than me. For all I knew it might be harmful, if it was just handed out. I didn't have enough information. The charm was so not leaving my body.

I lowered my left hand. One, it was twitching so badly, I wasn't a hundred percent sure I could hit anything with it. Two, I couldn't keep pointing guns if we weren't going to kill people. Three, my hand was hurting.

"Your word that if I give you a suitable gift, we all leave here in safety."

"You'd take the word of an ex-con, drug dealing, biker gang leader?"

"No, but I'll take the word of the Ulfric of the Broken Spear Clan. That I'll take." There were rules, and if he broke his word as Ulfric, he lost brownie points. He had to be on shaky ground anyway for a human, no matter how magically powerful, vargamor to have challenged his authority. He wouldn't give his word and break it, not in front of his pack.

"I am Ulfric of the Broken Spear Clan, and I give my word that you will all go in safety, if your gift is worthy."

I didn't like the wording on that last. "I didn't have time to stop at Tiffany's and pick up something for the little lady. Didn't get to hunt on the way here from the hospital. Cops frown on you shooting animals in town. The mystical shit is beyond me today."

"Then you have nothing worthy," he said, but he looked puzzled as though he was sure I had a gift of some kind.

"Let me see what's behind the bar, and I'll put up my guns and make tribute." I'd tried to put up the Firestar, but my left hand was shaking so badly that I couldn't raise the shirt and slide it inside my pants. I needed two hands for it. Which meant I needed to be able to holster the Browning.

"Done," he said. "Monstruo, rise, greet our guest."

It rose above the bar in a thin line of pale flesh like the rising of a crescent moon, then a face came into view. It was a woman's face with one eye gone stiff and dry like some kind of mummy. Face after face, rose brown and withered like a string of monstrous beads, strung together with pieces of body, arms, legs, and thick black thread like gigantic stitches holding it all together, holding the magic inside. It rose up and up until it towered against the ceiling, curving like a giant snake to stare down at me. I estimated forty heads, more, before I lost count, or lost heart to count anymore.

The werewolves had moved back further into the room like the tide retreating backwards. They feared the thing. I didn't blame them.

I heard Bernardo say, "Fuck."

Olaf said something in German, which meant he wasn't watching his part of the room. Only Edward remained silent and on the job, ever vigilant. I have to admit that if the werewolves had wanted to jump me while that thing rose above me like some demented snake I would have been slow. It was too much horror to leave room for anything else.

I'd only seen something like it once before. That monster had been made by the most powerful vaudun priestess I'd ever met. But hers had been formed of fresh zombies and pulled seamlessly together into one monstrous ball of flesh. Pure magic. This had been stitched together like Frankenstein's monster, and the bodies being dead like that, dried, deliberately mummified, or an after effect of the spell.

I dragged my gaze from the thing to the Nicky Baco still lying on the bar, gagged and bound and bloody. I heard my voice like a distant thing, "Why, Nicky, you bad, bad boy." I'd made a joke, when what I wanted to do was put a gun to his head and blow him away. Some things you did not do. Some things you simply did not do.

"You see why he's still alive," the Ulfric said.

"Too powerful to get rid of," I said, voice still oddly detached, as if I wasn't really concentrating on what I was saying.

"I used him as my threat. He would lay his magic on a wolf that was misbehaving, and they would be turned into what you see. And he would stitch them into the monstruo. But my wolves fear him now more than they fear me."

I was nodding over and over because I couldn't think of a good thing to say. Alive, they were alive when Nicky did his magic. I had a truly awful thought. Somehow it seemed wrong to be putting away the guns, but I needed my hands for other things. I raised the shirt and slid the Browning home, though it wasn't as smooth as it would have been if the holster had been familiar. But my left hand was pretty much gone. I had to raise the shirt with my right and very carefully tuck the Firestar into the front of my pants. Even after the hand was empty, it continued to twitch uncontrollably. There was nothing I could do but wait for it to calm down on its own. I cradled the hand against my body and walked towards the monster.

I stood on the other side of the bar from it, looking at one of those dried faces. The mouth had been sewn shut on this one. I didn't know why. I took a few deep cleansing breaths, and there was an odor of herbs to it, but mostly just a dry smell like tanned leather and dust. I reached out with my left hand. Even with the bandages and the muscle cramps this was still my power hand, the hand to sense magic with. Most people have a hand that is better for sensing stuff, usually the opposite hand from the one you write with. I have no idea what ambidextrous people do.

There was an amazing amount of power pushing out from the thing, but the bar was wide and I was hurt so my concentration wasn't good, and I still couldn't answer the one question I needed answered. I used my right hand to sort of jump-sit on the bar, then got onto my knees. There was a face at eye level with me, and this one had eyes. A man's face, I think, with pale grey wolf eyes trapped in a dried mummy face. Those eyes stared out at me, and there was someone home. The walking dead don't show fear. I knew what I'd feel before I stretched my hand out toward the face. There was Nicky's power like a warm blanket of worms, squirming over my skin. It was some of the most uncomfortable magic I'd ever felt, unclean, as if the power itself would eat your flesh if you stayed too close to it for too long. This was where Nicky's energy had gone, and this was why no matter how much energy he gathered, it would never be enough. Magic this negative, this evil, is like a drug. It takes more and more energy to get the same result with worse and worse effect on the spellcaster.

I sent my own magic into that mess, not to empower, but seeking. I felt the cool brush of a soul, and before I could pull back, my power ran up that column of trapped flesh, and the souls glowed behind my eyelids with cool white light. None of them had been dead when he did this to them. I wasn't a hundred percent sure they were dead now.

I opened my eye and pulled my hand back from the thing. His power sucked at my hand like invisible mud. I pulled free with an almost audible pop. The man's face moved its withered mouth, and made a long dry sound, twice. "Help," it said, "help."

I swallowed a wave of nausea and was very glad I'd missed breakfast. I crawled on one arm and my knees to Nicky. I bent over him and whispered, "Would burning it free their souls?"

He shook his head.

"Can you free their souls?"

He nodded.

I think if he'd said yes to the first question, I'd have put the Browning to his head and killed him. But I needed him to free them, and I added that to my list of things to do before I left town. But there was nothing I could do for them today, except stay alive, and strangely, keep Nicky Baco alive. One of life's little ironies, that last.

I sat on the bar with my legs dangling over the edge, hand cradled to my chest, dazed with the sheer evil of it. I'd seen my share, but this was near the top. This was near the top after what I'd seen in the hospital. At least the corpses were just eating bodies, not souls.

"You look like you've seen a ghost," the Ulfric said.

"You're closer than you know," I said.

"Where is our gift?" he said.

"Where's your lupa?"

He stroked the head of one of the wolves by his legs. "This is my lupa."

"I can't share the gift with anyone in animal form," I said.

He frowned, and it was very close to being angry. "You must honor us."

"I plan to." I rolled the sleeve of my jacket back over my left arm. The wrist sheath had to go. I undid the straps, propping the blade, sheath and all between my legs. The monster hovered behind me, peering curiously. It was distracting me. I couldn't save them today, and didn't want to see it anymore until I could fix it.

"Can you order it to leave the room?"

He looked at me. "Scared?"

"I can feel the souls crying out for help. It's sort of distracting."

He looked at me, and I watched the color drain from his face. "You mean that."

I smiled, but not like it was funny. "You didn't know that he's trapping their souls in that thing?"

"He said he was." His voice had gone softer.

"You didn't believe him," I said.

The Ulfric was gazing up at the thing as if he'd never seen it before. "You wouldn't believe something like that, would you?"

"I would." I shrugged, wished I hadn't, and said, "but then this is my line of work. Can you please send it away?"

He nodded, and spoke rapidly in Spanish. The thing folded down on itself and crept away on arms and legs and bodies like a broken centipede. Sitting on the bar, I could see it go down a trap door behind the bar. When the last segment of it had slithered out of sight, I turned back to the Ulfric. He still looked pale.

"Baco is the only one who can free their souls. Don't kill him until he's done that."

"I didn't plan to kill him," the man said.

"That was before you knew. I don't know you well enough to know if when I leave, you'll get all self-righteous and try to end this evil. Don't, please, or you condemn them all to an eternity of that."

He swallowed like he was having a little trouble keeping down his own breakfast. "I won't kill him."

"Good." I drew the knife from between my knees right-handed. "Now gather round, boys and girls, because I'm only going to do this trick once."

There was a general movement as the wolves moved forward. I spared a glance for the boys I'd come in with. They hadn't put their guns up, but they had them pointed at the floor or the ceiling. Edward was watching the wolves. Bernardo was watching the wolves, too, though he looked pale. Olaf was watching me. I really, really, didn't like him.

"I give honor to the Ulfric and lupa of the Broken Spear Clan. I give the most precious of gifts to the Ulfric, but not being true lukoi, I cannot share this gift with the lupa in her present form. For that, I apologize most sincerely. If I come back this way, I'll shop better." I sat the blade on the bar and leaned over the edge until I could reach a clean glass. One of those thick chunky ones that people are so fond of putting scotch in. It was a strain to get back into a sitting position on the bar, but I managed it with the glass in one hand. I put the glass beside me on the bar and picked the knife up. I laid the blade against my left arm, just above the wrist, and stared at the whole, pale, unscarred flesh. There were scars just above it where a shapeshifted witch had clawed me, and the cross-shaped burn scar that was now a little crooked from the claw marks, but this one patch was still pure. I hoped it didn't scar, but what was one more.

I took in a deep breath and sliced the blade down my skin. A sigh ran through the watching werewolves, and whimpers from a few of the furrier throats. I ignored them. I'd known it would get a crowd reaction. I kept looking at my flesh and the damage I'd just done to it. The wound didn't bleed immediately. It was just a thin red line, then the first drop spilled from the wound, and the rest of the wound spilled in crimson rivulets down my arm. Deeper than I'd wanted it, but probably about what was needed. I held the wound over the glass. Some of it splashed around the edges, trailing down the sides, but I managed to get it going into the cup. I didn't even need to squeeze the wound much to encourage the flow. Deeper than I wanted it, oh yeah.

The Ulfric had moved closer, close enough that he was standing with his body touching my legs. The wolf that he'd introduced as his lupa moved up to nuzzle at my knee, and he hit her. He backhanded her the way you'd hit a dog you didn't like much. Where was women's lib when you needed it? She went to her belly, crying in doggy fashion, telling him she hadn't meant any harm with her tail tight curled to her rump.

No one else tried to move forward. If the lupa couldn't share, the rest of them knew better than to try.

The Ulfric stayed pressed against my legs. "Let me take it out of your arm." He stared at my bleeding arm like I'd stripped for him, something beyond sex, beyond hunger, and yet a little of both. I raised the arm so the blood trickled down it in fast little streams of red, splashing down into the glass. His gaze followed the movement like a dog after a piece of food.

The truth was that letting people lick a wound directly tended to distract me. Through the marks I was bound to a werewolf and a vampire. Both of which found blood exciting. The thoughts that filled me when I shared blood with anyone were too primitive, too overwhelming. Especially now with my shields in ruins, I couldn't risk it. "Is the gift worthy?" I asked.

"You know it is," and his voice had that peculiar hoarseness that men get when sex is in the air.

"Then drink, Ulfric, drink. Don't waste it." I held the bloody glass out to him. He took it reverently in both hands. He drank, and I watched his throat convulse as he swallowed my blood. It should have bothered me more, I guess, but it didn't. The numbness was back, a distant almost comfortable feeling. I fished under the bar until I found a stack of clean napkins and pressed them to my arm. The napkins soaked crimson in moments.

The Ulfric had waded into the pack with my blood in his hands. They surrounded him, touching him, caressing, begging for him to share. He dipped his fingers in the nearly empty cup and held them down for the wolves to lick.

Edward came to stand near me. He said nothing, just helped me put pressure on the wound, got more napkins from under the bar and a clean cloth to tie it tight. Our eyes met, and he just shook his head, the faintest of smiles playing on his face. "Most people pay money for information."

"Money doesn't interest most of the people I deal with."

The Ulfric called back to me through the reaching werewolves. His mouth was bloodstained, his neat beard and mustache thick with my blood. He stared at me with his golden eyes and said, "If you want to talk to Nicky, help yourself."

"Thank you, Ulfric," I said. I hopped down off the bar, and Edward had to catch me or I'd have fallen. Fresh blood loss on top of everything else was not what I had needed. I waved him away, and he didn't argue.

Edward undid Nicky's gag, and took a step back. The werewolves had pulled back, giving us the illusion of privacy, though I knew that every werewolf in the room would hear us, even if we whispered.

"Hi, Nicky," I said.

He had to try twice before he said, "Anita."

"I was here before ten." I put my hands on the bar and propped my chin on them so he wouldn't have to strain. The movement hurt my back, but somehow I wanted to be on eye level with him. The bulky makeshift bandage seemed to be in the way, but I wanted to keep the arm elevated. Nicky looked even worse up close. One eye was completely closed, blackened and blood-filled. His nose looked broken, blood bubbling from it when he breathed.

"He came back into town early."

"I figured as much. You've been a very bad boy, Nicky. Pissing off your Ulfric, power play behind his back when you're just human, not even a werewolf, and that thing. That's not voodoo. How the hell did you do that?"

"Older magic than voodoo," he said.

"What kind of magic?" I asked.

"I thought you wanted to talk about the monster that's killing innocent citizens?" His voice was strained, pain-filled. Normally, I'm against torture, but I just couldn't find much pity in my heart for Nicky. I'd seen his creation, and I felt the torment of its parts. Nope, I just couldn't spare much sympathy for Nicky. He'd never take enough damage to make up for what he'd done, not at least while he was alive. Hell might be a very nasty place for Nicky Baco. I trusted the divine to have a better sense of justice and irony than I did.

"Okay, what do you really know about the thing that's out there?" I asked.

He lay there on the bar, wrists and ankles bound together, blood trickling from his mouth, and talked as if he were sitting behind a desk. Except for the little pain sounds he made every once in a while, which spoiled some of the effect.

"I felt it years ago, maybe ten. I felt it wake."

"What do you mean wake?"

"Have you had it in your mind yet?" he asked, and this time I heard the fear in his voice.

"Yeah," I said.

"It was sluggish at first, as if it had been asleep or imprisoned, dormant for a very long time. It grew stronger every year."

"Why didn't you tell the police?"

"Ten years ago the police didn't have any psychics or witches working for them. And I already had a criminal record." He coughed and spat blood, and a tooth out on the bar. It made me raise my head up, which forced Nicky to roll his head a little. "What was I going to tell them? That there was this thing out there somewhere, this voice in my head, and it was getting stronger. I didn't know what it could do at first. I didn't know what it was."

"What is it?"

"It's a god."

I raised eyebrows at him.

"It was worshipped as a god once. It wants to be worshipped again. It says that gods need tribute to survive."

"You got all this from just a voice in your head?"

"I've had ten years with the thing whispering in my head. What have you learned in less than that many days?"

I thought about that. I knew it was killing to feed, not just for sport. Though it enjoyed the slaughter, that I'd felt, too. I knew it both feared me and wanted me. It feared another death worker on the opposite side, but it wanted to drink my powers and would have if Leonora hadn't stopped it.

"Why has it just started to kill people now? Why after a decade?"

"I don't know," he said.

"Why does it slaughter some and skin others?"

"I don't know."

"What is it doing with the body parts that it takes away from the scenes?" Which was a detail that the police would not like me sharing with someone outside the investigation, but I wanted answers more than I wanted to be cautious.

"I don't know." He coughed again, but didn't spit out anything. Good. If he'd continued to spit blood, I'd have worried about internal injuries. I didn't want to have to persuade the pack to take him to the hospital. I didn't think I'd have much luck.

"Where is it?"

"I've never been there. But understand that what's been killing people is not the god. He's still trapped wherever he started. His servants have done all the murders, not him."

"What are you saying?"

"I'm saying that if you think you've got trouble now, you ain't seen nothing yet. I can feel him in the dark, lying like some kind of bloated thing, filling up with power. When he's full enough, he'll rise, and it'll be hell to pay."

"Why didn't you tell me all this before?"

"You had the police with you the first time. If you turn me over to them, I'm dead. You've seen what I do. There wouldn't even need to be a jury."

He had a point. "When this is over, you have to dismantle it. You have to free their souls, agreed?"

"When I can walk again, agreed."

I glanced at his legs and saw that there was a lump under his pants leg. It was the bone of the leg, a compound fracture. Jesus. Some days there are so many stones to throw in so many different directions that I don't even know where to start.

"Does this god have a name?"

"He calls himself the Red Woman's Husband."

"That can't be an original English phrase."

"I think he knows what his victims know. By the time he came to me, he spoke in English."

"So you think he's been here a long time."

"I think he's always been here."

"What do you mean, always? Like eternity, or a really, really long time."

"I don't know how long he's been here." Nicky closed his good eye, as if he were tired.

"Okay, Nicky, okay." I turned to the Ulfric. "Is he telling the truth?"

The man nodded. "He didn't lie."

"Great. Thank you for your hospitality and please don't kill him. We may need him in the next few days to help kill this thing, not to mention freeing the souls of your pack mates."

"I'll lay off on the beating."

It was the closest thing I was going to get to a "yes, we are going to let him go and make sure he isn't hurt anymore." "Great, I'll be in touch."

Edward stayed near me as we walked to the door. He didn't offer me his arm, but he stayed close enough that if I stumbled he'd be there. Bernardo already had the door open. Olaf just watched us walk towards them. I stumbled a little up the two steps to the door, and Olaf caught my arm. I looked up into his eyes, and it wasn't pride or honor or respect that I saw. It was . . . hunger, a desire so great it was a physical need, a hunger.

I pulled away from him and left a smear of blood on his hand. Edward was at my back, helping me towards the door. Olaf raised his hand to his mouth and pressed it to his mouth like a kiss, but he was doing the same thing that the wolves did. He was tasting my blood and liked it. There are all kinds of monsters. Most of them crave blood. Some for food, some for pleasure, but you're dead either way.

48

EVERYONE WAS QUIET in the car. Olaf consumed by his own thoughts, which I wanted no details about. Bernardo had finally said, "Where to?"

"My house," Edward said. "I don't think Anita's up to anything else today."

For once, I didn't argue. I was so tired, I was nauseated. If I could have found a comfortable position, I think I could have slept.

We drove out of Albuquerque and headed towards the distant mountains, bright and cheerful in the morning light. I wished for a pair of sunglasses, because I suddenly was neither cheerful nor bright.

"Did you learn anything worth getting out of the hospital early?" Edward asked.

"I learned that the thing has a name, the Red Woman's Husband. It is hiding some place that it can't move from, which means if we can track it, we can kill it." I added, because just in case, they needed to know. "Nicky says it was worshipped as a god once, and that it still thinks it is one."

"It can't be a god," Bernardo said, "not a real one."

"I'm the wrong person to ask," I said. "I'm a monotheist."

"Edward?" Bernardo made a question of his name.

"I've never met anything that was truly immortal. It's just a matter of figuring out how to kill it."

I actually had met a few things that seemed immortal. Maybe Edward was right, but I'd seen things that I still couldn't figure out how to kill. Lucky me, the naga had been a crime victim and not a bad guy, and the lamia had been converted to our side. But as far as I knew they were both immortal. Of course, I'd never shoved an incendiary grenade down their pants or tried to set them on fire. Maybe I just hadn't been trying hard enough. For all our sakes, I hoped Edward was right.

We pulled onto the long road that led, as far as I could tell, just to Edward's house. It had a steeper drop off than I'd noticed at night, enough of a drop off that being an all terrain vehicle didn't mean anything unless you could fly. A white truck pulled in behind us and started following us.

"Do you know them?" Olaf asked.

"No," Edward said.

I managed to turn in the seat far enough to watch the truck. It didn't try and overtake us or anything. There was nothing wrong with the truck except for the fact that it was on the road to Edward's house and he didn't recognize it. Add to that that all four of us were paranoid by profession, and it made for tension.

Edward pulled into the turnaround in front of his house. "Everybody into the house until we find out who it is."

Everyone was quicker out of the car than I was, but then I'd just managed to get the bleeding on my arm stopped. Lucky for me, Edward had a heavy duty first aid kit in the back seat. I had a nice big bandage taped to my arm, and the wrist sheath shoved in my pocket.

Edward was at the door, unlocking it. Olaf was behind him. Bernardo had actually waited for me, as if he would have liked to offer to help me out of the car, but was afraid to. I was actually feeling rough enough that I didn't mind the babysitting, which told you how truly bad I felt.

There was a small, sharp sound, a bolt being drawn back on a rifle, and everything happened at once. Edward had his gun out and pointed at the sound. Olaf's gun was out but not pointed. Bernardo had his gun pointed, using the door as a brace. I have to admit my gun was in my hand but not pointed. I just wasn't used to the new holster, and having to lift the shirt with a wounded left hand. Damn, I was slow.

Harold of the scarred face was leaning at the far end of Edward's house with a high-powered rifle pointed at Edward. He had most of his body hidden behind the house, and held the rifle like he knew what he was doing. If he'd wanted to drop Edward, he could have done it before Edward got the drop on him. That Harold hadn't shot anyone yet meant they had come for more than just killing. Probably.

Harold said, "Nobody panics, nobody gets hurt."

"Harold," Edward said, "when did you guys make bail?" He was still staring down the barrel of his Beretta at Harold. I could almost guarantee he was sighting on the top of the other man's head, his best killing target from what little he had to shoot at. Edward did not shoot to wound.

"Only Russell got arrested," Harold said, rifle settled comfortably against his shoulder.

Speak of the devil. Russell came around the corner behind Harold. His nose was packed with white cotton and covered in a hard bandage. I'd broken his nose. Great.

"I thought terrorizing women and children carried more time than this," I said. I kept the gun behind the open door. I didn't want to give anyone an excuse to start shooting.

The tall silent Newt came around the other side of the house with a large shiny revolver in his hands. He held it two-handed and moved in a cross-foot glide that said he knew what he was doing. There was a woman beside him, moving like a smooth oiled shadow. She was six foot if she was an inch, and the tank top she was wearing showed off shoulders and arms that made most of the men look puny. Only her breasts pressed against the shirt showed her braless and very much a girl.

Olaf pointed his gun at them. Bernardo moved up with his gun, and the woman turned to him. Olaf turned as Newt moved across in front of him like a long distance dance. The woman and Bernardo were more practical. They just stood a little bit apart and stared at each other over their guns.

Only Russell kept walking and didn't pull a gun. I tried pulling mine and pointing it at him. He did stop, but his smile got wider and the look in his eyes got worse, as if he had plans for me, and they were all about to come true.

"You shoot me and they shoot your friends. You're the only one our boss wants," Russell said.

"But we're not here to kill anyone," Harold said, very quickly, as if he wanted to be clear on that. If I were staring down a gun barrel that Edward was holding, I'd want to be clear, too.

Russell started walking towards me, even though I had the Browning pointed at his chest.

"Our boss just wants to talk to you, that's all," Harold said. "I promise he just wants to talk to the girl."

I was backing up with the gun held out. Russell was still walking forward very confident. Unless I was willing to shoot him, he wasn't stopping. I did not want to be the one who fired the first shot. People were going to die, and I couldn't control which people that would be.

I could hear the truck now, crunching over the gravel. I did the only thing I could think of, I turned and ran. I heard a surprised, "Hey," from behind me. But I was over the edge of the slope and down the other side. I suddenly wasn't worried about tearing my stitches up, or how tired I was. My heart was in my throat, and I found that not only could I walk without falling down, I could run. My mind seemed to be working fast and faster. I saw a dry wash at the base of the slope and a clump of trees to one side. I slid into the wash in a rush of small stones. I landed on all fours, heavy, and was scrambling to my feet before I felt the first trickle of blood down my back. I was behind the trees as I heard Russell slither down the slope behind me.

I couldn't shoot him, but there were other options. I was aiming for the clump of trees. But say what you liked about Russell, he could run, because I could hear him doing it. He wasn't going to give me enough time to hide. I ran past the trees and knew that I couldn't outrun him. The adrenaline was already beginning to fade, and the heat folded around me like a hand. I just wasn't up to a long chase today. I had to end it, soon.

I slowed, just a little, one to save energy, and one to let Russell catch up sooner. I took a big breath and prepared. I knew what I wanted to do. But my body had to do it. I couldn't hesitate because my back or my arm or anything else hurt. I risked a glance back, and Russell was almost there, almost on me. I kicked him, full out, straight in the balls. I did it without hesitating, almost without setting up for it, letting his own momentum carry him into me. The shock sent me hopping backward, and I did what I still wasn't smooth at in class, I did a reverse roundhouse kick, to where I thought his face would be, and it was. He'd crumbled, clutching himself, and he went to his knees with the kick. He stayed on all fours shaking his head, but he didn't go down. Dammit!

A voice yelled from up the slope. "I don't see them."

There was a long piece of bleached wood on the floor of the wash. I picked it up and hit him twice, hard. He finally slumped on the ground and didn't move. I didn't have time to check for a pulse. The wash stretched straight for about a hundred yards before brush filled the end of it. There was a place in the bank that had washed away more than the rest. It was like a shallow cave. I had a split second to decide which way to go. I took the knife sheath out of my back pocket, and threw it knife and all as far as I could towards the brush. I went for the cave, scrambling on feet and hands like a monkey, keeping low. I was in the cooler shade of the depression when I heard the men coming down the slope.

"I don't see them," the first man said.

"They went this way," a woman's voice. Could there be two female bad guys, I didn't think so. Did that mean that there was one less gun up with Edward and the others? I let the thought go. I had my own problems.

Rocks cascaded down over the overhang like a dry waterfall. At least one of them was coming down directly on top of me. Would the ceiling of the little cave hold the weight? I was already regretting hiding. But the wash stretched open and straight for too far. I'd have never made it to the place where it emptied and there was brush. I just wasn't that fast today. If they thought I'd gone that way and didn't see me, then it would be a good plan. If they turned and spotted me, it was a bad plan. I heard them coming, but the man's voice was right above me. It made me jump. He had to be standing just to the right of the roof. "Jesus, there's Russell." He jumped into the wash and started running towards the fallen man.

The woman was more cautious, sliding down into the wash, searching up and down the wash. She was so close, I could have reached out and touched the leg of her jeans. My heart was thundering in my throat, but I'd stopped breathing. I was holding my breath, willing her to go to the men, to walk away, and not look back.

"He's alive," the man said. Then he was up and moving towards the sheath I'd thrown. "She went this way." He went for the brush.

The woman walked towards him.

He was already at the brush, pushing into it.

"Maury, dammit, don't go in there." She had to jog to have any chance of catching him. She didn't look back to see me crouched in the hole. When her broad back vanished into the brush, and I heard the man curse, I crawled out of the hole and started up the slope on all fours. If the woman and Maury came out now, I would be caught like a black speck on a white sheet of paper. But they didn't come, and I made the top of the slope down from where I'd first entered, crawling on my belly to lie under the sage bushes that edged Edward's front yard.

Something slithered off to my right, and it wasn't human. A snake. A snake had slithered away deeper into the bushes. Shit. Thank you, dear God, that it left. One more problem and I was out of solutions. Of course, now every noise seemed to be reptilian, and crawling on my belly through the thick bushes, the smell of sage thick in the hot air was a little slice of nightmare. I kept waiting to hear that dry rattle that would tell me I'd used up all my luck. Every twig that brushed my leg seemed to have scales. The only thing that kept me from screaming was the knowledge that someone would probably shoot me before they knew it was me.

By the time I crawled to the very edge of the bushes one painful inch at a time, I was sweating and it was only partially from heat. The sweat stung on my back, and I knew that some of the thicker trickles were blood and not sweat. I could see the yard through the last screen of sage. Things had not improved.

The woman and the new man, Maury, had left the yard, but three others had taken their places. They had the men on their knees. Olaf had his hands laced on his bald head. Bernardo had his one good hand on his head, and his cast raised as high as he could. Edward was the closest to me. Newt was so close I could have put the knife into his foot. Harold was talking into a cell phone. He was waving one hand and had the rifle slung over one arm. He put the phone away from his mouth, and said, "He says search the house."

"What for?" one of the new men said, he had dark hair and a revolver.

"For an artifact, something the girl used against the monster."

"What kind of artifact?" the dark man asked.

"Just do it," Harold said.

Dark hair grumbled, but he motioned and the two men left to go into the open door of the house. Edward must have unlocked it for them. What the hell had been happening while I was crawling through the bushes?

The three men went into the house. Harold was still talking on the phone. That left just Newt with his .45, and he wasn't even pointing it at anyone's head. It would never get better than this. Any second now the others would come back up the wash or out of the house. I'd have liked to have at least gotten to my knees and plunged the knife into a vital area, but the bushes were too thick. I'd never push to my knees without making all kinds of noise.

If I fired a gun, I'd alert all the others. Shit. I had two knives. I had one idea. I slipped the blade out of my right arm sheath, making sure my left hand had a good grip. Newt's foot was still so temptingly close. I took the invitation. I stabbed the right-hand knife into the foot opposite from his gun. I felt the blade sink into the ground underneath his shoe, as he screamed. I was on my knees behind him, as he tried to twist and bring the gun on me, but he had the gun pointed for someone standing on his left side, and I wasn't there. I plunged the other knife up into his pants, into the front of his pants, my hand between his legs, and I missed. I didn't hit flesh. Fuck. I twitched the blade to the side and felt him, but he wasn't cut. But he was very, very still.

I hissed, "Don't move."

He didn't move. He stayed like some kind of awkward statue.

Harold started walking towards us. "What's wrong, Newt?"

Newt swallowed, and said, "N—nothing. Thought I saw a snake."

I whispered, "Good boy, Newt. If you want to keep the family jewels intact, very quietly hand me your gun." He let the .45 fall into my hand. I was close enough to whisper to Edward, "What do you want me to do?"

"Call Harold over."

"You heard him, Newt," I said.

The man never argued. "Hey, Harold, can you come over here a second?"

Harold sighed, snapping the cell phone shut. "What is it now, Newt?" He was almost even with Edward when he noticed that Newt's gun was gone. I was still hidden behind the larger man's body; even the blade was hidden in the cloth of his pants. "What the hell?"

Bernardo pulled one of the gold chopsticks out of his hair, and it was a blade that ended in Harold's arm. Edward hit him in the gut, doubled him over, and disarmed him. He stood over him with the rifle. Olaf and Bernardo were on their feet. I don't know what the plan would have been next because we heard the sirens. Police sirens.

"Did you call the cops, Harold?" Edward asked.

"Don't be an ass," Harold said.

"Anita," Edward said.

"I didn't call them. I've still got a .45 pointed at you, Newt. Don't get cute." But I withdrew the blade very carefully and stood up. I kept his gun pointed at his back, but I was beginning to doubt I'd have to shoot anybody. The sirens were almost here.

The three guys came out of the house with their guns in plain sight. They looked to Harold, saw him on the ground, and Edward had the rifle to his shoulder and was sighting down the barrel at them. Their eyes flicked to the cops coming at a fast pace, and back to Edward. They threw their guns down and laced their fingers on their heads without being told. I doubted it was the first time they'd had to do it.

It was an unmarked car with a marked car following it. They skidded to a stop on opposite sides of the black truck and four cops spilled out. Lieutenant Marks, Detective Ramirez, and two uniforms I didn't know. They had guns pointed but looked a little unsure who the bad guys were. Couldn't blame them. We had all the guns.

"Detective Ramirez," I said. "Thank God."

"What's going on?" Marks said, before Ramirez could answer me.

Edward told them that Harold and his men had jumped us and were trying to question us about the mutilation murders. Marks found that fascinating. Edward had known he would. Yes, Ted Forrester would press assault charges. Any good citizen would. There were enough handcuffs to go around, barely.

"There are two more out there somewhere," Edward said in his best helpful voice.

"There's one unconscious in the wash that way," I said.

Everyone looked at me. I didn't have to pretend to be uncomfortable. "He was chasing me. I thought they were going to kill the others." I shrugged and winced. "He's alive." It sounded like an excuse even to me.

They called for more men to search the area. They called for an ambulance for Harold, Newt, and Russell, when they found him. I'd sat down on the ground, waiting for everyone to do their jobs. I was using both hands to prop myself up. Now that the emergency seemed to be over, I wasn't feeling so good.

Marks was yelling at me. "You left the hospital against doctor's orders! I don't give a damn, but I want a statement. I want to know exactly what happened at that hospital."

I looked up at him, and he seemed to be taller than he was, further away somehow. "Are you saying that all the lights and sirens were because you were mad at me for not giving a statement before I left the hospital?"

A flush spread up his face, and I knew that that was exactly it. One of the uniforms called, "Lieutenant."

"I want that statement today." He turned and walked away. I hoped he stayed there.

Ramirez knelt beside me. He was wearing his usual, shirtsleeves rolled back, a striped tie at half-mast, around an open collar. "You all right?"

"No," I said.

"I went to the hospital today, and you were already gone. That night, the elevator had been turned off because of the fire alarms. I had to double back and get the stairs, and come up behind you. That's why I was late. That's why I wasn't there for you." For it to be almost the first thing out of his mouth, it must have been bugging him. I liked that.

I managed something close to a smile. "Thanks for telling me." I was so hot. The yard seemed to be swimming in heat, as if I were looking at the world through rippling glass.

He touched my back, I think to help me up. He drew his hand away from my shirt. His hand was bloody. He went on all fours, using one hand to raise my shirt. It was so blood-soaked that he had to peel it away from my skin. "Jesus, and Joseph, what the hell have you done to yourself?"

"It doesn't even hurt anymore." I heard myself saying it from a long way away, then I was sliding over into his arms, his lap. I heard someone call my name, and I finally passed out.

I woke up in the hospital. Doctor Cunningham was bending over me. I thought, "We have to stop meeting like this," but didn't even try to say it out loud.

"You've lost blood and had your stitches redone. Do you think you can stay in here long enough for me to actually release you this time?"

I think I smiled. "Yes, Doctor."

"Just in case you got any funny ideas about leaving, I've doped you up with enough pain killers to make you feel really good. So sleep, and I'll see you in the morning."

My eyes fluttered shut once, then opened. Edward was there. He bent over me and whispered, "Crawling through bushes on your belly, threatening to cut off a man's balls. Such a hard ass."

My voice came faintly even to me. "Had to save your ass."

He bent over me and kissed on my forehead, or maybe I dreamed that part.

49

SOME TIME DURING the second day in the hospital they lowered the meds, and I started having the dreams. I was wandering in a maze made up of high green hedges. I was wearing a long, heavy dress, made of white silk. There were heavy things under it, weighting it down. I could feel the tightness of a corset under the dress, and I knew it wasn't my dream. I would never dream of clothing that I had never worn. I stopped running through the green maze, looked up into a flawless blue sky, and shouted, "Jean-Claude!"

His voice came, rich, seductive. He could do things with his voice that most men couldn't do with their hands. "Where are you, ma petite? Where are you?"

"You promised to stay out of my dreams."

"We felt you dying. We felt the marks open. We worried."

I knew who "we" was. "Richard isn't invading my dreams, just you."

"I have come to warn you. If you had picked up a phone to call us, this would not be necessary."

I turned and there was a mirror in the middle of the grass and the hedges. It was a full-length mirror with a gilt edged frame. Very antique, very Louis XIV. My reflection was startling. It wasn't just the clothes. My hair was in some kind of complicated mound, with thick curls hanging down here and there. There was also more of it, and I knew at least some of it was a wig or at least hairpieces. There was even one of those beauty marks on my cheek. I expected to look ridiculous, but I didn't. I looked delicate, like a china doll, but it wasn't ridiculous. My reflection wavered, then grew taller, and it was Jean-Claude in the mirror, and my reflection had vanished.

He was tall, slender, dressed head to foot in white satin, in a suit that matched my dress. Gold brocade glittered down his sleeves, the seams of the pants. White boots rode over his knees tied with huge white and gold ribbons. It was a foppish outfit, sissy to use a modern word, but he didn't look foppish. He looked elegant and at ease like a man who'd pulled off his tie and slipped into something more comfortable. His hair fell in long black banana curls. Only the delicate masculinity of his face and his midnight blue eyes looked normal, familiar.

I shook my head, and the weight of the hair made it awkward. "I am so out of here," and I started to reach out to shred the dream.

"Wait, please, ma petite. Truly, I have a warning for you." He looked up as if seeing the mirror as a sort of prison. "This is to let you know that I will not touch you. I come only to talk."

"Then talk."

"Was it the Master of Albuquerque who harmed you?"

It seemed an odd question. "No, Itzpapalotl didn't hurt me."

He winced at her name. "Do not use her name aloud within this dream."

"Okay, but she didn't hurt me."

"But you have seen her?" he asked.

"Yes."

He looked puzzled, and he lifted a white hat and slapped it against his leg like it was a habitual gesture, though I'd never seen him do it before. But then I'd only seen him in clothes like this once before, and we'd been fighting for our lives, so there really hadn't been time to notice the small stuff.

"Albuquerque is taboo. The high council has declared the city off limits to all vampires and their minions."

"Why?"

"Because the Master of the City has slain every vampire or minion that has entered her city in the last fifty years."

I stared at him. "You're joking."

"No, ma petite, I do not joke." He looked worried, no, scared.

"She didn't try anything hostile, Jean-Claude, honest."

"Then there was a reason for it. Were the police with you?"

"No."

He shook his head, slapping the hat against his leg again. "Then she wants something from you."

"What could she want from me?"

"I do not know." He slapped the hat against his leg again and stared out at me through the glass wall.

"Has she really killed any vampire that just happened to be passing through?"

"Oui."

"Why hasn't the council sent someone to kick her ass?"

He looked down, then up, and the fear was in his eyes again. "The Council fears her, I believe."

Having met three of the council members personally, that raised my eyebrows as far as they would go. "Why? I mean I know she's powerful, but she's not that powerful."

"I do not know, ma petite, but I do know they decreed her territory taboo, rather than fight her."

That was just plain scary. "It would have been nice to know that before I got here."

"I know you value your privacy, ma petite. I have not contacted you in all these long months. I have respected your decision, but it is not merely our romance, or lack of it, that is important between us. You are my human servant whether you will or no. It means that you cannot simply enter another vampire's territory without some diplomacy."

"I'm here on police business. I thought I could enter anyone's territory as long as it was police business. I'm here as Anita Blake, preternatural expert, not as your human servant."

"Normally, that is true, but the Master whose lands you are in does not obey council decrees. She is a law unto herself."

"What does that mean for me here and now?"

"Perhaps she fears human law. Perhaps she will not harm you for fear of the humans destroying her. Your authorities can be very effective at times. Or she simply wants something from you. You've met her. What do you think?" he said.

It came to my lips before I thought about it. "Power, she's attracted to power."

"You are a necromancer."

I shook my head, and again the hairpieces made it awkward. I closed my eyes in the dream, and when I opened them, my hair just hung around my shoulders like normal. "The hair was heavy."

"It could be," he said, "I am happy that you left the dress. I cannot tell you how long I have wished to see you in something like it."

"Don't push it, Jean-Claude."

"My apologies," and he did a sweeping bow, using the hat in the gesture, so that it swept across his chest.

"I think it's more than the necromancy. She figured out that I was part of a triumvirate the first moment she met me. I felt her sift through the three of us, like unwinding a string. She knew. I think that's what she wants. She wants to figure out how it works."

"Could she repeat it?" he asked.

"She's got a human servant and jaguars are her animal to call. Theoretically, I guess she could, though can you make it a three-way when you've already got marks on a human, and no animal?"

"If the marks are recent, perhaps."

"No, not recent. They've been a couple a long time."

"Then no, her human's marks will be too entrenched to stretch for a third."

"So she may be interested in me for a power she can't have? If she finds out then I can't be of help to her?" I said.

"It would perhaps be best if she did not learn that, ma petite."

"You think she'd kill me."

"She has killed all that crossed her path for half a century. I do not see why she should change her ways now."

I was standing very close to the mirror now. Close enough that I could see the gold buttons on his jacket, and the rise and fall of his chest as he drew breath. This was the closest I'd been to him in months. It was just a dream, but we both knew it wasn't just a dream. He'd put the mirror barrier between us because once we'd used our dreams to enter each other's fantasies. He'd come like a demon lover in my dreams, in my sleep. We'd done the real thing, too, but the dreams had been sweet, sometimes a prelude to the real thing, sometimes an end in themselves.

The glass grew thinner, as if the glass were wearing away. It was like a thin pane of spun sugar. He touched fingertips to it, and the glass moved like clear plastic, giving at his touch.

My fingertips touched his, and the thin barrier vanished. Our fingers touched, and it was startling, electric. His fingers slid over mine, entwining, our palms touching, and even that one chaste touch sent my breath racing.

I stepped back but didn't let go of his hand, so the movement drew him out of the mirror. He stepped out of the golden frame and was suddenly standing in front of me, our hands still raised in front of us. I could feel his heart beating through his palm, feel the rise and pulse of his body through my hand as if all of him were contained in that one pale hand where it lay pressed against mine.

He leaned down towards me, as if to kiss me, and I started to pull away, afraid, but the dream shattered, and I was suddenly awake, staring up at the hospital ceiling. A nurse was in the room, checking my vitals. She'd woken me. I wasn't sure whether I was glad or sad.

The marks had been open for less than a week, and Jean-Claude was already pushing me. Okay, okay, I needed the warning, but . . . Oh, hell. My teacher, Marianne, had told me that I couldn't just ignore the boys, that that would be dangerous. I thought she meant ignoring the power that bound us, but maybe she meant more than that. I was Jean-Claude's human servant, and that made things complicated when I traveled. Each vampire's territory was like a foreign country. Sometimes you had diplomatic treaties between them. Sometimes you didn't. Occasionally, you just had a couple of master vamps that were enemies pure and simple, so if you belonged to one, you stayed the hell out of the other one's lands. By refusing to contact Jean-Claude, I could screw up, get myself killed or held hostage. But I'd thought I was safe as long as I was on police business or animating zombies. That was work. It had nothing to do with Jean-Claude and vampire politics. But I could always be wrong, like now.

Why, you may ask, did I believe Jean-Claude and his warning? Because it gained him nothing to lie about it. I'd also felt his fear. One of the things about the marks, you could usually tell what the other person was feeling. Sometimes that bugged me. Sometimes it was helpful.

The nurse shoved a thermometer with a little plastic sheath on it under my tongue. She took my pulse while we waited for the thermometer to beep. What really bugged me about the dream was how attracted to him I was. When I had the marks closed off, I'd have never touched him in the dream. Of course, I hadn't let him enter my dreams when I had the marks blocked off. With the barriers up, I'd policed my dreams, kept him and Richard out. I could still keep them out, but it took more work to do it. I was out of practice. I was going to have to get back into practice, fast.

The thermometer beeped. The nurse read the little monitor on her belt, gave me an empty smile that could have meant anything, and made a note. "I hear you're getting out of here today."

I looked up at her. "I am. Great."

"Doctor Cunningham will be in to see you before you leave." She smiled again. "He seems to want to oversee your release personally."

"I'm one of his favorite patients," I said.

The nurse's smile slipped just a touch. I think she knew exactly what Doctor Cunningham thought of me. "He should be in to see you soon."

"But I am definitely getting out of here today?" I asked.

"That's what I hear."

"Can I call a friend to come pick me up?"

"I can call them for you."

"If I'm getting out today, can't I have a phone?" The good doctor had made sure there was no phone in my room because he didn't want me trying to do work, any work, not even business phone calls. When I'd promised not to use the phone if he'd just give me one, he'd just looked at me, made some kind of note in his file, and left. I don't think he trusted me.

"If the doctor says you can have a phone, I'll bring you one, but just in case, give me the number and I'll contact your friend."

I gave her Edward's number. She wrote it down, smiled, and left.

There was a knock on the door. I expected Doctor Cunningham, but it was Detective Ramirez. His shirt today was a pale tan. The half-mast tie was deep brown with a small white and yellow design on it. But he'd also kept a brown suit jacket that matched his pants. It was the first time I'd seen him with an entire suit on at once. I wondered if the sleeves were rolled up underneath the jacket sleeves. He had a bouquet of shiny Mylar balloons with cartoon characters on them. The balloons said things like "get well soon," and "oh, bother." That was the Winnie the Pooh balloon.

I had to smile. "You already sent flowers." There was a small, but nice arrangement running long to daisies and miniature carnations on the bedside table.

"I wanted to bring something in person. I'm sorry I wasn't here sooner."

My smile wilted around the edges. "This level of apology is usually reserved for boyfriends or lovers, detective. Why are you feeling so guilty?"

"I keep having to remind you to call me Hernando."

"I keep forgetting."

"No, you don't. You keep trying to distance yourself."

I just looked at him. It was probably true. "Maybe."

"If I was your lover, I'd have followed you to the hospital and been by your side every minute," he said.

"Even with a murder investigation going on?" I asked.

He had the grace to shrug and look sheepish. "I'd have tried to be here every minute."

"What's been happening while I've been in here? My doctor has made sure I haven't found out anything."

Ramirez put the balloons beside the flowers. The balloons had one of those little weights on them to keep them from drifting away. "The last time I tried to see you, your doctor made me promise not to talk about the case."

"I didn't know you were here before."

"You were pretty out of it."

"Was I awake?"

He shook his head.

Great. I wondered how many other people had paraded through here while I was passed out cold. "I'm getting out today, so I think it's safe to talk about the case."

He looked at me, and the expression was enough. He didn't believe me.

"Doesn't anyone trust me?"

"You're like most of the cops I know. You never really get off work."

I raised my hand in the Boy Scout's salute. "Honest, the nurse told me I'm being released today."

He smiled. "I saw your back, remember. Even if you're being let out, you won't be going back on the case, not in person anyway."

"What? I'm going to look at pictures and listen to the clues that other people find?"

He nodded. "Something like that."

"Do I look like Nero Wolfe? I am not a staying at home, out of the firing line, kind of girl."

He laughed, and it was still a good laugh. A nice normal laugh. It had none of Jean-Claude's touchable sex appeal, but in some ways I liked it better for its very normalcy. But . . . but as nice and warm as Ramirez was, I had the memory of Jean-Claude's dream in my head. I could feel the touch of his hand on mine, a touch that lingered on my skin the way an expensive perfume will linger in a room long after the woman who wears it is gone.

Maybe it was love, but whatever it was, it was hard to find a man who could compete with it, no matter how much I wanted to find one. It was as if when he was with me, all other men just faded into the background, except Richard. Was that what it meant to be in love? Was it? I wish I knew.

"What are you thinking about?" Ramirez asked.

"Nothing."

"Whatever that nothing is, it makes you look very serious, almost sad." He'd moved very close to the bed, fingers touching the edge of the sheet. His face was gentle, questioning, very open. I realized in a way that Ramirez had my ticket. He knew what punched my buttons, partly just coincidence, partly he read me well. He read what I liked and what I hated in a man better than Jean-Claude had for years. I liked honesty, openness, and a sort of little boy charm. There were other things that led to lust, but for my heart that was the way. Jean-Claude was almost never open about anything. He always had a dozen different motives for everything he did. Honesty was not his best thing, and his little boy charm . . . nope. Jean-Claude had gotten there first, and for better or worse that was the way things were.

Maybe a little honesty would work here, too. "I'm wondering how different my life would be if I'd met you or someone like you first."

"First, that implies that you've already met someone."

"I told you I had two guys back home."

"You also said you couldn't decide between them. My grandmother always said that the only reason a woman hesitates between two men is that she hasn't met the right one."

"Your grandmother didn't say that."

He nodded. "Yes, she did. She was being courted by two men, sort of halfway engaged to both, then she met my grandfather and she knew why she'd been hesitating. She didn't love either of the two men."

I sighed. "Don't tell me I've got caught up in some family folklore?"

"You never said you were taken. Tell me I'm wasting my time and I'll stop."

I looked up at him, really looked at him, let my eye follow the smiling line of his face, the shining humor in his eyes. "You're wasting your time. I am sorry, but I think you are."

"Think?"

I shook my head. "Stop it, Hernando. I'm taken, okay."

"You're not taken until you make a final choice, but that's okay. I'm not the one. If I were, you'd know it. When you meet him, you won't have any doubts."

"Don't tell me you believe in true love, soul mate kind of stuff."

He shrugged, fingers running up and down the edge of the sheet. "What can I say? I was raised on stories about love at first sight. My grandmother, both my parents, even my great-grandfather said the same thing. They met that special person, and no one else existed after that."

"You're descended from a family of romantics," I said.

He nodded happily. "My great-grandfather, Poppy, talked about my great-grandmother like they were still school kids right up until he died."

"It sounds nice, really, but I don't believe in true love, Hernando. I don't believe that there's only one special person for your whole life's happiness."

"You don't want to believe it," he said.

I shook my head. "This is about to go from cute to irritating, Hernando."

"At least you're using my first name."

"Maybe because I don't see you as a threat anymore."

"A threat? Just because I like you? Just because I asked you out?" He frowned when he said it.

It was my turn to shrug. "Whatever I mean, Hernando, just cut the juice. It ain't going nowhere. Whatever I decide, it's between the two guys I have waiting for me back home."

"It sounds like you weren't sure of that until just now."

I thought about that for a heartbeat, or two. "You know, I think you're right. I think I've been looking around for someone else, anyone else. But it's no good."

"You don't sound happy about that. Love should make you happy, Anita."

I smiled and knew it was wistful. "If you think love makes you happy, Hernando, you've either never been in love, or never been in love long enough to have to start compromising."

"You're not old enough to be this cynical."

"It's not cynicism. It's reality."

His face was soft and sad. "You've lost your sense of romance."

"I never had a sense of romance. Trust me, the guys at home will back me on it."

"Then I'm even sorrier."

"Don't take this wrong, but hearing you go on about true love and romance, makes me sorry for you. You are setting yourself up for the big fall, Hernando."

"Not if it works out," he said.

I smiled and shook my head. "Isn't it against the rules for homicide detectives to be naïve?"

"You think it's naïve?" he asked.

"I know it is, but it's sweet. I wish you luck finding your Ms. Right."

The door opened and it was Doctor Cunningham. Ramirez asked, "Does she really get out today, Doctor?"

"Yes, she does."

"Why doesn't anyone believe me?" I asked.

They both looked at me. Funny how quickly people caught onto certain aspects of my personality. "I want to do one more check on your back, then you're free to go."

"You got a ride out of here?" Ramirez asked.

"I asked the nurse to call Ted, but I don't know if she did, or if he's home."

"I'll wait around to give you a ride." Before I could say anything, he added, "What are friends for?"

"Thanks, and this means you can fill me in on the case on the way out."

"You never give up, do you?"

"Not about a case," I said.

Ramirez walked out shaking his head, giving the doctor and me some privacy.

Dr. Cunningham poked and prodded, and finally just ran his hands over my back. It was nearly healed. "It's just impressive. I've treated lycanthropes before, Ms. Blake, and you're healing almost that fast."

I flexed my left hand, stretching the skin where the bite mark still showed where the flayed one had bitten me. The bite was pale pink, settling into a nice ordinary scar, only weeks ahead of schedule. I wondered if the scar would eventually disappear, or if it would be another permanent one.

"I've done blood work up on you. I even snuck some of your blood down to the genetics department and had them look for something not human."

"Genetic work takes weeks or months," I said.

"I've got a friend in the department."

"Some friend," I said.

He smiled and it was warmer than it should have been. "She is."

"So I'm free to go?"

"You are." His face got all serious again. "But I'd still like to know what the hell you are."

"You wouldn't believe human?"

"Forty-eight hours after your second injury, we had to remove the stitches from your back because the skin was starting to grow over them. No, I won't believe human."

"It's too long a story, Doc. If it was something I could teach you to use on other people, I'd tell, but it's not that kind of thing. You might call the healing a bonus for some other less pleasant shit that I put up with."

"Unless the other shit is really awful, the healing makes up for it. You'd never have survived the original injuries if you'd been human."

"Maybe."

"No maybe," he said.

"I'm glad to be alive. I'm glad to be nearly healed. I'm glad it didn't take months to recover. What more do you want me to say?"

He draped his stethoscope over his shoulders, holding onto the ends, frowning at me. "Nothing. I'll tell Detective Ramirez that he can tell you about the case now and that you are getting out today." He glanced at the flowers and the balloons. "You've been here, what, five days?"

"Something like that."

He touched a balloon, making them bounce on their strings. "You work fast."

"I don't think it's me that works fast."

He gave the balloons one more whack so they bobbed and weaved like some underwater creature. "Whatever, enjoy your stay in Albuquerque. Try to stay healthy." With that he left, and Ramirez came back in.

"Doctor says I can talk the case with you again."

"Yep."

"You're not going to like it." He looked all serious.

"What's happened?"

"There's been another murder, and not only are you not invited to the scene, neither am I."

50

"WHAT ARE YOU talking about?"

"Marks is in charge of the case. He has the right to use his resources as he sees fit."

"Stop talking political rhetoric and tell me what the little shithead has done now."

He smiled. "Okay. The men assigned to the case are one of those resources. He decided that I was best used at the police property room going over the items that we've confiscated from the victim's homes, and matching them to the pictures and video we have of some of the houses before the murders."

"Pictures and videos for what?" I asked.

"Insurance purposes. A lot of the houses hit had enough rare and antique pieces that they insured them, and that meant they needed proof that they had the pieces to begin with."

"What pieces did you find in the last scene I was at, the one on the Ranch?"

The smile didn't change, but the eyes did. They went from pleasant to shrewd. "It's not just that you're cute. I like the way you think."

"Just tell me."

"There were a lot of similar pieces since most of the people had collected things from this area, or the southwest in general, but nothing out of the ordinary. Except for this." He reached behind his back underneath the suit jacket and pulled a manila envelope out that must have been inside his belt underneath the jacket.

"I knew you had to be wearing the suit jacket for some reason."

He laughed. He unfolded the envelope and spilled out pictures into my lap. Half of them were semiprofessional shots of a small carved piece of turquoise. A glance and I wanted to say Mayan, Aztec, something like that. I still couldn't tell the difference at a glance. The second set were a few better shots of the object in the study of the man that had been killed. The one that had used salt to interrupt the critter. Then a series of Polaroids, taken from every angle.

"You took the Polaroids?" I asked.

He nodded. "This afternoon after he decided my best use was not at the murder site."

I lifted one of the first series of pictures. "These are sitting on a wooden surface, much better light, natural, I think. Insurance pictures?"

He nodded.

"Who did it belong to?"

"The first house you saw."

"The Bromwells'," I said.

He lifted another picture. “This one was from the Carsons’, and that’s it. Either no one else owned one, or they didn’t think to get it insured.”

“Did the people who didn’t try to get it insured, try to insure their other pieces?”

“Yes.”

“Shit,” I said. “I don’t know much about this stuff, but I know that it’s valuable. Why wouldn’t they try to insure it, if they owned one?

“What if they thought it was hot?”

“Illegal? Why would they think that?” I asked.

“Maybe because of the two houses we can prove had it, their history of the piece—where they got it and when—isn’t real.”

“What do you mean?”

“Something like this doesn’t just show up. It has to have a history if you want it insured. They gave their papers, what they’d been given to the insurance company, and just a little investigation showed that the people that were supposed to have unearthed the piece, sold the piece, had never heard of it.”

“They refused to insure it,” I said.

“Yes.” There was something in his face, a suppressed excitement like a kid with a secret.

“You’re holding something back. What is it?”

“You know what Riker is?”

“He’s a pot hunter, an illegal dealer in artifacts.”

“Why would he be so interested in you and this case?”

“I have no idea.” I looked at the pictures in my lap. “You’re saying that he sold these to the victims?”

“Not him personally, but Thad Bromwell, the teenage son, he was with his mother when she purchased it. It was a present for Mr. Bromwell’s birthday. They bought it from a shop that is a known associate of Riker. It takes pieces and makes them look legit.”

“Have you talked to the shop owners?”

“Unless you’ve got a ouija board, we’re not going to be talking to him.”

“He’s the newest victim,” I said.

Ramirez nodded, smiling. “You got it.”

I shook my head. “Okay, Riker is unusually interested in the case. He wanted to see me specifically about it. At least two of the victims are people who bought one of his pieces. The shop owner that sold it is dead now, too.” I looked up at him. “Is it enough for a warrant?”

“We already searched his house. Riker’s men are suspected in the killing of two local cops. It wasn’t hard to find a judge that would give us a warrant on the crap they pulled out at Ted’s house.”

“What the hell did the warrant give you permission to search for? They didn’t mention stolen artifacts at Ted’s house. They just pointed guns at us and said Riker wanted to talk about the case.”

“The warrant was to search for weapons.”

I shook my head. “So even if you found stolen artifacts, you wouldn’t be able to use them in court.”

“It was just an excuse to search the house, Anita. You know how that goes.”

“Did you find anything?”

"A few guns, two without license, but the warrant didn't allow us to knock down walls or destroy things. We couldn't pull up carpet or pull down shelves. Riker has a secret cache of artifacts, but we didn't find it."

"Was Ted with you on the search?"

"Yes, he was." He was frowning now.

"What's wrong?"

"Ted wanted to take a sledge hammer to some of the walls. He seemed pretty certain there was a hidden room in the lower areas, but we couldn't find a way to open it."

"And the warrant didn't allow you to tear up things," I said.

"No."

"What did Riker think of all the fun?"

"He had his lawyer screaming about harassment. Ted got up in his face, not yelling, but in his face, speaking real quiet. The lawyer said he threatened Riker, but Riker wouldn't back it up. He wouldn't say what Ted had said to him."

"You think he threatened him?"

"Oh, yeah."

It wasn't like Edward to threaten anyone, especially in front of the police. The case really was getting to him. "So what the hell are these little figures?"

"No one knows. According to experts, they are Aztec, but very late period like after the conquest."

"Wait a minute, you mean these were carved after the Spanish came and kicked the Aztecs' butts?"

"Not after, but right about the same time."

"Who was your expert?"

He mentioned a name I wasn't familiar with at the university. "Does it matter who it was?"

"I thought you were using Professor Dallas."

"Marks thinks she's spending too much time with the unholy demons."

"If he means Obsidian Butterfly, then I agree. Marks and I agreeing on anything. Jeez, that's almost scary."

"So you think she's a contaminated source, too."

"I think Dallas thinks the sun shines out of Itzpapalotl's butt, so yeah. Have you shown any of these pictures to Dallas?"

He nodded. "The ones from the Bromwells'."

"What did she say?"

"That it was a fake."

I raised eyebrows at him. "What's the other expert think?"

"That he understands why someone would think it was a fake just from pictures. The figure has rubies for eyes, and the Aztecs didn't have access to rubies. So just from pictures, you might assume it was a fake."

"I hear a 'but' coming," I said.

"Doctor Martinez got to hold it in his hand, look at it up close, and he thinks it's authentic, something made after the Spaniards arrived."

"I didn't think anything was made after the Spaniards arrived. Didn't they destroy everything?"

"If these are authentic, then apparently not. Doctor Martinez says that he'll need more tests to be a hundred percent sure."

"Cautious man."

"Most academics are."

I shrugged. Some were. Some weren't. "So let's say for argument's sake that Riker found these things, and he sold them to some people who knew they were hot, or suspected they were, and sold some to shops that passed them off as legit. Now something is killing off the customers and following the trail back to Riker. Is that what he's afraid of?"

"Sounds reasonable," Ramirez said.

I started looking through the Polaroids. They were back and front shots, not great pics, but from every angle. It looked like the figure was wearing armor, sort of. Its hands held long thick strings of things. "What did Martinez say this figure's holding?"

"He wasn't sure."

There were people curled around its feet, but they were thin and sticklike, not fat and square like the figure itself. The eyes were rubies, the mouth open and full of teeth. There was a long tongue coming out of the mouth, and what looked like blood pouring from the mouth. "Nasty looking."

"Yeah." He picked up one of the pictures from the sheet, staring at it as he spoke. "Do you think this thing is out there killing people?"

I looked at him. "An Aztec god, as in the real deal, out there slaughtering people?"

He nodded, still staring at the picture.

"If you mean a real god with a capital G, then I'm a monotheist, so no. If you mean some kind of preternatural nasty associated with this particular god, then why not?"

He looked up then. "Why not?"

I shrugged. "You were expecting a definitive yes or no? I don't know much about Aztec pantheon stuff, except that most of the deities are big and bad and required sacrifice, usually human. They don't have much in their pantheon that isn't a major god. Something big and bad enough that you don't fight it, you just try and stop it with magic or sacrifice, or you die. And whatever this thing is that's been doing the killings, it's not that bad."

I remembered what Nicky Baco had said, that the voice in his head was still trapped, that what had been doing the killings was just a minion, not the real deal.

"You're all serious again. What did you just think of?" Ramirez asked.

I looked up at him and tried to decide how much of a cop he was, and how much of a player he would be. I could never have told Dolph. He'd have used the info for strict cop stuff. "I have information from an informant that I don't want to name right now. But I think you need to know what was said."

His own face was solemn now. "Did you obtain this information legally?"

"I did nothing illegal to obtain this information."

"Not exactly a no," he said.

"Do you want it or not?"

He took a deep breath and blew it out slow. "Yeah, I want it."

I told him what Nicky had said about the voice and the thing being trapped. I finished with, "I don't believe in a real god, but I do believe there are things out there so terrible that once upon a time they were worshipped as gods."

"Are you saying that we haven't seen the worst of it?"

"If what is doing the killings is just a minion, and the master isn't up and around yet, then yeah, I'm saying the worst is yet to come."

"I'd really like to talk to this informant."

"You would be dandy, but Marks would have this informant up on charges so fast, we'd never find out what this person knew. Once you slap an automatic death sentence on someone, they tend not to cooperate."

We looked at each other. "There's only one person you've talked to that has a rep to get himself an automatic death sentence. That's Nicky Baco."

I didn't even blink. It wasn't like I hadn't known he'd figure it out. I was ready for it, and I'd gotten much better at lying. "You have no idea who I've talked to since I arrived. I've talked to at least three people that could be put up on charges with a death sentence attached."

"Three?" He made it a question.

I nodded. "At least."

"Either you are a better liar than I thought you were, or you're telling the truth."

I just looked up at him, giving him blank but earnest face. Even my eyes were quiet and able to meet his gaze, no flinching. There had been a time, not long ago, when I couldn't have pulled it off. But that was then, and I wasn't the same person anymore.

"All right, if there is some sort of Aztec god out there, what do we do about it?"

There was only one answer. "Itzpapalotl should know what this is."

"We questioned her about the killings."

"So did I."

He looked at me long and hard. "You went without police backup, and you didn't share what you found."

"I didn't find anything about the murders. She told me about what she told you, nothing. But when I talked to her, she stressed that no deity she knew of would flay people and keep them alive. Later I figured out that they were dead. She stressed that only through death could the sacrifice be a suitable messenger to the gods. She repeated almost word for word that she didn't know a being or god that would flay people and keep them alive. Maybe we should go back and ask her if she knows of any deity or creature that would flay people and not keep them alive."

"Oh, you're inviting the police now."

"I'm inviting you," I said.

He started picking up the pictures and shoving them back in the envelope. "I took the pictures out of the property room, but I signed for them. I brought Doctor Martinez in to see the statue, but it was official. I haven't done anything wrong, yet."

"Marks is going to be so pissed that you found out important stuff when he meant to just get you out of the way."

Ramirez smiled, but it wasn't exactly a pleased smile. "I've got better than that. Marks will take credit for the brilliant idea of putting one of his senior detectives on special detail to investigate the relics."

"You're kidding me."

"He did send me to the property room to look at what we took from the victims' houses."

"But he did it to humiliate you and get you out of the way."

"But that's not what he said out loud. Out loud it's going to make him seem inspired."

"He's done shit like this before, I take it."

Ramirez nodded. "He's a very good politician, and when he's not on his right-wing high horse, he's a good detective."

"Fine. You mentioned that I wasn't allowed on the murder scene either. What gives there?"

"Well, we all thought you were still out of the game, but he got Ted and company excluded by getting the powers that be to agree that Ted hadn't been a big help on the case, and that without you, his newest expert, Ted wasn't necessary on the murder scene."

"Oh, I bet Ted's going to love that."

Ramirez nodded. "He was very . . . unprofessional, or unlike himself when we searched Riker's place. I've never seen Ted so . . ." Ramirez shook his head. "I don't know, he just seemed different, close to the edge."

Edward had let a little of his real self peek out where the police could see. He had to be under immense pressure to be screwing up like that, or he thought that it was necessary. Either way, things were bad when Ted started losing focus and Edward's real self came through, accident or on purpose.

The door opened, no knock. It was Edward.

"Speak of the devil," I said.

His Edward face had been on, and I watched it move like liquid into Ted, smiling, but still weary around the eyes. "Detective Ramirez, I didn't know you were here."

They shook hands. "I was just filling Anita in on some of the things she's missed."

"You tell her about the search at Riker's?"

Ramirez nodded.

Edward hefted a gym bag. "Clothes."

"You didn't have time to drive from your house to here since the nurse called."

"I packed the bag the night you went in the hospital. I've been riding around with it in my Hummer ever since."

We looked at each other, and there was a weight of things unsaid and unsayable in front of company. Maybe it showed, or maybe Ramirez just felt it. "I'll leave you two alone. You probably have things to talk about. Mystery informants and things like that." He went for the door.

I called after him. "Don't go far, Hernando. When I'm dressed, we'll go see Obsidian Butterfly."

"Only if it's official, Anita. I go in, and we call for uniform backup."

It was our turn for solid eye contact and the weight of wills. I blinked first. "Fine, we go in with the cops like good little boys and girls."

He flashed that warm smile that he could draw from his bag anytime he wanted, or maybe it was real and my cynical nature was showing. "Good, I'll wait outside." He hesitated, then walked back and handed the envelope to Edward. He looked at me one more time then walked out.

Edward opened the envelope and looked inside. "What is this?"

"The link, I think." I explained what Ramirez and I had been discussing, about Riker and why he might be interested in the case on a very personal level.

"That would mean that Obsidian Butterfly lied to us," he said.

"No, she never lied. She said she knew of no deity or creature that would flay people and keep them alive. They aren't alive. They're dead. Technically, it wasn't a lie."

Edward smiled. "That is cutting it very thin."

"She's a nine hundred, nearly a thousand year old vampire. They tend to cut the truth pretty thin."

"I hope you like what I picked out for you to wear."

The way he said it made me start pulling things out of the gym bag. Black jeans, black scoop-neck T-shirt, black jogging socks, black Nikes, a black leather belt, my black suit jacket, the worse for being folded for two days, black bra, black satin panties—Jean-Claude had been a bad influence on my clothing—and under it all was the Browning, the Firestar, all the knives, an extra clip for the Browning, two boxes of ammo, and a new shoulder rig. It was one of the lightweight nylon ones with the holster itself angled for the front carry, downward draw that I favored. I always needed one with a very sharp downward angle to avoid scrapping my breast every time I drew the gun. I'd found that the millisecond I lost from the angle was made up for from the second I lost everytime I went past my breast and had the flinch reaction. Concealed carry is the art of compromise.

"I know you like leather, but most of those would have to be tailored down for you. The straps on the nylon ones can be adjusted down smaller," Edward said.

"Thanks, Edward. I was missing my rig." I looked at him, trying to read past the neutral baby blues. "Why this much ammo?"

"Better to not need and have it," he said.

I frowned at him. "Are we going some place where I'll need this much ammo?"

"If I thought that, I'd have packed the mini-Uzi and the sawed-off shotgun. This is just the normal stuff you carry."

I drew the big blade that would have normally rode down my back. "When they cut off the shoulder holster, they cut through the rig for this, too."

"Was it a specialty item?"

I nodded.

"I thought it must be because I asked around and no one had a sheath for concealment of something that large for the back, especially not when you throw in how damn narrow you are through the shoulders."

"It was a custom job." I laid the big knife back in the bag, almost sadly. "There's no way to conceal this thing without a rig for it."

"Did the best I could."

I smiled at him. "No, it's great. I mean it."

"Why are we taking the police in with us to Obsidian Butterfly?"

I told him what Jean-Claude had told me, though not how the message had gotten through. "With the police at our backs, she'll know it's not vampire politics and we'll probably be able to walk out without a fight."

He was leaning against the wall arms crossed. The white shirt didn't quite lay smooth over the front of him. His gun was showing but only if you knew what you were looking for. A paddle holster or a clip holster because the gun was riding outside the pants. It explained why the white shirt wasn't tucked in, and the fact that he was wearing a T-shirt under the shirt probably meant that he had something on him that would chafe without cloth between it and his skin.

"You still carrying that band of throwing darts?" I asked.

"You can't see it, not with the shirt untucked." He didn't even try to deny it. Why should he?

"Because you're wearing an undershirt, and because the shirt is untucked. I know, it's partially to hide the gun, but you never wear an undershirt, so you've got to be wearing something under the shirt that would chafe without the undershirt."

He smiled, and it was a pleased smile, almost proud, as if I'd done something smart. "I'm carrying two more guns, a knife, and a garrote. Tell me where they are and I'll give you a prize."

My eyes had gone wide. "A garrote. Even for you that's a little Psychos 'R Us."

"Give up?"

"No. Is there a time limit?"

He shook his head. "We've got all night."

"If I guess wrong, is there a penalty?"

He shook his head.

"What's the prize if I figure out where everything is?"

He smiled that close, secretive smile that said he knew things that I didn't. "It's a surprise prize."

"Get out so I can get dressed."

He touched the belt where it lay on the bed. "This buckle didn't come black. Who painted it?"

"I did."

"Why?"

He knew the answer. "So that if I'm out after dark, the buckle doesn't catch the light and give me away." I lifted the tail of his white shirt exposing the large ornate silver belt buckle. "This is like a freaking target after dark."

He looked down at me, making no move to lower the shirt. "It just clips on over the real buckle."

I let the shirt slide back. "The buckle underneath?"

"It's blacked," he said.

We smiled at each other. It went all the way to our eyes. We did like each other. We were friends. "Sometimes I think I don't want to be you when I grow up, Edward, sometimes I think it's too late, I'm already there."

The smile faded, leaving his eyes the color of winter skies and just as pitiless.

"Only you decide how far gone you are, Anita. Only you can decide how far you'll go."

I looked at the weapons and the black clothing like funeral clothes, even down to the things that touched my skin. "Maybe it would be a start if I bought something pink."

"Pink?" Edward said.

"Yeah, you know, pink, like Easter Bunny grass."

"Like cotton candy," he said. "Or almost everything women give each other at baby showers."

"When were you at a baby shower?" I asked.

"Donna's taken me to two of them. It's the new thing, couples baby showers."

I looked at him, eyes wide. "You, at a couples baby shower, Edward."

"You in something the color of children's candy and baby doll clothes." He shook his head. "Anita, you are one of the least pink women I've ever met."

"When I was a little girl, I'd have given a small body part to have a pink canopy bed, and ballerina wallpaper would have been perfect."

He gave me wide, surprised eyes. "You, in a pink canopy bed with ballerina wallpaper." He shook his head. "Just trying to imagine you in a room like that gives me a headache."

I looked at the things spread on the bed. "I was pink once, Edward."

"Most of us start off soft," he said, "but you can't stay that way, not and survive."

"There's got to be someplace I won't go, something I won't do, some line I won't cross, Edward."

"Why?" That one word held more curiosity than he usually allowed himself.

"Because if I don't have any lines, limits, then what kind of person does that make me?" I asked.

He shook his head, moving the cowboy hat low on his head. "You're having a crisis of conscience."

I nodded. "Yeah, I guess I am."

"Don't go soft, Anita, not on my dime. I need you to do what you do best, and what you do best isn't soft or gentle or kind. What you do best is what I do best."

"And what is that? What is it that we do best?" I asked, and I knew the anger came through in my voice. I was getting angry with Edward.

"We do what it takes, whatever it takes, to get the job done."

"There's got to be more to life than the ultimate practicality, Edward."

"If it makes you feel any better, we have different motives. I do what I do because I love it. It's not just what I do. It's who I am. You do the job to save lives, to keep the damage down." He looked at me with eyes gone as empty and bottomless as any vampire's. "But you love it, too, Anita. You love it, and that bothers you."

"Violence is one of my top three responses now, Edward, maybe my number one."

"And it's kept you alive."

"At what price?'

He shook his head, and now the blankness was replaced by anger. He was just suddenly moving forward. I caught his hand going under the shirt, and I was rolling off the bed, with the Browning in my hand. I had a round in the chamber and was falling back onto the floor with the gun pointed up, eyes searching for movement.

He was gone.

My heart was thudding so loudly that I could barely hear, and I was straining to hear. A movement, something. He had to be on the bed. It was the only place he could have gone. From my angle I couldn't see anything on top of the bed, just the corner of the mattress and the trail of sheet.

Knowing Edward, the ammo in the Browning was probably his homemade brew, which meant that it would pierce the bottom of the bed and go up into whatever lay on top of the bed. I felt the last of the air in my body slide outward, and I sighted on the underneath of the bed. The first bullet would either hit him or make him move, then I'd have a better idea of where he was.

"Don't shoot, Anita."

His voice made me move the gun barrel just a touch more right. It would take him mid-body because he was crouched up there, not lying down. I knew that without seeing it.

"It was a test, Anita. If I wanted to come against you, I'd warn you first, you know that."

I did know that, but . . . I heard the bed creak. "Don't move, Edward. I mean it."

"You think you can just decide to turn all this off. You can't. The genie is out of the bottle for you, Anita, just like it is for me. You can't unmake yourself. Think of all the effort, all the pain, that went into making you who you are. Do you really want to throw all that away?"

I was lying flat on my back, gun pointed two-handed. The floor was cold where the gown had gaped at my back. "No," I said, finally.

"If your heart starts bleeding for all the bad things you do, it won't be the last thing that bleeds."

"You really did this to test me. You son of a bitch."

"Can I move now?"

I took my finger off the trigger and sat up on the floor. "Yeah, you can move."

He eased back off the other side of the bed as I stood up on this one. "Did you see how fast you went for the gun? You knew where it was, you had the safety off and a round chambered, and you were looking for cover, and trying to target me." Again there was that pride, like a teacher with a favorite student.

I looked across at him. "Don't ever do anything like that again, Edward."

"A threat?" he asked.

I shook my head. "No threat, just instinct. I came so close to putting a bullet through the bed and into you."

"And while you were doing it, your conscience wasn't bothering you. You weren't thinking, 'It's Edward. I'm about to shoot my friend.' "

"No," I said. "I wasn't thinking anything but how to get the best shot possible before you had time to shoot me." It didn't make me happy to say it. It felt like I'd been mourning dead pieces of myself, and Edward's little demonstration had confirmed the deaths. It made me sad, and a little depressed, and not happy with Edward.

"I knew a man once who was as good as you are," Edward said. "He started second-guessing himself, worrying about whether he was a bad person. It got him killed. I don't want to see you dead because you hesitated. If I have to bury you, then I want it to be because someone was just that good or that lucky."

"I want to be cremated," I said, "not buried."

"Good little Christian, fallen Catholic, practicing Episcopalian, and you want to be cremated."

"I don't want anyone trying to raise me from the dead or stealing body parts for spells. Just burn it all, thanks."

"Cremated. I'll remember."

"How about you, Edward? Where do you want the body shipped?"

"It doesn't matter," he said. "I'll be dead, and I won't care."

"No family?"

"Just Donna and the kids."

"They are not your family, Edward."

"Maybe they will be."

I put the safety on the Browning. "We don't have time to discuss your love life and my moral crisis. Get out so I can get dressed."

He had his hand on the door when he turned. "Speaking of love life, Richard Zeeman called."

That got my attention. "What do you mean Richard called?"

"He seemed to know that something bad had happened to you. He was worried."

"When did he call?"

"Earlier tonight."

"Did he say anything else?"

"That he'd finally called Ronnie and had her track down Ted Forrester's unlisted number. He seemed to think that you leaving a forwarding number with him would be a good idea." His face was utterly blank, empty. Only his eyes held a faint hint of amusement.

So both the boys had finally grown frustrated at my silence. Richard had turned to my good friend, Ronnie, who happened to be a private investigator. Jean-Claude had taken a more direct route. But they'd both finally gotten hold of me on the same night. Would they compare notes?

"What did you tell Richard?" I laid the gun on the bed with the rest.

"That you were all right." Edward was looking around the room. "Doctor Cunningham still not allowing you a phone in here?"

"Nope," I said. I had managed to untie the back of the gown.

"Then how did Jean-Claude contact you?"

I stopped in mid-motion. The gown slid off one shoulder and I had to catch it with my hand. It caught me off guard and I'm never as good a liar on the spur of the moment. "I never said it was a phone call."

"Then what was it?"

I shook my head. "Just go, Edward. The night's not getting any younger."

He just stood there, looking at me. His face had gone all cold and suspicious.

I got the bra in one hand and turned my back on him. I let the gown slide to my waist, leaned back against the bed to hold it in place, and slipped the bra on. There was no sound from behind me. I got the panties and slipped them on underneath the gown. I had the jeans halfway up my legs under the cover of the gown when I heard the door hush open and close.

I turned and found the doorway empty. I finished dressing. I had my toiletries in the bathroom already, so I threw them in the gym bag along with the big knife, and the boxes of ammo. The new shoulder holster felt odd. I was used to a leather one which fit tight and secure. I guess nylon was secure, but it was almost too comfortable, as if it seemed less substantial than my leather one had. But it beat the heck out of sticking it down my jeans.

The knives went in the wrist sheaths. I checked to see what kind of ammo the Firestar had in it. Edward's homemade stuff. I checked the Browning, and it was his stuff, too. The backup clip for the Browning was the Homady XTP Silver-Edge. I changed the clip. We were going into the Obsidian Butterfly as cops, which meant if I had to shoot someone, I'd have to explain it to the authorities later. Which meant I didn't want to go in there with some possibly illegal homemade shit in my gun. Besides I'd seen what the Homady Silver-Edge could do to a vampire. It was enough.

The Firestar went into an Uncle Mike's inner pants holster, though truthfully the jeans were too tight for an inner pants holster. Maybe I wasn't spending enough time in the gym. I had been on the road more than I'd been home. The Kenpo was neat stuff, but it wasn't the same thing as a full workout with weights and running. Another thing to pay more attention to when I got back to St. Louis. I'd been letting a lot of things slide.

I finally transferred the Firestar to the small of my back and hated it, but it dug in something fierce in front. I have a slight sway to my back so there's always more room for a gun there, but it wasn't a quick place to draw from. Something about a woman's hip structure makes a gun at the small of the back not the best idea. That I kept the gun at the small of my back tells you just how tight the jeans were. Definitely going to have to get back into a regular gym schedule. The first five pounds are easy to get rid of, the second five are harder, and it gets even harder from there. I'd been chunky in junior high, close to fat, so I knew what I was talking about. So that no teenager out there will get the wrong idea and go all anorexic on me, I was a size thirteen in jeans, and that was at five foot nothing. See, I really was chunky. I hate women who complain about being fat when they're like a size five. Anything under size five isn't a woman. It's a boy with breasts.

I stared at the black jacket. Two days folded in a gym bag and it desperately needed to go to the dry cleaners. I decided to carry it folded over one arm, on the theory it would unwrinkle a little. I didn't really need to hide the weapons until we got to the club. The knives were illegal if I'd been a cop or a civvie, but I was a vampire executioner, and we got to carry knives. Gerald Mallory, the grandfather of our business, had testified before a senate subcommittee, or something like that, at how many times knives had saved his life. Mallory was well liked in Washington. It was his home base. So the law got changed to let us carry knives, even really big ones. If someone challenged me, all I had to do was whip out my executioner's license, and I was legal. Of course, that predicated on them knowing the loophole in the law. Not every cop on the beat is going to know. But my heart is pure because I'm legal.

Edward and Ramirez were waiting for me in the hallway. They both smiled and the smiles were so close to identical it was unnerving. Will the real good guys please stand up? But Edward's smile never faltered as I walked towards them. Ramirez's did. His gaze hesitated on the wrist sheath. The jacket hid the other one. I walked up to them smiling, and my eyes were shiny, too. I put a hand around Edward's waist and brushed my arm along the gun I'd thought was there at the small of his back.

"I've called for backup," Ramirez said.

Edward had given me a quick Ted hug and let me go, though he knew I'd found the gun. "Great. It's been a long time since I visited a Master of the City with the police."

"How do you usually do it?" Ramirez asked.

"Carefully," I said.

Edward turned his head away and coughed. I think he was trying not to laugh, but you can never tell with Edward. Maybe he just had a tickle in his throat. I watched him walk and wondered where in the world he was hiding the third gun.

51

ONE OF THE THINGS I liked about working with the police was that when you went into a business and asked to speak with the manager or owner, no one argued. Ramirez flashed his badge and asked to speak with the owner, Itzpapalotl, also known as Obsidian Butterfly.

The hostess, the same darkly elegant woman that had shown Edward and me to a table last time, took Ramirez's business card, showed us all to a table, and left us. The only difference was this time we didn't get any menus. The two uniforms stayed at the door, but kept us in sight. I'd put the wrinkled jacket on to cover the guns and knives, but I was glad the club was dark, because the jacket had seen better days.

Ramirez leaned over and asked, "How long do you think she'll keep us waiting?"

Funny how he didn't ask if she would keep us waiting. "Not sure, but a while. She's a goddess and you've just ordered her to appear before you. Her ego won't let her be quick."

Edward was leaning in on the other side. "Half hour, at least."

A waitress came. Ramirez and I ordered Cokes. Edward got water. The lights on the stage dimmed, then came up brighter. We settled back for the show. César had probably healed by now, but not by much. So it would either be a different wereanimal or a different show altogether.

There was what looked like a stone coffin propped up on the stage, sitting on its end with the carved lid staring out at the audience. Our table wasn't as good as last time. I spotted Professor Dallas at her usual table, alone this time. She didn't seem to mind.

The stone lid was carved in a crouching jaguar with a necklace of human skulls. The high priest Pinotl came onto the stage. He was dressed only in that skirt thing, a maxtlatl, that left the legs and most of the hips bare. I'd asked Dallas what the skirt was. His face was painted black with a stripe of white across the eyes and nose. His long black hair had been formed into individual strands curling at the ends. He wore a white crown, and it took me a second to realize it was made of bones. The stage lights flickered over the white bones, making them shimmer, and almost bleed white color when he moved his head. Finger bones had been restrung and formed a fan above the main band, reminiscent of the feathers I'd seen him wearing the first time. His ear spools of gold had been replaced by bones. He looked totally different from the first time, and yet the moment he stepped out on stage I knew it was him. No one else had had that aura of command.

I leaned into Ramirez. "You wearing a cross?"

"Yes, why?"

"His voice can be a little overwhelming without a little help."

"He's human, isn't he?"

"He's her human servant."

Ramirez turned his face full into mine, and we were too close. I had to move back to keep from bumping noses. "What?"

Did he really not know what a human servant was for a vampire? I didn't have time to give him a preternatural lesson, and this wasn't the place anyway. Far too many listening ears. I shook my head. "I'll explain later."

Two very Aztec-looking bouncers came on stage and lifted the lid of the coffin off. They moved to one side with it, and the way they shuffled, muscles in their arms and back working, it looked heavy. There was a cloth-draped body in the coffin. I didn't know for certain that it was a body, but it was shaped like a body. There just aren't that many things that are body-shaped.

Pinotl began to speak. "Those of you who have been with us before, know what it is to make sacrifice to the gods. You have shared in that glory, taken the offering into yourselves. But only the bravest, the most virtuous, are fit sacrifices. There are those that are not fit to feed the gods with their lives, but they, too, may serve." He drew the cloth off in one large movement, sending the black and sequined draped cloth spreading wide like a fisherman's net. As that glittering cloth fell to the stage, the contents of the coffin were revealed. Gasps, screams spread through the audience like ripples in a pool.

There was a body in the coffin. It was dried and wizened, as if the body had been buried in the desert and had mummified naturally. No artificial preservatives. The spotlight on the coffin seemed very bright, harsh. It showed every line in the dried skin. The skeletal shadow of bones underneath was painfully clear.

We were only three rows back, close enough to see more detail than I cared to see. At least this time they wouldn't be cutting anyone up. I really wasn't in the mood to see inside anyone's chest tonight. I was searching the crowd, trying to see if she was coming or if we were about to be surrounded by werejaguars.

I turned and looked. The dead mummy's eyes were open. I looked at Edward. He answered the question without me having to say it. "Its eyes just opened. Nobody touched it."

I stared at that skull trapped under dry parchment skin. The eyes were full of something dry and brown. There was no life to the eyes, but they were open. The mouth began to open slowly, as if the mouth were on a stiff hinge. As the mouth opened a sound came out of it, a sigh that grew into a scream. A scream that echoed through the room, reverberated off the ceiling, the walls, the inside of my head.

"It's a trick, right?" Ramirez said.

I just shook my head. It wasn't a trick. Dear God, it wasn't a trick. I looked at Edward, and he just shook his head. He'd never seen this particular act either.

The scream died, and there was a silence so thick you could have dropped a pin and heard it bounce. I think everyone was holding their breath, straining to hear. To hear what I didn't know, but I was doing it, too. I think I was trying to hear it breathe. I studied that skeletal chest, but it didn't rise and fall. It didn't move. I said a silent prayer of thanks.

"This one's energy went to feed our dark goddess, but she is merciful. What was taken shall be given back. This is Micapetlacalli, the box of death. I am Nextepeua. In legend I was the husband of Micapetlacalli, and I am still married to death. Death runs through my veins. My blood tastes of death. Only the blood of one consecrated to death will free this one of torment."

I realized that Pinotl's voice was just a voice, a good voice, like a good stage actor, but nothing more. Either he wasn't trying to bespell the audience, or I wasn't as susceptible tonight. The only change that I knew for certain was the marks. They were wide open now. I'd been told by my teacher and by Leonora Evans that the marks made me more vulnerable to psychic attack, but maybe on some things having a direct link to the boys helped me. Whatever it was, his voice didn't move me tonight. Great.

Pinotl drew an obsidian blade from behind his back. He'd probably been carrying it the way Edward and I were carrying guns, at the small of his back. He held his arm over the open coffin, over that gaping mouth. He drew the blade across his skin. It wasn't clear to the audience what he'd done. It would have been much better theater for Pinotl to slash his arm where the audience could see that first crimson slash. For him to hide it, there had to be some ritual significance, some importance, to those first drops of blood going into the corpse's mouth.

He dripped blood on the top of the thing's skull, dabbed it in the middle of that skull forehead, touched it to the throat, the chest, the stomach, the abdomen. He went down the line of chakras, energy points, of the body. I'd never believed in chakras until this year, when I'd found they were real, and they seemed to work. I hated all this new age stuff. I hated it worse when it worked. Of course, this wasn't new age stuff. This was very old stuff. With each touch of blood to that dried thing I felt magic. Each drop of blood made it grow, until the air hummed with it and my skin crept in waves of goosebumps.

Edward sat unmoved, but Ramirez was rubbing his arms, chasing goosebumps. "What's happening?"

He was at the very least a sensitive. I guess I couldn't possibly be attracted to a totally normal human being. I whispered, "Magic."

He looked at me, eyes showing too much white. "What kind?"

I shook my head. That I didn't know. I had a few clues, but I really had never seen anything like it, not exactly.

Pinotl walked around the coffin in a counter-clockwise motion, bleeding arm and bloody knife held apart, palm up while he chanted. The power built and built in the air like close thunder until my throat closed with it, and I was having trouble breathing. Pinotl came back to the front of the coffin where he'd begun. He made some kind of sign with his hands, then flung a spray of blood onto the body, and began to back slowly away. The lights dimmed until the only light was the harsh white light on the thing in the coffin.

The power had built to a screaming pitch. My skin was trying to crawl off my body and hide. The air was too thick to breathe, as if it had grown more solid, thick with magic.

Something was happening to the body. The power broke like a cloud bursting with rain, and that invisible rain broke over the body, over the room, over us all, but the focus was that dried thing. The skin began to move, to twitch. It filled out as if water flowed beneath it. Something liquid moved under that dry, wasted skin, and where it flowed the skin began to stretch. It was like watching one of those blow up dolls fill up. Flesh, flesh was flowing under the skin. It plumped like some obscene kind of dough. The body, the man, began to thrash and twist against the sides of the coffin. The chest finally rose, drawing in a great draught of air, as if he were struggling back from the dead. It was like the opposite of that death rattle where the breath flows away for the last time. Of course, that was exactly what it was: life returning, the last breath being drawn back in. When he had air to breathe, he began to scream. One long ragged shriek after another. As fast as his healing chest could bring in the air, he screamed.

The dry hair on his head turned curly, brown, and soft. His skin was tanned and young, smooth and flawless. He'd been under thirty when he went into the coffin. Who knew how long he'd been in there? Even after he looked human again, he kept shrieking, as if he had been waiting a very long time to scream.

A woman near the front screamed and took off running for the door. The vampires had moved up quietly through the tables. I hadn't sensed them over the suffocating flow of magic, and the sheer horror of the show. Careless of me. A vampire caught the running woman, held her, and she grew instantly still. He led her quietly back to her table, to the man that was standing, wondering what he should do. The vampires moved through the crowd touching someone here, stroking a hand there, soothing, soothing, telling the great lie. It was safe, it was peaceful, it was good.

Ramirez watched the vampires. He turned to me. "What are they doing?"

"Soothing the crowd so they don't all bolt for the exits."

"They aren't allowed to use one on one hypnosis."

"I don't think it's personal, more like crowd hypnosis." I looked back to the stage and found the man had collapsed onto the stage, pushing his way out of the coffin as soon as he got the strength. He was trying to crawl away.

Pinotl appeared in the growing circle of light. The man screamed and held his hands up in front of his face as if to ward off a blow. Pinotl spoke, and he didn't yell, so he must have been using a microphone of some kind. "Have you learned humility?" he asked.

The man whimpered and hid his face.

"Have you learned obedience?"

The man nodded his head over and over, still hiding his face. He started to cry, great sobs that made his shoulders shake. Three rows out and I could hear him sobbing.

Pinotl motioned and the two bouncers that had opened the coffin walked on stage. They lifted the weeping man up, carrying him between them. His legs didn't seem to move yet, so they carried him, with an arm on either of their shoulders, his feet dangling off the floor. He wasn't a small man, and again you got that sense of how strong the two men were. They were human, too, not wereanything.

Two werejaguars walked on stage in their spotted skin clothes, and between them they held another man. No, not a man, a wereanimal. It was Seth. He'd been stripped down to a G-string that left very little to the imagination. His long yellow hair was unbound, streaked with light and color. He didn't struggle as they brought him up on stage. The jaguar men had him kneel in front of Pinotl.

"Do you acknowledge our dark goddess as your one and true mistress?"

Seth nodded. "I do." His voice didn't have the resonance of the other man's, and I doubted that the people in the back could hear him.

"She has given you life, Seth, and it is right that she should ask you give that life back to her."

"Yes," Seth said.

"Then I will be her hand, and take that which is hers." He cradled Seth's face between his hands. It was gentle. The two jaguar men let go of Seth and backed away. But they stayed close, almost as if afraid that he might run. But his face was turned upward with a near beatific expression on it, as if this were wonderful. He'd been so afraid of being tortured by Itzpapalotl's four sisters weird, and yet now he seemed at peace with what they were about to do. I thought I knew, and I hoped I was wrong. Just once when I expect something truly hideous is about to happen, I'd like to be wrong. It would be a nice change.

It wasn't flashy. There was no fire or light or even a shimmer of heat. Lines appeared on Seth's twenty-something skin. The muscles under his skin began to shrink as though he had a wasting disease, but what should have taken months was happening in seconds. No matter how willing the sacrifice, it can still hurt. Seth started screaming as fast as he could draw breath. His lungs were working better than the other man's, and he drew breath so fast, it was like one continuous shriek. The skin darkened as it drew in and in like something were sucking him dry. It was like watching a balloon shrivel. Except there was muscle and when the muscle vanished, there was bone, and finally there was nothing but dried skin over bones, and still he screamed.

I've become something of a connoisseur of screams over the years, and I've heard some good ones. Some of them have even been mine, but I'd never heard anything like this. The sound stopped being human and became like the high-pitched sound of some wounded animal, but underneath it all you knew, knew at a level that you couldn't even explain, that it was a person.

Finally, there was no more air for screaming, but that dry, empty mouth kept opening and closing, opening and closing. Long after the screaming stopped, that skeletal thing was still writhing, still flinging its head from side to side.

Pinotl kept his hands pressed to Seth's face. He held him, and it looked gentle the whole time, but he had to be gripping with all the strength he had because he never lost his grip. While the flesh of that handsome face shriveled and died between his hands, Pinotl never moved. And through it all, Seth never once raised his hands up to save himself. He struggled because he couldn't not struggle, it hurt that much, but he never raised his hands against the other man. A willing sacrifice, a fit sacrifice.

My throat was tight, and something burned behind my eyes. I just wanted it over now. I just wanted it to stop. But it didn't stop. The skeletal thing that had been Seth kept twitching, opening and closing its mouth, as if trying to talk.

Pinotl looked up, breaking eye contact with Seth for a heartbeat. The two jaguar men that had escorted him onto the stage came into the light. One of them held a silver needle with black thread on it. The other held a pale green ball, tiny, the size of a marble maybe. If I'd been sitting much further out, I'd have never known what it was. Jade, I think, a jade ball. They placed it in that gaping mouth, and the mouth closed. The other jaguar began to sew his mouth shut, driving the silver needle through the dry lipless flesh, tugging it tight.

I looked at the table too, resting my forehead on the cool stone of the table. I would not faint. I never fainted. But I had a sudden flash of the creature that Nicky Baco had created out of the werewolves. Some of them had had their mouths sewn shut. I'd never seen a power like this. It was too big a coincidence that two people in one town could do it and not be connected.

Ramirez touched my shoulder. I raised my head and shook it. "I'm all right." I looked up and they were putting Seth in the coffin. I knew without trying to sense it that he was still in there. Still aware. He could not have understood what he was letting them do to him. He couldn't have. Could he?

Pinotl turned to the audience, and his eyes glowed with black fire the way a vampire's do when their power is high. Black flames licked around his eye sockets, and his skin seemed to glow with the power.

The thing that Seth had become was covered with the same black glittering cloth that had covered the last body. The jaguar assistants closed the coffin, securing the heavy lid. A collective sigh ran through the audience as if they were all relieved that it was covered. I wasn't the only one that didn't want to see it anymore.

Itzpapalotl glided on stage. She was wearing the same crimson cloak as before. Pinotl went to one knee in front of her, extending his hands. She put her delicate hands on his strong ones, and I felt the rush of power like the brush of bird's wings.

Pinotl stood, holding her hand, and they turned to the audience and now both of them had eyes of black flame, spreading over their faces like a mask.

Soft spotlights filled the darkness of the tables like giant, soft fireflies. Each light found one of the vampires. They were pale and wan, hungry, fasted maybe, because I wasn't the only one that could tell they hadn't fed. You heard the exclamations through the audience, how pale, how frightening, oh, my god. No, she wanted everyone to see them for what they truly were.

She and Pinotl stared off into that soft-lit dark and again I felt the rush of power, like a chittering flight of birds, brushing across my face, my skin, as if I had no clothes, and the swift passing of feathered things caressed my body. I felt it almost like a series of physical blows as the power hit each vampire, and their eyes filled with black fire. They became shining things with skin of alabaster, bronze, copper, all glowing, all beautiful with eyes filled with the light of black stars.

Then they fell into line and began to sing. A song of praise to her, their dark goddess. Diego, the vampire we'd seen whipped senseless, passed by our table with a leash in his hand. On the end of that leash was a tall, pale-skinned man with curly yellow hair. Was it Cristobal, one of the starved ones? There were no starved ones in line. All of them were glowing and well fed and filled to bursting with a dark, sweet power like overripe berries before they fall to the ground, when they are poised between the sweetest of ripeness and rotting. Life is often like that, the best balancing on a knife edge with the worst.

The vampires left the stage still singing her praises. Pinotl and she walked hand and hand down the steps, and I knew where they were coming, and I didn't want them near me. I could still feel the power as though I were standing in the middle of a cloud of butterflies, and they were beating at my skin with soft wings, beating at me, trying to come inside.

They came and stood in front of our table. Her face was smiling, soft as she gazed down at me. The black flames had quieted, but her eyes were still an empty blackness with a flicker of light in their depths. Pinotl's eyes echoed hers like a mirror, but it wasn't black flame. It was the blackness of endless night, and there were stars in her eyes, an endless fall of stars.

Edward had my arm. He had turned me to face him. We were both standing, though I didn't remember getting up. "Anita, are you okay?"

I had to swallow twice to find my voice. "I'm okay, I think. Yeah, I'm okay." But the power was still beating against me like frantic wings, birds crying that they've been shut out in the dark and they want inside to the light and the warmth. How could I leave them crying in the dark when all I had to do was open and they would be safe?

"Stop it," I said. I turned to face them. They were still smiling, still welcoming. She held her hand out to me, the other still holding Pinotl's hand. I knew if I took that hand that all this power would flow into me. That I could share it with them. It was an offering to share. But at what price, because there was always a price?

"What do you want?" I asked. I wasn't even sure who I was asking.

"I want the knowledge of how your triad of power was achieved."

"I can tell you that. You don't need to do this."

"You know that I cannot tell truth from lie. It is not one of my powers. Touch me and I will gain the knowledge from you."

The wings were flowing over my skin as if the flying things had found a current of air just above my body. "What do I gain?"

"Think of one question, and if I have the answer, you will draw it from my mind."

Ramirez was standing. He motioned and I knew without looking that the uniforms were coming this way. "I don't know what's happening, but we're not doing it."

"Answer one question first," I said.

"If I can," she said.

"Who is the Red Woman's Husband?"

Her face showed nothing, but her voice was puzzled. "The Red Woman was another term for blood among the Mexicanas, among the Aztecs. I truly do not know who the Red Woman's Husband would be."

I'd half reached out to her. I didn't really mean to. Three things happened almost together. Ramirez and Edward both grabbed me to pull me back, and Itzpapalotl grabbed my hand.

The wings erupted into a torrent of birds. My body opened, though I knew it didn't, and the winged things, only half-glimpsed spilled into that opening. The power flowed into me, through me, and out again. I was part of some great circuit, and I felt the connection with every vampire she'd touched. It was as if I flowed through them, and they through me like water coming together to form something larger. Then I was floating in the soothing dark, and there were stars, distant and glittering.

A voice, her voice came, "Ask one question, and it shall be yours."

I asked, though my mouth never moved, still I heard the words. "How did Nicky Baco learn to do what Pinotl did to Seth?" With the words came the image of Nicky's creature so clear I could smell the dryness of it, and hear that voice whispering, "Help me."

Images then, and they had force to them like things slamming into my body. I saw Itzpapalotl standing on the top of a pyramid temple surrounded by trees, jungle. I could smell the rich greenness of it, and hear the night call of a monkey, the scream of a jaguar. Pinotl knelt and fed from the bloody wound on her chest. He became her servant, and he gained power. Many powers, and one of them was this. And I understood how he'd taken Seth's essence. More than that I understood how it was done, and how it was undone. I knew how to unmake Nicky' s creature, though what he'd done to them might mean that to bring them back to flesh would kill them. We didn't need Nicky to undo the spell; I could do it. Pinotl could do it.

She didn't ask if I understood. She knew when I had it all. "Now for my question." And before I could say or think "Wait," she was inside my head. She drew the memories from me: images, pieces, and I couldn't stop her. She saw Jean-Claude mark me, and she saw Richard, and she saw the three of us calling power on purpose for the first time. She saw that last night when I'd taken the second and third mark to save our lives, all our lives.

I was suddenly back in my own skin, standing on one side of the table, still holding her hand. I was gasping, fast and faster, and I knew if I didn't get control, I was going to hyperventilate. She released my hand, and all I could do was concentrate on my own breathing. Ramirez was yelling at me, was I all right. Edward had his gun out, pointed at her. She and Pinotl just stood there, peaceful. I could see everything as though I were looking through crystal. The colors seemed darker, more vivid. Things stood out in bold relief, and it wasn't the things I would normally have noticed. The way the band in Edward's hat had a small ridge in it, and I knew where the garrote was.

When I could finally talk, I said, "It's all right. It's all right. I'm not hurt." I touched Edward's hand, lowering the gun to point at the table. "Chill, okay, I'm all right."

"She said it would harm you if we forced you to let go early," Edward said.

"It might have," I said. I'd expected to feel badly, drained, tired, but I didn't. I felt energized, exhilarated. "I feel great."

"You don't look great," Edward said, and there was something in his voice that made me look at him.

He grabbed my hand and started leading me through the tables towards the door. I tried to slow down and he jerked me with him, pulling me along.

"You're hurting my wrist," I said.

He pushed through the doors with the gun still naked in his hand, my wrist gripped in his other hand. He hit the lobby doors with his shoulders. I remembered it being darker in the lobby, but it wasn't dark now. It wasn't exactly light. It just wasn't dark. He pushed one of the wall hangings apart, and there was the men's room door. He pushed it open before I could say anything. The urinals stretched empty, and I was grateful. The lights were bright, made me squint.

Edward whirled me around to face the mirrors. My eyes were a solid shining black. There was no pupil, no white, nothing. I looked blind, yet I could see everything, every crack in the wall, the smallest dint on the edge of the mirror. I walked forward, and he let me go. I reached out until I could touch my reflection. I jumped when my fingers met the cool glass, as if I'd expected my hand to keep on going. I stared at my hand, and I could almost see the bones under my skin, the muscles working as I moved my fingers. Underneath that, I could see the flow of blood under my skin. I turned and looked at Edward. I looked at him slowly, and I could see the slight difference in the pants leg where the hilt of the knife was sticking out of his boot. There was the faintest line where the second knife was strapped to his thigh, and he could reach through his pants pocket and touch the hilt. There was a bulge in his other pocket, small, but I knew it was a gun, a derringer probably, but that last bit of knowledge was my knowledge. The rest was this extraordinary vision. It was like some fantasy spell of true seeing.

If this was how all vampires saw the world, then I should just stop trying to hide weapons. But I'd fooled vampires before, master-level vampires. So this was how she saw the world, but not necessarily how they all saw the world.

"Say something, Anita."

"I wish you could see what I'm seeing."

"I don't want to," he said.

"The garrote is in the band of your hat. You've got a knife in a sheath in your right boot, and a knife on your left thigh. You reach the hilt through your pants pocket. There's a derringer in your right pants pocket."

He paled, and I saw it. I saw the pulse in his throat beat faster. I could see the small changes in his body as the fear rushed through it. No wonder she'd been able to read me so easily. But it should have worked like a lie detector for her. That's what other vamps and wereanimals pick up on, the minute changes we all make when we lie. Even the smell changes, so Richard said. So why couldn't she tell if someone were lying?

The answer came in a wave of clarity that you usually have to meditate to have. She couldn't read things she didn't have inside herself. She wasn't a goddess. She was a vampire, not like any vampire I'd ever known before, but that was what she was. Yet she believed she was Itzpapalotl the living personification of the sacrificial knife, the obsidian blade. She was lying to herself, and thus she couldn't see a lie in someone else. She didn't understand what truth was, so she couldn't recognize that either. She was fooling herself on a cosmic scale, and it weakened her. But I wasn't going to march out there and point out the error of her ways. She was just a vampire and not a goddess, but I'd had a taste of her power and I did not want to be on her dirty list.

With her power flowing through me like a rising wind, warm and smelling of flowers that I did not recognize, I didn't even want to burst her bubble. I hadn't felt this good in days. I turned back to the mirror, and my eyes were still that spreading blackness. I should have been scared or screaming, but I wasn't scared, and all I could think was, cool.

"Shouldn't your eyes go back to normal?" he asked, and again I felt that tightness of fear in him.

"Eventually, but if we really want answers to our questions, we need to go back and ask her."

He gave one quick nod, after you, and I realized that Edward didn't trust me at his back. He thought that she had possessed me. I didn't argue with him. I just walked through the door first and went back to talk to Itzpapalotl. I hoped Ramirez hadn't tried to put handcuffs on her. She wouldn't like that, and what she didn't like, her followers didn't like, and there were a hundred and two vampires. I had no idea how many werejaguars she had. This was a feeding not meant for them. But it was a small army, and Ramirez hadn't brought that much backup.

52

RAMIREZ HADN'T PUT cuffs on anyone, but he had called for more backup. There were four more uniforms in the room, and about twenty werejaguars. The audience was watching it all as if it were part of the show. I guess if they could sit through what had been done to Seth, they could sit through a little police action.

I was ahead of Edward as we came into the room. He fell a step behind me, the way we often did when one of us was going to be in charge of the next few minutes. Maybe my eyes were glowing black pits, but Edward still trusted me to calm the situation. Good to know.

The werejaguars were moving through the tables, trying to flank the cops. The uniforms had their hands on their guns. The holsters were unbuckled. It wasn't going to take much to get a gun drawn and the shit to hit the fan. Be a shame to push this big a button when the vampires weren't trying to hurt anybody.

One of the jaguars was moving again, trying to close the circle around the police. I touched his arm. His power trembled over my hand, and it was more than just my own power, or the marks, that flared and answered that rush. He looked down at me and saw the eyes or felt her power, whatever it was, when I said, "Back up, go stand with the others." He did it. Progress. Now if only the police would be as reasonable.

I turned to the police and started walking towards them. One of the new uniforms said, "Shit," hand on gun, other hand out like a traffic stop. "Don't come any closer."

"Ramirez," I said, and made sure my voice carried.

"It's okay. She's with us," he said.

"But her eyes," the uniform said.

"She's with us. Let her through, now." Ramirez's voice was low, but the anger carried.

The uniforms parted like a curtain, very careful not to touch me as I went past. I guess I couldn't blame them, though I wanted to. I was finally at the table with Edward behind me, and the nervous uniforms beyond him. I faced Itzpapalotl across the table. Pinotl was at her side, but they were no longer holding hands. His eyes were still as black as mine, but hers were normal. Strangely, with the hood pushed back to show that delicate face and those normal seeming eyes, she looked the most human of the three of us.

Ramirez had laid some of the pictures on the table. "Tell me what this is." It sounded like a question he'd asked before.

She looked at me.

"Do you know what it is?" I asked.

"No, I truly do not. It does look like one of our artisans could have made it, but the eyes are stones that came with the Spaniards. I do not recognize all the elements of the symbolism."

"But you recognize some of them," I said.

"Yes."

"What do you recognize?"

"The bodies around the base could be the ones you drink."

"You mean like you did with Seth tonight?"

She nodded.

"What is it holding in its hands?"

"It could be many things, but I think it is the lesser things of the body. The heart is spoken for, as are the bones, and many other parts, but no god feeds on the . . ." she frowned searching for the word, ". . . intestines, and other viscera."

"That makes sense," I said.

I felt Ramirez shift beside me, as if he badly wanted to say it does. But he kept quiet because he was a good cop, and she was talking to me. Did it really matter why? Not right that second it didn't.

"You saw the creature that . . ." it was my turn to hesitate. If the police knew what Nicky had done, it was an automatic death sentence. But frankly, he deserved it. The werewolves that he had sucked dry hadn't been willing sacrifices. And he'd cut them up, knowing they were still alive, he'd cut them up and sewn them into that monster behind the bar. It was one of the worst things I'd come across, and that was saying a lot.

I made my decision and knew that it would eventually cost Nicky his life. "You saw the creature that Nicky Baco made?"

She nodded. "I saw. It is a corruption of a great gift."

"Does his master gain power through it just like you do?"

"Yes, and Nicky Baco gains power through it, much as Pinotl does. As you have."

"Can he pass that power to others, like maybe a werewolf pack?"

She seemed to think about that, head to one side, then finally nodded. "It would be possible to share with wereanimals if you had some bond with them of a mystical nature."

"He's vargamor for the local pack," I said.

"I am not familiar with the word vargamor."

It was a wolf term. "It's their witch, their brujo, and they are bound to the pack."

"Then certainly he could share the power with them."

"Nicky said he didn't know where this god lay."

"He lies," she said. "You do not gain this power without the touch of your god's hand."

I'd gotten that from the images that had filled me, but I wanted it confirmed.

"Then Nicky should be able to take us to the place where the god is hiding?"

She nodded. "He knows."

"Do you have a problem with us hunting down and killing a god from your pantheon?"

A look crossed her face that I didn't understand. "If it is a god, then you cannot kill it, and if you can kill it, then it is not a god. I do not mourn the death of false gods."

It was kind of funny coming from her, but I let it go. It wasn't my job to convince her what she was, or what she wasn't. "Thank you for your help, Itzpapalotl."

She gave me a long look, and I knew what she wanted, but . . . "You are indeed a goddess, but I cannot serve two masters," I said.

"His power is lust, and you deny him his power."

I felt the heat rush up my face and wondered what a blush looked like with glowing black eyes. It wasn't what she'd said. It was me knowing what she'd seen in my head. She knew more intimate details than my best friend. Just as I'd shared what she and Pinotl considered a very private and intimate moment of their sharing. Fair is fair, but somehow I didn't think Itzpapalotl blushed.

"I thought I was just denying him sex."

She looked at me the way you'd look a child that was deliberately misunderstanding a point. "Tell me, Anita, what is the base of my power?"

The question surprised me, but I answered it; the time for lying between us was past. "Power, you feed off of pure power regardless of the source."

She smiled, and that thread of power in me smiled with her, made me feel glowy all over. "Now, what is your master's base of power?"

I'd been running from this particular truth for a very long time. Not all master vampires had a secondary power base, another way to draw energy, other than blood or human servants or animals to call. But some did, and Jean-Claude was one of them.

"Anita," she said, as if reminding me that I was supposed to be saying something.

"Sex, his base of power is sex," I said.

Again, she smiled happily at me, and I felt that warm answering glow. It was good to be truthful. It was good to be smart. It was good to please her. And that of course was one of her dangers. If you stayed near her long enough, it might become an end in itself to please her. Even thinking it, I couldn't be afraid of her. Good that I didn't live in Albuquerque.

"By denying him and your wolf, you cripple not just the triad of power, but him. You have crippled him, Anita. You have crippled your master."

I heard myself say, "I'm sorry."

"It is not me that you must be sorry to. It is him. Go home and beg his forgiveness, lay yourself at his feet and feed his power."

I closed my eyes, because what I really wanted to do was nod and just agree. I was pretty sure the spell would wear off before I got home to St. Louis, but putting this woman and Jean-Claude together as a team would have been my undoing. Even now, I was glad he was hundreds of miles away, because I nodded, eyes still closed.

She took the nod as assent. "Good, very good. If your master is grateful for my aid in this matter, let him contact me. I know that we can come to an understanding."

And for the first time since she'd zapped me, I felt a thrill of fear. I looked at her through a veil of her power and was afraid of her.

She read it in me. "You should always be afraid of gods, Anita. If you are not afraid, then you are a fool and you are not a fool." She looked past me to Ramirez. "I believe that I have helped you all that I can, Detective Ramirez."

He said, "Anita?"

I nodded. "Yeah, it's time to go see Nicky Baco."

"If Nicky lied to us, then so did his pack leader," Edward said, "because he said Nicky was telling the truth about not knowing where the monster was."

"If Nicky can share this kind of power with the werewolves, then I know why the pack lied."

"The werewolves will fight to protect Nicky," Edward said.

We looked at each other. "It'll be a blood bath if the police go in force." I shook my head. "But what choice do we have?"

"Nicky isn't at the bar," Ramirez said.

We turned to him, said in unison, "Where is he?"

"In the hospital. Someone beat the shit out of him."

Edward and I exchanged glances, and we both smiled. "Back to the hospital, then," I said.

He nodded. "Back to the hospital."

I looked at Ramirez. "If that's all right with you?"

"Can you prove what you've been saying about Baco?" he asked.

"Yes," I said.

"Then it's a death sentence. He'll know that. I've seen Baco in an interrogation. He's tough, and he knows that he has nothing to gain and everything to lose by telling us the truth."

"Then we'll have to find something that he's more afraid of than being executed." I couldn't help it. I turned and looked at Itzpapalotl. I met her eyes and there was no pull to them now. Her own power protected me from her. No stars, no endless night, just a dark knowledge of what I was thinking, and her approval of the plan.

"We can't do anything illegal," Ramirez said.

"Of course not," I said.

"I mean it, Anita."

I looked at him, and watched him flinch when he met my eyes. "Would I do that to you?"

He searched my face as if trying to decipher it. It was the way I looked at Edward sometimes, or Jean-Claude. Finally, he said, "I don't know what you'd do." And that, for better or worse, was the truth.

53

EDWARD GOT HIS SUNGLASSES out of the glove compartment and handed them to me before we went inside the hospital. My eyes hadn't changed back, though I knew the effect was beginning to wear off, because the fact that my eyes were still black and glowy was beginning to worry me. It was a good sign.

Nicky Baco was not in a private room. The police had his roommate moved to a different room. Nicky was in traction, and wasn't going anywhere. He lay in the bed and looked smaller than I knew he was. The leg that had been badly broken was in a cast from toe to thigh. Little pulleys and cords held his leg up at an odd angle that must have been hell on the back.

Ramirez had been questioning Nicky for about thirty minutes and was getting nowhere. Edward and I leaned against the wall and watched the show. But Nicky had done exactly what we'd feared he'd do. He'd grasped his situation and his options right away. He was going to die. So why should he help us?

"We know where the monster you made is, Nicky. We know what you did. Help us stop this thing before it kills again."

"And what?" Nicky said. "I know the law. There's no life in prison for a witch that uses magic to kill. It's an automatic death sentence. You got nothing to offer me, Ramirez."

I pushed away from the wall and touched Ramirez's arm. He looked at me, and the frustration was already showing. He'd been informed that Lieutenant Marks was on the way. He wanted to crack Baco before Marks arrived so he would get credit and not his lieutenant. Political, but the reality in most police work.

"Can I ask a few questions, Detective?"

He took a breath, let it out slow. "Sure." He stepped back to let me stand beside the bed.

I looked down at Nicky. Someone had handcuffed one of his wrists to the bed rail. I wasn't sure it was necessary with the traction, but it made a nice point. "What would the Red Woman's Husband do if he knew you gave away his secret hideout?"

He stared up at me, and even through the sunglasses I could see the hate in his eyes. I could also see the fast rise and fall of his chest, the thud of the pulse in his neck. He was scared.

"Answer me, Nicky."

"He'd kill me."

"How?"

That made him frown. "What do you mean, how?"

"I mean what method of death would he use? How would he kill you?"

Nicky shifted in the bed, trying to find a comfortable spot. The leg pulled tight, and he jerked on the handcuffed wrist, making it rattle up and down the bar. There was no comfortable position for Nicky tonight.

"He'd probably send his monster after me. It'd cut me up and gut me like it's done to the others."

"His minion slaughtered all the witches or psychics, and skinned the mundanes. That's it, isn't it?"

"If you're so smart, you don't need to ask me. You have all the answers."

"Not all of them," I said. I touched the bed rail that he was cuffed to, wrapped my hands around it on either side of the cuff so he couldn't slide it without hitting one of my hands. "I've seen the bodies, Nicky. It's a bad way to go, but there are worse things."

He gave a harsh laugh. "Being gutted alive—doesn't get much worse than that," he said.

I took the sunglasses off and let him see the eyes.

He stopped breathing for a heartbeat. He just stared up at me, eyes growing wide, breath trapped in his throat.

I touched his hand, and he screamed. "Don't touch me! Don't you fucking touch me!" He was jerking on the handcuff frantically, over and over, as if that would help.

Ramirez came to stand on the other side of the bed across from me. He looked a question at me.

"I didn't hurt him, Hernando."

"Get her the fuck away from me."

"Tell us where the monster is, and I'll send her out of the room."

Nicky looked from one to the other of us, and the fear showed on his face now. You didn't have to have vampire vision to see it. "You can't do this to me. You're the cops."

"We're not doing anything to you," Ramirez said.

Nicky's eyes flicked back to me. "You're the cops. You can execute me, but you can't torture me. That's the law."

"You're right, Nicky. The police aren't allowed to torture prisoners." I leaned in close and whispered, "But I'm not the police."

He started tugging on the chain again, rattling it up and down the bar. "Get her away from me, now! I want a lawyer. I want a fucking lawyer."

Ramirez turned to the two uniformed cops waiting by the door. "Go call Mr. Baco a lawyer."

The two cops looked at each other. "Both of us?" one asked.

Ramirez nodded. "Yeah, both of you."

They exchanged another look and went for the door. The taller one asked, "How long you think this phone call should take?"

"A while, and knock before you come back in."

The uniforms left, and it was just Edward, Ramirez, Nicky, and me. Nicky was staring up at Ramirez. "You're a good cop, Ramirez. I've never heard any dirt on you. You won't let her hurt me. You're a good guy. You won't let her hurt me." His voice was high and frantic, but each time he said it, he seemed more sure of himself, more certain that Ramirez's goodness would be his shield.

He was probably right on one thing. Ramirez wouldn't let me hurt him, but I was willing to bet that Ramirez would let me scare him.

I reached out like I'd stroke Nicky's face. He jerked back, out of reach.

"Ramirez, shit, please, don't let her touch me."

"I'll be over there if you need me, Anita." He walked away from the bed and went to sit in a chair at the end of the room near Edward.

Nicky screamed after him, "Ramirez, please, please!"

I touched his mouth with fingertips, and he froze under that gentle touch. His eyes moved slowly, so slowly until he was looking up into mine. "Shhh," I said and lowered my face towards his, as if I'd kiss his forehead.

He opened his mouth, drew a breath, and shrieked. I grabbed his face between my hands the way I'd seen Pinotl do, but I knew that it didn't have to be the hands. I could suck him dry with a kiss. "Shut up, Nicky, shut up!"

He started to cry. "Please, oh, god, please don't."

"Did the werewolves beg like this?" I asked. "Did they, Nicky?" I pressed my hands into his face until the skin puckered.

"Yes," he said, voice squeezed by how tight I was holding his face. I had to force myself to release his face, or I was going to leave red marks. Couldn't mark him up. Couldn't give Marks a reason to punish Ramirez.

I leaned my arms on the bed rail that he was chained to. He pulled his hand to the length of the chain, but didn't struggle. He watched me the way mice watch cats when they know there's no way out. I leaned towards him. It was a very causal movement, but it put my face close to his, not close enough to touch but close enough that he got an up close look at the eyes.

"You see, Nicky, there are worse things."

"You need me to bring the others back. You do me, and I can't give them back their lives."

"You see, Nicky. I don't need you anymore. I know how to bring them back all by myself." I leaned over, balancing on tiptoe and my arms on the rail, leaning in, as if to whisper in his ear. "Your services are no longer needed."

"Please," he whispered.

I spoke with my mouth so close to his face that I could feel my breath coming back from his skin in a warm pulse. "The doctors will certify you dead, Nicky. They'll bury you in a box somewhere, and you'll hear every shovel full of dirt as it hits the coffin lid. You'll lie there in the dark and scream in your head, and no one will hear you. Maybe we'll have to put a jade bead in your mouth and sew it shut to make you lie still."

Tears trailed from his eyes, but his face was blank, as if he didn't know he was crying.

"Tell them where your master is, Nicky, or I swear I will do worse than kill you." I kissed him on the forehead, very gently.

He whimpered.

I kissed the tip of his nose, the way you do with children. I hovered over his mouth. "Tell them, Nicky." I lowered my mouth over his, our lips brushed, and he turned his head.

"I'll tell you. I'll tell you anything you want to know."

I moved away from the bed and let Ramirez move up to take his turn.

A phone rang, and Edward pulled his cell phone from his back pocket. He opened the door and went into the hall to take the call.

Ramirez's voice was not happy. "What do you mean you can't tell me how to get there?" He had his notebook open, his pen poised, and nothing written down.

I started to walk back toward the bed.

Nicky held his hands up as if to ward me off. "I swear to you that I can take you to it, but I can't give you directions and be sure you'll find it. I don't want to send you out into the dark, and have you not find it. You'd blame me, and it wouldn't be my fault."

Ramirez looked at me.

I nodded. He was too scared to lie, and it was too stupid a story to be made up.

"I can take you to it. If I'm there, I can take you to it."

"Of course, if you're there, you can warn your master," I said.

"I wouldn't do that." But I saw the change in his skin color, the rise in breathing, the flick of his eyes.

"Liar," I said.

"All right, but I'd be a fool not to try and get away. They're going to kill me, Anita. Why shouldn't I try to get away?"

I guess I couldn't blame him on that one. "Call Leonora Evans. She's a witch. Have her ward him, make sure that he can't contact his master by anything other than yelling."

"And the yelling?" Ramirez said.

"Gag him when the time comes," I said.

"You trust Leonora Evans to do this?"

"She saved my life, so I guess I do."

Ramirez nodded. "Okay, I'll call her in." He looked at the traction ropes. "The doctors aren't going to want him going anywhere tonight."

"Talk to them, Hernando. Explain what's at stake. Besides, what good does it do to heal him if you're just going to turn around and execute him?

Ramirez looked at me. "That was harsh."

"Yeah, it was, but it's still true."

Edward knocked and came in the door just far enough to say, "I need you out here."

I glanced at Ramirez. "I think we can take it from here, thank you," he said.

"My pleasure." I slipped the sunglasses back on as I followed Edward out into the hall. The moment I looked at Edward's face, I knew something bad had happened. He didn't show it the way a normal person would, but it was there, the tightness around his eyes, the way he held himself, carefully, as if he were afraid to move too suddenly or he'd break. I don't think I'd have seen it without the vampire vision.

"What's wrong?" I stepped in close, because something told me this was not for police consumption. With Edward it so seldom was.

He took me by the arm down the hallway, further away from the uniforms that were staring our way. "Riker has Donna's kids." His grip tightened, and I didn't tell him it hurt. "He has Peter and Becca. He's going to kill them if I don't bring you to him now. He knows we're at the hospital. He's given me an hour to make the drive, then he starts torturing them. If I'm not there in two hours, he'll kill them. If I bring the police in, he'll kill them."

I touched his arm. If it had been almost any other friend, I'd have hugged him. "Is Donna okay?"

He seemed to realize he was digging into my arm and let me go. "This is Donna's night at her group. I don't know if the babysitter's still alive, but Donna won't even be home for two, maybe three hours. She doesn't know."

"Let's go," I said.

We turned and started walking down the hallway. Ramirez yelled behind us. "Where are you two going? I thought you'd want to be in on it."

"Personal emergency," Edward said, and kept walking.

I turned around, walking backwards, trying to talk at the same time. "In two hours call Ted's house. The call will be forwarded to his cell phone. We'll join you on the monster hunt."

"Why two hours?" he asked.

"The emergency will be taken care of by then," I said. I had to touch Edward's arm, to keep walking backwards and not fall.

"Everything could be over two hours from now," Ramirez said.

"I'm sorry." Edward was at the doors that led into the next section of hallway. He pulled me through, the doors shut behind us. He was already punching numbers on the cell phone. "I'll have Olaf and Bernardo meet us at the turnoff to Riker's place."

I don't know which of them answered, but he gave a long list of things to bring, and he made them write it down. We were out of the hospital, through the parking lot and getting into his Hummer before he clicked the telephone off.

Edward drove, and all I had to do was think. Not a good thing. I was remembering last May when some bad guys kidnapped Richard's mother and younger brother. They'd sent us a box with a lock of his brother's hair, and his mother's finger in it. Everyone that had touched them was dead. Everyone that had hurt them would never hurt anyone again. I only had two regrets: one, that I hadn't gotten there in time to save them from being tortured; two, that the bad guys hadn't suffered enough before they died.

If Riker hurt Peter and Becca . . . I wasn't sure I wanted to see what Edward would do to him. I prayed as we rode through the darkness, "Please, God, don't let them be hurt. Let them be safe." Riker could be lying. They could already be dead, but I didn't think so. Maybe because I needed them to be alive. I remembered Becca in her sunflower dress with that sprig of lilacs in her hair, laughing in Edward's arms. I saw Peter's sullen resentment when Edward and his mother touched. I remembered the way Peter had stood up to Russell in the restaurant when he threatened Becca. He was a brave kid. I tried not to think about what could be happening to them right this second.

Edward had gone very, very quiet. When I looked at him, the dark crystal vision showed me further into him than I'd ever seen before. I didn't have to guess whether he cared for the children. I could see it. He loved them. As much as he was capable of it, he loved them. If someone hurt them, his vengeance was going to be a thing of great and awesome terror. I wouldn't be able to stop him no matter what he wanted to do to them. All I would be able to do was stand and watch and try not to get too much blood on my shoes.

54

IT WAS A DARK night. It didn't seem to be cloudy, just dark, as if something besides clouds was blocking the moon. Or maybe that was just my frame of mind. The one thing I'd wanted to avoid while I was doing my favor for Edward was dealing with Edward at his most illegal. We'd picked up Olaf and Bernardo at a crossroads in the middle of nowhere with those empty rolling hills stretching out and out into the darkness. There had been no cover except some scrub bushes, and when Edward stopped the car and cut the engine, I thought we'd have a wait ahead of us.

"Get out. We'll need to suit up." He'd gotten out without waiting to see if I was getting out or not.

I got out. The silence seemed as big as the sky overhead, an immense emptiness. A man stood up not five feet in front of me. I had the Browning pointed before the man held a flashlight under his face and I realized it was Bernardo.

Olaf had magically appeared on the other side of the road. There was no ditch on either side of the road. There was nothing on the side of the road. What was even more impressive was that they began lifting large black bags of equipment out of that same nowhere. If we'd had the time, I'd have asked how they did it, though I doubt I'd have understood the answer. Training probably. Training I didn't have, though it might be nice to get it.

Of course, most of the things I hid from could have heard Bernardo's and Olaf's heart beat no matter how well hidden they were. It was almost a relief to be up against mere humans. It meant you could at least hide in the dark.

Twenty minutes later we were on the road again, and Edward hadn't been joking on the suiting up part. I'd had to strip to my bra and put on a Kevlar vest. It was my size.

Which meant it had to be a special purchase because Kevlar doesn't come in my size off the rack.

"It's your prize for spotting all the weapons," Edward said. He always knows just what to buy me.

I needed to adjust the shoulder holster after putting on the vest, but I was told to do it in the car. I didn't argue. We had less than ten minutes to get to Riker's place. My T-shirt didn't quite fit over the body armor. I mean it did fit, but not well. Bernardo handed me a black, long-sleeved, man's shirt. "Put it on over the T-shirt. Button it up part way after you've got your holsters adjusted."

The shoulder holster was just a matter of readjusting straps. The inner pants holster just didn't work once the vest was on. I put the Firestar down the front of my jeans and angled it until I was as happy as I was going to get with the way it fit.

It still dug into my stomach, but I wanted it where I could get it fast. I could live with bruises tomorrow.

I practiced drawing the Browning through the half open shirt a few times, though it's hard to practice drawing from a sitting position, but we didn't have time for me to get out and practice standing.

"You guys are making me nervous, putting me in Kevlar."

"You didn't argue," Bernardo said.

"We don't have time to argue. Tell me what to do, I'll do it. But why the Kevlar?"

"Olaf," Edward said.

"Riker employs twenty men, ten are just hired muscle. We've met half of them already. But he's got ten that he keeps close to him. Three ex-seals, two ex-army rangers, one ex-police, and four guys who have black files. Which means whatever they do or did, it's top secret and maybe rogue."

I remembered what FBI Agent Bradford had said about Olaf. That he had a black file. "Isn't this a little too commando raidish for a pot hunter?"

Olaf continued like I hadn't said anything. Bernardo started showing me the contents of a large leather purse at the same time. I listened to Olaf and watched Bernardo.

"Riker has connections in South America that supply him with contraband. Suspicions are that he's running more than just artifacts. Maybe drugs. The locals have no idea how big a bad guy they've got here."

"When did you find all this out?"

"After they came to the house," Edward said.

"How did you find all this out?" I asked.

"If we told you, we'd have to kill you," Olaf said.

I started to smile, thinking it was a joke, but I caught a glimpse of his face as the only car we'd seen passed by, flashing lights over us as it passed. He didn't look like he was joking.

Bernardo said, "This looks like a can of hair spray. You can even squirt out a small amount of cresol." He demonstrated. "But lift here." He did and revealed a second layer of metal. "This is the pin. This is the depressor. It's an incendiary grenade. You pull the pin, let up on the depressor, and you have three seconds to get a minimum of fifty feet away from it. It's got white phosphorus in it. This shit burns under water. If you get a tiny piece on your sleeve, it will eat through the cloth, your skin, bone, all the way to the other side."

He clicked the secret compartment shut and handed it to me. "Damned heavy for hairspray," I said.

"Yeah, but how many ex-navy whatevers are going to notice?"

He had a point. Next was a small thing of breath freshener that was really heavy-duty mace. A key ring that when you hit the button on it, a four-inch blade popped out.

There was a heavy ink pen that actually wrote, that if you pressed the little switch, a six-inch blade came out the end. There was real perfume with a higher than normal alcohol content. "Go for the eyes," was the advice. A disposable lighter, because you never know when you might need some fire, and a package of cigarettes to explain the lighter. There was a transmitter in the collar of the black shirt that would allow them to find me inside the buildings or at least find the shirt. I was beginning to feel like I'd been shanghaied into a James Bond movie.

I lifted out a hairbrush with a heavier than normal handle. "What's this?"

"It's a hairbrush," Bernardo said.

Oh. I looked at Edward. The only thing he'd changed was putting a white Kevlar vest under his undershirt and white shirt. He was even still wearing his cowboy hat. Olaf and Bernardo were both dressed in commando black, and backpacks that looked full. They were bristling with weapons, blacked so they didn't show up at night, but not hidden.

"I take it that the guys here aren't going in the front door with us," I said.

"No," Edward said. He hit the brakes, and Olaf and Bernardo slipped out of the car and into the darkness. Because I knew what I was looking for, I could see them in a running crouch going over the hill. But if you hadn't been looking, you'd have missed them.

"You're scaring me, Edward. I'm not like a commando raid, James Bond kind of girl. Where the hell did you get a hairspray grenade?"

"A lot of female secret service now. It's a prototype."

"Nice to know where my tax dollars are going."

We were going down a long gravel driveway. There was a big house sitting up on a hill. Lights blazed out of the windows as if someone had gone through and hit every light, as if they were scared of the dark. If Riker really thought the monsters were coming, the analogy was accurate.

Edward outlined his plan as we drove the last few yards. I was to pretend to do a spell of protection for Riker. While I delayed, Olaf and Bernardo would try to find the kids. If they couldn't find them or couldn't get them out, Olaf was supposed to find a man and kill him as messily as possible in a short space of time, leave the body where it would be found, and hope to make Riker think the monsters had already gotten inside. They might take us to the point where the monster kill had been found to get my expert advice, which would put us and whoever was with us, hopefully Riker, near where Olaf and Bernardo could help us kill them. If that failed, Bernardo would start blowing things up. Which would create panic and hopefully allow us to find the kids. Unless Bernardo decided the structure wasn't sturdy enough to blow up and not cave in around us. Then we'd need another plan.

Edward stopped the car at a gravel turnaround near the crest of the hill. Men armed with automatic submachine guns walked towards the car. None of them were Harold or Russell. They moved like Olaf and Edward moved, like predators.

"You don't believe they're going to give back the kids, do you?"

"Do you?" he asked. He'd put his hands on the steering wheel at ten and two, in plain sight.

I raised my hands in the air where they could be seen. "No," I said.

"If the kids are okay, we'll do as little killing as possible, but if the kids aren't okay, it's zero survivors."

"The police are going to find out about this one, Edward. You will blow your Ted 'Good ol' boy' Forrester image all to hell."

"If the kids don't make it out, I don't give a damn."

"How will Olaf and Bernardo know whether to kill or not?"

"There's a wire worked into my vest. They've both got ear pieces, so they'll be able to hear."

"You're going to tell them to kill," I said.

"If I have to."

The machine-gun-toting men were at either side of the car. They made motions for us to get out. We did what they wanted, being sure to keep our hands in sight. We wouldn't want any misunderstandings.

55

THE MACHINE GUN GUY on my side wasn't that tall, five foot eight or maybe shorter, but his arms were corded with so much muscle that veins stood out against his skin like snakes. Some people vein up if they lift even a little, but most of the time you don't get that much popping up without some major effort. It was as if he was trying to make up for the lack of height by being obscenely strong. Most muscle-bound guys are slow and rarely know how to fight. They rely on sheer strength and just being a bully. But this one moved smoothly, almost gliding on his feet, sort of sideways, which hinted at some martial art training. He moved well, and his bicep was bigger than my neck. He was also pointing a very modern looking submachine gun at me. Muscle bound, trained fighter, and better armed than me—weren't there rules against that?

"Lean on the hood, assume the position," he said.

I put my hands on the hood and leaned. The engine was still warm, not hot, but warm. Muscle man kicked my legs. "Further apart." I did what he asked. I looked across the hood and met Edward's eyes. He was getting the same treatment on his side from a taller, slender man who wore silver frame glasses. Edward's eyes were at their empty, pitiless best. But somehow I knew he wasn't pleased. When I realized that, I realized I still had the sunglasses on, and my vision was still good through dark lenses at night. Funny, how neither Olaf nor Bernardo had asked in the car. There hadn't been time for many questions.

The vampire vision had toned down, but it was still there or I'd have been night blind with the glasses on. Wondered what Muscle Man would think of the eyes.

He kicked my right leg again, hard enough that it hurt. "I said, lean!" He had that drill sergeant voice going.

"If I lean any further, I'll be lying down."

I felt him move behind me and had my head turned to the side when he slapped me in the back of the head, hard enough that my cheek hit the hood. It would have hurt if it had been the front, nose, mouth. He'd meant it to hurt.

"Do what you're told, and you won't get hurt."

I was beginning not to believe him, but I leaned, cheek pressed to the hood, arms out flat like I was being nailed down, feet spread so far that one good foot sweep would have dumped me to the ground. But it was nice and unsteady, the way he wanted it apparently. In a way it was flattering. He was treating me as a dangerous person. A lot of bad guys don't. Usually, they live to regret it, but not always. If muscle man died tonight, it wasn't going to be because of carelessness.

He searched me, top to bottom, even running his fingers through my hair. He'd have found Bernardo's stiletto hairpins that the others had missed at the house. He took the sunglasses off and looked at them as if looking for things that I would never have thought to find in a pair of sunglasses. He didn't really look at my face, didn't catch the eyes, or maybe they weren't glowing black anymore. Muscle Man found everything but the transmitter that was sewn somewhere in the shirt and the contents of the purse. He did dump it out on the ground and shine a flashlight on every item. He made sure the ink pen wrote, that the hair-spray sprayed, and took the breath freshener mace as if he recognized it on sight. But that was all he took out of the purse, though once it was empty, he kneaded it with his left hand, the right still holding the submachine gun.

"This wouldn't be one of those with a compartment for a gun, would it?"

I'd raised my head enough to watch him empty the purse, so we could look at each other while he held the gun on me and glanced down at things. "No, it wouldn't be."

"I was betting it would be," he said.

"Nope," I said.

He finished by standing on the purse and stomping it flat. Glad it wasn't really my purse. "I guess there's no gun," he said.

"Told ya."

He took three big steps back, out of reach. He was treating me like I was dangerous. Darn. I sometimes counted on passing for harmless, but I guess I'd been packing too much hardware to pass for anything but dangerous.

"You can stand up."

I stood up.

He tossed the sunglasses to me. I caught them. My eyes were in the light from the house now, but he never flinched. Apparently, the glowy stuff had faded. He motioned with the gun for me to pick up the contents of the purse. I put everything back inside and almost put the sunglasses in, but decided to put them back on. Two reasons: one, when the night got too dark to wear them, I'd know the vampire stuff had left me completely; two, knowing Edward, they were probably expensive, and I didn't want to get them scratched up.

He motioned with the gun, and said, "Just walk slow, straight to the house, and it'll be all right."

"Why don't I believe you?" I asked.

He looked at me with eyes as dead and empty as a doll's. "I don't like smart mouths."

"You'll have to wait until I do the spell before you can shoot me," I said.

"So they tell me. Get moving."

The slender guy with glasses who had Edward at gunpoint was waiting for muscle man to get me moving. When I started walking, Glasses moved Edward forward. They kept us walking side by side, telling us to stay together. They kept us together so that if they had to start shooting they could kill us both with one spray of bullets. True professionals. I hoped Olaf and Bernardo were as good as they were supposed to be. If they weren't, we were in deep trouble.

The house was one of those nouveau architect homes that people with more money than taste are always hiring people to build. It looked like a giant had dumped white concrete in a free form slide putting windows and doors here and there like raisins in an oatmeal cookie. A nice surprise, but never where you expect to find them. The mismatched windows made the house look deformed. The door was off center but round, like a wide open mouth. The windows were not only round and mismatched, but the number of windows didn't seem to match the floor plan as if some of the windows looked into blank walls where no room could possibly be.

White steps led up to the round door like one of those cartoon tongues that spill out of mouths and go tumbling downstairs. The steps weren't wide enough for us to walk side by side, so Edward moved a couple of steps ahead. Neither of the men behind us protested, so we kept moving.

It had been so long since I carried a purse instead of a fanny pack that it felt awkward on my shoulder. I had to keep a hand on it to keep it from swinging around. I'd put it on the left shoulder, leaving my right hand uncompromised out of habit. Not that I had anything left to draw or pull or whatever. But it was always good to have your strong hand empty, just in case. So Edward and Dolph had always told me.

At the top of the porch in a spill of bright yellow light, they told us to stop. We stopped. They moved up to flank us and move a little back to either side. I didn't understand what they were doing at first, until the door opened and another man pointed the same kind of submachine gun at us. Muscle Man and Glasses had moved out of his line of fire and moved so they wouldn't catch him in their fire line. It is not easy to use three submachine guns in that small a space without crossing your own men, but they made it look easy, very smooth. The other men had carried an extra clip for the sub guns in a thigh holster, but this one had two clips at his waist.

The man in the door was African American and tall, like Olaf's height, very six foot plus. He was also completely bald just like Olaf. If they ever met, they'd look like light and dark versions of each other.

"What took so long?" he asked; his voice matched the body, deep.

"They were carrying a lot of hardware," Muscle Man said.

The new guy was smirking at me. "From the way Russell talked I expected you to look like Amanda. You're just a little bitch."

"Amanda the Amazon that came to Ted's house?" I asked.

He nodded.

I shrugged. "I wouldn't believe much that Russell said."

"He said you broke his nose, kicked him in the balls, and beat his head in with a piece of wood."

"Everything but the last bit. If I'd beaten his head in, he'd be dead."

"What's the hold up, Simon?" Muscle Man asked.

"Deuce is having some trouble locating the wand."

"Deuce would have trouble keeping track of his head if it wasn't attached," Muscle Man said.

"True, but we still wait." He was looking at both of us, the gun held easily in his big hands. "What's with the sunglasses, bitch?"

I let the name calling go. They had all the guns. "They look cool," I said.

He laughed then, a warm growly sound. A nice laugh if he hadn't been armed.

"What about you, Ted? I hear you are a bad dude."

Edward transformed into Ted, like a magician deciding he was going to have to perform after all. "I'm a bounty hunter. I kill monsters."

Simon looked at him, and there was something about the way he did it that said the Ted act wasn't fooling him. "Van Cleef recognized your picture, Undertaker."

Undertaker?

Ted smiled and shook his head. "I don't know anybody named Van Cleef."

Simon just looked at Glasses. Edward had time to turn his head so he took the blow on his shoulder. He moved a step, but didn't fall. Simon gave another look. Glasses hit his knee, and Edward collapsed onto one knee.

"We only need the girl up and running," Simon said. "So I'll ask you this just once, do you know Van Cleef?"

I stood there, not sure what to do. We were so totally covered by the guns, and the priority had to be getting the children out. So no heroics until they were safe. If we died, I wasn't a hundred percent sure that Bernardo and Olaf would risk their lives to get them out. So I stood there and looked at Edward kneeling on the porch, waiting for him to give me some kind of sign what I was supposed to do.

Edward looked up at Simon. "Yes."

"Yes, what, asshole?"

"Yes, I know Van Cleef."

Simon smiled broadly, obviously happy with himself. "Boys, this is the Undertaker, the man that still has the highest body count of anyone Van Cleef ever trained."

I felt, rather than saw, the two men twitch. The information not only made sense to them, but it scared them. It made them afraid of Edward. Who the hell was Van Cleef, and when had he trained Edward, and for what? I wanted to know the answers, but not badly enough to ask. Later, if we survived, I'd ask Edward. Maybe he'd even tell me. "I don't know you," Edward said.

"I came in just after you left," Simon said.

"Simon?" Edward made the name a question, and the big man seemed to understand what was being asked.

"As in whatever the fuck Simon says, you damn well better do."

How colorful, I thought, but didn't say out loud.

"Can I get up now?" Edward asked.

"If you can stand, then help yourself."

Edward got to his feet. If it hurt, it didn't show. His face was empty, eyes like bits of pale blue ice. I'd seen him kill with that face.

Simon's smile faltered around the edges. "You're supposed to be one mean son of a bitch."

"Van Cleef never said I was mean." He sounded very sure of that.

Simon's smile disappeared altogether. "No, he didn't. He said you were dangerous."

"What would Van Cleef say about you?" Edward asked.

"Same thing," Simon said.

"I doubt that," Edward said.

They looked at each other, and there was a weight and a testing like something nearly visible in the air between them. Muscle Man's nerve broke first. "Where the hell is Deuce with the wand?"

Simon blinked, and switched very cold brown eyes to the man behind me. "Shut up, Mickey."

Mickey? It didn't have quite the ring to it that the other nicknames did. Of course, Simon hadn't sounded too tough until it was explained.

"Van Cleef didn't recognize her picture."

"No reason he should," Edward said.

"The newspapers call her the Executioner."

"That's what the vampires call her."

"Why do they call her that?"

"Why do you think?"

Simon looked at me. "How many vampire kills you got, bitch?"

If I had a chance tonight, I was going to teach Simon some manners, but not right now. "I don't know exactly."

"Guess."

I thought about it. "I stopped keeping track around thirty."

Simon laughed. "Hell, every man on this porch has more kills than that."

More kills than thirty? Who the hell were these guys? I shrugged. "I didn't know it was a competition."

"Did you count the human kills?" Edward asked.

I shook my head. "He asked about vampire kills, not human."

"Add those in," he said.

That was harder. "Eleven, twelve maybe."

"Forty-three," Simon said, "you got Mickey beat, but not Rooster." Apparently, Rooster was Glasses.

"Add in the shapeshifters," Edward said.

It had turned into a competition. I wasn't really sure that I wanted to seem as dangerous as I really was, but I trusted Edward's judgment. "Oh, hell, Edward, I don't know." I started counting in my head. Finally, I said, "Seven."

"So fifty," he said.

Just hearing it out loud made me want to cringe. It sounded so Psychos 'R Us.

"I've still got you beat, bitch," Simon said.

He was beginning to get on my nerves. "The fifty only counts the people I did personally with a weapon."

"You mean it doesn't count the ones you killed barehanded?" He smiled when he said it, like he didn't believe it.

"No, I counted those."

The smile got positively condescending. "Then what didn't you count, little bitch."

"Witches, necromancers, things like that."

"Why not count them?" This from Mickey.

I shrugged.

"Because using magic to kill is an automatic death sentence," Edward said.

I frowned at him. "I never said anything about magic."

"We aren't friends," Simon said, "but you can be honest tonight, bitch. We won't tell the cops. Will we, boys?" He laughed and they laughed with him, with that same sort of nervous mirth that Itzpapalotl's vampires had had, like they were afraid not to laugh.

I shrugged. "Most of the fifty are sanctioned kills. The cops already know about them."

"You ever been on trial?" This from the until now silent Rooster.

"No."

"Fifty legal kills," Simon said.

"Give or take," I said.

Simon looked at Edward. They had another one of those weighted staring contests.

"Would Van Cleef like her?"

"Yes, but she wouldn't like him."

"Why not?"

"She's not big on orders and listening to people just because they've got an extra stripe on their shoulder."

"Not disciplined," Simon said.

"She's disciplined. You just got to have more than rank to get her to listen to you."

"She listens to you," Simon said. "She didn't want to talk about her kills, but she took your lead."

His saying that meant Simon was very observant, too observant for comfort actually. I'd underestimated him. Stupid of me. No, not stupid, careless.

Another man came up with the identical gun in his hands. He was just shy of six foot, but seemed smaller, delicate somehow. The hair was a deep brown, cut short, curly. The face was pretty in a girlish kind of way. His skin was that dark tan that isn't really tan at all. He had a set of small headphones around his neck, with wires connecting them to a metal box and a small flat . . . wand attached with a cord to the box. It had to be Deuce and the wand.

I didn't know what it was, but Edward went very still. He knew what it was, and he didn't like it. Not a good sign.

"Where the fuck have you been?" Mickey said.

"Mickey," Simon said, and he said 'Mickey' the way that Edward could say 'Olaf' and get perfect obedience. There was no more comment from the backup players. Simon looked at Deuce. "Do it."

Deuce slipped the headphones on, hit a switch and some knobs on the box, and a light went on on the box. He got a distracted inward look on his face as if he were listening to things we couldn't hear. He started at Edward's hat and worked down, hesitated over the chest area, then continued the sweep. He knelt on the ground beside Edward and waved the wand up the backside of Edward. He was careful to stay out of the line of fire of all three guns. His own gun was on a sling that he pushed far behind his back, keeping it out of the way with a well-placed elbow as he moved.

He stood, slipped the headphones off, and unplugged them from the box. "Listen to this." He waved the wand over Edward's chest. It beeped frantically.

"Take off the shirt," Simon said.

Edward didn't argue. He unbuttoned the shirt and handed it to Deuce, who waved the wand over it. The thing stayed silent.

Deuce waved the wand over Edward's chest again, and the wand beeped. He ran the wand over the shirt in his hand, no noise. Deuce shook his head.

"The undershirt," Simon said.

Edward had to take his hat off. He handed it to me, then lifted the undershirt over his head. The Kevlar looked very artificial and white. He handed the undershirt to Deuce, and we went through the same routine again.

"Take the vest off," Simon said.

"Tell me one thing first," Edward asked. "Are the kids all right?"

"Why the fuck do you care about some bitch's kids?"

Edward just looked at him, but there was something in that look that made Simon take a step back. He noticed what he'd done and took the step back, pointing the gun very solidly at Edward's chest. "Take off the damn vest."

"It's too hot for body armor anyway," Edward said. It seemed an odd thing to say for Edward man of few words, but you had to know Edward to know it was odd. I had the feeling that Edward had just put the word out for zero survivors. He undid the Velcro, slipped it over his head and handed it to Deuce.

Edward stood there naked from the waist up. He looked fragile beside the musclebound Mickey or the very tall Simon, but they saw in him what I saw in him because unarmed and half-naked they were still scared of him. It was there in the way Simon reacted to him. The way the others, except Deuce kept their distance. Deuce didn't seem to be working on the same instincts as the rest, though he never once crossed the fire line. He made Edward stretch out his hand, or he knelt under the direct line of fire. None of them were careless. It wasn't a good sign.

He ran the wand over the vest. When the wand beeped, he handed it to Simon. Then he ran the wand over Edward's bare chest. Silence. Good, because I think Simon would have said, "Skin," in the same voice he'd said, shirt, undershirt, vest. Just because Edward made him nervous didn't mean he wasn't scary all of his own.

"In the body armor, that's good," Simon said. "Most people, even if they have you strip, don't check the armor."

Edward just looked at him.

"Her next."

Deuce duck-walked in front of us. Just in case someone started shooting, he was safe. No one shot anyone. Of course the night was young. He stood on the other side of me. He didn't bother to put the earphones back on, just ran the wand over me. It beeped. "Hand the hat back to him, please."

Please—refreshing after hearing myself called bitch about a dozen times. "My pleasure," I said and handed Edward's hat back to him.

Deuce had looked up when I spoke, as if he wasn't used to politeness in others either. The wand ran over me, and it beeped at chest level.

"Take the shirt off, bitch," Simon said.

I untucked the shirt and started unbuttoning it. "My name's Anita, not bitch."

"Like I give a fuck," he said.

Fine, I'd tried being nice. I handed the shirt to Deuce and his magic wand. It beeped, but when he ran it back over me, nothing. He laid the box gently on the ground, the wand on top of it, and started looking at the shirt. In less than a minute he'd found a small wire with a slightly thicker head sewn into the collar of the shirt. "Looks like a transmitter, maybe a homing beacon."

Simon tossed the vest to Deuce. "Cut it open, find out what's inside."

Deuce pulled a gravity knife from his back pocket, did one of those quick wrist movements that spilled the blade open. He went over the vest with his hands first, eyes closed, then he started cutting. It was a longer wire, with a little box attached. "It's a receiver. Someone out there is hearing everything we say."

"Destroy the homer."

Deuce crushed mine under his heel. When it was a little metallic and plastic slimy place on the porch, he smiled up at us as if he'd done a good thing. Deuce was a few bricks shy of a load. Funny how many people that Edward introduced me to were.

"Who's out there, Undertaker?" Simon asked.

Edward had put his hat back on. It looked funny with the shirt gone, but he seemed perfectly at ease. If he was nervous, you couldn't tell it.

"I am going to ask you this, one more time nice, then it won't be so nice." He seemed to square his shoulders as if he were the one about to take a beating. "Who was on the other end of this wire? Who's out there?"

Edward shook his head.

Simon nodded.

Rooster hit him in the back, and it must have been hard because it drove him to his knees. Something on the butt of the gun broke the skin in two small cuts. He stayed on all fours for a few seconds as if it had stunned him, then he got up, on his feet and faced Simon.

"Answer the question, Undertaker."

Edward shook his head, again. He was ready for the next blow. It staggered him, but he didn't go down. There was a third small cut. The cuts weren't anything, but they showed how much force was being used. He was going to be bruised all to hell come morning.

"Maybe she knows," Mickey said.

"I don't know who they are," I said, and the lie fell smoothly off my tongue. "Edward said we needed backup. He found some."

"You'd come into a situation like this with unknown people at your back? You don't seem that stupid," Simon said.

"Edward vouched for them," I said.

"And you trust him?"

I nodded.

"You trust him with your life?"

"Yes," I said.

Simon looked at me, then back to Edward. "She your squeeze?"

Edward blinked, and I knew that was him trying to buy time to think what answer would be the least painful. "No."

"I'm not sure I believe you, either of you, but if we start beating up the bitch, and she gets too hurt to do the spell, Riker'd be pissed."

"Why don't you have Undertaker ask the backup to come in?" Deuce said.

Everyone sort of froze, then looked at him. Simon said, "What did you say?"

"If they can hear us, why not have him ask them to come up, hands up, that sort of thing."

Simon nodded, then turned back to Edward. "Tell them to come up to the house. Hands where we can see them."

"They won't come," Edward said.

"They'll come or we'll blow your fucking head off." Simon put the short-butted gun to his shoulder, and put the barrel against Edward's forehead. "Ask them to come into the house. Hands up. Throw their guns down."

It was funny how Simon had never once thought it might be the police out there, as if he didn't believe the Undertaker would bring the police to the party.

Edward stared down the barrel of that gun, looked past it, into Simon's eyes, and the look was his usual look. His eyes were cold and empty as winter skies. There was no fear. There was no anything. It was like he wasn't there at all.

Edward may have been calm, but I wasn't. I'd seen enough bad men to know that Simon meant it. More than that, he wanted to do it. He'd feel safer if Edward were dead. I was out of ideas, but I couldn't just stand here and watch it happen.

"Tell them, Undertaker, or I will blow your head all over this porch."

"Even if I asked, they wouldn't come."

Simon pressed the barrel in, so that Edward had to brace his feet against it to keep from being pushed backwards. "You better hope they come. We don't need you alive, just her."

"I need him alive," I said.

Simon's eyes flicked to me, then settled back on Edward. "Lying bitch."

"Are you a witch, Simon?" I asked, though I knew the answer. I'd have spotted it if he had been a practitioner.

"What the fuck does that matter?"

"Then you don't know what I need to do this spell, do you? Your boss would be pissed if you blew away someone I needed to keep him safe from the monsters."

"Why do you need him?" Deuce asked.

I swallowed and tried to think, nothing good was coming. I tried for truth. When I'm out of other options, it still works. "Riker said he wouldn't hurt the kids. He said he wouldn't hurt us. He said he just wanted me to save him from the monster. If you blow . . . Ted's brains into the next county, then I'm not going to believe any of Riker's other promises. The second I think that Riker is going to kill the kids and us once I do the job, then I don't have any incentive to help him."

Simon's eyes flicked to me again. "We can give you incentive." I didn't see him nod, but I felt Mickey moving behind me. I've never been good at taking a blow. I moved without thinking and he missed my shoulder, but I'd been right. He knew how to fight. I was turning towards him to do what, I'm not sure, when the butt of the gun caught me on the chin. I think I'd made him mad by ducking because he hit me hard.

The next thing I knew I was on the ground, looking up. Deuce was kneeling by me, stroking my face. I had the impression he'd been petting me for awhile, as if I'd passed out. I didn't remember passing out. The sunglasses were gone. I didn't know if Deuce took them off, or if they flew off when my head went back.

"She's awake," Deuce said, voice sort of dreamy. He gave me a gentle smile and kept stroking my face.

Simon knelt by me, blocking out the light. "What's your name?"

"Anita, Anita Blake."

"How many fingers?"

I watched his hand move back and forth, following it with my eyes. "Two."

"Can you sit up?"

It was a good question. "With help, maybe."

Deuce put his arm behind my back and lifted me. I let him take a lot of the weight, not because it was necessary, but because them thinking I was more hurt than I was might make them think I was less of a threat. We needed some sort of edge.

I rested against Deuce's shoulder. He was humming something tuneless under his breath, his hand cupping my face, stroking the skin, over and over. I was finally able to see everything. Edward was on his knees with his hands clasped on top of his cowboy hat. Rooster had a gun touching his head. Edward didn't look hurt. More like they'd done it to keep him from doing anything heroic.

Mickey had a bloody lip. He was carefully not making eye contact with anyone.

"Can you stand?" Simon asked.

"With help, yeah."

"Deuce."

Deuce helped me to my feet, and the world wavered. I clung to Deuce, hands digging in as the world tried to slide out my ear. Maybe I wasn't pretending to be hurt.

"Shit," Simon said. "Can you walk if Deuce helps you?"

I started to nod, and that made me nauseated. I had to breathe through it before I could answer him. "I think so."

"Good. Let's go." He backed into the house, eyes watching the darkness beyond, though with all the lights his night vision was probably shit. Deuce and I went next. He had Edward's wire hung around his neck like a doctor's stethoscope. Edward was next, hands still firmly on top of his head. Rooster, then Mickey bringing up the rear. They staggered us so that if someone started shooting, there was room to maneuver.

Simon started up a flight of stairs. I looked up the long flight and the world swam. Deuce called, "Simon, I'm not sure she's up to stairs."

"Mickey." The man in question moved up to the foot of the stairs. "Carry her."

"I don't want him touching me," I said.

"I didn't ask you, either of you," Simon said.

Mickey gave his gun to Simon, then took my arm. He pulled me too fast and I was suddenly airborne on his shoulder, my head hanging down. I couldn't breathe. The world was spinning, and I was going to be sick.

"I'm going to throw up."

He dumped me unceremoniously back to my feet, and I fell. It was Simon who caught me. "Are you too hurt to do the spell'?"

I knew the answer to that one—no. Because if Riker thought I couldn't help him, he would kill us all. "I can do it if Mickey here doesn't dangle me over his shoulder with my head hanging down. I need to stay upright, or it's not going to get any better."

"Carry her in your arms, not over your shoulders," Simon said. "All those muscles got to be good for something."

Mickey picked me up in his arms like you'd carry a small child. He stood there like I weighed nothing. He was strong but carrying like this is harder than it looks. We'd see how he did if there was more than one floor to climb. Here's hoping he didn't drop me.

I put my arm around his shoulders. I'd have clasped hands around his neck to be more secure, but I couldn't reach around his deltoids without straining. "How much do you bench press?"

"Three-ninety."

"I'm impressed," I said.

He preened a little. Mickey was dangerous, but if I could keep him from hitting me, he was the weak one. Rooster followed orders too well. Simon was Simon. Deuce seemed harmless, but there was something in those dreamy eyes that was a little scary. Maybe I was wrong, but I'd try Mickey before I tried Deuce, for trickery anyway. Arm wrestling, I'd take Deuce.

Mickey walked up the stairs with me in his arms, effortlessly. I could feel the muscles in his legs pushing, working. Again, I had the sense of immense physical potential and quickness.

"What's Mickey mean?" I asked.

"Nothing."

"Simon explained his nickname, I'm just wanting to know what yours means."

Deuce answered. "It's for Mickey Mouse."

"Shut up, Deuce."

"He's got a tattoo of Mickey on his butt," Deuce said as if Mickey hadn't spoken.

Mickey's face darkened, and he turned to glare at the other man. I just fought to keep my face blank. What kind of moron would have Mickey Mouse tattooed on his butt? But not out loud, not with those tree trunk arms wrapped around my tender body. If I hadn't had the marks on me, he'd have probably killed me with that one blow. No, I didn't want Mickey angry with me.

There was a landing, and a second flight of stairs. Mickey didn't even hesitate on the landing. He just went for the next set of stairs. His legs moved as easily up the second set as the first. He never paused to catch his breath. In fact, his breathing barely sped up. Whatever you could complain about Mickey, being out of shape wasn't part of it.

I told him so. "How far you jog a day?"

"Five miles, every other day. How'd you know?"

"A lot of body builders would be having trouble by now. They neglect the aerobic stuff, but you move like some kind of well-oiled machine. You're not even breathing hard." There was something very intimate about being carried in someone's arms like this, a reminder of childhood and your parents' arms maybe.

Mickey's hands tightened on me; the one on my thigh began to massage my leg. I didn't tell him not to. It's been my experience that if a man is interested in having sex with you, they hesitate to kill you before they've had the sex. This rule is not always true, but more often than not. The trick is to get the man thinking more about sex than violence, so he's a little confused. We needed a little confusion among our enemies right now.

We were in a wide white hallway that ran the length of the top of the house. There were white doors with silver knobs. Nothing differentiated one door from the other. Simon went to the furthest door, and Mickey followed with me in tow. I could see Deuce following, and Edward just topping the last stairs with Rooster behind him, walking well back out of arm's or leg's length. These guys were good. I'd gotten to where I counted on the bad guys not being this good. Even if they were vampires and werewolves they'd be unprofessional. But I'd never been around professional bad guys that were this professional. It cut our options from bad to worse.

Simon opened the door. We were here. We were still alive. The night still had possibilities.

56

MICKEY sat me down near the middle of a very nice Persian rug. He kept an arm around my shoulder, as if it had been his idea to carry me. I gave his arm a squeeze before I stepped away from him. Didn't want to be slutty, but wanted him hopeful in case it was useful. The room looked like the study of a prosperous academic. There were antique maps framed on the walls. Shelves lined almost every extra space of wall, a lot of books that looked well read and well used. There were books open on the big leather-topped desk with bookmarks in them and sticky notes covered in writing, as if we'd interrupted someone's research.

A man sat behind the desk. He was a big man, both tall and wide. Not fat exactly but headed that way. He rose from his chair with a smile and walked towards us, hand outstretched. He moved with a confident, easy stride, like an ex-athlete going soft with normal living. His dark hair was cut very short and mostly bald on top. His hands were big, and the new weight showed in the hands where a college ring was beginning to cut into his flesh. He had calluses on his hands like he wasn't afraid to do the real work himself, but the calluses were losing that hard edge, softening, smoothing back into his skin. He'd probably done some of his dirty work once, but no more.

He gripped my hand with both of his, when one of his hands could have swallowed both of mine. "So glad you're here, Ms. Blake." He said it like I'd been invited instead of blackmailed.

"I'm glad one of us is glad I'm here," I said.

The smile widened, and he let my hand go. "I am sorry for our little theatrics. Simon called up and said he thought Mickey had broken your neck. So happy that he exaggerated."

"Not by much, Mr. Riker."

"Are you feeling well enough to do the spell? We could have some tea first, let you rest."

I managed a smile. "I am grateful that we're being all civilized, and coffee would be great, but where are the children?"

His eyes flicked past me to Edward. He still had his hands clasped on top of his hat, but at least they hadn't made him kneel again. "Ah, yes, the children."

I didn't like the way he said it, like it was going to be bad news.

"Where are they?" Edward asked, and Rooster hit him in the back with the gun again. It staggered him, and he had to wait for it to pass before he straightened up. His hands never left his head, as if he knew they were looking for an excuse to hurt him again.

"You promised us that they wouldn't be harmed," I said.

"You were late," Riker said.

"No," Edward said.

"Don't," I said, as Rooster raised his arm back for another blow. He did it anyway. Fuck. I turned back to Riker. "Every cruel thing you do helps convince me that you have no intention of any of us getting out of here alive."

"I assure you, Ms. Blake, that I intend to let you go."

"What about the others?"

He gave a small shrug, and walked back behind his desk. "Unfortunately, my men think that Mr. Forrester is too dangerous to be allowed to live. I do regret that." He sat down at his nice swivel chair, elbows on the chair arms, thick fingers steepled. "But he will serve a useful purpose before he dies. If you are reluctant, we will take it out on Mr. Forrester. Since we intend to kill him anyway, we can do anything we want to him, and it doesn't really matter."

My stomach was a hard knot, my pulse beating in my throat hard enough that I had to try twice to talk. "What about the kids?"

"Do you really care?"

"I'm asking, aren't I?"

He reached behind the desk and pressed something. The rear walls of the room slid open, revealing enough equipment to make NASA proud. There were four blank TV screens, but somehow I didn't think this was Riker's new Digital Television system.

"What the hell is all that for?" I asked.

"That is not really your concern. I have signaled for additional men to be brought up. When they arrive, then I will show you the children."

"Why the additional men?" I asked.

"You'll see," he said.

We didn't have long to wait. Four men came through the door. Two I recognized: Harold of the scarred face and Newt who I'd nearly made a soprano. Harold had a shotgun, and Newt his big nickel-plated .45. But it was the two men behind them that were the problem.

One was tall and planed down to nothing but muscle and dark, burnished skin. He didn't have Mickey's bulk, but he didn't need it. He entered the room surrounded by a cloud of his own violent potential. He set my lizard sense screaming, as if it knew here was someone to avoid. He had the same gun the other pros were carrying, but he'd added knives. At his forearms, his upper arms, both hips, and even hilts sticking up from behind his shoulders. It was very primitive somehow and very effective. If he'd walked into a cell, you might have dropped to your knees and begged for mercy.

The other one was just medium height, medium brown hair cut short, not too dark, not too light, not too anything. He had a face that you wouldn't remember two seconds after you saw it, because he was not handsome enough or ugly enough to stand out. He was one of the most unmemorable people I'd ever seen, and yet when his brown eyes swept over me, met mine for a second, I felt a jolt all the way down to my feet. One flash, and I knew that of the two men, he would kill you quicker.

He had the same submachine gun the others had, but paired with what looked like a .10 mil automatic. I didn't recognize the brand. My hands aren't big enough for a .10 mil so I don't pay that much attention.

"Simon, I want two men on both of our guests."

"Make it four on him," Simon said.

"I bow to your expertise."

Rooster made Edward get on his knees. Simon made Mickey go to Edward. I guess he didn't want to risk the Muscle Man hitting me again. If they killed Edward early, they still had the kids to blackmail with. Simon sent the medium man to Edward, and Simon himself took up a post by Edward. They thought he was a very dangerous man, and they were right.

The nausea had been fading, but all the preparations were making me nervous. I was afraid of what we were going to see. If they hadn't been afraid to show us, they wouldn't have had four men on Edward. I was left with Deuce and the knife guy. Harold and Newt stayed near the door. Harold seemed nervous.

Deuce touched my arm, tracing the mound of scar tissue at my elbow. "What did it?"

"Vampire."

He raised his shirt up, and his stomach was a mass of white scars. "Mortar round."

I wasn't sure what I was supposed to say. But I was saved from the decision because the knife guy grabbed my arm and turned me to look at Riker. He kept his hand on my arm, and since his hand completely encircled my upper arm, it wasn't going to be easy to get away.

"Show time," Riker said. He hit another switch, and two of the monitors flickered to life. Black and white film of cells. At first, all I saw was Russell's back in one room, and the Amazon Amanda's back in the other room. Then my eyes saw legs sticking out from around the woman. Legs in jeans and jogging shoes, ankles tied together. Too big for Becca. Had to be Peter.

She'd stripped down to the waist, and that broad muscular back made everyone in this room look frail except for Mickey. It was only the length of her hair that made me guess her. She leaned forward, revealing more of Peter's body. She'd pulled his jeans and underwear down to his knees. She was playing with him.

I looked at the floor, then back up.

She tried to kiss him, and when he turned his head away, she slapped him twice hard, first one cheek then the other. There was already blood on his mouth as if it wasn't the first time she'd hit him. She leaned back in for the kiss, revealing small tight breasts to the camera. She kissed him and this time he let her. Her hand never stopped working on his body.

I turned slowly to look at the other monitor. Please, God, please, don't let Russell be doing the same thing to Becca. He wasn't, and I was grateful. He'd turned with her on his lap, as if he knew he had an audience to play to now. He cradled her like you'd hold any small child, but he'd pinned one small arm, and two of the fingers on the tiny hand were at a bad angle. He broke a third finger while we watched, and her mouth opened in a soundless scream.

"Shall we have sound?" Riker asked.

Becca was screaming high and piteous. Russell cradled her and murmured soothing things. He stroked her hair and looked directly at the camera. His nose was still packed and bandaged. He knew we were there.

Peter's voice came high. He'd never sounded more like a little boy. "Please, don't. Please stop!" His arms were tied behind his back, but he was still struggling.

She slapped him. "It'll feel good, I promise."

I looked at Edward. Simon had the gun against his head. The hat was on the ground. The medium-looking man had conjured a knife from somewhere and had it pressed to Edward's throat. A trickle of blood slid down his skin. I met his eyes, and I knew that everyone in this room, everyone in this house was dead. They just didn't know it yet.

Edward started to say something, but Simon said, "No, no talking from you or Shooter will slit your throat."

The medium guy must be Shooter. The name didn't suit him. He looked more like a Tom, Dick, or Harry.

They wouldn't let Edward talk, so it was my play, but we both knew where the game would end. Sudden death.

"Get them out of there, Riker."

"The children?" He gave a questioning lilt to his voice.

"Order them to leave the kids alone, now."

"And if I don't?"

I smiled. "Then the monster is going to come in here and gut you."

His eyes flinched. That bothered him. Good. "Knowing what is happening to them should speed up the spell of protection, I think."

"If you don't stop it, Riker, there won't be anything left to salvage."

"I don't know. I think the boy is enjoying himself, from the sound of things."

I'd been trying not to hear, but Peter's breath was coming faster and faster, frantic, but it wasn't the sound of pain. He screamed, "Don't, please don't."

I looked and I wished I hadn't. Some sights cut through your mind leaving a scar behind that never really heals. Watching Peter writhe caught between his first pleasure and the horror of it all, was one of those sights. I pride myself on never flinching. If someone is being tortured I don't look away. To look away only saves me pain, not them. If I can't save them the pain, then I watch as a kind of respect and as a punishment for myself, to remind me what happens to people when I fail them. But I failed Peter twice because I looked away just before a wordless scream tore form his mouth. It wasn't the sound of pain.

I turned away, and maybe I moved too fast for the head injury, or maybe it was something else, because the room swam in streamers of color. I tried to go to my knees, and the knife man jerked my arm, kept me on my feet. Fine, I threw up on him.

He jerked back, actually let go of my arm. I fell to my knees grateful to be low to the ground. Throwing up had brought a roaring headache. Riker's voice came through the next wave of nausea.

"Amanda, Russell, be so good as to leave the children alone. Our Ms. Blake is too squeamish to do her work while she fears for their safety."

I looked up at the monitors to make sure they actually left the rooms. Russell kissed Becca on the head, then left her huddled in the corner, crying for her mommy. Amanda blindfolded Peter while he begged her not to. She whispered something in his ear that caused him to curl into a ball. She left his pants down, picked up her shirt from the floor and walked out.

I huddled into my own version of a ball on the floor. I stayed on my knees while I tried to decide whether I was going to throw up again or not. Nausea like this is usually a sign of a concussion. The headache was another. But I think sheer nerves had pushed me over the edge. I used to throw up at crime scenes quite a bit. Apparently, there were still things I couldn't handle, like child abuse. Dear God, please give us some help here. Help us get them out of here safe.

There was a beeping, and Riker hit another button on his desk. "What is it?"

"We've got two dead down here. They were fucking butchered."

Riker went pale. "The monster."

"Knives, some kind of fucking big knife."

"You're sure of that?" Riker asked. "You are positive?"

"Yes, sir."

"It seems we have intruders." He looked at Simon. "What are you going to do about our company, Simon?"

"Kill them, sir."

"Then do it."

"Shooter, Rooster, stay with him and kill him as soon as Riker gives the word. Mickey, you're with me." He looked across at the two men by me. "You stay with her. Make sure no one else hits her. Harold, Newt, come with me."

Then they were gone, and we were down to two bad guys a piece, and Riker. It would never get better than this.

"Is there a bathroom?" I asked.

"Are you going to be ill again?"

"It's a thought."

"The two of you take her. And Deuce, if you can come up with something creative that won't leave a mark or physically harm Ms. Blake in any way, but will convince her that the children and Mr. Forrester are not the only ones that can be hurt, do so. Perhaps you can show her your namesake. You've got thirty minutes."

There aren't a lot of things you can do to a person that fulfilled Riker's requirements. The ones I could think of were mostly sexual. Usually, the talk of my impending rape upsets me, but all I could think of now was that I had thirty minutes with two men who might want to fuck me more than kill me. All I wanted to do was kill them. It made my options easier. But I said, "Is there a reason for torturing me, too, or is it just a hobby?"

He smiled, pleasant, confident. "I thought you would be worthy of my men, but I find you weak, Ms. Blake. Weakness should be punished. But it must be done carefully, so you can still do the spell, because I do want that."

"Isn't the line, these things must be done delicately or you injure the spell?"

Deuce laughed. Riker frowned at me. "It's from *The Wizard of Oz*," Deuce said. "The Wicked Witch of the West says it to Dorothy."

"Take her away, Deuce," he wrinkled his nose, "and clean yourself up, Blade. You're welcome to help in the punishment, but Deuce is in charge. I don't want her damaged."

Deuce grabbed my arm almost gently and helped me to my feet. The guy I'd thrown up on, Blade, followed us by a few steps. Evidently, he was taking no chances. At the door a man appeared. He was darkly Hispanic with longish hair, a shoulder holster, complete with .9 millimeter automatic. He looked like local hired muscle, but he wasn't. He vibrated with power. A shimmering energy flowed off of him. Psychic or maybe more.

"Ms. Blake, meet our resident expert on the supernatural, Alario. He was in charge of the protection spells on all my establishments. His art failed him recently at one of my shops, and my workers are dead. You will succeed where he has failed."

Alario watched me with cool dark eyes. His power flared over mine as Deuce led me past him. We recognized each other as powers, but there wasn't time for anything else, but there would be later. Which was what I was afraid of. Alario was the real deal, a practitioner of the arts. He'd figure out pretty quickly that I didn't know shit about spells of protection, at least not the kind Riker wanted.

Deuce led me down the white hall, with Blade trailing us. We were out of time. I couldn't go back into that room and fake a spell. Olaf had failed to make his kills horrendous enough to fool the bad guys. The only good thing he'd done was divide their forces, and I had to take advantage of that while it lasted. Which meant that if at all possible only one person was coming back from the bathroom. Hopefully, it would be me.

57

IT WAS ONE of those bathrooms with a double sink separate from the rest of the bathroom. Deuce led me into the little bathroom area, complete with shower. I managed to do some dry heaving, but that was the best I could do, and even that made my head ache. It hurt so much I closed my eyes trying to keep my brains from leaking out through them. If it wasn't a concussion, it was a hell of an imitation.

Deuce wet a washcloth and gave it to me.

"Thanks." I put it over my face and tried to think. So far, Deuce hadn't touched me. Blade was trying to clean up in the sink area, but he'd want the shower soon.

"I loved the look on Blade's face when you puked on him. It was priceless."

I put the wash rag to the back of my neck. I was thinking furiously about what was in the purse and what options I had. But my voice was calm, point for me. "Blade? As in the comic book character?"

He nodded. "Yeah, the vampire killer. They both carry knives."

"And they're both African American," I said.

"Yeah."

I looked into his face, wash cloth that he'd so kindly given me still on my neck. I tried to read behind those pleasant, slightly dreamy, brown eyes, but it was like trying to read Edward. I just couldn't read between the lines.

"I think that Blade actually used wooden knives and like a cross-bow in the comic books," I said.

Deuce shrugged. "You're either very brave, or you don't think I'll hurt you."

"I believe you'll hurt me, if you want to."

"Then you're brave," he said. He was leaning against the wall, fingers playing lightly with the gun on its sling at his shoulder.

It was my turn to shrug. "Yeah, but it's not really bravery that's keeping me calm."

He looked interested for the first time. "What is?"

"After what I saw being done to Becca and Peter, I just can't get too excited about myself."

Blade banged on the door. "We don't have all night, and I want a shower."

Deuce and I both jumped when he banged on the door. We shared one of those embarrassed smiles, then he opened the door and ushered me through.

Blade had tried to scrub at his clothes in the sink, but it hadn't helped. He tried to go through the door, and Deuce stepped in his way. "Riker won't like you taking a shower."

"He told me to get cleaned up."

"Simon told us to keep two people on her. We can't do that if you're in the shower."

Blade looked at me. "I think Simon overestimated her. Anyone that throws up after seeing mild torture like that, I'm not afraid of. Now get out of my way, Deuce."

Deuce moved to one side, moving just ahead and to one side of him. Blade brushed past us without a word, his anger trailing behind him like a loose coat. He slammed the door behind him.

I went to the sink and rewet the wash cloth. He was watching me in the mirror now. His eyes were still pleasant, but something else had crept in. Something that promised pain, the way the wind can bring the smell of rain against your skin just before it starts to pour.

I started fishing in the purse. "I've got some breath stuff in here somewhere."

"I could lock you in the room with Blade. He strips real pretty, and he's not very happy with you right now."

My hand closed on the pen with its hidden blade.

"You really think he could control himself enough to just rape me and not do other damage? Like you said, he's not very happy with me."

"You never asked about my nickname," he said.

The conversation was moving too fast for me. "I assumed it was some kind of card-playing thing."

He shook his head while I watched him in the mirror. Then he started unzipping his pants. He was too far away to touch me, or for me to fight back. All I could do was wait for him to come to me.

He slipped inside his open fly and lifted himself out in a smooth practiced movement. He was huge, impressive even limp and soft. If I hadn't seen Bernardo earlier, I'd have been more impressed. Of course, you could never be a hundred percent sure how big a man got when he was erect. Some barely changed size. Some grew a lot. Maybe he'd been very impressive. Then I realized he had a tattoo on it.

I had to turn and look, rather than trust to the mirror. "Am I supposed to run screaming or ask to touch it?" I wasn't even scared. It was too bizarre.

"Which do you want to do?"

I admit I was having a hard time looking at his face and not his penis because it was growing, and I could see the tattoo more clearly. "Can't rape the willing, hey?"

He smiled, as if this approach had worked before with women. It was certainly something a girl didn't get offered everyday. "I won't tell, if you don't."

"Is that the two of hearts on your . . . penis?"

His smile widened.

"Didn't that hurt?"

"Not as much as it's going to," Deuce said. He moved slowly towards me, so I could get a good look. He had a flair for theatrics, did Deuce. I didn't want him using his flair or anything else on me. I turned and stumbled on purpose. He caught me, as he'd caught me all the other times. I put the pen against his chest, just under the sternum, angled upward. I was a vampire hunter. If there was one thing I knew how to do, it was to find the heart with the first blow.

I pressed the button the second I touched him. There was no upward movement, no feel of shoving the blade, because the blade did its own work.

His eyes went wide, mouth opened, but no sound came out. I twisted the blade left, then right, making sure he'd never draw breath to warn the man in the other room.

Deuce started to slide down the cabinets. I caught him and lowered him gently to the floor, glad he was one of the smaller men. I'd have had trouble wrestling Mickey's body around. The water was still running in the shower. Blade probably wouldn't have heard the sound of the body hitting the ground over the shower, but better safe than sorry.

Deuce lay there on the floor, the blade sticking out of his chest, his pants still unzipped, his namesake naked to the world. He looked very sad lying there dead. If I had time before I left, I'd zip him up, but first Blade. I got the gun off Deuce's shoulder and put the sling around my shoulder. I checked to make sure I knew where the safety was, and that it was off. The switch on the side had three settings, not just two like the Uzi. I put the setting on high. Logic said it would make the most bullets come out in the shortest space of time. I got Duece's extra clip for the sub gun. A clip only holds twenty rounds. Normally, that sounded like a lot, but not tonight. There wasn't enough ammo in the world to make me feel safe tonight. I put the extra clips for both sub guns and the hand guns in the purse and crossed the purse straps across my chest.

Deuce's backup was a .9 mm Glock. Personally, I find Glocks awkward to shoot, though I know people that swear by them, once the learning curve was over at the firing range. But I was happy to see this one.

The guns were great, but they would make a lot of noise. If I shot Blade, it would bring the rest of the bad guys down on me, and worse yet, they might kill Edward before coming after me. They had three hostages. They only needed one.

I needed something quiet. Trouble was I didn't think I could take Blade with a blade. Hand to hand, forget it. That left me with the contents of the purse.

I pulled the blade out of Deuce's chest. Blood welled up darker than most, like heart blood is supposed to be. I cleaned the blade automatically on a sleeve of his shirt and slipped it into my front pocket.

One of his hands was lying against the cabinet doors far under the sink. Maybe I did have more than just what was in the purse. I moved his arm and looked. It's amazing how much lethal stuff people keep in their bathroom cabinets. Almost everything has hazardous warning labels, yelling poison, caustic agent, if accidental contact with eyes, flush with water immediately. But there was a pile of big, fluffy towels, and I had Deuce's handgun. Homemade silencer. But I was going to have to hold the gun at about waist level, close into my body, to keep the towels tight enough to act as a muffler. Holding the gun that way meant I'd want to get in close before I fired. If Blade were as good as the rest of them, he'd have his gun close. I'd only get one shot, and it had to count.

How do you get that close to a well-armed man? Answer—take off some clothes. I took off the T-shirt and the vest. It wouldn't stop a knife, and the idea was that he wouldn't get a shot off, right? Besides, I was trying for romance or at least lust. Kevlar just lacks that certain something.

I kept the bra. My nerves weren't that good. Besides, if he demanded I take some clothes off, it left me something besides my pants. It was like playing strip poker. More clothes give you more to work with.

The shower went off. Shit. My time had just run out. My heart was suddenly in my throat. But I had to get in there, before he came out here. If he saw the body, it wasn't rape I had to worry about.

I tucked the gun down the front of my pants, towels clutched to my chest and stomach, and opened the door. I closed the door with me leaning against it. Blade looked up. His dark skin was beaded with water, and Deuce had been right. Blade stripped real pretty. Under other circumstances, it would have been a pleasure to see him. Now, I was so scared I was having trouble breathing.

He reached for the gun that had been propped against the tub. His knife sheaths were draped across the back towel rack like you'd hang a wash rag, to keep them dry but handy. He stopped in mid-motion, fingers trailing on the gun.

"What do you want?"

"Deuce said to bring you towels." I let the fear slide into my voice, making it breathy.

"How'd he get you to strip down?"

I looked down, an embarrassed head bob. "He gave me a choice of him or you."

Blade laughed, and it was a purely masculine sound. "He show his deuce?"

I nodded. I didn't have to pretend to be embarrassed. I just didn't try and hide it.

"Take off the bra." He straightened up, hand going further away from the big gun, but still too close to the knives and his handgun on the towel rack.

I slid out of the straps, and pressed the towels to my chest, reached back and undid the snaps. I lifted the towels away from my body just enough to pull the bra out and let it fall to the floor. I kept the towels tight against me, for modesty's sake, and to hide the gun in my waistband.

He stepped out of the tub and started to take those three steps that would close the distance. I turned my body, sort of sideways, getting the gun out, still held behind the towels.

He was right in front of me, three steps away from all his weapons. He curled his fingers over the top of the towel and pushed them lower, exposing my breasts an inch at a time. He was less than ten inches away from me. His hand stroked the upper mound of my breast, and I fired. His body jerked, and I think he said, "Fuck." I kept pulling the trigger until he collapsed to his knees, eyes rolled back. His stomach and lower chest were a red ruin. The towels were shredded, and covered in black powder stains. The shots had been muffled, but not silenced. I waited there in the small room, the shots seeming to echo in the walls. I waited for cries of alarm. Nothing.

I picked up my bra, but didn't take time to put it on, before I opened the connecting door and listened. Silence. Great. I got dressed and took all the weapons. Blade's handgun was a Heckler and Koch. Nice gun. I tucked it in the front of my pants where the Firestar would have normally gone. I put both the big guns over the same shoulder, and the knife sheaths I draped over the other shoulder. I brought the sub-gun around, clicked the safety off, and I was as ready as I was going to be.

The last time I'd seen Edward, he'd been on his knees. His two guards had been standing. If I was careful and the gun didn't kick too much, I could take them out over Edward's head. My plan was to spray the room. As plans went, it was crude, and secrecy would be very lost if we were within hearing of anyone, but once I knew the noise wasn't going to get Edward killed, I didn't care as much.

They'd have killed Edward because he was a threat, and they'd want to take out the threat at their back before turning to face a new threat. The kids weren't a threat. If Riker was dead and couldn't give the order to hurt them, then they'd be okay until we reached them. That was the theory, and it was the best one I had.

Bristling with weapons, I listened at the outer door. Nothing. I opened it just a little. The hallway was empty. Better. I locked the door behind me so that when I shut it, people might assume it was occupied by more than dead people. The knives moved too much slung over my shoulder, so I set them down in a pile against the wall, being as quiet as I could. The corridor that had seemed so long, now seemed short because this was one of those plans that was either going to work really well or be a total disaster. In less than two minutes, I'd be at the door, and we'd see.

58

THE GUN HAD a short stock, but I braced it against my shoulder, and my arms were short enough that it was probably easier for me than the men I took them off. I was only steps from the open study door. Voices came out into the hallway.

"What do you mean that Antonio and Bandit are missing?" That was Riker. "I thought your men were good, Simon."

Shit. Was Simon back in the room? It didn't matter. It didn't change the plan. But I'd have preferred that Simon be elsewhere, at least until Edward was safe and armed. But Simon's voice came tinny and staticy. It was the intercom system. Shit, I didn't want them to hear the shots. The best I could do was wait until I didn't hear him using it. The longer I lurked in the hallway, the less chance the plan had. Someone was going to come up the stairs or out of the room or out of the study. If I lost surprise, it was over.

I was scared, really scared, not about killing or being killed, but about accidentally shooting Edward. I had an unfamiliar submachine gun in my hands. I'd never even seen one like this used. If you aim too high with a machine gun, more the full machine guns, but the subs, too, you can actually miss. If I fired into that room and missed everyone, I guess I deserved to get shot. I took the last deep breath and eased around the door frame. I know people always stand in the middle of the freaking door in the movies, but that's a good way to get killed. Use cover when you have it.

I had a split second to see the room. Rooster and Shooter had Edward covered, still on his knees. Alario the Witch had moved beside Riker's desk. I started firing almost before I'd finished looking. The sound was enormous, but the gun had almost no recoil. I had to adjust my aim because I'd been expecting to have to fight the gun, but it was smooth, for a sub gun. Shooter actually got a burst off, but it was angled wrong and took out the ceiling above me. Rooster turned, but that was it. Seconds for both of them to go down, seconds to move the gun in a continuous spray that took out the control panels and monitors, and Riker, sitting behind his desk. Alario was the furthest away, and he had time to dive to the floor.

I went for the floor, too, hitting on my stomach as I aimed for him. I was angled away from Edward. I didn't have to be careful. I kept the trigger down and hit Alario before he could get a shot off. His body danced with the slap of bullets. There was something fascinating about the way the bullets shredded him, or maybe I just couldn't let go of the trigger.

I caught movement out of the corner of my eye and rolled on one shoulder, gun pointed. I let off the trigger just in time. Edward was kneeling with a gun in his hand by the bodies of his guards. He had a hand out as if to ward off the bullets, as if he hadn't been sure I'd remember in time.

We stayed that way for a frozen second, me on my side, the sub-gun pointed at him, finger still on the trigger, but not pressing down. Him with his hand out, the automatic pistol in his hand but pointed down.

His mouth moved, but I couldn't hear him. Part shock, adrenaline, and part firing a submachine gun without ear protection in a closed room. I eased to a kneeling position and stopped pointing the gun at him. He seemed to realize I was having trouble hearing because he held up two fingers and did thumbs down. Rooster and Shooter were dead. Hurrah.

I knew Alario was dead. I'd gone way overboard on him. I looked across the room at Riker. He was sitting in his chair, mouth gaping open and closed like a landed fish. The front of his nice white shirt and suit jacket were stained red in a row across the entire front of his body, including his arms. He was sitting so that I could see his hands clearly. I don't know if the force of the shots had pushed the wheeled chair back or he'd started that way.

Edward pointed at Riker, and I heard one word of the sentence, "Guard." He wanted me to guard Riker, not kill him. Of course, we needed to know where the children were being held. I hoped he didn't die before he told us.

My hearing came back in stages. I could hear Riker saying, "Please, don't." It was what Peter had been saying on the monitor. It pleased me that Riker was begging. Edward came back from checking the hallway. He had one of the sub-guns in his hands. He'd closed the door so that if we had company, we'd get a little warning.

By the time he started asking Riker questions, I could hear, but there was a ringing echo in my head that didn't seem to want to go away.

"Tell me where to find Peter and Becca?" Edward said. He was leaning on the back of Riker's chair, face very close to his.

Riker rolled his eyes to look at him. There was bloody foam at his lips. I'd pierced at least one lung. If it had been both, he was dying. If only one, then maybe he could survive if he got to the hospital soon enough.

"Please," he managed to say again.

"Tell me where the children are being kept, and I'll let Anita call an ambulance."

"Promise?" he said, in a voice thick with things that should never be in a throat.

"I promise, just like you promised me," Edward said.

Either Riker didn't get the double entendre, or he didn't want to. People will believe a lot of things when they're afraid they're dying. He believed we'd call an ambulance because he gave directions in that thick wet voice. He told us where they were being held.

"Thank you," Edward said.

"Call now," Riker said.

Edward put his face almost next to Riker's. "You want to be safe from the monster?"

Riker swallowed, coughed blood, and nodded.

"I'll keep you safe from the monster. I'll keep you safe from everything." And he shot Riker in the head with the Beretta .9 mil he'd reclaimed from Rooster's body. My guns were still on Mickey somewhere out there.

Edward felt for Riker's pulse and didn't find it. He looked at me across the man's body. I'd always thought Edward killed with coldness, but his baby blues held a fine, heated rage, like a forest fire barely under control. He was still in control of himself, but for the first time I wondered if there would come a point tonight where he'd lose it. You can only stay cool and collected when things don't matter. And Peter and Becca mattered to Edward. They mattered more than I'd have ever thought anyone would matter to him. Them and Donna, his family.

He told me to reload the sub gun. I did what he asked. If Edward said I'd nearly emptied an entire clip in just a few seconds, I believed him. I added the extra clip from the dead man to the purse.

Edward went for the door, and I followed him. I'd thought that nothing could be scarier than Edward at his most cold. I was wrong. Edward the family man was downright terrifying.

59

HOURS LATER, THOUGH my watch said thirty minutes, I was plastered to a wall, crouched as low as I could get, trying not to get shot. I knew that I originally started out to rescue the kids, and I still planned to do that, but my immediate plan was just to avoid catching a bullet. That had been the plan for about five minutes. I'd heard the expression a hail of bullets, but I'd really never understood what it meant. It was as if the very air had turned into a moving, spattering thing, where tiny fast-moving objects peppered the air around you, bit into the solid rock wall beyond and left holes. There were two submachine guns down the hall, pinning us in cross fire. I'd never been shot at by fully automatic machine guns before. I was so impressed, I hadn't done anything in the last five minutes except hug the wall, and keep my head down.

The secret panel had been exactly where Riker said it would be. Edward had killed the guard on the other side with a knife, quick, efficient. We'd killed two more men before Simon and his crew, or what was left of it, found us and started fighting back. I'd thought I was good at killing people. I'd thought I was good in a gunfight. I was wrong. If what was happening to me now was a gunfight, then I'd never been in one before. I'd shot people and been shot, but that had been one on one with semi-auto pistols. The bullets whined by me in a near constant stream of noise and percussion. I was so *not* putting my face out there.

It was pure luck that I hadn't been shot before we got this far. The only thing I'd been doing right that had helped my chances was using every freaking bit of cover offered. The one comfort to my new-found cowardice was that Edward was crouched with me, though he kept peeking around the corner and firing short bursts at the shooters that had us pinned.

He reached around me, firing. I could feel the vibration of the gun against my body, the tremble of his arms as he held it. He darted back behind the wall, and a fresh burst of bullets thundered down at us. Edward held his hand out and I handed him another clip from the purse. I felt like a surgical nurse.

I leaned close to Edward's ear and whisper-screamed, "You want the vest? I'm not using it."

"I've got a vest on." Deuce had kindly left Edward's vest in the study.

"You could put mine on your head," I said.

He actually smiled at me as if I'd been joking. He motioned for me to scoot over, an acknowledgment from both of us that I wasn't doing much. He took up my post at the corner of the wall, and I flattened my back where he'd been. He went to his belly, firing around the corner. It only took seconds for him to peek around the corner, fire and come back, but while he was staring down the corridor

I saw the tiniest corner of a head peek round the bend of the stairs just above us. The head ducked back out of sight.

I started to touch Edward, to let him know we had company, when something came sailing through the air. Something small and roundish. I don't remember thinking about it. I was just on my knees, letting the sub-gun dangle. I caught the object in my hands and threw it back up the stairs, before my brain even had time to form the word grenade. I threw myself back to the floor, touching Edward's leg, and then there was an explosion. The world shuddered, and the stairway collapsed in a shower of rock and dust. Rock rained down on my arms where I'd curled them over my head. I thought that if the bad guys came running down the hall now, I wouldn't be much help, which made me raise my head enough to see the corner and Edward.

He had his head covered by one arm, but was looking round the corner, gun in one hand. Of course, nothing would make Edward forget the bad guys, certainly not a little thing like an explosion and the ceiling about to come down on us.

The silence came gradually full of creaks and groans from the stones around us. The dust lay like a thin mist in the air. I started to cough, and Edward's hand was just suddenly on my mouth. How had he known? He gave a small shake of his head.

I got the idea that he wanted me to be quiet, but I didn't know why. Of course, I didn't need to know.

We lay quiet, and the silence seemed to build. Finally, I heard the first scrape of a footstep coming down the hall. I tensed, and Edward's hand pressed on my shoulder. Easy, he was saying, easy. I swallowed as quietly as I could and tried to relax. Quiet I could do. Relaxed was not happening.

The movements were stealthy, very quiet. Someone was creeping down the hallway towards us. Wondering if we'd gotten blown up. We were pretending that we had, but once the man got down here, the jig would be up. We could kill him, but there was another man at the end of the hall. If he didn't run out of ammo, he could hold the hall against us. He didn't want to come to us, and we needed to go down that hall. Becca and Peter were in cells in the hall. The bad guys had the upper hand because we needed to move forward, and all they needed to do was hold position.

Of course, one of them was coming to us.

Edward pantomimed for me to go forward and lie down. I knew he wanted me to play dead, but that far out from the wall was kill zone. If they started firing, even flat on the ground, I might be hit. But . . . I crawled forward through the debris, being very, very careful not to scrape any weapons or the purse against the floor or make the rocks roll. I was further out than I wanted to be when I looked back, and Edward gave one nod. I lay down on the floor, quietly. I lay face down because my acting abilities aren't up to playing dead. My hair flung across my face and I left it there, the better to peek through. I kept the sub-gun in my hand, but Edward shook his head. I let the gun go, moved my hand minutely away from it, and played dead. If Edward were wrong, I wouldn't be playing for long. I'd never get to the gun in time. Once the man cleared the corner, it was over.

I lay there and strained to hear movement. Mostly, what I heard was the thudding of my heart. Whoever it was, was being even quieter than before. Maybe he'd chickened out. Maybe he wasn't coming at all, and they'd start shooting again. I had to fight to keep still, not to move, not to breathe too much. I willed myself to relax into the floor, and I'd almost succeeded when I caught movement in the hallway. I was far enough out from Edward that I had a better view at the end of the hall. Would he see the shine of my eyes through my hair? I took in a deep breath, closed my eyes, and held it. Either Edward would kill him, or he'd kill me. I trusted Edward. I trusted Edward. I trusted Edward.

Noises, soft, slithering noises, the brush of cloth. Then a sharp exhale of breath. Nothing you'd hear from the other end of the hallway. Silence so thick it was frightening, but if Edward hadn't won, there would have been gunfire. I opened my eyes a slit, then wider, because Edward was kneeling over Mickey's body, searching it.

I must not have been the only one who thought the silence was a long one because a man's voice sounded, "Mickey, you okay?"

Edward answered, and it didn't sound like his voice. It wasn't a perfect imitation but it was good. "All clear."

"What's the roger?" the man asked. I didn't recognize the voice. One of Simon's men we had yet to meet face to face.

Edward looked at me and shook his head. I didn't know what a roger was, but apparently, we couldn't fake it, though Edward tried. "Get the fuck down here and help me search the bodies."

The answer to that was gunfire. I was already as low as I could get to the ground, but I tried to get lower. The bullets sprayed over me into the wall beyond, and the only thing that kept me from screaming was pride.

Edward gave one abrupt motion. I thought I knew what he wanted. When the shots ended, I belly crawled back towards the wall. I was actually almost there when he fired again. I froze in place, face to the ground. The firing ended, and I put my back to the wall on the other side of Mickey's body from Edward.

Mickey was still carrying my guns. I took them back.

Edward had a canister in his hand that looked suspiciously like the incendiary grenade they'd put in my purse, minus the camouflaging hairspray can. My eyes widened. He shook his head, as if reading my mind, and mouthed, "Smoke."

Okay.

He leaned over the body, and I leaned into him. He whispered, "Cover me while I throw it. Belly crawl down the hall. When you see anyone through the smoke, shoot them." Then he leaned back, pulled the pin on the smoke grenade, and stood with the wall still hiding him.

I crawled to him, hugging the wall and his legs, sub-gun clutched tight. My heart was inside my head, pounding away. I had time to think, "Gee, the headache's gone," then Edward said, softly, "Now."

I peeked around the corner, my finger on the trigger, spraying down the hallway. Edward threw the smoke grenade. He jerked back around the corner, and so did I. Thick white smoke filled the hallway. I dropped to my belly, behind the wall, waiting for the smoke to find me. Edward motioned that he'd take the other side, but he pointed forward for me. He combat crawled and was almost immediately lost to the thick smoke. The smoke was bitter, like burning cotton soaked in something bad.

I crawled with the wall on my left, the sub-gun held out in front of me. I had two guns shoved down the front of my jeans now, and it wasn't comfortable for crawling, but nothing could have persuaded me to stop and adjust them. The purse stayed solid against my back like a bulky backpack. The world had narrowed down to soft rolling smoke, the feel of the floor under my arms and legs, the brush of the wall against my left elbow when I moved too close to it. There was nothing but me moving down the hall, eyes trying to see anything in the white mass of clouds.

Nothing moved but me.

Then bullets ripped through the smoke, and I was close enough to see the flash of the gun through the smoke. I was almost on top of him, and he was firing chest high into the smoke. I was about ankle high and looking up at him. I could actually see him like a shadowy figure above me when I pressed the trigger and watched that shadow jerk. I rolled onto my side to sweep my fire line up his body, still afraid to stand or even kneel until I knew he wasn't firing back.

He collapsed to his knees, face suddenly looming out of the smoke. I fired nearly point blank into his chest, and he fell backwards half vanishing in the fading smoke, like he'd fallen into clouds. I stayed low and realized I could see his feet. The smoke was almost gone at floor level, which was one of many reasons that Edward had had us crawl.

"It's me," Edward said, before he crawled out of the smoke. He was wise to have warned me. My finger was still on the trigger, and I was beginning to appreciate how you could accidentally shoot your friends in a combat situation, unless you were very careful.

He moved a little way, and the smoke was thinning enough that I could see him check the man's pulse. "Stay here," and he was gone into the dying smoke.

It pissed me off, but I stayed on the floor by the man I'd killed and waited. I might have been pissed off, but we were in a kind of fighting that I knew almost nothing about. I'd somehow fallen into Edward's other life, and he was better at surviving here than I was. I was going to do what I was told. It was pretty much my only hope for getting out alive.

Edward came back, walking instead of crawling. Probably a good sign. "The area's clear, but it won't be for long." He held the keys we'd taken from Riker. "Let's do it."

He unlocked the cell that was supposed to be Peter's and went across the hall to Becca's before he did more than push the door open. I guess I was getting Peter. I dropped to one knee and pushed the door open until it was flat against the wall. See, no one hiding behind it. If there had been someone in the room, they'd have probably shot over my head. Kneeling, I was a lot shorter than most people. But a glance showed the room was empty except for the narrow bed with Peter on it.

I stood, debated for a second whether to shut the door and risk someone locking it behind me, or leave it open and risk someone coming up behind me with a gun. I left it open, not because it was the best option, but because I just didn't want the door shut on me in the cell. Part claustrophobia, part just having been locked in too many places waiting for things to eat me. Sometimes I think that last part contributes to the claustrophobia.

It had been bad on the black and white monitor, but it was worse in person. Peter was curled into the tightest ball he could manage. His hands tied behind his back, tied ankles tucked up tight to his bare butt. His clothes were still bunched around his knees, and the expanse of pale flesh looked incredibly vulnerable.

She'd meant to humiliate him, leaving him like this. The blindfold was still in place, cutting a bright patch of color across his dark hair. His mouth was stained with drying blood, his lower lip already swollen, bruises beginning to spread across his face like ugly lipstick from an overzealous kiss.

I didn't try to be quiet. I tried to hurry. He heard me coming because he started talking through the gag. I could understand him.

"Please, don't, please don't." He kept saying it over and over in a progressively more frantic voice until his voice broke, not from adolescence, but from fear.

"It's me, Peter," I said.

He didn't seem to hear me, just kept begging over and over.

I touched his shoulder, and he screamed. "Peter, it's Anita."

I think he stopped breathing for a heart beat, then he said, "Anita?"

"Yeah, I'm here to get you out."

He started to cry, thin shoulders shaking. I drew one of Blade's blades and fitted it carefully between his wrists, jerking upward. The cord sliced clean under the sharp, sharp blade. I tried to lift the blindfold off of him, but it was too tight.

"I'm going to have to cut the blindfold off, Peter. Don't move."

His breathing slowed, and he held still while I slid the blade between the cloth and the side of his head. It was harder to cut than the rope because it was tighter to his skin and just a bad angle. But the blade finally sliced through it, and the cloth fell away. I had an impression of red marks in his skin where the blindfold had marked him. Then he flung himself on me, hugging me.

I hugged him back, knife in one hand.

He whispered, "She said she was going to cut it off when she came back." He didn't start crying again. He just held on. I rubbed his back with my free hand. I wanted to give him comfort, but we had to get out of here.

"She won't hurt you anymore, Peter. I promise that, but we've got to get out of here." I pulled back from his desperate arms until I could see his face and he could see mine. I held his face in my hands, the knife carefully pointed up. I looked into his eyes. They were wide and shocky, but there wasn't much I could do about it now.

"Peter, we have to go. Ted's getting Becca, and we're leaving."

Maybe it was his sister's name, but he blinked and gave a small nod. "I'm okay," he said, which was the best lie I'd heard all night.

But I accepted it and said, "Good." I had to stand to reach the ropes at his ankles. He was just that tall or I was that short. The hug had put him facing forward, and he seemed suddenly aware that he was exposed. He started grabbing at his underwear and pants while I tried to cut his ankles free.

I had to pull the knife back. "If you don't hold still, you're going to end up cut."

"I want my clothes on," he said.

I stood at the foot of the bed, and said, "Get dressed."

"Don't look," he said.

"I'm not looking."

"But you're looking at me," he said.

"But I'm not *looking* at you." But I couldn't explain it to him, so I turned and looked at the door while he struggled into his pants.

"You can look now."

He had everything zipped and buttoned, and just that had taken some of the raw terror out of his eyes. I cut his ankles free, sheathed the knife, and helped him to his feet. He jerked away from me, then almost fell because the ankles had been tied too tight for too long, and he didn't have all the feeling back. Only my hand on his arm kept him upright.

"You need to walk a little with help before you can run," I said.

He let me help him to the door, but he wouldn't look at me. His first reaction had been that of a child, grateful to be saved, wanting to hold on to someone, but his second reaction was older. He was embarrassed now. Embarrassed at what had happened, and probably at me seeing him nearly naked. He was fourteen, a trembling age between child and adult. Somehow, I think he'd been younger when he went into the cell than when he came out.

Edward met us in the hallway with Becca held in his arms. She looked pale and sick. Bruises had already started blooming on her face. But it was her hand that made me want to cry. That tiny hand that I'd held only days ago, while Edward and I swung her in the air. Three of the fingers looked crippled, at unnatural angles. They were swelling, the skin discolored. It was early for that, which meant they were bad breaks and wouldn't heal easily.

She said, "Anita, you came to save me, too." Her voice was high and thin. It made my throat tight.

"Yeah, sweetie, I came to save you, too."

Peter and Edward stood staring at each other. It was Edward that reached out first, just his hand, because the arm was underneath Becca's legs. Peter took that hand and hugged them both. His fingers hovered over Becca's hand, and fresh tears fell down his face, but there was no sobbing now, just tears so quiet you wouldn't have known he was crying if you hadn't seen them.

"She'll be all right," Edward said.

Peter looked up at him, as if he wasn't sure he believed, but he wanted to. But he stepped away from them, rubbed the tears from his face with his hands. "Can I have a gun?"

I opened my mouth to say, no, but Edward spoke first. "Give him your Firestar, Anita."

"You're kidding," I said.

"I've seen him shoot. He can handle it."

I'd been following Edward's orders for a while. He was usually right but . . .

"If we go down, I want him armed." Edward looked at me, and the weight in his eyes was enough. He didn't want Peter and Becca taken again. If he put a gun in Peter's hand, they'd kill him not torture him. If the worst happened, Edward had decided how the boy would go out. And, God help me, I agreed.

I pulled the gun out of the band of my jeans. "Why the Firestar?"

"Smallest grip."

I handed it to Peter, feeling vaguely like a child molester myself, or maybe a corrupter. "It holds nine if you carry one in the chamber. It's only holding eight. Safety's here."

He took the gun and popped the clip out to check it, then looked vaguely embarrassed. "Ted says to always check if something's loaded." He popped the clip back in, put a round in the chamber so it was ready to fire.

"Try not to shoot any of us," I said.

He clicked the safety on. "I won't."

Looking into his eyes, I believed him.

"I want to go home," Becca said.

"We're going home, honey," Edward said.

Edward led the way around the corner still carrying Becca. Peter went next, and I brought up the rear. I didn't burst anyone's bubble, but I knew we were a long way from safe. We had Simon and the rest of his men to get through, not to mention Harold and Newt and the local guys. Where were Russell and Amanda? I was really hoping to see them before we left. I'd promised Peter that she would never hurt him again. I always keep my promises.

60

THE HALLWAY SPILLED OUT into a large open space. Edward stopped, and Peter and I did, too. Becca was still being carried, so she didn't have much choice. I kept an eye on our back trail and waited for Edward to decide what to do. I couldn't see how big the open space was, so I figured it was big enough for Edward to worry about us being out in that much open. He finally moved slowly forward, hugging the left-hand wall. When I could see the room clearly, I realized why he'd hesitated. It wasn't just this huge open space. There were three tunnels leading off to the right, dark mouths where anything might lurk, like Simon and the rest of his men. But there was a fourth opening with stairs leading up. Up was what we needed.

I walked with my back to the solid wall behind me, trying to keep an eye on the hall we'd come out of and the three tunnels to the right. I left the stairs to Edward.

The stairway was narrow, barely broad enough for two slender people to walk abreast. It wound upward and had a sharp angle at the top, a blind corner. I kept watching behind us, because I knew that if shooters came up behind us, and in front of us at the same time, we were dead. It was a perfect place for an ambush.

Peter seemed to feel the tension because he moved closer to Edward, almost touching him as they moved up the stairs. We were about three fourths of the way up to that first blind corner, when Edward hesitated, staring down at the steps. Peter took one extra step. Edward hit him with his shoulder, knocking him back. He dropped Becca to the steps, still holding her good arm, trying to save her from the full fall. I think if he'd just dropped Becca, he might have gotten them all out of harm's way, but that last effort cost him the second he needed.

I saw a blur of movement, and there was a wooden stake sticking out of Edward's back. I started to go to him, but he said, "Up the stairs, now. Shoot them."

I didn't ask questions. I went up the last few steps as fast as I could go and threw myself around the corner on my side, and was shooting down the hallway before I saw what I was shooting at.

Harold, Russell, Newt, and Amanda were running down another level of stairs. I fired up into them, fighting the angle to make the spray pattern hit them. The three men went down, but Amanda turned and darted back around the corner they'd come from. I made sure the men weren't getting up, firing into their down bodies, then I got to my feet and ran up the stairs after her. I crouched at the corner, but the stairs were empty. Fuck. I didn't dare pursue her and leave the kids and Edward alone.

I went back down the steps and slipped on blood so that I ended up sitting down hard on the steps, my elbow hit Harold's body, and the body grunted.

I put the barrel of the gun against his chest as his eyes fluttered open. "Didn't make the ambush site in time. Simon's going to be pissed," he said, and the tone of his voice said he was hurting.

"I don't think you have to worry about Simon anymore, Harold. You're not going to be around to answer to him."

"Never approved of hurting kids," he said.

"But you didn't stop it," I said.

He took a breath and that seemed to hurt, too. "Simon called someone on the radio. Said he'd failed. Said they needed to clean up the mess. I think they're coming to kill us all."

"Who's coming?"

He opened his mouth, and I think he'd have told me, but his breath ran out in a long sigh. I felt for the pulse in his neck, but it wasn't there. I'd known he was dead, but still you check. I checked Russell and Newt just to be sure, but they were dead. I actually left everyone's guns because I just couldn't carry anymore.

I heard voices as I neared the bend that would take me back to Edward. Fuck. Then I recognized one of the voices. It was Olaf.

I came around the corner and found Olaf and Bernardo kneeling by Edward. Peter was sitting on the steps holding Becca. She was crying. He wasn't. He was staring at Edward, face white with shock.

Bernardo spotted me first. "Are they dead?"

I nodded. "Russell, Newt, and Harold. Amanda got away."

Peter's eyes flicked to me, and they were huge and dark in his pale, pale face. The bruised mouth stood out against his skin like it was makeup, too bright to be real.

Edward made a small sound, and Peter turned back to him. "I'm sorry, Ted," he said. "I'm sorry."

"It's all right, Pete. Just next time follow my lead better." His voice was strained, but Peter seemed to take heart from talk of a next time. I wasn't so sure.

Olaf and Bernardo had turned him so that you could see the sharpened end of the stake that had pierced his chest. It was upper chest, close to the left shoulder. It had missed the heart or he'd be dead, but it could have pierced the sack around the heart, and blood could be spilling into that sack as we watched. Or it could have missed it entirely. It was high enough up that it had probably missed the lungs. Probably.

"How'd you know that they were coming?" I asked.

"Heard them," and his voice reminded me of Harold's, pain stressed.

I was suddenly cold, and it wasn't the temperature. I started to kneel by them all, but Edward said, "Watch our backs."

So I stood up, put my back to the wall, and let my peripheral vision try to keep track of both up and down the stairs. But my eyes kept going back to him. Was he dying? Please, God, not like this. It wasn't just Edward. It was the look on Peter's face. If Edward died, Peter would blame himself. The boy was having a bad enough night. That kind of guilt he did not need.

"Give me your T-shirt," Olaf said.

I looked at him.

"We need to pack the wound and keep the stake from moving around. We can't remove it here. It's too close to his heart. He will need a hospital."

I agreed with that. "Someone else watch for bad guys while I undress."

Bernardo stood up and took my place at the wall. I noticed there was a blade sticking out of his cast like a spearhead. The blade was stained black with blood.

I pulled off my T-shirt and handed it to Olaf. He'd already stripped down to his black Kevlar vest, shoving his own shirt around the wound.

"Do you need mine?" Peter asked.

"Yes," Olaf said.

Peter moved Becca forward on his lap and took off his shirt. His upper body was thin and pale. He was tall, but the rest of him hadn't caught up. Olaf used pieces of Bernardo's shirt to hold the makeshift bandage in place. The wound looked terrible, but it wasn't bleeding much. I didn't know if that was a good sign or a bad one.

"We caught the other half of your ambush on its way to the stairs," Bernardo said.

"I wondered why there weren't more," I said. I remembered what Harold had said. "Before Harold died, he said that Simon called someone. Told them he'd failed and they needed to clean up the mess. Does that mean what I think it means?"

Edward looked up at me, as Olaf used more shirt strips to bind his left arm tight, so he wouldn't move it and risk jarring the stake into something vital. "They'll kill everything they find." His voice was almost normal, only slightly breathy, a touch tight. "They'll burn the place to ash. Maybe they even salt the earth." I think that last was the wound talking, but you never know with Edward.

Olaf lifted Edward to his feet, but the height difference was too much. Edward couldn't keep his arm over the big man' s shoulders. "Bernardo will have to help you."

"No, Anita can do it."

Olaf opened his mouth to argue, I think, but Edward said, "Bernardo only has one good arm. He needs that to shoot."

Olaf closed his mouth into a tight line, but he handed Edward over to me. Edward's arm went around my shoulders. I put my left arm around his waist. We tried a couple of steps, and it worked okay.

Olaf led the way. I came next with Edward, then Peter, carrying Becca wrapped around his body like a sad little monkey. Bernardo brought up the rear. Olaf looked at the bodies of the dead men as he passed. He spoke without looking back at me. "You did this?"

"Yeah." I'd have usually come up with something sarcastic like, "you see anyone else?" but I was too worried about Edward to waste the effort. Sweat had popped out on his face, as if it was taking a lot to keep going. Trouble was, a fireman's carry would disturb the stake, and if any of us could carry him just in his arms, it was Olaf, but it would mean not being able to shoot. We needed the gun.

"You okay, Edward?" I asked.

He swallowed before he said, "Fine."

I didn't believe him, but I didn't ask again. This was probably as good as it was going to get for awhile.

Edward tried to turn and say something to the kids, but it hurt, and I had to turn for him, moving us both to face backwards. "Cover Becca's eyes, Peter."

Peter had Becca bury her face against his shoulder and kept his hand pressed to the back of her head. He didn't have the Firestar in his hands. I wondered where it was but not enough to ask.

I turned Edward back around, and we started up the stairs again. Olaf was almost at the next bend in the stairs, when he stopped. He was looking down at the steps. I froze and said, "No one move."

"Is it a trap?" Edward asked.

"No," Olaf said.

I saw it then, thin rivulets of blood sliding down the steps towards us. It snaked around Olaf's feet and dripped its way toward Edward and me.

Peter wasn't that far behind us. He asked, "What is that?"

"Blood," Olaf said.

"Please tell me that this is your handiwork, Olaf," I said.

"No," he said.

I watched the blood flow around my Nikes and knew that our problems had just gotten worse.

61

I LEANED EDWARD up against the wall. He wanted me free to shoot if Olaf told me to. Olaf got to scout ahead and see what the problem was. He vanished around that corner, and I pressed myself to the wall and gave the briefest of looks ahead. The stairs ended just up ahead. The electric lights showed a cave, I think. The lights glistened on blood and bodies.

Olaf backed up, and came down to us again. "I can see the exit."

"What are the bodies?"

"Riker's men."

"What killed them?"

"I think it is our murderous beast. But there is no other way out. The other entrance has been blocked by an explosion. We must go out this way."

I figured if the murderous beast was up there waiting for us, Olaf would have been more excited. So I went back to Edward. His skin was the color of bad paste. His eyes were closed. They opened when I touched him, but they were brighter than they should have been. "We're almost out," I said.

He didn't say anything, just let me settle his arm over my shoulder. He was still holding on to me, but every step we took, my arm around his waist was taking more and more of his weight. "Hold on, Edward, just a little further."

His head jerked as if he'd just heard me, but his feet kept moving with me. We were going to make it, all of us. The blood got thicker the further up we walked. Edward slipped in it, and I had to catch him and barely managed to keep us both standing. But it was a sudden movement, and he let out a small sound of pain. Shit.

"Watch your step, Peter," I said. "It's slippery."

Olaf was waiting for us at the bodies. There were only three of them. One was a man I didn't recognize, but I recognized the gun near his body. He was one of Simon's men. Simon was lying in a pool of blood and darker fluids. The entire lower chest, stomach, abdomen were open. His intestines trailed out onto the cave floor, but his eyes were still blinking upward, still alive.

The third body was Amanda, and she was still moving, too. But Olaf had her covered, so I kept my attention on Simon. He smiled up at us. "At least I killed the Undertaker."

"He's not nearly as dead as you are," I said.

"You're all dead, bitch."

"We know you invited company," I said.

His eyes looked uncertain. "Fuck you." His hand inched towards his gun that was still lying beside him. Gutted, dying, in more pain than I could imagine, and he tried to go for his gun. I stepped on his hand, pinning it to the earth. Harder to do than normal with Edward hanging on me, but I managed. "Peter, you and Becca go up with Bernardo to the front of the cave."

Peter didn't argue. He just carried Becca past us, Bernardo trailing behind.

I pointed the gun barrel at Simon's head. I couldn't leave him behind because I didn't trust him at my back. Even this wounded, I wasn't willing to take the chance.

"I hope the monster guts you, Bitch."

"That's Ms. Bitch to you," I said and pulled the trigger. A short burst, but more shots echoed mine. I whirled, gun up, and found Peter standing over Amanda's body. He emptied the Firestar into her body while I watched. Olaf was just watching him do it. I looked for Bernardo and found him holding Becca near the cave mouth.

Edward started to slide to his knees. I knelt with him, trying to keep him upright. He whispered, "The kids, out, get them . . . out," and he fainted.

Olaf was there without me asking. He lifted Edward in his arms like a child. If the monster came now, we all had our hands full. Shit.

Peter had run out of bullets, but he was still squeezing the trigger, over and over and over. I went to him. "Peter, Peter, she's dead. You killed her. Ease down."

He didn't seem to hear me. I touched his hands, tried to lift the gun from him. He jerked away, violently, eyes wild. He kept dry firing into the woman's body. I shoved him back against the rock wall, hard, one arm across his throat, the other pinning his hands still wrapped around the Firestar. His eyes were wide and frightened, but he looked at me. "Peter, she's dead. You can't kill her anymore dead than she already is."

His voice shook when he said, "I wanted her to hurt."

"She did hurt. Being torn apart is a bad way to die."

He shook his head. "It's not enough."

"No," I said, "it isn't enough, but you killed her, Peter. That's as good as revenge gets. Once you kill them, there isn't any more."

I took the Firestar out of his hands, and he let me. I tried to hug him, but he pushed me away, then walked away. The time for that kind of comfort was past, but there were other kinds of comfort. Some of them came from the barrel of a gun. There is some comfort in killing that which has hurt you, but it is cold comfort. It'll destroy things inside of you that the original pain wouldn't have harmed. Sometimes it's not a question of whether a piece of your soul is going to go missing, only which piece it's going to be.

Peter carried Becca. Olaf carried Edward. Bernardo and I took the lead. We searched the spring darkness with our guns, back and forth, back and forth. Nothing moved. There was just the sound of wind in the tall line of sage bushes that bordered the back of the cave. The air felt so good against my face, and I realized that I'd not really expected to get out, not alive. Pessimism, it wasn't like me.

Bernardo led the way back to circle the house. We'd try for Edward's car, but we wanted to make sure no one or no thing was waiting to eat us when we went for the car. Olaf went second, carrying a very still Edward. I was praying hard that he'd be okay, though strangely it felt odd to pray to God for Edward, as if I were praying in the wrong direction. Peter and Becca were just ahead of me. He stumbled as we headed into the thicker brush. He had to be tired, but I couldn't afford to carry Becca. I needed to have my hands free to fight.

I felt the prickling brush of magic. I called, "Guys, something's out here."

Everyone stopped and started searching the darkness. "What did you see?" Olaf asked.

"Nothing, but something out here is doing magic."

Olaf made a noise in his throat like he didn't believe me. Then the first wave of fear washed over us. So much fear that it closed the throat, sent the heart thundering, made the palms of your hand sweat. Becca started struggling violently in Peter's arms.

I took two steps to help Peter control her, but she struggled free, fell to the ground, and ran like a rabbit into the brush. Peter yelled, "Becca!" and went after her.

"Peter, Becca! Oh, shit!" I ran into the brush after them. What else could I do? I heard them just up ahead, crashing through the brush, Peter calling Becca's name. I had a sense of movement to my right, and I saw something. It was bigger than a man, and even by moonlight you could see it was different colors. I fired into it as it opened a huge razored mouth, but the claw kept coming towards me, as if the bullets were nothing. The closed claw slammed into my head. It knocked me off my feet, and I hit the ground hard. Darkness swirled across my vision, and when I could see again, the thing was right above me. I kept my finger on the trigger, until it clicked empty. The monster never hesitated. It filled my vision with a face that was almost birdlike, and I had a moment to think it was pretty before it hit me again, and there was nothing but darkness.

62

I WOKE INSTANTLY, my skin jumping with a rush of magic that left me gasping. My body strained, writhing as the power rode over and through my body in a burning surge that just kept growing. My hands and legs strained against the chains that held me down. Chains? I turned and stared at my wrists, head still thrashing, my body jerking as the power roared through me. My arms and legs jerked, not because I was struggling against the chains but as a reaction to the power.

The magic began to fade, leaving my breath coming in pants. One thing I knew. If didn't get my breathing under control, I was going to hyperventilate. Passing out again would be bad. Heaven knew what I'd wake up to a second time. I concentrated on my breathing, forcing myself to be calm, and take deep, even, normal breaths. It's hard to be totally panic-stricken when you're doing breathing exercises. It poured a false calm over my body, and my mind. But it let me think, which was good.

I was lying on my back, chained to a smooth stone surface. There was a curve of cave wall beside me, and a ceiling lost to sight in the darkness above. I'd have loved to believe that Bernardo and Olaf had rescued me and we were back in the cave entrance, but the chains sort of ruined that pleasant thought. This cave was much taller, and without looking it just felt bigger. Firelight bounced in orange shadows along the cave, 1ike being in a ball of darkness and gold light.

I finally turned my head to the right and let myself see what was there. At first I thought it was Pinotl, Itzpapalotl's human servant. I had a few seconds of cursing myself for believing her when she said she didn't know about the monster, then I realized it wasn't him. It looked like him. Same square, chiseled face, dark, rich skin, and the black hair cut long and oddly square, but this man was narrow through the shoulders, thin, and there was no air of command to him. He was also wearing a pair of loose-fitting shorts instead of the nifty clothes that Pinotl wore.

There was a smooth rounded stone like the one at the Obsidian Butterfly. There was a body draped over that stone. Foreshortened legs and arms, short dark hair, and for a moment I thought it was Nicky Baco, then I saw the naked chest more clearly, and it was Paulina, Nicky's wife. There was a hole under her ribs like a great gaping mouth. They'd torn out her heart. The unknown man stood there holding the heart in his hands, above his head like an offering. His eyes looked black in the uncertain light. He lowered his arms, walking towards me with the heart cupped in his hands. His hands were so thick with blood that it looked like he was wearing red gloves. There were four men standing at attention around the altar. They were wearing some sort of soft leather on their bodies, hoods up and covering them from head to foot almost. There was something wrong with what they were wearing, but my eyes couldn't make sense of it, and I had other more immediate problems than what people were wearing.

I was still wearing the Kevlar vest and all the rest of my clothes. If they meant to take my heart, they'd have taken the clothes. It was a very comforting thought as the man, the priest, walked towards me with the heart in his hands. He held the heart over my chest and began to chant in a language that sounded like Spanish, but wasn't.

Blood dripped from the heart, splatted on the vest. It made me jump. The calm of the breathing exercises was wearing off. I did not want him to touch me with that thing. It wasn't even logic, fear of some spell or magic. It was pure revulsion. I did not want to be touched by a heart that had just been torn out of someone's body. I've put my share of stakes through hearts. I've even cut a few out for burning, but somehow this was different. Maybe it was being chained and helpless, or maybe it was Paulina's body lying limp over the altar, looking like a broken doll. The only time I'd met her she'd been so strong, threatening me with a gun, but lots of people had done that. Edward used to do that all the time. Starting out a relationship on the end of a gun didn't mean you couldn't be friends down the road. Unless one of you died. No friendship now. No nothing for Paulina.

The man ended the chant and began to lower the heart towards me.

I strained against the chains though I knew it was useless, and I said, "Don't touch me with that." It sounded sure and strong, but if he understood English, I couldn't tell it because he just kept lowering his bloody hands, closer and closer. He laid the heart on my chest, and I was almost as grateful that the Kevlar kept me from feeling that thing next to my skin, as I'd been for the extra protection from bullets earlier.

The heart lay on my chest like so much meat. There was no magic to it. It was just dead. Then the heart took a breath, or that's what it looked like. The skin rose and fell. It sat on my chest, naked and attached to nothing and pulsed. I was suddenly aware of my own heartbeat. The moment I noticed my heartbeat, Paulina's heart stuttered, then began to beat in time with mine. And the moment the rhythms were shared, I could hear a second heart beat. Except that Paulina's heart had no blood to pump, no chest to resonate in. It should have been a pale sound compared to the real thing, but it was a solid pulsing beat. It was as if the sound reached through the vest, through my skin, my ribs, and pierced my heart. The pain was sharp and immediate, stealing my breath, bowing my spine.

"Hold her," the man yelled.

The men who'd been standing by the altar ran to me, strong hands pressing on my legs, pinning my shoulders. My spine tried to bow with the pain, and a third set of hands pressed down on my thighs, three of them pinning me to the stone, forcing me to ride the pain and not struggle.

Paulina's heart was beating faster and faster, speeding, speeding, towards some grand climax. My heart thundered against my ribs, as if it were trying to tear loose of the tissue. It was as if a fist were beating on the inside of my chest, trying to smash its way out. I couldn't breathe, as if all of my chest was caught up in the frantic race, and there was no time for anything else.

The pain was centered in my chest, but it spread down my arms, my legs, filled my head until I thought that it might not be my heart that exploded. It might be the top of my head.

I could feel the two hearts like lovers separated by a wall, tearing it down between them until they would be able to touch. There was a moment when I felt them touch, felt the thick wet sides of the two organs slide into each other. Maybe it was just the pain. Then the heart stopped like a person caught in mid-motion, and my heart stopped with it. For a breathless moment my heart sat in my body and did nothing, as if waiting. Then it gave one beat, then another, and I drew air into my lungs in a frantic rush, and as soon as I had air, I screamed. Then I lay there, still listening to my heart beat, feeling the pain begin to fade like the memory of a nightmare. Minutes later, the pain was gone. My body didn't even hurt. In fact, I felt energized, wonderful.

The heart on my chest had shriveled into a gray, used up piece of flesh. It wasn't recognizable as a heart, just a dry ball smaller than my palm. I blinked up and saw the face of the man holding my shoulders down. I'm sure he'd been looking down at me for a while, but I hadn't seen him or hadn't understood what I was seeing.

He wore a mask over his face. Only his lips, eyes, and ears showed through the thin covering. His neck was bare, then a ragged bow neck of the same material of the mask covered him. I think part of me knew what I was looking at, before the rest of me would accept it. It wasn't until I turned my head as far as I could to one side, and saw the hands that I knew what he was wearing. The empty hands bunched at his wrists like limp, fleshly lace. It was human skin. I'd finally found out what had happened to some of the skin the flayed ones had lost.

The eyes that stared out of that horrible thing were brown and very human. I looked down the line of my body and found that the other two men holding my legs wore the same thing, but the skins weren't all the same colors. One dark, two light. The chests had thick cord sewn across it where the breasts and nipples would have been, so there was no clue to whether the skin had been male or female.

The first man I'd seen stepped forward. "How do you feel?" His English was heavily accented but clear.

I just looked at him for a second. He had to be kidding. "How am I supposed to feel? I just woke up in a cave where you just performed a human sacrifice." I glanced at the men still holding me down. "I'm being held down by men wearing flayed human skin suits. How the hell I am I supposed to feel?"

"I am asking after your bodily health. Nothing more," he said.

I started to say something else sarcastic, but stopped and really thought about his question. How did I feel? Actually, I felt good. I remembered that rush of energy and well-being that had spread over me when the spell finished. It was still there. I felt better than I'd felt in days. If it hadn't required human sacrifice, it would have been a great medical treatment.

"I feel okay."

"No pain in the head?"

"No."

"Good," he said. He motioned, and the skin guys moved away from me. They moved back to stand against the wall by the fourth man who hadn't been needed to hold me down. They stood there like good soldiers, waiting for their next orders.

I turned back to look at the other guy. Everyone in the room was scary, but at least he wasn't wearing someone else's skin. "What did you do to me?"

"We have saved your life. Our master's creature was overzealous. There was bleeding in your head. We needed you alive."

I thought about that. "You used Paulina's life force to heal me."

"Yes.

"I'm glad to be alive, honest." I looked past him at Paulina's body lying broken and forgotten. "But she didn't volunteer to trade her life for mine, did she?"

"Nicky Baco began to suspect what price he would have to pay for our master's blessing. She was a hostage to make sure he came to this our last meeting," the man said.

"Let me guess. He didn't show," I said.

"He no longer answers our master's call."

Apparently, Ramirez had taken my advice of having Leonora Evans do some sort of magical barrier around Nicky so he couldn't contact his master. Good to know it was working, but you try to do the right thing and it ends up getting someone else killed. Why is that always the way it works? But I admit that I was happier for me than sorry for Paulina. Not about her trading her life for mine, but if Nicky was being protected by magic, then he and the police were on their way. All I had to do was stall and keep them from doing whatever it was they had planned for me.

"So when Nicky didn't show up, you didn't need to keep her alive." My voice sounded calm, but better than that, I was calm. Not normal calm, but the cool distant calm that you either learn to do during the really bad stuff, or you run screaming. I'd done all the screaming I planned on doing tonight.

"Her life did not matter. Yours does."

"I'm glad to be alive, and don't take this wrong, but why do you give a damn if I live or die?"

"We need you," a male voice said from behind me. I had to arch my neck and crane my head backward to see the owner of that second voice. I didn't see the man at first because he was surrounded by the flayed ones. I'd known that Edward was worried that they'd missed some bodies. He had no idea. There must have been twenty-five, thirty-five animated corpses standing behind me. They'd been standing so quietly, I hadn't heard them or sensed them. They stood there now like robots with the switch turned off, waiting for life to return. Zombies never got that still, never went that empty. At the end, when they started to rot and you had to put them back in the grave before they melted into little puddles, they were more alive than this. I realized in that instant that the bodies were raised, but the person inside that body wasn't raised. The master ate that which made them individuals. He ate that which made them more than so much muscle and skin. He didn't eat the souls because I'd seen one of them in a house where two flayed ones had been made. But he took something out of their bodies, some memory or remnant that I left in when I raised the dead. They stood like rocks carved of flesh, utterly empty. At least the ones in the hospital had pretended to still be alive. There was no pretense here.

My eyes finally found the man. He wore a steel helmet and breastplate like the history books are always showing the conquistadors wearing, but the rest of the outfit was straight out of a nightmare.

He wore a necklace of tongues, and they were all still fresh and pink as if they'd just been cut out seconds ago. He wore a skirt of intestines that writhed and twisted like snakes, as if each thick glistening strand had an independent life of its own. His arms were bare, strong and muscled, and covered in the missing eyelids of the victims. As he moved close, the eyelids opened and closed. He came to stand beside me, next to the first man. The eyelids blinked at me and there were eye shaped holes underneath every lid that I saw. The holes held darkness and the cold light of stars.

I turned away because I was remembering Itzpapalotl's starry eyes. I didn't want to fall into these eyes. At that second if you had given me a choice, I'd have taken the vampire in town to the thing that was standing in front of me.

After what I'd seen at the murder scene, I expected to feel evil emanating from him, but there was no evil. There was power like being next to a battery the size of the Chrysler building. The energy hummed along my skin, but it was neutral energy. Neither good nor bad in and of itself, the way a gun is neither good nor bad but can be turned to evil purposes.

I stared up the line of his body, and the tongues were moving as if still trying to scream. He took off the helmet and showed a slender, handsome face that reminded me of Bernardo's, not the pure Aztec ethnicity I'd been expecting. He had turquoise ear spools in his lobes, and they matched the blue green of his eyes. He smiled down at me, looking like a fresh-faced twenty-something. I could feel the weight of the ages in his gaze like some vast weight pressing down on me, as if just being this close made it hard to breathe.

He reached out to touch my face, and I jerked back from him. That one movement seemed to break his hold over me. I could move. I could breathe. I could think. I'd been on the receiving end of enough magical glamour to know it when I felt it. You're either a god, or you're not. He was not. And it wasn't just my monotheism showing. I'd felt the magic of monsters and preternatural beasties of all sorts, and I knew one when I saw one. Power doesn't make you a deity. I don't know exactly what does, but power ain't it. Some spark of the divine was missing from the being that gazed down upon me. If he was just another monster, maybe we could deal.

"Who are you?" And I was happy that my voice was confident, normal.

"I am the Red Woman's Husband." He gazed down at me with eyes so patient, so kind. You think angels must have eyes like that.

"The Red Woman is the Aztec phrase for blood. What does it mean that you're blood's husband?"

"I am the body, and she is the life." He said it like it answered my question. It didn't.

Something wet and slimy touched my hand. I jerked back, but the chain didn't let me go far. The length of animated intestine followed my hand, nuzzling it like some obscene worm. I swallowed a scream, but I couldn't keep my pulse from speeding up.

He laughed at me.

It was a very ordinary laugh for a would-be god, but it was nicely condescending and maybe that's how would-be gods laughed. But it was a peculiarly masculine condescension, long gone out of style. The laugh says, "Silly little girl, don't you know I'm the big strong man, and you know nothing, and I know everything?" Or maybe I'm just too sensitive.

"Why intestines?" I asked.

The smile faded around the edges. His handsome face looked puzzled. "Are you making fun of me?" The intestine dropped away from my hand like a date that I'd rebuffed. Fine with me.

"No. I just wondered why intestines. You can obviously animate any body part. You can keep detached parts from decaying like the skins your men are wearing. With all that to choose from, why people's guts and not something else?" People love to talk about themselves. The bigger the ego, the more they enjoy it. I was hoping that the Red Woman's Husband was the same as everyone else, at least in this one thing.

"I wear the roots of their bodies so that all that see me will know that my enemies are empty shells and I have all that was theirs."

Ask a silly question. "Why the tongues?"

"So that the lies of my enemies will not be believed."

"Eyelids?"

"I will open the eyes of my enemies so that they may never again close their eyes to the truth."

He was answering questions so nicely that I decided to try for more. "How did you skin the people without using a tool of some kind?"

"Tlaloci, my priest, called the skin from their bodies."

"How?" I asked.

"My power," he said.

"Don't you mean Tlaloci's power?"

He frowned again. "All his power derives from me."

"Sure," I said.

"I am his master. He owes all to me."

"Sounds like you owe him."

"You do not know what you are saying." He was getting angry. Probably not what I wanted. I tried another more polite question.

"Why take the breasts and penises?"

"To feed my minion." He did nothing, but suddenly I felt the air in the cavern move, and it was as if the shadows themselves drew apart like a curtain revealing a tunnel about thirty feet from the foot of where I lay. Something crawled out of that tunnel. The first impression was of a brilliant iridescent green. The scales changed color at every turn of the light. First green, then blue, then blue and green all at once, then a pearl white glitter that I thought I must have imagined, until it turned its head and flashed a white underbelly. The green scales went closer to true blue as the color moved up towards the head, until the square snout was a clear pure blue the color of sky. There was a fringe of delicate feathers in a rainbow of colors around that face. It turned and stared at me, fanning the feathers around its scaled head into a display that would have been the envy of any peacock. Its eyes were round and huge, taking up most of its face like the eyes of a bird of prey. A pair of slender wings was folded along its back, rainbow colors of the fringe, but I knew without seeing that the underside of the wings would be white. It pushed forward on four legs. Counting the wings, it was a six-limbed animal.

It was a Quetzalcoatl Draconus Giganticus, or at least that was the last Latin classification I was aware of. Sometimes they were classed as a subspecies of dragons, sometimes as a subspecies of gargoyles, and sometimes they had their own group all to themselves. Whatever classification, the Giganticus was the biggest and supposedly extinct. The Spaniards had killed a lot of them to dishearten the natives to whom they were sacred, and because it was just the European thing to do. See a dragon, kill it. It was not a complex philosophy.

I'd only seen black and white photos, and the stuffed one in the Chicago Field Museum. The photos hadn't come close to doing it justice, and the stuffed one, well, maybe it was a bad taxidermy job.

It glided into the room in a shimmering roll of color and muscle. It was literally one of the most beautiful things I'd ever seen. It was also probably what had been gutting people. It opened that sky-blue snout and yawned showing rows of saw-like teeth. The sound of its claws clattered over the stone floor like some nightmarish dog.

Red Woman's Husband lay his Spanish helmet on the stone by my legs and went to greet the creature. It lowered its head to be petted, very like a dog. He stroked it just above the eye ridges and it made a low, rolling sound, eyes closing to slits. It was purring.

He sent it away with a playful push against one muscular shoulder. I watched it vanish back through the tunnel like it wasn't real. "I thought they were extinct."

"My minion helped bring us to this place, then it slept a magic sleep, waiting for me to awake."

"I didn't know Quetzalcoatls could hibernate."

He frowned at me again and came to stand by my head. "I know what your word hibernate means, but it was a magic sleep, done by the last of my warrior priests. The priest sacrificed himself, putting all of us in an enchanted sleep, knowing that there was no one to aid him, and that he would die alone in this alien place long before I rose."

Enchanted sleep. Sounded like Sleeping Beauty. "That's true loyalty, sacrifice yourself for the better good."

"I'm so glad you agree. It will make what has to happen much easier."

Didn't like the sound of that. Maybe flattery wasn't the way to go. I'd try something more normal for me—sarcasm—and see if that led us away from the topic of my impending doom. "I don't owe you any loyalty. I am not one of your followers."

"Only because you do not understand," he said, and those smiling eyes gazed down at me with a look of almost perfect peace.

"That's what Jim Jones said just before he gave every one the Kool-Aid."

"I do not know this name, Jim Jones." Then he turned his head to one side, and it reminded me of Itzpapalotl when she listened to voices I could not hear. Now I realized that it might just be a way to access other people's memories. "Ah, I know who he is now." He looked down at me with those calm, beatific eyes. "But I am no madman. I am a god."

He was getting distracted, as if it mattered to him for me to believe he was a god. If he had to convince me that he was divine before he killed me, then I was safe. He could kill me, but he'd never convince me he was a god.

He frowned. "You do not believe me." He sounded surprised again. And I realized that for all his power, he seemed young. The ages raged through the eyes on his arms as though you could see back through to the beginning of creation, but he, himself, seemed young. Or maybe he just wasn't used to people who didn't drop down and worship him. If that's all you'd known in your entire existence, then anyone not worshipping might be a shock.

"I am a god," he repeated, and his voice had that condescending tone again.

"Whatever you say." But I made sure my doubt showed in my voice.

The frown deepened, and again I was reminded forcibly of a pouting child. A spoiled, pouting child. "You must believe that I am a god. I am the Red Woman's Husband. I am the body that will be revenged on those that destroyed my people."

"You mean the Spanish Conquistadors?"

"Yes," he said.

"There aren't a lot of conquistadors in New Mexico," I said.

"Their blood still runs in the veins of their children's children's children."

"No offense, but you didn't get those turquoise blue eyes from anyone local."

He frowned again, and little lines formed between his eyes. If he kept talking to me, he was going to get frown lines. "I am a god created by my people's tears. I am the power that is left of the Aztecs, and I am the Spaniard's magic made flesh. We will use their own power to destroy them."

"Isn't it a little late to destroy them? About five hundred years too late."

"Gods do not reckon time as men do."

I believed that he believed what he was saying, but I also thought he was rationalizing. He'd have kicked the Spaniards' butts five hundred years ago if he'd been able to do it.

Maybe it showed on my face because he said, "I was a new god then, and I did not have the strength to defeat our enemies, so the Quetzalcoatl brought me here to wait until I grew strong enough for our purpose. I am ready to lead my army forward now."

"So you're saying that it took five hundred years for you to go from being a wee little god to a big bad god, the way soup needs to simmer for a really long time before it's soup?"

He laughed. "You think very strangely. I am sad that you will be dead soon. I would make you the first of my concubines, and the mother of gods, for children born of you would be great sorcerers, but sadly, I have need of your life."

We were back to killing me, and I didn't want to be there. His ego seemed pretty fragile for a deity. I'd see how fragile. "The offer doesn't sound very appealing, no offense."

He smiled down at me, fingers trailing along my arm. "That we will take your life is not an offer. It is a fact."

I gave him my best innocent eyes. "I thought you were offering to make me your concubine, the mother of gods?"

He frowned at me harder. "I did not offer you a chance to be my concubine."

"Oh," I said. "Sorry. I misunderstood you."

His fingers were still touching my arm, but they were still now, as if he'd forgotten he was touching me. "You would refuse my bed?" He sounded truly perplexed. Great.

"Yeah," I said.

"Is it your virtue you are protecting?"

"No, it's just your particular offer doesn't appeal to me."

He was really having trouble with the concept that I didn't find him attractive. He ran his fingers down my bare arm in a tickling brush. I just lay there and looked at him. I was giving him some of the best eye contact I'd given anyone this trip because if I looked anywhere else, I kept seeing severed body parts wiggling on their own. Hard to be tough as nails when you wanted to start screaming. He touched my face, and I let him this time. His fingers traced my face, delicately, gently. His eyes no longer looked peaceful. No, definitely disturbed.

He leaned into me as if he'd kiss me, and the eye lashes on his arms fluttered in butterfly kisses along my body. I gave a little shriek.

He drew back. "What is wrong?"

"Oh, I don't know. Severed eyelids fluttering against my skin, intestines that writhe like snakes around your waist, the necklace of tongues trying to lick me. Pick one."

"But that should not matter," he said. "You should see me as beautiful, desirable."

I did the best shrug I could with my hands chained higher than my shoulders. "Sorry, but I just can't get past what you're wearing."

"Tlaloci," he said.

The man in shorts came forward, and dropped to one knee before him. "Yes, my lord."

"Why does she not see me as wonderful?"

"Apparently, the aura of your godhood does not work on her."

"Why not?" And there was anger now in his voice, in that once peaceful face.

"I do not know, my lord."

"You said she could replace Nicky Baco. You said she was a nauhuli as he was. You said she had been touched by my magic, and it was the scent of my magic that drew the Quetzalcoatl to her. But she lies under the touch of my hands and does not feel for me. That is not possible if my magic clings to her."

I thought, what if it's not his magic, but I didn't say it out loud. What if it was Itzpapalotl's? The being standing in front of me had nearly killed me from a distance. He'd roared over my mind and taken me, and I hadn't been able to stop him. Now, he was touching me, and evidently trying things on me, and it wasn't working. The only thing that had changed was Itzpapalotl's power filling me for awhile. Had that made the difference?

Tlaloci stood, head still bowed. "There must be powerful magic at work here, my lord. First Nicky Baco is lost to us, and now this one is closed to your vision."

"She must be open to my power or she cannot be the perfect sacrifice," Red Woman's Husband said.

"I know, my lord."

"You are the magician, Tlaloci. How can I undo this magic?"

The magician put some serious thought into it. Several minutes passed while he thought. I just lay there trying not to draw their attention back to me. Finally, Tlaloci looked up. "To believe in your vision, she must believe in you."

"How do I convince her to believe that I am a god if she cannot feel my power?"

It was a good question, and I waited patiently for Tlaloci to answer it. The longer he thought about it, the more delay time I was getting. Ramirez was coming. I had to believe that because my options were limited unless I could figure out a way to get them to untie me.

I could feel the pen still in my pocket with its hidden blade. I was armed, if I could get my hands free, and if steel could hurt him. Of course, there were the four helpers, and Tlaloci, and a small army of flayed ones. So even if the god could die, I'd have to do something about everyone else. They'd probably be pissed if I killed their god. I just wasn't sure how to get out of this one.

If Ramirez didn't arrive with the cavalry, I was in deep shit. Edward wasn't out there looking for me this time. For the first time since I came to, I wondered was Edward alive. Please, God, let him be alive. But alive or not, Edward was out of the rescuing game for tonight. I admitted I needed help on this one, and the only hope I could count on was Ramirez and the police. He'd been late in the hospital. If he were late tonight, I probably wouldn't be around to complain.

Tlaloci motioned for his god to follow him a little away from me. I think they were whispering things they didn't want me to know. Why did it matter if I overheard them or not? What could they possibly be talking about that they needed to hide from me? They'd cheerfully told me they were going to kill me. It wasn't like they were trying to protect my feelings. So what was going on?

The Red Woman's Husband unfastened the necklace of tongues and handed it to the priest. He took off the steel breastplate and one of the skin guys came and took it from him, kneeling in front of him. He took off the skirt of intestines, and another skin guy hurried forward to take it. The "god" never asked them to help him, just sort of assumed that someone would be there to help. He was almost perfectly arrogant, but his ego was fragile, an arrogance that had never been tested in the outer world. He was like one of those fairy tale princesses that had been raised in an ivory tower with only people who told them how beautiful they were, how smart, how good, until the witch comes and lays her curse. Maybe I could be the witch, though truthfully I wouldn't have known a curse if it bit me on the butt. Maybe I could be the prince that comes and takes him away. At this point I wasn't picky.

The "god" was wearing a maxilatl like everyone at the Obsidian Butterfly had worn. But this one was black with a heavy fringe of golden thread hanging in front. He wore black sandals set with turquoise, which strangely I hadn't noticed when he was wearing all the severed body parts. Funny how you don't concentrate on the small details when you're scared.

He walked towards me, confidence showing in every step. The maxilatl left his lower body bare on the sides from waist to sandals. It was a nice length of thigh, but you know what they say. Pretty is as pretty does.

"Is this better?" he asked, his voice light, almost teasing, his eyes back to that peaceful contentment, as if things had always gone his way, and he didn't see why now should be different. Itzpapalotl had been arrogant, but not peaceful.

"Much better," I said. I thought about remarking on how much I liked seeing nearly naked men, but didn't want to take it to such an obviously sexual tone unless I ran out of other options.

He came to stand beside me again. The eyelids were still on his arms, blinking at me like the winking lights of fireflies, random, and alien.

"It's a big improvement," I said. "You can't do anything about the eyes on your arms, can you?"

He frowned again. "They are part of me."

"I see that," I said.

"But they are nothing to fear."

"If you say so."

"I want you to know me, Anita." It was the first time he'd used my name. I hadn't thought he knew it, until then. Of course, Paulina had known who I was. The Red Woman's Husband reached down to my right wrist, and he undid that little piece of metal that held the manacle closed.

The skinned man who was still standing on the other side of the stone took a step forward, hand on the knife at his belt. I froze, not sure if I was really going to be allowed to have my hand free.

The "god" lifted my hand free of the chain and laid his lips on the back of my hand. "Touch them. See that they are nothing to fear." It took me a second to figure out that "them" meant the eyes on his arms. I was relieved to realize he didn't mean anything below his waist, and so not happy that he meant all those eyes. I did not want to touch them. I wanted nothing to do with anything that had been carved off of a dead body, especially while that person had still been alive.

He held my wrist and tried to bring my hand over his arm, but I kept a tight fist. "Touch them, Anita, gently. They will not harm you." He began to pry my fingers open, and I couldn't fight him. I could have fought harder, maybe make him break a finger or two, to persuade me, but in the end I was going to lose this wrestling match, so I just let him spread my hand open. I didn't want anything broken if I could avoid it.

He guided my hand just above his arm, and the eyelids fluttered under my touch. I jumped every time one of them blinked, but the eyelids moving against my skin in a line of butterfly kisses wasn't as scary. The lids felt full, as if there was an eye behind them, and there wasn't. I'd seen that.

"What's inside them?" I asked.

"Everything," he said. Which told me nothing. "Explore them, Anita." He pressed one of my fingertips to the edge of an eye. Then he urged me to put the finger inside the eye.

I pushed my finger into that empty seeming eye, and there was a resistance like pushing against something thin and fleshy, then my finger was through and I could touch what was inside. Warm, a warmth that flowed through my hand, up my arm, and spread like a blanket over my body. I felt safe, warm. I stared up at him and wondered why I hadn't seen it before? He was so handsome, so kind, so . . . My finger was cold, so cold that it hurt. It had that stinging pain that you get just before you lose all feeling in the limb, and frostbite settles in and spills over your body, and you fall into that last gentle sleep, never to wake.

I jerked my hand back, and blinked awake, with a gasp.

"What is wrong?' he asked, and leaned over me, touching my face.

I jerked away from him, cradling my hand against my chest, staring up at him, afraid. "You're cold inside."

He took a step back from me, and the surprise showed on his face. "You should feel safe, warm." He leaned over me, trying to get me to gaze into his blue-green eyes.

I shook my head. Feeling was coming back into my finger in a stinging rush, the way circulation comes back after frostbite. The throbbing ache helped me think, helped me avoid his gaze. "I'm not safe," I said, "and I'm not warm." I looked away from him, which put me gazing at the skin-clad guy. But truthfully even that was better than staring at the "god." Itzpapalotl's touch was helping me, but it had limits. If I fell into his eyes, wherever they might be, they'd just kill me, and I might go willingly, eagerly into that last dark.

"You are making this difficult, Anita."

I kept my gaze on the far wall. "Sorry that I'm ruining your night."

He stroked the curve of my face. I flinched as if he'd hurt me. I'd thought what I was trying to delay was my death. Now I realized that I was trying to delay falling into his power. They'd kill me after that, but I'd be gone before the knife fell. Had Paulina went like that, willingly, eager to please the "god?" I hoped so, for her sake. For mine, I wasn't so sure.

"I want you to believe that your death will be for a great purpose."

"Sorry, not buying swampland today."

I could almost feel his puzzlement like a play of energy along my skin. I'd felt anger, lust, fear dance along my skin from vampires and wereanimals, but I'd never felt puzzlement before. I hadn't felt his emotions before I touched that damned eye. He was sucking me down a piece at a time.

He grabbed my hand.

"No." I said it through gritted teeth. He could break my fingers this time, but I wasn't just opening up and touching him again. I couldn't just cooperate with him anymore, not even to buy time. I had to start fighting him now, or there'd be nothing left of me. I'd had vampires roll my mind before, but I'd never felt anything like him. Once he got a really good hold on my mind, I wasn't a hundred percent sure I'd come back. There are a lot of ways to die. Being killed is only one of the more obvious ones. If he rolled my mind and there was nothing left of who I was, then I was dead or would wish I was.

I flexed my arm, hugging it to my chest, straining my muscles to keep it there. He lifted the wrist and my whole upper body with it, but I held the arm, fingers closed into a fist.

"Do not make me hurt you, Anita."

"I'm not making you do anything. Whatever you do, it's your choice to do it, not mine."

He laid me back down, gently. "I could crush your hand." It sounded like a threat, but his voice was still gentle.

"I won't touch you again, not like that, not voluntarily."

"But lay your hand upon my chest, above my heart. That is not a hard thing, Anita."

"No."

"You are a very stubborn woman."

"You're not the first one to say it," I said.

"I will not force you."

The skinned man moved forward until he was directly against the stone, mirroring his "god." He drew an obsidian blade and bent over me. I tensed, but I didn't say anything. I could not touch him again and promise I'd come out the other side. If I was going to die anyway, I'd die whole, not possessed by some would-be god.

But he didn't stab me. He slipped the tip of the blade under the shoulder of the Kevlar vest. Kevlar isn't meant to stop a stabbing motion, but it's not an easy thing to cut through, especially with a stone knife. The empty skin hand that decorated his wrist wobbled back and forth, back and forth, as he sawed. I stared past him at the far wall, but my peripheral vision just couldn't get rid of that flopping hand. I finally had to stare up at the ceiling, but it was just darkness. It's hard to stare into the dark when there are other things to look at, but I tried.

I almost asked them if they knew what Velcro was, but didn't. It would take them awhile to cut the vest off with an obsidian blade. Hell, I might not have to do anything else to delay them. It'd be morning by the time the obsidian cut through the material. Unfortunately, I wasn't the only one who figured that out.

The skin man put the blade back in his sheath and pulled a second knife out from a sheath behind his back, the way you'd carry a backup gun. When he raised it into the firelight, it glimmered silver, steel. With or without high silver content, it would still cut through the vest a lot quicker than the obsidian.

He slipped the tip under the shoulder seam of the vest. I finally had to say something. "You just planning to cut my heart out?"

"Your heart will remain in your chest where it belongs," the "god" said.

"Then why do you want the vest off?" I finally turned my head and looked at him, though not at any of his eyes.

"If you will not touch my chest with your hand, there are other parts of your body that can feel," he said.

It was almost enough to make me give him my hand, almost. I didn't trust what he might consider other parts of my body that could feel. But it would take time to get the vest off, and if I just gave up my hand, that wouldn't take any time at all. I needed the time.

The vest came off quicker than you'd think. It was not designed to stand up to a sawing blade. They pulled the pieces of the vest off me, tugging the last from under my back.

The Red Woman's Husband climbed up beside me. He knelt, staring down at me, and he wasn't staring at my face. He traced the outline of my bra with the tip of one finger. Trailing, oh, so lightly, along my skin. "What is this?" He traced under the bra back and forth, back and forth.

"Underwire," I said.

He traced the black lace at the top of the bra. "So many new things to learn."

"Glad you like it," I said. He didn't get the sarcasm. Maybe he was immune to it.

He did what I'd thought he'd do. He climbed on top of me. But he didn't get into a standard missionary position. He scooted lower until his chest was pressed against mine. With our height differences, that put his groin safely below mine. So it wasn't rape that we were doing. Maybe it was just me that worried so much about that. But somehow the knowledge that it wasn't sex he was after scared me more. There were worse things he could take from me than sex, like my mind.

His chest pressed against mine, smooth, warm, very human. Nothing bad happened. Funny, that didn't slow the frantic beat of my heart, or make me look him in the eyes.

"Do you feel it?" he asked.

I just kept staring at the far wall of the cave. "I don't know what you mean?"

His chest pressed harder against me. "Do you feel my heart beating?"

It wasn't the question I'd been expecting, so I actually thought about it. I tried to feel the answering beat of his heart against me, but all I could feel was my own panicked pulse.

"Sorry, all I can feel is mine."

"And that is the problem," he said.

I actually looked up at him then, getting a brief glimpse of his face, leaning so close below mine, the startling glimpse of his blue-green eyes in that dark face. I looked back to the wall. "What do you mean?"

"My heart does not beat."

I tried to feel his heart then, tried to sense the pulse of his life through the warm flesh of his chest. Concentrating on it slowed my own heart. You aren't always aware of a man's heart beating against your body, but when they're lying chest to chest, you usually feel it. But his chest pressed quiet above mine. I moved my free hand slowly toward him. He raised up, supporting himself with his hands, so I could press my hand against his chest.

His skin was warm and smooth, almost perfect, but nothing beat under my hand. Either he had no heart, or it wasn't beating.

"I am only body. The Red Woman does not live in me. My heart is not a fit sacrifice without her touch."

That made me look back at him. I looked into his peaceful eyes. "Sacrifice? You're going to sacrifice yourself?"

His eyes stayed gentle and hopeful. "I will be a sacrifice to the creator gods. They need to feed on the blood of a god as they did at the beginning of time."

I tried to read something in that peaceful handsome face. Some doubt, fear, anything I could understand.

"You're going to let your priest cut you up?"

"Yes, but I will be reborn."

"You're sure of that?" I said.

"My heart will be strong enough to beat outside my body, and when it is placed back within me, the old gods will return from the exile that your white Christ has cast them into." His face, more than his words, said that he did believe it.

I'd read enough of the conquest of Mexico by the Spanish to doubt that Christ had much to do with it, no matter how many things had been done in His name. "Don't blame Jesus Christ for what the Spanish did to your people. Our God gave us free choice, and that means we can choose evil. I believe that that's what happened to the men who conquered your people."

He looked down at me, and he was puzzled again. "You believe that. I can tell you believe that."

"With all my heart," I said. "No pun intended."

He sat up, sitting across my waist. "Most of the people I have taken as offerings did not believe in much of anything. The ones who did believe, did not believe in your white Christ." He touched my face. "But you do."

"Yeah," I said.

"How can you believe in a god that would allow you to be brought to this place and sacrificed to a foreign god?"

"If you only believe when it's easy, you don't really believe," I said.

"Is it not ironic that you, a follower of the God that destroyed us, will be what allows me to come into my power. When I have taken your essence, I will be strong enough to make the precious liquid, and I will be free of this place at last."

"What do you mean, take my essence?" I'd stopped being afraid because we'd just been talking so long, or maybe I just can't sustain fear for that long. Eventually, if you don't kill me or hurt me, I stop being afraid.

"I will but kiss you and you will become as light and dry as the aged maize. You will feed me as the corn feeds men." He began to lie down beside me on my right side, near my free hand.

I was suddenly scared again. I hoped I was wrong, but I was pretty sure I'd already seen what he meant to do to me at the Obsidian Butterfly. "You mean you'll suck the life out of me and I'll end up looking like a dried mummy."

He stroked a finger down my cheek, his eyes sad now, regretful. "It will hurt a great deal, and I am sorry for that, but even your pain will go to strengthen me." He leaned his face towards mine. I had a free hand and a knife in my pocket, but if I went for it too soon and failed, I was out of options. Where the hell was Ramirez?

"You're going to torture me. Great," I said.

He drew back from me, just a little. "It is not torture. It is the way all my priests waited for my waking."

"Who brought your priests back?" I asked.

"I wakened Tlaloci, but I was weak and I had no more blood to give the others. Then before we could raise the others the man you call Riker disturbed our place of rest." He stared off into space, as if he were seeing it over again. "He found what you called the mummies of my priests. Many were torn apart by his men, searching for jewels inside them." Anger darkened his face, stole the peacefulness from his eyes. "The Quetzalcoatl was not yet awake or we would have killed them all. They took things that belonged to my priests. It forced me to find a different way to give them back their lives."

"The skins," I said.

He looked down at me. "Yes, there are ways to make them give life."

"So you hunted down the people who desecrated your . . . sleeping place, and the people who bought the things that belonged to your people."

"Yes," he said.

I guess from a certain point of view it was fair. If you had no ability to feel mercy, then it was a dandy plan. "You killed and took the organs from the people who were gifted," I said.

"Gifted?" he made it a question.

"Witches, brujos."

"Ah, yes, I did not wish to leave them alive to hunt us before I came into my power." He was touching my face again, stroking it. I think he was getting back on track to give me his "kiss".

"What exactly does coming into your power mean?" I asked. As long as I could keep him talking, he wouldn't be killing me. I could think of questions all night long.

"I will be mortal and immortal."

I widened eyes at him. "What do you mean mortal?"

"Your blood will make me mortal. Your essence will make me immortal."

I frowned at him. "I don't understand what you mean."

He cupped my face in his hands like a lover. "How could you possibly understand the ways of gods." He held out his hand, and the skin-man handed him a long bone needle. Maybe I didn't know what he was going to do.

"What's that for?"

He held the needle, maybe four inches long, twirling it slowly between his fingers. "I will pierce your ear lobe and drink your blood. It will be a small pain."

"You keep saying you want me to believe in you, but you're the only one who never seems to be in pain. Your priests, the people who stole from you, all the sacrifices, everybody hurts but you."

He propped himself up on one elbow, his body snug against mine. "If my pain will convince you of my sincerity, then so be it." He jabbed the needle into his finger, deep, deep enough to touch bone. He drew the needle out slowly, making it hurt as much as he could. I waited for blood to come to the surface, but it didn't. He held the finger so I could see the hole the needle had left, but the hole was empty, no blood. As I watched, the wound closed like water smoothing, perfect once more. The knife wasn't going to do me any good, not against him.

"Does my pain make your pain less?" he asked.

"I'll let you know," I said.

He smiled, so patient, so kind. So full of it. He started moving the needle towards my left ear. I could have fought him with my free hand, but if all he was going to do was pierce my earlobe like I'd seen at the nightclub, then he could do that. I didn't like the idea, but I wasn't going to fight him. If I fought now, they might chain my hand back up. I wanted the free hand more than I wanted to keep him from sucking on my ear.

Truth is, I don't like needles, not just doctor needles, any of them. I have a phobia about small pointed things in my body. Knives don't seem to bother me, but needles do. Go figure. It was a phobia. To keep from struggling, I finally had to close my eyes because otherwise I'd have fought. I just couldn't help it.

The pain was sharp and immediate. I gasped opening my eyes, watching his face lean over me. For a second I thought I'd blown it. I thought he was going straight to the kiss, then his mouth passed by my mouth. He turned my face to the right, gently, exposing the ear, and the long line of my neck. It reminded me of vampires, except that this mouth licked my ear, one quick movement. He made a small sigh, as he swallowed the first blood, then his mouth closed over my earlobe, mouth working at the wound, tongue coaxing blood from the wound. He pressed his body the length of mine, one hand cupping my turned head, the other playing down the line of my body. Maybe it was just blood, but I never stroked my steak while I was eating it.

The line of his jaw was pressed to my face. I could feel his mouth moving as he swallowed. I'd had vampires take blood without me being under their spell, so it had hurt. This didn't hurt nearly as much. It was more like an overzealous lover with an ear fetish. Disturbing, but not really painful. His hand moved from my face to slide inside my bra. That I didn't like.

"I thought you said you weren't offering sex."

He drew his hand out of my bra and drew back from my ear. His eyes were wide and unfocused and drowning in turquoise glow like the eyes of any vampire when its bloodlust is up. "Forgive me," he said, "but it has been so very long since I felt life in my body."

I thought I understood what he meant, but I was asking every question I could think of tonight. Anything to keep him talking. "What do you mean?"

He laughed and rolled on his side to prop himself up on his elbow again. He jabbed the needle into his finger again, and gasped. Blood welled up from the wound, crimson blood. He laughed again. "Your blood runs through my body, and I am mortal once more, with all the appetites of a mortal man."

"You need blood to have blood pressure," I said. "You've got your first hard on in centuries. I get it."

He looked down at me with drowning eyes. "You could have it." He moved so that his body was pressed against mine, and I could feel him pressed against my jeans, eager, and ready.

I started to say my usual, no, then stopped. If my choices were being raped or being killed, when I thought that help was on the way . . . I debated, and I really don't know what I would have said, because another of the skin-men ran in from behind us where the silent flayed ones waited.

I heard the man's running footsteps and turned to watch him push his way through the flayed ones. He dropped to one knee in front of the Red Woman's Husband. "My lord, armed strangers are approaching. The little brujo is with them, leading them this way."

The Red Woman's Husband looked at him. "Kill them. Delay them. When I have come into my power, it will be too late."

The skin-men got weapons out of a chest and went running. I turned my head to watch the flayed ones trail after them. Only Tlaloci the priest stayed behind. It was just the three of us. Ramirez was coming. The police were coming. Surely, I could delay a few more minutes.

Fingers touched my face, moving me to look at him. "You could have been the first woman in centuries for me, but there is no time." He began to lower his face towards me. "I am sorry that I must take you as an unwilling sacrifice because you have not harmed me or mine."

I slipped my hand into my pocket. Fingers closed on the pen. I turned my head to the side so he couldn't kiss me, but I was really looking to see where Tlaloci was in the room. He'd moved back to the altar. He'd thrown Paulina's body off to one side like so much garbage. He was cleaning the altar, preparing I think for his god's death.

The Red Woman's Husband stroked my face, trying to turn me gently towards him. He whispered, breath warm against my face. "I will wear your heart on the necklace of tongues, so that all my followers may remember your sacrifice for all eternity."

"How romantic," I said. I started easing the pen out of my pocket.

"Turn to me, Anita. Do not make me hurt you." His fingers closed on my chin and began to turn my face slowly towards his. I felt his strength in his fingers and knew he could crush my jaw with only a flexing of his hand. I couldn't keep him from turning my face up to him. I couldn't stop it, but I had the pen in my hand now. I had my finger on the button that would release the blade. I just had to make sure it was over his heart.

Gunfire sounded from outside the cave, and it sounded close as if the entrance wasn't that far away. Then there was a sound like a roaring, and I knew what it was because I'd heard it before. The police had brought flame-throwers or found some National Guard to join the party. I wondered whose idea it had been. It was a good one. I hoped they all burned.

I stared up at him, his fingers keeping my face looking at him. "Does your heart really beat for me?" I asked.

"My heart beats. Blood runs through this body. You have given me life, and now you will give me immortality."

The Red Woman's Husband leaned over me like Prince Charming about to bestow the kiss that would make everything all right again. His mouth hovered an inch above mine. The memory of how Seth's body had dried, died, was too vivid. I must have rushed to get the pen in position just above his heart. He pulled back a fraction of an inch, eyes questioning. I hit the button, and the blade took him through the heart.

His eyes flew wide, all that turquoise fire fading, leaving his eyes human looking. "What have you done?"

"You're just another kind of vampire. I kill vampires."

He rolled off the stone, fell to the floor. He held a hand out to Tlaloci. The priest rushed over to him. I didn't wait to see if there was a cure for the "god." I undid my left wrist and reached down for my ankles.

The Red Woman's Husband collapsed to his knees, and the priest collapsed with him. He was crying. "No, no, no." He pressed his hands around the hilt, trying to stop the blood from pouring out. His "god" fell into convulsions on the floor. He tried to hold his hands over the wound, to staunch the blood.

I got my ankles freed and rolled off to the other side of the stone. Call it a hunch, but I thought that Tlaloci would be upset with me.

He rose to his feet, bloodstained hands held out in front of him. I'd never seen anyone look so horrified, so desolate, as if I had destroyed his world. And maybe I had.

He never said a word, just drew the obsidian blade at his waist and stalked towards me. But the rock I'd been chained to was the size of a large dining room table, and I kept it between him and me. I kept the distance between us even, and he couldn't catch me. The gunfire was coming closer. He must have heard it, too, because he suddenly rolled over the stone to slash at me with the knife. I ran away from the stone, out into the open, which was what he wanted.

I turned and faced him. He came for me in a crouch, knife held loose but firm, as if he knew what he was doing. I'd left the blade in the vampire. I faced him hands out from my body, not sure what to do, except not get cut. I thought of one thing. I screamed, "Ramirez!"

Tlaloci rushed me, blade slashing. I turned, feeling the rush of air as the blade passed. There were screams from the stairs, the sounds of in-close fighting. Tlaloci slashed at me like a madman. All I could do was keep backing up, trying to stay out of reach. I was bleeding from both arms, and one cut on my upper chest, when I realized he'd backed me up by the altar.

I tripped over Paulina's body about the second I started looking for it, to avoid it. I went down on my side, her body trapped under my legs. I kicked out at him without looking to see where he was, anything to keep him at a distance.

He grabbed my ankle, pinning my leg against his body. We stared at each other, and I saw my death in his face. He tossed the knife one-handed so that the grip changed from slashing, to a downward stab. He had my left leg pinned, but my right leg was still on the floor. I braced my upper body with my arms, leaned my shoulders downward and drew back my right leg. I lined up his kneecap.

Tlaloci started the downward stroke. I kicked the downward edge of his kneecap with everything I had. I saw the kneecap slide sideways, dislocated. His leg crumbled, he cried out in pain, but the blade kept coming.

Tlaloci's head exploded in a shower of brains, and bone. The pieces rained down on me, and the body fell to one side, obsidian blade scrapping along the stone floor as the hand convulsed around the hilt.

I stared across the cave and saw Olaf standing at the foot of the stone steps. He was still standing in his shooting stance, one-handed, gun still pointed at where the priest had been standing. He blinked, and I watched the concentration leave his face, watched something close to human spill across his face. He started walking towards me, gun at his side. The other hand held a knife, bloody to the hilt.

I was wiping Tlaloci's brains off my face when Olaf came to stand in front of me. "I never thought I'd say this, but damn I'm glad to see you."

He actually smiled. "I saved your life."

That made me smile. "I know."

Ramirez came down the stairs with what looked like a SWAT team in full battle gear behind him. They spilled out to either side, nasty-looking guns pointed at every inch of the cavern. Ramirez just stood there, gun in hand, looking for something to shoot. National Guardsmen in flame-thrower gear came next, nozzle of the flame-thrower pointed up at the ceiling.

Olaf cleaned his knife on his pants, sheathed it, and offered me a hand. The hand was stained red, but I took it. His skin was sticky with blood, but I squeezed his hand and let him pull me to my feet.

Bernardo came into the room with more cops behind him. His cast was red with blood, the blade sticking out of it so dark with blood, it looked black. He said, "You're alive."

I nodded. "Thanks to Olaf."

He gave a small pressure to my hand, then let me go.

"I was late again," Ramirez said.

I shook my head. "Does it matter who saves the day, as long as it gets saved?"

The other cops were starting to relax as they realized there was no one to shoot.

"Is this all?" one of the black-decked cops asked.

I looked back at the far tunnel. "There's a Quetzalcoatl down that tunnel."

"A what?"

"A . . . dragon."

Even through the battle gear you could see them all exchange glances.

"Monster, if you like the word better, but it's still down there."

They got into ranks and went past me to the tunnel at a crouched run. They hesitated at the tunnel entrance, then slipped through one at a time. For once I let them go. I'd done my part for one night. Besides, they were a hell of a lot better armed than I was. One of them ordered Ramirez and some of the other more civvie looking policemen to escort the civilians to the surface.

Ramirez came to stand in front of me. "You're bleeding." He touched the cut on my arm.

I turned so he could see some of the other cuts. "Pick one."

Bernardo and the other cops that had been ordered to stay behind came to look at the two dead men. "Where's this Red Woman's Husband that the little creep kept talking about?" one of the cops asked.

I pointed at the body with the blade sticking out of its chest.

Two of the cops went to stand over the body. "He doesn't look much like a god."

"He was a vampire," I said.

That got everyone's attention. "What did you say?" Ramirez asked.

"Let's concentrate on the important details here, boys. We need to make sure that body doesn't get back up. Trust me. He is one powerful son of a bitch. We want him to stay dead."

A cop kicked the body, which rolled limply as only the true dead move. "Looks dead to me."

Watching the body roll limply made me jump, as if I expected him to sit up and say, just kidding, I'm not really dead. The body stayed still, but it hadn't done my nerves any good.

"We need to take the head and cut out his heart. Then we burn them separately and scatter the ashes over different bodies of water. Then we burn the body to ash, and scatter it over a third body of water."

"You've got to be kidding," one of the cops said.

"The flayed ones just fell down and stopped moving," Ramirez said. "Did you do that?"

"Probably when I put the knife through his heart."

"Bullets hadn't worked on any of them until the flayed one fell down, then the bullets killed everything."

"She did that?" the cop asked. "She made our bullets work?"

"Yes," Ramirez said, and probably he was right. Probably it had been me. Regardless, I wasn't going to raise any doubts. I wanted them to listen to me. I wanted to make sure that the 'god' stayed dead.

"How exactly do we chop off the head?" the same cop asked.

Olaf went to the chest that the men had gotten their weapons out of and lifted a large flat club with bits of obsidian embedded in it. He holstered his gun and walked to the body.

"Shit, that's one of those damn things they used on us," the cop said.

"Nicely ironic to use it on their god, don't you think?" Bernardo asked.

Olaf knelt beside the body.

"Hey, we didn't say you could do that," the cop said.

Olaf looked at Ramirez. "What do you say, Ramirez?"

"I say we do whatever Anita says."

Olaf whirled the club as if getting the feel for it. It also made the cops back up. He looked at me. "I'll take the head."

I pulled the knife out of Tlaloci's hand. He wasn't going to be needing it anymore. "I'll take the heart." I walked toward him, blade in hand. The cops kept backing away from us.

I stood over the vampire. Olaf knelt on the other side, looking up at me. "If I'd let you get killed, Edward would have thought I failed."

"Edward's alive then?"

"Yes."

A tightness left my shoulders that I hadn't even realized was there. "Thank God."

"I don't fail," Olaf said.

"I believe you," I said.

We stared at each other, and there was still something in his eyes that I couldn't read or understand, a step beyond whatever I'd become. I stared into his dark eyes and knew that here was a monster, not as powerful as the one that lay on the ground, but just as deadly in the right circumstances. And I owed him my life.

"You take the head first."

"Why?"

"I'm afraid if I take the knife out while the body's still intact that he'll sit up and start breathing again."

Olaf raised eyebrows at me. "You are not joking me?"

"I never joke about vampires," I said.

He gave me another long look. "You would have made a good man."

I took the compliment because that's what it was, maybe the best compliment he'd ever given a woman.

"Thank you," I said.

The SWAT team came back out of the far tunnel. "There's nothing down there. It's empty."

"Then it got away," I said. I looked at the body still lying there. "Take the head. I want out of this damn cave."

The SWAT team leader didn't like us cutting up the body. He and Ramirez went into a yelling match. While everyone was watching the argument, I nodded to Olaf and he beheaded the corpse in one blow. Blood gushed out onto the cave floor.

"What the fuck are you doing?" one of the SWAT cops asked, bringing his gun pointed at us.

"My job," I said. I put the tip of the blade under the ribs.

The policeman brought the gun up to his shoulder. "Get away from the body until the captain tells you it's okay to do it."

I kept the knife against the body. "Olaf."

"Yes."

"If he shoots me, kill him."

"My pleasure." The big man turned his eyes to the policeman, and there was something in that gaze that made the heavily armed man take a step back.

The captain in question said, "Stand down, Reynolds. She's a vamp executioner. Let her do her job."

I plunged the blade into the skin, and it slid home. I cut a hole just below his ribs and reached into the hole. It was tight and wet and slick, and it took two hands to get the heart out, one to cut it free of the connecting tissue, and one to hold onto it. I drew it from the chest, blood stained to my elbows.

I caught Ramirez and Bernardo both looking at me, with nearly identical looks on their faces. I didn't think either of them would be wanting a date any time soon. They'd always remember watching me cut a man's heart out, and that memory would stain anything else. With Bernardo, I didn't give a shit. With Ramirez, it hurt to see that look in his eyes.

A hand touched the heart. I stared at that hand, then looked up to meet Olaf's eyes. He wasn't repulsed. He stroked the heart, hands sliding over mine. I pulled away, and we looked at each other over the body we'd butchered. No, Olaf wasn't repulsed. The look in his eyes was that pure darkness that only fills a man's eyes in the most intimate of situations. He raised the severed head up by the hair and held it almost as if he'd let me kiss it. Then I realized he was holding it over the heart, like a matched pair.

I had to turn away from what I saw in his face. "Does anyone have a bag that I can carry this in?"

Someone finally found an empty equipment bag and let me spill the heart into it. The policeman told me I could keep the bag. He didn't want it back.

No one offered Olaf a bag, and he never asked.

63

THEY FOUND MY GUNS in the chest with the rest of the weapons, though the holsters were missing. I just couldn't keep a holster intact on this job. But I stuffed the guns down my jeans. The knives weren't in the chest. Ramirez drove me personally to a crematorium so that I could see the heart and head burned down to ash. When I had two little containers of ash, it was almost dawn. I fell asleep in the seat beside him, or he'd have had a fight about taking me to the hospital. But he insisted that the doctors check me out. Amazingly enough, none of the cuts were even deep enough for stitches. I wouldn't even have any new scars. Miraculous.

One of the men had given me a jacket that said FBI on it to cover my nearly naked upper body. Several of the uniforms and most of the hospital staff assumed I was a federal agent. I kept having to correct people, and I finally realized that the emergency room doctor thought my denial meant I had a concussion and didn't know who I was. The more I argued the more concerned he got. He ordered a series of head X-rays, and I couldn't talk him out of it.

I was actually sitting in a wheelchair waiting to be escorted to X-ray when Bernardo came up. He touched the FBI jacket. "You're moving up in the world."

"When the nurse comes back, he'll be taking me down to X-ray."

"You okay?"

"Just precautionary," I said.

"I just came back from checking on the invalids."

"Olaf said Edward would live."

"He will."

"How are the kids?"

"Peter is okay. They put Becca in a room. She's got a cast to her elbow."

I stared at his cast stained a dirty brown. "That thing is going to start stinking with all that blood dried into it."

"The doc wants me to get a new cast, but I wanted to check on everyone first."

"Where's Olaf?"

Bernardo shrugged. "I don't know. He disappeared once the monsters were all dead and Ramirez had you in his car. He said something about the job being done. I guess he went back under whatever rock Edward found him under."

I started to nod, then remembered something that Edward had said. "Edward told you that you couldn't have a woman because he'd forbidden Olaf to have women, right?"

"Yeah, but the job's over, babe. I am headed for the first open bar."

I looked at him, nodding. "Maybe that's where Olaf is."

He frowned at me. "Olaf's at a bar?"

"No, he's out getting his ashes hauled, his way."

We both looked at each other, and there was a moment when horror dawned on Bernardo's face, and he whispered, "Oh, my god, he's out killing someone."

I shook my head. "If he's just out killing at random, there's no way to find him, but what if it's not random?"

"What do you mean?"

"Remember how he looked at Professor Dallas?"

Bernardo looked at me. "You don't think . . . I mean he wouldn't . . . oh, shit."

I got up out of the wheelchair and said, "I've got to tell Ramirez what we're thinking."

"You don't know he's there. You don't know he's doing anything wrong."

"Do you believe he just went home?" I asked.

Bernardo seemed to think about that for a second, then shook his head.

"Neither do I."

"He saved your life," Bernardo said.

"I know." We went to the elevator.

The elevator doors opened and Lieutenant Marks was standing there. "Where the fuck do you think you're going?"

"Marks, I think that Professor Dallas is in danger." I got into the elevator.

Bernardo followed.

"You think I'd believe anything you say, witch?" He hit the button that kept the doors open.

"Hate me if you want, but don't let her die."

"Your pet FBI agent kept me out of the big raid."

I didn't know what he meant, but I was pretty sure who he meant. "Whatever Bradley did, he did without me knowing, but that's not the point."

"I can make it the point."

"Did you hear that Dallas is in danger? Did you hear that part?" I asked.

"She's as corrupt as you are."

"So it's okay that she dies a horrible death," I said.

He just looked at me. I moved as if to go towards the buttons. Bernardo caught his clue. He hit Marks in the head with his cast. The man went down, and I hit the door closed button. The doors hushed closed as Bernardo lowered Marks to the floor.

"You want me to kill him?" Bernardo asked.

"No." But now if I went to Ramirez for help, Marks would think he'd been in on it. Shit. "Do you have Edward's car?"

"Yeah."

"How did Olaf drive off, then?"

Bernardo looked at me. "If he's really doing this, he'll steal a car and ditch it away from the murder scene. He won't chance using Edward's car."

"He'll go back to Edward's house for his goody bag," I said.

The doors opened on the floor that he'd parked on. We got out. "What do you mean goody bag?"

"If he's going to cut her up, then he'll want the tools he normally uses. Serial murderers are very anal when it comes to how the victims are treated. They spend a lot of time planning exactly what they'll do and how."

"So he's at Edward's?"

"How long has he been gone?"

"Three hours, maybe three and a half."

"No, he'll be at Dallas's, if that's where he is at all."

Bernardo opened the car, and we got in. I had to take the Browning out of my pants. The barrel's just too long for sitting down like that. I ended up holding it in my lap. I watched Bernardo drive with his cast-wrapped arm. "You need me to drive?"

"I'm fine. Just tell me where Dallas lives, and I'll drive us."

"Shit!"

He put the car in park and looked at me. "The police would know the address."

"When Marks wakes up, we'll be lucky to stay out of jail," I said.

"We don't even know that Olaf's at her house," he said.

"I got a better one. How to explain that we know he was a serial murderer and didn't warn the police sooner."

"Do you have Edward's cell phone?" I asked.

He didn't argue, just leaned across and opened the glove compartment. I got the phone out.

"Who you going to call?"

"Itzpapalotl. She'll know the address."

"She'll eat Olaf's face."

"Maybe, maybe not. Either way you better get us out of the parking area before Marks wakes up and starts screaming."

He drove us out of the parking lot and started slowly down the street. I dialed information, and the operator was happy to dial The Obsidian Butterfly for me. It was daylight. I knew better than to ask for Itzpapalotl herself, so I asked for Pinotl and told them it was an emergency and it was Anita Blake. I think it was my name that got me through, as if they'd been expecting the call.

Pinotl came on the line with his rich voice. "Anita, my mistress said you would call."

I was betting that she'd been wrong on the why, but . . . "Pinotl, I need the address for Professor Dallas's house."

Silence on the other end of the phone.

"She's in danger, Pinotl."

"Then we will take care of it."

"I'm going to have to call the police in on this, Pinotl. They'd shoot your werejaguars on sight."

"You are worried about our people?" he said.

"Give me the address, and I'll take care of it for you, Pinotl."

Silence except for his breathing.

"Tell your mistress, thanks for her help, Pinotl. I know I'm alive now because she helped me."

"You are not angry that she did not tell you all she knew?"

"She's a centuries old vampire. They can't help themselves sometimes."

"She is a goddess."

"We're just arguing semantics, Pinotl. We both know what she is. Please give me the address."

He gave it to me. I read the directions to Bernardo, and off we went.

64

I CALLED THE POLICE on the way. I made it an anonymous call. Saying I'd heard screams. I hung up without giving my name. If Olaf wasn't there, then they'd scare the hell out of Dallas, and I'd apologize. I'd even pay for any busted locks.

"Why didn't you tell them the truth?" Bernardo asked.

"What? I think that some serial killer is there murdering her. And how do you know this, ma'am? Well, officer, you see it's like this. I've known he was a serial killer for days now, but our mutual friend Ted Forrester had forbidden him from attacking women while he was here helping us solve the mutilation murders. You've heard of the mutilation murders. Who is this? It's Anita Blake, the vampire executioner. And what does an executioner know about serial murderers? More than you'd think." I looked at Bernardo.

"All right, all right. They'd still be asking questions when we arrived at the house."

"This way they'll send an Albuquerque PD car there ASAP. They'll get there before we can even come close."

"I didn't think you even liked Dallas when we met her."

"It doesn't matter if I like her or not."

"Yes, it does," he said.

"If I don't like her, then we just let Olaf butcher her, is that it?"

"He saved your life. He saved mine. We don't owe this woman anything."

I looked at him, trying to read his face from just the profile. "Are you saying that you won't back me on this, Bernardo? Because if you're not on my side on this, then I need to know because if we go up against Olaf, and you hesitate, then you're going to get yourself killed, and maybe me."

"If I go in, I'll go in ready to kill him."

"If?" I said.

"I owe him my life, Anita. While we were at Riker's, we saved each other's lives. We counted on each other and knew the other one would be there. I don't owe this Dallas chick anything."

"Then stay in the car." A thought occurred to me. "Or are you saying that you're on his side, really on his side?" I had the Browning out in my hand already. I clicked the safety off, and he heard it. I saw him stiffen.

"Well, that's not fair. If I take my left hand off to pull a gun, then we wreck."

"I didn't like the way the conversation was going," I said.

"All I'm saying, Anita, is that if we can save Dallas and let Olaf get away we should let him go. It'd make things even between us all."

"If Dallas is unharmed, I'll think about it. That's the best I can do. But let me remind you if you plan on killing me to help Olaf that Edward is going to live. He'd hunt you both down, and you know it."

"Hey, I never said anything about pulling down on you."

"Just trying to test the limits of our misunderstanding, Bernardo, because trust me, you don't want me to misunderstand you."

"There's no misunderstanding," Bernardo said, and there was no teasing in his voice, just a dry seriousness that reminded me of Edward. "I think it's shitty to turn Olaf in to the cops."

"They'll already be there, Bernardo."

"If there's only two uniforms, we can help him get away."

"Are you talking about killing the policemen?"

"I didn't say that."

"Don't. Don't go there because not only will I not follow you, I'll bury you there."

"For two cops you don't even know."

"Yeah, for two cops I don't even know."

"Why?" he said.

I shook my head. "Bernardo, if you have to ask that, you wouldn't understand the answer."

He glanced at me. "Edward said that you were one of the best shooters he'd seen, quick to kill. He said you only had two faults. You got too up close and personal with the monsters, and you thought too much like an honest cop."

"An honest cop, I like that," I said.

"I've seen you, Anita. You're as much a killer as Olaf, or me. You're not a cop. You never were."

"Whatever I am, we are not killing the cops on sight. If Dallas is unhurt, we'll discuss letting Olaf go, but if he's hurt her, then he pays. If you don't like the plan, then give up your weapons and wait in the car. I'll go in alone."

Bernardo looked at me. "What's to keep me from lying to you, keeping my guns, and shooting you in the back?"

"You're more afraid of Edward than you are grateful to Olaf."

"You know that for a fact," he said.

"I know that Olaf has more rules of honor than you do. If you'd really felt all that damn grateful you'd have said something before I called the cops. Being protective of Olaf wasn't your first thought, or your second, or even your third."

"Edward said you were one of the most loyal people he'd ever met. So why aren't you protecting Olaf?"

"He preys on women, Bernardo. He preys on them not because he's paid to or owes them vengeance, but because that's what he does. He's like a vicious dog that keeps attacking people. Eventually, you have to put it down."

"You're going in there planning to kill him," Bernardo said.

"No, no I'm not. Remember, if I kill either of you, I'll either owe Edward another favor, or I'll have to draw a gun on him and finally find out which of us is better. I don't think I'll survive the latter, and I have not had a good time honoring Edward's favor. I got a glimpse of his other life at Riker's place. I don't want to be in another firefight. It's not my cup of tea."

"It's not anyone's cup of tea," Bernardo said. "You just get used to it."

"You don't get used to shit like that."

"Like you don't get used to cutting out people's hearts? You did that like an old pro."

I shrugged. "Practice makes perfect."

"This is the street," Bernardo said.

The street had that just past dawn silence. The cars still sat unmoved in their driveways, but there were people standing in their driveways peering out at the marked police car that was sitting in front of Dallas's house. One of the doors was open, filling the quiet neighborhood with the radio squawk. The lights rotated pale and underdone like a child's toy in the heavy morning light.

Professor Dallas's house was a small ranch with those faux adobe walls that everyone was so fond of here. In the earlier morning light it looked almost golden, as if it glowed. Bernardo parked by the road.

"Well?" I asked.

"I'm with you." But before we could draw guns, the two uniforms came out of the house with Dallas in a robe. We sat there staring at her, smiling at the policemen while they apologized for bothering her. She looked up, noticed us. She looked puzzled but waved at us.

"Anita, look at the mailbox," Bernardo said,

Our car was almost right in front of the mailbox. There was a white envelope pinned to the front of the mailbox with a knife. My first name was printed in block letters on the front of the envelope. No one had noticed it yet, but us.

Edward's car was tall enough to hide it from the neighbors. "Can you help me hide it from the cops?"

"My pleasure."

I got out of the car, leaving the Browning on the seat because I couldn't figure out a way to put it down my pants without the police noticing me doing it, and I didn't have any ID on me. I might be able to fake being a Fed, but then again maybe not. And it's it a federal offense to impersonate a federal agent. Bernardo and I had assaulted a police officer. We didn't need any more charges.

Bernardo pulled the knife out, making the movement look natural. The envelope dropped into my hand, and I walked up to the house hitting my thigh with the envelope, as if I'd carried it from the car.

Neither of the cops yelled, "Halt, thief!" so I kept moving. I didn't know what Bernardo had done with the knife. It had just vanished. "Hi, Dallas, what's up?"

"Someone made a prank phone call about screams coming from my house."

"Who'd do such a dastardly thing?" Bernardo asked.

I frowned at him.

He smiled at me, pleased with himself

"Did you get a call, too?" she asked.

"I got it," Bernardo said. "They called Edward's cell phone, said you were in danger."

The uniform cops made the same mistake that the hospital staff had made. They introduced themselves by rank and name, and shook hands. I said, "Anita Blake. This is Bernardo Spotted-Horse."

"He's not a . . ." the policeman looked uncomfortable as soon as he started to say it.

"No, I'm not a federal agent," Bernardo said. There was bitterness in his voice. "It's the hair," I said. "They've never seen a male agent with long hair."

"Sure, it was the hair."

The uniforms went off, leaving us at Dallas' doorstep in the morning light with her curious neighbors coming out in drips and drabs to see what was happening at an hour past dawn on the quiet street.

"Would you like to come inside? I already started coffee."

"Sure."

Bernardo looked at me, but followed me in.

The kitchen was small, square, and neat like one that wasn't used much. But it was cheerful in a blaze of morning sunlight. "What's really going on, Anita?"

I sat down at her table and opened the envelope with my name on it. It was written in block letters.

ANITA,

I KNEW THAT MOMENT IN THE CAVE THAT YOU WOULD THINK AS I DID. I FELT THAT YOU WOULD KNOW WHERE I WOULD GO TO HUNT. NOW HERE YOU ARE. I AM NEARBY.

That made me look up. "He says he's nearby."

Bernardo drew his gun. He stood and began to watch the windows.

I went back to the note.

I HAVE WATCHED YOU COME TO THE GOOD PROFESSOR'S RESCUE. I WATCHED YOU TAKE THE ENVELOPE, AND I KNOW YOU ARE READING IT NOW. I BELITTLED EDWARD WHEN HE SPOKE OF SOUL MATES. I OWE HIM AN APOLOGY. WHEN I SAW YOU TAKE HIS HEART, SO PRACTICED, I KNEW THAT YOU WERE AS I AM. HOW MANY HAVE YOU KILLED? HOW MANY HEARTS HAVE YOU RIPPED OUT? HOW MANY HEADS HAVE YOU TAKEN? YOU'LL ARGUE WITH YOURSELF THAT YOU ARE NOT AS I AM. MAYBE YOU DON'T TAKE TROPHIES, BUT YOU STILL LIVE FOR THE KILL, ANITA. YOU WOULD WITHER AND DIE WITHOUT THE VIOLENCE. WHAT TRICK OF FATE HAS MADE YOU PHYSICALLY THE WOMAN I KILL OVER AND OVER AGAIN, AND YET PUT INSIDE THAT TINY BODY THE OTHER HALF OF MY SOUL? ARE MOST OF THE VAMPIRES YOU KILL MEN? DO YOU HAVE YOUR VICTIM PREFERENCE, ANITA?

I WOULD LOVE TO HUNT WITH YOU AT MY SIDE. I WOULD HUNT YOUR VICTIMS BECAUSE I KNOW YOU WILL NOT HUNT MINE. BUT WE WOULD STILL KILL TOGETHER AND CUT THE BODIES UP, AND THAT WOULD BE MORE THAN I EVER DREAMED OF SHARING WITH A WOMAN.

The note wasn't signed. Big surprise there, since I might have given it to the police.

"You look pale," Dallas said.

"What does the note say?" Bernardo asked.

I handed it to him. "I don't think he's out there to kill us or even her."

"Who are you talking about?" she asked.

I told her, and she laughed at me. "You know I'm a vampire executioner."

"Yes."

"I killed another vamp last night. One I think that Itzpapalotl wanted me to kill. She helped me do it. That's the heart that I took."

Bernardo read faster than I would have thought. "Jesus, Anita, Olaf has a crush on you."

"A crush," I said, "a crush. God, there's got to be another word for it."

Dallas asked, "Can I read it?"

"I think you should because he didn't wait just to catch a glimpse of me. He waited because if I hadn't shown up, he'd have come in here and butchered you."

She tried to laugh it off, but there must have been something in my face that choked the laughter and made her reach a shaking hand out for the letter. She read it and said, "Who is this?"

"Olaf," I said.

"But he was so nice."

Bernardo made a harsh sound.

"Trust me on this, Dallas. Olaf is not nice."

She looked from one to the other of us. "You're not kidding, are you?"

"He's a serial killer. I just don't think he's ever killed in this country."

"You should turn him in to the police," she said.

"I don't have any proof of what he's done."

"Besides," Bernardo said, "what if he was one of the vamps?"

"What do you mean?" Dallas asked.

"He means wouldn't you protect one of the vamps from the police because you'd know that the vamps would take care of it," I said.

"Well, yes, I guess."

"And we'll take care of this," Bernardo said.

She looked from one to the other of us, and for the first time she looked afraid.

"Will he be back?"

"For you, I don't think so," Bernardo said. He looked at me. "But I bet he'll find a reason to come to St. Louis."

I'd have liked to say he was wrong, but the cold tight feeling in my stomach agreed with Bernardo. I'd be seeing Olaf again. I just had to decide what I'd do when I met him. He hadn't done anything wrong on this trip. Not only couldn't I prove he was a serial killer, he hadn't done anything worse than I'd done this time round. Who was I to throw stones? Yet, yet, I hoped he stayed away from me. For more reasons than I wanted to admit, maybe. Maybe for the same reasons that I'd kill him if he came. Because maybe there was some truth to what he wrote. I had over fifty kills. What really separated me from people like Olaf? Motive, method? If those were the only differences, then Olaf was right, and I couldn't let him be right. I just could not accept that. Growing up to be Edward was a problem. Growing up to be Olaf was a nightmare.

EPILOGUE

MARKS TRIED TO PRESS assault charges, but Bernardo and I said we didn't know what he was talking about. Doctor Evans said that his injuries were inconsistent with being hit by a person. It wouldn't have worked except that Marks was in the doghouse about how he'd handled the case. He was in on the press conference where the public was assured that the danger was over, but Ramirez was standing up there beside him, along with Agent Bradford. And me. They put Ted and Bernardo up there, too. We didn't get to answer questions, but we got our picture in the papers. I'd have rather not, but I knew it would please Bert, my boss, and they did print it in several national papers that I was Anita Blake of Animators, Inc. Bert loved it.

Edward caught a secondary infection from something that had been smeared on the stake. He took a relapse, and I stayed. Donna and I took turns sitting by his bed. Sitting by Becca's bed. It got to the point where the little girl cried when I left.

Peter spent a lot of time playing games with her, trying to get her to smile. But his eyes had that hollow look you get when you're not sleeping well. He wouldn't talk to me or Donna. The only thing he'd admitted to her was the beating. He hadn't told her about the rape. I didn't betray his secret. First, I wasn't sure she could handle another shock. Second, it wasn't my secret to tell. Donna actually rose to the occasion. She was like this incredible pillar of strength for the kids, for Ted, even though he couldn't hear her talking to him. She never once turned to me in tears. It was like this new person had risen from the ashes of the person I'd first met. It saved me having to hurt her.

Ten days after the accident, Edward was awake and talking. Out of danger. I could finally go home. When I told them I was finally going home, Donna hugged me tight and cried and said, "You have to tell the kids good-bye."

I assured her I would, and she left us alone, to say our good-byes.

I pulled the chair up to the bedside and studied his face. He was still pale, but he looked like Edward again. That cold bleakness was back in his eyes when no one but me was looking.

"What's wrong?" he asked.

"It couldn't just be because you nearly died," I said.

"No," he said.

I smiled, but he didn't smile back.

"Bernardo came to see me, but Olaf never did," he said.

I realized then what he thought I'd waited around to tell him. "You think I killed Olaf, and I've been waiting for you to get healthy enough to give you the same choice you gave me after Harley died." I laughed. "Sweet Jesus, Edward."

"You didn't kill him." I watched him relax against his pillows, visibly relieved.

"No, I didn't kill him."

He managed a faint smile. "It wouldn't have been the same choice. But if you'd killed Olaf, you wouldn't have wanted to owe me another favor."

"You were afraid I'd press the point, make it the gunfight at the OK Corral?"

"Yes," he said.

"I thought you wanted to see which of us was better."

"I thought I was dying on the stairs. All I could think of was that Peter and Becca were going to die in there with me. Bernardo and Olaf were there, but you'd gone up the stairs and hadn't come back. When you came back around that corner, I knew you'd get the kids out. I knew you'd risk your life for theirs. Bernardo and Olaf would have tried, but the kids wouldn't have been their first priority. I knew they would be yours. When I passed out in the cave, I wasn't worried. I knew you'd see it right."

"What are you saying, Edward?"

"I'm saying if you had killed Olaf, I'd have given you a pass on it because Peter and Becca mean more to me than that."

I took Olaf's letter out of my back pocket and handed it to him. He read it while I watched his face. Nothing moved but his eyes. He had no reaction. "He's a good man at your back, Anita."

"You're not suggesting I date Olaf?"

He almost laughed. "No, fuck no. Stay as far away from him as you can. If he comes to St. Louis, kill him. Don't wait for him to deserve it. Just do it."

"I thought he was your friend."

"Not friend. Business associate. It's not the same thing."

"I agree someone needs to kill Olaf, but why are you so adamant all of a sudden? You trusted him enough to bring him here to your town."

"Olaf has never had a girlfriend. He's had whores and he's had victims. Maybe it's true love, but I think if he shows up and finds that you won't be his little serial killer pin-up girl, that he'll turn violent. You don't want to know what he's like when he's violent, Anita. You really, really don't."

"You're scared he'll come after me."

"If he shows in town, call me."

I nodded. "I will." I had other questions. "Riker's house sprang a mysterious gas leak and blew to Kingdom Come. No survivors, no bodies, no evidence that we did shit, or that Riker and his men did shit. Was it Van Cleef?"

"Not him personally," Edward said.

"You know the next question," I said.

"I know," he said.

"You're not going to tell me, are you?"

"I can't tell you, Anita. One of the conditions to leaving was to never talk about it with anyone. If I break that, they'll come after me."

"I wouldn't tell anyone."

He shook his head. "No, Anita, trust me on this one. Ignorance is bliss."

"That is incredibly frustrating," I said.

He smiled. "I know, and I'm sorry."

"No, you're not. You love keeping secrets."

"Not this one," he said. There was something close to sadness in his eyes, and for the first time I realized for sure that once there had been a kinder, gentler version of Edward. He hadn't been born this way. He'd been made like Frankenstein's monster.

"No answers, huh?"

"No," he said.

We stared at each other, but neither of us seemed impatient.

"Okay," I said.

"Okay, what?" he asked.

I shrugged. "You won't answer questions about your background, fine. Answer another one. Are you going to marry Donna?"

"If I say, yes, what will you do?"

I sighed. "I was willing to kill you to keep you away from them when I got here. But what is love, Edward? You're willing to give up your life for the kids. You'd do the same for Donna. She's convinced you're her dream man. It's a good act. Becca told her what you did, what we did. Peter backed it. So in a way they all three know what you are, who you are. Donna's cool with it." I stopped talking.

"Was there an answer to my question in there somewhere?"

"I won't do anything, Edward. You're willing to die for them. If that's not love, it's so close I can't tell the difference."

He nodded. "Nice that I have your blessing."

"You don't," I said. "But I don't have room to throw stones at your personal life. So do whatever you want."

"I will," he said.

"Peter hasn't told Donna what happened to him. He needs therapy for it."

"Why didn't you tell her?"

"It's not my secret to tell. Besides, you're his would-be stepfather, and you know. I trust you to do the right thing by him, Edward. If he doesn't want Donna to know, you'll find a way around it."

"You're treating me like his father," Edward said.

"How much did you see of what Peter did to Amanda?"

"Enough," Edward said.

"He emptied the clip into her, Edward. He turned her face into spaghetti. The look in his face . . ." I shook my head. "He's more your son than Donna's and has been since he blew away his father's killer when he was eight."

"You think he's like me?"

"Like us," I said, "like us. I don't know if you can rebuild someone that got that broken that early. I'm not a psychiatrist. Healing people's not my job."

"It's not mine either," he said.

"I never thought you missed the pieces of yourself that you gave up to be who and what you are, but when I see you with Donna and Becca and Peter, I see regret in you. You wonder what life might have been like if you hadn't met Van Cleef, or whoever the hell was first."

He looked at me, eyes cold. "It took me a long time to understand what I saw in Donna. How did you know?"

I shrugged. "Maybe, the same thing I thought I saw in Ramirez."

"It's not too late for you, Anita."

"It's too late for me to have the white picket fence, Edward. Maybe I can figure out something, but not that. It's too late for that."

"You think I'll fail with Donna," he said.

I shook my head. "I don't know. I just know it wouldn't work for me. I'm not the actor you are. Whoever I'm with has to know who I am, warts and all, or it won't work."

"You know which monster you're going to settle down with?"

"No, but I know I can't keep hiding from them. Hiding from them is like hiding from who I am. I'm not going to do that anymore."

"You think I'm running from myself by going with Donna."

"No, I think you always embraced the monster part of you. You're finding for the first time that not all of you is dead as you wanted it to be. Donna appeals to a part of you that you didn't know was left."

"Yes," he said. "And what do Richard and Jean-Claude represent for you?"

"I don't know, but it's time I found out."

He smiled, but it wasn't a happy smile. "Good luck."

"The same to you," I said.

"We're going to need it," he said.

I'd have liked to argue, but he was right.

I did call Itzpapalotl before I left for home. She was disappointed that I didn't come in person, but not angry. I think she knew why I didn't want to shake hands again. She'd killed every minion of every rival vamp that crossed her path for fifty years, but me she hadn't harmed a hair on my head. I thought she wanted the secret to the triumvirate, and that had interested her, but that hadn't been what saved me. She'd set me up to kill the Red Woman's Husband. She'd given me the power to both attract him and withstand his charms. I'd been her bait and her weapon. Now the other god was dead, and I was leaving her territory before she decided that I'd outlived my usefulness.

She extended an invitation to my master. "We could have much to discuss, your master and I."

I told her I'd pass along the invitation. I will, but they'll be ice skating in hell before I bring Jean-Claude down to meet Itzpapalotl. She'd gobble him up. Maybe Edward's right. Maybe Richard and I would survive Jean-Claude's death. But surviving his death and surviving whatever Itzpapalotl would do to him are two very different things.

There are so many easier ways to kill Jean-Claude. Ways that would be less risky to Richard and me. I know that's what Edward wants me to do. Several of my friends are voting that way. But I get presidential veto, and I don't want him dead. I'm not sure what I do want, but I know I want him walking around so I can decide.

I'm going home, and I'm going to start by seeing all the friends I've neglected for the past few months. So Ronnie is dating Richard's best friend. So what? She and I can still be friends. Catherine's had two years of honeymooning. Time I stopped using that as an excuse not to see her. I think I'm just uncomfortable with how terribly happy she is with a man that I found ordinary and a little boring. But she glows around him. I haven't done much glowing lately around either of my two men.

I'm going to start seeing the werewolves in Richard's pack again, and Jean-Claude's vamps. First renew friendships, then if that works out okay, I'll see the boys. It's a cautious plan, nay cowardly, but it's the best I can do. Okay, it's the best

I'm willing to do. Because the truth is that I am no closer to a solution to my love life than I was when I broke off with them over a year ago. The few times I fell off the celibacy wagon don't count because I was still trying to avoid them. I don't want to avoid them. I just want to know what exactly it is that I do want. Once I figure out what I want, who I want, the next question is can I have who I want or will the loser pull our little house down around us in bloody ruins. I would say it's the sixty-four thousand dollar question, but Richard and Jean-Claude are worth so much more than that to me. Maybe Ramirez is right. Maybe if I truly loved one of them, the choice would be easy. Or maybe Ramirez doesn't know what the hell he's talking about.

Edward loves Donna and Peter and Becca. They're all seeing a therapist together, but I think Peter is still lying about what really happened. You can't get good therapy if you lie to your therapist. But I think Peter is counting on Edward to be his therapist. Scary thought, isn't it?

Edward loves Donna. Do I love Richard? Yes. Do I love Jean-Claude? Maybe. If it's really yes for Richard, and maybe for Jean-Claude, then why don't I have my answer? Because maybe, just maybe, there is no one right answer. I'm beginning to worry that whatever I decide, I will be left mourning the one that got away. Once, I'd been afraid if I chose Richard that Jean-Claude would kill him rather than share me, but strangely the vampire seems willing to share, and Richard isn't. Maybe Jean-Claude loves the power of the triumvirate more than he loves me, or maybe Richard is just jealous. I certainly wouldn't share either of them with another woman. Fair is fair. Which brings me back to the original question: who is the love of my life? Maybe I don't have one. Maybe it's not love at all. But if it's not love, then what is it? I wish I knew.

NARCISSUS IN CHAINS

This one's for J., who renewed my faith in men,
love and happiness. Thank You.

Acknowledgments

To my writing group, who didn't get to see this one before it went to New York. Tom Drennan, Rett MacPherson, Deborah Millitello, Marella Sands, Sharon Shinn, and Mark Sumner. May this be the last book that doesn't get to go through the group due to time constraints, or any other reason. Thanks to Joan-Marie Knappenberger for letting Trinity come over to play with Melissa while I did last-minute things. Thanks to Darla Cook, who helps keep me sane, and Robin Bell, for almost the same reason. Thanks to all the fans for their enthusiasm. Anita and I, both, appreciate it.

1

JUNE HAD COME in like its usual hot, sweaty self, but a freak cold front had moved in during the night and the car radio had been full of the record low temperatures. It was only in the low sixties, not that cold, but after weeks of eighty- and ninety-plus, it felt downright frigid. My best friend, Ronnie Sims, and I were sitting in my Jeep with the windows down, letting the unseasonably cool air drift in on us. Ronnie had turned thirty tonight. We were talking about how she felt about the big 3-0 and other girl talk. Considering that she's a private detective and I raise the dead for a living it was pretty ordinary talk. Sex, guys, turning thirty, vampires, werewolves. You know, the usual.

We could have gone inside the house, but there is something about the intimacy of a car after dark that makes you want to linger. Or maybe it was the sweet smell of springlike air coming through the windows like the caress of some half-remembered lover.

"Okay, so he's a werewolf. No one's perfect," Ronnie said. "Date him, sleep with him, marry him. My vote's for Richard."

"I know you don't like Jean-Claude."

"Don't like him!" Her hands gripped the passenger-side door handle, squeezing it until I could see the tension in her shoulders. I think she was counting to ten. "If I killed as easily as you do, I'd have killed that son of a bitch two years ago and your life would be a lot less complicated now."

That last was an understatement. But . . . "I don't want him dead, Ronnie."

"He's a vampire, Anita. He *is* dead." She turned and looked at me in the dark. Her soft gray eyes and yellow hair had turned to silver and near white in the cold light of the stars. The shadows and bright reflected light left her face in bold relief, like some modern painting. But the look on her face was almost frightening. There was a fearful determination there.

If it had been me with that look on my face, I'd have warned me not to do anything stupid, like kill Jean-Claude. But Ronnie wasn't a shooter. She'd killed twice, both times to save my life. I owed her. But she wasn't a person who could hunt someone down in cold blood and kill him. Not even a vampire. I knew this about her, so I didn't have to caution her. "I used to think I knew what dead was or wasn't, Ronnie." I shook my head. "The line isn't so clear-cut."

"He seduced you," she said.

I looked away from her angry face and stared at the foil-wrapped swan in my lap. Deirdorfs and Hart, where we'd had dinner, got creative with their doggy bags: foil-wrapped animals. I couldn't argue with Ronnie, and I was getting tired of trying.

Finally, I said, "Every lover seduces you, Ronnie, that's the way it works."

She slammed her hands so hard onto the dashboard it startled me and must have hurt her. "Damn it, Anita, it's not the same."

I was starting to get angry, and I didn't want to be angry, not with Ronnie. I had taken her out to dinner to make her feel better, not to fight. Louis Fane, her steady boyfriend, was out of town at a conference, and she was bummed about that, and about turning thirty. So I'd tried to make her feel better, and she seemed determined to make me feel worse.

"Look, I haven't seen either Jean-Claude or Richard for six months. I'm not dating either of them, so we can skip the lecture on vampire ethics."

"Now that's an oxymoron," she said.

"What is?" I asked.

"Vampire ethics," she said.

I frowned at her. "That's not fair, Ronnie."

"You are a vampire executioner, Anita. You are the one who taught me that they aren't just people with fangs. They are monsters."

I'd had enough. I opened the car door and slid to the edge of the seat. Ronnie grabbed my shoulder. "Anita, I'm sorry. I'm sorry. Please don't be mad."

I didn't turn around. I sat there with my feet hanging out the door, the cool air creeping into the closer warmth of the car.

"Then drop it, Ronnie. I mean drop it."

She leaned over and gave me a quick hug from behind. "I'm sorry. It's none of my business who you sleep with."

I leaned into the hug for a moment. "That's right, it's not." Then I pulled away and got out of the car. My high heels crunched on the gravel of my driveway. Ronnie had wanted us to dress up, so we had. It was her birthday. It wasn't until after dinner that I'd realized her diabolical scheme. She'd had me wear heels and a nice little black skirt outfit. The top was actually, gasp, a well-fitted halter top. Or would that be backless evening wear? However pricey it was, it was still a very short skirt and a halter top. Ronnie had helped me pick the outfit out about a week ago. I should have known her innocent "oh, let's just both dress up" was a ruse. There had been other dresses that covered more skin and had longer hemlines, but none that camouflaged the belly-band holster that cut across my lower waist. I'd actually taken the holster along with us on the shopping trip, just to be sure. Ronnie thought I was being paranoid, but I don't go anywhere after dark unarmed. Period.

The skirt was just roomy enough and black enough to hide the fact that I wore the belly band and a Firestar 9 mm. The top was heavy enough material, what there was of it, that you really couldn't see the handle of the gun under the cloth. All I had to do was lift the bottom of the top and the gun was right there, ready to be drawn. It was the most user-friendly dressy outfit I'd ever owned. Made me wish they made it in a different color so I could have two of them.

Ronnie's plan had been to go to a club on her birthday. A dance club. Eek. I never went to clubs. I did not dance. But I went in with her. Yes, she got me out on the floor, mainly because her dancing alone was attracting too much unwanted male attention. At least with both of us dancing together the would-be Casanovas stayed at a distance. Though saying I danced was inaccurate. I stood there and sort of swayed. Ronnie danced. She danced like it was her last night on Earth and she had to put every muscle to good use. It was spectacular, and a little frightening. There was something almost desperate to it, as if Ronnie felt the cold hand of time creeping up faster and faster. Or maybe that was just me projecting my own insecurities. I'd turned twenty-six early in the year, and, frankly, at the rate I was going, I probably wouldn't have to worry about hitting thirty. Death cures all ills. Well, most of them.

There had been one man who had attached himself to me instead of Ronnie. I didn't understand why. She was a tall leggy blond, dancing like she was having sex with the music. But he offered me drinks. I don't drink. He tried to slow dance. I refused. I finally had to be rude. Ronnie told me to dance with him, at least he was human. I told her that birthday guilt only went so far, and she'd used hers up.

The last thing on God's green earth that I needed was another man in my life. I didn't have a clue what to do with the two I had already. The fact that they were, respectively, a Master Vampire and an Ulfric, werewolf king, was only part of the problem. That fact alone should let you know just how deep a hole I was digging. Or would that be, already have dug? Yeah, already dug. I was about halfway to China and still throwing dirt up in the air.

I'd been celibate for six months. So, as far as I knew, had they. Everyone was waiting for me to make up my mind. Waiting for me to choose, or decide, something, anything.

I'd been a rock for half a year, because I'd stayed away from them. I hadn't seen them, in the flesh anyway. I had returned no phone calls. I had run for the hills at the first hint of cologne. Why such drastic measures? Frankly, because almost every time I saw them, I fell off the chastity wagon. They both had my libido, but I was trying to decide who had my heart. I still didn't know. The only thing I had decided was that it was time to stop hiding. I had to see them and figure out what we were all going to do. I'd decided two weeks ago that I needed to see them. It was the day that I refilled my birth-control pill prescription, and started taking it again. The very last thing I needed was a surprise pregnancy. That the first thing I thought of when I thought of Richard and Jean-Claude was to go back on birth control tells you something about the effect they had on me.

You needed to be on the pill for at least a month to be safe, or as safe as you ever got. Four more weeks, five to be sure, then I'd call. Maybe.

I heard Ronnie's heels running on the gravel. "Anita, Anita, wait, don't be angry."

The thing was, I wasn't angry with her. I was angry with me. Angry that after all these months I still couldn't decide between the two men. I stopped walking and waited for her, huddled in my little black skirt outfit, the little foil swan in my hands. The night had turned cool enough to make me wish I'd worn a jacket. When Ronnie caught up with me I started walking again.

"I'm not mad, Ronnie, just tired. Tired of you, my family, Dolph, Zerbrowski, everyone being so damned judgmental." My heels hit the sidewalk with sharp *clacks*. Jean-Claude had once said he could tell if I was angry just by the sound of my heels on the floor. "Watch your step. You're wearing higher heels than I am." Ronnie was five feet eight, which meant with heels she was nearly six feet.

I was wearing two-inch heels, which put me at five five. I get a much better workout when Ronnie and I jog together than she does.

The phone was ringing as I juggled the key and the foil-wrapped leftovers. Ronnie took the leftovers, and I shoved the door open with my shoulder. I was running across the floor in my high heels before I remembered that I was on vacation. Which meant whatever emergency was calling at 2:05 in the morning was not my problem, not for another two weeks at least. But old habits die hard, and I was at the phone before I remembered. I actually let the machine pick up while I stood there, heart pounding. I was planning on ignoring it, but . . . but I still stood ready to grab the receiver just in case.

Loud, booming music, and a man's voice. I didn't recognize the music, but I recognized the voice. "Anita, it's Gregory. Nathaniel's in trouble."

Gregory was one of the wereleopards I'd inherited when I killed their alpha, their leader. As a human, I wasn't really up to the job, but until I found a replacement, even I was better than nothing. Wereanimals without a dominant to protect them were anyone's meat, and if someone moved in and slaughtered them, it would sort of be my fault. So I acted as their protector, but the job was more complicated than I'd ever dreamed. Nathaniel was the problem. All the others were rebuilding their lives since their old leader had been killed, but not Nathaniel. He'd had a hard life: abused, raped, pimped out, and topped. Topped meant he'd been someone's slave—as in sex and pain. He was one of the few true submissives I'd ever met, though, admittedly, my pool of acquaintance was limited.

I cursed softly and picked up the phone. "I'm here, Gregory, what's happened now?" Even to me, my voice sounded tired and half-angry.

"If I had anyone else to call, Anita, I'd call them, but you're it." He sounded tired and angry, too. Great.

"Where's Elizabeth? She was supposed to be riding herd on Nathaniel tonight." I'd finally agreed that Nathaniel could start going out to the dominance and submission clubs if he was accompanied by Elizabeth and at least one other wereleopard. Tonight it had been Gregory riding shotgun, but without Elizabeth, Gregory wasn't dominant enough to keep Nathaniel safe. A normal submissive would have been safe in one of the clubs with someone there to simply say, "no thanks, we'll pass." But Nathaniel was one of those rare subs who are almost incapable of saying no, and there had been hints made that his idea of pain and sex could be very extreme. Which meant that he might say yes to things that were very, very bad for him. Wereanimals can take a lot of injury and not be permanently damaged, but there is a limit. A healthy bottom will say *stop* when he's had too much or he feels something bad happening, but Nathaniel wasn't that healthy. So he had keepers with him to make sure no one really bad got ahold of him. But it was more than that. A good dominant trusts his sub to say *when* before the damage is too great. The dom trusts the sub to know his own body and have enough self-preservation to call out before he is in past what his body can take. Nathaniel did not come with that safety feature, which meant a dominant with the best of intentions could end up hurting him badly before realizing Nathaniel wouldn't help himself.

I actually had accompanied Nathaniel a few times. As his Nimir-ra it was sort of my job to interview prospective . . . keepers. I'd gone prepared for the clubs to be one of the lower circles of hell and had been pleasantly shocked. I'd had more trouble with sexual propositions in a normal bar on a Saturday night. In the clubs everyone was very careful not to impose on you or to be seen as pushy. It was a small community, and if you got a reputation for being obnoxious, you could find yourself blacklisted, with no one to play with. I'd found the people in the scene were polite, and once you made it clear you were not there to play, no one bothered you, except tourists. Tourists were posers, people not really into the scene, who liked to dress up and frequent the clubs. They didn't know the rules, and hadn't bothered to ask. They probably thought a woman who would come to a place like this would do anything. I'd persuaded them differently. But I'd had to stop going with Nathaniel. The other wereleopards said I gave off so much dominant vibe that no dominant would ever approach Nathaniel while I was with him. Though we'd had offers for ménage à trois of every description. I felt like I needed a button that said, "No, I don't want to have a bondage three-way with you, thanks for asking, though."

Elizabeth had supposedly been dominant, but not too much to take Nathaniel out and try to pick him up a . . . date.

"Elizabeth left," Gregory said.

"Without Nathaniel?" I made it a question.

"Yes."

"Well, that just fries my bacon," I said.

"What?" he asked.

"I'm angry with Elizabeth."

"It gets better," he said.

"How much better can it be, Gregory? You all assured me that these clubs were safe. A little bondage, a little light slap and tickle. You all convinced me that I couldn't keep Nathaniel away from it indefinitely. You said that they had ways to monitor the area so no one could possibly get hurt. That's what you and Zane and Cherry told me. Hell, I've seen it myself. There are safety monitors everywhere, it's safer than some dates I've had, so what could have possibly gone wrong?"

"We couldn't have anticipated this," he said.

"Just get to the end of the story, Gregory, the foreplay is getting tedious."

There was silence for longer than there should have been, just the overly loud music. "Gregory, are you still there?"

"Gregory is indisposed," a man's voice said.

"Who is this?"

"I am Marco, if that helps you, though I doubt that it does." His voice was cultured—American, but upper crusty.

"New in town are you?" I asked.

"Something like that," he said.

"Welcome to town. Make sure you go up in the Arch while you're here, it's a nice view. But what has your recent arrival in St. Louis got to do with me and mine?"

"We didn't realize it was your pet we had at first. He wasn't the one we were hunting for, but now that we have him, we're keeping him."

"You can't 'keep' him," I said.

"Come down and take him away from us, if you can." That strangely smooth voice made the threat all the more effective. There was no anger, nothing personal. It sounded like business, and I had no clue what it was about.

"Put Gregory back on," I said.

"I don't think so. He's enjoying some personal time with my friends right now."

"How do I know he's still alive?" My voice was as unemotional as his. I wasn't feeling anything yet; it was too sudden, too unexpected, like coming in on the middle of a movie.

"No one's dead, yet," the man said.

"How do I know that?"

He was quiet for a second, then, "What sort of people are you used to dealing with, that you would ask if we've killed him first thing?"

"It's been a rough year. Now put Gregory on the phone, because until I know he's alive, and he tells me the others are, this negotiation is stalled."

"How do you know we are negotiating?" Marco asked.

"Call it a hunch."

"My, you are direct."

"You have no idea how direct I can be, Marco. Put Gregory on the phone."

There was the music-filled silence, and more music, but no voices. "Gregory, Gregory, are you there? Is anyone there?" Shit, I thought.

"I'm afraid that your kitty-cat won't squawl for us. A point of pride, I think."

"Put the reciever to his ear and let me talk to him."

"As you wish."

More of the loud music. I spoke as if I was sure that Gregory was listening. "Gregory, I need to know you're alive. I need to know that Nathaniel and everyone else is alive. Talk to me, Gregory."

His voice came squeezed tight, as if he were gritting his teeth. "Yesss."

"Yes, what, they're all alive?"

"Yess."

"What are they doing to you?"

He screamed into the phone, and the sound raised the hairs on my neck and danced down my arms in goosebumps. The sound stopped abruptly. "Gregory, Gregory!" I was yelling against the techno-beat of the music, but no one was answering.

Marco came back on the line. "They are all alive, if not quite well. The one they call Nathaniel is a lovely young man, all that long auburn hair and the most extraordinary violet eyes. So pretty, it would be a shame to spoil all that beauty. Of course, this one is lovely too, blond, blue-eyed. Someone told me that they both work as strippers? Is that true?"

I wasn't numb anymore, I was scared, and angry, and I still had not a clue to why this was happening. My voice came out almost even, almost calm. "Yeah, it's true. You're new in town, Marco, so you don't know me. But trust me, you don't want to do this."

"Perhaps not, but my alpha does."

Ah, shapeshifter politics. I hated shapeshifter politics. "Why? The wereleopards are no threat to anyone."

"Ours is not to reason why, ours is but to do and die."

A literate kidnapper, refreshing. "What do you want, Marco?"

"My alpha wants you to come down and rescue your cats, if you can."

"What club are you at?"

"Narcissus in Chains." And he hung up.

2

"DAMN IT!"

"What's happened?" Ronnie asked. I'd almost forgotten her. She didn't belong in this part of my life, but there she was, leaning against the kitchen cabinets, searching my face, looking worried.

"I'll take care of it."

She gripped my arm. "You gave me this speech about wanting your friends back, about not wanting to push us all away. Did you mean it, or was it just talk?"

I took a deep breath and let it out. I told her what the other side of the conversation had been.

"And you don't have any clue what this is about?" she asked.

"No, I don't."

"That's odd. Usually stuff like this builds up, it doesn't just drop out of the blue."

I nodded. "I know."

"Star 69 will ring back whatever number just called you."

"What good will that do?"

"It will let you know if they're really at this club, or whether it's just a trap for you."

"Not just another pretty face, are you?" I said.

She smiled. "I'm a trained detective. We know about these things." The humor didn't quite reach her eyes, but she was trying.

I dialed, and the phone rang for what seemed forever, then another male voice answered, "Yeah."

"Is this Narcissus in Chains?"

"Yeah, who's this?"

"I need to speak with Gregory?"

"Don't know any Gregory," he said.

"Who is this?" I asked.

"This is a freaking pay phone, lady. I just picked up." Then he hung up, too. It seemed to be my night for it.

"They called from a pay phone at the club," I said.

"Well, at least you know where they are," Ronnie said.

"Do you know where the club is?" I asked.

Ronnie shook her head. "Not my kind of scene."

"Mine either." In fact the only card-carrying dominance and submission players that I knew personally were all at the club waiting to be saved.

Who did I know that might know where the club was, and something about its reputation? I couldn't trust what the wereleopards had told me about it being a safe place. Obviously, they'd been wrong.

One name sprang to mind. The only one I knew to call that might know where Narcissus in Chains was, and what kind of trouble I'd be in if I went inside. Jean-Claude. Since I was dealing with shapeshifter politics it might have made sense to call Richard, with him being a werewolf and all. But the shapeshifters were a very clannish lot. One type of animal rarely crossed boundaries to help another. Frustrating, but true. The exception was the treaty between the werewolves and the wererats, but everyone else was left to fend, and squabble, and bleed, among themselves. Oh, if some small group got out of hand and attracted too much unwanted police attention, the wolves and rats would discipline them, but short of that, no one seemed to want to interfere with each other. That was one of the reasons I was still stuck baby-sitting the wereleopards.

Also, Richard didn't know any more about the D and S subculture than I did, maybe less. If you're wanting to ask questions about the sexual fringe, Jean-Claude is definitely your guy. He may not participate, but he seems to know who's doing what, and to whom, and where. Or I hoped he did. If it had just been my life at stake, I probably wouldn't have called either of the boys, but if I got killed doing this, that left no one to rescue Nathaniel and the rest. Unacceptable.

Ronnie had kicked off her high heels. "I didn't bring my gun, but I'm sure you have a spare."

I shook my head. "You're not going."

Anger makes her gray eyes the color of storm clouds. "The hell I'm not."

"Ronnie, these are shapeshifters, and you're human."

"So are you," she said.

"Because of Jean-Claude's vampire marks, I'm a little more than that. I can take damage that would kill you."

"You can't go in there alone," she said. Her arms were crossed under her breasts, her face set in angry, stubborn lines.

"I don't plan on going in alone."

"It's because I'm not a shooter, isn't it?"

"You don't kill easily, Ronnie, no shame in that, but I can't take you into a gang of shapeshifters unless I know that you'll shoot to kill if you have to." I gripped her upper arms. She stayed stiff and angry under my touch. "It would kill a piece of me to lose you, Ronnie. It would kill a bigger piece to know that you died because of some shit of mine. You can't hesitate with these people. You can't treat them like they're human. If you do, you die."

She was shaking her head. "Call the police."

I stepped away from her. "No."

"Damn it, Anita, damn it!"

"Ronnie, there are rules, and one of those rules is you don't take pack or pard business to the police." The main reason for that rule was that the police tended to frown on fights for dominance that ended with dead bodies on the ground, but no need to tell Ronnie that.

"It's a stupid rule," she said.

"Maybe, but it's still the way business is done with the shifters, no matter what flavor they are."

She sat down at the small two-seater breakfast table, on its little raised platform. "Who's going to be your backup then? Richard doesn't kill any easier than I do."

That was half true, but I let it slide. "No, I want someone at my back tonight who will do what needs doing, no flinching."

Her eyes were dark, dark with anger. "Jean-Claude." She made his name a curse.

I nodded.

"Are you sure he didn't plan this to get you back into his life, excuse me, death?"

"He knows me too well to screw with my people. He knows what I'd do if he hurt them."

Puzzlement flowed through the anger, softening her eyes, her face. "I hate him, but I know you love him. Could you really kill him? Could you really stare down the barrel of a gun and pull the trigger on him?"

I just looked at her, and I knew without a mirror that my eyes had grown distant, cold. It's hard for brown eyes to be cold, but I'd been managing it lately.

Something very like fear slid behind her eyes. I don't know if she was afraid for me, or of me. I preferred the first to the last. "You could do it. Jesus, Anita. You've known Jean-Claude longer than I've known Louie. I could never hurt Louie, no matter what he did."

I shrugged. "It would destroy me to do it, I think. It's not like I'd live happily ever after, if I survived at all. There's a very real chance that the vampire marks would drag me down to the grave with him."

"Another good reason not to kill him," she said.

"If he's behind the scream that Gregory gave over the phone, then he'll need better reasons to keep breathing than love, or lust, or my possible death."

"I don't understand that, Anita. I don't understand that at all."

"I know," I said. And I thought to myself it was one of the reasons Ronnie and I hadn't been seeing as much of each other as we once had. I got tired of explaining myself to her. No, of justifying myself to her.

You're my friend, my best friend, I thought. But I don't understand you anymore.

"Ronnie, I can't arm wrestle shapeshifters and vampires. I will lose a fair fight. The only way I survive, the only way my leopards survive, is because the other shifters fear me. They fear my threat. I'm only as good as my threat, Ronnie."

"So you'll go down there and kill them."

"I didn't say that."

"But you will."

"I'll try to avoid it," I said.

She tucked her knees up, wrapping her arms around those long legs. She'd managed to get a tiny prick in one of the hose; the hole was shiny with clear nail polish. She'd carried the polish in her purse for just such emergencies. I'd carried a gun and hadn't even taken a purse.

"If you get arrested, call, and I'll bail you out."

I shook my head. "If I get caught wasting three or more people in a public area, there won't be any bail tonight. The police probably won't even finish questioning me until long past dawn."

"How can you be so calm about this?" she asked.

I was beginning to remember why Ronnie and I had started drifting apart. I'd had almost the exact conversation with Richard once when an assassin had come to town to kill me. I gave the same answer. "Having hysterics won't help anything, Ronnie."

"But you're not angry about it."

"Oh, I am angry," I said.

She shook her head. "No, I mean you're not outraged that this is happening. You don't seem surprised, not like . . ." She shrugged. "Not like you should be."

"You mean not like you would be." I held up a hand before she could answer. "I don't have time to debate moral philosophy, Ronnie." I picked up the phone. "I'm going to call Jean-Claude."

"I keep urging you to dump the vampire and marry Richard, but maybe there's more than one reason why you can't let him go."

I dialed the number for Circus of the Damned from memory, and Ronnie just kept talking to my back. "Maybe you're not willing to give up a lover who's colder than you are."

The phone was ringing. "There are clean sheets on the guest bed, Ronnie. Sorry I won't be able to share girl talk tonight." I kept my back to her.

I heard her stand in a crinkle of skirts and knew when she walked out. I kept my back facing the room until I knew she was gone. It wouldn't do either of us any good to let her see me cry.

3

JEAN-CLAUDE WASN'T AT the Circus of the Damned. The voice on the other end of the phone at the Circus didn't recognize me and wouldn't believe I was Anita Blake, Jean-Claude's sometimes sweetie. So I'd been reduced to calling his other businesses. I'd tried Guilty Pleasures, his strip club, but he wasn't there. I tried Danse Macabre, his newest enterprise, but I was beginning to wonder if Jean-Claude had simply told everyone that he wasn't in if I called.

The thought bothered me a lot. I'd worried that after so long Richard might finally tell me to go to hell, that he'd had enough of my indecision. It had never occurred to me that Jean-Claude might not wait. If I was so unsure how I felt about him, why was my stomach squeezed tight with a growing sense of loss? The feeling had nothing to do with the wereleopards and their problems. It had everything to do with me and the fact that I suddenly felt lost. But it turned out he was at Danse Macabre, and he took my call. I had a moment for my stomach to unclench and my breath to ease out, then he was on the phone, and I was struggling to keep my metaphysical shields in place.

I hated metaphysics. Preternatural biology is still biology, metaphysics is magic, and I'm still not comfortable with it. For six months when I wasn't working, I was meditating, studying with a very wise psychic named Marianne, learning ritual magic, so I could control my God-given abilities. And so I could block the marks that bound me to Richard and Jean-Claude. An aura is like your personal protection, your personal energy. When it's healthy it keeps you safe like skin, but you get a hole in it, and infection can get inside. My aura had two holes in it, one for each of the men. I suspected that their auras had holes in them, too. Which put us all at risk. I'd blocked up my holes. Then only a few weeks ago, I'd come up against a nasty creature, a would-be god, a new category, even for me. It had been powerful enough to strip all my careful work away, leaving me raw and open again. Only the intervention of a local witch had saved me from being eaten from the aura down. I didn't have six more months of celibacy, meditation, and patience in me. The holes were there, and the only way to fill them was with Jean-Claude and Richard. That's what Marianne said, and I trusted her in a way that I trusted few others.

Jean-Claude's voice hit me over the phone like a velvet slap. My breath caught in my throat, and I could do nothing but feel the flow of his voice, the presence of him, like something alive, flowing over my skin. His voice has always been one of Jean-Claude's best things, but this was ridiculous. This was over the phone. How could I possibly see him in person and maintain my shields, let alone my composure?

"I know you are there, *ma petite*. Did you call merely to hear the sound of my voice?"

That was closer to the truth than was comfortable. "No, no." I still couldn't gather my thoughts. I was like an athlete who had let her training go. I just couldn't lift the same amount of weight, and there was weight to wading through Jean-Claude's power.

When I still didn't say anything, he spoke again. "*Ma petite*, to what do I owe this honor? Why have you deigned to call me?" His voice was bland, but there was a hint of something in it. Reproach perhaps.

I guess I had it coming. I rallied the troops and tried to sound like an intelligent human being, not always one of my best things. "It's been six months . . ."

"I am aware of that, *ma petite*."

He was being condescending. I hated that. It made me a little angry. The anger helped clear my head a little. "If you'll stop interrupting, I'll tell you why I called."

"My heart is all aflutter with anticipation."

I wanted to hang up. He was being an asshole, and part of me thought I might deserve the treatment, which made me even angrier. I'm always angriest when I think I'm in the wrong. I'd been a coward for months, and I was still a coward. I was afraid to be close to him, afraid of what I'd do. Damn it, Anita, get ahold of yourself. "Sarcasm is my department," I said.

"And what is my department?"

"I'm about to ask you for a favor," I said.

"Really?" He said it as if he might not grant it.

"Please, Jean-Claude, I'm asking for help. I don't do that often."

"That is certainly true. What would you have of me, *ma petite*? You know that you have but to ask, and it will be yours. No matter how angry I may be with you."

I let that comment go, because I didn't know what to do about it. "Do you know a club called Narcissus in Chains?"

He was quiet for a second or two. "*Oui.*"

"Can you give me directions and meet me there?"

"Do you know what sort of a club this place is?"

"Yeah."

"Are you sure?"

"It's a bondage club, I know."

"Unless the last six months has changed you greatly, *ma petite*, that is not one of your preferences."

"Not mine, no."

"Your wereleopards are misbehaving again?"

"Something like that." I told him what had happened.

"I do not know this Marco."

"I didn't figure you did."

"But you did think that I knew where the club was?"

"I was hoping."

"I will meet you there with some of my people. Or will you allow only me to ride to your rescue?" He sounded amused now, which was better than angry, I guess.

"Bring who you need."

"You trust my judgment?"

"In this, yeah."

"But not in all things," he said softly.

"I don't trust anyone in all things, Jean-Claude."

He sighed. "So young to be so . . . jaded."

"I'm cynical, not jaded."

"And the difference is what, *ma petite*?"

"You're jaded."

He laughed then, the sound caressing me like the brush of a hand. It made things low in my body clench. "Ah," he said, "that explains all the differences."

"Just give me directions, please." I added the "please" to speed things along.

"They will not harm your wereleopards too greatly, I think. The club is run by shapeshifters, and they will smell too much blood and take matters into their own hands. It is one of the reasons Narcissus in Chains is no-man's-land, a neutral place for the fringe of our groups. Your leopards were right, it is usually a very safe place."

"Well, Gregory wasn't screaming because he felt safe."

"Perhaps not, but I know the owner. Narcissus would be very angry if someone became overzealous in his club."

"Narcissus, I don't know the name. Well, I know the Greek mythology stuff, but I don't recognize it as local."

"I would not expect you to. He does not often leave his club. But I will call him, and he will patrol your cats for you. He will not rescue them, but he will make sure no further damage is done."

"You trust Narcissus to do this?"

"*Oui.*"

Jean-Claude had his faults, but if he trusted someone, he was usually right. "Okay. And thank you."

"You are most welcome." He drew a breath, then said quietly, "Would you have called if you had not needed my help? Would you ever have called?"

I'd been dreading this question from either Jean-Claude or Richard. But I finally had an answer. "I'll answer your question as best I can, but call it a hunch, it may be a long conversation. I need to know my people are safe before we start dissecting our relationship."

"Relationship? Is that what we have?" His voice was very dry.

"Jean-Claude."

"No, no, *ma petite*, I will call Narcissus now and save your cats but only if you promise that when I call back we will finish this conversation.

"Promise."

"Your word," he said.

"Yes."

"Very well, *ma petite*, until we speak again." He hung up.

I hung up the phone and stood there. Was it cowardly to want to call someone else, anyone else, so the phone would be busy and we wouldn't have to have our little talk? Yeah, it was cowardly, but tempting. I hated talking about my personal life, especially to the people most intimately involved in it. I had just about enough time to change out of the skirt outfit when the phone rang. I jumped and answered it with my pulse in my throat. I was really dreading this conversation.

"Hello," I said.

"Narcissus will see to your cats' safety. Now, where were we?" He was silent for a heartbeat. "Oh, yes, would you ever have called if you had not needed my help?"

"The woman I'm studying with . . ."

"Marianne," he said.

"Yes, Marianne. Anyway, she says that I can't keep blocking the holes in my aura. That the only way to be safe from preternatural creepy-crawlies is to fill the holes with what they were meant to hold."

Silence on the other end of the phone. Silence for so long that I said, "Jean-Claude, you still there?"

"I am here."

"You don't sound happy about this."

"Do you know what you are saying, Anita?" It was always a bad sign when he used my real name.

"I think so."

"I want this very clear between us, *ma petite.* I do not want you coming back to me later, crying that you did not understand how tightly this would bind us. If you allow Richard and me to truly fill the marks upon your . . . body, we will share our auras. Our energy. Our magic."

"We're already doing that, Jean-Claude."

"In part, *ma petite,* but those are side effects of the marks. This will be a willing, knowledgeable joining. Once done, I do not think it can be undone without great damage to all of us."

It was my turn to sigh. "How many vampire challenges to your authority have there been while I've been off meditating?"

"A few," he said, voice cautious.

"More than a few I'd bet, because they sensed that your defenses are not complete. You had trouble backing them down without killing them, didn't you?"

"Let us say that I am glad that there were no serious challengers over the last year."

"You'd have lost without Richard and me to back you up, and you couldn't shield yourself without us there to touch. That worked when I was in town with you. Touching, being with each other helped us plug in to each other's power. It offset the problem."

"Oui," he said, softly.

"I didn't know, Jean-Claude. I'm not sure it would have made a difference, but I didn't know. God, Richard must be desperate—he doesn't kill like we do. His bluff is all that keeps the werewolves from tearing each other apart, and with two gaping holes in his most intimate defenses . . ." I let my voice trail off, but I still remembered the cold horror I'd felt when I realized how much I'd endangered all of us.

"Richard has had difficulties, *ma petite.* But we each have only one chink in our armor, the one that only you can heal. He was driven to merge his energies with mine. As you say, his bluff is very important to him."

"I didn't know, and I'm sorry for that. All I've been thinking about was how scared I was of being overwhelmed by the two of you. Marianne told me the truth when she thought I was ready to hear it."

"And are you done being frightened of us, *ma petite*?" His voice was careful when he asked, as if he were carrying a very full cup of very hot liquid up a long and narrow staircase.

I shook my head, realized he couldn't see it, and said, "I'm not brave. I'm pretty much terrified. Terrified that if I do this, there is no going back, that maybe I'm fooling myself about a choice. Maybe there is no choice and hasn't been for a long time. But however we end up arranging the bedrooms, I can't let us all go around with gaping metaphysical wounds. Too many things will sense the weakness and exploit it."

"Like the creature you met in New Mexico," he said, voice still as cautious as I'd ever heard it.

"Yeah," I said.

"Are you saying that tonight you will agree to letting us merge the marks, that we will at last close these, as you so colorfully put it, wounds?"

"If it doesn't endanger my leopards, yeah. We need to do it as soon as possible. I'd hate to make the big decision and then have one of us get killed before we could batten down the hatches."

I heard him sigh, as if some great tension had left him. "You do not know how long I have waited for you to understand all this."

"You could have told me."

"You would not have believed me. You would have thought it was another trick to bind you closer to me."

"You're right, I wouldn't have believed you."

"Will Richard be meeting us at the club, as well?"

I was quiet for a heartbeat. "No, I'm not going to call him."

"Why ever not? It is a shapeshifter difficulty more than a vampire one."

"You know why not."

"You fear he will be too squeamish to allow you to do what needs doing to save your leopards."

"Yeah."

"Perhaps," Jean-Claude said.

"You aren't going to tell me to call him?"

"Why would I ask you to invite my chief rival for your affections to this little tête-à-tête? That would be foolish. I am many things, but foolish is not one of them."

That was certainly true. "Okay, give me directions, and I'll meet you and your people at the club."

"First, *ma petite*, what are you wearing?"

"Excuse me?"

"Clothes, *ma petite*, what clothes are you wearing?"

"Is this a joke? Because I don't have time . . ."

"It is not an idle question, *ma petite*. The sooner you answer, the sooner we can all leave."

I wanted to argue, but if Jean-Claude said he had a point he probably did. I told him what I was wearing.

"You surprise me, *ma petite*. With a little effort it should do nicely."

"What effort?"

"I suggest you add boots to your ensemble. The ones I purchased for you would do very well."

"I am not wearing five-inch spikes anywhere, Jean-Claude. I'd break an ankle."

"I planned on you wearing those boots just for me, *ma petite.* I was thinking of the other boots with the milder heels that I bought when you were so very angry about the others."

Oh. "Why do I have to change shoes?"

"Because, delicate flower that you are, you have the eyes of a policeman, and so it would be better if you wore leather boots instead of high heels. It would be better if you remember that you are trying to move through the club as quickly and smoothly as possible. No one will help you find your leopards if they think you are an outsider, especially a policeman."

"Nobody ever mistakes me for a cop."

"No, but they begin to mistake you for something that smells of guns and death. Look harmless tonight, *ma petite,* until it is time to be dangerous."

"I thought this friend of yours, this Narcissus, would just escort us in."

"He is not my friend, and I told you the club is neutral ground. Narcissus will see that no great harm comes to your cats, but that is all. He will not let you come barging in to his world like the proverbial bull in the china shop. That, he will not allow, nor will he allow us to bring in a small army of our own. He is the leader of the werehyenas, and they are the only army allowed inside the club. There is no Ulfric, or Master of the City, within its walls. You have only the dominance you bring with you and your body to see you through."

"I'll have a gun," I said.

"But a gun will not get you into the upper rooms."

"What will?"

"Trust me, I will find a way."

I didn't like the sound of that at all. "Why is it that most of the time whenever I ask you for help, it's never a case where we can just run in and start shooting?"

"And why is it, *ma petite,* that when you do not invite me that it is almost always a case where you run in and shoot everything that moves?"

"Point taken," I said.

"What are your priorities for the night?" he asked.

I knew what he meant. "I want the wereleopards safe."

"And if they have been harmed?"

"I want vengeance."

"More than their safety?"

"No, safety first, vengeance is a luxury."

"Good. And if one, or more, is dead?"

"I don't want any of us going to jail, but eventually if not tonight, another night, they die." I listened to myself say it, and knew that I meant it.

"There is no mercy in you, *ma petite.*"

"You say that like it's a bad thing."

"No, it is merely an observation."

I stood there, holding the phone, waiting to be shocked at what I was proposing. But I wasn't. I said, "I don't want to kill anyone if I don't have to."

"That is not true, *ma petite.*"

"Fine, if they've killed my people, I want them dead. But I decided in New Mexico that I didn't want to be a sociopath, so I'm trying to act as if I'm not. So let's try to keep the body count low tonight, okay?"

"As you wish," he said. Then he added, "Do you really think that you can change the nature of what you are merely by wishing it?"

"Are you asking if I can stop being a sociopath, since I already am one?"

A moment of silence, then, "I think that is what I'm asking."

"I don't know, but if I don't pull myself back from the brink soon, Jean-Claude, there won't be any going back."

"I hear fear in your voice, *ma petite*."

"Yeah, you do."

"What do you fear?"

"I fear that by giving in to you and Richard that I'll lose myself. I fear that by not giving in to you and Richard I'll lose one of you. I fear that I'll get us killed because I'm thinking too much. I fear that I'm already a sociopath and there *is* no going back. Ronnie said that one of the reasons that I can't give you up and just settle down with Richard is that I can't give up a boyfriend who's colder than I am."

"I am sorry, *ma petite*." I wasn't sure exactly what he was apologizing for, but I accepted it anyway.

"Me, too. Give me directions to the club, I'll meet you there."

He gave me directions, and I read them back to him. We hung up. Neither of us said good-bye. Once upon a time we'd have ended the conversation with *je t'aime*, I love you. Once upon a time.

4

THE CLUB WAS over the river on the Illinois side, along with most of the other questionable clubs. Vampire-run businesses got a grandfather clause to operate in St. Louis proper, but the rest of the human-run clubs—and lycanthropes still counted legally as human—had to go into Illinois to avoid pesky zoning problems. Some of the zoning problems weren't even on the books, weren't even laws at all. But it was strange how many problems the bureaucrats could find when they didn't want a club in their fair city. If the vampires weren't such a big draw for tourists, the bureaucrats'd have probably found a way to get rid of them, too.

I finally found parking about two blocks from the club. It meant a walk to the club in an area of town that most women wouldn't want to be alone in after dark. Of course, most women wouldn't be armed. A gun doesn't cure all ills, but it's a start. I also had a knife sheath around each calf, very high up, so that the hilts came up on the side of my knees. I wasn't really comfortable that way, but I couldn't think of any other place to put knives so I could get to them easily. There was a very good chance I'd have bruises on my knees after tonight. Oh, well. I also had a black belt in Judo, and was making progress in Kenpo, a type of karate, one with fewer power moves and more moves using balance. I was as prepared as I could get for the wilds of the big city.

Of course, I usually don't walk around looking like bait. My skirt was so short that even with boots that came up to mid-thigh there was a good inch between the hem and the top of the boots. I'd put a jacket on for the drive, but had left it in the car because I didn't want to be carrying it around all night. I'd been in just enough clubs, whatever flavor they were, to know that inside it would be hot. So the goosebumps that traveled over my bare back and arms weren't from fear, but from the damp, chill air. I forced myself not to rub my arms as I walked and to at least look like I wasn't cold or uncomfortable. Actually the boots only had two-inch heels, and they were comfortable to walk in. Not as comfortable as my Nikes, but then, what is? But for dress shoes, the boots weren't bad. If I could have left the knives home, they'd have been peachy.

There was one other bit of protection that I'd added. Metaphysical shields come in different varieties. You can shield yourself with almost anything: metal, rock, plants, fire, water, wind, earth, etc. . . . Everyone has different shields because it's a very individual choice. It has to work for your own personal mind-set. You can have two psychics both using stone, but the shields won't be the same. Some people simply visualize rock, the thought of it, its essence, and that's sufficient. If something tries to attack them, they are safe behind the thought of rock.

Another psychic might see a stone wall, like a garden wall around an old house, and that would do the same thing. For me, the shield had to be a tower. All shields are like bubbles that surround you completely, just like circles of power. I'd always understood this when I raised the dead, but for shielding I needed to see it in my head. So I imagined a stone tower, completely enclosed, no windows, no chinks, smooth and dark inside with only what I allowed in or out. Talking about shielding always made me feel like I was having a psychotic break and sharing my delusions. But it worked, and when I didn't shield, things tried to hurt me. It had only been in the last two weeks that Marianne had discovered that I hadn't really understood shielding at all. I'd thought it was just a matter of how powerful your aura was and how you could reinforce it. She said the only reason I'd been able to get by with that for as long as I had was that I was simply that powerful. But the shielding goes *outside* the aura like a wall around a castle, an extra defense. The innermost defense is a healthy aura. Hopefully by the end of the night I'd have one of those.

I turned the corner and found a line of people that stretched down the block. Great, just what I needed. I didn't stop at the end of the line, I kept walking towards the door, hoping I'd think of something to tell the doorperson when I got there. I didn't have time to wait through all this. I was about halfway up the line when a figure pushed out of the crowd and called my name.

It took me a second to recognize Jason. First, he'd cut his baby-fine blond hair short, businessman short. Second, he was wearing a sheer silver mesh shirt and a pair of pants that seemed mostly made of the same stuff. Only a thin line of solid silver ran over his groin. The outfit was so eye-catching that it took me a moment to realize just how sheer the cloth was. What I was really seeing wasn't the silver, but Jason's skin through a veil of glitter. The outfit, which left precious little to the imagination, ended in calf-high gray boots.

I had to make myself look at his face, because I was still shaking my head over the outfit. The outfit didn't look comfortable, but of course, Jason rarely complained about his clothes. He was like Jean-Claude's little dress-up werewolf, as well as morning snack. Sometimes bodyguard and sometimes a fetch-and-carry boy. Who else could Jean-Claude get to stand out in the cold, nearly naked?

Jason's eyes looked bigger, bluer somehow, without all the hair to distract your eye. His face looked older with the shorter hair, the bone structure cleaner, and I realized that Jason was perilously close to that line between cute and handsome. He'd been nineteen when we met. Twenty-two looked better on him. But the outfit—there was nothing to do but grin at the outfit.

He was grinning at me, too. I think we were both happy to see each other. In leaving Richard and Jean-Claude I'd left their people behind, too. Jason was Richard's pack member, and Jean-Claude's lap wolf.

"You look like a pornographic space man. If you were wearing street clothes, you might have gotten a hug," I said.

His smile flashed even wider. "I guess I'm dressed for punishment. Jean-Claude told me to wait for you and take you in. My hand's already got a stamp on it so we can just go straight inside."

"A little cold for the clothes, isn't it?"

"Why do you think I was standing deep in the crowd?" He offered me his arm. "May I escort you inside, my lady?"

I took his arm with my left hand. Jason put his free hand on top of mine, doing a double hold. If that was the worst teasing he did tonight, then he'd grown up some. The silver cloth was rougher than it looked, scratchy where it rubbed against my arm.

As Jason led me up the steps, I had to look behind him. The cloth that covered his groin was only a thin thong at the back, leaving nothing but a fine glitter over his butt. The shirt was not attached to the pants, so as he moved I got glimpses of his stomach. In fact the shirt was loose enough through the shoulders that when he took my arm the shirt pulled to one side, revealing his smooth, pale shoulder.

The music hit me at the door like a giant's slap. It was almost a wall we had to move through. I hadn't expected Narcissus in Chains to be a dance club. But except for the patrons' clothing being more exotic and running high to leather, it looked like a lot of other clubs. The place was large, dimly lit, dark in the corners, with too many people pushed into too small a space, moving their bodies frantically to music that was way too loud.

My hand tightened just a touch on Jason's arm, because truthfully I always feel a little overwhelmed by places like this. At least for the first few minutes. It's like I need a depth chamber between the outside world and the inside world, a moment to breath deep and adjust. But these clubs are not designed to give you time. They just bombard you with sensory overload and figure you'll survive.

Speaking of sensory overload, Jean-Claude was standing near the wall just to one side of the dance floor. His long black hair fell in soft curls around his shoulders, nearly to his waist. I didn't remember his hair being that long. He had his head turned away from me, watching the dancers, so I couldn't really see his face, but it gave me time to look at the rest of him. He was dressed in a black vinyl shirt that looked poured on. It left his arms bare, and I realized I'd never seen him in anything that bared his arms before. His skin looked unbelievably white against the shiny black vinyl, almost as if it glowed with some inner light. I knew it didn't, though it could. Jean-Claude would never be so déclassé as to show such power in a public place. His pants were made of the same shiny vinyl, making the long lines of his body look like they had been dipped into liquid patent leather. Vinyl boots came up just over his knees, gleaming as if they'd been spit polished. Everything about him gleamed, the dark glow of his clothes, the shining whiteness of his skin. Then abruptly he turned as if he felt me gazing at him.

Staring full into his face, even from across a room, made me catch my breath. He was beautiful. That heartrending beauty that was masculine but treaded the line between what was male and what was female. Not exactly androgynous, but close to it.

But as he moved towards me, the movement was utterly male, graceful as if he heard music in his head that he quietly danced to. But the walk, the movement of his shoulders—women did not move like that.

Jason patted my hand.

I jumped, staring at him.

He put his mouth close enough to my ear to whisper-shout above the music, "Breathe, Anita, remember to breathe."

I blushed, because that was how Jean-Claude affected me—like I was fourteen and was having the crush of my life. Jason tightened his grip on me, as if he thought I might make a run for it. Not a bad idea. I looked back, and saw that Jean-Claude was very near. The first time I saw the blue-green roil of the Caribbean, I cried, because it was so beautiful. Jean-Claude made me feel like that, like I should weep at his beauty. It was like being offered an original da Vinci, not just to hang on your wall and admire, but to roll around on top of. It seemed wrong. Yet I stood there, clutching Jason's arm, my heart hammering so hard I almost couldn't hear the music. I was scared, but it wasn't knife-in-the-dark scared, it was rabbit-in-the-headlights scared. I was caught, as I usually was with Jean-Claude, between two disparate instincts. Part of me wanted to run to him, to close the distance and climb his body and pull it around me. The other part wanted to run screaming into the night and pray he didn't follow.

He stood in front of me, but made no move to touch me, to close that last small space. He seemed as unwilling to touch me as I was to touch him. Was he afraid of me? Or did he sense my own fear and fear he might scare me off? We stood there simply staring at each other. His eyes were still the same dark, dark blue, with a wealth of black lashes lacing them.

Jason kissed my cheek, lightly, like you'd kiss your sister. It still made me jump. "I'm feeling like a third wheel. You two play nice." And he pulled away from me, leaving Jean-Claude and me staring at each other.

I don't know what we would have said, because three men joined us before we could decide. The shortest of the three was only about five feet seven, and he was wearing more makeup on his pale triangular face than I was. The makeup was well done, but he wasn't trying to look like a woman. His black hair was cut very short, though you could tell that it would be curly if it was long. He was wearing a black lace dress, long-sleeved, fitted at the waist, showing a slender but muscular chest. The skirt spilled out around him, almost June Cleaverish, and his stockings were black, with a very delicate spiderweb pattern. He wore open-toed sandals with spike heels, and both his toenails and his fingernails were painted black. He looked . . . lovely. But what made the outfit was the sense of power in him. It hung around him like an expensive perfume, and I knew he was an alpha something.

Jean-Claude spoke first. "This is Narcissus, owner of this establishment."

Narcissus held out his hand. I was momentarily confused about whether I was supposed to shake the hand or kiss it. If he'd been trying to pass for a woman, I'd have known the kiss would have been appropriate, but he wasn't. He wasn't so much cross-dressing as just dressing the way he wanted. I shook his hand. The grip was strong, but not too strong. He didn't try and test my strength, which some lycanthropes will do. He was secure, was Narcissus.

The two men behind him loomed over all of us, each well over six feet. One had a wide, muscular chest that was left mostly bare through a complicated crisscross of black leather straps. He had blond hair, cut very short on the sides and gelled into short spikes on top. His eyes were pale, and the look in them was not friendly. The second man was slimmer, built more like a professional basketball player than a weightlifter. But the arms that showed from the leather vest were corded with muscle all the same. His skin was almost as dark as the leather he was wearing. All these two needed were a couple of tattoos apiece, and they would have screamed badass.

Narcissus said, "This is Ulysses and Ajax." Ajax was the blond, and Ulysses was the oh-so brunette.

"Greek myths, nice naming convention," I said.

Narcissus blinked large dark eyes at me. Either he didn't think I was funny, or he simply didn't care. The music stopped abruptly. We were suddenly standing in a great roaring silence, and it was shocking. Narcissus spoke at a level where I could hear him, but people nearby couldn't. He'd known the music would stop. "I know your reputation, Ms. Blake. I must have the gun."

I glanced at Jean-Claude.

"I did not tell him."

"Come, Ms. Blake, I can smell the gun, even over . . ." He sniffed the air, head tilted back just a little, "your Oscar de la Renta."

"I went to a different oil for cleaning, one with less odor," I said.

"It's not the oil. The gun is new, I can smell the . . . metal, like you would smell a new car."

Oh. "Did Jean-Claude explain the situation to you?"

Narcissus nodded. "Yes, but we do not play favorites in dominance struggles between different groups. We are neutral territory, and if we are to remain so, then no guns. If it is any comfort, we didn't let the ones who have your cats bring guns into the club either."

I widened my eyes at that. "Most shapeshifters don't carry guns."

"No, they do not." Narcissus's handsome face told me nothing. He was neither upset nor concerned. It was all just business to him—like Marco's voice on the phone.

I turned back to Jean-Claude. "I'm not getting into the club with my gun, am I?"

"I fear not, *ma petite.*"

I sighed and turned back to the waiting—what had Jean-Claude called them—werehyenas. They were the first I'd met, as far as I knew. There was no clue from looking at them what they became when the moon was full. "I'll give it up, but I'm not happy about this."

"That is not my problem," Narcissus said.

I met his eyes and felt my face slip into that look that could make a good cop flinch—my monster peeking out. Ulysses and Ajax started to move in front of Narcissus, but he waved them back. "Ms. Blake will behave herself. Won't you, Ms. Blake?"

I nodded, but said, "If my people get hurt because I don't have a gun, I can make it your problem."

"*Ma petite,*" Jean-Claude said, his voice warning me.

I shook my head. "I know, I know, they're like Switzerland, neutral. Personally, I think neutral is just another way of saving your own ass at the expense of someone else's."

Narcissus took a step closer, until only a few inches separated us. His otherworldly energy danced along my skin, and as had happened in New Mexico with a very different wereanimal, it called that piece of Richard's beast that seemed to live inside me. It brought that power in a rush down my skin, to jump the distance between us, and mingle with Narcissus's power. It startled me. I hadn't thought it could happen with shields in place. Marianne had said that my abilities lay with the dead, and that was why I couldn't control Richard's power as easily as I could Jean-Claude's. But I should have been able to shield against a stranger. It scared me a little that I couldn't.

It had been wereleopards and werejaguars in New Mexico. They had mistaken me for another lycanthrope. Narcissus made the same mistake. I saw his eyes widen, then narrow. He glanced at Jean-Claude, and he laughed. "Everyone says you're human, Anita." He raised a hand and caressed the air just above my face, touching the swirl of energy. "I think you should come out of the closet before someone gets hurt."

"I never said I was human, Narcissus. But I'm not a shapeshifter either."

He rubbed his hand along the front of his dress, as if trying to get the feeling of my power off his skin. "Then what are you?"

"If things go badly tonight, you'll find out."

His eyes narrowed again. "If you cannot protect your people without guns, then you should step down as their Nimir-Ra and let someone else have the job."

"I've got an interview set up day after tomorrow with a potential Nimir-Raj."

He looked genuinely surprised. "You know that you don't have the power to rule them?"

I nodded. "Oh, yeah, I'm only temporary until I can find someone else. If the rest of you weren't so damn species conscious, I'd have farmed them out to another group. But no one wants to play with an animal that isn't the same as them."

"It is our way, it has always been our way."

And I knew the "our" didn't mean just werehyenas but all the shifters. "Yeah, well it sucks."

He smiled then. "I don't know whether I like you, Anita, but you are different, and I always appreciate that. Now give up the gun like a good little girl, and you can enter my territory." He held his hand out.

I stared at the hand. I didn't want to give up my gun. What I'd told Ronnie was true. I couldn't arm wrestle them, and I would lose a fair fight. The gun was my equalizer. I had the two knives, but frankly, they were for emergencies.

"It is your choice, *ma petite.*"

"If it will help you make the choice," Narcissus said, "I have put two of my own personal guards in the room with your leopards. I have forbidden the others from causing further harm to your people until you arrive. Until you enter the upper room where they're waiting, nothing more will happen that they don't want to happen." Knowing Nathaniel, that wasn't as comforting as it could have been.

If anyone would understand the problem, it would be someone who ran a club like this. "Nathaniel is one of those bottoms that will ask for more punishment than he can survive. He has no stopping point, no ability to keep himself safe. Do you understand?"

Narcissus's eyes widened just a touch. "Then what was he doing here without a top of his own?"

"I sent him out with one that was supposed to watch over him tonight. But Gregory said that Elizabeth deserted Nathaniel early in the evening."

"Is she one of your leopards, too?"

I nodded.

"She's defying you."

"I know. The fact that Nathaniel suffers for it doesn't seem to bother her."

He studied my face. "I don't see anger in you about this."

"If I was angry at everything Elizabeth did to piss me off, I'd never be anything else." Truthfully, I was just tired. Tired of having to rescue the pack from one emergency after another. Tired of Elizabeth being up in my face and not taking care of the others, even though she was supposedly dominant to them. I'd avoided punishing her, because I couldn't beat her up, which was what she needed. The only thing I could do was shoot her. I'd been trying to avoid that, but she just may have pushed me far enough that I was out of options. I'd see what actual damage had been done. If anyone died because of her, then she would follow. I hated the fact that I didn't care whether I killed her. I'd known her off and on for over a year. I should have cared, but I didn't. I didn't like her, and she'd been asking for it for as long as I'd known her. My life would be simpler if she were dead. But there had to be a better reason to kill someone than that. Didn't there?

"Some advice," Narcissus said. "All dominance challenges, especially from your own people, must be handled quickly, or the problem will spread."

"Thanks. Actually, I knew that."

"Still she defies you."

"I've been trying to avoid killing her."

We looked at each other very quietly, and he gave a small nod. "Your gun, please."

I sighed and raised the front of my shirt, though the material was stiff enough that I had to roll it back to expose the butt of the gun. I lifted the gun out and checked the safety out of habit, though I knew it was on.

Narcissus took the gun. The two bodyguards had moved, blocking the crowd's view of us. I doubted most people knew what we'd just done. Narcissus smiled as I rolled my shirt back into place over the now-empty holster. "Truthfully, if I didn't know who you were and what your reputation was, I wouldn't have smelled the gun, because I wouldn't have been trying to. Your outfit doesn't look like it could hide a gun this big."

"Paranoia is the mother of invention," I said.

He gave a small bow of his head. "Now enter and enjoy the delights, and the terrors, of my world." With that rather cryptic phrase, he and his bodyguards moved through the crowd, taking my gun with them.

Jean-Claude trailed his fingers down my arm, and that one small movement turned me towards him, my skin shivering. Tonight was complicated enough without this level of sexual tension.

"Your cats are well until you enter the upper room. I suggest we do the mark now, first."

"Why?" I asked, my pulse suddenly in my throat.

"Let us go to our table, and I will explain." He moved off through the crowd, without touching me further. I followed and couldn't stop myself from watching the way the vinyl fit him from behind. I loved watching him walk, whether he was coming or going—a double threat.

The tables were small, and there weren't many of them crowded against the walls. But they'd cleared the dance floor so they could set up for some sort of show or demonstration. Men and women dressed in leather were setting up a framework of metal with lots of leather straps. I was reeeally hoping to be elsewhere before the show started.

Jean-Claude took me to one side before we got to the table that Jason and three complete strangers were gathered around. He stepped in so close to me that a hard thought would have made our bodies touch. I pressed myself against the wall and tried not to breathe. He put his mouth against my ear and spoke so low what came out was merely the soft sound of his breath against my skin. "We will all be safer when the marks are married, but there are other . . . benefits to it. I have many lesser vampires that I have brought into my territory in the last few months, *ma petite.* Without you at my side, I dared not bring in greater powers, for fear that I could not hold them. Once the marks are married between us, you will be able to sense those vampires that are mine. The exception, as always, is a Master Vampire. They can hide their allegiances better than the rest. The marriage of marks will also let my people know who you are, and what will happen to them if they overstep their bounds with you."

I spoke, lips barely moving, lower than he had spoken, because he could still hear me. "You've had to be very careful, haven't you?"

He rested his cheek against my face for a moment. "It has been a delicate dance to choreograph."

I had gone into this evening with my metaphysical shield tight in place. Marianne had taught me that with my aura ruptured, the other shielding was of paramount importance. I shielded with stone tonight, perfect, seamless stone. Nothing could get in, or out, without my permission. Except Narcissus's power had already danced inside my shields. I was afraid that touching Jean-Claude would be enough to shatter the stone, but it wasn't. I wasn't even aware of the shielding, unless I really concentrated. It could stay in place even when I slept. Only when you were attacked did you have to concentrate, if you were good at shielding. I'd spent a week at the beginning of the month in Tennessee with Marianne, working on nothing but this. I wasn't great at it, but I wasn't bad either.

My shields were in place. My emotions were drowning in Jean-Claude, but my psyche wasn't, which meant that Marianne was right. I could hold the dead outside my shield easier than the living. This gave me the courage to do a little more. I leaned my face against Jean-Claude's, and nothing happened. Oh, the feel of his skin against mine sent a thrill through my body, but my shields never wavered. I felt some tension that I hadn't even known was there ease out of me. I wanted him to hold me. It wasn't just sex. If that was all it was, I could have been rid of him long ago. He must have felt it, too, because his hands rested lightly on my bare arms. When I didn't protest, his hands caressed my skin, and that small movement brought my breath to a sigh.

I leaned into him, wrapping my arms around his waist, pressing the lines of our bodies together. I rested my head on his chest, and I could hear his heart beating. It didn't always beat, but tonight it did. We held each other, and it was nearly chaste, just a renewal of the fact that we were touching again. I'd worked on the metaphysical stuff so I could do this and not lose myself. It had been worth the effort.

He pulled back first, enough to look into my face. "We can marry the marks here, or find somewhere more private." He wasn't whispering as much as before. Apparently he didn't care now if others knew what we were doing.

"I'm not clear on what marrying the marks means."

"I thought your Marianne had explained it to you."

"She said we'll fit together like puzzle pieces and there'll be a release of power when it happens. But she also said that the manner in which it is done is individual to the participants."

"You sound as if you are quoting."

"I am."

He frowned, and even that small movement was somehow fascinating. "I do not want you to be unpleasantly surprised, *ma petite.* I am striving for honesty, since you value it so highly. I have never done this with anyone, but most things are sexual between us, whether we will or no, so it is likely this will be, too."

"I can't leave the leopards here long enough to grab a hotel room, Jean-Claude."

"They will not be harmed. Until you go upstairs, they will be safe."

I shook my head and pulled away from him. "I'm sorry, but I am not leaving here without them. If you want to do this afterwards, that's fine with me, but the leopards are priority. They're waiting for me to rescue them. I can't go off and have what amounts to metaphysical sex while they're afraid and bleeding somewhere."

"No, it cannot wait. I want us to have this done before the fight begins. I do not like that your gun is gone."

"Will this marriage of the marks give me more . . . abilities?"

"Yes."

"And you, what do you get out of it?" I was standing against the wall now, not touching him.

"My own defenses will be strong once more, and I will gain power, as well. You know that."

"Are there any surprises connected with this that I should know about?"

"As I said, I have never done this with anyone, nor have I seen it done. It will be as much a surprise to me as to you."

I stared up into his lovely eyes and wished I believed that.

"I see the distrust in your eyes, *ma petite.* But it is not me that you do not trust. It is your power. Nothing ever goes as it should with you, *ma petite,* because you are like no power come before you. You are wild magic, untamed. You throw the best of plans to the wind."

"I've been learning control, Jean-Claude."

"I hope it is enough."

"You're scaring me."

He sighed. "And that was the last thing I wished to do."

I shook my head. "Look, Jean-Claude, I know everyone keeps saying my people are fine, but I want to see for myself, so let's just get this done."

"This should be something special and mystical, *ma petite.*"

I looked around the club. "Then we need a different setting."

"I agree, but the setting was your choosing, not mine."

"But you're the one insisting on it having to be right now before all the fireworks start."

"True." He sighed and held out his hand to me. "Come, let us at least go to our table."

I actually thought about refusing his hand. Funny how quickly I could go from wanting to jump his bones to wanting to be rid of him. Of course, it wasn't exactly him, but more the complications that came with him. The mystical stuff between us was never simple. He said that was my fault, and maybe it was. Jean-Claude was a pretty standard Master Vampire, and Richard, a pretty standard Ulfric. They were both wonderfully powerful, but there was nothing too terribly extraordinary in their powers. Well, there was one thing about Jean-Claude. He could gain power by feeding off sexual energy. In another century he'd have been called an incubus. It's rare even for a Master Vamp to have a secondary way to gain power outside of blood. So it was impressive, sort of. The only other masters I'd met who could feed off of something other than blood had fed on terror. And of the two, I preferred lust. At least no one had to bleed for it. Usually. But I was the wild card, the one whose powers seemed to fit nothing but legends of necromancers long dead. Legends so old that no one believed they could be true, until I came along. Sad, but true.

The table had cleared out while we were whispering. Now just Jason and one other man were there. The man was dressed in brown leather, from what I could see of his pants to the zipped-front, sleeveless shirt he was wearing. He was also wearing one of those hoods that left your mouth, part of your nose, and your eyes bare, but covered the rest of your face. Frankly, I found the hoods creepy, but hey, it wasn't my bread that was being buttered. As long as he didn't try anything with me, we were cool. It wasn't until he looked up into my face that I recognized those pale, pale blue eyes—the startling ice blue eyes of a Siberian Husky. No human I'd ever met had eyes like that.

"Asher," I said.

He smiled then, and I recognized the curve of his lips. I knew why he'd worn the hood. It wasn't sexual preference, or at least I didn't think so. It was to hide the scars. Once, about two hundred years ago, some well-meaning church officials had tried to burn the devil out of Asher. They'd done it with holy water. Holy water is like acid on vampire flesh. He'd once been, in his own way, as breathtaking as Jean-Claude. Now half his face was a melted ruin, half his chest, most of the one thigh I'd seen. What I'd seen of the rest of him was perfect, as perfect as the day he died. And the parts I hadn't seen, I wasn't sure I wanted to know about. Through Jean-Claude's marks I had memories of Asher before. I knew what his body looked like in smooth perfection—every inch of it. Asher and his human servant, Julianna, had been part of a ménage à trois with Jean-Claude for about twenty years. She'd been burned as a witch, and Jean-Claude had only been able to save Asher after the damage had been done.

The events were over two hundred years old, yet they both still mourned Julianna, and each other. Asher was now Jean-Claude's second in command, but they were not lovers. And they were uneasy friends, because there was still too much left unspoken between them. Asher still blamed Jean-Claude for failing them, and Jean-Claude had a hard time arguing with that, because deep down he still blamed himself, too.

I leaned down and gave Asher a quick kiss on the leather cheek. "What did you do with all your long hair? Please tell me you haven't cut it."

He raised my hand to his mouth and laid a gentle kiss on it. "It is braided, and longer than ever."

"I can hardly wait to see it," I said. "Thanks for coming."

"I would move all of hell to reach your side, you know that."

"You French guys do talk pretty," I said.

He laughed softly.

Jason interrupted. "I think the show is about to start."

I turned and watched a woman being led towards the framework that had been erected. She was wearing a robe, and I really didn't want to see what was under it.

"Whatever we're going to do, let's do it and go get the leopards."

"You don't want to see the show?" Jason asked. His eyes were all innocent, but his smile was teasing.

I just frowned at him. But his eyes looked behind me, and I knew someone Jason didn't like was coming towards us. I turned to find Ajax standing there. He ignored me and spoke to Jean-Claude. "You have fifteen minutes, then the show starts."

Jean-Claude nodded. "Tell Narcissus I appreciate the notice."

Ajax gave a small head bow, much like his master had done before, then walked off through the tables.

"What was all that about?" I asked.

"It would be considered rude to do something magical during someone else's performance. I told Narcissus that we would be calling some . . . power."

I must have looked as suspicious as I felt. "You are beginning to piss me off with this cloak-and-dagger magic act."

"You are a necromancer, and I am the Master Vampire of this city. Do you really believe that we can merge our powers and not have every undead in this room, and more, notice it? I do not know if the shapeshifters will be able to feel it, but it is likely, since we are also both bound to a werewolf. Everything nonhuman in this club will feel something. I don't know how much, or exactly what, but *something, ma petite.* Narcissus would have taken it as a grave insult if we had interrupted this performance without warning him."

"I don't mean to rush you," Asher said, "but you will use up your time in talking if you are not quick about it."

Jean-Claude looked at him, and the look was not entirely friendly. What was happening between them that Jean-Claude would give such a look to Asher?

Jean-Claude held his hand out to me. I hesitated a second, then slid my hand into his and he led me to the wall near the table. "Now what?" I asked.

"Now you must drop your shields, *ma petite*, that so-strong barrier you have erected between me and your aura."

I just stared at him. "I don't want to do that."

"I would not ask if it were not necessary, *ma petite.* But even if I were able to do it, neither of us would enjoy me breaking down your shielding. We cannot merge our auras if my aura cannot touch yours."

I was suddenly scared. Really seriously scared. I didn't know what would happen if I dropped the shields with him right there. In times of crisis our auras flared together forming a unique whole. I didn't want to do this. I am a control freak, and everything about Jean-Claude ate at the part of me that most needed control.

"I'm not sure I can do this."

He sighed. "It is your choice. I will not force it, but I fear the consequences, *ma petite*. I do fear them."

Marianne had given me the lecture, and it was really too late to get cold feet. I could either move forward with this, or eventually one of us would die. Probably me. Part of my job was going up against preternatural monsters—things with enough magic to sense a hole in my defenses. Before I'd ever been able to sense auras, or at least before I knew that I was doing it, my aura had been intact. With my own natural talent, that had been enough. But lately I seemed to be running up against bigger, badder monsters. Eventually, I would lose. That, I might have been able to live with, sort of. But costing Jean-Claude or Richard their lives? That I couldn't handle. I knew all the reasons I should do this, and still I stood there gazing up at Jean-Claude, my heart beating in my throat, my shields tight in place. The front part of my brain knew this needed doing. The back part of my brain wasn't so sure.

"Once I drop my shield, then what?"

"We touch," he said.

I took a deep breath in and blew it out as if I were about to run a race. Then I dropped my shields. It wasn't like tearing down the stone walls; it was like absorbing them back into my psyche. The tower was just suddenly not there, and Jean-Claude's power crashed over me. It wasn't only that I felt the sexual attraction in full force, I could feel his heartbeat in my head. I could taste his skin in my mouth. I knew he'd fed tonight, though intellectually I'd known that when I heard his heart beating. Now, I could feel that he was well fed and full of someone else's blood.

His hand moved towards me, and I flattened against the wall. The hand kept moving, and I pulled away from it. I moved away because more than anything in the world at that moment I wanted him to touch me. I wanted to feel his hand against my bare skin. I wanted to rip the vinyl from his body and watch him, pale and perfect above me. The image was so clear that I closed my eyes against it, as if that would help.

I felt him in front of me, knew he was leaning close. I ducked under his arm and was suddenly standing by the table, leaving him near the wall. I kept backing up, and he kept watching me. Someone touched me, and I screamed.

Asher was holding my arm, gazing up at me with those pale eyes of his. I could feel him, too, feel the weight of his age, the heft of his power in my head. That was my power, but I realized in shielding so strongly from Jean-Claude I'd also cut myself off from some of my own powers. Shielding was a tricky thing. I guess I still didn't have the hang of it.

Jean-Claude moved away from the wall, holding one slender hand out to me. I backed up, Asher's hand sliding over my arm as I pulled away. I was shaking my head back and forth, back and forth.

Jean-Claude walked slowly towards me. His eyes had gone drowning blue, the pupil swallowed by his own power. I knew with a sudden clarity that it wasn't his power or lust that had called his eyes, it was mine. He could feel how my body tightened, moistened, as he moved towards me. It wasn't him I didn't trust. It was me.

I took one step backwards and fell on the small step leading down to the dance floor. Someone caught me before I hit the floor, strong arms around my waist, pressing me against the bare skin of a very masculine chest. I could feel that without looking. I was held effortlessly, feet dangling, and I knew those arms, the feel of that chest, the smell of his skin this close. I craned my head backwards and found myself staring at Richard.

5

I STOPPED BREATHING. To be suddenly inches away from him after all this time was too much. He leaned that painfully handsome face over mine, and the thick waves of his brown hair fell against my skin. His mouth hovered over mine, and I think I would have said, *no*, or moved, but two things happened at once. He tightened his one-armed hold around my waist, a movement that was almost painful. Then his newly free hand gripped my chin, held my face. The touch of his hands, the strength in them made me hesitate. One moment I was staring into his deep brown eyes, the next, his face was too close and he was kissing me.

I don't know what I expected, a chaste kiss, I think. It wasn't chaste. He kissed me hard enough to bruise, hard enough to force my mouth open, then he crawled inside, and I could feel the muscles in his mouth, his jaw, his neck working as he held me, explored me, possessed me. I should have been angry, pissed, but I wasn't. If he hadn't held me immobile I'd have turned in his arms, pressed the front of my body against his. But all I could do was taste his mouth, feel his lips, try to drink him down my throat, as if he were the finest of wines and I was dying of thirst.

He finally drew back from me, enough for me to see his face. I stared breathlessly at him, as if my eyes were hungry for the sight of those perfect cheekbones, the dimple that softened an utterly masculine face. There was nothing feminine about Richard. He was the ultimate male in so many ways. The electric lights caught strands of gold and copper, like metallic wire through the deep brown of his hair.

He lowered me slowly to the ground from his height of six one. His shoulders were broad, chest deep, waist tight and narrow, stomach flat, with a fine line of dark hair running down the middle of it and vanishing into the black vinyl pants he was wearing. More black vinyl! I was sensing a theme here, but my gaze traveled down his body just the same. Tracing the narrow hips, lingering where I shouldn't have been, noticing things I wished I hadn't, because we were in public, and I wasn't planning on seeing him naked tonight. Knee-high leather boots completed his outfit. The only things he was wearing on his upper body were leather and metal-studded "bracelets" and a matching collar.

A hand touched my back, and I jumped and whirled around, turning so I could face them both, because I knew who was behind me. Jean-Claude stood there, eyes having bled back to normal.

I finally found my voice. "You called him."

"We had an arrangement that whoever you called first would contact the other."

"You should have told me," I said.

Jean-Claude put his hands on his hips. "I am not taking the blame for this. He wished to be a surprise, against *my* wishes."

I looked at Richard. "Is that true?"

Richard nodded. "Yes."

"Why?"

"Because if I'd played fair I still wouldn't have gotten a kiss. I couldn't stand the thought of seeing you tonight and not touching you."

It wasn't so much his words as the look in his eyes, the heat in his face, that made me blush.

"I have played you fair tonight, *ma petite*, and yet I am punished, rather than rewarded." Jean-Claude held out his hand to me. "Shall we begin with a kiss?"

I was suddenly aware that we were standing on the dance floor near the metal framework and the waiting "actors." We had the audience's attention, and I didn't want that. I realized something I hadn't with the stone shield in place. Almost everyone in the room was a shapeshifter. I could feel their energy like the brush of warm electric fur, and they could feel ours.

I nodded. I suddenly wanted the privacy that Jean-Claude had offered earlier. But staring from Jean-Claude to Richard, I realized I didn't trust myself alone with them. If we had a room to ourselves I couldn't guarantee that the sex would be merely metaphysical. Admitting that even to myself was embarrassing. As uncomfortable as it was to do what we had to do in public, it was still better than in private. Here I knew I'd say *stop*, anywhere else I just wasn't sure. I wasn't thinking about the wereleopards. I was thinking about how large and bare my skin felt. Shit.

"A kiss, why not?"

"We can get a room," Richard said, voice low.

I shook my head. "No, no rooms."

He reached out as if to touch me, and one look was enough to make his hand drop. "You don't trust us."

"Or me," I said, softly.

Jean-Claude held out his hand to me. "Come, *ma petite*, we delay their show."

I stared at his hand for a space of heartbeats, then took it. I expected him to pull me in against his body, but he didn't. He stopped with the width of a handspan between us. I looked a question at him, and he touched my face, gently, tentatively, fingers hovering on either side of my face, like hesitant butterflies, as if he were afraid to touch me. He lowered his face towards me, as his fingertips found my skin. His hands slid on either side of my face, cupping it like something delicate and breakable.

I'd never felt him so tentative around me, so unsure. Even as his lips hovered over mine I wondered if he was doing it this way on purpose to contrast with Richard's forcefulness. Then his lips touched mine, and I stopped thinking. It was the barest of brushes, his mouth over mine. Then, softly, he kissed me. I kissed him back, being as tentative as he, my hands raising, covering his hands as they cradled my face. He'd thrown that surprisingly long black hair over one shoulder so that the right side of his face was bare to the lights and the hair didn't get in the way of the kiss. I ran one hand down the side of his jaw, tracing the shape of his face, ever so gently, as we kissed. He shuddered under that light brush of my hand, and the feel of him trembling under my hand brought a soft sound from low in my throat. Jean-Claude's mouth pressed against mine hard enough that I could feel the press of his fangs against my lip. I opened my mouth and let him inside me, ran my tongue between the delicate points. I'd learned how to French kiss a vampire, but it was a hazardous pleasure, one to be done with care, and I was out of practice.

In slipping my tongue between his fangs, I nicked myself. It was a quick, sharp pain, and Jean-Claude made a soft guttural sound, a heartbeat before I tasted blood.

His hands were suddenly at my back, pulling me against his body. The kiss never stopped, and the urgency of it grew, until it was as if he were feeding from my mouth, trying to drink me down.

I might have pulled away, I might not have, but the moment the front of our bodies touched, it was too late. There was no going back, no saying no, nothing but sensation. I felt that cool, shimmering wind that was his aura touch mine. For one trembling moment we were pressed together, our energy breathing against each other like the sides of two great beasts. Then the boundaries that held our auras in place gave way. Think of it as if you were making love and suddenly your skin slid away, spilling you against your partner, into your partner, giving you an intimacy that was never imagined, never planned, never wanted.

I screamed, and he echoed me. I felt us begin to fall to the floor, but Richard caught us, cradled us against his body, laid us gently on the floor. The power did not leap across to him, and I didn't know why.

Jean-Claude's body was on top of mine, pinning me to the floor, his groin pressed over mine. He drove his hips in against me, forcing my legs apart around the slick covering of his legs. I wanted him inside me, wanted him to ride me while the power rode us.

He struggled up on his arms, leaning up and away from me, forcing his lower body tighter against mine. And the power built in a skin-tingling rush, building, building, like that shining edge of orgasm when you can feel it growing large and overwhelming but can't quite reach it.

I saw Richard leaning over me like a dark shadow against the haze of the lights. I think I tried to say, *no, don't,* but no sound came. He kissed me, and the power flared, but still he wasn't part of it. He kissed my cheek, my chin, my neck, working lower, and I suddenly knew what he was doing. He was kissing his way down to the hole over my heart chakra, my energy center. Jean-Claude had already covered the one at my base, my groin. Richard's chest stretched above me, smooth, firm, so temptingly close, and I raised my mouth to his skin, so that as he kissed down my body he drew his naked chest across my tongue. I licked a wet line down his body. He buried his mouth inside the halter top and touched over my heart, and my mouth found his heart at the same moment.

The power didn't just build, it exploded. It was like lying at ground zero of a nuclear explosion, the shock waves shooting out, out, out into the room, while we melted together in the center. For one shining moment I felt both of them inside me, through me, as if they were wind, pure power, pouring through me, through us. Richard's electric warmth buzzed over us; Jean-Claude's cool power poured over and through like a chill wind; and I was something large and growing, holding the warmth of the living and the cold of the dead. I was both and neither. We were all and none.

I don't know if I passed out or if I just lost time for some metaphysical reason.

All I remembered was that I was suddenly lying on the floor with Richard collapsed beside me, pinning one of my arms, his body curled around my chest and head, his legs touching down the other side of my body. Jean-Claude was collapsed on top of me, his body pressing the length of mine, with his head to one side resting on Richard's leg. They both had their eyes closed, their breath coming in ragged pants, just like mine.

It took me two tries to say a breathless, "Get off me."

Jean-Claude rolled to one side without ever opening his eyes. The fall of his body forced Richard's legs to move a little farther out, so that Jean-Claude and I both lay in the semicircle of Richard's body.

The room was so quiet I thought we were the only ones left in it. As if all the others had fled in terror of what we'd done. Then the room thundered in applause and howling and other animal noises that I didn't have words for. The noise was deafening, beating against my body in waves as if I had nerves in places where I'd never had nerves before.

Asher was suddenly standing over us. He knelt beside me, touching the pulse in my neck. "Blink if you can hear me, Anita."

I blinked.

"Can you speak?"

"Yes."

He nodded and touched Jean-Claude next, stroking a hand down his cheek. Jean-Claude opened his eyes at the touch. He gave a smile that seemed to mean more to Asher than to me, because it made Asher laugh. The laugh was a very masculine one, as if they'd shared some dirty joke that I didn't understand. Asher crawled around me until he was kneeling by Richard's head. He lifted a handful of thick hair so he could see Richard's face clearly. Richard blinked at him, but didn't seem to be focusing.

Asher bent low over Richard, and I heard him say, "Can you hear me, *mon ami*?"

Richard swallowed, coughed, and said, "Yes."

"*Bon, bon.*"

It took me two tries but I had a smart-aleck comment, and I was going to make it. "Now, everyone who can stand, raise their hands." None of us moved. I felt distant, floating, my body too heavy to move. Or maybe my mind was too overwhelmed to make it move.

"Have no fears, *ma cherie*, we will attend you." Asher stood, and it was as if it were a signal. Figures moved out of the crowd. I recognized three of them. Jamil's waist length cornrows looked right at home with his black leather outfit. He was Richard's lead enforcer, or Sköff. Shang-Da didn't look comfortable in black leather, but the six-foot-plus Chinese never looked comfortable outside of nice dress clothes with polished wing tips. Shang-Da was the other enforcer for the pack, the Hati. Sylvie knelt beside me, looking splendid in vinyl, her short brown hair touched with burgundy highlights. Though it looked good, I knew she was conservative enough that it was probably a temporary color. She sold insurance when she wasn't being Richard's second in command, his Freki, and insurance salespeople didn't have hair the color of a good red wine.

She smiled at me, wearing more makeup than I'd ever seen her in. It looked great, but it didn't really look like Sylvie. For the first time I thought how pretty she was, and that she was almost as delicate-looking as me.

"I owed you a rescue," she said. Once upon a time a bunch of nasty vampires had come to town to teach Jean-Claude, Richard, and me a lesson. They'd taken prisoners along the way. Sylvie had been one of them. I'd gotten her out, and I'd kept my promise to see everyone who touched her dead. She did the actual killing, but I delivered them up to her for punishment. She kept a few bones as souvenirs. Sylvie would never complain that I was too violent. Maybe she could be my new best friend.

The werewolves took up positions around us, facing outward like good bodyguards. None of them were as physically imposing as Narcissus's bodyguards had been, but I'd seen the wolves fight, and muscles aren't everything. Skill counts, and a certain level of ruthlessness.

Two vampires came to stand with Asher and the wolves. I didn't recognize either of them. The woman was Asian, with shining black hair that fell barely to her shoulders. The hair was nearly the same color and brilliance as the vinyl cat suit that clung to nearly every inch of her body. The suit made sure you were aware of her high, tight breasts, her tiny waist, the swell of her shapely hips. She gave me an unfriendly look with her dark eyes, before she turned her back on me and stood, hands at her side, waiting. Waiting for what, I wasn't sure.

The second vampire was male, not much taller than the woman, with thick brown hair that had been shaved close to his head, except for a layer left on top that came about halfway to his eyes, shining and straight. He gazed down on me with a smile, eyes the color of new pennies, as if his brown eyes held just a trace of blood in them.

He turned his attention outward, arms crossed over the black leather of his chest. They too faced outward like good bodyguards, letting the crowd know that even though we couldn't stand up, we weren't helpless. Comforting, I guess.

Jason crawled in between their legs, head hanging down, as if he were almost too tired to move. He raised his blue eyes to me, and the look was almost as unfocused as I felt.

He gave a pale version of his usual grin and said, "Was it good for you?"

I was feeling better enough to try and sit up, but failed. Jean-Claude said, "Lie a little longer, *ma petite*."

Since I had no choice, I did what he suggested. I lay staring up at the dark, distant ceiling with its rows of lights. They'd turned off most of them, so that the club was nearly dark. Like the soft gloom that comes when you close the drapes during the day.

I felt Jason lay down on the other side of me, head resting on my thigh. Not long ago I'd have made him move, but I'd spent my time away learning how to be comfortable being close with the wereleopards. It had made me more tolerant of everyone, apparently. "Why are *you* tired?"

He rolled his head up to look at me without raising it from my leg, one hand curving over my calf as if to keep his balance. "You spill sex and magic through the whole club and you ask why I'm tired? You are such a tease."

I frowned at him. "One more comment like that and you'll have to move."

He snuggled his head on my hose. "I can see that your underwear matches."

"Get off of me, Jason."

He slid to the floor without being told twice. He could never leave well enough alone, our Jason. He always had to get the last joke, the last comment, that one bit too many. I worried that someday with someone else that little quirk might get him hurt, or worse.

Richard propped himself up on one elbow, moving slowly as if he wasn't sure everything was working. "I don't know if that felt better than anything else we've ever done, or worse."

"It feels like a combination of a hangover and mild flu to me," I said.

"And yet it feels good," Jean-Claude said.

I finally got upright and found that they both had a hand at my back to support me, as if their movements had been simultaneous.

I actually leaned in against their hands, rather than telling them to move. One, I was still shaky; two, I just didn't find the physical contact unpleasant. All these months of trying to forge the wereleopards into a cohesive, friendly unit, and it was me that had learned to be cohesive and friendly. Me that had learned that not every helping hand is a threat to my independence. Me that had learned that not every offer of physical closeness is a trap or a lie.

Richard sat up first, slowly, keeping his hand on my back. Then Jean-Claude sat up, keeping his hand very still against me. I felt them exchange glances. This was the moment that I usually pulled away. We'd have some fantastic sex, metaphysical or otherwise, and that was my cue to close down, hide. We were in public, all the more reason to do it.

I didn't pull away. Richard's arm slid cautiously up my back, over my shoulders. Jean-Claude's arm moved lower around my waist. They both pulled me into the curve of their bodies as if they were some huge, warm vinyl-covered chair with a pulse.

Some say that that moment during sex when you both have an orgasm your auras drop, you blend your energies, yourselves together. You share so much more than just your body during sex, it's one of the reasons you should be careful who you do it with. Just sitting there on the floor with them was like that. I could feel their energies moving through me, like a low-level current, a distant hum. In time I was pretty sure it would become white noise—something you can ignore, like psychic shielding when you no longer have to concentrate on it. But now it was like we would always walk, move, through that dreamy afterglow where you were still connected, still not quite back in your own skin. I didn't push them away, because I didn't want to. Pushing them away would have been redundant. We didn't need to touch to breach the barriers anymore. And that should have scared me more than anything else, but it didn't.

Narcissus walked out into the middle of the floor and a soft light fell upon him, growing ever so gradually brighter. "Well, my friends, we have had a treat tonight, have we not?"

More applause, screams, and animal noises filled the dimness. Narcissus held up his hands until the crowd fell quiet. "I think we have had our climax for the night." A smattering of laughter at that. "We will save our show until tomorrow, for to do less would be to dishonor what we have been offered here tonight."

The woman, who was still standing to the back of the dance floor in her robe, said, "I can't compete with that."

Narcissus blew her a kiss. "It is not a competition, sweet Miranda, it is that we all have our gifts. Some are merely more rare than others." He turned and stared at us as he said the last. His eyes were pale and oddly colored, and it took me a second or two to realize that Narcissus's eyes had bled to his beast. Hyena eyes, I guess, though truthfully, I didn't know what hyena eyes looked like. I just knew they weren't human eyes.

He knelt beside us, smoothing his dress down in an automatic and strangely odd gesture that I'd never seen a man make before. Of course, he was also the first man I'd ever seen in a dress. There was probably a cause and effect.

Narcissus lowered his voice. "I would love to speak with you in private about this."

"Of course," Jean-Claude said, "but first we have other business."

Narcissus leaned in close, lowering his voice until it was necessary to lean forward to hear him. "As I have two of my guards waiting with her leopards so no harm will come, there is time to talk. Or should I say, *your* leopards, for surely now, what belongs to one, belongs to all." He had leaned so far over that his cheek nearly touched Jean-Claude on one side and my face on the other.

"No," I said, "the leopards are mine."

"Really," Narcissus said. He turned his face that fraction of an inch and brushed his lips against mine. It might have been an accident, but I doubted it. "You don't share everything, then?"

I moved my face just far enough away so we weren't touching. "No."

"So good to know," he whispered. He leaned forward and pressed his mouth to Jean-Claude's lips. I was startled, frozen for a second wondering exactly what to do.

Jean-Claude knew exactly what to do. He put one finger in the man's chest and pushed, not with muscle, but with power. The power of the marks, the power that we had all just moments before solidified. Jean-Claude drew on it as if he'd done it a thousand times before, effortlessly, gracefully, commandingly.

Narcissus was pushed back from him by a rush of invisible power that I could feel tugging on my body. And I knew that most of the people in the room could feel it, as well. Narcissus stayed crouched on the floor, staring at Jean-Claude, staring at all of us. The look on his face was angry, but there was more hunger in it than rage, a hunger denied.

"We need to talk in private," Narcissus insisted.

Jean-Claude nodded. "That would be best, I think."

There was a weight of things left unsaid in that short exchange. I felt Richard's puzzlement mirror my own, before I turned my head to glance back at him. The movement put our faces close enough so that we could almost have kissed. I could tell just by the expression in his eyes that he didn't know what was going on. And he seemed to know that I could tell, because he didn't bother to shrug or make any outward acknowledgment. It wasn't telepathy, though to an outsider it might look that way. It was more extreme empathy, as if I could read every nuance on his face, the smallest change, and know what it meant.

I was still pressed in the circle of Richard's and Jean-Claude's arms, a strange amount of bare skin touching all of us—my back, Richard's chest and stomach, Jean-Claude's arm. There was something incredibly right about the touching, the closeness. I felt Jean-Claude's attention turn, before I moved my head to meet his eyes.

The look in those drowning eyes held worlds of things unsaid, unasked, all so tremblingly close. Because for once he didn't see in my eyes the barriers that kept all those words trapped. It had to be the marriage of the marks affecting me, but that night I think he could have asked me anything, anything, and I wasn't sure I'd say no.

What he finally said was, "Shall we retire to privacy to discuss business with Narcissus?" His voice had its usual smoothness. Only his eyes held uncertainty and a need so large he almost had no words for it. We'd all waited so long for my surrender. I knew that the phrasing wasn't mine. It sounded more like something Jean-Claude would think, but with Richard also pressed against my body I wasn't really sure who was thinking it. I only knew it hadn't been me.

Even before the marks had merged I'd had moments like this. Moments when their thoughts invaded mine, overrode mine. The images had been the worst—nightmare flashes of feeding on the warm bodies of animals, of drinking blood from people I didn't know. It had been this mingling, this loss of self, that had terrified me, sent me running for anything that would keep me whole—keep me myself. Tonight, that just didn't seem important. Definitely an aftereffect of the metaphysical union of marks. But knowing what it was didn't make it go away. It was a dangerous night.

Jean-Claude said, "*Ma petite*, are you well? I am feeling much better, energized in fact. Are you still ill?"

I shook my head. "No, I feel fine." *Fine* didn't really cover it. *Energized* was a good word for it, but there were others. How long could it take to rescue the wereleopards from yet another disaster? The night wasn't young, dawn would come, and I wanted to be alone with them before that. I realized with a jolt that ran all the way down my body, that tonight was it. If we could get some privacy and not be interrupted, all things would suddenly be possible.

Richard and Jean-Claude both stood up, in a boneless movement of grace for the vampire and pure energy for the werewolf. I gazed at them as they stood above me, and I was suddenly eager to have the other business done with. I wasn't as worried about the leopards as I should have been, and that did bother me. Whatever this effect was, it was distracting me from more important things. Saving the leopards was why I'd come. It was the first time I'd really thought of them in a while.

I shook my head trying to clear it of sex and magic and the weight of possibilities in Richard's eyes. Jean Claude's eyes were more cautious, but I'd taught him caution where I was concerned.

I held my hands up to both of them. I never asked for help to stand unless I was bleeding or something was broken. The two of them exchanged glances, then they held their hands out to me, again in perfect unison, like choreographed dancers who knew what the other would do.

They could feel my desire, but that had always been there; it told them nothing. I took their hands and let them lift me up. They were both still looking unsure, almost suspicious, as if they were waiting for me to recoil from them and run screaming from the intimacy of it all. I had to smile. "If we can get everyone all tucked in safe and sound before dawn, all things will be possible."

They exchanged another look between them. Jean-Claude made a small movement, as if encouraging Richard. It was a tiny, almost-push with his head, as if to say, *Go ahead, ask.* Normally, seeing them plot behind my back pissed me off, but not that night.

"Do you mean . . ." Richard let the thought trail off.

I nodded, and Richard's hand tightened on mine. Jean-Claude's hand was strangely quiet in mine. "You do realize, *ma petite*, that this new . . ." he hesitated, "willingness, may be a by-product of joining the marks tonight. I don't wish you to accuse us later of trickery."

"I know what it is, and I don't care." I should have, but I didn't. It was like being drunk, or drugged, and even thinking that made no difference.

I was looking at Jean-Claude, and I saw him let out the breath he'd been holding. I felt Richard do the same. It was as if a great weight had been taken from both of them. And I knew that I was that burden. I'd try not to be a burden from now on. "Let's get this over with and go get the leopards," I said.

Jean-Claude raised my hand to his mouth, brushing the knuckles across his lips. "And be gone from this place."

I nodded. "And be gone from this place," I said.

6

I'D BEEN COMPLAINING to Jean-Claude for years that his decorating scheme was too monochromatic, but one look at Narcissus's bedroom and I knew I owed Jean-Claude an apology. The room was done in black, and I mean *black*. The walls, the hardwood floor, the drawn drapes against one wall, the bed. The only color in the room was the silver chains and the silver-colored implements hanging from the wall. The color of the steel seemed to accentuate the blackness rather than relieve it. Chains dangled from the ceiling above the huge bed. It was bigger than king-sized. The only term that came to mind was *orgy-sized*. The bed was four-postered, with the largest, heaviest, darkest wood I'd ever seen. More chains dangled from the four posts, set in heavy permanent rings. If I'd been on a date, I'd have turned and run for it. But this wasn't a date, and in we all trooped.

My understanding about most people who were into D and S was that their bedrooms were separate from their "dungeons." Nearby perhaps, but not the same room. You needed somewhere to go to actually sleep. Maybe Narcissus just never rested from the fun and games.

There was a door in the opposite wall, and the drapes were drawn over the middle of one wall. Maybe his real bed was behind door number two or the drapes. I hoped so.

The only chair in the room had straps attached to it, so Narcissus offered us the bed to sit on. I don't know if I would have sat down or not, but first Jean-Claude, then Richard did. Jean-Claude settled against the black bedspread as he did everything, with grace, settling his body against the pillows as if he felt utterly comfortable. But it was Richard who surprised me. I expected to see in him some of the discomfort I felt about the room, but he didn't seem in the least uncomfortable. In fact, I realized for the first time that the heavy leather cuffs at his wrists and the collar at his throat had metal hooks in them, so they could be attached to chains or a leash. He'd probably worn them so he could blend into the club scene, as I'd worn the boots. But . . . but I could feel that he was calm about the room and everything in it. I wasn't.

I looked at Jean-Claude and Richard and knew I'd decided to sleep with both of them tonight, however we arranged it. But seeing them on the bed in the middle of all this, watching them at home in it, made me wonder about my decision. It made me think that maybe, after all this time, I still didn't know what I was getting myself into.

Asher was wandering the room looking at the things on the wall. I couldn't read him like I could read the others, but he, too, seemed unruffled, and I didn't think it was an act. Narcissus had swept into the room with Ajax at his back. He'd agreed to leave everyone else in the hallway, or downstairs, in exchange for us leaving our extra wolves outside the room. I guess for true privacy you did need less than a double digit worth of people in a room.

Richard held his hand out to me. "It's okay, Anita. Nothing in this room can hurt you without your permission, and you're not going to give that." That wasn't exactly the comforting comment I'd wanted, but I guess it was the truth. I used to believe that truth was good, but I'd begun to realize that it is neither good, nor bad. It's just the truth. Life had been simpler when I believed in black-and-white absolutes.

I took his hand and let him draw me to the bed, between Jean-Claude and himself. Well, Narcissus had already made a play for Jean-Claude, so I guess we needed to make the hands-off point. But it still bothered me that Richard put me between them, not simply beside him. The warm, fuzzy feeling I'd had from the marriage of the marks seemed to be receding at an alarming rate. Magic does that sometimes.

I felt stiff and uncomfortable on the black bed between my two men. "What is wrong, *ma petite*? You are suddenly very tense."

I looked at Jean-Claude, raising my eyebrows. "Am I the only one here that doesn't like this room?"

"Jean-Claude liked this room very much, once," Narcissus said.

I turned and looked at the werehyena as he paced the room in his stocking feet. "What do you mean?" I asked.

Jean-Claude answered, "Once, I submitted to unwanted advances because I was told to do so. But those days are past."

I stared at him, and he wouldn't meet my gaze. His eyes were all for Narcissus, as the other man paced around the bed.

"I don't remember you being unwilling," Narcissus said. He leaned against the far post of the bed.

"I learned long ago to make a virtue of necessity," Jean-Claude said. "Besides, Nikolaos, the old Master of the City, sent me to you. You remember how she was, Narcissus. Refusal of an order was not allowed."

I'd had the horror of meeting Nikolaos personally. She had been very, very scary.

"So I was an unpleasant duty." He sounded angry.

Jean-Claude shook his head. "Your body is pleasant, Narcissus. What you like doing with your lovers, if they can take the damage, is not . . ." Jean-Claude looked down as if searching for the right word, then raised his midnight blue eyes to Narcissus, and I saw the effect that his gaze had on the shapeshifter. Narcissus looked like he'd been hit between the eyes with a hammer—a handsome, charming hammer.

"Is not *what*?" Narcissus asked, his voice hoarse.

"Is not to my taste," Jean-Claude said. "Besides, I must not have pleased you very much, for you did not do what my late master wished you to do."

I was the reason that Nikolaos was the *late* Master of the City. She'd been trying to kill me, and I'd gotten lucky. She was dead, I wasn't. And now Jean-Claude got to be Master of the City. I hadn't planned that. How much of it Jean-Claude had planned was still up for debate. It is not just prejudice on my part that makes me trust him less than Richard.

Narcissus put one knee on the bed, one hand still around the bedpost. "You pleased me very much." The look on his face was too intimate. They should have been alone for this conversation. But, then again, watching the way Narcissus looked at Jean-Claude, maybe that wouldn't have been such a great idea. From Jean-Claude all I sensed was a desire to soothe any injured feelings. But I was betting if I could peek inside Narcissus's head I'd find a different kind of desire.

"Nikolaos thought I failed her and punished me for it."

"I could not ally myself with her—not even for you as my permanent toy."

Jean-Claude raised an eyebrow at that. "I do not remember that being part of the deal."

"When I first told her *no*, she sweetened the offer." Narcissus crawled onto the bed. He stayed crouched on all fours, as if he were expecting someone to come up behind him.

"In what way did she sweeten the offer?"

Narcissus started to crawl across the bed, slowly, his knees catching on the hem of his dress as he moved. "She offered you to me for always, to do with as I wished."

A thrill of terror ran through me from my toes to the top of my head. It took me a second to realize it wasn't my fear. Richard and I both turned to Jean-Claude. His face showed nothing. It was his usual polite, attractive, almost bored mask. But we could both feel the cold, screaming terror in his mind at the thought of how close he'd come to being Narcissus's permanent . . . guest.

It filled him with a fear that was larger than the shapeshifter. Images flashed through my mind, memories. Chained on my stomach on rough wood, the sound of a whip going back, the shock of it biting into my skin, and the knowledge that it was only the first blow. The wave of utter despair that followed that memory left me blinking back tears. I had a confused image of being tied to a wall, with a hand rotted to green pus caressing my body. Then the images stopped abruptly, like someone had thrown a switch. But the body the hand had been traveling down had been male. They were Jean-Claude's memories, not mine. He'd been projecting his memories on me and when he realized it, he'd blocked it.

I looked at him and couldn't keep the horror out of my eyes. My hair hid my face from Narcissus, and I was glad because I couldn't be blasé about what I'd just seen. Jean-Claude didn't look at me but kept his eyes on Narcissus. I was trying not to cry, and Jean-Claude's face betrayed nothing.

Jean-Claude hadn't been remembering Narcissus's abuse, but others, many, countless others. It wasn't the pain I carried away from the memories, but the despair. The thought that I . . . no, he. He had not owned his own body. He had never been a prostitute, or rather, he had never traded sex for money. But for power, the whim of whoever was his current master, and strangely for safety, he had traded sex for centuries. I'd known that, but I'd pictured him as the seducer. What I'd just seen had nothing to do with seduction.

A small sound came from Richard, and I turned to him. His eyes were shiny with unshed tears, and he had the same look of numb horror that I felt on my own face. We looked at each other for a long frozen moment, then a tear trickled down his face a second before a hot line of tears eased down my own.

He reached for my hand and I took it. And we both turned to Jean-Claude. He was still watching, even talking, though I hadn't heard any of it, with Narcissus. The other man had crawled all the way across that huge bed to be within touching distance of us all. But it wasn't *us all* that he wanted to touch.

"Sweet, sweet, Jean-Claude, I thought I had forgotten you, but seeing you tonight on the floor with the two of them made me remember." He reached out towards Jean-Claude, and Richard grabbed his wrist.

"Don't touch him. Don't ever touch him again."

Narcissus looked from Jean-Claude to Richard and finally back to Richard. "Such possessiveness, it must be true love." I had a ringside seat and watched the muscles in Richard's hands and forearm tense as he squeezed that dainty wrist.

Narcissus laughed, voice shaky, but not with pain. "Such strength, such passion, would he crush my wrist just for trying to touch your hair?" His voice held amusement and what I finally realized was excitement. Richard touching him, threatening him, hurting him . . . He was enjoying it.

I felt Richard realize it too, but he didn't let go. Instead he jerked the other man off balance until he fell against his body. Narcissus made a small surprised sound. Richard kept one hand on his wrist, and he put the other to the man's neck. Not squeezing, just there, large and dark against Narcissus's pale skin.

The bodyguard, Ajax, had moved away from the wall, and Asher had moved to meet him. Things could go very bad, very quickly here. It was usually me that lost my temper and made things worse, not Richard.

Narcissus had to sense rather than see the movement, because Richard had him facing away from the rest of the room. "It's alright, Ajax, it's alright. Richard is not hurting me." Then Richard did something that made Narcissus's breath stop in his throat and come out harsh. "You may crush my wrist, if it's foreplay, but if it's not, then my people will kill you, all of you." His words were reasonable, his tone was not. You could hear the pain in his voice, but there was also anticipation, as if whichever way Richard answered, it would excite him.

Jean-Claude spoke. "Do not give him an excuse to have us at his mercy, *mon ami*. We are in his territory tonight, his guests. We owe him a guest's duty to his host, as long as he does not forfeit that right."

I wasn't a hundred percent sure what a guest's duties to his host were, but I was willing to bet that crushing their limbs wasn't among them. I touched Richard's shoulder, and he jumped. Narcissus made a small protesting sound, as if Richard had involuntarily tightened his grip.

"Jean-Claude's right, Richard."

"Anita councils you to temperance, Richard, and she is one of the least temperate people I have ever known." Jean-Claude moved forward, laying his hand on Richard's other shoulder, so we both touched him. "Besides, *mon ami*, hurting this one will not undo the harm already done. No drop of blood less will have been spilt; no pound of flesh less will have been lost; no humiliation will have been stopped. It is over, memories cannot harm us."

For the first time I wondered if Richard and I had gotten the same memories in that flash of shared insight. What I'd seen had been horrible, but it hadn't affected me like it had him. Maybe it was a guy thing. Maybe a white, Anglo-Saxon, upper-middle-class male like Richard would take memories of being abused and raped harder than I would. I was a woman. I knew things like that could happen to me. Maybe he had never thought they could happen to him.

Richard spoke low, his voice fallen to a rolling growl, as if his beast lurked just behind that handsome throat. "Never touch him again, Narcissus, or we'll finish this." Then Richard slowly, carefully, slid his hands away from Narcissus. I expected him to scoot away, clutching his injured wrist, but I underestimated him, or maybe overestimated him.

Narcissus did cradle his wrist, but he stayed pressed against Richard's body. "You've torn ligaments in my wrist. They take longer to heal than bone."

"I know," Richard said softly. The level of anger in those two words made me flinch.

"With a thought I can tell my men to leave her wereleopards to the mercy of their captors."

Richard glanced at Jean-Claude, who nodded. "Narcissus can contact his . . . men mind-to-mind."

Richard put his hands on Narcissus's shoulders, to push him away I thought, but Narcissus said, "You've revoked your safe passage by injuring me against my will."

Richard froze, and I could see the tension in his back, feel the sudden uncertainty.

"What is he talking about?" I asked. I wasn't even sure who I was asking.

"Narcissus has a small army of werehyenas within this building and on the surrounding buildings as guards," Jean-Claude said.

"If the werehyenas are so powerful, then why doesn't everyone talk about them in the same breath with the wolves and the rats?" I asked.

"Because Narcissus prefers to be the power behind the throne, *ma petite.* It means that the other shapeshifters are constantly currying his favor with gifts."

"Like Nikolaos used you," I said.

He nodded.

I looked at Richard. "What have you been giving him?"

Richard eased away from Narcissus. "Nothing."

Narcissus turned on the bed, still cradling his wrist. "That's about to change."

"I don't think so," Richard said.

"Marcus and Raina had an arrangement with me. They and the rats dictated that my hyenas could never rise above fifty in number. To make this happen they used gifts, not threats."

"The threat was always there," Richard said. "War between you, us, and the rats, with you on the losing side."

Narcissus shrugged. "Perhaps, but have you not wondered what I've been doing since Marcus died and you took over? I wondered when the gifts would start arriving, but instead all gifts stopped, even the ones I'd begun to count on." He looked at me then. "Some of those gifts were yours to give, Nimir-Ra."

I must have looked as confused as I felt, because Jean-Claude said, "The wereleopards."

"Yes, Gabriel, their old alpha, was a dear, dear friend of mine," Narcissus said.

Since I'd killed Gabriel, I didn't like the way the conversation was going. "You mean that Gabriel gave some of the wereleopards to you?"

Narcissus's smile made me shiver. "All of them have spent time in my care, except Nathaniel." His smile faded. "I assumed Gabriel kept Nathaniel to himself because he was his personal favorite, but now that you've told me what Nathaniel is, I know that wasn't it." Narcissus leaned forward on his knees. "Gabriel was afraid to give me Nathaniel, afraid of what we might do together."

I swallowed hard. "You covered your reaction really well when I told you."

"I'm an accomplished liar, Anita. Best remember that." He looked up at Richard. "How long has it been since Marcus's death, a little over a year? When the gifts stopped coming, I assumed the pact was at an end."

"What are you saying?" Richard asked.

"There are over four hundred werehyenas now, some new, some recruited from out of state. But we rival the wererats and werewolves now. You will have to negotiate with us as equals instead of peons."

Richard said, "What do you . . ."

Jean-Claude interrupted. "Let us come to terms." I felt the fear that was behind his calm words, and so did Richard. You did not ask a sexual sadist what he wanted. You offered what you were willing to give up.

Narcissus looked at Richard. "Are they Jean-Claude's wolves now, Richard? Do you share your kingship?" The tone was mocking.

"I am Ulfric, and I will set the terms, no one else." But his voice was cautious, the temper slowed. I'd never seen Richard like this, and I wasn't sure I liked the change. He was reacting more like me. As I thought of it, I wondered . . . I channeled some of his beast, some of Jean-Claude's hunger, what did they gain from me?

"You know what I want," Narcissus said.

"You would be wise not to ask for it," Jean-Claude said.

"If I cannot have you, Jean-Claude, then perhaps to watch the three of you make love on my bed would be enough to wash this insult clean between us."

Richard and I said together, "No."

He looked at us, and there was something unpleasant in his eyes. "Then give me Nathaniel."

"No," I said.

"For one evening."

"No."

"For an hour," he said.

I shook my head.

"One of the other leopards?"

"I won't give you any of my people."

He looked at Richard. "And you, Ulfric, will you give me one of your wolves?"

"You know the answer, Narcissus," Richard said.

"Then what would you offer me, Ulfric?"

"Name something I'm willing to give."

Narcissus smiled, and I had a sense of Ajax and Asher circling each other as they felt the tension rising. "I want to be included in the conferences that run the shapeshifter community in this town."

Richard nodded. "Fine. Rafael and I thought you had no interest in politics, or you would already have been asked."

"The rat king does not know my heart, nor do the wolves."

Richard stood. "Anita needs to go to her people."

Narcissus smiled and shook his head. "Oh, no, Ulfric, it is not that easy."

Richard frowned. "You're to be included in decision making. That's what you wanted."

"But I still want gifts."

"No gifts pass between the rats and the wolves. We are allies. If you wish to be an ally then there will be no gifts, except that we will come to your aid when you need us."

Narcissus shook his head again. "I do not wish to be allies, to be dragged into every squabble between animals that do not concern me. No, Ulfric, you mistake me. I wish to be included in the conferences that set policy. But I do not wish to tie myself to anyone and be dragged into a war that is not of my own making."

"Then what are you asking?" Richard said.

"Gifts."

"Bribes, you mean," Richard said.

Narcissus shrugged. "Call it what you will."

"No," Richard said.

I felt Jean-Claude tense a moment before Richard said it. "*Mon ami* . . ."

"No," Richard said and turned to Jean-Claude. "Even if he could kill us all, which I doubt, my wolves, your vampires, they would rain down on this club and take it apart brick by brick. He won't risk that. Narcissus is a cautious leader. I learned from watching him deal with Marcus. He puts his own safety and comfort above all else."

"The comfort and safety of my people above all else," Narcissus said. He looked at me. "What of you, Nimir-Ra, how confident do you feel? Do you think if I had my people kill your kittens that the werewolves and vampires would lift a finger to avenge them?"

"You forget, Narcissus, she's also my lupa, my mate. The wolves will defend who she tells them to defend."

"Ah, yes, the human lupa, the human leopard queen. But not really human, is she?"

I met his gaze and said, "I need to go collect my leopards. Thanks for the hospitality." I pushed to my feet and stood beside Richard.

Narcissus looked at Jean-Claude, who still lounged on the bed. "Are they really such children?" he asked him.

Jean-Claude gave a graceful shrug. "They are not like us Narcissus. They still believe in right and wrong. And rules."

"Then let me teach them a new rule." He stared up at us, still kneeling on the bed, still wearing the black lace dress, and suddenly his power burst out before him in lines of heat. It slammed into my body like a giant hand, nearly staggering me. Richard reached out to steady me, and the moment we touched, his beast jumped between us, in a rush of warmth that raced through my body in goosebumps and shivers. Richard's body shuddered, and I felt his breath, our breath, catch. That otherworldly power curled between us, and for the first time I realized that the power came both ways. I'd thought what was inside me was an echo of Richard's beast, but it was more than that. Maybe it would have been different if I hadn't separated myself from him for so long. But now the power that had once been his was mine. The warmth spilled between us like two streams converging into a river, two scalding hot streams that spilled into a river that boiled over my skin. It was so hot that I half expected my skin to peel away and reveal the beast underneath.

"If she shifts, then my men are free to enter this fight." Narcissus's voice was shocking. I think I'd forgotten he was there, forgotten everything but the hot, hot power flowing between Richard and me. Narcissus's face began to grow longer. It was like watching sticks move behind clay.

Richard ran his hand just in front of my body, caressing the power that flowed off of my skin. There was a look of soft wonderment on his face. "She won't shift. You have my word," Richard said.

"Good enough. You always keep your word. I may be a sadist and a masochist, but I am still Oba of this clan." His voice had become a strange high-pitched growl. "You have insulted me and, through me, all that is mine." Claws slid out from his small fingers until he raised curved paws, not hands at all.

Jean-Claude came to stand beside us. "Come, *ma petite*, let them have room to maneuver." He touched my hand, and that scalding power poured from my skin to his. He collapsed to his knees, hand still pressed against my skin, as if the heat had welded it in place.

I knelt by him, and his gaze raised, drowning blue, the pupil lost in a rush of power, but not his power. He opened his mouth to speak, but no sound came out. He stared at me, and, judging by the look on his face, he felt lost, overwhelmed.

"What's wrong?" Asher asked from across the room, still facing Ajax.

"I'm not sure," I said.

"He seems in pain," Narcissus said. It made me glance up at him. Except for his face and hands, he was still in human form. The really powerful alphas could do that, partial changes.

"The power spills over him," Richard said, and his voice held that edge of growl. His throat was hidden behind the leather collar, but I knew if I could see it, that the skin would be smooth and perfect. His voice could howl from his mouth like a dog's without any change in his appearance.

"But he is a vampire," Narcissus said. "The power of the wolves should be closed to him."

"The wolf is his animal to call," Richard said.

I looked into Jean-Claude's face from inches away, watched him struggle through the hot, scalding power and knew why he wasn't dealing well with it. This was primal energy, the life and beat of the earth under our feet, the rush of wind in the trees, the stuff of life. And Jean-Claude for all that he walked and talked and flirted wasn't alive.

Richard knelt beside us, and Jean-Claude let out a low moan, half-collapsing against me. "Jean-Claude!"

Richard rolled him over into his arms, and Jean-Claude's spine bowed, his breath coming in ragged gasps.

Narcissus was above us on the bed. "What's wrong with him?"

"I don't know," Richard said.

I put a hand on Jean-Claude's throat. The pulse wasn't just racing, it was beating like a caged thing. I tried to use the ability I had to sense vampires, but all I could feel was the heat of the beast. There was nothing cold or dead in the circle of our arms.

"Lay him on the floor, Richard."

He looked at me.

"Do it!"

He laid Jean-Claude gently on the floor, hand still touching his shoulder.

"Move away from him." I did what I asked of Richard, standing and moving around the vampire, pushing Richard back with my body until Jean-Claude lay alone beside the bed.

Narcissus's body had re-formed, until he was the graceful man we'd met downstairs. He'd moved off the bed without being told, but moved around so he could still watch.

Jean-Claude rolled slowly onto his side, and moved his head to stare at us. He licked his lips and tried twice before he could speak. "What have you done to me?"

Richard and I still stood in a cocoon of heat. His hands brushed my arms, and I shuddered against him. His arms locked around my waist, and the more of our bodies that touched the more heat rose around us, until I thought the very air should tremble like the heat of a summer's day off a tar road.

"Shared Richard's power with you," I said.

"No," Jean-Claude said, and he rose slowly to sit, propped heavily on his arms. "Not just Richard, but you, *ma petite*, you. Richard and I have shared much, but it never did this. You are the bridge between the two worlds."

Asher spoke. "She bridges life and death."

Jean-Claude looked up at him sharply, a harsh look on his face. "*Exactement.*"

Narcissus spoke. "I knew Marcus and Raina could share their power, their beasts, but Anita is not a werewolf. You should not be able to share your beast with each other, wolf to leopard."

"I'm not a wereleopard," I said.

"Me thinks the lady doth protest too much," Narcissus said.

"Or wereanimal to vampire," Asher said.

I looked at Asher. "Don't *you* start."

He smiled at me. "I know that you are not a true shapeshifter, but your . . . magic has changed because of the addition of Richard. There is something about you, that if I did not know better, I would say you were indeed one of them."

"Richard said the wolf is Jean-Claude's animal to call," Narcissus said.

"That doesn't explain this," Asher said. He knelt by Jean-Claude, reaching towards him.

Jean-Claude caught his hand before it could touch his face, and Asher jerked back. "You're hot to the touch. Not just warm, hot."

"It is like the rush after we feed, but more . . . more alive." He gazed up at us, and his eyes were still drowning blue. "Go save your leopards, *ma petite*, and let us retire before dawn. I want to see how hot," he took a deep breath, and I knew he was drawing in the scent of us, "this power will grow."

"It is all very impressive," Narcissus said, "but I will have my pound of flesh."

"You're beginning to get on my nerves," I said.

He smiled. "Be that as it may, I still have a right to ask for the insult to be avenged."

I looked at Richard. He nodded. I sighed. "You know it's usually me that gets us into this kind of trouble."

"We're not in trouble yet," Richard said. "Narcissus is grandstanding. Why do you think I didn't change?" He stared at the smaller man.

Narcissus smiled. "And here I thought you were just decorative muscle standing behind Marcus."

"You won't fight unless you run out of options, Narcissus, so no more games."

There was a coldness in Richard's voice, a firmness that could not be crossed or reasoned with. Again it echoed me more than him. Just how tough had the last few months been on him and his wolves? There are only a few things that will harden you this fast. Death of those close to you; police work; or combat where people are actually dying around you. In civilian life, Richard was a junior high science teacher, so it wasn't police work. I think someone would have mentioned if he'd lost family members. That left combat. How many challengers had he fought? How many had he killed? Who had died?

I shook my head to clear away the thoughts. One problem at a time. "You can't have any of us, or our people, Narcissus. You're not going to start a war over the refusal, so where does that leave us?"

"I will take my men out of the room with your cats, Anita. I will do that." He came to stand in front of me, his back to the bedpost, one hand playing with the chains attached to it, making the metal jingle. "The . . . people that have them are not terribly creative, but they have a certain raw talent for pain." He stared at me with human eyes again.

"What do you want, Narcissus?" Richard said.

He wrapped the chain around one wrist over and over. "Something worth having, Richard, *someone* worth having."

Asher said, "Do you merely want someone to dominate, or are you interested in being dominated?"

Narcissus looked back at him. "Why?"

"Answer the question truthfully, Narcissus," Jean-Claude said. "You may find it worthwhile."

Narcissus looked from one vampire to the other, then back to Asher, standing there in his brown leather outfit. "I prefer to dominate, but with the right person I'll allow myself to be topped."

Asher walked towards us, making his tall, slender body sway. "I'll top you."

"You do not have to do this," Jean-Claude said.

"Don't do it, Asher," I said.

"We'll find another way," Richard said.

Asher looked at us with those pale, pale blue eyes. "I thought you'd be happy, Jean-Claude. I've finally agreed to take a lover. Isn't that what you wanted me to do?" His voice was mild, but the mockery came through just the same, the bitterness.

"I have offered you nearly all in my power, and you have refused all. Why him? Why now?" Jean-Claude got to his knees, and I offered him a hand up, not a hundred percent sure that I should.

He looked at the offered hand.

"If you think it's safe," I said.

He wrapped his hand around mine, and the power flowed in a burning rush down my hand over his, down his arm, and I felt it hit his heart like a blow. He closed his eyes, swayed for a second, then looked at me. "It was unexpected the first time." He started to stand, and Richard went to his other side, so that we held him between us.

"I don't know if this is good for you, or not," I said.

"You fill me with life, *ma petite*. You and Richard. How can it be bad?"

I didn't say the obvious, but I thought it really hard. If you could fill the walking dead with life, should you? And if you did, what would happen to that walking dead? So much of what we were doing between us magically had never been done before, or only once before. Unfortunately we'd had to kill the other triumvirate that consisted of a vamp, a werewolf, and a necromancer. They'd been trying to kill us, but still, they might have been able to answer questions that no one else could have answered. Now we were just swinging in the dark, hoping we didn't hurt each other.

"Look at you, Jean-Claude, between them like a candle with two wicks. You will burn yourself up," Asher said.

"That is my concern."

"Yes, and what I do is mine. You ask, 'Why him?' 'Why now?' First, you need me. Which of the three of you would be willing to do this?" Asher moved around Narcissus as if he weren't there, eyes on Jean-Claude, on us. "Oh, I know that you could have topped him. You can do it when you want, and make a virtue of necessity, but he's had you beneath him, and nothing less will satisfy him now." He stood close enough that the energy swirled outward, over him like a lip of hot ocean water. His breath came out in a shuddering sigh. "*Mon Dieu!*" He stepped back until his legs touched the bed, then he sat down on the black sheets. His brown leather didn't match as well as the rest of us had.

"Such power, Jean-Claude, and yet none of you wishes to pay the price for Richard's temper tantrum. But I will pay that price."

"You know my rule, Asher. I never ask of others what I'm not willing to do myself," I said.

He looked at me curiously, face unreadable behind the mask, except for his eyes. "Are you volunteering?"

I shook my head. "No. But you don't have to do this. We will find another way."

"And what if I want to do it?" he asked.

I looked at him for a second, then shrugged. "I don't know what to say to that."

"It disturbs you that I might want to do this, doesn't it?" His eyes were intense.

"Yes," I said.

That intense gaze moved past me to Jean-Claude. "It bothers him, too. He wonders if I am ruined and all that is left for me is pain."

"You once told me that everything worked. That you were scarred, but . . . functional," I said.

He blinked and looked at me. "Did I? Well, a man does not like to admit such things to a pretty woman. Or to a handsome man." He looked up at us, but the only person he was really looking at was Jean-Claude. "I will pay the toll for our handsome Monsieur Zeeman's display of strength. But I will not be the whipping boy. Not this time."

Not ever again, hung heavy in the air, unsaid, but there all the same. Asher had had two hundred years of being at the mercy of the people who had given Jean-Claude the memories that Richard and I had flashed on. Two centuries more of that kind of care and torment. When Asher had first come to us he'd been cruel occasionally. I thought we'd cured him of it. But watching the look in his eyes now, I knew we hadn't.

"And do you know the best part of all?" Asher asked.

Jean-Claude just shook his head.

"It will cause you pain to think of me with Narcissus. And even after I am with him, he will still not answer the question you have been wanting, so desperately, to have answered."

Jean-Claude stiffened, hand tightening on mine. I felt him slam his own shields into place, keeping us out of what he was thinking, feeling, at that moment. The warm, roiling power between us began to dissipate. Jean-Claude had made himself part of our circuit. Now he was shutting us down, though I didn't think it was on purpose. He just couldn't shield himself from us and keep the flow going.

His voice came out calm, his usual bored, yet cultured, tone, "How can you be so sure that he will not talk?"

"I can be sure of what I do. And I will not give him the answer you want."

"What answer?" I asked. "What are you guys talking about?"

The two vampires looked at each other. "Ask Jean-Claude," Asher said.

I looked at Jean-Claude, but he was staring at Asher. In a way, the rest of us were superfluous, an audience for a show that didn't need one.

"You're being petty, Asher," Richard said.

The vampire's gaze moved to the man on my other side, and the anger in those eyes made the blue spill across the pupils in a frosted gleam. He looked blind. "Have I not earned the right to be petty, Richard?"

Richard shook his head. "Just tell him the truth."

"There are three people in his power that I would strip for, that I would allow to touch me, and answer that so important question." He stood in one graceful movement, like a liquid puppet on strings. He stepped close enough for the power to spill around him, bringing his breath shuddering from his lips. The power recognized him, flared stronger, as if he could act as our third, if we weren't careful. Did the power just need a vampire, and not specifically Jean-Claude? Richard shut down his side of the power, clanging a shield in place that made me think of metal, strong and solid, uncompromising.

Asher caressed the air just above Richard's arm and had to step away, rubbing his hands on his arms. "The power fades." He shook himself like a dog coming out of water. "If you would say *yes*, his torment could end."

I frowned at them both, not sure I was following the conversation, not sure I wanted to.

Asher turned those pale, drowning eyes to me. "Oh, our fair Anita." He was already shaking his head. "But no, I know better than to ask. I have enjoyed shocking our so heterosexual Richard by my overtures. But Anita is not so easily teased." He came to stand in front of Jean-Claude. "And, of course, if he wanted the answer badly enough he could do it himself."

Jean-Claude's face was at its most arrogant. Its most hidden. "You know why I do not."

Asher moved back to stand in front of me. "He refuses my bed, because he fears that you would . . . what is the American word . . . dump him, if you knew he were sleeping with a man. Would you?"

I had to swallow before I could answer. "Yeah."

Asher smiled, but not like he was happy, more like it had been a predictable answer. "Then I will pleasure myself here with Narcissus, and Jean-Claude will still not know if I stay because I have become a lover of such things, or because this type of love is all that is left for me."

"I haven't agreed to this," Narcissus said. "Before I take second—no *fourth* choice—let me see what I'm buying."

Asher stood, turning so that his left side was towards the werehyena. He unzipped the mask and lifted it over his head. We were standing enough to one side so that I could see that perfect profile. His golden hair—and I mean golden—was braided along the back of his head so that nothing interfered with the view. I was used to looking at Asher through a film of hair. Without it, the lines of his face were like sculpture, something so smooth and lovely that you wanted to touch it, trace the movement of it with your hands, layer it with kisses. Even after the little show he'd put on, he was still beautiful. Nothing seemed to change that when I looked at Asher.

"Very nice," Narcissus said, "very, very nice, but I have many beautiful men at my beck and call. Perhaps not as beautiful, but still . . ."

Asher turned to face the man. Whatever Narcissus was about to say died in his throat. The right side of Asher's face looked like melted candle wax. The scars didn't start until well away from the midline of his face. It was as if his torturers all those centuries ago had wanted him to have enough left to remember the perfection he'd once been. His eyes were still golden-lashed, his nose perfect, his mouth full and kissable, but the rest . . . The rest was scarred. Not ruined, not spoiled, but scarred.

I remembered Asher's smooth perfection, the feel of that perfect body rubbing against mine. Not my memories. I had never seen Asher nude. I had never touched him that way. But Jean-Claude had about two hundred years ago. It made it impossible for me to look at Asher with unprejudiced eyes, because I remembered being in love with him, in fact, was still a little in love with him. Which meant that Jean-Claude was still a little in love with him. My personal life just can't get more complicated.

Narcissus drew a shuddering breath and said in a voice gone hoarse, eyes wide, "Oh, my."

Asher threw the hood on the bed and began to unzip the front of the leather shirt, very slowly. I'd seen his chest before and knew that it was much worse than his face. The right side of his chest was carved with deep runnels, the skin hard to the touch. The left side, like his face, still had that angelic beauty that had attracted the vampires to him long ago.

When the zipper was halfway down his body, baring his chest and upper stomach, Narcissus had to sit down on the bed as if his legs wouldn't hold him.

"I think, Narcissus," Jean-Claude said, "that after tonight you will owe us a favor." His voice was empty when he said it, devoid of anything. It was the voice he used when he was at his most careful, or his most pained.

Asher asked in a careful voice that didn't quite match the striptease he was doing, "What level of pain does Narcissus enjoy straight—how do you say—out of the box?"

"Rough," Jean-Claude said. "He can control his desire and not step outside the bounds of his submissive, but if he is to be topped, then rough, very rough. You do not need a warming up period for this one." Jean-Claude's voice was still empty.

Asher looked down at Narcissus. "Is that true? Do you like to start out with a . . . bang?" That last word was slow, seductive. One word, and it held worlds of promise within it.

Narcissus nodded slowly. "You can start with blood, if you've the balls for it."

"Most people have to work up to that for it to be pleasurable," Asher said.

"I don't," Narcissus said.

Asher finished unzipping and lowered the shirt off his arms, held it in his hands for a moment, then struck out with a movement so quick it was only an after-image blur. He slapped Narcissus across the face with the heavy zipper once, twice, three times, until blood showed at the corner of his mouth and his eyes looked unfocused.

I was so startled by all of it that I think I forgot to breathe. All I could do was stare. Jean-Claude had gone very still between Richard and me. It wasn't the utter stillness that he was capable of, that all the old masters were capable of, and I realized why. He couldn't sink into that black stillness of death with the lingering touch of the "life" we'd pumped through him.

Narcissus used the tip of his tongue to taste the blood on his mouth. "I am an accomplished liar, but I always give fair trade." He was suddenly more serious than he had been, as if the flippant tease was just a mask and underneath was a more solemn, thinking person. When he looked up, there was a person in his eyes that I knew was dangerous. The flirt was real, too, but it was partially camouflage to make everyone underestimate him. Looking into his eyes, I knew that to underestimate him would be a very bad thing.

He turned those newly serious eyes to Asher. "For this, I will owe you a favor, but only one favor, not three."

Asher reached up and undid his hair, letting the heavy sparkling waves fall around his face. He stared down at the smaller man, and I couldn't see the look he gave, but whatever it was, it made Narcissus look like a drowning man. "I am only worth one favor?" Asher said. "I think not."

Narcissus had to swallow twice before he could speak. "Perhaps more." He turned and looked at us, and his eyes were still raw, real. "Go, save your wereleopards, whoever they belong to. But know this, the ones inside are new to our community. They do not know our rules, and their own rules seem harsh by comparison."

"You warn us, Narcissus, thank you," Jean-Claude said.

"I think that this one would not like it if you were hurt, no matter how angry he is with you, Jean-Claude. I am about to let him bind me to this bed, or the wall, and do to me whatever he wishes."

"Whatever I wish?" Asher asked.

Narcissus's gaze flicked back to him. "No, not whatever, but until I use the safety word, yes." There was something almost childlike in the way he said the last, as if he were already thinking of what was to come, and not really concentrating on us.

"Safety word?" I asked.

Narcissus gazed at me. "If the pain grows too much, or if something is proposed that the slave does not want to do, you use the word agreed upon. Once the word is spoken the master must stop."

"But you'll be tied up, you won't be able to make him stop."

Narcissus's eyes were drowning, drowning in things that I didn't understand, and didn't want to. "It is both the trust and the element of uncertainty that makes the event, Anita."

"You trust that he'll stop when you say stop, but you like the thought that he might not stop, that he might just keep going," Richard said.

It made me stare at him, but I caught Narcissus's nod.

"Am I the only one in this room that doesn't understand how this game is played?"

"Remember, Anita," Richard said, "I was a virgin until Raina got me. She was my first lover, and her tastes ran . . . to the exotic."

Narcissus laughed then. "A virgin in Raina's hands, what a frightening image. Even I wouldn't let her top me, because you could see it in her eyes."

"See what?" I asked.

"That she had no stopping point."

Having almost been a star in one of her little bedroom dramas, saved only by the fact that I'd killed her first, I had to agree.

"Raina liked it better if you didn't want to do it," Richard said. "She was a sexual sadist, not a dominant. It took me a long time to realize how big a difference there is between the two."

I looked at his face, but he was safe behind his shields, I couldn't read him. He and Jean-Claude had more practice at shielding than I did. But, frankly, I didn't want to know what was behind the lost look on Richard's face. I realized with a start that I had Jean-Claude's memories but not Richard's. It had never occurred to me to ask why that was. But later, later. Right now I wanted to be out of this room. "I want out of here."

Jean-Claude pulled gently away from both of us to stand on his own. "Yes, the night is running out, and we have much to do."

I didn't look at him, or Richard. I'd pretty much promised that if dawn stayed at bay we'd have sex tonight. But somehow staring at Asher's naked back, with Narcissus gazing up at him with a look somewhere between adoration and terror, I just wasn't in the mood anymore.

7

THE UPPER HALLWAY stretched white and empty. There was a silver wallpaper border high up on the wall; more silver ran in thin lines down the walls, an opulent yet tasteful display. It looked like the hallway of some upscale hotel. I didn't know if it was camouflage or if Narcissus just liked it that way. After downstairs' black techno-punk and Narcissus's own Marquis de Sade bedroom, it was almost startling, as if we'd stepped from some dark nightmare into a quieter, more peaceful dream.

We were the ones who looked out of place. All of us in black, too much skin showing. Jamil paced up the stairs on point, his muscular upper body showing in tantalizing glimpses through a series of black leather straps. The pants fit his narrow hips like a second skin, and I'd learned long ago from watching Jean-Claude undress that you didn't get that smooth line if there was underwear between the skin and the pants. He turned, his waist-length cornrows flaring out around him. He was a contrast in darkness, the black of the leather, the dark, dark brown of his skin. He moved like a shadow in that white hallway.

Faust went next. He was the new male vampire I'd met downstairs. In the better light, his hair was obviously tinted burgundy, like a shade of red gone wrong, but somehow it suited him. His leather pants were covered in more zippers than seemed necessary to get them on and off, and his black shirt had a zipper up the front. It reminded me of Asher's shirt, except for the color. I tried not to think too much about what Asher might be doing right this moment. I still didn't know if Asher was pimping himself out for us or whether he truly wanted to be with Narcissus. I was more comfortable with the idea of self-sacrifice.

I brought up the middle with the two women behind me. Sylvie still didn't look like herself to me. The black skirt was so short that whoever was in back of her couldn't help but get a flash of whatever was under the skirt. The hose climbed her legs all the way up, making them look long and shapely, though she was only three inches taller than me. She was also wearing three-inch black spikes, which may have added to the illusion of long legs. Her leather top showed a very discreet line of flesh from neck to waist where a belt cinched in her tiny waist. Her breasts seemed to stay magically on either side of the line of skin, as if they were held in place by something more than a bra.

She smiled up at me, but her eyes had already bled to that pale wolfish color. They didn't match the careful makeup and the short, curly brown hair.

Meng Die brought up the rear. Where her pale flesh showed around the vinyl cat suit, colorless body glitter sparkled. There was a touch of glitter at the corner of each up-tilted eye, complementing pale eyeshadow and dramatic eyeliner. She was smaller than me, more delicate of bone, smaller of breast, more slender of waist, like a dainty bird. But the look she gave me was more vulture than canary. She didn't like me, and I didn't know why. But Jean-Claude had assured me she'd do the job. Jean-Claude had a lot of faults, but if he trusted Meng Die to keep me safe, then she'd do it. He was never careless with me, not in that way.

Faust just seemed to be amused as hell about it all. Everything made him smile, pleasantly. Most vampires went for arrogance to mask how they felt. He seemed to use mild amusement. Of course, maybe Faust was just a happy guy, and I was being too cynical.

Why weren't Jean-Claude and Richard with me? Because the wereleopards were mine. If I took other dominants with me, it would be seen as weakness. I was planning to interview other alphas to take over the wereleopards, but until I found someone to do that, I was all they had. If people began thinking I was weak, the leopards would be marked as anyone's meat. It wouldn't just be out-of-town shapeshifters that were trying to take them away from me, it would be every shapeshifter in town. It was funny how many shifters could be assholes unless you were strong enough to stop them.

I had to save the leopards, not Richard, not Jean-Claude, me. But I had to stay alive to do that, so I did take backup. I'm stubborn, not stupid. Though I know a few people who might argue that.

Each white door had a silver number on its surface. Again like a very discreet hotel. We were looking for room nine. There was absolutely no sound from behind the doors. The only noises I heard were the distant thud of the music downstairs and the faint whisper of leather and vinyl—our body movements. I'd never been so aware of how loud small noises could be. Maybe it was the eerie silence of the hallway, or maybe I'd gained something new from the marriage of the marks. Better hearing wouldn't be a bad thing, would it? So many of the "gifts" from the vampire marks tended to be double-edged swords, at best.

I shook off the gloomy thoughts and walked with my foursome of bodyguards down the carpeted hallway. I was trusting them to give their lives for mine. That's what a bodyguard does. Jamil had taken two shotgun blasts for me last summer. It hadn't been silver shot, so he'd healed, but he hadn't known that when he put himself between the gun barrel and me. Sylvie owed me one, and a woman her size doesn't get to be second in the pack hierarchy without being one tough werewolf. I didn't really trust the vampires to give up their undead lives for me. It's been my experience that the longer something semi-immortal lives, the more tightly it hugs its existence. So I counted on the wolves, and knew I could work around the vampires. It didn't matter that Jean-Claude trusted them. It mattered that I didn't. I'd have preferred to just bring along more werewolves, except if I showed up with nothing but wolves at my back, it would be like saying that I couldn't do this without Richard's pack. Not true. Or not completely true. We'd see how deep the shit was once we opened the door.

Room nine was nearly at the end of the long hallway. The building had been a warehouse, and the upstairs had simply been divided into long hallways with huge rooms scattered along them. Jamil was standing to one side of the door. Faust was standing in front of it. Not smart.

I stood to the other side of the door and said, "Faust, the werehyenas had to take guns off these guys."

The vampire raised an arched eyebrow at me.

"They may not have found all the guns," I said.

He still looked at me.

I sighed. Over a hundred years of "life," power enough to be a master vamp, and he was still an amateur. "It would be bad to be standing in the center of the door when a shotgun blast went off on the other side."

He blinked, and a little of that humor leaked away, showing that arrogance that most vamps acquire. "I think Narcissus would have found a shotgun."

I leaned my shoulder against the wall and smiled at him. "Do you know what a cop-killer is?"

He raised both eyebrows at me. "A person who kills policemen."

"No, it's a type of ammunition designed to go through body armor. The cops have no defense against it. You can carry armor-piercing bullets in handguns, Faust. I used the shotgun as an example, but it could be so many things. And they would all take out your heart, most of your spine, or all of your head, depending on where the shooter was aiming."

"Get out of the fucking doorway," Meng Die said.

He turned and looked at her, and it was not a friendly look. "You are not my master."

"Nor you mine," she said.

"Children," I said. They both looked at me. Great. "Faust if you're not going to be helpful then go back downstairs."

"What did I do?"

I glanced at Meng Die, shrugged, and said, "Get out of the fucking doorway."

I could see his shoulders tighten, but he gave a graceful bow at odds with the burgundy hair and leather. "As Jean-Claude's lady wishes, so shall it be." He stepped to the side closest to me. Sylvie moved up close to me, not exactly between us, but close. It made me feel better. Bossing around vampires was always chancy. You never knew when they'd try to boss back. I really, really wanted my gun back.

"What now?" Jamil asked. He was watching the vampires like he wasn't any happier with their company than I was. All good bodyguards are paranoid. It goes with the job.

"I guess we knock." I kept my body well to the side, extended just enough arm to get the job done, and gave three solid knocks. If they shot through the door, they'd probably miss me. But no one shot through the door. In fact, nothing happened. We waited for a few moments, but patience has never been my best thing. I started to knock again, but Jamil stopped me and said, "May I?"

I nodded.

He knocked hard and loud enough to shake the door. It was a solid door. If the door didn't open this time, they were deliberately ignoring us.

The door opened, revealing a brown-haired man as muscled as Ajax, but taller. What did Narcissus do, recruit from all the weight-lifting gyms in town? He frowned at us. "Yeah?"

"I'm Nimir-Ra for the wereleopards. I think you've been waiting for me."

"About fucking time," he said. He opened the door wide, pushing it flush against the wall, putting his back to it, arms crossed across his chest. His arms apparently weren't as muscular as they looked, if he could cross his arms that way. But he did demonstrate that there was no one hiding behind the door. Good to know.

The room was white—white floor, white ceiling, white walls—like a room carved of hard snow. There were blades on the walls—knives, swords, daggers, tiny glittering blades, swords the length of a tall man. The bodyguard by the door said, "Welcome to the room of swords." It sounded formal, like he was supposed to say it.

From the door I couldn't see anyone. I took a deep breath, let it out slowly, and walked inside. Jamil followed a step behind at my shoulder, Faust was at my other side. Sylvie and Meng Die brought up the rear.

A figure stepped into the middle of the room. At first glance I thought it was a man, but on second glance, not exactly. He was man-sized, almost six feet, broad shouldered, muscular, but what I'd thought was a golden tan was golden tan fur, very thin and fine. Covering the whole body. The face was almost human, though the bone structure was a little odd. A wide face, a lipless mouth that was almost a round muzzle. The eyes were a dark orange gold with an edge of blue in them, as if they, like the body, were only partly through their change. It was as if his body had frozen, stopping just short of attaining human form. I'd never seen anything like it. Pale skin showed in patches on his bare chest and stomach. I couldn't tell if the dark gold hair and edge of beard that encircled his face was actually hair or what was left of a mane. The longer I stared at him, the more like a lion he looked, until I couldn't see the man I'd thought I'd seen for the light coating of beast that covered him.

He gave a snarling smile. "Do you like what you see?"

"I've never seen anything like you," I said, nice, calm, even empty.

He didn't like that, my lack of reaction. His smile vanished and became only a snarl of very sharp, very white teeth.

"Welcome, Nimir-Ra, I am Marco, we have been waiting for you." He made a sweeping gesture to either side with his clawed human hands. I glanced around at the "we". They were small to medium-sized men with short black hair and dark skin. Most groups, prides, packs, whatever, were mixed ethnically. But there was a sameness to these dark men, almost a family look about them. Two on either side wore hooded cloaks, with the hoods thrown back, the wide cloaks spread like curtains. I glimpsed blond hair behind the blackness to the left. I couldn't see Nathaniel's hair over the blackness but I knew he had to be on the right.

There was blood on the white floor, pooling into a little depression in the concrete. A drain was in the middle so they could hose the floor down when they were finished. There was another guard in the far corner who looked very unhappy to be there. Three women that I did not know were chained to the wall on either side of the door. Two blonds on the right side, a brunette on the left. They weren't wereleopards, or at least none that were mine.

"Let me see my people," I said.

"Will you not greet us formally?" Marco asked.

"You're not the alpha anything, Marco. You get your head lion in here and I'll greet him, but you, I don't have to greet."

Marco gave a small bow, the gaze of those odd tawny eyes never leaving my face. It was the way you bow in martial arts when you're afraid the other person will hit you if you glance away.

Jamil had moved up beside me, not ahead of me, but close enough that our shoulders brushed. I didn't tell him to move back. He'd saved my life once, I'd let him do his job.

"Then greet me, Nimir-Ra." It was another male voice. He stepped out from behind the cloaks to the left. As he stepped out, the cloaks dropped and I could see Gregory clearly.

He was turned towards the wall, nude except for his pants that had been peeled down to his lower thighs, his boots still on. Chains held his wrists above his head, his legs were wide apart. His curling blond hair fell just below his shoulders. His body was slender but muscled, butt tight. You have to take care of your body if you're going to strip professionally. There was no mark on his body that I could see, but blood had spattered on the floor in front of him, below him, pooling, dark, drying. They hadn't cut anything on his back. My stomach clenched tight, my breath squeezing down in my throat.

"Gregory," I said, softly.

"He's gagged," said the man. I finally dragged my gaze away from Gregory, and the sight of the other man, the alpha, made me stare.

He wasn't a lion man, he was a snake man. His head was wider than my shoulders, covered in olive green scales with large black spots. One arm was bare, and it looked very human except for the scales and the hands that ended in twisted claws that would have made any predator proud. He turned his head to look at me with one large copper gold eye. A heavy black stripe stretched back from the corner of his eye to his temple. His movements were vaguely birdlike. Other black-cloaked figures stepped away from the walls, dropping hoods to show themselves scaled, with the same stripes near metallic eyes and hands with curling claws.

My people fanned out around me, two going to either side. "Who are you?"

"I am Coronus of the Black Water Clan, though I doubt that will mean anything to you."

"Marco mentioned you were new in town. I'm Anita Blake, Nimir-Ra of the Blooddrinkers Clan. By what right do you harm my people?" What I wanted to do was start screaming, but there are rules. I couldn't be furry, or scaly, but I could follow the rules.

Coronus walked to the wall and stood next to the brunette chained to it. She made small panicked sounds as he reached for her. Sylvie moved a little closer to him, to the girl, as if she was waiting for an excuse. Coronus traced a finger down the girl's cheek, the barest of touches, yet she closed her eyes and shivered.

"I came here seeking swanmanes, and I found three of them. They had already tied up the male. We thought it was their leader, their swanking, or we would not have harmed him. By the time we found we had the wrong animal, it was late in the game."

I glanced at the cloaks still held firmly in place, the impassive faces of the men as impossible to read as if they'd already become snakes. I noticed that one of the figures had breasts. It was nearly naked where they showed above a scoop neck T-shirt. I could see the chains reaching for the ceiling and down to the floor. There was more blood, a lot more blood, on that side.

"Let me see Nathaniel."

"Would you not like to see your blond leopard up close and personal first?"

I started to ask why. I didn't like the fact that he seemed reluctant for me to see Nathaniel. "You want me to see Gregory first?"

The man seemed to think about it, head to one side. The movement looked animal-like, yet not exactly snakelike. "Up close and personal, yes, yes, I do."

I didn't like the way he kept saying *personal,* but I let it go. "Then you've made a request of me, Coronus. If I do it, I can make one of you." Sometimes the rules are helpful. Rarely, but sometimes.

"What would you have of me?"

"I want him unchained."

"He was easily taken once by my people. I see no reason why not. Go, gaze upon him, touch him, then we will unchain him."

Jamil stayed at my side as I walked towards Gregory. My gut was tight. What had they done to him? I could still remember the scream over the phone. A glance from Jamil cleared the snake people away. They stood as far away as the room would allow them to, on either side. I had to step over the chains on the floor and under the ones that held Gregory's wrists up. I came around to look in his blue eyes. A black ball gag was stuffed in his mouth, the string tucked under his hair so it hadn't been visible from the back. His eyes were wide, panicked. His face was untouched, and my gaze followed down the line of his body almost against my will, as if I knew what I'd find. His groin was a red ruin, healing, covered in dried blood. They'd ripped him up. If he'd been human he'd have been ruined. I wasn't a hundred percent sure that he wasn't anyway. I had to close my eyes for a second. The room felt hot.

Jamil had let out a hissing breath when he saw what they'd done to Gregory, and his energy burned over my skin, fed by anger and horror. Strong emotions make shapeshifters leak all over you. My voice came out in a squeezed whisper, "Will he heal?"

Jamil had to come closer to inspect the wound. He touched it reluctantly, and Gregory writhed in pain at the gentlest of touches. "I think so, if they allow him to change form soon."

I tried to pull the gag out of Gregory's mouth and couldn't. It was too tight. I broke the leather string that held it in place and threw it on the floor.

Gregory took a sobbing breath and said, "Anita, I thought you weren't coming." His blue eyes glistened with unshed tears.

We were almost the same size, so I could touch my forehead to his, hands on either side of his face. I couldn't stand to see the tears in his eyes, and I couldn't afford to cry in front of the bad guys. "I'll always come for you Gregory, always." Seeing him like this, I meant it. I needed to find a real wereleopard to protect them. But how was I going to give them away like stray puppies to some stranger? But that was a problem for another night.

"Unchain him," I said.

Jamil moved to the manacles and seemed to know just how they worked. No key was needed. Great. Gregory sagged as soon as the first chain went, and I caught him, holding him under the arms. But when the second wrist restraint opened, his body fell against my leg and he screamed. Jamil undid the last ankle chain, and I lowered Gregory to the ground as gently as I could. I was stroking his hair, his upper body cradled in my arms, across my lap, when I had a sense of movement to either side.

Jamil couldn't guard both sides at the same time. The knives in my boots were trapped under Gregory's body. It was beautifully timed. I rolled over Gregory's body, and felt the cloak rush over me, as talons slashed where I'd been. I went for the boot knife, but never had a chance. I saw the clawed hand coming for me.

Everything slowed down, like images caught in crystal so that you see every detail. I seemed to have all the time in the world to draw the knife, or to try and dodge the slashing talons, yet a part of my brain was screaming that there was no time. I threw myself back onto the floor, felt the air rush over me as the snake man stumbled, so sure of its target that it hadn't been prepared for me to move. The rest was instinct. I foot-swept the snake, and it was suddenly on its back. I got a knife in my right hand, but the snake was on its feet, kicking upward like it had springs in its spine.

I felt more than saw something large and dark leap through the air over me, landing behind me. My attention was diverted for a fraction of a second, but that was enough. The one in front darted in, a movement so fast my eyes couldn't follow it. I put my left arm out, taking the blow, as my right tried to stab forward. My left arm went numb like it had been hit with a baseball bat. I could have stabbed into the stomach, but I caught movement out of the corner of my eye and threw myself on my side on the floor as the second claw swept over me. I slashed at the legs and opened a gash even through the boots. The snake screamed and limped away.

The second snake came for me, claws outstretched. I didn't have time to get off the floor or anything else. I held the knife ready, my left arm only partially useable, and watched the thing fall on me like an iridescent nightmare. A smaller black blur hit it from the side, and they both crashed into the wall. It was Meng Die. The claws ripped into her pale flesh as I watched.

I didn't have time to see more, because Coronus loomed up over me, blood dripping from his neck and shoulder, his shirt shredded. Sylvie was behind him, struggling with Marco, trying to get past him to follow Coronus. Her lovely hands had turned into claws, though the rest of her was still human. The really powerful shapeshifters could do that—partially change at will.

Jamil was in the far corner, fighting with two of the snake men. Gregory was flowing with fur, changing shape, helpless until he was finished. I didn't have time to look at the other half of the room. Coronus was almost on me, and I was out of time. I did the only thing I could think of. I up-ended the knife and threw it at him. I didn't wait to see if it would hit. I was already moving towards the nearest wall and the collection of blades. I had my hand on the hilt of a sword when Coronus slashed my back open. I fell to my knees screaming, but my right hand stayed on the sword, and I jerked it from the wall brackets as I fell. I turned, putting my left side to him. He sliced open my left shoulder, but it didn't hurt like my back had. Either the wound was deeper, or I was losing the feeling in that arm. I used the seconds I had—the ones he used to cut me—and it didn't hurt to turn the sword in my right hand and plunge it backwards, behind me without turning to see where he was. It was as if I could feel him behind me, as if I knew just where he stood. I felt the blade bite into flesh. I shoved upward, coming to my feet with the force of the blow, shoving the blade backwards, inwards, through him, as hard as I could. I had never done anything like that before, but the movement felt like old memory. And I knew it wasn't *my* memory. It wasn't my body that remembered how to turn the sword as I turned my body to do extra damage, scrambling internal organs as I drew the blade out, and raised it over the kneeling figure. I raised the sword one-handed. This I knew how to do. I'd been taking heads off of bodies for years. The blade was on its downward stroke when he screamed, "Enough!" I didn't stop or even hesitate.

It was Jamil who launched himself into me, over the man's bowed head. He pinned me to the wall, one hand on my wrist, while I fought him. "Anita, Anita!"

I looked up at him, and it was as if I was just realizing who he was, or what he was doing. I'd known, but only in theory, my body had been about to take the snake man's head. My body relaxed in Jamil's grip, but he didn't let me go.

"Talk to me, Anita."

"I'm alright."

"He gives. We win. You get your leopards." His hand went to my hand where it still gripped the sword. "Ease down, you won."

I tried to keep the sword, but Jamil wasn't happy until I let him take it. Then he moved slowly away from me, and I was left looking down at Coronus still kneeling on the floor, holding his claws against the blood that was flowing from his side. He looked up at me and coughed, a little blood touching his lips. He licked it off. "You nicked a lung."

"It's not silver. You'll heal."

He laughed, but it seemed to hurt him. "We'll all heal," he said.

"You better hope Gregory heals," I said.

His black eyes flicked up to me, and there was something in that look that I didn't like. "What is it, Coronus, what puts such unease in your eyes?" I went to my knees in front of him. My left arm hung nearly useless at my side, but it wasn't numb anymore. A deep burning pain was working its way from the wounds at my shoulder and lower back. I purposefully didn't look at them. I could feel the blood flowing down my skin in tickling lines. I kept my gaze on Coronus's eyes.

He met my eyes for a minute while Jamil loomed over us, then Coronus's gaze did a small slide to his right. I followed his look and saw Nathaniel across the wide room for the first time clearly. The world swam in streams of color, and I would have fallen to the floor if my right arm hadn't caught me. It was partly from blood loss and shock, but not all of it was from the wounds. I could hear Coronus speaking through the dizziness and the nausea.

His words were tripping over each other. "Remember that it was the hyenas who made us stop. They who decreed that nothing else was to be done until your arrival. We would never have been so cruel unless we intended to kill him."

My vision cleared, and all I could do was stare. Nathaniel was nude, hanging from his wrists, ankles chained like Gregory's had been. But Nathaniel was facing the room. Knives bisected each tricep. Smaller blades had been forced through each hand so he couldn't close his fingers around them. Thin knives had been forced through the bulk of the muscles just above each of his collarbones. Then the swords began.

Sword blades stuck out just below his collarbones. The blades gleamed silver, sprinkled with drying blood. Unlike the knives, the swords had been shoved in from behind so you couldn't see the hilts.

A wide curved sword stuck out of Nathaniel's right side, through the meat of his body. There were more, too big to be knives, too small to be swords, bisecting his thighs, his calves.

I was on my feet and didn't even remember standing up. I was walking towards him, my left arm hanging down, blood spilling from my fingers. The one thing that I hadn't expected when I saw the damage was his eyes. Those lilac eyes of his were open, staring at me, full of things that I didn't want to understand. A gag filled his mouth, cut across that long auburn hair. He watched me with wide eyes as I walked to him.

I stood in front of Nathaniel and tried to get the gag out of his mouth, but I couldn't do it one-handed. Faust was there, breaking the thong, helping me take it out gently. I touched Nathaniel's mouth, trying to stop him from making any noise. I looked down the length of his body. All the blood! All the blood drying, stiff and tacky against his skin. I couldn't not look at the blades, and from inches away I saw something that couldn't be true. I lowered my hand from his mouth towards the sword blade that protruded from his upper chest. I touched the dried blood, rubbed at it with my fingertips. Nathaniel made a small moan. I didn't stop, I had to be sure. I cleared the blood enough to see, enough to feel that his skin had closed around the blades. In the two hours it had taken me to get to this room, his body had reknit itself with the blades inside of him.

I dropped to my knees as if I'd been hit between the eyes. I tried to say something, but no sound came out. Jamil was there, kneeling beside me. I grabbed a handful of the leather straps across his chest. There was fresh blood on him, wounds in his arms and chest.

I finally managed to say, "How, how do we . . . fix this?"

He looked up at Nathaniel. "We pull the blades out."

I shook my head. "Help me up." The blood loss and the sheer horror were catching up with me. I felt sick, dizzy. Jamil helped me stand in front of Nathaniel. "Do you understand what we're going to have to do?"

Nathaniel looked at me with those purple eyes of his. "Yes," he said, softly, almost no sound at all.

I gripped the knife that was in his quadricep, hand wrapping around the hilt. My lower lip was trembling, and my eyes felt hot. I stared into his eyes, no flinching, no looking away. I took a deep breath, and I pulled it out. His eyes closed, his head thrust backwards, breath coming out in a hissing rush. The flesh clung to the blade. It wasn't like taking a knife out of a roast. The flesh hugged the blade as if it had grown around it.

The bloody knife fell from my hand, making a sharp sound on the cement floor. Nathaniel screamed. Jamil was behind him, and one of the swords was missing from Nathaniel's upper chest. The other sword sucked back through his body as I watched. Nathaniel screamed again. Blood welled from the wound and I turned away. I looked back at Coronus still crouched on the floor, two of his people crowded around him. Something in the look on my face must have frightened him, because his eyes widened, and I saw something like human fear cross his reptilian face.

"We would have taken the blades out, but the hyenas ordered us not to touch either of them again until you arrived."

I looked across the room at the guard that was closest to Nathaniel. The one that had looked unhappy to be there. He flinched under my gaze. "I was following orders."

"Is that an excuse or a defense?"

"We don't owe you an excuse," the other guard said, the tall brown-haired one that had let us into the room. He was standing by the closed door. He was arrogant, defiant, and I could taste his fear like candy on my tongue. He was afraid of what I'd do.

Gregory came to stand near me in half-leopard, half-man form. I'd never seen him like this, all spotted fur, taller than his human form, more muscled. His genitalia hung large and healed between his legs.

One of the snake men was on the floor, dragging its legs behind it. Its spine was broken, but it would heal. Another scream tore from behind me, from Nathaniel's throat. Another snake man was huddled against the far wall beside the chained brunette. Its arm was almost torn from its socket. Sylvie's dress was in shreds, baring her breasts to the world. She didn't seem to care, her hands still curled into claws, pale wolf eyes staring back at me.

"Take your leopards," Coronus said, "and go in peace."

Another scream came on the end of his words. "Peace," I said. I felt strangely numb, like part of me was folding away. I couldn't stand in this room and listen to Nathaniel's screams, and feel. Not and stay sane. A quietness that I sunk into when I killed spilled over me, and it felt so much better. There are worse things than emptiness.

"Who are the women?"

"Swanmanes," he said. "No concern of yours, Nimir-Ra."

I looked at him and felt a smile curl my lips. I knew it was an unpleasant smile. "What happens to them when we leave?"

"They'll heal," he said. "We don't want them dead."

My smile widened, I couldn't help it. I laughed, but it was a bad sound, even to me. "You expect me to leave them to your mercy?"

"They are swans not leopards. Why should you care?"

Nathaniel's voice came thick, and when I turned I saw tears sliding down his face. "Don't leave them. Please, don't leave them here."

Jamil pulled another blade out. Only three to go. Nathaniel didn't scream this time, just closed his eyes and shivered. "Please, Anita, they would never have come here if I hadn't asked them."

I looked at the three women, chained naked to the walls, gagged, surrounded by dozens of clean, unused blades. They watched me with wide eyes, their breath coming in quick shallow pants. Their fear slid down my throat as if it were wine and I could drink it down, deep and cool. Fear, like wine, goes good with food. And I knew just by looking that they were food. They were swans, not predators. They were not us. I was channeling Richard now. I was being a smorgasbord of the boys tonight, of their thoughts and feelings. But there was one thing that was my own. Rage. Not the hot rage that the wolves used when they killed. This was something colder and more sure of itself. It was a rage that had nothing to do with blood and everything to do with . . . death. I wanted them all dead for what they'd done to Nathaniel and Gregory. I wanted them dead. By the rules, I couldn't have them dead, but I'd do what I could. I'd cheat them of their other victims. I would not, could not, leave the three women here like this. I could not do it. Simple as that.

"Don't worry, Nathaniel, we won't leave them behind."

"You have no right to them," Coronus said.

Gregory growled at him. I touched Gregory's furred arm. "It's alright." I looked at Coronus surrounded by his snakes. "If I were you I wouldn't tell me what I have a right to. If I were you, I'd shut the fuck up and let us walk out of here with everyone we came for."

"No, they are ours until their swan king rescues them."

"Hey, he's not here, but I am, and I say to you, Coronus of the Black Water Clan, that I will take the swanmanes with me. I will not leave them behind."

"Why? Why do you care?"

"Why? Partly because I just don't like you. Partly because I want you dead and I can't do that tonight according to lycanthrope law. So I'll cheat you of your prize. That will have to suffice. But don't ever, *ever* get in my way again, because I *will* kill you, Coronus. I will kill you. In fact, I'd enjoy killing you." I realized that was true. I often killed cold, but there was something in me tonight that wanted him dead. Revenge maybe. I didn't question it, I just let it show in my eyes. I let the shapeshifter see it, because I knew he'd understand it. He wasn't human; he knew death when it looked at him.

He did know. I saw the knowledge in his eyes, tasted that fresh spurt of fear like a chemical rush. He looked suddenly tired. "I would give them up if I could, but I cannot. I must have something to show for this night's activities. I was hoping it would be the swans and the leopards, but if I cannot have one, I must have the other."

"Why do you care about either the swans or the leopards?" I asked. "They are nothing to you, you cannot make them part of your tribe."

His eyes shut down, unreadable. But that flash of fear grew, swelling in a rich odor of sweat and bitterness. He was very afraid. And it wasn't of me, not exactly, but of something that would happen if he didn't keep the swans. But what?

"I must keep them, Anita Blake."

"Tell me why?"

"I cannot." The fear was leaving him. Until that moment I never knew that resignation had a scent, but I could smell the quiet bitterness of defeat on him. It flared through me in a fierce wave, and I knew we'd won.

He shook his head. "I cannot give the swans up."

"You've already lost them. I can smell the defeat on you."

He bowed his head. "I would give them up if I could, but please, believe me, I cannot give them to you. I cannot."

"Cannot, or will not?" I asked.

He smiled, and it was bitter like the odor from his skin. "Cannot." Even his voice held reluctance, as if he wanted to just say *yes*, but couldn't.

"Do what's best for your people, Coronus, walk away from this." I knew in some indefinable way that we would win. My will to win was greater than his. We would carry this night in victory. Some of the snakes would die, because their leader had lost his nerve. Without his strength of will to buoy them, they could not win. They didn't want to be here. I looked at each of them, and in turn, they scented the air as I stared at them. Defeat hung over them like smoke; they had no will to win. They didn't want to be here. So why were they here? Their alpha, their leader, was here, and his will was theirs. So why were they all weak, as if something was missing inside their group, something that made them weak?

I realized with a start that this was what everyone had sensed from the leopards before I came to them . . . this smell of weakness and defeat. Nathaniel was weak. But now my will was his, and I was not weak. I turned to stare into his face, his eyes, and I saw through all the pain, the torture, that he was not hopeless. When I first met him, Nathaniel had had the most hopeless eyes I'd ever seen. But he knew I'd come. He'd known with an absolute certainty that I would not leave him here like this. Gregory could doubt, because he thought with that part of him that was human. But Nathaniel trusted me with something that had nothing to do with logic, and everything to do with truth.

I turned back to Coronus. "Run away from this, Coronus, or some of you won't see dawn."

He sighed heavily. "So be it." And then he did what he shouldn't have done. Something that had no logic to it, from a nonhuman point of view. He was going to lose, and he knew it. Yet he did a very human thing. He attacked us anyway. Only humans waste energy like that when they've been given an out.

The two snakes guarding Coronus suddenly launched themselves at me, and I was too close. I'd been so sure with my new werewolf senses that they wouldn't fight us. I'd been careless. I'd forgotten that in the end we're only half animal. And that human half will fuck you every time.

They came in a blur of speed too fast for me to do anything but start for the other boot knife. I knew I'd never reach it. Gregory leaped in a butter-colored streak, taking one snake out in midair, rolling on the floor. But the other one was on me, claws slashing down before I hit the ground with it riding me. I was already going numb; it didn't hurt. The claws ripped at my stomach, diving through the cloth of my shirt to the flesh underneath. I felt it digging for my heart. I raised my right hand to try and grab the wrist, but it felt like I was moving in slow motion. My hand seemed to weigh a thousand pounds, and distantly I knew I was hurt, badly hurt. Something bad had happened in that first blur of claws.

Gregory was suddenly there, pale fur caught between the multicolored snakes. He fell on top of me, with one of the things on top of him ripping him up. He never tried to defend himself; he clawed at the one riding me, tore it away from me, and the three of them fought on top of me. There was a moment when Gregory's eyes and that snarling mouth were inches from mine. We were pressed as close as lovers, and I knew that the claws in me were his. He'd fallen against me, been pushed into my flesh. Then other hands were pulling us all apart. I had a glimpse of Jamil's face, saw his lips move, but there was no sound. Then blackness swirled over my vision and ate everything but a dim, dim spot of light. Then even that vanished, and there was nothing but the dark.

8

I DREAMED I was running, being chased through the woods at night. I could hear them coming closer, closer, and I knew that what chased me wasn't human. Then I fell to the ground and I was running on four feet. I chased the pale thing that fled before me. The soft thing that had no claws, no teeth, and smelled wonderfully of fear. It fell, and its scream was shrill, it hurt my ears, and excited me. My fangs sank into flesh and did not stop until they tore meat. Blood poured scalding hot down my throat, and the dream faded.

I was in Narcissus's bedroom on the black bed. Jean-Claude was tied, standing between the posts at the end of the bed. His chest was bare, covered in claw marks, blood running down his skin. I crawled across the bed towards him, and I wasn't afraid, because all I could smell was the sweet copper scent of blood. He stared at me with eyes gone solid, drowning blue. "Kiss me, *ma petite*."

I rose on my knees, my mouth hovering over his lips. He moved towards me, but I stayed out of reach of those kissable lips. I moved my mouth lower, until it was just above his chest and the fresh wounds that decorated his skin. "Yes, *ma petite*, yes," he sighed.

I pressed my mouth to his chest and drank. I woke, eyes staring, heart thudding. It was Richard above me. He still had the leather collar on. I tried to raise my arms, to hold him, but my left arm was taped to a board. There was an I.V. in my arm. I looked at the darkened room and knew I wasn't in a hospital. I raised my right arm to touch his face, but it was heavy, too heavy to lift. Darkness spilled over my eyes like warm water rushing in, as my fingertips brushed his skin.

I heard his voice. "Rest, Anita, rest." I think he kissed me, gently, then there was nothing.

I was wading in water to my waist, clear, icy water. I knew I had to get out of the water or I'd die, the cold would steal me away. I could see the shore, dead trees, and snow. I ran for those distant trees, struggling in the icy water. Then my feet went out from under me, and I fell into a deep hole. The water closed over my face, and the shock of the cold hit me like a giant fist. I couldn't move, couldn't breathe. The light faded through the clear, shining water. I began to drift down, down into the cold dark water. I should have been scared, but I wasn't. I was so tired, so tired.

Pale hands reached for me, coming from the light. The sleeve of the white shirt billowed around his arm, and I moved my hand towards him. Jean-Claude's hand wrapped around mine, and he pulled me towards the light.

I was back in the dark room, but my skin was wet, and I was cold, so cold.

Jean-Claude was cradling me in his lap. He was still wearing the vinyl outfit. Then I remembered the fight. I'd been hurt. Jean-Claude leaned over and kissed my forehead, laying his face against mine. His skin was as cold as I felt—like ice pressed against me. The shivering was worse; my body danced in small involuntary movements.

"Cold," I said.

"I know, *ma petite*, we are both cold."

I frowned at him, because I didn't understand. He was looking at someone else in the room. "I have brought her back, but I cannot give her the warmth she needs to survive."

I managed to turn my head enough to look around the room. Richard was standing there with Jamil and Shang-Da and Gregory. Richard came to the bed; his hand touched my face. It was hot against my skin. It was too much, and I tried to move away from his hand.

"Anita, can you hear me?"

My teeth were chattering so hard, I could hardly get it out, but finally I said, "Yes."

"You've got a high fever, a very high fever. They put you in a shallow ice bath to bring it down. But your body reacted like a shapeshifter's. The low temperature while so much damage was healing almost killed you."

I frowned at him and finally managed to say, "Don't understand." The involuntary jerks were getting stronger, strong enough that it hurt the wounds. I was waking up enough to feel how very hurt I was. Things hurt that I didn't remember getting injured. My muscles ached.

"You need the high temperature to heal, just like we do."

I didn't understand who the "we" was. "Who . . ." and a spasm shook my body, tore a scream from my mouth. My body fell into convulsions and pain smashed through me. If I could have breathed, I'd have screamed more. My vision began to disappear in large gray patches.

"Get the doctor!" Richard's voice.

"You know what must be done, *mon ami*."

"If this works, then I've lost her."

My vision cleared for a few seconds. Richard was stripping out of the tight pants. It was the last thing I saw before the gray swept up over my eyes and sucked me down.

9

I THOUGHT I dreamed, but I wasn't sure. There were faces in the dark, some of them I knew, some of them I didn't. Cherry with her short blond hair, her face free of makeup, making her look years younger than either of us were. Gregory touching my face. Jamil resting beside me, curled like a dark dream. I drifted in and out, from face to face, body to body, because I could feel their bodies pressed against mine. Naked skin against naked skin. It wasn't sexual, or not overtly so. I woke, if I woke, enough to know it was Richard's arms wrapped around me, my body fitting like a spoon against his, his thick hair spilled across my eyes. I slept, knowing I was safe.

I woke slowly, in a cocoon of body heat and that prickling rush of lycanthrope energy. I tried to roll over and found the press of flesh kept me pinned on my side. I opened my eyes. The room was dark, with a small light near the wall like a child's night-light. My night vision was good enough to be able to see color by it. A man I didn't know was curled against the front of my body. His face was pressed into my shoulder just above my breasts, his breath hot against my skin. Normally, it would have been my cue to panic and run for the hills, but I just didn't feel like panicking. I felt warm and safe, and more . . . right than I'd felt in a long time, as if I were wearing a favorite pair of flannel jammies, wrapped in my favorite quilt. It was that kind of comfort, that kind of peacefulness. Even the sight of the arm around my waist from behind didn't disturb me. Maybe Dr. Lillian had slipped me some medicine that made everything feel okay. All I know was that I didn't want to move. It was like when you first wake in the morning and there's nowhere you have to be, nothing you have to do, and you can float in that half-awake, half-asleep, warm-nest-of-blankets feeling.

The arm around my waist was muscled, definitely masculine, but small, not just the hand, but the whole arm. The skin was tanned and looked darker than it should have against the paleness of my skin. I relaxed against the warm bulk of the body, where it lay spooned against mine. The fact that I was okay sleeping in a three-way naked sandwich, with me in the middle, told me beyond a doubt that I was on some kind of drug. I'd woken up wearing a lot more clothes, and been a whole lot more embarrassed.

I assumed they were both werewolves. It was a big pack, and I didn't know everyone on sight. I was bathed in their energy, as if hot invisible water flowed around the three of us. I remembered being hurt, the claws digging under my sternum. My gaze traveled down my own body and found a ragged circle of pinkish scar tissue where the snake had dug for my heart. There was a dull ache, but the scar was already pink and shiny, flat to my skin. How long had I been out?

I kept waiting for the panic to wash over me, the embarrassment. When it didn't, I looked at the first man, truly looking at him this time. He had rich brown curls cut short in the back, but long on top, so the curls tickled my skin as he made a small movement in his sleep. He was tanned so darkly that his skin almost matched his hair. The one eyebrow I could see had a tiny ring piercing it. One of his knees pinned my lower leg, one hand lay limply on my bare thigh. I think it was his leg being raised and a turn of his hips that saved me from seeing the whole show. What little modesty I had left was grateful. Whatever had kept me comfortable was beginning to wear off. Maybe I was simply waking up.

The rest of his front was pressed so close to me I couldn't see any details. The line of his back and buttocks was smooth, flawless. No tan lines. Nude sunbathing? The body looked young—early twenties—if that. He was taller than me—who wasn't?—but not by much. Five seven, maybe less. He stirred, the hand on my thigh flexing as if he dreamed, then suddenly I knew he was awake. A tension ran through his body that hadn't been there seconds before. I was suddenly wide awake, my heart thudding. I had about two seconds to wonder what the hell you say to someone you've never met when you wake up naked in bed beside him. He opened the eye I could see and moved his face enough to blink two solid brown eyes at me.

He gave a slow lazy smile, still half asleep. "I've never seen you awake before."

I said the only thing that came to mind. "I don't remember seeing you at *all* before. Who are you?"

"Caleb. I'm Caleb."

I nodded and started to sit up. I was getting out of this bed. The comforting warmth was still there, but my embarrassment was stronger. I just wasn't cool enough to keep talking to a strange, naked man, while I was naked, too. Nope, just not sophisticated enough for this one.

The arm around my waist tightened, holding me against the second man, and the bed. Caleb's knee on my leg got heavier, sliding farther between mine. I could suddenly feel parts of his body that I couldn't see. I think I'd have rather seen the whole show than had it pressed against my very upper thigh. Alright, groin, just not the right part to make me start hurting him, not yet. The hand that had been lying on my thigh was suddenly gripping it. It made my pulse speed up. It was too close to being trapped.

"Everybody be calm," I said, "but I need to get up and out of this bed now."

The body behind me moved. Even though I wasn't able to see it, I knew he was propped on one elbow, and the arm around my waist tightened. I was suddenly pressed very firmly against his body, and I knew several things. One, he was about my height, because he spooned perfectly against me; two, he was slender, muscular, and very happy to be pressed to my body. Eeek! I turned towards him like I was looking back at a noise in the dark at a horror movie—slowly, half-dreading. His face rose over my shoulder, long hair spilling to one side of his face in a thick mass that was so sleep-tousled I couldn't tell if it was waves or curls, only that it was a dark rich brown, darker than the first man's, almost brunette. His face was too triangular, almost too delicate, crossing that line into androgyny, the nose perky, a little less than perfect, his mouth wide, bottom lip thick and pouting. It was a sensual face. But it was the eyes that made the face, or ruined it. My first thought was that his eyes were yellow. But there was a thick ring of gray green around the pupil; the overall effect was a deep golden yellow-green set in a tanned face. They weren't human eyes, and don't ask me how I knew, but they weren't wolf eyes either.

I scrambled out from between them. My left arm protested the use, but it didn't hurt enough to outweigh my embarrassment. It wasn't a graceful exit, but at least I was standing at the foot of the bed staring down at the two men instead of sandwiched between them. Screw graceful, I wanted some clothes.

"Don't be afraid, Anita. We don't mean you any harm," the second man said.

I was trying to keep an eye on them and still search the dimly lit room for clothes. I didn't see any. The only cloth in the room seemed to be the sheet, and they were lying on that. I had a horrible urge to cover myself, but two hands weren't going to get the job done, and standing there with my hands cupped over my groin seemed somehow more embarrassing than just standing there. I suddenly didn't know what to do with my hands. My left arm ached in a line from my shoulder nearly to my wrist, a tracery of pink, flat scars down my flesh. "Who are you?" My voice came out a little breathy.

"I'm Micah Callahan." His voice was calm, ordinary, as he lay on his side completely naked. No one does comfortable nudity like a shapeshifter. His shoulders were narrow, everything about him slender, almost feminine. But muscles showed under his skin even at rest, lean muscle, not bulk. You knew at a glance he was strong, but if he were wearing clothes, you might not see it. There were other things you wouldn't see if he had his clothes on. And although the rest of him was slender, small, graceful in a way that women are graceful, parts of him were definitely not small, not slender. It seemed incongruous with the rest of him. As if mother nature had tried to make up for the feminine appearance by overcompensating in other areas. Noticing just how overcompensated he was brought heat in a rush up my face, and I glanced away, tried to both keep an eye on them in case they got off the bed and not look at them at the same time. It's hard to look and not to look, but I managed.

"This is Caleb," he said.

Caleb rolled onto his back and stretched like a big cat, making sure that, if I hadn't noticed already, he was naked, too. I had noticed. What looked like a tiny silver dumbbell pierced his belly button. That I hadn't seen. "We already introduced ourselves," Caleb said, that one innocent sentence sounding anything but innocent. Something in the tone he used, an inflection, while he rolled around on his back and waved himself at me, made the words obscene. I was willing to bet I wasn't going to like Caleb.

"Great, nice to meet you both." I still couldn't figure out what to do with my hands. "What are you doing here?"

"Sleeping with you," Caleb said.

The blush that had been almost gone flamed back to life. He laughed. Micah didn't. Point for him.

In fact, Micah sat up, bending a knee to cover himself, which earned him even more points. Caleb stayed on his back, flaunting himself. "There's a robe in the corner there," Micah said.

I glanced back where he was looking, and sure enough there was a robe. It was my robe, a deep, rich burgundy, with satin edgings, very masculine, like a long Victorian smoking jacket. When I lifted it up, there was a weight in one deep pocket. I had to fight the urge to turn my back to slip the robe on. They'd already seen the whole show. It wasn't like I could express my modesty now. When I had the robe belted in place, I slipped my hands into the pockets and my right hand closed around my derringer. Or at least I assumed it was mine; it *was* my robe. The only person I knew who'd think to leave a gun for me was Edward, and he, as far as I knew, was out of state. But someone had thought of it, and I was very glad. I had clothes and a weapon, life was good.

"Hi, Micah Callahan, nice to meet you. But the name doesn't tell me who you are."

"I am Nimir-Raj for the Maneater Clan," Micah said.

I blinked at him, trying to digest that little tidbit. I wasn't embarrassed anymore. Surprised, working on angry, maybe. "I am Nimir-Ra of the Blooddrinkers Clan, and I don't remember inviting you into my territory, Mr. Callahan."

"You didn't."

"Then what the hell are you doing here without my permission?" The first edge of anger threaded through my voice, and I was happy to hear it. Being angry made everything else easier to handle, even talking to two naked strangers.

"Elizabeth invited me," he said.

The anger rushed through me like a warm wind, and it touched that edge of beast that I'd thought was Richard's. I'd learned at the club however many nights ago it was that it was a permanent resident inside me now. Richard's beast, or mine, it flared through my body and raised above my skin like a sheen of invisible sweat. The men reacted to the power. Caleb sat up, his gaze suddenly intent on me, no teasing now. Micah sniffed at the air, nostril's flaring, his tongue running around the edge of his lips as if he could taste it against his skin.

Strong emotions always make the power worse, and I was so angry. I already owed Elizabeth for abandoning Nathaniel at the club. But now . . . she'd finally done something that I could not let slide.

Part of me was almost relieved, because things would be easier with Elizabeth dead. A tiny part of me was hoping not to have to kill her, but I just couldn't see how to avoid it anymore.

It must have shown on my face, because Callahan said, "I didn't know that her pard had a Nimir-Ra when I came here. She was their old alpha's second. It was within her rights to audition a new alpha for her pard."

"She just forgot to mention that the pard already had a Nimir-Ra, is that it?" I asked.

"That's it," he said.

"Really," I said, making sure the sarcasm was thick.

He stood beside the bed. I managed to keep the eye contact pure, but it was harder than it should have been. "I did not know until three nights ago when Cherry knocked on Elizabeth's door and asked her to come help heal you that you even existed."

"Bullshit," I said.

"I swear it," he said.

My hand closed around the derringer, felt its comforting weight. I had a moment to wonder what ammo it was loaded with; .38 or .22. I hoped it was .38, it had more stopping power. My left arm gave a twinge like the muscle was trying to jump apart. Tension, or had I permanently injured myself? I'd worry about it later, when I wasn't staring at two wereleopards that might, or might not, be my buddies. "You say you really didn't know about me before you hit town. Great, but why are you still here?"

"When I found out that Elizabeth had lied to me, I came here and tried to help, to make up for entering your territory without your permission. All my leopards took a turn in your bed, helping you heal."

"Bully for you."

He held his empty hands out towards me, palms up. A nice traditional gesture to show that you are unarmed and harmless. Yeah, right. "What can I do to make this right between us, Anita? I don't want war between our pards, and I have learned that you are interviewing alphas to take your place with your leopards. I'm a Nimir-Raj. Do you know how rare that is among the wereleopards? The best you're probably going to find elsewhere is a leopard *lionne*, a protector but not a true king."

"You applying for the job?"

He started walking towards me, and the room wasn't that big. "I'd be honored if you'd consider me for the job."

I tried to hold up my left hand, but the arm spasmed too badly to complete the gesture. But Micah got the idea; he stopped moving. "Let's start by you staying over there. I've had about as much up close and personal with the two of you as I can handle."

He just stood there, hands still in that open see-I-mean-no-harm position. "We caught you off guard, I understand."

I doubted he understood, but it was polite for him to pretend. I'd never met a shapeshifter that had a problem sleeping in a big naked pile, like puppies. Of course, I'd never met a brand-new one, yet. Surely, there was a learning curve for this sort of comfort level.

My left arm was twitching badly enough that I took my right hand off the gun, out of my pocket, and tried to calm the involuntary movements.

"You're hurt," he said.

Every jump of muscle sent sharp little pains through my arm. "Getting clawed up will do that to you."

"I can make it feel better."

I rolled eyes at him. "I bet you say that to all the girls."

He didn't even look embarrassed. "I told you, I am a Nimir-Raj. I can call flesh."

I must have looked as blank as I felt, because he explained. "I can heal wounds with my touch."

I just looked at him.

"What would it take to convince you that I'm telling the truth?" he asked.

"How about someone I know to vouch for you?"

"Easily done," he said, and a second later the door opened.

It was another stranger. The man was around six feet, broad shouldered, muscled, well built, and since he was nude, I knew for a fact that every inch of him was well proportioned. At least he wasn't erect. That was refreshing. He was pale, the first of the new ones without a tan. White hair with generous streaks of gray fell around his shoulders. He had a gray mustache and one of those tiny Vandyke beards. The hair was a clue that he was over fifty, probably. But what I could see of him didn't look old, or weak. He looked more like a lifer mercenary that would cut your heart out and take it back to someone in a box, for the right amount of money. A ragged scar nearly bisected his chest and stomach, curving in a vicious half-moon around his belly button and sinking towards his groin. The scar was white and looked old. Either he'd gotten the injury before he became a shapeshifter or—or I didn't know. Shapeshifters could scar, but it was rare; you almost had to do something wrong to the wound to get a scar that bad.

"I don't know him," I said.

"Anita Blake, this is Merle."

It was only after the introductions that Merle's eyes flicked to me. His eyes looked human, some pale gray color. His gaze went back to his Nimir-Raj's face almost immediately, like an obedient dog that wants to watch its master's face.

"Hi, Merle."

He nodded his head.

"Let her people in the room."

Merle shifted, and I knew instantly that he didn't want to do it. "Some, but not all?" he made it a question.

Micah looked at me.

"Why not all?" I asked.

Merle turned those pale eyes to me, and the look in them made me want to squirm. He stared at me as if he could see through to the other side and read everything in between. I knew it wasn't true, but it was a good stare. I managed not to flinch.

"Tell her," Micah said.

"Too many people in too small a room. I can't guarantee Micah's safety in a crowd of strangers."

"You must be his Skoll," I said.

His lips curled back in disgust—I think. "We are not wolves. We do not use their words."

"Fine, to my knowledge there's no equivalent word among the leopards, but you're still Micah's chief bodyguard, right?"

He stared at me, then gave a small nod.

"Okay. Do you really see my people as a threat to Micah?"

"It is my job to see them as a threat."

He had a point. "Fine. How many are you comfortable letting into the room?"

He blinked, that harsh gaze, shielded for a moment, his eyes uncertain. "You're not going to argue about it?" Again he made the statement into a question with the lilt of his voice.

"Why should I?"

"Most alphas will argue so they don't appear weak," he said.

I had to smile. "I'm not that insecure."

That made him smile. "Yes, those that hoard their power are often insecure."

"That's been my experience," I said.

He nodded again, face thoughtful. "Two."

"Fine."

"Do you have a preference who the two shall be?"

I shrugged. "Cherry and whoever else." I put Cherry in because she seemed to give the best after-action reports. Clearheaded was our Cherry, if not necessarily who you'd want at your back in a fight. But I needed information, not battle skills.

Merle gave me a slight bow, then his gaze flicked back to Micah, still standing by the bed. Micah waved him off. The big man opened the door and spoke quietly. Cherry was the first one through the door. She was tall and slender with well-formed breasts that led the eye to a very long waist, a swell of hips, and proof that she was indeed a natural blond. Wasn't anybody wearing clothes today?

Frankly, it was just nice to see another woman. Normally, I don't mind being the only girl, I do that a lot with the police, but nudity always makes me relieved to see another person without a penis.

She smiled when she saw me, relief so large in her eyes, her face, that it was almost embarrassing. She hugged me, and I let her, but I pulled away first. She touched my face as if she couldn't really believe her eyes.

"How do you feel?"

I shrugged, and the small movement tightened the muscles in my left arm until I had to press it against my body to keep it from jumping around. I spoke through the pain, teeth gritted a little. "Arm's giving me trouble, but other than that, I'm okay."

Cherry touched the arm, running her hand lightly over the sleeve of the robe. "The muscles are tightening up from the rapid healing. It will be alright in a few days."

"Am I not going to have the use of my left arm for a few days?"

"The spasms will come and go. Massage helps. Hot compresses may help. There must have been some severe muscle damage for this much spasming." Did I mention that Cherry was a nurse when she wasn't turning furry?

"I can give you the use of your arm today," Micah said.

We both turned and looked at him. "How?" Cherry asked.

"I can call flesh," he said again.

The look on her face said she knew what that meant, and she was impressed. And a second later, she looked doubtful, suspicious. That was my girl. Though truthfully, Cherry had had a hard enough life before I met her that she'd come with an overly active suspicion. I really couldn't take credit for it.

I was trying to remember what "calling the flesh" meant, when Nathaniel stepped through the door. The last time I'd seen him he'd been pierced with blades, his flesh grown around the steel. Now he was perfect—not even a scar.

I must have looked as pleased, and as astonished, as I felt, because he grinned at me. He did a little turn so I could see that back and front he was healed. I touched his upper chest where I'd pulled out one of the blades. The skin was smooth as if I'd only dreamed the knife. "I know you guys heal almost anything, but I never get over the surprise."

"Eventually, you'll get used to it," Merle said. There was something in his voice that made me look at him. Cherry's and Nathaniel's smiles faded. They looked suddenly serious.

"What's wrong?" I asked.

Cherry and Nathaniel exchanged glances, but it was Micah who spoke. "May I fix your arm?"

I turned to tell him to go to hell until I knew what was happening, but my left arm chose that moment to curl up from fingertips to shoulder, one massive, painful, charley horse that bent my knees. Only Cherry catching me kept me standing. My hand looked like that of a strychnine victim, the fingers convulsed, clawlike. It felt like my arm was trying to tear itself apart from the inside out. Cherry was supporting almost all my weight as I tried not to scream.

"Let him fix your arm, Anita, if he can," she said.

The muscles in my arm relaxed by painful inches, until the urge to scream was only a small voice in my head. My voice came out breathy from the strain, but it was clear, no whimpering. "What is calling flesh again?" I was leaning so heavily on Cherry that it was only politeness that kept her from picking me up in her arms. She was holding all my weight.

Micah came to stand by us. Merle hovered behind him like an overly anxious nursemaid. "I can heal damage in my pard with my body," Micah said.

I glanced up at Cherry and saw Nathaniel standing beside her. They both nodded at the same time, as if they'd heard my unasked question. "I've never seen a Nimir-Raj that could call flesh, but I've heard of it," Cherry said. "It is possible."

"You don't sound like you believe him," I said.

She gave a faint smile that left her eyes tired. "I don't believe in much of anyone." She smiled then. "Except you."

I stood, still leaning on her arm, but almost standing on my own. I squeezed her arm with my right hand, trying to put into my eyes what I was feeling. "I'll always do my best for you, Cherry."

She smiled again, and her eyes lightened a little, though that edge of cynicism never quite left them. "I know that."

"We all know that," Nathaniel said.

I smiled at him. I said the prayer I'd been saying since I inherited the wereleopards: Dear God, don't let me fail them.

I kept a tight grip on Cherry's arm, but turned to Micah. "Why is my arm the only thing that's hurting?"

"You don't hurt anywhere else?" he asked.

I started to say no, then had to think about it. "I ache, but nothing like the arm. Nothing else hurts like it does."

He nodded as if that meant something to him. "Your body and our energy healed the life-threatening injuries first, and the smaller ones like the marks on your back."

"I didn't think healing energy could be that selective," I said.

"It can when directed," he said.

"Who directed it?"

His eyes locked with mine. "I did."

I glanced at Cherry, and she nodded. "He is a Nimir-Raj. He was the dominant for us all. Him and Merle."

I glanced at the big man. "Do I owe you guys a thank-you?"

Merle shook his head. "You owe us nothing."

"Nothing," Micah said. "We were the ones who entered your territory without your permission. It was our transgression, not yours."

I looked at them both. "Okay, now what?"

"Can you stand unaided?"

I wasn't really sure, so I let go of Cherry in stages and found that I could stand on my own. Great. "Yeah, I guess I can."

"I need to touch the injuries to heal them."

"I know, I know, bare skin is best for healing among lycanthropes."

He gave a small frown. "Yes, it is."

I used my right hand to slide the robe off my left shoulder. I realized that it didn't bare enough of my arm. I started to wiggle my left arm out of the sleeve, and another spasm hit me. It was Micah who caught me this time as my arm tried to tear itself off my body and my hand gripped something that I could neither see nor feel. It wasn't just that it hurt. It was unnerving, like I had lost total control of my arm.

Micah whispered, "Scream, there's no shame in it."

I just shook my head, afraid to open my mouth, afraid I would scream. He lowered me to the floor. His hands going to the robe's sash. The spasm relaxed in stages again, leaving me gasping on the floor while he bared most of my left side. Once he'd revealed my left arm and shoulder, he pulled the robe back over me, covering everything I cared about, except for my left breast. I appreciated the gesture. Since I was now lying on the ground staring up at him, I also appreciated that he was no longer erect. That was somehow less threatening.

He was on his knees, tracing his fingers just above the skin of my arm. Except he wasn't touching my skin, he was touching that otherworldly energy that spilled off of my skin. His energy flowed from his hand and mingled with mine in a dance of electricity that sent goosebumps down my skin. For the first time I thought to ask, "Is this going to hurt?"

"No, it shouldn't."

I heard masculine laughter. I was looking up at all the men in the room except for one. I turned my head to see Caleb still sitting on the bed.

"Is there a joke I'm not getting?"

"Ignore him," Merle said.

I looked up at their so-serious eyes, while Caleb's laughter played background music. "Are you sure there isn't something you want to tell me about the calling of flesh?"

Micah shook his head, sending the tangle of curls sliding around his face. I realized that no one had turned on a light. We were still moving in the twilight of the night-light. "Can someone turn on a light?"

There was a flurry of eye flicks, one to the other, to the other, like they were playing hot potato with the glance. "What's wrong?"

"Why do you think anything is wrong?" Micah said.

"Don't fuck with me, I saw the glances. Why can't we turn on the lights?"

"You may be photosensitive because of the rapid healing," Cherry said.

I looked at her and could feel the suspicion on my face. "That's what all those looks were about?" I said.

"We're worried about how your body is . . . reacting to the injuries." She knelt beside me on the side opposite Micah. She stroked my hair like you'd pet a dog to soothe it. "We're worried about you."

"I got that." It was hard to be suspicious with her vibrating sincerity at me. I finally had to smile. "I guess we can do without the lights until after he heals me."

She smiled, and this time it did reach her eyes. "Good."

"You might want to give us some room here," Micah said. "Otherwise the energy can spread."

Cherry gave me a last touch then stood and moved back, taking Nathaniel with her. Micah stared up at Merle. "You, too."

Merle frowned, but he moved across the room with the others. They all ended up by the bed with Caleb. Strangely, I'd come as far across the room as I could get from the bed without leaving the room. Totally unconscious on my part, honest.

Micah stayed kneeling, but leaned back on the balls of his feet, hands open on his thighs, eyes closed, and I felt him open himself. His energy swirled over me like a thread of hot air that closed my throat, made it hard to breathe. He opened those alien eyes and looked at me, face slack, as if he were meditating or dreaming.

I expected him to lay hands on me, but his hands stayed on his thighs. He leaned his upper body towards my shoulder.

I put my right hand on his arm, and the moment I touched him, his beast curled through me. It was almost as if some great invisible cat were sliding in and out of my body, the way they'll entwine themselves around your legs, except this cat went places that not even a lover should be touching. It froze my words in my throat, and from the look on Micah's face, I could tell he was feeling it too. He looked as shell-shocked as I felt. But he continued to lean into me. My hand stayed on his arm, but it didn't stop him, and I couldn't think well enough to question him. His lips brushed my neck where the scars began, and it brought my breath in a shaky sigh. He pressed his mouth to my neck and forced that swirling, living power into me. It made me squirm, but it didn't hurt. In fact it felt so good that I pushed him backwards.

My voice squeezed out, faint, almost a whisper. "Wait a minute. What's with the mouth? I thought you were going to lay *hands* on me?"

"I said I could heal with my body," he said. The power stretched between us like taffy pulled between the hot sticky fingers of children. It was like if we touched we would melt into each other.

I dragged my hand away from him, and it was like my hand was moving through something—something real and almost solid. My voice was steady, and even I was impressed. "I thought that meant hands."

"If I'd meant hands, I would have said so." He lowered his face towards me, moving through the power, and it felt like waves in water when someone swims towards you. I grabbed a handful of those tangled curls. "Define body for me."

He smiled, and it was at the same time gentle, condescending, and somehow sad. He stayed kneeling over me, his face close enough to kiss, my hand in his hair, the power pulsing around us, building into something large. "Mouth, tongue, some hands, but it is body, my hands alone won't be enough. I am told that you can heal with your body, as well."

I took my hand out of his hair and tried to get some distance between us, but he didn't move back, so it didn't really work. Truth was I could heal with sex, or something so close to it that you didn't want to do it in public.

"Sort of," I said. I looked across the room, past Micah's head and found Cherry. "Is calling flesh like what I do when I call munin?" Munin were sort of the ancestral memories of the werewolves. Except that they were actually more like ghosts, the spirits of the dead. You could gain their knowledge, their skills, and their bad habits if you had the ability to channel them. I was a necromancer—all the dead liked me. The munin that liked me best of all was Raina, the wolf pack's old lupa. I'd been the one who killed her—to keep her from killing me—and she delighted in the fact that she could take me over. I'd gained the power to control Raina when I accepted her, warts and all. When I called her, I didn't fight her anymore. We'd worked out a sort of truce. But calling munin for healing was almost always sexual for me, because it had been sexual for Raina.

"It's not sexual," Cherry said. "Sensual, but not sexual."

I trusted Cherry's judgment on that. "Okay then, do it."

Micah looked at me, those strange yellow-green eyes so terribly close.

"Do it," I said.

He gave that wistful, sad, condescending smile again, like he was laughing at both of us, and crying for us, too. Unnerving, that smile. Then he lowered his mouth to my neck and the first of the scars. The first kiss was gentle against my throat; he breathed power against my skin, and it was suddenly hard to breathe. But the power hovered above my skin like cloth. Then the tip of his tongue slid along my skin, licking a hot, wet line down my neck. The power followed the line of that heat, sinking under my skin as he licked me. But it was when his mouth pressed over my skin, sealing him against me, sucking me into his mouth, between his teeth, that I felt the power shoved into me, forced into the scars. He literally breathed, bit, ate, the healing into me. I made small helpless movements. I couldn't help it. We all have our erogenous zones in addition to the normal ones, places where if we're touched our bodies react whether we want them to, or not. My neck and shoulders are two of my spots.

He leaned back, far enough from my neck to whisper, "Are you alright?" His breath was so hot against my skin.

I nodded, my face turned away from him.

He took me at my word, pressing his mouth back to my neck. There were no preliminaries this time; he bit me, hard enough that I gasped. My stomach knotted, twisting me onto my side, pulling me away from him.

"Anita, what's wrong?"

"My stomach," I said.

He slid the robe open, passing his hand over my stomach. "There was no wound here."

Another wave of pain tore through my gut, bending me over double, to writhe on the floor. The need tore through me like something alive trying to rip its way out from inside my body.

Micah was there, smoothing my hair back from my face, that power that was building between us rolling through my body like a cat wading through me. He bundled me into his arms, his lap, pressed my face against his chest. "Get the doctor."

His chest was smooth, warm. I could hear his heartbeat, feel it against my cheek. I could smell blood under his skin like some exotic candy that would melt on my tongue and glide down my throat. I worked my way up his body until I could see the big pulse in his neck. I watched that pulse like a man dying of thirst; my throat burned with the need, my lips dry, cracked from want of it. I had to feed. I knew in that instant that it wasn't my thought.

I stretched out that part of me that Jean-Claude claimed and found him. Found him sitting in a windowless cell. He looked up as if he could see me standing in front of him. He whispered, "*Ma petite*," and I knew where he was. I didn't know why, but I knew where. He was in the St. Louis city jail, in the rooms reserved for things that cannot stand the light of day. I stared into his eyes and watched them fill with blue fire, until they cast their own light in the dim cell.

He reached out towards me, as if we could touch, and it was Micah's power, Micah's beast rolling through my body that tore me away from Jean-Claude.

I opened my eyes to find my arms around Micah, my face pressed to his shoulder, my mouth very close to the long warmth of his neck. There was movement in the room, and I knew distantly that someone had run to get a doctor, but what I needed a doctor couldn't give me.

Micah's skin smelled clean, young. It was like I could tell just by scent how old he was. The blood was like icing spread just under the tenderness of his flesh; and the part of me that thought of Micah as meat wasn't Jean-Claude, it was Richard.

I didn't know how to put the need into words. Micah turned his face, looked into my eyes, and I felt something inside me open; some door that I hadn't even known existed swung wide. A wind blew through the door, a wind made of darkness and the stillness of the grave. A wind that held an edge of electric warmth like the rub of fur across bare skin. A wind that tasted of both my men. But I was the center, the thing that could hold both of them inside and not break. Life and death, lust and love.

"What *are* you?" Micah asked, his voice a surprised whisper.

I'd always thought that vampires took their victims—stole their will with their eyes and took them like magical rape. But in that instant I knew it was more complex than that, and more simple. I saw with Jean-Claude's eyes, his power. I stared into Micah's face from inches away, and I saw, felt, his own need. Lust was there, a horribly unsatisfied lust, and I knew it had been a long time for Micah. But underneath that was a greater need, a need for power and the shelter that power could provide. It was like I could smell his needs, roll them on my tongue. I stared into his yellow-green eyes in that so-human face, and Jean-Claude gave me the keys to Micah's soul.

"I am power, Nimir-Raj. Enough power to warm you on the coldest of nights." Power flowed off his skin like a scalding wind. That hot wind mingled with the power inside me, twisting together until it drove like a knife deep inside me. It tore a gasp from my throat, and Micah echoed it. The power turned into something gentler, something that caressed instead of stabbed, something that you would wait your whole life to have. I saw the sensation flow over Micah's face, knew that he felt it, too.

A wind stirred the edge of his hair. And the wind was moving between us like the point where cold and heat meet and form something larger than either can form alone, something huge and whirling, a wind so strong it can level houses and drive straw through telephone poles.

His arms tightened around me. "I am Nimir-Raj, mind games don't work on me."

I got to my knees still in the circle of his arms, and pressed my body down the front of his. We were almost exactly the same height, the eye contact was terribly intimate. The power pressed around us like a giant hand squeezing us together. His body responded, and he was large again, so hard pressed to my groin and stomach. This was my cue to be embarrassed, to panic, but I didn't. I knew that Jean-Claude fed off of lust as well as blood, but I'd never really understood what that meant until that moment when Micah's flesh touched mine. It wasn't just the naked press of him, hard and firm against my body, that made me shudder against him, it was the need in his body. I felt his hunger quiver through his flesh, as if I could read parts of him that were too primitive for words, needs that had nothing to do with language, and everything to do with naked flesh.

He closed his eyes, and a soft moan escaped him.

"What I offer isn't illusion, Nimir-Raj, it's real."

He shook his head. "Sex isn't enough."

"I'm not offering sex, not now." Even as I said it, I pressed my body against his. His entire body shuddered against me, and a sound very like a whimper crawled out of his throat.

"I'm offering a taste of power, Nimir-Raj, a small taste of all I can offer you." In my head I knew it was a lie, but in my heart I knew it was true. I could offer him power and flesh, the two things he wanted, needed, above all else. It was perfect bait, and it was wrong. I started to back down, to try and cram the power down, but Jean-Claude fought me. He thrust his power into me like an echo of his body, riding me. It was too late for me to feed as humans feed and give him back his strength. He'd avoided me for nights, because I was weak. I had grown strong again, and he had grown weak, and we had enemies in town. We could not afford weakness. All this, I knew in a heartbeat, his mind to mine. And it was that seed of doubt—*could we afford to be weak?*—that made me unable to shut him out.

"What do you want in return?" Micah asked it in a whisper that held an edge of desperation, as if we both knew that whatever I asked, he would do it.

"I want to drink the warm rush of your body, to have you fill my mouth with that hot liquid that beats just below here," and I rubbed my lips across his neck. The scent of blood so near the surface made my stomach twist, but we were close, so close, mustn't rush it, mustn't scare him. We were like fishermen. We had our net, all we needed was for the fish to stop fighting us and lay still.

My lips hovered over his neck as he spoke. "Show me you have enough power to make it worth my while, and I'll give you any body fluid you want."

I swept his hair to one side, and it slid back. I balled my hand into a fist of his curls to keep it out of the way, and even that movement brought a sound from his throat. I bared the long smooth line of his neck. He moved his head to one side as if he knew what I wanted now. I could see the big pulse in his neck, beating against his skin like something small and separate from him, something alive that I had to make free.

I licked my tongue across that throbbing skin. I meant to be gentle, I meant many things, but his skin was slick and flawless against my mouth; the smell of him intoxicated me like the sweetest perfume. His pulse throbbed against my mouth, and I sank my teeth around that frantic movement. I ate at his skin, dug my teeth into the flesh underneath, and into his power, his beast.

I felt my beast rise through my body, like some great shape rising from the ocean depths, a leviathan that grew and grew, swelling up inside me until my skin couldn't hold it, then it touched his beast, and it stopped, hovering in black water, hovering in my body like some huge thing. The two powers floated in that dark water, brushing huge, sleek sides down the length of their bodies, our bodies. It was a sensation like velvet rubbing inside me, except this velvet had muscles, flesh, and was hard even where it was soft. The imagery that kept flowing through my mind was of some great cat rubbing itself inside me, rolling through me, but bigger than that. I'd seen Richard's beast move through his eyes like some great shape half-seen in water, and it felt that large, that overwhelming. I drank Micah's power down but not just through my mouth and down my throat. Everywhere I touched him, I fed. I could feel his heart beating against my naked breasts. I could feel the blood rushing through his body, feel every inch of him pressed against me. Feel his need, his desire, and I ate at him. I fed at his neck as if his pulse were the center of some filled cake, as if once I gnawed away the flesh I would have something unutterably sweet. I drew blood, and with the first touch of sweet metallic flavor in my mouth, all pretense, all prettiness was wiped away, drowned in the scent of fresh blood, the taste of torn flesh, the feel of meat and blood in my mouth. The feel of his hands pressing my body against his, my legs wrapped around his waist, riding him. I was aware like some distant call that he wasn't inside me, that he was still pressed between our bodies, so hard, so ready that he quivered against my stomach. His breath came fast and faster. Someone was making small animal noises, and it was me.

Micah's fingernails dug into my body, an instant before he poured over me in a scalding wave, noises too primitive for words, and not loud enough for screams coming from his mouth.

I felt Jean-Claude down that long metaphysical cord that bonded us together. I felt him grow quiet and well fed, sated. I drew my mouth away from Micah's torn throat, putting my cheek against his bare shoulder, my legs and arms still wrapped around him. His arms still holding me tight. I was covered in fluid, my breasts thick with it. It ran down my body in heavy liquid lines, curling over my stomach, tracing down to my thighs.

He knelt there supporting both our weights, while our breathing quieted, and the massive pulse of our bodies subsided into silence. And in that silence there was nothing but the feel of his flesh, the raw scent of sex, and in the distance, the satisfaction of the vampire.

10

THE SHOWER WAS one of those group ones, like you'd find in a health club. But I was the only one in it. I'd cleaned off, scrubbed myself thoroughly, but I felt like Lady MacBeth screaming "out, out, damned spot!" Like I'd never really be clean again. I sat on the tiles under the hot, beating water, hugging my knees. I hadn't planned on crying, but I was. Slow tears that felt cool compared to the water pounding my body. I wasn't sure why I was crying. My mind was blank. Usually when I try to be blank, I can't, but just then, there was nothing but the water, the heat, the smooth tiles, and the little voice in my head that kept running round and round like a hamster on a wheel. I couldn't hear what the voice was saying—I think I didn't want to. All I knew was that it was screaming.

A noise behind me made me turn. It was Cherry, still naked. None of the leopards ever dressed unless I made them. I turned my head away from her. I didn't want her to see me cry. I was her Nimir-Ra, her rock. Rocks did not cry.

I knew she was standing over me, could feel it, even before the water's rhythm changed. She knelt over me, the water sluicing around her, leaving me shivering in the sudden touch of the cool, waterless air. I kept my face turned away from her. She touched my water-soaked hair. When I didn't protest she hugged me, arms going slowly around me, as if she expected me to complain.

I stayed stiff in her arms, with her body wrapped around me. She just held me, head pressed to the top of mine, her body sheltering me from the water, leaving me colder, even as her body stretched like heat against my wet skin. I leaned into her by painful inches until finally I let her hold me. I cried, and Cherry held me.

The crying never grew, or got loud. It remained slow tears while Cherry held me, and I let her. Finally, there were no more tears, just the sound of the water, the heat, the feel of Cherry's body around mine. There was comfort in the touch of flesh that went beyond sex. I pulled away, and she drew back. I stood and turned the water off. The silence was sudden and complete. I could feel the press of the night outside. Even without a window, I knew it was the wee hours of morning—maybe two, or even three. It would be dawn in a few short hours. I needed to know why Jean-Claude was in jail. Everything else could wait. We had enemies in town, and I needed to know who they were, what they wanted. After that I'd think about what had just happened, but not yet, not yet. Avoidance is one of my best things.

Cherry handed me a towel and kept one for herself. I wound the towel around my hair and retrieved a second towel for my body. We dried off in silence, no eye contact. It wasn't shower protocol; girls aren't as hung up about that as guys. I just didn't want to talk about what had happened. Not yet.

I wrapped the oversized towel securely around my body, and asked, "Why is Jean-Claude in jail?"

"For murdering you," she said.

I stared at her for a few seconds, and when I could talk, I said, "Pass that by me again. Slowly."

"Someone got pictures of Jean-Claude carrying you out of the club. You were covered in blood, Anita. He was covered in your blood." She shrugged, drying off a spot she'd missed on one long leg.

"But I'm alive," I said. It sounded almost silly saying it.

"And how would you explain that in less than a week you were healed of wounds that should have killed you?" She straightened, slinging the towel over one shoulder, not bothering to cover even an inch of her body.

"I don't want him in jail for something he didn't do," I said.

"If you go tonight, the police will want to know how you healed yourself. What are you going to tell them?" Her eyes were very direct. So direct it made me want to squirm.

"You're treating me like a lycanthrope who hasn't come out of the closet yet. I'm not a shapeshifter, Cherry."

She dropped her gaze then, wouldn't meet my eyes. It reminded me of the looks they'd all given each other in the room where I woke up. I touched her chin, having to reach up to do it. "What aren't you guys telling me?"

A man's voice came from outside the showers. "Can I please come in and clean off?" It was Micah. I'd planned on running for the hills the next time I saw him, but there was something in Cherry's eyes that kept me frozen. She was scared. And there was something else, something I couldn't quite read.

I yelled back, "Just a minute!" Then I continued."Cherry, tell me. Whatever it is, just tell me."

She shook her head. She was afraid, but of what? "Are you afraid of *me*?" I couldn't keep the surprise out of my voice.

She nodded, looking down again, avoiding my gaze.

"I would never hurt you, any of you."

"For this you might," she whispered.

I grabbed her arm. "Cherry, damn it, talk to me."

She opened her mouth, closed it, and turned towards the door a second before Micah Callahan walked through, as if she'd heard him before I had. He was still naked. I expected to be embarrassed, but I wasn't. I was beginning to have the proverbial bad feeling about whatever it was that Cherry didn't want to tell me.

Micah had combed his hair. It was definitely curls, not waves. The curls were tight, but not small. The color was that shade of dark, dark brown—almost black—that comes to people who start out white blond as children, then darken. The curls fell to just below his shoulders, and, following the line of hair, my eyes found his chest. I quickly moved them up so I could concentrate on his face. Eye contact. That was the ticket. I was getting back to the embarrassment.

"I told you we'd be out in a minute." My voice sounded grumpy, and I was glad. The fact that I was sort of clutching the towel to my body was purely coincidental.

"I heard you," he said. His face, voice, were neutral. Not as neutral as a vampire's can become. They are the champs of blank expression. But Micah was trying.

"Then wait outside until we're finished," I said.

"Cherry is afraid of you," he said.

I frowned at him, then at her. "Why, for God's sake?"

Cherry looked at him, and he gave a small nod. She moved away from me towards the door. She didn't leave the room, but she got as far away from me as she could.

"What in hell is going on?" I asked.

Micah was standing about four feet away, close, but not too close. I could see his eyes better now, and they were *so* not human. I knew at a glance that they didn't belong in his face. "She's afraid you'll kill the messenger," he said, voice soft.

"Look, all this tap dancing is getting old. Just tell me."

He nodded, winced as if it hurt. "The doctors seem to think that you've been infected with lycanthropy."

I shook my head. "Serpentine lycanthropy isn't really lycanthropy. It's not a disease that I can catch. You either are cursed by a witch into snake form, or it's inherited like a swanmane." That made me think of the three women I'd last seen chained to a wall in the room of swords. "By the way, what happened to the swanmanes in the club?"

Micah frowned. "I don't know what you're talking about."

Without warning, Nathaniel entered the shower. I was beginning to feel positively overdressed in my towel. "We rescued them."

"The snake leader changed his mind after I got hurt?"

"He changed it after Sylvie and Jamil nearly killed him."

Ah. "So they're okay," I said.

He nodded, but his face stayed serious, his eyes gentle, like someone who's about to tell you really bad news.

"Don't you start, too. I cannot catch serpentine shit. It doesn't work that way."

"Gregory isn't into serpentine shit," he said, the voice as gentle as his eyes.

I blinked at him. "What are you talking about?"

Nathaniel started to come farther into the room, but Cherry caught his arm, kept him near the door for a quick getaway—I think. Zane appeared in the doorway behind them. He was still the six-feet, pale, overly thin, but muscular guy I'd met when he was trashing a hospital emergency room. But he'd dyed his hair to an iridescent pale green, cut short, spiked. The fact that he was fully dressed actually looked odd to me. Of course, it was Zane's version of street clothes that ran to leather, no shirt, and vests.

I looked at the three of them in the doorway. They were so solemn. I remembered Gregory falling into me during the fight. His claws piercing me. "I've been cut up a lot worse by a wereleopard, and I didn't catch it," I said.

"Dr. Lillian thinks it may be because the wound was a deep piercing wound, instead of a surface cut," Cherry said, in a voice that was almost shaky. She was scared, scared of how I'd take the news, or scared of something else, but what?

"I am not going to be Nimir-Ra for real, guys. I can't catch lycanthropy. If I could . . . I've already been cut up enough . . . I'd have turned furry already."

The three of them just looked at me with wide eyes. I turned from them to Micah. His face was still neutral, careful, but there was a shadow in his eyes of . . . pity. Pity? I did not do pity, not as the object of it, anyway.

"You're serious," I said.

"You're exhibiting all the secondary symptoms," he said. "Rapid healing to the point that your muscles cramp. A temperature hot enough to boil the brain of a human. Yet when they lowered your temperature you nearly died. You needed to bake in the warmth, the heat of your pard to heal. That's how we healed you. It wouldn't have worked if you weren't one of us."

I shook my head. "I don't believe you."

"That's okay," he said, "you've got two weeks until the full moon. You won't change for the first time until then. You've got time."

"Time for what?" I asked.

"Time to mourn," he said.

I turned away from the compassion in his eyes, the pity. Shit. I still didn't believe it. "How about a blood test? That should prove it one way or the other."

Cherry answered, "Wolf lycanthropy shows up in the bloodstream anywhere from twenty-four to forty-eight hours, sometimes seventy-two. Leopard lycanthropy, most of the big cat lycanthropies, take anywhere from seventy-two hours to over eight days to show up in the bloodstream. A blood test won't prove anything yet."

I stared at them, trying to wrap my mind around it, and it just wouldn't wrap. I shook my head. "I can't deal with this right now."

"You're going to have to deal with it," Micah said.

I shook my head. "Tonight, I have to get Jean-Claude out of jail. I have to show the police he didn't murder me."

"Your pard told me that you wouldn't want to be outted. That you wouldn't want your police friends to know."

"I am not a wereleopard," I said. It sounded stubborn even to me.

Micah smiled, gently, and that pissed me off. "Don't look at me like that."

"Like what?" he asked.

"Like a poor little deluded girl. There are things you don't understand about me, about where my power comes from."

"You mean the vampire marks," he said.

I looked past him to the three wereleopards in the doorway. Something on my face made them all flinch. "So nice to know that we're just one big happy family with no secrets."

"I was in on the discussions with the doctors on whether your rapid healing could be merely a side effect of the vampire marks," he said.

"Of course it is," I said. But the first thread of doubt was worming its way through my stomach.

"If it will make you feel better," he said.

I stared into that compassionate face and felt anger wash over me in a line of heat, and with the anger came that trembling energy. Richard's beast . . . or mine? I let myself think the thought all the way through for the first time. Was it my beast that I'd felt with Micah? Was that why I hadn't gotten a sense of where Richard was, and what he was doing? I'd thought of him several times during all the hoopla, but had never felt the mark between us open completely. I'd assumed it was Richard's energy, because it was lycanthrope energy. But what if it hadn't been? What if it had been mine?

Someone touched my arm, and I jumped. It was Micah, his fingers barely touching my arm. "You look pale. Do you need to sit down?"

I took a step back and nearly stumbled. He had to grab my arm to keep me from falling on the slick, wet tile. I wanted to jerk away from him, but I was dizzy as if the world wasn't quite solid. He eased me to the floor.

"Put your head between your knees."

I sat Indian fashion on the floor, the wall to my back, my head bent over my folded legs while I waited for the light-headedness to pass. I never fainted. Not just from shock—occasionally from blood loss—but never from shock.

When I could think again, I raised up slowly. Micah was kneeling beside me, all attentive and compassionate, and I hated him. I laid my towel-wrapped head back against the wall, closed my eyes.

"Where are Elizabeth and Gregory?"

"Elizabeth wouldn't come to help," Micah said.

I opened my eyes at that, turning just my head to meet his eyes. "She give a reason for that?"

"She hates you," he said, simply.

"Yeah, she loved Gabriel, their old alpha, and I killed him. Hard to be friends after that."

"That's not why she hates you," he said.

I searched his face. "What do you mean?"

"She hates that you're a better alpha as a human than she is as a wereleopard. You make her feel weak."

"She is weak," I said.

He smiled, and it had humor in it this time. "Yes, she is."

"Where's Gregory?"

"Are you going to punish him for contaminating you?" Micah asked.

I glanced back at the other three waiting in the door, silent. I realized suddenly what the group dynamics meant. They were treating Micah as their Nimir-Raj, letting him deal with me, like calling in the husband when the wife has had one too many drinks. I didn't like that much. But if I concentrated just on the moment, the question at hand, no speculation, no looking for the future, maybe I'd survive.

"If Gregory hadn't interfered I'd be dead right now. They would have clawed out my heart. It was an accident that he fell into me during the fight." I was watching Micah's face, but I felt the relief sweep through the others, felt it from yards away. I glanced up at them, and it showed in the lines of their bodies.

"So where is he? Where's Gregory?"

The three of them did that hot-potato eye-flick game again. "Did he refuse to come help save me like Elizabeth?"

"No, of course not," Cherry said. But she didn't explain, didn't add to it.

I looked at Nathaniel. He met my gaze, no flinching, but I didn't like what I saw in his eyes. There was more bad news to come, you could smell it in the air.

I turned to Micah. "Fine, you tell me."

"When your Ulfric found out that Gregory had made you their Nimir-Ra in truth, he . . ." Micah spread his hands.

"He freaked." Zane said it.

I glanced at all of them. "What do you mean, he freaked?"

"He took Gregory," Cherry said.

"What do you mean, he took Gregory?"

"He treated Gregory as an enemy of the pack," Micah said.

I looked at him. "Go on."

"If you had been their lupa in truth, if someone injured you it is within the Ulfric's rights to declare them an enemy of the pack, a criminal."

I kept staring into those yellow green eyes. "What exactly does that mean?"

"It means that the wolves have your leopard, and they will pass judgment on him for injuring you."

"No way, I mean, even if I *am* turning into a wereleopard, which I'm not. It doesn't hurt me. I mean, I'm just going to be a shapeshifter like them now."

"Not like them," Micah said, "like us."

I tried to read his face, but I just didn't know him well enough yet. "You have a point, make it."

"You can't be the wolves' lupa *and* the leopard's Nimir-Ra."

"I've been both for a long time."

He shook his head, and again he winced as if his neck hurt. "No, you were a human dating the Ulfric, who declared you lupa. You were a human that was taking care of the wereleopards until you could find a true alpha leopard to take over the job. Now, you're truly Nimir-Ra, and the pack won't accept you as one of them."

"Are you saying Richard dumped me because I'm going to be a wereleopard?"

"No, I'm saying that the pack won't accept you as his lupa." Micah glanced down, then up. I could see him trying to put his thoughts into words. "My understanding of what's been happening with your local wolves is that your Ulfric has taken them from a monarchy where his word was law, to a democracy where the majority rules. He gets a decisive vote, but not the last word."

I nodded. It sounded like what Richard had wanted for the pack. "It sounds like something he'd do. I've sort of been out of touch for the last few months."

"He has succeeded too well. The vote went against him, against you. The pack will not accept you as lupa when you're wereleopard and not werewolf."

I looked past him at the others. "Is that true?"

They all nodded. "I'm so sorry, Anita," Cherry said.

I shook my head, trying to concentrate and not succeeding. "Alright, fine, fine. Richard can't make me lupa. I never wanted to be lupa, just his girlfriend. Fuck the wolves. But what have they done with Gregory?"

"Richard went ape-shit when he found out what Gregory had done," Zane said. "He thought Gregory had done it on purpose, because we were all afraid to lose you as our Nimir-Ra."

"He accused Gregory of doing it on purpose?" I asked.

Zane nodded. "Oh, yeah, then they took him."

"They, who?"

"Jamil, Sylvie, others." He wouldn't meet my eyes.

"Didn't anyone try and argue with him about this?"

"Sylvie tried to tell him it wasn't right, that you wouldn't like it. He hit her, told her never to argue with him again, that he was Ulfric, not her."

"Shit."

"Do not blame your leopards for not fighting the wolves," Micah said. "They are sorely outnumbered."

"They'd get their asses kicked, I know that. Besides, it's my job to deal with Richard, not theirs."

"Because you are their Nimir-Ra," he said.

"Because I am his girlfriend, sort of."

"Of course," he said.

I waved a hand at him. "Look, I can't deal with all of this right now, so I'm just going to concentrate on the important stuff, I mean the immediately important stuff. Where is Gregory, and how do I get him back?"

Micah smiled. "Very practical."

I looked at him and felt my eyes go cold. "You have no idea how practical I can be."

His eyes did change, but it wasn't fear in them, it was more interest, like my reaction intrigued him. "The situation is complex because you are the lupa that was injured. In effect, you must persuade yourself that Gregory meant no harm."

"That's too easy," I said. "I know he meant no harm. So why do I get the feeling that I can't just call Richard up and say, 'Hey, I'm coming to get Gregory'?"

"Because you must convince not just Richard, but the entire pack, that you have the right to Gregory."

"What do you mean 'right to Gregory'? He's my leopard. He's mine, not theirs."

Micah smiled, lowering long lashes over his eyes, as if he didn't want me to read his expression at that moment. "The Ulfric declared Gregory rogue for, in effect, killing their lupa."

"I'm alive, what . . . ?"

Micah held up a finger, and I let him finish. "You are dead to the pack—as their lupa. In effect, being a leopard makes you dead to them. You may share Richard's bed again, but you will never be their lupa again. They voted on it, and Richard has destroyed his own power structure to the point where he can't force a vote on them."

"You're saying that he is Ulfric but he doesn't really rule them," I said.

Micah seemed to think about that for a second, or two, then started to nod, stopped in mid-motion. "Yes, in fact, very well put."

"Thanks." A thought came to me, and I gripped his arm. "They aren't going to kill Gregory, are they?" Something passed over his face that tightened my grip on his arm. "They haven't killed him?"

"No," Micah said.

I let go of his arm and leaned back against the wall. "What are they doing to him, or what are they planning to do to him?"

"The penalty for killing the lupa is death in any pack. But the circumstances are strange enough that I think you will be allowed a chance to win him back."

"Win him back, how?" I asked.

"For that, you'll need to ask the Ulfric."

"I'll do that." I looked past him. "Someone get my cell phone out of my Jeep." Nathaniel went for the door without another word.

"What are you going to do?" Micah asked.

"I'm going to make sure that Gregory isn't being hurt. If he's okay for tonight, I'll go get Jean-Claude out of jail. If Gregory is in danger, then I get him out first."

"Priorities," he said, softly.

"Damn straight."

He smiled again. "I am very impressed. You've had several shocks in a very short space of time, yet you are clearheaded, and moving forward to solve the problems one at a time."

"I can only solve one problem at a time," I said.

"Most people let themselves be distracted."

"I'm not most people."

He gave that small smile again, shielding his eyes with his long lashes. "I've noticed."

Something about the way he said it made me suddenly aware that he was nude, and I was wearing nothing but a towel. It was time to get on my feet and get dressed. I stood, pushing away his offer of help. "I'm fine, Micah, thanks anyway." I looked past him at Cherry and Zane still standing in the doorway. "Do I have any clothes here?"

Cherry nodded. "Nathaniel brought your stuff from home. I'll go get it." She moved through the door.

"Weapons, too," I called after her.

She poked her head back around the doorway. "I know." That left just Zane standing in the doorway. "Do you have a job for me?"

"Not right now."

He flashed me a smile wide enough to show that he had dainty fangs upper and lower—kitty-cat fangs. Zane had spent a little too much time in animal form to come all the way back. "I'll go help Cherry then." He paused at the doorway. "I'm really glad you didn't die."

"Me too."

He grinned and left.

That left me alone with Micah. I looked into his yellow-green eyes and knew that they were also a sign that he'd spent too much time in animal form. We hadn't kissed, so I didn't know if he had dainty fangs like Zane. I hoped not, and wasn't sure why I cared.

"Do you mind if I start cleaning up?" he asked.

I shook my head. "Help yourself. I'm going to go look for my clothes." But Nathaniel came around the door with my cell phone.

I looked at the slim black phone. I'd only had it a few months. I'd tried not to buy one. If you had a cell phone and a beeper you were never truly free of the office. Of course, I was on vacation. Though, so far, it hadn't been all that relaxing.

I popped the phone open and dialed Richard's number from memory. There was no answer, just his machine. I left a message, then knew what I was going to do. I had to know what was happening with Gregory. I thought about Richard, the feel of his arms, the scent of his neck, the brush of his hair, and that prickling rush of energy rolled over my skin. I reached down the mark that bound me to Richard and found him standing on a podium. He was arguing with someone, but I couldn't see who. I never got as clear a visual through Richard as I did through Jean-Claude. Richard turned as if he could see me standing behind him, then he thrust me out, throwing up a shield so solid I couldn't feel him on the other side.

Nathaniel was holding my arm, steadying me. "Are you alright?"

I nodded. Being thrust out like that was always disorienting. Richard knew that. Fuck. "I'm okay." I pulled away from Nathaniel and had to call information for the number for The Lunatic Cafe. Richard was in the meeting room in the back of the restaurant. Raina had owned the restaurant, and according to pack law, it could have belonged to me, if I hadn't used a gun to kill her. It had to be mano-a-mano, hand-to-hand, or claws, or at least a knife before all that was hers would be mine. Possessions anyway. You can't get anyone's power by killing them. It just doesn't work that way. And anyway, who would want it to? Guns were considered cheating, so I didn't inherit all of Raina's stuff.

Richard picked up on the second ring, as if he'd been expecting the call. "Richard, it's Anita."

"I know." His voice was angry, closed, and tight.

"We need to talk."

"I'm in the middle of something here, Anita."

Fine, if he wanted to play it brusque and hostile, I'd play. "Where's Gregory?"

"I can't tell you that."

"Why?"

"Because, you might try and rescue him, and you're not lupa anymore. The pack would defend itself, and I don't want you shooting holes in my wolves."

"You leave my leopards alone, and I'll leave your wolves alone."

"Anita, it's not that simple."

"I got the explanation, Richard. You freaked when you found out Gregory may have infected me with leopard juice. You had your enforcers grab him, and you've charged him with killing your lupa. Which is just stupid, I'm not dead."

"Do you know what the pack is voting on right now, right this minute?"

"Not a clue."

"Whether I will be picking another lupa from the pack before the next full moon."

"I guess you'll need one," I said, and even hearing myself acknowledge it made my stomach clench.

"A *lover*, Anita, they're wanting to force me to pick a lover from the pack."

"You mean we can't date now?"

"That's the vote."

"Stephen, one of your wolves, and Vivian, one of my leopards, are living together. No one seems to care about that."

"Stephen is one of the least of us. They wouldn't tolerate cross-species dating for a dominant. And they certainly won't tolerate it for their Ulfric."

"Human is good enough to fuck, but not leopard," I said.

"We are human, Anita. But we aren't cats, we're wolves."

"So you won't be dating me, or anything, now?"

"Not if I want to stay Ulfric."

"What happens to the triumvirate?"

"I don't know."

"You're going to give me up just like that." I was suddenly cold, my stomach like a hard frozen knot.

"You've been out of my life for over half a year. How do I know that something else won't scare you off again?"

"I planned on dating you both, Richard, on being with you both." I realized as soon as I said it that I meant it. I'd made a decision and hadn't realized it.

"What about a week from now, or a month, or even a year? What will scare you off next time?"

"I don't plan on running anymore, Richard."

"Nice to know." I could feel his anger like something hot and touchable over the phone. Either his shield was leaking, or he'd lowered it.

"You don't want to be with me anymore?" My voice was soft, hurt, and I hated it. Hated it.

"I want to be with you, you know that. You drive me crazy, but I still want you."

"But you'll still give me up," I said. My voice was a little stronger, but not much. Richard was dumping me. Fine, it was his prerogative. I was a pain in the ass, I knew that. But my chest ached with it, damn it.

"I don't want to, Anita, but I'll do what I have to do. You taught me that."

My eyes were hot. I'd taught him that. Great. If we were really going to break up for good, then I would not cry or beg. I would not be weak. My voice came out more solid, more sure of itself. My stomach was still in cold knots, but it didn't show in my voice. The effort that it took to just sound normal over the phone made my chest tight. "You're Ulfric, wolf king. Your word is law in the pack."

"I've worked hard to make sure that everyone has an equal voice, Anita. I can't pull rank now. It would undo everything I've tried to change."

"Ideals are great in theory, Richard, but they don't work too well in real life."

"I disagree," he said. His anger was already leaking away. He just sounded tired.

"I'm not going to argue things we've been arguing since we met. I'm going to concentrate on the things I can change. And no matter how much we want to, we can't change each other, Richard. We are what we are." My voice was uncertain again, full of some of the emotion I was feeling. "So, is Gregory okay?"

"He's okay."

"I want him back, you know that."

"I know that." His anger was making a comeback.

"Now that I'm not lupa, not pack, how do I get him back?"

"You have to come to the lupanar tomorrow night and petition for him."

"What do you mean, 'petition for him?' "

"You have to prove yourself worthy. There'll be some kind of test."

"Like multiple choice, essay, what?"

"I don't know yet. We're . . . voting on it."

"Fuck, Richard, there's a reason why we have a representative democracy in this country, not a pure one. Pure one person, one vote, just doesn't work well. You can't decide anything that way."

"They're deciding, Anita. You're just not liking the way it's going."

"How could you take Gregory? How could you do that?"

"As soon as I realized what had happened, I knew that the pack would vote you out. Most of them weren't happy with you even before. You weren't pack, and they didn't like that. The fact that you've avoided them—all of them—for six months didn't help."

"I had to get my shit together before I could come back, Richard."

"And while you were getting your shit together, mine was falling apart."

"I'm sorry, Richard, I am. But I didn't know."

"Tomorrow night at the lupanar, about an hour after dark. You can bring all your wereleopards and any other shapeshifters that are your allies. If it were me, as Ulfric, I'd bring the wererats."

"I'm not lupa anymore, so they aren't my allies, are they?"

"No," he said, and the anger was gone again. Richard never could hold a grudge for long.

"What happens if I don't win Gregory back?"

He didn't answer me, just the sound of his breathing on the phone. "Richard, what happens to Gregory?"

"He'll be judged by the pack."

"And?"

"If he's convicted of killing our lupa, it's a death sentence."

"But I'm right here, Richard. I'm not dead. You can't kill Gregory for killing me, when he didn't do it."

"I delayed the judgment until you were well enough to attend. It was the best I could do."

"You know, Richard, sometimes it's good to be king. A king gets to pardon whomever he wants, a king gets to fuck whomever he wants."

"I know that."

"Then be king, Richard, really be king. Be their Ulfric, not their president."

"I'm doing what I think best for them all."

"Richard, you can't do this."

"It's already done."

"Richard, if I fail your little test, I will not let you execute Gregory. Do you understand me?"

"You won't be allowed to bring guns into the lupanar, just knives." His voice had gone very careful.

"I remember the rule. But Richard, are you listening to me? Are you understanding me?"

"If we try to execute Gregory tomorrow night, you'll fight us, I understand. But understand this, Anita, your leopards are no match for us, not even with Micah and his pard. We outnumber you five to one, maybe more."

"It doesn't matter, Richard. I can't stand by and watch Gregory die, not for something stupid like this."

"Will you try to save one of your cats and risk losing them all? Do you really want to see what would happen if they tried to fight their way out of the lupanar, through the pack? I wouldn't want to see it."

"This is . . . damn it, Richard, don't put me in a corner, you won't like it."

"Is that a threat?"

"Richard . . ." I had to stop in mid-sentence and count slowly under my breath. But counting to ten wasn't going to do it, maybe a bijillion. "Richard," my voice came out calmer, "I will save Gregory, whatever it takes. I will not let the wolves slaughter my leopards, whatever that takes. You lost your temper and took one of my leopards. You made your pack a freaking democracy, where you don't even have presidential veto. Are you really going to compound the mistakes by starting a war between your pack and my pard?"

"I still think that everyone having a voice is a good idea."

"It's a great idea, but it's not working, is it?" He was quiet again. "Richard, don't do this."

"It's out of my hands. I'm sorry, Anita, you don't know how sorry."

"Richard, you won't really let them execute Gregory. I mean, not really."

Silence again.

"Richard, talk to me."

"I'll do what I can, but I've lost the vote on it. I can't change that."

"Can you really stand by and watch him die for something he didn't do?"

"How do you know he didn't infect you on purpose?"

"I was there. He fell on top of me with two of the snake things riding him. It was an accident. He kept them from cutting out my heart. He saved my life, Richard, and this is damn poor payment."

"He couldn't have turned his claws aside at the last minute?" Richard asked.

"No, it all happened too fast."

He laughed, but it was bitter. "You've been around us so long, and you still don't understand what we are. I could turn aside in less than a blink of an eye. Gregory isn't slower than I am. As a leopard he's quicker, more agile."

"Are you saying he did this on purpose?"

"I'm saying that he had a fraction of a second to decide what he'd do, and he decided to keep you as their Nimir-Ra. He made the choice to take you from me."

"And you're going to make him pay for that. Is that it?"

"Yeah, that's it."

"With his life?"

He sighed. "I don't want him dead, Anita. But when I first found out what he'd done, I wanted to kill him myself. I wanted it so badly I didn't trust myself around him, so I had him taken somewhere safe until I could cool down. But Jacob got wind of it, and forced a vote."

"Who's Jacob?"

"My new Geri, third in charge behind Sylvie."

"I've never heard of him before."

"He's new."

"Damn, third in line, and he's new. He's either a very good fighter, or a very vicious one, to win that many fights in less than half a year."

"He's good, and he's vicious."

"Is he ambitious?" I asked.

"Why?"

"If Jacob hadn't forced a vote, would you have given Gregory back to me?"

He remained quiet so long, that I finally asked, "You still there?"

"I'm here. Yes, I would have given him back to you. I can't kill him for what he's done."

"So Jacob set in motion something that's stripped you of a powerful ally—me—and forced you to declare war on another group—the wereleopards. He's been a busy boy."

"He's just doing what he thinks is right."

"Jesus, Richard, how can you still be this naive?"

"You think he wants my job?"

"You *know* he wants your job. I can hear it in your voice."

"If I'm not strong enough to hold the pack, then it's Jacob's prerogative to challenge me. But he's got to defeat Sylvie first, and she's as good as he is—and as vicious."

"How big is Jacob?"

"My size, not as muscled."

"Sylvie is good, but she's five six, and slender, and a woman. And as much as I hate to say it, that makes a difference. Pound for pound you guys have the upper body strength on us. If the skill is equal, a larger person will beat a smaller one."

"Don't underestimate Sylvie," he said.

"Don't overestimate her, either. She's my friend, too, and I don't want her dead just because you're not willing to take care of business."

"What's that supposed to mean?"

"It means until he defeats Sylvie and becomes Freki, your second in command, you can kill him outside of a challenge. You can have him executed."

"And if Marcus had thought that about me, I'd be dead now."

"And Marcus would be alive, Richard. You're not helping your case."

"We aren't animals, Anita, we're people. And I can't just kill him because I think he's after my job."

"You don't just stand down as Ulfric, Richard, you fight to the death for it. I know theoretically if you both agree, it doesn't have to be death. But I've been asking around, and no werewolf I've talked to can remember a fight for Ulfric that wasn't to the death. He's not after your job, Richard, he's after your life."

"I can't control what Jacob does, only what I do."

I was beginning to remember why Richard and I didn't make a go of it as a couple. Oh, there had been a lot of reasons. I'd seen him eat Marcus, and that had made me run away. Then we got back together, and the marks were overwhelming. But there were other reasons. Reasons that made me feel tired and older than Richard, even though he was actually two years older than me. "You're being stupid, Richard."

"It's not really any of your business, Anita. You're not my lupa anymore."

"If you die, the marks may drag Jean-Claude and me down to die with you, so that sort of makes it my business."

"And you don't risk your life every time you go hunting vampires or preternatural creatures with the police? You almost died in New Mexico less than a month ago. You risked all of us."

"I was trying to save people's lives, Richard. You're trying to remake a political system. Ideology is great in a classroom or a debate, but it's flesh and blood that counts, Richard. It's life and death we're talking about here, not some outdated ideal you have in your head about what a better world you can make for the pack."

"If ideals mean nothing, Anita, then we are just animals."

"Richard, if Gregory dies for this, then *I* will kill Jacob, and anyone else who gets in my way. I'll destroy your lupanar and salt the ground, so help me. You explain to Jacob, and anyone else that needs convincing, that if they fuck with me, they will die."

"You can't fight the entire pack, Anita. Not and win."

"If you think the only thing I care about is winning, then you don't know me at all. I will save Gregory because I said I would."

"If you fail the tests, you can't save him."

"What sort of tests are we talking about?"

"Ones that only a shapeshifter could pass."

"Richard, Richard . . ." I wanted to scream and rant at him, but I was suddenly more tired than angry, more discouraged than enraged. "Mark me on this,

Richard, if I fail to save Gregory, then I will remake heaven into hell to avenge him. You explain that to Jacob, make sure he understands."

"Tell him yourself." There was silence and the sound of movement. Then a man's voice came on, a voice that I'd never heard before. The voice was pleasant, young, but not too young.

"Hello, I'm Jacob, I've heard a lot about you." His voice made it plain that he hadn't liked what he'd heard.

"Look, Jacob, we don't know each other, but I cannot allow you to kill Gregory for something he didn't do."

"The only way you can stop us is by winning him back."

"Richard explained that I'd have to pass a test to get Gregory back. He also said if I failed that you'd execute Gregory."

"It's pack law."

"Jacob, you don't want to make me your enemy."

"You are Nimir-Ra of a small leopard pard. We are the Thronnos Rokke Clan. We are the lukoi, and you are nothing to us."

"Yeah, I'm coming tomorrow night as Nimir-Ra of the Blooddrinker's Pard. But I'm Anita Blake. Ask the vampires and other shapeshifters around town about me. See what they say. You don't want to fuck with me, Jacob, you really don't."

"I've already asked around. I know your reputation."

"Then why are you pushing this?"

"That's my business," he said.

"Fine, you want to do this, we can do this. If you cause Gregory's death through voting or werewolf politics, I will bury you."

"If you can," he said. "You're a brand-new shapeshifter. You won't even change form until the full moon, and that's weeks away. You are no match for me."

"You say that like I'm going to offer to fight you one-on-one. I'm not. If Gregory dies, you die. Simple as that."

"If you shoot me, it won't reinstate you into the pack. If you could possibly win one-on-one against me, then maybe they'd vote you back to lupa. But if you just shoot me, you'll never be lupa again."

"I'm going to say this nice and slow, Jacob, so we understand each other. I don't give a shit about being lupa. I care about my friends, and the people I've promised to protect. Gregory is one of those people. If he dies, you die."

"I'm not going to kill him, Anita. I just made sure there was a vote about it."

"Do you like John Wayne movies, Jacob?"

He was quiet for a heartbeat. "I guess, I mean, what does that have to do with anything?"

"Your fault, my fault, nobody's fault, if Gregory dies, you die."

"Am I supposed to get the movie reference?" he asked. He sounded angry now.

"I guess not, but the point is this. I will blame you personally if anything happens to Gregory, for any reason. If he comes to harm, so will you. If he bleeds, so do you. If he dies . . ."

"I get the idea. But I don't have a deciding vote on this issue. I'm just one vote."

"Then you better think of something, Jacob. Because I give you my word that I mean everything I say."

"I heard that about you." He was quiet, and we stood on either end of the phone in silence, until he said, "What about Richard?"

"What about him?"

"If something happens to him what will you do?"

"If I tell you that I'll kill *you* if you kill *him*, that undercuts his authority as Ulfric. But I'll say this much, if you defeat him, then it better be a fair fight in a challenge circle. If you cheat in any way, no matter how small, I'll kill you." I wanted so badly to just give Richard blanket protection, but I couldn't. It would weaken his position, and his position was weak enough already.

"But if it's fair, you'll stay out of it?"

I leaned against the wall and tried to think. "I'll be honest, Jacob, I love Richard. I don't always understand him, or even agree with him, but I love him. I'm ready to kill you over someone who has never been my lover or even a good friend. So, yeah, you kill Richard, and I'm really, really going to want to kill you."

"But you won't," he said.

I didn't like how persistent he was about the issue. It made me nervous. "I'll make you a deal, you don't challenge Richard for Ulfric until after the next full moon, then whatever happens, as long as it's fair, I'll stay out of it."

"What if it's sooner?" he asked.

"Then I am going to rain all over your parade."

"You're undercutting Richard's authority," he said.

"No, Jacob, no I'm not. I wouldn't be killing you because I was lupa or any werewolf stuff. I'd be killing you because I am just that vindictive. Give me a few weeks until after the full moon, and you're in the clear on this one, if you've got the *cajones* to finish the job."

"You think Richard will kill me, instead?"

"He killed the last Ulfric, Jacob. That's how he got the job."

"If I don't agree to this, you'll just shoot me?"

"From a nice, safe distance, oh, yeah."

"I can promise that I won't challenge Richard until after the full moon, but I can't promise that the vote won't go against Gregory. He was one that Raina, the old lupa, used to help punish some members of the pack. There's more than one woman here that he helped rape."

"I know."

"Then how can you defend him?"

"He did what his old alpha told him to do, and what Raina, the wicked bitch of the west, told him to do. Gregory isn't a dominant, he's lesser, and he does what he's told, like a good submissive shapeshifter. Ever since I took over as his alpha, he's refused to rape and torture. As soon as he had a choice, he stopped doing it. Ask Sylvie. Gregory let himself be tortured instead of helping to rape her."

"She told the story to the pack."

"You don't sound impressed."

"It's not me you have to impress, Anita, it's the others."

"Help me figure out a way to impress them, Jacob."

"Are you serious? You want me to help you save the leopard?"

"Yeah."

"That's ridiculous. I'm Geri of Thronnos Rokke clan. I don't have to help a wereleopard that even *you* admit isn't a dominant."

"Don't go all class conscious on me, Jacob. Remember the early part of our conversation, the part about you dying? I blame you for the mess. And you will help me clean it up, or I will splatter your brains all over the walls."

"You can't bring guns into the lupanar."

I laughed, and even to me it was an unsettling sound, creepy even. "You going to spend the rest of your life inside the lupanar?"

"Jesus," he said, voice soft, "you're talking about assassinating me."

I laughed again. A small voice in my head was screaming at me, telling me I was being a very good sociopath. But Rebecca of Sunnybrook Farm wasn't going to cut it with Jacob. Maybe later I could afford to be soft. "I think we finally understand each other, Jacob. Here's my cell phone number. You call me before tomorrow night with a plan."

"What if I can't come up with one?"

"Not my problem."

"You'll kill me even if I try and save him—really try and save your leopard, but fail. You'll still kill me."

"Yes."

"You cold bitch."

"Sticks and stones will break your bones, but failure will get you killed. Call me, Jacob, make it soon." I hung up the phone.

11

"I SEE WHAT you mean about you being practical," Micah said. He was standing quietly watching me, face carefully neutral, but he couldn't quite keep everything off his face. He was pleased. Pleased with me, I think.

"You not going to run screaming because I'm a bloodthirsty sociopath?"

He smiled, and again his long lashes came down over his eyes. "I don't think you're a sociopath, Anita. I think you do what needs doing to protect your pard." He raised that yellow-green gaze to me. "I find that admirable, not something to criticize."

I sighed. "Good that someone approves."

He smiled, and it was that mixture of condescension, happiness, and sorrow, that I'd seen before. A complex smile, that. "The Ulfric means well."

"You know what they say about good intentions, Micah. If he's determined to take himself to hell, fine. But he has no right to drag the rest of us along with him."

"I agree."

It made me tired that Micah agreed with me. I wasn't in love with him. Why couldn't it be Richard who agreed with me? Of course, there was someone else. I needed to get to Jean-Claude while it was still dark.

"I had to put off the shower, first to be a gentleman, and let you go first, then so the noise wouldn't interrupt your phone call. I need to get clean now, if you don't mind."

"I'll give you some privacy." I turned towards the door.

"It wasn't privacy I was asking for, just explaining why I was turning the water on during our conversation," he said.

That turned me around at the door. "What conversation?"

He turned on the shower, testing the water with his hand, adjusting the heat, talking over his shoulder. "I've never felt another Nimir-Ra with the kind of power you put off. It was amazing."

"Glad you enjoyed it, but I've really got to go."

He turned to face me, stepping back into the water, throwing his head back for a second to wet his hair. The water hit his neck and he let out a hissing breath, bending over at the shoulders like it really hurt.

I went back into the room. "Are you alright?"

He nodded and stopped in mid-motion. "I will be."

I was close enough that when he raised his head I could see the water beaded on his face, clinging in thick drops to his lashes. I stood to one side, getting sprayed with just the faintest mist of the water. I got my first good look at the side of his neck. "Shit." I reached through the water to touch his face, turned him slowly so I could see the bite.

He had a perfect imprint of my teeth in the right side of his neck. The wound was still seeping blood, so the circle of toothmarks was filled with crimson. The tanned flesh of his neck was already bruising, dark colors swirling to the surface of his skin.

"God, Micah, I'm sorry."

"Don't be sorry, it is a love bite."

I dropped my hand from his face. "Yeah, right, it looks like I tried to eat your throat out." I frowned. "Why hasn't it started healing?"

"Wounds made by the teeth and claws of another lycanthrope heal slower than most, not as slow as silver, but slower than say, steel."

"I am sorry."

"And I said, don't be sorry."

"The last Ulfric I bit like this—and it wasn't nearly this bad, I didn't even break the skin—he considered it an insult. He said, it meant I considered myself higher in the pack than he was."

"We are not wolves. To the pard a wound on the neck from a Nimir-Ra is a sign that the sex was good."

That made me blush.

"I didn't mean to embarrass you, just to explain that you don't owe me an apology. I enjoyed it."

I blushed harder.

"Together we could do great things for our pard."

I shook my head. "We won't know for sure that I'm going to be Nimir-Ra for a few days. Let's take it slow until then."

"If you want to." His gaze was too direct, and I was suddenly aware that he was nude in a shower. I was getting better at ignoring, or at least not being bothered, around nudity. But there were moments when you had to be aware of it, when the look in the other person's eyes made you aware of it.

"I want to," I said.

He turned his back, lowering his head so the water beat on his shoulders, back, lower things. The spray widened as he moved through it, spattering on my face, shoulders, arms, legs, across the towel. It was time for me to leave, past time.

I was at the door again when he called after me. "Anita."

I turned back.

He was standing facing me, rubbing liquid soap from one of the wall dispensers on his body. He was doing his arms as I turned around, lathering his chest as he talked. "If you want us to go with you tomorrow, we would be honored."

"I can't let you drag your pard into our mess."

His hands slid downward, trailing white suds over his stomach, his hips, then slid between his legs, working the soap over himself. I knew from my own experience of getting the stuff off me that you had to scrub more where it had touched you, but his hands stayed, until he was slick, thick with bubbles, and partially erect by the time his hands slid to his thighs.

My mouth was dry, and I realized we hadn't said anything in several minutes. I'd just been watching him spread soap on himself. The thought brought heat in a rush up my face. Micah continued to soap his legs slowly, taking more time with each movement than he needed to. He was definitely doing it for my benefit. I needed to leave.

"If you are my Nimir-Ra, then your mess is my mess," he said, head still bent over his legs, face hidden from me, so that all I could see was the line of his body as he stood in the aisle, away from the water so the soap wouldn't rub off.

I had to clear my throat to say, "I don't want to pick out curtains, Micah."

"The power between us is enough that I'll agree to any arrangement you want." He stood up then, stretching his arm back to soap his shoulders. It made him stretch the front of his body in a long line, and I was painfully aware of him. I turned, really meaning to go out the door this time.

"Anita," he said.

I stopped in the doorway, but this time I didn't turn around. "What?" I sounded grumpy.

"It's alright to be attracted to me. You can't help yourself."

That made me laugh, a good normal laugh. "Oh, you don't have a high opinion of yourself, do you?" But I stayed facing away from him.

"It's not a high opinion of myself. You are a Nimir-Ra, and I am the first Nimir-Raj that you've ever met. Our power, our beasts are attracted to each other. We're *meant* to be attracted to each other."

I turned then, slowly, trying for eye contact and failing. He was turned away with the back of his body facing me. He was still spreading soap over his shoulders. The suds slid slowly down his skin towards his slim waist.

"We don't know yet that I'm a were-anything." My voice was breathy.

He managed to reach his entire back, his arms moving effortlessly over his skin, hands smoothing over the tightness of his buttocks. "You feel the call of my body, as I feel yours."

My pulse was beating way too hard. "You're an attractive man, naked, covered in soap. I'm human, so sue me."

He turned around, still soaped and slick. And he was huge.

My mouth went dry. My body tightened so hard and so suddenly, it almost hurt. It deepened my breathing, made me have to swallow my pulse.

"You're *not* human, that's the difference. That's why you keep looking even when you don't want to." He walked towards me, slowly, moving like all leopards could move when they wanted to. Like he had muscles in places that humans didn't. He glided towards me like some great, slinking cat, his nude body glistening with suds and water, his hair plastered in ringlets to his shoulders, around his face. Those huge yellow green eyes suddenly looked perfectly at home in his face.

"You don't understand yet how rare it is for two lycanthropes to share their beasts as we did." He was almost in front of me now. "They flowed in and out of our bodies." He stood there, not touching, not yet. "They were like two great cats, rubbing their furred sides against each other." He ran his hands slick with soap up my bare arms as he said it. I had to close my eyes. He was describing exactly how it had felt, as if he had read my mind, or had felt exactly the same thing.

His hands slid up my arms to my shoulders, to my neck, spreading slick and wet across my skin. His soapy hands cupped my face, and I felt his face moving towards mine before his lips touched me. The kiss was gentle, his body carefully not touching me.

He slid his fingers into the edge of the towel, gripping the cloth, pulling me forward. It made me open my eyes. It took a few steps to realize he was leading me towards the water.

"You'll need to wash the soap off," he said.

I was shaking my head, and finally stopped moving with him. He kept pulling on the towel and it unwrapped, starting to slide down my body. I grabbed it, holding it just below my suddenly bare breasts.

"No," I said, my voice strangled, but I repeated it. "No."

He stepped into me, pressing the slick hardness of him against my lower hand and arm. He tried to uncurl my fingers from the towel, and I held on for dear life. "Touch me, Anita, cup me in your hands."

"No."

"I know you want to. I can smell it," and he moved his face above my skin, drawing his breath in and out against my wet skin. "I can feel it." He rubbed his hands up my arms again, over my shoulders, down towards my breasts, but stopped without touching them. "I can taste it." He licked a slow line along the edge of my cheek. I shivered and wanted to step back, but it was like I was frozen in place. I couldn't move.

I found my voice, shaky, but mine. My hands clutched to my body, because I knew if I touched him we were in trouble. "This isn't like me, Micah. I'm not like this. You're a stranger. I don't do strangers."

"I'm not a stranger. I'm your Nimir-Raj, and you are my Nimir-Ra. We could never be strangers."

He kissed his way down my face to my neck, biting gently at me, and it made my knees weak. He came back up to my lips, and when he kissed me I could taste the soap from my skin. The feel of him pressed against the front of my body, close enough that if I opened my hand I'd be able to hold him, was overwhelming. I realized it was more than just sex. I wanted to feed off of him again, not with my teeth but with my body. I wanted to drink in the energy of him through my skin, my bare skin pressed to his. I wanted it so badly. His hands slid over my breasts, covering them in soap, making them slick, the nipples already tight and hard. My arms slid around his waist, using the pressure of our bodies to keep the towel in place. He moved against my body, and his chest was so slick, so smooth rubbing against my breasts.

He began to walk backwards with his arms locked behind me, moving us back towards the water. My hands moved over the slick hardness of his back, sliding dangerously lower. It was as if I wanted to press every inch of myself to him, to roll his body around me like a sheet and drink him in through the pores of my skin.

I opened that link with Jean-Claude and found him sitting, waiting, patient. I called for help, and distantly I heard his voice in my head. "It is all I can do, *ma petite*, to control my own appetites, you must control your own."

"What's happening to me?" Even as I asked, Micah moved his body that fraction away that allowed the towel to slide down, and when he quickly moved back, he was pressed against my groin and stomach, and it was déjà vu enough to draw a small sound out of my throat.

Jean-Claude looked up, and I knew that he saw what was happening with Micah, that with a thought he could feel what was happening, as if it were his hands sliding down the slick, soaped skin. My hand slid over the thick hardness of

Micah. He half-collapsed against me, as I caressed him, and I knew that it hadn't been my idea to touch him. Jean-Claude had wanted to know what it felt like. He drew away enough for me to move my hand, but the damage had been done. Micah dragged me into the water, surer now than ever that I would say yes.

Jean-Claude's voice in my head. "You can feed off his lust, but the price for that is that you will crave his lust, his sex. It is the double-edged sword of being incubus. The sword edge I have walked for centuries."

"Help me!"

"I cannot. You must ride this thing yourself. And you will either conquer it, or be conquered. You felt what happened when I interfered just now. Because I have denied myself feeding through my body. I knew you would not approve, so I denied myself. And being inside your body while you touch him, while you feed, would be my undoing. I crave you more than you will ever crave the man in your arms. I have wanted to take your body in the way that only I could take it. To feed from your sex, not from a vein. But I knew that would frighten you more than blood."

Micah turned me towards the wall, putting my hands up against the tile, pressing his body against my back. Jean-Claude's voice was soft in my head, more intimate than Micah's touch. "I did not know you would gain this demon from me, *ma petite*, and nothing I can say will convince you of that. I know that. I await you here, until you have wrestled the demon, whatever the outcome." And he shielded from me, hid himself away so he would not feel what was happening, left me alone to make my choice, if I was still capable of choosing.

I found I did have a voice and said, "Micah, stop, please stop."

Micah licked the back of my neck, and I shuddered, pressed against the wet wall.

"Please, Micah, I'm not on birth control." A clear thought at last.

He bit softly at the back of my neck. "I had myself fixed two years ago. You're safe with me, Anita."

"Please, Micah, please don't."

He bit harder, just this side of drawing blood, and my body went passive, calm. It was as if he'd hit a switch I didn't know I had. When he pressed himself inside me, he was slick, and I knew that sometime when I'd been paying attention to Jean-Claude inside my head, he'd spread more soap on himself, allowing that thick hardness to slide more easily inside me.

He pinned me to the wall and slid inside me, one tight inch at a time. It wasn't that he was long so much as he was wide—wide enough that it was just this side of pain to have him work himself inside me, even with the soap.

He pushed until most of him was inside me, and there was a stopping point. Then he began to draw himself out, slowly, so slowly. Then in again, slowly, still having to push himself, to work to make room for himself inside me. I stood pinned against the wall, passive, unmoving. It wasn't like me. I moved during sex. But I didn't want to move, didn't want to stop, and there was no thinking, just the feel of him moving in and out of me. I wasn't as tight now, and the soap had given way to my own wetness, so that he began to move more smoothly in and out of me. He was gentle, but he was so big that even gentle was almost overwhelming. He came to the end of my body before the full shaft of him was inside me. I could feel him bumping against my cervix at the end of each stroke. Most women find having their cervix bumped painful, but some women find it pleasurable. His size was intimidating, but when I realized it didn't hurt, in fact that it felt wonderful, a part of me that was still sane, still keeping track of some safety measures, relaxed and shut down. My last measure of control went away. I didn't want sex. That was just a means to an end. I wanted to feed. I wanted to eat his lust, drink his heat, bathe in his energy. The thought brought a sound low in my throat.

Micah braced himself against the wall, his body pinning mine completely, and began to find a rhythm, still gentle, but quicker. He was being so careful of me, and I didn't want him careful.

I heard a voice that didn't quite sound like mine. "Harder."

His voice came out squeezed tight. "It will hurt if I do it harder."

"Try me."

"No."

"Micah, please, just do it, please. If it hurts I'll tell you. Please." He'd been less controlled in the other room, and I realized why. He truly was afraid of hurting me because he was inside me. When he was just rubbing himself on my body, he hadn't had to worry about damaging me. Now he did. It gave him an edge of control that kept me from feeding. He was a Nimir-Raj, and he had enough power to keep me out. Unless he let down his guard. To do that he had to lose more control than this.

Even as I thought it, a part of me was swimming to the surface. I could think again, at least a little. I didn't want to do this. I didn't want to feed off of him. It was wrong, in so many ways it was wrong. I started to say, "Micah, stop, I can't do this." I got as far as, "Micah . . ." and he took me at my word. He thrust into me so hard and fast it tore a scream from my throat and brought that new part of me that was Jean-Claude's hunger in a raging wave of heat that rode my body and spilled out my mouth.

He'd stopped. "Are you alright?"

"Don't stop. Don't stop!"

He never asked again. He drove himself inside me so fast and hard that it left me gasping, unable to catch my breath. Small, helpless noises fell from my lips, spaced with the words, "Oh, God, yes, yes, Micah!" Every time he thrust as far as he could, smashing himself inside me, it rode that fine line between overwhelming pleasure and pain. And just as the pleasure began to turn to pain, he'd withdraw, and I'd be able to breathe again. Then he'd thrust himself inside me again, and it would start all over.

It felt like he filled me up as if I were a cup, until there was nothing inside me but the feel of his body, the feel of his flesh pounding into mine. It was tight, thick, like he'd plugged a hole with his body, and would never let it go. That sense of fullness inside me grew, grew, and spilled over me, through me, inside me, and tore out of my mouth in ragged, frantic screams, as my body spasmed around him. And it was only then that his control slipped away, letting me know that he had still been gentle. His control went when he did, and I drank him into me, through his chest pressed to my back, his hips thrusting against my butt. I drank him in, as he exploded inside me. I fed on him, drew him inside every pore of my skin, until it was as if our skins gave way and we spilled into each other, became for one shining moment one thing, one beast. And I could feel his beast inside mine, as if they were coupling within our bodies as our human shells merged. In that moment, I didn't doubt that I was truly his Nimir-Ra.

When we were finished and had slid to the floor, him still inside me, his arms hugging me to the front of his body, I started to cry. He was afraid he'd hurt me, but that wasn't it. I couldn't explain the tears to him, because I didn't want to say it out loud. But I knew. I'd tried not to be one of the monsters for so long, and now, in one fell swoop I was them, both of them. You couldn't be a bloodsucking vampire and be a lycanthrope at the same time. They canceled each other out as a disease or a curse. But I had felt my beast curl around Micah's. I had felt it like an embryo in a safe warm place, waiting. And I had fed off of him as surely as any vampire. I'd always thought I'd have to drink blood to be one of them. But I had been wrong, wrong about so many things. I let Micah hold me. I felt his heart pounding against my back and wept.

12

NATHANIEL DROVE BECAUSE I was too shaky to concentrate. I was functioning, moving forward, solving the problems one at a time, but it was as if the very ground I walked on, the air I breathed was precarious and new. As if everything had changed, because I had changed. I knew better. I knew that no matter how bad you feel, or what horrible thing happens to you, that the world just keeps on going. That the rest of the world doesn't even realize that the monsters are eating your heart. A long time ago it use to bother me that I could be in such confusion, such pain, and the world just didn't give a shit. The world, the creation as a whole, is designed to move forward, to keep on keeping on without any one individual person. It feels damned impersonal, and it is. But, then, if the world stopped rotating just because one of us was having a bad day, we'd all be floating out in space.

So I huddled in the passenger seat of my Jeep in the late darkness and knew that only I had changed. But it was just such a big change that it felt like the world should have changed its orbit, just a little.

June was back to its normal hot, sticky self. Nathaniel wore a ribbed tank top and silky jogging shorts. He'd tied his nearly ankle-length hair in a loose braid that curled on the seat beside his thigh. He'd found that if he let his hair fall onto the floorboard, sometimes it tangled around the pedals. He had to watch the gear shift between the seats, too. I'd never had hair that long.

Nathaniel had only had his driver's license for a few months, even though he was twenty. Gabriel, their old alpha, had not encouraged them to be independent. I sort of demanded it of them, as far as they were able. At first Nathaniel had been lost when I started to demand that he decide things for himself, but lately, he'd been doing better. It made me hopeful, and I needed some hope right now.

He'd picked out the clothes that he'd brought to the makeshift hospital for me. Black jeans, royal blue scoop neck T-shirt, a black bra that fit low enough to accommodate the low neckline, matching undies, black jogging socks, black Nikes, a short-sleeved black shirt to cover the shoulder rig with the Browning Hi-Power. People kept urging me to go shopping for a new main gun. They were probably right. There was probably something out there that would fit my hand better than the Browning. But I'd been putting it off. The Browning was like a piece of me. I felt incomplete without it, like I was missing a hand. It was going to take something more than a smaller grip to convince me to switch guns. So, for now, it was still me and the Browning.

Nathaniel had also brought my wrist sheaths and the matching silver knives. I was going to leave them in the car since the shirt was short-sleeved. They were a little too aggressive to wear into the police station. I had just replaced the back sheath I had ruined in New Mexico. It had been a special order, and it had cost mucho extra dinero to get a rush job on it, but it had been worth it. There really wasn't anywhere else on my body that I could carry a blade that large and still be able to sit down, without the hilt showing.

We drove in silence. Nathaniel hadn't even turned the radio on, which he liked to do. He rarely moved in silence if he could have music for background. But tonight he let the silence seep into the Jeep.

I finally asked a question I'd been wanting an answer for. "Who put the derringer in my robe pocket?" The derringer was in the glove compartment.

"I did."

"Thanks."

"The two things that you always do first is get dressed and get armed." His smile flashed in an instant of street light. "I'm not sure which is your highest priority."

I had to smile. "I'm not sure either."

"How are you doing?" His voice was very careful when he asked it, quiet in the rushing silence of the car.

"I don't want to talk about it."

"Okay." He was one of the few people that would actually take me at my word and not press. If I told Nathaniel I didn't want to talk, we didn't talk. The silence between us was no longer strained. In fact, silence with Nathaniel was one of the most relaxing sounds of my day.

Nathaniel parked the Jeep and we got out. I had my executioner's license with me, and most people knew me on sight. It occurred to me that they thought I was dead. As we walked towards the door, I realized I should probably have called ahead and given them a heads up, but it was too late now. I was a yard from the door. I wasn't using the cell phone now.

I was a familiar enough sight that I could usually just wave as I went past the desk, but tonight the officer's eyes got big as he waved me on to the left so I didn't have to go through the metal detector. But he was picking up a phone as he did it. I was betting he was calling ahead. You don't see people rise from the dead every night. Well, I guess *I* do, but most cops don't.

I was up the stairs leading to RPIT's headquarters when Detective Clive Perry opened the door and started down the stairs. He was slender, handsome, African-American, and the most unfailingly polite person I'd ever met. He actually missed the step and had to catch himself on the railing. Even then he leaned against the wall like his legs weren't working quite right. He looked shocked—no, scared.

"Anita." His voice was breathy. It was probably the second time in all the years we'd known each other that he had used my first name. It was usually Ms. Blake.

I responded in kind, smiling. "Clive, it's good to see you."

His eyes flicked from me to Nathaniel, then back to me. "You're supposed to be . . ." He straightened on the stairs. "I mean, we heard . . ." I watched him visibly try to rally. By the time we reached the step he was on, he looked almost normal. But his next question wasn't normal. "Did you die?"

I smiled, then felt the smile fade as I stared into his eyes. He was serious. I guess I did raise the dead for a living, so the question wasn't as ridiculous as it sounded, but I was realizing that some of his shock wasn't just from seeing me walking around. It was from his fear of what I was now. He thought I was the walking dead. In some ways he was closer to the mark than was comfortable, in others he was so far off.

"No, Clive, I didn't die."

He nodded, but there was a tightness around his eyes that made me wonder, if I tried to touch his arm, would he flinch? I didn't want to find out, so Nathaniel and I just walked past him, leaving him alone on the stairs.

I pushed into the squad room with its crowded desks and the busy clatter of people. RPIT had some of its busiest hours after three A.M. The noise died gradually like fading water rings, going out into the room, until I moved in silence between the desks and the staring faces. Nathaniel stayed at my back, moving like an attractive shadow.

I finally said, loud enough to carry through the room, "The rumors of my death are greatly exaggerated." And the room exploded into noise. I was suddenly surrounded by men, and a few women, hugging me, slapping me on the back, pumping my hand. Smiling faces, relieved eyes. No one else showed the reservations that Clive Perry had shown on the stairs, and it made me wonder about his religious background, or his metaphysical one. He wasn't a sensitive, but that didn't mean he hadn't grown up around people who were.

It was Zerbrowski who picked me completely off the ground in a huge bear hug. He's only five eight, and not that big, but he spun me around the room, finally putting me down, laughing and a little unsteady on my feet. "Damn, Anita, damn, I thought we were never going to see you come through that door again." He pushed a tangle of dark curls that were beginning to streak with gray from his forehead. He needed a haircut, but then he usually did. His clothes were the usual mismatch, as if he'd chosen his tie and shirt in the dark. He dressed like he was either color-blind or didn't give a shit. I was betting on the latter.

"It's good to see you, too. I hear you're actually holding someone on suspicion of having killed me."

His smile faded around the edges. "Yeah, Count Dracula's in a cell."

"Can you get him out, because as you see, I am very much alive."

Zerbrowski's eyes narrowed. "I saw the pictures, Anita. You were covered in blood."

I shrugged.

His eyes became cool, suspicious cop eyes. "It's been what, four nights? You're looking positively spry for suffering that much blood loss."

I could feel my own face grow neutral, distant, as cool and unreadable as any cop's. "Can you get Jean-Claude out and ready to go? I'd like to take him home before it gets light."

"Dolph's going to want to talk to you before you leave."

"I thought he might. Can you please start processing Jean-Claude while I talk to Dolph?"

"You going to take him to your house?"

"I'm going to drop him off at his place, not that it's any of your business. You're my friend, Zerbrowski, not my dad."

"I've never wanted to be your dad, Anita. That's Dolph's delusion, not mine."

I sighed. "Yeah." I looked up at Zerbrowski. "Will you please get Jean-Claude ready to go?"

He looked at me for a second or two, then nodded. "Okay." He looked past me to Nathaniel, who had moved to the side of the room to let the great reunion take place. "Who's that?"

"Nathaniel, a friend."

He looked back at me. "A little young, isn't he?"

"He's only six years younger than I am, Zerbrowski, but he drove me tonight, so I wouldn't have to."

His eyes looked worried. "You okay?"

"A little shaky, but it'll pass."

He touched my face, staring into my eyes, trying to read them, I think. "I'd like to know what the hell is going on with you."

I met his gaze, face, eyes blank. "So would I."

That seemed to surprise him, because he blinked and dropped his hand. "I'll get Count Dracula out of hock, you go talk to Dolph."

My shoulders hunched a little, and I had to concentrate to square them. I was not looking forward to talking with Dolph. Zerbrowski went to get Jean-Claude, and I left Nathaniel talking to a nice-enough seeming police woman and went to Dolph's office.

He was standing in the doorway like a small mountain. He's six eight and built like a pro wrestler. His dark hair was cut very short, leaving his ears stranded and bare. His suit looked pressed, tie neatly knotted. He'd probably already been on the job for nearly an eight-hour shift, but he still looked fresh out of the box.

His eyes were very careful when they looked at me. "I'm glad you're alive."

"Thanks, me, too."

He waved a hand and walked me down the hallway away from the office, away from the desks, towards the interrogation rooms. I guess he wanted privacy. Privacy that even the glass windows of his office wouldn't give him. It made my stomach tight and a little trickle of fear go through me. I wasn't afraid of Dolph the way I was afraid of a rogue shapeshifter or a vamp I had to kill. He wouldn't hurt me physically. But I was afraid of the tight set of his shoulders, the cautious, cold look of his eyes when he glanced back to make sure I was following.

I could feel how angry he was, almost like the energy off a shapeshifter. What had I done to deserve such rage?

Dolph held the door for me, and I squeezed past his bulk. "Have a seat," he said, as he closed the door behind us.

"I'll stand, thanks. I want to get Jean-Claude out of here before dawn."

"I heard you weren't dating him anymore," Dolph said.

"He's being held without charge on suspicion of killing me. I'm not dead, so I'd like to get him out of here."

Dolph just looked at me, eyes as cold and unreadable as if he were looking at a witness—no a suspect—that he didn't like much.

"Jean-Claude has a damn fine lawyer. How'd you keep him for over seventy-two hours without a charge?" I asked.

"You're a city treasure. I told everyone he'd killed you, and they helped me lose him for a while."

"Damn, Dolph, you're lucky some overzealous officer didn't put him in a cell with a window."

"Yeah, too bad."

I just stared at him not even sure what to say. "I'm alive, Dolph. He didn't hurt me."

"Who did?"

It was my turn to give *him* cool cop eyes.

He walked up to me, towering over me. He wasn't trying to intimidate me with his height; he knew that didn't work anyway. He was just that big. He touched my chin, tried to turn my face to the side. I jerked away.

"You've got scars on your neck that you didn't have a week ago. They're all shiny and nearly healed. How?"

"Would you believe I'm not sure?"

"No."

"Suit yourself."

"Let me see the scars."

I swept my hair to one side and let him trace one large finger down the healed wounds.

"I want to see the rest of the wounds."

"Don't we need a female officer in here for this?"

"Do you really want anyone else to see them?"

He had a point. "Why do you want to see, Dolph?"

"I can't force you to show me, but I need to see them."

"Why?"

"I don't know," he said, and his voice showed strain for the first time.

I shed the outer shirt and laid it on the table. I held my left arm out to him, pushing the sleeve of the T-shirt up.

He traced his finger over the marks. "What is it about your left arm? It's always where you get hit the most."

"I think it's because I'm right-handed. I'll let them chew on my left arm, while I grab a weapon with my right."

"Did you kill what did this to you?"

"No."

He looked at me, and the anger showed for a second. "I wish I believed you."

"Me, too, especially since I'm telling the truth."

"Who, or what, did this to you, Anita?"

I shook my head. "It's been taken care of."

"Damn it, Anita, how can I trust you when you won't talk to me?"

I shrugged.

"Is the arm all of it?"

"Almost."

"I want to see all of it."

There were a lot of men in my life that I'd have accused of just wanting to get my shirt off, but Dolph wasn't one of them. There'd never been that kind of tension between us. I stared at him, hoping he'd back down, but he didn't. I should have known he wouldn't.

I worked the shirt out of my pants and exposed my bra. I had to raise the edge of the underwire to show the round hole—now scar—over my heart.

He touched it like he had all the others, shaking his head. "It's like something tried to scoop your heart out." He raised his eyes to my face. "How the hell did you heal it, Anita?"

"Can I get dressed?"

There was a knock at the door, and Zerbrowski entered without waiting to be asked, while I was still struggling to get my breasts back behind the underwire. His eyes widened. "Am I interrupting?"

"We're finished," I said.

"Gee, and I thought Dolph would have more staying power."

We both glared at him. He grinned. "Count Dracula is processed and ready to go."

"His name is Jean-Claude."

"Whatever you say."

I had to bend over and rearrange my breasts so the bra would fit right again. Those underwires hurt if they ride up. They both watched me do it, and I stubbornly wouldn't turn away. Zerbrowski watched because he was a cheerful lech, Dolph, because he was angry.

"Would you take a blood test?" he asked.

"No."

"We can get a court order."

"On what grounds? I haven't done anything wrong, Dolph, except show up here not dead. If I didn't know better, I'd say you were disappointed."

"I'm glad you're alive," he said.

"But sorry you can't bust Jean-Claude's ass. Is that it?"

He looked away. I'd finally hit on it. "That's it, isn't it? You're sorry that you can't arrest Jean-Claude—get him executed. He didn't kill me, Dolph. Why do you want him dead?"

"He's already dead, Anita. He just doesn't know enough to lie down."

"Is that a threat?"

Dolph made a low exasperated sound. "He's a walking corpse, Anita."

"I know what Jean-Claude is, Dolph, probably better than you do."

"So I keep hearing," he said.

"What, you're angry because I'm dating him? You are not my father, Dolph. I can date who—or what—I want to date."

"How can you let him touch you?" And the anger was there again, rage.

"You want him dead because he's been my lover?" I couldn't keep the surprise out of my voice.

He wouldn't meet my eyes.

"You're not jealous of me, Dolph, I know that for a fact. It just bothers you that he's not human, is that it?"

"He's a vampire, Anita." He met my gaze then. "How can you fuck a corpse?"

The level of animosity was too personal, too intimate. And then it hit me. "What woman in your life is fucking the undead, Dolph?"

He took a step towards me, his entire body trembling, his huge hands balled into fists. The rage rushed up his face in a near purple wave. He spoke through gritted teeth. "Get out!"

I wanted to say something to make it better, but there was nothing to say. I moved carefully past him, keeping my eyes on him, afraid he'd make a grab for me. But he just stood there regaining control of himself. Zerbrowski walked me out and closed the door behind us.

If I'd been with another woman, we'd have talked about what just happened.

If I'd been with a lot of men in a different line of work, we'd have talked about it. But Zerbrowski was a cop. And that meant you didn't talk about the personal stuff. If you accidentally learned something truly painful, truly private, you left it the fuck alone—unless the man involved wanted to talk about it. Besides, I didn't know what to say. I didn't want to know that Dolph's wife was cheating on him with a corpse. He had two sons, no daughters, so who else could it be?

Zerbrowski walked me through the squad room in silence. A man turned as we entered the room. He was tall, dark-haired, with gray starting at the temples. The clean, strong lines of his face were beginning to soften around the edges, but it was still a handsome face in a manly man, Marlboro sort of way. He looked vaguely familiar. But it wasn't until he turned his head, exposing the claw scars on the side of his neck, that I recognized him. Orlando King had been one of the premiere bounty hunters in the country until a rogue shapeshifter had nearly killed him. The stories could never agree on what animal did it; some said wolf, others bear or leopard. The story had grown in the telling until I doubt anyone but King himself knew the truth. King and the shapeshifters that had nearly killed him, if they hadn't all died in the attempt, that is. He had a rep that he never lost a bounty, never stopped until his creature was dead. He earned good money lecturing across the country and in other countries. For his finale he'd take his shirt off and show his scars. It smacked a little too much of circus sideshow for my taste, but, hey, it wasn't my body. He also did some consulting with the police.

"Anita Blake, this is Orlando King," Zerbrowski said. "We brought him in to help convict Count Dracula of your murder."

I glared at Zerbrowski, who only smiled wider. He'd keep calling Jean-Claude by his pet names until it stopped getting a rise out of me. The quicker I ignored it the better.

"Ms. Blake," Orlando King said in the deep rolling voice that I remembered from his lectures, "so good to see you alive."

"It's good to be alive, Mr. King. Last I heard you were lecturing on the West Coast. I hope you didn't interrupt your tour to come solve my murder."

He shrugged, and there was something about the way he moved his shoulders that made him seem taller, broader than he was. "There are so few of us that truly pit ourselves against the monsters, how could I *not* come?"

"I'm flattered," I said. "I've heard you lecture."

"You came up and spoke to me afterwards," he said.

"I'm flattered again. You must meet thousands of people a year."

He smiled and touched my left arm, ever so lightly. "But not many with scars to rival mine. And none half so pretty in this line of business."

"Thanks." He was at least two generations removed from me, so I figured his complimenting me wasn't so much flirting as habit.

Zerbrowski was grinning at me, and his grin said he didn't think King was simply being polite. I shrugged and ignored it. I've found that if you pretend not to notice that a man is flirting with you, most of them will eventually grow tired and stop.

"It's good to meet you again, Ms. Blake. Especially alive. But I know that you must be in a hurry if you're going to rescue your vampire boyfriend before dawn." There was the faintest hesitation before the word *boyfriend*. I studied his face and found it neutral. There was no condemnation, nothing but a smile and goodwill. After Dolph's little fit, it was kind of nice.

"Thank you for understanding."

"I'd love a chance to talk to you before I leave town," he said.

Again, I wondered if he was flirting, and I said the only thing I could think of. "Compare notes, you mean?"

"Exactly," he said.

I just did not understand my effect on men. I wasn't that attractive—or maybe I just couldn't see it. We shook hands, and he didn't hold my hand any longer than necessary, didn't squeeze it, or any of those funky things men do when they're interested. Maybe I was just getting paranoid where men were concerned.

Zerbrowski led me through the sea of desks to fetch Nathaniel. The police woman, Detective Jessica Arnet, one of the newest members of the squad, was still entertaining Nathaniel at her desk. She was gazing into his lilac eyes as if there was some hypnotic power in them. There wasn't, but Nathaniel *was* a good listener. That's rare enough in men for it to be a bigger selling point than an attractive body.

"Come on, Nathaniel, we've got to go."

He stood instantly but tossed a smile towards Detective Arnet that made her eyes sparkle. Nathaniel's real-life job was as a stripper, so he flirted instinctively. He seemed both aware and unaware of his effect on women. When he concentrated, he understood what he was doing. But when he simply walked into a room and heads turned, he was oblivious.

I touched his arm. "Say good-bye to the nice detectives. We've got to hurry."

He said, "Good-bye, nice detectives." I gave him a small push towards the doors.

Zerbrowski followed us out. I think if Nathaniel hadn't been with us he'd have asked more questions. But he'd never met Nathaniel and wasn't sure of him. So we moved in silence to the Prisoner Processing, where Jean-Claude was sitting on one of the three chairs. Normally the processing area was full of people coming in, going out, and since its the size of a walk-in closet, that makes it seem crowded. The two vending machines took up room, but except for the prisoner processing clerk—the new name since turnkey fell out of fashion—behind his little barred bankteller window, the place was deserted. But it was 3:30 in the morning.

Jean-Claude rose when he saw me; his white shirt was stained, torn on one sleeve. He didn't look like he'd been beaten, or hurt. But he was usually a fanatic about his clothes. Only something drastic would have changed that. A struggle perhaps?

I did not run to him, but I did wrap my arms around him, press my ear to his chest, hold on to him as if he were the last solid thing in the world. He stroked my hair and murmured to me in French. I understood enough to know he was glad to see me and that he thought I looked beautiful. But beyond that it was just pretty noise.

It wasn't until I felt Zerbrowski behind me that I pulled away, but when Jean-Claude's hand found mine, I welcomed it.

Zerbrowski was looking at me as if he'd never seen me before. "What?" It came out hostile.

"I've never seen you be that . . . soft with anyone before."

It startled me. "You've seen me kiss Richard before."

He nodded. "That was lust. This is . . ." He shook his head, glancing up at Jean-Claude, then back to me. "He makes you feel safe."

I realized with a jolt that he was right. "You're smarter than you look, Zerbrowski."

"Katie reads self-help books to me. I just look at the pictures." He touched my right hand. "I'll talk to Dolph."

"I don't think it's going to help," I said.

He shrugged. "If Orlando King can have a conversion experience where the monsters are concerned, anybody can."

"What do you mean?" I asked.

"Have you ever read, or seen, any of his interviews before his accident?" Zerbrowski made little quote marks with his fingers when he said *accident*.

"No. That was before I was interested in the topic, I think."

He frowned at me. "I keep forgetting, you were still in diapers then."

I just shook my head. "So tell me."

"King was one of the shining lights behind trying to get lycanthropes declared nonhuman, so they could be executed just for existing, without a trial. Then he got cut up, and, lo and behold, he mellowed."

"Nearly dying will do that to you, Zerbrowski."

He grinned at me. "It didn't make me a better man." I'd held my hands over his stomach, kept his insides from spilling out, while we waited for an ambulance. It had happened just before Christmas about two years ago. Zerbrowski alive and well had been all I put on my list to Santa that year.

"If Katie couldn't make you a better man, then nothing could," I said.

He grinned wider, then his face sobered. "I'll talk to the boss for you, see if I can get him to mellow without a near-death experience."

I looked up into his serious face. "Just because you saw me hug Jean-Claude?"

"Yeah."

I gave Zerbrowski a quick hug. "Thank you."

He pushed me back towards Jean-Claude. "Better get him under wraps before dawn." He looked past me to the vampire. "Take care of her."

Jean-Claude gave a small bow from his neck. "I will take care of her as much as she allows it."

Zerbrowski laughed. "Oh, he does know you."

We left with Zerbrowski laughing, the clerk staring, and the night growing soft around us. Dawn was coming, and I had so many questions. Nathaniel drove. Jean-Claude and I rode in back.

13

I BUCKLED MY seat belt out of habit, but Jean-Claude stayed pressed to my side, arm around my shoulders. I'd started to shake and couldn't seem to stop. It was as if I'd been waiting for him so I could finally fall apart. I didn't cry, just let him hold me while I shook.

"It is alright, *ma petite*. We are both safe now."

I shook my head against the stained front of his shirt. "It's not that."

He touched my face, raised it to look at him in the soft-lighted darkness of the car. "Then what is it?"

"I had sex with Micah." I watched his face, waited for the anger, jealousy, something to flash through his eyes. What I saw was sympathy, and I didn't understand it.

"You are like a vampire newly risen. Even those of us who will be masters cannot fight our hunger the first night, or the first few nights. It is overwhelming. It is why many vampires feed on their nearest kin when they first rise. It is who they are thinking of in their hearts, and they are drawn to them. It is only with the aid of a master vampire that the hunger can be directed elsewhere."

"You're not angry?" I asked.

He laughed and hugged me. "I thought *you* would be angry with *me* for giving you the *ardeur*, the fire, the burning hunger."

I pushed back enough to see his face. "Why didn't you warn me that I couldn't control it?"

"I never underestimate you, *ma petite*. If anyone I have ever known in all these centuries could have withstood such a test, it was you. So I did not tell you you would fail, because I no longer try to predict what power will do to you, or through you. You are a law unto yourself so much of the time."

"I was . . . helpless. I . . . I didn't want to control it."

"Of course not."

I shook my head. "Is the *ardeur* permanent?"

"I do not know."

"How long until I can control it?"

"A few weeks. But even after you have control, you will have to be careful around those you most lust after. They will make the hunger flare like fire raging in your veins. There is no shame to it."

"So you say."

He held my face between his hands. "*Ma petite*, it has been over four hundred years since I first woke with the *ardeur* raging in me, but I remember. All these years, and I still remember that the cry for flesh was almost worse than the cry for blood."

I held his wrists, pressed his hands against my face. "I'm scared."

"Of course you are. You should be. But I will help you through this. I will be your guide. It may pass away in a few days, or come and go, I simply do not know. But I will help you through it, whatever happens."

Nathaniel pulled into the Circus of the Damned parking lot, beside the back door. It was still dark as we got out, but the air had that soft feel of predawn. You could taste the coming morning on the tip of your tongue.

Jason opened the outer door as if he'd been waiting for us. He probably had. Jean-Claude hurried past him to the door that led to the stairs. We followed, but Jean-Claude called back over his shoulder, "I must shower before dawn." With that he left us, running in a blur of motion. The rest of us walked more sedately down the stairs, able to walk three abreast, because none of us were large people.

"How are you feeling?" Jason asked.

I shrugged. "I'm pretty much healed."

"You look shook."

I shrugged, again.

"Okay, I can take a hint. You don't want to talk about it."

"No, I don't."

Jason glanced around me at Nathaniel. "You staying the night?"

"Am I?" I knew the question was directed at me.

"Sure, you may need to drive me home tomorrow, or rather, later today."

"Yes, I am staying."

"You can bunk with me then. God knows the bed is big enough and doesn't see many visitors."

I glanced at Jason. "Does Jean-Claude limit your social activities?"

He laughed. "No, not exactly, but the women who come down here are vampire freaks. They want to sleep in a bed under the ground at the Circus of the Damned. They don't want me, they want Jean-Claude's pet werewolf."

"I wouldn't think . . ." I stopped myself because I realized it was an insult.

"Go ahead and say it."

"I wouldn't think that you'd be that picky," I said.

"I wasn't when I first got here. But lately I just don't want to be with someone who just wants me so she can brag to her friends that she slept with a shapeshifter, or got to sleep where the vampires sleep. No matter how good it feels for a few minutes, it still makes me feel like they've just come to look at one of the freaks."

I slipped my arm through his, squeezed his arm. "Don't let anybody make you feel like that, Jason. You're not a freak."

He patted my hand. "Look who's talking."

I pulled away from him. "What's that supposed to mean?"

"Nothing, I'm sorry I said it."

"No, I want you to explain it."

He sighed and hurried down the steps, but I was in Nikes and could keep up. Nathaniel followed a few steps behind without saying a word. "Explain it, Jason."

"You hate the monsters. You hate being different."

"That's not true."

"You accept that you're different, but you don't like it."

I opened my mouth to argue with him, but had to stop myself, had to think. Was he right? Was he? Did I hate being different? Did I hate the monsters because they were different? "Maybe you're right."

He looked back at me, eyes wide. "Anita Blake admitting she may be wrong? Gasp!"

I tried to frown at him, but I could feel it held an edge of smile that ruined the effect. "I better get used to being one of the monsters, or so I hear."

His eyes went serious. "Are you really going to be a wereleopard?"

"We'll find out, won't we."

"You okay with it?"

It was my turn to laugh, but it sounded bitter. "No. No I'm not okay with it, but the damage is done. I can't change it."

"Fatalism," he said.

"Practicality," I said.

"Same thing," he said.

"No, it isn't."

Jason looked past me at Nathaniel who treaded softly a few steps behind me. "How do you feel about her being a wereleopard?"

"I think I'll keep my feelings to myself."

"You're happy about it, aren't you?" And there was an edge of hostility in his voice.

"No, I'm not."

"You get to keep her as your Nimir-Ra now."

"Maybe."

"Doesn't that make you happy?"

"Stop it, Jason. Richard's told me his little theory about Gregory marking me on purpose."

"You talked to Richard?" He made it a question.

"Unfortunately."

"You know what's happened, then?"

"About you guys taking Gregory, yeah. I talked to Jacob on the phone even."

Jason looked surprised. "What did you say to him?"

"Gregory dies, Jacob dies."

"Jacob wants to be Ulfric."

"We discussed that, too," I said.

"What did he say?"

"He won't challenge Richard until after the full moon this month. You better give Sylvie a heads up, because that means Jacob has to defeat her within the next two weeks."

"Why is he waiting for the full moon?"

"Because I told him I'd kill him if he didn't."

"You can't undercut Richard's authority like that."

"I don't need to, Jason, he's doing such a good job all on his own."

We were at the bottom of the stairs, the heavy door hanging open where Jean-Claude had rushed through. "Richard is my Ulfric."

"I'm not asking you to bad-mouth him, Jason. He's destroyed his power structure within the pack. It's not something to debate, it's just the truth."

Jason stopped me at the door. "Maybe if you had been here, you could have talked him out of it."

I was finally angry. "One, you have no right to question what I do, or don't do. Two, Richard is a big boy and makes his own decisions. Three, don't you ever, *ever* question me again."

"You're not my lupa anymore, Anita."

Anger flared through me like a scalding wave, tightening my shoulders, my arms, spilling into my hands. I'd never felt rage so quickly and so completely. I had to close my eyes to concentrate, so I wouldn't take a swing at him. What was wrong with me?

I felt Nathaniel at my back. "Are you alright?" he said.

I shook my head. "I don't think so."

"Look," Jason said, "I'm sorry, but I don't want Jacob in charge of the pack. I don't trust him. Richard may be a bleeding-heart, flag-waving right-winger, but he's also fair, and he really does try to put the best interests of the pack before his own. I don't want to lose that."

I looked at him, trying to swallow past the anger. My voice came out squeezed tight. "You're scared about what will happen to all of you if Jacob takes over."

He nodded. "Yes."

"Me, too," I said.

He looked into my face, studied it. "If Jacob kills Richard in a fair fight, what will you do?"

"Richard isn't my boyfriend anymore, and I'm not lupa. If it's a fair challenge fight, then I can't interfere. I told Jacob if the fight was fair, and after the full moon, I wouldn't take revenge on him."

"You won't avenge Richard's death?"

"If I kill Jacob, and Richard and Sylvie are already dead, who'll take over? I've seen what happens to a group of shapeshifters who don't have an alpha to lead them. I won't let what happened to the leopards happen to the wolves."

"If Jacob died before he fought Sylvie, then you wouldn't have to worry about it," Jason said.

The anger that had been leaking away made a comeback. "You can't have it both ways, Jason. Either I'm not your lupa—not dominant to you—and thus can't help you fix this, or I *am* still your lupa, still dominant to you, still someone you come to for this kind of help. Make up your mind which you want me to be before you get up in my face again."

"You can't be lupa, the pack voted you out. But you're right, it's not your fault. You had to try and fix yourself before you could fix anyone else. I'm sorry I got in your face."

"Apology accepted," I said. I started to go around him through the door, but he caught my arm.

"I didn't ask you to kill Jacob because you were my lupa, or dominant to me. I asked you because I know you've already thought of it. I asked you because I know if you think it's best for the pack, you'll do it."

"Pack business is no longer my concern, so everyone keeps telling me."

"They don't know you like I do," he said.

I pulled away from him, gently. "What's that supposed to mean?"

"It means that once you've given your friendship—your protection—to someone, you take care of them, even if they don't want you to."

"If I kill Jacob, Richard will never forgive me."

"He dumped you, right? What have you got to lose by killing Jacob? Nothing. But if you don't kill him, then you lose Sylvie and Richard."

I pushed past him. "I am getting really tired of doing everyone's dirty work."

"No one is better at dirty work than you are, Anita."

That stopped me, made me turn back around to face him. "What's *that* supposed to mean?"

"It doesn't mean anything. It's just the truth." I stared into his so-solemn eyes. I would have liked to argue, but I really couldn't.

I'd thought I couldn't feel worse about myself tonight. I'd been wrong. Watching the look in Jason's eyes, hearing him talk about me like that, made me feel worse. This night just couldn't get any more depressing.

14

DAWN WAS MINUTES away when Jean-Claude came through the door in a robe. "You may have the bed, *ma petite*, and I will take my coffin. I think your nerves are raw enough without me dying in your arms as the sun rises."

I'd have liked to argue, because I wanted him to hold me in the worst way, but he was right. I'd had enough shocks for one night. "Nathaniel will stay with me," I said.

A look passed over Jean-Claude's face. "And Jason, as well."

"Why?"

"I do not have the time to explain, *ma petite*, but please trust me that Jason should be here, too. It is for the best."

I could feel dawn trembling close, even so deep underground. "Okay, Jason can stay, too."

Jean-Claude was already edging out the door. "I will tell him on my way to the coffin room. I am sorry to leave you like this, *ma petite*."

"Go, it's almost dawn," I said.

He blew me a kiss then was gone, leaving the door slightly ajar. Nathaniel was sitting on the corner of the bed, neutral in face, eyes, even body language. He was very good at seeming nonthreatening, soothing almost.

I'd been sleeping off and on for almost four days, yet I was tired, unbelievably tired. I wasn't sure it was physical, more like I'd overused my mind, my emotions. I was wrung out. "Let's get some sleep."

He pulled off his tank top without another word, kicked off his shoes, pulled off his socks, and began to unbraid his hair. I knew that would take a while, so I went into the bathroom while he finished. It had been a long time since I'd seen Jean-Claude's bathroom, with its fancy black tub that was big enough for a small orgy. The silver swan that the water came out of always reminded me of a fountain. But no bath tonight. I just wanted to sleep and to forget. Forget everything.

Of course, I hadn't come away with jammies, and the shirt that Nathaniel had picked for me, though attractive and comfortable, was not long enough to be a sleep shirt. I could not sleep in jeans; it just wasn't comfortable. Damn, why should the small things be so important on a night when all the big things had gone to hell?

There was a knock on the bathroom door. "I'll be out in a minute, Nathaniel."

"It's Jason."

"What do you want?"

"Didn't Jean-Claude tell you that I was bunking with you tonight?"

"He mentioned it."

"He also sent me with pajamas for you. He figured you didn't pack an overnight case."

That got me to the door, and opening it. Jason stood there in a pair of blue silk boxers, baggy enough to be acceptable as sleepwear. Acceptable for him to wear while sharing a bed with me, I might add. Jason, left to his own devices, wore men's bikini underwear—or less—to bed.

He held out a folded piece of red satin. I took it and let it spill through my hands. It was actually two pieces, a loose top with spaghetti straps and a pair of shorts. It was obviously meant to be lingerie.

"He said to tell you that, of anything he had that would fit you, it covered the most, end quote," Jason said.

I sighed. "Thanks, Jason, I'll be right out." I closed the door without waiting for a reply. The top that had looked loose actually clung pretty tightly across my breasts. You'd certainly know whether I was cold or not. The shorts were cut so high on the sides that the legs almost met the waistband. It managed to cover everything and still not leave much to the imagination. Lingerie design at its best, I suppose.

I opened the door and turned off the bathroom light as I came out. Jason was already tucked into the covers on the right side of the bed. Nathaniel was still sitting on the other side. He got up as I came out, his unbound hair floating around him like a living curtain. "My turn," he said softly, turning on the bathroom light and closing the door.

"You look wonderful," Jason said.

"No compliments, Jason. I'm uncomfortable enough in the lingerie."

"Then by all means take it off."

I frowned at him.

He patted the bed beside him, grinning at me. "Come to bed."

"Piss me off enough and I'll send you back to your room."

"Jean-Claude told me to stay here today."

"I could insist." I had my gun on top of my folded clothes, tucked under one arm.

"If you'd shoot me just for teasing you, I'd have been dead a long time ago."

"Please, Jason, I have had a very hard night. Please, just behave yourself, just this once."

He raised his hand in the Boy Scout salute. "I won't bite, promise."

That made me think of Micah and caused me to blush, which was embarrassing under the circumstances.

Jason's eyes widened. "That's a better reaction than I've ever gotten from you. I'll have to remember the line."

"You reminded me of something embarrassing, that's all."

The grin faded to a smile. "I knew it wasn't because of me."

"I am not going to baby-sit your ego, too, Jason. You'll have to take care of it yourself."

"Always do." The smile had faded, leaving him serious. With his yellow hair and blue eyes, he looked somehow out of place against all the black silk, as if he needed a different color to frame him to best advantage. Of course, the bed wasn't meant to frame him to best advantage, it was meant to frame Jean-Claude.

The thought was enough. I felt him in his coffin, felt him dead to the world, gone away wherever vampires go when the sun rises. The feel of him so distant, unable to hold me, or help me, made me feel cold, and even more cut adrift.

I leaned against the heavy cherry wood post of the bed, one hand on it. But my hands were not big enough to encircle the wood. It was a big bed—at least king size.

"What's wrong, Anita?"

I shook my head. "I don't want to talk about it."

"I'm sorry. I will be good. I promise."

"No more teasing?" I asked.

He tried to stay serious, but a smile crept through. "I'd promise no more teasing if I thought I could live up to it, but I will promise to try and not tease you anymore today. How's that?"

I had to smile. "Honest, I guess." I sat down on the edge of the bed.

"You seem lost tonight," he said.

It was so close to what I was thinking that I turned and looked at him. "Is it that obvious?"

"Only to someone who knows you."

"Do you know me that well, Jason?"

"Sometimes. And sometimes you are totally confusing to me."

I pulled back the covers and crawled under the sheet, pushing the heavy satin coverlet away from me. I'd left a lot of distance between me and Jason. I slid my gun under the nearest pillow, safety on. And for extra precaution, since I was sleeping with non-gun users, no bullets were in the chamber.

"Honest, Anita, I'll behave myself, you can move closer."

"I know."

"And not just because Jean-Claude and Richard wouldn't like it."

"Richard isn't dating me anymore, Jason. He's not mine anymore." Just saying it out loud made my skin colder, my stomach clench tight.

"He may say that, but if he found out I tried anything tonight, anything serious, he'd make me pay for it."

"What do you mean?"

"He may not be dating you, but I'll bet my favorite body part that he wouldn't tolerate you dating any of the other werewolves. Him not being able to have you isn't the same thing as not wanting you."

I looked at him, sheet-covered knees hugged to my chest. "When did you get so smart?"

"I have my moments."

I had to smile. "Yeah, you do."

We were both smiling when Nathaniel came out of the bathroom. "Hit the lights, Nathaniel."

Nathaniel did what I asked, and the blackness was complete. The lights were on a timer and would come on softly in a few hours. But until then it was a darkness so complete it was like being dropped in ink. I'm not usually bothered by darkness, but just then it was claustrophobic, like some giant black hand pressing against me.

I felt Nathaniel by the bed. "Please, turn on the bathroom light, leave the door ajar." He went back and did it. One of the good things about Nathaniel was he didn't question orders much. It used to bug me. Now I counted on it, sometimes.

He left the door open a crack, just enough to let a slender finger of light fall into the room and slant along the bed.

Nathaniel lifted the sheet and crawled into bed without a word. But him crawling in meant I had to move over closer to Jason. I found the gun and moved it down a pillow with me. But Nathaniel didn't crowd me, and there was still space between us when we all tucked in for the night. Not as much space as I'd have liked, but still space. In fact I was able to roll over onto my side without bumping anyone. Of course, that wasn't how I slept at home. At home Nathaniel and the rest of the wereleopards cuddled into big piles. I'd slept most of the last six months among them. It was, sadly, getting to the point that when I slept alone I felt lonely.

Nathaniel had rolled automatically onto his side, his back to me, waiting for me to close the distance between us. He'd already moved his hair to one side like a blanket that had to be moved out of the way, leaving his back and part of his neck smooth and bare. I lay there for a second or two, then thought, screw it. I moved in against him, pressing myself to the smooth warmth of his body, my arm sliding around his waist. He was just a few inches taller than me, enough that I cuddled down just a little, pressing my face into his back, in the hollow behind his shoulder blade. It was the way we'd gone to sleep for a long time.

"Now I do feel left out," Jason said.

I sighed, clutching Nathaniel a little tighter. "Do you promise not to try anything?"

"I promise to be good."

"That's not what I asked."

He gave a small laugh. "You're better than you used to be at this game. Okay, I promise not to try anything."

"Then you can get closer, if you want to."

"You know I do," he said. I could feel him moving across the bed towards us.

"You also promised to be good."

"You have no idea how good I can be." He was very close when he said the last.

"You're pushing it, Jason."

"Sorry." But he didn't sound sorry. He curled against my back, his body spooning against me, his knees bending into a near perfect line behind mine. We were within an inch of being the same height, which made spooning easy. It also put certain parts of his anatomy up against my butt, and it was hard not to notice that he was happy to be there. Not too long ago, I'd have made him move, but I'd spent months learning shapeshifter etiquette. The men tried their best not to get erections, and not to use them when they did; the women tried to ignore the fact that they had them. That was the rule. It allowed everyone to pretend we were just a bunch of puppies sleeping in a nice friendly pile. To acknowledge anything else meant the system fell apart.

I realized that it didn't bother me. Over the months I'd learned that it was just one of those involuntary things that happened, nothing truly personal. I think Jason was disappointed that he didn't get more of a reaction from me. When I didn't react at all, he moved his hips just a fraction away from me, but snuggled the rest of himself against me more tightly.

I was effectively sandwiched between them, and it reminded me forcibly of waking up between Caleb and Micah. Not a comforting memory. But the smell of Nathaniel's skin was familiar. The vanilla scent of his hair where it edged my face and stretched under his body was comforting. I drew the scent of him around me like a blanket, pulled my body in as close to the warm curve of him as I could go and not come out the other side, and clung. I acknowledged in my head, though never aloud, that tonight I clung. I held him like he was the last solid thing in the world, the way I'd wanted to hold Jean-Claude and couldn't.

Jason's hand smoothed along my hip, but I'd forced his hand up from around my waist when I tucked so tightly against Nathaniel; there was really nowhere else for it to go. His hand was very still against my bare leg, and there was a tension to him, as if he was waiting for me to protest. When I didn't, he relaxed and even moved his entire body back against me. He'd managed to calm himself. Good for him.

Honestly, it was nice having Jason's weight at my back. Normally, I spooned Nathaniel—took the dominant position with my body protecting his—my back bare to the room. But I wasn't feeling particularly dominant. I wanted someone to have my back. And, if it couldn't be Jean-Claude, or Richard, Jason wasn't a bad choice. For all his teasing, he was my friend.

Nathaniel fell asleep first; he usually drifted off faster than I did. Somehow I knew that Jason was still awake pressed against my back, his hand on my thigh. I could feel a tension in him as I began to drift off, and strangely, it was comforting. Jason literally had my back. It meant I could sleep, and between the three of us, whatever came through the door, we could probably handle it. Probably.

15

I WAS DREAMING. Something confusing about bodies and running and a ringing noise that made the crowd run faster. Ringing noise? I woke up enough to feel Nathaniel move beside me. He groped over the side of the bed and came up with my cell phone from my pile of clothes. He handed the ringing phone to me. "It's for you."

Jason mumbled, "God, what time is it?"

I flipped the phone open and put it to my ear before anyone answered his question. "Yeah, it's me." I was only half awake.

"Anita?"

"Yes, who is this?"

"It's Rafael."

That made me sit up. Rafael was the wererat king. Their equivalent of an Ulfric. He was also Richard's ally. "I'm here, what's up?"

"First, my condolences. I hear you may be Nimir-Ra in truth next full moon."

"Gee, news does travel fast," I said, trying not to sound bitter, but failing.

"Second, I know the pack has one of your leopards, and that you must try and win him back from them tonight. You are allowed to bring allies with you, and I would be honored if you would allow the wererats to accompany you."

"I appreciate the gesture, Rafael, you don't know how much I appreciate it, but I'm not lupa anymore. Your treaty is with the pack, and I'm not pack anymore."

"True, but you risked yourself once to save me from torture, and possible death. I told you then that the wererats would not forget what you had done for us."

"What about your treaty with Richard?"

"It's with Richard, not the pack."

"Showing up at my back tonight is still a conflict of interests, don't you think?"

"I don't think so. I think it will make the point that if Richard is no longer Ulfric, the wererats will not be the werewolves' allies."

"You'll show up with me tonight to make it clear that your treaty is with Richard and not the pack?"

Jason sat up in the bed.

"Yes," Rafael said.

"Clever you."

"Thank you."

"So you don't like Jacob either?"

Jason moved closer to me, as if he could hear Rafael's side of the conversation. Maybe he could.

"No," Rafael said.

"Me either."

"So I will meet you at your home tonight before we drive to the lupanar."

"Just you?" I made it a question.

"Oh, no, we will be there in force so the point is not lost on Jacob's supporters."

"I like the way you think," I said.

"I wish Richard did," Rafael said.

"Have you tried to get him to execute Jacob, too?" I asked.

"I knew you would understand both the problem and the needed solution, Anita."

"Oh, I understand. I just wish Richard did."

"Yes," Rafael said, "yes. Jacob is not the man Richard is, but he has some qualities that I would wish on Richard if I could."

"Me too."

"I'll meet you tonight at your house at full dark."

"I'll be there. And Rafael . . ."

"Yes?"

"Thanks."

"No thanks are necessary. The rats owe you a debt. We pay our debts."

"And it allows you to make a threat to Jacob and his supporters without doing anything that could start a war," I said.

"As I said, Anita, you understand things that Richard does not. Until tonight."

"Until tonight," I said. He hung up. I hung up, flipping the phone closed. Jason was practically leaning over my shoulder.

"Did I just hear that Rafael and the wererats are going with you tonight to the lupanar?"

"You going to tattle to Richard?" I asked, staring at his face from inches away, his back touching my shoulder.

"No."

My eyes widened.

"Unless Richard specifically asks, 'Is Rafael going to be there tonight as Anita's ally?' then I don't have to answer. And I'm not volunteering the information."

"That's cutting your oath of obedience pretty close, isn't it?"

"My loyalty is to Richard. And having the rats with you tonight will help Richard, not hurt him."

I nodded. "Sometimes you have to keep things from Richard to help him."

"Unfortunately," Jason said.

I handed the phone to Nathaniel, who put it back on the floor with my clothes. I checked my watch. It was ten o'clock; we'd had a little over six hours of sleep. Time to start the day. Yippee! It was still hours before I could expect Jean-Claude to be awake.

I snuggled down into the covers on my back. Nathaniel rolled onto his side, hand going across my stomach, one leg entwined over my legs. His second favorite sleeping position, though one I often had to move him out of before I could go to sleep. But I wasn't sleeping, I was thinking, so it was okay.

He rubbed his cheek against my shoulder, and a small movement of his lower body pressed him against me. He was hard and firm under the silky shorts. It was morning, he was male, it was normal. Normally, I could ignore it, just one of those things that you pretended didn't happen, but today . . . Today the feel of him pressed against me made things low in my body clench tight. The need rode through my body like fire spilling through me, over me, inside me.

Nathaniel went very still beside me.

Jason was sitting up, rubbing his bare arms. "What was that?"

I tried not to move, not to breathe, to just be as still as Nathaniel. I tried to think of something besides the warmth of his body pressed against the length of mine. Tried not to feel the press of him hard and ready through the satin of the jogging shorts. I grabbed the sheet and jerked it off of us in one violent movement. I gazed down the length of his body, of our bodies, pressed together. The shorts clung like a second skin to the back of him. The *ardeur* rushed through me again like a new pulse I'd never felt before, and my beast rose up through the depths with it. It was as if they were tied together. I hungered, and my beast woke, rolling inside me like a lazy cat, stretching, eyeing the mouse. Except what this cat wanted to do to the mouse was not only against the laws of nature, but physically impossible. The trouble was this mouse smelled of vanilla and fur, and he was warm and full against me. I wanted to roll him over on his back and tear off the shorts and see what I was feeling. I wanted to lick down his chest, down his stomach, and . . . The visual was so strong that I had to close my eyes against the sight of him lying there. But sight wasn't my only problem. The smell of his skin was suddenly overwhelming, sweet. And I had a desire to roll my body on top of his, not for sex exactly, but to paint his scent on my body, to wear it like a dress.

"Anita," it was Jason. "What's happening?"

I opened my eyes to find him bending over me, propped on one elbow, and the *ardeur* widened to include him. It did not discriminate. I touched his face, ran my fingers down the edge of his cheek, traced the fullness of his lower lip with my thumb.

He moved his mouth back just enough to speak. "Jean-Claude said you'd inherited his need, his incubus. I don't think I believed him . . ." My hand traced down his face, his neck, his chest. ". . . until now," he whispered.

My hand stopped over his heart. It beat against my hand, and I could suddenly feel my pulse in my palm beating against his skin, as if my heart had spilled down my arm to cup against his body.

"Ask me why Jean-Claude insisted I stay in here today."

I just looked at him. I couldn't think, couldn't speak. I could feel his heart, almost caress it. His heart sped, beating faster. My heart sped to catch it, until our hearts were beating together, and it was hard to tell where one pulse stopped and the other began. I could taste his heartbeat in my mouth as if it pulsed inside me already, caressing the roof of my mouth as if I had already taken a bite of him.

I closed my eyes and tried to distance myself from the ebb and flow of his body, his warmth, his need.

"Jean-Claude was afraid you'd try to feed on Nathaniel. I'm supposed to keep that from happening." His voice was breathy.

I raised up, and Nathaniel's arms curled around my waist, pressing his face into my side. I sat up beside Jason with Nathaniel like a tempting weight wrapped around my body. My hand stayed on Jason's chest, cupping his heart. He should have moved away, but he didn't. I could feel his desire, feel the need in him. It was a pure desire, not for power, or anything else, just simply for me. It wasn't love, but it was purity of a sort. He simply wanted me. I stared into his blue eyes, and there was no deceit, no agenda. Jason didn't want to secure his power base, or gain mystical energy, he just wanted to have sex with me, to hold me in his arms.

I'd always treated Jason as lesser than a friend, young and amusing, not serious. Jean-Claude's *ardeur* let me see into his heart, and I found it the most pure of any that I'd looked into in a long time.

I stared down at Nathaniel where he lay clinging to me. I knew his heart, too. He wanted me physically, but more, he wanted me to want him. He wanted to belong to me in every way. He longed for safety, a home, someone to take care of him, and to take care of. He saw in me all the things that he'd lost over the years. But he didn't really see me; he saw an ideal of me that he wanted.

I ran my hand down his arm, and he snuggled against me. I looked back at Jason and let my other hand drop away from him, but it was like I pulled something out of him as it moved; his heart still beat inside my body. We didn't have to touch for that.

The fact that Jason wanted me just for me with no ulterior motives made me want to reward him. Made me love him just a little. It overrode the hunger, stilled my beast, helped me think.

"Get out, both of you, get out."

"Anita, is that you?"

"Go, Jason, take him with you, and go."

"I don't want to go," Nathaniel said.

I grabbed a handful of that thick hair and raised him to his knees with it. I expected to see fear in his eyes, or betrayal, but what I saw was eagerness. I used his hair as a handle and drew him to me until our faces almost touched. I felt his heart thudding, the thrill through his body as I drew him into me. Nathaniel would never tell me no.

If someone can't tell you no, it's rape, or something like it. The *ardeur* poured through me, taking my breath in a long shuddering line. I wanted to kiss Nathaniel, to fill his mouth with my tongue. And I knew if I did, it would be too late.

My voice came out strangled. "You will go when I tell you to go, now get out!" I released my hold on him so suddenly that he fell back against the bed.

Jason was on the other side of the bed, pulling Nathaniel away from me, pushing him towards the door. Watching them go made me want to cry, or scream. They were perfect for feeding. The room was thick with mutual desire, and I was sending them away. I could still feel their heartbeats like candy in my mouth, like a double echo of my own heart.

I covered my eyes with my hands and screamed, wordless, pain-filled. It was as if the hunger finally realized that I was truly going to let them go. It raged through me, tearing one ragged scream from my mouth after another, as fast as I could draw breath. I lay on the bed in the silk sheets, writhing, screaming. I had a sudden memory, and it wasn't mine, of this need denied, locked away in the dark where no hand could touch you, where no skin could melt into yours. I felt the faintest edge of Jean-Claude's madness after that particular punishment. He'd healed, but the memory was still raw.

Hands on me, holding me down. I opened my eyes to find Nathaniel and Jason holding me down. They each had a hand on one wrist and one leg. They could bench press small elephants, but as my body writhed against the bed, I raised them up, made them struggle to hold me.

"Anita, you're hurting yourself," Jason said.

I looked down my body and found bloody scratches on my arms and legs. I had to have done it, but I didn't remember doing it. The sight of those bloody scratches calmed me, made me lie still under their hands.

"I'm going to get something to tie you down with just until Jean-Claude rises," Jason said.

I nodded, afraid to speak, afraid of what I'd say.

He told Nathaniel to hold me, but the only way one person could do that was to hold my wrists while pressing against me with his lower body. It wasn't perfect control, but it kept me from hurting myself.

Nathaniel's hair fell around our bodies with a dry rushing sound, until I saw the world through a curtain of his hair. The scent of him was like some warm pressure between his upraised chest and mine. I could smell the fresh scent of blood, too. And my beast wanted to lick the wounds, wanted to feed on my own skin, or better yet, open wounds on Nathaniel and feed off of him. Just the thought tightened my body, made me writhe underneath him, until I'd freed my legs and he slid against me, only our clothing separating us. He made a small sound, half-protest, half-something else.

I raised my wrists off the bed, pushing against his grip on me. I felt his arms strain against me, forcing me back against the bed. It shouldn't have been a struggle for him to hold me here like this. I was gaining other things besides hunger through the marks, or the beast. Nathaniel was still stronger than I was, I could feel that. But there are things besides strength that count when you're struggling. I raised my arms from the bed again, only a few inches, and he forced me down again. But when I had enough room, I rotated my right wrist against his thumb, and my hand was free.

I raised up enough to kiss his chest, and he went very still above me. I knew in that instant that he wouldn't try and regain control of my arm. I bit him, gently, and his breath went out in a soft, sharp sound. I licked my way up his chest, with him still holding my left arm, his lower body still pinning mine. I ran my tongue over his nipple and felt his breathing quicken. I locked my mouth around his nipple and bit into the skin, the flesh underneath. He shuddered above me, his body jerking enough that I had to be careful not to break the skin. But I held on as he moaned above me, and when I drew back, I saw that I had left a near perfect imprint of my teeth behind.

I lay back against the bed and stared at the bite mark on his chest, with his nipple in the center of it, and a thrill went through me, a wave of pleasure at the sight of it, and a feeling of . . . possession. I'd marked him.

I drew my left wrist out of his hand, and he didn't fight me. He stayed propped above me on his arms, his hips pressed against me, his hair in a cascade around us. He stared down at me, and his face was raw with need. I didn't need anything else to tell me how much he wanted me to finish what I'd begun.

I raised up enough to kiss him, and his lips trembled against mine. The kiss was long and full, and a sound came low in his throat, and he suddenly collapsed against me, his full body weight pinning me to the bed, our mouths, our arms, our bodies locked together in a warm, vanilla-scented nest of his hair, like being rolled in warm satin. Nathaniel kissed me as if he would climb inside me through my mouth, and I opened for him, let him explore me, taste me, touch me. It wasn't his hand underneath my top, kneading my breast, that brought me to my senses. It was my hands down the back of his shorts, cupping the smooth curve of his buttocks. It helped me swim back into control, to fight down the desire, the hunger. Where the hell was Jason? I stopped kissing Nathaniel, stopped touching him, while his hands, his mouth, explored my body. His need was so strong, so strong. I could not leave the bed. I could not walk away. I was not that strong.

"Nathaniel, stop."

His mouth was on my breast through the satin of the top. He didn't seem to hear me.

"Nathaniel, stop!" I grabbed a handful of his hair and pulled him away from me. The front of the top was wet where his mouth had been. His eyes didn't seem to focus on me. It was as if he didn't see me at all.

"Nathaniel, can you hear me?"

He finally nodded. "Yes." Anyone else would have protested being stopped, but he simply looked at me, eyes beginning to focus. There was no resentment on his face, no anger. He simply did what I told him to do and waited for me to say more. I didn't understand Nathaniel; even knowing his heart's desires gave me no real understanding of him. We were too different, but today that difference might help us.

I would not, *could* not have sex with Nathaniel. But I couldn't stop completely either. I had to feed. I had to sink my teeth into his flesh, had to bathe in his lust, had to. "Get off me."

He rolled onto his back, gazing up at me, lying in a pool of his hair, like a shining auburn frame around his body. I wanted to see all of him framed against his hair, and all I had to do was drag his shorts down the curve of his hips. The image was so strong I had to close my eyes, take deep breaths. The need to touch him lashed through me, almost painful, as if the *ardeur* could force me to do it. And maybe it could. But I would control how I touched him. I would control at least that much.

I opened my eyes and found him gazing up at me with those impossible lilac eyes. "Roll over onto your stomach," I said, my voice hoarse.

He rolled over without a single question, and I was reminded how absolutely helpless he was with a dominant. He would do what he was told, whatever he was told. It helped steady me, to know that I had to be in charge. I had to have some control, because he would have none.

I picked up handfuls of that thick hair and pushed it to one side like a piled beast. I bared his back, in a clean smooth line. He turned his head to the side and gazed at me through the film of his hair. There was no fear in him, only a vast patience, an eagerness, and need.

I rose on all fours over him, straddling his body, and lowered my mouth to his skin. I licked across his shoulders, but it wasn't enough. I bit him, gently, and he made a small movement underneath me. I bit harder, and a tiny sound escaped his lips. I bit him hard enough that I felt his flesh fill my mouth, felt the grip of him, the meat of him. I wanted to tear at his flesh, to literally feed from him. The desire was almost overwhelming. I collapsed on top of him, my cheek against his back, until I could control myself. But the scent of his flesh, the smoothness of it under my cheek, the rise and fall of his breathing under my body, it was too much. I would not eat him literally, but I had to feed.

I bit the flesh of his back, drew him into my mouth, and this time I did not stop until I tasted the sweet metallic taste of blood. It was the beast that wanted to finish, blood was not enough. But I raised from the wound and moved on. I marked Nathaniel's back with near perfect imprints of my teeth, and more and more of them held blood. It was as if the longer I did it, the harder it was to control.

The scent of fresh blood tightened my body, filled me with heat and longings that had to do more with food than sex. I sat straddling his body looking down at his back, at my handy work. Blood ran in tiny drops from some of the wounds, but mostly it looked like tiny mouths pressed into his flesh. And it wasn't enough.

I slid my hands down the back of his shorts, drawing my nails delicately along his flesh. He writhed under the touch, started to rise from the bed, and I pushed him back down. "No, no," I said, and he went still under my hands.

I slid his shorts down his body until he lay nude underneath me. I spread his legs so I could kneel between them, lowered my mouth to that smooth, untouched skin, and marked him. There was more flesh to hold in my mouth here, tight, but more plentiful. I filled my mouth with him, drew blood in red, hot circles, until I heard him making small helpless noises. And I knew they weren't pain noises.

I rose on my knees above him, gazed down at the wounds I'd laid on his body, and I wanted more.

I slid my satin top off and wiggled out of the shorts. I laid my naked body on his and rolled along his back, his buttocks, rubbing the blood from the wounds on my body. Nathaniel was saying, "please, please, please," over and over under his breath. His need was like a pressing weight, a thick cloud that hovered over us. It was chokingly close, so overwhelming. He wanted this so badly. This, not sex, this. He'd waited so very long for me to dominate him, to take him.

Micah had wanted me, but his had been the want of a relative stranger. A man wanting an attractive and powerful mate. But with Nathaniel it was different. His desire had built over years, over a thousand intimacies, a thousand denials. It had built until it was a great weight in his body, in his mind. It was a thing that burdened him down, filled him up, and he could not be free of it. I understood why Jean-Claude had said that we would feed off those we were already attracted to. There was so much more to feed from with Nathaniel. Our history together made it not just a feeding, but a feast.

I worked my way back down his body, biting along his flesh, not drawing blood now. I lay with my cheek pressed against the curve of his buttocks, fighting with myself not to reach my hand around to the front of him. Fighting the growing need. I would not touch him, not like that. When I could trust myself, I spread his legs as far as they would go, and bit down, marking areas untouched, getting ever closer, until I could see him pressed between his body and the bed. I wanted to lick him there, roll his testicles in my mouth. But I didn't trust myself. I'd laid his back and buttocks bloody, I didn't trust myself, couldn't guarantee what I would do. I moved my mouth back without touching him, and the pressure of his lust and mine rode like summer lightning, almost there, almost there. I ran my tongue on the small ridge of skin just in back of his testicles, and Nathaniel cried out.

I sucked the skin, drew it into my mouth in a long line, working it with tongue and teeth, and the pressure broke over us like a storm released in one long thunderous burst. He called my name, and I raked his thighs with my nails and fought with two different hungers not to bite that delicate bit of skin away from his body. When it was over, I drew back from him just enough to see that I hadn't marked him, not even the mark of my teeth. I lay on the bed, between his legs, one arm on his thigh, the other folded beneath me, listening to the pounding of my heart.

He lay quiet except for his still frantic breathing. A sound raised me up to gaze over Nathaniel's leg, propping myself up on the smooth wounded flesh of his butt.

Jason was standing in the middle of the room with what looked like shackles in his arms. His eyes were wide, his own breathing a little too fast.

I should have been embarrassed, but the *ardeur* was sated, and my beast lay curled inside me like a contented cat. I was too well-pleased with myself to be embarrassed. "How long have you been watching?" Even my voice sounded lazy, content.

He had to clear his throat twice before he could say, "Long enough."

I climbed back up Nathaniel's body, until I was pressed against the length of him. I laid my cheek against his face, and whispered, "Are you alright?"

"Yes." It was a whisper.

"I didn't hurt you?"

"It was . . . wonderful. Oh, God, it was . . . better than I'd imagined it."

I raised up, stroking his hair, turning back to look at Jason, still standing in the middle of the floor. "Why didn't you try and stop me?"

"Jean-Claude was afraid you'd tear out Nathaniel's throat or something messy like that." Jason's voice was returning to normal, only the slightest edge of uncertainty in it. "But I watched you. Every time I thought I'd have to intervene, you drew back. Every time I thought you were going to lose control, you didn't. You rode the hunger, you tamed it."

I felt Jean-Claude waken, felt him take his first breath of the day. He sensed me, too, felt me still lying naked on Nathaniel's body, smelled the scent of fresh blood, felt that I had fed, and fed well. I felt him coming towards me, hurrying towards me, attracted to the scent of blood, and warm flesh, and sex, and me.

16

"JEAN-CLAUDE'S COMING," JASON said.

"I know," I said.

Jason walked to the foot of the bed and gazed down at us, at me. His eyes lingered on me. Most of my body was hidden beside Nathaniel, but he looked at what was revealed. If I hadn't had that glimpse into his heart, I'd have been mad, or told him to stop, but I didn't know what to say now. He wanted me, just me for me, not forever, but just for a night, a day, a week, just for sometimes. Jason's feelings for me might be the most uncomplicated of all the men in my life. Uncomplicated had its attractions, even with the *ardeur* gone. The moment I thought *gone*, I realized that wasn't true. The hunger was just below the surface; like something simmering in a pot, you have to keep the heat low, or it boils over. I'd had enough heat for one day.

Jason and I looked at each other. I don't know what we would have said, but just then the door opened. It was Asher. His room was closer than the coffin room, but I hadn't expected him. His golden hair lay in perfect waves around the shoulders of his robe. Vampires didn't move in their "sleep" so no morning hair problems. The robe was a rich, deep brown, open over matching pajama bottoms. His chest was bare, and the robe flared around him like a cape as he strode into the room.

He came to stand beside the bed, but his gaze went to Nathaniel's body, to the blood. "I felt . . ." He raised his eyes to my face, and I peered at him over Nathaniel's body. "I felt the call."

"I didn't call you," I said.

"The power did." He dropped to his knees beside the bed. "You did this?"

I nodded.

He reached out towards me, as if to touch my face, then jerked back. It was like he'd touched something in the air in front of me that had startled him. He raised his hand to his face and sniffed it, then licked it, as though there was something there to taste.

"May I taste your *pomme de sang?*" It was French for apple of blood, and it was a nickname for a person that was a regular donor to a particular vampire. Part of me wanted to argue with the phrase, but I had fed off of Nathaniel, even tasted his blood. To demand a different phrase was splitting hairs a little too finely for my conscience. We'd call a spade a spade.

"Define taste." I said.

"Lick the wounds."

The suggestion should have bothered me, but it didn't. I lowered my face enough to see Nathaniel's eyes. "Is it okay with you, Nathaniel?"

He nodded, face still pressed to the bed.

"Help yourself."

Asher lowered his mouth to Nathaniel's back, to a wound just above his waist. He kept those ice blue eyes rolled up towards me, the way you would watch someone on a judo mat—afraid that if you look away, they'll hurt you. It reminded me of watching lions drink from pools, with their eyes rolled up, watching for danger while they drank.

Nathaniel made a small sound as Asher licked the wound. It had stopped bleeding, but as the vampire traced the wound with his tongue, I saw blood well to the surface again. Vampires have an anticoagulant in their saliva, but I'd never seen its use demonstrated quite so well before.

It made me wonder. I curled closer to Nathaniel's body, one leg entwining over his. I didn't ask permission, because he was mine, and I knew him well enough to know he would not only not mind, but he would welcome it. I lowered my mouth to another of the wounds that had nearly stopped bleeding and licked. There was the sweet copper taste of blood, and the thick, rich taste of his skin, and a taste of . . . meat. As if I could tell what he would taste like if I ate him one bite at a time.

The beast flared over my skin like something trembling and alive. Nathaniel's beast responded to it, flaring, rolling, as if I could see it just below his skin, just below his ribs, as if I could feel where it lay in the heart of his body. In that moment I knew I could call his beast, could coax him to change when the moon was far from full. I was his Nimir-Ra, and that meant so much more than merely being his dominant.

Asher's eyes had drowned in pale blue fire, so he looked blind as he licked at the wound. He gazed into my face, directly across Nathaniel's body, our eyes at the same level as we tasted the wounds. My wound bled a little bit more, but not as much as Asher's did. I was not truly a blood drinker—I fed on other things—and staring across Nathaniel's body, feeling his breathing quicken as the two of us touched him, I knew that those other things were here for the taking.

Asher's hand slid over Nathaniel's body, until he touched my thigh where it curved over Nathaniel's leg. The moment he touched me something rushed between us. It was as if the *ardeur* recognized him, as if it had touched him before.

It made me raise up from the wound, drew me back into myself a little. Something on my face made Asher take his hand back.

Jean-Claude entered then. He was wearing a black robe with black fur at collar, lapel, and sleeves. His black hair melted into the fur, so you couldn't tell where one blackness stopped and the other began. The last time I'd seen him in the robe, I'd told him there better be something under the robe besides skin. Now, I hoped there wasn't.

Seeing him brought the *ardeur* boiling over me again. It made me catch my breath, things lower than my stomach clenching tight enough to draw a sound from my throat.

"She holds your incubus," Asher said, and his voice tore my gaze from Jean-Claude to him.

"*Oui.*" Jean-Claude glided around the room to the opposite side of the bed from where Asher knelt.

"She tastes of you, and of Belle Morte."

"*Oui,*" Jean-Claude said. He walked around the bed to the other side, and I rolled away from Nathaniel so I could see Jean-Claude move. The movement exposed the front of my body, and I had enough of myself left to roll onto my stomach.

Jason said, "Awww."

I ignored him.

Jean-Claude lifted the robe so he could crawl onto the bed. The movement revealed a long, pale line of skin from his shoulders to his stomach. The glimpse of that white flesh caught between the blackness of the fur made me want to untie the sash and expose his entire body. But I stayed where I was, half-leaning against Nathaniel, because I was afraid to move. Afraid to go to Jean-Claude, because I didn't trust myself.

There was just enough of *me* left not to want to make love to Jean-Claude in front of the other men. But it was a razor-thin part, something that glittered in the darkness but didn't quite believe itself anymore.

"The hunger recognizes Asher. Is it because it's yours, or because it's hers?" I asked.

"Hers?" he asked.

"Belle Morte."

"I do not know," he said. And he was close enough now that the edge of the robe brushed my body. I could see a thin line of pale skin below the waist where the robe gaped. A thin, thin line of white, but it was enough to let me know that there was nothing under the robe but Jean-Claude.

I wanted to open the robe, to see all of him. I said it without thinking, as if I hadn't meant to say it out loud. "Open the robe." It startled me as if I didn't know my own voice.

I closed my eyes, tried to think.

"It is alright, *ma petite*. Once taken, blood fills your stomach, but lust . . ." Fur brushed in a teasing line down my arm. "Lust is always there, never vanquished completely, never satisfied." He brushed the edge of his furred cuff down my waist, my hip, my thigh, my calf. When he brushed it along my foot, he started back up, but this time on the back of my body, so that the teasing brush touched my buttocks, my back, my shoulder.

I lay wordless, breathless, under his touch. When he curved the fur around my face, I grabbed the edge of the robe and held him away from me. "Make everyone leave." My voice was barely above a whisper.

"I can do nothing until I have fed, *ma petite*, you know that."

"I know. Blood pressure." I was having a hard time thinking. "Then do it, but . . ."

"Hurry," he said softly.

I nodded.

He drew his sleeve out of my grip and looked down the bed to Jason, who was still standing there, watching the show. "Come, *pomme de sang*, come and enjoy the rewards of your sacrifice."

The phrase was oddly formal, and I'd never heard it put that way before. I expected Jason to go around the bed to the same side as Jean-Claude, but he didn't. He rolled over the foot of the bed in a movement so liquid it was like watching water flow, as if his skin barely contained some elemental energy that had nothing to do with the flesh and bone body I was seeing. He ended on his knees on the opposite side from Jean-Claude. I could taste the movement of his body in my mouth, not just his heart, but as if every throb and beat of him was trying to slide over my tongue and down my throat. I could feel his eagerness, not for me, but for what Jean-Claude had to offer. He came eagerly to the vampire, in that breathless rush that you usually save for sex. They mirrored each other, both on their knees, gazing at each other across my body.

"I will leave you alone with your *pomme de sangs* and each other." Asher was standing next to the bed, belting the sash at his waist, securing the robe around him. He stood very straight with that perfect posture that all the old nobles seemed to have, but still he huddled inside the robe.

I rolled onto my stomach, gazing at him, trying to read his face, his body. The discomfort I could read, and even pain. And it must have shown on my face, because Asher dropped his gaze, that wonderful golden hair sliding over the scarred side of his face, so that when he looked up, you could see nothing but the perfect half of him, that one ice-blue eye.

I had a sudden memory of lying in a different bed in a huge dark room surrounded by dozens of candles until the shadows moved and rippled with every small breath of air, every movement of a pale arm. I lay in that trembling golden darkness in the embrace of a pale, dark-haired woman. I gazed up at her, and her face was like something carved of alabaster, with lips red and perfect, hair like the darkness of night made into furred silk, falling around her nude perfection like a veil. Her eyes were pale brown, like dark honey. I knew it was Belle Morte, as if I'd always known her face.

The door opened, and Asher entered, wearing a robe more elaborate, heavier than the one he wore now. But still he huddled in it, held it around his body, afraid. I saw the scars on his face—fresh, raw—and it was . . . painful. My chest went tight with the sight of his ruin. I went to my knees, reaching out to him, moving a body that I'd never been inside. Jean-Claude reaching out to Asher all those centuries ago. But she lay there nude and perfect showing every curve, every secret place to the candlelight, and turned him away. I couldn't remember the words she used, only the look on her face, the utter arrogance, the distaste. The look on Asher's face as he turned from her to Jean-Claude, to me. The look of pain, and he let that glorious hair fall forward, hiding his face, and it was the first time we'd seen him do that, hide from us.

I felt her hands on our body as she turned back to us, as if Asher were no longer there, but we remembered the look on his face, the line of his body as he left that room. I blinked and was back in Jean-Claude's bedroom, watching Asher in his brown silk robe walking towards the door. And the line of his shoulders, the way he held himself, made my chest tight, closed my throat, made my eyes hot with things unsaid and unshed.

"Don't go." I heard myself say it, and I glanced up at Jean-Claude. His face was careful, unreadable, but for just a moment I saw his eyes, and the pain I was feeling was only an echo of what filled his eyes.

Asher stopped at the door and turned, his hair falling over his face, the robe covering everything else. He said nothing, just looked back at me, at us.

I repeated, "Don't go, Asher, don't go."

"Why not?" he asked, his voice as careful and neutral as he could make it.

I couldn't tell him about the shared memory. It would sound like pity, and it wasn't that—not exactly. I couldn't think of a good lie. But this wasn't really the time for lies, anyway. Only truth would heal this. "I can't stand to watch you walk away like this."

He moved his gaze from me to Jean-Claude, and there was anger in him now. "You had no right to share that memory with her."

"I do not choose what *ma petite* knows and what she does not."

"Very well," Asher said. "Now you know how she cast me out of her bed. How she cast me out of his bed."

"That was your choice," Jean-Claude said.

"How could you bear to touch me? I couldn't bear to touch me." He stayed near the door with his head turned to one side, so all you could see was a wave of golden hair. His voice held bitterness the way it could sometimes hold joy—a bitterness that was hard to swallow, like choking on broken glass. Asher's voice and laugh weren't as good as Jean-Claude's, but he seemed better at sharing sorrow and regret than Jean-Claude.

"Why?" I asked, already knowing the answer.

"Why what?"

"Why did she cast you out?"

Jean-Claude moved beside me, and I realized two things. One, he was shielding from me, from all of us, so I couldn't sense him, and two, his body movement alone let me know he wasn't happy.

Asher grabbed his hair, forced it back from his face, showed the scars to the light. "This, *this*. Our mistress was a collector of beauty, and I am no longer beautiful. It pained her visibly to see me."

"You are beautiful, Asher. That she couldn't see that isn't your fault."

He let his hair fall back. It slid over the scars, hiding them. He had almost stopped doing that when he was here in the Circus. I'd forgotten how, when he first arrived in St. Louis, he had automatically hidden whenever you looked directly at him. He had used every shadow, every fall of light to hide the scars and highlight the beauty that remained untouched. He had stopped doing that around me.

It hurt my heart to see him hide. I tried to keep the sheet over me as I crawled towards the edge of the bed, but it was all tangled and trapped under Jason's and Jean-Claude's weight. Screw it, everyone here had seen the show. I wanted to wipe that hurt look from Asher's face more than I wanted to be modest.

Jason moved out of my way without uttering a single teasing comment. Unheard of! I crawled off the bed and walked towards Asher, and other memories spilled over me like cards thrown in the air. How many times had he watched Jean-Claude and Belle Morte and Julianna and so many others walk towards him nude and eager. Even Jean-Claude had failed him. There had been that shadow in his eyes formed of guilt. Guilt at failing to save Julianna, failing to save Asher. But Asher had assumed it was rejection and that Jean-Claude touched him only out of pity. It hadn't been pity—I had the memory of it—it had been pain. They had become constant reminders of how each had failed the other. A constant reminder of the woman they'd both loved, and lost. Until the pain was all they had left. Asher had turned it into hate, and Jean-Claude had simply turned away.

I walked through the memories like moving through cobwebs, things that brushed me, clung to me, but did not stop me. His hands were behind his back, his body leaning against the door, pinning them, and I knew why. Through Jean-Claude's "gift" I knew that Asher wanted to touch me and didn't trust himself enough to have his hands out in front of him. But it wasn't me he wanted to touch. In a way he was like Nathaniel; he saw in me what he needed to see, not exactly what was there.

I touched his hair where it hid his face. He flinched. I swept the hair back from his face, standing on tip-toe to reach him, putting one hand lightly on his chest for balance. He moved away from me, taking a step into the room. I grabbed his robe, but he stayed turned away as the robe pulled back from the perfect half of his chest. "Look at me, Asher, please."

He stayed turned away, and I finally had to walk those few steps to him. I was short enough that, standing right in front of him, I could look up underneath the hair into his face. He turned away again, and I stretched up, putting a hand on either side of his face, turning him to look at me. It put my body against his just for balance, and I felt the reluctance in his body, the need to move away. But he stayed immobile under my touch. He kept his hands behind his back, as if I'd tied them there.

The skin under one hand was so smooth, the other so rough. He could have fought me, but he didn't. He let me turn his face to me. I wrapped my hands in the thickness of his golden hair, holding it back from his face. I stared into his upturned face. The eyes, that impossible pale blue, were unreal, like the eyes of a husky. His lips were still full and kissable, his nose still a perfect profile. Even the scars that started far on the right side of his face were just another part of Asher—just another piece of him that I loved. I'd always assumed that any emotions I felt for Asher were from Jean-Claude's memories of him when they were lovers, companions for over twenty years. But staring at him now, I realized that that was only part of it.

I held memories of his body smooth and perfect. But that wasn't what I thought of when I thought of Asher. I pictured him as he was now, and I still loved him. It wasn't the way I felt about Jean-Claude, or Richard, but it was real, and it was mine. Maybe it wouldn't have existed if I hadn't had Jean-Claude's memories and emotions to build on, but whatever the foundation, I had feelings for Asher that were all mine, no one else's. I realized with something like a shock that it wasn't just everyone else's heart I could see into. I turned and looked back at Jean-Claude, tried to ask with my eyes what I was thinking.

"To know another's heart, you must first know your own, *ma petite.*" His voice was soft, no reproach.

I turned back to Asher, and there was something in his eyes—half wonderment, half pain—as if he expected me to hurt him in some way. He was probably right. But if so, I wouldn't mean to do it. Sometimes the greatest wounds are the ones we try the hardest not to inflict.

I let what I was feeling fill my eyes, my face. It was the only gift I had to give him. His expression softened, and what I saw in those lovely eyes was at the same time wonderful and painful. He dropped to his knees, one tear trailing down his smooth cheek. The look on his face was full of so many things. "The look in your eyes heals a part of my heart, *ma cherie*, and wounds another."

"Love is such a bitch," I said.

He laughed and hugged me around the waist, the roughness of his right cheek pressed into my belly, and I valued that more than anything else he could have done. I stroked his hair and held him against me. I looked across the room to Jean-Claude, and the look on his face was drowning deep, a longing so immense that there were no words to hold it. He wanted Asher and me. He wanted what he had had so many centuries ago. He'd once told Asher that he'd once almost been happy, and that had been when he was in Asher's and Julianna's arms. Before she died and Asher was saved but no longer Belle Morte's perfect golden boy. Jean-Claude had been forced to take Asher back to the vampire Council to have him healed. Jean-Claude had traded a hundred years of his own freedom to the Council for the favor of them saving Asher's life. Then Jean-Claude had fled, and Asher had stayed behind, blaming Jean-Claude for Julianna's death and for his ruin. Jean-Claude had gone from being in love, and being loved by two people, to losing one lover and having the other one hate him.

We gazed at each other. The look in Jean-Claude's eyes was so raw, like a fresh wound that still bled. He wanted to secure his power base with the triumvirate. He did want that—needed it—but there were other things that he wanted, almost needed. And one of those was hugging my waist, pressing his face to my stomach.

Jean-Claude lowered his eyes as if he couldn't control what was in them. He was the master of blank, careful expression. The fact that what he felt was too strong to hide said more than anything else. He couldn't shield his emotions right now. They were too strong; they shattered all his careful control, and a part of me was glad.

In that moment I wanted to give him what he most desired. I wanted to do it because I loved him, but it was more than that. I suddenly realized that with Richard gone from our bed, other things were suddenly possible. I turned back to Asher, gazing down on the top of his head, and knew that to be held in the circle of both our arms would heal something inside him that might never heal any other way.

The *ardeur* flared through me, hot, so hot, as if my skin must feel feverish. Asher drew back from me, letting his arms drop slowly to his sides. He gazed up at me, and the look in his eyes was enough. I knew he felt the hunger, too.

"It feels hot," I said. "Always before your power has felt cool, or cold even. It's Richard's beast that holds the heat."

"Lust is warm, *ma petite*, even among the cold-blooded."

I turned towards the bed and was suddenly very aware that I was nude. I was really going to have to get a robe. It wasn't Jean-Claude's gaze that made me look away, it was Nathaniel and Jason. Everyone in this room responded to me, in different ways, for very different reasons. But it was all fodder for this . . . need inside me.

Asher made some small movement that drew my attention back to him. I started to reach for him, to push his robe from his shoulders, to watch it fall to the floor. I hugged my arms to me, as if I was cold, but I wasn't cold. It was my turn not to trust where my hands were. The temptation was so thick everywhere I looked that there seemed no place to walk in safety. I felt trapped. Trapped, not in the room, but in the desire.

When I was sure I could talk without sounding as confused as I felt, I asked, "Is this thing permanent, or will it go away when we all adjust to the marks being married?"

"I do not know, *ma petite.* I wish I could tell you something more certain. If you were truly of my get, truly vampire, then I would say, yes, it is permanent. But you are my human servant. You have manifested powers in the past, and some have come and gone." He raised his hands. "There is no way to be sure."

"Is it always like this, never satisfied, never finished?"

"No, you can sate yourself, but it takes much to do it. Usually, one must be content with enough to keep the desire from overwhelming you."

"And you haven't fed like this in months, because you thought I would disapprove?"

"Years. And yes."

I stared at him across the room with Asher still kneeling in front of me. I'd always thought of Jean-Claude as the weaker-willed of the three of us—Richard, him, and me. Now I stood there afraid to move, afraid not to move, wanting to do things that were not me, not mine, not even Jean-Claude's. I'd known that the lycanthropes spoke of their animal half as something separate from them—their beast—but I'd never understood that some of the vampires' powers were the same way. Desires, hungers, so strong and overwhelming that they were like separate beings trapped inside your head, your body, your blood.

Asher made a small movement, and I turned to him. My hand reached out to stroke his hair before I'd turned completely to face him, as if my body had been moving without my eyes or my brain. His hair was thicker textured, more like mine, not the baby-fine curls of Jean-Claude or Jason, or the velvet silk of Nathaniel. I bundled my hands into Asher's hair as if I'd memorize the feel of it. Somewhere between mine and Richard's, somewhere in the middle, but not warm like Richard's was to the touch. Asher hadn't fed today, and he had no warmth to give. His skin was cool under my fingertips as I traced his cheek.

I spoke without looking at Jean-Claude. "How have you stood it? How could you fight the need all this time?"

"You are a fledgling, *ma petite.* Your control will never be weaker than now. I have had centuries to practice my control."

I made myself stop petting Asher. But he took my hand as I moved it back and laid a gentle kiss on my knuckles. Even that small touch made me catch my breath. My voice came out weak. "So you can go without feeding the desire."

"No, *ma petite.*"

I turned and stared at him, and Asher rubbed his thumb in small circles on my hand. I remembered that small touch as precious, a habit he had no matter which of us he held hands with. "You said you hadn't fed like this."

"I have had no sex, nor touched anyone in such a complete manner as you have done with Nathaniel. But I must feed the desire, just as I must take blood."

"What happens if you don't?"

"You remember what happened to Sabin when he stopped taking human blood?"

I nodded. Asher's thumb continued its small circle on my hand, and it made things low in my body tighten. "Sabin started to rot while he was still alive." I stared into Jean-Claude's perfect face. "Is that what would happen to you?"

He sat back on the bed in his black robe. Jason had moved against the headboard as if watching a show, and Nathaniel still lay on his stomach where I'd left him, watching us with pale eyes. "There was a vampire of Belle's lineage who renounced the lust. He took only animals, as well, and I believe would have rotted as Sabin did, but he did not have the time. He began to age in a matter of days. When he was a wizened thing, Belle had him killed."

"But you haven't aged, what have you been doing?" It wasn't accusatory. I simply wanted to know, because I could feel Asher on the end of my hand like something huge and . . . like something I couldn't live without. I'd wanted Nathaniel, I'd wanted Jason, I'd wanted Micah, but not like this. I think it was Jean-Claude's feelings that made this so much more.

"It is possible to feed from a distance without touching," Jean-Claude said.

"That's why a strip club was your first business. You were feeding off the lust."

"*Oui, ma petite.*"

"Teach me to feed from a distance." Even as I said *distance* Asher drew my hand to his cheek and rubbed against it like a cat. I had to close my eyes for a second, but I didn't tell him to stop.

"Feeding from a distance is a poor substitute for a true feeding."

I opened my eyes and stared at him across the room, and now I could feel him. I could feel his need—for blood, sex, love, and the touch of our flesh against his. He wrapped his arms around his body, as if he were cold, or didn't trust himself not to leave the bed and come to us.

"Teach me anyway," I said.

"I cannot, not this soon. In a few nights I will instruct you, but your control is not . . . complete enough yet."

I started to say, "try me," but Asher drew my finger into his mouth in one long, wet line, and I suddenly couldn't think.

"Come to bed, *ma petite*," Jean-Claude said. "If you feed here, there is a chance you may be sated enough that you will not press our so-stubborn Richard."

The thought was enough to dim the desire for a moment or two. I drew my hand away from Asher, and he didn't protest. The sheer horror of what I'd be like around Richard with this inside me helped me think. Being around him normally made me want sex, but now . . . "My God, I'll be lucky if I don't just strip down and do him in the lupanar." I stared at Jean-Claude. "What do I do?"

"I say again, *ma petite*, if you feed now off of such rich fare, you may be too full to need to feed again so soon. It is all I can offer you for tonight. You could simply delay the meeting for a few nights."

I shook my head. "They'll kill Gregory. I have to get him out tonight."

"Then come and feed."

"Define feed?"

"Drink their lust," he said.

I looked at Jason and Nathaniel, and they weren't even trying for neutral. The looks on their faces brought heat in a rush up my face. I shook my head.

"You do not have to have intercourse to feed from them, as you have discovered."

"Aww," Jason said, but the look on his face didn't match the light teasing of his voice. They were responding to my need, the way I'd responded for so long to Jean-Claude's, drawn like a moth to a flame. You just couldn't help wanting to touch it, even when you knew it would burn.

Asher stood. "I will leave you alone. But with permission, I would feed on Nathaniel as my *pomme de sang* for the day."

"No," I said.

His eyes widened just a touch, face going neutral, eyes empty and cool as a spring sky. I felt him draw away from me. "As you wish." He turned for the door.

I grabbed his hand, slid my fingers between his. "Come to bed, Asher."

I'd thought his face was as blank and careful as it could get. I was wrong. His voice held nothing when he asked, "What do you mean?"

"I can't give you back what you had. I can't even give you . . ." I stopped and tried again. "But I can let you feed together again."

"How?"

"If Nathaniel says it's okay, you can take blood from him, and Jean-Claude will take blood from Jason. You can feed together."

"Do you know how intimate a thing it is to feed together on your *pomme de sang*? A *pomme de sang* is not a casual feeding, it is intimate, to be shared only with intimate companions."

I entwined my fingers around his hand. "I know." I took a step towards the bed, drawing him with me. "Let us feed on your lust, Asher, as in days of old."

Asher stared past me at Jean-Claude. "The last time two fed from my desire, it was Belle and you."

"I remember," Jean-Claude said softly.

He held his hand out to Asher from across the room, and I was reminded of him reaching for Asher all those centuries ago. "Let it be again as it was before, but better this time. Anita loves you as you are now, not as some ideal thing like a butterfly on a pin to be tossed aside if a wing falls away. Come to us, Asher, come to us both."

Asher smiled, then took a step to be beside me. He offered me his arm in a very old-fashioned gesture. I wanted to take his arm, to have an excuse to rub my body against his as we walked, and that was why I asked, "How about the use of your robe, as well as your hand?"

He gave a low and perfect bow, so low that his hair almost swept the floor. "That you had to prompt me to offer you my robe proves I am not a gentleman." He slipped it off as he stood, and held it for me like a coat. Asher is six feet, so the sleeves hung over my hands and the hem pooled around my feet. I pushed the sleeves up and got the sash tied, but the only thing to do for the length was just to bundle it in one hand like you would an overly long dress. But it covered almost every inch of me, and I felt better for it. The sweet scent of Asher's cologne clung to the robe, and that soft, masculine scent made me turn back to him. Made my eyes seek him out. Seeing Asher with no shirt on didn't make me feel better. I had the urge to caress his bare skin, to lick the scars. I never remembered being this orally fixated before, and wondered if it was the beast talking or the vampire. But to ask the question would be to admit the desire, and I didn't want to know that badly.

I laid my hand in Asher's, partially because he was holding his hand out to me, and partially because even that small touch was satisfying. I wanted to touch him, wanted to wrap myself around him and answer that question that Jean-Claude was so desperate to answer. Was all this beauty and heat ruined? Was Asher unable to function as a man now? I closed my eyes as he led me forward, because the visuals were just too strong. Through Jean-Claude I knew exactly what Asher had looked like nude, before the scars. I held memories of his body bathed in firelight as he lay rampant on a rug in a room in a country that I had never seen. I knew the play of moonlight on his back as I touched him.

I tripped on the hem of the robe, and he had to catch me to keep me from falling. I was suddenly pressed against his chest with the feel of his arms solid against my back. My face was suddenly uptilted, as if I were waiting for a kiss, and there was one of those moments when you become aware of each other painfully and suddenly aware of the possibilities of the next few seconds. He picked me up in his arms, carrying me easily, smoothly forward. I'd have told him to put me down, but my heart had filled my throat, and I couldn't speak around it.

17

ASHER STRODE TO the bed and laid me on it, leaning over Nathaniel's nude body to do so. I lay on my back and felt movement from every direction. Jean-Claude crawled up beside me, and Jason moved down beside him from the head of the bed. Nathaniel rolled over until we were lying beside each other with him on his side. His eyes told me nothing, except he would not say no, but I asked anyway.

"Do you want Asher to feed from you?"

"Oh, yes," Nathaniel said, and there was something in his voice that I rarely heard—surety. In this moment he knew what he wanted. There was no doubt in him, and the strength of his desire made him . . . stronger.

Asher slid in against Nathaniel's back, so that their bodies spooned together. I turned in time to see Jean-Claude mirror the movement with Jason. Jason reached out, touched my arm, and it was like a door had been burst open. I thought I'd felt desire before this, but it had been a dim echo. It roared over me like something huge and burning, except this fire did not burn, it fed me energy, as if I were not the wood on which it fed, but I was the flame. I was the thing that fed and grew and consumed.

I found Jason's mouth and kissed him, kissed him with lips and tongue and teeth, biting at his lips, pulling him into my mouth. And his body was suddenly pressed against mine, his arms pinning me to him, and Nathaniel slid in behind my back. I was pinned between them, and I didn't care.

My leg slid over Jason's hip, my leg touching Jean-Claude on the other side of him. Jason was suddenly pressed between my legs, with only the silk of his shorts between us. It should have been enough to stop me, but it wasn't. I needed him. Nathaniel raised my hair, bit gently at the back of my neck, and a sound drew from my throat. The two of them fell on me, hands, mouths, bodies, like they were fire to my wood, but this wood drew them in, drank them, almost. Jason pushed against me, and the shorts were baggy enough, the silk thin enough that he entered me. The barest of touches, but it was enough to bring me up for air, to make me draw back from him.

He drew back enough to whisper, "Sorry."

My voice sounded as breathless as his when I said, "I'm not on birth control."

Everyone froze. Jean-Claude peered over Jason's shoulder. "What did you say, *ma petite*?"

"I stopped taking the pill six months ago. I've only been on it for two weeks. No guarantee for another two to four weeks."

"You made love to the Nimir-Raj."

"He's been fixed."

Asher said, "She did what?"

Jean-Claude looked across the bed at him. "Her hunger woke for the first time with the new Nimir-Raj. You have not met him."

"You have," Asher said.

"*Oui.*"

Jason was looking at me, and I had to put a hand over his eyes, close them; And the embarrassment helped, but the *ardeur* only withdrew momentarily, like a wave pulling back from the shore, I could feel it rushing towards us again. Jean-Claude was right, every time I said no, the next time was harder to deny.

Jean-Claude rolled off the bed, and I heard a drawer open. He came back into sight with foil-wrapped packages and wordlessly handed them to Jason and Nathaniel.

That did it. I crawled out from between them to huddle against the headboard. "No, no, no, you said no intercourse."

"I said, that you do not need intercourse to feed."

"No, oh, so no." I tucked the robe around my legs and covered everything I could, which was pretty much all of me.

"We are not planning on them having intercourse with you, *ma petite*. But I have both fed on desire and been fed off of by Belle Morte. There comes a time in the feeding where you lose yourself and cannot always think clearly. I do not want regrets if we get carried away."

"I am not going to have sex with Nathaniel, or Jason. Keep this up, and you won't even be on the list."

"I would rather have you angry with me and not in my bed than accidentally pregnant by one of them."

"I think I can keep from fucking them." I sounded angry, but it wasn't anger that I felt, it was a seed of doubt. That hesitation made the anger worse. I always hid behind anger when I could.

"And before this morning, you would have sworn even more strongly that you would not fuck a strange man you had just met."

The blush was so hot, it almost hurt. "I didn't mean to." That sounded weak even to me. "I couldn't . . ."

"You could not control yourself, *ma petite*, I know. But if you lose control again, would you not rather be safe?"

I shook my head. "If I can't control myself better than this, we're not going to do this."

"And if you do not feed from the lust in this room, how will you go into the lupanar tonight? How will you see your wereleopard lover tonight when he accompanies you to the lupanar without losing your precious control? How will you stand this close to our Richard and not offer yourself to him? *Ma petite*, you have had sex with a stranger."

"He is her Nimir-Raj," Nathaniel said. "They are meant to be a mated pair."

"Pretty to think so," Jean-Claude said, "but I have been where *ma petite* is right now. I have felt the hunger for centuries, and I tell you that you will not be able to go among the shapeshifters tonight unless you are sated. I ask again, can you delay this meeting for a few nights?"

"I might be able to delay it for a night," I said.

He shook his head. "No, *ma petite*, one night will not suffice. You are drawn to

Richard and now to the Nimir-Raj. I think you will be unable to think around them unless you have fed. Your wereleopard's life is at stake. Can you afford to be that distracted? Can you bear the thought of being that out of control in a public setting, among potential enemies?"

"Damn you," I said.

He nodded. "Yes, perhaps, but is anything I have said untrue?"

"No." I shook my head. "I hate it, but no."

"Then let us at least take precautions, *ma petite*. It is luck alone that had the Nimir-Raj made safe. Our lives are complicated enough without that."

I knew what "that" meant. An accidental pregnancy. The thought of it made my blood run colder than anything else had. I hid my face in my hands. "I can't do this."

"Then you must call Richard and tell him you cannot come tonight. You cannot go as you are, *ma petite*. The need will only worsen the longer you deny it."

I raised my face and stared at him. "How much worse?"

He lowered his gaze. "Bad enough."

I crawled across the bed to him, made him look at me. "How bad?"

He tried not to meet my gaze. His shields were back in place, and I couldn't tell what he was feeling. "You would be attracted to all the men. You would . . . I cannot guarantee what you would do, *ma petite*, or who you would do it with."

I just stared at him. "No. No, I would never . . ."

He touched my mouth with his fingertip. "*Ma petite*, if you have not found my memories of my first days with this inside my body, then it is a blessing. I was a wanton thing before I became a vampire. But what I did when the desire first fell upon me . . . The desire did not hit me at once, because I craved blood first, then when that quieted, the desire rose inside me." He took my hands in his, pressed them against the cool flesh of his chest. "I did things, *ma petite*, things that even to a hardened libertine were humilating. A look, a glance, and it was enough to bring me to them."

"Didn't Belle Morte try to protect you?"

"I did not meet Belle until I had been dead nearly five years."

I stared at him. "I thought Belle was your, whatever, that she made you into a vamp."

"Lissette was my creator. She was of Belle's line, but not a master vampire, not by any stretch of the definition. In France it is customary that every kiss of vampires has at least one vampire belonging to each of the council bloodlines. Lissette was the only one of her kind in a nest descended mostly of far less pleasant vampires. Julian was her Master of the City, and he was my first true master. He brought in people for me, but not people I would have chosen. He brought in . . ." Jean-Claude shook his head. "He amused himself at my expense, because he knew I would take whatever he offered, because I would have no choice. I thought I had no room for embarrassment, but he taught me that there were things I did not want to do, and I did them anyway."

I think if he hadn't been shielding so strongly that I would have seen what he was remembering, but he didn't want me to see.

"Let me spare you such degradation, *ma petite*. You are not as I was. You have never given yourself freely. I fear what you would do, or think of yourself, if you did these things. I do not think your sense of yourself would survive intact."

"You're scaring me," I said.

"Good, you should be frightened. Asher met me before I had mastered the *ardeur*. He can tell you what I was like then."

I just looked at Asher.

"I had seen the *ardeur* rise in others before Jean-Claude, and I have watched it since, but I have never seen anyone so crazed by it," said Asher.

"So you helped him learn how to control the *ardeur*."

"*Non*. Lissette sent to Belle, telling her of Jean-Claude's beauty. I was sent to, how would you say, look him over for Belle. I advised Belle not to bring Jean-Claude and his master to court."

"Why?" I asked.

"I was jealous of his beauty and his prowess. After ten years she was growing bored with me, or so I feared. And I did not wish the competition."

"I learned to control the *ardeur* without the aid of another who had experienced it. For five years I fed on flesh as I fed on blood. Only then did I master the ability to feed from a distance."

"Five years!" I said.

"Belle taught me true control of the *ardeur*, and I was not hers until I had been dead five years. But I will be there for you from the beginning. It will not be as it was for me." Jean-Claude hugged me against him, and that scared me more. "I would never have married the marks with you if I had thought you could inherit my incubus. I would not knowingly have done this to you."

I pushed away from him and found him crying, and the fear sat like stale metal on my tongue. I was so scared my body went quiet, not racing, but almost as if every beat of my body, every breath, had simply stopped, and all there was to fill me was fear.

"What have you done to me?"

"I thought at first that you were not vampire, and it would not be a true hunger. But watching you today, I know that it is as it was for me. You *must* feed. You must not deny yourself. To do so is to court madness, or worse."

"No," I said.

"If you had withstood the Nimir-Raj's advances, then I would say that your strength of will might conquer it. If you had withstood the desire to feed on Nathaniel, I would say you would master it. But you fed on him."

"I did not have sex with Nathaniel."

"No. And wasn't what you did instead more satisfying to some part of you than mere intercourse would have been?"

I started to say no and stopped. I could still feel Nathaniel's flesh in my mouth, the touch of his skin under my hands, the taste of his blood on my tongue. The memory brought the hunger over me in a hot rush. Not merely the lust, but Jean-Claude's craving for blood, and Richard's beast—or my beast—wanting to take that last bite and tear flesh for real, no pretending, no holding back.

I had an awful idea. "If I deny one hunger all of them grow worse, don't they?"

"If I deny the lust, I need more blood, and the reverse is true."

"I don't just have your blood lust, Jean-Claude, I have Richard's beast—or mine. I wanted to tear Nathaniel up. I wanted to feed on him for real, the way an animal does. Will that grow worse, too?"

His face started to slip back into careful, neutral lines. I grabbed his shoulders, shook him. "No! No more hiding. Will it grow worse?"

"I have no way of knowing for certain."

"No more games! Will it grow worse?"

"I believe so." His voice was very soft as he said it.

I drew back from him, huddled against the headboard, stared at him, waiting for him to say, "sorry, just kidding," but he just met my eyes. I stared at him, because I didn't want to see anyone else's face. If I saw pity, it might make me cry. If I saw lust, it'd make me mad.

I finally said, "What am I going to do?" There was no inflection in my voice, just a dragging tiredness.

"You will feed, and we will help you. We will keep you safe."

I finally glanced at the others. Every face was either carefully neutral or, in Nathaniel's case, staring down at the bed, as if he didn't trust me to see his eyes. Probably smart of him.

"Fine, but I think we can do better than condoms."

"What do you mean, *ma petite*?"

"Nathaniel can put his shorts on, and I'll find my jammies."

"I still think . . ."

I held a hand up, and Jean-Claude fell silent. "They can put them on underneath their clothes, just in case, but I know that if I tell Nathaniel not to . . . that he won't." I frowned at Jason.

"I'll be good," he said.

"I am not afraid that Nathaniel will disobey you, *ma petite*."

The tone in his voice turned me from Jason's face to his. "What do you mean?"

"I am worried that he will indeed do everything you tell him to do."

We stared at each other for a long space of my heartbeats. I understood what he meant now. It wasn't the boys he didn't trust, it was me. I would have liked to say, I would never ask them—either of them—to do that to me, but there was something in Jean-Claude's eyes, some knowledge, some sorrow, that kept me from saying it.

"How much control am I going to lose?" I asked finally.

"I do not know."

"I'm getting really tired of hearing you say that."

"And I of saying it."

I finally asked what I had to ask, "What do we do now?"

"Our *pomme de sangs* fetch their clothing and yours, and we feed."

And as much as I hated it, as much as I wanted to deny it, I knew he was right. I'd been trying not to be a sociopath because it made me a monster. I just hadn't known what I was saying. I needed to feed off humans, lust instead of blood and flesh, but it was still feeding. Being a sociopath was beginning not to sound so bad.

18

SOMEWHERE DURING THE dressing process I came to my senses. I stayed up against the headboard, Asher's robe belted securely over the red pajamas, my face averted, forehead pressed to the wood. Control was the heart of who I thought I was. I could do this, or rather not do this. I had to try and let this pass me by, because to do anything else . . . I could not do this.

The bed moved, and just the sensation of the men moving around on the bed was enough to tighten my body, speed my pulse. Dear God, help me. This couldn't be happening. I'd feared ending up as a vampire. I'd come close many times, but I'd never thought it would happen like this. I was still alive, still human, but the hunger rose inside me like some great beast trying to dig its way out of me, and all that kept it from surfacing was my fingers digging into the wood, my forehead pressed against the carvings. I wasn't sure which hunger I was fighting. But the *ardeur* colored all of it, whether I was craving flesh, or blood, the sex was there in all of it. I couldn't separate them, and that was scary all on its own.

I felt someone crawling towards me, and I knew without looking that it was Jean-Claude. I could just feel him.

"*Ma petite*, all is prepared, we need only you."

I spoke with my face still pressed into the wood, my fingers clinging to it. "Well, then you'll just have to do without."

I felt his hand hovering over my shoulder, and I said, "Don't touch me!"

"*Ma petite, ma petite*, I would change this if I could, but I cannot. We must make the best of what is given us."

That made me look at him. His face was too close, eyes that intense midnight blue, hair a dark glory around his pale face. I flashed on another face just as pale, just as perfect, with a wealth of black hair, but with eyes a rich brown like dark amber. They grew in my vision until the world drowned in the dark honey of her eyes, as if it were poured over my eyes, over my skin, my body, until it filled me, and when I raised my eyes to Jean-Claude's worried face, his hand on my arm, I saw something close to terror in his eyes.

He scrambled back from me, and when I turned and stared at Asher, he spilled off the bed, to stand shaking. Jason and Nathaniel stayed on the bed because they didn't know any better. "What's wrong?" Jason asked.

Nathaniel whispered, "Her eyes."

I turned and caught sight of myself in the standing mirror in the corner. My es had filled with pale brown fire, not the darkness of my own eyes, but hers.

"No," I said, softly. I felt her thousands of miles away. Her pleasure at my ter-lled through my body, raised my beast and sent me falling onto the bed. My hands strained for something to hold on to, some help, but there was nothing to fight; it was power and it was inside me.

She explored me, raising my beast until it rolled just under the surface of my skin. She touched that part of Richard that was still inside me and raised his beast, until the two energies entwined and my body started to convulse.

I heard yelling. "She's going to change!" Hands holding me down to the bed.

But Belle had learned what she wanted and let them slide back into my body. She separated out the powers inside me like you'd sort a deck of cards. She touched Jean-Claude's link to me and it puzzled her, I could feel it. Until that moment she'd assumed I was a vampire, and now she knew I wasn't. She let what puzzled her slide back deep inside me, then she called the *ardeur*, the incubus, and the moment I thought it, I realized it was the wrong word. Succubus, she whispered in my head, succubus. The hands that had been holding me down, poured over my body, responding to the *ardeur*. It was like being covered in pure lust, rolled in it, like flour on a piece of meat before you cook it.

Hands slid along my skin, a mouth closed on my mouth, and I couldn't see who was right above me, kissing me. I could feel the weight of their body, another set of hands, but I could see nothing but a shining amber light.

Belle kept the *ardeur* on the surface, because it amused her. I couldn't see whose hands were where, or who was doing what, all I could do was feel them; the brush of silk, the press of flesh, a curtain of hair, the scent of vanilla, but I could not see. Belle Morte was using my eyes for other things. She touched that part of me that allowed me to raise the dead. She caressed my necromancy, tried to bring it to the surface as she had the two; beasts and the *ardeur*, but everything else she had explored was hers to call, it was all in some way part of her lineage, her blood. But the necromancy was all mine.

My magic welled up through me, pushing her back, but I couldn't cast her out, not with just the raw power. It was as if she floated near the surface of some dark pool and I sat at the bottom trying to push her out. I couldn't cast her out, but I could see again, think again.

I was nude from the waist up. Nathaniel's mouth closed on my nipple drawing it in. I cried out, and Jason lowered his mouth to my other breast. There was a moment when I stared down at the two of them pressed to my body, the blond head, the auburn, their mouths working at my breasts, the line of their bodies pressed along mine, the marks of my teeth still visible in Nathaniel's flesh, when the *ardeur*, when Belle Morte spilled over me again. Jason's hand slid down the front of the red silk bottoms, his fingers finding me as if he'd always known just where to touch me. I writhed under his touch, their touch.

I grabbed Jason's wrist, tried to pull his hand away, but he fought me and it was a tender place to fight over. I screamed, "Jean-Claude! Asher!"

"Ma petite?" Jean-Claude made the name a question as if he wasn't sure it was really me. I found the vampires standing beside the bed, not helping, not hindering, just watching. But I understood; the *ardeur* called to them too. They were afraid to touch us.

"Feed," I said.

"Non, ma petite."

"I can't fight her and the hunger. Feed, and let me feed."

"You cannot break free of her, *ma petite*."

"Help me!"

He looked across the bed at Asher, and I watched something pass between them, something built of sorrow and old regrets. "She is right, *mon ami*, she cannot fight Belle and the *ardeur*."

"She doesn't understand what she's asking," Jean-Claude said.

"No, but she asks, and if we do not do it, we will always wonder. I would rather try and fail, than regret having never tried at all."

They stared at each other for a second or two, then Asher crawled onto the bed and Jean-Claude followed him. Asher stretched out beside Nathaniel, and Jean-Claude mirrored him with Jason. Belle Morte's joy flared through me, filled my eyes with honey-colored flames, and I lost my grip on Jason's wrist. His hand slid back over me, but when I turned to look, I could see Jean-Claude through the dark glass of her eyes and Asher on the other side. I knew that once they touched either *pomme de sang* they would be caught in the desire, and they would not break free. It was a trap. I opened my mouth to say, don't, but three things happened all at once. They each struck into the neck of the man on their side, as if they'd known exactly what the other would do, and Jason forced me over that shining edge of orgasm. I screamed, body bucking against the bed, and only their weight kept me from sitting up, from clawing the air, because it wasn't just my own pleasure I was feeling. I felt Asher's fangs in Nathaniel's neck, felt Nathaniel's body build, build, and finally release in a rush of pleasure that made him bite down on my breast, made me score not his back, but Asher's with my nails. Jason drew his mouth back from me and screamed. The vampires rode their bodies, and I knew with Belle Morte's awareness that the only reason they didn't orgasm with us was the blood pressure wasn't there yet. But the pleasure was. The five of us were locked into wave after wave of pleasure. Like the heat the *ardeur* was named for, it passed over and through us again and again. It was like floating, skinless, formless, just above the bed, and I could feel their heartbeats inside my body. Finally I could feel Jean-Claude and Asher, feel their hearts give a massive beat and feel the life flood through their bodies and spill in a long, hot, line of pleasure that seemed to be pulled from the soles of their feet to the tops of their heads, as if every piece of their bodies, every atom, exploded in pleasure at once. Nathaniel, Jason, and I screamed for them, because their mouths were still locked on the blood, still drinking, still feeding. Then it was over, and the five of us lay motionless, except for the frantic rise and fall of our chests, trying to breath, trying to remember what it was like to be inside our own skins, with just one heart inside us, instead of five. We melted back into our own skins, only the faint dew of sweat and the panicked thunder of our pulses beating against each other's bodies.

Jean-Claude and Asher pulled back from Nathaniel and Jason just as they'd bitten them—together, in a synchronization as perfect now as it had been two centuries ago. Belle Morte filled my mind with images—images of the two of them making love to her before Asher was scored, when they were her perfectly matched pair. I had a confused image of them making love to her at the same time. The feel of them pushing inside her, as perfectly aware then as now of where each her's bodies were, and of exactly what they would do. She missed them, and it partially my love of Asher, my seeing him as beautiful, that made her regret. aring wasn't only one way; she was getting my feelings, too. But I was my-. The desire had been well fed, sated, so now I could do what I did best.

I called my magic, pulled it around me like a breath of cool wind against my sweat-soaked skin. Nathaniel and Jason pulled back from me, eyes still unfocused.

Jean-Claude and Asher raised up above each of the smaller men, their eyes as out of focus as the lycanthropes', but Jean-Claude said, "*Ma petite*, what . . ."

I reached for him. "Take my hand."

"*Ma petite* . . ."

"Now!"

Belle's power cut through me like a whip in a practiced hand. She'd been using it to tickle my skin; now she meant it to hurt. I writhed on the bed, only Jason's and Nathaniel's weight keeping me from flailing. My vision was being consumed by brown flames.

A hand in mine, cool flesh, and the moment Jean-Claude touched me I could see again. I was his human servant, he was my master, we were part of a triumvirate of power. If Richard had been here we could have chased her back to the hell she crawled out of. I sent the call in my head, screaming psychically for Richard, but the answer came against my skin. Jason stared at me, confused. He said, "Anita . . ." I felt Richard's power in Jason, the link of their pack. The power of the triumvirate leaped between Jean-Claude's hand, my hand, and Jason's body. It would work, it had to work, because I could feel Belle Morte rising inside me again, and I wasn't sure I had it in me to chase her back.

I drew my necromancy like a great dark cloud, a storm ready to break, filling the room with the tingling brush of magic. Nathaniel drew back, whispered, "Nimir-Ra."

The power pressed like lightning in a bottle, but the bottle was my body, and there was no release without one more thing . . . blood. The last time we'd done overt triumvirate magic I'd asked the boys to give me blood, watched as Jean-Claude had sunk fangs into Richard for the first time, but not today. Today *I* needed the blood, *I* wanted the blood. I would not share.

I used my free hand to lower Jason's face towards me, but I didn't kiss him. My mouth moved down the side of his cheek, and I whispered, "I need blood, Jason. Say yes."

He'd been holding himself off of me with his arms, but he whispered, "Yes," and collapsed his upper body across my breasts, his hand sliding along my stomach as if he meant to do other things. I could smell the blood just below the surface of his neck, could taste his pulse like candy on my tongue, and I bit him. I wasn't a vampire. There were no mind tricks to make it pleasant. We weren't having sex anymore, there was no distraction, only my teeth tearing his flesh, his blood pouring into my mouth, and the moment the blood poured over me the necromancy flared and I pushed it into that honeyed touch. She laughed at me, at us, then the laughter stopped, because she felt the push of my power. I was a necromancer, and she was just another kind of vampire. My magic didn't differentiate between her and any other corpse. I shoved her out, cast her back, locked her outside us. I'd been training in witchcraft this year, so I bound her from us, bound her from harming us in any way, bound her from contacting us through her power. My last thought to her was, *If you want to find out what the fuck is going on, pick up a phone*. Then she was gone.

19

I WAS NAKED again. It seemed to be a theme that night. The five of us lay in a heap, breathing hard, bodies tingling, with that rush that magic will leave behind sometimes—where you feel both tired and exhilarated at the same time—sort of like sex. Asher and Nathaniel lay on the bed just out of my reach. My mouth, chin, and neck were covered in Jason's blood. He lay with his head on my chest, his head turned so I could see the neck wound. I'd marked Nathaniel and Micah, but there was a piece of meat missing from Jason's neck. It wasn't a big piece, but it was a missing piece of flesh, nonetheless.

I swallowed hard, taking deep, even breaths. I would not throw up. I would not throw up. I would not throw up. I was going to throw up. I pushed everyone off the bed and ran for the bathroom. I threw up, and the flesh—about the size of a fifty-cent piece—came up just like it had gone down—whole. There was something about seeing it, about having my worst fears confirmed that brought nausea in a burning wave. I threw up until I thought my head would explode and I was dry heaving.

There was a knock on the door. "*Ma petite*, may I come in?" He hadn't asked if I was alright. Smart vampire. I didn't answer him, just stayed kneeling with my head against the cool bathtub edge, wondering if I was going to throw up again or my head would fall off first. My head hurt worse than my stomach.

I heard the door open. "*Ma petite?*"

"I'm here," I said, my voice sounding thick, as if I'd been crying. I kept my head down. I didn't want to see him, or anyone.

I saw the edge of the black robe, then more of it as he knelt down in front of me. "Is there anything I can get you?"

A dozen answers flew through my mind, most of them sarcastic, but I settled for, "Some aspirin and a toothbrush."

"You could ask me to cut my heart out at this moment, and I might do it. Instead you ask for aspirin and a toothbrush." He leaned in and laid the gentlest of kisses on the top of my head. "I will get what you ask." He stood, and again I heard a drawer opening and closing.

I looked up and watched him move efficiently around the bathroom, setting out a bottle of aspirin and a toothbrush and a choice of toothpastes. It was absurdly domestic, and the black-furred robe didn't fit the part. Jean-Claude looked like someone who should have servants, and he did. But mostly around me he'd always done for himself, and for me. When I wasn't around he probably had fifty dancing girls waiting on him hand and foot. But with me, it was often just him.

He brought me the aspirin and a glass of water. I took them, and there was a moment when I wasn't sure my stomach would keep them down, but it passed. Jean-Claude helped me stand, and I let him. It wasn't just that my legs were shaky—though they were—it was more like all of me was shaky, uncertain.

I started to shiver and couldn't stop. Jean-Claude held me against his robe in the circle of his arms. My breast hurt where it rubbed against the cloth. I pulled back enough to look down at my body. There was a perfect imprint of Nathaniel's teeth encircling my breast around the areola. He'd only drawn blood in a few places, but the rest was a deep red-purple. It was going to be a hell of a bruise if my body didn't heal it first.

Jean-Claude traced his finger across the upper part of the bite mark, and I winced. "Why is it things like this never hurt while you're doing them?"

"The question is its own answer, *ma petite*."

Strangely, I understood what he meant. "It's almost a mirror of what I did to his chest."

"Nathaniel is being cautious, I think."

"What do you mean?"

"He did nothing to you that you had not done to him first."

"I thought they were both carried away with the *ardeur* and Belle Morte."

"The first time you feel the call of her power it is heady stuff. But the fact that Jason did something that he knew you would not allow, and Nathaniel did not, may mean that Nathaniel has more control of himself than Jason does."

"I would have thought it was the other way around."

"I know," he said, and the way he said it made me look at him.

"What's that supposed to mean?"

"It means, *ma petite*, that you may know Nathaniel's heart's desire, but I do not think you truly know *him*."

"He doesn't know himself," I said.

"In part that is true, but I think he will surprise you."

"Are you hiding something from me?"

"About Nathaniel, no."

I sighed. "You know on another day I'd make you tell me what that cryptic remark meant, but damn it, I want a little comfort from someone right now, and I guess you're it."

His eyebrows raised. "When you ask in so flattering a manner, how can I refuse?"

"No games, please, Jean-Claude, please, just hold me."

He drew me back into the circle of his arms, and I moved so that the bite mark wasn't hurting, or rather wasn't hurting more than it already did. It had turned into a throbbing pain, sharp when touched. It did hurt, but a part of me found that satisfying. It was a comfirmation of what we'd done, a painful souvenir of something that had been amazing. If my morals hadn't gotten in the way, I could have just marveled at the whole thing.

"Why am I pleased that Nathaniel marked me?" I asked it in a small voice, because I wasn't a hundred percent sure Jean-Claude shouldn't have been jealous about it.

He stroked my hair, as his other arm held me close. "I can think of many reasons." His voice vibrated through his chest against my ear, mingling with the sound of his heartbeat.

"One that makes sense to me would be enough," I said.

"Ah, one that makes sense to *you*, now that is a different question."

I squeezed my arms around his waist. "No games, remember, just tell me."

"It could be that you are truly becoming his Nimir-Ra." His arm tightened around me. "I do feel something different in you, *ma petite*, some wildness that was not there before. It does not feel like Richard's beast feels, but it is a difference. It may simply be that as Nathaniel's Nimir-Ra you want closer contact with him."

It made sense. It was hard to argue with the logic of it, but I wanted to. "What could be the other reasons?"

"Belle Morte treated you as a vampire of her line. If through the marks or your necromancy you have some of the powers of a vampire, you may have others. It could be that leopards will be your animal to call. I admit that the first is the more likely reason, but the second is also possible."

I leaned back enough to see his face. "Are you attracted to the wolves?" I asked.

"I find it pleasant to have the wolves around me. It is comforting to touch them like a . . . pet, or lover."

I wasn't sure how I felt about him using pet and lover in the same sentence, but I let it go. "So you want to have sex with the werewolves?"

"Do you want to have sex with Nathaniel?"

"No . . . not exactly."

"But you want to touch him and be touched?"

I had to think about that for a few seconds. "I guess so."

"In a true joining of animal and vampire, there is a desire in both to touch, for one to serve and the other to take care of them."

"Padma, the Master of Beasts, treated his animals like shit."

"One of the many reasons that Padma will always be a secondary power on the Council is his belief that all power must be taken, that all power must come through fear. True power comes when others offer it to you and you merely accept it as a gift, not as the spoils of some personal war."

"So the fact that you treat your wolves better than most is just, what, a political decision?"

He shrugged, still holding me against him. "I do not know how other vampires feel. I know only that Belle Morte felt attracted to her cats and I feel the same for my wolves. Perhaps it is only her line that turns the bond between animal and vampire into something like lovers? Much of her power fed into sex, or at least, attraction, and perhaps that is not how others feel?" He frowned. "I had not truly thought about that before. Perhaps it is another benefit of her lineage—or a shortfall of it—that most of my powers turn to something resembling sex."

"Does Asher feel the same way about his animal to call?"

"He has no animal to call."

I widened my eyes. "I thought all master vamps over a certain age had an animal to call."

"Most of the time they do, but not always. Just as his bite can give true sexual release and mine cannot. We have different powers."

"But not having an animal to call is like a major . . ."

"It means he is weaker than I am."

"But he could still be Master of the City somewhere else. I mean I've met Masters of the City that had no animal to call before."

"If there was a territory vacant in this country, and he would be willing to leave us, then yes, he might rise to Master of the City."

I started to ask, *Then why doesn't he go?* But I was pretty sure I knew the answer, and it was a painful answer, so I left it unsaid. Maybe I was growing up at last. Not every thought that came into my head had to come out of my mouth.

"Or it could simply be that you've wanted Nathaniel for a very long time. There is satisfaction in finally giving in to the desire."

I pushed away from him. "You know, you're not very good at this comforting stuff."

"You said no games. Isn't a lie the same as playing a game?"

I frowned at him. "I did not have sex with Nathaniel."

"Come, *ma petite*, you did not have intercourse, but to say you did not have sex is splitting the hair a little too fine, no?"

I glared at him and tried to be angry, but there was something closer to panic than anger making my heart beat faster. "Are you saying that what we just did qualifies as sex?"

"Are you saying that it did not?"

I turned so I couldn't see his face, hugging my arms around myself. I finally turned back to look at him. I tried leaning against the wall, but the tiles were cold and I was still naked. I needed my clothes, but they were out in the other room, and I was so not ready to see the other men again.

"So you're saying that we had sex—all of us?"

He took a deep breath. "What answer do you want, *ma petite*?"

"Truth would be nice."

"No, you do not want the truth. I thought that you did, or I would have taken better care about what I said." He looked tired. "I am glad you are the woman that you are, but there are moments when I wish that you could simply enjoy something without being chased around the room by your guilt and your morals afterwards. What we did tonight is a glorious thing. A thing to be shared and treasured, not something to be ashamed of."

"I was doing better with it before you told me it counts as sex."

"And the fact that I had to tell you that it counts as sex means you are still lying to yourself more than I have ever tried to lie to you."

"What's that supposed to mean?"

He held up a hand. "I will say no more about this. You do not want the truth, and you told me not to lie. I am out of options."

I hugged myself and frowned at the floor. I tried to wrap my mind around what he'd said, what we'd done, and I just couldn't do it. We needed a change of topic, fast.

"Jason acted like a power substitute for Richard," I said.

"*Oui.*" He let me change the subject without a word or a change in expression.

"I didn't know we could do that."

"Nor did I." He took those few gliding steps that put him beside me again. "If it is comfort that you want, more than truth, then I can do that." He touched my chin, raised my face so that our gazes met. "But you must tell me when you do not want the truth, *ma petite*. It is usually your greatest demand on me."

I stared up into his beautiful face and understood what he was offering—comfort, but not honesty. Comforting lies, because I didn't want to hear the truth.

"I don't want you to lie to me, but I'm about at my limit for hard truths for the day. I need a breather."

"You want a space of calm to think about everything. I understand that. I can even give it to you for a few hours, but you have to confront Richard at the lupanar tonight, and I fear that more hard truths await you there."

I put my face against his chest, cuddled into the smoothness of his skin, caught between the furred lapels. "Your bringing up Richard isn't going to make me feel better."

"My apologies." He was rubbing my back with his hands, over and over. The movement made the fur on the sleeves rub up and down my body, from my butt to my shoulders. It was soothing and not soothing at the same time. I looked up at him and didn't know whether to cry or scream. "I thought I fed the *ardeur*."

His hands went still against my body. "You have, and you have fed it well, but it is always just below the surface. Like being full but still admiring a beautifully made dessert."

I didn't really like the analogy, but couldn't think of a better one. I pressed my body into his robe, let him cradle me against his body, and listened to the comforting beat of his heart.

I spoke with my face pressed against his chest, the black furred edge of the lapels tickling my lips. "Why didn't you warn me that she could do that?"

"If you were a vampire of my line, then I would have warned you, but you are not vampire, you are human, and it should not work that way for you."

I leaned back enough to see his face. "Can she enter any of her . . . children?"

"No, her ability to look in upon her children only lasts for a few nights. Once the new vampire is strong enough to control its own hunger, then she is unable to enter, as if some door closes that was held open before."

"She called my beast, or beasts, or whatever the hell is going on with me. She called it to the surface like she knew what she was doing."

"Her animal to call is all great cats."

"So, leopards," I said.

He nodded. "Among other things."

"I thought only the Master of Beasts could call more than one animal."

"It was the ability he came with from almost the beginning, but many of the oldest grow into a variety of powers. She began, as I understand it, able to call only leopards, then one by one the other great cats answered to her."

"If I really am a wereleopard, will she be able to control me—if she meets me?"

"You cast her out, *ma petite*. You can answer your own question, can you not?"

"You're saying I kicked her butt once, I can do it again."

"Something like that, *oui*."

I pushed away from him, my fingers trailing down his arms under the heavy robe until our hands touched. "Trust me, Jean-Claude, one victory doesn't guarantee you'll win the war."

"This was not a small victory, *ma petite*. Never in all her two thousand years of life has any of her line defied her as you just did." He'd bent at the waist just a little to kiss my hands, showing a long, thin triangle of his chest and upper stomach. My gaze followed that line of pale flesh down into the shadow that hid the rest of him. For once I didn't want to undo the robe. Part of it was that I was well . . . satisfied, and part of it—most of it—was that I had just had sex with four men at once, and my discomfort level was just a little too high to think about any sex for a while.

"I knew that vampires could make the bite pleasant, but I never dreamed it felt like that," I said.

"It is one of Asher's gifts to make his bite orgasmic."

I looked at him.

He nodded. "*Oui, ma petite*, I can make it pleasant, but not that pleasant."

"Asher bit me once, and it wasn't orgasmic."

"He drew back when he realized he had rolled your mind without intending to. He . . . behaved himself."

I raised my eyebrows at that. If tonight was the real thing, he'd more than behaved himself. "You fed off of it, too, and Belle Morte, as well."

"It was a feast, was it not?" And something in the way he said it made me blush. "I do not mean to embarrass you, *ma petite*, but it *was* glorious. I have not shared Asher's gift in over two hundred years. I had almost made myself forget what it was like."

"So you can't do this without Belle Morte."

"One of her gifts is to be a bridge, a connection, between her children. That allowed the sharing of gifts."

"I cast her out, Jean-Claude, it won't be happening again."

"And we are both thrilled. I do not think you understand the risk we all took, *ma petite*. If you had failed to cast her out, then she could have done things to us, even from such a distance. We are the only two of her line that ever left her side willingly. Some were exiled, but none simply left, and she is not a woman that takes rejection well."

That was an understatement. "She saw Asher through my eyes. I felt her regret that she'd let him go, that she hadn't seen him the way I did."

He turned his head to one side. "Then perhaps even a very old dog can learn new tricks."

I swallowed, and something about it made me very aware of the taste of blood and other things in my mouth. I had to get cleaned up.

I went to the sink and watched him in the mirror behind me. I'd known I was nude, but it wasn't until I saw myself in the mirror that I really noticed it. I'd managed to wipe most of the blood off my mouth with toilet paper, but it was still clinging to my chest and my neck. "I really need a robe of my own," I said.

"I would offer you mine," he said.

I shook my head, reaching for the toothbrush. Normally, I would have washed the blood off first, but I wanted that taste out of my mouth more. "You naked around me right now is not what I need."

"I will send . . ." he hesitated, "Asher for a robe for you."

"You started to say Jason, didn't you?"

He looked at me in the mirror.

"I know he'll heal, but . . . I could have really hurt him," I said.

"But you didn't, and that is what matters."

"Pretty to think so," I said.

He smiled, but not like he was happy. "I will send Asher for a robe."

"Great. Thank you."

I squeezed toothpaste onto the brush as he went for the door. He stopped with his hand on the doorknob. "Normally you would owe your *pomme de sangs* some gift or show of gratitude for serving you."

"I think they've had all the gratitude they're getting from me for one day."

He laughed, and the sound rode over my body like a caress of silk. "Oh, yes, *ma petite*, and I think they would agree, but I tell you this for later. You must reward your *pomme de sang* for his, or her, services."

"Money wouldn't do it?" I asked.

The look on his face said he was truly insulted, outraged, in fact. "You have just shared something more intimate than most people will ever know with another being. They have given us a great gift this day, and they are not whores, Anita." My real name, I was in trouble. "They are *pomme de sangs*, think of them as beloved mistresses."

I frowned at him.

"Today the sharing of pleasure was reward enough, but you will need to feed the *ardeur* every day, and unless it is a feeding worthy of the thirst, more than once a day for a few weeks."

"What are you saying?" I asked.

"I am saying that it would be best if you chose a *pomme de sang* and kept him near you, for you do not truly know yet what your hunger is like. It may be a light thing, easily tended, or it may not."

"You're saying I'll need to do this every day?"

"Yes."

"Fuck."

He shook his head. "Was today so horrible, *ma petite*? Was the pleasure you gained so very small?"

"It's not that. It was glorious, and you know it. But we'll never be able to duplicate that, not without Belle Morte, and I don't want a return visit from her."

"Nor do I. But there are many things that can be done to feed, and when you have some control I will teach you to feed from a distance."

"When?"

"A few weeks."

"Shit." I turned back to the mirror, not looking at him. "How do I pick a *pomme de sang*?"

"I think you already have," he said.

I looked at him. "You mean Nathaniel."

He nodded.

"No, I . . . I don't trust myself not to lose control and . . . you know what I mean."

"He is lovely to the eye, and he cares for you. Would it be so very wrong?"

"Yes, yes, it would be like child molesting. He can't say no. If a person can't say no, then it's the same as rape."

"Perhaps what you do not wish to acknowledge, *ma petite*, is that Nathaniel knows exactly what he wants, and what he wants is you."

"He wants me to dominate him in every sense of the word."

"It is best if a *pomme de sang* is submissive to you."

I shook my head.

"Then who else would you want to risk being carried away with, your Nimir-Raj?" This time there was something in his voice.

"You are jealous."

"The Nimir-Raj is not a *pomme de sang*, a mistress, a dessert, no matter how delectable. He is an entrée, a very, very main course, and I wish to be the only entrée at your table."

"You were sharing me with Richard, and he certainly wasn't just dessert."

"Very true, but he also had ties to me. He is my wolf to call, and that is a different . . . relationship to me, to you, than some stranger."

"I know it was the *ardeur*, but damn, I've never . . ."

"You are not a woman of casual lusts. No, *ma petite*, you are not. And I fear that this Nimir-Raj is no more casual than the rest of your lusts." He looked so serious when he said it, solemn.

"What do you mean?"

"If you are truly his Nimir-Ra, then you will be drawn to him. There is no help for it. And truthfully, I cannot fault your taste. He is not as fair of face as our Richard, but he does have certain compensations." The look on his face made me blush again.

I turned to the sink and started brushing my teeth, and he took it as a dismissal. He went out laughing. When the door was closed behind him and I was alone I stood for a long time looking at myself in the mirror. It still looked like me. But I could taste Jason's blood underneath the toothpaste. I started scrubbing and spitting and running the cold water, listening to the sound of the water instead of the screaming inside my head.

When Jean-Claude came back into the room I was rinsing the blood out of the washrag I'd used and had three different kinds of mouthwash sitting beside the sink. I'd used all three, and I couldn't taste anything but minty freshness. You could scrub yourself clean of the blood and the taste of it in your mouth, but the stains that really mattered were the ones that no amount of soap or water could touch. I'd have said that things couldn't get any worse, but I knew they could, and rapidly. If I locked myself away for a few days until I could control the *ardeur*, the werewolves would vote without me there, and they'd execute Gregory. If they killed Gregory, it wasn't just Jacob that I'd kill. It would be war between me, my pard, and Richard's pack. Richard was just Boy Scout enough to get in my way, and maybe force me to kill him. Something inside of me would die if Richard died, and if I pulled the trigger . . . some things you recover from, some things you don't. Killing Richard would be one of those things I wouldn't recover from.

Jean-Claude said softly, "Are you alright, *ma petite*?"

I shook my head, but said, "Sure."

He held a bundle of blue satin out to me. "Then you need to get dressed, and I will escort you back outside."

I looked at him. "Is it that obvious that I don't want to go back out there?"

"Jason has been taken to his room. He will heal. But we thought it would upset you to see him. Nathaniel awaits your pleasure, since he did drive you."

"What about Asher?"

"He took Jason away."

"You know we have the answer to the question you've been wanting to know," I said.

We looked at each other. "I felt his release, *ma petite*. I know that he has been tormenting me, allowing me to believe he was ruined. But we still do not know how badly scarred he is, and that is a ruin of a different sort."

"You mean he may feel he's so scarred that he doesn't want anyone to see him, or touch him?"

"*Oui.*"

"Until the two of you touched the boys, the *ardeur* didn't spread to you. Belle Morte didn't spread to you. It's like a disease," I said.

"I have seen that particular disease set loose in a banquet room the size of a football field and spread from person to person until all fell upon each other in a . . . well, orgy is too mild a word."

"What did she gain from making a whole room of humans lose control like that?"

"She gains power from every feeding around her, but it was not that alone. She wished to see if there were limits to the number of people she could spread the desire through."

"Did she find her limit?"

"No."

"So hundreds of people," I said.

He nodded.

"And she fed off of the lust from them all?"

"*Oui.*"

"What did she do with all that power?"

"She helped a marquis seduce a king and changed the trade routes and alliances of three countries."

I widened my eyes. "Well, at least it didn't go to waste."

"Belle has many faults, but the wasting of an advantage is not one of them."

"What did she gain through all the political maneuvering?"

"Land, titles, and a king that adored her. Remember, *ma petite*, that this was at a time in history when to be king of a nation meant to be absolute monarch. His word was life and death, and she ruled him through the sweet secrets of her body."

"No one is that good in bed."

A look passed over his face—a small smile that he tried to hide.

"If she was that wonderful, then why did you and Asher leave her the first time?"

"Asher had been with Belle for many years before I arrived, and more beyond that before he found Julianna. He and I were in the circle of innermost power, where many strived for centuries to get to and failed. We were her favorites until Asher found Julianna. It did not occur to me until decades later that Belle was jealous, but I think in a way that was it. She slept with other men, other vampires, and she was content that Asher and I shared each other's beds, and that we went to the vampires she chose to share us with. But another woman that we chose ourselves—that was different. But it is one of our most sacred laws not to harm another's human servant, so Belle did nothing. Then Asher offered Julianna to me, and we became a ménage à trois, and that raised the question of Julianna sleeping with others."

He looked down at the floor, then up again. "Arturo was one of her favorites, as well. He desired Julianna, but Asher refused him."

"Asher refused him, not Julianna," I said.

"She was his servant. She could not deny if he had consented."

"Ick," I said.

He shrugged. "It was a different century, *ma petite*, and Julianna was a different woman than you are."

"So why did Asher refuse?" I asked.

"He feared for Julianna's safety. We both did."

"Arturo liked it rough?"

"Mother Nature had made it almost impossible for Arturo to have it any way but rough."

I looked at him. "What do you mean?"

He gave that graceful shrug again. "Arturo is still the most well-endowed man I have ever seen."

It was my turn to shrug. "So?"

He shook his head. "You do not understand, *ma petite*. He is *bien outille*, well tooled. Ah, what is the English? . . . Hung like a horse."

I started to point out that Richard was pretty well-endowed, but it's bad form to point out to boyfriend A that boyfriend B is bigger. Micah was better endowed even than Richard, but again, it didn't seem the thing to mention. I was finally left with, "I've seen two men that were hung like horses, as you say, and it was intimidating, but . . . you're implying that you feared for Julianna's safety because he was so big."

"That is exactly what I am saying."

"No one's *that* big."

"Arturo makes even our Richard and your Nimir-Raj seem ungraced."

I blushed and wished I hadn't. "Those weren't the two men I was referring to."

He raised an eyebrow at me. "Indeed?"

The way he said it made me blush harder. "In New Mexico, one of Edward's backups, and one of the bad guys."

"And how did you happen to see just how well-graced they were, *ma petite*?" There was something in his voice, a hint of warmth, like the beginnings of anger.

"I did not have sex with anyone."

"Then how did you see them nude?" His voice still held that warm edge, and I couldn't really blame him.

"Bernardo, Edward's backup, and I got questioned by a local biker gang, uh club. They didn't believe he was my boyfriend. They asked if he was circumcised, and I said yes. I figured I had a better than fifty-fifty chance in America. They made him drop his pants to prove it."

"Under some threat, I assume." He was looking more amused than angry now.

"Yeah."

"And the other one?"

"He tried to rape me."

Jean-Claude's eyes went wide. "What became of him?"

"I killed him."

He touched my face, gently. "I have only recently understood why I was so very attracted to you from almost the first time I heard you interact with the police."

"Not love at first sight," I said, "but love at first hearing. I don't have that good a voice."

"Do not underestimate the dulcet sounds of your voice, *ma petite*, but it was not the sound of your voice that fascinated me. It was your words. I knew from the moment I heard you, the moment I saw the gun and realized that this lovely, petite woman was the executioner, that you would never die waiting for me to save you—that you would save yourself."

I cupped his hand against my cheek, looked into his eyes and saw again that sorrow for failing to save Julianna that never quite left him. "So you wanted me because I was such a tough broad?"

He let me make the joke. He even smiled, but it never reached his eyes. *"Oui, ma petite."*

My voice was soft when I said, "So Arturo wanted Julianna."

He took his hand back, slowly. "And she feared him, and we feared for her. This is two hundred years ago, a little more now. Asher was not as powerful as he is now, and we feared that his human servant would not survive Arturo's attentions."

"I've got to ask, how big was he?"

Jean-Claude spaced his hands apart like you'd measure a fish. "Like this big." It looked to be about six inches.

"That's not so big."

"That is how wide he was," Jean-Claude said.

I just gaped at him. "You're exaggerating."

"No, *ma petite*, believe me, I remember."

"Then how *long* was he?"

He made another measuring movement. I laughed because I didn't believe him. "Oh, please. You're saying he was what, about six inches wide and over a foot long? No way."

"Yes, way, *ma petite*."

"You said Arturo was one of Belle's favorites. Does that mean she . . ."

"Had sex with him, *oui*."

I frowned, couldn't think of a slick way to say it, so just blurted out, "Didn't that hurt her?"

"She was a woman with a large capacity for men in every way."

Gee, that was polite. "Most women wouldn't be able to . . . accommodate that," I said.

"No," he agreed.

"Did she want to kill Julianna?"

"No, she believed Arturo would not harm her."

"Why?"

He licked his lips, which he rarely did, and looked uncomfortable, which he did even less often. "Let us say that something that Belle Morte taught Asher and me to take pleasure in, we also did with Julianna."

I frowned at him, because I so did not have a clue. "If you're hinting, I'm not getting it."

"I would rather not discuss it, now. Perhaps at a later time."

I frowned harder. "What aren't you telling me?"

He shook his head. "I think, *ma petite*, that you would rather not know."

I looked at him. "You know, Jean-Claude, there was a time—not that long ago—that I'd have thrown a fit and made you tell me everything. But now if you tell me I don't want to know, then I'll just believe you. I really am not up to hearing intimate and shocking details about your vampire sex life. I've had enough shocks in that area for one day."

"*Ma petite*, I think you are growing up at last."

"Don't push it. And I'm not growing up, I'm just getting tired."

"As are we all, *ma petite*, as are we all."

I let the royal blue satin robe fall from my hands. It had wide lace sleeves and more lace at what passed for the lapels, to curve in flowers down the sides. It was beautiful and fit me perfectly. Most robes are too long for me. He'd probably bought it with me in mind. I belted it in place and didn't want to ask any more questions about the *ardeur* and sex and vampire stuff. But some things had to be clear between us.

"I need to get this straight, Jean-Claude."

"*Oui, ma petite.*"

"You say that what we did was sex, so in effect I had sex with everyone?"

He just nodded.

"You don't seem at all jealous about that."

"I was participating, *ma petite*. Why should I be jealous?"

The answer confused me more. I frowned up at him. "Okay, let me try this again. You say the *ardeur* may need to be fed more than once a day. We can't count on you being Johnny-on-the-spot when it happens. I can sleep over here, but . . ."

"You may need to feed when I am not awake. This is very possible, in fact, it is likely."

"Okay, then what are the rules?"

It was his turn to frown. "What do you mean, *ma petite*?"

"Rules. I mean like what will make you jealous and what won't? What, or who, am I supposed to stay away from?"

He started to smile, then stopped. "You are one of the most cynical people I have ever met, the most practical in a life-and-death context, and if you knew some of the people I had met, you would understand the compliment that is. But you are also very earnest, like a child. It is a type of innocence that I do not think you will ever outgrow. But I find it hard to deal with."

"It's a fair question."

"Indeed it is, but most people would not need to ask it so blandly. They would either ignore it and do the best they could when the need arose, or they would ask who among my people will I allow you to have sex with, without becoming angry."

It made me wince to hear him say it, but . . . "I like the way I phrased the question better."

"I know. You are simultaneously one of the most direct women I know, and one of the most self-deluding."

"I am really not liking where this conversation's going."

"Fine, but I will answer my question, because it is the truth. If Nathaniel is your *pomme de sang*, then I will let intimacy with him pass. Jason as my *pomme de sang* is within his rights to make love with my human servant. It is considered a great gift for a vampire to share his servant with another, and Jason has earned that. He has served me faithfully for many years."

"I'm not a prize to be given away."

He held up a hand. "Hush, *ma petite*, I will answer the question, and I will try for truth, even though you do not want to hear it today. There are many things I would have told you today, if you had been in the mood for truth. But you are right, this we must have clear between us. I would simply have urged you to keep Nathaniel close at hand and let the cards fall as they may, but if you insist on a list, then I will give it to you, but not without reasons. Because I want it clear that I do not share you lightly, and there are men I will not share you with at all."

He was angry now, and his eyes had bled to sapphire flame. The rest of his body was very still, but the eyes gave it all away. He was in the grip of some strong emotion, probably anger, but I wasn't sure. And he was shielding like a son of a bitch, so something he was feeling, or thinking, he didn't want me to share.

"Asher is acceptable."

He didn't give the reasons for that one, and I didn't ask, because there were too many of them, most of them painful.

"If Richard comes to his senses, then of course." He smoothed his hands down the front of his robe; he often checked his clothes when he was nervous. "The Nimir-Raj will have to be acceptable, because he calls to you. Richard's beast calls to you through my marks, my ties to him, to it, but the Nimir-Raj, he calls to you, Anita." My real name again. He was not happy. "He calls to something in you, in your power. It may be that you are truly Nimir-Ra, and the full moon will see it true. Or it may be that, as with Nathaniel, you have found your animal to call. If you are drawn more strongly to all the leopards, then it could be for either reason. Be wary if the leopards are yours to call. It may not merely be Nathaniel and the Nimir-Raj that beckon."

"Please, don't tell me that I'm going to turn into slut-girl."

He smiled. "I do not think you need to fear that. You are stronger willed than that."

"You just said I might be tempted by the other wereleopards."

"If the Nimir-Raj or Nathaniel are not near you when the *ardeur* rises, then my advice is to give in to it instantly."

I gave him wide eyes.

"If you fight it, *ma petite*, it grows. If it grows large enough, then you may indeed turn into slut-girl. If you give in and feed immediately, then you will have sex with one person, not several, and it will be more a person of your choosing."

"So the real advice is, keep the men I prefer within easy reach."

"I would make Nathaniel, or someone of your choosing, your constant companion."

I swallowed hard and searched his face, but it was pleasantly blank—his expression when he didn't want me to know what he was thinking. His eyes had bled back to normal.

Something occurred to me. "I haven't seen Damian around."

"I speak of sex, and you think of Damian." His voice was still pleasant but the words held something harsh.

"You give me this list of people to sleep with, and not to sleep with, but you leave him off either list. And he wasn't at the club, and he didn't come to the bedroom, attracted by the power like Asher. Where is he?"

Jean-Claude rubbed his hands over his face. "I was going to tell you, then you decided you wanted no more hard truths today." He lowered his hands and looked at me.

"He's alive, I'd know it if he wasn't."

"Yes, I believe you would. There was a time when my first master made my heart beat. Her power suffused me, made me live. But her power came from her Master of the City, so it was in reality his power that filled me. Each master vampire that I belonged to demanded blood oaths, and each one in turn made my blood course, my heart move. Then Belle, herself, the head of my line, brought me in, and she filled me. She was like the pounding of the ocean, and all others before her were but rivers seeking to drown in her embrace. Gradually, I filled with my own power. But even now it is her lineage that makes me live. The power that made her is what keeps me alive. Damian is descended from her line, not from Belle herself, but from one of her children, as I am. I am Master of the City and the power that animates me, animates Damian. When he took the oaths that bound him to me, that made him loyal to me, it became my power that filled him, my power that made his heart beat. And I broke the tie with She who made him."

"You make all the vampires under you alive?" I made it a question.

"The power comes through me, yes, but only if they are of my line, my lineage. If they are descended from other than Belle's children, then no, the blood oaths do not bind as tightly."

"What about Asher? You don't make his heart beat."

He nodded. "Very good, *ma petite*. No, I do not. A Master Vampire is a vampire that has become enough of a power that they fill themselves up. It is one of the things that being a master means, and one of the reasons that many of the older vampire masters still kill their children when they feel that tie break."

"You're volunteering an awful lot of information, and don't think I'm not grateful, it's fascinating, but what does this all have to do with Damian?"

"You have raised Damian from his coffin once, filling him with your necromancy like a zombie. You have saved his life twice with your necromancy. You have forged a tie between him and you."

Actually, I knew that, but out loud I said, "He said that he couldn't tell me no if I gave him a direct order. That he wanted to serve me. It scared him."

"It should have."

"I didn't mean to do it, Jean-Claude. I didn't even know it was possible."

"Legends speak of necromancers that could control all types of undead, not merely zombies. It was at one time Council policy to slay all necromancers on sight."

"Gee, glad the policy changed."

"Yes," he said. "But you severed my tie with Damian. I did not realize it at first, but when he returned from Tennessee, it was not my power that made his heart beat, it was yours."

I remembered feeling that in Tennessee, feeling the tie between us. "It wasn't done deliberately," I said.

"I know that, but you left me with a problem when you went away for over half a year. Damian is over a thousand years old. Though not a Master Vampire, he is still powerful. He no longer had ties to any vampire hierarchy. It freed him of all blood oaths, of all mystically bound loyalties. He was yours, but you did not come to claim him."

"You should have told me."

"And what would you have done? Taken him home to live in your basement? You did not have the power or control six months ago to deal with him."

"Now I do. Is that what you're saying?"

"You cast out Belle Morte. One of the most powerful of the Council. If you can do that, *ma petite*, then you can handle Damian."

"This is all great, but where is Damian?"

"I could no longer count on his loyalty. I no longer controlled him, do you understand, *ma petite*? I had a vampire that was more than twice my age, and I could not control him. It both made me look weak in others' eyes when I could not afford to appear weak, and it was dangerous, because he knew when you healed over your aura and shielded so tight. It wasn't only Richard and me who felt the loss of you. You cut Damian off, and he went a little . . . mad."

I was scared now, my heart beginning to climb up my throat. "*Where is Damian?*"

"First, *ma petite*, understand that you cannot take him with you tonight, because to tend him will be a full-time job for the first few hours."

"Just tell me," I said.

"I had to lock him away, *ma petite*."

I stared at him. "Lock him away, how?"

He just looked at me, and it was eloquent.

"He's been locked in a cross-wrapped coffin for six months?"

"About that, yes."

"You bastard."

"I could have killed him, *ma petite*, that's what others would have done."

"Why didn't you?"

"Because it was partially my fault for exposing him to you. Damian was mine to protect, and I failed him."

"He's mine, mine to protect," I said.

"Yet, you deserted him."

"I didn't know. You should have told me."

"And six months ago would you have believed me? Or would you have thought it was some ploy to get you back into my life?"

I started to tell him, of course I'd have believed him, but I stopped and thought about it. "I don't know if I'd have believed you or not."

"I hoped that I would find a way to reestablish my dominance over him, but he is closed to me."

I swallowed hard and looked at him. "If he's mine, then why didn't I feel him when my shielding broke all to hell in New Mexico?"

"I have been blocking you from sensing him, and it has not been easy."

I closed my eyes and counted to ten, but it didn't help. I was so angry my skin felt hot. "You had no right to do that."

"Without the marks being married, I think Damian would have seduced you. Because you would have been drawn to him as you are drawn to Nathaniel now, or perhaps even the Nimir-Raj."

"I would not have fucked Damian without the *ardeur* helping me, and I didn't have that six months ago."

"You may have your vampire back tomorrow night. I will help you nurse him back to health."

"I'm coming back tonight to get him."

"Talk to Asher, *ma petite.* Ask him what it will take to nurse a vampire back from six months in the coffin. Damian is not a master; he has had no ability to feed or gain energy. He will come out of the coffin a starved, crazed thing. There will be very little left of him, at first." He was so calm while he said it.

I didn't know what to say. I wanted to hit him, but it wouldn't change anything. I wasn't even sure it would make me feel better. "I want him out tonight, when I get back from the lupanar."

"You will not be able to tend both your injured wereleopard and Damian tonight. Ask Asher, and he will tell you how much work goes into such as this. One more night will not make a difference to Damian, and tonight you are trying to prevent war between the leopards and the wolves. More than that, you are trying to make a strong enough show of force to convince Richard's enemies that he is too well-allied to be killed. You must concentrate on these things tonight, *ma petite.*"

"I don't believe you," I said.

He shrugged. "Believe what you like, but it will take hours of care to make Damian sane again. It will take days of care, and blood, and warmth, to bring him back to himself."

"How could you know that and still do this to him?" My voice didn't even sound angry, just tired.

"I learned the lessons of the cross-wrapped coffin personally, *ma petite.* I have not done to Damian anything that has not been done to me."

"You were in it for a few days until I killed the old Master of the City."

He shook his head. "When I returned to the Council with Asher and bargained with them, the price for them saving his life was my freedom. I spent two years inside a coffin, unable to feed, unable to sit up, unable . . ." He was hugging his arms, holding himself. "I know that what I have done to Damian is a terrible thing, but my only alternative was to kill him. Would you have preferred that?"

"No."

"Yet, I see the accusation in your eyes. I am a monster because of what I have done to him. But you would feel me more a monster if I had killed him. Or perhaps you would have preferred that I let him go into the city streets and slaughter people."

"Damian would never do that."

"He went mad, *ma petite.* He became an alien. Do you remember the couple that was slaughtered about six months ago?"

"I saw several slaughtered couples over the last year. You'll need to be more specific."

He was angry now, too. Great, we could be angry together. "They were in a car, at a stoplight. The front of the car was dented as if they had hit a body, but no body was found."

"Yeah, I remember that one. They had their throats torn out. The woman had tried to defend herself. She had wounds on her arms where something had clawed at her."

"Asher found Damian wandering a few blocks from the car. He was covered in blood. He fought Asher, and it took over half a dozen of us to bind him and bring him home. Was I supposed to let him wander the streets after that?"

"You should have called me," I said.

"And what? You would have executed him? If insanity is a viable plea in your court system, then he cannot be held accountable. But your court system does not give us the same privileges it gives humans. We cannot plead insanity and live."

"I saw that crime scene. It didn't look like a vampire did it. It looked more like a shapeshifter, but . . . but the marks were wrong." I shook my head. "It was vicious, a vicious animal."

"*Oui*, and so I locked him away and hoped that you would come home to us, or sense his plight. At first I did nothing to block him from reaching you, but you did not come."

"I didn't know."

"You knew that Damian was yours, and yet you did not ask about him. You cast him away."

"I didn't know," I said, again, each word tight with anger.

"And I had no choice, Anita. I had to put him away."

"Do you think the insanity is permanent?"

He shrugged, arms still hugging his body. "If you were a vampire and he your vampire child, I would say no. But you are not vampire, you are necromancer, and I simply do not know."

"If he stays that crazy . . ."

"He will have to be destroyed," Jean-Claude said, voice soft.

"I didn't mean for this to happen."

"Nor did I."

We stood there for a few moments while I thought about everything and Jean-Claude either thought about it, too, or just stood there. "If all you're saying is true, then you had no choice," I said.

"But you are still angry with me. You will still punish me for it."

I glared up at him. "What do you want me to say? That knowing you've shoved him in a box for six months takes the sparkle out of our relationship? Yeah, it bothers me."

"Under normal circumstances you would rescue Damian and avoid me for a time until your anger cooled."

I nodded. "Yeah, that's about right."

"But you will need me, *ma petite*, in these first few nights. You will need another vampire with the same hungers to teach you control."

"Can't live with you, can't live without you, is that it?"

"I hope your anger cools before you need my help again, but I fear it will not. Remember this, *ma petite*, that the *ardeur* is not bound by morals, or even by your preferences. If you fight it long enough, hard enough, you will eventually give in, and it will be out of your control who it chooses. So do this one thing for me, if you cannot forgive me right away, keep always by your side either Nathaniel or the Nimir-Raj. Not for my sake, but for yours. For I think, of the two of us, I would forgive you sooner for sleeping with strangers than you would."

We pretty much left the conversation there. I found Asher and had him confirm the story. Hell, I waited for Willie McCoy to climb out of his coffin and heard the story from him. Damian had gone ape-shit and killed a couple that apparently hit him with their car. The man had gotten out to check on whoever they hit. They had hurt him and Damian struck out, killing the man. But the woman . . . he'd climbed into the car after her. We might have to kill him, because I hadn't understood what my magic meant to Damian. I hadn't understood a lot of things.

I drove out in the soft summer dusk with Nathaniel riding beside me. It had been a very long day. I was going to go home and pick up Rafael and the wererats, and Micah and his pard. He'd left a number at the shapeshifter hospital, and I'd called for it. I almost didn't call, but we needed backup tonight. My embarrassment was a small price to pay. If I had been in contact with Jean-Claude and Richard for the last half year, I probably could have talked Richard out of doing all the shit he'd done to his pack. I'd come home to try and reestablish a relationship, or two, but I was mostly cleaning up the mess that my absence had made. Richard might be dead at the full moon, and Jacob, Ulfric. Damian might be permanently crazy and have to be destroyed. The couple that had hit him with their car would have been alive if I'd known what the hell my magic was doing.

I'd avoided a lot of Marianne's teachings because it was too much like pure witchcraft for my monotheistic beliefs, but I knew now that I had to understand how my powers worked. I couldn't afford to be squeamish. God kept telling me I was okay with Him. I wasn't evil. But at some level I didn't believe it. At some level I thought that witchcraft, raising the dead, wasn't very Christian. If God was okay with me doing it, then what was my problem? I'd prayed about it often enough and gotten the answer more than once. The answer was to do it, that this was what I needed to be doing. If God was for it, then who was I to question it? Look where my arrogance had gotten us. Two dead, one crazy, and if Richard lost the pack . . . there'd be a lot more dead.

I felt a quietness inside me as I drove. Usually the touch of God is golden and warm, but sometimes when I've been really slow and not picked up on what He's wanted for me, I get this kind of quiet sadness, like a parent watching a child learn a necessary hard lesson. I'd never once prayed to God about Richard and Jean-Claude—not about who to choose anyway. It just hadn't seemed right to ask God to help me choose a lover, especially when I thought I knew who He'd pick. I mean vampires are evil, right?

But driving through the falling darkness, feeling His soft presence fill the car, I realized that I hadn't asked because I'd been afraid of the answer. I drove and I prayed, and I didn't get an answer, but I knew He heard me.

20

IT WAS FULL dark when we pulled up in front of my house. Almost every light in the house was on, like I was giving a party and no one had bothered to tell me. The driveway was full and overflowing onto the road. One of the reasons I'd rented the house was because I had no near neighbors to get caught up in whatever crisis I was having. My crises usually involved gunfire, so no neighbors to get hurt had been my primary requisite in a house. There was no one around to peek out a window and wonder what the hell was going on next door. Just trees and the lonely road, neither of which cared what I did. Or at least I didn't think the trees cared, though Marianne might tell me I'm wrong on that one. You never know.

I ended up parking quite a ways down from the house, with nothing but trees on either side of the road. I turned off the engine, and Nathaniel and I sat in the dark, listening to the engine tick. He hadn't said much since I came back out of the bathroom at Jean-Claude's—nothing at all on the forty-minute drive here. But then, neither had I.

I'd left Jean-Claude in a huff with a firm date to come back tomorrow night and get Damian out of hock. It wasn't just Damian locked away all these months that made me not want to be with Jean-Claude, it was that he had finally changed me into one of the monsters. I already knew that sex with him bound the marks closer, but now that the marks were married . . . what would sex do to us now? How much closer could the marks bind us all? Was it just changes with Jean-Claude, or did I have mystical surprises coming up tonight with Richard, too? Chances were likely, and Jean-Claude really had no clue what the surprises might be. He didn't know what he was doing. He really didn't. Since I didn't know what the hell *I* was doing either, and Richard had no clue. That left us in a bad place. I'd call Marianne tomorrow on the theory that one magic is much like another, but until then I was on my own. Big surprise.

Of course, I wasn't exactly alone. I looked across the front seat at Nathaniel. He looked back at me, face peaceful, hands in his lap, seat belt still in place. He'd pulled his hair back into a thick braid, leaving his face very plain and unadorned. In the moonlight his eyes looked pale gray, instead of their usual vibrant violet. Without the hair or the eyes showing, he looked closer to normal than I'd ever seen him. He was suddenly a person sitting across from me, and I realized with a shock that I didn't really think of Nathaniel as a person. Not as a grown-up separate human being kind of person anyway. He was more a burden than a person to me. Someone to be rescued, helped. He was a cause, a project, but not a person.

The heat began to press in around the Jeep. If we sat here much longer I'd have to turn the air conditioning back on. If Jean-Claude was right, then I'd had sex with Nathaniel earlier tonight. I was hoping Jean-Claude wasn't right, because I still considered Nathaniel a child, an abused child. You took care of them, you did not have sex with them, not even if they wanted you to.

My breast was aching, faintly, from his teeth marks. We'd shared a bed so often that it felt odd when he wasn't beside me. But I still didn't see him as a grown-up. Sad, but true.

"Jean-Claude is pretty sure that the *ardeur* is well fed enough that it won't be an issue for the rest of the night," I said.

Nathaniel nodded. "You won't need to feed again until you've slept for a few hours. Jean-Claude explained it to me, a little."

That pissed me off. "He did, did he?"

He shook his head. "Anita, he's worried about you."

"I'll bet."

"You really aren't going to sleep at the Circus tonight, are you?"

"No," I said. I was sitting back in the seat with my arms crossed over my stomach. I'm sure I looked as stubborn as I felt.

"And when you get up tomorrow, what then?" His voice was very soft in the hot, dark car.

"I don't know what you mean."

"Yes, you do," he said.

I sighed. "I don't want to do this, Nathaniel. I don't want to have Jean-Claude's incubus inside me. I'd rather be Nimir-Ra for real than have to feed off of others."

"And if you're both?" he asked, voice even softer.

I shrugged, arms still crossed, but hugging me more than being stubborn now. "I don't know."

"I'll be there for you, Anita."

"Be where?" I looked at him.

"Tomorrow, when you wake."

"What else did Jean-Claude tell you while I was running around trying to find out about Damian?"

Nathaniel's gaze never wavered, never changed. He wasn't embarrassed or bothered in the least about the conversation. "That he wouldn't hold a grudge if you had real sex with me."

I studied his face. "You don't consider what we did today sex?" I made it half-question, half-statement.

"No," he said.

"I don't either, but . . ." I was glad it was dark, because I was blushing, but damn it I wanted someone else to answer this question. "I know why I don't think today was actual sex, but why don't you?"

He smiled and did look away. He answered looking down at the floorboard. "What we did the first time with you marking my back, that was closer to real sex for me."

"So it was the dominance/submission thing?"

"No," he said, still looking down. "If we'd really needed the condoms, then it would have been sex."

"You mean intercourse," I said.

He nodded, still not looking at me.

"That's how I feel too. Jean-Claude said I was fooling myself."

Nathaniel flashed me a small smile, then went back to staring at nothing. "He told me I was being very American, very male, and very young."

"You are American, male, and twenty," I said. "What else are you supposed to be?"

He looked at me for a moment, then looked away again. He was definitely uncomfortable now.

"What else did Jean-Claude say?" I asked.

"You'll be mad."

"Just tell me, Nathaniel."

He shrugged, the thin straps of the tank top showing most of his shoulders as he did it. "He's hoping you'll choose me as your *pomme de sang*. He said he mentioned it to you."

"He mentioned it."

"Can I undo the seat belt?" he asked.

"Be my guest."

He let the belt slide to one side and turned so he was facing me, one leg drawn up into the seat, his braid curled over one shoulder. "Jean-Claude said that the more you fight the *ardeur* the stronger it grows, but if you feed when it first arises, then it's not such a big deal."

"He told me," I said.

"He's afraid you'll try and tough it out tomorrow without him. He's afraid you'll fight it all day, then only give in when you have to."

"Sounds like a plan to me," I said.

Nathaniel shook his head. "Don't be tough on this one, Anita, don't fight. I'm afraid of what will happen if you do."

"What, I'm supposed to roll over tomorrow morning and fall into your arms?" I couldn't keep the sarcasm out of my voice, though it brought a hurt look to his face, and made me want to apologize. "It's nothing personal, Nathaniel. It's not you, it's having to do it that I don't like."

"I know that." He lowered his face, not meeting my eyes again. "Just promise me that when the hunger rises tomorrow that you'll turn to me, or to someone, early and not try to be so . . . tough."

"What were you really going to say on the end of that sentence?"

He smiled. "Stubborn."

I had to smile. "I don't think I can just roll over the first time the *ardeur* hits me. I just can't give in that quickly, Nathaniel. Do you understand that?"

"You have to prove you're tougher than it is," he said.

"No, I have to be who I am, and who I am doesn't just give in to anyone, or anything."

He grinned at me. "That's an understatement."

"You're making fun of me," I said.

"A little," he said.

"You saw what I did to Jason's neck, Nathaniel. What if I hurt you? I mean really hurt you?"

"Jason will heal, Anita, and he wasn't complaining when Asher took him away." Nathaniel grinned and looked away as if he were trying not to laugh.

"What?"

He shook his head. "You'll get mad, and he didn't mean it that way."

"What did he say, Nathaniel?"

"Ask him yourself. He always seems to be able to say outrageous things to you and you think it's cute. When I say them, you just get mad."

"What if I ordered you to tell me?"

He seemed to think about it for a second, then flashed me another smile. It was a good smile, young, relaxed, real. When I'd first met Nathaniel he'd forgotten how to smile like that. "No, no I wouldn't."

"Some submissive you are," I said.

The smile widened to a grin. "You didn't like me submissive. It made you uncomfortable."

"So you're changing to please me?"

The smile faded, but not like he wasn't happy, more like his expression had shifted from humor to thoughtful. "At first, but lately some of it's to please me, too."

That made me smile. "That's the best news I've had all night."

"I'm glad," he said.

I undid my own seat belt. "Let's get out of this car before we melt." I opened the door and knew he'd do the same. We closed the doors, and I hit the button on my key chain that locked the Jeep. It made the little beeping sound, and I walked around the cars to the road, where the walking was smoother. Nathaniel and I started walking down the line of cars towards my house. His braid fell along his spine like a long, thick tail, moving as he walked.

Cherry and Zane came out from between the cars just ahead of us. "We thought you'd gotten lost," she said, smiling.

"You guys let everyone into the house?" I asked.

Her smile faded. "Yes, I hope that was okay."

I smiled. "It's okay, Cherry, really. If I'd been thinking, I'd have arranged for someone to let them in."

She relaxed visibly and dropped to her knees in front of me. I offered her my left hand. I was keeping my right hand free in case I had to draw my gun. Not likely, but you never know. Cherry gripped my hand in both of hers and rubbed her face against it like a cat marking its scent. The other formal greeting involved licking, but I'd finally convinced all of my cats that face rubbing was about all I was comfy with.

Zane went to his knees beside Cherry but didn't try to grab my right hand. He waited until she was done with my left. I'd also broken them of being grabby with my gun hand. He rubbed his face on my hand, and there was the faintest roughness alongside his jaw, as if he'd missed a spot when he shaved.

Cherry rubbed herself against my legs while Zane greeted me. It was like being body-rubbed by a really big cat that just happened, at the moment, to be in human form. The first few times it had happened, I'd freaked. But it just didn't strike me as that strange anymore. I wasn't sure if that was good or sort of sad.

When the greeting was over, Zane said, "We've got the extra key, so we took care of the company." They were both standing now, like good little people alright, good *tall* people, whatever.

"Good, though I had no idea we'd have this big a crowd."

They fell into step, one on either side of us, and I could feel Cherry beside me. I could feel her energy like a vibrating line against my body. I'd never sensed her this strongly before. Just another nail in the coffin on the Nimir-Ra question. The evidence was getting thick enough that if I hadn't been so damn good at self-delusion, I'd have had to admit it by now. But I'd had enough for one day. I needed a pass on this one tonight. So I ignored it, and if Cherry felt anything different, she didn't say.

It was Zane who put his face next to Nathaniel and sniffed him as we walked. "You smell like fresh wounds." He touched Nathaniel's back where it showed above the tank top. I knew there were bite marks up around his shoulders, all the way up to his neck. I should have known we couldn't hide it. Hell, even with clothes covering it, they'd have smelled it.

"What have you been doing?" Zane asked. "Or should I say who?"

Nathaniel didn't even glance at me. He was going to leave it all to me—what was said and what wasn't. Smart of him. Or maybe he just didn't know what to say either. I tried to think of a lie that would explain it, and nothing that didn't make Nathaniel sound slutty came to mind. Either he'd had sex with some strange woman, or . . . or what? The truth? I didn't want to tell the truth until I was sure how I felt about it. Knowing me, that could take at least a couple of days.

Cherry and Zane circled Nathaniel in ever-tightening circles, until their bodies brushed him as they moved around him. They bumped him continuously, like a shark testing to see if you're good to eat.

"Come on guys, we don't have time for this. We need to get to the lupanar and rescue Gregory."

Zane dropped to his knees beside Nathaniel, running his hands over the smaller man's body. Zane's hands slid under Nathaniel's tank top.

"Zane, get up," I said.

Cherry stepped very close to Nathaniel, looking down at him, putting a hand under his chin to lift his face to her, as if she meant to kiss him. "Who was it?"

"That's Nathaniel's business," I said. Nathaniel glanced at me, sort of sideways. The look was enough. I was being a coward. My pulse was going way too fast in my neck, like I'd tried to swallow something while it was still trying to get away.

"If it were Zane, or me, yes," Cherry said. "But while you were in the hospital these last few days we decided that Nathaniel has to run all girlfriends past the pard before he does anything intimate with them."

"As Nimir-Ra, don't I have like presidential veto?"

Cherry looked at me. "Of course, but you have to agree with checking out people for Nathaniel. He nearly got you killed again."

I did agree, but just not that night. That night, of all nights, I wanted everyone to mind their own business. No one cared a damn who slept with whom—until now. It figures. I make my first indiscreet move with one of them, and I was going to have to confess, even though I still didn't know how I felt about it. I opened my mouth to say, *It was me*, but I stopped when I saw the next wereleopard coming down the street. Of all of them, she was the one I least wanted to talk in front of about intimate matters.

It was Elizabeth. Her walk was always a cross between a strut and a glide, the ultimate hooker's walk. She strode from between the cars on Caleb's arm, and there was a self-satisfied smile on her face that said either she didn't know I was angry with her or she was confident I couldn't do anything about it. She was taller than Caleb by nearly five inches. Her hair fell in curls to her waist, a brunette so dark you would have called it black if you didn't have my hair to compare it to. She was pretty in a pouting, lush sort of way, like some sort of tropical plant with thick, fleshy leaves and beautiful but deadly blossoms.

She was wearing a skirt so short the tops of her black hose and the garters that held them up showed. Her shoes were black sandals with a lower heel than she usually wore. After all, we were going to be tramping through the woods. The shirt was sheer enough that even by starlight you could see she wasn't wearing a bra, and she, like me, was a woman who needed one.

Caleb was wearing a pair of bell-bottom jeans, no shoes, no shirt. The jeans were cut low enough to show off his belly-button ring. I was too young to remember wearing bell-bottoms personally, but I did remember my older cousins competing to see who could get the widest bell. Even as a child I'd thought the pants were ugly. Time had not changed my opinion.

Caleb looked pretty satisfied himself. I was betting they'd had sex together, but it wasn't any of my business who they fucked. Honest it wasn't.

"I'm glad you've had a good night, Elizabeth."

She squeezed Caleb's arm. "Oh, it's been a very, *very* good night."

"I'm glad, because it's about to get very, very bad," I said.

She fake-pouted at me. "Oh, did our little Nimir-Ra get her feelings hurt because I wouldn't come and sleep naked beside her?"

I had to laugh.

"What's so funny?" she asked. Caleb started moving away from her, pulling free.

"Why is it that you don't think I'll kill you, Elizabeth?"

"For what?" she asked.

"Oh, maybe for deserting Nathaniel at the club and letting the bad guys get him, which led to *me* nearly getting killed, and maybe becoming Nimir-Ra for real."

"I'm tired of baby-sitting him," she said. "He used to be a lot of fun, but not anymore. He's got standards now."

"Meaning that he won't fuck you anymore," I said.

The first touch of real anger slid across her face. "We used to have some real good times, Nathaniel and me."

"Not good enough, apparently," I said.

She strode up to stand beside Cherry, which put her very close to me. She truly wasn't afraid of me, and I knew why—or thought I did. She'd been insulting, arrogant, and a downright pain in the ass since I took over the pard and I hadn't hurt her. I'd let it all slide, because, as she was so happy to point out, I could shoot her, but I couldn't really punish her. *Punish* to a shapeshifter means either beat the shit out of them or do some mystical crap that scares the shit out of them. She was right. I couldn't do the shapeshifter stuff. It had taken me a while to realize why I let Elizabeth slide so much. I'd killed her sweetie, the man she loved. It made me feel bad. Gabriel had earned death, but she had loved him, and I sympathized. But she'd used up the last of my sympathy when I saw Nathaniel hanging from those chains with the swords grown into his flesh. The rules had changed, and Elizabeth didn't know it. Yet.

The other wereleopards glided out of the trees, trailed down the road. Merle's hair gleamed white in the darkness, his beard and mustache silvered. He was wearing straight-legged jeans and cowboy boots with silver-tipped toes. An open leather jacket did more to frame his chest than cover it. He had a woman with him.

She was tall—six feet or maybe a little over. She was wearing jogging shoes, jeans, and a baggy T-shirt that hung to mid-thigh. The baggy T-shirt couldn't hide the fact that she was leggy and well built. Her hair was almost black, straight, thick, cut just above her shoulders. She wore no makeup, and the bones of her face made her look sculpted—almost harsh. Her eyes were pale, her lips, thin. She had one of those faces that would have been beautiful with a little makeup, but was still striking. It was a face you wouldn't forget or grow tired of. Merle was holding her hand, but not like they were a couple, more like a father holds a daughter's hand—a comforting gesture.

She vibrated with that otherworldly energy that all the leopards had to some degree. But this one made my skin dance from yards away. When they got close enough for me to see that her eyes were pale, I could also see that she was afraid. Her eyes had that wincing look of a person who's been abused once too often.

Merle introduced her, "This is Gina."

"Hi, Gina," I said.

She looked at me, and the fear in her eyes was replaced by disdain. "She's a little short for a Nimir-Ra."

"Micah and I are the same height," I said.

She shrugged. "Like I said." But her bravado didn't ring true. It was more like someone whistling in the dark. But I let it go. Gina wasn't my problem tonight.

Vivian was the last of my leopards, and she came alone down the street. She was one of the few women who made me feel protective and made me think of adjectives like *doll-like* and *delicate*. She was simply one of the most beautiful women I'd ever seen, and the casual shorts and striped tank top with sandals couldn't hide that. She was African-American by way of Ireland, and her skin was that flawless pale cocoa shade that you only get with that particular mixture. She looked sort of lost, and I realized why. I hadn't seen her without Stephen at her side in over a year. Stephen was Gregory's identical twin, also a stripper at Guilty Pleasures. Stephen and Vivian were living together and seemed very happy doing it. But Stephen was at the lupanar tonight like all good werewolves, and she was here with the leopards. Poor Vivian. Poor Stephen. I hadn't really thought until that moment that Stephen might lose a brother tonight. Shit.

Vivian dropped to her knees in front of me, and I offered her my hands. She took them in her hands, then rubbed her face against them, as Cherry and Zane had done. Elizabeth hadn't offered a greeting, and it was an insult. The others weren't my leopards, but she was. And she'd deliberately snubbed me. It was the first time in front of company. I didn't usually insist on it, because I didn't like Elizabeth touching me, but I watched Caleb's face as Vivian rose from her greeting. He'd noticed the oversight.

"How you doing, Vivian?"

"A real Nimir-Ra wouldn't have to ask," Elizabeth said.

I squeezed Vivian's hands and helped her stand. "Are you going to help us rescue Gregory, or just be a big pain in the ass?" I asked Elizabeth.

"I want Gregory safe," she said.

"Then shut the fuck up."

She started to say something, and Cherry gripped her arm. "That's enough, Elizabeth."

"You're not dominant to me," Elizabeth said.

"I'm trying to be your friend," Cherry said.

"You want me to leave her alone?"

"Please," Cherry said.

"Fine," Elizabeth said. She turned back to Nathaniel. "I can smell fresh blood on you, Nathaniel." She put her arms on either side of his neck, hands clasped together, her body pressed the length of his, moving Cherry back. "You finally find someone to top you?"

"Yes," he said.

"Who?" Cherry asked.

"We really don't have time for this," I said. "We need to get to the lupanar."

Merle had to add his two cents worth. "The only reason that Elizabeth treats you the way she does is that you let her. Disobedience must be punished immediately, or the power structure cannot survive—much like your local Ulfric and his pack."

"I control my leopards," I said.

Elizabeth laughed, planting a big kiss on Nathaniel's forehead and leaving a red lipstick print behind. "He fucked someone tonight, when he'd been forbidden to be with anyone without pard approval. And you're going to let *that* slide, too. You are *so* weak."

I took a deep breath and let it out. "He didn't fuck anyone tonight."

Caleb had joined the others crawling around Nathaniel. He plunged his face into Nathaniel's groin. Elizabeth moved back so he could do it. "I smell sperm, but not pussy." This after I knew that Nathaniel had washed thoroughly. Caleb stood, and Elizabeth moved back. He put his hand behind Nathaniel's neck and moved their faces together as if they were going to kiss, but he stopped just short of their lips touching. "I don't smell pussy here either. I don't think he had sex."

Zane raised Nathaniel's shirt as far as he could reach from his knees, then stood pushing the shirt up to Nathaniel's neck. The bite marks were almost black in the starlight. There was a bite mark on almost every inch of his back; the edges didn't touch, but I hadn't missed much. It made me blush.

Vivian looked at me, and I realized that she could probably smell the blood rushing to my cheeks.

Zane said, "He might not have had sex, but he had something."

Caleb came around to gaze at Nathaniel's naked back. "Someone had fun."

"Look at this," Elizabeth said. She drew them around to the front and the bite mark around his nipple. They ran their fingers over it, and Zane pulled Nathaniel's shirt off and threw it on the hood of the nearest car. Everyone but Merle, Gina, and Vivian swarmed Nathaniel, touching the wounds with fingers, hands, and tongues. Nathaniel's head went back, eyes closed, and I knew he wasn't exactly having a bad time, but . . .

"That's enough," I said.

Elizabeth pulled Nathaniel's shorts down, and I got a glimpse of just how not-unhappy he was.

I yelled, "That's enough!"

Elizabeth turned on her knees, her hands on his butt. "Whoever did this could have just as easily done more damage. They could have cut him up bad, and he would have let them do it. Wouldn't you have, Nathaniel?"

"I would have let her do anything she wanted," he said.

Shit.

"You can't let him do this," Cherry said, standing and coming to me. "You can't let him skate on this, Anita. Or the next time whoever she is might just kill him."

"She won't kill him," I said.

"You know who it is?" she asked.

I nodded.

"Why didn't you say so?" Merle asked.

I took a deep breath and blew it out. "Because I'm not comfortable with it yet. But that's my problem not Nathaniel's." I held my hand out to him. "Nathaniel."

He pulled his shorts up so he could walk and came to me, squeezing my hand as he took it. I put him behind me, the line of our bodies touching. Physical contact was a way of saying he was under my protection. "I marked him."

Elizabeth laughed still on her knees. "I know he's your favorite, but I never thought you'd outright lie for him."

"At least some of you can smell it if I lie. I marked his body, my teeth marks."

"Your anxiety level has been high since we got here. I can't tell if you're lying," Merle said. "And if I can't tell, then no one else here is alpha enough to be sure."

"It's gotten so that your scent doesn't change when you lie," Cherry said.

I'd heard of lying with your eyes, but never with your scent. "I didn't know you could do that, lie with your smell."

"I think lying just doesn't make you anxious anymore," she said.

Oh. "Being a sociopath does have its benefits," I said.

Caleb crawled towards us, in that gliding crawl the leopards could do. It was inhumanly graceful. He came close enough to put his face against my leg. I let him, because I figured that they'd get around to smelling me if I claimed Nathaniel. I just hadn't planned on it being one of Micah's cats first.

"He does have her scent on his skin."

"They sleep in the same bed most nights," Elizabeth said. She was on her feet, hadn't even snagged her hose.

Caleb rubbed his face against my leg. "She smells of wolf and . . . vampire." He gazed up at me. "Did you do your Ulfric and your master last night? Is that why Nathaniel doesn't smell like pussy, because there wasn't a hole left for him?"

I'd tried to keep my version of an open mind, but I decided then and there that I didn't like Caleb. "The pard has a right to question who Nathaniel sleeps with, because he doesn't have good judgment. None of you have the right to question me."

Caleb moved in one of those too-fast-to-see motions and shoved his face into my groin, hard enough that it almost hurt. I pulled the Browning without thinking about it and had it pressed against his skull before I realized it. Faster than normal—even for me.

Caleb raised his head back so that his forehead was pressed against the end of the gun. He stared up at me. "You don't smell like dick. Don't tell me you had at least three men with you in a bed and nobody got to fuck you."

"Caleb, I'm really beginning not to like you."

He grinned. "But you won't shoot me, because that would make Micah mad."

"You're right, I shouldn't have pulled the gun. I'm just not used to being able to draw a gun before I have time to think about it."

"I've never seen you move that fast," Zane said.

I shrugged. "Benefits of the change, I guess." I put the Browning back. I wasn't going to shoot him for just being obnoxious.

Caleb rested his cheek against my thigh, and I let him. My struggling would just amuse him, and he was behaving himself, relatively speaking.

Vivian touched my arm. "Are you really going to be one of us?"

"We'll know in about two weeks," I said.

"I am sorry," she said.

I smiled at her. "Thanks."

"You didn't top Nathaniel," Elizabeth said. "You're too squeamish to use your teeth on him like that."

I looked at her, and I let the darkness fill my eyes that was my own version of a beast. The look that said just how far down the well I'd fallen. "I'm not as squeamish as I used to be, Elizabeth. You might want to remember that."

"No," she said, "no, you're protecting him. He's been teacher's pet since day one. You're just afraid of what Micah will do. Afraid of what a real Nimir-Raj will do to him now that he's disobeyed a direct order." She stalked over to us. "And you should be afraid, Anita, you should be very afraid, because Micah's strong, strong the way Gabriel was strong. He doesn't flinch."

"I've heard enough about Gabriel to wonder if that's a compliment." Micah came out of the woods with a tall man beside him. Before Micah, I'd never slept with a man that I'd just met. I'd never slept with anyone that didn't make my heart beat faster, my skin react to the sight of him. As Micah glided from the trees, he was graceful and handsome, but I wasn't in love with him, and my body didn't react like I was. I was both relieved and a little ashamed of that.

He was wearing shorts that had been cut off and allowed to go ragged at the hem. A white tank top seemed to glow in the dark, making his tan look even darker. A wide leather belt encircled his slender waist. He'd tied his hair back in a ponytail, but it was so curly that it didn't give the illusion of short hair; you knew even from the front that there was a lot more hair behind him. He seemed more delicate in clothes than he had without them. Maybe I just hadn't been paying attention to how small boned he was. There was something graceful in the way he was made, fine bones, smooth skin, very . . . refined, especially for a man. Jean-Claude was prettier, but he was too tall to ever be called delicate. Micah was delicate. The only thing that saved him from looking fragile was the play of muscles in his arms, the way he walked, like the world was his and everywhere he moved he was the center of the universe. It wasn't so much confidence as surety. So much potential in such a small package. He reminded me of somebody.

The man trailing behind Micah was dark complected, with very short, close cut hair, and there was something about his skin tone, even by starlight, that didn't look tan. He was handsome in a young, almost preppy sort of way, but muscled and very alert. That explained why Merle hadn't been glued to Micah's side. We'd had a change of guard. Micah introduced him as Noah.

I'd dreaded seeing Micah again—wondered what I'd say, how I'd feel. I wasn't nearly as uncomfortable as I'd thought I'd be. Maybe I'd have been more so if I hadn't been trying to defend Nathaniel's honor. Maybe because I didn't give any sign of what we'd done, Micah didn't either. Or maybe he was as confused as I was about it. Or maybe that's how casual sex works. I just didn't know.

"What is everyone so tense about?" Micah asked.

"Show him, Nathaniel."

Nathaniel never questioned, just stepped out from behind me and showed his back to the two men.

The bodyguard gave a sharp whistle. Micah's eyes widened, and he looked over Nathaniel's shoulder at me.

"You did this?"

I nodded.

"She didn't," Elizabeth said.

Caleb had risen as far as he could on his knees and was sniffing my stomach, his face pointed towards other things, but he was careful not to touch them. I don't think he would have sniffed my groin in front of Micah. Elizabeth was right on one thing. The leopards just weren't as afraid of me as they were of Micah.

"She smells of blood, too," Caleb said.

"Get away from me," I said.

He smirked, but he crawled away.

"Are you saying she has a wound on her like what he has on his back?" Elizabeth asked.

Caleb nodded as he crawled.

"Then she's lying. Whoever did his back, did her, too."

I sighed. "Am I really going to have to prove this?"

"I would take your word," Micah said, "but apparently your pard won't."

"It's just that we've wanted you to take one of us like this for so long," Cherry said. "And now . . . I think we'd have believed sex but not this. It just doesn't look like your work, and Elizabeth's right about one thing. Nathaniel is your favorite, and you do protect him."

Great, no one believed me. "Fine, just fine," I said. I started sliding out of the shoulder holster to let it flop at my back. Pulling my shirt out of my jeans wasn't a problem, even taking it off and laying it beside Nathaniel's shirt on the car hood wasn't a problem. I was wearing a very nice black bra. It was meant to be seen. Jean-Claude had been a very bad influence on my wardrobe. The problem was taking off the bra. I really didn't want to do that.

I undid the back, but held the front in place. "What happens when you see the bite mark?"

"If you show me a bite mark on your breast that doesn't have fang marks in it, I'll believe it was Nathaniel," Micah said.

Everyone had crowded close. I never liked being the center of attention, not for this kind of thing. "Give me a little breathing space guys."

They moved back a fraction of a step, and I thought, screw it. Everyone here, except Elizabeth and maybe the new bodyguard, had seen me naked. Oh, hell. I slipped the bra off and laid it on the hood with my shirt. I made absolutely no eye contact.

A hand came into view, and I grabbed the wrist. It was Caleb. "Nathaniel gets to take a bite, and I can't even touch it."

"No, you can't," I said.

Micah didn't come any closer. "Why did you mark him?"

I met his eyes, expecting to see accusation, or disdain, or something negative. But his face was very still. "I needed to sink my teeth into something. I needed . . ." I shook my head and looked away. "It wasn't sex I wanted. I wanted to feed."

"No." Elizabeth came crowding close. "No, you can't be Nimir-Ra for real, not for real." There was something close to panic on her face. I could smell her fear. She moved close enough that our bodies almost touched, and I could hear her heart thundering.

"Be afraid, Elizabeth, be very afraid," I said.

She half-turned away from me, and Micah said something at the same time, which is my only excuse for not seeing her fist coming. She rocked me back against the side of the Jeep, filling my mouth with blood and making my knees go weak. Only Cherry catching me around the waist kept me standing. The world swam in black and white streamers for a second. When my vision cleared, Elizabeth was being held by Micah and Noah, the bodyguard.

I pushed myself upright and stepped away from Cherry. She kept hold of my arm, and I let her for a second while I let the last of the vertigo slip away. I put a hand to my mouth and came away with blood.

Merle moved up to take Elizabeth's arm, and Micah came to stand in front of me. "Are you alright?"

"I'll be okay."

He touched my bare arms. It was the lightest brush of fingertips, but it made me shiver. My nipples grew hard, and there was nothing I could do to hide the sudden reaction.

I looked at him, and I didn't have to look up for it, not even an inch. "I don't know you, why . . ."

His arms slid behind my back, pressed our bodies together, and I suddenly couldn't get enough air. "I am your Nimir-Raj, Anita. There is no shame in that."

"You say *Nimir-Raj* like other people say *husband*."

He ran one hand through my hair, until his fingers were tight to my scalp, the other hand at the small of my back. "Our souls resonate like the sound of two perfect bells," he whispered, as his mouth hovered over mine. The comment was so romantic it was stupid, and I should have laughed at it, but I didn't.

He kissed me, a push of his lips, then his tongue slipped into my mouth. I knew when he tasted my blood, because his hands tightened on my body and his body reacted against me. He was too large for me not to feel him grow hard between our bodies.

I ran my hands over his arms, his shirt, and it wasn't enough. I wanted to touch his bare skin to mine, to drink in every inch of him, into every inch of me.

He kissed me as if he would drink me in, and I knew that part of the excitement was the fresh blood. I pulled his shirt out of his pants and ran my hands up his back. But it wasn't enough.

He drew back from the kiss, and I pulled his shirt over his head. Just pressing our bare chests against each other was better. It was as if my skin craved his skin. I'd never felt anything like it.

We held each other, both breathing too hard, our arms locked around each other, faces pressed to each other's shoulders, his breath hot on my neck.

"We don't have time for more," he whispered.

I nodded, my head still against his neck. It wasn't like I'd been planning on more, but . . . "I had to touch my skin to yours, why?"

"I told you, you are my Nimir-Ra, and I am your Nimir-Raj."

I pulled back enough to see his face. "That doesn't explain it to me."

He held my face in his hands, making very serious eye contact. "We are a mated pair, Anita. It's legend among the leopards that you can find your perfect mate, and from the first moment you have sex you're bound, more than marriage, more than law. We will always crave each other. Our souls will always call to each other. Our beasts will always hunt together."

It should have scared me, but it didn't. It should have made me angry, but it didn't. I should have felt a lot of things, but all I really felt was that he was right, and I didn't even want to try and talk him out of it.

"Richard's going to *love* this," Elizabeth said.

Merle and Noah took her down to her knees, in an abrupt gesture that had to hurt a little. I looked at her. "Thanks for reminding me what I was about to do, Elizabeth. I got distracted." I drew away from Micah, my fingers trailing down his arm, as if I couldn't quite bare to let go of him.

"Let her go, boys. She's my problem, not yours."

They looked to Micah, who nodded. Elizabeth stayed on her knees, as if uncertain what to do. She tried to get one of them to help her to her feet, but they ignored her and left her to stand on her own.

I took time to put my bra on as I walked back to my Jeep, the shoulder holster still flapping around my waist. I slipped it over my naked skin, and it was not comfortable, but I didn't want to take the time to put my shirt on. I knew what I was going to do now.

I walked to my Jeep, and everyone waited in the dark while I unlocked the door, scooted into the passenger seat, opened my glove compartment, and got out a spare clip of lead bullets. I'd started carrying an extra clip of lead bullets in the Jeep since I ran afoul of a few rogue fairies. You can shoot the fey with silver all day and it won't do much. But lead, they didn't like lead. Lead also had other uses, because it wouldn't kill a wereanimal. Only silver would do that. I walked back towards them, popping out the clip that was in the gun as I moved. I put the clip in my pocket, though it didn't fit well, and shoved the new clip home until it clicked.

Elizabeth finally started looking worried when I was about two cars away. Anyone else would probably have been running, but common sense wasn't one of Elizabeth's strong suits. I had actually pointed the gun at her while I very calmly walked closer, before she said, "You wouldn't dare."

I stared down the barrel of the gun at her, and I felt nothing. It was a big, cold empty place inside me—utterly calm, peaceful. But at the center of that empty peacefulness was a tiny kernel of satisfaction. I'd been wanting to do this for a long time.

I shot her twice in the chest, while she was still telling me I wouldn't shoot her. She went over backwards, spine bowing, hands scrabbling at the road, legs kicking while she tried to breathe.

Everyone had cleared a big space around her. I stood over her and stared down while she tried to breathe, and her heart struggled to beat around the hole I'd put in it. "You keep saying I can't kill you like a real Nimir-Ra by tearing your throat out, or gutting you. Maybe that's going to change soon, but until then I can shoot you, and you'll be just as dead."

Her eyes rolled desperately, while her body tried to cope with the damage. Blood welled out of her mouth.

"This time it wasn't silver. But fail me again, Elizabeth, in anything large or small, fail any member of this pard, and I will kill you."

She'd finally gotten enough air to talk. She spat out blood and the words, "Bitch, you don't even . . ." more blood, "have the guts . . ." dark blood from her mouth, "to shoot me for real."

Staring down at her, I realized something I hadn't before. Elizabeth wanted me to kill her. She wanted me to send her to wherever Gabriel was. She probably didn't realize that's what she wanted, but if it wasn't a death wish, it was close enough.

She lay there and healed, and cursed me, and told me how weak I was. I shot her in the chest again. She writhed and jerked, and the pool of blood just grew wider underneath her body.

I let the ammo clip fall into my hand from the gun, put it in my other pocket and got my main clip back in the gun. "Silver now, Elizabeth. Any more smart remarks?" I waited until she had healed enough to talk. "Answer me, Elizabeth."

She stared up at me, and there was something in her eyes, something that said we finally had an understanding. She was afraid of me, and sometimes that's the best you can do with people. I'd tried kindness. I'd tried friendship. I'd tried respect. But when all else fails, fear will do the job.

"Good, Elizabeth, I'm glad we understand each other." I turned to the others. They were staring at me like I'd sprouted a second head—a nasty one. Micah held out my clothes to me, and I slipped the shoulder holster off and the clothes on. No one said anything while I dressed.

When everything was back in place, I said, "Shall we go to the house now?"

Caleb looked positively ill. Micah looked pleased. So did Merle, and Gina, and all my leopards.

"You will not be allowed guns tonight in the lupanar," Merle said.

"That's what the knives are for," I said.

He looked at me as if he wasn't sure whether I was serious or not.

"Smile, Merle, she'll heal."

"I'm beginning to agree with what the wererats said."

"And what was that?"

"That you were scary enough all on your own without being Nimir-Ra."

"This isn't even close to as scary as I get," I said.

He raised his eyebrows at me. "Really?"

It was Nathaniel who said, "Really." My other cats echoed him, nodding.

"Then why aren't you afraid of her?" Gina asked.

"Because she doesn't try to be scary to us," Zane said. He looked down at Elizabeth on the ground, still unable to move much. "Of course, maybe the rules have changed."

"Only for bad little leopards," I said, "Let's get to the rats and go see the wolves."

"And the swans," Micah said.

"Swans?" I asked.

He smiled. "You just keep making conquests, Anita, even when you don't mean to do it." He held his hand out to me. I hesitated, then, slowly, I took it. Our fingers interlaced, and we walked together hand-in-hand down the road, and it felt good, and right, like I'd found a piece of myself that was missing. I left Zane behind to make sure Elizabeth didn't get run over by a car. We'd send Dr. Lillian back for her. The rest of the leopards followed behind Micah and me, and for the first time since I'd inherited the cats, I felt like I really was Nimir-Ra. And maybe, just maybe, I wouldn't fail them.

21

RAFAEL THE RAT king had a black limo. He'd never struck me as a limo kind of guy, and I said as much. He said, "Marcus and Raina used to put on quite a show for things like this. I and my rats are not willing to make a spectacle of ourselves, so the limo."

"Hey, I wore makeup," I said. That had made him smile.

We were riding in the back of the limo, with one of his wererats driving. Merle and Zane were in the front with the driver. Merle, because he'd objected to us all being split up among people he didn't know, and Zane, because I just didn't completely trust Merle yet. Though I had no illusions about which of them would win the fight, if it came to that. Richard had a werewolf or two that I would have bet on against Merle, but there was something downright scary about Micah's head bodyguard, a "something" that all of my leopards lacked. Not ruthlessness, more an ultimate practicality. You just knew Merle would do whatever needed to be done, no hesitation, no sympathy, just business. When that's pretty much how you operate yourself, you begin to recognize it in other people, and you watch them closely.

All the leaders got to ride in the back of the limo, which smacked of elitism to me, but it did allow us all to talk together, and no one else seemed to have a problem with it. I wasn't sure why it bugged me, but it did.

Rafael was tall, dark, handsome, and strongly Mexican. He spoke with no trace of an accent, or rather he sounded like he was from Missouri. He sat facing us. Yes, us. Micah and I sat across from him. We were not holding hands. We were not casting longing glances at each other. In fact, strangely, once I was away from the other leopards, I was uncomfortable around him. Maybe it was my usual discomfort that always set in after intimacy. But I wasn't sure, it felt different. Or maybe it was the closer we got to seeing Richard, the more I wondered what the hell I was doing. Was I really going to tell Richard that I'd taken a lover, another shapeshifter? We'd broken up before and gotten back together, but if Richard thought I'd taken a permanent lover besides Jean-Claude, it was over. I didn't want it to be over, though part of me wasn't at all sure that dating Richard was healthy for either of us. We weren't really good for each other. Love is like that sometimes.

I pushed away serious thoughts and looked at the last member of our little party. Donovan Reece was the new swan king in town. He was about six feet tall, though it was hard to tell exactly while he was sitting down. His skin was that flawless milk and cream complexion that the beauty aids promise when tan is out for a year or two, but Donovan's was the real deal. He was whiter than I was, as white as Jean-Claude, but there was a slight pink flush to Donovan's cheeks, like perfectly applied blush. You could almost see the blood flowing under his skin, as if it were nearly transluscent. He not only looked alive, but *very* alive, as if he'd be hot to the touch.

His eyes were a pale blue-gray that shifted with his moods like a summer sky that couldn't make up its mind whether it wanted to be peaceful with fluffy white clouds or rain all over your head. He was handsome in a clean-cut, preppy sort of way, as if he should have been on a college campus somewhere pledging to a frat and chugging beers. Instead he was going with us into a gathering of werewolves where he would be the only nonpredator there. That didn't sound like a good idea to me.

"You saved my swanmanes, Ms. Blake. You nearly got yourself killed doing it. I couldn't risk the girls coming, they are not . . ." He looked down at his folded hands, then raised those changeable eyes to me. "They are like your Nathaniel—victims."

"Nathaniel is driving my Jeep with the rest of my people in it," I said.

Reece nodded. "Yes, but the shape of his beast is a predator. My girls are not. If they lost control and changed during the meeting, they would be meat."

"I agree with you, Mr. Reece, but doesn't the same logic apply to you?"

"I am a swan king, Ms. Blake, I will not change shape unless I will it so."

Will it so. I'd never heard anyone put it quite that way. Donovan Reece had a bad case of arrogance. I wasn't going to talk him out of this. Rafael had been trying to before I arrived. Micah never offered. He'd been very good about letting me do all the talking. I liked that in a man.

"Can you fight?" I asked.

"I will not be a burden, Ms. Blake, don't worry."

I was worried, because I could smell the blood just under his skin. I could almost see it flowing under his flesh. He smelled like meat and blood, and heat. He smelled like food. I'd been around shapeshifters that were prey animals, but I'd never realized you could tell by smell what wasn't a predator. I knew by the gentle scent of him that Reece's beast was something soft and easily killed. Something that would struggle but not hurt me. I had to swallow hard, trying to slow my pulse, but it would not slow. I wanted to drop on my knees in front of him and sniff his skin, rub my face against his bare arms until the short sleeves of his button-up shirt stopped me. A white undershirt peeked out the top of the blue and white striped shirt. I wanted to rip the shirt open, send the buttons popping through the air, take a knife from my wrist sheath and slit the undershirt, bare his naked chest and stomach. But it wasn't the *ardeur*, it wasn't sex I was thinking about. I wanted to see his stomach bare, to feel the soft tissue under my mouth, my teeth, to bite into . . .

I covered my eyes with my hands, and shook my head. What was wrong with me?

Micah touched my arm, gently. "Anita, what's wrong?"

I lowered my hands and looked at him. "He smells like food."

Micah nodded. "Yes."

I shook my head again. "You don't understand what I'm thinking. It's . . . frightening." I couldn't say it out loud. I wanted to feed on him, or at least sink my teeth into his flesh. I think I could keep from actually feeding, but the urge to mark that flawless skin was so strong that I almost didn't trust myself.

"When you told me why you marked Nathaniel I knew it was the hunger." Micah said the last word like it should have been in capital letters. "It usually takes a few days, or weeks, before your first full moon, to have the hunger become a problem. It's okay to have thoughts, images in your head about feeding. It's normal."

"Normal." I laughed, but it was a harsh sound. "What I'm thinking isn't even close to normal." Again I couldn't bring myself to say it out loud.

"What do you want to do to Reece?" Rafael asked.

I looked across the seat at him. I opened my mouth to say, then glanced at Reece and stopped. "No, it's like telling a sexual fantasy in front of the stranger you just had the fantasy about. It feels that intimate."

"It *is* that intimate," Rafael said.

I looked back at him, and his dark eyes held my gaze. "If you tell Mr. Reece what you're wanting to do to him, then maybe he'll fly home."

"A rat is a prey animal, too," Reece said.

"Everything that is smaller is a prey animal," Rafael said, "but rats are omniverous. They eat anything that crosses their path, including humans, if they can't get away. A wererat is not a small thing, Mr. Reece, we are large enough to be the predators that our namesakes cannot be."

Reece was scowling at us all now. He shook his head angrily and leaned forward and shoved his wrist into my face. "Get a good whiff, all of you seem to like it."

"I wouldn't do that, if I were you," Rafael said.

"Listen to him, Reece," Micah said.

I didn't say anything because the scent of his flesh so close was intoxicating. It was like the most exotic perfume spread across silk sheets, with an undertone of fresh baked bread and some sweet jelly spread over flesh. I had no words for it, but it smelled better than anything I'd ever smelled in my life.

I was holding his wrist, pressing the thin skin against my lips, before I realized what I was doing. The skin was so tender, and I could smell the blood under that paper-thin layer of skin. I wanted to do more than smell it. I wanted to taste it, to feel his flesh give under my teeth, to have the blood gush warm in my mouth, to . . . I jerked away from him and crawled across Micah, across the seat to huddle in the far corner as far away from the swan king as I could get and not jump out the door.

There must have been something on my face, in my eyes that scared him, because his eyes widened, his full mouth opened slightly. "My God, your control really is that bad."

I managed to say, "Sorry."

"Do you really want to put yourself in the midst of hundreds of us?" Rafael asked.

"I won't be bluffed," Reece said. "You won't hurt me. From everything I've heard about Anita, and you, Rafael, you're the good guys." His gaze flicked to Micah. "Him, I don't know, but I do know that the swans have never thrown their allegiance to anyone. We've been autonomous. The fact that I'm supporting Anita and her pard will mean something to the wolves. We are weak as battle allies, but that any animal other than her own would ally with her pard will mean something to their Ulfric."

I huddled on the far corner of the seat, arms hugging my legs to my chest, a position not really meant to be performed while wearing a shoulder holster. But I was literally holding on to myself, hugging my control and my body. How was I ever going to get through tonight without doing something embarrassing, or deadly? How much worse was my control going to get?

"Your last swan king answered to their now-deceased lupa," Rafael said.

"So I've heard. Though technically he was a swan prince, not a king. I don't know what he owed the old lupa, but I'd guess it was something blackmailable, because I've found some polaroids that would make you blush."

I had to clear my throat twice before I could talk. "Kaspar refused to be in Raina's dirty movies, but the price for that was that he helped audition people for the films."

Reece looked at me. "Audition, what do you mean?"

I huddled and talked, but I was talking over the pulse in my head, the rush of blood in my body. I wanted to be next to Reece. I wanted to take a bite. Instead, I talked. "Kaspar could change form from swan to man at will. Raina used him to see if non-shapeshifters freaked when he changed in the middle of sex."

I felt Micah's reaction even from a distance. Reece looked horrified. "You saw this?"

"No, but Raina took great delight in telling me about it in detail. She tried to get me to watch one of his auditions, but I had better things to do."

"He did this willingly?" Reece asked.

"No," I said. "It was most definitely not his choice. He seemed to hate it."

"We see the fact that we can change forms at will as a great gift. We're one of the few shapeshifters that can do it with ease."

"Is that because your gift is either a curse or a born talent, rather than a disease?"

"We think so," he said.

"Kaspar was under a curse," I said.

"Are you wondering about me?"

Actually I was watching the way his Adam's apple bobbed when he talked, and wondering what it would feel like to fix teeth in his throat, but that was probably a fact best kept to myself. I kept talking, but I think both Micah and Rafael knew how ragged my control was. I hugged myself and kept talking, because silence filled with awful images, terrible desires.

"Yeah, I'm wondering," I said.

"I was born a swan king."

"You were born a swan king, not a swanmane. Does that mean you're male? Is swanmane only used for women?"

He looked at me, studying my face. "I was born to be their king. I'm the first king in over a century."

"Everybody else is chosen to lead, or fights for the right, but you make it sound like a hereditary monarchy," I said.

"It is, but it's not bloodlines that makes the difference, though being a swanmane either runs in your family or it doesn't. But I didn't inherit the title."

"Then how did you know?" I asked.

His eyes had gotten dark, dark gray like storm clouds. "The answer to that is somewhat intimate."

"I'm sorry, I didn't know."

"I'll give you the answer you seek, if you answer a rather delicate question for me."

We stared at each other. My heart rate was almost normal again. I could look at him without smelling the blood under his skin. Talking, listening, doing somewhat normal things had helped. I was a *person*, with speech and higher functions, not an animal. I could do this. Really. I eased out of my little ball, slowly.

"Ask and I'll let you know," I said.

"Did you kill Kaspar Gunderson, the last swan king?"

I blinked at him. That was unexpected. The sheer surprise made my pulse rate speed up a touch. "No, no, I didn't."

"Do you know who did?"

I blinked at him again. I wondered if I could lie and if he would be able to tell, or not. I finally stuck to the truth. "Yes."

"Who?"

I shook my head. "That I won't answer."

"Why not?"

"Because I would have killed Kaspar myself if he hadn't gotten away."

"I know he was responsible for several deaths, and that he tried to kill you and some of your friends," Reece said.

"It was a little more diabolical than that," I said. "He was taking money from hunters and supplying them with shifters."

Reece nodded. "He also made the swanmanes in his care into victims. I think that's what he and the old lupa shared—sexual sadism."

"That's why your girls, as you put it, were at the club with Nathaniel."

"Yes, I don't play those sorts of games, and they've grown to crave it."

I nodded. "I sympathize," I said.

"You've answered my questions truthfully, I can do no less." He started unbuttoning his shirt.

I looked at Micah, who shrugged. I looked at Rafael, who shook his head. Nice that none of us knew why he was undressing.

He left the overshirt tucked in but started pulling the undershirt out of his pants. He was about to bare his soft underbelly, and I wasn't a hundred percent sure my control was up to seeing it. My pulse was in my throat again. Since apparently neither of the men was going to ask, I asked, "Why are you undressing?"

"To show you the symbol of my kingship."

I stared at him. "Excuse me?"

Reece frowned at me. "Don't worry, Ms. Blake, I'm not about to flash you."

"I'm not worried about you flashing me, Reece, it's that . . ." but I never finished, because he'd bared the white, white skin of his stomach. In the darkened car I could still see the pulse just behind his belly button. Hell, I could almost taste it in my mouth, as if I'd already sunk teeth into that tender flesh, as if I was already eating my way through to more vital things. Something was odd about the hair on his chest. It was almost too fine, too thin, too delicate, running in a dainty white line down the center of his chest and spreading in an upside down triangle around his belly button then down into his pants.

I was on the floorboard crawling towards him, and I didn't remember getting there. I stopped, pressed against Micah's legs. "I don't remember leaving my seat. I'm losing time."

Micah put his hands on my shoulders. "It happens when your beast controls you, at first. The first few full moons will be almost complete blackouts, until you can begin to access the memories, and that will take work."

Reece had leaned back across the seat, half-reclining, and started to undo his belt.

This close I could see, or thought I saw what was wrong with the hair on his chest and stomach. I tried to move forward, but Micah held me, hands tightening on my shoulders. I stretched out my hand and could brush fingertips over Reece's stomach. The light touch of my fingers over his skin made him stop fussing with his belt, made him look at me.

It wasn't hair. "Feathers," I said, softly, "like the down on a baby chicken, so soft." I wanted to run my hands over the surprising texture of it, to roll my body across the feathers and the heat of his skin. I could hear his heart in his chest pounding, and when I looked up, I met his gaze. His pulse was in his neck, like a trapped thing, and I could taste his fear. That one touch of my hand, the soft, dreamy quality of my voice had frightened him.

Micah's arms wrapped around my neck and shoulders and drew me in against his body with his legs on either side of me. He leaned over me, his face pressed to mine, and said, "Ssshhh, Anita, ssshhh." But it was more than a soothing voice. I could feel his beast calling to mine, as if he'd rolled his hand through my body, but so much larger. And that touch made my body tighten, grow wet. It brought my own pulse into my throat.

"What did you do?" I sounded breathless.

"The hunger can be turned to sex," Micah said.

"I wasn't going to feed," I said.

"Your skin went hot. Our bodies spike a temperature just before we change, like a human before a seizure."

I turned, still held in his arms, half-pinned between his knees. "You thought I was going to change?"

"It usually takes weeks, or at least the first full moon, for the first shape change. But you seem to be gaining problems faster than normal. If you changed for the first time here, I don't think either Rafael or I would be able to keep you from tearing Reece up."

"The first change is very violent," Rafael said, "and even the backseat of a limo doesn't have much room to hide or to run in."

Reece looked at me from only inches away, held in Micah's arms, his body, and I knew that it wasn't romantic. He was holding on in case the sex as distraction didn't work. "She's been Nimir-Ra for over a year," Reece said.

"But still human, until recently," Rafael said.

Reece stared at me for a second or two, then said, "Very well, I have a birthmark in the shape of a swan. My family knew from my birth what I was meant to be."

"I've heard of such things," Micah said, "but I thought it was legend."

Reece shook his head. "It's very true." He sat back in his seat, tucking his undershirt down in front.

"Kaspar had feathers instead of hair on his head," I said.

"I'm told that if I live long enough that gradually that will happen to me." There was something in his voice that said he wasn't looking forward to the prospect.

"You don't sound happy," I said.

He frowned at me, rebuttoning his shirt. "You were human once, Ms. Blake, I've never been human. I was born a swan king. I was raised to take my place as their king from my earliest memories. You have no idea what that's like. I insisted on going to college, on getting a degree, but I may never get to use it, because going from place to place caring for the other swans keeps me very busy."

I stayed in the circle of Micah's body, but the tension was draining away. "I saw my first soul when I was ten, and my first ghost earlier than that, Reece. At thirteen I accidentally raised my dog that had died. I've never been human, Reece, trust me on that."

"You sound bitter about it," he said.

I nodded. "Oh, yeah."

"You must both accept who and what you are, or you will make yourselves miserable," Rafael said.

We both looked at him, and I don't think either look was friendly. "Give me a week or two to come to terms with being a kitty cat," I said.

"I am not referring to you being Nimir-Ra for real," Rafael said. "From the moment I met you, Anita, you have half hated what you are. As Richard has run from his beast, so you have run from your own gifts."

"I don't need a philosophy lesson, Rafael."

"I think you do, and badly, but I'll let that go, if it bothers you so very much."

"Don't even start on me," Reece said. "I've had people preach to me all my life that I'm blessed and not cursed. If my entire family couldn't convince me of it, you might as well not even try."

Rafael shrugged, then turned back to me. "Let's pick a different topic, because we are only minutes away from the lupanar, and I saw Micah's beast—his energy—pass through you, and your beast responded."

"You saw it?" I asked.

He nodded. "His energy is very blue, and yours is very red, and they mingled."

"So you got what, purple?" I said.

Micah hugged me a little tighter, a warning I think not to be flippant, but Rafael was more direct. "No jokes, Anita, if I saw it, so will Richard."

"He's my Nimir-Raj," I said.

"You don't understand, Anita. Micah said he thought birthmarks in the shape of your beast was legend. Well, until just now, I believed talk of a perfect mate was legend. Like true fated love, just a romantic story." Rafael's already serious face got even more solemn. "You recognize some bond from the beginning, so the stories go, but it's only after you have sex for the first time that your beasts can roll through each other's bodies. Only physical intimacy will allow such metaphysical intimacy."

I glanced down from those hard, demanding eyes, but finally made myself look back up. "What are you asking, Rafael?"

"Not really asking, telling. Telling you that I know you had sex with Micah, and that, even though Richard has dumped you and publicly declared that you and he are no longer a couple, he won't like it."

That was an understatement. I pulled away from Micah, and he let me go, no lingering touches. I moved away, and he allowed it. It earned him brownie points. "Richard dumped me, Rafael, not the other way around. He doesn't have any right to bitch about what I do."

"If he dumped her, then she's free to do what she wants," Reece said. "The Ulfric has only himself to blame."

"Logically, you're right, but when has logic dictated how a man acts when he sees the love of his life in someone else's arms?" The bitter way Rafael said it made me look at him, study his face. He sounded like he was speaking from experience.

"As Ulfric to my Nimir-Ra, he has no authority over me."

"Tonight is going to be dangerous enough, Anita. You don't need to make Richard angry."

"I don't want to make things worse. God knows they're bad enough as they are."

"You're angry with him for dumping you," Rafael said.

I started to say *no*, then realized he might be right. "Maybe."

"You want to hurt him."

I started to say *no*, then stopped and tried to think—really think—about how I felt. I was angry and hurt that he could just cast me aside. Okay, it hadn't been that simple, but still . . . "Yeah, I'm hurt, and maybe a part of me wants to punish Richard for that, but it's not just him dumping me. It's the mess he's made of the pack. He's endangered people I care about, and he's doing his usual Boy Scout shit that doesn't even work well in the human world, let alone with a bunch of werewolves. I'm tired, Rafael, I'm tired of it, and him."

"It sounds like you might have dumped him if he hadn't beat you to it."

"I came back to make it work. To see if we could make some sense of it all. But he has to give up that moral code of his that has never worked for him or anyone around him."

"To give up his moral code is to give up being who he is."

I nodded. "I know." And just saying that made me feel worse. "He can't change, and staying who he is is going to get him killed."

"And maybe you and Jean-Claude with him," Rafael said.

"Does everyone know that part?"

"It's standard that if you kill a vampire's human servant, the vampire may not survive the death. And if you kill a vampire, their human servants either die or go crazy. Logic dictates that killing either of you endangers the other."

I still didn't like that everyone knew that to kill one of us might kill all of us. Made it too damn easy for assassins. "What do you want me to say, Rafael? That Richard and I have a fundamental difference of philosophy in nearly every important area? There's more than one reason we didn't get married and live happily ever after. That maybe he's going to have to choose between survival or his morals? That I'm afraid he'd almost rather die than compromise those morals? Yeah, I'm afraid. It's going to kill a little piece of him to see me with Micah. I'd spare him if I could, but I didn't choose any of this."

"You take no blame in this," Rafael said.

I sighed. "If I hadn't left for six months maybe I could have talked him out of the democracy with his pack. Maybe if I'd been here a lot of things would be different, but I wasn't here, and I can't change that. All I can do is try and fix what got broke."

"You think you can fix this, all of it?" Rafael asked.

I shrugged. "Ask me again after I've met Jacob and seen how Richard deals as Ulfric with all of them. I need a feel for the dynamics before I say if it's fixable."

"How would you fix it?" Micah asked.

I glanced back at him. "If Jacob and a few others are the problem, then it's fixable."

"Killing the ones who stand against Richard won't fix things, Anita," Rafael said. "The experiment in democracy must end. Richard must begin being harsher to those who would stand against him. He must be frightening to them, or there will be another Jacob, and another after that."

I nodded. "You're preaching to the choir here, Rafael."

"If you are not his girlfriend, or his lover, then I fear that your influence over Richard will be slight."

"I'm not sure I had a lot of influence over him when we were dating."

"If you cannot talk sense into him, then eventually Richard will die and someone else, probably Jacob, will take over the pack. The first thing any good conqueror does is kill those closest and most loyal to the executed leader."

"You think Jacob is that practical?" I asked.

"Yes," Rafael said.

"What do you want me to do?"

"I want you to hide the fact that you and Micah are lovers."

I glanced behind me at Micah. He shrugged, face peaceful. "I told you I wanted you on any terms that you wished, Anita. What do I have to do to convince you I meant that?"

I searched his face, tried to find something false in it, and couldn't. Maybe he was that good a liar. Maybe I was just being too suspicious. "When we were with the leopards, just the leopards, I was completely comfortable with you. It felt right and . . . why doesn't it feel that way now?"

"You're having second thoughts," Reece said.

"No," Rafael said. He looked at Micah, and the two of them had major eye contact.

The staring contest went on so long that I had to interrupt. "One of you better start talking," I said.

Rafael inclined his head at Micah, as if to say, go ahead. I turned to Micah. "Alright," he said, and he seemed to be choosing his words carefully. I was almost positive I wasn't going to like this conversation. "Every pard, every group of shifters that is healthy has a group mind."

"You mean a group identity?" I asked.

"Not exactly. It's more . . ." He frowned. "It's more like a coven that's worked magic together for a while. They begin to be parts of a whole when it comes to working magic or healing. Together they form more than they form separately."

"Okay, but what's that have to do with why I felt more comfortable when it was just us leopards?"

"If you feel differently when the leopards are around you, then we're forming a group mind. It usually takes months to forge that kind of bond between shifters. Maybe it's just a bond with your own leopards. The change coming on could have set it in motion."

"But you think it's more than that, don't you?"

He nodded. "I think you're forming a group mind with my pard, that in effect, the decision to join our pards into one unit has already been made."

"I haven't decided anything."

"Haven't you?" he asked. He looked so reasonable sitting there, hands clasped in front of him, leaning a little towards me. So earnest.

"Look, the sex was great. But I'm not ready to pick out china patterns here, you do understand that?" There was a feeling very close to panic in the pit of my stomach.

"Sometimes your beast picks for you," Rafael said.

I looked at him. "What does that mean?"

"If you are already a part of a group mind with his pard, then your beast has chosen for you, Anita. It's more intimate than being his lover, because it's not just him that you have a commitment to."

I gave him wide eyes. "Are you saying that I'm going to feel responsible for the safety and well-being of all his wereleopards as well as my own?"

Rafael nodded. "Probably."

I looked back at Micah. "How about you? You feel responsible for my people?"

He sighed, and it was heavy, not happy at all. "I didn't expect to form a bond this quickly. I've never seen it work this fast."

"And?" I said.

His mouth moved, almost a smile. "And, if we've really formed a group mind, then yes, I'll feel responsible for your people."

"You don't sound happy about that."

"Nothing personal, but your cats are a mess."

"Yours are so much healthier," I said, "Gina looks like someone who's been kicked once too often."

Micah's eyes hardened, and he searched my face. "No one talked to you. They wouldn't dare."

"No one tattled, Micah, but I could see it on her, smell the defeat. Someone's damn near broken her, and it's recent, or ongoing. She got a bad boyfriend?"

His face closed down. He didn't like that I'd figured that out. "Something like that." But his pulse had sped up, and I knew he was hiding something from me, something that scared him.

"What aren't you telling me, Micah?"

His gaze flicked past me to Rafael. "Will she be able to read my people more easily as time goes on."

"And you hers," Rafael said.

"Her people are pretty easy to read now," he said.

I was watching his face. He was controlling his body, keeping the tension out of it, but I could taste the speed of his pulse, and the fear. It wasn't just a small fear either. The thought that I could read his people so completely almost terrified him.

I laid my hand over his clasped ones, and he turned serious, guarded eyes to me. "Why does it scare you that I knew that Gina is being abused?"

He tensed under my hand and pulled away, gently, but he definitely didn't want me to touch him. "Gina wouldn't like it if you knew."

"As her Nimir-Raj, aren't you supposed to protect her from abusive assholes?"

"I've done my best for her," he said, but it sounded defensive.

"Kick the guy's ass and forbid her to see him again. It's a simple problem, don't complicate it. Or is she in love with him?"

He shook his head, eyes down, his hands clutching so tight that the skin mottled. His voice came out even, normal, but that terrible tension shook through his hands. "No, she's not in love with him."

"Then what's the problem?"

"It's more complicated than you could ever imagine." He looked up, and there was anger in his eyes now.

I started to reach out, to touch him, then let my hand fall back. "If we really are forming one pard. If I really am her Nimir-Raj, then no one's allowed to hurt her. No one hurts my people."

"The wolves took your Gregory," he said. The anger was still in his eyes, trembling down his hands.

"And we're going to get him back."

"I know you've had a hard life. I've heard some of the stories, but you talk as if you're young and naive. Sometimes no matter how hard you try, you can't save everyone."

It was my turn to look down. "I've lost people. I've failed people, and they've gotten hurt, and dead." I raised my eyes to meet his gaze. "But the people who hurt them, killed them, they're dead too. Maybe I can't keep everyone safe, but I'm damn fine at revenge."

"But the harm still happens. The dead don't really walk again. Zombies are just corpses, Anita. They aren't the people you lost."

"I know that last better than you do, Micah."

He nodded. Some of the terrible tension had eased away from him, but it left his eyes haunted with some old pain that was still raw.

"I've done everything I can for Gina and the others, and it's still not enough. It will never be enough."

I touched his hands, and this time he let me slide my hands over his. "Maybe together we can be enough for them all."

He searched my face. "You really mean that, don't you?"

"Anita rarely says anything she doesn't mean," Rafael said, "but if I were her, I'd ask first what the problems are before I promised to fix them."

I had to smile. "I was just about to ask, what is Gina into that's got you so terrified?"

He turned his hands so he was holding mine tight. He looked into my eyes. The look was not love, or even lust, but so serious. "Let's save your leopard first, then ask me again, and I'll tell you all of it."

The car slowed and turned. Gravel sounded under the tires. It was the turnoff to the farm that fronted the woods around the lupanar.

"Tell me some of it now, Micah. I need something here, now."

He sighed, looked down at his clasped hands, then up, slowly to meet my eyes. "Once we were taken over by a very bad man. He still wants us, and I'm searching for a home strong enough to keep us safe."

"Why are you afraid to tell me?"

His eyes widened a little. "Most pards don't want that kind of trouble."

I smiled. "*Trouble* is my middle name."

He looked a little puzzled. I guess I was the only one who liked film noir. "I'm not going to kick you guys out because of some asshole alpha. Let me know which way the danger's coming from, and I'll deal with it."

"I wish I had your confidence."

There was a weight to his gaze of such sorrow, such horrible loss. It made me shiver to see it, and he let go of my hands, sliding away from me just before Merle opened the door and offered a hand out. He didn't take the hand, but he slid out into the dark.

Reece followed him with a look at Rafael, as if the rat king had told him to get out and give us some privacy. I turned to Rafael. "You have something to say?"

"Be careful of that one, Anita. None of us know him, or his people."

"Funny, I was pretty much thinking the same thing."

"Even though he can make your beast roil through your body?"

I met his dark, dark eyes. "Maybe especially because of that."

Rafael smiled. "I should know by now that you are not a person to let her affections cloud her vision."

"Oh, it can be clouded, but never for long."

"You sound wistful," he said.

"Sometimes I wonder what it would be like to actually be able to just fall in love and not weigh the risks first."

"If it works out, it's the best thing in the world. If it doesn't work out, it's like having your heart torn out and chopped up into little pieces while you watch. It leaves a big hollow space that never really heals."

I looked at him, unsure what to say, but finally, "You sound like experience talking."

"I've got an ex-wife and a son. They live in a different state, as far away from me as she could drag him."

"What went wrong, if you don't mind me asking?"

"She wasn't strong enough to handle what I am. I didn't hide anything from her. She knew everything before we married. If I hadn't been so much in love with her, I'd have seen that she was weak. It's my job as king to know who's strong and who isn't. But she fooled me, because I wanted to be fooled. I know that now. She is what she is—not her fault. I can't even regret her getting pregnant right away. I love my son."

"Do you ever get to see him?"

He shook his head. "I get to fly in twice a year and have suprervised visits. She's made him afraid of me."

I started to reach out to him, hesitated, then thought, what the hell. I took his hand, and he looked startled, then smiled. "I'm sorry, Rafael, more than I can ever say."

He squeezed my hand then moved back from me. "Just thought you ought to know that falling blindly in love isn't at all the way all those poems and songs make it sound. It hurts like hell."

"I did fall in love like that once," I said.

He raised his eyebrows at me. "Not since I've known you."

"No, in college. I was engaged, thought it was true love."

"What happened?"

"His mom found out my mother was Mexican, and she didn't want her little blond-haired, blue-eyed, family tree getting contaminated."

"You were engaged before they'd met your family?"

"They'd met my father and his second wife, but they are both good little Aryans, very nordic. My stepmother didn't like pictures of my mother being out, so they were all in my room. I wasn't hiding it, but that's how my almost mother-in-law took it. Funny thing, her son knew. I'd told him the whole story. It hadn't mattered until his mom threatened to cut him off from the family money."

"Now *I'm* sorry."

"Your story is more pitiful."

"That doesn't make me feel better," he said, smiling.

I smiled back, but neither of us really looked happy. "Ain't love grand?" I said.

"You can answer your own question after you see Richard and Micah in the lupanar together."

I shook my head. "I don't love Micah, not really, not yet."

"But," he said.

I sighed. "But I almost wish I did. It would make seeing Richard less painful. I don't know how I'm going to feel seeing him tonight and knowing that he's not mine anymore."

"Probably about the same way he'll feel when he sees you."

"Is that supposed to make me feel better?"

"No, it's just the truth. Remember that cutting you out of his life was forced on him. He loves you, Anita, for better or worse."

"I love him, but I won't let him kill Gregory. And I won't let him cost Sylvie her life. I won't let him take the pack down to wrack and ruin because of some idealistic set of rules that only he is paying attention to."

"If you kill Jacob and his followers without Richard's permission, then he may send the pack after you and your leopards. If you are not lukoi, not lupa, then to let their deaths go unpunished would make him appear so weak you might as well let Jacob kill him."

"Then what am I supposed to do?"

"I don't know."

Merle stuck his head in the car. "We've got wolves out here. Your rats are holding them back, but they're getting impatient."

"We're coming," Rafael said. He looked across the seat at me. "Shall we?"

I nodded. "I guess it'd be silly not to get out of the car."

He slid out to the edge of the seat, then hesitated, holding his arm out for me. Normally, I wouldn't have taken it, but tonight we were trying for a show of solidarity and style. So I stepped out of the car on the rat king's arm, like a trophy wife—except for the wrist sheaths and the two folding knives hidden in my clothing. Somehow I think trophy wives wear more makeup and less cutlery. But, hey, I haven't ever met a trophy wife, maybe I'm wrong. Maybe they know what I know, that the true way to a man's heart is six inches of metal between his ribs. Sometimes four inches will do the job, but to be really sure, I like to have six. Funny how phallic objects are always more useful the bigger they are. Anyone who tells you size doesn't matter has been seeing too many small knives.

22

THE CLEARING WAS huge, but not huge enough. The cars, trucks, and vans filled most of the available ground; some parked so far under the trees that the paint jobs had to have gotten scratched all to hell. There wasn't room for all the wererats to park, and the cars filled the gravel drive, until it was just another parking lot. Some people ended up parked beside the road, or so they said, as they drifted up through the trees. Rafael had brought all his rats—about two hundred of them. The treaty between the rats and wolves dictated that their numbers had to top at two hundred. Rafael had agreed to that on the understanding that the much larger werewolf pack—six hundred or so—would come to his aid if needed. No questions asked. Your enemies are my enemies sort of thing. He'd explained that in the last few minutes, and it meant that he was risking a great deal tonight. Made me feel guilty. Made me wish I'd found a way to sneak a gun into the lupanar. Truthfully, I hadn't even tried. Was I growing soft, overconfident, or just tired?

The tallest woman I'd ever seen came to stand beside Rafael and me. She was at least six feet six inches, broad-shouldered, and had the muscles that only serious weight lifting will give you. She was wearing a black sports bra across her tanned chest and a pair of faded black jeans. Her dark hair was caught back in a tight ponytail, leaving her face clean and startling with not a touch of makeup on it.

"This is Claudia. She's going to be one of your enforcers for the night," Rafael said.

I opened my mouth to protest, but he stared me into silence. His face so serious. "You have wereleopards, but only Micah has bodyguards. We can't afford to lose you Anita, not for something stupid like this."

"If I can't take care of myself, then what good is my threat?"

"Richard will have his Skoll and Hati. I will have my guards. Micah has his. Only you are without escort. Raina kept the wereleopards as an adjunct to the werewolves. They never really grew into a full pard, not really. Even Micah's people added to yours don't have the right personnel for a working pard. You have too many submissives and not enough dominants. So tonight you will have Claudia and Igor."

Zane said, "We can take care of Anita."

"No we can't," Nathaniel said.

I stared at him. He touched my arm. "Take the help, Anita, please."

"We can protect her," Micah said.

Merle echoed him.

"And if you have to choose between saving Micah, or saving Anita, which one will you choose?" Rafael asked.

Merle looked away, but Noah said, "Micah."

"Exactly."

"Won't your rats feel just as torn between you and Anita as my leopards would?" Micah asked.

"No, because I'll have bodyguards. My rodere, my gang, runs high to enforcers and professional soldiers. Why do you think that Raina and Marcus agreed to the treaty when Richard brought it to them? They'd never have allied with us if we weren't stronger than just our numbers."

"I don't . . ."

He actually touched my mouth with his finger. "No, Anita. When this is over, and you are truly Nimir-Ra, then you will need to advertise for enforcers of your own. Until then, I'll share."

I moved his hand away from my mouth. "I don't think this is necessary."

"I do," he said.

"I agree," Cherry said.

Finally, Micah said, "Agreed." Merle and Noah both gave him a funny look, then exchanged glances with each other.

"I haven't agreed to this," I said.

Nathaniel leaned into me, and said, "If you don't give in on this we'll still be standing here an hour from now."

I frowned at him.

He smiled and shrugged.

I turned to the bodyguard in question. She just looked at me, face impassive, as if it didn't matter to her one way or another. A man moved up beside her. He was about two inches shorter than she was, broader through the shoulders, and had so many tattoos that for a second I thought he was wearing a colorful long-sleeved shirt. His tank top was small and strained over the swell of his chest. Jeans and work boots completed his outfit. He was bald, with a tattoo of a dragon curling around his ears and the back of his skull. Even by starlight you could see the design of the tat was oriental and well done.

"How do you guys feel about putting your life on the line for someone you just met?"

"You saved our king's life," the man said. "We owe you a life."

"Even if it's your own," I said.

"Them's the breaks," he said.

I stared up at the woman. "You agree with that?"

"Like Igor says, we owe you one."

It always made me uncomfortable when people were willing to put my safety ahead of their own. I just wasn't really comfy with the concept of bodyguards, but, what the hell? I put my hand out. They exchanged glances between them, then shook my hand. Igor touched me like he was afraid I'd break, and Claudia tried to squeeze hard enough to make me cry uncle. I didn't. I smiled pleasantly at her, because I knew she wouldn't really hurt me. She just wanted to see if I'd squirm. My pleasant smile made her frown, but she let go of my hand. My hand actually ached just a little, and if my healing powers weren't up to it, I'd be bruised in the morning. Damn.

Rafael turned to some of his rats, giving instructions, leaving me alone with the two bodyguards. "Is Igor your real name?" I asked.

"Nickname," he said.

"What's your real name?"

He smiled and shook his head.

"What could be worse than Igor?" I asked.

His smile widened to a grin. "Wouldn't you like to know?"

It made me smile, and some tightness in my chest eased. You'd almost think I was relieved to have bodyguards of my own. Naw, not me. I didn't need no stinking bodyguards. I probably wouldn't need them, but extra muscle is like extra ammunition. If you need it, it's good to have it, if you don't need it, then it can always go back in the box.

Truth was, I felt more protective of my leopards than protected by them. Sad, but true. And I didn't entirely trust Merle, or Noah, or even Micah. He was keeping things from me, and I didn't like that. Some women are just never satisfied.

Rafael moved off through his people, giving them soft-voiced instructions. Micah moved up closer to me, with Merle and Noah at a very attentive distance. I looked at Micah and suddenly couldn't be this close and not touch him. I reached my hand out to him, his eyes widened, but he took my hand. His hand slid over mine in a play of pulsing warmth that almost took my breath away. I watched a similar reaction play on his face. What was going on? I drew my hand out of his, and it was like pulling it through melted taffy, so thick.

I looked up to find that, except for Claudia and Igor, we were surrounded by wereleopards, his and mine. The moment I met Nathaniel's eyes the power jolted through me. I turned from him to Cherry, and her pale eyes widened. The power was so thick it was like trying to breath something liquid, as if it hurt for the air to go down. The power leaped between me and Zane, Vivian, and Caleb, who was next in the circle. Caleb, who I didn't particularly like. But as soon as I searched his face, the power leaped between us, just as it had with the others.

He gasped, hand going to his chest, as if he'd felt it like a blow there. His voice came out strangled. "What are you doing?"

"She is being Nimir-Ra," Micah said.

I turned back to him, but in the turning crossed Noah's gaze first. The power stretched between me and this stranger, and the fear showed on his face. I was strangely calm; it felt right, good. Gina moved closer to Merle, and that drew my gaze. The power swung through her, from her. We were all like some great circuit of energy, sharing, flowing, growing. Tears trailed down Gina's face; she cried softly, clinging to Merle's arm. I met his eyes last, as if I was supposed to, and he tried to turn away, but it wasn't a matter of locking gazes, it was a matter of my attention going to him. The power, my power, my beast, noticing him.

The power lashed through him, because he fought it. He tried to shield, but he couldn't shield from this. It wasn't that I was strong enough to force him. I didn't try to push. It was more that the power recognized him, and something, maybe his beast, resonated with the power. He turned slowly to stare at me, and the look on his face was pained. It didn't hurt, it felt warm and good and frightening.

The power grew, wound tight and tighter, until it filled the air around us.

Claudia said, "What the hell are you doing?"

"Bonding," Rafael said, and he drew the two wererats out of our circle. The instant they were gone, the circle tightened, and it was like the pressure of a storm; my ears needed to pop, as if the pressure of the air had changed.

Micah moved to stand in front of me. The others formed a circle around us as if someone had choreographed it. We stared at each other and then reached a hand towards each other. It was hard to move forward, as if the air had grown solid and we had to push our way through. Our fingertips touched, and our hands slid together, quickly, easily, like a fish breaking through water into open air. We spilled around each other, our arms, our bodies touching completely, as if we could walk into the other's body like it was an open door. His mouth hovered over mine, and the power was there, breathing, pulsing, hot against my lips. I tried to be afraid. Tried to draw back, but I didn't want to. It was as if a part of me that I hadn't even known existed was in charge, and no amount of common sense—or doubts—could stop it.

It wasn't a kiss, it was a melding. The power poured in a scalding wave from his mouth to mine, from my mouth to his. I could feel the others, like lines of heat running out like spokes of a wheel, and Micah and I were the hub of that wheel. The power ran between us all, back and forth, liquid, burning, growing, growing, and melting. Melting boundaries, borders that kept us separate as people. It was as if Micah's body and mine were a door and we stepped into each other, closer than flesh could touch, closer than hearts could beat, and I felt his beast and mine roll through us, around us, as if the two great animals bound us together like a rope that ran through our flesh, our skin, our minds. And the beasts flared outward, traveled down those lines of power and smashed into each of the others. I felt it as a physical blow, felt them stagger as our twinned beasts traveled the circle and caressed their beasts in turn. And our beasts came home in a rush of heat, like standing in the middle of a bonfire, but it was also a glorious rush, a joyousness like nothing I'd ever felt. I caught, with that rush of power, glimpses into all the others.

I saw Gina tied to a bed and a man above her like a shadow, something evil that the power could not see clearly; Merle covered in wounds and blood, huddled against a wall, weeping; Caleb standing alone, covered in blood, his eyes haunted; Noah running down a hallway with screams chasing him, making him run faster; Cherry lying in a huge heap of warm bodies, beside Zane and Nathaniel and me; Zane's memory was of sitting at my kitchen table eating, laughing with Nathaniel; Vivian lying in Stephen's arms in their bed; Nathaniel's memory was of me marking his back, but the sense of peace I got from him with the memory was stronger than the sense of sex, as if some great burden had lifted from him; and I saw Gregory bound wrist-to-ankle behind his back, gagged, blindfolded, terrifed. He lay naked on a bed of bones. I knew this was not a memory, this was what was happening to Gregory right this minute. And I could see it, feel his terror, and I still didn't know where he was.

The power burst over us all in a wave of skin-rushing, nerve-caressing contentment, as if we'd all walked into a strange room and suddenly realized that everything in it was familiar, every corner of the room was a key to our hearts, and the word that washed over me, was *home*.

Micah drew back first, shaking. I was crying, and didn't remember when it had started. I heard other people crying in the dark, and I looked beyond us and found that it wasn't just our people. Some of the wererats were crying, faces turned towards us with something like awe—or fear—in their eyes.

Something made me look past all of them to the wood's edge. Richard stood shirtless, dressed in nothing but jeans and whatever shoes he was wearing. The sight of him there painted with starlight and shadows made me catch my breath, not because he was beautiful, or because I wanted him—that always went without saying with Richard—but because he was suddenly, for the first time, wild. It wasn't his anger that made the difference. I saw him at the edge of the woods, the way you'd come unexpectedly upon a wild animal, like glimpsing deer in the twilight, or that flash as something large and furred raced in front of your headlights, and you knew it wasn't a dog and it was too big to be a fox. Richard stood there, and when our eyes met, it sent a jolt through me from the top of my head to the soles of my feet, and into the ground beyond. Whatever else Richard had been doing to screw up his pack's structure, one thing he'd done right, he'd embraced his beast. You could see it on him like a coat that he'd finally grown into, something that fit him, tailor-made.

Marcus, the old Ulfric, had always insisted on dressing up, so at a glance you'd know he was king. Richard stood there with no clothes to distinguish him, yet you knew he was king. Power makes you a monarch, and all the fancy robes in the world won't do the job without it.

We stared at each other across the clearing. Underneath that new veneer of comfortable power, the look on his face made my chest so tight it hurt. If I could have thought of anything to say that would have made things less painful, I'd have said it, but I couldn't think of any words that would help.

Jamil and Shang-Da came up on either side of him, and there was a look of anger on Shang-Da's face. Anger at me, I think. Jamil looked at Richard, as if he wished there was some way for him to guard Richard from this, as well as from bullets and claws. But with some things, even a really good bodyguard can't take the hit for you. This was one of those things.

Richard's voice came deep, loud, clear, untouched by the look on his face. "Welcome rat king of the Dark Crown Clan. Welcome Nimir-Ra and Nimir-Raj of the Blooddrinkers Clan. Welcome to the lands of the Thronnos Rokke Clan. The leopards have shown us this night what it truly means to be a clan, be they pard, lukoi, or rodere. They show us what we all strive for—a true melding of all our parts into a whole." Bitterness crept in at the last, but on the whole, it was a lovely speech, and more heartfelt than pleasant.

"Now join us at our lupanar, and we will see if you can win back your lost cat." There was anger in his voice, and I wondered if Gregory was about to pay the price for Richard's anger with me.

Richard turned and melted into the trees with Shang-Da at his side. Jamil spared a glance back at me, then followed.

Micah leaned close and whispered, "I owe you several apologies. I'm sorry your Ulfric had to see us this way."

"Me, too," I said.

"I said your cats were a mess, and I was wrong. You have made a home for your cats, and mine have nowhere to hide."

"What is wrong with all of you?" It wasn't perhaps the most diplomatic question, but it covered things.

"That is a very long story."

Merle leaned over us. He spoke so low that I almost couldn't hear him. "Be very careful for all our sakes."

They had some very serious eye contact. I said, "What is going on?"

Micah raised my hand and laid a brief kiss on the knuckles. "Let's save your Gregory. That has to be priority tonight, right?"

He smiled and tried to charm his way out of the stare I was giving him. I stared at him until the smile faded from his face and he dropped my hand. "Yeah, saving Gregory is priority for tonight, but I want to know what's going on."

"One problem at a time," Micah said.

I was getting the very distinct feeling that if they all could have lied to me forever, they would have. It wasn't lying, as much as hiding things from me. Things that had to do with blood and pain, and no matter how powerful they all were, Micah's pard wasn't a family, wasn't whole. Strangely, as messed up as me and my leopards were, we were a family. More so than Richard and his wolves, even. Richard was so busy fighting his moral battles and his power structure problems that there wasn't time for mending other things.

"Give me the *Reader's Digest* condensed version, Micah" I said.

"Gregory is waiting for you to rescue him."

"So give me a couple of sentences, but make it the truth, Micah."

"Micah," Merle said softly, but with force to his voice. It was a warning.

I looked at the big man. "What are you guys hiding, Merle?"

Micah touched my arm, brought my attention back to his face. "I told you that once we were taken over by a very bad man, who still wants us. I'm searching for someplace strong enough to keep us safe."

"Are you saying this guy will come looking for you here in St. Louis?"

"Yes," he said.

"Most alphas can take a hint," I said.

Micah shook his head. "This one won't. He will never give us up." He gripped my arm. "If you take us on, you'll have to deal with him eventually."

"Is he bulletproof?" I asked.

The question seemed to confuse him, because he frowned. "No, I mean, no, I guess not."

I shrugged. "Not a problem then."

He looked at me. "What do you mean? That you'll just kill him?"

It was my turn to look at him. "Is there any reason I shouldn't?"

He almost smiled, stopped, then frowned again. "Just kill him, just like that." It was almost as if he were thinking it over, as if it had never occurred to him.

Merle said, "He's a hard man to kill."

"Unless he's faster than a silver bullet, Merle, nobody's that hard to kill."

Rafael came slowly through the leopards, Claudia and Igor trailing him. "We've all been thinking of your leopards as lesser than us. What I just saw makes me envious."

"I know how the wolves work," I said. "And I know that they don't have a sense of home. First Raina and Marcus made them afraid of each other, now Richard's morals have him struggling to be safe. But you and yours seem pretty secure. How different is what I've done with my leopards from what everyone else is doing?"

"I've benefited from your loyalty, your sheer stubbornness. What I didn't realize until tonight is that you didn't save me just because I was your friend, or just because it was the right thing to do. You didn't risk yourself and your people to save me from torture because of the kind of moral rightness that Richard is fond of. You saved me because you could not bear the thought of leaving me behind." He touched my face, very gently. "Not from a sense of right and wrong, but because you are just that tenderhearted."

I looked at him. "I've been called a lot of things, but never that."

He chucked me under the chin like you would a child. "Don't make light of one of your better qualities. You love your people like a mother is supposed to love her children. You want what's best for them, even if that makes you uncomfortable, even if you don't like their choices."

I had to look away from the wonderment on his face, like he was looking at somebody else that couldn't be me. "You have never been their leopard queen in body, but you shamed us all tonight. It's not seeing your closeness to Micah that will torment Richard, though that will burn. It's that you gave us a glimpse of what we are all striving for, for our clans. Richard believes his moral rightness will get him where your leopards already are."

I looked up at him. "My pard is not a democracy, and I have a hell of a lot more than just presidential veto when it comes to decisions."

"Richard knows that, better probably than anyone, and that will gall him, Anita. It will make him doubt himself."

I shook my head. "Richard always doubts himself when it comes to the lukoi. He'll never have surety about them until he has surety about who and what he is."

"First I have to accept the fact that you're kindhearted, now I have to accept the fact that you're insightful as well. I knew you were powerful, ruthless, and pretty, but that you have a mind and a heart besides is going to take some getting used to."

"Does everyone pretty much think I'm just a sociopath who happens to have magical abilities?"

"It's all you let people see," he said, "until now." He gazed out towards the circle of faces still turned to us. I saw a kind of hunger in their faces, and I knew that they had felt what I'd felt, a sense of true belonging, of being home within the circle—not of bricks or mortar—but of flesh, of hands to grasp, arms to hold, smiles to share. So simple, so rare.

All these months I'd been worried I'd fail the wereleopards. I thought failure meant them dying, or getting hurt. What I realized suddenly was that the true failure would have been if I hadn't given a damn. You can bandage a wound, set a broken bone, but not caring . . . you can't cure that, and you can't recover from it.

23

THE LUPANAR WAS a large clearing 100 yards by 150 yards. The clearing appeared to be flat, but actually it sat in a large smooth valley between hills. You couldn't notice it at night, but I knew that just beyond the trees that ringed the far side of the lupanar were steep hills. It had taken me more than one visit to find what lay beyond the trees.

Now all vision stopped at the far edge of the clearing. Torches that rose man-high were stuck into the ground on either side of the stone throne. The throne was a huge chair carved of rock, so old that there were places on the arms where countless generations of Ulfrics had touched it and worn away the stone. Probably the back and seat of the chair were worn as well, but they were covered by a spill of purple silk, suitably royal. There was something very primitive about the huge stone chair and its spill of cloth caught between the wavering golden light of the torches. It looked like a throne for some ancient barbaric king, someone who should wear animal skins and a crown of iron.

Werewolves, most—but not all—in human form, stood or crouched in a huge circle. There was one opening in the circle, which we walked through. The werewolves flowed behind us, like a door of flesh closing. The wererats spread around behind us and to either side, but we all knew if it came to a fight, we were outmatched, and outflanked.

Rafael and two very large wererats stood to one side of me. Donovan Reece, the swan king, was on the other side. Rafael had kindly given him a quartet of bodyguards. Micah stood just a little behind me, and my newly acquired bodyguards were just behind him. Our leopards had spilled out in a rough knot behind us, like a line of defense, before the main show of wererats.

Someone had hung cloth in the trees to one side of the throne. Black cloth, like a curtain, and it took a movement of the wind to draw my attention to it. It was held aside, and Sylvie came through, followed by a tall man I didn't know. Her face was less refined with no makeup, less soft. Her short hair curled neatly, but carelessly. She was dressed in the first pair of jeans I'd ever seen her in, with a pale blue tanktop and white jogging shoes.

The tall man was thin the way basketball players are thin—all arms and legs and lanky muscle. Most of that lanky muscle showed because all he wore was a pair of cutoff jean shorts. But he, like Richard, didn't need finery. He moved in a circle of his own grace and power, like a tiger stalking into view. Except there were no bars to hide behind, and I'd had to leave my gun at home.

He had short, dark hair that curled a little thicker than Sylvie's. His face was one of those that you couldn't decide was attractive or plain. It was made up of strong bones, long lines, thin lips on a wide mouth. I'd just about decided he was plain when he looked at me, and the moment I saw those dark eyes I knew I was wrong. Intelligence burned in there, intelligence and some dark emotion. He let anger flow over his face, and I realized the very force of his personality made him so striking that he *was* handsome, though it was the kind of handsome that would never come across in a still photo, because it needed movement, his vibrating energy to make it work.

I knew without being told that this was Jacob, and I knew something else. We were in trouble.

Richard came next, and he moved in his own vibrating spill of power. He glided as gracefully, filled with as much anger as Jacob, but he still lacked something, some edge that the other man had. An edge of darkness, maybe. All I knew for sure was that Jacob was ruthless. I could almost smell it on him. And Richard, for better, or worse, still was not.

I sighed. I'd thought if he could just once embrace his beast he'd be alright. He sat on the throne with the firelight playing in the loose waves of his hair, turning it to spun copper and burnished gold, the fire shadows playing on the muscles of his chest, shoulders, arms. He looked the part of the barbarian king, but there was still something in him, something . . . soft. And if I could taste it, then so could Jacob.

I had one of those moments of clarity that comes sometimes. There was nothing that any of us could do to Richard to make him truly harsh. He might act in anger, like he'd taken Gregory, but no matter what the world did to him, there would still be something in him that flinched. His only hope for survival was to surround himself with loyal people who *wouldn't* flinch.

Jamil and Shang-Da stood together to one side of the throne, not too close, but not too far either. Shang-Da was back in his usual monochrome black business dress: black slacks, black shirt, black suit jacket, and the polished black shoes. He always looked very *GQ*, even in the woods.

Jamil could dress up with the best of them, but he tried to be appropriate to the situation. He had on jeans that looked freshly pressed and a red muscle tank top that looked splendid against the darkness of his skin. He'd changed the beads in his waist-length cornrowed hair to red and black. The beads gleamed softly in the torchlight, as if they might be made of semiprecious stones.

Jamil caught my glance. He didn't exactly nod, but he acknowledged me with his eyes. Shang-Da avoided my gaze, searching the crowd, but never quite looking at me. I think if Richard would have allowed it the two of them would have done whatever was necessary to secure his throne. But they were hamstrung by Richard, and the best they could do was work within his honorable trap.

Sylvie and I stared at each other for a few heartbeats. I'd seen her collection of bones of her enemies. She got them out periodically and handled them. She said it was comforting to run her hands over them. I personally liked a good stuffed toy and some really fine coffee, but, hey, whatever makes you feel better. Sylvie would do whatever needed doing, if Richard would only let her.

And if I'd still been lupa, hell, we had enough ruthless people to get the job done, if Richard would just get out of our way. We were so close, and at the same time we weren't even in the ballpark. It was more than frustrating. It was like watching a train race towards Richard, and we were all yelling, "Get off the tracks, get off the tracks!" Hell, we were trying to drag him off the tracks, and he was fighting us.

If Jacob was the train, then I could kill him and Richard would be safe. But Rafael was right. If it wasn't Jacob, it'd be someone else. Jacob wasn't the train hurtling to destroy Richard. Richard was.

His voice filled the clearing. "We gather here tonight to say good-bye to our lupa and to choose another."

There was a rash of howls and applause from about half of the pack. But dozens of the werewolves stood silent, watching. It didn't mean they were on my side. Maybe they were neutral, but it was good to notice who wasn't a rousing supporter of my being kicked out of the pack.

"We are here to stand in final judgment for one who has wronged our pack by taking our lupa from us."

There was less applause, fewer howls. It looked like the vote to condemn Gregory had been a close one. That made me feel better, not much, but a little. Though if Gregory died, I guess it really didn't matter.

"We are also here to give the leopards' Nimir-Ra a last chance to win back her cat."

The howls and applause stayed at about fifty–fifty, but the general atmosphere was definitely cooler. The pack wasn't lost, and it certainly wasn't wholeheartedly on Jacob's side. I said a little prayer for guidance, because this was more a political problem, and that wasn't one of my best things.

"It is business between the lukoi and the pard. Why are the rodere here, Rafael?" Richard asked. He talked like he didn't know us, very political, very distant.

"The Nimir-Ra saved my life once. The rodere owe her a great debt."

"Does this mean that your treaty with us is null and void?"

"I formed a treaty with you, Richard, and I will hold to that, because I know you are a man that honors his obligations and remembers his duty to his allies, but I owe Anita a personal debt, and I am honor-bound to uphold that as well."

"If it comes to fighting, who will you fight with, us or the leopards?"

"I hope most sincerely that it does not come to that, but I came with the leopards, and we will go with them, under whatever circumstances that leave-taking will be."

"You have destroyed your people," Jacob said.

Richard turned on him. "I am Ulfric here, Jacob, not you. I say what will be destroyed and what will not."

"I meant no offense, Ulfric." But his voice made the words a lie. "I meant only that if it comes to a fight the rats cannot defeat us. Perhaps their king would like to reconsider who he owes a debt of honor to."

"A debt of honor exists whether you want it to or not," Rafael said. "Richard understands what it means to owe an honor-debt. That is why I know that Richard will honor our treaty. I have no such assurances when it comes to other members of this pack."

There, he'd said it. It was as close to saying, *I don't trust you, Jacob*, as he could get. A spreading well of silence filled the clearing, so that the brush of cloth, the shift of a furred body was suddenly loud.

Richard's hands tightened on the arms of his throne. I watched him, because he was shielding so tight against me that I couldn't feel him, but I could watch,

watch him think. "Are you saying that if I am no longer Ulfric that the treaty no longer holds?"

"Yes, that is what I'm saying."

Richard and Rafael stared at each other for a long time, then the faintest of smiles played on Richard's lips. "I have no plans to step down as Ulfric, so the treaty should be secure for a while, unless Jacob has other plans."

That one statement sent a wave of unease through the waiting werewolves. You could feel it, see it spreading out through them, as if they smelled a trap of some kind.

Jacob looked surprised, shocked. He was a perfect stranger, but I watched the confusion play over his face, as he tried to think of what to say. If he said he had no designs on the throne, then he would be foresworn, and the shapeshifters were a little touchy about things like that.

Jacob was either going to have to lie or declare his intentions, and the look on his face said clearly he wasn't ready to do that.

A woman's voice came from the right, clear and ringing like she'd had stage training. "Aren't we getting distracted from the business at hand? I for one am very interested in choosing the new lupa."

The woman was tall, but built all of curves, voluptuous the way that movie stars in the fifties had been. She seemed soft, feminine, yet she stalked over the ground in a swaying glide, half sex on the hoof and half predatory, like she'd lure you in by playing victim, fuck you till you cried for mercy, then eat your face off.

She was even wearing a dress, one that clung to her curves and had a neckline so low that you knew she had to be wearing a bra. Breasts that size didn't do perky without some help. She stalked barefoot, her deep red hair styled and perfect, falling just above her shoulders in a burnished shine.

"We'll get around to choosing the new lupa," Richard said.

She dropped to her knees in front of the throne, folding the dress under her thighs, very ladylike, though making sure to lean forward enough for Richard to look straight down her cleavage. I didn't like her much.

"You can't blame us for being eager, Ulfric. One of us," and she hesitated, making it clear that the "us" was for politeness' sake, "will be chosen lupa and become your mate all in one glorious night." Her voice had dropped to a sultry murmur, still loud enough to be heard.

Nope, didn't like her. I had no room to bitch with Micah standing beside me, but that didn't matter. Logic had nothing to do with it. I wanted to grab a handful of that bottle-dyed red hair and hurt her. It wasn't until Micah touched my arm that I realized I'd been caressing one of the knives in its wrist sheath. Sometimes I touch my weapons when I'm nervous; sometimes my body just betrays my thoughts. I forced my hands to be still, but I was so not happy.

"Go back with the other candidates, Paris," Richard said. He was carefully not looking at her, as if he were afraid to. That didn't make it better; it made it worse.

She leaned forward, putting a hand on his knee. He jumped. "You can't blame us for being eager, Ulfric. We've all wanted you for so *very* long."

Richard's face had thinned down with anger. "Sylvie," he said.

Sylvie smiled, and it was a smile of pure evil pleasure. She grabbed Paris's wrist and dragged her, none too gently, to her feet. Paris was a good two inches taller, but Sylvie's power, her beast, made her seem ten feet tall.

"The Ulfric told you to go back and stand with the other candidates. Do it." She gave Paris a little shove towards the crowd. The woman stumbled, but regained her composure, smoothing the tight dress down over her thighs.

Sylvie had turned to walk back to her place at Richard's side, when Paris said, "I heard you liked it rough."

Sylvie froze, and I didn't need to see her face to feel the instant rage that radiated from her. I knew before she turned, slowly, muscles tense, that her eyes had bled to wolf amber. "What did you say?"

"Sylvie," Richard said, voice soft. It wasn't a command, it was a request. I think if he'd made it a command, she'd have fought it, demanded some sort of satisfaction. But it was a request . . . She turned back to Richard.

"Yes, Ulfric."

"Take your place, please."

She went back to take her place as Freki on his right side. But the anger boiled around her like nearly visible heat off a summer road.

"I apologize to the swan king, for not recognizing him sooner, but we've only met once."

"Yes," Donovon Reece said, "I remember."

"Welcome to our lupanar. I would give you safe passage among us, but I have to know why you are here before I can do that."

"I am here because the Nimir-Ra rescued my swanmanes from the people that nearly killed her. She risked her life for them. I am here at her side tonight as an ally."

"I can't grant you safe passage, Donovan, because if things go badly it will be a fight. If you're Anita's ally, you'll be in the middle of it."

"She risked her life for my people, I can do no less."

Richard nodded, and I watched an understanding pass between them. Birds of an honorable feather, so to speak.

"Does she save every shapeshifter she comes across in trouble?" Jacob asked, and he made it derisive.

Richard started to say something, and Sylvie stepped forward, touching his arm. He gave a small nod, and let her speak. "How many of us has Anita saved from torture or death?" She raised her own hand.

Jamil stepped out from around the throne and raised his own. All my leopards raised their hands like a small forest of gratitude. Rafael raised his hand. I finally spotted Louie, his lieutenant, and Ronnie's boyfriend. He gave a small nod to me and raised his own hand.

Richard stood and raised his hand. There were other hands here and there. Then Irving Griswold, mild-mannered reporter—and werewolf—stepped forward. His glasses reflected the firelight so that he looked blind. He looked like a tall, slightly balding cherub with eyes of flame.

"What would have happened if Anita hadn't saved Sylvie from the vampire council's torture? Sylvie's strong, but what if she had broken? She's dominant enough to call most of us in, to have forced us to give ourselves over to the vampire council." Irving raised his hand. "She saved us all."

Hands went up among the werewolves until nearly half of them were holding a hand up. It made my throat tight, my eyes burn. I wasn't going to cry, but if someone hugged me, I couldn't be sure of that.

Louie stepped forward, small, dark, and handsome, with his short black hair cut neat. "Rafael is a strong king, so strong that if the vampire council had broken him, none of us could have refused his call. We would all have been at their mercy. You all saw what they did to him and how long it took him to heal. Anita saved all the rodere in this city."

The rats raised their hands—all of them.

Sylvie said, "Look around you, do you really want to lose Anita as our lupa? Most of you remember what it was like with Raina. Do you want to go back to that?"

"She's not lukoi," Jacob said.

A few others said the same thing, but not many. "If your only objection to her is that she's not a werewolf," Sylvie said, "then that's a poor excuse for losing Anita."

"Losing her," Jacob said, "this is the first time I've ever seen her. I've been with this pack for five months and this is the first time I've set eyes on your precious lupa. We can't lose something we never had."

There was a lot of support for that, a lot of howls, cries of *yeah*, applause even. I couldn't blame them on this one. I stepped forward, moving until I stood alone between my allies and the throne. Silence fell around the clearing, until you could hear the torches sizzling.

Richard stared down at me. I could meet his eyes now. I made sure my voice carried when I said, "Jacob's right."

Sylvie looked startled. So did Jacob. And there was movement behind me as people startled. "I haven't been much of a lupa to the Thronnos Rokke Clan, but I didn't know I was supposed to be. I was just the Ulfric's girlfriend. I had my hands full with the wereleopards, and I trusted Richard to take care of the wolves. The leopards had no one but me." I turned and faced the crowd. "I was human, not fit to be lupa, or Nimir-Ra." The crowd's murmur was louder this time.

"I don't know if you've all heard, but there was an accident in the fight that saved the swanmanes. I may be Nimir-Ra for real in a few weeks. We won't know for sure, but it seems likely."

They were quiet now, watching me, human eyes, wolf eyes, rats, leopards, but every face held intelligence, a burning concentration. "There's nothing I can do about that. We'll just have to wait and see, but my leopard did not injure me on purpose. I will stake my word of honor on that. I'm told that Gregory stands accused of killing your lupa." I raised my hands out from my body. "Here I stand, alive and well. If you lose me as your lupa, it won't be because Gregory took me from you, it will be because you choose to let me go. If that's what you want, fine. I don't blame you. Until tonight, until just a few minutes ago, I didn't think I was doing a very good job as Nimir-Ra, let alone trying to be human lupa. Now, I think maybe I was wrong. Maybe if I'd stayed around more, things would be better. I did what I thought was right at the time. If you don't want me as lupa, that's your right, but don't punish a fellow shapeshifter for an accident that happened during a fight where he saved me from getting my heart dug out of my chest."

"A pretty speech," Jacob said, "but we've already voted, and your leopard has to pay the price, unless you're shapeshifter enough to win him back."

I looked back, not at Jacob, but at Richard. "Richard, please."

He shook his head. "I can't undo the vote, Anita. I would if I could." He sounded tired.

I sighed. "Fine, how do I win Gregory back?"

"She needs to stop being lupa, before she can be Nimir-Ra." This from Paris, who though back in the crowd, still managed to make her voice ring over the clearing.

"I thought you voted me out as lupa," I said.

"They have," Richard said, "but to make it official by our laws, there's a ceremony that will sever your ties to us."

"Is it a long ceremony?" I asked.

"It can be," he said.

"Let me get Gregory out first, then I'll do whatever lukoi ceremony you want me to do."

"You have the right to refuse to step down," Sylvie said.

I looked at Richard.

"You have that right." His face, his voice, were neutral as he said it. I couldn't tell if he was happy or sad about the idea.

"What happens if I refuse?"

"You'd have to defend your right to be lupa, either by one-on-one combat with any dominant that wants the job . . ." And he stopped there.

Sylvie looked at him, but it was Jacob who finished. "Or you can prove that you're lupa enough to keep the job by annointing the throne."

I just looked at him and shrugged. "Annointing the throne—what does that mean?"

"You fuck the Ulfric on the throne in front of all of us."

I was already shaking my head. "Somehow I don't think either Richard or I are up to public sex."

"It's a little more complicated than that," Richard said. He looked at me, and there was so much in his eyes—anger, pain—that it hurt to hold his gaze.

"Sex alone isn't enough. We'd have to have a mystical connection between our beasts." He was quiet, and I thought he'd finished, but he hadn't. "Like you have with your Nimir-Raj."

We stared at each other. I couldn't think of anything good to say, but I had to say something. "I'm sorry." My voice came out soft, almost sad.

"Don't apologize," he said.

"Why not?"

"It's not your fault, it's mine."

That made me widen my eyes at him. "How so?"

"I should have known you'd have that kind of bond with your mate. You're more powerful as a human than most true lupas."

I looked at him. "What are you saying, Richard? That you wish you'd made me one of you while you had the chance?"

He lowered his eyes as if he couldn't bear for me to see his expression anymore. I stepped closer, close enough to touch him, close enough so that his vibrating energy spilled like a march of insects across my skin. It made me shiver. But I felt something else, something I'd never felt before, not with Richard.

My beast spilled over my skin and reached out like a playful kitten to swat at Richard's power. The energies sparked against each other, and I could almost see the play of colors in my head, like flint and steel being struck against one another, except in technicolor.

I heard Richard catch his breath; his eyes were very wide. His voice came hoarse, almost strangled. "Did you do that on purpose?"

I shook my head. I didn't trust myself to speak. The sparks had quieted, and it was as if I were leaning against a nearly solid wall of power, his and mine, as if I could have leaned against that energy and it alone would have kept us from touching. I finally found my voice, but it was a whisper. "What's happening?"

"The marriage of the marks, I think," he said, voice almost equally soft.

I wanted so badly to reach through that power and touch him, to see if the beasts would roll through each other like they did for Micah and me. I knew it was silly, he was wolf, and apparently I was leopard, so our beasts wouldn't recognize each other. But I'd loved Richard for so long, and we were bound to each other by Jean-Claude's marks, and I carried a piece of his beast inside me. I had to know. I had to know if I could have with Richard what I had with Micah.

My hand moved through the power, and it was like shoving it into an electric socket. The energy was so strong, it bit along my skin. I was reaching for his shoulder, a nice neutral place to touch someone, when he rolled off the side of the throne and was suddenly standing beside it. He'd moved so fast I couldn't follow with my eyes. I'd seen the beginning of the movement and the end, but the middle—I'd blinked and missed it.

"No, Anita," he said, "no, if we can't ever touch again, I don't want to feel your beast. We may not be the same animal, but it will be more than anything we've ever had between us. I couldn't bear it."

I let my hand fall to my side and stepped back far enough from the throne for him to regain his seat. I wasn't apologizing again, but I wanted to. I wanted to cry for both of us, or scream. I know the universe has a sense of irony, and sometimes you get reminded just how sadistic that can be.

I would finally have to accept his furry half, because I'd have one of my own. I could be Richard's nearly perfect lover, at long last, and we could never touch each other again.

24

RICHARD WAS SITTING on his throne again, and I was standing back far enough for him to feel safe. Rafael, Micah, and Reece had all moved up beside me, a half-circle of kings at my back. It should have made me feel secure. It didn't. I was tired, so terribly tired, so terribly sad. Even with Micah at my back, I couldn't stop looking at Richard, couldn't stop wondering, *what if*. Oh, I knew, I'd never have allowed him to make me a werewolf on purpose, but a small part of me wondered. But I told that small part to shut up, and I got down to business.

"I want Gregory back unharmed. How do I do that, according to lukoi law?"

Richard said, "Jacob." That one word sounded as tired as I felt.

Jacob stepped forward, obviously pleased with himself. "Your leopard is here on our land, and we've done nothing to hide his scent trail. If you can track him, you can take him home."

I raised my eyebrows at him. "I have to follow a scent trail like a dog?"

"If you were a true shapeshifter, you could do it," Jacob said.

"This isn't a fair test," Rafael said. "She hasn't had her first change. Most of our secondary powers don't appear until after our first full moon."

"It doesn't have to be scenting," Richard said, "but it must be something that only a shapeshifter could do. Something that only a shifter powerful enough to truly be Nimir-Ra, or lupa, could do." He was looking at me when he said it, and there was something in his eyes, something he was trying to tell me.

"That doesn't sound very fair either," Micah said.

Richard kept looking at me, willing me to understand him. I didn't know why he didn't just drop his shields and let me see his mind.

Almost as if Richard had read my mind, he said, "No werewolf or wererat or wereleopard, no one can aid you in finding your leopard. If anyone interferes in any way, then the test is invalid, and he'll die."

"Even if that help is metaphysical?" I asked.

Richard nodded. "Even if."

I looked at him, studied his face, and frowned. I finally shook my head. I'd had a vision of where Gregory was, and under what circumstances, but it gave me no real clue. All I really needed to do was ask someone where a hole was with bones at the bottom. But I couldn't ask anyone there. Then I had an idea.

"Can I use my own metaphysical abilities to aid me?"

Richard nodded.

I looked at Jacob, because I knew the objection would come from him, if anyone. "I don't think your necromancy is going to help you locate your leopard."

Actually, it might have. If the bones Gregory was lying on were the largest burial sight in the area, then I might be able to track the bones and find him. Or I might spend all night chasing after piles of buried animals or old Indian graves. I had a faster way, maybe not better, but faster.

I sat down on the ground, Indian fashion, resting my hands lightly on my knees.

"What are you doing?" Jacob asked.

"I'm going to call the munin," I said.

He laughed, a loud bray of sound. "Oh, this should be good."

I closed my eyes, and I opened that part of me that dealt with the dead. I've heard Marianne and her friends describe it to be like opening a door, but it's so much a part of me that it's more like unclenching a hand, like opening something in my body that is as natural as reaching across the table for the salt. That might sound like an awfully mundane description of something mystical, but the mystical stuff truly is a part of everyday life. It's always there, we just choose to ignore it.

The munin are the spirits of the dead, put into a sort of racial memory bank that can be accessed by lukoi who have the ability to speak with them. It's a rare ability; to my knowledge no one in Richard's pack could do it. But I could. The munin are just another type of dead, and I'm good with the dead.

In Tennessee, the munin of Verne and Marianne's pack had come quickly and eagerly—so very close to being real ghosts, crowding around me, eager to speak. I'd practiced until I could pick and choose who would join with me and be able to communicate. It was close enough to channeling or mediumship that Marianne had suggested I could probably do this with normal ghosts, if I wanted. I didn't want to. I didn't like sharing my body with another being, dead or alive. Creeped me out, yes it did.

I waited to feel the press of the munin spreading around me, like a ghostly card deck that I could shuffle and pick the very card I wanted. Nothing happened. The munin did not come. Or rather a gathering of munin did not come. There was always one munin that came when I called, and sometimes when I didn't.

Raina was the only munin of Richard's pack that traveled with me always. Even in Tennessee, surrounded by munin from a different clan line, Raina was still there. Marianne said that Raina and I had a etheric bond, though she wasn't sure why. I'd managed to call munin hundreds of years old, and Raina, the very recently dead, came with more than ease. But Marcus, the previous Ulfric, remained elusive. I'd thought with my newfound control I'd be able to call him, but not only was Marcus not there, no one was there. The clearing was empty of spirits. It shouldn't have been. This was the spot where they consumed their dead, each pack member eating the flesh to take on the memories and courage, or faults, of the recently dead. They could choose not to feed, but it was like the ultimate excommunication. Raina had been a bad person, and I wondered sometimes what exactly you had to do to get excommunicated from the lukoi. Raina had been so bad that I would have let her go, but she was powerful. Maybe that's why she was still hanging around.

Though hanging around implied she was like the phantoms of Verne's pack, and she wasn't. She was internal to me, as if she poured out from inside my body, rather than pouring into me from outside. Marianne still couldn't explain why it worked that way for Raina and me. Some things you just accept and work around, because to do anything else is to butt your head against a brick wall; the wall will not break first.

Raina filled me like a hand inside a glove, and I was the glove. But I'd worked a long time to be able to control her. We'd worked out a deal of sorts. I used her memories and powers, and I let her have some fun. The problem was that Raina had been a sexually sadistic nymphomaniac when alive, and death hadn't changed her much.

I opened my eyes and felt her smile curve my lips, felt my face take on her expression. I rose to my feet in a graceful line, and even my walk was different. Once I'd hated that; now I shrugged it off as the price of doing business.

She laughed, full throated, the kind of laugh that makes a man look in a bar. Her laugh was deeper than mine, contralto, a practiced seduction of sound.

Richard went pale, hands gripping the arms of his throne. "Anita?" he made it a question.

"Guess again, my honey wolf."

He flinched at the nickname. In wolf form Richard is a ginger color, like red honey, though I'd never really thought of it like that before. Trust Raina to think of something thick and sticky when she looked at a man.

Her words came out of my mouth. "Don't be bitchy, when you called me for help."

I nodded, and it was my voice that explained to Richard's confused frown. "I was thinking something less than charitable about her. She didn't like it."

Jacob walked towards me and stopped when I looked at him with Raina's expression. "You can't have called munin. You're not lukoi."

Strange, but it hadn't even occurred to me that being a leopard might mean I couldn't call munin. It might explain why the other munin hadn't come when I called. "You said my necromancy wouldn't help me, Jacob, can't have it both ways. Either I'm lukoi enough to call the munin, or I'm necromancer enough to help myself."

We—Raina and me—stalked towards the tall, shirtless man. Raina liked him. Raina liked most men. Especially if the man was someone she'd never had sex with, and among the pack that had been a short list. But Jacob and more than twenty others were new. She looked out over the pack and picked out the new faces. She hesitated over Paris and didn't like her either. You can't have too many alpha bitches in one pack without them fighting amongst themselves.

I felt something I hadn't felt before from Raina—caution. She didn't like how many new people Richard had allowed into the pack in such a short space of time. It worried her. I realized for the first time that it hadn't just been love that made Marcus put up with her as lupa. She was powerful, but more than that, in her own twisted way she did care about the pack, and she and I were in perfect agreement on one thing: Richard had been careless with it. But we both felt we could fix it. It was almost scary that the wicked bitch of the west and I were in such perfect agreement. Either I had been corrupted, or Raina had never been quite as corrupt as I thought. I wasn't sure which idea bothered me more.

Of course, she thought we should seduce Richard into letting us kill a few select people, and I was still hoping that a slightly less sweet reason would prevail. Raina thought I was a fool, and I wasn't sure I didn't agree with her. Scarier and scarier.

"Anita." Richard said my name again, hesitant, as if he wasn't sure I was in there.

I turned, one hand coming up to my hair, flinging it back from my face. It was

Raina's gesture, and I watched that one movement make not only Richard, but Sylvie and Jamil behind her, nervous. No, frightened.

I could smell their fear. Raina's laugh bubbled out of my mouth, because she liked it. I didn't. I never liked it when my friends were afraid of me. My enemies, fine, but not my friends.

"I'm here, Richard, I'm here."

He stared at me. "The last time I saw you call Raina's munin you weren't able to think like yourself with her inside you."

"I really didn't leave you for all these months just because I was afraid of how close we all were. I left to get my shit together, and part of that was learning how to control the munin."

Raina said, "Control me? You wish." She hadn't said it aloud, only in my head. It had taken me a long time to realize that some things were said out loud and some things weren't. It was confusing, but you got used to it.

I said aloud what I'd seen in vision. "I saw Gregory in a hole, naked, tied up, lying on a bed of bones. Where is it?"

Raina showed me in images. It was like a fast-forward picture show, but the images came with emotions, smashing into me, one after the other. I saw a metal cap that screwed down with a tiny airway on top that let in enough light for you to see, if the sun was high enough. There was a rope ladder that spilled down into the dark and was taken up when it wasn't needed. I was Raina kneeling on a bed of bones, a human skull next to my knee. I had a syringe and injected its contents into a dark-haired man that was chained like I'd seen Gregory chained, ankles to wrists. He was gagged and blindfolded. When the needle went in, he whimpered and started to cry. The drugs were to keep him from changing.

I turned him over on his side and saw that a bone fragment had cut into his naked groin. I bent towards the smell of fresh blood, fresh meat, and the absolutely intoxicating stink of fear that came off the man. Not man, lukoi. I clawed my way up from my memory before Raina pressed our lips over him. I shoved it away from me, but I could still smell the fear, the drugs sweated out on his skin, the smell of soap from where Raina had cleaned him up, daily, before the abuse began. I knew his name had been Todd, and he'd talked to a reporter about the lukoi, helped them set up a blind with a camera on a full moon, for money. Maybe he had deserved to die, but not like that. No one deserved to die like that.

I came to myself lying on the ground in front of the throne, tears drying on my face. Jamil and Shang-Da were standing between me and the crowd that had moved to help me. Claudia and Igor were facing off with them, and Rafael had Micah by the arm, trying to convince him not to fight his way to me. Merle and Noah were moving up to join Claudia and Igor. This was all about to go to hell.

I propped myself up on my arms, and that small movement froze everyone in place. My voice came out hoarse, but mine. "I'm okay. I'm okay."

I'm not sure they believed me, but the tension level started to drop almost immediately. Good, I had enough problems tonight without a free-for-all breaking out.

I looked up at Richard, and all I could feel was anger. "Is that how you're going to kill Gregory, just leave him down in the oubliette until he rots?" My voice came out soft, because if I lost control of it, I wasn't sure how much other control I'd lose. I knew Raina. She wasn't gone. She'd want her "reward" first. She'd done her job. I knew where Gregory was. I even knew how to get there. She'd earned her prize. I didn't dare lose control of myself with her waiting like a shark just under the water.

"I told them to put Gregory some place far away from me. I didn't tell them to put him there."

I got to my feet slowly, even my body movements controlled, muscles almost stiff with adrenaline and the need to lash out. "But you left him there. Who's been going down and pumping him full of drugs to keep him from turning? You don't have Raina to do the dirty work anymore. Who was it? WHO WAS IT!" I screamed it into his face, and the rage was all she needed. She poured over me, and the last control I might have had drowned because I wanted to hurt Richard. I wanted to do it.

I hit him, closed-fist, turning my body into it, twisting my hand at the end, putting all I had into it. I did what they taught us to do in martial arts class if it was for real. I aimed not at Richard's face, but at a point two inches inside his face; that was the real goal.

I was back in a protective stance before Jamil and Shang-Da had time to react. I felt them move towards me and felt others move forward, too. The very thing I'd been trying to avoid, and I'd set it off. Raina was laughing in my head, laughing at us all.

25

RICHARD WAS LEANING over the arm of his throne, hair covering his face, when Sylvie grabbed me. I didn't fight her. Her fingers dug into my arms, and I knew I'd be bruised in the morning. Or maybe not. Maybe I'd heal it. Jacob was watching it all astonished and pleased.

I glanced back and found the bodyguards fighting. The leopards and rats were spreading out, the wolves beginning to close around them. I opened my mouth to yell something, but Richard's voice boomed over the clearing.

"Enough!" That one word froze us all, and we turned shocked faces to him. He was standing in front of his throne, blood spattered across one shoulder and on his upper chest. One side of his mouth was a red ruin. I'd never been able to do that kind of damage before.

He spat blood and said, "I'm not hurt. Some of you here have been inside the oubliette. You know what it was when Raina still lived. Can you blame the Nimir-Ra for hating me for putting her leopard down there?"

You could feel the tension begin to ease as the wolves pulled back. Richard had to order Jamil and Shang-Da to back off, and they and Claudia and Igor pushed at each other, like bullies that still didn't know who was tougher. I hadn't realized that Claudia was nearly six inches taller than Jamil, until they drew away from each other and he had to stare up at her to glare into her eyes.

Sylvie whispered in my ear, "Are you okay?"

I looked up at Richard. He was still bleeding. "Other than embarrassed, yeah."

She let me go, slowly, as if not sure that I was safe to let loose. She hovered right next to me, between me and Richard, until he motioned her back.

He stood in front of me, and we stared at each other. Blood still dripped from his mouth. "You pack a hell of a punch now," he said.

I nodded. "If you'd been human, what would that have done to you?"

"Broken my jaw, or maybe my neck."

"I didn't mean it," I said.

"Your Nimir-Raj will teach you how to judge your strength. You might stop going to your martial arts classes for a while, until you understand how your body works now."

"Good advice," I said.

He put his hand to his mouth, and it came away bright with blood. I had the urge to take his hand and lick the blood off of it. I wanted to climb his body and press my mouth to his and drink him down. The image was so vivid that I had to shut my eyes, so I couldn't see him standing there half-naked, bloodied, as if that would help me not want him. It didn't. I could smell his skin, the scent of him, and the fresh blood, like icing on a cake that I couldn't have.

"Go get your leopard, Anita."

I opened my eyes and looked up at him. "The oubliette was one of the things you fought against under Marcus. You said it was inhuman. I don't understand how you could use it."

"He was in there for nearly a day before I asked where they'd put him. That was my fault."

"But who's idea was it to put him there?" I asked.

Richard looked at Jacob. The look said it all.

I walked over to the tall man. "You never called me, Jacob."

"You got your leopard back, so what does it matter?"

"If you ever touch one of my people again, I'll kill you."

"You going to pit your kitty-cats against our pack?"

I shook my head. "No, Jacob, this is personal, between me and you. I know the rules. I make this a personal challenge between you and me, and that means that no one can help you."

"Or you," he said. He stared down at me trying to use his height to intimidate me. It didn't work. I was used to being short. I gave him dead eyes until the smirk on his face faltered and he took one step back, which pissed him off. But he didn't retake that step. Jacob might be able to kill Richard in a fair fight for dominance, but he'd never be a true Ulfric.

I stepped up close to him, close enough that a good insult would have made us touch. "There's something weak in you Jacob. I can smell it, and so can they. You may challenge Richard and win, but the pack will never accept you as Ulfric. You winning will tear them apart—it'll be a civil war."

Something flashed through his eyes.

"That doesn't scare you. You don't care," I said.

He stepped back from me, averting his eyes, his face. "You heard the Ulfric. Go fetch your cat before we change our minds."

"You couldn't change your mind with a hundred watt bulb and a team of helpers."

He frowned at me then. Sometimes my humor is a little esoteric, or maybe it's just not funny. Jacob didn't find it funny.

"Go with her, Sylvie, make sure she gets everything she needs to get him out of there and back to the cars safely," Richard said.

"Are you sure you want me to go?" she asked.

"We'll stay with him," Jamil said. None of them tried to hide the fact that they were looking at Jacob while they said it. Not only didn't they not trust him, but they didn't care that he knew that they didn't trust him. How had things downgraded to that? What had been happening in the pack that no one had told me about yet? Plenty, from the looks on everyone's faces.

"She can't go home until after the ceremony to break her ties with the pack," Jacob said.

"She will go home when I say she goes home," Richard said, voice low and full of that deep tone he got just before his voice crawled to something growling and inhuman.

"The candidates have all come prepared tonight, Ulfric, dressed to please you."

"Then they can dress to please me another night."

"You disappoint . . ."

"You are about to overstep yourself, Jacob." There must have been something in the way he said it, because Jacob finally shut up and gave a small bow. But he managed to make the movement mocking, and even from a distance you could tell he didn't mean it. But he lowered his eyes with his head, as he bent at the waist. It's a mistake to take your eyes off your opponent.

I asked, "Am I still lupa until the ceremony?"

"I suppose," Richard said.

"Yes," Sylvie said. And they looked at each other.

"Good." I kicked Jacob in the face, though not as hard as I'd hit Richard. You didn't have to kick as hard to do the same kind of damage.

I watched who in the pack made movements towards us and who didn't. I didn't see what everybody did, but I saw enough. Nobody near the throne made a single move to stop me, or help him.

Jacob staggered to his feet. His nose had burst like a piece of overripe fruit. Blood poured from his face, over his hands, like crimson water. He yelled at me, voice thick with the blood running down his throat. "You broke my nose!"

I was in a defensive stance, the one I'd learned in kenpo, just in case, but he didn't try to hit me back. I think he knew that there were too many people close at hand aching for an excuse to hurt him. Jacob was weak, but he was smarter than he looked, and not quite as arrogant.

"I am lupa of the Thronnos Rokke Clan. Maybe just for tonight, but I am lupa here. And he is Ulfric, and you will by God show some respect!"

"You have no right to question the Geri of this clan. I've *earned* my place. You just fucked the Ulfric."

I laughed, and it startled him, made him unsure. "I know pack law, Jacob. It doesn't matter how I got the job. All that matters is that I am lupa, and that means that except for the Ulfric, my word is law."

His eyes looked uncertain, and the first faint trace of fear showed, like a bitter scent on the wind. "You are about to be dethroned as lupa. Your word means nothing here."

"I am Ulfric here, Jacob, not you, and I say whose word means something and whose does not. Until we have the ceremony breaking her ties with our pack, Anita is still lupa, and I will support what she says."

"And I," Sylvie said.

"And I," Jamil said.

Shang-Da said, "I support my Ulfric in all things."

"Then let's have a little irony," I said. "Since it was Jacob's idea to put Gregory down in the oubliette, let him take Gregory's place."

Jacob started to protest, hands still trying to stop the blood flow from his nose. "You can't do that."

"Oh, but she can," Richard said, and there was a coldness in him that I'd never seen before. He wouldn't have come up with the idea himself, but he liked it. It let me know just how frustrated he'd been with Jacob.

"Great," I said. "Shall we all walk like civilized wereanimals to the oubliette and rescue Gregory?"

"I will not go willingly down in that hole," Jacob said. His voice sounded a little funny, what with all the blood and his nose smashed to hell, but he sounded sure of himself. He shouldn't have been.

"Your Ulfric and your lupa have both decreed you will go," Sylvie said. "To refuse the order is to refuse their authority."

Jamil continued, "To refuse their authority is to be declared outlaw from the clan."

Jacob glared at me when he said, "I will obey my Ulfric, but I do not acknowledge the Nimir-Ra as my lupa."

"If I say she is lupa, then to deny that is to question my authority as Ulfric," Richard said.

Jacob's eyes flicked to Richard. "We voted her out as our lupa."

"I'm voting her back in," Richard said, voice deep and quiet, but loud enough that it carried.

"Take another vote," Jacob said, still trying to slow the blood from his face. "It will go against her again."

"No, Jacob, you misunderstand me. I said, I am voting her back in, not you, not anyone else, just me."

Jacob's eyes widened. "You've preached about democracy in action since I joined this clan. Are you going back on all of it now?"

"Not on all of it, but we don't vote for Freki, or Geri, or for Hati and Skoll. We don't vote for Ulfric. Why should we vote for lupa?"

"She's fucking the Nimir-Raj. For that alone she should be cast out as lupa."

"That's my problem, not yours, not the pack's."

"You going to fuck her, too? You think the Nimir-Raj will share?"

Richard started to say something, but Micah spoke first, taking a step from the rest, his guards flanking him. "Why don't you ask the Nimir-Raj?"

Richard looked at me, a question in his eyes. I shrugged.

"Ask him, Jacob," Richard said. The blood had almost stopped dripping from Richard's mouth.

"You mind if the Ulfric fucks your Nimir-Ra?" Jacob was still bleeding like a stuck pig. His chest, stomach, even the front of his shorts were soaked with blood.

"I've agreed to any arrangement that Anita wishes, as long as she remains my Nimir-Ra and lover."

"You'd share her with another man?" Jacob said, voice thick with disbelief.

"With two other men," Micah said.

That got almost everybody staring at him. I glanced at him, but mostly watched everyone else's reaction, especially Richard's. The others looked shocked, Richard looked thoughtful, as if Micah had finally done something he didn't hate.

"She is the Master of the City's human servant. Being my Nimir-Ra has not changed that. I've felt the mark that binds them together, and it is not something that will break, as, apparently, the mark that binds her to the Ulfric will not break."

"Nothing binds her to the Ulfric but her stubbornness, and his," Jacob said.

"You think so?" Micah made it a question.

Jacob looked uncertain. The blood from his nose was finally beginning to slow. "You've seen more than I've seen, if you think they still have a special bond."

"More than any of us have seen." This from Paris, who had pushed her way to the front of the crowd.

"I am Nimir-Raj, of course I see more than you do." His voice made it so logical, so matter of fact.

"I am Geri, third in line to the throne."

"Noah is my third in line. I think if you ask him he will say he did not see what I saw either. Third in line to be Nimir-Raj, or Ulfric, is not the same as being the real thing."

I fought not to give Micah the look of gratitude that I wanted to give him. We were still deep in bluff territory, and not safely out the other side yet.

"You can't mean to share your lupa with two other men," Paris said. She'd pushed her way to stand in front of Richard, with her back to me. She was either being insulting, or stupid. Maybe both.

Richard looked down at her, and it wasn't a friendly look. Somehow I didn't think Paris ever had a very good shot at being lupa, not with Richard in charge anyway. "What I and my lupa do, or don't do, is none of your business."

I saw her back stiffen, as if he'd hit her, and maybe he had hit her pride. She'd really believed she could seduce him into picking her. I could have told her that sex wasn't the key to Richard's heart. He liked it well enough, but it wasn't one of his top priorities, not if it interfered with other things that were. It had been the same mistake that Raina had made with him, or one of the mistakes she'd made with him. Raina had never really understood Richard, either.

"You can't just arbitrarily decide you don't need a vote for this," Jacob said.

"Yes," Richard said, "I can."

I stepped up beside Jacob. "That's what being Ulfric means, Jacob."

"You're going back to a dictatorship after all the high-minded talk," Jacob said.

"For tonight, it's sufficient that Anita is my lupa, and that's not going to change. We'll discuss everything else later."

"I say we put it to a vote whether the pack wants to go back to being a dictatorship," Jacob said.

"If you don't have someone set that nose, it may heal crooked," I said.

He glared at me. "You stay out of this."

Richard called up a man with short brown hair and a neat mustache. He shrugged a backpack off his shoulders and began taking out medical supplies. "Fix his nose," Richard said and then turned to Sylvie. "When he's bandaged up, pick some people and escort Jacob to the oubliette."

There were murmurings in the crowd. One clear voice that I hadn't heard before said, "You can't do that."

Richard looked up, searching the crowd, and they fell silent under his gaze. His power rolled out from him like a burning invisible fog, something that clung to your skin and made it hard to breath. They avoided his eyes; some even dropped down into submissive postures, their bodies low to the ground, eyes rolled up, arms and legs held close, making themselves seem small and defenseless, clearly asking not to be hurt.

"I am Ulfric here. If there is any among you that disagree with that, then you are free to challenge the next in line, and the next after that, until you are Freki, then declare yourself Fenrir, and you can challenge me. If you kill me then you can be Ulfric, and you can set any damn policy you want. Until that time, shut the fuck up and follow my orders."

I don't think I'd ever heard Richard cuss. The silence was thick enough to cut. It was Jacob who cut it, like I knew he would. He pushed the mustached doctor away impatiently, while the shorter man tried to pack his nose with what looked like gauze. "Anita shows back up, and so does your backbone. Does she kill and torture for you like Raina did for Marcus?"

Richard's fist struck out in a blur that I couldn't follow. It was almost magical. One moment Jacob was standing, the next moment he was on the ground with his eyes rolled back inside his head.

Richard turned to the rest of them, the dried blood decorating his nude upper body, his hair turned to spun bronze in the torchlight. His eyes had gone wolf amber, and looked more gold than normal against his darker than usual summer tan. "I thought we were people, not animals. I thought we could change the old ways and make something better. But we all felt it tonight when Anita and her leopards melded. Something safe and good. I've tried to be temperate and kind, and look where it's gotten us. Jacob said Anita is my backbone. No, but she's doing something right, something that I've missed. If you won't take kindness, then we'll have to try something else." He looked at me with those alien eyes, and said, "Let's go get your leopard. We need to get him out of the oubliette before Jacob comes to." And he stalked off through the trees and left the rest of us to trail after. There was no question about what to do next. We followed Richard into the trees. We followed the Ulfric, because you're supposed to follow your king, if he's worthy of the name. For the first time ever I thought maybe, just maybe, Richard was going to be Ulfric after all.

26

THE OUBLIETTE WAS a rounded metal lid set in the ground. The metal lid sat in the middle of a clearing scattered with tall, thin trees. Honeysuckle bushes ringed the lid on one side; leaves were so thick on the ground that the area looked untouched. I would never have found it if I hadn't known it was there.

Oubliette is French for a little place of forgetting, but that's not a direct translation. Oubliette simply means little forgetting, but what it is, is a place where you put people when you don't plan on ever letting them out. Traditionally it's a hole where once you push someone in they can't get out. You don't feed them, or water them, or talk to them, or anything to them. You just walk away. There's a Scottish castle where they found an oubliette that had literally been walled up and forgotten, discovered only during modern remodeling. The floor was littered with bones and had an eighteenth-century pocket watch in among the debris. It had an opening where you could see the main dining hall, could have smelled the food, while you starved to death. I remembered wondering if you could hear the person screaming from the dining hall while you ate. Most oubliettes are more isolated, so that once you put him away, you never have to worry about the prisoner again.

Two of the werewolves in nice human form knelt by the metal and began unscrewing two huge bolts in the lid. There was no key. You screwed the lid in place and just walked away. Fuck.

The lid lifted off, and it took both of them to carry it away. Heavy, just in case the drugs didn't keep the adrenaline from pumping enough and cause the change. Even in animal form you'd still have a hard time getting through the lid.

I walked to the edge of the hole, and the smell drove me back. It smelled like an outhouse. I don't know why it surprised me. Gregory had been down there for what, three days, four? In the movies they talk about you starving to death, the romantic stuff—if such horror is really romantic—but no one ever talks about your bowels moving, or the fact that when you have to go, you have to go. It's not romantic, it's just humiliating.

Jamil brought a rope ladder and attached it with large metal clips to the side of the hole. The ladder fell away into the darkness with a dry, slithery sound. I forced myself to crawl back to the edge of the oubliette. I was prepared now for the smell, and underneath the ripe smell of life in too small a space was a dry smell, a dry, dusty smell. The smell of old bones, old death.

Gregory wasn't the strongest person I knew, not even one of the top hundred. What had it done to him to lie there in the dark with the stench of old bones, old death, pressed against his body? Had they explained to him how they'd leave him there to die? Had they told him every time they screwed the lid back in place that they weren't coming back, except to drug him?

The hole was like a perfect blackness, darker than the star-filled night sky, darker than anything I'd seen in a long time. It was wide enough for Richard's broad shoulders to have scooted down into the dark, but barely. The longer I stared at it, the narrower it seemed to become, as if it were some great black mouth waiting to swallow me down. Have I mentioned that I'm claustrophobic?

Richard came to stand beside me, peering down into the hole. He had an unlit flashlight in his hand. Something must have shown on my face, because he said, "Even we need some light to see by."

I held my hand out for the flashlight.

He shook his head. "I let this happen. I'll get him out."

I shook my head. "No. He's mine."

He knelt beside me and spoke softly, "I can smell your fear. I know you don't like close places."

I stared back into the hole and let myself acknowledge just how afraid I was. So afraid that I could taste something flat and metallic on my tongue. So afraid that my pulse was hammering in my throat, like a trapped thing. My voice came out calm, normal. I was glad. "It doesn't matter that I'm afraid." I touched the flashlight, tried to pull it from his hand, but he held on. And, short of playing tug of war—which I would probably lose—I wasn't getting it away from him.

"Why do you have to be the toughest, the bravest? Why can't you, just once, let me do something for you? Going down in the hole doesn't scare me. Let me do this for you. Please." His voice was still soft, and he was leaning into me enough so that I could smell the drying blood on him, the richness of fresh blood in his mouth, as if some small cut had not healed completely.

I shook my head. "I have to do it, Richard."

"Why?" and his voice held the first hint of anger, like a slap of warmth.

"Because it scares me, and I have to know if I can."

"Can what?"

"If I can crawl down into that hole."

"Why? Why do you need to know that? You've proven to me and everyone here that you're tough. You don't have anything left to prove to us."

"To me, Richard, I have something left to prove to me."

"What difference would it make if you couldn't climb down in that stinking hole? You'll never have to do it again, Anita. Just don't do it."

I looked at him, at the puzzlement in his face, his eyes, which had bled back to their normal, perfect brown. I'd been trying to explain shit like this to Richard for a few years now. I finally realized that he would never understand and I was tired of trying to explain myself, not just to Richard, to everybody.

"Give me the flashlight, Richard."

He held on with both hands. "Why do you have to do this? Just tell me that. You're so scared your mouth is dry. I can taste it on your breath."

"And I can taste fresh blood on yours, but I have to do it because it scares me."

He shook his head. "This isn't courage, Anita, this is stubbornness."

I shrugged. "Maybe, but I still have to do it."

He clutched the flashlight tighter. "Why?" And somehow I thought the question was about more than the oubliette and why I had to climb inside it.

I sighed. "Less and less scares me, Richard. So when I find something that does bother me, I have to test it. I have to see if I can do it."

"Why?" He studied my face like he'd memorize it.

"Just to see if I can."

"Why?" and the anger was more than a faint hint now.

I shook my head. "I'm not competing with you, Richard, or anyone else. I don't give a shit who's better or faster or braver."

"Then why do it?"

"The only person I compete against is me, Richard, and I'll think less of me if I let you, or anyone else, climb down in that hole first. Gregory is my boy, not yours, and I have to rescue him."

"You've already rescued him, Anita. It doesn't matter who climbs in the damn hole."

I almost smiled, but not like it was funny. "Give me the flashlight, please, Richard. I can't explain this to you."

"Does your Nimir-Raj understand it?" The anger burned along my skin, like a swarm of stings. It damn near hurt.

I frowned at him. "Ask him yourself, now give me the damn flashlight." If you get angry at me, it never takes me long to respond.

"I want to be your Ulfric, Anita, your guy, whatever the hell that means. Why won't you let me be . . . ?" He stopped talking, looking away from me.

"*The man*. Was that what you were going to say?"

He looked back at me and nodded.

"Look, if we keep dating, or whatever the hell we're going to do, we have to get one thing straight. Your ego is no longer my problem. Don't be the man for me, Richard, be the person I need. You don't have to be bigger and braver than I am to be my man. I've got male friends that spend most of their time trying to prove they have bigger, brassier balls than I do. I don't need that from you."

"What if I need to be braver than you for myself, not for you?"

I thought about that for a second or two, then said, "You're not afraid of going down into the oubliette, are you?"

"I don't want to go down, and I don't want to see what they've done to Gregory, but I'm not as afraid as you are, no."

"Then it doesn't make you braver than me to go down into the hole, does it? Because it doesn't cost you anything to go down there."

He leaned very, very close to my ear, then breathed the barest of sounds against my skin. "Like it would cost you nothing to kill Jacob for me."

I stiffened beside him, then turned, trying to keep the shock off my face.

"I knew that was what you were thinking the moment I saw you look at him," Richard said.

"You'd let me do that?" I asked, voice soft, but not as soft as his had been.

"I don't know yet. But wouldn't your reasoning be that it would cost you nothing to do it and it would cost me dear?"

We stared at each other. I finally nodded.

He smiled. "Then let me go down the fucking hole."

"When did you start using the F-word?"

"While you were away. I think I missed hearing it." He grinned at me suddenly, a bright flash of smile in the dark.

I couldn't not smile back. Kneeling by that horrible black opening, fear still flat on my tongue, his anger still riding the air between us, and we smiled at each other. "I'll let you go down the hole first," I said.

The smile widened until it filled his eyes, and even by starlight I could see them gleam with humor. "Okay."

I leaned into him and gave him a quick kiss. Too quick for the powers to move between us, too quick to taste the blood in his mouth, too quick to find out if our beasts would roil through each other's bodies. I kissed him just because I wanted to, because for the first time I thought we might both be willing to bend a little. Would it be enough? Who the hell knew? But I was hopeful. For the first time in a long time, I was truly hopeful. Without hope, love dies and parts of you wither. I didn't know what it meant for Micah that I had hope for Richard and me. We'd talked openly about sharing, but I didn't know how much of that had been for public show and how much had been real. But right that second, I didn't care, I clutched that positive emotion to me and held on. Later, later, we'd worry about other things. I'd let Richard climb down first, but I'd still be going down, and I wanted that small warm hope inside my chest along with the fear.

27

RICHARD'S WEIGHT ON the rope ladder kept it tight under my hands. He'd put his flashlight on a strap around his wrist. I watched the pool of yellow light vanishing down into that narrow darkness and realized that I was still barely on the ladder, my head still aboveground.

Micah was kneeling beside the hole. "It'll be alright," he said.

I swallowed and looked at him, knowing my eyes were just a little wide. "I know," but my voice came out breathy.

"You really don't have to do this," he said, voice soft, and as neutral as he could make it.

I frowned at him. "Don't *you* start."

"Then you better catch up with him." His voice was a little less neutral, but I couldn't tell what tone it held.

I started climbing down the soft roughness of the rope ladder, moving quickly, angrily. I wasn't angry with Micah, not really. I was angry with me. The anger got me well down into the dark where the light from the flashlight below me seemed very yellow and very stark against the earthen walls.

I clung there for a second or two, staring at that hard-packed earth. I gazed up slowly and found Micah staring down at me from a distance so far away that I couldn't tell what color his eyes or hair were. I knew it was him from the shape of his face and shoulders. My God, how deep did this pit go?

It seemed like the earthen walls were curving in towards me, like a hand about to close into a fist and crush me, so that I couldn't breath enough of the stale, flat air to fill my lungs. I closed my eyes and forced myself to move one hand off the ladder and touch the wall. It was farther away than I'd thought, and when I finally touched it, it startled me. The earth was surprisingly cool against my hand, and I realized it was cool in the pit, even with early summer heat up above. I opened my eyes, and the walls were still about six feet circular, just like they'd always been. The earth wasn't closing in around me, only my phobia was doing that.

I started climbing down again, and this time I didn't stop until I felt the ladder loosen under my body and it was suddenly harder to climb down without bumping into the dirt walls. Richard's weight was no longer steadying the ladder for me. If I hadn't been such a pain in the ass, I might have asked for him to hold it steady until I got down to the end. Instead I hugged the ladder frantically and kept moving downward. It's hard to cling to something while you're climbing down it, but I managed.

The world narrowed down to the feel of the rope under my hands, my feet trying to find purchase—just the simple act of moving downward. It got to the point that I stopped jumping every time my body bumped the walls. Hands touched my waist, and I let out that little yip that is only a girl sound. I always hated when I did it.

They were Richard's hands around my waist, of course. He steadied me the last few feet, while my heart tried to jump out of my chest. I stepped down onto a floor that crunched and rolled with bones. They were deep yet you didn't sink into them, rather walked on top of them like a saint treading on water.

The narrow shaft opened into a small, cramped, cave-like hole in the earth. Richard had to stand bent almost in two. I could stand up if I was careful, though the top of my hair brushed the ceiling solidly enough that ducking a little was a good idea.

Micah called from way, way above us, "Are you alright?"

It took me two tries to be able to say, "Fine, we're fine."

Micah pulled back from the opening, a dark dot against the paler grayness. "My God, how far down are we?"

"Sixty feet, give or take." There was something in his voice that made me turn to him.

He shook his head and looked to one side, shining the flashlight on something small and hunched. It was Gregory.

He was on his stomach, hog-tied, his arms and legs at such acute angles that I couldn't imagine lying there like that for three days. He was nude, a white cloth blindfold cutting across his face, knotted in a tangle of long blond hair, as if even that had been done to hurt, and not merely to blind. As Richard's light played over Gregory's body, he made small helpless sounds. He could see the light through the cloth, if nothing else. I knelt beside him, seeing where the silver chains had dug into his wrists and ankles. The wounds were raw and bloody where he'd struggled against them.

"The chains have rubbed him raw," Richard said, voice soft.

"He struggled," I said.

"No, he's not powerful enough to take this much silver against his skin. The chains ate their way into his skin."

I stared at the raw wounds and didn't know what to say. I touched Gregory's shoulder, and he screamed through the gag I hadn't seen. His hair had hidden it. But there was a dark rag stuffed in his mouth. He screamed again and tried to worm away from me.

"Gregory, Gregroy, it's Anita." I touched him as gently as I could, and he screamed once more. I looked up at Richard. "He doesn't seem to hear me."

Richard knelt and raised a tangle of Gregory's hair. Gregory struggled harder, and Richard handed me the flashlight so he could use one hand to steady the smaller man's face and the other to keep the hair out of the way. There was more cloth stuffed in his ears. Richard pulled out the cloth and found a black earplug deeper in the channel. They were never meant to be pushed in that far, and when Richard pulled it free, fresh blood trickled from his ear.

I just stared, my mind frozen for a second, not wanting to understand. But finally, I heard myself say it. "They burst his eardrums. Why, for God's sake? Wasn't the blindfold and gag enough sensory deprivation?"

Richard held the earplug up to the light. I had to shine the flashlight directly on it to see that it had a metal point.

"What is that?"

"Silver," he said.

"Oh, God, they were designed for this?"

"Remember, Marcus was a doctor. He knew all kinds of medical supply places. Places that would make things." The look on Richard's face told me he was lost in memory and something darker.

I glanced back at the marks on Gregory's arms and legs. "Dear God, did the silver tear up his ear canals the way it did his skin?"

"I don't know. It's good that it's still bleeding. It means if he shapeshifts soon, he'll probably heal." Richard's voice was thick.

I wasn't close to crying, the horror too overwhelming for tears. I wanted Jacob down here, and whoever had helped him, because you didn't do this to a shapeshifter without help, not one-on-one.

Richard tried to take off the blindfold, but it was tied so tight he couldn't get a good hold on it. I handed him the flashlight and drew the knife from my left wrist sheath. "Hold him, the knives are sharp, I don't want to cut him if he struggles."

Richard held Gregory's head between his two hands like a vise, and Gregory struggled harder, screaming through the gag. But Richard held him firm while I slid the knife carefully between the cloth and Gregory's hair. One quick slice downward and the blindfold eased away from his skin, but it had been tied so tight for so long that Richard had to peel it away.

Gregory blinked at the light and saw Richard and screamed more. Something died on Richard's face when he did it, like it had killed something inside him to have anyone be that terrified of him.

I leaned over, placing my hand carefully on the pile of bones and watched Gregory's eyes finally see me. He stopped screaming, but he didn't look relieved enough. I pulled the gag out of his mouth, and it peeled away, taking bits of lip skin with it. He worked his mouth slowly, and for some odd reason I was reminded of the scene from *The Wizard of Oz* where Dorothy puts oil on the Tin Man's jaw after he'd been rusted. The image should have made me smile, but it didn't.

There was a padlock on the chains around each of his limbs. Richard crawled around me, letting me stay where Gregory could see me. I was saying over and over again, "It's going to be alright. It's going to be alright." He couldn't hear me, but it was the best I knew how to do.

Richard snapped the lock on one wrist, and pain showed on Gregory's face like it hurt for the arm to move at all. Richard freed both wrists and then began to slowly uncurl Gregory's body.

Gregory screamed, but not from fear this time, from pain. I tried to cradle him, but moving at all seemed to hurt. It took both of us crawling around to get him unbent enough to lay in my lap. He was never going to be able to climb the ladder.

The bends of both of his arms were covered in needle marks; none of them had healed. "The needle marks, why haven't they healed?"

"Silver needles in direct contact with the bloodstream. A sedative to keep the adrenaline low so you can't change, but not so much that you can't feel, or know where you are, and what's happening. That's how Raina used to do it."

"This is how she used to tie them up and exactly what she used to do to them. How did Jacob know that?" I asked.

"One of my people told him," Richard said. He stayed on his knees rather than stand bent over. His face was calm, almost serene.

"I want them down here. Whoever helped Jacob. Whoever brought out those damn earplugs. I want them down here."

He turned those calm eyes to me, and I saw the anger at the bottom of that calm. "Could you do this to someone? Could you plunge these things in their cars? Could you do all this to *anyone*?"

I thought about that, really thought about it. I was angry, sickened. I wanted to punish someone, but . . . "No, no, I could shoot them, kill them, but I couldn't do this."

"Neither could I," he said.

"You knew Gregory was in the oubliette, but you didn't know what they'd done to him, did you?"

He shook his head, kneeling on the bones, still staring down at the bloody earplug, like it held answers to questions too hard to ask out loud. "Jacob knew."

"You're Ulfric, Richard, you should know what's done in your pack's name."

The anger flared so hot and tight that it filled the little cave like water just this side of boiling. Gregory whimpered and watched Richard with fearful eyes.

"I know, Anita, I know."

"So you're not going to put Jacob down here?"

"I am, but not like this. He can stay down here, but not chained, not tortured." Richard glanced around the tiny space. "Being down here at all is torture enough."

I didn't even try to argue that one. "What about whoever helped him?"

Richard looked at me. "I'll find out who helped him."

"Then what?"

He closed his eyes, and it wasn't until he opened his hand and I saw the flash of blood that I realized he'd pressed the silver point into his palm. He pulled it out and stared at the bright flash of blood.

"You just keep pushing, don't you, Anita."

"The pack knows you well enough, Richard. They know you didn't mean for anyone to be put down here, especially not with all Raina's old accoutrements. Doing this at all was a challenge to your authority."

"I know that."

"I don't want to fight, Richard, but you have to punish them for this. If you don't, then you lose more ground to Jacob. Even if you put him down here, it won't stop things. Everyone that touched this has to suffer."

"You're not angry now," he said, and he looked puzzled. "I thought you wanted revenge, but you seem cold about it all, now."

"I wanted revenge, but you're right, I couldn't do this to anyone, and I can't order done what I wouldn't do myself. Just a rule I've got. But the pack is a mess, and if you want to stop the downward slide and keep them from a civil war, werewolf against werewolf, you must be harsh. You must make it clear that is not acceptable."

"It isn't," he said.

"There's only one way for them to know that, Richard."

"Punishment," he said, and he made the word sound like a curse.

"Yes," I said.

"I've worked for months—no, years—to try and get away from a punitive system. You want me to throw away all that I've worked for and go back to the way it was."

Gregory's hand came up, slowly, painfully, to clutch weakly at my arm. I stroked his matted hair, and his voice came out hoarse, abused, as if even through the gag, he'd been screaming for days. "I want . . . out of . . . here. Please."

I nodded my head so he could see it, and a relief so large it was beyond words flashed through his eyes.

I looked up at Richard. "If your system worked better than the old one, then I'd support it, but it's not working. I'm sorry that it's not working, Richard, but it's not. If you continue this . . . experiment in democracy and gentler, kinder laws, people are going to die. Not just you, but Sylvie, and Jamil, and Shang-Da, and every wolf that supports you. But it's worse than that, Richard. I watched the pack. They're divided almost evenly. It will be civil war, and they will tear each other to bits—Jacob's followers and the ones who won't follow him. Hundreds will die, and the Thronnos Rokke Clan may die with it. Look at the throne you're sitting on as Ulfric. It's ancient, you can feel it. Don't let everything that it stands for be destroyed."

He stared down at the still-bleeding wound in his hand. "Let's get Gregory out of here."

"You'll punish Jacob, but not the others," I said, and my voice was tired.

"I'll find out who they are first, then we'll see."

I shook my head. "I love you, Richard."

"I hear a 'but,' coming."

"But I value the people who count on me for their safety more than I value that love." It felt cold and awful saying it out loud, but it was true.

"What does that say about your love?" he asked.

"Don't go all sanctimonious on me, Richard. You dropped me like yesterday's news when the pack voted me out. You could have said, screw it, take the throne, I want Anita more, but you didn't."

"You really think Jacob would have let me walk away?"

"I don't know, but you didn't make the offer. It didn't even occur to you to make the offer, did it?"

He looked away, then back, and his eyes held such sadness that I wanted to take it back, but I couldn't. It was time we talked. It was like the old joke about the elephant in the living room. No one acknowledged it existed until the shit was so deep they couldn't walk. Glancing down at Gregory, I knew the shit was too deep to ignore. We were out of options except for the truth, no matter how brutal.

"If I'd stepped down as Ulfric, even if Jacob had let me do it, it would still have been civil war. He'd have still executed those closest to me. It would have been deserting them. I'd rather die, than just walk away and leave them to be slaughtered."

"If that's how you really feel, Richard, then I've got a better plan. Make an example of Jacob and his followers."

"It's not that simple, Anita. Jacob's got enough support that it might still be war."

"Not if it's bloody enough."

"What are you saying?"

"Make them fear you, Richard. Make them fear you. Machiavelli said it nearly six hundred years ago, but it's still true. Every ruler should strive for his people to love him. But if they cannot love you, then make them fear you. Love is better, but fear will do the job."

He swallowed hard, and there was something close to fear in his eyes. "I think I could kill Jacob, and even execute one or two of his people, but you don't think that's enough, do you?"

"Depends on how you execute them."

"What are you asking me to do, Anita?"

I sighed and stroked Gregory's cheek. "I'm asking you to do what needs doing, Richard. If you want to hold this pack together and save hundreds of lives, then I'm telling you how you can do it with the minimum amount of bloodshed."

"I can kill Jacob, but I can't do what you're asking. I can't do something so terrible that the entire pack would fear me." He looked at me, and there was a wildness, a panic in his face, like a trapped thing that finally realizes there is no escape.

I could feel my face grow calm, and I felt myself sinking into that place where there is nothing but white noise and the solid, almost comforting surety that I felt nothing. I said, softly, "I can."

He turned away from me, as if I hadn't spoken, and called up for them to lower the harness. We slid the harness around Gregory, talking only about the task at hand—no metaphysics, no politics. There was a second harness on the rope, and Richard made me put it on. I'd get to cradle Gregory, protecting him with my body so he didn't get scraped up too badly.

"I've never done this before," I said.

"I'm too broad through the shoulders to add Gregory's bulk to mine. It has to be you. Besides, you'll keep him safe, I know you will." There was something in his eyes that made me want to say something, but he jerked on the rope and we started rising into the air.

Richard watched us, face upturned, his flashlight casting odd shadows around the small room as he knelt on the bones. Then we were up inside the tunnel, and I couldn't see him anymore. I had my arms full, literally and figuratively, trying to keep Gregory from crashing into the walls. His arms and legs were still almost useless. I wasn't sure if it was because of the long confinement or the drugs he'd been given, or both. Probably both.

Gregory kept saying "thank you, thank you, thank you" under his breath.

By the time we reached the top, there were tears drying on my cheeks. Regardless of what Richard decided, someone was going to pay.

Jacob was there, already bound in silver chains, carried like a piece of struggling luggage between three werewolves. They let him keep his cutoff shorts. No nudity for the good guys. I guess there has to be some differences, or how do you tell which side you're on?

Cherry was already checking Gregory over. She had to keep chasing the other leopards back. They kept trying to touch him.

I stared across the clearing at Jacob. The look in his eyes was enough. Richard could be squeamish if he wanted to be, but if I let what had been done to Gregory stand unchallenged, then Jacob and his followers would see it as weakness. They'd turn and destroy us once Jacob secured his power base. Because there was one way for Jacob to avoid a civil war, and that was by doing what I was encouraging

Richard to do. If he did something so terrible that the others were afraid to fight, then he could be Ulfric without a bloodbath. I'd seen what he'd done to Gregory. Call it a hunch, but I was willing to bet Jacob would do what needed doing. He didn't strike me as the squeamish sort.

Richard climbed out of the hole. "Put him in."

"Do you want the drugs used?" Sylvie asked.

Richard nodded.

"What about the blindfold and the rest?"

Richard shook his head. "Not necessary."

Jacob started struggling again. "You can't do this!"

Richard knelt in front of him, holding him by his thick hair. The grip looked painful. "Who showed you where these were?" He held his hand out with the silver-tipped earplugs in his palm.

"Oh, my God," Sylvie whispered.

Others asked, "What is it?"

"Who, Jacob? Who told you our dirty little secrets?"

Jacob just stared at him.

"I could have them used on you," Richard said.

Jacob paled a little, but he didn't answer. His jaw was so tense that I could see the muscles pulsing, but he didn't give up who'd helped him. He didn't even ask if answering the question would save him from the oubliette. I had to admire that, at least, but I didn't have to like it.

"You wouldn't do that." It was Paris, looking a lot less confident than she had by the throne. She looked downright unsure of herself in her skintight dress.

Richard looked at her for a long time, or maybe it just seemed long, and something in his eyes made her look away.

"You're right, I can't use them on Jacob, or anyone." He looked around the clearing at the scattered wolves and at the ones waiting in the trees beyond. "But hear me, if there are anymore of these things around, I want them destroyed. When Jacob comes out of the oubliette, it is to be sealed up forever. You have learned nothing from me, if any of you could do this, you have learned nothing." He signaled Sylvie, and she came forward with a syringe.

The three werewolves had to hold Jacob against the ground for her to give him the shot. They held him until his limbs went limp and his eyes fluttered shut.

"He'll wake up in the oubliette," Richard said. His voice held not just tiredness, but defeat. He turned to me as they carried Jacob towards the hole. "Take your leopards, and your allies, and go home, Anita."

"I'm lupa, remember, you can't kick me out of pack business."

He smiled, but it left his eyes empty and tired. "You're still lupa, but for tonight you're also Nimir-Ra, and your leopards need you. Take care of Gregory, and for what it's worth, I'm sorry about all of this."

"Sorry is worth something, Richard, but it doesn't change things."

"It never does," he said.

I couldn't read his mood. He wasn't sad exactly, or worried, or, anything I had a name for, except defeated. It was like he'd already lost the battle.

"What are you going to do?" I asked.

"I'm going to find out who helped Jacob do this."

"How?" I asked.

He smiled and shook his head. "Go home, Anita."

I stood and looked at him for a heartbeat or two, then turned back to my leopards. Gregory was on a stretcher, and Zane and Noah were carrying it. Cherry was talking to the werewolf doctor that had packed Jacob's nose. She was doing a lot of nodding. Instructions, maybe.

Micah was standing at the edge of the group watching me. I met his eyes, but neither of us smiled. I looked back but Richard was already moving off through the trees with Jamil and Shang-Da at his back. Micah's face was very neutral as I walked towards him. I wasn't hopeful anymore. I could have played it cool, but I didn't want to. I was tired, so terribly tired. My clothes smelled like an outhouse, and probably so did my skin. I wanted a shower, clean clothes, and to make the lost look in Gregory's eyes go away. The shower and clothes were the easy part. I didn't even know how to begin to make Gregory's pain go away.

I held out my hand to Micah, not because of otherworldly energy, apparently depression dampens that, but because I wanted the touch of another hand. I wanted the comfort, and I didn't want to have to think about it. I just wanted to be held.

He widened his eyes, but took my hand, squeezing it gently. I started walking towards the trees, leading him by the hand. The others followed us. Even the swan king and the wererats. Anita Blake, preternatural pied piper. The thought should have made me smile. But it didn't.

28

TWO HOURS LATER I'd had a shower and Gregory had had a bath, though I'd showered by myself, and Gregory had had company. He still didn't have complete use of his arms and legs. I didn't think that Cherry, Zane, and Nathaniel needed to get naked and in the tub with him, but, hey, I wasn't offering to help, so who was I to complain? Besides, it never became sexual; it was as if the touch of their flesh on his was necessary, part of the healing process. Maybe it was.

I was sitting at my new kitchen table. My old two-seater table just hadn't been roomy enough for all the wereleopards to have bagels and cream cheese at the same time. The new table was pale pine, varnished to a golden glow. There still wasn't enough room at the table for everyone to sit and drink coffee, but it was closer. I'd have needed a banquet table to have that much room, and the kitchen wasn't long enough for it. There was more than one reason that feudal lords had had great big castles—you needed the room just to feed and care for all your people.

The only person sitting in the dimly lit kitchen was Dr. Lillian. Elizabeth had been transported to the secret hospital that the shapeshifters kept in St. Louis. All my other leopards were tending to Gregory. Micah and his cats wandered around the periphery of it all. Caleb had tried to include himself in the bath and had been refused. The rest of Micah's pard seemed unsettled, nervous, not knowing what to do with themselves. I had my priority for the evening—taking care of Gregory. Everything else could wait. One disaster at a time, or you lose your way, and your mind.

Dr. Lillian was a small woman with gray hair cut straight just above her shoulders. Her hair was longer than the first time I met her, but everything else was the same. I'd never seen her wear makeup, and her face still looked pleasant and attractive in a fifty-plus sort of way—though I'd discovered she was actually well over sixty. She certainly didn't look it.

"The drugs are still in his system," Dr. Lillian said.

"Drugs, plural?" I asked.

She nodded. "Our metabolism is so fast that it takes quite a cocktail of chemicals to keep us sedated for any length of time."

"Gregory wasn't sedated. He seemed very much aware of everything that was happening," I said.

"But his heart, his breathing, his involuntary reflexes were all subdued. If you can't access the full effects of an adrenaline rush, you can't change shape."

"Why not?'

Lillian shrugged, taking a small sip of her coffee. "We don't know, but there is something in the extremes of the fight or flight response that opens the way for our beast. If you can deprive a shapeshifter of that response, then you can keep them from shifting."

"Indefinitely?" I asked.

"No, the full moon will bring it on, no matter what drugs you pump into someone."

"How long until Gregory's back to normal?"

Her eyes flicked downward, then up, and I didn't like that she'd needed that second to school her eyes, as if something bad were coming.

"The drugs will probably wear off in about eight hours, maybe more, maybe less. It depends on so many things."

"So he stays here until the drugs wear off, then he shapeshifts and he's fine, right?" I put a lilt at the end, making it a question, because I knew the atmosphere was too serious for it to be that easy.

"I'm afraid not," she said.

"What's wrong, doc, why so solemn?"

She gave a small smile. "In eight hours the damage to Gregory's ears may be permanent."

I blinked at her. "You mean he'll stay deaf?"

"Yes."

"That's not acceptable," I said.

Her smile widened. "You say that as if by sheer will you can change things, Anita. It makes you seem very young."

"Are you telling me that there's nothing we can do to heal him?"

"No, I'm not saying that."

"Please, doc, just tell me."

"If you were truly Nimir-Ra, then you might be able to call his beast out of his flesh and force the change, even with the drugs in his system."

"If someone can tell me how to do it, I'm willing to give it a shot."

"So you believe that you will be Nimir-Ra in truth come full moon?" Lillian asked.

I shrugged and sipped my coffee. "Not a hundred percent sure, no, but the evidence is sort of mounting up."

"How do you feel about that?"

"Being Nimir Ra for real?" I asked.

She nodded.

"I'm trying really hard not to think too much about it."

"Ignoring it won't make it go away, Anita."

"I know that, but worrying about it won't change things either."

"Very practical of you, if you can pull it off."

"What, not worrying?"

She nodded again.

I shrugged. "I'll worry about each disaster as it happens."

"Can you really compartmentalize to that degree?"

"How do we fix Gregory?"

"I take that as a yes," she said.

I smiled. "Yes."

"As I said, if you were a Nimir-Ra in full power, you might be able to call his beast, even through the drugs."

"But since I haven't shifted yet, I can't?"

"I doubt it. It's a rather specialized skill, even among full shapeshifters."

"Can Rafael do it?"

She smiled, the smile that most of the wererats got when you asked about their king. It was a smile that held warmth and pride. They liked and respected him. Let's hear it for good leadership.

"No."

That surprised me, and it must have shown on my face.

"I told you, it is a rare talent. Your Ulfric can do it."

I looked at her. "You mean Richard?"

"Do you have another Ulfric?" she asked, smiling.

I almost smiled back. "No, but we need someone who can call leopards, right?"

She nodded.

"How about Micah?"

"I've already asked him. Neither he nor Merle can call another's beast. Micah did offer to try and heal Gregory by calling flesh, but the injuries are beyond him."

"When did Micah try and heal Gregory?"

"While you were cleaning up," she said.

"I took a quick shower."

"It didn't take long for him to be certain that Gregory's injuries were above his abilities."

"You wouldn't be belaboring the point if there wasn't some hope."

"I can use other drugs to try and overcome the effects."

"But . . ." I said.

"But the mix of the drugs could explode his heart or rupture enough blood vessels in other major organs to kill him."

I stared at her for a heartbeat or two. "How bad are the odds?"

"Bad enough that I need his Nimir-Ra's permission before trying."

"Has Gregory given his permission?"

"He's terrifed. He wants to be able to hear again. Of course he wants me to try, but I'm not sure he's thinking clearly."

"So you're coming to me like you'd go to a parent for a child," I said.

"I need someone who is thinking clearly to make a decision on Gregory's behalf."

"He has a brother." I frowned, because I realized I hadn't seen Stephen at the lupanar. "Where *is* Stephen?"

"I've been told that the Ulfric ordered Gregory's brother not to attend tonight. Something about it being unfair for him to watch his own brother be executed. Vivian has gone to get him."

"My, that was big of Richard."

"You sound bitter."

"Do I?" And that sounded bitter even to me. I sighed. "I'm just frustrated, Lillian. Richard is going to get people I care about slaughtered, not to mention himself."

"Which risks both you and the Master of the City."

I frowned at her. "I guess everyone does know that part."

"I think so," she said.

"Yeah, he's risking us all for his high moral ideals."

"Ideals are worth sacrifice, Anita."

"Maybe, but I'm not a hundred percent sure I've ever held an ideal close enough to trade the people I love for it. Ideals can die, but they don't breathe, they don't bleed, they don't cry."

"So you would trade all your ideals for the people you care about?" she asked.

"I'm not sure I have any ideals anymore."

"You're still Christian, aren't you?"

"My religion isn't an ideal. Ideals are abstract things that you can't touch or see. My religion isn't abstract, it's very 'stract,' very real."

"You can't see God," she said. "You can't hold Him in your hand."

"How many angels can dance on the head of a pin, huh?"

She smiled. "Something like that."

"I've held a cross while it flared so bright it blinded me until all the world was just white fire. I've seen a copy of the Talmud go up in flames in a vampire's hands, and even after the book had burned to ash, the vampire kept burning until it died. I've stood in the presence of a demon and recited holy script, and the demon could not touch me." I shook my head. "Religion isn't an abstract thing, Dr. Lillian, it is a living, breathing, growing, organic thing."

"Organic sounds more Wiccan than Christian," she said.

I shrugged. "I've been studying with a psychic and some of her Wiccan friends for about a year, hard not to soak some of it up."

"Doesn't studying Wicca put you in an awkward position?"

"You mean because I'm a monotheist?"

She nodded.

"I have God-given abilities and not enough training to control those abilities. Most denominations of the church frown on psychics, let alone someone who raises the dead. I need training, so I've found people to train me. The fact that they're not Christian I see as a failing of the church, not a failing of theirs."

"There are Christian witches," she said.

"I've met some of them. They all seem to be zealots, as if they have to be more Christian than anyone else to prove that they're good enough to be Christian at all. I don't like zealots."

"Neither do I," she said.

We looked at each other in the darkened kitchen. She raised her coffee mug. I'd given her the one with a tiny knight and a large dragon that said, "No guts, no glory."

Lillian said, "Down with zealots."

I raised my own mug in the air. It was the baby penguin mug, still a favorite. "Down with zealots."

We drank. She set her mug on the coaster and said, "Do I have your permission to try the drugs on Gregory?"

I took a deep breath and let it out slowly, then nodded. "If he agrees, do it."

She pushed back from the table and stood. "I'll get everything ready."

I nodded, but stayed sitting. I was praying when I felt someone come into the room. Without opening my eyes, I knew it was Micah.

He waited until I raised my head, opened my eyes. "I didn't mean to interrupt," he said.

"I'm finished," I said.

He nodded and gave that smile of his that was part amusement, part sorrow, and part something else. "You were praying?" He made it a question.

"Yes."

Some trick of the light made his eyes gleam in the dark, like there was a spark of hidden fire down deep in their green gold depths. The illusion lost his eyes and most of his face to shadow and darkness. Only that shimmering gleam remained, as if the color dancing in his eyes was more real than the rest of him.

Without seeing his face, I knew he was upset. I could feel it like a tension down my spine. "What's wrong?" I asked.

"I can't remember the last time I prayed."

I shrugged. "A lot of people don't pray."

"Why does it surprise me that you do?" he asked.

I shrugged again.

He took a step forward, and the light fell upon his face and that odd, mixed smile of his.

"I have to go."

"What's wrong?" I asked.

"What makes you think anything's wrong?"

"Tension level between you and your cats. What's up, Micah?"

He pressed his thumb and forefinger against his eyes, rubbing, as if he were tired. He blinked those jewel-like eyes at me. "A pard emergency. We've got one member that couldn't come tonight, and she's got herself in trouble."

"What kind of trouble?"

"Violet is our version of your Nathaniel, the least dominant of us." He left it at that, as if it explained everything. It did, and it didn't.

"And?" I said.

"And I have to go help her."

"I don't like secrets, Micah."

He sighed, running his fingers through his hair. He ripped the ponytail holder out, threw it on the floor, ran his hands through the shoulder-length curls, over and over, as if he'd been wanting to do it all night. The movement was harsh, frantic with tension.

He looked down at me, dark brown hair in disarray around his face, eyes gleaming. In an instant he went from being this nice, attractive man to something feral and alien. It wasn't just the hair or the kitty-cat eyes. His beast bubbled against my skin like boiling water. I'd felt his power, but not like this, almost hot enough to scald. Then I realized that I could see that heat, *see* it. It flowed over him, invisible, but almost not, like something half-seen out of the corner of your eye. I could almost see the shape of something monstrous looming around him, like heat rising off of summer pavement, a rippling thing. I'd been around shapeshifters for years and never seen anything like it.

Merle appeared in the doorway. "Nimir-Raj, is anything wrong?"

Micah turned, and I got a swimming afterimage, as if something large and almost invisible moved around and just above his body. His voice came out low and growling. "Wrong, what could possibly be wrong?"

Gina pushed past Merle. "We've got to go, Micah."

Micah put his hands up, and the afterimage moved with him. I couldn't actually see claws and fur, just hints of it, swimming around him. He covered his eyes with his hands, and I saw those ghostly claws go through, into, *past* his face. Watching it made me dizzy, and I looked down at the tabletop to steady myself and reality.

I'd heard Marianne say she could see auras of power around people and lycanthropes, but I'd never been able to see one before.

I felt his power folding away, the heat, the skin-ruffling sensation pulling away, like the ocean going back from the shore. I raised my face to see, and that seen-not-seen shape was gone, swallowed back into his body.

He stared down at me. "You look like you've seen a ghost."

"You're closer than you think," I said.

"She's afraid of your power," Gina said, and there was scorn in her voice.

I looked up at her. "I saw his aura, saw it like a white phantom around his body."

"You say that like you've never seen it before," Micah said.

"I haven't, not a visual."

Gina took his arm, gently but firmly, and tried pulling him towards the door. He just looked at her, and I felt his presence, his personality, for lack of a better word, like something almost touchable. She dropped to the floor, gripping his hand, rubbing her cheek against it. "I meant no offense, Micah."

The look on his face was cold. His power, his force began to trickle through the room again.

"Nimir-Raj," Merle said, "if you are going, then you must go. If you are not going . . ." His voice was careful, almost gentle, a pitying tone of voice, and I didn't understand why.

Micah growled at Merle, I think. Then his voice came out normal, human. "I know my duty as Nimir-Raj, Merle."

"I would never presume to tell you the duties of a Nimir-Raj, Micah," he said.

Micah suddenly looked tired again, all that energy draining away. He helped Gina to her feet, though it looked awkward since she was more than a head taller. "Let's go."

They all turned towards the door. "I hope your leopard is alright," I said.

Micah glanced back. "Would Nathaniel be, if he'd called for help?"

I shook my head. "No."

He nodded and turned back for the door. "Mine either." He hesitated and said without turning around, "I'll take Noah and Gina with me, but if it's alright I'll leave Merle and Caleb here?"

"Won't you need them with you?"

He looked back, smiling. "I just need to pick up Violet. I don't need muscle for that, and you might want some extra muscle."

"You mean in case Jacob's people get pesky?"

His smile widened. "Pesky, yeah, in case they get pesky."

Then they were gone into the other room, and I was left alone at the table. Lillian came back in, her eyes narrowed.

"What?" I asked.

She just shook her head. "None of my business."

"That's right," I said.

"But if it were . . ."

"But it's not," I said.

She smiled. "But if it were, I'd say two things."

"You're going to say them anyway, aren't you?"

"Yes," she said.

I waved her to go ahead.

"First, it's nice to see you letting yourself follow your heart with someone new. Second, you don't know this man very well. Be careful who you give your heart to, Anita."

"I haven't given anyone my heart, yet."

"Not yet," she said.

I frowned at her. "You do realize that you've told me to follow my heart and not to follow my heart."

She nodded.

"Those are contradictory bits of advice," I said.

"I'm aware of that."

"Then which piece of advice do you want me to follow?"

"Both, of course."

I shook my head. "Let's go save Gregory and worry about my ever-sordid love life later."

"I can't promise that we'll save Gregory, Anita."

I held up a hand. "I remember the odds, doc." I followed her out and into the darkened living room and tried to believe, really believe, in miracles.

29

WE DECIDED TO do it on the deck out back. My deck backed to a couple of acres of mature woodland. No neighbors. No one to see us. The deck was also twice the size of the kitchen, which was the only part of the house without carpeting. Once a shapeshifter changed on carpet it was either steam clean it yourself, or hire it done. I was not the one who suggested that Gregory would ruin the carpet; it was actually Nathaniel. He was, after all, the person most likely to be vacuuming between housekeeper visits. I wasn't even sure I knew where the vacuum was.

Gregory was curled in the center of the deck, his head in his brother's lap, his arms wrapped around the other man's naked waist. Only the curling yellow hair, paled by moonlight, covered Stephen's upper body. He'd stripped to the waist in preparation for the change. He was going to go out into the woods with his brother. This presupposed that Gregory would survive the change. We had a fifty-fifty chance, not bad odds, if all you were about to lose was money, but when it was someone's life, fifty-fifty just didn't sound that good.

Stephen looked up at me. His cornflower blue eyes were silvered with moonlight. He looked pale and ethereal. His face was raw with emotion; his eyes held an intelligence and a demand that Stephen didn't often show. He was submissive, fragile in every walk of his life, but in that moment he laid a demand on me with his eyes, his face, the pain that showed in the set of his shoulders, the fierce way he touched his brother, who was still huddled in his lap, just a fall of long pale curls and paler skin. Gregory was naked in the hot summer night, and until that moment I hadn't noticed. The nudity didn't make me think of sex, it made me think how terribly vulnerable he was.

Stephen looked up at me and asked with every line of his body, the desperation in his eyes, what he was too submissive to say out loud. I didn't need to be telepathic to know what he wanted. Save him, save my brother, he screamed at me from his eyes. To say it out loud would have been redundant.

Vivian, who was as fragile as Stephen, as submissive, said it out loud anyway. "Please, try and call his beast, at least try before they use the drugs."

I looked at her, and there must have been something in my face that frightened her, because she dropped to her knees and crawled towards me. It wasn't that graceful stalk that the leopards could do. It was like a human crawling, awkward, slow, head down, eyes rolled up. She was displaying the leopard version of submissive behavior, and I hated it. Hated her feeling the need, like I was some ogre that needed placating, but I let her do it. Richard had shown me what happened in a were-group when the dominant refused to be dominant.

She leaned against my legs, pushing her body against me, head down. Normally, leopards would roll around my legs like huge cats, but tonight Vivian just pressed against my legs more like a frightened dog than a luxuriating cat. I leaned over to touch her hair and heard her murmuring under her breath, so soft, "Please, please, please." You would have had to be colder than even I was to ignore that soft pleading.

"It's okay, Vivian, I'll try."

Rubbing her cheek along my jeans as she raised her head, her eyes rolled up to me, again like a frightened dog. Vivian had always been timid around me, but I'd never seen this level of fear before. I didn't think it was Gregory's torture that had made the difference. I think it was the fact that I'd shot Elizabeth full of holes. Yeah, that probably did it. And I couldn't undermine the lesson by reassuring Vivian now that I wouldn't shoot her. Merle and Caleb were listening, and if we were really going to combine our pards, being feared was not a bad way for me to start.

I looked across the deck and found Merle watching me. He was still fully dressed, jeans, boots, jean jacket over bare chest, the scar showing like a flash of moonlit lightning across his stomach. We stared at each other, and the force in his gaze, the physical potential that shimmered around him, made the hair on the back of my neck crawl. I'd spent years around dangerous men, and dangerous monsters; Merle was both. If I could make him truly afraid of me, that would be a good thing.

Caleb on the other hand had started stripping off his clothes when everyone else did, and only my protest, backed by Merle, had kept his pants on. He walked barefoot, moonlight catching in the rings in his nipple and the edge of his belly button. He had to look directly at me for the ring in his eyebrow to spark. He was circling Cherry, who had never dressed after helping Gregory in his bath. She stood tall and comfortably nude, ignoring him.

The fact that he was paying attention to her nudity was a breach of protocol among the shapeshifters. You only noticed nudity if you'd been invited to have sex. Short of that, you pretended everyone was as neuter as a Barbie doll.

Zane stepped between Cherry and the circling Caleb, giving a low growl. Caleb laughed and backed off. I did not need another pain in the ass in my pard, and that's what Caleb was.

Dr. Lillian was standing behind us holding a huge needle all ready to go. The two wererat bodyguards, Claudia and Igor, were behind her. They'd surprised me by putting on guns in the car on the way over. Guns weren't allowed in the lupanar, but they were bodyguards, and guns were a good thing for bodyguards. Claudia had a 10 millimeter Beretta tucked behind her back. The fact that she could carry a 10 mil anything said how much larger her hands were than mine. Igor had a shoulder rig with a Glock 9 mil. They were both good guns, and the two wererats handled them like they knew what they were doing. Rafael had insisted that they stay just in case Jacob, or his allies, got some wild idea about a preemptive strike.

Claudia and Igor stood in typical bodyguard pose, hands clasped in front of them, one hand holding the opposite wrist. It's usually a guy thing to stand like that, or a jock thing, but bodyguards do it too. It's like they hold their own hands for reasurrance.

Their faces were neutral. They were here to protect me, not Gregory. Didn't matter to them, or didn't seem to.

Nathaniel leaned against the railing, wearing a pair of shorts, his hair hanging like a dark curtain around his body, still wet from the bath. It took forever for his hair to dry naturally. His face was serene. It reflected an almost zen-like pleasantness, as if he trusted me to make everything alright. Of all their faces, his was the most unnerving. I was used to people being afraid of me, eventually, but soft adoration—that I was not used to.

I looked back down at Vivian, still pressed against my legs. There was fear in her eyes, but there was also hope.

I touched her face and managed a smile. "I'll do what I can."

She smiled, and it was radiant. She was always beautiful, but when she smiled like that there was a little girl peeking out, someone more joyous and more free than the Vivian I knew. I valued that little girl smile from her, because I saw it so rarely.

I walked the few feet to the two men. Stephen was still kneeling, his brother huddled against him. He watched me with cautious eyes. He was rubbing his hand on Gregory's bare back over and over in small circles, the way you stroke a sick child when they want some touch to let them know they're going to be alright. Looking into Stephen's eyes, I knew he didn't believe that. He didn't believe Gregory would be alright, and it terrified him.

I knelt beside them and was almost the same height as Stephen. I met that pale gaze, that demand, and said, "I'm going to try and heal him."

It was Caleb who said, "If Micah couldn't heal him, why do you think you can?"

I didn't even bother glancing back at him. "It doesn't hurt to try."

"You haven't seen your first full moon," Merle said. "You can't call flesh and heal him, not yet, maybe not ever. Calling flesh to heal is a rare talent."

I did look at Merle. "I'm not going to call flesh, I'm not even sure how that works."

"Then how will you heal him?" Merle asked.

"With the munin."

"How will a werewolf ghost help you heal a wereleopard?"

I shook my head. "I've healed the leopards before using the munin."

"You've healed Nathaniel," Cherry said, "twice, but no one else."

"If it works for one of you, it should work for all of you," I said.

Cherry was frowning.

"What's wrong?"

"You heal with Raina, everything was sex with her, and you want Nathaniel in that way. You've never been attracted to Gregory."

I shrugged. She was pretty much voicing the same doubts that I had, but hearing them out loud made them sound worse. I felt more doubtful that I could do it and more slutty because I needed sexual attraction to heal. But I was getting over the slutty feeling. If I could save both Gregory's hearing and his life, a little embarrassment wasn't too high a price to pay.

I looked down at Gregory, still huddled in a tight fetal ball around Stephen's lap and waist. He held on as if his brother were the last solid thing in the universe, as if, if he let go he'd swirl away and be lost.

I touched his hair, lightly, and he moved his face so that he could see me through a tangle of pale curls. I swept the curls away from his face. It was a gesture you used for a child. I'd hated Gregory once because of some things he'd done when Raina and Gabriel were still alive. But the moment they were dead and he knew he had a choice, he'd stopped doing most of them. Had he made me Nimir-Ra on purpose? Staring into his wide blue eyes I didn't believe that. It wasn't naïveté, it was a surety that Gregory just wasn't that dominant. To decide, even in a split second, to change the status quo that profoundly was just beyond him. He'd debate, or ask advice, or ask permission, but he wouldn't make a unilateral decision without some feedback. I knew this about Gregory. Richard didn't.

I touched his face, cupping it, raising it so he'd meet my eyes without having to do that eye roll that unnerved me. Just too subservient for my taste. I stared into that beautiful face, let my gaze glide over the fall of curls, the line of his back, the curl of his hip, but I felt nothing. I could appreciate his beauty, but I tried very hard to think of my leopards as neuter. You can be someone's friend and have sex with them. The trick is you have to want their emotional and physical well-being more than you want to fuck them. If you cross that line and want sex more than their happiness, then you aren't their friend. Their lover maybe, but not their friend.

But it was more than that. Cherry was right, Gregory had never moved me in that way. I sighed and moved my hand back from him. "What's wrong?" Stephen asked.

"He's pretty to look at, but . . ."

Stephen almost smiled. "But you need more than just a pretty face to lust after."

I shrugged. "Sometimes my life would be simpler if I didn't, but yeah."

"I remember I had to talk you through the first time you healed Nathaniel," he said, voice soft.

I nodded. "I remember too."

Gregory sat up, watching us both, trying to read our lips, I think. There was something frantic about the way he tried to decipher what we were saying. God, please let me help him. He was so scared.

"I think of him more like a child, no offense."

"You think more like a parent than a seducer; that's a good thing," Stephen said. "Don't apologize for it."

Cherry joined us, kneeling on her heels, long body curved in graceful lines. "You called Raina in the lupanar without any lust, right?"

I nodded. "I can call Raina's munin, sometimes even if I don't want to, but she always demands a price before she leaves."

"You didn't seduce anyone at the lupanar tonight," she said.

"No, but I damn near started a fight by hitting Richard, and that was part Raina's doing. She enjoyed my loss of control, and . . . and she was worried about the pack tonight. She doesn't like what Richard's done. I think she toned down her demands because of that."

"And she doesn't care about us like she does the wolves."

"No, she doesn't."

"What are you afraid of?" Stephen asked. "That you'll molest Gregory."

I shook my head. "No, I'm afraid Raina will."

"You healed Nathaniel in the woods and didn't do anything awful to him," Cherry said.

"No, but I had Richard and the pack there to balance me, to help me control her through the marks. Without extra help in that area, Raina's idea of payment can get a little messy."

"Define messy," Stephen said.

"Sex, violence—" I shrugged—"messy."

"You have the pard here now," Cherry said. "You can use us for balance."

Truth was, without Micah here I wasn't sure I could do that. Just as Richard was my door to the wolves, Micah was my door to the leopards. Or was he? I was treating this like I treated Richard and Jean-Claude, like I was the outsider and they were my ticket in. But what if I really was the leopard queen? If I really was Nimir-Ra, then I should be able to do this without Micah. I realized the moment I doubted that, I was still hoping I wasn't going to be furry next full moon. No matter how much evidence to the contrary, I still didn't believe it. Maybe I didn't want to believe it. But I wanted to heal Gregory, that I did want.

I looked at them all and knew Cherry was right. If I was Nimir-Ra, then I had all I needed to balance me. If I wasn't Nimir-Ra, then it wouldn't work. What did we have to lose? I looked at Stephen and Gregory, their mirror faces, their frightened eyes, and knew exactly what we had to lose if I didn't try.

I took the Uncle Mike's sidekick holster complete with Firestar out of the front of my jeans and looked around. If I was going to be calling on the leopards, I didn't want them having to worry about the gun. I motioned Claudia the wererat over. Since I was still kneeling, she towered over me, only two inches shorter than Dolph. I had to admit it was impressive, even more so because she was a woman.

I handed the holstered gun to her, and she took it. "Make sure no one gets shot with it."

She frowned down at me. "You think someone is going to try and get the gun?"

"Me, maybe."

The frown deepened. "I don't understand."

"Raina's amused by violence. I don't want to be carrying a gun when I call her munin."

Claudia's eyebrows raised. "You mean she'd try to get you to use it on someone?"

I nodded.

"She's tried before?'

I nodded again. "In Tennessee when I was practicing with the munin, yeah."

Claudia shook her head. "You didn't seem that worried at the lupanar."

"I can call her once and be okay, probably. But if I call her too often, too close together, it's like she grows—" I hesitated—"stronger, or maybe I just get tired of fighting."

"She was a bitch when she was alive," Claudia said.

"Being dead hasn't changed her much," I added.

The tall woman shivered. "I'm glad the wererats don't have anything like the munin. The thought of some entity inside me just creeps me out."

"Me too," I said.

She looked down at me, thoughtful now. "I'll keep the gun safe. Is there anything else Igor and I can do to help?"

I tried to think of something, but only one thing came to mind. "If the leopards can't control me, make sure I don't hurt anyone."

"How bad is this going to be?" she asked.

I shrugged. "Normally, I wouldn't be this worried, but last time I called her she didn't get her bit of flesh, or sex. Hitting Richard made her happy, but . . ." I tried to explain. "I called her three times in a row for practice, without molesting or hurting anyone. My teacher, Marianne, and I both thought it was a sign that I was gaining control of Raina. Then the fourth time I called her, it was worse than it had ever been. You either pay as you go with Raina, or you end up owing her, and owing comes with interest, and the interest is hell to pay."

"Should you give me the knives, too, then?" Claudia asked.

She had a point, no pun intended. I took the wrist sheaths off, folded them up, and handed them to her.

"I thought you could control this shit." Caleb was standing just a little behind and to one side of Claudia. He was looking up at the tall woman as if wondering what she'd do if he tried to climb her. I almost wanted him to try, because I was pretty sure what would happen, and even more sure that I'd enjoy watching it. Caleb needed a good lesson from someone.

"I can."

"Then why all the precautions?"

I could have told him about the time in Tennessee when Raina's munin nearly started a riot among Verne's pack in a sort of game of rape tag, with me as the rapee, but I didn't. Instead, I said, "If you're not going to be helpful, stand over to the side and shut the fuck up."

He opened his mouth as if to protest, but Merle said, "Caleb, do what she says." His voice was quiet, a deep rumble of sound, but that mild tone seemed to work on Caleb like a charm.

"Sure, Merle, anything you say." He went to stand over to one side, near Dr. Lillian and Igor.

I glanced at Merle. "Thanks," I said.

He just bowed his head at me.

Dr. Lillian said, "I take this to mean that you want me to wait on the injection."

I nodded. "Yeah."

She turned and walked back through the sliding glass doors, into the darkened house. Everyone else stayed where they were, looking at me. Even Caleb, sulking by the railing with his arms crossed, was still watching the show.

I slipped my shirt off and felt rather than saw all my people react, like wind through a wheat field, involuntary. I never undressed in front of people unless I absolutely had to. The black bra I was wearing covered more than most swim suits, but there's something about letting people see you in your underwear that just makes all us good little girls squirm.

"Black lace, I like it," Caleb said.

I started to say something, but Merle beat me to it. "Shut up, Caleb, and don't make me tell you again."

Caleb settled back against the rail, arms hugging himself, face crinkled into a sulk that made him look even younger than he was.

"Go on," Merle said, "he won't interrupt again."

I looked at him. It was bad that he kept interfering. It undermined my authority, but since I wasn't entirely sure I had any authority over Caleb, it was okay, I guess. But it bugged me. I just wasn't sure what to do about it.

"I appreciate the help, but if our pards really do merge, then Caleb is going to have to learn to respect me, not you."

"You don't want my help?" He made it a question.

"Priority tonight is Gregory, but Caleb and I are going to have to come to an understanding."

"Are you going to shoot him too?"

I tried to read Merle's face and failed. A sort of blank hostility was all that showed. "You think I'll have to?"

Merle gave a very small smile. "Maybe."

It made me smile, a little. "Great, just what I need, another discipline problem in my pard."

His smile vanished like a hand had wiped it away. "We're not your cats, Anita, not yet."

I shrugged. "Whatever you say."

"We are not yours," he said.

I watched his face and saw something cross it in the moonlight. Maybe if I'd had better light I could have deciphered it. "Why does the thought of me being in charge bother you so much?"

He shook his head. "It's not you being in charge that bothers me."

"Then what is it?"

He shook his head again. "What bothers me is you trying to be in charge and failing—failing really, really badly."

"I do my best, Merle, that's all I can do."

He nodded. "I believe you, but I've seen a lot of people try their best and still not make it."

I shrugged and let it go. "Be pessimistic on your own time, Merle, we need a little hope here, not negativity."

"I'll just shut up then," he said, which implied that if he couldn't be negative he had nothing to say. Fine by me.

I turned back to Gregory and his wide, frightened eyes. I touched his face, gently, trying to ease some of that fear, but he flinched ever so slightly when I touched him. You get enough abuse in your life, and you begin to think that every offered hand is a blow waiting to strike.

"It'll be alright, Gregory," I said. Since he couldn't hear me, I must have been saying it to reassure myself. It didn't seem to do a damn thing for Gregory.

I tried to see Gregory as a lust object, and I failed. I ran my hands over the smooth skin of his back, I grabbed a handful of those yellow curls, looked into those lovely eyes, but all I could feel was pity. All I could feel was protective towards him and how much I wanted to keep him safe. He was totally nude, sitting in front of me, and he was lovely. There was nothing wrong with the way he looked, except that I didn't see Gregory in that way. Trust me to find a way to make virtue a problem.

I turned to Stephen, who was still kneeling beside us. "I'm sorry, he's beautiful, but I want to hold him, keep him safe, not have sex with him, and protective intincts are not going to get Raina to come out."

Cherry said, "You simply called Raina at the lupanar. Why is this different?"

I looked up at her, standing nude and comfortable against the deck railing. Zane was next to her, clothed, and just as comfortable.

"I can call Raina, but I can't guarantee she'll help me heal Gregory. The healing usually comes with lust, not without."

"Call her," Stephen said. "Once she's here maybe the rest will come."

"You mean call her munin, then get *her* in the mood, not me."

He looked very solemn, but he nodded.

"You know what her idea of sex is, Stephen."

He nodded again. "Trust me," he said.

Strangely, I did. He wasn't dominant, in fact was very often a victim, but Stephen did what he said he'd do, at almost any cost. There was a desperate stubbornness in him, no matter how often you knocked him down.

"I'll call the munin."

"And I'll make sure that Raina sees Gregory the way she needs to see him."

We looked at each other and had one of those moments of near perfect understanding. Stephen would do anything to save his brother, and I would do almost anything to help him do that.

30

I SAT BACK on my heels in front of Gregory, and I opened myself to the munin, dropped that barrier that kept Raina out, and she spilled up through me like warm water filling a pipe, up, up, riding on a wave of eagerness that she hadn't had at the lupanar. A thrill of fear went through me. I knew it was a bad sign, but I didn't fight her. I let her come, let her fill me up, let her laugh bubble from my throat.

When she looked at Gregory, she had no trouble seeing him as a sexual object, but then Raina saw almost everyone as a sexual object, so no big surprise.

I touched his face, caressed the line of his jaw. Gregory's eyes widened. I realized in that moment that he might not know what the hell we were doing, or what had changed. I could call Raina and think rationally. I'd fought long and hard to be able to do that. I could be distant while my hand glided down Gregory's bare chest. I could stop my hand—our hand—at his slender waist, and Raina couldn't force me lower. She snarled in my head, giving me a visual of her in wolf shape, snapping at me. But it was just a visual, like a dream; it couldn't hurt me, or anyone.

Raina spoke in my head. "This wolf still has teeth, Anita."

"You know the rules," I said.

"What?" Stephen asked.

I shook my head. "I'm talking to Raina."

"That is just creepy," Zane said.

I agreed with him, wholeheartedly, but Raina was already talking in my head, and I couldn't answer him. "I know the rules, Anita, do you?"

"Yeah."

"I do whatever I please . . ."

"And I try to stop you," I finished for her.

"Like old times," the voice in my head said.

It did sound like the relationship we'd had when she was alive. She wanted to kiss Gregory, and I didn't fight it. The kiss was openmouthed, but soft, nothing that would scare me too badly. In her own way Raina was learning how to work me, too.

I'd never kissed Gregory before, never wanted to. I still didn't want to. Kissing, in some ways, is more intimate than intercourse, more special. I pulled away from his lips, and Raina was just as happy to kiss the side of his neck. His skin was warm and smelled like soap. I buried my face under his hair at the back of his ear and found the hair still damp, smelling of my shampoo.

I tried to call healing from Raina, but she fought me. "No, not until after my reward."

I actually had leaned back from Gregory, and must have said it out loud, because Stephen asked, "What reward?"

I shook my head. "Raina won't heal him until after she's been . . . fed." It was a type of feeding; in her own way Raina was like the *ardeur*, except she only needed feeding when I called her—her craving, not mine.

"What do you want?" I asked it out loud, because I still wasn't comfortable with having silent conversations in my head.

She gave me a visual of kissing down his chest, of forcing him onto his back on the deck, and the next thing I remembered clearly was laying a gentle kiss beside Gregory's belly button. He was lying on his back, watching me with unfocused eyes. I was lying across his body, pinning his legs, my nearly naked chest pressed over his groin. I didn't remember getting there. Shit.

I rolled off of him, and Raina came like heat, racing through my body, drawing my mouth down to his hip, licking along that small hollow just where the waist meets groin. Gregory writhed under the stroke of my mouth, and as much as I'd tried to ignore it, drew our gaze to his groin.

He was hard, ready, but the sight of him pushed Raina back, left me in control, not because it was embarrassing, but because I had never seen Gregory erect before. He was still lovely to look at, but he was an odd shape, almost hooked at the end. I didn't know that men could be made that way, and it stopped me cold.

Raina screamed in my head, roared over me in a rush of body memory. The memory was of being on all fours with a man riding me from behind, riding Raina. I couldn't see who it was; all I could do was feel. They'd found that spot in a woman's body, and the rush of orgasm was close. Raina threw her—our—head back, a rush of auburn hair flinging free of our face, and I saw Gregory's reflection in the room's mirror.

Raina whispered in my head, "It's always like that with him from behind, because of his shape."

I tore free of the memory and found myself on all fours beside Gregory, one hand on his body. I fell back from him, because the shared memories didn't work without body contact.

I turned my face away so I wouldn't see him nude and ready, because I could still feel the memory of him inside my body, Raina's body. A hand touched my bare arm, and the rush of memories this time was overwhelming. I was there.

He filled my mouth, my throat, came inside my mouth in a spill of thick heat, and with his body trembling, thrashing, teeth tore into thick, tender flesh, and we ate him. Blood poured upwards, and Raina bathed in it.

I fought free of it, screaming, shrieking, and someone else was screaming. It was Gregory. For one awful second I opened my eyes, because the memory was so strong I couldn't tell the difference between it and reality. But when I could see again, he was whole, crawling away from me, from the shared memory. Because that was one of Raina's gifts, the ability to share the horror.

I could still feel the thickness of meat in my mouth, taste blood and thicker things. I crawled to the railing, pulled myself up and lost everything I'd eaten that day.

Someone came up behind me, and I put out a hand, head still dangling over the dark edge of the deck. "Don't touch me."

"Anita, it's Merle. Nathaniel said that no one was to touch you that had ever shared a . . ." he hesitated, "moment with the old lupa. I didn't know her. She can't hurt you through me."

I held my head in my hands. It felt like it was going to split apart. "He's right."

His grip on my shoulders was as hesitant as his words. I pushed away from the railing and the world swam. Merle caught me, held me against his chest. "It's alright."

"I can still taste meat and blood and . . . oh, God! God!" I screamed it, and it didn't help, not for this. Merle held me against his chest, tight, my hands pinned to my sides, as if I'd tried to hurt myself. I didn't think I had, but I didn't know anymore. Months of practice, and Raina could still do this to me.

I screamed wordlessly over and over again, as if I could scream the memory out of me. Every time I drew breath I could hear Merle whispering, "It's alright, it's alright, Anita, it's alright."

But it wasn't alright. What Raina had just shown me would never be alright. Merle carried me into the bathroom, and I didn't protest. Caleb wet a cloth and put it on my forehead without a word of teasing. A small miracle, but not the one we needed.

31

RAINA HAD GONE, fled laughing, pleased with herself. God, I hated that woman. I'd already killed her; it wasn't like I could do anything else to her, but I wanted to. I wanted her to hurt like she'd hurt so many others, but I guess it was a little late for that.

Dr. Lillian was shining a tiny light in my eyes and trying to get me to follow her fingers. I wasn't doing a good enough job apparently, because she wasn't happy. "You are in shock, Anita, and so is Gregory. He was a little shocky before you began, but damn it."

I blinked and tried to focus on her. My eyes just couldn't settle on anything, as if the world were trembling, but that made no sense. Maybe I was the one that was trembling? I couldn't tell. I clutched the cover they'd put around me, huddling on my white couch amid the multicolored pillows, and couldn't get warm. "What are you saying, doc?"

"I'm saying that Gregory's chances are worse than fifty-fifty now."

I blinked and fought to look at her, meet her eyes, to think. "How bad?"

"Seventy-thirty, maybe. He's curled on the deck in a blanket, shivering worse than you are."

I shook my head, and couldn't seem to stop. I closed my eyes, forced myself to be still for a second, a heartbeat. I spoke without opening my eyes. "I saw . . . how did Gregory heal . . ." I stopped, tried again. "How did he survive . . . what she did to him?"

"We can regrow any body part short of decapitation, unless fire is added to the wound to close it. We can't heal burns, unless the burned flesh is completely removed, in effect making a new wound." Her voice was bitter, fierce. I'd never heard her so angry.

I looked up at her. "What's wrong with you?"

Lillian looked down, wouldn't meet my eyes. "I was the doctor on call the night she did that to Gregory. I saw the reality, not just a memory."

I shook my head, and had to bury my chin on my knees to stop the movement. "It isn't a memory with the munin, doc, it's real. It's like . . . it's like a live-action movie, but with me in the movie." I hugged my knees and tried desperately not to think, not to revisit what I'd experienced. I was actually having some luck being absolutely blank. Even my mind had finally found something so terrible it couldn't cope with it. In a bizarre way, it was comforting. I'd finally found a line that I could not cross.

"If I try to force Gregory into animal form now, it'll probably kill him," Dr. Lillian said.

I buried my face into my knees, hiding. I spoke with my mouth buried against the thick covers. "I can't try again."

"No one is asking you to call that bitch again."

"Anita." It was Nathaniel.

It wasn't his voice that made me look up, it was the rich, bitter smell of coffee. I found him holding my baby penguin mug full of fresh coffee. It was very pale, lots of sugar, lots of cream; good for shock. Hell, good for everything.

He helped me rescue my hands from the blanket and wrap them around the mug. I held the mug tight, and it took several seconds to realize I was burning my hands. I didn't panic, just handed the mug back to Nathaniel. He took it, and I stared at my pink, red hands. I had first-degree burns, and I hadn't felt the heat until it was too late.

"Damn," I said, softly.

Lillian sighed. "I'll get some ice." She left us alone.

Nathaniel knelt in front of me, being careful not to spill the coffee. Merle and Cherry glided into the living room while I was still staring at my reddened hands. Cherry sat beside me on the couch. She was still nude, but it didn't matter. Nothing seemed to matter. Merle stayed standing, and I didn't even bother trying to look up at him. All I could see were the silver toes of his boots.

"Nathaniel said that you touched his beast when you marked his back," Cherry said.

I blinked at her, meeting her pale eyes. I nodded. I remembered a shining moment, after I'd marked his back actually, where I'd felt his beast roiling under the touch of my power, and I'd been sure I could call that part of him, make him shapeshift for me. I was still nodding, and made myself stop, saying, "I remember."

Lillian came back out and applied bags of ice wrapped in a small towel to my hands. "Try not to hurt yourself for a few minutes. I'm going back to check on Gregory." She left me with the three leopards and my ice.

"If you touched Nathaniel's beast, there's a chance you could call Gregory's now."

I shook my head. "I don't think so."

Cherry gripped my arm. "Don't fall apart on us now, Anita, Gregory needs you."

The first flare of anger pushed through the shock. "I have done my fucking best for him tonight."

She dropped her hand away from my arm, but didn't look away. "Anita, please, Merle thinks you may be strong enough to call Gregory's beast, even before your first full moon."

I clutched the towel-covered ice to my chest. The sudden cold across my nearly naked chest helped clear my head. "I thought that wasn't possible before I shifted for the first time."

"With you, Anita," Merle said, "I would be a fool to say what you can and can't do."

I let the ice fall on the coverlet in my lap and looked up at the big man. "Why the change of heart? I failed Gregory out there on the deck."

"You risked yourself for one of your cats. It is the very best a Nimira-Ra, or -Raj, has in them, to take great risks for their people."

I touched the towel, found one corner wet, and knew the plastic bag hadn't sealed completely. I moved the bag rightside up so it wouldn't spill anymore. "What do you want from me?" My voice sounded as tired as I felt.

Merle knelt in front of me, and I met his eyes. There was a look in them that I didn't want right now. He seemed to trust me, and I didn't feel trustworthy. I felt scared.

"Call Gregory's beast."

"I don't know how. When I was with Nathaniel, it was . . ." I sighed.

"It was sexual," Cherry finished for me.

I nodded. "I am not trying for that kind of mood with Gregory again tonight. I don't think either he, or I, could handle it if it went wrong again."

"Calling the beast doesn't have to be sexual," Merle said.

I met his strangely trusting gaze. I was beyond tired. I just didn't have anything left tonight, not for Gregory. I did not want to touch him again tonight. Part of me was afraid that Raina would make an unplanned appearance, though I knew that was almost impossible for her now. I did have better control than that. But . . . "How can I ever touch Gregory again and not remember that?"

"I don't know," Cherry said, "but please, Anita, please help him."

"How do I call his beast without getting in the mood?" I asked.

"You need to talk to someone who can call the beast from their people," Merle said.

I looked at him. "You got someone in mind?"

"I am told your Ulfric can call the beast from his wolves."

I nodded. "So I hear."

"If he called a wolf into form, while you watched, then he might be able to show you how to do it."

"You really think it will work?" I asked him.

"I don't know," he said, "but isn't it worth trying?"

I handed him the leaking bag of ice. "Sure, if Richard will come."

Nathaniel answered that one. "Richard blames himself for Gregory's injuries. If we offer him a chance to heal him, he'll come."

I stared at Nathaniel, watched the intelligence in those flower-colored eyes. It was one of the most insightful things I'd ever heard him say. It gave me just a little hope, that indeed Nathaniel could be made whole—that he was getting better. I needed some hope just then, but it was still unnerving for Nathaniel to know Richard so well, to be that observant. It meant that I'd underestimated Nathaniel. I kept equating submissiveness with being inferior, and that wasn't really the case. Some people choose to be bottoms, to serve; it doesn't make them less, just different. I looked into his face and wondered what else I'd missed, or what else he'd show me? It was a night for revelations, so why the hell not have Richard join us? How much worse could it get? Please, no one answer that.

32

I BRUSHED MY teeth and sat at the kitchen table in the dark, drinking coffee while we waited. Nathaniel padded barefoot into the room, his hair swinging loose around his bare chest and the jean shorts he'd put on.

"How's Gregory?" I asked.

"Dr. Lillian put an IV in him, to help with the shock, she said." He stopped beside the table, not quite in front of me.

"An IV. Richard will be here within an hour or less. If she put an IV in then . . ." I let my voice trail off.

Nathaniel finished for me. "Gregory's very hurt."

I looked up at him in the darkened kitchen. The only light was the small one over the sink. It left most of the room in thick shadows. "You don't mean the injuries he got from the wolves, do you?"

He shook his head, all that hair sliding around his body. A long heavy strand slid over one shoulder, and he tossed his head to flip it back behind him. I'd never been around a man that had such long hair, who was so comfortable with it.

"He kept talking about Raina," Nathaniel said, "kept swearing under his breath." His voice had dropped low, almost a whisper. He was staring over my head at things I couldn't see, and probably didn't want to.

I touched his arm. "You alright?"

He looked down at me, smiled, but not like he was happy. He moved his hand so he was holding mine. His grip was tight like he needed the comfort.

"Talk to me, Nathaniel."

"I gave you copies of three of my movies." He smiled, wide this time, before I could say anything. "I know you've never watched them. When I gave them to you, I still thought you were like Gabriel and Raina, that it had to be sex, that you would like that they were porn. I understand now that you'll take care of us no matter what, not because you lust after us or because you love one of us, but just—because." He went to his knees, still holding my hand, pressing it against his chest with both his own. He laid his head on my lap, his face turned away from me. I moved a thick line of hair away from his face, so I could see his profile as he leaned against me.

We sat there for a few moments, me waiting for him to continue, him maybe waiting for me to prompt him, but the silence wasn't strained. One of us would fill it when we were ready, and we both knew that. He was the one who sighed, keeping one hand on my hand, pressed to him, his other hand curling around my leg. I could feel the beat of his heart against the back of my hand.

"I did more movies than just those three. Most of them with Raina. Gabriel wouldn't let her have me as a lover, or a slave. I think he knew she'd kill me, but on film where things could be controlled . . ." He hugged his body against mine, clinging.

"What happened?" I said, softly.

"She did that to Gregory on her own, as a kind of . . . fun. But when he survived it, she wanted to do a version of it on film."

I went very still for a second or two. I think I stopped breathing, because when my breath finally did come out, it shook. "You?" I made it a question.

He nodded his head, cheek still pressed to my thigh. "Me."

I stroked his hair, stared down into that young face. He was six years younger than me, almost seven, but it seemed like there should have been decades between us. He was so much a victim, so much anyone's meat.

"Gregory wouldn't do it again, said he'd kill himself first, and Gabriel must have believed him."

I kept petting his hair because I didn't know what else to do. What do you say while someone whispers horrors in your ear, tells you their most intimate, nightmarish secrets? You sit and you listen. And you give them the only thing you can—the silence and the safety to talk and to be heard.

His voice dropped soft, softer, until I had to lean my face over his to hear him. "They chained me down, and I knew the script. I knew what was about to happen, and I was excited. The fear made the anticipation almost unbearable."

I laid my cheek against his, felt his mouth move as he spoke, and I kept very, very quiet. I had nothing to offer but my silence, and my touch.

He whispered, "I like teeth, biting, I like a lot of damage. It was wonderful until . . ." He closed his eyes, turned his face into my jeans, as if even now he couldn't look at the memory. I had lifted my head up when he moved, but laid a gentle kiss on the back of his head. "It's okay, Nathaniel, it's okay."

He said something, but I couldn't understand it.

"What?"

He moved his head just enough so that his mouth wasn't buried against my leg. "God, it hurt. She took it in pieces, wanted it to last longer than it had with Gregory."

His whole body gave one great shiver, and I leaned over him, my free hand across his back, smoothing the hair away so I could reach his skin. I stroked over his back, and found all the little bite marks I'd left in his skin. I hadn't felt bad for marking him, until now. Now I felt like I'd used him like everyone else had.

I curled my body over his, hugging him into my lap, holding him as close as I could. "I am sorry, Nathaniel, so sorry."

"You don't have anything to be sorry about, Anita. You've never hurt me."

"Yes, I have."

He raised up enough to meet my eyes. He looked so young, eyes wide. "I love that you've marked me, don't be sorry about that." He gave a small smile. "If you start feeling guilty about it, you won't do it again, and I want you to, I want that very much."

"If I feed on you, Nathaniel, for the *ardeur*, or the flesh, or whatever, I'm using you. I don't use people."

He held my hand so tight that it almost hurt. "Don't do this to me."

"Do what?"

"Don't punish me for telling you about how Raina hurt me."

"I'm not punishing you."

"I tell you this horrible thing, and you start feeling protective of me, and guilty. I know you, Anita, you'll let your head get in the way of what we both need."

"And what exactly is that?" And even I could hear the impatience, almost anger, in my voice.

He raised up farther, bringing his face close to mine, because I'd sat up, distancing myself from him. "You need to feed the *ardeur*, and I need to have a place to belong."

"You are welcome in my house as long as you need it, Nathaniel."

He shook his head, pushing the hair back impatiently, letting go of my hand, putting his hands on my knees, half-crawling under the table so that he was kneeling between my legs, though only his hands touched the tops of my knees. He stared up at me. "No, you tolerate me. I do some housework, errands, but I don't belong. You don't go through your day thinking about me. I'm here, but I'm not part of your life, I know that. If I am your *pomme de sang*, then I will be. I'll finally belong to you in a way that both of us can live with."

I shook my head. "No, Nathaniel, no."

He grabbed the legs of the chair and picked the entire thing up with me on it from a kneeling position and moved it backwards with a bump, so he could fit under the table better. He hadn't even strained when he did it. He put his hands on the chair arms, slid his lower body against the chair, putting my knees on either side of his hips.

"And who else are you going to feed off of every day? Richard? Jean-Claude? Micah?"

"The *ardeur* may be temporary," I said.

He put a hand on either side of my waist. "If it's temporary, then feed on me until it goes away. If it's permanent . . ."

"I don't want to feed on anyone."

His hands slid around my waist, his head going to my lap, and I realized he was crying. "Please, don't do this, Anita, please don't do this."

I stroked his hair, his face, and didn't know what to say. What was I going to do if the *ardeur* was permanent? Richard didn't let anyone feed off of him for any reason—same rule I had. Jean-Claude would be literally dead to the world when I most needed to feed. Micah was still a question mark. But in some ways, feeding off of Nathaniel because he was the only one that would let me, was almost worse.

I lifted his face from my lap, a hand on either side. Tears glittered on his cheeks in the faint light. I kissed his forehead, kissed his closed eyes, the way you would a child's.

"Did I get here just in time, or am I interrupting?" It was Richard standing in the doorway. Perfect fucking timing, as always.

33

I FROZE WITH Nathaniel's face cradled in my hands, him kneeling between my legs with the table hiding most of him, having just risen from kissing him, and knew how it looked. I wasn't sure I could explain it to Richard's satisfaction. To my knowledge Richard didn't know about the *ardeur* yet, and right then I didn't want to tell him.

I laid another gentle kiss on Nathaniel's forehead and leaned back. I wasn't going to act like I'd done something wrong when I hadn't. Nathaniel took his cue from me, laying his head back in my lap, which I realized meant he was invisible from the doorway, the table hiding what he was doing.

Richard strode into the kitchen like an angry wind, his power biting along my skin. He came to stand where he could see that Nathaniel had his cheek against my thigh, gazing up at the larger man, as he towered over both of us.

Jamil and Shang-Da were hanging back by the doorway. They were good bodyguards, but some things bodyguards can't keep you safe from.

I felt my face go neutral, empty, vaguely pleasant. "I was comforting one of my leopards, something wrong with that?"

"He looks very comfortable," Richard said, voice mild enough, but his power was hot, like opening the door to an oven.

I licked my lips. I was going to have to explain the ardeur, sooner or later, and since I wanted him to help us save Gregory, tonight was probably the right time. "Nathaniel and I were discussing some side effects of marrying the vampire marks."

"You mean the *ardeur*," he said.

I was surprised and let it show. "Who told you?"

"Jean-Claude thought I should know. He encouraged me to come over and be here for you in the morning."

"And you said?" I kept my voice as neutral as I could, but not as neutral as I wanted it to be.

"I don't let him, or Asher, or any of them, feed off of me, blood or anything else. I don't see why I should change that rule just because it's you and it's sex instead of blood."

"Did he explain that if I don't feed off of you, or him, I still have to feed off of someone?"

"There's always your Nimir-Raj." The contempt in his voice was thick enough to walk on.

"Micah's been called away on pard business."

"You really think he won't be back before morning so you can fuck him? I do."

I stared up at him, still sitting in the face of his burning power and the sheer physical presence of him. Richard was one of those big men who never seemed big unless he was angry. He seemed big now, and I wasn't impressed.

I started petting Nathaniel's hair, and he snuggled in against my legs, letting the tension ease out of his body. "You dumped me, remember?"

"And did you fuck him for the first time before or after you found out I'd dumped you?"

I had to think about that for a second or two. "After," I said.

"You mourned my loss for, what, half a second?"

I felt heat crawl up my face. I was out of moral high ground, and explaining that it was the *ardeur* just wasn't good enough for Richard.

"It took all three of us to get into this mess, don't make it worse."

"Don't you mean four of us, or is it five now?"

I must have looked as blank as I felt. "I don't know what you're talking about."

He grabbed the table and shoved it backwards with a scream of wood on wood. Nathaniel stayed curled around my legs and just looked up at him. I'd never gotten my gun back from the wererats. I had gotten my knives back, but I wasn't really willing to cut Richard up, not yet, not for this. I couldn't arm wrestle Richard, not and win, so really my only option was to sit, look perfectly calm, and tell him by my facial expression what a fucking asshole he was being.

He shoved the table again, making the wood scream, then he knelt beside Nathaniel and pushed his long hair back. He bared his back and stared at the bite marks.

"Is that all?" he asked, voice fierce, his power so high it was like treading in boiling water, up to my chin, and still rising.

"No," I said.

Richard gripped the back of Nathaniel's shorts and pulled, the movement so violent that Nathaniel's entire body moved with it. I heard the button from the top of the shorts bounce along the floor. Richard jerked down the shorts and stared at the bite marks, where they trailed ever lower.

Richard leaned over Nathaniel, not quite touching, but he was like some huge presence, and I felt Nathaniel cower against me.

Richard hissed into his ear, "Did she suck you off? She's good at that."

"That's enough, Richard."

Nathaniel answered, "No."

"You're so scared of me I can't tell if you're lying or not." He grabbed a handful of Nathaniel's hair and pulled him backwards, peeling him away from me. I had one of the wrist sheath knives in my hand and didn't remember drawing it. The point was pressed against the long line of Richard's throat, and even I was breathless at the speed of it. It must have been a blur of movement. It wasn't human speed.

Everything froze.

Shang-Da and Jamil moved into the room. I pressed the point deeper against Richard's neck. "Don't interfere, boys."

They stopped moving. I met Richard's gaze and found his eyes had gone wolf amber. "Let go of him, Richard." My voice was low, but it seemed to fill the room.

"You wouldn't kill me for this." His voice was low, careful, too.

"Kill, no, but bleed? Oh, yes."

"You need me to help you save Gregory."

I could feel his pulse beating against the tip of my knife. "I won't let you hurt Nathaniel to save Gregory."

His grip actually tightened on Nathaniel's hair, and I pressed the point in enough to draw the first crimson drop. "Would you be this upset if it wasn't Nathaniel?" he said.

"This is the only warning I will ever give you, Richard. Never touch one of my people again."

"Or what? You'll kill me? I don't think you'll do it."

I realized in that moment that if I wasn't willing to kill him, I had no threat. And I really wasn't willing to kill him, not over this, not yet.

I drew the blade back from his neck and watched him relax, the tension easing away from him, his hand still in Nathaniel's hair. I moved without thinking, and I was fast enough that the knife cut across his forearm before he could react. He jerked away, came to his feet, and took a step back, holding his bleeding arm. The cut was deeper than I'd meant for it to be, because I'd rushed it. Blood dripped from between his fingers. Jamil and Shang-Da moved into the room.

I stood and drew Nathaniel with me, as he pulled up his shorts to cover himself. I put the French doors at our backs. "You are never to lay a hand in anger on my leopards, Richard, you or any of your wolves."

Jamil was helping Richard press a towel to the wound. Shang-Da had gone for Dr. Lillian. "It would serve you right if I just walked out and left you and your leopards to fend for yourselves."

"You'd leave Gregory to be permanently deaf, or dead, because we had a fight? He's in danger because you couldn't control your temper, or your wolves."

"It's my fault, right, all my fault."

I just looked at him, Nathaniel behind me, the bloody knife still in my hand.

Richard gave a laugh that sounded more out of pain than humor. "I've let everyone down tonight." He looked at me, and there was something fierce in his face that wasn't his beast but just sheer emotion. Anger, pain, so deep it was like anquish. "I'll help you save Gregory, because you're right, it *is* my fault. I'll take this," he raised the wounded arm, while Jamil still held it, "because you're right again, I had no right to touch one of your people. I wouldn't have let you abuse one of my wolves either."

Dr. Lillian came in, took one look and started scolding us for being children who couldn't play well together. "He's going to need stitches. Shame on you both."

Richard stared over her head as she cleaned the wound. I think he wasn't really glaring at me, he was glaring at Nathaniel. He was genuinely jealous. Jealous in a way that he shouldn't have been. What had Jean-Claude told him about the *ardeur* and about Nathaniel, and about what we'd all done together at the Circus? Jean-Claude wouldn't actually lie, but he might make things sound worse if it suited his purposes. But what purpose did it serve to make Richard jealous of Nathaniel? I would have to ask Jean-Claude about that. I had time to call while Richard got stitched up.

34

JEAN-CLAUDE ADMITTED ONLY to telling the absolute truth. But, he added, if because of that Monsieur Zeeman was jealous of Nathaniel, this wasn't an altogether bad thing. "He will share you with me, because he must, and he will share you with Micah also, because he must, but we are both alphas, dominants. To share you with someone like Nathaniel—that is different."

"You changed something about the story to make Nathaniel sound like more of a threat, didn't you?"

"No, *ma petite,* I merely told the truth without leaving anything out. He is not entirely happy with Jason either."

"Jean-Claude, you can't do this to Richard. You'll drive him mad."

"Mad enough, perhaps, to finally acknowledge that he cannot live without you, and that he must come to terms with our triumvirate."

"You Machiavellian shithead, you're playing with him."

"I am trying to maneuver him into doing what must be done if we are to survive. If that be Machiavellian, so be it."

"You are making things worse," I said.

"I don't believe so. I think, *ma petite,* that you still do not understand men. Many men will give up a woman if they are unhappy with her. But let another man try to claim her, and often, they find they still do want her."

"You and Micah aren't competition enough?" I asked.

"As I explained, we are his equals. Nathaniel is lesser, and that will prick his pride more."

"I didn't think Richard had that kind of destructive guy pride."

"I think there are many things you do not know about our Richard."

"And you do?"

"I am, after all, a man, *ma petite*. I believe I understand the male psyche a tiny bit better than you do."

I couldn't argue with that. "Well, give me a heads-up next time you plan to do any maneuvering. You could have gotten one of us killed."

He sighed. "I do keep underestimating the stubbornness of both of you. My apologies for that."

I leaned my forehead against the kitchen wall. "Jean-Claude . . ."

"Yes, *ma petite*."

I closed my eyes. "Tell me exactly what you think Richard thinks about Nathaniel and me."

"I told him the absolute truth, *ma petite*, nothing more, and nothing less."

I turned around, put my back to the wall, looked out at the empty kitchen.

Richard was in the downstairs bathroom getting stitched up. Nathaniel was with the other leopards. I'd given strict orders that he was not to be left alone. I just wasn't up to Richard and him actually having a fight. It would be too . . . ridiculous, or pathetic.

"And what does that mean, that you told the truth, no more, no less?"

"You will not like it."

"I don't like it now, just tell me, Jean-Claude."

"I told him what had happened with the *ardeur*, and added my own belief that the reason you so often find Nathaniel around when sex is in the air is that you find him sexually attractive."

"That did not make Richard come over here and start a fight."

"I do remember adding that you might find a less-demanding male refreshing after the two of us. Someone who did not make so many demands on you, someone who merely accepted you as you are."

"You do that," I said.

"So good of you to notice," he said. "But it is not I that has been living in your home for months, and from what I smell on Nathaniel when he comes into work, sharing your bed."

"Any of the wereleopards are welcome in the bedroom when they stay here. It's like a big pile of puppies—it's not sexual."

"If you say so." His voice was soft, mocking.

"Damn you, Jean-Claude, you know I don't see Nathaniel that way."

He sighed, and it was heavy. "I think it is not me that you lie to, *ma petite*, but yourself."

"I am not in love with Nathaniel."

"Did I ever say you were?"

"Then what are you talking about?"

He made a small exasperated sound. "*Ma petite*, you still believe that you must love every man that you come to physically. It is not so. You can have very pleasant, even wondrous sex with a friend. It does not have to be love."

I was shaking my head, realized he couldn't see it, and said, "I don't do casual sex, Jean-Claude, you know that."

"Whatever you are doing with Nathaniel, *ma petite*, it is not casual."

"I can't use him as my *pomme de sang*. I can't."

"Your morals have reared their ugly heads, *ma petite*, do not let them make you foolish."

I opened my mouth to protest everything he'd said, but closed it and just thought about what he'd said for a few seconds. Did I find Nathaniel attractive? Well, yeah. But I found a lot of men attractive. That didn't mean I had to be intimate with them.

"*Ma petite*, I can hear you breathing. What are you thinking?"

What he said made me think a new thought. "When we first married the marks I could almost read your mind, unless you concentrated to keep me out. Now it's not like that. Maybe the *ardeur* will be temporary, too."

"Perhaps, we can but hope."

"If I have the *ardeur*, I'll have to have sex. Isn't that what you wanted?"

"I would be a fool to deny that your enforced chastity is burdensome, but I would never willingly inflict the *ardeur* on anyone. It is a . . . curse, *ma petite*. The blood lust that I feel can be sated. My body can only hold so much. But the *ardeur*, oh, *ma petite,* it is never truly satisfied. There is always that ache, that need. How could I wish that upon you? Though if our Monsieur Zeeman would cooperate, it might be the answer for the two of you to finally reach some permanent arrangement."

"What, move in together?"

"Perhaps." His voice was very careful when he said that one word.

"Richard and I can't be in a room for an hour without arguing, unless we are having sex. Somehow I don't think that makes for domestic bliss."

I felt the first emotion he'd let me feel over the phone—relief. He was relieved. "I want what is best for all of us, *ma petite,* but as things grow more complex, I am no longer certain what 'best' would be."

"Don't tell me your machinations didn't include some backup plan to cover every eventuality. You are the ultimate plotter, don't tell me you missed a trick."

"I watched Belle Morte fill your eyes with her fire. You are acquiring powers as if you were a Master Vampire, or a Master Lycanthrope. How could I have planned for any of this?"

There was a cold knot of fear in the center of my gut. "So you finally admit that you don't know what the hell is going on either."

"*Oui,* does that please you?" I heard the first stirrings of anger in his voice. "Are you happy now, *ma petite?* I am well and truly out of my depth. No one has ever tried to forge an alliance such as we have, an alliance not of master and two slaves, but of three equals. I do not think you appreciate how gentle I am when it comes to hoarding my power. The wolves are my animal to call. Many masters would have forced them to simply be an adjunct to their own vampires."

"Nikolaos's animal to call was rats, not wolves," I said. "By the time you took over as Master of the City, Marcus and Raina's pack was too strong for you to make them an adjunct to your power. Hell, until you replenished the vamps that I killed, they were probably more powerful than you and your vampires."

"Are you implying that the only reason I am not a tyrant is because I didn't have the strength of arms to make it so?"

I thought about that for a second, then said, "I'm not implying it, I'm saying it."

"You think so little of me?"

"I know what you were like two, almost three years ago, and I think then you would have consolidated your power base with very little regard for anyone that got in your way."

"Are you saying I am ruthless?"

"Practical," I said.

It was his turn to be quiet for a second or two, then, "Practical, yes, I am that, as are you, *ma petite.*"

"I know what I am, Jean-Claude, it's you I'm not sure of."

"I would never willingly hurt you, *ma petite.*"

"I believe you," I said.

"I am not sure the same can be said of you," he said, quietly.

"I don't want to hurt either of you. But Richard cannot harm my leopards, and if you do anything stupid, don't blame me for what happens next."

"I would never underestimate your level of . . . practicality, *ma petite,* though I think Richard might."

"He told me I wouldn't kill him just for roughing up Nathaniel."

"How rough was Richard to little Nathaniel?"

"Don't talk about him like he's a child, Jean-Claude, and rough enough that I cut Richard's arm open."

"How badly?"

"The doc's stitching him up, even as we speak."

"Oh, dear," he said, and sighed, and this time the sound eased down my skin. I realized that he'd been behaving himself until now, at least about using his voice.

"No more games, Jean-Claude. I want to put Richard on the phone, and you tell him you did this on purpose."

"But I cannot tell him that I lied about Nathaniel, now can I?"

"You fix this, Jean-Claude, now, tonight. I need Richard to teach me how to call Gregory's beast. I don't have time for him to sulk."

"What am I to tell him, *ma petite*? What surety can I give him that you will not be in Nathaniel's arms tomorrow morning? I believe that I can maneuver Richard into staying the night, having him there at your side when the *ardeur* rises."

"Richard's already made his position clear, Jean-Claude. He doesn't let you, or Asher, or anyone, feed off of him. He doesn't see why the rules change just because it's me and sex, instead of blood."

"He said that?" Jean-Claude gave a questioning lilt to his voice.

"Yeah, he said that, almost word-for-word."

Jean-Claude sighed, and it sounded tired. "What am I to do with the two of you?"

"Don't ask me," I said, "I just work here."

"And what, exactly, does that mean, *ma petite*?"

"It means that we don't have a boss. It's great being equals, if that's what we are, but none of us knows what the hell is going on, and that isn't good, Jean-Claude. We are messing with some very serious stuff here, metaphysically and emotionally and just plain physically. We need some clue as to what we should be doing with all of it."

"And who should we be asking advice of, *ma petite*? If any vampire on the Council were to suspect that I have not given you both the fourth mark, they would destroy us, for fear that with the fourth mark we would become an even greater power."

"I've talked to Marianne and her friends. They're witches, Wiccan."

"So we find, what, a local coven, and ask their guidance?" He sounded patronizing.

"I resent the tone, Jean-Claude, especially since I don't hear you offering any better suggestions. Don't criticize unless you can do better."

"Very true, *ma petite*, and very wise. My deepest and most sincere apologies. You are quite right. I do not have a suggestion for whom we might turn to for advice, or guidance. I will think upon your suggestion to find a friendly witch to speak with."

"I have a friendly one to speak to. She just might need to see the three of us together to see how things work."

"You mean your Marianne?"

"Yeah."

"I thought she was more psychic than witch."

"There's not all that much difference," I said.

"I will take your word on that. I do not have much business with either."

I realized I'd been planning to call Marianne since I woke up sandwiched between Caleb and Micah. Funny how it had slipped my mind.

"Is there anything you can say to Richard that will help smooth things on this end?"

"Do you wish me to lie?"

"Damn it, Jean-Claude . . ."

"I can point out to him that if he does not meet the *ardeur*'s appetite that someone else must."

"I've already pointed that out to him." I thought about that for a few heartbeats. "He accused me of having . . ." I found I couldn't quite say it. "He accused me of doing worse with Nathaniel than I've done, and he was crude about it. I'm not sure I want to have sex with him right now."

"You are angry with him," Jean-Claude said.

"Oh, yeah."

"So angry that if he asked, you would refuse his bed?"

I started to say *yes*, then stopped myself. I was tired. Tired of all of it, of both of them, if the truth be known. Couldn't live with them, or without them. I wanted Richard's body like an ache in my heart, but when he wanted to be, he could be ugly, and his mood tonight was ugly. I didn't want to have sex with him when he was like this. Hell, I didn't want to be around him when he was like this.

"I don't know," I said.

"Well, that was honest, and does not bode well. If you refuse Richard, and Nathaniel, and your Nimir-Raj does not return tonight, what will you do in the morning, *ma petite*? Please, think carefully on this. I beg you to choose the lesser evil, whatever that may be, rather than wait until the hunger overrides your common sense, or even your need for survival."

"What are you saying?"

"I am saying what I have said before—that to deny the *ardeur* is to worsen it. Deny it long enough and hard enough, and it will begin to erode all that you are, or thought yourself to be. I survived what I did to feed it in those first weeks, but my moral degradation had been accomplished years before I died. I say again, *ma petite*, that you will not take it as well as I did. I believe it will compromise your sense of who you are."

"And fucking Nathaniel isn't going to compromise me?"

He sighed. "Put that way, I do see your point. But how much more compromising would it be to seduce a stranger?"

"I would never do that."

"Is that not exactly what you did with the Nimir-Raj?" His voice was very quiet as he said it, very careful not to be accusatory.

I would have loved to have argued the point, but I hate to lose, and I was going to lose this one. "Alright, you've made your point."

"I hope so, Anita, I do hope so." He never used my name unless something was very wrong. Damn.

"You know, just once it might be nice to have normal problems."

"And what, exactly, is a normal problem, *ma petite*?"

Another point for Jean-Claude. "I don't know anymore."

"You sound tired, *ma petite.*"

"It's only a few hours until dawn. I've been up all night, so yeah, I'm tired." Just acknowledging it seemed to bring it on in a rush that left me rubbing my eyes, which smeared the eye shadow I'd put on onto my fingers and probably around my eyelids. I wore makeup so seldomly that I often forgot I was wearing it.

Richard came back into the kitchen with his bodyguards and the wererats in tow. He gave me a look, and it was not a friendly one.

"I've got to go," I said to Jean-Claude.

"Do you wish me to speak to Richard?"

"No, I think you've done enough damage for one night."

"I meant only to help."

"Sure you did."

"Ma petite."

"Yes."

"Be careful, and remember what I have said about the *ardeur*. There is no shame in it."

"Even you don't believe that," I said.

"Ah, you have found me out. There is no shame in feeding, if you feed immediately on a person of your own choosing. If you fight, then you will find yourself feeding on someone not of your choosing, in a place not of your choosing. I do not think you would enjoy that, *ma petite.*"

He was right about that anyway. "I'll talk to you tomorrow after you get up. I haven't forgotten Damian, you know."

"I did not think that you had, *ma petite*. I will look forward to your call."

I hung up without saying good-bye, mainly because I was angry, and scared. Not only did I have Richard to deal with tonight and Gregory to save, but tomorrow morning when I woke up, the *ardeur* would be there, waiting. There was a chance that it wouldn't be, that the one day was the only time I'd have it, but I couldn't count on that. I had to plan for the worst-case scenario. Worst case was I would wake up tomorrow and need to feed just like I had this morning. The big question was, who would I feed on, and could I live with myself after I'd done it?

35

I HATE BEING awake at three in the morning. It is the godforsaken heart of darkness when the body runs slow, and the brain runs slower, and all you want to do is sleep. But I had promises to keep, and miles to go before I could sleep. Or at least a couple of miracles to perform before I could go to bed.

Dr. Lillian had unhooked Gregory's IV, but he was still bundled in the quilts. He sat on the picnic table on the deck, cradled between Zane and Cherry. Dr. Lillian kept touching Gregory, checking his pulse, how clammy his skin was. She was frowning and clearly not happy. Nathaniel stayed by them, keeping the picnic table between him and Richard. Richard hadn't tried to hurt him again; in fact, he'd ignored him studiously. The other cats milled around near the sliding glass doors. The two wererat bodyguards, Claudia and Igor, were standing to one side of me as I leaned on the railing. They started following me around when Richard came out with his bandaged arm and Jamil and Shang-Da at his back.

Richard's power crept on the summer darkness like close thunder, making the hot, sticky night even thicker and making it harder to breathe. I think it was the press of his power, the edge of his anger, that made the wererats start acting like bodyguards. I'd tried telling them that Richard wouldn't hurt me, but Claudia had shrugged, and said, "Rafael told us to keep you safe, and that's what we're going to do."

"Even if I tell you that there is no threat?"

She shrugged again. "I'd say, you're a little too close to this one to make a sound judgment call."

I'd glanced at Igor. "You agree with her?"

"I never argue with a lady, especially one that can beat me at arm wrestling."

Igor's logic was hard to argue with, but it meant that I had acquired two tall, muscular shadows, and it irritated me. But neither of them gave a damn whether I was happy or not. They were following Rafael's orders, and my wishes didn't count.

So Richard and his bodyguards, and me, with mine, stood on the deck, facing Stephen, who had stripped off in preparation for the change. If you made the change with clothes on, you ruined them. Shapeshifters either haunted the thrift shops, looking for old clothes to wear on the night of the full moon, or went nude.

We all stood there in the circle of Richard's power. The energy built around us like invisible lightning lashing around us. The power literally crackled, raising the hair on our arms, raising the hair on our heads, like the hackles on a dog.

Jamil said, "Richard . . ." But one glance from Richard stopped him in mid-sentence. The power rose another notch, squeezing around us like some kind of giant hand.

"What's wrong, Richard? What's with the power display?" I asked.

He turned to me, and the anger in his face made me want to step back, but I didn't. I stood my ground, but it took effort.

"Do you want to save your cat?" he asked, voice thick with the emotion that showed on his face, that crackled in his power.

My voice was almost a whisper, "Yes."

"Then watch," he said.

He spread his hands in front of Stephen, keeping them about eight inches away from the smaller man's shoulders. The energy squeezed tight, and tighter, until I had to swallow to try and clear my ears, as if there'd been a pressure change. But swallowing didn't help. It wasn't that kind of pressure.

Richard's hands convulsed, as if his fingers were digging into something invisible just in front of Stephen. He staggered towards Richard, one step, and I was close enough to hear a small pained sound come from him. Richard balled his hands into fists, and something shimmered between them like heat caught in the close summer darkness. The bones in my face ached with the building power. The air was almost too thick to breathe, as if it had weight.

Richard made one abrupt movement with his hands and the pressure broke, like a storm finally bursting to life. For a second or two, I thought the heavy, clear liquid that burst around us was rain, but it was hot like blood, and it didn't fall from the sky. It burst from Stephen's body. I'd seen dozens of shapeshifters change, but nothing like this. It was as if Stephen's body blew apart in a rain of hot, thick fluids and small bits of flesh. The beast usually pulls itself from the human body, like a butterfly from a chrysalis, but not this time. Stephen's body folded over on itself, and his man-wolf shape was just suddenly standing there. It collapsed to its knees, panting, shivering.

I was left standing, not even breathing, covered in the rapidly cooling bits and pieces of Stephen's body. When I could breathe again, I gasped. "Jesus Christ."

Stephen's fur was the color of dark, golden honey. He crouched, shivering at Richard's feet. Again, the change may hurt while the person is going through it, but once it's over, they usually stand up and start moving around. Stephen seemed disoriented, almost like he was in pain. What the hell was happening?

He crawled the last few steps to Richard, laying his long, teeth-filled snout against his wolf king's jogging shoes. He was almost in a fetal position, great, muscular arms wrapped around golden fur, lying at his Ulfric's feet. It was extreme submissive behavior, and I didn't know why. Stephen hadn't done anything wrong.

I looked up at Richard. His white shirt was plastered to his body with the thick fluids. He turned his face to look at me, and the faint light of stars glistened in the wetness on his face. A thick piece of something slid down his cheek as he glared at me. The look on his face was defiant, as if he expected me to be angry with him.

I raised a shaking hand and wiped the worst of the gunk off of my face, flinging it onto the deck where it hit with a wet splat. I looked at the bodyguards. They too were spattered with the thick stuff, but not nearly as messy as Richard and I. They hadn't been standing as close. They all stared at Richard, stared at him with a mixture of horror and anger and astonishment on their faces, which let me know that something was very, very wrong.

I had to try twice before I could speak, and even then my voice was breathy. "I've seen a lot of shapeshifters change into their beasts, but I've never seen anything like that. Was it different because you called Stephen's beast instead of him doing it on his own?"

"No," Richard said.

I waited for more, but that was all he said, and it looked like all he intended to say. But *no* just didn't cover it. I looked at the others. "Okay, someone tell me what just happened here."

Jamil started to speak, then stopped and looked at Richard. "With my Ulfric's permission." The words were polite, but the tone was angry, almost defiant.

Richard looked at him. I couldn't see his face, but whatever look he gave Jamil, it was something that made the other man flinch. Jamil dropped to one knee in the spreading pool of thick liquid. He bowed his head. "I mean no offense, Ulfric."

"That's a lie," Richard said, and his voice was lower than normal, just a tone or two above a growl.

Jamil darted a glance upward, then bowed his head again. "I don't know what you want me to say, Ulfric. Tell me, and I will say it."

Richard turned back to me, leaving Jamil kneeling. "I didn't just call Stephen's beast, I tore it from his body."

I glanced down at Stephen, who was still crouched at Richard's feet. "Why?" I asked.

"It's usually punishment to do it this way."

"What did Stephen do?"

"Nothing." Richard's voice was harsh, almost as harsh as the look on his face.

"Then why punish him?"

"Because I could." His chin lifted when he said it, and that arrogance was back.

"What the hell is wrong with you, Richard?"

He laughed, and the sound was so inappropriate that it made me jump. He laughed, but it was too loud, too harsh. "Didn't this teach you how to call Gregory's beast?"

"I didn't learn a damn thing except that you're in a foul mood and taking it out on other people."

"You want to know what's wrong? You really want to know?"

"Yeah, I do."

"Get out of the way, Stephen," he said, and Stephen didn't even ask why, he just crawled out from between us.

We were left staring at each other, not quite two feet apart. What he'd done to Stephen seemed to have taken the edge off his power, but it was still there like some great slumbering thing pressing against the surface.

"Open the marks, Anita, feel what I'm feeling."

"I opened the marks already. I figured I had to, to learn how to do this."

"So it's just my shielding?" He made it a question.

I nodded. "I can feel your rage, Richard, I just don't know why."

"Just my shields between us and . . ." He shook his head, almost smiling, then he dropped his shields. It hit me like a physical force, drove me back a step. Anger so raw it filled my throat with bile; a self-loathing so deep that it drew tears down my cheeks in two hot lines. I stood there for a minute feeling Richard's pain, and it was suffocating.

I stared up at him, the tears still wet on my cheeks. "Richard, oh my God."

"Don't feel sorry for me, don't you *dare* feel pity for me!" He grabbed my arms when he said it, and the moment we touched, our beasts poured up from inside us and spread across our skins in a hot dance of power. His beast crashed through me, invisible, metaphysical claws ripping through my body. It was as if Richard's beast was trying to eat his way through my body. I screamed, and thrust my beast into his, and I felt claws ripping into meat. There was nothing to see with the eye, but I could feel it, feel fur and muscle and meat under claws and teeth. I screamed not just from the pain, but from the sensations of cutting Richard up. He hurt me, and I wanted to hurt him back. There was no more reasoning, no more thinking, just reacting.

Our beasts tore through each other, rolling, clawing, tearing. We collapsed on the deck, screaming. Dimly I could still feel Richard's hands locked on my arms as if he couldn't let go.

There was movement all around us. People hovering, but no one interfered, no one touched us. When we fell, they scattered, as if afraid to touch us. Voices shouting above our screams, "What's wrong? What's happening? Anita, Anita! Richard, control it!"

His beast was suddenly like a weight inside me, but it didn't hurt. The two energies lay quiet, leaning against each other, not mingling, just leaning. I could almost feel the solid push of his beast against something inside of me that had bones and fur, and wasn't me. I couldn't hear anything but the thundering of the blood in my own head. I felt Richard's weight on top of me, before I looked down to find him collapsed over me. His head rested on my chest. I could feel the pulse of the blood in his body, his heart racing against the skin of my stomach. I was covered in the cool slime from Stephen's body. One, I was lying in a pool of it; two, Richard had been covered in it, and he'd slid down my body. I was going to have to shower before I could go to bed, even if it was dawn. And I ached, ached as if I'd been beaten. I knew I'd be stiff when I moved.

Everyone was standing in a ring above us, staring down. I found my voice, hoarse, almost raspy, but clear. "Get off of me."

Richard raised his head, slowly, as if he hurt, too. "I'm sorry."

"You're always sorry, Richard, now get off of me."

He didn't move, in fact he settled heavier, hands curving at the edges of my waist. "Do you still want to help Gregory?"

"That's what this whole show is about, so yeah."

"Then let's try again."

I tensed, and started trying to wriggle out from under him. His hands tightened at my waist. "Easy, Anita, it won't hurt. I don't think."

"Says you. It hurt like a son of a bitch. Let me go, Richard." My voice held the beginnings of anger, and fear. I liked the anger, could have done without the fear.

"You fought me to a standoff. It's over," he said.

I stopped struggling and stared at him. "What are you talking about?"

"We're not the same kind of animal, Anita. They had to find out who's . . . tougher."

I stared down the line of my body into those brown eyes. "Are you saying this was some kind of dominance display?"

"Not exactly."

Strangely, it was Merle who answered. "When two such different beasts meet, and they are both strong dominants—such as a true Nimir-Ra, and a true Ulfric—the two animals must fight and test each other. I have seen it before. It is a type of taming of one beast by the other."

I looked way up at the tall man. "No one tamed anyone."

Merle knelt beside us. "I think you are right. It is as the Ulfric has said, a standoff. He could have kept fighting until one of you won, or lost, but he chose to let it be."

I remembered someone telling Richard to control it, *it* being his beast. I looked at Richard. "You stopped, didn't you?"

"I don't care which of us is more dominant, Anita. Those kind of games have never meant anything to me, unless people forced me to play them."

"You said something about helping Gregory. What did you mean?"

He started working his way a little higher up my body, sliding his body along mine. I could feel the slime from his shirt recoating my bare stomach and nearly bare chest. My disgust must have shown on my face, because he asked, "What's wrong?"

"Your shirt is covered in slime, and I'm lying in a pool of it. I didn't just want you to get off me to be off of me, I wanted to get up out of this mess."

He came to his knees, his legs on either side of mine. I could feel our beasts stretched between us like something that should have been visible, as if each of their heads was buried in the other's chest. He offered me a hand. I stared up at him.

"I know you don't need the help, Anita. But our beasts are touching now. It's a close connection and physical contact will help us keep it until we finish with Gregory."

I didn't need the earnest look on his face to know he was telling the truth. The marks were still open between us. I knew he was telling the truth.

I took his hand and he lifted me to my feet. Standing up hurt, and either he felt it or saw it on my face. "I hurt you," he said softly.

"We hurt each other." I could feel that he was stiff, aching, but he moved like he wasn't, and I still moved human stiff.

He raised the bottom of his shirt, still holding my hand. "Touch me."

I looked up at him, and he laughed. "Just keep physical contact, Anita. I don't mean anything by it. But I need both my hands."

I laid a hand on his side, very tentatively.

He shook his head. "I'm going to take my shirt off."

If you can't touch a person's hands, arms, or much of their upper body, you run out of polite places to touch. I settled for sliding my hand under the wet shirt, touching the smooth firmness of his side. Even his skin was damp from the shirt having molded to it.

Richard drew the shirt over his head, and I was left standing inches from him as he revealed the flat plains of his stomach, the muscular swell of his chest, and arched his back to draw the shirt over his head. The sight of him, the pull of the lust that always came when I saw him without clothes pushed my beast against his. I felt furred sides roll against each other, a tentative roll of power that felt like someone had taken velvet and caressed the most intimate part of me.

Richard gasped.

I concentrated hard to stop the movement, but that I'd done it without thinking brought heat in a wash up my face. I looked at the ground; my hand was still only touching his side, just above his jeans, but the touch felt suddenly intimate. I wanted to take my hand away, and his hand covered mine before I could move. He pressed my hand to him, firm, but not forceful.

He touched my chin, raised my face until I had to look at him. "It's alright, Anita. I love the fact that just seeing me moves you like that."

The blush that had been fading, blazed harder. He laughed, soft, low, with that edge that a man's laugh gets when he's thinking intimate things. "I have missed you, Anita."

I looked up at him. "I missed you, too."

His beast moved through me in a wash of power and sensation that left me gasping. My beast responded to his. I couldn't seem to stop it. Maybe I didn't want to. Those shadow forms rolled in and out of each other, through us, until I couldn't breathe, couldn't think. It was Richard who drew back first, and said, "Dear God, I never thought . . ." I felt the effort it cost him to draw back from me, to stop. His face showed a businesslike, no-nonsense look, but I could feel the trembling of other things inside him. His voice came out brisk. "I'll call Jamil's beast, the way it's supposed to be done. Feel what I do, how I use my beast to call his."

My voice was a little breathy. "Then I'll do Gregory."

He nodded. "Or I can call Shang-Da's beast, if you need to see it one more time."

I nodded. "Okay."

He slid a hand around my waist, drawing me against him. It didn't seem as intimate as the roil of our beasts inside us. Jamil stood facing us. He'd stripped off his shirt and shoes, but kept on his pants. It occurred to me for the first time that I'd never seen him nude, except when he'd been injured and near death. Jamil didn't do casual nudity. One of the few modest shapeshifters I knew.

"I'm ready, Ulfric."

After what Richard had done to Stephen I thought Jamil was being awful trusting. But then, everyone trusted Richard; he was very trustworthy. No, lack of trust wasn't the problem.

"I don't need to physically touch anyone to do this, but it's easier that way, so I'll touch him, so you can understand better how it works."

I nodded, wrapped in the circle of his arm, the firmness of his body, the velvet roll of our beasts like another arm to hold us against each other.

Richard touched Jamil's bare shoulder, and I felt his power move outward like a warm wind. It caressed Jamil's skin, and Richard's beast flowed with it, pulling mine along for the ride. Richard's power teased along Jamil, coaxing, and the best analogy I could think of was like someone trying to lure a cat down out of a tree. Beckoning, talking sweetly, promising caresses, and treats, if only it would come down. But Jamil's beast didn't come down, it came out. It rolled out of the center of his being like a pale golden fog, an almost shape. I saw his beast like I'd seen Micah's earlier, for an instant, then Jamil collapsed to the deck, and his bare back began to ripple like water under a strong wind. The wolf drew out of his back in a long wet line, and his body dissolved into that dark furred shape, so that his human body became the wolf, like flipping over a coin, heads, tails, but still the same coin. I felt the rightness of it, the harmony of it. Jamil embraced what he was; there was no conflict between him and his beast. I'd never seen him in wolf form, man-wolf, but not this pony-sized black beast. He was like Little Red Riding Hood's worst nightmare.

The wolf shook himself, and I realized that his fur was dry. There was more of that clear goop all over the deck, but very little of it had clung to the wolf itself. Yet another metaphysical mystery: How do werewolves stay dry when shapeshifting is such a mess?

I turned without a word, drawing Richard with me. I went to Gregory, still sitting on the picnic table, only Cherry and Dr. Lillian with him now. Zane had come to see what the matter was when Richard and I started writhing on the deck.

Gregory looked at me, blue eyes silvered in the moonlight. I smiled and touched his cheek, cupped the side of his face against my hand. I reached for his beast, not with my hand, but with that shadowy thing that swirled through Richard and me. I sent it shivering across Gregory's skin, and he sat up, letting the quilt fall away from his bare upper body. Cherry moved away just enough so they wouldn't touch, as if she was afraid to touch him now.

I tried to coax his beast, to call it with sweet caresses and gentle persuasion, but it remained stubbornly just under the surface, trapped by the drugs that still made Gregory's body a prison and the shock that had further dampened everything I needed to call. But I knew that it didn't have to be gentle. I might not have been along for the ride when Richard brought Stephen's beast, but I'd seen it, and I knew enough of power to guess what he'd done.

"I'll try not to hurt you," I said, but I thrust my power into Gregory. I felt it hit his chest and sink into him like a large flesh-and-fur blade.

Gregory gasped, back arching, just a little.

I found his beast like a curled cat, asleep, sluggish, and I grabbed it in my hand, sank claws in it and pulled it screaming into the air. I ripped his beast out of him, and Gregory shifted, as Stephen had shifted in an explosion of blood, flesh, and fluid. I was covered in it, so thick I had to scoop it out of my eyes to see. To see that yellow and black spotted man-leopard lying hunched on the table. I watched Stephen come to sniff along his brother's shivering body.

"Gregory, Gregory, can you hear me?" I asked, and my voice was softer than I meant it to be.

Gregory blinked leopard eyes at me, but a growling voice came out of that furred throat. "I can hear you."

Stephen threw his head back and bayed. Jamil echoed him, and the leopards' screams of triumph filled the night.

36

DAWN WAS SLIDING through the trees in a wash of white, white light that left the trees looking like black paper cutouts against the shining sky when I pulled the curtains and filled the bedroom with twilight dimness. I'd put very heavy curtains in the room when Jean-Claude had been a frequent visitor. The bedside lamp seemed dim after the glow of sunrise. Nathaniel sat on the edge of the bed by the lamp. He was wearing the bottoms of silk pajama shorts. They were a pale lavender silk that echoed his eyes and looked too delicate a color for men's sleepwear. I always suspected the shorts were originally designed for a woman, but shorts were shorts.

The lamplight caught red highlights in his auburn hair, where it gleamed down the side of his body like something warm and alive, almost separate. Strangely, in wereleopard form, he was a black panther, so that auburn hair vanished once he left human form.

Nathaniel was the only one of the wereleopards still in human form. So he was the only one that got to share my bed. If they were kitty-cats, they had to sleep elsewhere, but in human form we tried to be a big pile of puppies. Somehow it was less comfy with only Nathaniel than it would have been with more of them. Maybe it was the fact that his right nipple still had a circle of my teeth marks.

"Shouldn't the bite marks have healed by now?" I asked.

"I don't heal as quickly as some," he said softly. "And marks made by another shapeshifter, or even a vampire, heal more slowly."

"Why is that?"

He shrugged. "Why does silver kill us, and steel not?"

"Point taken," I said. I ran my hand through my still-damp hair. I'd showered and was actually wearing pajamas, not an oversized T-shirt, which was my usual sleep attire. Though *pajamas* may have been too big a word for the emerald green camisole and matching short-shorts. There was a floor-length robe in the same vibrant green, so everything was covered, but Nathaniel knew I hadn't dressed up for him. Or at least I hoped he did.

He watched me pacing the room with careful eyes. We had crossed a line, he and I, and the mark on his chest just kept reminding me of it. I didn't think that Richard would tolerate Nathaniel and me sharing the bed alone, not that I really expected the three of us to bunk together, either. Oh, hell, I didn't know what I expected. I had expected Richard to come to me after his shower. But he was a no-show, and it was dawn, and I was tired.

There was a firm knock on the door. I said, "Come in," with my heart beating a little too fast. Merle opened the door, and I hoped my disappointment didn't show on my face. His own face registered nothing, so I couldn't judge what he saw on mine.

"The Ulfric is in the kitchen." He did look uncomfortable then. "He is crying."

I felt my eyes widen. "Excuse me?"

Merle looked down, then up, almost defiant. "He has ordered his bodyguard out of the room, and he is crying. I do not know why."

I sighed. Although I was tired, I was excited at the thought of Richard being in the house, of him coming to me, maybe. Instead of sex we were going to have another session of hand-holding, and shoulder-crying. Damn it.

I felt my shoulders slump and forced myself to stand upright again. I didn't have to ask why Merle had told me. Who else would Richard take comfort from? I wasn't even a hundred percent sure he'd take comfort from me.

I went for the door. Merle held it open for me, and I walked under his arm without having to duck. "Thanks for telling me, Merle," I muttered as I went out into the darkened living room.

Shang-Da was leaning against the wall by the open doorway that led into the kitchen. He looked as uncomfortable as I'd ever seen him. He wouldn't meet my eyes. What was going on?

Caleb was settled on the couch with a blanket and an extra pillow. He was sitting up, the blanket bunched in his lap. He was nude from the waist up and probably nude from the waist down if no one had made him wear jammies. I hoped someone had remembered to put a sheet on the couch. He watched me walk across the room, and even in the dim light from the kitchen I didn't like the way his eyes followed me.

"Nice robe," he said.

I ignored him and went for the doorway. Richard sat at the kitchen table. He'd opened all the curtains so that the room was filled with the soft light of dawn. His shoulder-length hair had been blow-dried to a soft, fluffy mass. I could never blow-dry my hair without it turning to something thick and awful-looking. The early morning light made his hair look more golden than normal, less brown. He looked up, and I realized the gold glow was a halo effect of the rising sun. It painted a nimbus of shining gold around him, leaving his hair light brown around his face, making the skin at the center of his body look even darker than it was, almost like it was in shadow.

I had a moment to see the shine of tears on his shadowed face, then he lowered his head and twisted in his chair so I couldn't see. The movement placed more of his body in the burning golden light, but the illusion of halos and shadow was gone.

I walked to the table, stood close enough to touch his bare shoulder, not sure if I should. "Richard, what's wrong?"

He shook his head, still not looking at me.

I reached out, touched the smoothness of his shoulder gently. He didn't tell me to go away, and he didn't pull away. Okay. I touched the tears on the cheek closest to me, smoothed them away with my hand. It reminded me of comforting Nathaniel earlier.

I touched Richard's chin, turned his face to me, and dried the tears on his other cheek with the sleeve of my robe. "Talk to me, Richard, please."

He smiled. Maybe it was the "please." I didn't use that word often. "I've never seen this before." He touched the sleeve very gently.

I wasn't going to be distracted, not even by him noticing what I'd worn with him in mind. "You have to be as tired as I am, Richard. What's keeping you up?"

He looked down, then up, and there was such sorrow in his dark eyes, that I almost said, *no, don't*, but he needed to talk. "Louisa is in jail, and Guy is dead."

I frowned. "I don't know the names."

"Louisa is one of our newest wolves." He looked down again, not meeting my eyes. "Guy is her fiancé . . . husband. *Was* her husband." He covered his face with his hands, shaking his head over and over and over.

I held his wrists, lowered his hands so I could see his eyes. "Richard, talk to me."

His hands turned in my grip, holding my hands. We held hands while I watched the pain in his eyes spill out in words. "Louisa killed Guy on their honeymoon, yesterday. I got the call just before I came here."

"I still don't understand. It's awful, tragic, but . . ." I said.

"I was her sponsor. I trained her to control her beast, and she lost that control on her honeymoon in the middle of . . ." He lowered his head, and raised my hands so that his forehead rested against the back of my hands.

"She lost control in the middle of sex," I finished for him.

He nodded, his face still pressed to my hands. "Losing her virginity," he said, voice muffled, low.

"Did you say virginity?"

He pulled away from me then, dropped his hands in his lap, and I noticed for the first time that he was wearing a towel knotted at his waist. "Yes."

"You mean she'd never tried to control her beast during intercourse?" I asked.

He shook his head. "They'd been engaged for more than two years before Louisa was attacked and became one of us. They both wanted to wait for the wedding night."

"Commendable," I said. "And orgasm, to a certain extent, is orgasm. If she could control herself during nonintercourse orgasm, then she should have been able to control herself during intercourse, too." I touched his shoulder again. "You did all you could for her."

He jerked away as if I'd burned him, coming to his feet so suddenly that the chair crashed back against the kitchen island, then the floor. I sensed rather than saw people in the doorway. I said, "We're alright." I turned to see Shang-Da, Merle, and the two wererats, still hesitating in the doorway. "We're alright, go away." They all pulled back, but I knew now that we had an audience, because they wouldn't go far.

Richard stood in the middle of my kitchen wearing nothing but a towel and the golden first light of dawn. Normally it would have distracted me from anything reasonable, but not this morning. The pain in his face was more important than his body right now. Looking at him, standing there so defiant, so hurt, I had an idea, an awful idea.

"Please tell me you don't mean she wanted to wait for *any* sexual contact until the honeymoon?"

His chin raised, and that arrogance tried to slide over him. But it was a mask, and I saw through it now. Underneath he was scared and guilty. "I taught her to control the beast during anger, sadness, fear, pain, every extreme of emotion, but not sex. I respected her convictions."

I stared at him. It was so something Richard would do. Theoretically, I even approved, but theory and practice aren't the same. In real life it had been a bad idea, and Richard should have known that better than I did.

I felt my face go blank, empty. It was a good cop face. I didn't want anything I was thinking to show for this. "So this Louisa shifted in the middle of sex and killed her husband, and the cops caught her." I didn't add that I was surprised they hadn't shot her on sight. Finding the big bad wolf eating the body of the nice little human would be cause enough for shooting to kill.

"Louisa turned herself in. I think if she didn't think suicide was a sin, she'd have killed herself." He turned my way walking to the sliding glass doors, leaning his forehead against the glass, as if he was tired.

I wished I could have said it wasn't his fault, but it was. He was her sponsor, the one who was supposed to teach her how to be a shapeshifter. I'd learned from dealing with the wereleopards, and Richard, and Verne's pack in Tennessee that orgasm of any kind was one of the true tests of their control. Orgasm was supposed to be a release, but to truly give up all control meant shifting form, and that was the ultimate nightmare when you had a human lover. Richard had lectured me often enough when we were dating that he didn't trust himself the night of the full moon, or even the day before. He didn't fear losing control and killing me, just losing control and scaring me to death. Or more honestly, grossing me out. He had shifted on top of me once, and that had had nothing to do with sex. And that one experience had sent me running to Jean-Claude. Well, Richard changing on top of me and seeing him eat someone.

I didn't know what to say. All I knew was that I had to say something, that silence was almost worse than anything.

He spoke without turning around. "Go ahead, Anita, tell me I'm a fool. Tell me I sacrificed both of them on the altar of my ideals." His voice was bitter enough to choke on, just hearing the pain in it.

"Louisa and her husband wanted to hold true to who they were. You wanted to help them do that. It's perfectly, logically you." My voice was empty, but at least it wasn't reproachful. It was the best I could do. Because it was a waste, a waste because Richard and the girl and her fiancé had been more worried about appearance than reality. Or maybe I'm just cynical, and tired, oh, so tired.

It was like any really good tragedy—entirely dependent on the personalities of the people involved. If Richard had been more practical and less idealistic; if Louisa and her late husband had been less religious, less pure; hell, if the husband really brought her to orgasm with just intercourse, then if he'd only been less talented. So many things had gone into making all the good intentions go horribly wrong.

"Yes, it was perfectly, logically me, and I was wrong. I should have at least forced her to have her first experience with Guy where the pack could oversee it, save him. But Louisa was so . . . delicate about it. I just couldn't insist. I just couldn't make her strip down in front of strangers and have her most intimate moment witnessed. I just couldn't do it."

I didn't know what to say. I did the only thing I could think of to comfort him. I went to him and put my arms around his waist, put my cheek against the smooth firmness of his back, and held him. "I am so sorry, Richard, so very sorry."

His body started to shake, and I realized he was crying again, still soundlessly, but not gently. Great racking sobs shook his body, but the only sound he allowed himself was the harsh shaking of his breath as he gasped, trying to get enough air.

He slid slowly to his knees, his hands making harsh sounds down the glass of the door, as if he were taking skin off as his hand slid down the glass. I stayed standing, leaning over him, cradling his head against my body, my hands on his shoulders and chest, trying to hold him.

He fell backwards, and I was suddenly trying to hold all his weight as he went for the floor. I tripped on the hem of the robe, and we ended in a heap on the floor, with his head and shoulders in my lap and me struggling to sit up. The knot on the towel had loosened, and a long, uninterrupted line of his body showed from his waist down his hip to his foot. The towel was still in place, but it was losing the battle.

His mouth opened in a soundless cry, then suddenly there was sound. He gave one ragged, tear-choked scream, and the sound seemed to free something inside him. Because the sobbing was suddenly loud, full of small, awful, painful sounds. He sobbed, and whimpered, and screamed, and clutched at my arms, hard enough that I knew I'd be bruised. And all I could do was hold on, touch him, rock him, until he quieted. He finally lay on his side, his upper body as far into my lap as he would fit, the rest of him curled up so that one thigh covered him. The towel formed a heap on the floor underneath him. I didn't even know when the towel had fallen away. I was sort of proud of that, because usually when I see Richard naked, I lose about forty points of IQ and most of my reasoning ability. But now, his pain was so raw, that that took precedence. It was comfort he needed, not sex.

He finally lay quiet in my arms, his breathing slowed almost to normal. His eyelids had fluttered shut, and for a moment I thought he was asleep. Then he spoke, eyes still closed. "I appointed an Eros and Eranthe for the pack." His voice was still thick with all the crying.

Eros was the Greek god of love, or lust, and Eranthe was the muse of erotic poetry; in werewolf lore they were the names for sexual surrogates. A man and a woman that did what needed doing when a werewolf's sponsor was too squeamish. Verne's pack had them, because Verne's lupa was very jealous of her Ulfric, and sometimes you just needed someone who isn't emotionally involved.

"That's good, Richard. I think it will make things easier."

He opened his eyes, and they were bleak. It made my chest ache to see that look in his eyes. "There are other positions that would make a lot of things easier," he said, voice thick and low.

I tensed up. I couldn't help it, because I knew that there were titles among the lukoi that would make all the problems he'd created in the pack fixable. There were titles that amounted to executioners, torturers. The lukoi have a long history through some very harsh times. Very few packs fill these slots anymore. Most don't see the need, but then most Ulfrics are good little tyrants; they don't need to delegate the rough stuff.

"Do you know what Bolverk means?" Richard asked softly.

"It's one of the names of Odin. It means worker of evil." My voice was almost as soft as his.

"You didn't remember that from a semester of comparative religion back in college."

"No," I said. My pulse had sped up. I couldn't help it. Bolverk was the title for what amounted to someone who did the Ulfric's evil deeds. It could be anything from trickery, to lies, to murder.

"You asked Verne about it, didn't you?"

"Yes." I kept my voice low. I was afraid to be loud, afraid he'd stop talking. I thought I knew where the conversation was going, and I wanted to get there.

"Jacob is going to challenge Sylvie," Richard said, and his voice was growing stronger, "and he'll kill her. She's good, but I've seen Jacob fight. She can't win."

"I haven't seen him fight, but I think you're right."

"If I made you Bolverk . . ." He stopped. I wanted to yell at him to finish, but I didn't dare. All I could do was sit there, very still, and try not to do anything that would change his mind.

He started over. "If I made you Bolverk, what would you do?" That last was soft again, as if he couldn't quite believe he was saying it.

I let out a breath I hadn't even realized I was holding and tried to think. Think before I spoke, because I'd only get one shot at this. I knew Richard, and if what I said didn't meet with his approval, the offer would go away, and he might never be willing to ask for this kind of help again. I'd seldom been so eager to speak and so afraid at the same time. I prayed for wisdom, diplomacy, help.

"First, you'd need to announce my new title to the pack, then I'd choose some helpers. I'm allowed three, Baugi, Suttung, and Guunlod."

Richard said, "The two giants Bolverk tricked to get the mead of poetry, and Guunlod, the giant's daughter, who he seduced for it."

"Yes."

He rolled his upper body over, so he was looking up at me. "You spent almost every weekend of the last six months in Tennessee. I thought you were just studying with Marianne, learning how to use your talents, but you were studying the lukoi, too, weren't you?"

I tried to be very careful, as I said, "Verne's pack runs very smoothly. He's helped me make the wereleopards into a true pard."

"You don't need a Bolverk or a Guunlod to make the leopards into a pard." His gaze was very direct, and I couldn't lie to him.

"I was still your lupa, but not a werewolf, the least I could do was learn about your culture."

He smiled then, and it reached his eyes, just a little—chased that lost look away. "You didn't care about the culture."

That pissed me off. "Yes, I did."

His smile widened, his eyes filling with light, the way the sun filled the sky as it rose above the edge of the world. "Alright, you cared about the culture, but that wasn't why you wanted to know about Bolverk, the evildoer."

I looked down, feeling just a little embarrassed. "Maybe not."

He touched my face lightly, turning me to look down at him again, to meet his gaze. "You said you didn't know about Jacob before you talked with him on the phone."

"I didn't," I said.

"Then why ask Verne about Bolverk?"

I stared down into those true-brown eyes and spoke the truth. "Because you are kind and fair and just, and those are lovely things to have in a king, but the world is not kind, or fair, or just. The reason Verne's pack runs smoothly, the reason my pard runs smoothly, is because Verne and I are ruthless when we need to be. I don't know if you could be ruthless if you had to be. But I think it would break you, if you managed to pull it off."

"Having you be ruthless for me is going to break something inside of me, Anita. Something that's important to me."

I stroked his hair, feeling the thick softness of it. "But me doing it won't break as much, or as badly, as you doing it, Richard."

He nodded slowly. "I know, and I hate myself for that."

I leaned over and kissed his forehead, very gently. I spoke with my lips touching his skin. "The only true happiness, Richard, lies in knowing who you are—what you are—and making peace with it."

His arm curved up around me, holding me against him. He spoke with his mouth against the hollow of my throat. "And are you at peace with what you are?"

"I'm working on it," I said.

He kissed my throat, very softly. "Me too."

I drew back enough to see his face, and his hand thrust upward through my hair, pulled my face down to his. We kissed, soft, then harder, his lips, his tongue, his mouth working at mine. I cupped his face in my hands and kissed him—kissed him long and hard. When I drew back, breathless, I found that he'd rolled his lower body over and lay on his back, nude. He laughed at the expression on my face and pulled me down towards him. I lost that forty points of intelligence and all my reasoning skills as he undid my robe and I ran my hands down the long line of his body.

I had just enough self-possession left to say, "Not here. We've got an audience in the living room."

His hand slid under the green satin of the camisole, curving around to my back, pulling me against him. "There's no place in the house that they won't hear us, smell us."

I pulled back from him before he could kiss me. "Gee, Richard, that makes me feel a lot better."

He propped himself up on one arm, staring down at me. "We can go into the bedroom if you want, but we won't be fooling anybody."

I didn't like that, and it must have shown on my face, because Richard drew his hand out from under my top, and said, "Do you want to stop?"

We hadn't really gotten started, but I knew what he meant. I looked into the solid brown of his eyes, traced the edge of his jaw with my gaze, the fullness of his lips, the curve of his throat, the spread of his shoulders, the way his hair fell around him, catching the early morning light, bringing out shades of gold and copper in his hair, the swell of his chest, his nipples already dark and hard, the flat line of his stomach with that thin, dark line of hair that went from his belly button to . . . the skin was darker, richer, you could almost smell the blood that pumped him full and hard. He looked ripe, like he was something full to bursting with life. I wanted to touch him, to squeeze, oh so delicately. I lay on the floor with my hands at my sides, my pulse beating in my throat, and said, "No, I don't want to stop." My voice was almost a whisper.

His eyes filled with that dark heat that spills into a man's face when he's almost a hundred percent sure of what's about to happen. His voice was deeper, that low note that most men's voices get when the excitement runs deep. "Here, or the bedroom?"

I tore my gaze away from him to look at the open doorway to the living room. There was no door to close. I needed more privacy than this. Even if they could hear us, even smell us in the bedroom, at least they wouldn't be able to see us. Maybe it was only an illusion of delicacy, but sometimes illusion is all you've got.

I looked back at him. "Bedroom."

"Good choice," he said, and got to his knees, taking my hand, so that when he got to his feet, he half-pulled me to mine. The movement startled me, and I fell against him. The height difference was enough that it put my hand on his hip and so very close to other things. It embarrassed me how very much I wanted to touch him, hold him. I started to pull away, because I was so close to losing all decorum and groping him right there in the kitchen. I wasn't entirely sure that if I grabbed him we'd make it to the bedroom. I wanted that door between us and everyone else.

He put his arms around my waist and lifted me off my feet, until our faces were even and I didn't know what to do with my legs. If I'd been sure we wouldn't be using the kitchen table I'd have wrapped my legs around his waist, but I didn't trust either of us that far. He put his arms under my butt, so that my head was slightly above his, and I rested in his arms almost like I was in a swing. I could still feel him pressed hard and firm against my body, but it had a certain decorum to it that straddling his waist lacked. He started walking for the door, carrying me, his eyes so intent on my face that he almost tripped on a chair. It made me laugh, until his eyes came back to meet mine, and I saw the need in those dark eyes. That one look robbed me of speech, and all I could do was stare into his eyes as he carried me into the bedroom.

37

THE BEDROOM WAS empty when he kicked the door shut behind us. I didn't know if the living room was empty or not. I couldn't remember anything but Richard's eyes from the kitchen to the bedroom. Every room might have been empty, for all I'd seen.

We kissed just inside the door; my hands were full of the rich thickness of his hair, the firm warmth of his neck. I explored his face with my hands, my mouth, tasted, teased, caressed, just his face.

He drew back from my mouth enough to say, "If I don't sit down, I'm going to fall down. My knees are weak."

I laughed, full-throated, and said, "Then put me down."

He half-walked, half-staggered to the bed, laying me on it, going to his knees beside it. He was laughing as he crawled onto the bed beside me. He lay beside me, his knees hanging over the side of the bed, though since he was tall enough for his feet to actually touch the floor when he lay like that, maybe *hanging* wasn't the right word. We lay beside each other on the bed, laughing softly, not touching.

We turned our heads to look at each other at the same moment. His eyes sparkled with the laughter, his whole face almost shining with it. I reached out and traced the lines of laughter around his mouth. The laughter began to fade as soon as I touched him, his eyes filling up with something darker, more serious, but no less precious. He rolled onto his side. The movement put my hand along the side of his face. He rubbed his face into my hand, eyes closed, lips half parted.

I rolled onto my stomach, and moved towards him, my hand still on his face. He opened his eyes, watching me crawl towards him. I propped myself up on hands and knees and watched his eyes as I leaned in towards his mouth. There was eagerness there, but there was also something else, something fragile. Did my eyes mirror that look, half-eager, half-fearful, wanting, afraid to want, needing, and afraid to need?

My mouth hovered over his, our lips touching, delicate as butterflies blown by a warm summer wind, touching, not touching, sliding along each other, gliding away. His hand grabbed the back of my neck, forced my mouth to press against his, hard, firm. He used his tongue and lips to force my mouth open. I opened to him, and we took turns exploring each other's mouths. He came to his knees, hand still pressed to the back of my neck, our mouths still locked together. He drew back, crawling backwards to the head of the bed, leaving me kneeling alone in the center of the bed. He reached under the covers, drew out pillows, propped himself up, watching me. There was something almost decadent about him naked, propped up, watching me.

I knelt looking back at him, having a little trouble focusing, thinking. I finally managed to say, "What's wrong?"

"Nothing," he said, voice deep, lower than normal. It wasn't the growl of his beast, it was a peculiarly male sound. "I want to run my beast through you, Anita."

For a split second, I thought it was a euphemism, then I realized he meant exactly what he'd said. "Richard, I don't know."

"I know you don't like otherworldly stuff during sex, but Anita . . ." he settled into the pillows in a strange smoothing motion that somehow reminded me that he wasn't human, "I felt your beast. It rolled through me."

Just hearing it out loud took a little of the glow off for me. I slumped back against the bed, still on my knees, but no longer upright, hands limp in my lap. "Richard, I haven't had time to think this through. I don't know how I feel about it yet."

"It's not all bad, Anita. Some of it can be wondrous."

This from the man who had hated his beast for the entire time I'd known him. But I didn't say that out loud. I just looked at him.

He smiled. "I know how strange that sounds coming from me."

I looked at him harder.

He laughed, settling lower on the pillows until he was sprawled in front of me. One leg bent up so he wouldn't touch me, but close enough that I could have touched him. He lay there unself-consciously nude, which I'd seen before, but it was more than that. He seemed bathed in a comfortableness that was rare for Richard. I'd seen it at the lupanar, that he'd accepted his beast. But it was more than that; he'd accepted himself.

"What do you want from me, Richard?"

This was his cue to get serious, to demand I be less bloodthirsty, or a half dozen other impossible things. He didn't. "I want this," he said, and I felt the prickling rush of his power a second before it passed through me like a warm ghost.

I shuddered with it. "I don't know, Richard. I don't know if this is a good idea." It would have sounded better if my voice hadn't had a tremble in it.

I expected him to question, or talk, but he didn't. I felt his power like a brush of thunder a second before it smashed into me. I had a second of panic, a moment to wonder if his beast and mine would claw me apart, then his power rubbed through me like a velvet glove. My beast rose as if from a great, warm, wet depth, up, up to meet the warm, burning rush of Richard's energy. He pushed his beast through me, and I could feel it, impossibly huge, the brush of fur so deep inside me that I cried out. I felt his beast as if it had crawled inside me and was caressing things from the inside that his hands would never have touched. My power seemed less certain than his, less solid. But it rose around the hard, muscled fur like velvet mist, swirling through his power, through my own body. Until it felt as if something huge was growing inside me, something I'd never felt before, swelling inside me. It felt larger than my body, as if I couldn't hold it inside myself, like a cup filled to the brim with something hot and scalding, but the liquid kept pouring in, and still I held it, held it, held it, until it burst over me, through me, out of me, in a roar of power that turned the world golden and slow, drew my body to its knees, curved my back, sent my hands clawing at the air trying to hold on to something, anything, while my body spilled apart and remade itself on the bed. For a space of labored heartbeats I thought he'd brought on the change, and I had slipped my skin for real, but it wasn't that. I felt like I was floating and only gradually felt my body again. I lay on my back, my knees folded under me, hands limp at my sides, so relaxed it was like being drugged.

I felt the bed move under me, and a moment later, Richard appeared above me. He was on all fours, looming over me, and I had trouble focusing on his face. He cradled my face, staring into my eyes, while I tried to look at him. "Anita, are you alright?"

I laughed then, slow and lazy. "Help me get my knees straightened out, and I'll be fine."

He helped me straighten my legs, and even then all I wanted to do was just lay there. "What did you do to me?"

He lay down beside me, propped on one elbow. "I brought you, using the beasts."

I blinked at him, licked my lips, and tried to think of an intelligent question, gave up, and settled for what I wanted to know. "Is it always like that between lycanthropes?"

"No," he said and leaned over me, until his face filled my vision. "No, only a true lupa, or a true Nimir-Ra, can respond to my Ulfric the way you just did."

I touched his chest enough to back him up so I could see his face clearly. "You've never done that with anyone before?"

He looked down then, a curtain of his hair sliding over his face, hiding it from me. I pushed his hair back so I could see that nearly perfect profile. "Who?" I asked.

Heat washed up his neck and face. I wasn't sure I'd ever seen him blush before. "It was Raina, wasn't it?"

He nodded. "Yes."

I let his hair fall back in place and lay there for a few seconds thinking about it. Then I was laughing, laughing and couldn't stop.

He was back at my shoulder, peering down at me. "Anita?"

The laughter faded as I looked into his worried eyes. "When you forced Raina to give you up all those years ago, did you know that she was the only one that could do this with you?"

He nodded, face solemn. "Raina pointed out the downside to not being her pet."

I took his hand and slid it down the front of my satin bottoms. His fingertips found the wetness that had soaked through the satin, and I didn't have to guide his hand anymore. He cupped that big hand of his over my groin, and the cloth was soaked through. He traced fingertips across my inner thigh and the skin was wet, wet down to my knees.

"How did you give it up?" My voice came out in a whisper.

His finger slid up the inside of my thigh, in the hollow just below. He leaned in to kiss me as his finger slid slowly, slowly, upward across the moist skin, under the wet satin. His mouth stayed just above mine, so close that a sharp breath would have made us touch. He spoke, his breath warm on my skin, as his finger caressed the edge of me. "No amount of pleasure was worth her price." Two things happened at once; he kissed me, and his finger slid inside of me. I screamed against his mouth, back arching, fingernails digging into his shoulder, as his finger found that small spot and thrust over and over it, until he brought me again. The world had soft, white edges, like seeing through gauze.

I felt the bed move, but couldn't focus, couldn't see, wasn't sure I cared what was happening. Hands fumbled at my shorts. I blinked up to see Richard kneeling over me. He slid my shorts down, spread my legs, and knelt between them. He leaned over me raising the satin camisole, baring my breasts. He ran his hands across them, made me writhe, then moved his hands down the line of my body, his hands gripping my thighs, bringing me in a harsh jerk against his body.

The moment he rubbed against the outside of me, I felt the rubbery latex of the condom. I looked up at his face, and asked, "How did you know?"

He moved so that his lower body was lying between my legs, but still pressed against the outside of my body. Most of his weight was supported by his arms like a modified push-up position. "Do you really think Jean-Claude would warn me about the *ardeur* and not warn me that you weren't on birth control?"

"Good point," I said.

"No," he said, "this is." I felt the movement of his hips, seconds before he thrust inside me, in one powerful motion that drove sounds from my mouth, somewhere between a scream and a shout.

He lowered his head enough to see my face. I lay gasping under him, but whatever he saw there reassured him, because he arched his back, his face looking somewhere in the distance, and drew himself out of me, slowly, inch by inch, until I made small noises. He drew himself out until he was barely touching inside me. I gazed down the length of my body to see him stretched hard and ready. He'd always been careful of me, because he wasn't small; that one first thrust had been more force than he'd ever before allowed himself. He, like Micah, filled me up, hit that point deep inside that was either pain or pleasure. I saw his back and hips flex a second before he thrust into me. I watched him thrust into me, saw every inch of him plunge into me, until it bowed my back, my neck, and I couldn't watch because I was writhing underneath him, my hands scrambling at the bedspread, digging fingers into the covers.

He drew himself out of me again, and I stopped him with a hand on his stomach. "Wait, wait." I was having trouble breathing.

"It's not hurting you. I can tell by your face, your eyes, your body."

I swallowed, took a shaky breath, and said, "No, it's not hurting me. It feels wonderful, but you've always been so careful, even when I asked you not to be. What's changed?"

He looked down at me, his hair falling around his face like a silken frame. "I was always afraid of hurting you before. But I felt your beast."

"I haven't changed yet, Richard, we don't know for sure."

"Anita," he said softly, and I knew he was chiding me. Maybe it was a case of the lady protesting too much, but still . . .

"I'm still human, Richard, I haven't changed yet."

He leaned over me, his hair gliding around my face as he kissed me gently on the cheek. "Even before the first full moon, we can take more damage. The change has already begun, Anita."

I pushed against his chest until he drew back enough for me to see his face. "You've always been holding back, haven't you?"

"Yes," he said.

I searched his face and saw such need in his eyes, and I knew why he'd been so angry at Gregory. He'd said that he almost regretted not making me his lupa in truth, now that he'd seen me be Nimir-Ra, but it was more than that. I looked into his brown eyes in the spill of early morning light and knew that he'd wanted me to be what he was, even though he hated it, that at some level he'd been tempted to make me his lupa for real. Somewhere in the lovemaking where he had to be so careful, he'd thought of it, more than once. It was there in eyes, his face. He started to look away as if he could feel that I saw it all, but he made himself look back, meet my gaze. He was almost defiant.

"How careful have you been of me, Richard?"

He did look away then, using his hair as a shield. I reached through that thick hair to touch his face, to turn him to look at me. "Richard, how careful have you been of me?"

There was something close to pain in his eyes. He whispered, "Very."

I held his face between my hands. "You don't have to be careful anymore."

A look of soft wonderment crossed his face, and he bent his head down, and we kissed, kissed as we had earlier, propping, exploring, taking turns at thrusting into each other. He drew slowly back from the kiss, and I felt the tip of him touch my opening. I stared down the length of our bodies so I could watch as his body flexed above me, and he thrust himself inside me harder this time, quicker. It brought my breath in a soundless scream.

"Anita . . ."

I opened my eyes, not realizing I'd closed them. I gazed up at him. "Don't be careful anymore, Richard, don't be careful."

He smiled, gave me a quick kiss, then he was back, arched above me, and this time he didn't stop. He thrust every inch of himself into me as hard and as fast as he could. The sound of flesh into flesh became a constant sound, a wet hammering. I realized it hadn't been just his size that made him careful, but his strength. He could have bench-pressed the bed we lay on, and that strength lay not just in his arms, or back, but in his legs, his thighs, in the body he was pressing inside me, over and over again. For the first time ever, I began to appreciate the full power of him.

I'd felt the strength in his hands, his arms, when he held me, but it was nothing to this. He made of our bodies one body, one pounding, sweating, soaking, drenching piece of flesh. I was vaguely aware that it did hurt, that I was bruising, and I didn't care.

I called out his name as my body tightened around his, squeezing, and I spasmed underneath him, body slamming against the bed, not from Richard's thrusts, but from the power of the orgasm itself; screams spilled from my throat as my body rocked underneath him. It felt good, better than almost anything, but it was almost violence, almost pain, almost frightening. Somewhere in the midst of it all I was aware that he came, too. He screamed my name, but held his place, while I continued to writhe and fight underneath him. It wasn't until I lay quiet that he allowed himself to collapse on top of me, slightly to one side, so my face wouldn't be pressed into his chest.

We lay in a sweating, breathless heap, waiting for our hearts to slow enough to speak. He found his voice first. "Thank you, thank you for trusting me."

I laughed. "You're thanking me." I raised his hand to my mouth and kissed the palm, then rested his hand against my face. "Trust me, Richard, it was my pleasure."

He laughed, that rich throaty sound that is purely male, and purely sexual. "We're going to need another shower."

"Whichever of us can walk first can have the first shower," I said.

He laughed and hugged me. I wasn't even sure my legs would work enough to shower at all. Maybe a bath.

38

I WOKE JUST enough to feel the weight of someone at my back. I snuggled against that warmth, wrapping sleep back around me. An arm spilled over my shoulder, and I wriggled into the circle of arm and body. It wasn't the warmth, or the feel of him that woke me; the wereleopards had gotten me used to all that. It was the scent of his skin. By the scent alone, I knew it was Richard. I opened my eyes and snuggled deeper against him, curling that dark, muscled arm tighter around my body like drawing a cozy blanket around me. Of course, a blanket didn't have the hard weight of Richard, or the silken glide of his naked skin against mine, or the ability to cuddle back, to use hands to pull my body tighter in against him. He closed the distance, worked until, even with the height difference, his chest, stomach, and hips were curled around me. He gave one last movement, and I could feel him pressed hard and ready against the back of my body. It was morning, he was male, but it wasn't something embarrassing to be ignored. I could pay as much, or as little, attention to it as I wanted, and I wanted.

I started to roll over in the almost tight circle of his body and found I was stiff. My lower body felt bruised, aching, but in a good way. I laughed as he opened his arms enough for me to roll onto my back.

"What's so funny?" Richard asked.

I stared up at him, still laughing, I think to keep from groaning. "I'm stiff."

He wiggled his eyebrows at me. "So am I."

I blushed, and he kissed my nose, then my mouth, but still chaste, still not really sexual. It made me laugh. If it had been anyone but me, I'd have said I giggled.

The next kiss wasn't chaste, and the one after that pressed me back against the bed. He slid his leg between my thighs, until his knee touched me, and I winced.

He drew back. "Are you too sore for this?"

"I'm willing to give it the ol' college try," I said, "but honestly, maybe."

He stayed propped above me, fingers moving a lock of my hair from my cheek. "What I did last night would have broken things inside an ordinary human."

I didn't need a mirror to feel my eyes go cool. I'd really been trying not to think about it.

"I'm sorry," he said. "I didn't mean to ruin the mood." He smiled suddenly and looked younger, more relaxed than I'd seen him in a long time. "I'm just glad to be with someone I don't have to worry about hurting."

I had to smile at him. "I'm not hurt, but we might have to try something a little more gentle this morning."

The humor faded, and something else filled his eyes, as he lowered his face for another kiss. He spoke as he moved towards me. "I think we can come up with something." He kissed my lips, then worked one kiss at a time down my neck, my shoulders. He got distracted at my breasts, covering them in kisses, his tongue licking a quick, wet line across one nipple. He cupped one breast in his hands, holding it in the circle of his warmth, sliding his mouth over the nipple, taking as much of the breast into his mouth as he could. He sucked me into his mouth until he held over half my breast in the wet warmth. And with that touch, the *ardeur* flared up through my body from wherever it had been hiding.

Richard drew back from my breast, hands still cradling it. "What was that?" There were goosebumps on his arms.

"The *ardeur*," I said, voice soft.

He licked his lips, and I saw real fear in his eyes. "Jean-Claude told me about it, even let me feel his own version of it, but I didn't really believe it. I don't think I wanted to believe it."

My beast had awoken with the *ardeur*, as if one hunger fed the other. I felt it uncurl inside me and stretch for all the world, like some great cat waking from a nap. It rolled through me, reaching out to Richard, and his beast woke to it. One hand was on the solid warmth of his chest, but I could feel something else in there, something moving around as if his chest were hollow and there was something caged inside.

He gripped my hand, moved it back from his chest. "What are you doing?"

"The *ardeur* calls to our beasts, Richard." I snuggled down underneath him, my hand sliding down his body, tracing the flatness of his stomach, the curve of his hip. He grabbed my hand just before I could touch him. He had both my hands now, trapped in his larger ones. It didn't bother me, because I knew that I could touch him with things other than my hands, or even my body. I remembered the feel of his beast thrusting through me, and I spilled mine into him in a hot push of energy.

He jumped off of me, rolled out of the bed in a movement that was almost too quick to follow with the eyes. He stood by the bed, breath coming in ragged gasps, as if he'd been running. I could feel his fear like fine champagne. It added to the sex, brought me to my knees, to crawl from the tangle of covers to the edge of the bed. I could smell how warm he was; the scent of his skin came to me on the air, the faint sweetness of the cologne he'd put on the day before. My gaze wandered over the beauty of him. His sleep-tousled hair hung in a heavy mass over one side of his face. He brushed the thickness of it back from his face with one hand and a toss of his head, and that one simple movement made things low in my body tighten. But underneath the sex was the thought of what all that smooth, hard skin would feel like under my teeth. I wanted to mark him as I'd marked Nathaniel. I wanted to sink my teeth into his flesh and bite. I had a flash of what it felt like to taste him like so much meat, to feel his body respond, not just to the sex but to the hunger, and I knew for the first time why shapeshifters spoke of the hunger like it should be in all capital letters. Raina had risen her lascivious head. The *ardeur* overrode, or overpowered her, but she was there, supplying images to the things I was feeling. I slid off the bed, and Richard backed up.

I could see his pulse in his neck, beating like a trapped thing. His beast was trapped, too, trapped by his control, his fear. I could feel it, as if it were literally pacing inside his body, like a wolf in a cage at the zoo; pacing, pacing, never free. It might be a large, roomy cage, but it was still a cage. Raina gave me a visual that drove me to my knees. I saw Richard pinned under my body, chained to a bed, and when he came inside me, he shifted at the same moment. That was release for the shapeshifters; anything else was holding back.

Richard knelt in front of me. "Are you alright?" He touched my arm, and that was a bad thing. My beast roared across our skins, hit his in a blow that I felt physically in my stomach and ribs, like a punch. It staggered Richard, made him fall forward into me, and we clung for a second, arms around each other, our bodies pressed together. The *ardeur* flared over us like invisible flame, and we knelt in the heart of that fire like the wick of a candle. His heart beat against my arms, where they lay pressed to his chest, as if my skin had become a drum and he beat inside me, filled me with the rythmn of his body. My own heartbeat found a home inside Richard's body. We were filled with the rise and fall, the pulse and beat of each other, until I couldn't tell whose heart was in my chest, whose blood rushed through us. For a trembling moment we pressed above one another, as if our skin would give way and we would finally be what the marks had promised—one being, one body, one soul. The power broke apart, as Richard struggled against it, like a drowning man, breaking apart the power like arms shatter water; you can move it, disrupt it, but it flows back around you, swells over you, engulfs you. Richard screamed, and I felt him fall back.

I opened my eyes as his hand pulled away, and my hand tried to hold him. His hand was almost free, only his fingers still caught in mine, when the *ardeur* pressed around us, and I knew his control was fragile enough that I would feed. I felt his confusion, felt him struggling to decide what to hold on to and what to let go. I realized that the shields had come down long ago, because he couldn't hold the marks closed, keep himself in human form, and keep me from feeding, all at the same time. He screamed again, and I felt Richard decide, felt the conscious choice of the lesser evil. He shoved his beast down, down, deep inside himself, and he shut the marks between us like slamming a door. It was so sudden that it felt like the world had lurched. I had a moment of dizziness, was almost sick, then the *ardeur* rode over us, through us, like a thundering thing to trample us both underfoot, until we were just flesh, bone, blood, just meat, just need. I saw Richard's back arch, his head fling back, and through the *ardeur* I felt the growing pressure, tightness in his body, seconds before that hot release spilled over him, and I held his hand while his body rocked with the strength of it, and the pleasure of it drew me to my knees, almost as if the power itself lifted me up for a second, held me, rocked me, and I fed, I fed, and fed, and fed, until we were left lying on the floor, sweat-covered, breathing in gasps, our hands still locked together.

Richard pulled away first. He lay there, eyes unfocused, breathing labored, his heart beating too fast, filling his throat. He swallowed hard enough that it sounded like it hurt. I felt weighted, heavy with the feeding, almost like I could sleep again, like a snake after a big meal.

Richard found his voice first. "You had no right to feed off me."

"I thought that was the idea of you staying until morning," I said.

He sat up slowly, as if he were stiff now. "It was."

"You never said *no*." I rolled onto my side, but didn't try and sit up yet.

He nodded. "I know that. I'm not blaming you."

He was, but at least he was trying not to. "You could have stopped me, Richard. All you had to do was either leave the marks open between us or let your beast go. You could have held the *ardeur* out. You made your choice on what to control."

"I know that, too." But he wouldn't look at me.

I propped myself up on my arms, almost sitting. "Then what's wrong?"

He shook his head and got to his feet. He was a little unsteady, but he went for the door. "I'm leaving, Anita."

"You make that sound awfully permanent, Richard."

He turned and looked at me. "No one feeds off me, no one."

He'd closed himself so tight that I couldn't tell what he was feeling, but it was plain on his face. Pain. His eyes held some deep pain, and he'd pulled so far away in his mind, his heart, that I couldn't tell what it was, only that it hurt him.

"So, you won't be here tomorrow morning when the *ardeur* comes again?" My voice sounded almost neutral when I asked.

He shook his head, all that heavy hair sliding around his shoulders. His hand was on the doorknob, his body turned away enough that he hid himself from me as much as he could. "I can't do this again, Anita. For God's sake, you have the same rule. No one feeds on you either."

I sat up, arms wrapping around my knees, holding them tight to my chest. I guess I was covering my nakedness, too. "You've felt the *ardeur* now, Richard. If I can't feed off of you, then who? Who do you want me to share this with?"

"Jean-Claude . . ." But his voice dropped off before he could finish.

"It's a little after noon and he's still dead to the world. He won't wake in time to share the *ardeur* with me."

His hand tightened on the doorknob hard enough for me to see the muscles in his arm tense. "The Nimir-Raj, then. I'm told you've already fed on him once anyway."

"I don't know Micah that well, Richard." I took a deep breath and said, "I don't love him, Richard. I love you. I want you."

"You want to feed off me? You want me to be your cow?"

"No," I said, "no."

"I am not food, Anita, not for you or anyone else. I am Ulfric of the Thronnos Rokke Clan, and I am not cattle. I am the thing that eats the cattle."

"If you had shifted, then you could have blocked the *ardeur*, kept me from feeding, why didn't you?"

He leaned his forehead against the door. "I don't know."

"Honesty, Richard, at least with yourself."

He turned then, and his anger flared across my skin like a whip. "You want honesty, fine, we can have honesty. I hate what I am. I want a life, Anita. I want a real life. I want free of all this shit. I don't want to be Ulfric. I don't want to be a werewolf. I just want a life."

"You have a life, Richard, it's just not the life you thought it would be."

"And I don't want to love someone who is more at home with the monsters than I am."

I just looked at him, hugging my knees to my bare chest, my back pressed up against the bed. I looked at him, because I couldn't think of a damned thing to say.

"I'm sorry, Anita, but I can't . . . *won't* do this." He opened the door then. He opened the door, and he walked out, closing it behind him. The door closed with a soft, firm click. I sat there for a few seconds not moving. I don't even think I was breathing, then slowly the tears squeezed out, and my first breath was a ragged gasp that hurt my throat. I rolled slowly to the floor, lying in a tight, tight ball. I lay on the floor and cried until I was cold and shivering.

That's how Nathaniel found me. He pulled the blanket from the bed and wrapped it around me, picked me up, and climbed onto the bed with me in his arms. He held me in the curve of his body, spooned against me, and I couldn't feel him through the thick blanket. He held me and stroked my hair. I felt the bed move and opened my eyes to find Cherry and Zane crawling around me. They touched my face, took my tears with the tips of their fingers, and curled around me on the other side until I was cupped in their warmth.

Gregory and Vivian came next and climbed onto the bed until we all lay in a warm, thick nest of bodies and covers. And I was hot and had to peel the blanket back, and their hands spilled over me, touching, holding. I realized that I was still naked and so were they. No one ever put on clothes unless I made them. But the touching wasn't sexual, it was comfort, the warm pile of puppies, and everyone in that pile loved me in their way. Maybe it wasn't the way I wanted to be loved, but love is love and sometimes I think I'd thrown away more love than most people ever get a chance at. I was trying to be more careful lately.

They held me until I fell asleep, exhausted with crying, skin hot. But down in the center of my being was a cold, icy spot that they couldn't touch. It was the place where I loved Richard, had always loved Richard, almost from the first time I'd seen him. But he was right on one thing. We couldn't keep doing this. I wouldn't keep doing this. It was over. It had to be over. He hated what he was, and now he hated what I was. He said he wanted someone that he wouldn't have to worry about hurting, and he did want that, but he also wanted someone human, ordinary. He couldn't have both, but that didn't keep him from wanting both. I couldn't be ordinary, and I wasn't sure I'd ever been human. I couldn't be what Richard wanted me to be, and he couldn't stop wanting it. Richard was a riddle with no answer, and I was tired of playing a game I couldn't win.

39

I SLEPT LIKE I was drugged, heavy, with harsh, fragmented dreams, or nothingness. I don't know when I would have woken, but someone was licking my cheek. If they'd shaken me or called my name, I might have been able to ignore it, but someone was licking my cheek in long languorous movements that I couldn't ignore.

I opened my eyes and found Cherry's face so close I couldn't focus on it. She moved back just enough so I wouldn't feel cross-eyed looking at her, then said, "You were having a nightmare. I thought we should wake you."

Her voice was neutral, her face blank, cheerful in an anonymous sort of way. It was her nurse face, cheerful, comforting, telling you nothing. The fact that she was naked, lying on her side, propped up on one elbow so that her body showed in one long line didn't seem to distract from her professionalism. I could never pull that off naked. No matter what else was happening I was always aware that I didn't have clothes on.

"I don't remember what I was dreaming," I said. I raised a hand to smooth the wetness along my cheek.

"You taste salty from all the crying," she said.

The bed moved, and Zane peeked around my other shoulder. "Can I lick the other cheek?"

It made me laugh, and that was almost miracle enough to let him do it, almost. I sat up and instantly regretted it. My whole body felt stiff and abused, aching, as if I'd been beaten. Hell, I'd felt better after some of the beatings I'd taken over the years. I hugged the blanket to me, partially to cover my nakedness, partially because I was cold.

I leaned against the head of the bed, frowning. "You said nightmare. What time is it?"

"About five," Cherry said. "I could say *daymare*, if you like, but either way, you were—" she hesitated—"whimpering in your sleep."

I hugged the blanket tighter. "I don't remember."

She sat up, patting my knee under the blanket. "Are you hungry?"

I shook my head.

She and Zane exchanged one of those looks that say just how worried about you people are. It made me angry.

"Look, I'm okay."

They both looked at me.

I frowned at them. "I'll be okay, alright."

They didn't look convinced.

"I need to get dressed."

They both just lay there staring at me.

"Which means get out and give me some space."

They exchanged another of those looks, which bugged me, but at a nod from Cherry, they both got up off the bed and went for the door. "And put some clothes on," I said.

"If it'll make you feel better," Cherry said.

"It will," I said.

Zane gave a little salute. "Your wish is our command."

That was actually a little too close to the truth, but I let it go. When they were gone, I picked out some clothes, some weapons, and made it to the bathroom without seeing anyone. I wouldn't have put it past Cherry to make sure I had a clear shot to the bathroom. They were managing me, but this morning, make that afternoon, I didn't care enough to complain.

I was as quick in the bathroom as I could be, and for some reason I didn't like looking in the mirror. I was trying not to think, and seeing my eyes staring back at me like those of a shock victim made it hard not to think about why I looked so pale, so shell-shocked.

I put on my usual black undies and matching bra. It was getting to the point where I didn't own a white bra. Jean-Claude's fault. Black jogging socks, black jeans, black polo shirt, shoulder rig, complete with Browning Hi-Power, the Firestar in its interpants holster in front almost lost against the black shirt. I even added the wrist sheaths and the two silver knives. I didn't need this much firepower for walking around the house, especially with so many shapeshifters running around, but I was feeling shaky, as if my world was less solid today than yesterday. I'd always thought that Richard and I would work something out. I wasn't sure what, but something. Now, I didn't believe that. We weren't going to work anything out. We weren't going to be anything, except the bare miniumum to each other. I wasn't even sure his invitation to be Bolverk was still on the table. I hoped so. I could lose him as my lover, but I couldn't let him send the pack to rack and ruin. If he didn't cooperate, I wasn't sure how I was going to stop it, but that was a problem for another day. Today my goal was just to survive, just to get through the day. I huddled my weapons around me like comfort objects. If I'd been alone in the house, or if it had just been Nathaniel, I would have carried Sigmund, my stuffed toy penguin, around with me. That was how bad a day it was.

I did have a moment when I caught a glimpse of myself in the mirror in my bedroom where I stopped and had to smile. I looked like I was dressed in casual assassin chic. I'd teased some of my friends who were assassins or bounty hunters about assassin chic, but sometimes you gotta go with the stereotypes. Besides, I look great in black. The black-on-black look made my skin look almost translucent, like it should have glowed. My eyes were swimmingly dark. I looked almost ethereal, like a wingless angel on a bad day. Alright, maybe a fallen angel, but the effect was still striking. I'd learned long ago that if you're feeling unloved by the man in your life, the best revenge is to look good. If I'd really wanted to follow the strategy completely, I'd have put on makeup, but screw that. I was still on vacation. I didn't wear makeup on vacation.

There was a crowd in the kitchen. The order for everyone to wear clothes had been taken to heart. Cherry had on cutoff jean shorts and a white men's shirt with the sleeves torn off, so that little bits of thread decorated the arm holes. She'd tied the ends of the shirt so her stomach showed as she moved around the kitchen. Zane's gaze followed her wherever she moved. I wasn't sure how Cherry felt about him, but Zane was beginning to act like a man in love, or at least very serious lust. He sat at the table wearing the leather pants he'd taken off last night, ignoring his coffee and watching Cherry.

Caleb leaned against the counter in his jeans, with the top button unbuttoned so that his belly-button ring showed. He sipped coffee and watched Zane watch Cherry with an odd look on his face. I couldn't decipher it, but I didn't like it, as if he were trying to think how to cause trouble between them. Caleb struck me as one of those who liked to cause trouble.

Nathaniel was sitting at the table, his long hair in a braid down his back, chest bare, but I knew without checking that he'd have something on. He knew me well enough to know I liked my houseguests clothed.

Igor and Claudia stood when I came into the room. His tattoos were even more striking in the full light of day. They graced his arms, what I could see of his chest through the white tank top, and the sides of his neck, like liquid jewels, brilliant, eye-catching. Even from a distance they were beautiful against his pale skin. I wasn't much into tattoos but I couldn't picture Igor without them—the look just worked for him. He'd put on the shoulder rig, and it still looked like it should chaff with the tank top, but, hey, it wasn't my skin. The Glock sat under his arm, a black spot on all that pretty color, like an imperfection on a Picasso.

Claudia looked positively ordinary beside him—if a woman that was so damn close to seven feet and muscled better than most men could look ordinary. The gun at the small of her back wasn't nearly as noticeable as Igor's. Her black hair was still pulled back in a tight ponytail, leaving her face clean and empty, and that included her eyes. Claudia had cop eyes, or bad-guy eyes, the eyes of someone who doesn't let you see what's inside. I didn't meet many women with eyes like that, outside of the police. If her face had been a little softer, she'd have been beautiful. But there was something in the set of her jaw, the way she held that full mouth that said, back off, no touching. It robbed her of something that would have changed everything about her.

The two of them came to take up posts to either side and a little behind me. I would have protested, but I'd discovered last night that it didn't do much good. They took orders from Rafael, not me. He'd said, "Keep her safe," and that was what they were going to do. I was too . . . whatever the hell I was to waste energy on telling them to back off. They could follow me around if it made them feel better. This afternoon I just didn't care.

Merle was standing in the corner of the cabinets, near enough to the coffeemaker that Igor crowded him while I poured my coffee. I didn't know who had made a fresh pot, and I didn't care; just the sight and smell of it made me feel better.

Merle was wearing the cowboy boots, jeans, and jean jacket over bare chest that he'd had on last night. He was sipping coffee out of one of the few plain mugs I owned. The scar on his chest was very white, ragged, pitted in one spot as if that had been the deepest part of the wound. It did look like lightning carved into his chest and stomach. I wanted to ask what had happened, but there was a look to his eyes as he watched the kitchen that said he probably wouldn't tell me, and he'd definitely see it as intrusive. None of my business anyway.

The only chairs open at the table gave their backs to the bay window and the sliding glass door. I hated sitting with my back to a window or a door—especially a door. Nathaniel touched Zane's arm. He glanced back at me then got up, coffee cup and all, and went around to the chair that backed the door. Cherry sat beside him, though her chair had been Claudia's, and it was turned so that she had the view of both doors. Cherry moved the chair closer to Zane, giving her back to all that glass.

There'd been a time when I wasn't this careful, especially at home, but today was going to be one of my paranoid days. Insecurity had that effect on me, even emotional insecurity.

Claudia sat beside me. Igor leaned against the island behind me, keeping an eye on Merle, I think. They didn't seem to like each other.

I took the first sip of coffee, hot, black, and let the warmth fill me for a few seconds, before I asked, "Where's Gregory?"

"Stephen and Vivian took him back to their apartment," Cherry said.

"But he's alright?" I asked.

She nodded, smiling that smile that made her look years younger than we both were. "He's healed, Anita. You healed him."

"I called his beast, I didn't heal him."

She shrugged. "Same difference."

I shook my head. "No, I couldn't heal him last night."

She frowned, and even that was pretty. She was buzzed today, shining with it. I glanced at Zane, who was still gazing at her. Maybe it was love for both of them. Something had certainly put a twinkle in her eye.

"For heaven's sake, Anita, you saved him, does it really matter how you did it?"

It was my turn to shrug. "I just don't like the fact that Raina's munin seems to be interfering more and more when I try to heal."

The doorbell rang, and I jumped like I'd been shot. Nervous—who me?

"I ordered take-out," Nathaniel said.

I looked at him. "Please tell me it's Chinese."

He nodded, smiling, I think at my pleased expression. We'd discovered that though no Chinese restaurant would ordinarily deliver out this far, that for a sizable tip, and I mean sizable, they'd make an exception for us. Nathaniel got up, but Caleb pushed away from the door. "I'll get it. I don't seem to be much use for anything else." He set his mug on the island and threaded his way between us to vanish into the living room.

"What's his problem today?" I asked.

Igor answered, "He tried to get friendly with Claudia."

"And me," Cherry said.

I looked from Cherry's smiling face to Claudia's frown. "And he's not bleeding or bruised?"

"It wasn't necessary to hurt him," Claudia said, "only to be very, very clear." The tone in her voice and the look in her eyes made my own eyes go cold. I don't know if I'd ever met a woman that had that effect on me. It made me feel sexist to say that it was more unnerving because she was a woman, but it was still true.

Her nostrils flared, and I watched all of them sniff the air. Everyone moved at once, scattering around the room. Claudia stood, grabbed my arm—my gun arm—and pulled me back towards the far side of the kitchen and the wall. She already had her gun out in her right hand. I jerked my gun arm free as Igor moved with her and they stood in front of me, blocking my view. Igor had his gun out, too. I was about to ask what the hell was going on, when I smelled it. The acrid, musty scent of snakes.

I had the Browning out and pointed at the door, sighted two-handed when the first snake man came through the kitchen doorway with Caleb in front of him, a sawed-off shotgun pressed into the angle of his jaw. "Anyone moves, and he dies."

40

EVERYONE FROZE, AS if we'd all taken a collective breath and held it. "No one has to die here," the snake man said. He looked at me with a huge copper-colored eye. The strong black stripe that edged the eyes looked like dramatic makeup. There were no scars on this one's face. He was shorter and seemed younger. His scaled face almost managed a smile, but the jaw of a snake is just not made for smiling. His eyes were as empty and alien as the rest of him. "Our boss just wants to talk to Ms. Blake, that's all."

"Have him pick up the damn phone and make an appointment," I said. I was staring down the barrel of the Browning at a point near the center of his chest, far enough up from Caleb's head that I wasn't worried about shooting him, but close enough to the throat that with the ammo I had in the gun it might pretty much decapitate him. If he ever moved the gun barrel out of Caleb's jaw. A sawed-off shotgun, with silver shot at touching range, and Caleb would be gone. I didn't much like him, but I couldn't let the bad guys blow his head off, could I?

"He didn't think you'd come," the snake man said.

"You go away, have him call, and I promise to give it the consideration it deserves." My voice was quiet because I was stilling my breath as much as I could, waiting for that one shot, if it ever came.

The snake man ground the barrel into Caleb's neck, until he forced a small pain sound from him. "This is silver shot, Ms. Blake. At this range it'll take his head."

"The second after he dies, so do you." Claudia said it, her voice as quiet and steady as the arm that held the gun that was pointed at the snake man's head.

He gave a hissing laugh, and it was echoed from behind him. More of the things started to move up in the open doorway. I caught a flash of silver metal, more guns. "No one else comes through that doorway, or I'll blow you away and let Caleb take his chances."

He pushed the barrel of the shotgun into Caleb's jaw until the smaller man had to rise on tiptoe, and I saw the first hints of panic on his face. "I don't think she likes you very much," the snake man hissed.

"Doesn't matter," I said. "I'm not letting you bring more guns into this room."

"You promise not to hurt Anita." It was Merle. I'd almost forgotten him standing to one side and behind us.

"We won't harm a hair on her head."

"We can smell that you're lying," Claudia said.

The snake head turned to one side, birdlike. "Most people can't smell changes in us, can't smell anything but the stink of snake."

Cherry's voice. "Anita."

My eyes flickered to her, and I saw movement outside the sliding glass doors. They were trying to flank us. "We've got movement on this side," Igor said.

For once other people had guns, and they seemed to know what they were doing. How refreshing. My gaze turned back to the snake man in time to see him motion with the barrel of the gun towards the glass. "We have the house surrounded. There is no need for all of you to die."

Claudia fired a second before I did. Her bullet hit him in the face, mine took him high on the chest, low on the neck. His head vanished in a welter of blood and thicker things. My ears rang with the shots in the small space. The snake's body jerked back; the shotgun went off as his hand convulsed. Caleb threw himself to the floor towards us. Two more snake men came through the door shoulder-to-shoulder, both with shotguns. Claudia said, "Left."

I shot the one on the right, and she took the one on the left. Both of us hit what we aimed at, and the two fell to the floor, one shotgun skidding across the floor towards us.

Another shotgun blast exploded to our left. I turned towards the noise, I couldn't help it. The sliding glass door had shattered, and I hadn't heard the sound of falling glass, just the shotgun roaring. Igor was kneeling, using the island as cover, as he put two shots into the chest of a man. The man fell to his knees, abruptly, like a puppet whose strings had been cut.

"Incoming," Claudia said, and I turned back to the other door. I could see the barrel of a shiny revolver, something nickel plated. Claudia was standing with her body pressed to the cabinets on the near wall, almost hidden from the door. She fired twice at that shiny barrel, and there was a scream that overrode the ringing in my ears. A screaming that went on and on like the squeal of a baby rabbit when a cat gets it. Dimly, I heard someone yell, "Shut up, Felix!"

Shots showered into the room from the side of the inner door that neither Claudia nor I could see and still stay hidden. Someone touched my arm, and I whirled, smacking into Nathaniel with the barrel of the Browning. He pointed. Igor was on the floor, on his side, with the first hint of crimson trickling across the floor. I saw Zane and Cherry under the table, hugging the ground. I caught a glimpse of Merle farther back, tucked into the corner of the cabinets, probably better hidden than any of us. What do you do in a gunfight if you have no gun, hide? I had a moment of meeting Merle's eyes, before I turned back to the wreckage.

A man stepped through the broken sliding glass door, a pump-action shotgun in his hands. He pumped a round in as he stepped through the door. I shot him three times before his knees collapsed from under him. He should have had the round pumped in before he stepped through the door.

Claudia was putting bullets into the inner door. I don't think she was hitting anything now, but she was keeping them from rushing us. Nothing else moved in the broken door, but I stayed crouched, gun aimed two-handed at the opening.

Bullets rained down from the inner door, and Claudia and I hugged the cabinets. I kept an eye on the far door, but I couldn't keep aimed and take cover at the same time. Another shotgun blast roared through the room from the little window above the sink. It took a big bite out of the island cabinets. I was as low to the ground as I could get, on my butt, pressed to the cabinets, but I kept the Browning on the sliding glass door. The shotgun sent another blast through the little window, and the shots from the living room came one after the other, not aiming, just keeping us where we were. I kept my eyes and my gun on the far door. They were shooting to cover something, and that was the only door left.

Three of them came through the sliding door, and everything slowed down. I was seeing the world through crystal, everything sharp edged. I had all the time in the world to see the two snakes and the lion man Marco come through in a blur of movement that was so fast I knew that none of them was human. I saw the shotguns, long and black, barrels impossibly long; the lion, Marco, had a 9 mil in each hand. I had an impression of blond and golden fur, before my first bullet took him in the side, spun him around. Claudia fired into one of the snakes, dropped him, but the other shotgun roared, and I felt her stagger above me.

I put two shots into the man's chest, and he collapsed on the kitchen table, shotgun falling soundlessly to the floor.

A bullet hit right next to me, and I saw Marco aiming from a prone position. I brought the Browning around to aim at him, but I was going to be too late. I watched him squeezing off the shot and knew he had me. There wasn't time to be scared, just a calm thought, that he was going to shoot me, and I couldn't stop him. Then a black blur was on his back, jerking him backwards, as the shot skidded along the floor in front of me. A wereleopard in man form threw the man out of the door and vanished after him.

I kept my eye on the door, but nothing moved. Something dripped on my face, warm, almost hot. Claudia slumped down the cabinets, to sit, legs sprawled out in front of her, gun still gripped in her hand, but loosely. I gave myself a second to see that her right shoulder and arm was a mass of red, then I turned back to the sliding glass door. I hugged the cabinet beside her. If they came through from the living room, then I could get some of them. If they rushed us from both doors at once, it was over.

I saw movement in the far corner and found Merle on his feet with a shotgun in one hand and a snake in the other. He'd pulled him through the window. It was another pump, and he pumped a round in the chamber with one hand, tearing his fingers through the throat of the snake with the other.

I saw his mouth move more than heard him and knew the lack of sound wasn't just shock, it was too much gunfire in a small room. I thought he said, "I've got this door." I eased around Claudia and tried to cover the living room, having to trust that Merle really could handle the other door. Claudia's eyes rolled as I moved around her. Her mouth moved, but I couldn't hear her. She began to reach her left hand towards her motionless right, as if the right hand couldn't move. I kept an eye on the door, but felt her painfully slow movements as she transferred the gun to her left hand. Since I was pressed just above her body, I hoped that she practiced left-handed. I'd hate to get shot by accident, when I was so much more likely to get shot on purpose.

Nothing happened for what seemed like forever; the silence was utterly still. My hearing came back in stages. I heard Caleb muttering over and over again, "Mother fucking son of a bitch, mother fucking son of a bitch." He was curled against the far cabinets behind me, making as small a target of himself as he could. Nathaniel actually had Igor's dropped handgun and was pointing it at the sliding glass door. I'd taught Nathaniel the basics of guns. I had too many around for him not to know something about them, but watching him lean against the island cabinets above Igor's body, the gun held two-handed, his left arm steadied against the cabinet edge, I knew he'd shoot whoever came through that door. If he was actually going to start picking up guns during fights, I was going to have to take him out to the range with me more.

Of course, that presupposed we would all live to do anything else. The silence stretched, until the wind sighing through the trees outside the broken glass seemed loud.

A voice came from the direction of the deck. "It's me, it's Micah." The voice was a deep, growling bass.

"It doesn't sound like Micah," I called back.

"It sounds like me when I'm not in human form," the voice said.

I said, "Merle?"

"It's Micah," he said.

"Come into the doorway, slowly," I said.

The black wereleopard eased through the broken doorway, claws held in the air. The dark shape seemed to fill the doorway. In leopardman form he was over six feet, broader through the shoulders, bulkier all over, as if he had muscles in this shape that he didn't have in human form. His fur gleamed like ebony, sunlight caressed his side, bringing out black-on-black rosettes like sable flowers crushed into velvet. Pale skin showed through at his chest, stomach, lower. In the movies the wolfmen are sexless, smooth as a Barbie doll. In real life, they are very much male. Somehow it was easier to see him naked in half-human form and not be the least bit embarrassed. I just didn't see the shapeshifters as sex objects once the fur started to flow.

"Where's the guy you threw out the door?" I asked.

"He got away."

"I don't hear anyone in the living room," Merle said.

"They all went out the front door," Zane said, "or at least the room looks clear." He and Cherry were still crouched under the kitchen table, flat to the ground.

"I'll check the living room," Micah said.

"These bad guys have silver bullets. I wouldn't be so cavalier about it," I said.

He nodded and his head was mostly leopard, very little left of the man he was, except, strangely, those chartreuse eyes. They marked him as alien, other, in human form, but as that furred and muscled body stalked past me, those same eyes marked him as Micah. The color was richer. Encircled with black fur, the eyes were even more striking. He hesitated in the doorway, then crept through, going low, making as small a target of himself as he could. It was rare to see a lycanthrope that took advantage of cover. Most of them seemed to see themselves as invulnerable, which was usually true, but not today. Igor was very still on the floor, and Claudia's shoulder looked like so much meat. She was slumped against the cabinets. Her left hand still gripped the gun, though the hand was motionless on the floor, as if she had no use of the arm.

When I glanced down, the gun was pointed somewhere in the direction of the sliding glass doors. The hand wavered enough that I was nervous crouching over her, but she fought that shaking limb so that she never quite compromised the line of my body. The right side of her body was soaked with blood, and her eyes were having trouble focusing. I think only shear stubbornness was keeping her conscious.

My gaze flicked to Igor's still form and the bodies piled in the doorways. If Igor was breathing, I couldn't see it. "Check his pulse, Nathaniel."

Nathaniel glanced down at the man, gave me a second of eye contact, then turned back to staring at the broken sliding door. "I'd hear his heart if it was still beating. Hear the blood in his body if it was still moving. It's not." He said all that with his head turned away from me. It made it somehow worse, more unnerving.

Micah appeared in the far doorway. "There's no one left alive in here." He stepped over the pile of bodies in the door, and even that movement was gliding, his balance forward on the feet, which were somewhere between human and leopard. Was I really going to be a leopard when the moon came full this month? Was this dark, graceful shape, this muscular shadow, what I had inside of me?

I pushed the question away; we had other more pressing problems, like the wounded. I'd concentrate on the emergencies and try to let everything else go. It was one of my specialties. I put my fingers against Claudia's neck, trying to check her pulse. She shrugged her shoulders, moving just enough so I couldn't check it. "I'm fine," she said, voice harsh. "I'm fine."

That was so obviously not true, I didn't even argue. Until I checked the house personally, I wouldn't believe we had the all-clear, but my industrial size first-aid kit was in the pantry, and I knew the immediate area was safe. "Cherry crawl out from under the table on this side and get the first-aid kit." I stood up and moved around the cabinets so I'd be able to see both the living room and the sliding glass door, not to mention the bay window over the breakfast nook.

Cherry glanced once at Zane, then crawled out from among the chair legs. She stayed low until she got to the pantry closet. She had to make Caleb move, scooting at him, gently, with her feet. He finally unwound from his tight fetal position and crawled about a foot away so Cherry could get the kit.

Cherry went to Igor first. She was a wereleopard; her hearing was just as good as Nathaniel's, but she went through all the motions, then turned to Claudia. Claudia tried to push her away with her left hand, gun still in it.

"Claudia, let Cherry help you," I said.

"Damn it!"

Cherry took that for a yes and started inspecting the shoulder. Claudia didn't fight her anymore, and I was glad. Shock can make you do and say funny things. I didn't really want to arm wrestle the wererat, wounded or not. Of course, Micah was here and he could probably arm wrestle Claudia and win, at least while she was wounded.

I was still keeping a peripheral sense of the open spaces, but as the time dragged on quietly, there was only the wind in the trees, the noise of summer locusts thrumming through the open living room door and the splintered glass of the back door. I began to relax by inches. That tension in my shoulders that I always get during a fight and never really notice until the adrenaline lets down, let me know that I thought we were safe, for now.

Then I heard something over the summer silence—sirens. Police sirens wailing, getting closer. I didn't have any near neighbors. You heard gunshots in Jefferson County pretty regularly, so who the hell reported the gunshots?

Micah turned that strangely rounded face towards me. "Are they coming here?"

I shrugged. "I don't know for sure, but it seems likely."

We both glanced down at the bodies on the floor, then looked at each other. "We don't have time to hide the bodies," he said.

"No, we don't," I said. I looked at everybody. Merle was still watching the kitchen window, the borrowed shotgun in his big hands. Zane had crawled out from under the table to play nurse for Cherry, handing her things as she asked for them. She had packed Claudia's arm.

Cherry looked up at me. "She could partially heal herself if she shapeshifted, but she'd still need medical attention."

"The police tend to shoot shapeshifters in animal form," I said.

"I'll stay," Claudia said, teeth gritted just a little. "The more wounded we have on our side, the better the police will like it."

She had a point. I looked at Micah. The sirens were very near now, almost in front of the house.

"You better go, Micah."

"Why?"

"The police are about to burst in here, see a lot of bodies, a lot of blood. Anything in animal form stands a good chance of getting shot."

"That's not a problem," he said. The fur began to recede, like water pulling back from the shore. As human skin was revealed, his bones slid out of sight into it, like hard things thrown in wax, covered, melted. I'd never seen anyone change so casually, so easily. It was almost as if he were merely changing clothes, except for the clear fluid that ran down his body like a liquid sheet, the sound of bones popping, reforming, even the sound of flesh boiling over him. Only his eyes remained the same, unchanging, like two jewels fixed in the center of the universe. Then he was suddenly human again, body covered in that thick, watery fluid. I'd never seen so much of the liquid before from only one change. I was standing in a pool of it and hadn't noticed.

He slumped suddenly, trying to catch himself on the cabinet, but I was in the way and had to grab him around the waist to keep him from falling to the floor. "Rapid change comes with a price."

"I've never seen anyone change back that quickly," Cherry said.

"And he won't fall into a coma-sleep either," Merle said. "Give him a few minutes and he'll be fine, messy, but fine." There was admiration in the big man's voice, and something else—almost jealousy.

The sirens wailed to a stop outside the house, then silence. "Everybody put the guns down. Don't want to get shot by accident," I said.

Nathaniel did as I asked, instantly. I had to press Micah closer into my body, one-handed, so I could put my own gun back on the cabinet. Micah's body shuddered against me. I looked at him, about to ask if he was alright, but the look in his eyes stopped me. It wasn't pain I saw in his eyes. I slid my other hand around his waist so that I held him more securely against me. His skin was slick under my hands. He managed to put a hand on the cabinet behind us. I stared into his eyes from inches away, and there were worlds to drown in, in those eyes, needs and hopes, everything.

A man's voice yelled, "Police!"

I yelled back, "Don't shoot, the bad guys are gone. We've got wounded." I moved Micah so he could prop himself against the cabinet, then put my hands on my head and moved carefully into the doorway. I had to step over the bodies in the kitchen door to come into the line of sight of the two officers crouched in the doorway. If I'd been a large imposing man, they might still have fired, not on purpose exactly, but you don't see three bodies in a doorway in Jefferson County, Missouri, every day. But I was small, female, and looked fairly benign, unarmed. But I kept talking as I moved anyway. Things like, "They attacked us. We've got wounded. We need an ambulance. Thank God you guys came when you did. The sirens scared them away." I kept babbling until I was sure that they weren't going to shoot me, then the really hard part started. How do you explain five bodies in your kitchen, some of which even in death didn't look very human? Beats the hell out of me.

41

TWO HOURS LATER I was sitting on my couch, talking to Zerbrowski. He looked, as he usually did, like he'd dressed in a hurry, in the dark, so that nothing quite matched, and he'd grabbed the tie with the stain on it, instead of the one that he probably meant to wear. His wife, Katie, was a neat, orderly sort of person, and I'd never figured out why she allowed Zerbrowski to leave the house dressed like a walking disaster. Of course, maybe it wasn't a matter of allowing him to do anything; maybe it was just one of those battles you just gave up on after a few years.

Caleb sat on the far end of the couch huddled in a blanket we'd gotten off the bed. The paramedics that had taken Claudia away had said he was in shock. I was betting that this was the first time he'd been on the wrong end of a shotgun. Only the top of his curls and a thin slit of brown eyes showed above the blanket. He looked about ten years old, huddled like that. I would have offered comfort but Zerbrowski wouldn't let me talk to him or anyone else. Merle stood against the wall at the end of the couch, watching everything with unreadable eyes. The cops kept giving him little eye flicks as they moved around the room. He made most of them uncomfortable for the same reason he made me uncomfortable; he wore the potential for violence like an expensive cologne.

Zerbrowski pushed his glasses more firmly on his nose, shoved his hands in his pants pockets, and looked down at me. He was standing, I was sitting, the looking down part was easy. "So let me get this straight, these guys just burst in here, and you don't have the first idea why."

"That's right," I said.

He stared at me. I stared back. If he thought I was going to break under the pressure of his steely gaze, he was wrong. It helped that I really didn't have the faintest idea what was going on. I sat. He stood. We stared at each other. Caleb shuddered on his end of the couch. Merle watched all the people scurrying back and forth.

There were a lot of people. They moved around the house behind Zerbrowski, going in and out of the kitchen, like huge, ambitious ants. There's always too many people at a crime scene, not gawkers either. You always have too many cops around, way more than you need. But you never know which pair of eyes or hands will find that vital clue. Frankly, I thought more evidence was probably lost with all the traffic than found with the extra help, but that was me. I'm just not the social type.

We stood in our own little well of silence. The bedroom door opened behind us. I glanced back to see Micah come out of the room. He was wearing a pair of my sweatpants. Since they were men's sweats anyway and we were the same height, they fit perfectly. I'd never had a boyfriend that I could trade clothes with before. You just didn't find that many grown men my size.

The police hadn't let him shower, so his long hair had dried in messy clumps to his shoulders. The drying liquid was beginning to flake off in patches. His chartreuse eyes flicked towards me, but they stayed neutral. Dolph came right behind him, looming over Micah the way he loomed over me. Dolph's eyes weren't neutral; they were angry. He'd been angry since he stepped through the door. He'd separated us all into different rooms. Nathaniel was being questioned by his friend from the police station, Detective Jessica Arnet. They were in the guest room upstairs. Detective Perry had questioned Caleb and was still questioning Zane. Dolph had done Merle and Micah. Zerbrowski hadn't so much questioned me as simply stood there and made sure I didn't talk to any of the others. Call it a hunch, but I was betting Dolph planned on questioning me personally.

We did have five bodies on the ground, three of which even in death hadn't changed back to human form. The three snake things had stayed snakey. Shapeshifters always change back to their original form in death. Always. Which raised the question, if they weren't shapeshifters, what the hell were they?

"Anita," Dolph said. One word, but I knew what he meant. I got up and went for the bedroom. Micah brushed his fingertips across my hand as I passed him. Dolph's eyes tightened, and I knew he'd noticed.

He held the door for me, and I walked past him into my bedroom. I resented them using my house, my bedroom, to question me, but it beat the hell out of going downtown. So I kept my complaints to myself. Dolph had every reason to take us all downtown. We had dead bodies, and I wasn't even denying I had killed them. Oh, I might have tried to deny it if I thought I could get away with it, but I couldn't, so I didn't.

He motioned me to the kitchen chair that had been moved into the bedroom. He stayed standing, all six-feet-eight of him. "Tell me," he said.

I told him exactly what had happened. I told the truth, all of it. Of course, I didn't know enough to need to lie. They'd carted Igor's body away, all those bright tattoos still vibrant, more alive than the rest of him. We had one dead and one wounded. It was my house. It was obviously a case of self-defense. The only difference from the other two times I'd had to kill people in my house was the number of bodies and that some of them were so not-human. Other than that, I'd walked on much more questionable occasions. So why was Dolph treating this one more seriously? I didn't have a clue.

Dolph stared down at me. He has a much better steely gaze than Zerbrowski, but I gave him calm, blank eyes. I could look innocent this time, because I was.

"And you don't know why they wanted to take you?"

Actually, I had a thought on that one, but I didn't share it, couldn't. They might have come hunting me because I nearly killed their leader. One of the problems with withholding evidence from the police is that later you can't always explain yourself without confessing that you've withheld evidence. This was one of those moments. I hadn't told Dolph about the half-men half-snakes taking Nathaniel and the fight afterwards. I could have told him now, but . . . but there were too many things that I'd have had to tell him, like that maybe I was going to be a wereleopard. Dolph hated the monsters. I wasn't ready to share that with him.

I gave him an innocent face and said, "Nope."

"They wanted you pretty damn bad, Anita, to come in here with this kind of firepower."

I shrugged. "I guess so."

The anger filled his eyes, thinned his lips to a tight line. "You are lying to me."

I widened my eyes. "Would I do that?"

He whirled and slammed his hand into the top of my dresser, hard enough that the mirror thudded against the wall. The glass shivered, and for a second I thought it might shatter. It didn't, but the door opened and Zerbrowski stuck his head in the door. "Everything alright in here?"

Dolph glared at him, but Zerbrowski didn't flinch. "Maybe I should finish questioning Anita."

Dolph shook his head. "Get out, Zerbrowski."

Brave man that he was, he looked at me. "You okay with that, Anita?"

I nodded, but Dolph was already yelling, "Get the fuck out!"

Zerbrowski gave us both a last look and closed the door, saying, "Yell if you need anything." The door closed, and in the sudden silence I could hear Dolph's breathing, heavy, labored. I could smell the sweat on his skin, faint, not unpleasant, but a sure sign that he was in distress. What was going on?

"Dolph?" I made his name a question.

He spoke without turning around. "I am taking a lot of heat for you, Anita."

"Not on this you're not," I said. "Everybody that you took out of this house won't be human. The laws may cover shapeshifters as human, but I know how it works. What's one more dead monster?"

He turned then, leaning his big body against the dresser, arms crossed. "I thought that shapeshifters changed back to human form when they died."

"They do," I said.

"The snake things didn't."

"No, they didn't."

We looked at each other. "You're saying they weren't shapeshifters?"

"No, I'm saying I don't know what the hell they are. There are snake men in a lot of different mythologies. Hindu, vaudun. They could be something that was never human to begin with."

"You mean like the naga you pulled out of the river two years ago?" he said.

"The naga was truly immortal. These things, whatever they are, couldn't stand up to silver bullets."

He closed his eyes for a second, and when he looked at me again, I saw how tired he was. Not a physical tiredness, but a tiredness of the heart, as if he'd been carrying some emotional burden around a little too long.

"What's wrong, Dolph? What's got you so . . . riled up?"

He gave a small smile. "Riled up." He shook his head and pushed away from the dresser. He sat on the edge of the bed, and I turned in the chair, so I was straddling the back of it and could see him better.

"You asked what woman in my life was sleeping with the undead."

"I shouldn't have said that. I'm sorry."

He shook his head. "No, I was being a bastard." His eyes were fierce again. "I don't understand how you can let that . . . thing touch you." His revulsion was so strong that I could almost feel it against my skin.

"We've had this discussion before. You're not my father."

"But I am Darrin's father."

I gave him wide eyes. "Your oldest, the lawyer?" I asked.

He nodded.

I watched his face, tried to catch a clue, afraid to say anything. Afraid I'd misunderstood him. "What about Darrin?"

"He's engaged."

I watched the terrible seriousness of his face. "Why do I get the idea that congratulations aren't in order?"

"She's a vampire, Anita, a fucking vampire."

I blinked at him. I didn't know what to say.

Those angry eyes glared at me. "Say something."

"I don't know what you want me to say, Dolph. Darrin's older than I am. He's a big boy. He has the right to be with whoever he wants to be with."

"She's a corpse, Anita. She is a walking corpse."

I nodded. "Yeah."

He stood, pacing the room in long angry strides. "She's dead, Anita, she's fucking dead, and you can't get grandchildren from a corpse."

I almost laughed at that, but my sense of self-preservation is stronger than that. I finally said, "I'm sorry, Dolph, I . . . it's true that, as far as I know, female vamps can't carry a baby to term. But your youngest, Paul, the engineer, he's married."

Dolph shook his head. "They can't have kids."

I watched him pace the room, back and forth, back and forth. "I didn't know. I'm sorry."

He sat back down on the bed, broad shoulders slumping suddenly. "No grandchildren, Anita."

I didn't know what to say, again. I couldn't remember Dolph ever sharing this much of his personal life with me, or anyone for that matter. I was both flattered and almost panicked. I am not a natural caregiver, and I just didn't know what to do. If he had been Nathaniel or one of the leopards, or even one of the wolves, I'd have hugged him, petted him, but he was Dolph, and I just wasn't sure he was a petting kind of guy.

He just sat there staring blindly at the floor, his big hands limp in his lap. He looked so lost. I got up from the chair and went to stand beside him. He never moved. I touched his shoulder. "I'm so sorry, Dolph."

He nodded. "Lucille cried herself to sleep after Darrin made his little announcement."

"Is it the vampire issue or the no-grandchildren issue?" I asked.

"She says she's too young to be a grandmother, but . . ." He looked up suddenly, and what I saw in his eyes was so raw, I wanted to look away. I had to force myself to meet that pained gaze, to hold it and take in everything that he was offering. Dolph was letting me see further inside him than ever before, and I had to honor that. I had to look at him, let him see that I saw it all. If he had been a girlfriend, I'd have hugged him. If he had been most any of my male friends, I'd have hugged him, but he was Dolph, and I just wasn't sure.

He turned his face away, and only then, when he'd given me all the pain in his eyes, did I try to hug him. He didn't let me do it. He stood up, moving away from me. But I'd tried, and that was the best I could do.

When he turned back towards me, his eyes were blank, his face set in that mask he usually wore, his cop face. "If you are holding out on me, Anita, I will bust your ass."

I nodded, my own face falling back into a mask as empty as his. The moment of sharing was over, and he was uncomfortable with it, so we'd go back to familiar ground. Fine with me. I hadn't known what to say anyway. But I'd remember he let me see inside. I'd remember, though I wasn't sure what good it would do either of us.

"A group of shapeshifters, or whatever, attacks me in my own home, kills one of my guests, wounds another, and you'll bust *me*. What the hell for?"

He shook his head. "You are holding out on me, Anita. Sometimes I think you do it out of habit, sometimes just to be a pain in the ass, but you don't tell me everything anymore."

I shrugged again. "I'm not saying I'm holding out anything about today, but I tell you what I can, Dolph, when I can."

"How about the new boyfriend with the cat eyes?"

I blinked at him. "I don't know what you mean."

"Micah Callahan. I saw him touch you."

"He brushed my hand, Dolph."

He shook his head. "It was the way he touched you, the way your face softened when he did it."

It was my turn to look down. I didn't look up until I was sure I could keep an empty face. "I'm not sure I'd call Micah my boyfriend."

"What would you call him?"

"I appreciate you sharing your personal life with me, Dolph, I really do, but I don't have to return the favor."

His eyes hardened. "What is it with you and the monsters, Anita? Us poor humans not good enough for you?"

"It's none of your business who I date, Dolph."

"I don't mind the dating, but I still don't know how you can stand for them to touch you."

"If it's none of your business who I date, it sure as hell isn't any of your business who I have sex with."

"You fucking Micah Callahan?" he asked.

I met his angry eyes with my own, and said, "Yeah, yeah I am."

He stood trembling in front of me, big hands in fists at his side, and for just a second, I thought he might do something, something violent, something we'd both regret. Then he turned his back on me. "Get out, Anita, just get out."

I started to reach out, to touch him, then let my hand drop. I wanted to apologize, but that would have made it worse. I was uncomfortable with the fact that I had sex with Micah, and that made me touchy. Dolph deserved better. I did the best I could to make up for it. "The heart wants what the heart wants, Dolph. You don't plan on making your life complicated, it just happens, and you don't do it on purpose, and you don't do it to hurt the people who love you. It just turns out that way sometimes."

He nodded, still turned away from me. "Lucille wants to call you and talk about vampires sometime—wants to understand them better."

"I'd be happy to answer any questions she has."

He nodded again, but wouldn't look at me. "I'll tell her to call."

"I'll look for the call."

We both stood there, him still not looking at me. The silence stretched between us, and it wasn't companionable, it was strained. "I don't have any more questions, Anita. Go on out."

I stopped at the door, looked back at him. He was still carefully turned away, and I wondered if he was crying. I might have been able to sniff the air and use my newfound leopard senses to answer the question, but I didn't. He'd turned away so I wouldn't see, wouldn't know. I respected that. I opened the door and closed it quietly behind me, leaving him alone with his grief and his anger. Whether Dolph cried or not was his business, not mine.

42

WHEN THE LAST policeman had wandered away, the last emergency vehicle driven off, the summer silence settled over the house. The kitchen was a mess—broken glass ground into the floor, blood drying to black-red puddles on the polished wood. I'd never get all the blood out from the crevices in the wood. It would be there forever, a reminder that superior fire power had prevailed, but not without cost.

I was going to have to call Rafael and tell him I'd gotten his man killed and his woman wounded. I had to admit that it had been a damn good thing I'd had them. The two extra guns had made the difference. If I'd been the only one armed, things might have gone differently. Okay, I might be dead.

A noise behind me whirled me around. Nathaniel stood in the doorway with a broom, a dustpan, and a small bucket. "I thought I'd clean up the glass."

I nodded, my heart in my throat too much to talk. I hadn't heard him come up behind me. He was only in the doorway, not so close, but close enough if he'd been a bad guy with a gun.

I had been utterly calm through everything. I hadn't fallen apart when the police were here, but suddenly I was shaking, a faint trembling. A nice delayed reaction, damn.

Nathaniel set the dustpan and the bucket on the table, propped the broom against a chair, and walked slowly to me. He peered into my face, lilac eyes concerned. "Are you alright?"

I started to open my mouth and lie, but a small sound came out when my lips parted, almost a whimper. I closed my mouth tight to hold the sounds in, but the shaking got worse. If you're too damn stubborn to let yourself cry, then your body finds other ways to let it out.

Nathaniel touched my shoulder, tentatively, as if not sure he was welcome. For some reason that made my eyes burn, my chest tighten. I clutched my arms tight around myself, as if by holding tight I could keep the tears squeezed inside. He started to move in, started to hug me. I pulled away, because I knew that if he held me I'd cry. I'd already cried once today; that was all I was allowed. Hell, if I cried every time someone tried to kill me, I'd have drowned in my tears by now.

Nathaniel sighed. "If you found me like this, you'd hold me, make me feel better. Let me do the same for you."

My voice came out squeezed tight. "I fell apart once today. Once is enough."

He grabbed my arm. Almost anyone else I'd have been watching for it, but not Nathaniel. I thought of him as safe. His fingers squeezed my arm, not hard enough to hurt, but hard enough to let me know he was serious. I stopped shaking, like a switch had been thrown. I was focused, not even close to tears.

He shook me by the arm, hard enough to have me glare at him. "You wouldn't take a hug. I knew that this," he squeezed the arm a little harder, "would help."

"Let go of me, Nathaniel, now." My voice was low and careful, purring with anger. Nathaniel had never laid hands on me before in any way that was close to violent. Underneath the anger was sadness. He was supposed to be safe, and now he wasn't. He was becoming a person, not just a submissive mess, and it hadn't occurred to me until just this moment that I might not like everything that Nathaniel would grow into.

I felt movement, as if the very air had changed current, just before Micah stepped through the doorway of the kitchen. His hair was still wet from the shower, slicked back from his face, giving me the first real glimpse I'd ever had of that face without the curls to distract the eyes.

His face was as delicate as the rest of him. I'd assumed the long curls only made him seem more delicate, but it was bone structure, just him. If you could ignore the broadening of his shoulders, going down into that slender waist, the straight line of his hips, you might almost say, *girl.* He wasn't really anymore feminine looking than Jean-Claude, but he was more delicately boned, slighter. It was just easier to pull off being masculine when you were an inch away from six feet than when you were an inch away from five-feet-five. Only one thing ruined the delicacy of his face. His nose wasn't quite perfectly straight; it had been badly broken once upon a time and not healed quite right. It should have ruined the near-perfection of his face, but it didn't. It, like his eyes, seemed to add to Micah, make him more interesting, not less attractive. Maybe I'd just had my fill of perfect men.

He'd added an oversized T-shirt to the sweatpants. The shirt hit him at mid-thigh, which hid more of his body than it showed, but even covered, I was aware of him. Aware of him in a way that I was aware of Richard and Jean-Claude. I'd always assumed it was love mixed with lust, but I didn't know Micah well enough to love him. Either pure lust felt pretty much like love, or there was more than one kind of love. It was too confusing for me.

"What's wrong?" he asked.

Nathaniel went back to his broom, bucket, and dustpan. He picked them up and began to sweep the glass up, ignoring us.

"Nothing, what's up?"

He frowned at me. "You're both upset."

I shrugged. "We'll get over it."

He closed the distance between us, but the movement was too sudden after Nathaniel's grab, and I backed up.

Micah stopped, looked at me, clearly puzzled. "What happened? You didn't look this spooked when the guns were out."

I glanced at Nathaniel, who was kneeling, sweeping glass into the dustpan. He was studiously avoiding looking at me, at us. "We had a disagreement."

Nathaniel stiffened then, his whole body reacting to what I'd said. He turned slowly around until he looked up at me with those flower-colored eyes. "That wasn't fair, Anita. I've never disagreed with you in anything."

I sighed, not because he was right, but because of the hurt in his eyes. I went to him, balanced on my heels, because I didn't dare try to kneel in the glass. I touched his bare shoulder, the side of his face. "I'm sorry, Nathaniel, you just caught me off guard."

"Why won't you let me in, Anita, why? I know you want to."

I touched his back where the bite marks had almost healed, dim reddish circles. "I don't let anyone in without a fight, Nathaniel. You should know that by now."

"Not everything has to be a fight," he said. His eyes were very wide, glittering.

"For me it does."

He shook his head, closing his eyes, and tears trailed down his cheeks. I helped him stand, because I was still worried about the glass. When we were standing, I eased my arms around him until my face touched his bare skin, my mouth pressed into the hollow of his shoulder where the collarbone spoons inward. His arms wrapped around me, held me close. His skin was so soft, so warm. I took a deep shaking breath. He smelled of vanilla, like always. I was never sure whether it was soap, shampoo, cologne, or just him. But underneath was a ranker scent—one that no perfume-maker in the world would bottle. Something feral and far too real, the scent of leopard, of pard.

I felt Micah at my back. I knew the feel of his body, like a line of heat before he pressed himself against me. But his arms didn't encircle me, they touched Nathaniel. Micah's body spooned against mine as we stood, but his hands, his arms traced mine, holding Nathaniel to us, embracing him.

Nathaniel let out a trembling breath. A deep, rumbling sound came out of Micah's throat, and it took me a second to realize he was purring, a deep rhythm of contentment. The purr vibrated against my back. Nathaniel started to cry, and I heard myself say, "We're here, Nathaniel, we're here." We're here. Pressed into the rich vanilla of Nathaniel's skin, Micah's purr thrumming against my body, the feel of both their bodies so solid, so real, and I did cry. I held Nathaniel, Micah held both of us, we cried, and it was okay.

43

SOMEONE CLEARED THEIR throat loudly from the doorway. I blinked through the soft tears and found Zane standing there. "Sorry to interrupt, but we've got a crowd out here."

"What do you mean?" Micah asked.

"The swan king, his swanmanes, and pretty much at least one representative from every other wereanimal in the city, as far as I can tell."

Nathaniel and Micah pulled away from me. We all rubbed at our faces; even Micah had been crying. I wasn't sure why; maybe he was just an emotional kind of guy. "What do they want?" I asked.

"To see you, Anita."

"Why?"

Zane shrugged. "The swan king won't talk to us flunkies. He insists that he talk to Anita, and her Nimir-Raj, if she pleases."

Micah and I exchanged glances. We both looked as puzzled as I felt. "Tell Reece that I need a bit more info before I grant an interview. I'm a little preoccupied."

Zane grinned wide enough to flash his upper and lower cat fangs. "We deny him entrance to the house until he tells us peons what he wants. I like it, but he won't."

I sighed. "I don't want to start a fight just because he shows up without calling. Shit." I started to walk out, but Micah caught my hand as I went by. I turned back to look at him.

"May your Nimir-Raj accompany you?"

I smiled, partly because he'd asked, rather than assumed, and partly because looking at him made me smile. I squeezed his hand, and his hand closed around mine, pressing back. What I wanted to say was, "I'd love the company," what came out was, "Sure."

He smiled, and for the first time it wasn't mixed, it was just a smile. He raised my hand to his lips and pressed his mouth against my knuckles. The gesture reminded me of Jean-Claude. How was it going to be to have Micah and Jean-Claude in the same room at the same time with me?

Micah frowned. "You don't look happy now. Did I do something wrong?"

I shook my head, squeezed his hand, and led him towards the living room. He pulled me back towards him. "No, you thought of something that bothered you. What was it?"

I sighed. "Truth?"

He nodded. "Truth."

"Just wondering how awkward it's going to be when you and I are in the same room with Jean-Claude."

He pulled on my hand, drawing me against him. I put a hand up to keep our bodies from touching completely, and found his heartbeat under the palm of my hand. Even through the cotton shirt, I could feel the thud of his body, as if his heart were naked in my hand. I had to raise my head just a little to meet the green gold depths of his eyes.

His voice came out a little breathy. "I told you, I want to be your Nimir-Raj, whatever that means, whatever it takes."

My own voice wasn't doing much better than his. "Even if that means sharing me with someone else?"

"I knew that coming in."

I felt a frown forming between my eyes. "You know what they say about things that are too good to be true, don't you?"

He touched his fingertips to my face and bent towards me, speaking softly as he moved. "Am I too good to be true, Anita?" He whispered my name against my lips, and we kissed. Gentle, soft, wet. His heart was beating so fast under my hand, my pulse was in my throat, and I think I'd forgotten to breathe.

He drew back first. I was breathless and a little disoriented. There was a look on his face—delight, I think—with the effect the kiss had had on me.

It took me two tries to find my voice. "Too good to be true, oh, yeah, definitely."

He laughed then, and I wasn't sure I'd ever heard him laugh before. It was a good sound. "I can't tell you how much it means to see that look in your eyes."

"What look?"

He smiled, and he was suddenly all male, pride, pleased with himself, and something else—almost embarrassed. He touched my face. "I love the way you look at me."

It made me lower my eyes, and I blushed, even though I wasn't thinking a damn thing that was sexual.

He laughed again, a surprised burst of sound that held so much joy. He laughed the way children laugh before they learn to hide how they feel. He picked me up around the waist and swung me around the kitchen.

I would have told him to put me down, but I was laughing too hard.

"I hate to interrupt," Donovan Reece, the swan king, said from the doorway, "but I told them you'd help us." He frowned at us, his pale, pale skin, showing almost no lines, as if his skin was like the water that his alter form swam upon. He had obviously decided not to wait outside.

I asked, still held above the ground in Micah's arms, "Help you do what?"

He shrugged. "Nothing important, just find some missing alphas and try to convince the Kadru of the werecobras that her Kashyapa, her mate, isn't dead, just missing with the rest. Trouble is," Reece said, "I think she's right. I think he's dead."

Micah let me slide back to the ground. I wondered if my face looked as grim as his. Marianne tells me that the universe/deity loves me and wants me to be happy. So why is it that every time I get a little happy all hell breaks loose? The message seems clear, and it's not about love.

44

DONOVAN REECE HAD curled up on the far end of my white couch. He was dressed in blue jeans so faded they were almost white. His pale pink shirt brought out the natural pink and blue undertones of his near translucent skin. He was beautiful, but not in the way a man or woman is beautiful, in the way a statue or a painting is beautiful, as if he wasn't quite real. Maybe it was because I knew that he had baby swan feathers on his chest, but of all the people in the room he seemed the most surrealistic.

A tall woman with hair almost as white as his sat on the arm of the couch by him. Her pants were black leather, her loose-fitting blouse a pink that matched his shirt, almost. I'm not sure I would have remembered the woman if the other two hadn't been kneeling on the floor at their feet. The second blond's hair was pale yellow and matched her long summer dress. The brunette's hair fell like a curtain around a navy blue dress with tiny white daisies all over it. The swanmanes that we'd saved from the club were all looking at me with large, almost fearful eyes.

I only recognized one person other than the swan king and his entourage. I'd met Christine for the first time at the Lunatic Cafe back when Raina still owned it, and Marcus, her Ulfric, was still trying to control all the other wereanimals in town and make himself high supreme commander, whether everyone else agreed or not. Christine's hair was still blond, short, professional. She was dressed in a navy business suit. Her powder blue shirt was partially unbuttoned, as if she'd removed a tie, though I don't think she had. She was perched on the other end of the couch from Donovan, her sensible navy pumps still on. Almost everyone else had gotten casual. There were a pile of shoes near my front door.

"Hi, Christine, it's been a while," I said.

She looked up at me, and it wasn't a friendly look. "I'm impressed you remembered my name."

"I tend to remember people I meet under stressful situations."

I got the tiniest smile out of her. "Well, we do seem to meet under less than pleasant circumstances," she said.

Donovan took over then, introducing me to the man and woman sitting between them. They were both dark-complected. Their bone structure was pure middle America, nothing special, but their eyes were too big, too dark, the hair truly black. There was something exotic about them that straight European just doesn't give you. They also looked amazingly alike, like male and female versions of each other. They were Ethan and Olivia MacNair, respectively.

The man in my white chair was bulky, not muscled, or fat, just big. He had the fullest beard I'd ever seen. The thick hair covered most of his face and neck. He was introduced as Boone, and the moment he turned small dark eyes to me, I knew he was something that would eat me if it could. Not wolf, not cat, but something with teeth.

His voice was a rumbling bass, so low it almost hurt to hear it. "Ms. Blake."

I nodded. "Mr. Boone."

He shook his head, the dark beard rubbing back and forth over his white shirt. "Just Boone, no mister."

"Boone," I said.

Nathaniel, Zane, and Cherry were bringing in kitchen chairs so the last four people could sit down. Two women, two men, were left. One man was slender with golden red hair, and strangely up-tilted green eyes. He sat on the floor, huddled against the side of the couch as if he were hiding.

"That's Gilbert," Donovan said.

"Gil," he said, voice almost too soft to hear.

The woman was tall, nearly six feet, broad-shouldered, strong-looking. Her hair was brown, streaked with gray, pulled back from her face in a loose ponytail. Her face was bare of makeup. She offered me a hand, and gave me one of the best handshakes I've ever had from another woman. Her brown eyes were deep with worry, as she said, "I'm Janet Talbot. It's good of you to see us all on such short notice."

"I didn't come here to make small talk." This from a woman who was standing on the far side of the room, near the big picture window. She was looking out through the closed sheers, hands gripping her elbows, nervous tension singing along her straight spine, as she turned to face the room. I could see where Ethan and Olivia had gotten the dark skin and their exotic look. Nilisha MacNair was about my size but even more delicately put together, so that she seemed smaller. A man might think words like *birdlike*, *kittenish*, until he looked in her eyes. Once you looked into those dark, dark eyes, you knew better. The eyes gave the lie to the packaging. She was hell on wheels and used to getting her own way.

A man stood near her, but not too near. He was as tall, as blond, as pale, as she was small, black-haired, and dark. He was also muscled in a way that nature does not do. His shoulders were broad, waist narrow, hands large enough to palm her entire head, yet he was clearly afraid of her. Oh, it was bodyguard deferential, but there was real fear there, too.

Merle was leaning casually near the big blond man. I didn't know where Caleb was, and didn't care.

"I am the Kadra, and the Kashyapa, who is dead, is my husband." Nilisha MacNair let out a sudden breath that shook, then she regained control like a mountain squeezing downward. "*Was* my husband."

"Father is not dead," Olivia said. "I won't let you make him dead by giving up."

Her brother, Ethan, touched her arm, as if trying to soothe her or tell her to shut up. She ignored him.

But the damage was done; the fight was on. "How dare you? How dare you say that I would make him dead? I am merely facing the truth."

Olivia stood up, shaking off her brother's hand. "You just can't stand the fact that he was with another woman when it happened."

The fight went downhill from there. Apparently Henry MacNair, patriarch of the clan, had been leaving his mistress and fellow werecobra's house, when someone had taken him. No body was found, but a lot of blood was left behind. There had been signs of a struggle, a car on its side, a good-sized tree torn up. When wereanimals struggle, they struggle.

I actually learned quite a bit from the fight, but when it was reduced to the two women screaming at each other from less than a foot away, some of it not even in English, I'd had enough.

I looked across the room at Donovan. He had brought them to my house, after all. He shrugged. Basically, he didn't know what to do either.

I had visions of dumping water over their heads, but decided that it might just work better to leave the room. I motioned the others into the kitchen, and they all trooped out. It was as the last of them were leaving the room that the shouting began to die down. Then Nilisha's voice. "Where are you all going?"

Janet Talbot spoke for all of us. "Some place quieter."

I couldn't see the women's faces, but I could almost smell the embarrassment on the air. Not wereanimal ability, just a good guess.

"Please," Olivia said, "please, I do apologize. Please come back."

Everyone started trickling back into the room. Nilisha actually took a chair with the blond bodyguard behind her. "We are all very worried about my husband."

"Worried about him, Mama?" Olivia said.

The woman nodded, smiled. "Yes, worried."

"He's not dead," the girl said.

"If you can have hope, so can I."

They smiled at each other like bright mirrors, so alike in that one moment. Ethan looked relieved, but he didn't smile.

"Alright, besides Henry MacNair, who else is missing?"

"My son, Andy," Janet Talbot said. She handed me a snapshot of a young man with her brown hair, cut short, but his features were softer than hers. He was handsome, bordering on pretty. "He looks like his father." She said it, as if strangers had remarked on the lack of resemblance before. I wouldn't have said a damn thing.

"Our Ursa," Boone said, "I didn't think to bring a picture."

"Ursa, bear, your queen?" I made it a question.

He nodded that massive, bearded head, and I wondered how I'd missed it. "She went out to pick up a few things at the store and never came back. No signs of a struggle, just gone."

I looked at Gil of the green eyes. "Who'd you misplace?"

He shook his head. "No one, I'm just scared."

I looked at Christine. "How 'bout you?"

"I'm here as a representative for the weres that only have one or two members. Those of us who have chosen St. Louis because there were no others like us. I'm the only weretiger in town, so I haven't lost anybody, but we've lost one werelion."

"I don't suppose the missing lion is named Marco?"

Christine shook her head. "No, Joseph, why?"

Donovan answered, "The lion man was named Marco."

"Oh" she said.

"And," Donovan added, "Joseph isn't able to change that close to human. No one I know of can change that close to human and hold it without changing."

Christine continued as if I hadn't spoken. Focused, Christine was always focused. "Joseph's mate is pregnant. Amber would be here but she's under complete bed rest until the baby is born."

"Until she loses it, you mean," Cherry said.

I glanced at her. "You say that like she's lost some before."

"This is her third try," Cherry said.

"I'm sorry to hear that. Losing her . . . mate must not be helping her stress levels."

"That is an understatement," Christine said.

"She's a fool to keep trying," Cherry said. "We can't carry a baby to term, and that's that."

I looked at her again. "Pass that by me again, slowly."

"The change is too violent, it causes miscarriage." Cherry said it matter of factly, then I watched her understand what she'd just said, and she whispered, "Anita, I didn't . . . you shouldn't have had to find out this way. I'm sorry."

I shrugged, then shook my head. "But the MacNairs have two children. I'm looking at them. Janet has a son."

"My type of shapeshifting is inherited," Janet said. "It's not tied to the moon. I avoided shapeshifting until after Andy was born."

I looked at Nilisha. "I am a werecobra. I can choose to try and carry a baby like a mammal or like a snake."

"You laid eggs?" I made that one a big question.

She nodded. "I couldn't have carried them in my body. The change is too hard. But I had other options."

The unspoken, *but you don't*, hung on the air. It was too hard to think about. It wasn't like I'd ever considered having children. I mean, get real, with my life? Out loud, I said, "One problem at a time. So who disappeared first?"

Henry MacNair was the first victim, and had had the most struggle. Then, the werelion, Joseph; Andy Talbot, weredog, as it turned out; and last the Ursa of the bears, Rebecca Morton.

The last time we'd had this many wereanimals missing, it had been the old swan king who was delivering them over to be hunted by illegal thrill seekers.

I looked at Donovan Reece. He either read my mind or anticipated it. "Interesting coincidence that I come into town about the same time everyone goes missing, isn't it."

"Gee, Donovan, you read my mind."

"I swear to you that I know nothing of this."

Nilisha said, "I know all about the betrayal of the last swan king. But I am betting my husband's life that Donovan is innocent of all this."

I shrugged. "We'll see."

"You do not trust my judgment," she said.

"I don't trust much of anyone's judgment but mine. Nothing personal."

Olivia touched her arm. "Mother."

Nilisha took a deep breath and calmed down. The day was looking up.

"The first thing I'm going to suggest is that we call in the police."

Nobody liked that idea. "Look, they have resources that I don't, computer searches, forensics."

"No," Nilisha said, "no, we must handle this among ourselves."

"I know the rule is that we don't bring in the human authorities, but guys, we have four missing, and they made a run at the swans and the leopards already."

"You think the snake people and their pet lion are behind this?" Donovan asked.

"It would be too big a coincidence if they weren't," I said.

"I agree," Micah said. He'd been very quiet through everything, carefully not standing or sitting too close, as if he didn't want to confuse things. He was letting me be in charge without hovering.

"Okay, then who are these guys, and what the hell would they want with a variety of shapeshifters?"

We talked for a couple of hours but didn't come up with anything brilliant. The snakemen were behind it. But why? Why would any wereanimals give a shit about other wereanimals that weren't their kind? If it had just been the werecobras targeted, then maybe it could be a reptile turf war, though frankly, it was unusual to have a fight even between two different kinds of snakes. The town was big enough for everybody as long as they weren't the same species.

I thought Nilisha MacNair was right and her husband was dead. If people kidnap someone and don't want money, they want worse things, usually things that include blood, pain, and, eventually, death. They were probably all dead, and if they weren't, we needed the police in on it to keep them alive.

It turned out that everyone had reported their people missing, neglecting to mention the part about being wereanimals. "But don't you see, the police have a twenty-one-year-old college senior missing, a forty-five-year-old husband, a thirty-something single woman, and a thirty-something married man. Other than the fact that they're all Caucasian, there is no common denominator to link up these cases. But if I can tell the police they are all wereanimals, then that's the link. You guys live all over the city. You have different police units working on each case. They'll never make the connection, unless we tell them what the connection is."

Janet Talbot nodded first. "Andy's almost got his pre-med degree. If they find out what he is, he'll never be a doctor, but I want him safe more than I want anything right now. So I agree, go to the police."

"I can't speak for Amber," Christine said, "but I'm pretty sure she'd agree."

"I should ask the others first, but the hell with it, find Rebecca for us, even if that means bringing in the cops," Boone said.

We all turned to Nilisha MacNair. "No, if they find out, we are all ruined."

Olivia took her hand. Ethan knelt in front of her. "Mother, without father, what does it matter?"

I wasn't sure she'd agree since he'd been cheating on her, but she nodded, and she agreed. Love is a funny thing sometimes. But whatever the motive, it meant I could talk to Dolph, and I wouldn't even have to lie.

45

DOLPH ANSWERED ON the second ring. "Dolph." He never said, Regional Preternatural Investigation Team, or even police, just his name, not even his last name, not even his full first name, just "Dolph," or "Dolph, here." Did anyone ever complain? Somehow I doubted it.

He sounded as close to surprised as he ever gets. "Anita, I didn't expect to hear from you until we'd at least finished the paperwork on the last batch of bodies." I heard a man's voice, but couldn't tell what was said. Dolph came back on. "Zerbrowski says that if you killed someone else just hide the body, he's not starting over on the paperwork."

"I know enough about procedure to know that he'd have to start a new report anyway. Separate crime, separate report, right?"

"Do you really have a fresh body out there?" He sounded tired, but not surprised.

"No," I said.

"Then how do we rate a call?"

"I have information pertaining to several crimes and the permission of those involved to tell you the truth, the whole truth. Now, isn't that refreshing?"

I could almost feel him sitting up over the phone. "I'm a cop, truth is always refreshing, so dazzle me."

I told him. As I'd suspected, the MacNair case was already on the roster for Dolph and the gang, but it was the first he'd heard of the others.

"I interviewed the wife personally. She kept saying she had no idea why some monster would attack her husband. It might have helped us find him if we'd known."

"Dolph, they run a restaurant. If it gets out that they're shapeshifters, they may lose it."

"Board of Health can't shut them down for this."

"No, but word will get out, and the customers will start to worry. You know it, and I know it."

"No one will find out from my people. You have my word on it."

"Yeah, but how many other departments are involved? How many nonpolice are at every crime scene, not to mention clerical workers? It'll come out, Dolph, eventually it'll come out."

"I'll keep a lid on it, Anita, but I can only guarantee my people."

"I know, Dolph, but Andy Talbot wants to be a doctor. He'll never get into med school once this comes out. Rebecca Morton is a chiropractor. If they find out what she is, they'll yank her license."

"Why is it that most of these people go in for professions where this is a problem?"

I shrugged, knew he couldn't see it. "Just lucky, I guess."

"I think it's stubbornness," Dolph said.

"What do you mean?"

"Tell anyone that they can't do something, and they'll want to do it."

He had a good point. "Makes sense."

"How do these disappearances tie in to the attack on your house?"

Damn, the whole truth, I'd said. There was my chance to prove it. I took a deep breath and told him almost all of the truth. I told him that Gregory had called for help, leaving out why he'd call me. Dolph never questioned that I'd be a good choice when calling for rescue from the monsters. He did say, "He could have called the police."

"It hasn't been that long since the police killed wereanimals on sight, Dolph. You can't really blame them for being leery of you guys."

"Why didn't you tell me all this when you were in for questioning?"

"You were mad at me," I said, as if that explained it. And it sort of did, though it made me sound childish.

"What are you leaving out?" he asked.

"I tell you the truth, and you still doubt me. That really hurts, Dolph."

"Not as much as it's going to if I find out you withheld evidence on this."

"It's not like you to make threats, Dolph."

"I'm tired," he said.

I was quiet for a second. "You should get some rest, Dolph."

"Yeah, if you can keep from killing anyone else, maybe I'll catch up on the paperwork."

"I'll do my best," I said.

"You do that." I heard him take a deep breath. "Is this all the information you're going to give me on this?"

"Yep."

"I'll go back and interview the families again. Do you know how much extra work this is going to be, just because they fucking lied the first time?"

"They didn't mean to make your job hard, Dolph, they were just scared."

"Yeah, so isn't everyone?" With that, he hung up.

I stared at the buzzing phone. The man was not in a good mood. I knew why, now, and I was probably one of the few outside his family that did know why. I wondered how much grouchier he was going to get, and if it would start affecting his job, if it hadn't already. If his hatred of the monsters took away his objectivity, then he was going to be useless as the head of the Regional Preternatural Investigation Team. Shit. It was a problem for another day. I could add it to the list of things I'd worry about later. At the rate the list was growing, I'd never have time to worry about everything on it. Maybe I could throw a dart and make what it stuck in the problem of the day. Or maybe I could just ignore the list. Yeah, ignoring sounded good.

46

THE MACNAIRS, PLUS bodyguard, promised to drive straight to RPIT's headquarters and give statements. Janet Talbot went with them. Christine didn't really know anything about the werelion's disappearance, so she just went home, promising to be careful. I offered to let her stay at my place until the bad guy, or guys, was caught, but she turned me down flat.

Donovan Reece said, "She is an independent creature."

I could admire that. "I hope her independence doesn't get her hurt."

He shrugged, getting to his feet. I noticed a lump under the front of his pink shirt. "You're armed," I said.

He glanced down at the place where his gun was trying and failing to hide. "I won't let my girls be taken again."

"People, call them people," I said.

He gave me a smile. "They are all girls."

"Humor me," I said.

He gave a small bow of his head. "My people, fine, but I won't let them be taken again."

"Or you either, Donovan. Remember everyone that's vanished has been a leader, not a follower. They chained Nathaniel up because they thought he was you; your people being taken was just incidental."

He met my eyes, suddenly very serious. "You're right. How did you know I was armed?"

"If you're going to tuck a gun into the front of your pants, wear a darker-colored shirt, and maybe one that's a size bigger."

He nodded. "I've never carried a gun before."

"Do you know how to use it?"

"I know how to shoot. I just don't usually carry concealed."

"Do you have a license to carry?"

He blinked at me.

"I take that as a no."

"No," he said.

"Then if you use it and kill someone, it's going to be a headache in court. Carrying concealed without a license will make it an illegal weapon. Depending on the judge, you might see jail time."

"How long does it take to get a license?"

"Longer than you'll want to wait. But check your county and start the process. Or don't start the process, and when you get arrested you can try and claim ignorance of the law. It's not a legal excuse, but it might sway a judge. I don't know. I'd apply for a license and hope it goes through."

"What do I have to do to apply?"

"It differs from county to county. Check with your local police. They'll know who you have to see."

He nodded again. "I'll do that." He looked at me, gray eyes so serious. "Thank you, Anita."

I shrugged. "Just doing my job."

He shook his head. "This isn't your job. You're no one's alpha here. You could have just refused to help us."

"And what good would that have done?" I asked.

"Most of the wereanimals won't help each other."

"You know of all the furry—and feathered—politics, that's the one I understand the least. Just like now, what happens to one group can affect the others. If you guys had been talking to each other, then you'd have known that Henry MacNair went missing, violently missing. It might have put all of you on guard."

"You think it would have prevented the other disappearances?"

"I don't know, but it might have helped. People would have been more cautious, maybe not gone out alone. We might have at least had witnesses."

"It was after my girls—people—got taken and you helped us that Christine came to me. She knew about the bears' Ursa having gone missing. It was Ethan MacNair, not his mother, that told us about his father."

"I bet he paid for going outside his mother's orders," I said.

"Probably," Donovan said, "but you're right, if we'd just bloody talk to each other, we could help each other more."

"Not just in emergencies either," I said.

His eyes narrowed. "You mean a coalition of wereanimals?"

I shrugged. "I hadn't thought that far ahead, but why not? Something where we share information. We've got a lion working with a bunch of snakes. Why should the bad guys get along better than we do?"

"Every time one of the animals talks about joining forces they always mean that they'll be top . . . dog. You want to be everybody's Nimir-Ra, Anita?"

"I'm not talking sharing authority. That'll never work without a war. I'm just saying share information, help each other more. When one of the leopards or wolves gets hurt, he, or she, has a place to stay until they're well. That kind of thing."

"Someone would need to be in charge of it."

I felt like grabbing him by the front of the shirt and shaking him. "Why, Donovan, why does anyone have to be in charge? Something happens to one of your swans, you pick up the phone and call me, or Ethan, or Christine. We call someone else. We try to help each other. We don't need a hierarchy, just a willingness to cooperate."

He looked unhappy, almost suspicious. "You don't want to be in charge."

I shook my head. "Donovan, I don't even want to be in charge of what I'm in charge of now. I sure as hell don't want to add to it."

It was Micah, who had been leaning against the wall, so still, so calm that you forgot he was there, who said, "She's offering you friendship, Donovan."

"Friendship?" He made it sound like a foreign concept.

Micah nodded, pushing away from the wall to stand beside me. "If something goes wrong and you need help, you call your friends."

Donovan frowned hard enough that he formed lines in that flawless skin. "Wereanimals aren't even friends with each other, let alone across species lines."

"That's not true," I said. "Richard," I paused after I'd said his name, as if it hurt, or I was waiting for it to hurt. Micah touched my shoulder, and I put my hand over his, held on. I tried again. "Richard's best friend is one of Rafael's rats. My leopard Vivian is living with, and in love with, Stephen, one of Richard's wolves."

"That's different."

"Why?"

"Because the wolves and rats have a treaty, and through you the leopards and the wolves are joined."

I shook my head. "You're quibbling, Donovan, or deliberately missing the point. Let's just agree to try and help each other, that's all. I don't have any ulterior motives. I'm just trying to keep the damage to a minimum."

"It's true you didn't have to save my girls. It nearly cost you your life."

"And you didn't have to go to the lupanar with me. But you did. That's how it works, cooperation."

He thought for a moment, then nodded. "Agreed. I'll try to get the others to agree also. You're right, you are right. If we'd just talk to each other, we could prevent a lot of bad things from happening."

"Great," I said, and let out a breath I hadn't realized I was holding. I wanted this. I wanted them to talk to each other, to help each other.

Someone cleared their throat, softly. It made us all look at Gil. He was still huddled beside the couch, where he'd been the entire time. "You have something to say?" Donovan asked.

"How far does this new spirit of cooperation go?" he asked. His uptilted green eyes were almost round with anxiety. He gripped his knees so hard his hands were mottled. He was scared; you could smell it on him, that and a neck-ruffling scent that I didn't recognize.

"What do you mean?" Donovan asked.

"I'm actually talking to Anita," Gil said.

I glanced at Micah then back to the man huddled on the floor. "What do you want to know?" I asked.

"I'm the only werefox in town. I don't have an alpha, or any family." He stopped there and licked his lips nervously.

"And?" I said.

"How much help are you willing to give?"

"How much do you need?"

"Can I stay with you until this thing, or whatever, is caught?"

I felt my eyes go wide. I opened my mouth, closed it, exchanged a look with Micah. He shrugged. "It has to be your call. It's your house."

Point. I turned back to Gil. "I don't know you at all. If you are a bad person, and you do bad things to my people, I will kill you, but if you really just want someplace to hide for a few days, you can stay."

He seemed to get smaller, more huddled. “I won’t hurt anybody. I just want to feel safe again, that’s all.”

I looked at Donovan. “Do you know anything about him?”

“He’s scared of his own shadow. I wouldn’t trust him to help in an emergency. I think he’d save himself first.”

Gil didn’t argue with Donovan’s estimation of him, he just huddled, trembling. “If we only help the strong ones, then we’re not helping ourselves,” I said.

“You’ll take him in, knowing he can’t help you in a fight, and would probably run to save his own skin?” Donovan asked.

I looked at those wide, terror-filled eyes and saw something besides fear, a pleading. They said, “Please, please help me.”

“You can stay, and we’ll protect you, but if there is an emergency I expect you to do your best. You don’t have to fight, but don’t be a hindrance.”

“What’s that mean?” he asked.

“It means if the guns come out, hide under something, get low to the ground. Don’t make yourself a target. If my people get hurt and you have a chance to drag them to safety but leave them to die instead, you’ll be next.”

“I’m not brave, Anita, I’m not even a little bit brave.”

“Don’t be brave, Gil, just do what you’re told, do your best whatever that is, but understand the rules. Keep yourself out of the line of fire because we won’t have time to worry about you when the fighting starts. Help if you can, stay out of the way if you can’t. Simple.”

He nodded, rubbing his chin between his knees, over and over. “Simple,” he whispered, “I wish life were simple.”

“Life isn’t simple, Gil, but a fight is.” I knelt in front of him, and I hated the weakness that radiated from him. Dear God, the last thing I needed was another emotional cripple following me around. But I couldn’t kick him out. Anita the bleeding heart. who’d have thought it? I stared at him, until his frightened eyes met mine. “A fight is simple, Gil. You protect yourself, your people, and you kill the bad guys. You do whatever it takes to get yourself and your people out alive.”

“How do you know who the bad guys are?” he asked, voice almost a whisper.

“Anyone in the room that isn’t us,” I said.

“And you kill them, just like that?”

I nodded. “Exactly,” I said.

“I don’t think I could kill anyone.”

“Then hide.”

He did that chin-rubbing nod thing again, like he was scent marking his own knees. “I can hide, I know how to do that.”

I touched his face very gently. He flinched, then relaxed a little. All the animals liked to be touched. “I’m not very good at hiding, maybe you can teach me.”

“Why would you need to know how to hide?” he asked.

“Because there’s always someone, or something, bigger and badder than you are.”

“I can teach you how to hide, but I don’t know if I can learn how to kill.”

Where had I heard that before? Oh, I knew—Richard. But even he had learned how, in the end. “You’d be surprised what you can learn, Gil, if you have to.”

He hugged himself again. “I don’t think I want to learn how to kill people.”

"Now that," I said, "is a different problem altogether."

"I don't want to," he said.

I stared down at him. "Then don't, but don't let your squeamishness get any of my people killed."

"It's more likely to kill me."

"True, but that's your choice—get yourself killed if you want, but don't bring harm to me or mine because of some moral high ground."

"Would you really kill me for it?"

I knelt back in front of him. "You can stay with me and I'll keep you safe, or die trying, but if you fuck up and cause the death of one of my leopards, or my friends, I will kill you. I don't want you to be crying later and saying you didn't understand. Because if you've earned it, I will shoot you while you beg me not to."

"But who decides whether I deserve it?" he asked.

"I do."

He stared up at me as if he weren't sure if he was safer with me or without me. I watched him think it through and felt nothing, no pity. Because Gil the werefox was a liability. In a combat situation he was a fucking casualty waiting to happen. I was civilized enough to give him protection when he asked, but not civilized enough to pay in the blood of those I held dear. In that moment I knew I wasn't a sociopath, because if I had been, I'd have kicked his ass out the door. Oh, hell, I'd have shot him and put him out of everyone's misery. Instead I offered him a hand, and pulled him to his feet.

"Do you understand the rules?" I asked.

"I understand," he whispered.

"You willing to live by them?"

He gave one small nod.

"You willing to die by them?"

He took a shaky breath, then gave another nod.

I smiled and knew it never reached my eyes. "Then welcome to the club, and keep your head down. There's some business we have to take care of tonight. You can come along." Even I wasn't sure if that was an invitation or a threat.

47

THERE WAS STILL a thread of light in the sky, like a slender golden ribbon, glowing against the push of dark, dark clouds when we parked in the back of the Circus of the Damned. The back parking lot was for employees. It was dark, bare, not the least bit entertaining, unlike the front, which was like a carnival. I'd driven past the bright lights and dramatic posters without a second glance.

"Did the clowns up front have fangs?" Caleb asked.

It wasn't until he asked that that I realized that none of them had ever been to the Circus. I undid my seat belt and leaned around so I could see him in the middle section of seats. He was sitting pressed against the door with Merle's broad shoulders crowding him. Nathaniel was on the other side of Merle. Cherry and Zane were in the back seats with Gil. Micah was sitting up front with me. Until we knew my house wasn't a free-fire zone we'd keep everybody together. Rafael had sent two new bodyguards over, but they'd arrived just as we were leaving, and I wouldn't make anyone in the Jeep move. They followed us, not happy, but taking orders, which was good.

I answered Caleb's question. "Yeah, the big spinning clowns on top of the sign have fangs."

"I saw a poster for zombie raisings. Do you do that?" Merle asked.

I shook my head. "I don't believe in using God-given gifts for entertainment purposes."

"I didn't mean to insult you," he said.

I shrugged. "Sorry, I'm a little touchy about shit like that. I don't approve of a lot of things some of my fellow animators do for money."

"You raise the dead for money," Caleb said.

I nodded. "Yeah, but I've turned down more money than I've taken."

"Turned down, why?" he asked.

I shrugged. "Local money who wanted to have his Halloween party in a cemetery so I could raise zombies at midnight. Or the guy that had offered a million if I could raise Marilyn Monroe and guarantee that she'd do anything he asked for a night." I shuddered. "I told that one if I even heard a rumor that he'd gotten someone to do the job, I'd see his ass in prison."

Caleb's eyes were a little wide. I think I'd shocked him. Good to know that I could. "You're deeply moral," Merle said, a tone in his voice like he was surprised.

"My own version of it, yeah."

"You hold to your own rules no matter what?" Merle made it a question.

I nodded. "Most of the time."

"What will make you break your own moral code?"

"Harm to my people, survival, the usual."

Merle's eyes flicked to Micah, sitting beside me. It was a small movement. If I hadn't been looking directly at him, I'd have missed it.

"What?" I asked, glancing from one to the other.

Merle answered, "You sound like Micah."

"You make that sound like a bad thing," I said.

He shook his head. "Not a bad thing, Anita, not a bad thing at all, just . . . unexpected."

"You still don't sound entirely happy about it," I said.

"Merle worries too much," Micah said.

I glanced at him, but he was watching the big man. Micah had tied his hair back while it was still wet, so that it lay flat to his head, utterly straight until it spilled out into the long ponytail, where the curls spilled like froth along his spine. His hair lay like brown velvet against the charcoal gray of his shirt.

"What does Merle worry about?" I asked.

"Taking care of me, mostly, and now, I think, you."

I looked at the big man. "Is that what you're worrying about?"

"Something like that," Merle said. He'd put a clean white T-shirt underneath his jean jacket, but other than that, he was wearing an identical outfit to the first one I'd ever seen him in. If he'd been wearing more leather, he'd have looked like an aging biker.

Micah turned towards me. His shirt made that rich, slithery sound that silk makes against leather seats. The dark gray shirt was short-sleeved, button-up, dressy. The color brought out the gold-green of his eyes, made his skin look even darker. He'd matched the shirt with black jeans, black belt, silver buckle, soft black tie-up shoes. It occurred to me for the first time that he looked like he'd dressed for a date. Had he dressed to impress me or Jean-Claude? It was a semiformal occasion for any alpha to meet the Master of the City. But especially one that was fucking the Master's human servant. I just wasn't sure how to handle the whole situation. Jean-Claude had taken Micah in stride in theory, but how would he react to seeing him in the flesh? How would Micah react to seeing Jean-Claude?

Damn it, I had enough to worry about without having to juggle male egos.

"You're frowning again," Micah said.

I shook my head. "It's nothing. Let's get this over with."

"Why do you sound less than thrilled?"

I had my door open and turned back around to say, "We're here to rescue Damian. I don't know what shape he's going to be in. Why would I be thrilled?"

"I know you're worried about your friend, but are you sure that that's really what's bothering you?"

I frowned at him. "What are you talking about?"

"I'm nervous about meeting the Master of the City, too."

It was almost like he'd read my mind. We didn't know each other well enough for him to really read me, but . . . he was either telepathic, which I didn't believe, or he *could* read me that well. I wasn't sure which thought bothered me more.

I let out a breath and half slumped in the seat. "Yeah, I'm a little nervous about introducing you to Jean-Claude. He was cool about you in the abstract, even knowing that we've been together, but seeing you in the flesh . . ." I tried to think how to word it. "I don't know how he'll feel about that."

"Will it make you feel any better if I promise to behave myself."

"Maybe, if you can pull it off."

"I can pull it off," he said, giving me very serious eye contact. He certainly vibrated sincerity.

"Don't take this wrong, Micah, but I've been disappointed pretty badly recently by the men in my life. It's a little hard to trust that anyone can pull it off."

He reached out to touch me, then let his hand fall back, as if something in my face hadn't been friendly. "I'll do my best tonight, Anita, that I can promise."

I sighed. "I believe you."

"But," he said.

I had to smile. "Your intentions are good, my intentions are good, Jean-Claude's intentions are probably good." I shrugged. "You know what they say about good intentions."

"My best is all I can offer," he said.

"And it's all I can ask, but let's say I'm not exactly sure how to handle this. I'd barely gotten to where I could deal with Richard and Jean-Claude at the same time, and now here *you* are. I just don't know."

"I can go back to your house," he said.

"No, Jean-Claude asked to meet you."

Micah looked at me. "And that makes you nervous."

I half-laughed. "Oh, yeah."

"Why?"

"If Jean-Claude were having sex with someone else, I wouldn't want to meet them."

Micah shrugged. "Do you think he means me harm?"

"No," I said, "no, nothing like that." I tried to put it into words and couldn't. Maybe it was just my lack of sophistication. How do you introduce boyfriend C to boyfriend A, after boyfriend A has been such a good sport, of late, about boyfriend B, who is no longer in the picture? Or maybe it was the way Jean-Claude had asked for him. "Bring your Nimir-Raj, *ma petite*, I would like to meet him."

"Why?" I'd asked.

"Am I not entitled to meet the other man in your bed?"

It had made me blush. But here Micah was, and here we were outside the Circus. Jean-Claude was inside, waiting. I was actually more scared about introducing the two of them than I was worried about Damian. If Jean-Claude didn't try and kill Micah, *then* I'd worry about Damian. I was ninety-nine percent sure that Jean-Claude wouldn't start a fight. It was the last one percent that clenched my gut into a tight knot as we moved out into the darkness.

The two new bodyguards came up to flank me as I walked towards the back door. They were both over six feet, male, and radiated bodyguard badass. Other than that they were almost opposites. Cris (no h, it's short for Cristiano) was mid-twenty-something, skin tanned a soft gold, eyes a pale shade of gray blue. His hair was that shade of pale brown that some people call blond. Bobby Lee was over forty, very short hair, gone white gray, eyebrows still black above startling blue eyes, like bits of water-blue sapphires. He had a neatly trimmed mustache and beard that were also black, with the first streaks of white and gray running through them.

Cris had no accent whatsoever, but Bobby Lee's voice was thick as hominy, and twice as Southern.

Nathaniel tried to stand next to me, and Cris moved to keep him away. "He's with me," I said.

"We were ordered to keep you safe. I don't know him."

"Look, both of you, we don't have time for major introductions here. He's one of my wereleopards, so are the two blonds. Micah's the one with the ponytail, the two men with him his leopards."

"Who's the redhead?" Bobby Lee asked.

"Gil, he's a werefox, and he's under my protection, too."

"They're like walking cannon fodder," Cris said.

I frowned up at him. "Most of this cannon fodder are friends, or more, to me. If the shit hits the fan and you save me at the expense of their lives, you will follow them."

"Our orders are to keep you safe, ma'am, no one else," Bobby Lee said.

I shook my head and drew Nathaniel into the crook of my arm. "What would Rafael do if you protected him but got his people slaughtered?"

They glanced at each other. Bobby Lee finally spoke. "It would depend on the situation."

"Yeah, maybe, but I'm armed, and can take care of myself most of the time. I need backup, not interference."

"We weren't told to be backup," Bobby Lee said.

"I know, but tonight there may be a certain amount of grandstanding. Jean-Claude won't let me get hurt, but he might play with some of the others, even me. Don't overreact, okay."

"You're making it so we can't do our job," Cris said.

I shrugged, hugging Nathaniel to me. "I appreciate you being here. I appreciate the help. I might be dead right now if Igor and Claudia hadn't been with me. But there are people who I would risk my life to keep safe, and some of them are with me tonight. All I'm saying is keep cool, don't overreact, don't jump the gun."

Again they looked at each other. I sighed. Bobby Lee was wearing a sleeveless jean jacket over his T-shirt. Cris wore a short-sleeved dress shirt and oversized black tank top untucked, sloppy over his khaki pants. It was too hot to wear a coat. But I was wearing a black silk shirt, open over a black tank top myself. I had my shirt tucked in, and the Firestar 9mm in a front draw across the front of all that black. Most people wouldn't see it, black on black. But the long-sleeved shirt was hiding guns and knives. I was betting that Bobby Lee had at least one gun under his jacket, probably at the small of his back, because there was no bulge, no matter how slight, under either arm. It was hard to see the bulge under Cris's left arm. He'd chosen a shirt with a lot of print on it, bright patterns to distract the eye, but a hot wind blew his shirt back, and I caught a glimpse of his shoulder holster. I couldn't be sure what was under the untucked tank top, but I was betting at least one more gun, in front for a cross-draw, just like mine.

"You cannot shoot anyone tonight unless I say so, how's that for clear?"

"We have our orders," Bobby Lee said, "and they aren't from you."

"Then you can go back to Rafael and tell him I refused your help."

Cris's eyes widened a touch. Bobby Lee's expression never changed. Those pretty blue eyes were as empty as glass, no one home. "Why are you so afraid of taking us inside?" he asked.

I sighed again and tried to put it into words they'd understand and I was willing to share. I couldn't come up with anything, so I tried the truth. "I am about to introduce my Nimir-Raj to the Master of the City for the first time."

"You fucking both of them?" Bobby Lee asked, and the phrase seemed wrong with that Scarlett O'Hara accent.

I started to protest, or bitch, but let it go. "Yeah, I am, and I'm a little worried about how the introduction's going to go."

"You think the Master will try and kill your Nimir-Raj?" Cris asked.

"No, but he may want to play with him, and a vampire's idea of fun and games can get a little odd."

Bobby Lee laughed. "Odd, she says, odd." He laughed again, and it sounded warm and deep and rumbly. The laughter filled his eyes, made them more real. "What she is trying to say, Cris, is that we are about to be entertained just like when the rats meet the hyenas. A show of force with no danger, but maybe a little discomfort."

"Yeah, what he just said."

Cris nodded. "So tonight isn't real."

"It's real," I said, "but it's just not dangerous in any way you can protect me from."

"We're supposed to protect you, period," Cris said.

Bobby Lee clamped him on the shoulder. "We can't protect her from her own love life, Cris. We're supposed to keep her body intact, not her heart."

"Oh," Cris said, and he looked suddenly much younger—early twenties, at best.

Bobby Lee turned to me. "We'll hang back tonight, unless you're in real physical danger."

"I'm glad we understand each other."

His eyes went empty again, the smile still curving his lips. "Oh, we don't understand each other at all, ma'am, I can almost guarantee that, but we'll do what we're told, until we decide not to."

I didn't exactly like the sound of that, but, looking into his empty blue eyes, I knew it was the best I was going to get.

48

THE STEPS LEADING down into the bowels of the Circus are wide enough for three small people to walk abreast, but the steps themselves are oddly spaced, as if whatever the steps were originally built for wasn't two-legged, or at least wasn't human sized.

We were following Ernie down the steps. The first time I'd met him he'd had one of those long hair cuts with the sides shaved. The sides had grown out, and he'd cut the rest, so he had a fairly standard short haircut, with a little more on top, so he could gel it into soft spikes, sort of executive punk. The short hair also left his neck bare so you could see two fang marks on the right side.

He wasn't feeding Jean-Claude. I don't think the Master of the City fed off humans anymore, not when he could have lycanthrope. But there were other vampires under the Circus, and they had to eat, too.

Micah walked beside me. Merle, Bobby Lee, and Cris had a disagreement about exactly where they were going to walk. They finally settled on Cris walking with Ernie ahead of us and Merle and Bobby Lee walking just behind us. Everyone else sort of trailed behind, including Caleb. None of the bodyguards seemed to give a shit if the others lived or died. I was pretty sure that the bodyguard thing was going to get on my nerves soon, like tonight.

The huge metal door at the end of the stairs was open, waiting. It was usually kept locked for security purposes. My stomach clenched so tight that it hurt. I just didn't know how to handle this. Did I kiss Jean-Claude hello? Did I touch Micah in front of him? Oh, hell.

"Did you say something?" Micah asked.

"Not on purpose," I said.

He looked a question at me, and that did it. I would behave like I always did. I would do exactly what I'd do if the other one wasn't there. To do anything else was going to have us all walking on pins and needles. Besides, I'd been careful with Richard and Jean-Claude, and look where that ended up. I didn't want the same mistakes again. Maybe we could make new ones.

49

THERE WERE SILVER drapes just inside the door. That was new. Ernie parted the drapes and led us into Jean-Claude's living room. Once upon a time it had been black and white drapes, and a smaller area, but now it was white, silver, and gold. White drapes, silk and sheer, hung like a hallway that led into something that looked like a huge fairytale tent. The stone walls and ceiling that I knew were there, were hidden by yards and yards of gold and silver cloth. It was like standing in the middle of a jewel box. The coffee table had been painted gold and white and made to look antique, or maybe it was the real deal. A crystal bowl sat in the center of the table with a spill of white carnations and baby's breath.

A huge white couch sat against the far drapes, so covered in silver and gold pillows that some of the pillows had fallen to the white carpeted floor. Two overstuffed chairs were in opposite corners, one gold, one silver, with white pillows on each.

The fireplace looked real, but I knew it wasn't because it had been added later, but it was everything a fireplace should have been, except it was painted white. There was even a new marble mantel that was white with veins of silver and gold, ordered to match.

The only thing that hadn't changed was the portrait above the fireplace. The first thing you saw was Julianna, sitting, dressed in silver and white, half-laughing, brown hair done in careful ringlets. Asher stood behind her in gold and white, his face still perfect, his gold hair in ringlets longer than hers, his mustache and Vandyke beard a blond so dark it was almost brown. Jean Claude sat behind Julianna, the only one of the three not smiling, solemn, dressed in black and silver. He'd designed the room around the painting—silver and gold and white.

"Wow." Caleb said it for us all.

I'd seen Jean-Claude's sense of style before, but every once in a while he'd amaze even me. Then I felt him coming towards us. I felt him coming and that wasn't a good thing. I'd expected anger, jealousy, but what was moving towards me was simply lust, need. He could shield better than this. Was this my punishment, to be drowned in his lust? If so, he'd misjudged me, because it was just going to piss me off.

He pushed through white and silver drapes, and for a moment I couldn't see where his clothes began and the cloth ended. He was wearing a silver frock coat with white edging, white buttons. His shirt was a spill of white froth, the pants, what I could see of them, were white, but the white leather boots covered almost all of his long legs. The leather looked soft, pettable, held in place with small silver buckles going from just above his ankles to his very upper thigh.

I stared because I couldn't do anything else. Even if he hadn't been projecting sex inside my head, he'd have made me think of it. His hair fell in loose curls nearly to his waist, a black glory on all that silver and white.

Bobby Lee said, "Well, aren't you just pretty as a picture."

Jean-Claude didn't even look at him. He looked at me, and I was walking towards him across the so-soft carpet without a thought, except that I had to touch him.

He closed his eyes, held out his hand. "No, *ma petite*, do not come closer."

I hesitated for a second, then started walking again. I could already smell his cologne, sweet, spicy. I wanted to run my hands through his hair, wrap the scent of him on my hands.

He stumbled back, half-tripping in the drapes. There was something like panic on his face. "*Ma petite*, I thought I could shield you from the *ardeur*, but I cannot."

That did stop me. I had to frown at him. I couldn't seem to think. That kept me where I was, almost close enough to touch him, but not quite. "What's happening, Jean-Claude?"

"I have fed this night, but I have not fed the *ardeur*."

"That's what I'm feeling," I said, "the *ardeur*."

"*Oui*, I am shielding as hard as I can, yet you are picking up on it. That has never happened before."

"Is it because I've got my own *ardeur*?"

"That is all that has changed, so yes, I believe so."

"You're not going to be in any shape to help with Damian, are you?"

He sighed and looked down. "I need to feed all my hungers, *ma petite*. I have not had this much difficulty with the *ardeur* in centuries. Something about sharing it with you has affected me. I did not know until I felt you enter the building that it had changed."

"You mean your control is better farther away from me?"

He nodded.

"What the hell is this 'ardoo-whatever'?" Bobby Lee asked.

I glanced back at him. "When we want to share, I'll let you know."

Bobby Lee raised his eyebrows at that, then made a small pushing motion. "You're the boss, ma'am . . . for now."

I let that slide and turned back to Jean-Claude. "What do we do?"

Nathaniel offered a suggestion. "Feed him."

I looked back at him, and the look must have been enough, because he put his hands out empty, and went to stand by the fireplace. Everyone else had taken a seat, except for Gil, who was huddled beside one of the chairs on the floor, clutching a pillow.

I turned to Jean-Claude, and it was Micah's voice that turned me back again. "I've seen Anita in the—" he changed whatever he was going to say—"grip of the *ardeur*, and this doesn't look like it. She's way too calm."

Jean-Claude looked past me at him, seeing him, I think, for the first time, at least in person. His gaze traveled up and down his body, an assessing look, like he was thinking of buying or was trying to be deliberately insulting.

Micah either didn't catch the insult or was proof against it, because he started walking towards us. He moved in a well of his own power, as if even here, surrounded by Jean-Claude's things, he was supremely confident, totally at ease. He moved like a dancer, compact, graceful, strong. The sight of him tightened things low in my body. Jean-Claude made a small sound. I started to turn towards him, but it was too late, his shields shattered and the *ardeur* roared over me. My skin ran with heat, my breath stopped, my vision was gone in streamers of color. Jean-Claude's need marched over me, through me, inside me. It screamed in my head, danced down my nerves, flowed through my veins. In that instant if he had asked anything, anything at all, I would have said *yes*.

My vision cleared and I found Jean-Claude on the floor, half-caught in a spill of draperies that he'd pulled from their hangers, so that he sat in a nest of white and silver. His face was almost slack with need, his eyes already a spill of blind blue fire.

I was on my knees, too, and didn't remember falling. Micah was there, taking my arm, I think to help me stand, but the moment he touched me the *ardeur* leaped, and he fell to the floor beside me, like someone had struck him with a hammer; his legs just stopped holding him. He whispered, "Oh, my God."

The bodyguards moved in then, and I had to scream, "No!" There must have been something in my voice, because all three of them froze in mid-motion. "No one touches us, no one." My voice was high, frantic. There was a very real chance that the *ardeur* could spread through the whole room, one touch at a time. We had enough problems without that.

Micah had released my arm, his hands nerveless in his lap, but the tie had been made, and the act of touching, or not, didn't change it.

Jean-Claude crawled from the bed of glittering cloth, slowly, every move something graceful and dangerous. He'd never looked more predatory than he did at that moment.

"Jean-Claude," I whispered, "don't." But I couldn't move. I watched him like a tiny bird fascinated as the serpent glides closer, caught between terror and the sheer beauty of him.

Asher was suddenly there in the space between the cloth. Jean-Claude froze, but it wasn't that stillness that the old vampires could fall into, there was a thrumming energy to him, more like a big cat about to pounce than something cold and reptilian.

"Jean-Claude, you must control the *ardeur* better than this." He was hugging his arms as if he felt at least a brush of it himself. He'd noticed the new faces and used a practiced shake of his head to spill his golden hair across the scars, only revealing the perfect half.

Jean-Claude's voice came low and harsh. "I cannot."

I'd been afraid; now it was sheer terror. I looked up at Asher and saw him through a film of all the times we'd touched him, all that beauty, all the beauty that I still saw. I whispered, "Help us!"

Asher was shaking his head. "If I am dragged in as well, it will help no one."

"Asher, please!"

"Once he feeds, all will be well, simply let him feed."

I shook my head. "Not here, not like this."

Micah said, "If it will help, why not let him feed?"

I looked at him, and just turning to him made my mouth part, my breath catch. It was almost like the *ardeur* remembered him, like a succulent food that it wanted to taste again.

It took two tries to say, "You don't understand."

Zane said, "Anita doesn't let Jean-Claude feed off of her." He and Cherry were sitting on the far edge of the couch, watching with wide eyes, not coming near us.

"I thought she was his human servant," Micah said.

"She is." Jean-Claude whispered it.

Something in those two words made me look at him, made me stare into those glittering blue eyes. He couldn't trap me with his gaze anymore, because I was his human servant, but tonight there was a pull to those eyes. I wanted to cradle his face in my hands, wanted to taste those half-parted lips.

"Anita!" Asher's voice jerked me around, made me look at him.

"Help me."

"He can feed on me." Micah said it, voice soft. We all turned and stared at him.

He looked a little less sure. I think something he saw on our faces made him hesitate, but he said it again. "If a little blood will cure this, then I'm willing."

"He has fed on blood tonight already," Asher said. "It is not blood he needs but . . . *voir les anges*."

"English, Asher, even I didn't understand that one," I said.

He waved his hands as if erasing what he'd said. "He needs release, a . . ." He said several things in rapid French, and I couldn't follow it. Asher was in great distress if his English had abandoned him.

I was careful not to look at Micah when I tried to explain. "It's the *ardeur* that Jean-Claude needs fed."

"He needs sex, not blood," Nathaniel said. His voice was soft, but a glance showed him standing as far across the room as he could get. I didn't blame him a bit.

"The first time you fed on me it wasn't intercourse, just contact," he said.

I nodded, still trying not to look at any of the men. "I remember."

"Contact is okay," Micah said.

I had to look at him, and the surprise was great enough that for just a second I almost fought free of the ardeur, I could almost think. "What kind of contact?"

"Sexual contact." His face was very serious, eyes solemn, as if he, too, could think again. "I said I would do anything to be your Nimir-Raj, Anita. What do I have to do to convince you I mean it?"

"What are you offering, Micah?"

"Whatever you need." He looked past me to Jean-Claude. "Whatever you both need."

I felt Jean-Claude's attention sharpen, almost like a physical force, and the *ardeur* was back, thick enough to drown in. My breath froze in my throat, my pulse was too fast to swallow. Jean-Claude's voice came, I think in my head, because his lips never moved. "Be careful what you offer, *mon ami*, my control is poor tonight."

Micah answered, as if he'd heard Jean-Claude too. "You were a ménage à trois with the Ulfric. He's gone. I'm here, and I'm staying. I will be Anita's Nimir-Raj, whatever that means."

I managed to say, "Who said that we were a ménage à trois?"

"Everyone," he said.

I wondered who everyone was, because I knew it *wasn't* everyone.

Jean-Claude was moving forward again, painfully slow, every movement so full of energy, so full of potential violence and grace, that it almost hurt to watch. It made my pulse race, my breath hard to take—made my body run moist. Oh, shit, oh, shit, oh, shit.

"Jean-Claude, no," but my voice was a whisper.

His mouth hovered over mine, then his face turned for a second to Micah. I watched the two of them gaze at each other from inches away and felt the power pulsing in the air between. Jean-Claude moved so slowly to close the distance between them that it was like watching slow motion. Micah sat there, waiting. He didn't move in to him, but he didn't move away either. I thought at first they'd kissed, then some trick of the light let me see a thin line of space between their mouths. Not touching, not yet. I watched their lips so tremblingly close, and part of me wanted them to touch, but Jean-Claude held his place, held his place until Micah closed his eyes, as if he couldn't stand to meet those glowing orbs, like looking away from the sun, too brilliant to bear.

And still Jean-Claude did not close that small distance. It was the distance of a breath, the flick of a tongue and still he held himself almost touching, almost there, but not quite. The tension grew, grew, grew, until I wanted to scream. I didn't realize that I'd moved in towards them, until they both turned at once and looked at me from inches away. My eyes flicked from one to the other. Eyes like blue fire; eyes like yellow-green clouds. Micah's eyes grew more green as I watched, until they were pale, pale green, like spring leaves. He focused on me. I couldn't explain it, but I knew that this was the look he hunted with, that sharp focus, the pupil nearly lost in the color of his eyes.

I realized that I'd pushed the *ardeur* back. I was attracted to both, but I could think again, feel something besides the burn. You practice one kind of metaphysical control, and I guess it gives you an edge on all of them. The relief made me feel weak, as if I could have curled on the floor and slept. We weren't going to fall on each other like ravening lust-monsters. Yippee.

I eased away, started to crawl backwards. Jean-Claude's gaze followed me, but he made no move to touch me. There was something about the way he stayed on all fours that let me know the *ardeur* was still riding him. But if I could keep from touching him, we'd be alright. He watched me, like a starving man, who was watching his first meal in days crawl away. But he played fair, he stayed where he was, he let me crawl away. He knew the rules. Micah didn't.

He reached for me, and I threw myself back to the floor in a blur of speed that I'd never had before, but Micah wasn't human either. He followed me in a movement that was too fast for my eyes to follow, so that he was above me before my mind could see that he'd moved. It was magical.

He was frozen just above me, his body balanced on hands and feet, almost like he was doing a push-up. I reached out, around him, trying not to touch him. I had time to say, "No, don't," then two things happened at once. Micah dropped his body on top of mine, and Jean-Claude took my outreached hand. Maybe he thought I was reaching for him, I don't know. But the moment we touched the heat ran over us, through us, and there was nothing but the need.

50

WE KISSED, AND it was like melting from the mouth down. My hands slid over the silk of Micah's shirt, and it wasn't enough. I ripped at it, tore it from his body until my hands spilled over the solid smoothness of his chest, his skin like warm satin under my fingers. Micah was suddenly grinding me into the floor, so heavy. I opened my eyes and found Jean-Claude above us, over Micah, pressing us both into the floor. I had a moment of meeting his eyes, a moment to see the rage in that blind blue fire, then his arms were around Micah, and he was jerking the smaller man backwards.

I sat up, watching them roll across the floor, fighting. Anger, frustration, and just sheer tiredness welled up inside me until there was no room for the *ardeur*. I was tired of fighting, so tired of it.

I smelled blood like a hot spike through the center of my body; the smell was almost sexual. That was enough. I drew the Browning and sighted around the room. For a split second, I had the two of them at the end of the barrel. For a split second it occurred to me. Then I moved the gun around the room, registering for the first time that there was no one left in the room but us. Good to know we didn't have an audience. I pointed the gun at the overstuffed white couch and fired. One of the small gold and silver pillows jumped upward with the impact. The noise was thunderous in the stone room, as if the heavy drapes caught the sound, held it around us.

They froze. Micah's hands were claws, shredding across Jean-Claude's back, because that was all he could reach. Jean-Claude's face was buried in Micah's neck, his body wrapped around him, so that everything vital was hidden while he tried to tear Micah's throat out.

I sighted on them. "Stop it, stop it, both of you, or the next one goes in one of you. I swear, by God, that I will shoot you."

Jean-Claude raised up, blood in a crimson wash across his mouth, chin, down his neck. There was so much blood, it made me afraid to look at Micah's neck. Micah's claws stayed in Jean-Claude's back. I could see the tension as if every muscle were poised to drive the claws farther in.

"The Nimir-Raj holds me in place, *ma petite.* I cannot move."

"Micah, let him up."

Micah didn't move, and I guess I couldn't blame him, but . . . I aimed the gun at his head because that was the only clear shot I had. I had a small spurt of panic that I might have to pull the trigger, then a calmness welled over me, and I stood in that well of silence, that buzzing white noise that I went to when I killed. There was no feeling here, there was almost nothing here.

"I . . . will . . . kill you, Micah." My voice sounded as empty as I felt.

Micah turned his head slowly to look at me. Blood flowed from the left side of his neck down his shoulder, his chest. He was drenched in his own blood. I could see more of it welling up, sliding down, but not constant; the blood pumped out with his pulse. Shit.

"Let him up, Micah, he's pierced your carotid." I lowered the gun and started to close the distance between them.

Micah looked up at the vampire, still poised with his claws in Jean-Claude's flesh. "If I die, I want him to go with me."

"It should be simple enough for a Nimir-Raj of your power to heal such a small wound," Jean-Claude said, still pressed around the other man's body, intimate.

Micah withdrew the claws from Jean-Claude's back. Jean-Claude moved enough to prop himself up on his hands. I saw Micah tense a second before his arm swung in that unbelievable speed, so fast, so fast. Jean-Claude's throat hadn't even started to bleed when Micah's hand was back at his side. Then blood spilled in a fountain from Jean-Claude's throat.

"Heal *that*," Micah said.

I was left standing there, watching them both bleed to death. Mother fucking son of a bitch.

51

JEAN-CLAUDE HALF FELL, half moved off of Micah. Blood sprayed in a red rain as he knelt on all fours, coughing, as if he were trying to clear his throat. It made the blood pump faster.

I screamed, at first wordless, then I thought of something better. I screamed, "Asher!"

Micah was already rolling in black fur, bones sliding in and out, muscles rolling in glimpses of pinkish flesh. He'd shapeshift and heal himself, but Jean-Claude couldn't shapeshift.

I grabbed Jean-Claude's arm, and the moment I touched him the marks flared between us. I was choking on my own blood, drowning in it. Strong hands were digging into my arms, fingers like cold stone. I blinked and found Jean-Claude's face glowing like carved alabaster with white light inside it. His skin glowed behind the coating of blood on his lower face, like rubies spread across diamonds. His eyes were pools of molten sapphire flame, if fire could be cold, achingly cold. A wind sprang from his body, from our bodies, and it was the cold of the grave that danced around us, fluttered our hair around our faces. We reached that cold power out, out, to find Richard, and as before the answer came against our skin. Jason was kneeling beside us. I didn't have time to marvel that he was healed. He touched us and the mark that was Richard flared through his body, a warmth to dance with our coldness. And I knew Micah was kneeling behind me, furred and clawed. I felt him at my back the way I felt Jason, as if he were tied to us.

Micah fell back, screaming, "Nooo!" The tie was cut and for a second I swayed, as if part of my support was gone, then Nathaniel was there, and the world was solid again.

We knelt, bound by flesh, magic, and blood. I watched the flesh in Jean-Claude's throat reknit, reform, remake, reshape itself until the flesh was perfect and white, surrounded by a coating of wet blood. He'd healed so fast that the blood hadn't had time to dry.

I smelled roses, not the faint perfume of potpourri, but thick, melt-on-your-tongue, old-fashioned garden roses, as if I were drowning in the cloying sweetness of them. It was like being dipped in honey that you knew had poison in it.

Honey, honey brown eyes. I remembered the pale honey brown of Belle Morte's eyes. "Do you smell the roses?" I asked.

Jean-Claude turned drowning blue eyes to me. "Roses? I smell nothing but the scent of your perfume, and skin." He scented the air, "And blood."

Nathaniel and Jason were lost in the wonder of the power rush, but no one smelled roses but me. Once upon a time I'd smelled perfume when a certain Master Vampire had been using her magic. My friend and fellow animator, Larry Kirkland, had smelled the perfume, too, but no one else around us had been able to scent it.

I looked into Jean-Claude's eyes, not with my sight, but with my magic, and found something, something that wasn't him. It was subtle. What she'd done with me earlier had been like a sledgehammer between the eyes; this was a stiletto in the dark.

I found the thread of her power coiled in him, and the moment my magic, my necromancy, hit it, the power uncoiled, opened, and it was like a window thrown wide. I saw her sitting in her room by fire and candlelight, as if electricity hadn't been invented. She was dressed in a white lace dressing gown, all that black hair falling around her, and a bowl of pink roses next to her pale hand. She turned those huge pale brown eyes to me, and I saw the surprise on her face, the shock. She saw me kneeling with the men, as I saw her before her dressing table with her roses.

I cut her off, cast her out of Jean-Claude, as I'd cast her out of me earlier. It was easier, because she hadn't tried to possess him, only to tamper with him, to be that dark voice in his ear that pushed him a little over the edge.

Jean-Claude slumped suddenly, as if dizzy. He raised eyes to me that were as normal as they ever got, his usual midnight blue. There was fear on his face, no hiding it. "I thought I saw Belle, sitting before her mirror."

I nodded. "You did."

He looked at me, and I think that only all our hands on him kept him from falling to the floor. "She weakened my control of the *ardeur*."

"And your control of your temper," I said.

"What has happened?" Asher asked.

I looked up to find that everyone was back in the room. "Any of this blood yours, ma'am?" Bobby Lee asked.

I shook my head. "Not a scratch on me."

"Then I guess we won't get blacklisted from the bodyguard union for leaving you alone with a shapeshifter and a vampire, so they could fight over you." He was shaking his head. "The next time you ask us to leave you alone because it's your love life, we aren't going to listen to you."

I shook my head, again. "We'll talk about it later."

"No, ma'am," he said, "we won't."

I let the argument go. There was always time to fight later. Besides, he was too close to right. If I'd gotten between them at the wrong moment, who knew what accident might have happened?

Jean-Claude spoke softly, voice urgent, to Asher. They were speaking French and I still didn't know enough to catch more than a word here and there. I heard Belle, clearly, several times.

In English Asher said, "Do you remember Marcel?"

"*Oui*. He went mad one night and slew his entire household."

"Including his human servant," Asher said, "which is what killed him."

The two vampires stared at each other. "No one ever understood what had caused it," Jean-Claude said.

"So fortuitous," Asher said, "only two nights before he would have fought Belle for her Council seat."

Jean-Claude took Asher's offered hand and let him help him to his feet. Asher had to steady Jean-Claude with a hand on his elbow. "So fortuitous that many tried to prove she had poisoned him, or some such," Asher said.

Jean-Claude nodded, passing a hand over his face, as if he were still dizzy. I felt nothing, as if my necromancy protected me from whatever Belle had done to him. "The Council themselves tried to prove her at fault and failed," Jean-Claude said.

"Did they hire a witch to look into the magic angle?" I asked. I stood on my own, just fine. Nathaniel and Jason got to their feet, again with no ill-effects, except for Jason's stupid grin, which he often wore after a power rush.

The vampires looked at me. "*Non,*" Asher said, "no one thought of it."

"Why the hell not?"

"Because, *ma petite*, she should not be able to do what she did to a Master of the City, even one of her own bloodline. That she could do this to a Master of the City that was *not* her bloodline would be unthinkable."

"Impossible," Asher added.

"I think it's like real possible," I said. "I caught her in the act."

"Who's Belle?" Micah asked in his growling leopard voice.

I turned to him, slowly, and something must have shown on my face, because Merle moved in front of him, and suddenly the two wererats were alert, starting to move up beside me. I don't know what I was about to say, probably something really angry, because Micah beat me to it.

"He pierced my jugular vein, Anita. I'm allowed to defend myself when someone tries to eat my throat out."

"Remember I'm his human servant. He dies, so might I."

He stalked around Merle, gliding on bent legs and kitty-cat feet. "So I'm just supposed to let him kill me?"

"No," I said, "no, but your wound wasn't life-threatening. You proved that already. There's not a scratch on you now."

"I healed it, yes, but not every shapeshifter could have healed it. A vampire wound is a lot like silver, it can kill, and most of us heal from those wounds like we were human." He was standing very close to me, those green-gold eyes sparkling with anger. "He meant to kill me, Anita, don't think he didn't."

"He is right, *ma petite*, if he had not held me off more, I would have torn his throat out."

I turned back to Jean-Claude. "What are you saying?"

"I saw him on top of you, and I was drowning in jealousy. I meant him harm, *ma petite.* He defended himself."

"He didn't have to do that last blow. The fight had stopped."

Jean-Claude looked past me at Micah, and there was something on his face—respect, I think. "If he had done to me what I did to him, then I would have had no choice but to make my point," he seemed to consider several words and settled for, "strongly."

"Strongly? He damn near slit your throat."

"After I had tried to do the same to him."

I was shaking my head. "No, no, I don't . . ."

"What, *ma petite*, are you truly saying that if someone had torn your throat out, tried for your life that you wouldn't have shot them?"

I opened my mouth to argue, closed it, tried again, and stopped. I looked at him, then back at Micah, then back to Jean-Claude. "Well, damn."

"The Nimir-Raj has made his point, *ma petite.* He is willing to be accommodating up to a point—beyond that point there is no compromise."

Micah nodded, and the movement looked awkward in his furred body. "Yes."

"You have the same rule, *ma petite*, as do I. The three of us merely have different places where the line is drawn. But the line is there for all of us."

"How can you both be so reasonable about this? You both nearly just killed each other?"

They looked at each other, around me, again, and there was something in that look. It was something masculine and arcane, as if the fact that I was a girl meant I wouldn't get it, and they couldn't explain it to me. Which did explain it to me.

"Oh, great, great, you guys nearly kill each other, and that makes you buddies."

Jean-Claude gave that wonderful Gallic shrug, his face still covered in Micah's blood. "Let us say we have an understanding."

Micah agreed.

"Jesus, only men could get a friendship out of something like this."

"You are friends with Monsieur Edward. Did you not both begin by trying to kill each other?" Jean-Claude asked.

"That's different," I said.

"How?"

I tried to argue, but stopped because I would have looked silly. "Fine, fine, so what, the two of you kiss and make up?"

They looked at each other, and again there was weight to the gaze, but it was a different weight. "Shit," I said.

"I think we begin by apologizing," Jean-Claude said. "I am truly sorry for my lack of control."

"Me, too," Micah said, then added, "and I'm sorry that I had to try and kill you." It was interesting phrasing, not I'm sorry I nearly killed you, but sorry I had to try and kill you. I was seeing Micah's ruthless streak. It wasn't really any bigger than my own, but it bothered me anyway. Wasn't sure why, but it did.

I didn't know what to do, so I decided to move on, we had other business. "Are you well enough to help get Damian out of his coffin?"

"I have used up all my reserves, *ma petite.* I will need to feed again." He raised a hand. "But not the *ardeur*, merely blood."

Merely, he says.

"I offered to let you feed on me earlier. The offer still stands," Micah said.

"No, Micah," Merle said.

Micah touched the taller man's arm. "It's alright."

"Are you not afraid I will try and tear your throat out again? I would listen to your bodyguard."

"You said we had an understanding."

"That is true."

They were watching each other, and I could almost feel the testosterone rise.

Micah smiled, or tried to. In the half-leopard form it was a snarl of white fangs in black fur. "Besides, the next time you bite me like that, it better be foreplay, or I will kill you."

"If it pleases you, my pleasure," Jean-Claude said. He laughed then, that touchable sound that caressed my skin, made me shiver. Micah reacted to it, eyes wide. He'd never heard Jean-Claude's laugh before. If he thought the *laugh* was something special, well, the best truly was yet to come.

"I thank you for your most generous offer,"Jean-Claude said, "but I prefer my food without fur."

"No problem," Micah said. Micah released Merle's arm, and did that magically quick change. His tanned skin seemed to absorb the fur like rocks sinking into water. He stood naked and perfect, no mark of the fight on that smooth skin. Neither his clothing nor the tie in his hair had survived the change. But strangely the hair fell straight around his face, as if it were affected by the fact that he'd pulled it back tight while it was still wet. The hair was still thick, but it framed his face better, was less overwhelming, so that you could still see the delicate bone structure, those wondrous eyes.

I heard someone catch their breath, and it wasn't me. I don't think it was Jean-Claude, but I wasn't sure. Didn't matter, didn't want to know.

"You are not even dizzy, are you?" Jean-Claude asked.

Micah shook his head.

Jean-Claude raised his eyebrows, lowered his eyes, fought to control his face, until he could give a perfect blank expression, but it took him a few seconds. "I will clean this," he made a vague motion at his gore-soaked clothes, "before taking such a bounty, if that is alright?"

Micah gave a small nod.

"You are not taking a bath," I said.

"I will be quick, *ma petite*."

"You have never taken a quick bath in your entire life."

Asher laughed, then tried to smother it, but was only partially successful. He spread his hands. "*Mon cheri*, she is right."

"Would I touch that for the first time covered in this?"

Asher's face sobered instantly, like someone had thrown a switch. He turned that serious, blank face to stare at Micah, who stared back. If he was uncomfortable under the scrutiny, it didn't show.

Asher sighed. "I suppose not."

"And what are we supposed to do for the hour that it takes you to soak in the tub?" I asked.

"I will be quick, *ma petite*, my word on it."

I crossed my arms over my stomach. "I'll believe it when I see it."

"*Ma petite*, I have given my word."

"On important stuff, your word is great, but when it comes to primping, you have no sense of time."

"I thought that was the man's line," Bobby Lee said.

I glanced at him then back to the vampire. "Couldn't prove it by me."

Bobby Lee laughed, but no one else did.

52

I SAT ON the white couch with its brand-new bullet hole. Micah sat down beside me, and since he was naked, that was . . . interesting. Uncomfortable, and sort of titillating all at the same time. He kept insisting on trying to talk to me, and I found it hard to keep eye contact, and that was embarrassing.

Bobby Lee and Cris stayed near me, hovering behind and to one side, because I made them move from right behind me. I just don't like armed people at my back, not unless I know them really well. The wererats were there to protect me. I believed they'd do the job, because Rafael told them to, but I still didn't want them standing armed at my back. Merle lounged near the fireplace, keeping an eye on Micah and the other bodyguards. Gil was actually hiding in the corner, or nearly—not a stable guy—the others milled around the room. Except for Asher.

He sat in the chair opposite the couch and watched us. He had shaken that glorious hair over his face so that only the perfect side was visible, and only one pale blue eye looked at us. His face showed nothing, but I could still feel the weight of his gaze, like a hand pushing. His face may have shown nothing, but he was giving us way too much attention.

I might have asked why, but Jean-Claude walked back through the gap in the drapes. I had to check my watch. Only twenty minutes had passed. I'd dated him off and on for nearly three years; a twenty-minute cleanup was nothing short of miraculous. Of course, his black hair was still wet and heavy; he hadn't taken time to blow-dry it. He was wearing one of my favorite robes, the black one with the black furred edging. The fur outlined a wonderful expanse of pale perfect chest. The robe was open enough that the cross-shaped burn scar showed, and as he glided into the room you caught glimpses of his upper stomach through the fur. The robe was very loosely tied, not at all the way he usually wore it.

He had that smile on his face that said he knew he looked wonderful, and he knew just what effect he had on me, then his gaze slid to Micah. I was close enough to see Micah's pulse speed up, jumping under the skin of his neck. He tried to meet Jean-Claude's eyes, but finally had to look down, and he blushed.

His reaction made *my* pulse speed up. I looked back at Jean-Claude gliding towards us, catching a glimpse of his pale feet under the black robe, against the white carpet. The look on his face was all for Micah. It made me go up on one knee, my butt against the arm of the couch. I felt oddly possessive, almost jealous, as if I should be defending Micah's honor. I'd never felt like this with Richard and Jean-Claude, but then, Jean-Claude had never looked at Richard in quite that way. Because Richard would have hurt him.

Micah had nearly killed Jean-Claude over an insult that Richard would not have fought back over, yet here he sat blushing, uncomfortable, but not angry.

Jean-Claude was standing in front of us, so close that the furred hem of the robe brushed Micah's bare leg. "Have you changed your mind, *mon minet*?"

Micah shook his head, then raised his face up to look at the vampire. There was both vulnerability and warning in that look. "I haven't changed my mind."

"*Bon.*" Jean-Claude went to his knees in front of him. "You are powerful in your own right, and you are not my animal to call. I may not be able to cloud your mind and make this tasting a pleasure. You may be able to keep me out of your mind."

Micah nodded, thick hair falling around his face. "I understand."

"Do you have a preference on where the blood is taken from?"

"The neck hurts less," Micah said.

Jean-Claude raised an eyebrow. "You've done this before?"

Micah gave a smile that managed not to be happy. "I've done a lot of things before."

Jean-Claude raised both eyebrows at that and looked at me. I shrugged.

"Very well, *mon minet*." He stood in one graceful movement, swinging the robe around him like a dress, giving the slightest glimpse of bare legs as he stalked behind the couch. He stopped just behind Micah, putting a hand on either of his shoulders. He didn't caress, or squeeze, just rested his hands on that smooth, warm flesh for a moment.

"Get on with it," Merle said.

Micah turned his head to look at the other wereleopard. "Merle." One word, but it made the big man lean back harder on the fireplace, arms crossed over his chest, face sullen, a very unhappy bodyguard. But he did what he was told.

Jean-Claude slid one arm around the front of Micah's shoulders, across his very upper chest. He used his free hand to smooth Micah's hair back, exposing the side of his face and the long clean line of his throat. Micah moved his head a little to the side, giving Jean-Claude a better angle. The small movement was like a woman coming to her tiptoes for a kiss, a helpful movement.

"Maybe we could have a little privacy," I said, and it made both men look at me.

"As you like, *ma petite*." Everyone left except Merle, Bobby Lee, and Asher. They were the minimum that might be needed to keep us from killing each other. After what had just happened, I really couldn't work up a good argument for leaving us completely alone. When everyone had settled down, Jean-Claude turned back to Micah.

Jean-Claude's fingers stroked Micah's hair so that it fell behind his ear, exposing the entire side of his face, the shape of his ear. He pressed the back of Micah's head gently against his chest, drawing the exposed neck in an even longer line. Micah was utterly passive, eyes closed, face peaceful; only the pulse in his neck beating like a trapped thing gave lie to all that calmness.

Jean-Claude bent over him, mouth open, lips going back, but even this close I got only the barest glimpse of teeth. He bit down, sharp, sudden. Micah gasped, breath catching in his throat. Jean-Claude's grip tightened at Micah's head, his shoulders, pressing him in against his body. I could see the muscles in Jean-Claude's jaws working, his throat swallowing convulsively. One of them was making small noises low in his throat, and I wasn't sure who it was.

Jean-Claude reared back, bringing Micah with him, drawing him half over the couch. Micah cried out, his hands going to Jean-Claude's arm, holding on, as the vampire rocked his body backwards. Jean-Claude moved his hand from Micah's face to his waist, as if he knew the other man wouldn't move away now. He held Micah, arms across his chest and waist, Micah's hands on Jean-Claude's arm. He stretched Micah's body backwards as he'd lengthened the man's neck earlier, so that Micah's body showed in a long, clean line, back curved against Jean-Claude's body, so that both of them were bowed backwards.

I was left kneeling on the couch, staring up the line of Micah's nude body, seeing without doubt that what was happening was making his body happy. His face was slack with need, pleasure. His hands convulsed over Jean-Claude's arm, and he half-screamed, half-shouted, "God!"

Jean-Claude's body began to straighten up, slowly. He eased Micah back over the couch. He raised his mouth from Micah's neck; his eyes were drowning blue, sightless, inhuman. His lips were full, red, but not with spilled blood, red like someone who's been kissing too much. He released Micah slowly, letting his body slide against the back of the couch, until the wereleopard half-collapsed on his side. His head spilled into my lap, and I jumped. Micah raised his head, slowly, heavy. He propped himself up on one arm and turned unfocused eyes to me. His pupils were enormous, drowning black in the circle of his green-yellow eyes. I watched his pupils spiral downward to small dots so that the color almost overwhelmed them, like a vampire's eyes. I could feel him staring at me, the weight of his gaze like something pushing against me. He leaned in towards me, slowly, lips half-parted.

I stayed where I was, frozen, unsure what to do. It wasn't that he was any less lovely than he had been. It was just . . . oh, hell, I didn't know what to do. I didn't even know what I wanted to do.

"Didn't you need to get Damian out of his coffin?" Asher's voice came dry, making me draw back from Micah.

Jean-Claude snarled at him, looking more inhuman than the entire time he was feeding.

Asher stood in one smooth motion, like a puppet pulled up by strings. "Fine, but if you are going to have sex, then I don't have to watch."

I stood, Micah's hands sliding down my body as I moved away from the couch. I faced Asher. "Look, I am so far over my comfort zone right now that I can't think, but I'll tell you one thing. I am not going to salve your male ego while the little voice in my brain is still screaming, run away, run away. So, put the attitude on ice, Asher, I can't deal with it right now."

He was suddenly vibrating with anger, his eyes like icy blue pools. "So sorry that my discomfort annoys you."

"Fuck you, Asher."

He was suddenly moving forward in a blur of speed. I backed up so fast that I fell against the couch. Micah caught me, or I'd have fallen to the floor. I had time to draw a gun, or a knife, but I didn't even try. Asher wasn't trying to hurt my body, just my feelings. He bent at the waist, looming over me and Micah, though I think that part was accidental. He put a hand on either side of us and leaned into my face, so close that I had to pull back to focus on those chilling blue eyes. "Don't offer things you're not willing to do, *ma cherie*, because that is annoying."

He stood up abruptly and stalked from the room.

Micah's voice was soft. "What was all that about?" His hands were still on my arms, half-holding me, protective.

I shook my head. "Ask Jean-Claude." I pushed to my feet. "I'm going to go get Damian."

"I will accompany you, *ma petite.*"

"Fine." I started walking. I could feel them following me, feel them both behind me. I almost turned around to see if they were holding hands, but if they were, I wasn't ready to see it.

Bobby Lee trailed behind without a word. Smart man.

53

THE ROOM WAS bare stone walls. There was no pretense of comfort. It was the vampire's version of prison, and it looked like one. There were half a dozen coffins sitting on bare, raised platforms with silver chains around them, waiting to be raised and locked in place with crosses. The only crosses in the room were on the two closed coffins. Two? Two chained coffins. Damian was in one. Who the hell was in the other?

"Which one is your boy?" Bobby Lee asked.

I shook my head. "Don't know."

"I thought you were supposed to be this boy's master."

"That's the theory."

"Then shouldn't you be able to tell which box is which?"

I glanced at him, gave a small nod. "Point." I looked back at the door but it was still empty, just us. I didn't know where everyone had gone to, and I was so trying not to speculate on what might have distracted Micah and Jean-Claude.

I tried to concentrate on who was in the coffins, but I couldn't. Once upon a time I could sense Damian even before he woke in his coffin, but I got nothing from either coffin, except that there were vampires in them. I went to the closest coffin. The wood was pale and smooth. Not the most expensive, but not cheap either, heavy, well made. I passed my hands across the smooth wood, fingers caressing the coolness of the chains. Something banged against the lid of the coffin. I jumped.

Bobby Lee laughed.

I frowned at him, then turned back to the coffin, but I wasn't touching it anymore. I knew it wasn't possible with a blessed cross attached to the lid, but I'd had this sudden image of an arm tearing through the wood and grabbing me. Damian was supposed to be homicidally crazy. Better cautious than dead.

I put my hands just above the coffin, not quite touching. I drew my necromancy, like drawing a breath, and breathed it out through my body, not exactly through my hands, but everywhere. The necromancy was part of *what* I was, not just who I was. I started to push my power into the coffin, but it was pulled in, like water pouring into a hole. The water falls down because gravity pulls it down, and there is no stopping it; it's natural, automatic. My necromancy spilled into that coffin, and into Damian. I felt him lying in the dark, his body pressed against the thin satin. I saw his eyes stare up into mine, felt something flare inside him, something that recognized my power, but I couldn't feel him. There was no personality there, no Damian. I knew it was him, but there was no thought in him, nothing but that tiny spark of recognition, and barely that. I tried to reconcile the thing I felt to what I knew Damian had been, and it was like he had become something else. I said a quick prayer, and I didn't even feel odd praying to God about a vampire. I'd had to give up my narrow ideas of God a long time ago, or give up church and everything I held dear about my religion. The deal was, if God was okay with what I was doing, then I had to be, too.

"Where is everybody?" I asked it aloud, so Bobby Lee answered.

"I don't know, but if you come with me, we'll go look."

I shook my head staring at the other coffin. Who was in there locked in the dark? I had to know, and if I could, I'd get them out. I didn't approve of torture, and being locked in a coffin where you would never starve to death, but always go hungry, never die of thirst, but burn with the need for liquid, be trapped in a space so small you couldn't even turn onto your side, were all good definitions of torture in my book. I liked most of Jean-Claude's vamps, and I wouldn't leave them like this, not if I could presuade him that they'd been punished enough. I was pretty stubborn about things like that, and Jean-Claude was wanting to please me right now; I could probably get whoever it was out. I'd do my best. But who was it? Admittedly, there were vampires that I'd make more of an effort to save, just like people.

I went to stand beside the other coffin and pushed my magic into it. I had to push this time; it wasn't like Damian. Whatever was in this box didn't welcome me in. It wasn't anyone I had a connection with. I felt something, and I knew it was a kind of undead, but it didn't feel like a vampire. It felt emptier than that. It was fully dark outside; there should have been movement, life, of a sort, but there was nothing. I pushed farther into the thing, and found the faintest answering pulse. It was as if whatever was in there was a lot more dead than alive, yet not truly dead.

A sound turned me towards the door. Jean-Claude glided into the room, his robe tied tight now, like a signal that he was ready to get down to business. He was alone.

"Where's Micah?" I asked.

"Jason has taken him to get some clothing. They should be able to find something that will fit him."

"Who is in this coffin?" I'd almost said, *what*, but I was betting it was a vampire, just not like one I'd ever sensed before.

His face was already careful, neutral. "I would think, *ma petite*, that you have enough to be concerned over with Damian?"

"You know and I know that I am not moving until I know who's in here."

He sighed. "Yes, I know." He actually looked down at the floor, as if he were tired, and because his face showed nothing, the gesture looked half-finished, like bad acting. But I knew that for him to be working so hard at keeping anything off his face, only to let his body betray him meant he was very unhappy. Which meant that I was really not going to like the answer.

"Who, Jean-Claude?"

"Gretchen," he said, finally meeting my eyes. His face told me nothing, the one word empty.

Once upon a time Gretchen had tried to kill me because she wanted Jean-Claude for herself. "When did she get back in town?"

"Back?" He gave it that little lilt that made it a question.

"Don't be coy, Jean-Claude. She came back to town still out for my blood, and you put her in here, so when?"

His face became like a sculpture, except with less movement in it. He was hiding as much of himself as he could, and the shields were like armor. "I say again, *ma petite*, she had gone nowhere."

"What's that supposed to mean?"

He looked at me with that perfect face, so unreadable. "It means that from the moment you watched me put her in the coffin in my office at Guilty Pleasures, she has always been here."

I blinked, frowned, opened my mouth, closed it, tried again, failed. I must have looked like a landed fish, because I couldn't think of a damn thing to say. He just stood there, not helping.

I found my voice, and it was breathy. "You're saying that Gretchen has been in a coffin for two, no three years?"

He just looked at me. He'd stopped breathing. There was no sense of movement to him at all, as if, if I looked away I'd never find him again; he'd be invisible.

"Answer me, damn it! Has she been in a coffin for three years?"

He gave the smallest of nods.

"Jesus, Jesus." I paced the room, because if I didn't do something physical, I was going to hit him or start screaming. I finally ended up standing in front of him, hands in fists at my sides. "You bastard." My voice was a hoarse whisper, squeezed out of my throat because to do anything else would have had me ranting at him.

"She tried to kill my human servant, who I also loved. Most masters would have simply killed her."

"That would have been better than this," I said, voice still a hissing whisper.

"I doubt Gretchen would agree."

"Let's open the coffin and see," I said.

He shook his head. "Not tonight, *ma petite.* I knew you would feel this way, and we can try and release her, though I have poor hope for it."

"What's that supposed to mean?"

"She was not the most stable of women when she went in. This will not have strengthened her grasp of reality."

"How could you have done this to her?"

"I told you before, *ma petite*, she earned her punishment."

"Not three years," I said. My voice was beginning to sound normal again. I wasn't going to hit him, great.

"Three years for nearly killing you. I could leave her in for three more years, and it would not be punishment enough."

"I'm not going to argue whether the punishment was justified or excessive, or anything. All I can say is that I want her out of there. I won't let her stay in there another night. There's barely anything left now."

He glanced at the coffin. "You have not opened it, how do you know what is inside?"

"I wanted to know how Damian was. I used a little magic to explore what was inside both coffins."

"And what did you discover?" he asked.

"That my necromancy recognizes Damian. That Damian isn't there. It's like his personality is missing. Whatever made him, him, is missing."

Jean-Claude nodded. "With the vampires that are not master strength and never will be, it is often the Master of the City, or their creator, that enables them to exist as strong presences. Cut off from that, they often fade."

Fade, he called it, like he was talking about curtains that had been in sunlight too long, instead of a living being. Well, a sort-of-living being.

"Well, Gretchen is way past faded. There's almost nothing left. We leave her in even one more night and she may not be there."

"She cannot die."

"Maybe not, but the damage . . ." I shook my head. "We have to get her out now, tonight, or we might as well put a bullet in her."

"Leave Damian in for one more night, and I will agree to release Gretchen."

"No," I said. "Damian is like one of those feral vamps. The longer he's like this, the greater the likelihood that he'll never be anything else."

"Do you really believe that one more night will damage him irreparably?" Jean-Claude asked.

"I don't know, but I know that if I wait until tomorrow night to get him out and the damage is permanent, I'll always wonder if that one extra night made the difference."

"Then we have a problem, *ma petite.* A hot bath is being run now in preparation for one released vampire. We only have one place suitable here at the Circus for such a recovery."

"Why a bath?" I asked.

"They must be brought back to life, to warmth. The process must be done carefully, or the risk is one of true death."

"Wait a minute. A vamp can be in the coffin locked away forever and never die, but getting them out can kill them? That doesn't make sense."

"They have adjusted to the coffin, *ma petite*. To bring them out after a length of time is a shock to their system. I have seen vampires die of it."

I knew he wouldn't lie; he was too unhappy about having to say it. "So we throw them both in the same tub, no big."

"But it is a big, *ma petite.* The attention and power needed to bring one back must not be divided between them. It will take all that I have to bring one at a time back. I cannot divide my efforts without risking them both."

"I know that you made Gretchen, but you didn't make Damian. His ties to you as Master of the City broke when he became mine, so you aren't his master in any way. I am."

"Yes," he said.

"Then isn't it my job to bring Damian back—my mystical connection with him, not yours?"

"If you were truly his master, another vampire, I would agree. But you are, for all your talents, still human. There are things you cannot do for him, and there are many things you will not know to do for him."

"Like what?"

He shook his head. "It is a complex process, requiring specialized skills."

"And you have those skills," I said.

"Do not sound so skeptical, *ma petite.* I was part of our mistress's emergency . . . crew," he said. "She would punish others and we would be left to deal with the aftermath. It was often her way."

"We?" I asked.

"Asher and myself."

"So Asher knows how to do this," I said.

"*Oui*, but he is not Damian's master either."

"No, but I am. If Damian still has one, I'm it. So you take care of Gretchen, you loan me Asher, and he tells me what to do for Damian."

"After his little display in the other room, you would trust him?"

"I'd trust him with my life, and so would you."

"But not our hearts," Jean-Claude said.

"Why did it bother him so much to see you with Micah?" I asked. "He's seen almost as bad with Richard, and me."

"I believe that you as my human servant and Richard as my wolf to call were possessions, mine by right, and you were already in place when Asher arrived in St. Louis. Micah is not my animal to call. He has no ties directly to me. He is your Nimir-Raj, but nothing to me."

"And?" I asked.

"Asher was willing to share me with you and Richard because you were mine. But this Nimir-Raj is simply another man that has my favor when Asher does not."

"Micah doesn't have your favor, exactly, yet."

Jean-Claude gave a small smile. "True, but Asher does not see it that way."

"If it weren't for my . . . social qualms would you be doing Asher right now?"

He laughed, an abrupt sound that didn't dance along my body; it just filled his face with glee. The closest I'd ever seen to real laughter from him. "Social qualms—ah, *ma petite*, that is precious."

I frowned at him. "Just answer the question."

The laughter faded, almost like a person, instead of that abrupt change he usually did. "Asher and I would likely have come to an understanding if it would not have cost me you, *ma petite*."

"An understanding. Now who's being coy?" I said.

He gave that Gallic shrug that meant everything and nothing. "You would not be comfortable with brutal honesty, *ma petite*."

"Fine, if I could have stomached it, would you have taken Asher back as your lover by now?"

He thought about it, then finally, "I do not know, *ma petite*."

"I know you love him."

"*Oui*, but that does not mean we could be lovers again. When he and I were happiest, it was with Julianna. You might be able to stand us as lovers out of your sight, as long as we did not act like lovers in front of you. I do not think you would like watching Asher and me hold hands in front of you."

Put that way, he was right. "What are you saying?"

"I am saying that Asher deserves better than a hidden relationship where we could never show public affection for fear of hurting you. I would rather give him up completely to someone else, male or female, than force him to play second—or lower—to you forever."

I opened my mouth to say that I liked Asher, even loved him in a way, but I didn't, because I didn't want to raise the possibility of a true ménage à trois. What

I'd seen with Micah and Jean-Claude had already bugged me a lot. I just couldn't deal with two men and me. Yeah, yeah, it was the Midwestern, middle-class value system, but it was the way I looked at the world. I couldn't change that, could I? And if I could, did I want to?

I didn't know. I just didn't know. The fact that the thought didn't make me run screaming into the night bothered me, but not as much as I thought it should have.

54

JEAN-CLAUDE GAVE JASON the keys to the locks on the silver chains. He'd spent the last hour explaining everyone's job. Jason would be the appetizer, oh, sorry, Gretchen's first feeding. It couldn't be someone human because the first feeding after being in the box could be quite . . . *traumatic.* Jean-Claude's choice of words, not mine. So basically Jason got to be point man and take the first damage. Then it was Jean-Claude's turn to donate blood. The vamp's master gave a feeding and rebound the vamp to the blood oaths that connected them either to the Master of the City, their bloodline, their maker, or, in Jean-Claude's case, all three. All three was better; the stronger the original connection, the greater chance the vampire had of healing the damage.

That last part made me worry for Damian. I wasn't his maker, I wasn't his bloodline, or his Master of the City. I wasn't sure exactly what I was to him. To that question, Jean-Claude had said, "You are his master, *ma petite*. Whatever that means for a necromancer, that is what you are to him. If taking blood from you doesn't reconnect him, then Asher will try. Failing that, they will fetch me from Gretchen. Damian must rebind his ties to one of us, or he is lost."

"Define lost," I said.

"The madness may be permanent."

"Shit."

"Oui."

But first Gretchen, so that I could see it done, understand the process better.

Jason unlocked the chains. They fell off the coffin and clunked against the wood, a dull, harsh sound. It made me jump. Gretchen had tried to kill me when she only *thought* I was dating Jean-Claude. She might rise from the coffin bent on killing me. I'd been her advocate, demanding Jean-Claude let her out. Now as Jason undid the locks on the lid itself, my chest was tight, and I had to fight to keep my hand away from my gun. It would be stupid—not to mention ironic—if I had to kill her the moment she rose. I could just hear Jean-Claude's dry, *And this is an improvement, ma petite?* I said a quick prayer that it wouldn't come to that. I didn't want to kill her, I wanted to save her. Wanting to do the last didn't mean I wouldn't do the first, but it did mean I would try to avoid it.

Jason raised the lid, slowly. Not because it was heavy, but because, I think, he was scared, too. The idea of being Gretchen's first meal had made him laugh, that anticipatory sound that is half grown-up male, and half little boy. The sound that men reserve for things that combine sex and usually sports, cars, technology, or danger—depends on your man. I'm sure there are men out there that would give that purring, excited laugh at the thought of gardening, or poetry, but I haven't met them. Might be an interesting change, though.

The lid went back in that halfway position that coffin lids do. Nothing moved. There was just Jason standing there in his cutoff jean shorts, bare back to the room. Gretchen didn't come bounding out and eat anybody, and I let out a breath I hadn't known I was holding.

Jason stayed there, gazing down, unmoving, hands frozen on the lid. He finally turned towards the rest of us, and there was a look on his face that I'd never seen. It was a mixture of horror and pity. His spring blue eyes were wide, and there was a glitter of tears, I thought. Jason and Gretchen hadn't been close. The reaction couldn't be personal. What was in that coffin to put that look on Jason's face?

I was moving forward without realizing it. "*Ma petite,* do not go closer."

I looked at him. "What's the matter with her? Why does Jason look so . . . stricken?"

Jason answered, "I've never seen anything like this."

I had to see now, I had to. I kept walking towards the coffin. Jean-Claude met me, blocked my path. "Please, *ma petite,* do not go closer."

"I'm supposed to watch the process, right? I'm going to have to see what she looks like sooner or later, Jean-Claude. Might as well be sooner."

He studied my face, as if he'd memorize it. "I did not anticipate that she would be so . . ." He shook his head. "You will not be happy with me after you see her."

"You don't know what she looks like either," I said.

"No, but Jason's reaction tells me many things I do not wish to know."

"What's that supposed to mean?"

He just stepped aside. "Gaze upon her, *ma petite,* and when you have forgiven me, come back to me."

Forgiven him? I did not like the phrasing. I'd been scared of Gretchen pouncing out and trying to kill me; now I was more frightened of looking at her, of what horror awaited me inside that coffin. My pulse was trying to climb out my throat, and I couldn't breathe past it. Jason's face, Jean-Claude's sorrow, and the utter stillness from the coffin had left me so scared my mouth was dry.

Jason moved to one side, turning away from the coffin, leaning his butt against it, arms hugging his sides. He looked pale and ill. I wondered if he'd changed his mind about letting Gretchen touch him.

I stood just far enough back that I couldn't see into the coffin. I didn't want to see something so horrible that it made Jason pale. I didn't want to see it, but I had to.

I stepped up to the coffin, like stepping up to the plate, knowing that the ball coming at you is going a hundred-plus miles an hour and you have no chance to swing. My eyes couldn't make sense of what I saw at first. My mind simply refused to understand. It's a safety feature that we all have. If something is too horrendous, sometimes our brain just says, nope, not going to see this, not going to record this, nope, it would break us. But if you stare long enough, the mind says, well damn, we're not turning away, and finally, finally, you'll see it, and once you see it, you'll never be able to unsee it.

It lay against white satin so that the dry, brown color was very stark, painfully outlined. It looked like a wizened mummy, one of those bodies they find every once in a while in the desert, where the dryness makes natural mummies. The brown skin had molded to the bones, there was no muscle under it, just bones and skin. The mouth was open wide, as if the jaw hinge had broken. The fangs were dry, but white like a skull. The entire head had dried down to just the skull covered by a light coating of brown skin. Patches of bright blond hair clung to that skull, and the bright color made it worse, more obscene somehow. The eyes opened. I jumped, but the eyes that stared back at me were filled with something brown and dried, like big raisins. They blinked once, slowly, and a sound like wind sighing came out of the mouth.

I fell back from the coffin, fell to my knees. Jason grabbed my arm, drew me to my feet. I shook his hand off and went for Jean-Claude. He stood there, face patient, empty. I hit him without ever breaking stride. Maybe he expected me to stop, take a stance, but I hit him in the face, closed fist, like it was a continuation of the movement of my body. I twisted my fist—my whole body—into it, and he was suddenly on the floor, looking up at me, with blood on his face.

55

"YOU BASTARD, YOU fed off her energy while she was in there." I had to stalk away from him to keep from kicking him. Some things you did not do; some lines you did not cross.

He touched the back of his hand to his mouth. "What if I had nothing to do with it?"

"What if?" I came to stand over him. "What if? Are you really going to try and tell me that you didn't feed off of her?" I pointed back towards the coffin and must have glanced back, because the next thing I knew he had my legs, and I was suddenly falling towards the ground. I slapped the hard stones with my arms like I'd been taught in Judo. That took some of the impact, kept my head from hitting the stone floor, but it took concentration. By the time my body hit the ground, Jean-Claude was on top of me, pinning my arms to the floor with his forearms, the rest of his body trapping the rest of mine.

"Get off of me."

"*Non, ma petite,* not until you hear me out."

I tried to raise my arms, not because I thought I could outmuscle him, but because I had to try. I've never been able not to struggle even when I know it's a lost cause.

I was able to raise my arms a little—not enough to get away, but enough to make him bear down, enough to widen his eyes, enough to make him tense. Good to know the marks were helping me gain useful things like strength and not just crap.

Blood was a bright surprise against that pale skin. The blood dripped from an open cut on his mouth. "How do you know that this is not what all vampires would be reduced to after years?"

I glared up at him because I couldn't do much else. "Liar."

"How are you so certain?" He pressed himself harder against me for emphasis I think because he wasn't happy to be there; his body was all about anger not sex. "How do you know, Anita?"

He'd used my real name. "I'm a necromancer, remember?"

His face clearly said he didn't believe the answer was that simple, and he was right. I was remembering my visit to New Mexico and what I'd learned there. A monster rising above the bar in a club in Albuquerque. It rose above the bar in a thin line of pale flesh, like the rising of a crescent moon, then a face came into view. It was a woman's face with one eye gone stiff and dry like some kind of mummy. Face after face rose brown and withered, like a string of monstrous beads strung together with pieces of body, arms, legs, and thick black thread like gigantic stitches holding it all together, holding the magic inside. It rose up and up until it towered against the ceiling, curving like a giant snake to stare down at me. I estimated forty heads, more, before I lost count, or lost the heart to count anymore.

There had been another club in that town, and it had been worse in some ways, because the torture was part of the entertainment . . . Lines had appeared on the man's skin. The muscles under his skin began to shrink, as though he had a wasting disease, but what should have taken months was happening in seconds. No matter how willing the sacrifice, it can still hurt. The man started screaming as fast as he could draw breath. His lungs were working better than the first man's, and he drew breath so fast, it was like one continuous shriek. His skin darkened as it drew in and in, like something was sucking him dry. It was like watching a balloon shrivel. Except there was muscle, and when the muscle vanished, there was bone, and finally there was nothing but dried skin over bones. And still he screamed.

The last insult, or gift, or horror, had been the Master of the City of Albuquerque's power. Her power had beat against me like frantic wings, birds crying that they've been shut out in the dark and they want inside to the light and the warmth. How could I leave them crying in the dark, when all I had to do was open and they would be safe? I'd fought it, but in the end the wings erupted into a torrent of birds. My body seemed to open, though I knew it didn't. And the winged things—only half-glimpsed—spilled into that opening. The power flowed into me, through me, and out again. I was part of some great circuit, and I felt the connection with every vampire she'd touched. It was as if I flowed through them, and they through me, like water coming together to form something larger. Then I was floating in the soothing dark, and there were stars, distant and glittering.

Images then, and they had force to them like things slamming into my body. I saw the Master of the City standing on the top of a pyramid temple surrounded by trees, jungle. I could smell the rich greenness of it and hear the night call of a monkey, the scream of a jaguar. Her human servant knelt and fed from the bloody wound on her chest. He became her servant, and he gained power, many powers. And one of them was this—how to take the life force of something, someone, and feed upon it, without killing it. And I understood how he'd taken the man's essence, during that terrible entertainment. More than that, I understood how it was done, and how it was undone. I knew how to unmake the creature in the bar, though what had been done, being sewn together into a Frankenstein nightmare, might mean that to bring them back to flesh would kill them. I didn't need the necromancer who had trapped them to undo the spell; I could do it myself.

The memories were so vivid, it was like reliving them. I came back to the present almost with a jolt, staring up into Jean-Claude's eyes, still trapped under his body, still in the punishment room thousands of miles away from Obsidian Butterfly and her small army. But it was the look on Jean-Claude's face that caught my breath in my throat.

His eyes were wide, and I knew in that moment that he'd seen my memories, that he'd shared them the way I sometimes shared his. Fuck.

His voice had a shakiness to it that I rarely heard. "*Ma petite,* you were a busy girl while you were away from us."

"You saw what I saw, and you know how I feel about what you did to Gretchen."

His hands tightened on my arms, fingers digging into my skin just a little. "I know how you feel, *ma petite.* But I will not take this blame gently. I am the Master of the City, my vampires live through me. Unless they are masters themselves, their life force comes through the line that bred them, until they take blood oath to a Master of the City. Then that master makes their hearts beat. If I run short of power, then some will simply not wake in the night, or they will become revenants, animals to be destroyed as Damian has become."

I moved under him. "I don't . . ."

"Shhh, *ma petite,* I will not be condemned without a hearing, not this time. Perhaps you can save Damian, but he is over a thousand years old. Even though not a master, that is a long time, long enough to accumulate power enough to survive. But vampires like Willie and Hannah who are not masters and not that old, they would fade or go mad, and there would be no saving them." He shook me, digging into my arms, raising his elbows so that I could have gone for a weapon if I'd wanted, but I just watched him and listened.

"Is that what you want, Anita? Which of them would you sacrifice to save Gretchen? Gretchen whom you hate. I took power from her because you denied it to me."

"Don't blame this on me," I said.

He moved suddenly, sitting up on his knees, his body straddling my legs. He lifted me into a sitting position, fingers brushing against my arms. "The system of master and servant has worked well for thousands of years, but you keep fighting it, and you keep forcing me to do things I do not wish to do." He raised me up close to his face, and I watched his eyes bleed to burning blue from inches away. He shook me more violently this time, almost hard enough to scare me.

"If I could have fed the *ardeur* as it was meant to be fed, then this would not have been necessary. If I could have fed through my human servant, this would not have been necessary. If I could have fed through my animal to call, this would not have been necessary. But you and Richard bind me 'round with rules, you cripple me with your morality, and you force me to do such as I swore I would never do. I have been in the box and been food for my master, and it was the worst thing I have ever endured. And now because you and he had your moral high ground to keep you pure, you have forced me to be more practical than I have ever wanted to be."

He released me so suddenly I fell back against the floor, slamming an elbow into the stones. He stood over me, as angry as I'd ever seen him, and I had no anger to give back. I finally said, "I didn't know."

"That is becoming a poor excuse, *ma petite.*" He went to the coffin and gazed down at what lay inside. "I gave her my protection once, and this is not protection." He turned and glared at me. "I do what I must, *ma petite,* but I take no pleasure from it, and I tire of the necessity of it. If you would but meet me even halfway, we could avoid so much pain."

I sat up, fighting the urge to rub my elbow. "Do you want me to say I'm sorry? I am. Do you want permission to feed off of me, is that it?"

"The *ardeur*, yes," he said. "But in truth, if you are in the mood for it, simply having the marks open and married gains me much."

He held his hand out to Jason, and for one of only a few times, I saw Jason hesitate before taking Jean-Claude's hand. Jean-Claude didn't even look at him, as if his obedience was simply a fact, like gravity. "If she were stronger it would be a more dangerous feeding, but she is very weak, so it will not be so very bad." The words were comforting, but he never looked at Jason as he lowered the younger man's wrist towards what lay in that coffin.

I got to my feet, watching Jason's face. He was pale, eyes wide, breath coming too short, too fast. He didn't normally have a problem letting vamps feed on him, but I understood. What lay in that coffin was something out of a nightmare. Most of the time if you saw a vamp looking like something made of dried sticks, it was well and truly dead.

Jason pulled on his arm, keeping himself just out of reach, I think. Jean-Claude turned to him, but there was no anger. He kept the one hand on Jason's arm, and the other he touched to his face, gently. "Would you have me take your mind, before she strikes?"

Jason nodded, wordlessly.

Jean-Claude cradled his hand against Jason's face. They stared into each other's eyes, one of those long, lingering stares, like lovers, except I felt the moment that Jason slipped away. I felt his mind release, his will evaporate. His face went slack, his mouth half-parted, eyes fluttering. Jean-Claude kept his hand on the other man's face, as he guided the wrist into the coffin.

Jason's body tensed, and I knew that Gretchen had bitten him. But his eyes stayed closed, his face pleasant. I found myself beside the coffin without meaning to be. The dried stick hands raised as I watched, clutching at Jason's arm, holding him against the mouth. Jean-Claude moved his hand back, as the thing in the coffin pressed Jason's wrist to its mouth. Blood flowed over that brown skin, soaked the white satin pillow, and still that lipless mouth fed.

The room was suddenly too warm, almost hot. I turned away and found Micah watching me. I couldn't read his expression, wasn't sure I wanted to. I looked away from whatever was in his eyes. I didn't want to meet anyone's eyes right now. I'd fought so long and so hard not to be what I was. Not to be Jean-Claude's human servant, not to be Richard's lupa, not to be anything to anyone. Everyone seemed to be paying the price for that. I hated having other people pay the price for my problems. It was against the rules somehow.

Jean-Claude's voice drew me back to the coffin. "Drink, Gretchen, drink of my blood. I gave you life once, let it be so again." Jason was sitting slumped beside the coffin, cradling his bloody wrist with a beatific expression on his face. The dried thing was sitting up with Jean-Claude's arm behind its shoulders. It looked . . . better, but still not alive, not even quite real. He offered the pale flesh of his wrist to that lipless mouth, still red with Jason's blood, and it bit down. I heard Jean-Claude sigh, but that was the only sign that it might hurt.

"Blood to blood, flesh to flesh." Jean-Claude spoke the words, and with each word, with each suck of blood, I felt the power grow, felt it curl in my stomach, shorten my breath. Gretchen's body began to stretch and fill. The pieces of hair thickened and began to flow around her. The dried things in her eye sockets filled and began to have a hint of blue to them. When Jean-Claude moved his wrist from her mouth, they were full-pouting lips. She had blue eyes and a wealth of yellow hair. She was thin, her bones showing under the near translucent paleness of her skin. Her eyes were filled with fire, nothing human. Her hands were still painfully thin, her body fragile, but she looked almost like the vampire that had tried to kill me years ago.

He picked her up in his arms; her body didn't fill out the clothes that hung from her frame. "Breath to breath," he said and leaned in towards her. They kissed, and I felt the power pass between them. I knew that that kiss could have drained her life away again, but it didn't. When he raised back from her, her face was full and rounded, human looking. It was like Prince Charming waking Sleeping Beauty, except that this beauty's eyes found me, and the hatred in them was a burning thing.

I sighed. Some people never learn. I met that hateful gaze and said, "Gretchen, I promise you two things, you'll never have to go back in that box, and if you try to hurt me or mine again, I'll kill you. And that would be a damn shame since I'm the one who persuaded Jean-Claude to let you out in the first place."

She just looked at me the way that tigers behind bars watch the visitors, biding their time. Jean-Claude hugged her to him. "If you try and harm my human servant again, I will see you destroyed, Gretal." *Gretal* had been her original name, so I'd been told.

"I hear you, Jean-Claude." Her voice sounded rough, as if the time in the coffin had damaged it.

"Come, Jason, we need to warm this one." Jason got to his feet like an obedient puppy, still bleeding, still happy.

Jean-Claude paused in the doorway looking, not at me, but at Asher. "I must take this one to the bath, or all the work will be undone. But Damian is a revenant now."

Asher raised a hand, which had been hidden along his body. He had a gun, a .10-millimeter Browning, the big brother of my own gun. "I will do what needs doing."

"We are not going to kill Damian," I said.

Jean-Claude looked at me, then at Micah, and Nathaniel, and Gil, and the other wereleopards, and even the bodyguards. His gaze seemed to take everyone in, then he looked at me again. "I ask again, *ma petite*, who will you sacrifice for your high ideals?"

"You think he can't be saved, don't you?"

"I know that once the madness takes a vampire, even the master who bore him cannot always bring him back to his senses."

"Is there anything I can do that might bring him back to himself?"

"Let him feed, try to see he does not kill that which he eats, and hope when he tastes your blood, he regains his senses. If your blood does not sate him, then Asher will try to feed him. If that fails . . ." He gave that shrug that meant everything and nothing; even holding Gretchen it looked graceful.

"I don't want him to die because of me."

"If he dies, *ma petite*, it will be because he tried to kill someone in this room." With that he walked out, Jason trailing behind.

I think, perhaps, I'd used up Jean-Claude's patience with me, or maybe seeing what he'd done to Gretchen had bothered him that much. Whatever the cause, he left me in the room with everyone looking to me as to how to proceed. And I didn't have a clue. Who was I willing to put next to the coffin? Who was I willing to risk?

56

THE ANSWER, OF course, was no one, but we finally decided who got to be the first victim. I was pretty useless for the discussion, because I would have put myself first in line. Never ask of anyone what you're not willing to do yourself. But Asher pointed out that I couldn't be the first feed if I had any chance of being Damian's master. So they decided among themselves, and it was Zane left standing next to the coffin.

Everybody but me that had a gun had it out with a round chambered. I needed my hands free to offer up a body part to get gnawed on. Come to think of it, I didn't much like that job description either. But it wasn't watching Zane's pale back as he unfastened the chain that bothered me, it was watching Cherry's face as she watched him do it. That much fear for someone's safety, that much importance attached to one other being meant that it was love for her, too. They loved each other, and he was about to cry, cry for help, and loose the carrion birds to feed, and feed, and feed.

The lid of the coffin was only half raised when Zane jerked forward and pale hands showed around him, holding him. Blood sprayed the white satin of the coffin, spattered over Zane's shoulders, and the only thing we could see of Damian was pale hands and arms latched around Zane's back. There was no shot to take.

Someone was screaming. I think it was Cherry. I had my gun out, but there was no way to fire without killing Zane first. Micah and Merle were at the coffin, trying to pry Zane free. Zane fell back, his throat a gaping wound, and something that was all bloody fangs and wild red hair grabbed Merle and folded around him, tearing at the big man's throat. The wererats and Asher were standing back, waiting for a clear shot, but there wasn't going to be one, not before someone else died.

I pushed forward, trying to shove Micah out of the way while I pressed the gun to Damian's face, but Micah was trying to pry the vampire off of Merle, and in the struggle I couldn't get my gun steady. The barrel slipped in the blood against Damian's skin, and suddenly green eyes turned to me, and there was nothing in them but hunger. Damian was already dead. I just hadn't pulled the trigger yet.

Then he was on me, faster than anything I'd ever seen. I was pressed back against the satin of the coffin, my hips and legs sticking out. He didn't go for my neck; he buried his fangs in my upper chest. I screamed past the pain and pressed the barrel of the Browning against his temple. Asher was yelling, "Don't fire, you'll hit Anita!"

I screamed again and had to adjust the angle of the gun, because if I'd pulled the trigger, the bullet would have gone through his head into my chest. I moved the gun a fraction while he savaged me. My finger curled on the trigger when he raised his green eyes to me. I watched his eyes fill up with knowledge, intelligence—with him. He raised his mouth back from my chest. He looked scared. “Anita, what’s happening?” He seemed to see my bloody chest for the first time, and his eyes went wide. “What’s happening to me?”

The moment he spoke, the moment there was something in him besides monster, I felt the connection between us click into place, like a perfectly tuned string on a harp. The power flowed between us like warm water, filling him up, filling me up, and I drew him down to me, my blood still on his lips.

I heard Asher saying, “Stay back, it’s alright, let her finish.”

I whispered as I drew Damian down to me, “Blood of my blood, flesh of my flesh, breath to breath, my heart to yours.”

And just before our lips met and his fate was sealed, he whispered, “Yes, oh, yes.”

57

I WAS SHOULDER-DEEP in water so hot it made my skin pink. I was so hot I was almost ill, because I was still fully dressed, including all my guns. Damian leaned up against the front of my body, my arms wrapped around him, holding him close. His body folded in against mine, his arms holding mine across his bare chest.

How did I end up being guardian of the bathtub for Damian once we reached my house? He'd gone into convulsions, and only my touch had calmed him. We'd gotten him to my house with Nathaniel riding in the back, cradling Damian. They'd filled the bathtub with hot, hot water, and I'd left Asher in charge of Damian's care. I'd done my part, I'd brought him back to himself. I had a bandage over my left breast to prove that I'd donated my piece of flesh and blood for the night. Zane and Merle were on their way to the lycanthrope hospital, with Micah and Cherry to oversee them. Everyone else had trooped back to my house, and everything had seemed fine, until screams from the bathroom brought me running.

Damian had been beating himself against the floor, convulsing like he'd tear himself apart, vomiting blood on the tile. Asher and Nathaniel had been fighting to hold him down, to keep him from hurting himself, but they couldn't hold him. I knelt to help, and the moment I touched him, he quieted. I'd withdrawn my hand, and his body had bucked again, hands scrambling at the slick tile. I'd touched his shoulder, and he calmed. We'd tried letting him take blood from Caleb, but the moment I stopped touching him, his body rejected the blood, and everything else. The last time I'd stopped touching him, Damian had simply gone quiet, and I had felt him beginning to fade, to die.

We'd dragged Damian into the steaming bath water, and I'd held him. He had recovered, but only with me holding him while my clothes stuck to my body.

"What's wrong with him?" I asked.

Asher had answered, "I've only seen this reaction between master and servant."

"I'm Damian's master, so what? It shouldn't cause this, should it?"

"No, *ma cherie,* not merely master, but master vampire and human servant."

"Damian is not my master," I said.

"Damian is no one's master," Asher said quietly, gazing down at us from the edge of the tub. He was sitting in a pool of the blood that had poured out of Damian.

"What are you saying, Asher?"

"You have made him your servant."

"He can't be a human servant, he's a vampire," I said.

"I did not say human servant, *ma cherie*."

"Then what are you talking about?"

"A . . . vampire servant for a master necromancer, I think."

"You think?" I made it a question.

"We are dealing with things of legend, *ma cherie*, things that should not be possible. I am having to . . . guess at this."

"Guess?" I said.

He sighed. "If I said that I knew for certain what has happened, it would be a lie. I would never lie to you on purpose."

I had protested, demanded, but nothing I could do or say made it untrue. I had a vampire servant, and that was impossible. But impossible or not, Damian lay against my body, clinging to me, like I was the last hope he had.

Asher glided back into the bathroom, wearing a beach towel wrapped around him. The towel was big enough to cover him from armpits to mid-calf, effectively hiding his body. Hiding the scars. "My clothes are covered in blood. I hope you do not mind."

I hated wearing bloody clothes myself, so, "Fine, glad you found a towel you liked."

He glanced down at the colorful towel. "I do not fit in your robe."

I was sorry Asher felt like he had to hide himself away, but I had other things to worry about. "I think if I don't get cooler soon I'm either going to throw up or pass out."

He knelt by the tub, smoothing the long towel under his knees in a gesture that you don't see much in men. He touched my face lightly. "You are flushed." He touched Damian. "His skin is still cooler than it should be." He frowned. "You need to take off some of your clothing, especially the jeans, I would think."

Normally, I go to great lengths not to be unclothed in front of all the boys, but tonight I was willing to strip down a little. "How do I undress and still hold him?"

"I believe that one of us could hold him against you while you disrobed."

"You really think that he'll go into convulsions again?"

"You could release him, and we could find out," Asher said, voice soft.

I shook my head. "I'm tired of cleaning up blood. Just help me hold him."

Asher's eyes went a little wide. "I will call Nathaniel."

The heat had gone to my head in a pounding headache. "Just jump in, Asher, I promise not to peek."

He curled beside the tub, tucking every piece of him he could underneath the towel. "If I dropped this towel to the floor, would you really not look?"

His question stopped me. I opened my mouth, closed it, and tried to think through the heat, the headache, the growing nausea, and finally just said the truth. "I wouldn't mean to look, but no, you're right. If you're naked I'm going to look. I don't think I could stop myself."

"Like a car accident, you cannot turn away," he said.

I looked up then and found he'd turned away, hiding his face with that fall of golden hair. Damn it, I didn't have time to hold everybody's hand. "Asher, please, I didn't mean that."

He wouldn't look at me. I extracted one arm from Damian, who moved around the remaining arm like a child settling in his sleep around his favorite

Teddy bear. I grabbed Asher's arm through the towel. "Yes, I'd look just for sheer curiosity's sake, how could I help it? You've teased and taunted about how bad your injuries are. You've set it up so that I'll have to look, have to see."

He was looking at me now, those pale eyes, empty, hidden from me.

I dug my fingers into his arm, trying to grip him through the towel, and finding mostly cloth. "But if you don't know by now that I just want to see you nude, then you haven't been paying attention."

His face told me nothing, that blank politeness that both he and Jean-Claude could pull off when they wanted to. "Now help me get some of these clothes off before I melt."

He gave a low chuckling laugh that danced over my skin and brought my pulse to my throat. I was too hot to have goosebumps. "You offering to disrobe without any magic to push you, I believe that is a first."

I had to laugh, because he was right. But the laugh forced me to close my eyes, because it felt like the pulsing of the headache was going to shove my eyeballs out of their sockets. I let go of his arm and pressed my hand to my forehead to try and keep my head from falling into pieces. "Please, Asher, I am going to be sick."

I heard the water splashing, felt it push against me as someone climbed into the tub. I opened my eyes slowly, trying to hold the headache inside and found Nathaniel kneeling in the water. His hair was still bound in a loose braid that trailed behind him, curling through the water like something separate and alive. The swirling braid brought my gaze low on his body, and I had a peripheral sense that Nathaniel wasn't getting any clothes wet whatsoever, but I didn't care. The headache had reached a point where I was afraid I was going to start throwing up if I didn't get cooler.

He answered my question without me asking it. "Asher wants Damian to try to take blood again, see if it will stay down."

Asher was still perched on the edge of the tub wrapped in the towel. "Damian must be able to keep down blood, or he will perish. I believe that if you stay in constant contact with him that he will be able to keep a feeding down."

"If I have to stay in constant contact then I have to get cooler first."

"Nathaniel will help you," he said.

I glanced up at Asher, and even in the dim glow of a night light, it hurt my head. "Fine."

Damian made small protesting movements as Nathaniel tried to take some of his weight off of me. We finally leaned him up against the edge of the tub with Asher supporting some of his weight, but letting him keep my arm pressed to his chest. Nathaniel undid my belt and helped me slip the shoulder holster off one arm, but I needed the other arm free to slip it out of the other strap. Damian fought us, slowly, stubbornly, as if he were sleepwalking. But he was a vampire; he could have torn his way through the wall of my bathroom with his bare hands. If he didn't want to let go of my arm, we couldn't make him, not unless we were willing to break his fingers one at a time, and we weren't willing to do that.

"What do we do?" Nathaniel asked.

"I have to get out of this heat," I said. "Can we like run cold water in the tub, or something?"

"No," Asher said, "we must keep him as warm as possible, until after he has retained some of the blood. We don't dare allow him to be chilled."

"Then get these clothes off me."

I felt rather than saw the two of them exchange glances. "How do you want me to do it?" Nathaniel asked.

I leaned my head forward, resting against the top of Damian's wet hair. His skin was the coldest thing in the tub. I was so hot I was about to be sick, yet Damian's skin was still cool to the touch. The headache overwhelmed me and spilled out my mouth. I did my best to crawl out on the edge of the tub before I vomited. Damian had managed to miss the water every time he threw up; at least I could do the same. But he clung to me, and only Asher's hand on my arm kept me high enough from the water to keep it clean.

My head was screaming, the pain so strong that it impacted my vision in explosions of color. Asher got me a cool cloth and wiped my mouth. He laid another cool cloth across my forehead. Then Nathaniel gripped the back of my shirt and ripped. He tore it off of me in pieces. Asher draped a wet towel over my shoulders that was so cold it made me whisper, "Shit."

Asher and Nathaniel took my weight and Damian's and moved us back to the far edge of the tub, as Gil came in and started cleaning up the mess. Gil had cleaned up a lot of messes tonight, and he'd never bitched, not once. He did a double take at the pieces of my shirt floating in the water, but never commented aloud. He made a good flunkie. Did what he was told and didn't ask questions.

Nathaniel tried to tear my jeans off the way he'd done the shirt. He managed to rip the top, but Damian's weight kept pushing me under the water, and he couldn't get the leverage he needed. Asher fastened the towel as securely as he could and climbed gingerly into the water. He knelt and slid his arms around Damian and me and lifted, standing, holding us both upright. I was still touching bottom, but he was still holding both our weights, because my legs still weren't working quite right. He held us both effortlessly.

Nathaniel put a hand on either side of the rip he'd made in my jeans and pulled. The heavy wet cloth came apart under his hands with a sound like tearing flesh, but heavier—a wet, harsh sound. The force of it jerked my body, and only Asher's strength kept me standing.

I felt the air on my bare skin and realized that in ripping away the jeans he'd taken my undies with them, but I didn't care. The air on my skin was still suffocatingly hot. I couldn't breathe. The last thing I remember thinking was, I'm going to pass out, then nothing.

58

I WOKE LYING on the edge of the tub with only one arm in the water with Damian. Cold towels covered me from head to foot. The one on my face lifted, and I saw that Nathaniel was in the water, holding Damian upright. I blinked up through a strand of wet hair and found Asher spreading a fresh cold towel against my face. He left enough of my face uncovered so I could look at him, sideways.

"How are you feeling?"

I had to think about that. "Better." He replaced the towels down the length of my body, and I realized I was completely nude. I shivered with the cold cloth and didn't care about anything except that I was finally cool. "How long was I out?"

"Not long," Asher said, smoothing the towel so that it molded to my legs.

I looked at Nathaniel, kneeling in the tub, pinning Damian to the edge, so the vampire could hold on to me. "I've never seen a shapeshifter pass out from heat exhaustion before," he said.

"A first time for everything," I said.

Damian turned his head slowly to look at me. His eyes were clear, bright, alive again. His eyes were the color of emeralds, and it wasn't caused by vampire powers, it was his natural eye color, as if his mother had fooled around with a cat to get him here. People just didn't have that color of eyes.

I smiled at him. "You look better."

"I fed."

I glanced at Nathaniel. He turned his head so I could see the neat bite marks in the side of his throat.

"I think I can support myself," Damian said.

Nathaniel looked a question at Asher, who must have nodded, because Nathaniel backed off. Damian settled against me, still holding my arm across his chest, but lightly now. One hand gently on my wrist, the other hand stroked my arm.

"I hear you're my master."

I looked into those calm eyes. "You don't seem upset."

He rubbed his chin and cheek against my arm. It was catlike, and intimate, a lover's gesture. I studied his face, tried to read past those peaceful emerald eyes. Then I realized I didn't have to read his face. The barest thought and I knew that the peacefulness in his eyes went all the way through. He was filled with a great calmness, a sense of rightness. Calm and peace had never been my reaction to Jean-Claude binding *me* closer to him.

I could feel what Damian was feeling, knew his heart almost better than my own, but I didn't understand him. In that moment staring into those beautiful, peaceful eyes, I simply had no clue. I would have run for the hills, fought, screamed, hated. I would not have gone quietly into any kind of servitude, no matter how potentially beneficent the ruler. Truthfully, I wasn't a hundred percent sure I was a beneficent ruler. I mean I was easy to get along with as long as everything went my way, but cross me, and I wasn't easy. I was close to being the hardest person I knew, and I know some hard people. I was trying to be softer lately, but trying to be softer and actually being softer, aren't the same. I looked into Damian's eyes and knew that if it were me, tied to me as master, I'd be scared.

Damian turned in the water, kneeling at the tub edge. He leaned in and laid a gentle kiss on my forehead. "You saved me, again."

He was right, but as his lips touched my skin, I wondered how long he'd be grateful and when he'd finally realize how screwed we both were.

59

ASHER TOOK DAMIAN down to the basement for the day, settling them both in just before dawn. Micah had called, saying that both Merle and Zane would survive. Cherry was going to stay there with Zane, and he had to go check on the rest of his wereleopards. I invited him to bring his leopards over to my house, and he said he'd ask. We didn't say "I love you" at the end of the conversation, which was unnerving. I wasn't used to sleeping with someone that I didn't love or didn't say I love you to. But I was too tired to think that hard, so I pushed it down where all the other things I don't want to think about live. The place is getting damned crowded. Nathaniel helped me dress in the coolest jammies I had—a silky spaghetti strap nightshirt that would have been too revealing if I hadn't been so damn short. Then Nathaniel cuddled in beside me in a pair of jogging shorts. Gil slept in the guest room. The two wererat bodyguards divided the night up between the couch and sleeping on the floor in front of the door of my bedroom, which meant if I had to go to the bathroom after we bedded down I'd have to step over them. Bobby Lee said, "It'll wake us up, make sure you don't go wandering around alone."

I couldn't persuade Bobby Lee or Cris that I didn't need that much watching, but truthfully I was too tired to do much arguing. So we all settled down for a long summer's nap. Nathaniel had closed the heavy curtains so that the room lay in a heavy gray twilight.

I settled down in the air-conditioned hush of the bedroom with Nathaniel curled up against my side and fell almost immediately into a deep, dreamless sleep. When the bedside phone shrilled, I knew what it was, but it took me several seconds to wake up enough to move. Nathaniel had actually reached across me and answered, "Blake residence," before I opened my eyes.

He was quiet, face very serious, then he cupped his hand over the receiver and said, "It's Ulysses, Narcissus's bodyguard. He wants to speak with you."

I took the phone, still lying flat on my back. "This is Anita, what do you want?"

"My Oba wishes to meet with you."

I moved my head enough to see the clock and groaned. I'd barely had two hours of sleep. I could manage an hour nap and feel okay, or go without sleep, but somewhere between two and three hours just felt worse. "I work the night shift, Ulysses, whatever Narcissus wants can wait until later in the day."

"The word went out yesterday that any information about the missing lycanthropes was to go through you."

That woke me up a little. I blinked and tried to be more awake than I felt. "What information?"

"He will only talk directly to you."

"Then put him on the phone, I'm all ears."

"He insists that you come down to his club, now."

"I have had less than two hours of sleep, Ulysses. I am not dragging my ass over to the Illinois side of the river at the crack of dawn. If he has information that can help us save shapeshifters' lives, just give it to me, and I'll see that the info gets to where it needs to go."

"My Oba insists that if you do not come down to the club now, he will not share the information at all."

I sat up, leaning against the headboard, closing my eyes. "Why now?"

"It is not my way to question my orders."

"Maybe you should work on that," I said.

There was silence on the other end of the phone. I didn't know if he was puzzled and didn't get my comment, or if it had struck too close to home. He finally said in a quiet voice, "Right now the lions' Rex is alive. That may not be the case in a few hours."

I sat up, eyes wide, completely awake at last. "How do you know that?"

"My Oba knows many things."

"Narcissus would really let the lions' Rex die, just because I won't come down to the club at the ass crack of dawn?"

"My master is very insistent."

"Shit," I said softly and with feeling. "Tell him I'll be down, but tell him this, too. The next time he's in trouble, maybe no one will help him either."

"This is more help than he has ever been to any other animal clan."

There was something in Ulysses's voice now, something. He was lying. I could hear it in his voice. I didn't know if it was vampire powers or werewolf, or wereleopard, and I didn't care. The question was, why lie about the fact that the werehyenas had helped no other shapeshifter group more than this? Why was that worth a lie at all?

"Narcissus helps out more than he wants people to know, doesn't he?" I said.

"What makes you say that?" There was a thread of fear, almost panic, in Ulysses's voice.

"What would it hurt if the lycanthrope community knew that the werehyenas were helping other animals out?" I asked.

His breath came out in a long sigh. "Narcissus would never want anyone to think that about the werehyenas. It would . . ." he hesitated, "be bad for business."

"If Narcissus is so concerned about Joseph the lion, then why not give me the info over the phone?"

Ulysses laughed, abrupt, amused. "Narcissus has never given anything away for nothing. There's always a price with him."

"So my dragging down to his club on no sleep is the price?"

"Something like that."

"Can I bring my people?"

"My master would love to see any of your people you care to bring."

I didn't like the phrasing on that. "How big of him."

"When will you be here?" Ulysses asked.

"How do you know I'm coming?"

"Because you know that he's enough of an egotist that if you don't come now he may not share the information at all. You know he'd let the lions' Rex die just because he's not the same animal we are, and you not coming down now would be an insult."

"This clannish shit has got to stop, Ulysses. We need to start helping each other more."

"Not my place to change the system, Anita. I'm just trying to survive in it."

He sounded sad. "I don't mean to yell at the messenger, Ulysses, I'm just tired of the system."

He laughed again, but not like he was happy. "*You're* tired of the system. Jesus, you have no idea. When can I tell him to expect you?"

"An hour. Less, if I can manage it. I want Joseph alive to see his baby."

"His mate will probably lose it like all the others."

"I thought you hyenas didn't talk to the lions or anyone else. How do you know about Joseph's baby woes?"

"Narcissus keeps track of things like that."

"Why would he care?"

"He wants a baby."

That made me raise my eyebrows. "I've never pictured Narcissus as the paternal type."

"Try maternal."

"What?"

"We'll be waiting for you, Anita. Don't keep him waiting. He doesn't like to be kept waiting." I heard sorrow in his voice, sorrow bordering on grief. I almost asked what was wrong, but he'd already hung up. What had Narcissus done to him to put that tone in his voice? Did I really want to know? Probably not. Not unless there was something I could do about it, and there wasn't. If I started a war with every harsh lycanthrope master in town, I'd have to kill them all, or almost. The only one who wasn't harsh was Richard, and that was going to get *him* killed. I complained about Narcissus being too harsh and Richard being too soft. I guess I was just never satisfied.

I hung up the phone and told Nathaniel what was happening while I picked out clothes. Nathaniel threw a tank top over the jogging shorts he'd slept in, added jogging shoes, no socks. He knew better than to try and dress, because he'd insist on unbraiding his hair and combing it out, which would take all the time the rest of us would need to get dressed. I was wrong. Nathaniel wasn't even close to done with his hair when the rest of us were dressed and ready to go. Bobby Lee and Cris just threw on their shirts and shoes, ran fingers through their short hair, put the holsters back on, and they were ready to go. Gil came down in jeans, jogging shoes, and an untucked men's dress shirt. The shirt looked new, but he didn't keep us waiting. Caleb came down in jeans and nothing else. I didn't bother to tell him to throw a shirt on, or shoes. Somehow I didn't think that Narcissus would deny us service because Caleb was underdressed.

I actually took the longest getting dressed: black jeans, red polo shirt, black Nikes, every blade I had, including the new back sheath I'd had made for the largest knife that ran along my spine. The first sheath had gotten cut to pieces by emergency room personnel, while they were trying to save my life. I also brought my two handguns, though I wasn't sure that any of us would be allowed to bring guns into the club. But just in case I brought them, and I warned Cris and Bobby Lee about the no-guns rule. They flashed their own set of wicked-looking blades—about three apiece—and we were ready to go.

I thought about calling Christine the weretiger, but figured since it wasn't quite seven that I'd let somebody sleep in today. Besides, I didn't know shit yet. When I knew something worth sharing, I'd share.

I was halfway to the club when I realized that the *ardeur* hadn't set in. It was morning. I was awake. There wasn't a stir from the *ardeur*. Hope flared through me in a warm, fuzzy wash. Maybe the *ardeur* was going to be temporary. Dear God, I hoped so. I said a brief prayer of thanks and kept monitoring myself for the first hints of unbridled lust.

We arrived at Narcissus in Chains with me grumpy, but not the least bit lustful. It was a good day.

60

I WAS ABLE to park right in front of Narcissus in Chains. Not only was there no line at 8:00 A.M., there were no other people in front of the club. The wide sidewalk stretched empty, almost golden, in the early morning light. If I'd had time for coffee, I might even have said it was pretty, but I hadn't had time for coffee, so the sunlight was just bright. I had finally broken down and bought sunglasses a few weeks ago. I huddled behind them, wishing I was still in bed. I was so tired, I felt fuzzy-headed. I'm usually pretty good at going without sleep. The only thing I could blame the fuzziness on was the heat exhaustion from the night before. Maybe I needed more than three hours to recover from it. It made me wonder how bad off I'd have been if I hadn't had all my preternatural powers. A person can die of heatstroke.

Nathaniel was at my side, Bobby Lee and Cris, a step behind and to either side. Gil and Caleb brought up the rear. The door opened before we could knock. Ulysses ushered us into the darkened club. He was still wearing his leather and metal harness. The smell of it made me wonder if it was the exact same outfit he'd been wearing, was it five or six days ago? The tall, dark, and handsome man that I'd met looked hollow-eyed. His strong hands gripped his elbows, hugging his body. When he moved a hand to motion us inside, it shook. What the hell had been going on?

Half a dozen other muscular men of varying races and heights stood in the shadows waiting for Ulysses to tell them what to do. The tension in the room was so thick you could have choked on it.

Cris made a hissing sound at my back, and I couldn't blame him. I decided then and there that unless we got some really good explanations, we were keeping the guns. There was an air of desperation about all the werehyenas, as if something really bad had happened.

The door was shut behind us, but we were close to it, and no one was between us and it. I wanted to save the lion Joseph, but not enough to risk myself and my people. If it was a choice, I knew who I'd choose. Cold, maybe, but I'd never met Joseph the werelion. He wasn't real to me yet, and everyone with me was.

Ulysses must have seen, or smelled, something on us, because he explained. "Our master has seen fit to punish us."

"What for?" I asked.

He shook his head. "That is personal."

"Fine, let's talk to Narcissus, and you guys can get back to punishing yourselves."

"We are not punishing ourselves," Ulysses said.

I shrugged. "Look, I don't believe in letting anyone push me around to this degree, but it's not my deal, it's yours. So let's share information and let us get out of here."

Something crossed Ulysses's face, some emotion that I couldn't read. "No guns in the club, that's the rule."

"I think we'll keep our guns," Bobby Lee said.

I glanced at him, and the look was enough. He shut up but smiled at me. "Actually, I agree with him. We're not giving up our guns today."

Ulysses shook his head. "I can't fail my master in this, Anita. You have no idea what he'll do to us if we let you inside with guns."

I glanced at the men standing around in the shadowed room. Fear rolled off of them in waves; their bodies were tight with tension. I'd never seen so many men so thoroughly whipped before. They would do exactly what they were told to do, because they were terrified to do anything else. I'd been told that a good dominant was a caring partner. Maybe Narcissus wasn't a good dom, maybe he was a bad one.

"I'm sorry, Ulysses, really, I don't want to cause you pain, but if Narcissus has gone crazy enough to make all of you this scared, then we keep the guns."

"Please, Anita, please." He must have seen something on my face that let him know I wasn't going to give in, because he dropped to his knees in front of me. The sound of his knees hitting the floor was sharp, made me wince. He'd kept his hands wrapped on his arms, so that he just dropped without catching himself at all. "Please, Anita."

I shook my head, staring into those haunted eyes.

Tears glimmered down his cheeks. "Please, Anita, please, you don't know what he'll do to our lovers if we fail him."

"Lovers?" I made it a question.

It took him two tries to say, "Ajax is my . . . lover. We've been together four years. Please, Anita. I don't have any right to ask this, but please give up your guns."

I shook my head. "I'm sorry, Ulysses, really I am, but the more you talk the more I want to keep my guns."

He moved so suddenly that I didn't have time to react, and Cris and Bobby Lee both cleared their guns, but Ulysses wasn't trying to hurt me. He wrapped his arms around me, buried his face in my chest, and wept and begged. He stank of fear and blood and worse things.

"Put up the guns, boys, he's not trying to hurt me."

They put their guns up, but they didn't look happy. But then, neither, I suppose, did I. I touched Ulysses's head, but he just kept saying, "Please, please, please."

"You guys can all come with us, just walk out with us."

Bobby Lee whispered, "This is not a good idea."

"I don't care. Nobody deserves to be treated like this."

"What'cha gonna do, Anita, offer them all sanctuary? We didn't bring that many guns," he said.

"If the other werehyenas object, we leave them. I didn't bring us out here to get killed, but if we can, we take them with us."

Bobby Lee shook his head. "You make your life hard, Anita, you make your life very hard."

"So I've been told."

Ulysses just clung to me, crying, begging. I had to grab his face and make him look at me, and even then his eyes didn't focus. It took almost a full minute for him to see me. "You can come with us, Ulysses, all of you, just walk out."

He shook his head. "They have our lovers. You don't know what they'll do, you can't know."

"They?"

A rifle shot exploded from somewhere in the room. I had the Browning halfway out of its holster when Cris staggered backwards. Blood sprayed out his back onto Caleb and Gil. Gil started screaming. I had to turn away before Cris hit the floor.

Bobby Lee said, "Three on the catwalk with rifles. Fuck, girl, we've walked into it."

I looked where he was looking and could barely make out the shapes. If I was supposed to be the kitty-cat, why did the rat have better night vision?

Ulysses was whispering over and over, "I'm sorry, I'm sorry, I'm sorry."

I put the barrel against his forehead. "Whatever else happens, Ulysses, you die next."

A man's voice came out of the darkness. He was speaking over a sound system, that much I could tell. "If you pull the trigger, we will kill your other bodyguard. Rifles with silver shot, Ms. Blake, and I assure you that my people are dead shots. Now, put your guns down, and we'll talk."

I kept my gun and told Ulysses, "Get away from me, now!" He crawled away, still crying.

I picked out the shadowy form on my side of the catwalk. Bobby Lee was aimed to the other side, which left one man in the middle without a gun on him. But from this distance, with them above us, we had to make each shot count, which meant that we had to kill what we could, then hope we could do something with the last one. "Who the hell are you?" I asked.

"Drop your guns, Ms. Blake, and I'll tell you."

"We keep our guns, girl," Bobby Lee said. "He's going to kill us either way."

I agreed.

"We don't want you dead, Ms. Blake, but we don't give a shit about your friends. We can just keep picking them off until you change your mind."

I moved to stand in front of everyone, so that the middle shot was harder. From the above angle, I couldn't block them completely, but it was the best I could do. "Everybody get down." Only Bobby Lee hesitated. "They don't want me dead, and I need your gun." He glanced at me, then dropped to one knee, using me to shield himself from the middle gunman. He'd grasped my plan. Everyone else was hugging the floor. There was no cover, and the door was close but not close enough, what with three rifles on us.

"What are you doing, Ms. Blake?" the voice asked.

"Just testing a theory," I said.

"Don't be stupid, Ms. Blake."

"Bobby Lee," I said.

"Yes, ma'am."

"How good are you?"

"Give the word, we'll find out."

I felt my body go very, very still, so that the world narrowed down to the end of my gun and that shape crouched on the catwalk. It was about ten yards. I'd hit targets farther away than that. But that was target shooting. I'd never tried to drop a man with a handgun from this distance. I let out the last of my breath so that I was just stillness, just the gun, just the point of the gun, just the aim of the gun, and with the last, barest touch of my voice, I whispered, "Word."

Our guns went off almost simultaneously. I didn't shoot just once, I fired as fast as I could pull the trigger. My figure jerked, the target came out of his crouch, then fell slowly off the catwalk. I turned my gun before the body hit the ground and found the man in the middle standing up. I saw the shadow of his rifle. I heard the voice shouting over the explosion of gunshots, "Don't hit her, don't you dare."

The rifle plowed up floor inches from me—two shots—trying to get me to move and give him a shot at Bobby Lee, but I stood my ground and fired back. Bobby was firing with me, and the shadow form jerked, staggered, then slumped forward, his rifle falling to land on the floor with the other two bodies of the now-dead riflemen.

The voice said, "Boys, do not disappoint me."

The werehyenas rushed us. Bobby Lee and I started shooting. We divided the six werehyenas up between us, smooth, no cross fires, no taking the other's hit—my side of the room, his side of the room. I took two, I think he took one, and we both clicked empty. I drew the Firestar left-handed, which made it about two seconds slower than it needed to be, but it was probably faster than popping the clip on the Browning and reloading. If I survived, I'd have to time which one was faster.

It was Ulysses who was almost upon me like a dark shape of doom. A gun exploded at my back, and Ulysses fell backwards onto the floor. I whirled to find Nathaniel with a gun. His eyes were wide, his lips parted, a look of astonishment on his face. He'd picked up Cris's dropped weapon. Movement turned me back to the fight. Metal flashed as Bobby Lee waded into the last two werehyenas. The fight was too intense. I couldn't get a clear shot.

The far doors opened, and men poured out. I rushed the fight around Bobby Lee and fired almost point blank into someone's back. The man shuddered and dropped, putting me face-to-face with Bobby Lee. It had startled him, and I had to fire across his body into the last of the fightees. I pointed the Firestar at the werehyenas pouring towards us. I emptied the gun into them, as we all started backing for the door. I wasn't as good left-handed. I don't think I killed anyone, but I wounded someone with every shot, and it slowed them, made them hesitate.

Gil, Caleb, and Nathaniel were already at the doors. Daylight spilled in, and I was dazzled for a second, because my sunglasses were still tucked across the front of my shirt. I dropped the Firestar, popped the empty clip from the Browning and had the second clip pounded home before we made the sidewalk. I still couldn't hear the noise of the clips hitting home, but I saw Bobby Lee making the same movement with his gun that I'd made with mine. I knew he was locked and loaded.

I yelled, "Nathaniel! Jeep, get it running!" I knew he knew where the extra set of keys were. I remembered Narcissus saying that there were over five hundred werehyenas. We had to get out of there before they decided to pick up more guns or just overwhelm us with numbers. Shooting them would slow them down, but whoever that voice had been, he had them terrified. I could kill them, but I couldn't terrorize them. Whether they poured out of that door in a wave would depend on whether they feared death or terror more.

I glanced back to find Nathaniel in the Jeep, with Caleb and Gil in the back. The engine roared to life. Bobby Lee and I started for the Jeep, and the werehyenas rolled out into the sunlight, too many to count, almost too many to aim at. I fired into the mass of bodies, and I yelled, "Run!"

Bobby Lee and I were running for the Jeep, which meant our aim wasn't what it should have been, but the men were packed so tight that we kept hitting them anyway. They'd fall, then there'd be screams, sounds, a chittering laughter that raised the hair at the back of my neck, and the wounded rose as hyenamen, muscled, pale-furred, spotted, with a muzzle full of fangs and claws like black knives. We weren't whittling them down, we were giving them better weapons to use against us.

Nathaniel yelled, "Get in!"

I glanced back to find the doors open front and middle. I slid into the rear seat, Bobby Lee slid in front. The doors were shut, locked, and Nathaniel was pulling away from the curb when they poured over us. They swarmed the car, covering the windows. Nathaniel hit the gas and the Jeep roared forward. An arm smashed through the window beside me. The sound of breaking glass was everywhere. They were trying to hold on and get inside. I fired through my window into the man beyond, and he fell away. Bobby Lee was firing into the hyenaman that was trying to crawl through the windshield.

But there were at least three others smashing at the glass, trying to crawl through. I fired the Browning into the one on the opposite window from mine. It took four shots before he fell away. The Browning had to be close to empty, but I'd lost count. The last two werehyenas were halfway through the windows; one of them spilled into the back of the Jeep. He launched himself at me, and I fired two more bullets almost point blank into him. The gun clicked empty. The man fell, apparently dead at my knees, because I was kneeling in the back of the Jeep, which meant that I'd crawled over the seat to meet his charge. I didn't remember doing it.

The last one was in half-man form. He was having trouble tearing his way through the window. I think he'd caught something painful on the glass. I drew the blade that I wore down my back. My right knee was down, leg flat to the floorboard, my left, raised on the ball of my foot. It was a swordsman's stance for when you couldn't stand—balanced. I struck in a blur of speed, feeling the strength in my body like nothing I'd ever felt before. He looked up at the last second just before the blade bit into the side of his face and split his head open. Blood splattered on my arms, across my face. The body slumped forward, most of its lower parts still dangling out the window. The upper part of his head from just above the jaw was gone, spilling out onto the carpet, soaking into the leg of my jeans. I had a heartbeat to think, holy shit, then I heard the sounds on the roof.

Bobby Lee said, "Persistent bastards."

I didn't answer, just knelt by the wheel well opposite the bodies. Edward, assassin to the undead, and the only person I knew of with a higher kill count for monsters than me, had talked me into letting a friend of his remodel my Jeep. The wheel well held a secret compartment. Inside there was an extra Browning Hi-

Power, two extra clips, and a mini-Uzi with a mushroom clip. The clip barely fit inside the compartment, but it nearly tripled the round capacity, so it was worth the tight fit.

Claws ripped through the roof of the Jeep and started peeling it back, like opening a tin can. I threw myself onto my back and fired up into the roof. Animal howls, one body fell past the windows, but the other one stayed on the roof, the half-animal arm shoved through the metal. I went to my knees, firing just in back of the arm. The hyenaman rolled off the back of the Jeep and bounced in the road. The arm stayed in the hole in the roof, caught on the metal.

When the ringing in my ears toned down enough for me to hear something besides the pounding of my own blood, I could hear Caleb saying, "Fuck, fuck, fuck," over and over. Gil was huddled beside him on the floorboard, screaming, a high piteous sound, his hands over his ears, eyes closed. I leaned on the seat, but didn't try to climb back over. My back was covered in blood and worse things from rolling around on the floor.

I yelled, "Gil, Gil!"

He just kept screaming. I tapped the top of his head with the gun barrel. That made him open his eyes. I pointed the gun at the ceiling while he stared at me. "Stop screaming."

He nodded, hands lowering slowly. He kept nodding over and over again. Caleb had stopped cursing under his breath. He was breathing so hard I thought he might hyperventilate, but I had other things to worry about.

"What kind of clip ya got on that Uzi?" Bobby Lee asked.

"It's called a mushroom clip. It about triples the ammo capacity."

He shook his head. "Damn, girl, where have you been living that you need that kind of firepower?"

"Welcome to my life," I said. I looked down at Gil. "Next time I tell you to stay home, stay home."

"Yes, ma'am," he whispered.

"Slow it down, boy," Bobby Lee said, "we don't want to get picked up by the cops with bodies in the car."

"The damage may be a tip-off," I said.

The arm dangling from the ceiling had changed back to human shape. It flopped bonelessly as Nathaniel turned a corner. I looked away from it and found the now-human with his head bisected. His brains had leaked out in pieces. I was suddenly hot, dizzy. I couldn't remember what I'd done with the big blade. I must have dropped it, but I didn't remember doing it. I wedged myself into a corner, the Uzi raised to the ceiling, my body held on three sides by metal and the seat back. It was as close to being held as I could manage. I closed my eyes, so I couldn't see what I'd done. But the smell was still there: fresh blood, butchered meat, and that outhouse smell that let you know someone's bowels had let loose. I started to choke, and the Jeep pulled off the road. That made me look up, gave me something else to concentrate on.

Nathaniel was pulling onto a gravel road in the middle of nowhere. There were trees, a floodplain, green grass, and beyond that, the shine of the river. It was a peaceful spot. He drove until we weren't easily visible from the road, then stopped.

"What's going on?" I asked.

Bobby Lee answered, "I think if we drive around in traffic with legs sticking out, someone will notify the police."

I nodded. It was a good point. "I should have thought of it," I said.

"No, you've done your work for the day. Let me do the thinking 'til your head clears."

"My head's clear," I said.

He climbed out of the car and spoke through one of the broken windows as he moved towards the legs. "I know pangs of conscience when I see them, girl."

"Stop calling me 'girl'."

He grinned at me. "Yes, ma'am." He grabbed the legs and shoved the body through the glass. It landed with a thick sound on top of the first body. A sound came out of the body on the bottom. It might have just been air escaping—it happened sometimes—but then again . . .

I was on my knees, Uzi pointed at the bodies. Bobby Lee said, "Don't hit the gas tank, ma'am, we don't want to blow ourselves up." He had his gun back out.

I shifted my angle so that I'd shoot through the dark head that lay at the bottom of the pile. Did two bodies constitute a pile? Did it matter? Something brushed my hair and I jerked the gun up, only to find that I'd brushed the fingers on the arm hanging from the ceiling. It was coming loose, sliding lower on its own. Great.

I pressed the barrel of the Uzi against the top of the head. "If you're alive, don't move, if you're dead, don't worry about it."

Bobby Lee opened the back of the Jeep, his gun angled down for a shot at the "body."

"If I fire into the top of his head, the bullets may cut your legs out from under you."

He moved off to one side, gun steady. "My deepest apologies, ma'am, I know better than that."

I pressed the gun barrel more securely into the top of the head and began to reach slowly towards the neck that was just visible under the very dead top body.

"I'm alive." The voice made me jump and nearly made me squeeze the trigger.

"Shit," I said.

"Why don't you finish it?" the man asked. His voice was pain-filled, but not thick. I'd missed heart and lungs. Careless of me.

"Because that wasn't Narcissus's voice over the speaker system, and Ulysses said they had your lovers. That we didn't know what they'd do to your lovers if you guys failed them. Who is the guy over the speaker? Who is 'they'? Where the fuck is Narcissus? Why would the werehyenas let anyone take them over like this?"

"You're not going to kill me?" He made it a question.

"You answer our questions, and I give you my word that we won't kill you."

"May I move?"

"If you can."

He moved slowly, painfully onto his side. His hair was curly, dark, cut very short, skin pale. He turned until he could see my eyes, and the effort left him shaking, his lips blue, which made me think maybe we didn't have much time to ask our questions, that maybe we'd already killed him, just not fast enough.

His eyes were a strange shade of gold. "I'm Bacchus," he said in that pain-filled voice.

"Nice to meet you. I'm Anita, that's Bobby Lee, now start talking."

"Ask me anything."

I started asking. Bacchus started answering. He didn't die. By the time we crossed the bridge into Missouri, his lips were pink and healthy and the dazed look had left his eyes. I was really going to have to start packing better ammo.

61

BACCHUS ACTUALLY DIDN'T know all that much. Narcissus had introduced his new gentleman fair, Chimera, and they'd seemed to be having a wonderful time together. If not true love, then the rough trade they both wanted. Then Narcissus had gone into one of the rooms and not come back out. For twenty-four hours the werehyenas had thought it was just sex, but after that, they stopped believing Chimera's assurances that Narcissus was alright. Ajax had managed to get inside, and that's when it went bad.

"Ajax told us Narcissus was being tortured, really tortured."

"Why didn't you rescue him?" I asked.

"Chimera came with his own bodyguards. They took . . ." Bacchus had to stop and fight to take a deep breath, as if something inside him was hurting. "You don't know what they've done to our people. You don't know what they've threatened to do to them if we fail them."

"Tell us, then we'll know," I said.

"Have you met Ajax?" he asked.

I nodded.

"They cut his arms and legs off and burned the ends of the wounds so he couldn't heal the damage. Chimera said they'd put him in a metal box and just get him out on special occasions." Bacchus choked, and I wasn't sure if it was from injuries or horror.

Bobby Lee said, "He's upset enough that I can't tell if he's lying or not, but I think he's telling the truth." His voice was a little hoarse, as if he were seeing the images in his head that I was trying very hard not to imagine. I'd gotten better lately at simply refusing to let my imagination run away with me. Maybe it had something to do with being a sociopath; if so, let's hear it for dementia. I sat there in the Jeep, my mind carefully blank, no visuals. Bobby Lee looked ill.

"How many bodyguards does this Chimera have?" I asked.

"About twenty-five, before you started killing them."

"I thought there were like five hundred of you guys. How could twenty-five men keep you down?"

Bacchus looked at me with stricken eyes. "If someone had your Ulfric, Richard, and was cutting pieces off of him, crippling him, wouldn't you do anything to save him?"

I stayed quiet and thought about that one. I gave the only truthful answer that I could. "I don't know. It would depend on what 'anything' covered. I see your point, but why didn't you just rush them?"

Bacchus propped himself up against the side of the Jeep. Nathaniel took a corner a little fast, and Bacchus tried to grab something so he wouldn't slide. I gave him my hand, caught him, and he looked both grateful and uncertain. He kept hold of my hand and gave really good eye contact. "We didn't have an alpha. Ajax and Ulysses were the next in command, and once they started cutting up Ajax, Ulysses told us to do what they said." He squeezed my hand, not too tight. "The rest of us aren't leaders, Anita. Our alphas were all telling us to cooperate with Chimera. We're followers, that's it, that's all. We need an alpha with a plan."

My eyes widened. "What are you saying, Bacchus?"

He drew me close to him with our clasped hands. "There are still almost one hundred and fifty ablebodied hyenas. God knows what they'll do to the prisoners now that we've failed them."

"Why do they want Ms. Blake?" Bobby Lee asked.

"Chimera wants Anita for his mate."

That raised my eyebrows. "What are you talking about?"

"He's got a real hard-on where you're concerned. I don't know why."

I tried to draw my hand out of Bacchus's grip, but he kept me close. "He's tried to kill me at least twice. That doesn't sound so friendly."

"He wanted you dead, now he doesn't, I don't know why. Chimera's crazy, he doesn't need a reason to change his mind." He gazed up at me, still holding my hand. "Please help us."

"Can you guarantee that the other hyenas will follow Ms. Blake?" Bobby Lee asked.

Bacchus looked down, his grip loosened, then it tightened, and he looked up again. "I know that if we'd had any alphas that would have stood up for us all, we'd have taken these guys out by now. But Ulysses loves Ajax, really loves him. He didn't know what to do."

"What about Narcissus? He's not still all mushy about Chimera, right?" I said.

"No, but the only time we've been allowed to see Narcissus, he was gagged."

"Narcissus has a reputation," Bobby Lee said, "of being a tough bastard. I don't think he would have rolled over for them."

Bacchus shrugged, and I finally freed my hand. "I don't know," the werehyena said, "but he couldn't tell us to attack them. For all I know Chimera may have taken his tongue. He did that to Dionysus, my . . . lover." He hugged himself, head down, eyes closed. "He gave me the tongue in a box wrapped with a ribbon."

I'd been given a box once with pieces of people I cared about in it. I'd killed the ones who'd hurt them, killed them all. But the damage done to my friends had been permanent. Nothing I could do would fix it, because they'd been human; they didn't grow back lost body parts.

Bacchus kept his eyes closed, his face very still, as if he were holding himself tight, afraid to lose control. I didn't know what to say in the face of his pain. How did I go from trying to kill him to feeling bad for him? Maybe it was a girl thing, or maybe I'd been oversocialized as a child. Whatever the reason, I found myself wanting to help him, but not wanting to risk any of my own people. Cris was dead on the floor of Narcissus in Chains. I hadn't known Cris long; his loss wasn't that great to me, it just wasn't. But if I went in there in force, I'd be risking people I would miss.

Still . . . "Can you draw a plan, a layout of the club, mark where everybody is being held?"

He opened his eyes, his expression surprised, the tears he'd been holding back trailing down his cheeks, forgotten. "You'll help us?"

I shrugged, uncomfortable at the frantic relief in his eyes. "I'm not sure yet, but it doesn't hurt to find out what we'd be up against."

Bacchus took my hand again, pressed it to his cheek. I thought at first it was going to be some kind of hyena greeting, but he laid a soft kiss on my hand and let me go. "Thank you."

"Don't thank me yet, Bacchus, don't thank me yet." I didn't say out loud that if the club looked too hard to take, like it would cost too many lives, I wouldn't do it. I kept it to myself, because he might lie, make it seem easier. The person he loved was being tortured. People will do a lot of things for the person they love, even stupid things.

62

BOBBY LEE INSISTED on calling Rafael first thing. Nathaniel and Caleb helped me get Bacchus settled in the kitchen. He was still walking like things hurt. Gil had sat down at the end of the couch first thing, huddling. He'd been withdrawn since I told him to stop screaming. Normally, I'd have asked what was wrong, but screw it, I didn't have time to baby-sit him right now.

The kitchen was dim and depressing with all the windows and the sliding glass door boarded over. We had to turn on all the lights. My sunny kitchen had been turned into a cave.

An hour later we had a fair map of the inside of the club. Bacchus knew the guard schedule for the hyenas but not for Chimera's men. He did the best he could but said, "Chimera changes his routine, sometimes every day, at least every three days. One day he kept changing his orders every hour or so. It was weird, weirder even than normal for Chimera."

"How unstable is he?" Bobby Lee asked.

Bacchus actually seemed to think about that for a second or two. I'd thought it was a rhetorical question; maybe I was wrong. "Sometimes he seems fine. Sometimes he's so crazy it scares me. I think it even scares his own people." Bacchus frowned then said, "I heard them say things, like he literally was getting crazier and they were afraid of him, too."

The doorbell rang. It made me jump. Nathaniel jumped off the kitchen counter, where he'd been sitting. "I'll get it."

"Check and see who it is first," I said.

He looked back over his shoulder, the look on his face clearly saying that I was telling him something he already knew. After months of sharing room and board with me, he knew to check the door before he opened it.

"You used to just open the door," I said.

"I know better now," he said and vanished into the living room.

He came back almost immediately. "It's the werewolf that was at Narcissus in Chains, the one called Zeke." Nathaniel looked a little pale.

Bobby Lee and I both had guns in our hands. I didn't really remember drawing mine. I was looking at the boarded-up windows. The wood was a little more protection than the glass had been, but we couldn't see through the wood either. The bad guys could sneak up on us better. "Is he alone?" I asked.

"He's the only one standing on the porch," Nathaniel said, "but that doesn't mean he's alone." His eyes were a touch wide when he said, "I don't smell snakes or lions." I could see the pulse in his neck jumping under his skin.

"It's going to be alright, Nathaniel," I said.

He nodded, but the look on his face told me he wasn't convinced. Gil joined us in the kitchen. "What's happening?"

"Bad guys," I said.

"More of them?" he said, voice plaintive.

"You might have been safer on your own, Gil," I said.

He nodded. "I'm beginning to see that." His eyes were so wide it looked painful.

I had brought the mini-Uzi in from the car and had reloaded it from the gun safe upstairs. I took it off the kitchen cabinet and debated between it and the Browning. The doorbell rang again. I didn't jump this time. I hung the Uzi over my shoulder by its strap and settled the Browning more comfortably in my hand. The Uzi was really an emergency weapon. The fact that I'd even thought about answering my door with it on my person was probably a bad sign. If I needed more than a 9mm to answer my own front door, I should just leave town.

I peered out at the living room, but there was nothing to see but the closed front door. I was going to have to look out the side window to see what was waiting on the porch. I approached the door with the Browning in a two-handed grip, staying to one side of the door. I was ready in case they started shooting through the door. Of course, last time they'd shot through the windows, too, but the drapes were drawn, and it was the best I was going to be able to do, as far as safety went.

I knelt by the window, because most people shoot for the chest or head, and on my knees I'm a lot shorter. I eased the drape to one side, and something slapped against the glass. I jumped back, bringing the gun up, but nothing else happened. I had an image in my head of what it had been, and it hadn't been a gun. I thought it had been a picture. I eased the drape back and found myself staring at a Polaroid of a man chained to a wall. He was nude, covered in bloody scratches, blood covering most of his body so it was hard to see at first exactly who it was. Then gradually my eyes made sense of it, and I realized it was Micah. I sat back abruptly on the floor, almost like I'd fallen. My hand dragged at the drape, keeping it open. The gun wasn't where it was supposed to be, but hovered in the air, half-forgotten. A gag cut across that wide mouth, the delicate face covered in blood and swollen flesh. The long hair was mounded to one side, as if it were so sticky with blood that it no longer moved freely. His eyes were closed, and I wondered for a second that lasted forever if he was dead. But there was something about the way he hung in the chains that said *alive*. Even in a picture there is a stillness to death that the live cannot mimic. Or maybe I'd just seen enough bodies to know.

Bobby Lee was beside me. "What is it, what's wrong?" Then he saw the picture, and I heard his breath go in sharp. "That's your Nimir-Raj, isn't it?"

I nodded, because I still wasn't breathing, which made it hard to talk. I closed my eyes for a moment, took a deep cleansing breath, and let it out slowly. It shook as it left my body. I cursed silently. "Get a handle on it, Anita, you can do better than this."

"What?" Bobby Lee asked.

I realized I'd said the last aloud and shook my head, letting the drape fall back into place. I got to my feet. "Let him in, let's see what he's got to say."

Bobby Lee was giving me a funny look. "You can't shoot him until after we know what's happening."

I nodded. "I know."

He touched my shoulder, turned me to look at him. "There is a look on your face, girl, that is as bleak as a winter's dawn. People kill other people while they're wearing that look. I don't want you to let your emotions get in the way of business."

Something that was almost a smile touched my lips. "Don't worry, Bobby Lee, I won't let anything interfere with business."

His hand dropped away slowly. "Girl, the look in your eyes now scares me."

"Then don't look," I said, "and *don't* call me 'girl'."

He nodded. "Yes, ma'am."

"Now open the damn door, and let's get this done."

He didn't argue again. He just went for the door and let the big, bad wolf inside.

63

WHEN WE OPENED the door, Zeke had a picture of Cherry in front of his chest. His first words were, "Shoot me and they both are worse than dead."

So he took a seat on my white couch, still breathing, though if he said the wrong thing, I was hoping to change that.

"What do you want?" I asked.

"I was sent to fetch you for my master."

"Define 'fetch'," I said. I was sitting on the low wood coffee table in front of him. Bobby Lee was standing in back of him with a gun pressed to his spine. At that range with silver ammo there wasn't an alpha in the world that would survive, or at least none that I'd met, and I'd met a few.

"He wants you to be his mate."

I shook my head. "I heard that, but didn't he try, twice, to have you guys kill me?"

Zeke nodded. "Yes."

"And he suddenly wants me to be his honey bun."

Zeke nodded again. The gesture looked odd in the wolfman form, kind of like a golden retriever that was nodding sagely.

"Why the change of heart?" I asked. The fact that I was asking calm questions while the Polaroids of Cherry and Micah sat beside me on the coffee table was a testament to both my patience and my lack of sanity. If I'd really been sane I couldn't have been calm, but I'd hit that switch in my head that let me think when awful things were happening. The same switch that let me kill without much remorse. Being able to divorce myself from my emotions kept me from shooting pieces off Zeke's body until he told me where Micah and Cherry were. Besides, there was always the very real possibility that we could do it later. Talk reasonably first, torture only if you had to, conservation of energy.

"Chimera was told that you would be a panwere like himself."

I raised eyebrows at that. "Panwere, what the hell is that?"

"A lycanthrope that can take more than one form," Zeke said.

"Not possible," I said.

Bacchus spoke from the kitchen doorway. He'd stayed as far away from Zeke as he could and remain in the room. "Chimera can take more than one form, I've seen it."

I looked back at Zeke. "Okay, fine, he's a panwere. Why would someone tell him that I was one, too?"

"Before I answer that question, I have someone waiting in a nearby car. I would like her to come in and speak with you."

"Who?" For a wild moment I thought he might mean Cherry, but he didn't.

"Gina."

"Micah's Gina?" I asked.

Zeke nodded.

I looked behind him at Bobby Lee. "Do we trust him to go back out and come back in without reinforcements?"

Bobby Lee shook his head.

I shook my head, too. "Sorry, Zeke, but we don't trust you."

"Send Caleb then." He looked at the wereleopard, who had been very quiet throughout everything. Caleb was sitting in the far corner of the room, keeping away from Zeke, a lot like Bacchus, come to think of it. But then Gil was huddled in a different corner. I'd assumed I was surrounded by scaredy-cats, hyenas, and foxes, but now . . .

"How did you know his name?" I asked.

"I know a lot of things about Caleb."

"Explain," I said.

The doorbell rang again. I didn't jump this time. I was in that far away place where I didn't get nerves, though the Browning was pointed at the door. Did that count as nerves?

I went to the door, and Bobby Lee stayed with his gun pressed to Zeke's back. "Y'all better hope that that is someone friendly," Bobby Lee drawled.

Zeke's wide nose flared, scenting the wind. "It's Gina."

Call me paranoid, but I didn't trust him. I peeked out the window. This time there were no nasty surprises, just Gina standing on the small porch, a thick gray shawl hugged around her upper body. It was nearly ninety outside, what the hell was the shawl for? I let out a deep breath. The shawl was thick enough to hide all sorts of unpleasant surprises. Damn.

"What's she got under the shawl?" I asked Zeke.

"You might say a message from Chimera."

I glanced back at him. "Talk like that isn't going to get the door opened."

Zeke moved his shoulders, and Bobby Lee must have pressed the gun barrel deeper into his back, because he stopped moving abruptly. "She's been tortured. Chimera sent her with me to show what will happen to your leopard if you don't come with me."

"Why the shawl?" I asked again.

Zeke closed his eyes, as if he wanted to look away but was afraid Bobby Lee would take it wrong. "It's to cover her, Anita, just to cover up her nakedness." He sounded weary, not just tired, but weary. "Please, let her inside, she's in a great deal of pain."

"He smells like he's telling the truth," Bobby Lee said.

I sighed. That was probably as good an assurance as we were going to get. I opened the door, gun at the ready, staying out of the sight of anyone who might be watching from the yard. Because I was hiding behind the door, I didn't see Gina until she was well into the room. I closed the door behind her, and she jumped, then gasped, as if the sudden movement had hurt her badly. When she looked at me, it was all I could do to keep from gasping. I thought at first she had two black eyes, then realized it was just hollows under her eyes so deep they looked like bruises. Her skin was so pale with an undertone of gray, and I understood for the first time what they meant by ashen. She was ashen, as if her body was covered by something thinner, more delicate, than skin. Her tall body was hunched in on itself, as if standing upright would hurt. Her lips were nearly bloodless, but it was her eyes that hurt me the most. They were filled with horror as if she were still seeing whatever had been done to her, as if she might always see that awful thing over and over again.

She spoke in a voice that was hollow, hopeless. "I got worried."

I didn't need to see what was under the shawl to believe that she'd been tortured. I didn't need to see anything but her face.

"Can she sit down before she falls down?" Zeke asked.

I nodded a little too rapidly, realizing that I had been staring. "Please, sit down."

Gina looked at Bobby Lee, standing behind Zeke. "Have you told them?"

"I wanted you here to back up my story," Zeke said.

She nodded once, then moved to sit beside him on the couch. She sat close to him, almost touching. If he'd had anything to do with what had happened to her, I don't think she'd have been so cozy.

In fact she was so cozy that I was almost certain she knew Zeke. Knew him not just for Chimera's fun and games, but knew him before. How did one of Micah's cats end up friendly with Chimera's top goon?

I asked. "You two seem to know each other." Alright, maybe that wasn't a question, but it would do.

They exchanged a look, then Zeke turned to me. I wished that he was in human form. Even after years of dealing with lycanthropes, I still had trouble reading their expressions when they were in animal form. The fact that his eyes were human helped some, but you never realize how much of the expression isn't really the eyes but the facial movements around the eyes, until you don't have them as clues.

"Let me start by saying that Chimera wants you alive and well and in his care in less than two hours or he will start doing permanent damage to Micah and your leopard."

I felt my eyes go a little dead. "We have a deadline then," I said. "Talk faster."

"Shortest version that I know is this. Chimera has always been a harsh master, but never sadistic, until the last few weeks. He's unstable, and I believe he's going mad and will kill us all if he remains in charge."

"This is the short version?" Bobby Lee asked.

"I agree," I said, "speed it up."

"I want you to help me stage a palace revolt, Ms. Blake. Is that quick enough for you?"

"Maybe that was a little too quick," I said. "Why do you want to revolt, and why do you want my help?"

"I told you, I fear that Chimera will destroy us all. The only way to prevent that is to kill him."

Well, that was blunt. "So, why my help?"

"You have a certain reputation for deadly force."

"You talk like an English professor," I said, "or an expensive lawyer. Why not just kill him yourself?"

"The others that follow him, fear him, they would not trust that I alone could guarantee his death."

"And I can?"

"You and your people, yes."

"My leopards are not going inside."

Nathaniel said, "Anita . . ."

I shook my head. "No, I won't endanger the rest of you to save one of you."

"What kind of pard would we be if we allowed our Nimir-Ra to go into danger alone?"

"A pard that obeyed orders," I said.

He leaned back against the wall, but there was an unusually stubborn set to his face that said maybe, just maybe, he'd been picking up more than just weapons skill from hanging around with me. Was stubbornness catching?

"Not your leopards, but the wolves, and the rats."

"The rats aren't mine." *And I'm not the wolves' lupa anymore.*

"Rafael is already on his way here with some of our people," Bobby Lee said.

I frowned at him. "Well, nice you mentioned that."

He shrugged. If he was getting tired of pressing the gun into Zeke's back, it didn't show. "Rafael is my alpha, not you, ma'am."

"I understand that, but if we're going to get along, you still need to keep me informed. I've had enough surprises for one day."

"Amen to that," he said.

"Where are Micah and Cherry being held?" I asked.

Zeke shook his great wolfish head. "No, not until you agree to help us."

"Chimera wanted to blackmail me into being his sweetie, you want to blackmail me into helping you kill him. I don't see much difference."

"The only way to stop Chimera and those still loyal to him is their death. I propose that we pool our resources and accomplish that."

"You talk awful pretty for a goon."

"I am his goon because when he conquered my small pack of wolves, he forced me into this form and kept me in it. When he allowed me to try and change back, this was the best I could do."

I looked into those human eyes. "Only your eyes," I said.

"Only my eyes."

The eyes were usually one of the first things to go animal if you stayed in beast form too long at a time. His eyes being the only thing human was odd. But I didn't ask him to explain, because we were eating up our time and I wanted Micah and Cherry back.

"In this form," Zeke said, "I can be nothing else but a goon, an enforcer. I cannot be human."

I didn't try to argue that he was human. I let it go. "Let's cut to the chase. Bobby Lee, will Rafael help on this?"

"I think so. He's coming with enough soldiers to make a good show."

I looked at Bacchus. "Will the werehyenas join forces with their, what, oppressors? Will you guys help Zeke and his people?"

"Zeke always tried to save us pain. He always spoke for moderation." Bacchus nodded. "I think the others will agree to work with him, but whether they'll agree to let everyone live afterwards, that I can't promise."

"If we help you destroy him," Zeke said, "then you turn around and slaughter us, we have gained nothing."

In looking between Bacchus and Zeke I'd glanced back over the photos. I'd spent the last few minutes not thinking about them. I'd managed to concentrate on other things, but it was as if that one glance had torn through all the barriers that usually kept me from doing stupid shit. I stood up, abruptly enough that everyone looked at me.

"Would you kill Zeke?" I asked.

"No, but Marco, he has to die," Bacchus said.

"Why?" I asked.

"He and the snake men have to die," Bacchus said.

"Agreed," Zeke said. Then he looked up at me. "And I think I know a way to have the wolves involved."

"I'm listening."

"Chimera is wolf, hyena, leopard, lion, bear, and snake."

"He's behind the disappearances of the other alphas," I said.

Zeke nodded.

"Are they alive?"

"The lion and the dog are. Chimera hasn't been able to force them to change form yet. He never kills anyone unless he can break them first."

"Is Narcissus alive?" This from Bacchus.

"Yes," Zeke said. "Chimera has not been able to break him either."

"How will any of this interest the wolves?" I asked. I'd gone to stand on the other side of the kitchen doorway, opposite Bacchus. I couldn't see the pictures from there.

"Chimera's never been able to find a dominant animal group that was weak enough to be taken over by outsiders before, until he heard of your wolf pack."

I stood up straighter, pushing away from the wall. "What do you mean?"

"Jacob, Paris, and a few others are what's left of my pack. Chimera couldn't send me because my condition would raise questions."

"Are you saying that as soon as Jacob becomes Ulfric, he turns the pack over to Chimera?"

"That was the plan," Zeke said.

"And now?" I asked.

"Now either Jacob and the others agree to leave your pack where it is, or they die."

"You'd kill what's left of your own pack, just like that?" I said.

"They stopped being my pack a long time ago."

"So let me get this straight," Bobby Lee said, "you want the rats, the wolves, and the leopards to join forces with the hyenas and whatever people of yours will join you and destroy the rest."

"Yes," Zeke said.

"And if we don't?" Bobby Lee asked.

"You talk as if you have many choices here," Zeke said. "You do not. Chimera will do worse than kill your leopards. What he has allowed done to the hyenas is beyond any civilized tolerance. His sanity is slipping away, and there are those among his people that will do terrible things without a master to tell them no."

"It takes time to arrange an offensive like this," Bobby Lee said.

Zeke said, "I do not see a clock but time is running out. Anita must be in Chimera's presence before two hours is over, or it will go badly for Micah and the leopard."

"You keep saying Micah and the leopard," I said, "like you know Micah." I had an awful thought, and I'd been slow not to think of it before. "Jacob was supposed to get the wolves for Chimera, and Micah was supposed to get the leopards." I said it in an empty voice. My body felt empty, as if I were falling away inside myself, drowning in that great white static that allowed me to kill and not to think.

"We thought their alpha was dead and it would be easy enough." He looked at me. "We didn't know about you, or rather didn't understand what you were."

Gina spoke. "Once Micah met you, he knew it wouldn't work. He tried to get Chimera to leave you and yours alone, but when you went up against Jacob, you became too big a threat. Chimera ordered you killed. Micah didn't find out about the order until after everyone had left to come after you. He saved you."

I just looked at her. My mind was still trying to process the thought that Micah had lied to me the entire time I'd known him.

"Micah told Chimera that you were going to be a panwere like him, and he might never find another one like himself. That's why you can control the leopards and the wolves both."

I blinked at her. "I guess that's one theory." My voice sounded distant even to me.

"Don't you understand, Anita? I don't think Micah believed it, but it was all he could think of to keep you alive and him alive, and not to get the rest of us tortured." She stood up, and pain tore across her face. Zeke steadied her, then she stood straight and she let the shawl fall away.

Burns traced her pale shoulders. The rest of her chest was bare and lovely and unharmed, but as she turned to show her back, Gil gasped. Her back was patterned with burns, no, not burns, brands. Someone had branded her over and over again. The burns were fresh, some of them bloody raw, some with crisp blackened skin, as if the pressure hadn't been even every time. Some of the marks were smeared around the edges, as if she'd moved, struggled.

She turned back to face me, tears glittering in her eyes. "Every time Chimera sent Micah out he had Violet or me with him. If Micah didn't do what he was told to do, then he'd hurt us." She started walking towards me, hands holding her arms, as if to hold herself steady, but every step hurt, and it showed in the flinching of her eyes. "What would you do to keep this from happening to Nathaniel?"

I met her eyes, but it took effort. "I'd do a lot, but I wouldn't betray anyone."

The tears started slowly down her face, as if she were fighting not to cry. "He tortured Micah because Micah refused to help lure you into the ambush. Chimera is going to kill him, because he says that Micah is no longer his cat, but yours, that the wiles of a woman have won his loyalty." She sobbed, and the movement must have hurt, because she bent forward, body spasming. I caught her by the arms to keep her from falling.

"Oh, God," she whispered, "it hurts."

My throat was tight. I held her elbows until she could stand again.

"I'm Chimera's message to you, Anita. He says he'll do this to your leopard if you don't come back with us."

"You're not going back there," I said.

"He still has Cherry and Micah. If I don't go back he'll do this to her. I don't think she'd survive it." I understood what Gina meant. Not Cherry's body, but her mind.

She began to collapse towards the floor, slowly, me supporting her as gently as I could. "Micah knew what would happen to him when he refused to help trap you, but he still did it." She was on her knees now, her hands gripping my arms tight, tight enough to hurt. "I would have lied and agreed to do anything to keep this from happening to me." She sobbed again, and I held her arms to keep her from falling backwards onto her back on the floor. I held her while she shook in pain, and when she quieted, she said, in a voice more tears than noise, "I would have betrayed anyone to stop him from hurting me. But he didn't want anything from me. Nothing I could say, or do, would stop it. Chimera promised Micah that only he would suffer for refusing, then once he was chained up and couldn't get away they brought me in and made him watch." She looked at me, eyes wide, full of awful things. "Chimera would have made Cherry or me take animal form. He said he'd never had a female beast before."

"That's what he calls those of us trapped between forms," Zeke said.

Gina's fingers dug into my arm, just a little. "Micah took our place. He's alpha enough to have kept human form. He risked his human form for us. Merle was our Nimir-Raj but he wouldn't risk his humanity for us. Micah took his place, our place. He's our Nimir-Raj because he loves us, all of us. Micah offered to betray you to stop them from hurting me, but Chimera said he could smell that Micah was lying and that he would just get away and warn you. So he sent me with Zeke, because he trusts Zeke."

I looked at Zeke over her slowly collapsing form, trying to cradle her as she slid down, and not hurt her, but everything seemed to hurt. She was making small mewling sounds by the time I helped her lower herself to the floor. There was something in Zeke's human eyes that didn't need facial expressions to interpret.

"Chimera must be stopped," Zeke said, softly. "He must be stopped."

"Yes," I said, still holding one of Gina's hands, "yes, he must be stopped."

"Stopped, hell," Bobby Lee said, "we need to kill his ass."

I nodded. "That, too."

64

WE MADE IT back to the club with a little time to spare. The wererats had arrived in force at my house, and d left Rafael in charge of the rescue, because that's what it would be. I was letting Zeke take me into the bad guy's lair unarmed. Zeke would be carrying my weapons, and theoretically he'd give them back to me if I needed them, theoretically. But theory and practice aren't always the same thing. Zeke had tried to kill me once; now I was supposed to trust him with my life. It seemed a bad idea, but I was still going to do it. With enough time maybe we could have come up with a better plan, but we didn't have the time. Not if we hoped to save Cherry and Micah.

It seemed like I'd spent most of the last four years arriving too late. Too late to save people, too late to keep the monsters away. I was cleanup crew, someone that came after the bodies were scattered around and mopped up the mess. I killed the monsters, but only after they'd done terrible things. Even now, Chimera had already butchered and tortured, but I could confess to myself, if to no one else, that part of me didn't give a damn about the others. I mean, I was sorry for Gina's pain and Bacchus's lover, and Ajax getting chopped up, but they were abstract to me. Cherry and Micah were real. How very quickly Micah had become that real to me frightened me, but if I didn't look too closely at it, I could keep moving forward, could keep thinking clearly, could keep breathing normally. Thinking too much tended to make my thoughts jump around, my breath come a little too fast.

The main part of the club had been dark and empty. The party, as they say, was upstairs. It was the room at the end of the big white hallway that we'd gone down to rescue Nathaniel and Gregory days ago. Chimera waited outside the door in his black hood, and his eye slits were unzipped so I could see pale gray eyes. He wore a rather ordinary looking suit, complete with tightly knotted tie and white shirt that met oddly with the black leather of the hood. He had his hands behind him, leaning against his arms. He was trying for casual and failing. He was nervous, and I didn't need any lycanthrope powers to notice.

Gina had needed help from two of the werehyenas to make the steps. Zeke and I could have helped her, but he was pretending to guard me, and Gina had a note under her shawl to slip the hyenas. The note was from Bacchus, asking one of them to let him in the secret entrance. Apparently Chimera had never asked if there was a secret entrance to the club, so no one had told him.

Chimera's eyes looked past me to her. "Gina . . ." He shook his head. "Take her away, get her some medical care."

The two hyenas didn't argue, just turned and went back down the hallway. The snake man that had been with them stayed where he was, his black-and-green striped eyes never leaving Chimera's face. I would have said he stood at attention like a good soldier, but it was more than that. There was something on his face that went beyond that, as if standing there waiting for Chimera's orders was the most wonderful thing in the world. That look of patient adoration was creepy all on its own, and I knew why Bacchus had said the snakes had to die. Not because of what they'd done to the hyenas, not revenge, but because people who worship their kings as gods don't participate in palace revolts.

"I wasn't sure you'd come, Ms. Blake."

The voice was familiar, but I couldn't quite place from where. "You didn't give me much choice."

"And for that I am sorry."

"Sorry enough to let me take my leopards and go home?"

He almost smiled, but shook his head. "Micah is not your leopard, he's mine, Ms. Blake."

Again, the voice rang familiar, but I couldn't place it. I shrugged. "You got me down here with the understanding that both Cherry and Micah would be set free, unhurt. Sounds like they're both mine."

He shook his head again. "To give up Micah I would have to give up all my leopards, and I am not willing to do that."

"Then you lied to get me down here."

"No, Ms. Blake." He took his hands out from behind his back. He wore black leather gloves. "Join your pard to ours, strengthen us."

I shook my head. "I came down here to free my people, not to join your club."

He looked at Zeke. "Didn't you explain to her what I wanted?"

Zeke shifted beside me. "You told me that if she came down here unarmed you would free Micah and the other wereleopard. That is all you told me."

Chimera frowned; even through the hood I could see it. He rubbed at his face behind the leather as if something hurt. "I know I told you that I wanted her to join us."

"You have said many things over the last few weeks," Zeke said, voice very careful.

"How long have you been the leopard's Nimir-Ra?" he asked. The voice was normal, ordinary, though his hands kept rubbing at his face.

"About a year."

"Then you must see as I do that there needs to be a joining together of all the different forms. The only thing that has allowed us to move in to every city and take over the smaller groups is the fact that the larger groups won't help them. They're like city neighbors who only call the police if it's their own apartment being robbed. They let anyone who isn't like them go to hell."

"I agree that the lycanthrope community could use a little togetherness, but I'm not sure torture and blackmail is the way to get it done."

He clamped his hands over his eyes, back bowing, as if he were in pain. The snake man touched him with small dark hands. Chimera shuddered, then raised up, the snake man still touching him, comforting him, I think.

Chimera looked at me, eyes very direct. He grasped the leather hood and pulled it over his head. His dark hair stood on end, sweaty, needing to be combed. The touch of gray at the temples wasn't distinguished anymore. It looked more like mad-scientist hair, as if he'd done something awful and it had changed colors over night. I could see the scars at the side of his neck now. Orlando King, alias Chimera, looked down at me.

I just gaped at him. I was too surprised for anything else.

"I see that you didn't recognize me, Ms. Blake."

I shook my head, and tried twice before I could say, "I didn't expect to see you here." That sounded lame even to me, but what I meant was Orlando King, bounty hunter extraordinaire, should not have been the leader of a group of rogue shapeshifters. It wasn't doable somehow.

"That's why you knew about all the shapeshifters in town, because they came to you for help."

He nodded. "I have been known, since my accident, to hunt down rogue lycanthropes and not inform the authorities. A few bad apples don't have to spoil the entire barrel."

I looked at him and tried to think. "People thought your near-death experience had mellowed you, but you contracted lycanthropy, that's why you stopped being a bounty hunter."

"It seemed wrong to hunt other unfortunates," he said. "People who had less to do with the accident that made them what they were than I did. At least I was hunting the werewolf that almost killed me. I was trying to hurt it. Most people who survive an attack are just innocents."

"I know that," I said, voice soft, because knowing Chimera was Orlando King didn't help solve the mystery for me; it deepened it. I was more confused than when I walked in the damn building.

"But my change of heart, as you put it, came later. Wolf lycanthropy showed up in my bloodstream within forty-eight hours of my attack. I decided I would take out as many monsters as I could and let them take me out before the first full moon." He stared past me, eyes distant with remembering. "I took the most dangerous jobs I could find, until I ended up trying to kill an entire tribe of weresnakes in the depths of the Amazon basin." He looked at the small dark man still at his side. "I decided that dozens of any animal would surely kill me, and if not, then at the first full moon I would be in an area devoid of any human except the people I'd come to kill."

"Logical, I guess," I said, because it seemed appropriate to say something.

His gaze flicked to me. "I had planned my death, Ms. Blake, but every animal I tried to kill just wasn't up to killing me. By the time I had my first full moon I'd been infected by a great many forms of predatory lycanthropy. And on that first moon, I changed into what Abuta and his people are, then a wolf, then a bear, then a leopard, then a lion, so forth, and so on." He was looking at Abuta, and his face held some of the religious fervor that the smaller man seemed to emanate. "They thought I was a god because I could take so many forms. They worshipped me, and they sent half their tribe to accompany me back to civilization." He laughed then. It was abrupt and unpleasant. Something about that laugh raised the hairs on my arms.

"You've killed all but three of them, Anita. I may call you Anita, mightn't I?"

I nodded, almost afraid to speak, because emotions were chasing across King's face, emotions that didn't match his calm words, as if he were feeling things that he wasn't aware of. It was like watching a badly dubbed film, except it was body actions that were out of step, not the words.

A prickling rush of energy came off him like heat, and his eyes turned. One pale greenish leopard, one wolf amber. It wasn't just the colors of the irises that didn't match, it was the shape of the pupils; the entire set of each eye socket was slightly different from the other. I hadn't noticed the bone structure shifting; it had been that fast.

A smile curled his lips. The entire expression of face, body, everything changed, and it wasn't shapeshifting; it was as if another person just settled into King's skin. Chimera's voice was slightly southern, thick and round-voweled. It was the voice I'd heard over the loudspeaker when they tried to ambush us in the club. "Poor Orlando, he just can't cope anymore. He hates what he's become."

I think I stopped breathing for a few heartbeats, which made my next breath harsh. I'd dealt with sociopaths, pychopaths, serial killers, crazies of all ilk, but this was my first multiple personality.

Chimera jerked at the tight tie, tore it off, unbuttoned the collar, rotated his neck, and smiled. "There, that's much better, don't you agree?"

My voice came out breathy. "Always good to be comfortable."

He stepped closer to me, and I backed up, bumping into Zeke. Chimera stepped in very close, almost touching and sniffed just above the skin of my face. This close his power rode over me like thousands of ants biting along my skin.

"You smell of fear, Anita. I didn't think a little eye shift would spook you."

I licked my lips, staring into those mismatched eyes from inches away. "The eyes don't bother me."

"Then what does?" he asked, still hovering over me.

I licked my lips again and didn't know what to say. Or rather, couldn't think of a safe thing to say. I thought of several smart alec remarks, but you should humor crazy people when you're at their mercy; it's a rule. Of course, I also had a rule never to put myself at the mercy of sadistic serial killers suffering from multiple personality disorder. I hoped we all lived to regret my breaking that rule. Truly insane people are often unpredictable and hard to negotiate with.

"I'm waiting for an answer," he said in a sing-song voice.

I just couldn't think of a good lie, so I tried mild truth. "The fact that I was talking to Orlando King and now I'm not, but it's the same body talking at me."

He laughed and stepped back. Then he went very still, as if he were listening to things I couldn't hear. Was it the rescue, this soon? It couldn't be. He looked down at me, smiling that unpleasant smile and ran his hands down his own body. "I make better use of the body than Orlando does."

Okeydokey, things were not improving. I looked up at Zeke and tried to tell him with my eyes that he should have told me that Chimera was this crazy.

Chimera grabbed my wrist, jerked me close. I'd been so busy trying to get eye contact with Zeke that I hadn't even seen it coming. "I was always inside Orlando. I was that part of him that allowed him to slaughter other human beings and feel nothing but hatred. He rarely took a shifter in animal form. It was safer in human form, and Orlando was a very big believer in safety, at least for himself." He drew me against his body using my wrist like a handle. He wasn't hurting me, but the strength in his grip was like a promise, a threat. He could have crushed my wrist and we both knew it.

"King had a reputation for getting the job done," I said.

"The job was to kill other people, women as well as men. Then he'd cut off their heads, burn the bodies, make sure they weren't coming back. I was the part of him that enjoyed the work, and when he became what he hated most in the world, I protected him from himself."

"How?" I asked, softly.

"By doing the things he was too weak to do himself, but still wanted done."

"Like what?" I asked. Rescue was coming; it was just a matter of stalling until help arrived. It had been the original plan, and the fact that Chimera was Orlando King and crazier than a June beetle on crack didn't really change the plan. Just keep him talking. All men love to talk about themselves, even the ones who are completely buggers. Being insane doesn't change that, or at least it never had before. It was just the multiple personality stuff that was freaking me out. If I treated Chimera like any other homicidal maniac, we'd be fine. At least that's what I kept telling myself. My pulse stayed too fast, my chest stayed tight, the fear stayed high; I don't think I believed myself.

"You want to know how I helped Orlando?" he asked.

I nodded "Yeah."

"You really want to know what I've done for him?"

I nodded again, but I was beginning not to like the way he kept phrasing things.

He smiled, and just the smile promised painful, unpleasant things. "You know what they say. Talk is cheap. Let me show you, Anita, let me show you what I've done." With that he reached behind him to the doorknob, turned it, and pulled me into the room beyond.

65

THE ROOM WAS black, utterly black, like being flung into blindness, nothingness, like a cave. Chimera released my arm. It was like being cut adrift, lost in the blackness. I stumbled in the darkness. I reached out blindly to catch myself and touched something. I grabbed at it, trying to hold on to something, anything. Then the flesh gave under my hand, and I realized it was human and not where it should have been. It was too high up to be someone's calf. I jerked back, and something else brushed my back. I let out a little squeal, hands out, stumbling in the dark, and smacked into something else that swung as I hit it. I realized whatever it was, was hanging from the ceiling. I moved away from it and ran face first into the next surprise. The solid smack of flesh on flesh let me know it was a body. The scream let me know it was still alive. I'd hit hard enough that the man swung into me again, and I tried to back away and bumped into another one. That one didn't make any noise. I kept my hands out in front of me and fought to get free of them, but my hand kept touching bodies and body parts—hips, thighs, groins, buttocks. I moved faster, trying to force my way out of the forest of hanging bodies, but moving fast made them start to swing and crash into me. Screams came out of the dark, as if I'd started them all bumping into each other. Men screaming in the dark; by the sound of the voices I knew there were no women. One body hit me hard enough that I fell, and dangling feet brushed against me. I tried to crawl away from them, but they were everywhere, touching me, brushing me, some struggling against my back. I lay down on the floor trying to get away, to get clear, swatting at them with my hands, frantic not to be touched. I crawled on my back, using my feet and hands to try and get under them, but their heights were all different, and I couldn't get free of them.

I felt a scream building in my gut and knew if I screamed once I'd just keep on. My hand landed in a pool of something warm and liquid, and it stopped me. Even in the dark I knew what blood felt like. This was probably the point where most people would have definitely started screaming, but somehow the feel of the blood calmed me. I knew about blood and letting it out of a man until he died. I pressed my hand into that still-warm pool and it steadied me.

I lay back on the floor with my hand in blood and my head resting in God knows what and relearned how to breathe. If I lay very still and didn't try and move, the feet didn't touch me, nothing touched me. So I lay in the dark and closed my eyes and tried to use my other senses, because my eyes were useless. I've got pretty good night vision, but even a cat needs some light, and there was nothing, nothing but the darkness.

The chains creaked as the bodies still swung heavily above me. There were tiny air currents. A warm drop hit my cheek. All the movement had started fresh bleeding from someone. I kept my eyes closed and forced myself to take steady, even breaths. One man was screaming, "God, God, God!" over and over again, as fast as he could draw breath. He'd lost it, and I didn't blame him. I'd come damn close myself, and I wasn't hanging nude from the ceiling, bleeding.

Chimera's voice came out of the darkness. "Shut up, shut the fuck up!"

The man stopped screaming almost instantly, but his breath came in whimpers, as if he had to make some sound.

"Anita," Chimera said. "Anita, where are you?"

Even he couldn't see in the pitch blackness, and the smell of blood, sweat, and flesh masked my odor apparently. Great, he didn't know where I was. I wished I could think of something good to do with that information. But I just lay in the dark on the foul floor, my hand in the pool of cooling blood, another drop of fresh, warm blood hitting my cheek, and did nothing. All I had to do was stall until the cavalry arrived. I'd tried talking to Chimera and that hadn't worked so well. I'd try silence.

"Anita, Anita, answer me."

I didn't answer. If he wanted to find me he could damn well turn on the light. I thought I wanted some light. But then I thought maybe I didn't really want to see what hung above me in this room. Maybe it would be one of those sights that blasts the mind, one you never really recover from. But I badly wanted to see something, almost anything. I lay in the dark, the way I used to huddle under the sheets as a child, afraid of the dark, afraid of what I could not see.

"Answer me, Anita!" He screamed it this time, voice harsh.

A male voice from above me. "Answer him if you can, you don't want him angry with you."

Another man gave a sound like a choking laugh. It sounded thick, as if there were blood in his mouth and throat.

The dark was suddenly full of voices saying, "Answer him, answer him." It was like the wind had found a voice and was giving me instructions in the dark.

Another drop of blood fell on my cheek and began to slide slowly down my skin. I didn't wipe it off. I didn't move. I was afraid any movement would let Chimera know where I was, and I didn't want that.

"Shut up!" Chimera yelled, and I heard him move farther into the room. The voices above me fell silent. But I could still feel them hanging there like weight above me, like a rock ceiling pressing down on me. I took a deep breath, let it out slowly. My claustrophobia was trying to scream in my head that I couldn't breathe, but it was a lie. The dark did not have weight to it; that was the fear talking. If Chimera wanted to let me lie in the dark for the next hour until help arrived, I'd let him. I would not panic. It wouldn't help anything for me to start crawling frantically across the floor with feet brushing my back. If I did that, I would start screaming, and I wouldn't stop for a long, long time.

The blood oozed along my neck into my hair, and I kept my eyes closed and concentrated on breathing shallow, quiet.

"Answer me, Anita, or I will start cutting on the men hanging above you," Chimera said. His voice was closer, but not too close. He was still outside the forest of hanging bodies.

I still didn't answer.

"You don't believe me? Let me prove it to you."

A man screamed, high, piteous, hopeless.

"Don't," I said.

"Don't what?"

"Don't hurt them."

"They're nothing to you, not your animal, not your friend. Why do you care?"

"Orlando King knows the answer to your question."

"I'm asking you," Chimera said.

"You already know the answer," I said.

"No, no! Orlando knows the answer. I don't. I don't understand. Why do you care about strangers?" The other man screamed again.

"Stop it, Chimera."

"Or what?" he asked. "What will you do if I don't stop? What will you do if I stand here in the dark and cut pieces off this man? How will you stop me?"

The man was shrieking, "No, don't, not that, nooo!" The scream fell off, which meant the man was either dead, or he'd fainted. I hoped he'd fainted, but either way I couldn't do much about it.

"Can you taste the fear, Anita? Roll it on your tongue like the strong spice it is."

Right then my mouth was so dry I couldn't have tasted a damn thing. But I could sense their fear, smell it on them. All of them were afraid now, fresh terror, pouring out of their skin. "It's easy to scare people in the dark, Chimera. Everybody's afraid of the dark."

"Even you?"

I avoided the question. "I was told if I came down here that you'd let Cherry and Micah go."

"I did tell Zeke that."

And in that moment I knew he had no intention of letting them go. It shouldn't have surprised me, but it did. Had I really expected fair dealings from him? Maybe. It offended some part of me to know that he wasn't going to do what he'd said. It meant all deals were off. I'd gone from having something to bargain with, to nothing. Just on a whim, he could kill Cherry and Micah before help arrived. My pulse was speeding up again, and I fought to keep my breathing steady. I took my hand out of the cooling pool of blood. I might as well move. He'd locate me soon through my voice.

I laid my hands on my stomach and tried to think of what I could do, unarmed, against a man who outweighed me by more than a hundred pounds and was strong enough to break through brick walls. Nothing useful came to mind. Maybe violence wasn't the way to stall. What did that leave? Sex? Sweet reason? Witty repartee? Dear God, a little help here.

"You don't feel the need to talk, do you?" he asked, voice calmer than it had been, more "normal."

"Not unless I have something to say."

"That's unusual in a woman. Most of them can't stand the thought of silence. They talk and talk and talk." He was sounding calmer. In fact, he sounded like we should have been sitting across a table in some nice restaurant on a blind date. Since we were in a pitch-black torture room with blood on the floor, the matter-of-fact voice was more frightening than the ranting had been. He was supposed to rant and rave, but calm small talk, that was really crazy.

His voice got calmer, but it never sounded exactly like Orlando King's. It was as if there was another voice coming out of him, another personality, maybe. I didn't know, and I didn't care. If it kept him from cutting people up, then yea.

"Would you like to see your leopard now?" the calm voice asked.

"Yes."

The lights exploded across my vision, and I was as blind with the brilliance as I had been with the dark. I put a hand over my eyes to shield them, then slowly lowered it as my spotty vision cleared.

I was staring up at a pair of feet, legs. My gaze went up the line of the man's body to find fresh claw marks on his buttocks and thighs. Another drop of blood trailed from his bare foot to land on my hand. My gaze went slowly to the next pair of legs, and the next, and the next . . . Dozens of men hung like obscene ornaments. For the first time I let myself wonder, was Micah hanging somewhere in the forest of bodies?

"Do you want to stand up or are you enjoying the view from there?" The calm voice spoke from only about two feet away from me. It made me jump badly. I rolled my head back to see Chimera standing two hanging men away from me.

"I'll stand, if you don't mind."

"Allow me to help you." He pushed one of the hanging men to the side like you'd move a drape, like the pale blue eyes weren't open, staring, like the man didn't shudder as Chimera touched him.

I was on my feet, carefully avoiding the body nearest me, before Chimera could push aside another one and help me stand. I really didn't want him to touch me.

Chimera's eyes had bled back to human gray. His face was blank, ordinary. That nearly diabolical smile was gone, but I wasn't looking at Orlando King either. It was somebody else. The question was, was the new personality going to be more helpful or more dangerous?

He pushed back the bodies like holding open a door so I could walk out. I let him do it, but I kept my attention on him, as if I expected him to try and grab me. I guess I did. When I stepped out into a clear space a breath went out of me that I hadn't even known I was holding.

Chimera stepped beside me, and I moved just a little away from him. Movement caught my attention but it was only the hanging men swinging slowly from where Chimera had moved them. All of them bore marks of some kind; claws, blades, burns. One of them was missing his legs below the knees. I turned back to the man in front of me, and I knew I looked pale. I couldn't help that. I hadn't screamed. I hadn't panicked, much. I couldn't control the involuntary stuff. I was having enough trouble with the voluntary.

"Where are my leopards?" I asked, and my voice sounded almost normal. I got a zillion brownie points for that.

"Your leopard is here," he said and moved to a heavy white curtain that took up almost all of the near wall. He pulled on a cord and the curtain parted. Behind it was an alcove, and Cherry was chained by her wrists and ankles to the stone wall. A leather ball gag filled her mouth. Her pale eyes were wide. Tears stained the dried blood on her face. Her face looked untouched, but the blood had come from somewhere.

"She's healed everything we did to her," Chimera said. Abuta the snake appeared at Chimera's side, as if he'd been summoned. The bigger man stroked the snake man's head, like you'd pet a dog that you liked a lot. "Abuta has shown quite a talent for this sort of thing."

I swallowed hard and tried not to get angry. Anger wouldn't help anyone. Help was coming. I just had to stall until it got here. I glanced around the room. There were men chained to the wall all the way around. I didn't recognize any of them. There was a certain uniformity to them—youngish, or at least not old, well built, some slender, some muscular, all races, all physical types, all attractive. I wondered how long it had taken Narcissus to find this many good-looking men?

Micah wasn't along the wall. The room in the Polaroid had looked more like the alcove that Cherry was in. I glanced at the still unopened part of the curtain. Was he behind there?

I had moved closer to Cherry without realizing it, because she made a small movement in her chains, and I startled. I turned back to find her looking at Chimera, not me. He hadn't moved as far as I could see, but something he'd done had frightened her, and I finally realized what. His eyes has gone animal again, and that eerie smile was back. It was Chimera again, and call it a hunch, but I was betting he did most of the pain work for the other two personalities.

"Unchain her," I said, like I was positive he'd do what I asked. I so wasn't sure.

He reached out a hand towards her face, and I grabbed his wrist. "Unchain her."

He smiled that unpleasant smile at me. "I'd hate to lose one of the only women we've got up here. Narcissus may go both ways, but he keeps the women out of his pack. Real spotted hyenas are matriarchal. He's afraid if he brings women in that instinct will take over and he'll lose his pack, because he's not woman enough to keep it."

"I always enjoy learning new zoological facts," I said, "but let's unchain Cherry and get her out of here."

"But what of your lover? What of Micah?"

I met those mismatched animal eyes and fought to keep the fear out of my face. "I figured you were saving him for last, a sort of finale." My voice had gone from calm to jaded. From the tone, you'd have thought that it didn't matter to me one way or another, but I couldn't stop my pulse from jumping in my neck.

His smile deepened, and I watched a human expression fill those animal eyes. Anticipation, anticipation of my pain, I think.

He opened the curtain slowly, revealing Micah chained by his wrists and ankles to the wall, just like Cherry. But unlike her, his wounds hadn't healed. The right side of his face had been beaten badly. His eye was swollen completely shut, encrusted with dried blood. That delicate curve of jaw was so swollen it didn't look real. The swelling had twisted his lip to one side. It was so swollen that I could see the pink inside of his mouth and glimpse teeth where his mouth no longer closed completely.

I heard a small sound, and it was me. It was close to a sob, and I couldn't afford that. If Chimera knew how much this cut me up, he'd just hurt Micah more. I couldn't stop myself from touching him. I had to touch him, because only then would he be real to me. Seeing was never quite believing with me.

I touched my fingertips to the whole side of his face. His good eye fluttered open. There was a moment of relief, then I think he saw Chimera, and his eye widened. He tried to speak but couldn't open his mouth. He made small hurt noises.

Chimera touched his bruises, lightly, but Micah winced anyway. I grabbed his wrist, as I had for Cherry, and moved my body in between the two men. "Unchain him."

"I broke his jaw personally for lying to me."

"He didn't lie to you," I said.

"He told me you were going to be a panwere like me, but you're not." He leaned into me sniffing. "I'd smell it if you were. You're *something*, and it's not human. It smells of leopard and wolf." He took a deep breath just above the skin of my face. "But it also smells like vampire. You aren't what I am, Anita." He looked at Micah. "He was just trying to keep me from hurting him or his cats after he saved you from my people, when they came to your house."

"So I'm not a panwere. Does that mean you don't want me for your mate?"

He laughed then. "Oh, I don't know, I enjoy rape, adds spice." I think he said it just to shock me, but I wasn't sure. Had he raped Cherry? Had he touched her? I tried to keep the thought off my face, because with the thought came a white, hot wash of anger.

"Oh, you don't like that idea, do you?" He tried to touch my hair, and I stepped away from him out of the alcove so I'd have room to maneuver. Help was on its way, but a glance at my watch showed another twenty minutes of the hour still left. Maybe the troops would come sooner, maybe they wouldn't. I couldn't afford to count on it.

He didn't try and follow me, just let me inch away. "I could rape you in front of Micah. I don't think either of you would like that. Though truthfully I might prefer it the other way around. Orlando is homophobic. I wonder why that would be?"

I spoke as I inched down the curtain, drawing him away from Cherry and Micah. "We dislike most in others what we hate most in ourselves," I said.

"Bravo," Chimera said. "Yes, I keep a lot of Orlando safe from Orlando."

"That must be hard," I said.

"What?" he asked.

"Keeping secrets when you share the same body."

He followed me slowly around the edge of the wall. "At first he didn't want to know what we did, but lately he's become . . . unhappy with us. I think he'd have done himself harm if I hadn't stopped him." Chimera motioned towards the hanging men. "He woke up in the dark in the middle of them. He screamed like a girl." Chimera put his fingers to his lips and said, "Oops, excuse me, you didn't scream at all. He screamed like a baby until I came and rescued him, but he didn't seem all that grateful. Like he blamed me." Chimera looked puzzled, and again I had that impression that he was listening to things I couldn't hear.

He stared at me. "Do you hear that?"

I widened my eyes at him and shrugged. "What?"

He looked off past the hanging men, and I looked around for a weapon. All this damage and cutting people up, there had to be a blade around here somewhere. But the room stretched white and empty, except for the chained men. Weren't there supposed to be pokers, maces, fucking weapons? What kind of dungeon was this, victims but no instruments of torture?

I heard it then, screams, fighting. The battle was on. Though it was still distant. The good news was that help was on its way, the bad news was that Chimera knew what was happening and I was alone with him. Alright, not alone, but nobody chained to the stone was going to be able to help me.

He turned a face so full of rage to me that it was almost bestial, without any shifting of form.

"Why did you take all the alphas?" I asked. I was still going to try and keep him talking; it was all I had.

"So I could rule their groups." His words came out low and growling through clenched teeth.

"Your snakes are anacondas. The alpha you took was a cobra. You can't rule over a type of snake you're not."

"Why not?" he asked, and he started to stalk towards me, still in human form, but with that tense grace that is more animal than human.

I didn't have a good answer for that one. "Are the alphas alive?"

He shook his head. "I hear fighting, Anita. What have you done?"

"I haven't done anything."

"You're lying. I can smell it."

Okay. Maybe truth would help. "The sounds you hear are the cavalry riding to the rescue."

"Who?" he asked, voice almost pure growl. He was still stalking towards me, and I was still backing up.

"Rafael and his wererats, probably the werewolves by now."

"There are hundreds of werehyenas in this building. Your cavalry cannot get through them in time to save you."

I shrugged, afraid to tell the truth, afraid he'd take it out on the werehyenas' lovers. And I didn't dare try to lie; he'd smell it. So I just kept backing up. We were almost to the door. If I could get it open, maybe he'd chase me. Maybe I could lead him into an ambush of my own.

Abuta moved in front of the door. I'd forgotten him, and that was careless. Not fatal, not yet, but careless.

I pressed my back to the wall so I could keep an eye on both of them. Abuta stayed by the door, the message clear that if I kept away from the door he'd keep away from me. Chimera, on the other hand, kept stalking closer. I was between a panwere and a snake—not actually a rock and a hard place, but close.

Chimera flowed into his other form. I've seen shapeshifters change for years, and it was always violent, or messy. But this, this was almost . . . breathtaking. Scales flowed over him as if they were water. There was no clear fluid, no blood, nothing but the change, as if he stepped from one form into another, like Clark Kent changes into Superman. It was so quick it was almost instantaneous. He didn't even miss a step. His clothes folded away like the petals of a flower falling to the earth, and he stepped out in the snake form of Coronus. The big snake man stopped moving. He froze in that stillness that reptiles love. I froze when he did. He finally turned his head so he could look at me with a copper eye. It must have played hell with his depth-perception having to do that.

"I remember you. Chimera told us to kill you." He looked around at the dark room and said slowly, "Where are we?"

Then he bent over as if in pain, and the next form was human but not Orlando's body. He was Boone and before Boone's eyes had lost their confused look, he was a lion man. For a second I thought it would be Marco, but of course he couldn't be both Marco and Coronus; not even Chimera could pull that one off.

He was golden, tawny, muscled, masculine, with a mane around his half-human face that was almost black. The claws on his hands were like black daggers.

"This form is truly mine," he growled. "The snake and the bear are like Orlando, they still believe in themselves. But I am all there is, and there is nothing but Chimera." He reached for me, and I bolted. I ran towards the hanging men, because I knew they'd slow him down, then turned at the last second, so fast I fell on the ground and skittered away on hands and feet like a monkey. They would slow him down, but he'd cut them up to get at me. I couldn't let that happen.

He cornered me on the far side of the room—farthest away from the door and Micah. I think he could have caught me sooner but he wasn't rushing. I don't know why. The sounds of fighting were closer, but not close enough.

Chimera came at me like grace contained in violence, a mountain of tawny muscle and fur that gleamed in the lights. He opened his mouth and roared, a sound I'd never heard outside of a zoo before. That coughing roar made me stand a little straighter. Zeke and Bacchus had promised to come get us out of here before the rest of the fighting started. They'd failed, or lied, but I wasn't going down without a fight, and I wasn't going down screaming. I watched him come towards me, like a slow-motion nightmare, beautiful and terrible, like some kind of beastial angel.

Suddenly, the *ardeur* rose inside me like a warm wave, spilling along my skin, drawing a gasp from my throat. The last time it had risen because of Richard's nearness. This time . . . maybe it was just time to feed again. The moment I thought *feed* I knew Jean-Claude had awakened, and with his rising, down in the depths of the Circus, the *ardeur* had risen inside me.

Chimera stopped where he was, shaking his great maned head. "What is that?" he growled.

My voice came breathy. "The *ardeur*."

"The what?"

"The *ardeur*, the fire, the need," I said. With each word the *ardeur* grew like a weight, and that weight brushed against my beast. It spilled upward from that tight curled place inside me, and the two separate heats rose up inside, spilling along my body, drawing me forward towards Chimera. I wasn't afraid of him anymore, because I could smell his fear. You never had to be afraid of anything that was afraid of you. Part of me knew that wasn't true, that a scared man with a gun is more likely to shoot you than a brave one, but the parts of me that were able to think were sliding away, leaving behind only instinct. What was left liked the smell of fear. It reminded me of food and sex.

Chimera backed away, and we began a slow walk back the way we'd come, this time with me advancing slowly on him. I stalked him as he'd stalked me, and part of me noticed that I was placing my feet one atop the other, almost stepping in my own footsteps, like a cat. The walk was oddly graceful, swaying my hips. My spine was very straight, shoulders back, arms almost motionless at my sides, but there was a tension running through my upper body, an anticipation of action, of violence. Always before the *ardeur* had overridden the beast's hunger, but as I stalked Chimera, watched that huge muscular form back away from me, it was meat I was thinking of. Teeth and claws, flesh to rend, to bite, to tear. I could almost taste his blood—hot, almost scalding in my mouth, down my throat. It wasn't just my beast's hunger, but Jean-Claude's blood thirst and Richard's craving for flesh. It was all that and the *ardeur* running through all of it, so that one hunger fed into the next in an endless chain, a snake eating its own tail, an Ouroboros of desires.

Chimera stopped running, pressing himself up against the white curtain. We were almost back to Cherry and Micah. There was solid wall behind Chimera, behind the curtain. "What are you?" he asked in a voice that was strangled, full of the fear that rose off of him in waves. He scented the air, nostrils flaring. "You don't even smell the same."

"What do I smell like?" I touched his chest with just my fingertips, not sure what he'd do. But he didn't pull away. I pressed my palm over his heart and felt that thick, heavy beat rise against my hand, as if I could have caressed it, like running your hand over the head of a drum. I knew in that moment what he wanted most of all. He wanted to die. Whoever was at the core, whatever was left of who Orlando King had been, he wanted to end it. He'd been trying to kill himself since the moment he learned he was going to be a werewolf. He'd never changed his mind. He just couldn't bring himself to commit suicide, not directly anyway.

I leaned in close to him, pressing our bodies together, lightly, both hands on his chest. "I'll help you," I whispered.

"Help me, how?" But his voice was fearful, as if he already knew.

Pain lanced through my chest. My knees collapsed and Chimera caught me, carefully, in those clawed hands. I think it was an automatic gesture. I saw through Richard's eyes for a moment, saw a werehyena snarling in his face, felt the claws ripping through his chest. The pain was sharp, bones breaking, then numbness, and Richard didn't fight it. He let the numbness roll over him. I knew in that instant that Richard wanted to die, or rather he didn't want to live as he was. The pain had made him reach out for me, but his hands were slow, slow to defend himself. He would never admit he'd let himself die, but he wanted it, and it made him slow. Slow enough to have the hyena man carve his chest open like cracking a melon.

Shang-Da was there pulling the hyena off of him, then I was back in my own body, airborne, thrown into the curtain and the alcove beyond. The curtain cushioned some of the fall, and the last remnants of Richard's numbness made my body limp, so it didn't really hurt. I lay for a second in a spill of curtain. My hand brushed outward and hit metal. I raised the edge of the curtain and found that this alcove was full of weapons. I'd found the blades. Chimera had thrown me into them, and the shock of Richard's injury had squelched the ardeur. My hand closed on a knife that was longer than my forearm. I raised it to the light and knew silver when I saw it. The *ardeur* was gone without my feeding it, and I was armed. Life was good.

Then I heard the sound of claws, or blades, in flesh; a thick, tearing sound of something sharp going through meat. You hear the sound often enough, you know what it is.

I could see the hanging men from here, and they were untouched. My stomach clenched tight and cold, because I knew where Chimera was. I just didn't know which of them he was cutting up.

I pushed the curtain away from me, started to stand, and Abuta was in front of me. I kept one hand balled in the curtain and flung it at him. He did what anyone would do. He flinched, and I drove the silver blade through the middle of his body, angling up, hunting for the heart.

Abuta screamed, hand reaching back towards where Chimera was cutting up my people. He said something in a language I didn't understand. As his body collapsed, I kept twisting the blade trying to find his damn heart, but the blade was stuck on his ribs and wider than my usual knives. It wouldn't move where I wanted it to go. I got a glimpse of a golden-colored blur moments before Chimera smashed a hand into me and sent me flying back into the hanging men. I hit solid, and they cried out, then I was on the ground trying to relearn how to breathe. His arm had taken me across one shoulder, and it was numb from the impact.

Chimera knelt over the snake man, cradling him in his arms. Movement turned my gaze towards Micah and Cherry. The front of Cherry's body was bloody ribbons, as if he'd racked claws down either side of her as deep as he could go, as much damage as he could do in as little time as possible. Her ruined chest rose and fell frantically; she was alive.

Micah's body was spilled open like something ripe that had been thrown against a wall. His intestines glittered like something separate and alive. I could see things inside his body that were never meant to see the light of day. He convulsed, jerking against the chains.

I screamed, and something about my panic opened me to Richard again. He was lying on the floor downstairs, and he was dying, and more than that I felt that his giving up had hurt the wolves. He was their Ulfric, their heart and their head, and his will was weak, and it made them weak. The hyenas and the halfmen that fought for Chimera were fighting for what they believed in, or fighting for the ones they loved. The wolves had nothing but Richard's willingness to die.

And I knew in that moment that if he died like that it wouldn't just be Jean-Claude and me who would join him, it would be all the wolves. Something had gone terribly wrong with Bacchus and Zeke's plan. The hyenas and the halfmen would slaughter our pack. All of them, all of them would die.

I screamed again, and Chimera was in front of me, one hand balled in my shirt, his claws ripping shallow wounds in my upper chest. He drew the other hand back, and time seemed to slow. I had all the time in the world to decide what to do, and yet, I had no time left. I felt Richard's breath rattling in his chest, felt him begin to die. Micah's body gave one last shudder, then he went very still.

I screamed, wordless, reaching for something, anything to save them. My power came, *my* power, and the one thing I could do to save us all. It was one of the worst things I'd ever seen done and I didn't hesitate.

I didn't call my power—there was no time. I *became* my power. It flowed up, through me, instantly, spilled into my hands. I touched one hand to the furred arm that held me, then blocked his other arm as it swept down towards me in a blur of motion. Blocked the blow and swept my free hand up over Chimera's arm, so that both my hands touched his arms. The moment enough of me touched enough of him, I called the power I'd learned in New Mexico. When I raised a zombie I put energy into the corpse, helped what lay in the grave to be solid and real. This was the reverse of that. I took energy out, sucked it away, made the lion man less real, less alive.

The fur flowed under my hands until I touched human skin. It was Orlando King's body that collapsed to its knees in front of me. Orlando's eyes that raised horrified gray to search my face, to beseech me, maybe. But he never asked me to stop, and truthfully I wasn't sure I knew how to stop.

He started to scream just before his skin began to run with fine lines, like watching decades catch up with him in one fell swoop. I fed on him, fed on his essence, fed on what he was. It rushed through my body, thrilling along my skin, singing through my bones, cascading in a rush of joy through every fiber of my being, and beyond. I felt the energy flow outward to Micah, down that link that made me want to touch him every time we were close. The power found Richard and made him breathe. It spilled outward to all the wolves, and they were no longer dependent on Richard's broken will, they had mine, and I wanted to live. I wanted us all to live. We would live. We would live, and our enemies would die. I willed it so. I made it so. I used Orlando King's life to fill my leopards, my wolves, and distantly, my vampires, with will. Will to live, to fight, to survive.

And through all of it, Orlando King shrieked. He screamed as his body drained away into my hands. His skin was like dirty tissue paper on skeleton sticks when I finally let him go. He collapsed on his side, that large body turned to something light as air, but still he screamed. One ragged horror of a sound after another, and I felt no pity. I felt only the rush of power like a flight of bird wings inside my head.

Micah was beside me in black, furred leopard man form. The center of his body was whole, healed, only partially due to his shifting. A huge spotted leopard the size of a pony stalked around us, hissing at what was left of Orlando. Cherry was whole in her furred coat, not even bloody.

I must have stood there longer than I knew, draining Orlando King's life away. Long enough for them to tear the chains off, long enough for them to shapeshift and heal. The hanging men were changing form, too. And with the change, they broke their chains, healed most of the damage that had been done to them, and dropped to the ground in spotted fur and claws. They sniffed around what was left of Orlando. They gave strange barking sounds as the thing continued to scream.

Micah's voice came furry, rough with his new shape. "Your eyes are like a night-filled sky with stars in it."

I didn't need to see a mirror to know what he meant. My eyes were black, swimming and dark with the distant glow of stars in that darkness. Obsidian Butterfly's eyes had been like that, and my eyes had mirrored hers after she touched me with her power.

The far door opened and the wolves poured in. Shang-Da and Jamil were holding Richard between them. He was still in human form, still refusing to shift and help the power heal him.

The wolves, some in human form, some not, came to touch me, lick me, abase themselves before me. They growled and snapped at the dried thing that still screamed on the floor.

Jamil and Shang-Da helped Richard around the room until he stood facing me and Micah. It was only when he was that close that I realized his eyes were black with the play of cold stars in them, too. I wondered if Jean-Claude's eyes looked the same, and a thought let me know that it was so. Jean-Claude was basking in the rush of power. Richard stared at me like I'd run over his mother. The pain on his face had nothing to do with the healing wounds. I'd taken just a little bit more of his humanity, or so he felt.

He gazed down at the screaming thing on the floor with those black star-filled eyes and said, "How could you do it?"

"I did what I had to do," I said.

He was shaking his head. "I didn't want to live this badly."

"I did," Micah said.

The two men looked at each other; yellow-green eyes to black. Something seemed to pass between them, then Richard looked back at me. "Is he dying?"

"Not exactly."

He closed his eyes, and I got a glimpse inside him before he threw up his shields. It wasn't the horror that made him blanch, it was the fact that the power rush had felt better than almost anything else he'd ever experienced. Then the shields tightened, but his eyes stayed a swimming blackness.

"Get me out of here," he said.

"Change shape, Richard, heal yourself," I said.

He just shook his head. "No."

"Damn it, Richard."

He just said, "No," then Jamil and Shang-Da helped him towards the door. I watched him go but didn't try and call him back. I did my best to ignore him as I knelt by the skeletal thing that I'd made out of Orlando King. I knew how to give him back his energy, and that too would have been a rush in it's own way, but Orlando wanted to die, and Chimera was too dangerous to be kept alive. I did what Orlando wanted, and I passed judgment on Chimera. I called my magic one more time and spilled it into that struggling, screaming thing, and I released the soul. It fluttered past me like an invisible bird, and the body gave that long harsh breath that is often the very last sound. Orlando King died unrecognizable, unless you had dental records.

Micah helped me to my feet. He was back in human form. Before I'd seen Chimera, I would have said that Micah's change was smoother than anyone's I'd ever seen. He pulled me into the circle of his arms, and I pressed my face against the bare skin of his neck, caught the scent of his skin, and the *ardeur* welled up inside me, as if it had been waiting. Goosebumps ran up his bare arms, and he gave a nervous laugh. "I don't know if I'm up to it. I've had a hard day."

I wrapped my arms around his back, pressed my face against his chest, to hear the beating of his heart strong and steady. And for no reason that I could figure out, I started to cry, and the *ardeur* flowed away on a wash of tears, and hands. Hands not just Micah's, but hands of wolves, hyenas, and the leopards that had disobeyed me and come for the fight. And finally Zeke and the halfmen who had joined him. They all touched me, marked me with their scent, their tears, their laughter. We laughed and cried, howled and roared, made every noise you could make. Richard missed a hell of a victory party.

Epilogue

RICHARD DID MAKE me his Bolverk. But I was no longer his girlfriend. I'm not even sure I'm upset about that. He's free to find another lupa, though I'm not sure the pack will agree with him; they seem to like me just fine. As Bolverk of the Thronnos Rokke Clan, my first order of business was to execute Jacob. Paris is still alive at Richard's insistence. I think it's a mistake, but he is Ulfric. Oh, well.

I did not turn furry with the full moon. Apparently, Jean-Claude was right about the leopards being my animal to call, just as Damian is my vampire servant. I'm gaining powers like a master vampire. Go figure.

The snake men and Marco died during the fighting. The remainder of Chimera's people have joined their appropriate animal groups. We have a shapeshifter coalition to promote better understanding among the groups. I'm chairman, though I tried not to be. Micah and his pard stayed in town.

Micah and I are still dating, if you can call sharing a bed and my house dating. But I haven't left Jean-Claude. I'm dating them both. I am Jean-Claude's human servant, and I can't hide from that anymore. Jean-Claude wasn't horrified by what I did to Orlando King, either. He was pleased. Pleased we won, pleased we all survived. He and Micah seem to be getting along, so far. I keep waiting for the other shoe to drop and all hell to break loose between them, but so far, so good.

We rescued Joseph, the lions' Rex, and his wife is still pregnant, four months and counting—a record. Narcissus turned out to be a hermaphrodite, and he's pregnant, too. I'm not sure Narcissus should be breeding, especially knowing who the father is, but it's not my choice.

The cobras' king and son were both dead. Killed after Chimera had broken them.

I wake up pressed between Micah and Nathaniel. You can't feed the *ardeur* off of the same person every day, not even a lycanthrope. That's why they used to say that succubi and incubuses killed their victims. You can literally love someone to death. So, I feed on Micah and Nathaniel. Micah as my Nimir-Raj, and Nathaniel as my *pomme de sang*. No, I'm not having intercourse with Nathaniel. Both of them seem peaceful with the arrangement, though I'm still a little weirded out by it. I'm still hoping the *ardeur* is temporary.

Belle Morte's people contacted Jean-Claude. They're negotiating for Musette, one of Belle's lieutenants, to come for a visit. The mention of Musette's name made Asher and Jean-Claude go pale.

Ronnie is horrified that I came so close to getting killed, but it hasn't made her any more reasonable on the subject of my love life. We're back to not seeing a whole lot of each other. Maybe Micah can be my new workout partner, no pun intended.

I still love Richard, but it doesn't matter. It won't work. He can't accept what he is, or what I am. Neither of us can change our nature, and I don't even want to anymore. Micah accepts me for what I am, all of me. He loves me, from my toy penguin collection to my cold-blooded practicality. He doesn't mind bodies on the ground, and neither does Jean-Claude. I hope Richard makes peace with himself someday, but it's not really my problem anymore. I'll keep the pack safe with or without him.

As for the rest, if I wake up to silk sheets I know I'm at Jean-Claude's place. If I wake up on pure cotton sheets, I'm at home. But wherever I am, Micah is beside me. I go to sleep against the smooth warmth of him, breathing in the honeyed sweetness of his skin. Sometimes the sheets smell of Jean-Claude's cologne, sometimes they don't. Sometimes Micah's body bears two neat fang marks, and I feel Jean-Claude in his coffin, settling down for the day, content and well-fed, full of my sex and Micah's blood. Life really is good, even if you are dead.

ABOUT THE AUTHOR

LAURELL K. HAMILTON is a full-time writer and mother. Her bestselling Anita Blake, Vampire Hunter novels include *Obsidian Butterfly, Blue Moon, Burnt Offerings, The Killing Dance, Bloody Bones, The Lunatic Cafe, Circus of the Damned, The Laughing Corpse*, and *Guilty Pleasures*. She is also the author of *A Kiss of Shadows*, She lives in a suburb of St. Louis with her family.